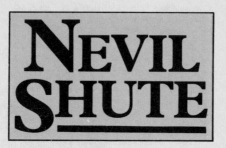

NEVIL SHUTE

A TOWN LIKE ALICE

PIED PIPER

THE FAR COUNTRY

THE CHEQUER BOARD

NO HIGHWAY

Heinemann/Octopus

A Town like Alice first published in Great Britain in 1950
Pied Piper first published in Great Britain in 1942
The Far Country first published in Great Britain in 1952
The Chequer Board first published in Great Britain in 1947
No Highway first published in Great Britain in 1948

This edition first published in 1976 by
William Heinemann Limited
15–16 Queen Street, London W1

in association with

Octopus Books Limited
59 Grosvenor Street, London W1

ISBN 0 7064 0574 9

Printed in Great Britain by
Jarrold & Sons Ltd., Norwich

CONTENTS

NEVIL SHUTE

A TOWN LIKE ALICE

How many loved your moments of glad grace,
And loved your beauty with love false or true;
But one man loved the pilgrim soul in you,
And loved the sorrows of your changing face.

W. B. Yeats

I

James Macfadden died in March 1905 when he was forty-seven years old; he was riding in the Driffield Point-to-Point.

He left the bulk of his money to his son Douglas. The Macfaddens and the Dalhousies at that time lived in Perth, and Douglas was a school friend of Jock Dalhousie, who was a young man then, and had gone to London to become junior partner in a firm of solicitors in Chancery Lane, Owen, Dalhousie, and Peters. I am now the senior partner, and Owen and Dalhousie and Peters have been dead for many years, but I never changed the name of the firm.

It was natural that Douglas Macfadden should put his affairs into the hands of Jock Dalhousie, and Mr Dalhousie handled them personally till he died in 1928. In splitting up the work I took Mr Macfadden on to my list of clients, and forgot about him in the pressure of other matters.

It was not until 1935 that any business for him came up. I had a letter from him then, from an address in Ayr. He said that his brother-in-law, Arthur Paget, had been killed in a motor car accident in Malaya and so he wanted to redraft his will to make a trust in favour of his sister Jean and her two children. I am sorry to say that I was so ignorant of this client that I did not even know he was unmarried and had no issue of his own. He finished up by saying that he was too unwell to travel down to London, and he suggested that perhaps a junior member of the firm might be sent up to see him and arrange the matter.

This fitted in with my arrangements fairly well, because when I got this letter I was just leaving for a fortnight's fishing holiday on Loch Shiel. I wrote and told him that I would visit him on my way south, and I put the file concerning his affairs in the bottom of my suitcase to study one evening during my vacation.

When I got to Ayr I took a room at the Station Hotel, because in our correspondence there had been no suggestion that he could put me up. I changed out of my plus-fours into a dark business suit, and went to call upon my client.

He did not live at all in the manner I had expected. I did not know much about his estate except that it was probably well over twenty thousand pounds, and I had expected to find my client living in a house with a servant or two. Instead, I discovered that he had a bedroom and a sitting-room on the same floor of a small private hotel just off the sea front. He was evidently leading the life of an invalid though he was hardly more than fifty years old at that time, ten years younger than I was myself. He was as frail as an old lady of eighty, and he had a peculiar grey look about him which didn't look at all good to me. All the windows of his sitting-room were shut and after the clean air of the lochs and moors I found his room stuffy and close; he had a number of budgerigars in cages in the window, and the smell of these birds made the room very unpleasant. It was clear from the furnishings that he had lived in that hotel and in that room for a good many years.

He told me something about his life as we discussed the will; he was quite affable, and pleased that I had been able to come to visit him myself. He seemed to be an educated man, though he spoke with a marked Scots accent. 'I live very quietly, Mr Strachan,' he said. 'My health will not permit me to go far abroad. Whiles I get out upon the front on a fine day and sit for a time, and then again Maggie–that's the daughter of Mrs Doyle who keeps the house–Maggie wheels me out in the chair. They are very good to me here.'

Turning to the matter of the will, he told me that he had no close relatives at all except his sister, Jean Paget. 'Forbye my father might have left what you might call an indiscretion or two in Australia,' he said. 'I would not say that there might not be some of those about, 'though I have never met one, or corresponded. Jean told me once that my mother had been sore distressed. Women talk about these things, of course, and my father was a lusty type of man.'

His sister Jean had been an officer in the W.A.A.C.s in the 1914–18 War, and she had married a Captain Paget in the spring of 1917. 'It was not a very usual sort of marriage,' he said thoughtfully. 'You must remember that my sister Jean had never been out of Scotland till she joined the army, and the greater part of her life had been spent in Perth. Arthur Paget was an Englishman from Southampton, in Hampshire. I have nothing against Arthur, but we had all naturally thought that Jean would have married a Scot. Still, I would not say but it has been a happy marriage, or as happy as most.'

After the war was over Arthur Paget had got a job upon a rubber estate in Malaya somewhere near Taiping, and Jean, of course, went out there with him. From that time Douglas Macfadden had seen little of his sister; she had been home on leave in 1926 and again in 1932. She had two children, Donald born in 1918 and Jean born in 1921; these children had been left in England in 1932 to live with the Paget parents and to go to school in Southampton, while their mother returned to Malaya. My client had seen them only once, in 1932 when their mother brought them up to Scotland.

The present position was that Arthur Paget had been killed in a motor accident somewhere near Ipoh; he had been driving home at night from Kuala Lumpur and had driven off the road at a high speed and hit a tree. Probably he fell asleep. His widow, Jean Paget, was in England; she had come home a year or so before his death and she had taken a small house in Bassett just outside Southampton to make a home for the children and to be near their schools. It was a sensible arrangement, of course, but it seemed to me to be a pity that the brother and the sister could not have arranged to live nearer to each other. I fancy that my client regretted the distance that separated them, because he referred to it more than once.

He wanted to revise his will. His existing will was a very simple one, in which he left his entire estate to his sister Jean. 'I would not alter that,' he said. 'But you must understand that Arthur Paget was alive when I made that will, and that in the nature of things I expected him to be alive when Jean inherited from me, and I expected that he would be there to guide her in matters of business. I shall not make old bones.'

He seemed to have a fixed idea that all women were unworldly creatures and incapable of looking after money; they were irresponsible, and at the mercy of any adventurer. Accordingly, although he wanted his sister to have the full use of his money after his death, he wanted to create a trust to ensure that her son Donald, at that time a schoolboy, should inherit the whole estate intact after his mother's death. There was, of course, no special difficulty in that. I presented to him the various pros and cons of a trust such as he envisaged, and I reminded him that a small legacy to Mrs Doyle, in whose house he had lived for so many years, might not be out of place provided that he was still living with them at the time of his death. He agreed to that. He told me then that he had no close relations living, and he asked me if I would undertake to be the sole trustee of his estate and the executor of his will. That is the sort of business a family solicitor frequently takes on his shoulders, of course. I told him that in view of my age he should appoint a co-trustee, and he agreed to the insertion of our junior partner, Mr Lester Robinson, to be co-trustee with me. He also agreed to a charging clause for our professional services in connection with the trust.

There only remained to tidy up the loose ends of what was, after all, a fairly simple will. I asked him what should happen if both he and his sister were to die before the boy Donald was twenty-one, and I suggested that the trust should terminate and the boy should inherit the estate absolutely when he reached his majority. He agreed to this, and I made another note upon my pad.

'Supposing then,' I said, 'that Donald should die before his mother, or if Donald and his mother should die in some way before you. The estate would then pass to the girl, Jean. Again, I take it that the trust would terminate when she reached her majority?'

'Ye mean,' he asked, 'when she became twenty-one?'

I nodded. 'Yes. That is what we decided in the case of her brother.'

He shook his head. 'I think that would be most imprudent, Mr Strachan, if I may say so. No lassie would be fit to administer her own estate when she was twenty-one. A lassie of that age is at the mercy of her sex, Mr Strachan, at the mercy of her sex. I would want the trust to continue for much longer than that. Till she was forty, at the very least.'

From various past experiences I could not help agreeing with him that twenty-one was a bit young for a girl to have absolute control over a large sum of money, but forty seemed to me to be excessively old. I stated my own view that twenty-five would be a reasonable age, and very reluctantly he receded to thirty-five. I could not move him from that position, and as he was obviously tiring and growing irritable I accepted that as the maximum duration of our trust. It meant that in those very unlikely circumstances the trust would continue for twenty-one years from that date, since the girl Jean had been born in 1921 and it was then 1935. That finished our business and I left him and went back to London to draft out the will, which I sent to him for signature. I never saw my client again.

It was my fault that I lost touch with him. It had been my habit for a great many years to take my holiday in the spring, when I would go with my wife to Scotland for a fortnight's fishing, usually to Loch Shiel. I thought that this was going on for ever, as one does, and that next year I would call again upon this client on my way down from the north to see if there was any other business I could do for him. But things turn out differently, sometimes. In the winter of 1935 Lucy died. I don't want to dwell on that, but we had been married for twenty-seven years and–well, it was very painful. Both our sons were abroad, Harry in his submarine on the China station and Martin in his oil company at Basra. I hadn't the heart to go back to Loch Shiel, and I have never been to

Scotland since. I had a sale and got rid of most of our furniture, and I sold our house on Wimbledon Common; one has to make an effort at a time like that, and a clean break. It's no good going on living in the ashes of a dead happiness.

I took a flat in Buckingham Gate opposite the Palace stables and just across the park from my club in Pall Mall. I furnished it with a few things out of the Wimbledon house and got a woman to come in and cook my breakfast and clean for me in the mornings, and here I set out to re-create my life. I knew the pattern well enough from the experience of others in the club. Breakfast in my flat. Walk through the Park and up the Strand to my office in Chancery Lane. Work all day, with a light lunch at my desk. To the club at six o'clock to read the periodicals, and gossip, and dine, and after dinner a rubber of bridge. That is the routine that I fell into in the spring of 1936, and I am in it still.

All this, as I say, took my mind from Douglas Macfadden; with more than half my mind upon my own affairs I could only manage to attend to those clients who had urgent business with my office. And presently another interest grew upon me. It was quite obvious that war was coming, and some of us in the club who were too old for active military service began to get very interested in Air Raid Precautions. Cutting the long story short, Civil Defence as it came to be called absorbed the whole of my leisure for the next eight years. I became a Warden, and I was on duty in my district of Westminster all through the London blitz and the long, slow years of war that followed it. Practically all my staff went on service, and I had to run the office almost single-handed. In those years I never took a holiday, and I doubt if I slept more than five hours in any night. When finally peace came in 1945 my hair was white and my head shaky, and though I improved a little in the years that followed I had definitely joined the ranks of the old men.

One afternoon in January 1948 I got a telegram from Ayr. It read,

Regret Mr Douglas Macfadden passed away last night please instruct re funeral.
Doyle, Balmoral Hotel, Ayr.

I had to search my memory, I am afraid, to recollect through the war years who Mr Douglas Macfadden was, and then I had to turn to the file and the will to refresh my memory with the details of what had happened thirteen years before. It seemed rather odd to me that there was nobody at Ayr who could manage the funeral business. I put in a trunk call to Ayr right away and very soon I was speaking to Mrs Doyle. It was a bad line, but I understood that she knew of no relations; apparently Mr Macfadden had had no visitors for a very long time. Clearly, I should have to go to Ayr myself, or else send somebody. I had no urgent engagements for the next two days and the matter seemed to be a little difficult. I had a talk with Lester Robinson, my partner, who had come back from the war as a brigadier, and cleared my desk, and took the sleeper up to Glasgow after dinner that night. In the morning I went down in a slow train to Ayr.

When I got to the Balmoral Hotel I found the landlord and his wife in mourning and obviously distressed; they had been fond of their queer lodger and it was probably due in a great part to their ministrations that he had lived so long. There was no mystery about the cause of death. I had a talk with the doctor and heard all about his trouble; the doctor had been with him at the end, for he lived only two doors away, and the death certificate was already signed. I took a brief look at the body for identification and went through the various formalities of death. It was all perfectly straightforward, except that there were no relations.

'I doubt he had any,' said Mr Doyle. 'His sister used to write to him at one time, and she came to see him in 1938, I think it was. She lived in Southampton. But he's had no letters except just a bill or two for the last two years.'

His wife said, 'Surely, the sister died, didn't she? Don't you remember him telling us, sometime towards the end of the war?'

'Well, I don't know,' he said. 'So much was happening about that time. Maybe she did die.'

Relations or not, arrangements had to be made for the funeral, and I made them that afternoon. When that was done I settled down to look through the papers in his desk. One or two of the figures in an account book and on the back of the counterfoils of his cheque book made me open my eyes; clearly I should have to have a talk with the bank manager first thing next morning. I found a letter from his sister dated in 1941 about the lease of her house. It threw no light, of course, upon her death, if she was dead, but it did reveal significant news about the children. Both of them were in Malaya at that time. The boy Donald, who must have been twenty-three years old at that time, was working on a rubber plantation near Kuala Selangor. His sister Jean had gone out to him in the winter of 1939, and was working in an office in Kuala Lumpur.

At about five o'clock I put in a trunk call to my office in London, standing in the cramped box of the hotel, and spoke to my partner. 'Look, Lester,' I said. 'I told you that there was some difficulty about the relations. I am completely at a loss up here, I'm sorry to say. Provisionally, I have arranged the funeral for the day after tomorrow, at two o'clock, at St Enoch's cemetery. The only relations that I know of live, or used to live, in Southampton. The sister, Mrs Arthur Paget, was living in 1941 at No 17 St Ronans Road, Bassett–that's just by Southampton somewhere. There were some other Paget relations in the district, the parents of Arthur Paget. Mrs Arthur Paget–her Christian name was Jean–yes, she was the deceased's sister. She had two children, Donald and Jean Paget, but they were both in Malaya in 1941. God knows what became of them. I wouldn't waste much time just now looking for them, but would you get Harris to do what he can to find some of these Southampton Pagets and tell them about the funeral? He'd better take the telephone book and talk to all the Pagets in Southampton one by one. I don't suppose there are so very many.'

Lester came on the telephone to me next morning just after I got back from the bank. 'I've nothing very definite, I'm afraid, Noel,' he said. 'I did discover one thing. Mrs Paget died in 1942, so she's out of it. She died of pneumonia through going out to the air raid shelter–Harris got that from the hospital. About the other Pagets, there are seven in the telephone directory and we've rung them all up, and they're none of them anything to do with your family. But one of them, Mrs Eustace Paget, thinks the family you're looking for are the Edward Pagets, and that they moved to North Wales after the first Southampton blitz.'

'Any idea whereabouts in North Wales?' I asked.

'Not a clue,' he said. 'I think the only thing that you can do now is to proceed with the funeral.'

'I think it is,' I replied. 'But tell Harris to go on all the same, because apart from the funeral we've got to find the heirs. I've just been to the bank, and there is quite a sizeable estate. We're the trustees, you know.'

I spent the rest of that day packing up all personal belongings, and letters, and papers, to take down to my office. Furniture at that time was in short supply, and I arranged to store the furniture of the two rooms, since that might be wanted by the heirs. I gave the clothes to Mr Doyle to give away to needy people in Ayr. Only two of the budgerigars were left; I gave those to the Doyles, who seemed to be attached to them. Next morning I had another interview with the bank manager and telephoned to book my sleeper on the night mail down to London. And in the afternoon we buried Douglas Macfadden.

It was very cold and bleak and grey in the cemetery, that January afternoon. The only mourners were the Doyles, father, mother, and daughter, and myself, and I remember thinking that it was queer how little any of us knew about the man that we were burying. I had a great respect for the Doyle family by that time. They had been overwhelmed when I told them of the small legacy that Mr Macfadden had left them and at first they were genuinely unwilling to take it; they said that they had been well paid for his two rooms and board for many years, and anything else that they had done for him had been because they liked him. It was something, on that bitter January afternoon beside the grave, to feel that he had friends at the last ceremonies.

So that was the end of it, and I drove back with the Doyles and had tea with them in their sitting-room beside the kitchen. And after tea I left for Glasgow and the night train down to London, taking with me two suitcases of papers and small personal effects to be examined at my leisure if the tracing of the heir proved to be troublesome, and later to be handed over as a part of the inheritance.

In fact, he found the heir without much difficulty. Young Harris got a line on it within a week, and presently we got a letter from a Miss Agatha Paget, who was the headmistress of a girls' school in Colwyn Bay. She was a sister of Arthur Paget, who had been killed in the motor accident in Malaya. She confirmed that his wife, Jean, had died in Southampton in the year 1942, and she added the fresh information that the son, Donald, was also dead. He had been a prisoner of war in Malaya, and had died in captivity. Her niece, Jean, however, was alive and in the London district. The headmistress did not know her home address because she lived in rooms and had changed them once or twice, so she usually wrote to her addressing her letters to her firm. She was employed in the office of a concern called Pack and Levy Ltd., whose address was The Hyde, Perivale, London, N.W.

I got this letter in the morning mail; I ran through the others and cleared them out of the way, and then picked up this one and read it again. Then I got my secretary to bring me the Macfadden box and I read the will through again, and went through some other papers and my notes on the estate. Finally I reached out for the telephone directory and looked up Pack and Levy Ltd, to find out what they did.

Presently I got up from my desk and stood for a time looking out of the window at the bleak, grey, January London street. I like to think a bit before taking any precipitate action. Then I turned and went through into Robinson's office; he was dictating, and I stood warming myself at his fire till he had finished and the girl had left the room.

'I've got that Macfadden heir,' I said. 'I'll tell Harris.'

'All right,' he replied. 'You've found the son?'

'No,' I said. 'I've found the daughter. The son's dead.'

He laughed. 'Bad luck. That means we're trustees for the estate until she's thirty-five, doesn't it?'

I nodded.

'How old is she now?'

I calculated for a minute. 'Twenty-six or twenty-seven.'

'Old enough to make a packet of trouble for us.'

'I know.'

'Where is she? What's she doing?'

'She's employed as a clerk or typist with a firm of handbag manufacturers in Perivale,' I said. 'I'm just about to concoct a letter to her.'

He smiled. 'Fairy Godfather.'

'Exactly,' I replied.

I went back into my room and sat for some time thinking out that letter; it seemed to me to be important to set a formal tone when writing to this young woman for the first time. Finally I wrote,

DEAR MADAM,

It is with regret that we have to inform you of the death of Mr Douglas Macfadden at Ayr on January 21st. As Executors to his will we have experienced some difficulty in tracing the beneficiaries, but if you are the daughter of Jean (*nee* Macfadden) and Arthur Paget formerly resident in Southampton and in Malaya, it would appear that you may be entitled to a share in the estate.

May we ask you to telephone for an appointment to call upon us at your convenience to discuss the matter further? It will be necessary for you to produce evidence of identity at an early stage, such as your birth certificate, National Registration Identity Card, and any other documents that may occur to you.

> I am,
> Yours truly,
> for Owen, Dalhousie and Peters,
> N. H. STRACHAN

She rang me up the next day. She had quite a pleasant voice, the voice of a well-trained secretary. She said, 'Mr Strachan, this is Miss Jean Paget speaking. I've got your letter of the 29th. I wonder–do you work on Saturday mornings? I'm in a job, so Saturday would be the best day for me.'

I replied, 'Oh yes, we work on Saturday mornings. What time would be convenient for you?'

'Should we say ten-thirty?'

I made a note upon my pad. 'That's all right. Have you got your birth certificate?'

'Yes, I've got that. Another thing I've got is my mother's marriage certificate, if that helps.'

I said, 'Oh yes, bring that along. All right, Miss Paget, I shall look forward to meeting you on Saturday. Ask for me by name, Mr Noel Strachan. I am the senior partner.'

She was shown into my office punctually at ten-thirty on Saturday. She was a girl or woman of a medium height, dark-haired. She was good-looking in a quiet way; she had a tranquillity about her that I find it difficult to describe except by saying that it was the grace that you see frequently in women of a Scottish descent. She was dressed in a dark blue coat and skirt. I got up and shook hands with her, and gave her the chair in front of my desk, and went round and sat down myself. I had the papers ready.

'Well, Miss Paget,' I said. 'I heard about you from your aunt – I think she is your aunt? Miss Agatha Paget, at Colwyn Bay.'

She inclined her head. 'Aunt Aggie wrote and told me that she had had a letter from you. Yes, she's my aunt.'

'And I take it that you are the daughter of Arthur and Jean Paget, who lived in Southampton and Malaya?'

She nodded. 'That's right. I've got the birth certificate and mother's birth certificate, as well as her marriage certificate.' She took them from her bag and put them on my desk, with her identity card.

I opened these documents and read them through carefully. There was no doubt about it; she was the person I was looking for. I leaned back in my chair presently and took off my spectacles. 'Tell me, Miss Paget,' I said. 'Did you ever meet your uncle, who died recently? Mr Douglas Macfadden?'

She hesitated. 'I've been thinking about that a lot,' she said candidly. 'I couldn't honestly swear that I have ever met him, but I think it must have been him that mother took me to see once in Scotland, when I was about ten years old. We all went together, Mother and I and Donald. I remember an old man in a very stuffy room with a lot of birds in cages. I think that was Uncle Douglas, but I'm not quite sure.'

That fitted in with what he had told me, the visit of his sister with her children in 1932. This girl would have been eleven years old then. 'Tell me about your brother Donald, Miss Paget,' I asked. 'Is he still alive?'

She shook her head. 'He died in 1943, while he was a prisoner. He was taken by the Japs in Singapore when we surrendered, and then he was sent to the railway.'

I was puzzled. 'The railway?'

She looked at me coolly, and I thought I saw tolerance for the ignorance of those who stayed in England in her glance. 'The railway that the Japs built with Asiatic and prisoner-of-war labour between Siam and Burma. One man died for every sleeper that was laid, and it was about two hundred miles long. Donald was one of them.'

There was a little pause. 'I am so sorry,' I said at last. 'One thing I have to ask you, I am afraid. Was there a death certificate?'

She stared at me. 'I shouldn't think so.'

'Oh . . .' I leaned back in my chair and took up the will. 'This is the will of Mr Douglas Macfadden,' I said. 'I have a copy for you, Miss Paget, but I think I'd better tell you what it contains in ordinary, non-legal language. Your uncle made two small bequests. The whole of the residue of the estate was left in trust for your brother Donald. The terms of the trust were to the effect that your mother was to enjoy the income from the trust until her death. If she died before your brother attained his majority, the trust was to continue until he was twenty-one, when he would inherit absolutely and the trust would be discharged. If your brother died before inheriting, then you were to inherit the residuary estate after your mother's time, but in that event the trust was to continue till the year 1956, when you would be thirty-five years old. You will appreciate that it is necessary for us to obtain legal evidence of your brother's death.'

She hesitated, and then she said, 'Mr Strachan, I'm afraid I'm terribly stupid. I understand you want some proof that Donald is dead. But after that is done, do you mean that I inherit everything that Uncle Douglas left?'

'Broadly speaking–yes,' I replied. 'You would only receive the income from the estate until the year 1956. After that, the capital would be yours to do what you like with.'

'How much did he leave?'

I picked up a slip of paper from the documents before me and ran my eye down the figures for a final check. 'After paying death duties and legacies,' I said carefully, 'the residuary estate would be worth about fifty-three thousand pounds at present-day prices. I must make it clear that that is at present-day prices, Miss Paget. You must not assume that you would inherit that sum in 1956. A falling stock market affects even trustee securities.'

She stared at me. 'Fifty-three thousand pounds?'

I nodded. 'That seems to be about the figure.'

'How much a year would that amount of capital yield, Mr Strachan?'

I glanced at the figures on the slip before me. 'Invested in trustee stocks, as at present–about £1550 a year, gross income. Then income tax has to be deducted. You would have about nine hundred a year to spend, Miss Paget.'

'Oh . . .'' There was a long silence; she sat staring at the desk in front of her. Then she looked up at me, and smiled. 'It takes a bit of getting used to,' she remarked. 'I mean, I've always worked for my living, Mr Strachan. I've never thought that I'd do anything else unless I married, and that's only a different sort of work. But this means that I need never work again–unless I want to.'

She had hit the nail on the head with her last sentence. 'That's exactly it,' I replied. 'Unless you want to.'

'I don't know what I'd do if I didn't have to go to the office,' she said. 'I haven't got any other life . . .'

'Then I should go on going to the office,' I observed.

She laughed. 'I suppose that's the only thing to do.'

I leaned back in my chair. 'I'm an old man now, Miss Paget' I've made plenty of mistakes in my time and I've learned one thing from them, that it's never very wise to do anything in a great hurry. I take it that this legacy will mean a considerable change in your circumstances. If I may offer my advice, I should continue in your present employment for the time, at any rate, and I should refrain from talking about your legacy in the office just yet. For one thing, it will be some months before you get possession even of the income from the estate. First we have to obtain legal proof of the death of your brother, and then we have to obtain the confirmation of the executors in Scotland and realize a portion of the securities to meet estate and succession duties. Tell me, what are you doing with this firm Pack and Levy?'

'I'm a shorthand typist,' she said. 'I'm working now as secretary to Mr Pack.'

'Where do you live, Miss Paget?'

She said, 'I've got a bed-sitting-room at No. 43 Campion Road, just off Ealing Common. It's quite convenient, but of course I have a lot of my meals out. There's a Lyons just round the corner.'

I thought for a minute. 'Have you got many friends in Ealing? How long have you been there?'

'I don't know very many people,' she replied. 'One or two families, people who work in the firm, you know. I've been there over two years now, ever since I was repatriated. I was out in Malaya, you know, Mr Strachan, and I was a sort of prisoner of war for three and a half years. Then when I got home I got this job with Pack and Levy.'

I made a note of her address upon my pad. 'Well, Miss Paget,' I said, 'I should go on just as usual for the time being. I will consult the War Office on Monday morning and obtain this evidence about your brother as quickly as I can. Tell me his name, and number, and unit.' She did so, and I wrote them down. 'As soon as I get that, I shall submit the will for probate. When that is proved, then the trust commences and continues till the year 1956, when you will inherit absolutely.'

She looked up at me. 'Tell me about this trust,' she asked. 'I'm afraid I'm not very very good at legal matters.'

I nodded. 'Of course not. Well, you'll find it all in legal language in the copy of the will which I shall give you, but what it means is this, Miss Paget. Your uncle, when he made this will, had a very poor opinion of the ability of women to manage their own money. I'm sorry to have to say such a thing, but it is better for you to know the whole of the facts.'

She laughed. 'Please don't apologize for him, Mr Strachan. Go on.'

'At first, he was quite unwilling that you should inherit the capital of the estate till you were forty years old,' I said. 'I contested that view, but I was unable to get him to agree to any less period than the present arrangement in the will. Now, the object of a trust is this. The testator appoints trustees—in this case, myself and my partner—who undertake to do their best to preserve the capital intact and hand it over to the legatee—to you—when the trust expires.'

'I see. Uncle Douglas was afraid that I might spend the fifty-three thousand all at once.'

I nodded. 'That was in his mind. He did not know you, of course, Miss Paget, so there was nothing personal about it. He felt that in general women were less fit than men to handle large sums of money at an early age.'

She said quietly, 'He may have been right.' She thought for a minute, and then she said, 'So you're going to look after the money for me till I'm thirty-five and give me the interest to spend in the meantime? Nine hundred a year?'

'If you wish us to conduct your income-tax affairs for you, that would be about the figure,' I said. 'We can arrange the payments in any way that you prefer, as a quarterly or a monthly cheque, for example. You would get a formal statement of account half-yearly.'

She asked curiously, 'How do you get paid for doing all this for me, Mr Strachan?'

I smiled. 'That is a very prudent question, Miss Paget. You will find a clause in the will, No. 8, I think which entitles us to charge for our professional services against the income from the trust. Of course, if you get into any legal trouble we should be glad to act for you and help you in any way we could. In that case we should charge you on the normal scale of fees.'

She said unexpectedly, 'I couldn't ask for anybody better.' And then she glanced at me, and said mischievously, 'I made some enquiries about this firm yesterday.'

'Oh . . . I hope they were satisfactory?'

'Very.' She did not tell me then what she told me later, that her informant had described us as, "as solid as the Bank of England, and as sticky as treacle". 'I know I'm going to be in very good hands, Mr Strachan.'

I inclined my head. 'I hope so. I am afraid that at times you may find this trust irksome, Miss Paget; I can assure you that I shall do my utmost to prevent it from becoming so. You will see in the will that the testator gave certain powers to the trustees to realize capital for the benefit of the legatee in cases where they were satisfied that it would be genuinely for her advantage.'

'You mean, if I really needed a lot of money–for an operation or something–you could let me have it, if you approved?'

She was quick, that girl. 'I think that is a very good example. In case of illness, if the income were insufficient, I should certainly realize some of your capital for your benefit.'

She smiled at me, and said, 'It's rather like being a ward in Chancery, or something.'

I was a little touched by the comparison. I said, 'I should feel very much honoured if you care to look at it that way, Miss Paget. Inevitably this legacy is going to make an upset in your condition of life, and if I can do anything to help you in the transition I should be only too pleased.' I handed her her copy of the will. 'Well, there is the will, and I suggest you take it away and read it quietly by yourself. I'll keep the certificates for the time being. After you've thought things over for a day or two I am sure that there will be a great many questions to which you will want answers. Would you like to come and see me again?'

She said, 'I would. I know there'll be all sorts of things I want to ask about, but I can't think of them now. It's all so sudden.'

I turned to my engagement diary. 'Well, suppose we meet again about the middle of next week.' I stared at the pages. 'Of course, you're working. What time do you get off from your office, Miss Paget?'

She said, 'Five o'clock.'

'Would six o'clock on Wednesday evening suit you, then? I shall hope to have got somewhere with the matter of your brother by that time.'

She said, 'Well, that's all right for me, Mr Strachan, but isn't it a bit late for you? Don't you want to get home?'

I said absently, 'I only go to the club. No, Wednesday at six would suit me very well.' I made a note upon my pad, and then I hesitated. 'Perhaps if you are doing nothing after that you might like to come on to the club and have dinner in the Ladies Annexe,' I said. 'I'm afraid it's not a very gay place, but the food is good.'

She smiled, and said warmly, 'I'd love to do that, Mr Strachan. It's very kind of you to ask me.'

I got to my feet. 'Very well, then, Miss Paget–six o'clock on Wednesday. And in the meantime, don't do anything in a great hurry. It never pays to be impetuous . . .''

She went away, and I cleared my desk and took a taxi to the club for lunch. After lunch I had a cup of coffee and slept for ten minutes in a chair before the fire, and when I woke up I thought I ought to get some exercise. So I put on my hat and coat and went out and walked rather aimlessly up St James's Street and along Piccadilly to the Park. As I walked, I wondered how that fresh young woman was spending her weekend. Was she telling her friends all about her good luck, or was she sitting somewhere warm and quiet, nursing and cherishing her own anticipations, or was she on a spending spree already? Or was she out with a young man? She would have plenty of men now to choose from, I thought cynically, and then it struck me that she probably had those already because she was a very marriageable girl. Indeed, considering her appearance and her evident good nature, I was rather surprised that she was not married already.

I had a little talk that evening in the club with a man who is in the Home Office about the procedure for establishing the death of a prisoner of war, and on Monday I had a number of telephone conversations with the War Office and the Home Office about the case. I found, as I had suspected, that there was an extraordinary procedure for proving death which could be invoked, but where a doctor was available who had attended the deceased in the prison camp the normal certification of death was the procedure to adopt. In this instance there was a general practitioner called Ferris in practice at Beckenham who had been a doctor in Camp 206 in the Takunan district on the Burma-Siam railway, and the official at the War Office advised me that this doctor would be in a position to give the normal death certificate.

I rang him up next morning, and he was out upon his rounds. I tried to make his wife understand what I wanted but I think it was too complicated for her; she suggested that I should call and see him after the evening surgery, at half past six. I hesitated over that because Beckenham is a good long way out, but I was anxious to get these formalities over quickly for the sake of the girl. So I went out to see this doctor that evening.

He was a cheerful, fresh-faced man not more than thirty-five years old; he had a keen sense of humour, if rather a macabre one at times. He looked as healthy and fit as if he had spent the whole of his life in England in a country practice. I got to him just as he was finishing off the last of his patients, and he had leisure to talk for a little.

'Lieutenant Paget,' he said thoughtfully. 'Oh yes, I know. Donald Paget—was his name Donald?' I said it was. 'Oh, of course, I remember him quite well. Yes, I can write a death certificate. I'd like to do that for him, though I don't suppose it'll do him much good.'

'It will help his sister,' I remarked. 'There is a question of an inheritance, and the shorter we can make the necessary formalities the better for her.'

He reached for his pad of forms. 'I wonder if she's got as much guts as her brother.'

'Was he a good chap?'

He nodded. 'Yes,' he said. 'He was a delicate-looking man, dark and rather pale, you know, but he was a very good type. I think he was a planter in civil life—anyway, he was in the Malay volunteers. He spoke Malay very well, and he got along in Siamese all right. With those languages, of course, he was a very useful man to have in the camp. We used to do a lot of black market with the villagers, the Siamese outside, you know. But quite apart from that, he was the sort of officer the men like. It was a great loss when he went.'

'What did he die of?' I asked.

He paused with his pen poised over the paper. 'Well, you could take your pick of half a dozen things. I hadn't time to do a post mortem, of course. Between you and me, I don't really know. I think he just died. But he'd recovered from enough to kill a dozen ordinary men, so I don't know that it really matters what one puts down on the certificate. No legal point depends upon the cause of death, does it?'

'Oh, no,' I said. 'All I want is the death certified.'

He still paused, in recollection. 'He had a huge tropical ulcer on his left leg that we were treating, and that was certainly poisoning the whole system. I think if he'd gone on we'd have had to have taken that leg off. He got that because he was one of those chaps who won't report sick while they can walk.

Well, while he was in hospital with the ulcer, he got cerebral malaria. We had nothing to treat that damn thing with till we got around to making our own quinine solutions for intravenous injection; we took a frightful risk with that, but there was nothing else to do. We got a lot through it with that, and Paget was one of them. He got over it quite well. That was just before we got the cholera. Cholera went right through the camp – hospital and everything. We couldn't isolate the cases, or anything like that. I never want to see a show like that again. We'd got nothing, *nothing*, not even saline. No drugs to speak of, and no equipment. We were making bed-pans out of old kerosene tins. Paget got that, and would you believe it, he got over cholera. We got some prophylactic injections from the Nips and we gave him those; that may have helped. At least, I think we gave him that – I'm not sure. He was very weak when that left him, of course, and the ulcer wasn't any too good. And about a week after that, he just died in the night. Heart, I fancy. I'll tell you what I'll do. I'll put down for Cause of Death – Cholera. There you are, sir. I'm sorry you had to come all this way for it.'

As I took the certificate I asked curiously, 'Did you get any of those things yourself?'

He laughed. 'I was one of the lucky ones. All I got was the usual dysentery and malaria, the ordinary type malaria, not cerebral. Overwork was *my* trouble, but other people had that, too. We were in such a jam, for so long. We had hundreds of cases just lying on the floor or bamboo charpoys in palm huts – it was raining almost all the time. No beds, no linen, no equipment, and precious few drugs. You just couldn't rest. You worked till you dropped asleep, and then you got up and went on working. You never came to an end. There was never half an hour when you could slack off and sit and have a smoke, or go for a walk, except by neglecting some poor sod who needed you very badly.'

He paused. I sat silent, thinking how easy by comparison my own war had been. 'It went on like that for nearly two years,' he said. 'You got a bit depressed at times, because you couldn't even take time off to go and hear a lecture.'

'Did you have lectures?' I asked.

'Oh yes, we used to have a lot of lectures by the chaps in camp. How to grow Cox's Orange Pippins, or the TT motorcycle races, or Life in Hollywood. They made a difference to the men, the lectures did. But we doctors usually couldn't get to them. I mean, it's not much of an alibi when someone's in convulsions if you're listening to a lecture on Cox's Orange Pippins at the other end of the camp.'

I said, 'It must have been a terrible experience.'

He paused, reflecting. 'It was so beautiful,' he said. 'The Three Pagodas Pass must be one of the loveliest places in the world. You've got this broad valley with the river running down it, and the jungle forest, and the mountains . . . We used to sit by the river and watch the sun setting behind the mountains, sometimes, and say what a marvellous place it would be to come to for a holiday. However terrible a prison camp may be, it makes a difference if it's beautiful.'

When Jean Paget came to see me on Wednesday evening I was ready to report the progress I had made. First I went through one or two formal matters connected with the winding up of the estate, and then I showed her the schedule of the furniture that I had put in store at Ayr. She was not much interested in that. 'I should think it had all better be sold, hadn't it?' she remarked. 'Could we put it in an auction?'

'Perhaps it would be as well to wait a little before doing that,' I suggested. 'You may want to set up a house or a flat of your own.'

She wrinkled up her nose. 'I can't see myself wanting to furnish it with any of Uncle Douglas's stuff, if I did,' she said.

However, she agreed not to do anything about that till her own plans were more definite, and we turned to other matters. 'I've got your brother's death certificate,' I said, and I was going on to tell her what I had done with it when she stopped me.

'What did Donald die of, Mr Strachan?' she asked.

I hesitated for a moment. I did not want to tell so young a woman the unpleasant story I had heard from Dr Ferris. 'The cause of death was cholera,' I said at last.

She nodded, as if she had been expecting that. 'Poor old boy,' she said softly. 'Not a very nice way to die.'

I felt that I must say something to alleviate her distress. 'I had a long talk with the doctor who attended him,' I told her. 'He died quite peacefully, in his sleep.'

She stared at me. 'Well then, it wasn't cholera,' she said. 'That's not the way you die of cholera.'

I was a little at a loss in my endeavour to spare her unnecessary pain. 'He had cholera first, but he recovered. The actual cause of death was probably heart failure, induced by the cholera.'

She considered this for a minute. 'Did he have anything else?' she asked.

Well, then of course there was nothing for it but to tell her everything I knew. I was amazed at the matter-of-fact way in which she took the unpleasant details and at her knowledge of the treatment of such things as tropical ulcers, until I recollected that this girl had been a prisoner of the Japanese in Malaya, too. 'Damn bad luck the ulcer didn't go a bit quicker,' she said coolly.. 'If there'd been an amputation they'd have had to evacuate him from the railway, and then he wouldn't have got the cerebral malaria or the cholera.'

'He must have had a wonderfully strong constitution to have survived so much,' I said.

'He hadn't,' she said positively. 'Donald was always getting coughs and colds and things. What he *had* got was a wonderfully strong sense of humour. I always thought he'd come through, just because of that. Everything that happened to him was a joke.'

When I was a young man, girls didn't know about cholera or great ulcers, and I didn't quite know how to deal with her. I turned the conversation back to legal matters, where I was on firmer ground, and showed her how her case for probate was progressing. And presently I took her downstairs and we got a taxi and went over to the club to dine.

I had a reason for entertaining her, that first evening. It was obvious that I was going to have a good deal to do with this young woman in the next few years, and I wanted to find out about her. I knew practically nothing of her education or her background at that time; her knowledge of tropical diseases, for example, had already confused me. I wanted to give her a good dinner with a little wine and get her talking; it was going to make my job as trustee a great deal easier if I knew what her interests were, and how her mind worked. And so I took her to the Ladies Annexe at my club, a decent place where we could dine in our own time without music and talk quietly for a little time after dinner. I find that I get tired if there is a lot of noise and bustling about, as in a restaurant.

I showed her where she could go to wash and tidy up, and while she was doing that I ordered her a sherry. I got up from the table in the drawing-room when she came to me, and gave her a cigarette, and lit it for her. 'What did you do over the weekend?' I asked as we sat down. 'Did you go out and celebrate?'

She shook her head. 'I didn't do anything very much. I'd arranged to meet one of the girls in the office for lunch on Saturday and to go and see the new Bette Davis film at the Curzon, so we did that.'

'Did you tell her about your good fortune?'

She shook her head. 'I haven't told anybody.' She paused, and sipped her sherry; she was managing that and her cigarette quite nicely. 'It seems such an improbable story,' she said, laughing. 'I don't know that I really believe in it myself.'

I smiled with her. 'Nothing is real till it happens,' I observed. 'You'll believe that this is true when we send you the first cheque. It would be a great mistake to believe in it too hard before that happens.'

'I don't,' she laughed. 'Except for one thing. I don't believe you'd be wasting so much time on my affairs unless there was something in it.'

'It's true enough for that.' I paused, and then I said, 'Have you thought yet what you are going to do in a month or two when the income from the trust begins? Your monthly cheque, after the tax has been deducted, will be about seventy-five pounds. I take it that you will hardly wish to go on with your present employment when those cheques begin to come in?'

'No . . .' She sat staring for a minute at the smoke rising from her cigarette. 'I don't want to stop working. I wouldn't mind a bit going on with Pack and Levy just as if nothing had happened, if it was a job worth doing,' she said. 'But–well, it's not. We make ladies' shoes and handbags, Mr Strachan, and small ornamental attaché cases for the high-class trade–the sort that sells for thirty guineas in a Bond Street shop to stupid women with more money than sense. Fitted vanity cases in rare leathers, and all that sort of thing. It's all right if you've got to earn your living, working in that sort of place. And it's been interesting, too, learning all about that trade.'

'Most jobs are interesting when you are learning them,' I said.

She turned to me. 'That's true. I've quite enjoyed my time there. But I couldn't go on now, with all this money. One ought to do something more worth while, but I don't know what.' She drank a little sherry. 'I've got no profession, you see–only shorthand and typing, and a bit of book-keeping. I never had any real education–technical education, I mean. Taking a degree, or anything like that.'

I thought for a moment. 'May I ask a very personal question, Miss Paget?'

'Of course.'

'Do you think it likely that you will marry in the near future?'

She smiled. 'No, Mr Strachan, I don't think it's very likely that I shall marry at all. One can't say for certain, of course, but I don't think so.'

I nodded without comment. 'Well then, had you thought about taking a university course?'

Her eyes opened wide. 'No–I hadn't thought of that. I couldn't do it, Mr Strachan–I'm not clever enough. I couldn't get into a university.' She paused.

'I was never higher than the middle of my class at school, and I never got into the Sixth.'

'It was just a thought,' I said. 'I wondered if that might attract you.'

She shook her head. 'I couldn't go back to school again now. I'm much too old.'

I smiled at her. 'Not quite such an old woman as all that,' I observed.

For some reason the little compliment fell flat. 'When I compare myself with some of the girls in the office,' she said quietly, and there was no laughter in her now, 'I know I'm about seventy.'

I was finding out something about her now, but to ease the situation I suggested that we should go into dinner. When the ordering was done, I said, 'Tell me what happened to you in the war. You were out in Malaya, weren't you?'

She nodded. 'I had a job in an office, with the Kuala Perak Plantation Company. That was the company my father worked for, you know. Donald was with them, too.'

'What happened to you in the war?' I asked. 'Were you a prisoner?'

'A sort of prisoner,' she said.

'In a camp?'

'No,' she replied. 'They left us pretty free.' And then she changed the conversation very positively, and said, 'What happened to you, Mr Strachan? Were you in London all the time?'

I could not press her to talk about her war experiences if she didn't want to, and so I told her about mine—such as they were. And from that, presently, I found myself telling her about my two sons, Harry on the China station and Martin in Basra, and their war records, and their families and children. 'I'm a grandfather three times over,' I said ruefully. 'There's going to be a fourth soon, I believe.'

She laughed. 'What does it feel like?'

'Just like it did before,' I told her. 'You don't feel any different as you get older. Only, you can't do so much.'

Presently I got the conversation back on to her own affairs. I pointed out to her what sort of life she would be able to lead upon nine hundred a year. As an instance, I told her that she could have a country cottage in Devonshire and a little car, and a daily maid, and still have money to spare for a moderate amount of foreign travel. 'I wouldn't know what to do with myself unless I worked at something,' she said. 'I've always worked at something, all my life.'

I knew of several charitable appeals who would have found a first-class shorthand typist, unpaid, a perfect god-send, and I told her so. She was inclinded to be critical about those. 'Surely if a thing is really worth while, it'll pay,' she said. She evidently had quite a strong business instinct latent in her. 'It wouldn't need to have an unpaid secretary.'

'Charitable organizations like to keep the overheads down,' I remarked.

'I shouldn't have thought organizations that haven't got enough margin to pay a secretary can possibly do very much good,' she said. 'If I'm going to work at anything, I want it to be something really worth while.'

I told her about the almoner's job at a hospital, and she was very much interested in that. 'That's much more like it, Mr Strachan,' she said. 'I think that's the sort of job one might get stuck into and take really seriously. But I wish it hadn't got to do with sick people. Either you've got a mission for sick people or you haven't, and I think I'm one of the ones who hasn't. But it's worth thinking about.'

'Well, you can take your time,' I said. 'You don't have to do anything in a hurry.'

She laughed at me. 'I believe that's your guiding rule in life–never do anything in a hurry.'

I smiled. 'You might have a worse rule than that.'

With the coffee after dinner I tried her out on the Arts. She knew nothing about music, except that she liked listening to the radio while she sewed. She knew nothing about literature, except that she liked novels with a happy ending. She liked paintings that were a reproduction of something that she knew, but she had never been to the Academy. She knew nothing whatsoever about sculpture. For a young woman with nine hundred a year, in London, she knew little of the arts and graces of social life, which seemed to me to be a pity.

'Would you like to come to the opera one night?' I asked.

She smiled. 'Would I understand it?'

'Oh yes. I'll look and see what's on. I'll pick something light, and in English.'

She said, 'It's terribly nice of you to ask me, but I'm sure you'd be much happier playing bridge.'

'Not a bit,' I said. 'I haven't been to the opera or anything like that for years.'

She smiled. 'Well, of course I'd love to come,' she said. 'I've never seen an opera in my life. I don't even know what happens.'

We sat talking about these things for an hour or more, till it was half-past nine and she got up to go; she had three-quarters of an hour to travel out to her suburban lodgings. I went with her, because she was going from St James's Park station, and I didn't care about the thought of so young a woman walking across the park alone late at night. At the station, standing on the dark, wet pavement by the brightly lit canopy, she put out her hand.

'Thank you so much, Mr Strachan, for the dinner, and for everything you're doing for me,' she said.

'It has been a very great pleasure to me, Miss Paget,' I replied, and I meant it.

She hesitated, and then she said, smiling, 'Mr Strachan, we're going to have a good deal to do with each other. My name is Jean. I'll go crackers if you keep on calling me Miss Paget.'

'You can't teach an old dog new tricks,' I said awkwardly.

She laughed. 'You said just now you don't feel any different as you get older. You can try and learn.'

'I'll bear it in mind,' I said. 'Sure you can manage all right now?'

'Of course. Goodnight, Mr Strachan.'

'Goodnight,' I said, lifting my hat and dodging the issue. 'I'll let you know about the opera.'

In the following weeks while probate was being granted I took her to a good many things. We went together to the opera several times, to the Albert Hall on Sunday afternoons, and to art galleries and exhibitions of paintings. In return, she took me to the cinema once or twice. I cannot really say that she developed any very great artistic appreciation. She liked paintings more than concerts. If it had to be music she preferred it in the form of opera and the lighter the better; she liked to have something to look at while her ears were assailed. We went twice to Kew Garden as the spring came on. In the course of these excursions she came several times to my flat in Buckingham Gate; she got to know the kitchen, and made tea once or twice when we came in from some outing together. I had never entertained a lady in that flat before except my daughters-in-law, who sometimes come and use my spare room for a night or two in London.

Her business was concluded in March, and I was able to send her her first cheque. She did not give up her job at once, but continued to go to the office as usual. She wanted, very wisely, to build up a small reserve of capital from her monthly cheques before starting to live on them; moreover, at that time she had not made up her mind what she wanted to do.

That was the position one Sunday in April. I had arranged a little jaunt for her that day; she was to come to lunch at the flat and after that we were going down to Hampton Court, which she had never seen. I thought that the old palace and the spring flowers would please her, and I had been looking forward to this trip for several days. And then, of course, it rained.

She came to the flat just before lunch, dripping in her dark blue raincoat, carrying a very wet umbrella. I took the coat from her and hung it up in the kitchen. She went into my spare room and tidied herself; then she came to me in the lounge and we stood watching the rain beat against the Palace stables opposite, wondering what we should do instead that afternoon.

We had not got that settled when we sat down to coffee before the fire after lunch. I had mentioned one or two things but she seemed to be thinking about other matters. Over the coffee it came out, and she said,

'I've made up my mind what I want to do first of all, Mr Strachan.'

'Oh?' I asked. 'What's that?'

She hesitated. 'I know you're going to think this very odd. You may think it very foolish of me, to go spending money in this way. But – well, it's what I want to do. I think perhaps I'd better tell you about it now, before we go out.'

It was warm and comfortable before the fire. Outside the sky was dark, and the rain streamed down on the wet pavements.

'Of course, Jean,' I replied. I don't suppose it's foolish at all. What is it that you want to do?'

She said, 'I want to go back to Malaya, Mr Strachan. To dig a well.'

2

I suppose there was a long pause after she said that. I remember being completely taken aback, and seeking refuge in my habit of saying nothing when you don't know what to say. She must have felt reproof in my silence, I suppose, because she leaned towards me, and she said, 'I know it's a funny thing to want to do. May I tell you about it?'

I said, 'Of course. Is this something to do with your experiences in the war?'

She nodded. 'I've never told you about that. It's not that I mind talking about it, but I hardly ever think about it now. It all seems so remote, as if it was something that happened to another person, years ago – something that you'd read in a book. As if it wasn't me at all.'

'Isn't it better to leave it so?'

She shook her head. 'Not now, now that I've got this money.' She paused. 'You've been so very kind to me,' she said. 'I do want to try and make you understand.'

Her life, she said, had fallen into three parts, the first two so separate from the rest that she could hardly reconcile them with her present self. First, she had been a schoolgirl living with her mother in Southampton. They lived in a small, three-bedroomed house in a suburban street. There had been a period before that when they had all lived in Malaya, but they had left Malaya for good when she was eleven and her brother Donald was fourteen, and she had only confused memories of that earlier time. Apparently Arthur Paget had been living alone in Malaya when he met his death, his wife having brought the children home.

They lived the life of normal suburban English children, school and holidays passing in a gentle rhythm with the one great annual excitement of three weeks holiday in August in the Isle of Wight, at Seaview or at Freshwater. One thing differentiated them slightly from other families, in that they all spoke Malay. The children had learned it from the amah, of course, and their mother encouraged them to continue talking it in England, first as a joke and as a secret family language, but later for a very definite reason. When Arthur Paget drove his car into the tree near Ipoh he was travelling on the business of his company, and his widow became entitled to a pension under the company scheme. He had been a competent and a valuable man. The directors of the Kuala Perak Plantation Company, linking compassion with their quest for first-class staff, wrote to the widow offering to keep a position for the boy Donald as soon as he became nineteen. This was a good opening and one that they all welcomed; it meant that Donald was headed for Malaya and for rubber-planting as a career. The Malay language became a matter of importance in giving him a good start, for very few boys of nineteen going to the East for their first job can speak an Oriental language. That shrewd Scotswoman, their mother, saw to it that the children did not forget Malay.

Jean had liked Southampton well enough, and she had had a happy childhood there in a gentle orbit of home, school, the Regal cinema, and the ice-skating rink. Of all these influences the one that she remembered best was the ice rink, connected in her mind inevitably with Waldteufel's Skaters Waltz. 'It was a lovely place,' she said, staring reminiscently into the fire. 'I suppose it wasn't much, really—it was a wooden building, I think, converted out of something that had been put up in the first war. We skated there about twice a week ever since I can remember, and it was always lovely. The music, and the clean, swift movement, and all the boys and girls. The coloured lights, the crowd, and the ring of skates. I got quite good at it. Mummy got me a costume—black tights and bodice, and a little short skirt, you know. Dancing was wonderful upon the ice . . .'

She turned to me. 'You know, out in Malaya, when we were dying of malaria and dysentery, shivering with fever in the rain, with no clothes and no food and nowhere to go, because no one wanted us, I used to think about the rink at Southampton more than anything. It was a sort of symbol of the life that used to be—something to hold on to in one's mind.' She paused. 'Directly I got back to England I went back to Southampton, as soon as I could—I had something or other to do down there, but really it was because all through those years I had promised myself that one day I would go back and skate there again. And it had been blitzed. It was just a blackened and a burnt-out shell–there's no rink in Southampton now. I stood there on the pavement with the taxi waiting behind me with my boots and skates in my hand, and I couldn't keep from crying with the disappointment. I don't know what the taxi-driver thought of me.'

Her brother had gone out to Malaya in 1937 when Jean was sixteen. She left school at the age of seventeen and went to a commercial college in Southampton, and emerged from it six months later with a diploma as a shorthand typist. She worked then for about a year in a solicitor's office in the town, but during this year a future for her in Malaya was taking shape. Her mother had kept in contact with the chairman of the Kuala Perak Plantation Company, and the chairman was very satisfied with the reports he had of Donald from the plantation manager. Unmarried girls were never very plentiful in Malaya, and when Mrs Paget approached the chairman with a proposal that he should find a job for Jean in the head office at Kuala Lumpur it was considered seriously. It was deemed undesirable by the Company that their manager should marry or contract liaisons with native women, and the obvious way to prevent it was to encourage unmarried girls to come out from England. Here was a girl who was not only of a family that they knew but who could also speak Malay, a rare accomplishment in a shorthand typist from England. So Jean got her job.

The war broke out while all this was in train, and to begin with, in England, this war was a phoney war. There seemed no reason to upset Jean's career for such a trivial matter; moreover in Mrs Paget's view Jean was much better in Malaya if war was to flare up in England. So Jean left for Malaya in the winter of 1939.

For over eighteen months she had a marvellous time. Her office was just round the corner from the Secretariat. The Secretariat is a huge building built in the more spacious days to demonstrate the power of the British Raj; it forms one side of a square facing the Club across the cricket ground, with a perfect example of an English village church to one side. Here everybody lived a very English life with tropical amenities; plenty of leisure, plenty of games, plenty of parties, plenty of dances, all made smooth and easy by plenty of servants. Jean boarded with one of the managers of the Company for the first few weeks; later she got a room in the Tudor Rose, a small private hotel run by an Englishwoman which was, in fact, more or less a chummery for unmarried girls employed in the offices and the Secretariat.

'It was just too good to be true, she said. 'There was a dance or a party every single night of the week. One had to cry off doing something in order to find time to write a letter home.'

When war came with Japan it hardly registered with her as any real danger, nor with any of her set. December the 7th, 1941, brought America into the war and so was a good thing; it meant nothing to the parties in Kuala Lumpur except that young men began to take leave from their work and to appear in uniform, itself a pleasurable excitement. Even when the Japanese landed in the north of Malaya there was little thought of danger in Kuala Lumpur; three hundred miles of mountain and jungle was itself a barrier against invasion from the north. The sinking of the *Prince of Wales* and the *Repulse* was a catastrophe that didn't mean a thing to a girl of nineteen who had just rejected her first proposal.

Soon the married women and the children were evacuated to Singapore, in theory at any rate. As the Japanese made headway down the peninsula with swift encirclements through the jungle that no troops had ever penetrated before, the situation began to appear serious. There came a morning when Jean's chief, a Mr Merriman, called her into the office and told her bluntly that the office was closing down. She was to pack a suitcase and go to the station and take the first train down to Singapore. He gave her the name of their representative at an address off Raffles Place, and told her to report there for a passage home. Five other girls employed in the office got the same orders.

The Japanese at that time were reported to be near Ipoh, about a hundred miles to the north.

The serious nature of the position was obvious to everyone by then. Jean went to the bank and drew out all her money, about six hundred Straits dollars. She did not go to the station, however; if she had, it is doubtful whether she would have been able to get down to Singapore because the line by that time was completely blocked with military traffic coming up to the Front. She might have got away by road. Instead of that, she went to Batu Tasik to see Mrs Holland.

Batu Tasik is a place about twenty miles north-west of Kuala Lumpur, and Mr Holland was a man of forty, the manager of an opencast tin mine. He lived in quite a pleasant bungalow beside the mine with his wife Eileen and their three children, Freddie aged seven, Jane aged four, and Robin, who was ten months old. Eileen Holland was a comfortable, motherly woman between thirty and thirty-five years old. The Hollands never went to parties or to dances; they were not that sort. They stayed quietly at home and let the world go by them. They had invited Jean to come and stay with them soon after she arrived, and she had found their company restful. She had been to see them several times after that, and once, when she had had a slight attack of dengue, she had spent a week with them recuperating. In Kuala Lumpur on the previous day she had heard that Mr Holland had brought his family into the station but had been unable to get them on the train, so they had all gone home again. Jean felt she could not leave without seeing the Hollands and offering her help with the children; Eileen Holland was a good mother and a first-rate housewife, but singularly unfitted to travel by herself with three children in the turmoil of evacuation.

Jean got to Batu Tasik fairly easily in a native bus; she arrived about lunch-time and she found Mrs Holland alone with the children. All trucks and cars belonging to the mine had been taken by the army, and the Hollands were left with their old Austin Twelve with one tyre worn down to the canvas and one very doubtful one with a large blister on the wall. This was the only vehicle that they now had for their evacuation, and it didn't look too good for taking the family to Singapore. Mr Holland had gone into Kuala Lumpur to get two new outer covers; he had gone in at dawn and Mrs Holland was already in a state of flutter that he had not come back.

In the bungalow everything was in confusion. The amah had gone home or had been given notice, and the house was full of suitcases half packed, or packed and opened again. Freddie had been in the pond and was all muddy, Jane was sitting on her pot amongst the suitcases, crying, and Mrs Holland was nursing the baby and directing the cooking of lunch and attending to Jane and worrying about her husband all at the same time. Jean turned to and cleaned up Freddie and attended to Jane, and presently they all had lunch together.

Bill Holland did not come till nearly sunset, and he came empty-handed. All tyre stocks in Kuala Lumpur had been commandeered. He found out, however, that a native bus was leaving for Singapore at eight in the morning, and he had reserved seats for his family on that. He had had to walk the last five miles for lack of any other transport, and walking five miles down a tarmac road in the middle of the afternoon in the heat of the tropics is no joke; he was soaked to the skin and with a raging thirst, and utterly exhausted.

It would have been better if they had started for Kuala Lumpur that night, but they didn't. All movement on the roads at night was prohibited by the military, and to start out in the Austin in the dark would have been to risk a burst of fire from trigger-happy sentries. They decided to leave at dawn, which would give plenty of time to get to Kuala Lumpur before eight. Jean stayed the night with them in the bungalow, wakeful and uneasy. Once in the middle of the night she heard Bill Holland get up and go out into the veranda; peering out through her mosquito net she could see him standing motionless against the stars. She climbed out from under the net and slipped on her kimono; in Malaya one sleeps with very little on. She walked along the veranda to him. 'What is it?' she whispered.

'Nothing,' he said. 'Just thought I heard something, that's all.'

'Someone in the compound?'

'No—not that.'

'What?'

'I thought I heard guns firing, very far away,' he said. 'Must have been fancy.' They stood tense and listening against the great noise of the crickets and the frogs. 'God,' he said presently, 'I wish it was dawn.'

They went back to bed. That night the Japanese advanced patrols infiltrated behind our forces lining the Bidor and penetrated as far as Slim River, less than fifty miles away.

They were all up before dawn and loading up the Austin with the first grey light; with three adults and three children and the luggage for all of them the Austin was well loaded down. Mr Holland paid the boys off and they started down the road for Kuala Lumpur, but before they had gone two miles the tyre that was showing canvas burst. There was a strained pause then while they worked to put the spare on, the one with the blister on the wall; this took them for another half mile only before going flat. In desperation Mr Holland went on on the rim; the wire wheel collapsed after another two miles, and the Austin had run to its end. They were then about fifteen miles from Kuala Lumpur, and it was half past seven.

Mr Holland left them with the car and hurried down the road to a plantation bungalow about a mile away; there was no transport there, and the manager had left the day before. He came back disappointed and anxious, to find the children fretful and his wife only concerned to get back to their bungalow. In the circumstances it seemed the best thing to do. Each of the adults took one child, and carrying or leading it they set out to walk the five miles home again, leaving the luggage in the car, which they locked.

They reached home in the first heat of the day, utterly exhausted. After cold drinks from the refrigerator they all lay down for a little to recover. An hour later they were roused by a truck stopping at the bungalow; a young officer came hurrying into the house.

'You've got to leave this place,' he said. 'I'll take you in the truck. How many of you are there?'

Jean said, 'Six, counting the children. Can you take us into Kuala Lumpur? Our car broke down.'

The officer laughed shortly. 'No I can't. The Japs are at Kerling, or they were when I last heard. They may be further south by now.' Kerling was only twenty miles away. 'I'm taking you to Panong. You'll get a boat from there to get you down to Singapore.' He refused to take the truck back for their luggage, probably rightly; it was already loaded with a number of families who had messed up their evacuation, and the Austin was five miles in the direction of the enemy.

Kuala means the mouth of a river, and Kuala Panong is a small town at the entrance to the Panong River. There is a District Commissioner stationed there. By the time the truck reached his office it was loaded with about forty men, women, and children picked up for forcible evacuation from the surrounding estates. Most of these were Englishwomen of relatively humble birth, the wives of foremen engineers at the tin mines or gangers on the railway. Few of them had been able to appreciate the swiftness and the danger of the Japanese advance. Plantation managers and those in the Secretariat and other Government positions had had better sources of information and more money to spend, and these had got their families away to Singapore in good time. Those who were left to be picked up by truck at the last moment were the least competent.

The truck halted at the D.C.'s office and the subaltern went inside; the D.C. came out presently, a very worried man, and looked at the crowded women and children, and the few men amongst them. 'Christ,' he said quietly as he realized the extent of the new responsibility. 'Well, drive them to the accounts office over there; they must sit in the veranda for an hour or two and I'll try and get something fixed up for them. Tell them not to wander about too much.' He turned back into the office. 'I can send them down in fishing-boats, I think,' he said. 'There are some of those left. That's the best I can do. I haven't got a launch.'

The party were unloaded on to the veranda of the accounts office, and here they were able to stretch and sort themselves out a little. There were chatties of cold water in the office and the veranda was shady and cool. Jean and Bill Holland left Eileen sitting on the veranda with her back against the wall with the children about her, and walked into the village to buy what they could to replace the luggage they had lost. They were able to get a feeding-bottle for the baby, a little quinine, some salts for dysentery, and two tins of biscuits and three of tinned meat; they tried for mosquito nets, but they were all sold out. Jean got herself a few needles and thread, and seeing a large canvas haversack she bought that, too. She carried that haversack for the next three years.

They went back to the veranda about teatime and displayed their purchases, and had a little meal of biscuits and lemon squash.

Towards sunset the lighthouse-keepers at the river mouth telephoned to the D.C. that the *Osprey* was coming into the river. The *Osprey* was the customs launch that ran up and down the coast looking for smugglers from Sumatra across the Malacca Strait; she was a large Diesel-engined vessel about a hundred and thirty feet long, normally stationed at Penang; a powerful, seagoing ship. The D.C.'s face lit up; here was the solution to his problems. Whatever was the mission of the *Osprey* she must take his evacuees on board, and run them down the coast out of harm's way. Presently he left his office, and walked down to the quay to meet the vessel as she berthed, to interview the captain.

She came round the bend in the river, and he saw that she was loaded with troops, small stocky men in grey-green uniforms with rifles and fixed bayonets taller than themselves. With a sick heart he watched her as she came alongside, realizing that this was the end of all his endeavour.

The Japanese came rushing ashore and arrested him immediately, and walked him back up the jetty to his office with guns at his back, ready to shoot him at the slightest show of resistance. But there were no troops there to resist; even the officer with the truck had driven off in an attempt to join his unit. The soldiers spread out and occupied the place without a shot; they came to the evacuees sitting numbly in the veranda of the accounts office. Immediately, with rifles and bayonets levelled, they were ordered to give up all fountain-pens and wristwatches and rings. Advised by their men folk, the women did so silently, and suffered no other molestation. Jean lost her watch and had her bag searched for a fountain-pen, but she had packed it in her luggage.

An officer came presently, when night had fallen, and inspected the crowd on the veranda in the light of a hurricane lamp; he walked down the veranda thrusting his lamp forward at each group, a couple of soldiers hard on his heels with rifles at the ready and bayonets fixed. Most of the children started crying. The inspection finished, he made a little speech in broken English. 'Now you are prisoners,' he said. 'You stay here tonight. Tomorrow you go to prisoner camp perhaps. You do good things, obedience to orders, you will receive good from Japanese soldiers. You do bad things, you will be shot directly. So, do good things always. When officer come, you stand up and bow, always. That is good thing. Now you sleep.'

One of the men asked, 'May we have beds and mosquito nets?'

'Japanese soldiers have no beds, no mosquito nets. Perhaps tomorrow you have beds and nets.'

Another said, 'Can we have some supper?' This had to be explained. 'Food.'

'Tomorrow you have food.' The officer walked away, leaving two sentries on guard at each end of the veranda.

Kuala Panong lies in a marshy district of mangrove swamps at the entrance to a muddy river; the mosquitoes are intense. All night the children moaned and wailed fretfully, preventing what sleep might have been possible for the adults. The night passed slowly, wearily on the hard floor of the veranda; between the crushing misery of captivity and defeat and the torment of the mosquitoes few of the prisoners slept at all. Jean dozed a little in the early hours and woke stiff and aching and with swollen face and arms as a fresh outburst from the children heralded the more intense attack from the mosquitoes that comes in the hour before the dawn. When the first light came the prisoners were in a very unhappy state.

There was a latrine behind the accounts office, inadequate for the numbers that had to use it. They made the best of that, and there was nothing then to do but to sit and wait for what would happen. Holland and Eileen made sandwiches for the children of tinned meat and sweet biscuits, and after this small breakfast they felt better. Many of the others had some small supplies of food, and those that had none were fed by those who had. Nothing was provided for the prisoners that morning by the Japanese.

In the middle of the morning an interrogation began. The prisoners were taken by families to the D.C.'s office, where a Japanese captain, whom Jean was to know later as Captain Yoniata, sat with a lieutenant at his side, who made notes in a child's penny exercise book. Jean went in with the Hollands; when the captain enquired who she was she explained that she was a friend of the family travelling with them, and told him what her job was in Kuala Lumpur. It did not take very long. At the end the captain said, 'Men go to prisoner camp today, womans and childs stay here. Men leave in afternoon, so you will now say farewell till this afternoon. Thank you.'

They had feared this, and had discussed it in the veranda, but they had not expected it would come so soon. Holland asked, 'May we know where the women and children will be sent to? Where will their camp be?'

The officer said, 'The Imperial Japanese Army do not make war on womans and on childs. Perhaps not go to camp at all, if they do good things, perhaps live in homes. Japanese soldiers always kind to womans and to childs.'

They went back to the veranda and discussed the position with the other families. There was nothing to be done about it, for it is usual in war for men to be interned in separate camps from women and children, but none the less it was hard to bear. Jean felt her presence was unwanted with the Holland family, and went and sat alone on the edge of the veranda, feeling hungry and wondering, with gloom tempered by the buoyancy of youth, what lay ahead of her. One thing was certain; if they were to spend another night upon the veranda she must get hold of some mosquito repellent. There was a chemist's shop just up the village that they had visited the afternoon before; it was probable that in such a district he had some repellent.

As an experiment she attracted the attention of the sentry and pointed to her mosquito bites; then she pointed to the village and got down from the veranda on to the ground. Immediately he brought his bayonet to the ready and advanced towards her; she got back on to the veranda in a hurry. That evidently wouldn't do. He scowled at her suspiciously, and went back to his position.

There was another way. The latrine was behind the building up against a wall; there was no sentry there because the wall prevented any exit from the accounts office except by going round the building to the front. She moved after a time and went out of the back door. Sheltered from the view of the sentries by the building, she looked around. There were some children playing in the middle distance.

She called softly in Malay, 'Girl. You, you girl. Come here.'

The child came towards her; she was about twelve years old. Jean asked, 'What is your name?'

She giggled shyly, 'Halijah.'

Jean said, 'Do you know the shop that sells medicine? Where a Chinese sells medicine?'

She nodded. 'Chan Kok Fuan.'

Jean said, 'Go to Chan Kok Fuan, and if you give my message to him so that he comes to me, I will give you ten cents. Say that the Mem has Nyamok bites'–she showed her bites–'and he should bring ointments to the veranda, and he will sell many to the Mems. Do this, and if he comes with ointments I will give you ten cents.'

The child nodded and went off. Jean went back to the veranda and waited; presently the Chinaman appeared carrying a tray loaded with little tubes and pots. He approached the sentry and spoke to him, indicating his wish to sell his wares; after some hesitation the sentry agreed. Jean got six tubes of repellent and the rest was swiftly taken by the other women. Halijah got ten cents.

Presently a Japanese orderly brought two buckets of a thin fish soup and another half full of boiled rice, dirty and unappetizing. There were no bowls or utensils to eat with. There was nothing to be done but to eat as best they could; at that time they had not fallen into the prisoner's mode of life in which all food is strictly shared out and divided scrupulously, so that some got much more than others, who got little or none. There were still food supplies, however, so they fell back on the biscuits and the private stocks to supplement the ration.

That afternoon the men were separated from their families, and marched off under guard. Bill Holland turned from his fat, motherly wife, his eyes moist. 'Goodbye, Jean,' he said heavily. 'Good luck.' And then he said, 'Stick with them, if you can, won't you?'

She nodded. 'I'll do that. We'll all be in the same camp together.'

The men were formed up together, seven of them, and marched off under guard.

The party then consisted of eleven married women, and two girls, Jean and an anaemic girl called Ellen Forbes who had been living with one of the families; she had come out to be married, but it hadn't worked out. Besides these there were nineteen children varying in age from a girl of fourteen to babies in arms; thirty-two persons in all. Most of the women could speak no language but their own; a few of them, including Eileen Holland, could speak enough Malay to control their servants, but no more.

They stayed in the accounts office for forty-one days.

The second night was similar to the first, except that the doors of the offices were opened for them and they were allowed to use the rooms. A second meal of fish soup was given to them in the evening, but nothing else whatever was provided for their use—no beds, no blankets, and no nets. Some of the women had their luggage with them and had blankets, but there were far too few to go round. A stern-faced woman, Mrs Horsefall, asked to see the officer; when Captain Yoniata came she protested at the conditions and asked for beds and nets.

'No nets, no beds,' he said. 'Very sorry for you. Japanese womans sleep on mat on floor. All Japanese sleep on mat. You put away proud thoughts, very bad thing. You sleep on mat like Japanese womans.'

'But we're English,' she said indignantly. 'We don't sleep on the floor like animals!'

His eyes hardened; he motioned to the sentries, who gripped her by each arm. Then he hit her four stinging blows upon the face with the flat of his hand. 'Very bad thoughts,' he said, and turned upon his heel, and left them. No more was said about beds.

He came to inspect them the next morning and Mrs Horsefall, undaunted, asked for a water supply; she pointed out that washing was necessary for the babies and desirable for everyone. A barrel was brought into the smallest office that afternoon and was kept filled by coolies; they turned this room into a bathroom and washhouse. In those early days most of the women had money, and following the example of Chan Kok Fuan the shopkeepers of the village came to sell to the prisoners, so they accumulated the bare essentials for existence.

Gradually they grew accustomed to their hardships. The children quickly learned to sleep upon the floor without complaint; the younger women took a good deal longer, and the women over thirty seldom slept for more than half an hour without waking in pain–but they did sleep. It was explained to them by Captain Yoniata that until the campaign was over the victorious Japanese had no time to construct prison camps for women. When all Malaya had been conquered they would be moved into a commodious and beautiful camp which would be built for them in the Cameron Highlands, a noted health resort up in the hills. There they would find beds and mosquito nets and all the amenities to which they were accustomed, but to earn these delights they must stay where they were and do good things. Doing good things meant getting up and bowing whenever he approached. After a few faces had been slapped and shins had been kicked by Captain Yoniata's army boots, they learned to do this good thing.

The food issued to them was the bare minimum that would support life, and was an unvarying issue of fish soup and rice, given to them twice a day. Complaint was useless and even dangerous; in the view of Captain Yoniata these were proud thoughts that had to be checked for the moral good of the complainant. Meals, however, could be supplied by a small Chinese restaurant in the village, and while money was available most of the families ordered one cooked meal a day from this restaurant.

They received no medical attention and no drugs whatsoever. At the end of a week dysentery attacked them, and the nights were made hideous by screaming children stumbling with their mothers to the latrine. Malaria was always in the background, held in check by the quinine that they could still buy from Chan Kok Fuan at an ever increasing price. To check the dysentery Captain Yoniata reduced the soup and increased the rice ration, adding to the rice some of the dried, putrescent fish that had formerly made the soup. Later, he added to the diet a bucket of tea in the afternoon, as a concession to English manners.

Through all this time, Jean shared with Mrs Holland the care of the three Holland children. She suffered a great deal from weakness and a feeling of lassitude induced, no doubt, by the change in diet, but she slept soundly most nights until wakened, which was frequently. Eileen Holland suffered much more. She was older, and could not sleep so readily upon the floor, and she had lost much of the resilience of her youth. She lost weight rapidly.

On the thirty-fifth day, Esmé Harrison died.

Esmé was a child of eight. She had had dysentery for some time and was growing very thin and weak; she slept little and cried a great deal. Presently she got fever, and for two days ran a temperature of a hundred and four as the malaria rose in her. Mrs Horsefall told Captain Yoniata that the child must see a doctor and go to hospital. He said he was very sorry, but there was no hospital. He would try and get a doctor, but the doctors were all fighting with the victorious army of the Emperor. That evening Esmé entered on a series of convulsions, and shortly before dawn she died.

She was buried that morning in the Moslem cemetery behind the village; her mother and one other woman were allowed to attend the burial. They read a little of the service out of a prayer book before the uncomprehending soldiers and Malays, and then it was over. Life went on as before in the accounts office, but the children now had nightmares of death to follow them to sleep.

At the end of six weeks Captain Yoniata faced them after the morning inspection. The women stood worn and draggled in the shade of the veranda facing him, holding the children by the hand. Many of the adults, and most of the children, by that time were thin and ill.

He said, 'Ladies, the Imperial Japanese Army has entered Singapore, and all Malaya is free. Now prisoner camps are being built for men and also for womans and childs. Prisoner camps are at Singapore and you go there. I am very sad your life here has been uncomfortable, but now will be better. Tomorrow you start to Kuala Lumpur, not more than you can go each day. From Kuala Lumpur you go by train to Singapore, I think. In Singapore you will be very happy. Thank you.'

From Panong to Kuala Lumpur is forty-seven miles; it took a minute for his meaning to sink in. Then Mrs Horsefall said, 'How are we to travel to Kuala Lumpur? Will there be a truck?'

He said, 'Very sorry, no truck. You walk, easy journeys, not more than you can go each day. Japanese soldier help you.'

She said, 'We can't walk, with these children. We *must* have a truck.'

These were bad thoughts, and his eyes hardened. 'You walk,' he repeated.

'But what are we to do with all the luggage?'

He said, 'You carry what you can. Presently the luggage is sent after you.' He turned, and went away.

For the remainder of the day they sat in stunned desperation; those who had luggage sorted hopelessly through their things, trying to make packs that would hold the essentials and yet which would not be too heavy. Mrs Horsefall, who had been a schoolmistress in her time and had assumed the position of leader, moved among them, helping and advising. She had one child herself, a boy of ten called John; her own position was better than most, for it was possible for a woman to carry the necessities for one boy of that age. The position of the mothers with several younger children was bad indeed.

Jean and Mrs Holland had less of a problem, for having lost their luggage they had less to start with and the problem of selection did not arise. They had few clothes to change into, and what they had could easily go into Jean's haversack. They had acquired two blankets and three food bowls between them, and three spoons, and a knife and fork; they decided to make a bundle of these small possessions in the blankets, and they had a piece of cord to tie the bundle with and to make a sling, so that one could carry the haversack and one the bundle. Their biggest problem was their shoes, which had once been fashionable and were quite unsuitable for marching in.

Towards evening, when the children had left them and they were alone with the baby in a corner, Mrs Holland said quietly, 'My dear, I shan't give up, but I don't think I can walk very far. I've been so poorly lately.'

Jean said, 'It'll be all right,' although deep in her mind she knew that it was not going to be all right at all. 'You're much fitter than some of the others,' and this possibly was true. 'We'll have to take it very slowly, because of the children. We'll take several days over it.'

'I know, my dear. But where are we going to stay at night? What *are* they going to do about that?'

Nobody had an answer to that one.

Rice came to them soon after dawn, and at about eight o'clock Captain Yoniata appeared with four soldiers, who were to be their guard upon the journey. 'Today you walk to Ayer Penchis,' he said. 'Fine day, easy journey. Good dinner when you get to Ayer Penchis. You will be very happy.'

Jean asked Mrs Horsefall, 'How far is Ayer Penchis?'

'Twelve or fifteen miles, I should think. Some of us will never get that far.'

Jean said, 'We'd better do what the soldiers do, have a rest every hour. Hadn't we?'

'If they'll let us.'

It took an hour to get the last child out of the latrine and get the women ready for the march. The guards squatted on their heels; it was a small matter to them when the march started. Finally Captain Yoniata appeared again, his eyes hard and angry. 'You walk now,' he said. 'Womans remaining here are beaten, beaten very bad. You do good thing and be happy. Walk now.'

There was nothing for it but to start. They formed into a little group and walked down the tarmac road in the hot sun, seeking the shade of trees wherever they occurred. Jean walked with Mrs Holland carrying the bundle of blankets slung across her shoulders as the hottest and the heaviest load, and leading the four-year-old Jane by the hand. Seven-year-old Freddie walked beside his mother, who carried the baby, Robin, and the haversack. Ahead of them strolled the Japanese sergeant; behind came the three privates.

The women went very slowly, with frequent halts as a mother and child retired into the bushes by the roadside. There was no question of walking continuously for an hour and then resting; the dysentery saw to that. For those who were not afflicted at the moment the journey became one of endless, wearisome waits by the roadside in the hot sun, for the sergeant refused to allow the party to move on while any remained behind. Within the limits of their duty the Japanese soldiers were humane and helpful; before many hours had passed each was carrying a child.

Slowly the day wore on. The sergeant made it very clear at an early stage that there would be no food and no shelter for the party till they got to Ayer Penchis, and it seemed to be a matter of indifference to him how long they took to get there. They seldom covered more than a mile and a half in the hour, on that first day. As the day went on they all began to suffer from their feet, the older women especially. Their shoes were quite unsuitable for walking long distances, and the heat of the tarmac swelled their feet, so that before long many of them were limping with foot pains. Some of the children went barefoot and got along very well. Jean watched them for a time, then stooped and took her own shoes off, savouring the unaccustomed road surface gingerly with her bare feet. She walked on carrying her shoes, picking her way with her eyes upon the ground, and her feet ceased to pain her though from time to time the tarmac grits hurt her soft soles. She got along better barefoot, but Eileen Holland refused to try it.

They stumbled into Ayer Penchis at about six o'clock that evening, shortly before dark. This place was a Malay village which housed the labour for a number of rubber plantations in the vicinity. The latex-processing plant of one stood near at hand and by it was a sort of palm thatch barn, used normally for smoking sheets of the raw rubber hung on horizontal laths. It was empty now and the women were herded into this. They sank down wearily in a stupor of fatigue; presently the soldiers brought a bucket of tea and a bucket of rice and dried fish. Most of them drank cup after cup of the tea, but few had any appetite for the food.

With the last of the light Jean strolled outside and looked around. The guards were busy cooking over a small fire; she approached the sergeant and asked if she might go into the village. He understood that, and nodded; away from Captain Yoniata discipline was lax.

In the village she found one or two small shops, selling clothes, sweets, cigarettes, and fruit. She saw mangoes for sale, and bought a dozen, chaffering over the price with the Malay woman to conserve her slender cash. She ate one at once and felt better for it; at Kuala Panong they had eaten little fruit. She went back to the barn and found that the soldiers had provided one small lamp with an open wick fed by coconut oil.

She distributed her mangoes to Eileen and the Holland children and to others, and found they were a great success. Armed with money from the women she went down to the village again and got four dozen more, and presently all the women and children were in mango up to their ears. The soldiers came in with another bucket of tea and got a mango each for their pains, and so refreshed the women were able to eat most of the rice. Presently, they slept, exhausted, weak, and ill.

The barn was full of rats, which ran over them and round them all night through. In the morning it was found that several of the children had been bitten.

They woke aching in new places with the stiffness and fatigue of the day before; it did not seem possible that they could march again. The sergeant drove them on; this time the stage was to a place called Asahan. It was a shorter stage than the day before, about ten miles, and it had need to be, because they took as long getting to it. This time the delay was chiefly due to Mrs Collard. She was a heavy woman of about forty-five with two children, Harry and Ben, aged about ten and seven. She had suffered from both malaria and dysentery at Panong, and she was now very weak; she had to stop and rest every ten minutes, and when she stopped they all stopped since the sergeant would not allow them to separate. She was relieved of all load and the younger women took turns to walk by her and help her along.

By the afternoon she had visibly changed colour; her somewhat ruddy face had now gone a mottled blue, and she was complaining constantly of pains in her chest. When they finally reached Asahan she was practically incapable of walking alone. Their accommodation was another rubber-curing barn. They half carried Mrs Collard into it and sat her up against the wall, for she said that lying down hurt her, and she could not breathe. Somebody went to fetch some water, and bathed her face, and she said, 'Thank you, dearie. Give some of that to Harry and Ben, there's a dear.' The woman took the children outside to wash them, and when she came back Mrs Collard had fallen over on her side, and was unconscious. Half an hour later she died.

That evening Jean got more fruit for them, mangoes and bananas, and some sweets for the children. The Malay woman who supplied the sweets refused to take money for them. 'No, mem,' she said. 'It is bad that Nippon soldiers treat you so. This is our gift.' Jean went back to the barn and told the others what had happened, and it helped.

In the flickering light of the cooking fire outside the barn Mrs Horsefall and

Jean held a conference with the sergeant, who spoke only a very few words of English. They illustrated their meaning with pantomime. 'Not walk tomorrow,' they said. 'No. Not walk. Rest–sleep–tomorrow. Walk tomorrow, more women die. Rest tomorrow. Walk one day, rest one day.'

They could not make out if he understood or not. 'Tomorrow,' he said, 'woman in earth.'

It would be necessary to bury Mrs Collard in the morning. This would prevent an early start, and would make a ten-mile stage almost impossible. They seized upon this as an excuse. 'Tomorrow bury woman in earth,' they said. 'Stay here tomorrow.'

They had to leave it so, uncertain whether he understood or not; he squatted down on his heels before the fire with the three privates. Later he came to Jean, his face alight with intelligence. 'Walk one day, sleep one day,' he said. 'Womans not die.' He nodded vigorously and she called Mrs Horsefall, and they all nodded vigorously together, beaming with good nature. They were all so pleased with each other and with the diplomatic victory that they gave him a banana as a token of esteem.

All that day Jean had walked barefoot; she had stubbed her toes two or three times and had broken her toenails; but she felt fresher that evening than she had felt for a long time. The effect of the march upon the women began to show itself that night in very different forms, according to their age. The women under thirty, and the children, were in most cases actually in better condition than when they left Panong; they were cheered by the easier discipline, and stimulated by the exercise and by the improvement in the diet brought by fruit and sweets. The older women were in much worse case. For them exhaustion outweighed these benefits; they lay or sat listlessly in the darkness, plagued by their children and too tired to eat. In many cases they were too tired even to sleep.

In the morning they buried Mrs Collard. There was no burial ground at hand but the Malay headman showed them where they could dig the grave, in a corner of the compound, near a rubbish heap. The sergeant got two coolies and they dug a shallow grave; they lowered Mrs Collard into it covered by a blanket, and Mrs Horsefall read a little out of the Prayer Book. Then they took away the blanket because they could not spare that, and the earth was filled in. Jean found a carpenter who nailed a little wooden cross together for them, and refused payment; he was a Moslem or perhaps merely an animist, but he knew what the Tuans did for a Christian burial. They wrote JULIA COLLARD on it and the date of death with an indelible pencil, hoping it would survive the rain, and then they had a long discussion over the text to put underneath it. This interested every woman in the party, and kept them happy and mentally stimulated for half an hour. Mrs Holland, rather surprisingly, suggested Romans, xiv, 4; "Who art thou that judgest another man's servant? to his own master he standeth or falleth", meaning the sergeant who had made them march that day. But the other women did not care for that, and finally they compromised on "Peace, perfect peace, with loved ones far away". That pleased everybody.

They sat around and washed their clothes after the burial was over. Soap was getting very scarce amongst them, but so was money. Mrs Horsefall held a sort of meeting after rice and examined the money situation; half the women had no money left at all, and the rest had only about fifteen dollars between them. She suggested pooling this, but the mothers who had money left preferred to keep it for their own children; as there was so little in any case it did not seem worth while to worry them by making an issue of it. They all agreed, however, to share rations equally, and after that their feeding times were much better organized.

Captain Yoniata turned up about midday, driving into Kuala Lumpur in the District Commissioner's car. He stopped and got out, angry to find that they were not upon the road. He abused the sergeant for some minutes in Japanese; the man stood stiffly to attention, not saying a word in explanation or defence. Then he turned to the women. 'Why you not walk?' he demanded angrily. 'Very bad thing. You not walk, no food.'

Mrs Horsefall faced him. 'Mrs Collard died last night. We buried her this morning over there. If you make us walk every day like this, we shall all die. These women aren't fit to march at all. You know that.'

'What woman die of?' he inquired. 'What illness?'

'She had dysentery and malaria, as most of us have had. She died of exhaustion after yesterday's march. You'd better come inside and look at Mrs Frith and Judy Thomson. They couldn't possibly have marched today.'

He walked into the barn, and stood looking at two or three women sitting listless in the semi-darkness. Then he said something to the sergeant and walked back to his car. At the door he turned to Mrs Horsefall. 'Very sad woman die,' he said. 'Perhaps I get a truck in Kuala Lumpur. I will ask.' He got into the car and drove away.

His words went round the women quickly; he had gone to get a truck for them, and they would finish the journey to Kuala Lumpur by truck; there would be no more marching. Things weren't so bad, after all. They would be sent by rail from Kuala Lumpur to Singapore, and there they would be put into a proper camp with other Englishwomen, where they could settle down and organize their lives properly, and get into a routine that would enable them to look after the children. A prison camp would have a doctor, too, and there was always some kind of a hospital for those who were really ill. They became much more cheerful, and the most listless ones revived, and came out and washed and made themselves a little more presentable. Their appearance was a great concern to them that afternoon. Kuala Lumpur was their shopping town where people knew them; they must get tidy before the truck came for them.

Captain Yoniata appeared again about an hour before sunset; again he spoke to the sergeant, who saluted. Then he turned to the women. 'You not go to Kuala Lumpur,' he said. 'You go to Port Swettenham. English destroy bridges, so railway to Singapore no good. You go to Port Swettenham now, and then ship to Singapore.'

There was a stunned silence. Then Mrs Horsefall asked, 'Is there going to be a truck to take us to Port Swettenham?'

He said, 'Very sorry no truck. You walk slow, easy stages. Two days, three days, you walk to Port Swettenham. Then ship take you to Singapore.'

From Asahan to Port Swettenham is about thirty miles. She said, 'Captain Yoniata, please be reasonable. Many of us are quite unfit to walk any further. Can't you get some transport for the children, anyway?'

He said, 'Englishwomans have proud thoughts, always. Too good to walk like Japanese womans. Tomorrow you walk to Bakri.' He got into his car and went away; that was the last they ever saw of him.

Bakri is eleven miles in the general direction of Port Swettenham. The change in programme was the deepest disappointment to them, the more so as it showed irresolution in their destiny. Mrs Holland said despairingly, 'I don't see why he shouldn't have known at Panong that the bridges were down, and not sent us to Kuala Lumpur at all. It makes one wonder if there's going to be a ship when we get to Port Swettenham. . . .''

There was nothing for it, and next morning they started on the road again. They found that two of the privates had been taken away, and one remained to guard them, with the sergeant. This was of no consequence to their security because they had no desire to attempt to escape, but it reduced by half the help the guards had given them in carrying the younger children, so that it threw an extra burden on the mothers.

That day for the first time Jean carried the baby, Robin: Mrs Holland was walking so badly that she had to be relieved. She still carried the haversack and looked after Freddie, but Jean carried the bundle of blankets and small articles, and the baby, and led Jane by the hand. She went barefoot as before; after some experiments she found that the easiest way to carry the baby was to perch him on her hip, as the Malay women did.

The baby, curiously, gave them the least anxiety of any of the children. They fed it on rice and gravy from the fish soup or stew, and it did well. Once in the six weeks it had seemed to be developing dysentery and they had given it a tiny dose or two of Glauber's salt, and it recovered. Mosquitoes never seemed to worry it, and it had not had fever. The other children were less fortunate. Both had had dysentery from time to time, and though they seemed now to be free of it they had gone very thin.

They slept that night in the bungalow that had belonged to the manager of the Bakri tin mine, an Englishman. In the seven or eight weeks since he had abandoned it it had been occupied by troops of both sides and looted by the Malays; now little remained of it but the bare walls. Marvellously, however, the bath was still in order though filthily dirty, and there was a store of cut wood for the furnace that heated water. The sergeant, true to his promise, allowed them a day of rest here, and they made the most of the hot water for washing their clothes and themselves. With the small improvement in conditions their spirits revived.

'I should think there'd be hot water on the ship,' said Mrs Holland. 'There usually is, isn't there?'

They marched again next day to a place called Dilit; this was mostly a day spent marching down cart tracks in the rubber plantations. The tracks were mostly in the shade of the trees and this made it pleasant for them, and even the older women found the day bearable. They had some difficulty in finding the way. The sergeant spoke little Malay and had difficulty in understanding the Malay women latex-tappers that he asked for directions from time to time. Jean found that she could understand the answers that the women gave, and could converse with them, but having got the directions they required she had some difficulty in making the sergeant understand. They reached an agreement by the end of the day that she should talk to the women, who talked to her less shyly in any case, and she developed a sign language which the sergeant understood. From that time onwards Jean was largely responsible for finding the shortest way for the party to go.

In the middle of the afternoon Ben Collard, the younger son of Mrs Collard who had died, trod on something while walking barefoot in the grass that bit him with poison fangs and got away. He said afterwards that it looked like a big beetle; possibly it was a scorpion. Mrs Horsefall took charge and laid him on the ground and sucked the wound to draw the poison from it, but the foot swelled quickly and the inflammation travelled up the leg to the knee. It was obviously painful and he cried a great deal. There was nothing to be done but carry him, and this was no easy matter for the women in their feeble condition because he was a boy of seven and weighed five stone. Mrs Horsefall carried him for an hour and after that the sergeant took him and carried him the rest of the way. By the time they got to Dilit the ankle was enormous and the knee was stiff.

At Dilit there was no accommodation for them and no food. The place was a typical Malay village, the houses built of wood and palm thatch raised about four feet from the ground on posts, leaving a space beneath where dogs slept and fowls nested. They stood or sat wearily while the sergeant negotiated with the Malay headman: very soon he called for Jean, and she joined the tri-lingual discussion. The village had rice and could prepare a meal for them, but the headman wanted payment, and was only with difficulty induced to agree to provide rice for so many on the word of the sergeant that they would be paid some day. As regards accommodation he said flatly that there was none, and the party must sleep under the houses with the dogs and poultry; later he agreed to move the people from one house, so that the thirty prisoners had a roof to sleep under on a floor about fifteen feet square.

Jean secured a corner for their party, and Eileen Holland settled into it with the children and the baby. A few feet from them Mrs Horsefall was working on Ben Collard. Somebody had some permanganate crystals and someone else an old razor blade; with this they cut the wound open a little, in spite of the child's screams, and put in crystals and bound it up; then they applied hot fomentations. There was nothing Jean could do, and she wandered outside.

There was a sort of village kitchen, and here the Japanese private was superintending the activities of women of the village who were preparing rice. At a house nearby the headman was sitting at the head of the steps leading up to his house, squatting on his heels and smoking a long pipe: he was a grey-haired old man wearing a sarong and what once had been a khaki drill jacket. Jean crossed to him and said rather shyly in Malay, 'I am sorry we have been forced to come here, and have made trouble for you.'

He stood up and bowed to the Mem. 'It is no trouble,' he said. 'We are sorry to see Mems in such a state. Have you come far?'

She said, 'From Bakri today.'

He made her come up into the house: there was no chair and she sat with him on the floor at the doorless entrance. He asked their history, and she told him what had happened, and he grunted. Presently the wife came from within the house bearing two cups of coffee without sugar or milk; Jean thanked her in Malay, and she smiled shyly, and withdrew into the house again.

Presently the headman said, 'The Short One'—he meant the Japanese sergeant—'says you must stay here tomorrow.'

Jean said, 'We are too weak to march each day. The Japanese allow us to rest a day between each day of marching. If we may stay here tomorrow it will help us a great deal. The sergeant says he can get money for the food.'

'The Short Ones never pay for food,' the headman said. 'Nevertheless you shall stay.'

She said, 'I can do nothing but thank you.'

He raised his grey old head. 'It is written in the Fourth Surah, "Men's souls are naturally inclined to covetousness; but if ye be kind towards women and fear to wrong them, God is well acquainted with what ye do".'

She sat with the old man till rice was ready; then she left him and went to her meal. The other women looked at her curiously. 'I saw you sitting with the headman, chatting away,' said one. 'Just as if you were old chums.'

Jean smiled. 'He gave me a cup of coffee.'

'Just fancy that! There's something in knowing how to talk to them in their own language, isn't there? What did he talk about?'

Jean thought for a minute. 'This and that–about our journey. He talked about God a little.'

The women stared at her. 'You mean, his own God? Not the real God?'

'He didn't differentiate,' Jean said. 'Just God.'

They rested all next day and then marched to Klang, three or four miles outside Port Swettenham. Little Ben Collard was neither better nor worse: the leg was very much swollen. The chief trouble with him now was physical weakness: he had eaten nothing since the injury for nothing would stay down, and none of the children by that time had any reserves of strength. The headman directed the villagers to make a litter for him in the form of a stretcher of two long bamboo poles with spreaders and a woven palm mat between and they put him upon this and took turns at carrying it.

They got to Klang that afternoon, and here there was an empty schoolhouse: the sergeant put them into this and went off to a Japanese encampment near at hand, to report and to arrange rations for them.

Presently an officer arrived to inspect them, marching at the head of a guard of six soldiers. This officer, whom they came to know as Major Nemu, spoke good English. He said, 'Who are you people? What do you want here?'

They stared at him. Mrs Horsefall said, 'We are prisoners, from Panong. We are on our way to the prisoner-of-war camp in Singapore. Captain Yoniata in Panong sent us here under guard, to be put on a ship to Singapore.'

'There are no ships here,' he said. 'You should have stayed in Panong.'

It was no good arguing, nor had they the energy. 'We were sent here,' she repeated dully.

'They had no right to send you here,' he said angrily. 'There is no prison camp here.'

There was a long, awkward silence: the women stared at him in blank despair. Mrs Horsefall summoned up her flagging energy again. 'May we see a doctor?' she asked. 'Some of us are very ill–one child especially. One woman died upon the way.'

'What did she die of?' he asked quickly. 'Plague?'

'Nothing infectious. She died of exhaustion.'

'I will send a doctor to examine you all. You will stay here for tonight, but you cannot stay for long. I have not got sufficient rations for my own command, let alone feeding prisoners.' He turned and walked back to the camp.

A new guard was placed upon the schoolhouse: they never saw the friendly sergeant or the private again. Presumably they were sent back to Panong. A Japanese doctor, very young, came to them within an hour; he had them all up one by one and examined them for infectious disease. Then he was about to take his departure, but they made him stay and look at little Ben Collard's leg. He ordered them to continue with the hot fomentations. When they asked if he could not be taken into hospital he shrugged his shoulders and said, 'I inquire.'

They stayed in that schoolhouse under guard, day after day. On the third day they sent for the doctor again, for Ben Collard was obviously worse. Reluctantly the doctor ordered his removal to the hospital in a truck. On the sixth day they heard that he had died.

Jean Paget crouched down on the floor beside the fire in my sitting-room; outside a change of wind had brought the London rain beating against the window.

'People who spent the war in prison camps have written a lot of books about what a bad time they had,' she said quietly, staring into the embers. 'They don't know what it was like, not being in a camp.'

3

They stayed in Klang eleven days, not knowing what was to become of them. The food was bad and insufficient, and there were no shops in the vicinity: if there had been shops they could not have done much with them, because their money was now practically gone. On the twelfth day Major Nemu paraded them at half an hour's notice, allocated one corporal to look after them, and told them to walk to Port Dickson. He said that there might be a ship there to take them down to Singapore; if there was not they would be walking in the general direction of the prison camps.

That was about the middle of March 1942. From Klang to Port Dickson is about fifty miles, but by this time they were travelling more slowly than ever. It took them till the end of the month; they had to wait several days in one village because Mrs Horsefall went down with malaria and ran a temperature of a hundred and five for some time. She recovered and was walking, or rather tottering, within a week, but she never recovered her vigour and from that time onwards the leadership fell more and more upon Jean's shoulders.

By the time they reached Port Dickson their clothes were in a deplorable condition. Very few of the women had a change of any sort, because burdens had been reduced to an absolute minimum. Jean and Mrs Holland had nothing but the thin cotton frocks that they had worn since they were taken; these were now torn and ragged from washing. Jean had gone barefoot since the early stages of the march and intended to go on without shoes: she now took another step towards the costume of the Malay woman. She sold a little brooch for thirteen dollars to an Indian jeweller in Salak, and with two of the precious dollars she bought a cheap sarong.

A sarong is a skirt made of a tube of cloth about three feet in diameter; you get into it and wrap it round your waist like a towel, the surplus material falling into pleats that permit free movement. When you sleep you undo the roll around your waist and it then lies over you as a loose covering that you cannot roll out of. It is the lightest and coolest of all garments for the tropics, and the most practical, being simple to make and to wash. For a top, she cut down her cotton frock into a sort of tunic which got rid of the most tattered part, the skirt, and from that time she was cooler and more at ease than any of them. At first the other women strongly disapproved of this descent to native dress: later most of them followed her example as their clothes became worn out.

There was no haven for them at Port Dickson, and no ship. They were allowed to stay there, living under desultory guard in a copra barn, for about ten days; the Japanese commander then decided that they were a nuisance, and put them on the road to Seremban. He reasoned, apparently, that they were not his prisoners and so not his responsibility; it was the duty of those who had captured them to put them into camp. His obvious course was to get rid of them and get them out of his area before, by their continued presence, they forced him to divert food and troops and medical supplies from the Imperial Japanese Army to sustain them.

At Siliau, between Port Dickson and Seremban, tragedy touched the Holland family, because Jane died. They had stayed for their day of rest in a rubber-smoking shed: she had developed fever during the day's march and one of the two Japanese guards they had at that time had carried her for much of the day. Their thermometer had been broken in an accident a few days before and they had now no means of telling the temperature of malaria patients, but she was very hot. They had a little quinine left and tried to give it to her, but they could not get her to take much of it till she grew too weak to resist, and then it was too late. They persuaded the Japanese sergeant to allow them to stay at Siliau rather than to risk moving the child, and Jean and Eileen Holland stayed up with her, sleepless, fighting for her life in that dim, smelly place where the rats scurried round at night and hens walked in and out by day. On the evening of the second day she died.

Mrs Holland stood it far better than Jean had expected that she would. 'It's God's will, my dear,' she said quietly, 'and He'll give her Daddy strength to bear it when he hears, just as He's giving us all strength to bear our trials now.' She stood dry-eyed beside the little grave, and helped to make the little wooden cross. Dry-eyed she picked the text for the cross: 'Suffer little children to come unto Me'. She said quietly, 'I think her Daddy would like that one.'

Jean woke that night in the darkness, and heard her weeping.

Through all this the baby, Robin, throve. It was entirely fortuitous that he ate and drank nothing but food that had been recently boiled; living on rice and soup, that happened automatically, but may have explained his relative freedom from stomach disorders. Jean carried him every day, and her own health was definitely better than when they had left Panong. She had had five days of fever at Klang, but dysentery had not troubled her for some time, and she was eating well. With the continual exposure to the sun she was getting very brown, and the baby that she carried on her hip got browner.

Seremban lies on the railway, and they had hoped that when they got there there would be a train down to Singapore. They got to Seremban about the middle of April, but there was no train for them; the railway was running in a limited fashion but probably not through to Singapore. Before very long they were put upon the road to Tampin, but not till they had lost another member of the party.

Ellen Forbes was the unmarried girl who had come out to get married and hadn't, a circumstance that Jean could well understand by the time she had lived in close contact with her for a couple of months. Ellen was a vacuous, undisciplined girl, good humoured, and much too free with Japanese troops for the liking of the other women. At Seremban they were accommodated in a schoolhouse on the outskirts of the town, which was full of soldiers. In the morning Ellen simply wasn't there, and they never saw her again.

Jean and Mrs Horsefall asked to see the officer and stated their case, that a member of their party had disappeared, probably abducted by the soldiers. The officer promised to make inquiries, and nothing happened. Two days later they received orders to march down the road to Tampin, and were moved off under guard.

They stayed at Tampin for some days, and got so little food there that they practically starved; at their urgent entreaty the local commandant sent them down under guard to Malacca, where they hoped to get a ship. But there was no ship at Malacca and the officer in charge there sent them back to Tampin. They plodded back there in despair; at Alor Gajah Judy Thomson died. To stay at Tampin meant more deaths, inevitably, so they suggested it was better for them to continue down to Singapore on foot, and a corporal was detailed to take them on the road to Gemas.

In the middle of May, at Ayer Kuning, on the way to Gemas, Mrs Horsefall died. She had never really recovered from her attack of malaria or whatever fever it was that had attacked her two months previously; she had had recurrent attacks of low fever which had made Jean wonder sometimes if it was malaria that she had had at all. Whatever it was it had made her very weak; at Ayer Kuning she developed dysentery again, and died in two days, probably of heart failure or exhaustion. The faded little woman Mrs Frith, who was over fifty and always seemed to be upon the point of death and never quite made it, took over the care of Johnnie Horsefall and it did her a world of good; from that day Mrs Frith improved and gave up moaning in the night.

They got to Gemas three days later; here as usual in towns they were put into the schoolhouse. The Japanese town major, a Captain Nisui, came to inspect them that evening; he had known nothing about them till they appeared in his town. This was quite usual and Jean was ready for it; she explained that they were prisoners being marched to camp in Singapore.

He said, 'Prisoner not go Singapore. Strict order. Where you come from?'

She told him. 'We've been travelling for over two months,' she said, with the calmness borne of many disappointments. 'We must get into a camp, or we shall die. Seven of us have died upon the road already—there were thirty-two when we were taken prisoner. Now there are twenty-five. We can't go on like this. We *must* get into camp at Singapore. You must see that.'

He said, 'No more prisoner to Singapore. Very sorry for you, but strict order. Too many prisoner in Singapore.'

She said, 'But, Captain Nisui, that can't mean women. That means men prisoners, surely.'

'No more prisoner to Singapore,' he said. 'Strict order.'

'Well, can we stay here and make ourselves a camp, and have a doctor here?'

His eyes narrowed. 'No prisoner stay here.'

'But what are we to do? Where can we go?'

'Very sad for you,' he said. 'I tell you where you go tomorrow.'

She went back to the women after he had gone. 'You heard all that,' she said calmly. 'He says we aren't to go to Singapore after all.'

The news meant very little to the women; they had fallen into the habit of

living from day to day, and Singapore was very far away. 'Looks as if they don't
want us anywhere,' Mrs Price said heavily. 'Bobbie, if I see you teasing Amy
again I'll wallop you just like your father. Straight, I will.'

Mrs Frith said, 'If they'd just let us alone we could find a little place like one
of them villages and live till it's all over.'

Jean stared at her. 'They couldn't feed us,' she said slowly. 'We depend upon
the Nips for food.' But it was the germ of an idea, and she put it in the back of
her mind.

'Precious little food we get,' said Mrs Frith. 'I'll never forget that terrible
place Tampin in all my born days.'

Captain Nisui came the next day. 'You go now to Kuantan,' he said.
'Woman camp in Kuantan, very good. You will be very glad.'

Jean did not know where Kuantan was. She asked, 'Where is Kuantan? Is it
far away?'

'Kuantan on coast,' he said. 'You go there now.'

Behind her someone said, 'It's hundreds of miles away. It's on the east coast.'

'Okay,' said Captain Nisui. 'On east coast.'

'Can we go there by railway?' Jean inquired.

'Sorry, no railway. You walk, ten, fifteen miles each day. You get there soon.
You will be very happy.'

She said quietly, 'Seven of us are dead already with this marching, Captain.
If you make us march to this place Kuantan more of us will die. Can we have a
truck to take us there?'

'Sorry, no truck,' he said. 'You get there very soon.'

He wanted them to start immediately, but it was then eleven in the morning
and they rebelled. With patient negotiation Jean got him to agree that they
should start at dawn next day; this was the most that she could do. She did,
however, get him to provide a good supper for them that night, a sort of meat
stew with the rice, and a banana each.

From Gemas to Kuantan is about a hundred and seventy miles; there is no
direct road. They left Gemas in the last week of May; on the basis of their
previous rate of progress Jean reckoned that it would take them six weeks to do
the journey. It was by far the longest they had had to tackle; always before there
had been hope of transport of some sort at the end of fifty miles or so. Now six
weeks of travelling lay ahead of them, with only a vague hope of rest at the end.
None of them really believed that there were prison camps for them at
Kuantan.

'You made a mistake, dearie,' said Mrs Frith, 'saying what you did about us
staying and making a camp here. I could see he didn't like that.'

'He just wants to get rid of us,' Jean said wearily. 'They don't want to bother
with us – just get us out of the way.'

They left next morning with a sergeant and a private as a guard. Gemas is a
railway junction and the East Coast railway runs north from there; the railway
was not being used at all at that time, and there was a rumour that the track was
being taken up and sent to some unknown strategic destination in the north.
The women were not concerned with that; what concerned them was that they
had to walk along the railway line, which meant nearly walking in the sun most
of each day, and there was no possibility of getting a ride in a train.

They went on for a week, marching about ten miles every other day; then
fever broke out among the children. They never really knew what it was; it

started with little Amy Price, who came out in a rash and ran a high temperature, with a running nose. It may have been measles. It was impossible in the conditions of their life to keep the children segregated, and in the weeks that followed it spread from child to child. Amy Price slowly recovered, but by the time she was fit to walk again seven of the other children were down with it. There was nothing they could do except to keep the tired, sweating little faces bathed and cool, and change the soaked clothes for what fresh ones they could muster. They were at a place called Bahau when the sickness was at its height, living at the station in the ticket office and the waiting-room, and on the platform. They had bad luck because there had been a doctor in Bahau three days before they arrived, a Japanese army doctor. But he had gone on in his truck in the direction of Kuala Klawang, and though they got the headman to send runners after him they never made contact with him. So they had no help.

At Bahau four children died, Harry Collard, Susan Fletcher, Doris Simmonds, who was only three, and Freddie Holland. Jean was most concerned with Freddie, as was natural, but there was so little she could do. She guessed from the first day of fever that he was going to die; by that time she had amassed a store of sad experience. There was something in the attitude of people, even tiny children, to their illness that told when death was coming to them, a listlessness, as if they were too tired to make the effort to live. By that time they had all grown hardened to the fact of death. Grief and mourning had ceased to trouble them; death was a reality to be avoided and fought, but when it came—well, it was just one of those things. After a person had died there were certain things that had to be done, the straightening of the limbs, the grave, the cross, the entry in a diary saying who had died and just exactly where the grave was. That was the end of it; they had no energy for afterthoughts.

Jean's care now was for Mrs Holland. After Freddie was buried she tried to get Eileen to care for the baby; for the last few weeks the baby had been left to Jean to feed and tend and carry, and she had grown very much attached to it. With both the older children dead Jean gave the baby, Robin, back to its mother, not so much because she wanted to get rid of it as because she felt that an interest must be found for Eileen Holland, and the baby would supply it. But the experiment was not a great success; Eileen by that time was so weak that she could not carry the baby on the march, and she could not summon the energy to play with it. Moreover, the baby obviously preferred the younger woman to its mother, having been carried by her for so long.

'Seems as if he doesn't really belong to me,' Mrs Holland said once. 'You take him, dear. He likes being with you.' From that time on they shared the baby; it got its rice and soup from Eileen, but it got its fun from Jean.

They left four tiny graves behind the signal box at Bahau and went on down the line carrying two litters of bamboo poles; the weakest children took turns in these. As was common on this journey, they found the Japanese guards to be humane and reasonable men, uncouth in their habits and mentally far removed from western ideas, but tolerant to the weaknesses of women and deeply devoted to children. For hours the sergeant would plod along carrying one child piggyback and at the same time carrying one end of the stretcher, his rifle laid beside the resting child. There was the usual language difficulty. The women by that time were acquiring a few words of Japanese, but the only one who could talk Malay fluently was Jean, and it was she who made inquiries at the villages and sometimes acted as interpreter for the Japanese.

Mrs Frith surprised Jean very much. She was a faded, anaemic little woman of over fifty. In the early stages of the journey she had been very weak and something of a nuisance to them with her continued prognostications of evil; they had trouble enough in the daily round without looking forward and anticipating more. Since she had adopted Johnnie Horsefall Mrs Frith had taken on a new lease of life; her health had improved and she now marched as strongly as any of them. She had lived in Malaya for about fifteen years; she could speak only a few words of the language but she had a considerable knowledge of the country and its diseases. She was quite happy that they were going to Kuantan. 'Nice over there, it is,' she said. 'Much healthier than in the west, and nicer people. We'll be all right once we get over there. You see.'

As time went on, Jean turned to Mrs Frith more and more for comfort and advice in their predicaments.

At Ayer Kring Mrs Holland came to the end of her strength. She had fallen twice on the march and they had taken turns in helping her along. It was impossible to put her on the litter; even in her emaciated state she weighed eight stone, and they were none of them strong enough by that time to carry such a load very far. Moreover, to put her on a litter meant turning a child off it, and she refused even to consider such a thing. She stumbled into the village on her own feet, but by the time she got there she was changing colour as Mrs Collard had before her, and that was a bad sign.

Ayer Kring is a small village at a railway station; there were no station buildings here, and by negotiation the headman turned the people out of one house for them, as had been done several times before. They laid Mrs Holland in a shady corner and made a pillow for her head and bathed her face; they had no brandy or any other stimulant to give her. She could not rest lying down and insisted on sitting up, so they put her in a corner where she could be supported by the walls. She took a little soup that evening but refused all food. She knew herself it was the end.

'I'm so sorry, my dear,' she whispered late in the night. 'Sorry to make so much trouble for you. Sorry for Bill. If you see Bill again, tell him not to fret. And tell him not to mind about marrying again, if he can find somebody nice. It's not as if he was an old man.'

An hour or two later she said, 'I do think it's lovely the way baby's taken to you. It *is* lucky, isn't it?'

In the morning she was still alive, but unconscious. They did what they could, which wasn't very much, but her breathing got weaker and weaker, and at about midday she died. They buried her in the Moslem village cemetery that evening.

At Ayer Kring they entered the most unhealthy district they had passed through yet. The central mountains of Malaya were now on their left, to the west of them as they marched north, and they were coming to the head waters of the Pahang river, which runs down to the east coast. Here the river spreads out into numerous tributaries, the Menkuang, the Pertang, the Belengu, and many others, and these tributaries running through flat country make a marshy place of swamps and mangroves that stretched for forty miles along their route, a country full of snakes and crocodiles, and infested with mosquitoes. By day it was steamy and hot and breathless; at night a cold wet mist came up and chilled them unmercifully.

By the time they had been two days in this country several of them were

A Town like Alice

suffering from fever, a fever that did not seem quite like the malaria that they were used to, in that the temperature did not rise so high; it may have been dengue. They had little by that time to treat it with, not so much because they were short of money as because there were no drugs at all in the jungly villages that they were passing through. Jean consulted with the sergeant, who advised them to press on, and get out of this bad country as soon as possible. Jean was running a fever herself at the time and everything was moving about her in a blur; she had a cracking headache and it was difficult to focus her eyes. She consulted with Mrs Frith, who was remarkably well.

'What he says is right, dearie,' Mrs Frith declared. 'We won't get any better staying in this swampy place. I think we ought to walk each day, if you ask me.'

Jean forced herself to concentrate. 'What about Mrs Simmonds?'

'Maybe the soldiers would carry her, if she gets any worse. I don't know, I'm sure. It's cruel hard, but if we've got to go we'd better go and get it over. That's what I say. We shan't do any good hanging around here in this nasty place.'

They marched each day after that, stumbling along in fever, weak, and ill. The baby, Robin Holland, that Jean carried, got the fever; this was the first ailment he had had. She showed him to the headman in the village of Mentri, and his wife produced a hot infusion of some bark in a dirty coconut shell; Jean tasted it and it was very bitter, so she judged it to be a form of quinine. She gave a little to the baby and took some herself; it seemed to do them both good during the night. Before the day's march began several of the women took it, and it helped.

It took them eleven days to get through the swamps to the higher ground past Temerloh. They left Mrs Simmonds and Mrs Fletcher behind them, and little Gillian Thomson. When they emerged into the higher, healthier country and dared to stay a day to rest, Jean was very weak but the fever had left her. The baby was still alive, though obviously ill; it cried almost incessantly during its waking hours.

It was Mrs Frith who now buoyed them up, as she had depressed them in the earlier days. 'It should be getting better all the time from now on,' she told them. 'As we get nearer to the coast it should get better. It's lovely on the east coast, nice beaches to bathe on, and always a sea breeze. It's healthy, too.'

They came presently to a very jungly village on a hilltop; they never learned its name. It stood above the river Jengka. By this time they had left the railway and were heading more or less eastwards on a jungle track that would at some time join a main road that led down to Kuantan. This village was cool and airy, and the people kind and hospitable; they gave the women a house to sleep in and provided food and fresh fruit, and the same bark infusion that was good for fever. They stayed there for six days revelling in the fresh, cool breeze and the clear, healthy nights, and when they finally marched on they were in better shape. They left a little gold brooch that had belonged to Mrs Fletcher with the headman as payment for the food and kindness that they had received, thinking that the dead woman would not have objected to that.

Four days later, in the evening, they came to Maran. A tarmac road runs through Maran crossing the Malay peninsula from Kuantan to Kerling. The road runs through the village, which has perhaps fifty houses, a school, and a few native shops. They came out upon the road half a mile or so to the north of the village; after five weeks upon the railway track and jungle paths it overjoyed them to see evidence of civilization in this road. They walked down to the village with a fresher step. And there, in front of them, they saw two trucks and two white men working on them while Japanese guards stood by.

They marched quickly towards the trucks, which were both heavily loaded with railway lines and sleepers; they stood pointing in the direction of Kuantan. One of them was jacked up on sleepers taken from the load, and both of the white men were underneath it working on the back axle. They wore shorts and army boots without socks; their bodies were brown with sunburn and very dirty with the muck from the back axle. But they were healthy and muscular men, lean, but in good physical condition. And they were white, the first white men that the women had seen for five months.

They crowded round the trucks; their guard began to talk in staccato Japanese with the truck guards. One of the men lying on his back under the axle, shifting spanner in hand, glanced at the bare feet and the sarongs within his range of vision and said slowly, 'Tell the mucking Nip to get those mucking women shifted back so we can get some light.'

Some of the women laughed, and Mrs Frith said, 'Don't you go using that language to me, young man.'

The men rolled out from under the truck and sat staring at the women and the children, at the brown skins, the sarongs, the bare feet. 'Who said that?' asked the man with the spanner. 'Which of you speaks English?' He spoke deliberately in a slow drawl, with something of a pause between each word.

Jean said laughing, 'We're all English.'

He stared at her, noting the black hair plaited in a pigtail, the brown arms and feet, the sarong, the brown baby on her hip. There was a line of white skin showing on her chest at the V of her tattered blouse. 'Straits-born?' he hazarded.

'No, real English—all of us,' she said. 'We're prisoners.'

He got to his feet; he was a fair-haired powerfully built man about twenty-seven or twenty-eight years old. 'Dinky-die?' he said.

She did not understand that. 'Are you prisoners?' she asked.

He smiled slowly. 'Are we prisoners?' he repeated. 'Oh my word.'

There was something about this man that she had never met before. 'Are you English?' she asked.

'No fear,' he said in his deliberate way. 'We're Aussies.'

She said, 'Are you in camp here?'

He shook his head. 'We come from Kuantan,' he said. 'But we're driving trucks all day, fetching this stuff down to the coast.'

She said, 'We're going to Kuantan, to the women's camp there.'

He stared at her. 'That's crook for a start,' he said slowly. 'There isn't any women's camp at Kuantan. There isn't any regular prisoner camp at all, just a little temporary camp for us because we're truck drivers. Who told you that there was a women's camp at Kuantan?'

'The Japanese told us. They're supposed to be sending us there.' She sighed. 'It's just another lie.'

'The bloody Nips say anything.' He smiled slowly. 'I thought you were a lot of boongs,' he said. 'You say you're English, dinky-die? All the way from England?'

She nodded. 'That's right. Some of us have been out here for ten or fifteen years, but we're all English.'

'And the kiddies—they all English too?'

'All of them,' she said.

He smiled slowly. 'I never thought the first time that I spoke to an English lady she'd be looking like you.'

'You aren't exactly an oil painting yourself,' Jean said.

The other man was talking to a group of the women; Mrs Frith and Mrs Price were with Jean. The Australian turned to them. 'Where do you come from?' he inquired.

Mrs Frith said, 'We got took in Panong, over on the west coast, waiting for a boat to get away.'

'But where did you come from now?'

Jean said, 'We're being marched to Kuantan.'

'Not all the way from Panong?'

She laughed shortly. 'We've been everywhere–Port Swettenham, Port Dickson–everywhere. Nobody wants us. I reckon that we've walked nearly five hundred miles.'

'Oh my word,' he said. 'That sounds a crook deal to me. How do you go on for tucker, if you aren't in a camp?'

She did not understand him. 'Tucker?'

'What do you get to eat?'

'We stay each night in a village,' she said. 'We'll have to find somewhere to stay here. Probably in a place like this it'll be the school. We eat what we can get in the village.'

'For Christ's sake,' he said. 'Wait while I tell my cobber.' He swung round to the other. 'You heard about the crook deal that they got?' he said. 'Been walking all the time since they got taken. Never been inside a prison camp at all.'

'They've been telling me,' the other said. 'The way these bloody Nips go on. Makes you chunda.'

The first man turned back to Jean. 'What happens if any of you get sick?'

She said cynically, 'When you get sick, you get well or you die. We haven't seen a doctor for the last three months and we've got practically no medicines left, so we mostly die. There were thirty-two of us when we were taken. Now we're seventeen.'

The Australian said softly, 'Oh my word.'

Jean said, 'Will you be staying here tonight?'

He said, 'Will you?'

'We shall stay here,' she said. 'We shall be here tomorrow too, unless they'll let us ride down on your trucks. We can't march the children every day. We walk one day and rest the next.'

He said, 'If you're staying, Mrs Boong, we're staying too. We can fix this bloody axle so it will never roll again, if needs be.' He paused in slow thought. 'You got no medicines?' he said. 'What do you want?'

She said quickly, 'Have you got any Glauber's salt?'

He shook his head. 'Is that what you want?'

'We haven't got any salts at all,' she said. 'We want quinine, and something for all these skin diseases that the children have got. Can we get those here?'

He said slowly, 'I'll have a try. Have you got any money?'

Mrs Frith snorted, 'After being six months with the Japs? They took everything we had. Even our wedding rings.'

Jean said, 'We've got a few little bits of jewellery left, if we could sell some of those.'

He said, 'I'll have a go first, and see what I can do. You get fixed up with somewhere to sleep, and I'll see you later.'

'All right.'

She went back to their sergeant and bowed to him because that pleased him and made things easier for them. She said, 'Gunso, where yasme tonight? Children must yasme. We see headman about yasme and mishi?'

He came with her and they found the headman, and negotiated for the loan of the school building for the prisoners, and for the supply of rice for mishi. They did not now experience the blank refusals that they formerly had met when the party was thirty strong; the lesser numbers had made accommodation and food much easier for them. They settled into the school building and began the routine of chores and washing that occupied the bulk of their spare time. The news that there was no women prisoners' camp in Kuantan was what they had all secretly expected, but it was a disappointment, none the less. The novelty of the two Australians made up for this, because by that time they were living strictly from day to day.

At the trucks the Aussies got back to their work. With heads close together under the axle, the fair-haired man that Jean had talked to said to his cobber, 'I never heard such a crook deal. What can we do to fix this bastard so as we stay here tonight? I said I'd try and get some medicines for them.'

They had already rectified the binding brake that had heated up the near side hub and caused the stoppage. The other said, 'Take the whole bloody hub off for a dekko, 'n pull out the shaft from the diff. That makes a good show of dirty bits. Means sleeping in the trucks.'

'I said I'd try and get some medicines.' They worked on for a little.

'How you going to do that?'

'Petrol, I suppose. That's easiest.'

It was already growing dark when they extracted four feet of heavy metal shafting, splined at both ends, from the back axle; dripping with black oil they showed it to the Japanese corporal in charge of them as evidence of their industry. 'Yasme here tonight,' they said. The guard was suspicious, but agreed; indeed, he could do nothing else. He went off to arrange for rice for them, leaving them in charge of the private who was with him.

On the excuse of a benjo, the fair-haired man left the trucks and in the half light retired behind a house. He slipped quickly down behind a row of houses, and came out into the street a couple of hundred yards down, towards the end of the village. Here there was a Chinaman who ran a decrepit bus; the Australian had noted this place on various journeys through Maran; they plied regularly up and down this road.

In his deliberate manner he said quietly, 'Johnnie, you buy petrol? How much you give?' It is extraordinary how little barrier an unknown language makes between a willing buyer and a willing seller. At one point in the negotiation they resorted to the written word, and the Australian wrote GLAUBER'S SALT and QUININE and SKIN DISEASE OINTMENT in block letters on a scrap of wrapping paper.

He slunk back behind the houses carrying three two-gallon cans and a length of rubber hose, which he hid behind the latrine. He came back to the trucks presently, ostentatiously buttoning his shorts.

In the darkness, early in the night, he came to the schoolhouse; it may have been about ten o'clock. One of the Japanese soldiers was supposed to be on guard all night, but in the five weeks that they had been with this pair of guards the women had not shown the slightest inclination to escape, and their guards had long given up watching them at night. The Australian had made sure where they were, however, and when he had seen them squatting with the truck guards he came silently to the school.

At the open door he paused, and said quietly, 'Which of you ladies was I talking to this afternoon? The one with the baby.'

Jean was asleep; they woke her and she pulled up her sarong and slipped her top on, and came to the door. He had several little packages for her. 'That's quinine,' he said. 'I can get more of that if you want it. I couldn't get Glauber's, but this is what the Chinese take for dysentery. It's all written in Chinese, but what he says it means is three of these leaves powdered up in warm water every four hours. That'll be for a grown-up person. If it's any good, keep the label and maybe you could get some more in a Chinese drug shop. I got this Zam-Buk for the skin, and there's more of that if you want it.'

She took them gratefully from him. 'That's marvellous,' she said softly. 'How much did it all cost?'

'That's all right,' he said in his deliberate manner. 'The Nips paid, but they don't know it.'

She thanked him again. 'What are you doing here?' she asked. 'Where are you going with the trucks?'

'Kuantan,' he said. 'We should be back there tonight, but Ben Leggatt–he's my cobber–he got the truck in bits so we had to give it away. Get down there tomorrow, or we might stretch it another day if it suits, though it'ld be risky, I think.' He told her that there were six of them driving six trucks for the Japanese; they drove regularly from Kuantan up-country to a place upon the railway called Jerantut, a distance of about a hundred and thirty miles. They would drive up one day and load the truck with sleepers and railway lines taken up from the track, and drive back to Kuantan the next day, where the railway material was unloaded on to the quayside to be taken away by ship to some unknown destination. 'Building another railway somewhere, I suppose,' he said. A hundred and thirty miles is a long way to drive a heavily loaded truck in a day in tropical conditions, and they sometimes failed to reach Kuantan before dark; when that happened they spent the night in a village. Their absence would not be remarked particularly at Kuantan.

He had been taken somewhere in Johore, and had been driving trucks from Kuantan for about two months. 'Better than being in a camp,' he said.

She sat down on the top step of the three that led up to the school, and he squatted down before her on the ground. His manner of sitting intrigued her, because he sat down on one heel somewhat in the manner of a native, but with his left leg extended. 'Are you a truck driver in Australia?' she asked.

'No bloody fear,' he said. 'I'm a ringer.'

She asked, 'What's a ringer?'

'A stockman,' he said. 'I was born in Queensland out behind Cloncurry, and my people, they're all Queenslanders. My dad, he came from London, from a place called Hammersmith. He used to drive a cab and so he knew about horses, and he came out to Queensland to work for Cobb and Co., and met Ma. But I've not been back to the Curry for some time. I was working in the Territory over to the west, on a station called Wollara. That's about a hundred and ten miles south-west of the Springs.'

She smiled. 'Where's the Springs, then?'

'Alice,' he said. 'Alice Springs. Right in the middle of Australia, half way between Darwin and Adelaide.'

She said, 'I thought the middle of Australia was all desert?'

He was concerned at her ignorance. 'Oh my word,' he said deliberately. 'Alice is a bonza place. Plenty of water in Alice; people living there, they leave the sprinkler on all night, watering the lawn. That's right, they leave the sprinkler on all night. Course, the Territory's dry in most parts, but there's usually good feed along the creeks. Come to that, there's water all over if you look for it. You take a creek that only runs in the wet, now, say a couple of months in the year, or else not that. You get a sandy billabong, and you'll get water there by digging not a foot below the surface, like as not—even in the middle of the dry.' His slow, even tones were strangely comforting. 'You go to a place like that and you'll find little diggings all over in the sand, where the kangaroos and euros have dug for water. They know where to go. There's water all over in the outback, but you've got to know where to find it.'

'What do you do at this place Wollara?' she asked. 'Do you look after sheep?'

He shook his head. 'You don't find sheep around the Alice region,' he said. 'It'd be too hot for them. Wollara is a cattle station.'

'How many cattle have you got?'

'About eighteen thousand when I come away,' he said. 'It goes up and down, according to the wet, you know.'

'Eighteen thousand? How big is it?'

'Wollara? About two thousand seven hundred.'

'Two thousand seven hundred acres,' she said. 'That's a big place.'

He stared at her. 'Not acres,' he said. 'Square miles. Wollara's two thousand seven hundred square miles.'

She was startled. 'But is that all one place—one farm, I mean?'

'It's one station,' he replied. 'One property.'

'But however many of you does it take to run it?'

His mind ran lovingly around the well-remembered scene. 'There's Mr Duveen, Tommy Duveen—he's the manager, and then me—I'm the head stockman, or I was. Tommy said he'd keep a place for me when I got back. I'd like to get back to Wollara again, one day . . .'' He mused a little. 'We had three other ringers—whites,' he said. 'Then there was Happy, and Moonlight, and Nugget, and Snowy, and Tarmac . . .' He thought for a minute. 'Nine boongs we had,' he said. 'That's all.'

'Nine what?'

'Black boys—black stockmen. Abos.'

'But that's only thirteen men,' she said.

'That's right. Fourteen if you count Mr Duveen.'

'But can fourteen men look after all those cattle?' she asked.

'Oh yes,' he said thoughtfully. 'Wollara is an easy station, in a way, because it hasn't got any fences. It's fences make the work. We've got the Palmer River and the Levi Range to the north, and the sand country over to the west; the cattle don't go there. Then there's the Kernot Range to the south and Mount Ormerod and the Twins to the east. Fourteen men is all right for a station like that; it would be easier if we had more whites, but you can't get them. These bloody boongs, they're always going walkabout.'

'What's that?' she asked.

'Walkabout? Why, an Abo ringer, he'll come up one day and he'll say, "Boss, I go walkabout now." You can't keep him. He'll leave the station and go wandering off just in a pair of pants and an old hat with a gun if he's got one, or a spear and a throwing stick, maybe, and he'll be away two or three months.'

'But where does he go to?' she asked.

'Just travels. They go a long way on a walkabout–oh my word,' he said. 'Four or five hundred miles, maybe. Then when he's had enough, he'll come back to the station and join up for work again. But the trouble with the boongs is, you never know if they'll be there next week.'

There was a short silence; they sat quietly in the tropic night together on the steps of the atap schoolhouse, exiles far from their homes. Over their heads the flying foxes swept in the moonlight with a dry rustling of leathery wings.

'Eighteen thousand cattle . . .' she said thoughtfully.

'More or less,' he said. 'Get a good wet, and it'll maybe rise to twenty-one or twenty-two thousand. Then you get a dry year, and it'll go right down to twelve or thirteen thousand. I reckon we lose about three thousand every year by drought.'

'But can't you get them to water?'

He smiled slowly. 'Not with fourteen men. There's enough cattle die of thirst each year in the Territory and Northern Queensland to feed the whole of England. Course, the horses make it worse on Wollara.'

'Horses?'

'Oh my word,' he said. 'We've got about three thousand brumbies, but you can't do nothing with them–they're vermin. Wollara used to be a horse station years ago, selling horses to the Indian Army, but you can't sell horses now. We use a few, of course–maybe a hundred, with packhorses and that. You can't get rid of them except by shooting, and you'll never get a ringer to shoot horses. They eat the feed the cattle ought to get, and spoil it, too. Cattle don't like feeding where a horse has been.'

She asked, 'How big is Wollara–how long, and how wide?'

He said, 'Oh, I'd say about ninety miles from east to west, and maybe forty-five to fifty, north to south, at the widest part. But it's a good station to manage, because the homestead is near the middle, so it's not so far in any one way. Over to the Kernot Range is the furthest; that's about sixty miles.'

'Sixty miles from the homestead? That's where you live?'

'That's right.'

'Are there any other homesteads on it?'

He stared at her. 'There's only the one homestead on each station. Some have an outstation, a shack of some kind where the boys can leave blankets and maybe a little tucker, but not many.'

'How long does it take you to get to the furthest point, then–to the Kernot Range?'

'Over to the Range? Oh well, to go there and come back might take about a week. That's with horses; in a utility you might do it in a day and a half. But horses are best, although they're a bit slow. You never take a packhorse faster'n a walk, not if you can help it. It isn't like you see it on the movies, people galloping their horses everywhere–oh my word. You'd soon wear out a horse if you used him that way in the Territory.'

They sat together for over an hour, talking quietly at the entrance to the schoolhouse. At the end the ringer got up from his strange posture on the ground, and said, 'I mustn't stay any longer, case those Nips come back and start creating. My cobber, too–he'll be wondering what happened to me. I left him to boil up.'

Jean got to her feet. 'It's been terribly kind of you to get us these things. You don't know what they mean to us. Tell me, what's your name?'

'Joe Harman,' he said. 'Sergeant Harman–Ringer Harman, some of them call me.' He hesitated. 'Sorry I called you Mrs Boong today,' he said awkwardly. 'It was a silly kind of joke.'

She said, 'My name's Jean Paget.'

'That sounds like a Scotch name.'

'It is,' she said. 'I'm not Scotch myself, but my mother came from Perth.'

'My mother's family was Scotch,' he said. 'They came from Inverness.'

She put out her hand. 'Goodnight, Sergeant,' she said. 'It's been lovely talking to another white person.'

He took her hand; there was great comfort for her in his masculine handshake. 'Look, Mrs Paget,' he said. 'I'll try if I can get the Nips to let your party ride down on the truck with us. If the little bastards won't wear it, then we'll have to give it away. In that case I'll see you on the road again before you get to Kuantan, and I'll make darn sure there's something crook with the truck. What else do you want?'

'Soap,' she said. 'Could you possibly get us soap?'

'Should be able to,' he said.

'We've got no soap at all,' she observed. 'I've got a little gold locket that one of the women had who died, a thing with a bit of hair in it. I was going to see if I could sell that here, and get some soap.'

'Keep it,' he said. 'I'll see you get soap.'

'We want that more than anything, now that you've got these medicines for us,' she said.

'You'll have it.' He hesitated, and then said, 'Sorry I talked so much, boring you with the outback and all that. There's times when you get down a bit–can't make yourself believe you'll ever see it again.'

'I wasn't bored,' she said softly. 'Goodnight, Sergeant.'

'Goodnight.'

In the morning Jean showed the women what she had got. 'I heard you talking to him ever so long,' Mrs Price said. 'Nice young man, I'd say.'

'He's a very homesick young man,' Jean said. 'He loves talking about the cattle station he comes from.'

'Homesick!' Mrs Price said. 'Aren't we all?'

The Australians had a smart argument with their guard that morning, who refused point-blank to let the women ride down on the trucks. There was some reason in this from their point of view, because the weight of seventeen women and children added to two grossly overloaded trucks might well be the last straw that would bring final breakdown, in which case the guards themselves would have been lucky to escape with a flogging at the hands of their officer. Harman and Leggatt had to put the back axle together again; they were finished and ready for the road about the middle of the morning.

Joe Harman said, 'Keep that little bastard busy for a minute while I loose off the union.' He indicated the Jap guard. Presently they started, Harman in the lead, dribbling a little petrol from a loosened pipe joint, unnoticed by the guard. It was just as well to have an alibi when they ran out of fuel, having parted with six gallons to the Chinaman.

From Maran to Kuantan is fifty-five miles. The women rested that day at Maran, and next day began the march down the tarmac road. They reached a village called Buan that night. Jean had looked for Joe Harman's truck all day, expecting to see it returning; she was not to know that it had been stranded overnight at Pohoi, short of petrol, and was a day late in the return journey. They stayed next day at Buan in an atap shed; the women took turns with Jean watching for the truck. Their health already was somewhat improved. After the railway track and the jungle paths the tarmac road was easy walking, and the medicines were already having an effect. The country, too, was growing higher and healthier, and the more imaginative of them were already saying they could smell the sea. And finally their contact with the two Australians had had a marked effect on their morale.

They did not see Joe Harman's truck as it passed through. Instead, a Malay girl came to them in the evening with a brown paper parcel of six cakes of Lifebuoy soap; it was addressed to Mrs Paget. Written on the parcel was a note which read,

DEAR LADY,
I send some soap which is all that we can find just at present but I will get more later on. I am sorry not to see you but the Nip won't let us stop so I have given this to the Chinaman at Maran and he says he will get it to you. Look out for us on the way back and I will try and stop then.
JOE HARMAN

The women were delighted. 'Lifebuoy,' said Mrs Warner, sniffing it ecstatically. 'You can just smell the carbolic in it! My dear, wherever do you think they got it?'

'I'd have two guesses,' Jean replied. 'Either they stole it, or they stole something to buy it with.' In fact, the latter was correct. At Pohoi their Japanese guard had taken off his boots to wash his feet at the village well; he washed his feet for about thirty seconds and turned round, but the boots had vanished; it could not have been either of the Australians because they both appeared immediately from the other direction. The mystery was never cleared up. Ben Leggatt, however, was most helpful and stole a pair from a sleeping Japanese that evening and gave them to their guard, who was so relieved that he gave Ben a dollar.

The next day the women marched to Berkapor. They were coming out into much better country now, a pleasant, relatively healthy part where the road wound round hillsides and was mostly shaded by the overhanging trees. That day for the first time they got coconuts. Mrs Price had an old worn-out pair of slippers that had belonged to Mrs Horsefall; she had carried them for weeks and had never really used them; they traded these at Berkapor as soon as they got in for milk coconuts, one for each member of the party, thinking that the vitamins contained in the fluid would be good for them. At Berkapor they were accommodated in a large atap copra shed beside the road, and just before dusk the two familiar trucks drew up in the village, driven by Ben Leggatt and Joe Harman. As before, they were headed for the coast and loaded high with railway lines and sleepers.

Jean and several of the others walked across the road to meet them, with the Japanese sergeant; the Japanese guards fell into conversation together. Joe Harman turned to Jean. 'We couldn't get loaded at Jerantut in time to make it down to Kuantan tonight,' he said. 'Ben's got a pig.'

'A pig?' They crowded round Ben's truck. The corpse was lying upon the top of the load, a black, long-nosed Oriental pig, somewhat mauled and already covered in flies. Somewhere near the Tekam River Ben, whose truck was in the lead, had found this pig upon the road and had chased it with the truck for a quarter of a mile. The Japanese guard beside him had fired six shots at it from his rifle and had missed it every time till with the seventh he had wounded it and so enabled Ben to run over it with one of the front wheels. They had stopped and Harman coming close behind them had stopped too, and the two Aussies and the Japanese guard had heaved the pig on to the load and got moving again before the infuriated Chinese storekeeper had caught up with them to claim his property. Harman said quietly to Jean, 'We'll have to let the bloody Nips eat all they can and carry away a bit. Leave it to me; I'll see there's some for you.'

That night the women got about thirty-five pounds of boiled pig meat, conveyed to them surreptitiously in several instalments. They made a fire of coconut shells behind the copra store and made a stew with their rice ration, and ate all of this that seemed prudent to them; at that there was enough meat left for the three meals that they would have before they took the road again. They sat about in the shed or at the roadside after they had finished, replete with the first really nourishing meal that they had had for months, and presently the Australians came across to talk to them.

Joe Harman came to Jean. 'Sorry I couldn't send over more of that pig,' he said in his slow Queensland drawl. 'I had to let the bloody Nips have most of it.'

She said, 'It's been splendid, Joe. We've been eating and eating, and there's still lots left for tomorrow. I don't know when we last had such a meal.'

'I'd say that's what you need,' he observed. 'There's not a lot of flesh on any of you, if I may say so.'

He squatted down upon the ground beside the women, sitting on one heel in his peculiar way.

'I know we're pretty thin,' Jean said. 'But we're a darned sight better than we were. That Chinese stuff you got us as the substitute for Glauber's salt—that's doing the trick all right. It's stopping it.'

'Fine,' he said. 'Maybe we could get some more of that in Kuantan.'

'The pig was a god-send,' she said. 'That, and the fruit—we got some green coconuts today. We've been very lucky so far that we've had no beriberi, or that sort of thing.'

'It's because we've had fresh rice,' said Mrs Frith unexpectedly. 'Being in the country parts we've had fresh rice all through. It's old rice that gives you beriberi.'

The Australian sat thoughtful, chewing a piece of stick. 'Funny sort of a life for you ladies,' he said at last. 'Living in a place like this, and eating like the boongs. These Nips'll have something coming to them, when it's all added up.'

He turned to Jean. 'What were you all doing in Malaya?' he asked.

'Most of us were married,' she said. 'Our husbands had jobs here.'

Mrs Frith said, 'My hubby's District Engineer on the railway. We had ever such a nice bungalow at Kajang.'

Harman said, 'All the husbands got interned separately, I suppose?'

'That's right,' said Mrs Price. 'My Arthur's in Singapore. I heard about him when we was in Port Dickson. I think they're all in Singapore.'

'All comfortable in a camp while you go walking round the country,' he said.

'That's right,' said Mrs Frith. 'Still, it's nice to know that they're all right, when all's said and done.'

'It seems to me,' said Harman, 'the way they're kicking you around, they just don't know what they can do with you. It might not be too difficult for you to just stay in one place, as it might be this, and live till the war's over.'

Mrs Frith said, 'That's what I've been thinking.'

Jean said, 'I know. I've thought of this ever since Mrs Frith suggested it. The trouble is, the Japs feed us – or they make the village feed us. The village never gets paid. We'd have to earn our keep somehow, and I don't see how we could do it.'

Harman said, 'It was just an idea.'

He said presently, 'I believe I know where I could get a chicken or two. If I can I'll drop them off for you when we come up-country, day after tomorrow.'

Jean said, 'We haven't paid you for the soap yet.'

'Forget about it,' he said slowly. 'I didn't pay cash for it myself. I swapped it for a pair of Nip rubber boots.' With slow, dry humour he told them about the boots. 'You got the soap, the Nip got another pair of boots, and Ben got a dollar,' he said. 'Everybody's happy and satisfied.'

Jean said, 'Is that how you're going to get the chicken?'

'I'll get a chicken for you, one way or another,' he said. 'You ladies need feeding up.'

She said, 'Don't take any risks.'

'You attend to your own business, Mrs Boong,' he said, 'and take what you get. That's what you have to do when you're a prisoner, just take what you can get.'

She smiled, and said, 'All right.' The fact that he had called her Mrs Boong pleased her; it was a little tenuous bond between herself and this strange man that he should pull her leg about her sunburn, her native dress, and the baby that she carried on her hip like a Malay woman. The word boong put Australia into her mind, and the aboriginal stockmen, and she asked a question that had occurred to her, partly from curiosity and partly because she knew it pleased him to talk about his own country. 'Tell me,' she said, 'is it very hot in Australia, the part you come from? Hotter than this?'

'It's hot,' he said. 'Oh my word, it can be hot when it tries. At Wollara it can go to a hundred and eighteen – that's a hot day, that is. But it's not like this heat here. It's a kind of a dry heat, so you don't sweat like you do here.' He thought for a minute. 'I got thrown once,' he said, 'breaking in a brumby to the saddle. I broke my thigh, and after it was set in the hospital they used to point a sort of lamp at it, a sunray lamp they called it, to tone up the muscles or something. Do you have those things in England?'

She nodded. 'It's like that, is it?'

'That's right,' he said. 'It's a kind of warm, dry heat, the sort that does you good and makes you thirsty for cold beer.'

'What does the country look like?' she inquired. It pleased the man to talk about his own place and she wanted to please him; he had been so very kind to them.

'It's red,' he said. 'Red around Alice and where I come from, red earth and then, the mountains are all red. The Macdonnells and the Levis and the Kernots, great red ranges of bare hills against the blue sky. Evenings they go purple and all sorts of colours. After the wet there's green all over them. In the dry, parts of them go silvery white with the spinifex.' He paused. 'I suppose everybody likes his own place,' he said quietly. 'The country round about the Springs is my place. People come up on the 'Ghan from Adelaide and places in the south, and they say Alice is a lousy town. I only went to Adelaide once, and I thought that was lousy. The country round about the Springs is beautiful to me.'

He mused. 'Artists come up from the south and try and paint it in pictures,' he said. 'I only met one that ever got it right, and he was an Abo, an Abo called Albert out at Hermannsburg. Somebody gave him a brush and some paints one time, and he started in and got it better than any of them, oh my word, he did. But he's an Abo, and he's painting his own place. I suppose that makes a difference.'

He turned to Jean. 'What's your place?' he asked. 'Where do you come from?'

She said, 'Southampton.'

'Where the liners go to?'

'That's it,' she said.

'What's it like there?' he asked.

She shifted the baby on her hip, and moved her feet in the sarong. 'It's quiet, and cool, and happy,' she said thoughtfully. 'It's not particularly beautiful, although there's lovely country round about–the New Forest, and the Isle of Wight. It's my place, like the Springs is yours, and I shall go back there if I live through this time, because I love it so.' She paused for a moment. 'There was an ice rink there,' she said. 'I used to dance upon the ice, when I was a girl at school. One day I'll get back there and dance again.'

'I've never seen an ice rink,' said the man from Alice. 'I've seen pictures of them, and on the movies.'

She said, 'It was such fun . . .'

Presently he got up to go; she walked across the road with him towards the trucks, the baby on her hip, as always. 'I shan't be able to see you tomorrow,' he said. 'We start at dawn. But I'll be coming back up the road the day after.'

'We shall be walking to Pohoi that day, I think,' she said.

'I'll see if I can get you those chickens,' he said.

She turned and faced him, standing beside her in the moonlit road, in all the noises of the tropic night. 'Look, Joe,' she said. 'We don't want meat if it's going to mean trouble. It was grand of you to get that soap for us, but you did take a fearful risk, pinching that chap's boots.'

'That's nothing,' he said slowly. 'You can run rings round these Nips when you learn how.'

'You've done a lot for us,' she said. 'This pig, and the medicines, and the soap. It's made a world of difference to us in these last few days. I know you've taken risks to do these things. Do, please, be careful.'

'Don't worry about me,' he said. 'I'll try and get the chickens, but if I find things getting hot I'll give it away. I won't go sticking out my neck.'

'You'll promise that?' she asked.

'Don't worry about me,' he said. 'You've got enough troubles on your own plate, my word. But we'll come out all right, so long as we just keep alive, that's all we got to do. Just keep alive another two years, till the war's over.'

'You think that it will be as long as that?' she asked.

'Ben knows a lot more than I do about things like that,' he said. 'He thinks about two years.' He grinned down at her. 'You'd better have those chickens.'

'I'll leave that with you,' she said. 'I'd never forgive myself if you got caught in anything, and bought it.'

'I won't,' he said. He put out his hand as if to take her own, and then dropped it again. 'Goodnight, Mrs Boong,' he said.

She laughed. 'I'll crack you with a coconut if you say Mrs Boong again. Goodnight, Joe.'

'Goodnight.'

They did not see him next morning, though they heard the trucks go off. They rested that day at Berkapor, as was their custom, and the next day they marched on to Pohoi. The two trucks driven by Harman and Leggatt passed them on the road about midday going up empty to Jerantut; each driver waved to the women as they passed, and they waved back. The Japanese guards seated beside the drivers scowled a little. No chickens dropped from the trucks and the trucks did not stop; in one way Jean was rather relieved. She knew something of the temper of these men by now, and she knew very well that they would stop at nothing, would be deterred by no risk, to get what they considered to be helpful for the women. No chickens meant no trouble, and she marched on for the rest of the day with an easy mind.

That evening, in the house that they had been put into at Pohoi, a little Malay boy came to Jean with a green canvas sack; he said that he had been sent by a Chinaman in Gambang. In the sack were five black cockerels, alive, with their feet tied. Poultry is usually transported in the East alive.

Their arrival put Jean in a difficulty, and she consulted with Mrs Frith. It was impossible for them to kill, pluck and cook five cockerels without drawing the attention of their guards to what was going on, and the first thing that the guards would ask was, where had the cockerels come from? If Jean had known the answer to that one herself it would have been easier to frame a lie. It would be possible, they thought, to say that they had bought them with money given to them by the Australians, but that was difficult if the sergeant wanted to know where they had bought them in Pohoi. It was unfortunate that Pohoi was a somewhat unfriendly village; it had been genuinely difficult for the village to evacuate a house for the women, and it was not to be expected that they would get much co-operation from the villagers in any deceit. Finally they decided to say that they had bought them with money given to them by the Australians, and that they had arranged at Berkapor for the poultry to be sent to them at Pohoi from a village called Limau, two or three miles off the road. It was a thin tale and one that would not stand up to a great deal of investigation, but they saw no reason why any investigation should take place.

They decided regretfully that they would have to part with one of the five cockerels to their guards; the gift of a chicken would make the sergeant sweet and involve him in the affair, rendering any serious investigation unlikely. Accordingly Jean took the sack and went to find the sergeant.

She bowed to him, to put him in a good temper. 'Gunso,' she said, 'good mishi tonight. We buy chickens.' She opened the sack and showed him the fowls lying in the bottom. Then she reached down and pulled out one. 'For you.' She smiled at him with all the innocence that she could muster.

It was a great surprise to him. He had not known that they had so much money; they had never been able to buy anything but coconuts or bananas before, since he had been with them. 'You buy?' he asked.

She nodded. 'From Limau. Very good mishi for us all tonight.'

'Where get money?' he inquired. Suspicion had not dawned, for they had never deceived him before; he was just curious.

For one fleeting moment Jean toyed with the idea of saying they had sold some jewellery, with a quick, intuitive feeling that it would be better not to mention the Australians. But she put the idea away; she must stick to the story that they had prepared and considered from all angles. 'Man prisoner give us money for chicken,' she said. 'They say we too thin. Now we have good mishi tonight, Japanese and prisoner also.'

He put up two fingers. 'Two.'

She went up in a sheet of flame. 'One, not two, gunso,' she said. 'This is a present for you, because you have been kind and carried children, and allowed us to walk slowly. Five only, five.' She showed him the sack, and he counted them carefully. It was only then that she took note of the fact that the birds were rather unusually large for the East, and jet black all over. 'One for you, four for us.'

He let the sack fall, and nodded; then he smiled at her, tucked the cockerel under his arm, and walked off with it towards the kitchen where his meal was in preparation.

That day there was a considerable row in progress at Kuantan. The local commanding officer was a Captain Sugamo, who was executed by the Allied War Crimes Tribunal in the year 1946 after trial for atrocities committed at Camp 302 on the Burma-Siam railway in the years 1943 and 1944: his duty in Kuantan at that time was to see to the evacuation of the railway material from the eastern railway in Malaya and to its shipment to Siam. He lived in the house formerly occupied by the District Commissioner of Kuantan, and the District Commissioner had kept a fine little flock of about twenty black Leghorn fowls, specially imported from England in 1939. When Captain Sugamo woke up that morning, five of his twenty black Leghorns were missing, with a green sack that had once held the mail for the District Commissioner, and was now used to store grain for the fowls.

Captain Sugamo was a very angry man. He called the Military Police and set them to work; their suspicion fell at once upon the Australian truck drivers, who had a record for petty larceny in that district. Moreover, they had considerable opportunities, because the nature of their work allowed them a great deal of freedom; trucks had to be serviced and refuelled, often in the hours of darkness when it was difficult to ascertain exactly where each man might be. Their camp was searched that day for any sign of telltale feathers, or the sack, but nothing was discovered but a cache of tinned foods and cigarettes stolen from the quartermaster's store.

Captain Sugamo was not satisfied and he became more angry than ever. A question of face was now involved, because this theft from the commanding officer was a clear insult to his position, and so to the Imperial Japanese Army. He ordered a search of the entire town of Kuantan: on the following day every house was entered by troops working under the directions of the military Police to look for signs of the black feathers or the green sack. It yielded no result.

Brooding over the insults levelled at his uniform, the captain ordered the barracks of the company of soldiers under his command to be searched. There was no result from that.

There remained one further avenue. Three of the trucks, driven by

Australians, were up-country on the road to or from Jerantut. Next day Sugamo dispatched a light truck up the road manned by four men of his military police, to search these trucks and to interrogate the drivers and the guards, and anybody else who might have knowledge of the matter. Between Pohoi and Blat they came upon a crowd of women and children walking down the road loaded with bundles; ahead of them marched a Japanese sergeant with his rifle slung over one shoulder and a green sack over the other. The truck stopped with a squeal of brakes.

For the next two hours Jean stuck to her story, that the Australian had given her money and she had bought the fowls from Limau. They put her through a sort of third degree there on the road, with an insistent reiteration of questions: when they felt that her attention was wandering they slapped her face, kicked her shins, or stamped on her bare feet with army boots. She stuck to it with desperate resolution, knowing that it was a rotten story, knowing that they disbelieved her, not knowing what else she could say. At the end of that time a convoy of three trucks came down the road; the driver of the second one, Joe Harman, was recognized by the sergeant immediately, and brought before Jean at the point of the bayonet. The sergeant of the Military Police said, 'Is this man?'

Jean said desperately, 'I've been telling them about the four dollars you gave me to buy the chickens with, Joe, but they won't believe me.'

The military policeman said, 'You steal chickens from the shoko. Here is bag.'

The ringer looked at the girl's bleeding face and at her bleeding feet. 'Leave her alone, you bloody mucking bastards,' he said angrily in his slow Queensland drawl. 'I stole those mucking chickens, and I gave them to her. So what?'

Darkness was closing down in my London sitting-room, the early darkness of a stormy afternoon. The rain still beat upon the window. The girl sat staring into the fire, immersed in her sad memories. 'They crucified him,' she said quietly. 'They took us all down to Kuantan, and they nailed his hands to a tree, and beat him to death. They kept us there, and made us look on while they did it.'

4

'My dear,' I said. 'I am so very sorry.'

She raised her head. 'You don't have to be sorry,' she replied. 'It was one of those things that seem to happen in a war. It's a long time ago, now—nearly six years. And Captain Sugamo was hung—not for that, but for what he did upon the railway. It's all over and done with now, and nearly forgotten.'

There was, of course, no women's camp in Kuantan, and Captain Sugamo was not the man to be bothered with a lot of women and children. The execution took place at midday at a tree that stood beside the recreation ground overlooking the tennis courts: as soon as the maimed, bleeding body hanging by its hands had ceased to twitch Captain Sugamo stood them in parade before him.

'You very-bad people,' he said. 'No place here for you. I send you to Kota Bahru. You walk now.'

They stumbled off without a word, in desperate hurry to get clear of that place of horror. The same sergeant that had escorted them from Gemas was sent with them, for he also was disgraced as having shared the chickens. It was as a punishment that he was ordered to continue with them, because all prisoners are disgraceful and dishonourable creatures in the eyes of the Japanese, and to guard them and escort them is an insulting and a menial job fit only for the lowest type of man. An honourable Japanese would kill himself rather than be taken prisoner. Perhaps to emphasize this point the private soldier was taken away, so that from Kuantan onwards the sergeant was their only guard.

So they took up their journey again, living from day to day. They left Kuantan about the middle of July. It is about two hundred miles from Kuantan to Kota Bahru: allowing for halts of several days for illness Jean anticipated it would take them two months at least to get there.

They got to Besarah on the first day: this is a fishing village on the sea, with white coral sand and palm trees at the head of the beach. It is a very lovely place but they slept little, for most of the children were awake and crying in the night with memories of the horror they had seen. They could not bear to stay so close to Kuantan and travelled on next day another short stage to Balok, another fishing village on another beach with more palm trees. Here they rested for a day.

Gradually they came to realize that they had entered a new land. The north-east coast of Malaya is a very lovely country, and comparatively healthy. It is beautiful, with rocky headlands and long, sweeping, sandy beaches fringed with palm trees, and usually there is a fresh wind from the sea. Moreover there is an abundance of fresh fish in all the villages. For the first time since they left Panong the women had sufficient protein with their rice, and their health began to show an improvement at once. Most of them bathed in the warm sea at least once every day, and certain of the skin diseases that they suffered from began to heal with this salt water treatment, though not all. For the first time in months the children had sufficient energy to play.

They all improved, in fact, except the sergeant. The sergeant was suspicious of them now; he seldom carried a child or helped them in any way. He seemed to feel the reproofs that he had been given very much, and he had now no companion of his own race to talk to. He moped a great deal, sitting sullenly aloof from them in the evenings; once or twice Jean caught herself consciously trying to cheer him up, a queer reversal of the role of prisoner and guard. Upon this route they met very few Japanese. Occasionally they would find a detachment stationed in a river village or at an airstrip; when they came to such a unit the sergeant would smarten himself up and go and report to the officer in charge, who would usually come and inspect them. But there is very little industry between Kuantan and Kota Bahru and no town larger than a fishing village, nor was there any prospect of an enemy attack upon the eastern side of the Malay Peninsula. On several occasions a week passed without the women seeing any Japanese at all except the sergeant.

As they travelled slowly up the coast the condition of the women and the children altered greatly for the better. They were now a very different party from the helpless people who had started off from Panong nearly six months before. Death had ruthlessly eliminated the weakest members and reduced them to about half the original numbers, which made all problems of billeting and feeding in the villages far easier. They were infinitely more experienced by that time, too. They had learned to use the native remedies for malaria and dysentery, to clothe themselves and wash and sleep in the native manner; in consequence they now had far more leisure than when they had been fighting to maintain a western style of life in primitive conditions. The march of ten miles every other day was now no longer a great burden; in the intervening day they had more time for the children. Presently Mrs Warner, who at one time had been an elementary schoolmistress, started a class for the children, and school became a regular institution on their day of rest.

Jean began to teach her baby, Robin Holland, how to walk. He was quite fit and healthy again, and getting quite a weight for her to carry, for he was now sixteen months old. She never burdened him with any clothes in that warm climate, and he crawled about naked in the shade of palm or casuarina trees, or in the sun upon the sand, like any Malay baby. He got nearly as brown as one, too.

In the weeks that followed they moved slowly northwards up the coast, through all the many fishing villages, Ular and Chendar and Kalong and Penunjok and Kemasik and many others. They had a little sickness and spent a few days here and there while various members of the party sweated out a fever, but they had no more deaths. The final horror at Kuantan was a matter that they never spoke about at all, each fearing to recall it to the memory of the others, but each was secretly of the opinion that it had changed their luck.

With Mrs Frith this impression struck much deeper. She was a devout little woman who said her prayers morning and evening with the greatest regularity. It was Mrs Frith who always knew when Sunday was: on that day she would read the Prayer Book and the Bible for an hour aloud to anyone who came to listen to her. If it was their rest day she would hold this service at eleven o'clock as near as she could guess it, because that was the correct time for Matins.

Mrs Frith sought for the hand of God in everything that happened to them. Brooding over their experiences with this in mind, she was struck by certain similarities. She had read repeatedly about one Crucifixion; now there had been another. The Australian, in her mind, had had the power of healing, because the medicines he brought had cured her dysentery and Johnnie Horsefall's ringworm. It was beyond all doubt that they had been blessed in every way since his death for them. God had sent down His Son to earth in Palestine. What if He had done it again in Malaya?

Men and women who are in great and prolonged distress and forced into an entirely novel way of life, divorced entirely from their previous association, frequently develop curious mental traits. Mrs Frith did not thrust her views upon them, yet inevitably the matter that she was beginning to believe herself became known to the other women. It was received with incredulity at first, but as a matter that required the most deep and serious thought. Most of the women had been churchgoers when they got the chance, mostly of Low Church sects; deep in their hearts they had been longing for the help of God. As their physical health improved throughout these weeks, their capacity for religious thought increased, and, as the weeks went on, accurate memory of the Australian began to fade, and was replaced by an awed and roseate memory of the man he had not been. If this incredible event that Mrs Frith believed could possibly be true, it meant indeed that they were in the hand of God; nothing could touch them then; they would win through and live through all their troubles and one day they would regain their homes, their husbands, and their western way of life. They marched on with renewed strength.

Jean did nothing to dispel these fancies, which were evidently helpful to the women, but she was not herself impressed. She was the youngest of all of them, and the only one unmarried; she had formed a very different idea of Joe Harman. She knew him for a very human, very normal man; she had grown prettier, she knew, when he had come to talk to her, and more attractive. It had been a subconscious measure of defence that had led her to allow him to continue to refer to her as Mrs Boong; if the baby on her hip had misled him into classing her with all the other married women, that was just as well. In those villages, in the hot tropic nights when they wore little clothing, in that place of extraordinary standards or no standards at all, she knew that anything might have happened between them if he had known that she was an unmarried girl, and it might well have happened very quickly. Her grief for him was more real and far deeper than that of the other women, and it was not in the least because she thought that he had been divine. She was entirely certain in her own mind that he wasn't.

Toward the end of August they were in a village called Kuala Telang about half way between Kuantan and Kota Bahru. The Telang is a short, muddy river that wanders through a flat country of rice fields to the sea; the village stands on the south bank of the river just inside the sand bar at the mouth. It is a pretty place of palm and casuarina trees and long white beaches on which the rollers of the South China Sea break in surf. The village lives upon the fishing and on the rice fields. About fifteen fishing-boats operate from the river, big open sailing-boats with strange, high, flat figureheads at bow and stern. There is a sort of village square with wood and palm-leaf native shops grouped round about it; behind this stands a godown for the rice beside the river bank. This godown was empty at the time, and it was here that the party was accommodated.

The Japanese sergeant fell ill with fever here, probably malaria. He had not been himself since Kuantan; he had been sullen and depressed, and he seemed to feel the lack of companionship very much. As the women had grown stronger so he had grown weaker, and this was strange to them at first, because he had never been ill before. At first they had been pleased and relieved that this queer, ugly, uncouth little man was in eclipse, but as he grew more unhappy they suffered a strange reversal of feeling. He had been with them for a long time and he had done what was possible within the limits of his duty to alleviate their lot; he had carried their children willingly and he had wept when children died. When it was obvious that he had fever they took turns at carrying his rifle and his tunic and his boots and his pack for him, so that they arrived in the village as a queer procession, Mrs Warner leading the little yellow man clad only in his trousers, stumbling about in a daze. He walked more comfortably barefoot. Behind them came the other women carrying all his equipment as well as their own burdens.

Jean found the headman, a man of about fifty called Mat Amin bin Taib, and explained the situation to him. 'We are prisoners,' she said, 'marching from

Kuantan to Kota Bharu, and this Japanese is our guard. He is ill with fever, and we must find a shady house for him to lie in. He has authority to sign chits in the name of the Imperial Japanese Army for our food and accommodation, and he will do this for you when he recovers; he will give you a paper. We must have a place to sleep ourselves, and food.'

Mat Amin said, 'I have no place where white Mems would like to sleep.'

Jean said, 'We are not white mems any longer; we are prisoners and we are accustomed to living as your women live. All we need is a shelter and a floor to sleep on, and the use of cooking pots, and rice, and a little fish or meat and vegetables.'

'You can have what we have ourselves,' he said, 'but it is strange to see mems living so.'

He took the sergeant into his own house and produced a mattress stuffed with coconut fibre and a pillow of the same material; he had a mosquito net which was evidently his own and he offered this, but the women refused it because they knew the sergeant needed all the cooling breezes he could get. They made him take his trousers off and get into a sarong and lie down on the bed. They had no quinine left, but the headman produced a draught of his own concoction and they gave the sergeant some of this, and left him in the care of the headman's wife, and went to find their own quarters and food.

The fever was high all that night; in the morning when they came to see how he was getting on they did not like the look of him at all. He was still in a high fever and he was very much weaker than he had been; it seemed to them that he was giving up, and that was a bad sign. They took turns all that day to sit with him and bathe his face, and wash him; from time to time they talked to him to try and stimulate his interest, but without a great deal of success. In the evening Jean was sitting with him; he lay inert upon his back, sweating profusely; he did not answer anything she said.

Looking for something to attract his interest, she pulled his tunic to her and felt in the pocket for his paybook. She found a photograph in it, a photograph of a Japanese woman and four children standing by the entrance to a house. She said, 'Your children, gunso?' and gave it to him. He took it without speaking and looked at it; then he gave it back to her and motioned to her to put it away again.

When she had laid the jacket down she looked at him and saw that tears were oozing from his eyes and falling down to mingle with the sweat beads on his cheeks. Very gently she wiped them away.

He grew weaker and weaker, and two days later he died in the night. There seemed no particular reason why he should have died, but the disgrace of Kuantan was heavy on him and he seemed to have lost interest and the will to live. They buried him that day in the Moslem cemetery outside the village, and most of them wept a little for him as an old and valued friend.

The death of the sergeant left them in a most unusual position, for they were now prisoners without a guard. They discussed it at some length that evening after the funeral. 'I don't see why we shouldn't stay here, where we are,' said Mrs Frith. 'It's a nice place, this is, as nice as any that we've come to. That's what He said, we ought to find a place where we'd be out of the way, and just live there.'

Jean said, 'I know. There's two things we'd have to settle though. First, the Japs are bound to find out sometime that we're living here, and then the headman will get into trouble for having allowed us to stay here without telling them. They'd probably kill him. You know what they are.'

'Maybe they wouldn't find us, after all,' said Mrs Price.

'I don't believe Mat Amin is the man to take that risk,' Jean said. 'There isn't any reason why he should. If we stay he'll go straight to the Japanese and tell them that we're here.' She paused. 'The other thing is that we can't expect this village to go on feeding seventeen of us for ever just because we're white mems. They'll go and tell the Japs about us just to get rid of us.'

Mrs Frith said, 'If we were growing rice like that, maybe perhaps. Half the paddy fields we walked by coming in haven't been planted this year.'

Jean stared at her. 'That's quite right—they haven't. I wonder why that is?'

'All the men must have gone to the war,' said Mrs Warner. 'Working as coolies taking up that railway line, or something of that.'

Jean said slowly, 'What would you think of this? Suppose I go and tell Mat Amin that we'll work in the rice fields if he'll let us stay here? What would you think of that?'

Mrs Price laughed. 'Me, with my figure? Walking about in mud and water up to the knee planting them little seedlings in the mud, like you see the Malay girls doing?'

Jean said apologetically, 'It was just a thought.'

'And a very good one, too,' said Mrs Warner. 'I wouldn't mind working in the paddy fields if we could stay here and live comfortable and settled.'

Mrs Frith said, 'If we were growing rice like that, maybe they'd let us stay here—the Japs I mean. After all, in that way we'd be doing something useful, instead of walking all over the country like a lot of whipped dogs with no home.'

Next morning Jean went to the headman. She put her hands together in the praying gesture of greeting, and smiled at him and said in Malay, 'Mat Amin, why do we see the paddy fields not sown this year? We saw so many of them as we came to this place, not sown at all.'

He said, 'Most of the men, except the fishermen, are working for the army.' He meant the Japanese Army.

'On the railway?'

'No. They are at Gong Kedak. They are making a long piece of land flat, and making roads, and covering the land they have made flat with tar and stones, so that aeroplanes can come down there.'

'Are they coming back soon to plant paddy?'

'It is in the hand of God, but I do not think they will come back for many months. I have heard that after they have done this thing at Gong Kedak, there is another such place to be made at Machang, and another at Tan Yongmat. Once a man falls into the power of the Japanese it is not easy for him to escape and come back to his home.'

'Who, then, will plant the paddy, and reap it?'

'The women will do what they can. Rice will be short next year, not here, because we shall not sell the paddy that we need to eat ourselves. We shall not have enough to sell to the Japanese. I do not know what they are going to eat, but it will not be rice.'

Jean said, 'Mat Amin, I have serious matters to discuss with you. If there were a man amongst us I would send him to talk for us, but there is no man. You will not be offended if I ask you to talk business with a woman, on behalf of women?' She now knew something of the right approach to a Mohammedan.

He bowed to her, and led her to his house. There was a small rickety veranda; they went up to this and sat down upon the floor facing each other. He was a level-eyed old man with close-cropped hair and a small, clipped moustache, naked to the waist and wearing a sarong; his face was firm, but not unkind. He called sharply to his wife within the house to bring out coffee.

Jean waited till the coffee appeared, making small talk for politeness; she knew the form after six months in the villages. It came in two thick glasses, without milk and sweet with sugar. She bowed to him, and lifted her glass and sipped, and set it down again. 'We are in a difficulty,' she said frankly. 'Our guard is dead, and what now will become of us is in our own hands–and in yours. You know our story. We were taken prisoner at Panong, and since then we have walked many hundreds of miles to this place. No Japanese commander will receive us and put us in a camp and feed us and attend to us in illness, because each commander thinks that these things are the duty of the other; so they march us under guard from town to town. This has been going on now for more than six months, and in that time half of our party have died upon the road.'

He inclined his head.

'Now that our gunso is dead,' she said, 'what shall we do? If we go on until we find a Japanese officer and report to him, he will not want us; nobody in all this country wants us. They will not kill us quickly, as they might if we were men. They will get us out of the way by marching us on to some other place, perhaps into a country of swamps such as we have come through. So we shall grow ill again, and one by one we shall all die. That is what lies ahead of us, if we report now to the Japanese.'

He replied, 'It is written that the angels said, "Every soul shall taste of death, and we will prove you with evil and with good for a trial of you, and unto us shall ye return."'

She thought quickly; the words of the headman at Dilit came into her mind. She said, 'It is also written, "If ye be kind towards women and fear to wrong them, God is well acquainted with what ye do."'

He eyed her steadily. 'Where is that written?'

She said, 'In the Fourth Surah.'

'Are you of the Faith?' he asked incredulously.

She shook her head. 'I do not want to deceive you. I am a Christian; we are all Christians. The headman of a village on our road was kind to us, and when I thanked him he said that to me. I do not know the Koran.'

'You are a very clever woman,' he said. 'Tell me what you want.'

'I want our party to stay here, in this village,' she said, 'and go to work in the paddy fields, as your women do.' He stared at her, astonished. 'This will be dangerous for you,' she said. 'We know that very well. If Japanese officers find us in this place before you have reported to them that we are here, they will be very angry. And so, I want you to do this. I want you to let us go to work at once with one or two of your women to show us what to do. We will work all day for our food alone and a place to sleep. When we have worked so for two weeks, I will go myself and find an officer and report to him, and tell him what we are doing. And you shall come with me, as headman of this village, and you shall tell the officer that more rice will be grown for the Japanese if we are allowed to continue working in the rice fields. These are the things I want.'

'I have never heard of white mems working in the paddy fields,' he said.

She asked, 'Have you ever heard of white mems marching and dying as we have marched and died?'

He was silent.

'We are in your hands,' she said. 'If you say, go upon your way and walk on to some other place, then we must go, and going we must die. That will then be a matter between you and God. If you allow us to stay and cultivate your fields and live with you in peace and safety, you will get great honour when the English Tuans return to this country after their victory. Because they will win this war in the end; these Short Ones are in power now, but they cannot win against the Americans and all the free peoples of the world. One day the English Tuans will come back.'

He said, 'I shall be glad to see that day.'

They sat in silence for a time, sipping the glasses of coffee. Presently the headman said, 'This is a matter not to be decided lightly, for it concerns the whole village. I will think about it and I will talk it over with my brothers.'

Jean went away, and that evening after the hour of evening prayer she saw a gathering of men squatting with the headman in front of his house; they were all old men, because there were very few young ones in Kuala Telang at that time, and young ones probably would not have been admitted to the conference in any case. Later that evening Mat Amin came to the godown and asked for Mem Paget; Jean came out to him, carrying the baby. She stood talking to him in the light of a small oil lamp.

'We have discussed this matter that we talked about,' he said. 'It is a strange thing, that white mems should work in our rice fields, and some of my brothers are afraid that the white Tuans will not understand when they come back, and that they will be angry, saying we have made you work for us against your will.'

Jean said, 'We will give you a letter now, that you can show them if they should say that.'

He shook his head. 'It is not necessary. It is sufficient if you tell the Tuans when they come back that this thing was done because you wished it so.'

She said, 'That we will do.'

They went to work next day. There were six married women in the party at that time, and Jean, and ten children including Jean's baby. The headman took them out to the fields with two Malay girls, Fatimah binti Darus and Raihana binti Hassan. He gave them seven small fields covered in weeds to start upon, an area that was easily within their power to manage. There was a roofed platform nearby in the fields for resting in the shade; they left the youngest children here and went to work.

The seven women were all fairly robust; the journey had eliminated the ones who would have been unable to stand agricultural work. Those who were left were women of determination and grit, with high morale and a good sense of humour. As soon as they became accustomed to the novelty of working ankle-deep in mud and water they did not find the work exacting, and presently as they became accustomed to it they were seized with an ambition to show the village that white mems could do as much work as Malay women, or more.

Paddy is grown in little fields surrounded by a low wall of earth, so that water from a stream can be led into the field at will to turn it into a shallow pool. When the water is let out again the earth bottom is soft mud, and weeds can be pulled out by hand and the ground hoed and prepared for the seedlings. The seedlings are raised by scattering the rice in a similar nursery field, and they are then transplanted in rows into the muddy field. The field is then flooded again for a few days while the seedlings stand with their heads above the water in the hot sun, and the water is let out again for a few days to let the sun get to the roots. With alternating flood and dry in that hot climate the plants grow very quickly to about the height of wheat, with feathery ears of rice on top of the stalks. The rice is harvested by cutting off the ears with a little knife, leaving the straw standing, and is taken in sacks to the village to be winnowed. Water buffaloes are then turned in to eat the straw and fertilize the ground and tramp it all about, and the ground is ready for sowing again to repeat the cycle. Two crops a year are normally got from the rice fields, and there is no rotation of crop.

Working in these fields is not unpleasant when you get accustomed to it. There are worse things to do in a very hot country than to put on a large conical sun-hat of plaited palm leaves and take off most of your clothes, and play about with mud and water, damming and diverting little trickling streams. By the end of the fortnight the women had settled down to it and quite liked the work, and all the children loved it from the first. No Japanese came near the village in that time.

On the sixteenth day Jean started out with the headman, Mat Amin, to go and look for the Japanese; they carried the sergeant's rifle and equipment, and his uniform, and his paybook. There was a place called Kuala Rakit twenty-seven miles away where a Japanese detachment was stationed, and they went there.

They took two days to walk this distance, staying overnight at a place called Bukit Perah. They stayed with the headman there, Jean sleeping in the back quarters with the women. They went on next day and came to Kuala Rakit in the evening; it was a very large village, or small town. Here Mat Amin took her to see an official of the Malay administration at his house, Tungku Bentara Raja. Tungku Bentara was a little thin Malay who spoke excellent English; he was genuinely concerned at the story that he heard from Mat Amin and from Jean.

'I am very, very sorry,' he said at last. 'I cannot do much to help you directly, because the Japanese control everything we do. It is terrible that you should have to work in the rice fields.'

'That's not terrible at all,' Jean said. 'As a matter of fact, we rather like it. We want to stay there, with Mat Amin here. If the Japanese have got a camp for women in this district I suppose they'll put us into that, but if they haven't, we don't want to go on marching all over Malaya. Half of us have died already doing that.'

'You must stay with us tonight,' he said. 'Tomorrow I will have a talk with the Japanese Civil Administrator. There is no camp here for women, anyway.'

That night Jean slept in a bed for the first time in nearly seven months. She did not care for it much; having grown used to sleeping on the floor she found it cooler to sleep so than to sleep on a mattress. She did not actually get out of bed and sleep upon the floor, but she came very near to it. The bath and shower after the bath taken by holding a gourd full of water over her head, however, were a joy, and she spent a long time washing.

In the morning she went with Tungku Bentara and Mat Amin to the Japanese Civil Administrator, and told her tale again. The Civil Administrator had been to the State University of California and spoke first-class American English; he was sympathetic, but declared that prisoners were nothing to do with him, being the concern of the Army. He came with them, however, to see the military commanding officer, a Colonel Matisaka, and Jean told her tale once more.

It was quite clear that Colonel Matisaka considered women prisoners to be a nuisance, and he had no intention whatsoever of diverting any portion of his force to guarding them. Left to himself he would probably have sent them marching on, but with Tungku Bentara and the Civil Administrator in his office and acquainted with the facts he could hardly do that. In the end he washed his hands of the whole thing and told the Civil Administrator to make what arrangements he thought best. The Civil Administrator told Bentara that the women could stay where they were for the time being, and Jean started back for Kuala Telang with Mat Amin.

They lived there for three years.

'It was three years wasted, just chopped out of one's life,' she said. She raised her head and looked at me, hesitantly. 'At least–I suppose it was. I know a lot about Malays, but that's not worth much here in England.'

'You won't know if it was wasted until you come to an end of your life,' I said. 'Perhaps not then.'

She nodded. 'I suppose that's right.' She took up the poker and began scraping the ash from the bars of the grate. 'They were so very kind to us,' she said. 'They couldn't have been nicer, within the limits of what they are and what they've got. Fatimah, the girl who showed us what to do in the rice fields in those first weeks–she was a perfect dear. I got to know her very well indeed.'

'Is that where you want to go back to?' I asked.

She nodded. 'I would like to do something for them, now that I've got this money. We lived with them for three years, and they did everything for us. We'd have all died before the war was ended if they hadn't taken us in and let us stay with them. And now I've got so much, and they so very, very little . . .'

'Don't forget you haven't got as much as all that,' I said. 'Travelling to Malaya is a very expensive journey.'

She smiled. 'I know. What I want to do for them won't cost so very much–not more than fifty pounds, if that. We had to carry water in that village–that's the women's work–and it's a fearful job. You see, the river's tidal at the village so the water's brackish; you can use it for washing in or rinsing out your clothes, but drinking water has to be fetched from the spring, nearly a mile away. We used to go for it with gourds, two in each hand with a stick between them, morning and evening–a mile there and a mile back–four miles a day. Fatimah and the other girls didn't think about it; it's what the village has done always, generation after generation.'

'That's why you want to dig a well?'

She nodded. 'It's something I could do for them, for the women–something that would make life easier for them, as they made life easier for us. A well right in the middle of the village, within a couple of hundred yards of every house. It's what they ought to have. I'm sure it wouldn't have to be more than about ten feet deep, because there's water all about. The water level can't be more than about ten feet down, or fifteen feet at the most. I thought if I went back there and offered to engage a gang of well-diggers to do this for them, it'd sort of wind things up. And after that I could enjoy this money with a clear conscience.' She looked up at me again. 'You don't think that's silly, do you?'

'No,' I said. 'I don't think that. The only thing is, I wish it wasn't quite so far away. Travelling there and back will make a very big hole in a year's income.'

'I know that,' she said. 'If I run out of money, I'll take a job in Singapore or somewhere for a few months and save up a bit.'

'As a matter of interest,' I said, 'why didn't you stay out there and get a job? You know the country so well.'

She said, 'I had a scunner of it, then—in 1945. We were all dying to get home. They sent three trucks for us from Kota Bahru, and we were taken to the airfield there and flown down to Singapore in a Dakota with an Australian crew. And there I met Bill Holland, and I had to tell him about Eileen, and Freddie and Jane.' Her voice dropped. 'All the family, except Robin; he was four years old by that time, and quite a sturdy little chap. They let me travel home with Bill and Robin, to look after Robin. He looked on me as his mother, of course.'

She smiled a little. 'Bill wanted to make it permanent,' she said. 'I couldn't do that. I couldn't have been the sort of wife he wanted.'

I said nothing.

'When we landed, England was so green and beautiful,' she said. 'I wanted to forget about the war, and forget about the East, and grow to be an ordinary person again. I got this job with Pack and Levy and I've been there two years now—ladies' handbags and attaché cases for the luxury trade, nothing to do with wars or sickness or death. I've had a happy time there, on the whole.'

She was very much alone when she got home. She had cabled to her mother directly she reached Singapore; there was a long delay, and then she got a cable in reply from her Aunt Agatha in Colwyn Bay, breaking to her the news that her mother was dead. Before she left Singapore she heard that her brother Donald had died upon the Burma-Siam railway. She must have felt very much alone in the world when she regained her freedom; it seemed to me that she had shown great strength of character in refusing an offer of marriage at that time. She landed at Liverpool, and went to stay for a few weeks with her Aunt Agatha at Colwyn Bay; then she went down to London to look for a job.

I asked her why she had not got in touch with her uncle, the old man at Ayr. 'Quite honestly,' she said, 'I forgot all about him; or if I thought of him at all I thought he was dead, too. I only saw him once, that time when I was eleven years old, and he looked about dead then. It never entered my head that he would still be alive. Mother's estate was all wound up, and there were very few of her personal papers left, because they were all in the Pagets' house in Southampton when that got blitzed. If I had thought about Uncle Douglas I wouldn't have known where he lived . . .'

It was still pouring with rain. We decided to give up the idea of going out that afternoon, and to have tea in my flat. She went out into my little kitchen and began getting it, and I busied myself with laying the tea table and cutting bread and butter. When she came in with the tray, I asked, 'When do you think of going to Malaya, then?'

She said, 'I thought I'd book my passage for the end of May, and go on working at Pack and Levy up till then,' she said. 'That's about another six weeks. By then I'll have enough saved up to pay my passage out and home, and I'll still have about sixty pounds I saved out of my wages in this last two years.' She had been into the cost of her journey, and had found a line of intermediate class cargo ships that took about a dozen passengers for a relatively modest fare to Singapore. 'I think I'll have to fly to Kota Bahru from Singapore,' she said.

'Malayan Airways go to Kuantan and then to Kota Bahru. I don't know how I'll get from Kota Bahru to Kuala Telang, but I expect there'll be something.'

She was quite capable of walking it, I thought; a journey through the heart of Malaya could mean little to her now. I had had the atlas out while she had been telling me her story to see where the places were, and I looked at it again now. 'You could get off the aeroplane at Kuantan,' I said. 'It's shorter from there.'

'I know,' she said, 'I know it's a bit shorter. But I couldn't bear to go back there again.' There was distress in her voice.

To ease the situation I said idly, 'It would take me years to learn how to remember these Malay names.'

'It's all right when you know what they mean,' she said. 'They're just like English names. Bahru means New, and Kota means a fort. It's only Newcastle, in Malay.'

She went on with her work at Perivale, and I went on with mine in Chancery Lane, but I was unable to get her story out of my mind. There is a man called Wright, a member of my club, who was in the Malayan Police and was a prisoner of the Japanese during their occupation of Malaya, I think in Changi gaol. I sat next to him at dinner one night, and I could not resist sounding him about it. 'One of my clients told me an extraordinary story about Malaya the other day,' I said. 'She was one of a party of women that the Japanese refused to put into a camp.'

He laid his knife down. 'Not the party who were taken at Panong and marched across Malaya?'

'That was it,' I said. 'You know about them, do you?'

'Oh yes,' he said. 'It was a most extraordinary thing, as you say. The Japanese commanders marched them from place to place, till finally they were allowed to settle in a village on the east coast somewhere, and they lived there for the rest of the war. There was a very fine girl who was their leader; she spoke Malay fluently. She wasn't anybody notable; she'd been a shorthand typist in an office in Kuala Lumpur. A very fine type.'

I nodded. 'She's my client.'

'Is she! I always wondered what had happened to her. What's she doing now?'

I said dryly, 'She's a shorthand typist again, working in a handbag factory at Perivale.'

'Really!' He ate a mouthful or two, and then he said, 'I always thought that girl ought to have got a decoration of some sort. Unfortunately, there's nothing you can give to people like that. But if she hadn't been with them, all those women and children would have died. There was no one else in the party of that calibre at all.'

'I understand that half of them did die,' I said.

He nodded. 'I believe that's true. She got them settled down and working in the rice fields in the end, and after that they were all right.'

I saw Jean Paget from time to time in the six weeks before she left this country. She booked her passage to sail from London docks on June 2nd, and she gave notice to her firm to leave at the end of May. She told me that they were rather upset about it, and they offered her a ten shilling rise at once; in view of that she had told Mr Pack about her legacy, and he had accepted the inevitable.

I made arrangements for her income for the months of July and August and September to be available to her in Singapore, and I opened an account for her with the Chartered Bank for that purpose. As the time for her departure drew

closer I became worried for her, not because I was afraid that she would
overspend her income, but because I was afraid she would get into some
difficulty due to her expenses being higher than she thought they would be.
Nine hundred a year does not go very far in these days for a person travelling
about the east.

I mentioned that to her about a week before she left. 'Don't forget that you're
a fairly wealthy woman now,' I said. 'You're quite right to live within your
income and, indeed, I have to see you do. But don't forget that I have fairly
wide discretionary powers under your uncle's will. If you get into any
difficulty, or if you really need money, let me have a cable at once. As, for
example, if you should get ill.'

She smiled. 'That's very sweet of you,' she said. 'But honestly, I think I'll be
all right. I'm counting upon taking a job if I find I'm running short. After all, I
haven't got to get back here to England by a given date, or anything like that.'

I said, 'Don't stay too long away.'

She smiled. 'I shan't Mr Strachan,' she said. 'There's nothing to keep me in
Malaya once I've done this thing.'

She was giving up her room in Ealing, of course, and she asked if she might
leave a trunk and a suitcase in the box-room of my flat till she came back to
England. She brought them round the day before she sailed, and with them a
pair of skating boots with skates attached, which wouldn't go into the trunk.
She told me then that she was only taking one suitcase as her luggage.

'But what about your tropical kit?' I asked. 'Have you had that sent on?'

She smiled. 'I've got it with me in the suitcase,' she said. 'Fifty Paludrine
tablets and a hundred Sulphatriads, some repellent, and my old sarong. I'm not
going out to be a lady in Malaya.'

She had nobody but me to go down to the docks with her to see her off; she
was very much alone in the world, and friends she had who might have liked to
come were all working in jobs, and couldn't get the time off. I drove her down
in a taxi. She took her journey very much as a matter of course; she seemed to
have made no more preparation for a voyage half way round the world than a
girl of my generation would have made for a weekend at Chislehurst. The ship
was a new one and everything was bright and clean. When the steward opened
the door of her cabin she stood back amazed, because he had arranged the
flowers all round the little room, and there were plenty of them. 'Oh Noel,
look!' she said. 'Just look at all the flowers!' She turned to the steward.
'Wherever did they come from? Not from the Company?'

'They come in three big boxes yesterday evening,' he replied. 'Make a nice
show, don't they, Miss?'

She swung round on me. 'I believe you sent them.' And then she said, 'Oh,
how perfectly sweet of you!'

'English flowers,' I said. 'Just to remind you to come back to England soon.'
I must have had a premonition, even then, that she was never going to come
back.

Before I could realize what she was doing, she had slipped an arm round my
shoulders and kissed me on the lips. 'That's for the flowers, Noel,' she said
softly. 'For the flowers, and for everything you've done for me.' And I was so
dumbfounded and confused that all I could find to say to her was, 'I'll have
another of those when you come back.'

I didn't wait to see her ship go off, because partings are stupid things and best got over quickly. I went back in the taxi to my flat alone, and I remember that I stood for a long time at the window of my room watching the ornamented wall of the stables opposite and thinking of her fine new steamer going down the river past Gravesend and Tilbury, past Shoebury and the North Foreland, taking her away. And then I woke myself up and went and shifted her trunk and her suitcase to a corner of the box-room by themselves, and I stood for some time with her boots and skates in my hand, personal things of hers, wondering where they had better go. Finally I took them to my bedroom and put them in the bottom of my wardrobe, because I should never have forgiven myself if they had been stolen. She was just such a girl as one would have liked to have for a daughter, but we never had a daughter at all.

She travelled across half the world in her tramp steamer and she wrote to me from most of the ports she called at, from Marseilles and Naples, from Alexandria and Aden, from Colombo, from Rangoon, and from Penang. Wright was always very interested in her because he had known about her in Malaya, and I got into the habit of carrying her latest letter about with me and telling him about her voyage and how she was getting on. He knew the British Adviser to the Raja at Kota Bahru quite well, a Mr Wilson-Hays, and I got him to write out to Wilson-Hays by air mail telling him about Jean Paget and asking him to do what he could for her. He told me that that was rather necessary, because there was nowhere a lady could stay in Kota Bahru except with one of the British people who were living there. We got a very friendly letter back from Wilson-Hays saying that he was expecting her, and I was able to get a letter out to her by air mail to meet her at the Chartered Bank telling her what we had done.

She only stayed one night in Singapore, and took the morning plane to Kota Bahru; the Dakota wandered about all over Malaya calling at various places, and put her down upon the air-strip at Kota Bahru early in the afternoon. She got out of the Dakota wearing the same light grey coat and skirt in which she had left London, and Wilson-Hays was there himself to meet the aeroplane, with his wife.

I met Wilson-Hays at the United University Club a year later, when he was on leave. He was a tall, dark, quiet man with rather a long face. He said that she had been a little embarrassed to find that he had come to the airstrip to meet her personally; she did not seem to realize that she was quite a well-known person in that part of Malaya. Wilson-Hays knew all about her long before we wrote to him although, of course, he had heard nothing of her since the end of the war. He had sent word to Mat Amin when he got our letter to tell him that she was coming back to see them, and he had arranged to lend her his jeep with a driver to take her the hundred miles or só to Kuala Telang. I thought that very decent of him, and I told him so. He said that the prestige of the British was higher in the Kuala Telang district after the war was over than it was before, due solely to the presence of this girl and her party; he thought she'd earned the use of a jeep for a few days.

She stayed in the Residency two nights, and bought a few simple articles in the native shops. When she left in the jeep next morning she was wearing native clothes; she left her suitcase and most of her things with Mrs Wilson-Hays. She took with her only what a native woman of good class would take; she wore a faded old blue and white chequered sarong with a white coatee. She wore sandals as a concession to the softness of her feet, and she carried a plain tan

Chinese type umbrella as a sunshade. She had done her hair up on top of her head in the native style with a large comb in the middle of it. She carried a small palm-leaf basket, but Mrs Wilson-Hays told her husband there was very little in it; she took a toothbrush but no toothpaste; she took a towel and a cake of antiseptic soap and a few drugs. She took one change of clothes, a new sarong and a flowered cotton top to match; she took three small Woolworth brooches and two rings as little presents for her friends, but she took no cosmetics. That was about all she had.

'I thought her very wise to go like that,' said Wilson-Hays. 'If she had gone dressed as an Englishwoman she'd have made them embarrassed. Some of the English residents were quite upset when they heard she'd gone off in native dress–old school tie, and letting down the side, and all that sort of thing. I must say, when I saw her go I thought it was rather a good thing to do.' He paused. 'After all, it's how she was dressed all through the war, and nobody talks about her letting down the side then.'

It is a long day in a jeep from Kota Bahru to Kuala Telang; the roads are very poor, and there are four main rivers to be crossed which necessitate ferrying the jeep over in a boat, apart from a large number of fords. It took her fourteen hours to cover the hundred miles, and it was dark when they drove into Kuala Telang. There was a buzz of excitement as the jeep drove through the shadowy village, and people came out of their houses doing up their sarongs; there was a full moon that night, so that there was light enough to see to drive. They stopped in front of the headman's house, and she got out of the jeep a little wearily, and went to him, and put her hands up in the praying gesture, and said in Malay, 'I have come back, Mat Amin, lest you should think the white mems have forgotten all about you when their need is past.'

He said, 'We have thought and talked about you ever since you went.' And then there were people thronging about them, and she saw Fatimah approaching with a baby in her arms and a toddler hanging on to her sarong, and she pushed through the crowd and took her by the hand, and said, 'It is too long since we met.' And there was Raihana, and Safirah binti Yacob, and Safirah binti Taib, and little Ibrahim who squinted, now grown into a young man, and his brother Samat, and old Zubeidah, and Meriam, and many others, some of whom she did not know, because the men had come back from the labour gangs soon after she left Malaya, and there were a number of new faces.

Fatimah was married to a young man called Derahman bin Ismail, and she brought him forward and presented him to the white mem; Jean bowed before him and wished that she had brought a shawl to pull over her face, as would have been polite when being introduced to a strange man. She put her hand up to her face, and said, 'Excuse me that I have no veil.' He bowed to her and said, 'It is no matter,' and Fatimah broke in and said, 'He knows and everybody knows that the white mems never veiled their faces when they lived with us, because different people have different ways. Oh Djeen, we are so happy that you have come back.'

She made arrangements with Mat Amin for the accommodation of the driver, and then went with Fatimah to her husband's house. They asked if she had eaten, and she said no, and they made her a supper of rice and blachan, the highly-spiced paste of ripe prawns and fish that the Malays preserve in an up-ended concrete drain pipe. And presently, tired out, she made a pillow of her palm-leaf bag and lay down on a mat as she had done a thousand times before, and loosened the sarong around her waist, and slept. It would not be entirely accurate to say that she slept well upon the floor after sleeping in a bed for three years. She woke many times throughout the night, and listened to the noises of the night, and watched the moonlight creep around the house, and she was happy.

She had a talk with Fatimah and Meriam and old Zubeidah next morning, squatting round the cooking-pots behind the house out of the way of the men. 'Every day that I have been away I have thought of this place,' she said; it was not precisely true, but near enough. 'I have thought of you all living and working as I lived and worked. I was working in England, in an office at books in the way that women have to work in my country, because, as you know, I am a poor woman and I have had to work all my life to earn my living till I find a husband who suits me, and I am very particular.' The women laughed, and old Zubeidah said, 'It is very strange that a woman should earn her living in that way.'

Meriam said, 'There is a woman of our people working in the bank at Kuala Rakit. I saw her through the window. She was doing something with her fingers on a machine, and it went clock-click-click.'

Jean nodded. 'That is how I earn my living in my country, working a machine like that to make a printed letter for the Tuan. But recently my uncle died; he lived far away from me and I have only met him once, but he had no other relatives and I inherited his money, so that now I need not work unless I want to.' A murmur of appreciation went around the women. Two or three more had drifted up to enlarge the circle. 'And now, having money of my own for the first time in my life, I thought more of you here in Kuala Telang than ever before, and of your kindness to us when we lived with you as prisoners. And it came to me that I should give a thankoffering to this place, and that this thankoffering should be a present from a woman to the women of Kuala Telang, nothing to do with the men.'

There was a pleased and excited little buzz amongst the women who surrounded her. Old Zubeidah said, 'It is true, the men get everything.' One or two of the women looked shocked at this heresy.

'I have thought many times,' Jean said, 'that there should be a well in this place, so that you should not have to fetch fresh water from the spring morning and evening, but you could walk out of your houses only fifty paces at the most and there would be a well of fresh water with a bucket that you could go to and draw water at any time of the day whenever you had the need of cool, fresh water.' There was a little buzz of appreciation again. 'There would be smooth stones around the well where you could sit and talk while the young men work the bucket for you. And close beside the well, I would have an atap house for washing clothes with long slabs of smooth stone or concrete arranged so that you could face each other while you wash, and talk, but all surrounded by an atap wall so that the men will not be able to see.' The buzz rose to an excited clamour. 'This is what I want to do, as a thankoffering. I will engage a gang of well-diggers, and they shall dig the well, and I will pay masons for the stonework round the top, and I will pay carpenters to build the washing-house. But for the arrangement inside the house I shall want two or three women of experience to advise me how it should be devised, for the height of the slabs, for concrete pools or channels for the water, and so on. This is the gift of a woman for women, and in this thing the men shall do what women say.'

There was a long clamour of discussion. Some of the women were doubtful if the men would ever allow such a thing, and some were doubtful whether it was not impious to wish to alter the arrangements that had satisfied their mothers and their grandmothers before them. But most were avid for the innovation if it could be achieved; once they were used to the idea they savoured it and turned it over, examining it in every detail and discussing where the well should be and where the washhouse, and where the concrete pools should be, and where the drain. At the end of a couple of hours they had accepted the idea wholeheartedly, and Jean was satisfied that it would fill a real need, and that there was nothing that they would have preferred her to give.

That evening she sat opposite Mat Amin on the small veranda before his house, as she had sat so many times before when matters that concerned the women had to be discussed. She sipped her coffee. 'I have come to talk with you,' she said, 'because I want to give a thankoffering to this place, that people may remember when the white women came here, and you were kind to them.'

He said, 'The wife has been talking of nothing else all day, with other women. They say you want to make a well.'

Jean said, 'That is true. This is a thankoffering from all the English mems to Kuala Telang, but because we are women it is fitting that it should be a present for the women of this place. When we lived here it was a great labour, morning and evening, to fetch water from the spring and I was sorry for your women when I thought of them, in England, fetching water all that way. That is why I want my thankoffering to be a well in the middle of the village.'

He said, 'The spring was good enough for their mothers and their grandmothers before them. They will get ideas above their station in life if they have a well.'

She said patiently, 'They will have more energy to serve you faithfully and kindly if they have this well, Mat Amin. Do you remember Raihana binti Ismail who lost her baby when she was three months' pregnant, carrying this water?' He was shocked that she should speak of such a thing, but English mems would speak of anything. 'She was ill for a year after that, and I don't think she was any good to her husband ever again. If the women had had this well I want to give you as a thankoffering, that accident would not have happened.'

He said, 'God disposes of the lives of women as well as those of men.'

She smiled gently, 'Do I have to remind you, Mat Amin, that it is written, "Men's souls are naturally inclined to covetousness; but if ye be kind towards women and fear to wrong them, God is well acquainted with what ye do."'

He laughed and slapped his thigh. 'You said that to me many times when you lived here, whenever you wanted anything, but I have not heard it since.'

'It would be kind to let the women have their well,' she said.

He replied, still laughing, 'I say this to you, Si-Jean; that when women want a thing as badly as they want this well that you have promised them, they usually get it. But this is a matter which concerns the village as a whole, and I must consult my brothers.'

The men sat in conference next morning, squatting on their heels in the shade of the atap market house. Presently they sent for Jean and she squatted down with them a little to one side as is fitting for a woman, and they asked her where the well was to be put, and where the atap washhouse. She said that everything was in their hands, but it would be convenient for the women if it was on the patch of ground in front of Chai San's shop, with the atap washhouse west of it and pointing towards Ahmed's house. They all got up then and went to see the ground and discuss it from all angles, and all the women of the village stood around and watched their lords making this important decision, and Djeen talking with them almost as if she was an equal.

She did not hurry them; she had lived three years in this village and she knew the slowness of their mental processes, the caution with which all innovations were approached. It took them two days to make up their minds that the well would be a good thing to have, and that the Wrath of God would not descend upon them if they put the work in hand.

Well-digging is a skilled craft, and there was one family only on the coast who could be entrusted with the work; they lived about five miles from Kuantan. Mat Amin dictated a letter for the Imam to write in the Jawi script, and then they took it into Kuala Rakit and posted it. Jean sent for five sacks of cement from Kota Bahru, and settled down to wait for several weeks while the situation developed.

She spent much of the time with the fishermen on their boats, or sitting on the beach and playing with the children. She taught them to build sand castles and to play Noughts and Crosses on a chequer drawn with the finger in the sand; she bathed and swam a good deal, and worked for a week in the rice fields at the time of harvest. She had lived so long with these people that she was patient about the passage of time; moreover, she had a use for time to consider what she was going to do with her life now that she had no further need to work. She waited there for three weeks in idleness, and she did not find it tedious.

The well-diggers and the cement arrived about the same time, and work commenced. The diggers were a family of an old grey-bearded father, Suleiman, and his two sons, Yacob and Hussein. They spent a day surveying the land and all the arguments for the site chosen for the well had to be gone over once again to satisfy these experts; when work finally began it was done quickly and well. The diggers worked from dawn till dusk, with one at the bottom of the shaft and the other two disposing of the soil on top; they bricked it downwards from the top as they worked, supporting the brickwork upon stakes driven into the earth sides.

Old Suleiman, the father, was a mine of information to the village, for he travelled up and down the east coast of Malaya building and repairing wells, and so visited most villages from time to time. The men and women of Kuala Telang used to sit around watching the progress of the new well and gossiping with the old man, getting news of their acquaintances and relatives up and down the coast. Jean was sitting there one afternoon, and said to him, 'You are from Kuantan?'

'From Batu Sawah,' said the old man. 'That is two hours' walk from Kuantan. Our home is there, but we are great travellers.'

She was silent for a moment; then she said, 'Do you remember the Japanese officer in charge at Kuantan in the first year of the war, Captain Sugamo?'

'Assuredly,' the old man replied. 'He is a very bad man, and we were glad when he went away. Captain Ichino who came after him was better.'

Jean was surprised that he did not seem to know the Sugamo was dead; she had supposed that the War Crimes Commission would have taken evidence in Kuantan. She told him, 'Captain Sugamo is dead now. He was sent to the Burma-Siam railway, and there he caused many atrocities, and many murders.

But the Allies caught him when the war was over, and he was tried for murder, and executed in Penang.'

'I am glad to hear it,' the old man replied. 'I will tell my sons.' He called down the well with the news; it was discussed a little, and then the men went on with their work.

Jean asked, 'Did he do many evil things in Kuantan?' There was one still hideously fresh in her mind, but she could not bring herself to speak of it directly.

Suleiman said, 'Many people were tortured.'

She nodded. 'I saw one myself.' It had to come out, and it did not matter what she said to this old man. 'When we were starving and ill, a soldier who was a prisoner helped us. The Japanese caught him, and they crucified him with nails through his hands, and they beat him to death.'

'I remember that,' the old man said. 'He was in hospital at Kuantan.'

Jean stared at him. 'Old man, when was he in hospital? He died.'

'Perhaps there were two.' He called down the well to Yacob. 'The English soldier who was crucified and beaten at Kuantan in the first year of the war. The English mem knew him. Tell us, did that man die?'

Hussein broke in. 'The one who was beaten was an Australian, not English. He was beaten because he stole chickens.'

'Assuredly,' the old man said. 'It was for stealing the black chickens. But did he live or die?'

Yacob called up from the bottom of the well. 'Captain Sugamo had him taken down that night; they pulled the nails out of his hands. He lived.'

5

In Kuantan, in the evening of that day in July 1942, a sergeant had come to Captain Sugamo in the District Commissioner's house, and had reported that the Australian was still alive. Captain Sugamo found this curious and interesting, and as there was still half an hour before his evening rice, he strolled down to the recreation ground to have a look.

The body still hung by its hands, facing the tree. Blood had drained from the blackened mess that was its back and had run down the legs to form a black pool on the ground, now dried and oxidized by the hot sun. A great mass of flies covered the body and the blood. But the man undoubtedly was still alive; when Captain Sugamo approached the face the eyes opened, and looked at him with recognition.

It is doubtful if the West can ever fully understand the working of a Japanese mind. When Captain Sugamo saw that the Australian recognized him from the threshold of death, he bowed reverently to the torn body, and he said with complete sincerity, 'Is there anything that I can get for you before you die?'

The ringer said distinctly, 'You bloody bastard. I'll have one of your black chickens and a bottle of beer.'

Captain Sugamo stood looking at the wreck of the man nailed to the tree, and his face was completely expressionless. Presently he turned upon his heel and went back to his house. He called for his orderly as he went into the shade, and he told him to fetch a bottle of beer and a glass, but not to open the bottle. The man protested that there was no beer. Captain Sugamo already knew that, but he sent his orderly to the town to visit all the Chinese eating-houses to see if he could find a bottle of beer anywhere in Kuantan. In an hour the man came back; Captain Sugamo was sitting in exactly the same attitude as when he had gone out to find the beer. With considerable apprehension he informed his officer that there was no beer in all Kuantan. He was dismissed, and went away gladly.

Death to Captain Sugamo was a ritual. There had been an element of holiness in his approach to the Australian, and having offered in the hearing of his men to implement the last wishes of his victim he was personally dedicated to see that those last wishes were provided. If a bottle of beer had been available he would have sacrificed one of his remaining black Leghorns and sent the cooked meat and the beer down to the dying body on the tree; he might even have carried the tray down himself. By doing so he would have set an example of chivalry and Bushido to the troops under his command. Unfortunately, it was impossible for him to provide the bottle of beer, and since the beer was missing and the soldier's dying wish could not be met in full, there was no point in sacrificing one of the remaining black Leghorns. He could not carry out his own part in the ritual; he could not show Bushido by granting the man's dying wish. Therefore, the Australian could not be allowed to die, or he himself would be disgraced.

He called for his sergeant. When the man came, he ordered him to take a party with a stretcher to the recreation ground. They were to pull the nails out and take the man down from the tree without injuring him any further, and put him face downwards on the stretcher, and take him to the hospital.

To Jean, the news that the Australian was still alive came like the opening of a door. She slipped away and went and sat in the shade of a casuarina tree at the head of the beach to consider this incredible fact. The sun glinted on the surf and the beach was so white, the sea so blue, that it was almost ecstasy to look at them. She felt as if she had suddenly come out of a dark tunnel that she had walked down for six years. She tried to pray, but she had never been religious and she didn't know how to put what she was feeling into a prayer. The best she could do was to recollect the words of a prayer that they had used at school sometimes. 'Lighten our darkness, oh Lord, and of Thy great mercy . . .' That was all she could remember, and she repeated it over and over to herself that afternoon. Her darkness had been lightened by the well-diggers.

She went back that evening and spoke to Suleiman again about the matter, but neither he nor his sons could supply much further information. The Australian had been in the hospital at Kuantan for a long time, but how long they did not know. Yacob said that he had been there for a year, but she soon found that he only meant a very long time. Hussein said three months, and Suleiman did not know how long he had been there, but said that he was sent down on a ship to Singapore to a prison camp, and he was then walking with two sticks. She could not find out from them when that was.

So she had to leave it, and she stayed on in Kuala Telang till the well and washhouse were completed. She had already started the carpenters upon the washhouse after long consultations with the elder women, and the concrete work was now completed in the shuttering, and drying out. On the day that water was reached at the bottom of the well the carpenters began to erect the posts for the atap house, and the well and the house were finished about the same time. Two days were spent in baling out the muddy water from the well till it ran clean, and then they had an opening ceremony when Jean washed her own sarong and all the women crowded into the washhouse laughing, and the men stood round in a tolerant circle at a distance, wondering if they had been quite wise to allow anything that made the women laugh so much.

On the next day she sent a telegram by runner to Kuala Rakit to be dispatched to Wilson-Hays asking him to send the jeep for her, and a day or two later it arrived. She left in a flurry of shy good wishes with some moisture in her eyes; she was going back to her own place and her own people, but she was leaving three years of her life behind her, and that is never a very easy thing to do.

She got back to the Residency at Kota Bahru after dark that night, too tired to eat. Mrs Wilson-Hays sent her up a cup of tea and a little fruit to her bedroom, and she had a long, warm bath, putting off her native clothes for the last time. She lay on the bed in the cool, spacious room under the mosquito net, rested and growing sleepy, and what she thought about was Ringer Harman, and the red country he had told her of round Alice Springs, and euros, and wild horses.

She walked with Wilson-Hays in the garden of the Residency next morning after breakfast in the cool of the day. She told him what she had done in Kuala Telang; he asked her where she had got the idea of the washhouse from. 'It's obvious that's what they need,' she said. 'Women don't like washing their clothes in public, especially Moslem women.'

He thought about it for a minute. 'You've probably started something,' he remarked at last. 'Every village will want one now. Where did you get the plan of it—the arrangement of the sinks and all that sort sort of thing?'

'We worked it out ourselves,' she said. 'They knew what they wanted all right.'

They strolled along by the river, brown and muddy and half a mile wide, running its way down to the sea. As they walked she told him about the Australian, because she could talk freely about that now. She told him what had happened. 'His name was Joe Harman,' she said, 'and he came from a place near Alice Springs. I would like to get in touch with him again. Do you think I could find out anything about him in Singapore?'

He shook his head. 'I shouldn't think so, not now that S.E.A.C. is disbanded. I shouldn't think there's any record of prisoners of war in Singapore now.'

'How would one find out about him, then?'

'You say he was an Australian?'

She nodded.

'I think you'd have to write to Canberra,' he said. 'They ought to have a record of all prisoners there. I suppose you don't happen to know his unit?'

She shook her head. 'I'm afraid I don't.'

'That might make it difficult, of course—there may be several Joe Harmans. I should start off by writing to the Minister for the Army—that's what they call him, the head of the War Office. Just address your letter to the Minister for the Army, Canberra, Australia. Something might come of that. What you want is an address where you could write to him, I suppose?'

Jean stared across the river at the rubber trees and coconut palms. 'I suppose so. As a matter of fact, I've got an address of a sort. He used to work before the war on a cattle station called Wollara, near a place called Alice Springs. He said that they were keeping his job open for him there.'

'If you've got that address,' he observed, 'I should write there. You're much more likely to find him that way than by writing to Canberra.'

'I might do that,' she said slowly. 'I would like to see him again. You see, it was because of us that it all happened . . .'

It had been her intention to go back to Singapore and wait there for a boat to England; if she had to wait long for a cheap passage she intended to try and find a job for a few weeks or months. Malayan Airways called at Koto Bahru next day, and the Dakota landed at Kuantan on the way down to Singapore. She spoke to Wilson-Hays again that evening after dinner.

'Do you think there would be a hotel or anything at Kuantan if I stopped there for a day?' she asked.

He looked at her kindly. 'Do you want to go back there?' he asked.

'I think I do,' she said. 'I'd like to go and see the people at the hospital and find out what I can.'

He said, 'You'd better stay with David and Joyce Bowen. Bowen is the District Commissioner; he'd be glad to put you up.'

'I don't want to be a nuisance to people,' she said. 'Isn't there a resthouse that I could stay in? After all, I know this country fairly well.'

'That's why Bowen would like to meet you,' he remarked. 'You must realize that you're quite a well-known person in these parts. He would be very disappointed if you stayed at the resthouse.'

She looked at him in wonder. 'Do people think of me like that? I only did what anybody could have done.'

'That's as it may be,' he replied. 'The fact is, that you did it.'

She flew on down to Kuantan next day. Someone must have told the crew of the aircraft about her, because the Malay stewardess came to her after half an hour and said, 'We're just coming up to Kuala Telang, Miss Paget. Captain Philby wants to know if you would care to come forward to the cockpit and see it.' So she went forward through the door and stood between the pilots; they brought the Dakota down to about seven hundred feet and circled the village; she could see the well and the new atap roof of the washhouse, and she could see people standing gazing up at the machine. Fatimah and Zubeidah and Mat Amin. Then they straightened up and flew on down the coast, and Kuala Telang was left behind.

The Bowens met her at the airstrip, which is ten miles from the town of Kuantan; Wilson-Hays had sent them a signal that morning. They were a friendly unsophisticated couple, and she had no difficulty in telling them a little about the Australian soldier who had been tortured when they were sitting in the D.C.'s house, where Captain Sugamo had sat so often, over a cup of tea. They said that Sister Frost was now in charge of the hospital, but it was doubtful if there was anybody now upon the staff who was there in 1942. They drove down after tea to see Sister Frost.

She received them in the matron's room, very hygienic and smelling strongly of disinfectant. She was an Englishwoman about forty years of age. 'There's nobody here now who was on the staff then,' she said. 'Nurses in a place like this—they're always leaving to get married. We never seem to keep them longer than about two years. I don't know what to suggest.'

Bowen said, 'What about Phyllis Williams? She was a nurse here, wasn't she?'

'Oh, her,' the sister said disparagingly. 'She was here for the first part of the war until she married that man. She might know something about it.'

They left the hospital, and as they drove to find Phyllis Williams Mrs Bowen enlightened Jean. 'She's a Eurasian,' she said. 'Very dark, almost as dark as a Malay. She married a Chinese, a man called Bun Tai Lin who runs the cinema. What you'd call a mixed marriage, but they seem to get along all right. She's a Roman Catholic, of course.' Jean never fathomed the 'of course'.

The Bun Tai Lins lived in a rickety wooden house up the hill overlooking the harbour. They could not get the car to the house, but left it in the road and walked up a short lane littered with garbage. They found Phyllis Williams at home, a merry-faced, brown woman with four children around her and evidently about to produce a fifth. She was glad to see them and took them into a shabby room, the chief decorations of which were a set of pewter beer-mugs and a large oleograph of the King and Queen in coronation robes.

She spoke very good English. 'Oh yes, I remember that poor boy,' she said. 'Joe Harman, that was his name. I nursed him for three or four months—he *was* in a state when he came in. We none of us thought he'd live. But he got over it. He must have led a very healthy life, because his flesh healed wonderfully. He said that he was like a dog, he healed so well.'

She turned to Jean. 'Are you the lady that was leading the party of women and children from Panong?' she asked. 'I thought you must be. Fancy you coming here again! You know, he was always wanting to know about you and your party, if anybody knew the way you'd gone. And of course, *we* didn't know, and with that Captain Sugamo in the mood he was nobody was going to go round asking questions to find out.'

She turned to Jean. 'I forget your name?'

'Paget. Jean Paget.'

The Eurasian looked puzzled. 'That wasn't it. I wonder now, was he talking about someone different? I can't remember now what he called her, but it wasn't that. I thought it would have been you.'

'Mrs Frith?'

She shook her head. 'I'll remember presently.'

She could not tell them very much more than Jean knew already. The Australian had been sent down to a prison camp in Singapore as soon as he was fit to travel; they heard no more of him. They thought that he would make a good recovery in the end, though it would be years before the muscles of his back got back their strength if, indeed, they ever would. She knew no more than that.

They left presently and went down the garbage-strewn lane towards the car. When they were nearly at the bottom the woman called to them from the veranda. 'I just remembered that name. Mrs Boong. That's who he was always talking about, Mrs Boong. Was that one of your party?'

Jean laughed, and called back to her. 'That's what he used to call me!'

The woman was satisfied. 'I thought it must have been you that he was always talking about.'

On the way back to the D.C.'s house in the car, they passed the recreation ground. There were tennis nets rigged and one or two couples playing; there was a white young man playing a brown girl. The tree still stood overlooking the courts, and underneath it a couple of Malay women sat exactly where the feet of the tortured man had hung, on ground that had been soaked in blood, and gossiped while their children played around. It all looked very peaceful in the evening light.

Jean spent that night with the Bowens, and went on to Singapore next day in the Dakota. Wilson-Hays had advised her about hotels, and she stayed at the Adelphi opposite the Cathedral.

She wrote to me from there a couple of days later. It was a long letter, about eight pages long, written in ink smudged a little with the sweat that had formed on her hand as she wrote in that humid place. First she told me what had happened in Kuala Telang; she told me about the well-diggers and that Joe Harman was still alive. And then she went on,

'I've been puzzling over what I could do to get in touch with him again. You see, it was all because of us that it happened. He stole the chickens for us, and he must have known the sort of man that Captain Sugamo was, and the risk that he was taking. I must find out where he is living now, and if he's all right; I can't believe that he can be able to work as a stockrider after having been so terribly injured. I think he was a man who'd always fall upon his feet somehow or other if he was well enough, but I can't bear the thought that he might be still in hospital, perhaps, and likely to stay there for ever with his injuries.

I did think of writing to him at this place Wollara that he told me about, the cattle station that he worked on, somewhere near Alice Springs. But thinking it over, if he can't work he can't be there, and I don't suppose I'd ever get an answer to a letter from a place like that, or not for ages, anyway. I thought of writing to Canberra to try and find out something, but that's almost as bad. And this brings me to what I wanted to tell you when I started this letter, Noel, and I hope it won't be too much of a shock. I'm going on to Australia from here.

Don't think me absolutely crazy for doing this. The fare from here to Darwin costs sixty pounds by the Constellation, and you can get a bus from Darwin to Alice Springs; it takes two or three days but it ought to be much cheaper than flying. After paying the hotel bill here I shall still have about a hundred and seven pounds, not counting next month's money. I thought I'd go to Alice Springs and get to this place Wollara and find out about him there; someone in that district is bound to know what happened to him, and where he is now.

There are some merchant service officers staying here, very nice young men, and they tell me I can get a cabin on a merchant ship back to England probably from Townsville, that's on the east coast of Australia in Queensland, and if there isn't a ship there I'd certainly get one at Brisbane. I've been talking to a man in the Chartered Bank here in Raffles Place who is very helpful, and I've arranged with him to transfer my next month's money to the Bank of New South Wales in Alice Springs, and so I'll have money to get me across to Townsville or Brisbane. Write to me care of the Bank of New South Wales in Alice Springs, because I know I'm going to feel a long way from home when I get there.

I'm leaving here on Thursday by the Constellation, so I'll be in Australia somewhere by the time you get this letter. I have a feeling that I'm being a terrible nuisance to you, Noel, but I'll have an awful lot to tell you when I get back home. I don't think the trip home from Townsville or Brisbane can take longer than three months at the outside, so I shall be home in England in time for Christmas at the very latest.

I sat there reading and re-reading this, bitterly disappointed. I had been making plans for entertainments for her when she came back, I suppose—in fact, I know I had been. Old men who lead a somewhat empty life get rather stupid over things like that. Lester Robinson came into my office with a sheaf of papers in his hand as I was reading her letter for the third time; I laid the letter down. 'My Paget girl,' I said. 'You know—that Macfadden estate that we're trustees for. She's not coming home after all. She's gone on from Malaya to Australia.'

He glanced at me, and I suppose the disappointment that I felt showed in my face, because he said gently, 'I told you she was old enough to make a packet of trouble for us.' I looked up at him quickly to see what he meant by that, but he began talking about an unadopted road in Colchester, and the moment passed.

I went on with my work, but the black mood persisted and it was with me when I reached the club that night. I settled down after dinner in the library with a volume of Horace because I thought the mental exercise required to read the Latin would take my mind off things and put me in a better frame of mind. But I had forgotten my Horace, I suppose, because a phrase I had not read or thought about for forty years suddenly stared up at me from the page and brought me up with a round turn,

> −*Dulce ridentem Lalagen amabo,*
> *Dulce loquentum.*

It had been a part of my youth, that phrase, as I suppose it is a part of the youth of many young men who have been in love. I could not bear to go on reading Horace after that, and I sat thinking of sweetly smiling, soft-spoken Lalage on her way to Alice Springs in a long-distance bus, until I broke away from morbid fancies and got up and put the book back in the shelf.

It must have been about a week after that that Derek Harris came into my room as the client went out. Derek is one of our two articled clerks, and one day I expect to make him a partner; a pleasant fresh-faced lad. He said, 'Could you spare a few minutes for a stranger, sir?'

'What sort of stranger?' I inquired.

He said, 'A man called Harman. He came about an hour ago without any appointment and asked to see you. Sergeant Gunning asked if I would see him as you were engaged, and I had a talk with him, but it's you that he wants to see. I understand that it's something to do with Miss Paget.'

I knew now where I had heard that name before, but it was quite incredible. I asked, 'What sort of a man is he?'

He grinned broadly. 'Some sort of a colonial, I should think. Probably Australian. He's an outdoor type, anyway.'

'Is he a reasonable person?'

'Oh, I think so, sir. He's some sort of a countryman, I should say.'

It was all beginning to fit in, and yet it was incredible that an Australian stockman should have found his way to my office in Chancery Lane. 'Is his name Joseph, by any chance?' I asked.

'You know him, do you, sir? Joe Harman. Shall I ask him to come up?'

I nodded. 'I'll see him now.' Harris went down to fetch him, and I stood by my window looking out into the grey street, wondering what this visit meant and how it had come about, and how much of my client's business could I tell this man.

Harris showed him in, and I turned from the window to meet him.

He was a fair-haired man, about five feet ten in height. He was thickset but not fat; I judged him to be between thirty and thirty-five years old. His face was deeply tanned but his skin was clear; he had very bright blue eyes. He was not a handsome man; his face was too square and positive for that, but it was a simple and good natured face. He walked towards me with a curious stiff gait.

I shook hands with him. 'Mr Harman?' I said. 'My name is Strachan. Do you want to see me?' And as I spoke I was unable to resist the temptation to look down at his hand. There was a huge scar on the back of it.

He said a little awkwardly, 'I don't want to keep you long.' He was ill at ease and obviously embarrassed.

'Not at all,' I said. 'Sit down, Mr Harman, and tell me what I can do for you.' I put him in the client's chair before my desk and gave him a cigarette. He pulled from his pocket a tin box of wax matches of a style that was strange to me, and cracked one expertly with his thumbnail without burning himself. He was wearing a very ready-made suit, quite new, and an unusually ornamental tie for London wear.

'I was wondering if you could tell me about Miss Jean Paget,' he said. 'Where she lives, or anything like that.'

I smiled. 'Miss Paget is a client of mine, Mr Harman,' I said. 'You evidently know that. But a client's business is entirely confidential, you know. Are you a friend of hers?'

The question seemed to embarrass him still further. 'Sort of,' he replied. 'We met once in the war, in Malaya that was. I'll have to tell you who I am, of course. I'm a Queenslander. I run a station in the Gulf country, about twenty miles from Willstown.' He spoke very slowly and deliberately, not from embarrassment but because that seemed to be his way. 'I mean the homestead is twenty miles from the town, but one limb of the land runs down the creek to within five miles. Midhurst, that's the name of my station. Midhurst, Willstown, is the address.'

I made a note upon my pad, and smiled at him again. 'You're a long way from home, Mr Harman,' I said.

'Too right,' he replied. 'I don't know nobody in England except Miss Paget and a cobber I met in the prison camp who lives at a place called Gateshead in the north of England. I came here for a holiday, you might say, and I thought perhaps Miss Paget might be glad to know that I'm in England, but I don't know her address.'

'Rather a long way to come for a holiday?' I observed.

He smiled a little sheepishly. 'I struck it lucky. I won the Casket.'

'The Casket?'

'The Golden Casket. Don't you have that here?'

I shook my head. 'I'm afraid I've never heard of it.'

'Oh my word,' he said. 'We couldn't get along without the Casket in Queensland. It's the State lottery that gets the money to build hospitals.'

'I see,' I said. 'Did you win a prize in the lottery?'

'Oh my word,' he repeated. 'Did I win a prize. I won a thousand pounds–not English pounds, of course, Australian pounds, but it's a thousand pounds to us. I always take a ticket in every Casket like everybody else because if you don't get a prize you get a hospital and there's times when that's more useful. You ought to see the hospital the Casket built at Willstown. Three wards it's got, with two beds in each, and two rooms for the sisters, and a separate house for the doctor only we can't get a doctor to come yet because Willstown's a bit isolated, you see. We've got an X-ray apparatus there and a wireless so that the sister can call for the Cairns Ambulance–the aeroplane, you know. We couldn't do without the Casket.'

I must say I was a little bit interested. 'Does the Casket pay for the aeroplane, too?'

He shook his head. 'You pay seven pounds ten a year to the Cairns Ambulance, each family, that is. Then if you get sick and have to go to Cairns the sister calls Cairns on the wireless and the aeroplane comes out to take you into Cairns to hospital. That's free, provided that you pay the seven pounds ten each year.'

'How far are you from Cairns?'

'About three hundred miles.'

I reverted to the business in hand. 'Tell me, Mr Harman,' I said, 'how did you get to know that I was Miss Paget's solicitor?'

'She told me in Malaya when we met, she lived in Southampton,' he said. 'I didn't know any address, so I went there and stayed in a hotel, because I thought maybe she'd like to know I was in England. I never saw a city that had been bombed before—oh my word. Well, then I looked in the telephone book and asked a lot of people but I couldn't find out nothing except she had an aunt that lived in Wales at a place called Colwyn Bay. So then I went to Colwyn Bay.'

'You went right up there, did you?'

He nodded. 'I think her aunt thought I was up to some crook game or other,' he said simply. 'She wouldn't tell me where she lived or anything. All she said was that you were her trustee, whatever that means. So I came here.'

'When did you arrive in England?' I asked.

'Last Thursday. Five days ago.'

'You landed at Southampton, did you?'

He shook his head. 'I flew from Australia, by Qantas. You see, I got a good stockman looking after Midhurst for me, but I can't afford to be away so long. Jim Lennon's all right for a time, but I wouldn't want to be away from Midhurst more'n three months. You see, this is a slack time in the Gulf country. We mustered in March this year on account of the late season and drove the stock down Julia Creek in April—that's railhead, you know. I had about fourteen hundred stores I sold down to Rockhampton for fattening. Well, after getting them on rail I had to get back up to Midhurst on account of the bore crew. I got Mrs Spears—she's the owner of Midhurst—I got her to agree we sink a bore at Willow Creek, that's about twenty miles south-east of the homestead, to get water down at that end in the dry, and we got a bonza bore, we did. She's flowing over thirty thousand gallons a day; it's going to make a lot of difference down at that end. Well, that took up to about three weeks ago before I got that finished up, and I must be back at Midhurst by the end of October for getting in the stores and that before the wet begins at Christmas. So I thought that coming on this holiday I'd better fly.'

Flying to England, I thought, must have made a considerable hole in his thousand pounds. 'You came to London, then, and went straight down to Southampton?'

'That's right,' he said.

'And from there you went up to North Wales. And from there you came here?'

'That's right.'

I looked him in the eyes, and smiled. 'You must want to see Miss Paget very much.'

He met my gaze. 'I do.'

I leaned back in my chair. 'I've got a disappointment for you, I'm afraid, Mr Harman. Miss Paget is abroad.'

He stared down at his hat for a moment. Then he raised his head. 'Is she far away?' he asked. 'I mean, is it France or anything like that, where I could get to see her?'

I shook my head. 'She's travelling in the East.'

He said quietly, 'I see.'

I couldn't help liking and respecting this man. It was perfectly obvious that he had come twelve thousand miles or so to find Jean Paget, and now he wasn't going to find her. It was bad luck, to say the least of it, and he was taking it well. I felt that I wanted a little time to consider this affair.

'The most that I can do for you,' I said, 'is to forward a letter. I can do that, if you care to write one, and I'll send it to her by air mail. But I'm afraid that you may have to wait a month or so before you get an answer.'

He brightened. 'I'd like to do that. I never thought that after coming all this way I'd find that she'd gone walkabout.'

He thought for a minute. 'What address should I put upon the letter.'

'I can't give you my client's address, Mr Harman,' I said. 'What I suggest that you do is to write her a letter and bring it in to me here tomorrow morning. I will send it on with a short covering note explaining how it came into my hands. Then if she wants to see you she will get in touch with you herself.'

'You don't think she'll want to see me?' he said heavily.

I smiled. 'I didn't say anything of the sort, Mr Harman. I'm quite sure that when she hears you've been in England looking for her she will write to you. What I'm saying is that I have her interests to consider, and I'm not going to give her address to anyone who comes into this office and cares to ask for it.' I paused. 'There's one thing that you'd better know,' I said. 'Miss Paget is a fairly wealthy woman. Women who have command of a good deal of money are apt to be troubled by touts. I'm not saying that you're a tout or that you're after her money. I *am* saying that you must write to her first of all, and then let her decide if she wants to meet you. If you're a friend of hers you'll see that that's reasonable.'

He stared at me. 'I never knew that she had money. She told me she was just a typist in an office.'

'That's quite true,' I said. 'She inherited some money recently.'

He was silent.

'Suppose you come back tomorrow morning, Mr Harman,' I said. I glanced at my engagement diary. 'Say, twelve o'clock tomorrow morning. Write her a letter saying whatever it is you want to say, and bring it here then. I will forward it to her tomorrow evening.'

'All right,' he said. He got up and I got up with him. 'Where are you staying, Mr Harman?' I asked.

'At the Kingsway Palace Hotel.'

'All right, Mr Harman,' I said. 'I shall expect you tomorrow morning, at twelve o'clock.'

I spent most of that evening wondering if I had done the right thing in refusing Mr Harman the address. I thought ruefully that Jean would have been very angry if she had known I had done such a thing, especially when she was looking for him all over Australia. At the same time, what I had done would not delay a letter from him reaching her, and there was no sense in putting all her cards upon the table for him to see just at present. One thing that puzzled me a little was, why had he suddenly awoken to the fact that he wanted to meet Jean Paget again, after six years? A question or two upon that point seemed to be in order, and I prepared a small interrogation for him when he came to see me with his letter.

Twelve o'clock next morning came, and he didn't turn up for his appointment. I waited in for him till one o'clock, and then I went to lunch.

By three o'clock I was a little bit concerned. The initiative had passed into his hands. If he should vanish into thin air now and never come back to see me again, Jean Paget would be very cross with me, and rightly so. Between clients I put in a telephone call to the Kingsway Palace Hotel and asked to speak to Mr Joseph Harman. The answer was that Mr Harman had gone out after breakfast, and had left no message at the desk. I left one for him, asking him to ring me as soon as he came in.

He did not ring that day.

At half past ten that night I rang the hotel again, but I was told that Mr Harman was not in.

At eight o'clock next morning I rang again. They told me that Mr Harman had not checked out and his luggage was still in his room, but that he had not slept in the room that night.

As soon as I got into the office I sent for Derek Harris. 'Harris,' I said. 'I want you to try and find that man Harman. He's an Australian.' I told him briefly what had happened. 'I should try the hotel again, and if you draw a blank, ring round the various police courts. I think I may have given him some rather unwelcome news, and it's quite possible he's been out on a blind.'

He came back in a quarter of an hour. 'You must have second sight, sir,' he said. 'He's coming up at Bow Street this morning, drunk and disorderly. They had him in the cooler for the night.'

'He's a friend of Miss Paget's,' I said. 'Get along down to Bow Street, Harris, and make yourself known to him. Which court is he coming up in?'

'Mr Horler's.'

I glanced at my watch. 'Get along down there right away. Stay with Harman and pay the fine if he hasn't got any money. Then give me a ring, and if it's all in order take him in a taxi to my flat. I'll meet you there.'

There was nothing on my desk that day that could not be postponed or handled by Lester. I got back to my flat in time to catch my charwoman at work and tell her to make up the spare room bed. I told her I should want food in the flat for three or four meals, and I gave her money and sent her out to buy whatever food she could get off the ration.

Harris arrived with Harman half an hour later, and the Australian looked a little bit the worse for wear. He was cheerful and sober after his night in the cells, but he had lost one shoe and he had lost his collar stud and his hat. I met him in the hall. 'Morning, Mr Harman,' I said. 'I thought perhaps you'd rather come round here and clean up. You'd better not go back to the hotel looking like that.'

He looked me in the eyes. 'I've been on the grog,' he said.

'So I see. The water's hot for a bath if you want one, and there's a razor in the bathroom.' I took him and showed him the geography of the house. 'You can use this room.' I looked him up and down, smiling. 'I'll get you a clean shirt and collar. You can try a pair of my shoes; if they're too small I'll send out for a pair.'

He wagged his head. 'I dunno why you want to do this for me. I'll be all right.'

'You'll be righter when you've had a bath and a shave,' I said. 'Miss Paget would never forgive me if I let a friend of hers go wandering about the streets like that.'

He looked at me curiously, but I left him and went back to the sitting-room. Harris was waiting for me there. 'Thanks, Derek,' I said. 'There was a fine, I suppose?'

'Forty shillings,' he said. 'I paid it.'

I gave him the money. 'He was cleaned out?'

'He's got four and fourpence halfpenny,' he replied. 'He thinks he had about seventy pounds, but he's not sure.'

'It doesn't seem to worry him,' I said.

He laughed. 'I don't think it does. He seems quite cheerful over it.'

I sent Harris back to the office and settled down to write a few letters while Harman was in the bath. He came into the sitting-room presently looking a bit sheepish, and again I noticed the curious, stiff gait with which he walked. 'I dunno what to say,' he said in his slow way. 'Those jokers I was with got all the money I had on me so Mr Harris had to pay the fine. But I got some more. I got a thing called a letter of credit that the bank in Brisbane gave me. I can get some money on that and pay him back.'

'That's all right,' I said. 'Have you had any breakfast?'

'No.'

'Want any?'

'Well, I dunno. Maybe I'll get something round at the hotel.'

'You don't have to do that,' I said. 'My woman's here still; she'll get you some breakfast.' I went out and organized this, and then I came back and found him standing by the window. 'You didn't come back with that letter,' I observed.

'I changed my mind,' he said. 'I'm going to give it away.'

'Give it away?'

'That's right,' he said. 'I won't be writing any letter.'

'That's seems rather a pity,' I said quietly.

'Maybe. I had a good long think about it, and I won't be writing any letter. I decided that. That's why I didn't come back at the time you said.'

'As you like,' I said. 'Perhaps you'd like to tell me a bit more about it when you've had some breakfast.'

I left him to his breakfast and went on with my letters. My woman took it to the dining-room and he went in there to eat it; a quarter of an hour later he came back to me in the sitting-room.

'I'd better be getting along now,' he said awkwardly. 'Will it be all right if I come round later in the day and leave these shoes with the woman?'

I got up and offered him a cigarette. 'Will you tell me a bit more about yourself before you go?' I asked. 'You see, I shall be writing to Miss Paget in a day or two, and she's sure to want to know all about you.'

He stared at me, cigarette in hand. 'You're going to write and tell her I've been here?'

'Of course.'

He stood silent for a moment, and then said in his slow Queensland way, 'It would be better to forget about it, Mr Strachan. Just don't say nothing at all.'

I struck a match and lit his cigarette for him. 'Is this because I told you about her inheritance?'

'You mean, the money?'

'Yes.'

He grinned. 'I wouldn't mind about her having money, same as any man. No, it's Willstown.'

That was rather less intelligible than Greek to me, of course. I said, 'Look, Joe, it won't hurt you to sit down for a few minutes and tell me one or two things.' I called him Joe because I thought that it might make him loosen up.

'I dunno as there's much to tell,' he said sheepishly.

'Sit down, anyway.' I thought for a moment, and then I said. 'I'm right in thinking that you met Miss Paget first in the war?'

'That's right,' he said.

'That was in Malaya, when you were both prisoners?'

'That's right.'

'Some time in 1942?'

'That's right.'

'And you've never met her since, nor written to her?'

'That's right.'

'Well, what I don't understand is this,' I said. 'Why do you want to meet her now so very badly? After all, it's six years since you met her. Why the sudden urge to get in touch with her now?' It was still vaguely in my mind that he had somehow heard about her money.

He looked up at me, grinning. 'I thought she was a married woman.'

I stared at him. 'I see. . . . When did you find out that she wasn't married?'

'I only found out that this May. I met the pilot that had flown her out from a place in Malaya called Kota Bahru. At Julia Creek, that was.'

He had driven his fourteen hundred cattle down from Midhurst station to Julia Creek with Jim Lennon and two Abo stockriders to help. From Midhurst to Julia Creek is about three hundred miles by way of the Norman River, the Saxby River and the Flinders River. They left Midhurst at the end of March and got the herd to railhead at Julia Creek on the third of May, moving them at the rate of about ten miles a day. The beasts were corralled in the stockyards of the railway, and they set to work to load them into trains; this took about three days.

During this time Jim and Joe lived in the Post Office Hotel at Julia Creek. It was very hot and they were working fourteen hours a day to load the cattle into trucks; whenever they were not working they were standing in the bar of the hotel drinking hugely at the cold Australian light beer that does no harm to people sweating freely at hard manual work. One evening while they were standing so two dapper men in uniform came into the bar and shouted a couple of rounds; these were the pilots of a Trans-Australia Airline Dakota which had stopped there for the night with an oil leak in the starboard engine.

Harman found himself next to the chief pilot. Joe was wearing an old green linen sun hat that had once belonged to the American Army, a cotton singlet, a pair of dirty khaki shorts, and boots without socks; his appearance contrasted strangely with the neatness of the airman, but the pilot was accustomed to the outback. They fell into conversation about the war and soon discovered they had both served in Malaya. Joe showed the scars upon his hands and the pilots examined them with interest; he told them how he had been nailed up to be beaten, and they shouted another grog for him.

'The funniest do I ever struck,' said the chief pilot presently, 'was a party of women and children that never got into a prison camp at all. They spent most of the war in a Malay village working in the paddy fields.'

Joe said quickly, 'Where was that in Malaya? I met that party.'

The pilot said, 'It was somewhere between Kuantan and Kota Bahru. When we got back they were taken in trucks to Kota Bahru, and I flew them down to Singapore. All English, they were, but they looked just like Malays. All the women were in native clothes, and brown as anything.'

Joe said, 'Was there a Mrs Paget with them then?' It was vastly important to him to hear if Jean had survived the war.

The pilot said, 'There was a *Miss* Paget. She was the hell of a fine girl; she was their leader.'

Joe said, 'Mrs. A dark-haired girl, with a baby.'

The pilot said, 'That's right—a dark-haired girl. She had a little boy about four years old that she was looking after, but it wasn't hers. It belonged to one of the other women, one who died. I know that, because she was the only unmarried girl among the lot of them, and she was their leader. Just a typist in Kuala Lumpur before the war. Miss Jean Paget.'

Joe stared at him. 'I thought she was a married woman.'

'She wasn't married. I know she wasn't, because the Japs had taken all their wedding rings so they had to be sorted out and that was quite easy, because they were all Mrs So and So except this one girl, and she was Miss Jean Paget.'

'That's right,' the ringer said slowly. 'Jean was her name.'

He left the bar presently, and went out to the veranda and stood looking up at the stars. Presently he left the pub and strolled towards the stockyards; he found a gate to lean upon and stood there for a long time in the night, thinking things over. He told me a little about what he had been thinking, that morning in my London flat.

'She was a bonza girl,' he said simply. 'If ever I got married it would have to be with somebody like her.'

I smiled. 'I see,' I said. 'That's why you came to England?'

'That's right,' he said simply. He had ridden back with Jim Lennon and the Abo stockmen to Midhurst, a journey that took them about ten days, leading their string of fifteen packhorses; since they had started mustering on the station in February he had been in the saddle almost continuously for three months. 'Then there was the bore to see to,' he said. 'I'd made such a point of that with Mrs Spears that I couldn't hardly leave before that was finished, but then I got away and I went into Cairns one Wednesday with John Duffy on the Milk Run'—I found out later that he meant the weekly Dakota air mail service—'and so down to Brisbane. And from Brisbane I came here.'

'What about the Golden Casket?' I inquired.

He said a little awkwardly, 'I didn't tell you right about that. I *did* win the Casket, but not this year. I won it in 1946, the year after I got back to Queensland. I won a thousand pounds then, like I said.'

'I see,' I observed. 'You hadn't spent it?'

He shook his head. 'I was saving it, in case some day I got to have a station of my own, or do a deal with cattle, or something.'

'How much do you think you've got left now?'

He said, 'There's five hundred pounds of our money on the letter of credit, and I suppose that's all I've got. Four hundred pounds of yours. There's my pay as manager goes into the bank at Willstown each month, of course.'

I sat smoking for a time in silence, and I couldn't help being sorry for this man. Since he had met Jean Paget six years previously he had held the image of her in his mind hoping to find somebody a little like her. When he had heard that she was not a married woman he had drawn the whole of his small savings and hurried expensively half across the world to England, hoping to find her and to find that she was still unmarried. It was a gambler's action, but his whole life had probably been made up of gambles; it could hardly be otherwise in the outback. Clearly he thought little of his money if it could buy a chance for him of marrying Jean Paget.

It was ironical to think that she was at that moment busy looking for him in his own country. I did not feel that I was quite prepared to tell him that.

'I still don't quite understand why you've given up the idea of writing to Miss Paget,' I said at last. 'You said something about Willstown.'

'Yes.' There was a pause, and then he said in his slow way, 'I thought a lot about things after I left you, Mr Strachan. Maybe I'd have done better to have done some thinking before ever I left Midhurst. I told you, I got none of them high-falutin ideas about not marrying a girl with money. So long as she was the right girl, I'd be tickled to death if she had money, same as any man. But there's more to it than that.'

He paused again. 'I come from the outback,' he said slowly. 'Running a cattle station is the only work I know, and it's where I like to be. I couldn't make out in any of the big cities, Brisbane or Sydney. I couldn't make out even in Cairns for very long, and anyway, there'd be no work there I could do. I never got a lot of schooling, living on a station like we did. I don't say that I won't make money. I can run a station better'n most ringers, and I seem to do all right with selling the stock too. I'll hope to get a station of my own one day, and there's plenty of station owners finish up with fifty thousand pounds. But if I get that far, it'll be staying in the outback and doing what I'm cut out for. And I tell you, Mr Strachan, the outback is a crook place for a woman.'

'In what way?' I asked quietly. We were really getting down to something now.

He smiled a little wryly. 'Take Willstown, as an example. There's no radio station to listen to, only the short wave stuff from Brisbane and that comes and goes with static. There's no shop where you can buy fruit or fresh vegetables. The sister says that it's because of that so many of the old folk get this pellagra. There's no fresh milk. There's no dress shop, only what a woman can get in Bill Duncan's Store along with the dried peas and Jeyes Fluid and that. There's no ice-cream in Willstown. There's nowhere that a woman can buy a paper or a magazine or a book, and there's no doctor because we can't get one to come to Willstown. There's no telephone. There's no swimming-pool where a girl could sit around in a pretty bathing dress, although it can be hot there, oh my word. There's no other young women. I don't believe there's more'n five women in the district between the age of seventeen and forty; as soon as they're old enough to leave home they're off out of it, and down to the city. To get to Cairns to do a bit of shopping you can either fly, which costs money, or you can drive for four days in a jeep, and after that you'll find the jeep needs a new set of tyres.' He paused. 'It's a grand country for a man to live and work in, and good money, too. But it's a crook place for a woman.'

'I see,' I said. 'Are all the outback towns like that?'

'Most of them,' he said. 'You get the bigger ones, like the Curry, they're better, of course. But Camooweal and Normanton and Burketown and Croydon and Georgetown–they're all just the same as Willstown.' He paused for a moment in thought. 'There's only one good one for a woman,' he said. 'Alice Springs. Alice is a bonza place, oh my word. A girl's got everything in Alice–two picture houses, shops for everything, fruit, ice-cream, fresh milk, Eddie Maclean's swimming-pool, plenty of girls and young married women in the place, and nice houses to live in. Alice is a bonza town,' he said, 'but that's the only one.'

'Why is that?' I asked. 'What makes Alice different from the others?'

He scratched his head. 'I dunno,' he said. 'It's just that it's got bigger, I suppose.'

I left that one. 'What you mean is that if you got Miss Paget to agree to marry you, she wouldn't have a very happy life in Willstown.'

He nodded. 'That's right,' he said, and there was pain in his eyes. 'It all seemed sort of different when I met her in Malaya. You see, she was a prisoner and she hadn't got nothing, and I hadn't got nothing either, so there was a pair of us. When I got to know there was a chance she wouldn't be married I was so much in a hurry to get over here I didn't stop to think about the outback, or if I did I thought of her as someone who'd got nothing so she'd be all right in Willstown. See what I mean?' He looked at me appealingly. 'But then I come to England and I see Southampton and the sort of way people live there, bombed and muggered up although it is, and I been in London and I been in Colwyn Bay. Then when you told me she'd come into money I got thinking about how she would be living and the sort of things that she'd be used to and she wouldn't get in Willstown, and then I thought I'd acted a bit hasty. I never know it to work, for a girl to come straight out from England to the outback. And for a girl with money of her own, it'ld be worse still.' He paused, and grinned at me. 'So I went out on the grog.'

In all the circumstances, it now seemed to me that he had taken a very reasonable line of action, but it was a pity it had cost him seventy pounds. 'Look, Joe,' I said. 'We want to think about this thing a bit. I think I'll have to write and tell Miss Paget that I've met you. You see, she thought you were dead.'

He stared at me. 'You knew about me, then?'

'Not very much,' I said. 'I know that you stole chickens for her, and the Japs nailed you up and beat you. She thought you died.'

'I bloody near did,' he said grinning. 'She told you that, did she?'

I nodded. 'It's been a very deep grief to her,' I said quietly. 'You wouldn't want her to go on like that? You see, she thinks it was her fault.'

'It wasn't her fault at all,' he said in his slow way. 'She told me not to stick my neck out, and I went and bought it. It wasn't her fault at all.'

'I think you ought to write to her,' I repeated.

There was a long pause.

'I dunno what in hell I'd say to her if I did,' he muttered.

There was no point in going on agonizing about it. I got up. 'Look, Joe,' I said. 'Take a bit of time to think it over. When have you got to be back in Australia?'

'I wouldn't be doing right by Mrs Spears unless I get back on the station by the end of October,' he said. 'I don't want to serve her a crook deal.'

'That gives you two and a half months,' I said. 'How much did your airline ticket cost you when you came here?'

'Three hundred and twenty-five pounds,' he said.

'And you've got five hundred pounds left, on your letter of credit.'

'That's right.'

'Do you want to go back by air, or would you rather go by sea? I could find out about sea passages for you, if you like. I think it would cost about eighty pounds on a tramp steamer, but you'd have to leave pretty soon–within a fortnight, say.'

'There don't seem to be much point in staying here,' he said a little wearily. 'There wouldn't be no chance that she'll be coming back to England?'

'Not in that time, I'm afraid.'

'I'd better go back by sea, and save what's left of the money.'

'I think that's wise,' I said. 'I'll get my office on to finding out about the passage. In the meantime, why don't you move in here? You're welcome to use that spare room till you go, and it will be cheaper for you than living in the hotel.'

'Wouldn't I be in your way?'

'Not in the least,' I said. 'I'm out most of the day, and I'd be very glad for you to stay here if you'd like to.'

He agreed to that, and I asked him what he wanted most to see in England in his brief visit. He wanted to see No 19 Acacia Road, Hammersmith, where his father had been born. He wanted to see a live broadcast of 'Much-Binding-in-the-Marsh' which he listened to on short wave from Brisbane when the static permitted. ('They've got a bonza radio at Alice,' he said wistfully. 'A local station, right in the town.') He wanted to see all he could of thoroughbred horses and thoroughbred cattle. He was interested in saddlery, but he didn't think that we had much to teach them about that.

There was no difficulty about Hammersmith, of course; I put him in a bus that afternoon, and went into my office to deal with my neglected work. Apart from the clients who came to see me, I had plenty to think about. Whether Jean Paget chose to marry this man when she met him was entirely her own affair, but it was quite a possibility that she would do so. Whatever one might think about the suitability of such a match, there was no denying that Joe Harman had some very solid virtues; he seemed to be hard-working, thrifty if one excepts the great extravagance of flying half across the world to look for the girl he loved, and likely to make a success of his life; quite certainly he was a kind man who would make a good husband.

There was another aspect of the matter which was worth investigation. Whether she knew it or not, Jean Paget had Australia in her ancestry. She had never mentioned her grandfather, James Macfadden, to me and it seemed quite possible that she had never thought about him much. And yet, he was the original source of her money, and apparently he had made it in Australia before coming home to England to break his neck while riding in a point-to-point in Yorkshire. It would be interesting, I thought, to find out a little more about James Macfadden. Had he made his money on an outback cattle station, too? Had he been just such another as Joe Harman?

I sent my girl that afternoon to bring me the Macfadden box, and I sat looking through the old deeds and wills after my last client had gone. The only clue I found was in the Will of James Macfadden dated September 18th, 1903, which began, 'I, James Nelson Macfadden of Lowdale Manor, Kirkby

Moorside, in the County of Yorkshire, and of Hall's Creek in Western Australia, do hereby revoke all former wills . . . etc.' I knew nothing of Hall's Creek at that time, but I noted the name for future investigation. That is all there was.

I got Marcus Fernie on the telephone that afternoon at his office at the BBC and asked if I could have a ticket for 'Much-Binding-in-the-Marsh'. I had to tell him something about Joe Harman in order to get it because there seemed to be considerable competition, and he came back at once with a demand that Harman should be interviewed for the programme 'In Town Tonight'. I said I'd see him about that, and he promised to send over a ticket. Then I got on to old Sir Dennis Frampton who has a herd of pedigree Herefords at his place down by Taunton and told him about Joe Harman, and he very kindly invited him down for a couple of nights.

I got back to my flat at about seven o'clock; I had arranged for dinner there. Joe Harman was there, and he had been to the Bank and the hotel, and he had brought his suitcase round to my spare room. I asked if he had found his father's house at Hammersmith.

'I found it,' he said. 'Oh my word, I did.'

'Pretty bad?'

He grinned. 'That's putting it mild. We got some slums in Australia, but nothing like that. Dad did all right for himself when he come away from that and out to Queensland.'

I offered him a glass of sherry, but he preferred a beer; I went and got him a bottle. 'When did your father leave this country?' I inquired.

'1904,' he said. 'He went out to the Curry, to Cobb and Co. They used to run the stage coaches, before motors came. He must have been about fifteen then. He fought in the first war with the Aussies at Gallipoli.'

'He's dead now, is he?'

'Aye,' he said. 'He died in 1940, soon after I joined the army.' He paused. 'Mother's still alive. She lives with my sister Amy at the Curry.'

'Tell me,' I said, 'do you know a place called Hall's Creek?'

'Where the gold was? Over by Wyndham, in West Australia?'

'That will be the place,' I said. 'There are gold mines there, are there?'

'I don't think they work it now,' he said. 'There was a lot of gold there in the nineties, like in Queensland, in the Gulf country. I've never been to Hall's Creek, but I've always thought that it would be like Croydon. There was a lot of gold at Croydon, oh my word. It lasted for about ten years, and then they had to go so deep for it, it didn't pay any longer. Croydon had thirty thousand people one time, so they say. Now it's got two hundred. It's the same at Normanton and Burketown—Willstown's the same. All gold towns at one time, they were.'

'You never heard of anybody called Macfadden over at Hall's Creek, did you?'

He shook his head. 'I never heard the name.'

I told him I was getting a ticket for 'Much-Binding-in-the-Marsh', and that they wanted him to broadcast on Saturday night. He agreed diffidently to do this; when the time came I listened in and thought he did it surprisingly well. The announcer shepherded him along quite skilfully, and Harman spoke for about six or seven minutes about the Midhurst cattle station and the country down below the Gulf of Carpentaria that he called the Gulf country. Marcus Fernie took the trouble to ring me up next day to tell me how well it had gone. 'I only wish we could get more chaps like him now and then,' he said. 'It makes a difference when you hear the real McCoy.'

I put him on the train on Sunday down to Taunton to see Sir Dennis Frampton's cows. He had not much time left, because a ship of the Shaw Savill line was leaving on the following Friday morning for New Zealand and Australia, and I had managed to get him a cheap berth on that. He came back on the Wednesday full of what he had seen. 'He's got a bonza herd there, oh my word,' he said. 'I learned more about raising up the quality of stock there in two days than I'd have learned in ten years in the Gulf country. Of course, you couldn't do the things that he does on a station like Midhurst, but I got plenty to think about.'

'You mean about breeding?'

'We don't breed for quality at all in the Gulf,' he said. 'Not like you set about it here in England. All we do is go out and shoot the scrub bulls when you see them so you keep the best ones breeding. I'd like to see a herd of pedigree stock out there, like he's got. I never see such beasts outside a show.'

After dinner I had a word with him about Miss Paget. 'I shall write to her in a day or two and give her your address,' I said. 'I know that she'll be very sorry to have missed you, and I should think you'd find a letter from her waiting for you at Midhurst when you get there. In fact, I know you will, because I shall write air mail, and she's certain to write air mail to you.'

He brightened considerably at the thought. 'I don't think I'll write to her from here,' he said. 'If you're going to do that I'll wait and write when I hear from her. I'm glad I didn't meet her over here, in a way. It's probably all turning out for the best.'

It was on the tip of my tongue to tell him then that she was in Australia, but I refrained. I had written to her in Alice Springs the day before Joe Harman had come to me, and I was expecting a letter from her any day now, because she used to write once a week, very regularly. If necessary, I could cable her to tell her his address in order that she might not leave Australia without seeing him, but there was no reason to lay all her cards before him at this stage.

I saw him off at the docks two days later, as I had seen Jean Paget a few months before. As I turned to go down the gangway he said gruffly, 'Thank you for doing so much for me, Mr Strachan. I'll be writing from Midhurst.' And he shook my hand with a grip that made me wince, for all the injury his hand had suffered.

I turned to go down the gangway. 'That's all right, Joe. You'll find a letter from Miss Paget when you get back home. You might even find more than that.'

I had reason for that last remark, because I had a letter from her in my pocket that had come by that day's post, and it was postmarked Willstown.

6

When Jean Paget stepped down the gangway from the Constellation on to Darwin airport she was wildly and unreasonably happy. It is a fact, I think, that till that time she had never really recovered from the war. She had come to England when she was repatriated and she had done her job efficiently and well with Pack and Levy for two years or so, but she had done it in the manner of a woman of fifty. She lived, but she had very little zest for life. Deep in the background of her mind remained the tragedy of Kuantan, killing her youth. She had only been speaking the truth when she had told me once that she felt about seventy years old.

She landed at about eight-fifteen at night, after dark; as she was getting off the plane at Darwin, Qantas had booked a room for her at the Darwin Hotel. She stepped on to the concrete and was marshalled to the Customs office in the hangar; at the foot of the gangway there were three young men who scrutinized her carefully. At the time she took them for officials of the airport. It was only later that she found out that they were reporters on the staff of various Australian newspapers engaged in what must surely be the worst assignment in all journalism, meeting every aeroplane that lands on Darwin airport in the hope of finding a Prime Minister on board, or a woman with two heads.

One of them came up to her as soon as she was through the Customs; there had been nothing to make a story in this load of passengers. A happy-looking girl was a small dividend, however. He said, 'Miss Paget? The stewardess tells me that you're getting off here and you're staying at the Darwin Hotel. Can I give you a lift into town? My name is Stuart Hopkinson; I represent the *Sydney Monitor* up here.'

She said, 'That's terribly kind of you, Mr Hopkinson. I don't want to take you out of your way, though.'

He said, 'I'm staying there myself.' He had a small Vauxhall parked outside the hangar; he took her suitcase and put it in the back seat and they got in, chatting about the Constellation and the journey from Singapore. And presently, as they drove past the remains of Vestey's meatworks, he said, 'You're English, aren't you, Miss Paget?' She agreed. 'Would you like to tell me why you're visiting Australia?'

She laughed. 'Not very much, Mr Hopkinson. It's only something personal—it wouldn't make a story. Is this where I get out and walk?'

'You don't have to do that,' he said. 'It was just a thought. I haven't filed a story for a week.'

'Would it help if I said that I thought Darwin was just wonderful? "London Typist thinks Darwin wonderful"?'

'We can't go panning London, not in the *Monitor*. Is that what you are, a typist?'

She nodded.

'Come out to get married?'

'I don't think so.'

He sighed. 'I'm afraid you're not much good to me for a story.'

'Tell me, Mr Hopkinson,' she said, 'how do the buses go from here to Alice Springs? I want to go down there, and I haven't got much money, so I thought I'd go by bus. That's possible, isn't it?'

'Sure,' he said. 'One went this morning. You'll have to wait till Monday now; they don't run over the weekend.'

'How long does it take?'

'Two days. You start on Monday, stop at Daly Waters Monday night, and get in late on Tuesday. It's not too bad a journey, but it can be hot, you know.'

He put her down at the hotel and carried her bag into the lobby for her. She was lucky in that overcrowded place to get a room to herself, a room with a balcony overlooking the harbour. It was hot in Darwin, with a damp enervating heat that brought her out in streams of perspiration at the slightest movement. This was no novelty to her because she was accustomed to the tropics; she bolted the door and took off her clothes and had a shower, and washed some things in the hand basin, and lay down to sleep with a bare minimum of covering.

She woke early next morning and lay for some time in the cool of the dawn considering her position. It was imperative to her that she should find Joe Harman and talk to him; at the same time the meeting with Mr Hopkinson had warned her that there were certain difficulties ahead. However pleasant these young men might be, their duty was to get a story for the paper, and she had no desire whatever to figure in the headlines, as she certainly would do if the truth of her intentions became known. 'Girl flies from Britain to seek soldier crucified for her . . .' It would be far easier if she were a man.

However, she wasn't. She set to work to invent a story for herself, and finally decided that she was going out to Adelaide to stay with her sister who was married to a man called Holmes who worked in the Post Office; that seemed a fairly safe one. She was travelling by way of Darwin and Alice Springs because a second cousin called Joe Harman was supposed to be working there but hadn't written home for nine years, and her uncle wanted to know if he was still alive. From Alice she would take the train down to Adelaide.

It didn't quite explain why she had come to Darwin in a Constellation, except that there is no other way to get to Darwin. Lying on her bed and cogitating this it seemed a pretty waterproof tale; when she got up and went downstairs for breakfast she decided to try it out on Stuart Hopkinson. She got her chance that morning as he showed her the way to the bus booking-office; she let it out in little artistic snippets over half an hour of conversation, and the representative of the *Sydney Monitor* swallowed it without question so that she became a little ashamed of herself.

He took her into a milk bar and stood her a Coca-Cola. 'Joe Harman . . .' he said. 'What was he doing at Alice nine years ago?'

She sucked her straw. 'He was a cowboy on a cattle farm,' she said innocently, and hoped she wasn't overdoing it.

'A stockman? Do you remember the name of the station?'

'Wollara,' she said. 'That's the name, Wollara. That's near Alice Springs, isn't it?'

'I don't know,' he said. 'I'll try and find out.'

He came back to her after lunch with Hal Porter of the *Adelaide Herald.* 'Wollara's a good long way from Alice Springs,' said Mr Porter. 'The homestead must be nearly a hundred and twenty miles away. You mean Tommy Duveen's place?'

'I think that's it,' she said. 'Is there a bus there from Alice Springs?'

'There's no bus or any way of getting there except to drive there in a truck or a utility.'

Hopkinson said. 'It's on one of Eddie Maclean's rounds, isn't it?'

'Now you mention it, I think it is.' Porter turned to Jean. 'Maclean Airways run around most of those stations once a week, delivering the mail,' he said. 'You may find that you could get there by plane. If so, that's much the easiest.'

Her ideas about reporters had been moulded by the cinema; it was a surprise to her to find that in real life they could be kind and helpful people with good manners. She thanked them with sincere gratitude, and they took her out for a run round Darwin in a car. She exclaimed at the marvellous, white sand beaches and the azure blue of the sea, and suggested that a bathing party might be a good thing.

'There's one or two objections,' Mr Porter said. 'One is the sharks. They'll take you if you go out more than knee deep. Another is the alligators. Then there's the stone fish—he lies on the beach and looks just like a stone until you tread on him, and he squirts about a pint of poison into you. The Portuguese Men-o'-War aren't so good, either. But the thing that really puts me off is Coral Ear.'

'What's that?'

'A sort of growth inside your head that comes from getting this fine coral sand into your ear.'

Jean came to the conclusion that perhaps she wouldn't bathe in Darwin after all.

She got her bathe, however, because on Sunday they drove her forty miles or so southwards down the one road to a place called Berry Springs, a deep water hole in a river where the bathing was good. The reporters eyed her curiously when she appeared in her two-piece costume because the weeks that she had spent in native clothes in Kuala Telang had left her body tanned with sunburn in unusual places. It was the first mistake that she had made, and for the first time a dim suspicion crossed their minds that this girl held a story for them if they could only get it out of her.

'Joe Harman . . .' said Hal Porter thoughtfully to Stuart Hopkinson. 'I'm sure I've heard that name before somewhere, but I can't place it.'

As they drove back from the bathe the reporters told her about Darwin, and the picture they painted was a gloomy one. 'Everything that happens here goes crook,' Hal Porter said. 'The meatworks has been closed for years because of labour troubles—they got so many strikes they had to close it down. The railway was intended to go south to Alice and join up with the one from Alice down to Adelaide—go from north to south of the continent. It might have been some good if it had done that, but it got as far as Birdum and then stopped. God knows what it does now. This road has just about put the railway out of business—what business it ever had. There used to be an ice factory, but that's closed down.' He paused. 'Everywhere you go round here you'll see ruins of things that have been tried and failed.'

'Why is that?' Jean asked. 'It's not a bad place, this. It's got a marvellous harbour.'

'Of course it has. It ought to be a great big port, this place–a port like Singapore. It's the only town of any size at all on the north coast. I don't know. I've been up here too long. It gives me the willies.'

Stuart Hopkinson said cynically, 'It's got outbackitis.' He smiled at Jean. 'You'll see a lot of this in Australia, specially in the north.'

She asked, 'Is Alice Springs like this?' It was so very different from the glowing recollections of Alice that Joe Harman had poured out to her, six years before.

'Oh, well,' said Hopkinson, 'Alice is different. Alice is all right.'

'Why is it different?' she asked.

'I don't really know. It's railhead, of course, for trucking cattle down to Adelaide–that's one thing. But it's a go-ahead place is Alice; all sorts of things go on there. I wish to God the *Monitor*'ld send me there instead of here.'

She said goodbye to her two friends that night, and started at dawn next morning in the bus for Alice Springs. The bus was a big, modern Bedford, heavily streamlined; it towed a trailer carrying goods and luggage. It was comfortable enough although not air-conditioned; it cruised down the wide, empty tarmac road at fifty miles an hour, hour after hour, manned by ex-naval crew.

As far as Katherine, where the bus stopped for lunch, the country was well wooded with rather stunted eucalyptus trees, which Jean discovered were called gums. Between these trees were open meadows of wild land, ungrazed, unused, and uninhabited. She discussed this country with a fellow traveller, a bank inspector on his way to Tennant Creek, and she was told that all this coastal belt was useless for farming for some reason that she could not understand. After Katherine the country gradually became more arid, the trees more scattered and desiccated, till by the evening they were running through a country that was near to desert.

At dusk they stopped for the night at a place called Daly Waters. Daly Waters, she discovered, was a hotel, a post office, a large aerodrome, and nothing else whatsoever. The hotel was a rambling collection of single-storey wooden huts or dormitories for men and for women, strange to Jean but comfortable enough. She strolled outside before tea, in the dusk, and looked around. In front of the hotel three young men were squatting on their heels with one leg extended in the peculiar attitude that Joe Harman had used; they wore a sort of jodhpur trouser and elastic-sided boots with a very thin sole, and they were playing cards upon the ground, intent upon their game. She realized that she was looking at her first ringers.

She studied them with interest; that was how Joe Harman would have looked before he joined the army. She resisted an absurd temptation to go up to one of them and ask if they knew anything about him.

The bus started at dawn next day, and drove on southwards down the tarmac road, past Milners Lagoon and Newcastle Waters and Muckety Bore to Tennant Creek. As they went the vegetation grew sparser and the sun grew hotter, till by the time they stopped at Tennant Creek for a meal and a rest the country had become pure sand desert. They went on after an hour, driving at fifty to fifty-five miles an hour down the scorching road past tiny places of two or three houses dignified with a name, Wauchope and Barrow Creek and

Aileron. Toward evening they found themselves running towards the Macdonnell Ranges, lines of bare red hills against the pale blue sky, and at about dusk they ran slowly into Alice Springs and drew up at the Talbot Arms Hotel.

Jean went into the hotel and got a room opening on to a balcony, the hotel being a bungalow-type building with a single storey, like practically every other building in Alice Springs. Tea was served immediately after they arrived, and she had already learned that in Australian country hotels unless you are punctual for your meals you will get nothing. She changed her dress and strolled out in the town after tea, walking very slowly down the broad suburban roads, examining the town.

She found it as Joe Harman had described it to her, a pleasant place with plenty of young people in it. In spite of its tropical surroundings and the bungalow nature of the houses there was a faint suggestion of an English suburb in Alice Springs which made her feel at home. There were the houses standing each in a small garden fenced around or bordered by a hedge for privacy; the streets were laid out in the way of English streets with shade trees planted along the kerbs. Shutting her eyes to the Macdonnell Ranges, she could almost imagine she was back in Bassett as a child. She could now see well what everybody meant by saying Alice was a bonza place. She knew that she could build a happy life for herself in this town, living in one of these suburban houses, with two or three children, perhaps.

She found her way back to the main street and strolled up it looking at the shops. It was quite true; this town had everything a reasonable girl could want—a hairdressing saloon, a good dress shop or two, two picture houses. . . . She turned into the milk bar at about nine o'clock and bought herself an ice-cream soda. If this was the outback, she thought, there were a great many worse places.

Next morning, after breakfast, she went and found the manageress, a Mrs Driver, in the hotel office. She said, 'I want to try and get in touch with a second cousin of mine, who hasn't written home for ten years.' She told her story about being on her way from London to Adelaide to stay with her sister. 'I told my uncle that I'd come this way and stop in Alice Springs and try and find out something about Joe.'

Mrs Driver was interested. 'What's his name?'

'Joe Harman.'

'Joe Harman! Worked out at Wollara?'

'That's right,' Jean said. 'Do you know if he's there still?'

The woman shook her head. 'He used to come in here a lot just after the war, but he was only here about six months. I only came here in the war; I don't know about before that. He was a prisoner of the Japs, he was. They treated him terribly. Came back with scars on his hands where they'd put nails right through, crucified him, or something.'

Jean expressed surprise and horror. 'Do you know where he is now?'

'I don't know, I'm sure. Maybe one of the boys would know.'

Old Art Foster, the general handyman who had lived in Alice Springs for thirty years said, 'Joe Harman? He went back to Queensland where he come from. He was at Wollara for about six months after the war, and then he got a job as station manager at some place up in the Gulf country.'

Jean asked, 'You don't know his address?'

'I don't. Tommy Duveen would know it, out at Wollara.'

'Does he come into town much?'

'Aye, he was in town on Friday. He comes about once every three or four weeks.'

Jean asked innocently, 'I suppose Joe Harman took his family with him when he went to Queensland. They aren't living here still, are they?'

The old man stared at her. 'I never heard Joe Harman had a family. He wasn't married, not so far as I know.'

She said defensively. 'My uncle back in England thinks he's married.'

'I never heard nothing of a wife,' the old man said.

Jean thought about this for a minute, and then said to Mrs Driver, 'Is there a telephone at Wollara? I mean, if Mr Duveen knows his address, I'd like to ring him up and get it.'

'There isn't any telephone,' she said. 'They'll be speaking on the radio schedule morning and evening from Wollara, of course.' There was an extensive radio network operated by the Flying Doctor service from the hospital; morning and evening an operator at the hospital sat down to call up forty or fifty stations on the radio telephone to transmit messages, pass news, and generally ascertain that all was well. The station housewife operated the other end. 'Mrs Duveen is sure to be on the air tonight because her sister Amy is in hospital here for a baby and Edith'll want to know if it's come off yet. If you write out a telegram and take it down to Mr Taylor at the hospital, he'll pass it to them tonight.'

Jean went back to her room and wrote out a suitable cable and took it down to the hospital to Mr Taylor, who agreed to pass it to Wollara. 'Come back at about eight o'clock, and I may have the answer if they know the address right off; if they've got to look it up they'll probably transmit it on the schedule tomorrow morning.' That freed her for the remainder of the day, and she went back to the milk bar for another ice-cream.

In the milk bar she made a friend, a girl called Rose Sawyer. Miss Sawyer was about eighteen and had an Aberdeen terrier on a lead; she worked in the dress shop in the afternoons. She was very interested to hear that Jean came from England, and they talked about England for a time. 'How do you like Alice?' she asked presently, and there was a touch of conventional scorn in her tone.

'I like it,' Jean said candidly. 'I've seen many worse places. I should think you could have a pretty good time here.'

The girl said, 'Well, I like it all right. We were in Newcastle before, and then Daddy got the job of being bank manager here and we all thought it would be awful. All my friends said these outback places were just terrible. I thought I wouldn't be able to stick it, but I've been here fifteen months now and it's not so bad.'

'Alice is better than most, isn't it?'

'That's what they say—I haven't been in any of the others. Of course, all this has come quite recently. There weren't any of these shops before the war, they say.'

Jean learned a little of the history of the town and she was surprised at the rapidity of its growth. In 1928 it was about three houses and a pub; that was the year when the railway reached it from Oodnadatta. The Flying Doctor service started about 1930 and small hospitals were placed about in the surrounding districts. The sisters married furiously, and Jean learned that most of the older families were those of these sisters. By 1939 the population was about three hundred; when the war came the town became a military staging point. After the war the population had risen to about seven hundred and fifty in 1945, and when Jean was there it was about twelve hundred. 'All these new houses and shops going up,' Miss Sawyer said. 'People seem to be coming in here all the time now.'

She suggested that Jean should come swimming in the late afternoon. 'Mrs Maclean's got a lovely swimming-pool, just out by the aerodrome,' she said. 'I'll ring her up and ask if I can bring you.'

She called for Jean that afternoon at five o'clock and Jean joined the swimming party at the pool; sitting and basking in the evening sun and looking at the gaunt line of Mount Ertwa, she become absorbed into the social life of Alice Springs. Most of the girls and married women were under thirty; she found them kindly, hospitable people, well educated and avid for news of England. Some spoke quite naturally of England as 'home' though none of them had ever been there; each of them cherished the ambition that one day she would be able to go 'home' for a trip. By the end of the evening Jean was in a humble frame of mind; these pleasant people knew so much about her country, and she knew so very little about theirs.

She strolled down to the hospital in the cool night, after tea. Mrs Duveen had not been able to give Joe Harman's address offhand, but she confirmed that he was managing a station somewhere in the Gulf country. She would ask her husband and send a message on the morning schedule.

That night Jean thought a good deal about what she would do when she did get the address. It was clear now that her first apprehensions were unfounded; Joe Harman had made a good recovery from his injuries, and was able to carry on his work in the outback. She was amazed that this could be so, but the man was tough. Though there was no compelling need for her to find him now, she felt that it would be impossible to leave Australia without seeing him again; too much had passed between them. She did not fear embarrassment when she met him. She felt that she could tell him the truth frankly; that she had heard of his survival and had come to satisfy herself that he was quite all right. If anything should happen after that, well, that would be just one of those things.

She drifted into sleep, smiling a little.

She went down to the hospital in the morning after the radio schedule and learned that Joe Harman was the manager of Midhurst station, near Willstown. She had never heard of Willstown before; Mr Taylor obligingly got out a map of Australia designed to show the various radio facilities and frequencies of the outback stations, and showed her Willstown at the mouth of the Gilbert River on the Gulf of Carpentaria.

'What sort of a place is it?' she asked him. 'Is it a place like this?'

He laughed. 'It's a fair cow up there.' He studied the map. 'It's got an airstrip, anyway. I don't suppose it's got much else. I've never been there, and I've never heard of anyone who had.'

'I'm going there,' she said. 'I've got to see Joe Harman, after coming all this way.'

'It's likely to be rough living,' he said. 'Oh my word.'

'Would there be a hotel?'

'Oh, there'll be a hotel. They've got to have their grog.'

She left the hospital and went thoughtfully to the milk bar; as she ordered her ice-cream soda, it occurred to her that it might be a long time before she had another. When she had finished her soda she walked up the street a little way and turned into the magazine and book shop, and bought a map of Australia and a bus timetable and an airline timetable. Then she went back to the milk bar and had another ice-cream soda while she studied this literature.

Presently Rose Sawyer came into the milk bar with her dog. Jean said, 'I've found out where Joe Harman lives. Now I've got to find out how to get there. There doesn't seem to be a bus going that way at all.'

They studied the timetables together. 'It's going to be much easiest to fly,' said Rose. 'That's how everybody goes, these days. It's more expensive, but it may not be in the long run because you've got so many meals and hotels if you try and go by land. I should take the Maclean service to Cloncurry, next Monday.'

It meant staying a few days more in Alice Springs, but it seemed the best thing to do. 'You could come and stay with us,' said Rose. 'Daddy and Mummy would love to have somebody from England. It's not very nice in the hotel, is it? I've never been in there, of course.'

'It's a bit beery,' said Jean. She was already aware of the strict Australian code, that makes it impossible for a woman to go into a bar. 'I would like to do that, if you're sure it wouldn't be a lot of trouble.'

'We'd love to have you. It's so seldom one can talk to anyone that comes from England.' They walked round to the Sawyers' house; on the way they met Mrs Maclean, fair-haired and youthful, pushing her pram. They stopped, and Jean said, 'I've got to go to Willstown in the Gulf country to see Joe Harman. Can I get a seat on your plane on Monday as far as Cloncurry?'

'I should think you could. I'm just going to the office; I'll tell them to put you down for Monday. Shall I ask them to arrange the passage for you from Cloncurry on to Willstown? I think you can get there direct from the Curry, but they'll find out that and make the booking if you want.'

'That's awfully good of you,' said Jean. 'I would like them to do that.'

'Okay. Coming down to the pool this evening?'

'Yes, please.'

They went on to the Sawyer house, a pleasant bungalow with a rambler rose climbing over it, standing in a small garden full of English flowers, with a sprinkler playing on the lawn. Mrs Sawyer was grey-haired and practical; she made Jean welcome. 'Much better for you to be here with us than in that nasty place,' she said, with all of an Australian woman's aversion to hotels. 'It'll be nice having you, Miss Paget. Rose was telling us about you yesterday. It's nice to meet somebody from home.'

She went back to the hotel to pack her suitcase, and on the way she stopped at the Post Office. She spent a quarter of an hour sucking the end of a pencil, trying to word a telegram to Joe Harman to tell him that she was coming to see him. Finally she said,

Heard of your recovery from Kuantan atrocity quite recently perfectly delighted stop I am in Australia now and coming up to Willstown to see you next week.

JEAN PAGET

She took her suitcase round to the Sawyers' house in a taxi, and settled in with them. She stayed with these kind people for four days. On the third day she could not bear to go on lying to them; she told Rose and her mother what had happened in Malaya, and why she was looking for Joe Harman. She begged them not to spread the story; she was terribly afraid that it would get into the papers. They agreed to this, but asked her to tell her story again to Mr Sawyer when he came back from the office.

Mr Sawyer had a lot to say that interested her that evening. 'Joe Harman may be on to a good thing up there,' he said. 'The Gulf country's not much just at present, but he's a young man, and things can happen very quickly in Australia. This town was nothing twenty years ago, and look at it now! The Gulf's got one thing in its favour, and that's rain. We get about six or seven inches a year up here–about a quarter of what London gets. Up where Joe Harman is they probably get thirty inches–more than England does. That's bound to tell in the long run, you know.'

He sucked at his pipe. 'Mind you,' he said, 'it's not much good to them, that rainfall, because it all comes in two months and runs off into the sea. It's not spread out all the year round, like yours is in England. But I met a chap from home last year, and he said most of your water would run off into the sea, in England, if you hadn't got a weir every three miles or so on every river. That's what Australia hasn't got around to yet–water conservation on the stations. They're doing a little at it, but not much.'

In the days she spent with the Sawyers, Jean inevitably heard about Rose Sawyer's love life, which was not so far very serious. It chiefly centred round a Mr Billy Wakeling, who built roads when he could get a road to build. 'He did awfully well in the war,' she told Jean. 'He was a captain when he was twenty-three. But he's nothing to compare with your Joe Harman. He hasn't been crucified for me yet . . .'

'I'm not in love with Joe Harman,' Jean said with some dignity. 'I just want to know that he's all right.'

Rose was still looking round for work that would suit her.

'I like a shop,' she said. 'I couldn't ever learn shorthand, like you do. I like a shop all right, but I don't know that the dress shop is much catch. I can never tell what suits a person till I see it on, so I don't think I'll ever be a dress designer. I'd like to run a milk bar, that's what I'd like to do. I think it must be ever such fun, running a milk bar . . .'

Jean visited Mr Sawyer at the bank in his professional capacity, and arranged for him to transfer to Willstown any credits that might come for her account after she had gone. She left Alice Springs on Monday morning with regret, and the Sawyers and Macleans were sorry to see her go.

She flew all that day in a Dragonfly, and it was a very instructive day for her. The machine did not go directly to Cloncurry, but zigzagged to and fro across the wastes of Central Australia, depositing small bags of mail at cattle stations and picking up stockmen and travellers to drop them off after a hundred or a hundred and fifty miles. They landed eight or ten times in the course of the day, at Ammaroo and Hatches Creek and Kurundi and Rockhampton Downs and many other stations; at each place they would get out of the plane and drink a cup of tea and gossip with the station manager or owner, and get back into the plane and go on their way. By the end of the day Jean Paget knew exactly what the homestead of a cattle station looked like, and she was beginning to have a very good idea of what went on there.

They got to Cloncurry at dusk, a fairly extensive town on a railway that ran eastward to the sea at Townsville. Here she was in Queensland, and she heard for the first time the slow, deliberate speech of the Queenslander that reminded her of Joe Harman at once. She was driven into town in a very old open car and deposited at the Post Office Hotel; she got a bedroom but tea was over, and she had to go down the wide, dusty main street to a café for her evening meal. Cloncurry, she found, had none of the clean glamour of Alice Springs; it was a town redolent of cattle, with wide streets through which to drive the herds down to the stockyards, many hotels, and a few shops. All the houses were of wood with red-painted corrugated iron roofs; the hotels were of two storeys, but very few of the other houses were more than bungalows.

She had to spend a day here, because the air service to Normanton and Willstown ran weekly on a Wednesday. She went out after breakfast while the air was still cool and walked up the huge main street for half a mile till she came to the end of the town, and she walked down it a quarter of a mile till she came to the other end. Then she went and had a look at the railway station, and, having seen the aerodrome, with that she had exhausted the sights of Cloncurry. She looked in at a shop that sold toys and newspapers, but they were sold out of all reading matter except a few dressmaking journals; as the day was starting to warm up she went back to the hotel. She managed to borrow a copy of the Australian *Women's Weekly* from the manageress of the hotel and took it up to her room, and took off most of her clothes and lay down on her bed to sweat it out during the heat of the day. Most of the other citizens of Cloncurry seemed to be doing the same thing.

She revived shortly before tea and had a shower, and went out to the café for an ice-cream soda. Stupefied by the heavy meal of roast beef and plum pudding that the Queenslanders call 'tea' she sat in a deckchair for a little in the dusk of the veranda, and went to bed again at about eight o'clock.

She was called before dawn, and was out at the aerodrome with the first light. The aircraft this time was a vintage Dragon, which wandered round the cattle stations as on the previous flight, Canobie and Wandoola and Milgarra. About midday, after four or five landings, they came to the sea, a desolate marshy coast, and shortly after that they put down at Normanton. Half an hour later they were in the air again for Constance Downs station; they had a cup of tea here and a chat with the manager's wife, and took off on the last leg to Willstown.

They got there about the middle of the afternoon, and Jean got a bird's-eye view of the place as they circled for a landing. The country was well wooded with gum trees and fairly green; the Gilbert River ran into the sea about three miles below the town. There was deep, permanent water in it as far up as Willstown and beyond, because she could see a wooden jetty, and the river ran inland out of sight into the heat haze with water in it as far as she could see. All the other watercourses, however, seemed to be dry.

The town itself consisted of about thirty buildings, very widely scattered on two enormous intersecting streets or areas of land, for the streets were not paved. Only one building, which she later learned to be the hotel, was of two storeys. From the town dirt tracks ran out into the country in various directions. That was all that one could see of Willstown, that and a magnificent aerodrome put there in the war for defence purposes, with three enormous tarmac runways each a mile long.

They landed upon one of these huge runways, and taxied towards a truck parked at the runway intersection; this truck was loaded with two barrels of petrol and a semi-rotary pump for refuelling. The pilot said to Jean as he came down the cabin, 'You're getting off here, Miss Paget? Is anyone meeting you?'

She shook her head. 'I want to see a man who's living in this district, on one of the stations. I'll have to go to the hotel, I think.'

'Who is it? Al Burns, the Shell agent out there on the truck, he knows everybody here.'

She said, 'Oh, that's a good idea. I want to see Mr Joe Harman. He's manager of Midhurst station.'

They got out of the aeroplane together. 'Morning, Al,' the pilot said. 'She'll take about forty gallons. I'll have a look at the oil in a minute. Is Joe Harman in town?'

'Joe Harman?' said the man in the truck. He was a lean, dark-haired man of forty or so. 'Joe Harman's in England. Went there for a holiday.'

Jean blinked, and tried to collect her thoughts. She had been prepared to hear that Harman was out on his property or even that he was away in Cairns or Townsville, but it was absurd to be told that he was in England. She was staggered for a moment, and then she wanted to laugh. She realized that the men were looking at her curiously. 'I sent him a telegram to say that I was coming,' she said foolishly. 'I suppose he didn't get that.'

'Couldn't have done,' said Al Burns slowly. 'When did you send it?'

'About four or five days ago, from Alice Springs.'

'Oh no, he wouldn't have got that. Jim Lennon might have it, out at Midhurst station.'

'That's dinky-die is it?' the pilot asked. 'He's gone to England?'

'Went about a month ago,' the man said. 'Jim Lennon said the other night that he'd be back about the end of October.'

The pilot turned to Jean. 'What will you do, Miss Paget? Do you want to stay here now? It's not much of a place, you know.'

She bit her lip in thought. 'When will you be taking off?' she asked. 'You're going back to Cloncurry?'

'That's right,' he replied. 'We're going back to Normanton tonight and night-stopping there, and back to the Curry tomorrow morning. I'm going into town now while Al fills her up. Take off in about half an hour.'

Cloncurry was the last place that she wanted to go back to. 'I'll have to think about this,' she said. 'I'll have to stay in Australia, till I've seen Joe Harman. Cairns is a nice place to stay, isn't it?'

'Oh, Cairns is a bonza town,' he said. 'Townsville, too. If you've got to wait six or eight weeks you don't want to wait here, Miss Paget.'

'How could I get to Cairns?' she asked.

'Well,' he said. 'You could come back with me to Cloncurry and then go by train to Townsville and up to Cairns. I don't quite know how long that would take in the train—it must be between six and seven hundred miles. Or you could wait here till next Wednesday, today week, and go by the Dakota straight to Cairns in about two and a half hours.'

'How long would the train take, from Cloncurry to Cairns?'

'Oh, I don't know about that. I don't think they go every day from Townsville to Cairns, but I'm not really sure. I think you'd have to allow three days.' He paused. 'Of course, the best way would be to fly from Cloncurry to Townsville and then fly up to Cairns.'

'I know.' She was getting very sensitive of the cost of flying these vast distances, but the alternative of three days in an outback train in sweltering heat was almost unbearable. 'It'ld be much cheaper to stay here and go by the Dakota next week, wouldn't it?'

The pilot said, 'Oh, much. From here to Cairns would cost you ten pounds fifteen shillings. Flying back to Cloncurry and then on to Townsville and Cairns would be about thirty pounds.'

'I suppose the hotel here is quite cheap?'

'About twelve and six a day, I should think.' He turned to the Shell agent, busy with the fuel. 'Al, how much does Mrs Connor charge?'

'Ten and six.'

Jean did a rapid mental calculation; by staying in this place and waiting for the Dakota in a week's time she would save sixteen pounds. 'I think I'll stay here,' she said. 'It's much cheaper than going back with you. I'll stay here and see Jim Lennon and wait for the Dakota next week.'

'You know what it's going to be like, Miss Paget?'

'Like the Post Office Hotel at Cloncurry?'

'It's a bit more primitive than that. The whatnot's out in the back yard.'

She laughed. 'Will I have to lock myself in my room and take a revolver to bed with me?'

He was a little shocked. 'Oh, you'll find it quite respectable. But, well, you may find it a little primitive, you know.'

'I expect I'll survive.'

By that time another truck had appeared, a lorry with a couple of men in it; they stared at Jean curiously. The pilot took her suitcase and put it in the back; the driver helped her up into the cab beside him. It was a relief to get out of the blazing sunshine into the shade again.

The driver said, 'Staying in Willstown?'

'I wanted to see Joe Harman, but they say he's away. I'm staying here till next week if Mrs Connor can have me, and going on to Cairns in the Dakota.'

He looked at her curiously. 'Joe Harman's gone to England. You're English, aren't you?'

The truck moved off down the wide tarmac runway. 'That's right,' she replied.

He beamed at her. 'My mother and my dad, they both came from England. My dad, he was born in Lewisham, that's part of London, I think, and my mother, she came from Hull.' He paused. 'My name's Small,' he said. 'Sam Small, like the chap with the musket.'

The truck left the runway and began bumping and swaying over the earth track leading to the town. Dust rose into the cab, the engine roared, and blue fumes enveloped them; every item of the structure creaked and rattled. 'Why did Joe Harman go to England?' she shouted above the din. 'What did he go for?'

'Just took a fancy, I think,' Mr Small replied. 'He won the Casket couple of years back.' This was Greek to her. 'There's not a lot to do upon the stations, this time of the year.'

She shouted, 'Do you know if there's a room vacant at the hotel?'

'Oh, aye, there'll be a room for you. You just out from England?'

'Yes.'

'What's the rationing like at home, now?'

She shouted her information to him as the truck bumped and swayed across the landscape to the town. A wooden shack appeared on one side of the track, and fifty yards on there was another on the left; there was another some distance ahead, and they were in the main street. They drew up in front of a two-storeyed building with a faded signboard on the first-floor veranda, AUSTRALIAN HOTEL. 'This is it,' said Mr Small. 'Come on in, and I'll find Mrs Connor.'

The Australian Hotel was a fair-sized building with about ten small bedrooms opening on to the top floor veranda. It had wooden floors and wooden doors; the whole of the rest of it was built of corrugated iron on a wood framework. Jean was accustomed by that time to the universal corrugated iron roofs, but a corrugated iron wall to her bedroom was a novelty.

She waited on the upstairs veranda while Mr Small went to find Mrs Connor; the veranda had one or two beds on it. When the landlady appeared she was evidently only just awake; she was a tall, grey-haired determined woman of about fifty.

Jean said, 'Good afternoon. My name's Jean Paget, and I've got to stop here till next week. Have you got a room?'

The woman looked her up and down. 'Well, I don't know, I'm sure. You travelling alone?'

'Yes. I really came to see Joe Harman, but they tell me he's away. I'm going on to Cairns.'

'You just missed the Cairns aeroplane.'

'I know. They say I'll have to wait a week for the next one.'

'That's right.' The woman looked around. 'Well, I don't know. You see, the men sleep out on this balcony, often as not. That wouldn't be very nice for you.'

Sam Small said, 'What about the two back rooms, Ma?'

'Aye, she could go there.' She turned to Jean. 'It's on the back balcony, looks out over the yard. You'll see the boys all going to the gents, but I can't help that.'

Jean said, 'I expect I'll survive that.'

'You been in outback towns before?'

She shook her head. 'I've only just come out from England.'

'Is that so! What's it like in England now? Do you get enough to eat?'

Jean said her piece again.

'I got a sister married to an Englishman,' the woman said. 'Living at a place called Goole. I send her home a parcel every month.'

She took Jean and showed her the room. It was clean and with a good mosquito net; it was small, but the passage door was opposite the double window opening on to the balcony, giving a clear draught through. 'Nobody don't come along this balcony, except Anne—she's the maid. She sleeps in this other room, and if you hear any goings on at night I hope you'll let me know. I got my eye upon that girl.' She reverted to the ventilation. 'You leave your door open a chink, prop your case against it so that no one can't come barging in by mistake, and have the windows open, and you'll get a nice draught through. I never had no difficulty sleeping in this place.'

She glanced down at Jean's hand. 'You ain't married?'

'No.'

'Well, there'll be every ringer in this district coming into town to have a look at you. You better be prepared for that.'

Jean laughed. 'I will.'

'You a friend of Joe Harman, then?'

'I met him in the war,' Jean said. 'In Singapore, when we were both waiting for a passage home.' It was nearer to the truth than her last lie, anyway. 'Then as I was in Australia I sent him a telegram to say I'd come and see him. I didn't get an answer so I came here anyway. But he's gone walkabout.'

The woman smiled. 'You picked up some Aussie slang.'

'Joe Harman taught me that one, when I met him in the war.'

Sam Small brought up her suitcase; she thanked him, and he turned away, embarrassed. She went into her room and changed her damp clothes for dry ones, and went along to the bathroom and had a shower, and was ready for tea at half past six when the bell echoed through the corrugated iron building.

She found her way down to the dining-room. Three or four men were seated there already and they looked at her curiously; a well-developed girl of sixteen whom she came to know as Annie indicated a separate small table laid for one. 'Roast beef, roast lamb, roast pork, roast turkey,' she said. 'Tea or coffee?'

It was swelteringly hot still. Flies were everywhere in the dining-room; they lighted on Jean's face, her lips, her hands. 'Roast turkey,' she said; time enough to try for a light meal tomorrow, when she knew the form. 'Tea.'

A plate was brought to her heaped high with meat and vegetables, hot and greasy and already an attraction for the flies. Tea came, with milk out of a tin; the potatoes seemed to be fresh, but the carrots and the turnips were evidently tinned. She thought philosophically that the flies would probably result in dysentry but she knew what to do about that; she had plenty of sulphatriad to see her through the week. She ate about a quarter of the huge plate of food and drank two cups of tea; then she was defeated.

She got outside into the open air as soon as possible; escaping from the flies. On the downstairs veranda three feet above the level of the ground there were two or three deckchairs, a little distance from the entrance to the bar. She had seen nowhere else in the hotel where she could sit and she already knew enough about Australian conventions not to go near the bar; she went and sat down in one of these chairs wondering if by doing so she was offending against local manners.

She lit a cigarette and sat there smoking, looking at the scene. It was evening but the sun was still strong; the dusty great expanse that served as a street was flooded with a golden light. On the opposite side of the road, more than a hundred yards away, there was a fairly extensive single-storey building that had been built on to from time to time; this was labelled–Wm Duncan, General Merchant. There was no sign of any other shop in the town. Outside Mr Duncan's establishment three coloured Abo stockmen were gossiping together; one held the bridle of a horse. They were big, well-set-up young men, very like Negroes in appearance and, like Negroes, they seemed to have plenty to laugh about.

Further along the other side of the great street a six-inch pipe rose vertically from the ground to a height of about eight feet. A fountain of water gushed up from the top of this pipe and the water seemed to be boiling hot, because a cloud of steam surrounded the fountain, and the stream running away into the background was steaming along its length. A quarter of a mile away a small hut was built across the course of the stream so that the stream ran into the hut and out the other side, but Jean had yet to discover the purpose of this edifice.

A low murmur of voices reached her from the bar; from time to time a man passed her and went in through the open door. She saw no women in the place.

Presently a young man, passing by upon the road, smiled at her and said, 'Good evening.' She smiled back at him, and said, 'Good evening.'

He checked immediately, and she knew that she had started something. He said, 'I saw you come in with Sam Small this afternoon. Came in the aeroplane, didn't you?'

He was a clean-looking young yokel; he walked with the typical swaying gait of the ringer, and he wore the green jodhpurs and the elastic-sided boots that marked his calling. It was no good trying to be standoffish. 'That's right,' she said. 'I came up from Cloncurry. Tell me, is that water natural?'

He looked where she was pointing. 'Natural? That's a bore. Never seen one before?'

She shook her head. 'I've only just come out from England.'

'From England? Oh my word.' He spoke in the slow manner of the outback. 'What's it like in England? Do you get enough to eat?'

She said her piece again. 'My Dad came from England,' he said. 'From a place called Wolverhampton. Is that near where you live?'

'About two hundred miles,' she replied.

'Oh, quite close. You'll know the family then. Fletcher is the name. I'm Pete Fletcher.'

She explained to Pete that there were quite a lot of people in England, and reverted to the subject of the bore. 'Does all the water that you get from bores come up hot like that?'

'Too right,' he said. 'It's mineral, too—you couldn't drink that water. There's gas comes up with it as well. I'll light it for you if you'd like to see.' He explained that it would make a flame five or six feet hight. 'Wait till it gets a bit darker, and I'll light it for you then.'

She said that was terribly kind of him, and he looked embarrassed. Al Burn, the Shell agent and truck repairer came by and stopped to join them. 'Got fixed up all right, Miss Paget?'

'Yes, thank you. I'm staying here till Wednesday and then going on to Cairns.'

'Good-oh. We don't see too many strange faces, here in Willstown.'

'I was asking Pete here about the bore. Pete, do the cattle drink that water?'

The boy laughed. 'When they can't get nothing sweeter they'll drink that. You'll see that they won't touch it in the wet, but then in the dry you'll see them drinking it all right.'

'Some bores they won't touch,' said Al. He was rolling himself a cigarette. 'They sunk a bore on Invergordon, that's a station between here and Normanton—over to the south a bit. They had to go down close on three thousand feet before they got the water and did it cost them something, oh my word. The bore crew, they were there close on three months. Then when they got the water it was stinking with the minerals and the cattle wouldn't touch it, not even in the dry. What's more, it wouldn't grow grass, either.'

Two more men had drifted up and joined the little gathering about her chair. 'Tell me,' she said, 'why is this town so spread out? Why aren't the houses closer together?'

One of the newcomers, a man of forty that she later learned to know as Tim Whelan, a carpenter, said, 'There was houses all along here once. I got a photograph of this town took in 1905. I'll bring it and show you tomorrow.'

'Were there more people living here then?'

Al Burns said, 'Oh my word. This was one of the gold towns, Miss Paget. Maybe you wouldn't know about that, but there was thirty thousand people living here one time.'

The other newcomer said, 'Eight thousand. I saw that in a book.'

Al Burns said stubbornly, 'My Dad always said there was thirty thousand when he come here first.'

It was evidently an old argument. Jean asked, 'How many are there now?'

'Oh, I dunno.' Al turned to the others. 'How many would you say now, Tim?' To Jean, aside, he said, 'He builds the coffins so he ought to know.'

'A hundred and fifty,' said Mr Whelan.

Sam Small had joined them on the veranda. 'There's not a hundred and fifty living in Willstown now. There's not more than a hundred and twenty.' He paused. 'Living here in the town, not the stations, of course. Living right here in the town, not counting boongs.'

A slow wrangle developed, so they set to work to count them; Jean sat amused while the evening light faded and the census was taken. The result was a hundred and forty-six, and by the time that that had been determined she had heard the name and occupation of most people in the town.

'Were there goldmines here?' she asked.

'That's right,' said Mr Small. 'They had claims by the hundred one time, all up and down these creeks, oh my word. There were seventeen hotels here, seventeen.'

Somebody else said, 'Steamers used to come here from Brisbane in those days–all around Cape York and right up the river to the landing stage. I never see them myself, but that's what my old man told me.'

Jean asked, 'What happened? Did the gold come to an end?'

'Aye. They got the stuff out of the creeks and the surface reefs, the stuff that was easy got. Then when they had to go deep and use a lot of machinery and that, it didn't pay. It's the same in all these towns. Croydon was the same, and Normanton.'

'They say they're going to start the mine in Croydon–open it again.' said somebody.

'They been talking like that ever since I can remember.'

Jean asked, 'But what happened to the houses? Did the people go away?'

'The houses just fell down, or were pulled down to patch up others.' Al told her. 'The people didn't stay here when the gold was done–they couldn't. There's only the cattle stations here now.'

The talk developed among the men, with Jean throwing in an occasional remark or question. 'Ghost towns,' somebody said. 'That's what they called the Gulf towns in a book that I read once. Ghost towns. That's because they're ghosts of what they were once, when the gold was on.'

'It didn't last for long,' somebody said. '1893 was the year that the first gold here was found, and there wasn't many people still living here in 1905.'

Jean sat while the men talked, trying to visualize this derelict little place as a town with eight thousand inhabitants, or thirty thousand; a place with seventeen hotels and houses thickly clustered in the angles of the streets. Whoever had planned the layout had dreamed a great dream; with people streaming in to take up claims and the population doubling itself every few days, the planner had had some excuse for dreaming of a New York of the Gulf of Carpentaria. Now all that remained was a network of rectangular tracks where once there had been streets of wooden houses; odd buildings alone remained among this network to show what had been the dream.

As the light faded Pete and Al went out and lit the bore for Jean. They struck half a dozen matches and got it to light; a flame shot upwards from it and lit up the whole town, playing and flickering amongst the water and the steam till finally it was extinguished by a vomit of water. They lit it again, and Jean admired it duly; it was clear that this was the one entertainment that the town provided, and they were doing their best to give her a good time. 'It's wonderful,' she said. 'I've never seen anything like that in England.'

They were duly modest. 'Most towns around here have a bore like that, that you can light,' they said.

She was tired with her day of flying; at nine o'clock she excused herself from their company and they all wished her goodnight. She drew Al Burns a little to one side before she went. 'Al,' she said. 'I'd like to see Jim Lennon–he's the man at Midhurst, isn't he? I'd like to see him before I go on Wednesday. Will he be coming into town?'

'Saturday he might be in,' Al said. 'I'd say that he'd be in here Saturday for his grog. If I hear of anybody going out that way I'll send him word and say that you're in town, and want to see him.'

'Do they work a radio schedule at Midhurst?'

He shook his head. 'It's too close in town, it wouldn't be worth it. If anyone gets sick or has an accident they can get him into town here in an hour or so, and the sister has a radio at the hospital.' He paused. 'There'll be someone going out that way in the next day or so. If not, and if Jim Lennon doesn't come in on Saturday, I'll run you out there in the truck on Sunday.'

'That's awfully kind of you,' she said. 'I don't want to put you to that trouble.'

'It's no trouble,' he said. 'Make a bit of a change.'

She went up to bed. The hotel was lit by electric light made in the backyard by an oil engine and generator set that thumped steadily outside her room till she heard the bar close at ten o'clock; at five past ten the engine stopped and all the lights went out. Willstown slept.

She was roused at five o'clock with the first light with the sounds of people getting up and washing; she lay dozing, listening to the early morning sounds. Breakfast was not till half past seven; she got up and had a shower and was punctual in the dining-room. She found that the standard breakfast in Willstown was half a pound of steak with two fried eggs on top of it; she surprised Annie very much by asking for one fried egg and no steak. 'Breakfast is steak and eggs,' Annie explained patiently to this queer Englishwoman.

'I know it is,' said Jean. 'But I don't want the steak.'

'Well, you don't have to eat it.' The girl was obviously puzzled.

'Could I have just one fried egg, and no steak?' asked Jean.

'You mean, just one fried egg on a plate by itself?'

'That's right.'

Food conversation in Willstown was evidently quite a new idea. 'I'll ask Mrs Connor,' said Annie. She came back from the kitchen with a steak with two fried eggs on top. 'We've only got the one breakfast,' she explained. Jean gave up the struggle.

She ventured out to the kitchen after breakfast and found Mrs Connor. 'I've got a few things to wash,' she said. 'Could I use your washtub, do you think? And–have you got an iron?'

'Annie'll do them for you,' Mrs Connor said. 'Just give them to her.'

Jean had no intention of trusting her clothes to Annie. 'She's got a lot of work to do,' she said, 'and I've got nothing. I'll do them myself if I can borrow the tub.'

'Good-oh.'

Jean spent the morning washing and ironing in the back ground-floor veranda just outside the kitchen; in that dry, torrid place clothes hung out on a line were dry in ten minutes. In the kitchen the temperature must have been close on a hundred and twenty Fahrenheit; Jean made quick rushes in there to fetch her irons from the stove, and wondered at the fortitude of women who cooked three hot meals a day in such conditions. Annie came presently and stood around on the back veranda, furtively examining Jean's washing.

She picked up a carton of soap flakes. 'How much of this do you put in the water?'

Jean said, 'I think it's an ounce to a gallon of water, isn't it! I used to know. I put in just a bit. It tells you on the packet.'

The girl turned the packet over in her hands, scrutinizing it. 'Where it says, DIRECTIONS FOR USE,' said Jean.

From the door behind her Mrs Connor said, 'Annie don't read very well.'

The girl said, 'I can read.'

'Oh, can you? Well then, read us out what's written on that packet.'

The girl put the carton down. 'I ain't had much practice lately. I could read all right when I was at school.'

To ease the situation Jean said, 'All you do is just go on putting in the soap flakes till the water lathers properly. It's different with different sorts of water, because of the hardness.'

'I use ordinary soap,' said Annie. 'It don't come up so well as this.'

Presently the girl said, 'Are you a nurse?'

Jean shook her head. 'I'm a typist.'

'Oh, I thought you might be a nurse. Most women that come to Willstown are nurses. They don't stay here long. Six months, and then they've had enough.'

There was a pause. 'If you'd been a nurse,' the girl said, 'I'd have asked you for some medicine. I've been feeling ever so ill lately just after getting up. I was sick this morning.'

'That's bad,' said Jean cautiously. There did not seem to be much else to say.

'I think I'll go up to the hospital,' said Annie, 'and ask Sister Douglas for some medicine.'

'I should do that,' said Jean.

In the course of the day she met most of the notable citizens of Willstown. She walked across to the store to try and buy some cigarettes, but only succeeded in buying a tin of tobacco and a packet of papers. While she was chatting to Mr Bill Duncan in the store and examining the piece of quartz with gold in it that he showed her, Miss Kenroy came in, the schoolteacher. Half an hour later, as Jean was walking back across the road to the hotel, Al Burns met her and wanted to introduce her to Mr Carter, the Shire Clerk.

She slept most of the afternoon upon her bed, in common with the rest of

Willstown; when the day cooled off she came down to the lower veranda and sat there in a deckchair, as she had the previous evening. She had not long to wait before the ringers found her; they came one by one, diffidently, unsure of themselves before this English girl, and yet unable to keep away. She had a little circle of them squatting with her on the veranda presently.

She got them to talk about themselves; it seemed the best way to put them at their ease. 'It's all right here,' said one. 'It's good cattle country; more rain here than what you get down further south. But I'm off out of it next year. My brother, he's down at Rockhampton working on the railway. He said he'd get me in the gang if I went down and joined him.'

Jean asked, 'Is it better pay down there?'

'Well, no. I don't think it's so good. We get five pounds seventeen and six here–that's all found, of course. That's for an ordinary stockrider.'

She was surprised. 'That's not bad pay, is it? For a single man?'

Pete Fletcher said, 'The pay's all right. Trouble is this place. There's nothing to do here.'

'Do you get a cinema here ever?'

'There's a chap supposed to come here every fortnight and show films in the Shire Hall–that building over there.' She saw a low, barnlike wooden structure. 'He hasn't been for a month, but he's coming next week, Mr Carter says.'

'What about dances?' Jean asked.

There was a cynical laugh. 'They try it sometimes, but it's a crook place for a dance. Not enough girls.'

Pete Fletcher said, 'There's about fifty of us stockmen come into Willstown, Miss Paget, and there's two unmarried girls to dance with, Doris Nash and Susie Anderson. That's between the age of seventeen and twenty-two, say. Not counting the kids and the married women.'

One of the ringers laughed sourly. 'Susie's more than twenty-two.'

Jean asked, 'But what happens to all the girls? There must be more than that around here?'

'They all go to the cities for a job,' said somebody. 'There's nothing for a girl to do in Willstown. They go to Townsville and Rockhampton–Brisbane, too.'

Pete Fletcher said, 'That's where I'm going, Brisbane.'

Jean said, 'Don't you like it on a cattle station, then?' She was thinking of Joe Harman and his love for the outback.

'Oh, the station's all right,' said Pete. He hesitated, uncertain how to put what he felt to this Englishwoman without incautiously using a rude word. 'I mean,' he said, 'a fellow's got a right to have a girl and marry, like anybody else.'

She stared at him. 'It's really like that, is it?'

'It's a fair cow,' said somebody. 'It's a fair cow up here. No kidding, lady. It's two unmarried girls for fifty men in Willstown. A fellow hasn't got a chance of marrying up here.'

Somebody else explained to her, 'You see, Miss Paget, if a girl's a normal girl and got her head screwed on right–say, like it might be you–you wouldn't stay here. Soon as you were old enough to go away from home you'd be off to some place where you could get a job and make your own living, not have to depend on your folks all the time. My word, you would. The only girls that stay in Willstown are the ones who are a bit stupid and couldn't make out in any other place, or else ones who feel they've got to stay and look after the old folks.'

Somebody else said, 'That kind take the old folks with them down to the city. Like Elsie Freeman.'

Jean laughed. 'You mean, that if you stay in Willstown you'll finish up by marrying a girl who's not so hot.'

They looked over their shoulders, embarrassed. 'Well, a fellow wants to look around a bit . . .'

'Who's going to run the stations if you all go down to the cities, looking round a bit?' Jean said.

'That's the manager's headache,' said Pete. 'I've got headaches of my own.'

That evening shortly before tea a utility drove up, a battered old Chevrolet with a cab front and an open, truck-like body behind. It was driven by a man of about fifty with lean, sensitive features. Beside him sat a brown girl of twenty or twenty-five with a smooth skin and a serene face; she was not pure native, but probably a quarter white. She wore a bright red dress, and she carried a kitten, which was evidently a great amusement and interest to her. They passed into the hotel, the man carrying their bags; evidently they were staying for the night. At teatime Jean saw them in the dining-room sitting with the men at the other table, but they were keeping very much to themselves.

Jean asked Mrs Connor who they were, after tea. 'That's Eddie Page,' she said. 'He's manager of a station called Carlisle about a hundred miles out. The lubra's his wife; they've come in to buy stores.'

'Real wife?' asked Jean.

'Oh yes, he married her properly. One of the Bush Brothers was round that way last year, Brother Copeland, and he married them. They come in here from time to time. I must say, she never makes any trouble. She can't read or write, of course, and she doesn't speak much. Always got a kitten or a puppy along with her; that's what she likes.'

The picture of the man's sensitive, intelligent face came incongruously into Jean's mind. 'I wonder what made him do that?'

Mrs Connor shrugged her shoulders. 'Got lonely, I suppose.'

That night, when Jean went up to her bedroom, she saw a figure standing by the rail of the balcony that overlooked the backyard. There were two bedrooms only that opened on that balcony, her own and Annie's. In the dim light as she was going in at her window, she said, 'Goodnight, Annie.'

The girl came towards her. 'I been feeling awful bad,' she muttered. 'Mind if I ask you something, Miss Paget?'

Jean stopped. 'Of course, Annie. What's the matter?'

'Do you know how to get rid of a baby, Miss Paget?'

Jean had been prepared for that one by the morning's conversation; a deep pity for the child welled up in her. 'I'm terribly sorry, Annie, but I don't. I don't think it's a very good thing to do, you know.'

'I went up to Sister Douglas and she said that's what's the matter with me. Pa'll beat the daylights out of me when he hears.'

Jean took her hand, and drew her into the bedroom. 'Come in here and tell me about it.'

Annie said, 'I know there's things you can do like eating something or riding on a horse or something like that. I thought perhaps you might have had to do it, and you'd know.'

'I've never had to do it, Annie. I don't know. Why don't you ask him to marry you and have it normally?'

The girl said, 'I don't know how you'd tell which one it was. They'd all say it was one of the others, wouldn't they?'

It was a problem that Jean had never had to face. 'I suppose they would.'

'I think I'll ask my sister Bessie. She might know. She had two kids afore getting married.'

It did not look as if Bessie's knowledge had been very useful to her. Jean asked, 'Wouldn't the sister do anything to help you?'

'All she did was call me a wicked girl. That don't help much. Suppose I am a wicked girl. There's nothing else to do in a crook place like this.'

Jean did what she could to comfort her with words, but words were little good to Annie. Her interests were not moral, but practical. 'Pa will be mad as anything when he gets to know about it,' she said apprehensively. 'He'll beat the daylights out o' me.'

There was nothing Jean could do to help the girl, and presently they went to bed. Jean lay awake for a long time beset by human suffering.

She continued for the next two days in Willstown, sitting on the veranda and talking to the ringers, and visiting the various establishments in the town. Miss Kenroy took her and showed her the school. Sister Douglas showed her the hospital. Mr Carter showed her the Shire Hall with the pathetically few books that constituted the public library; Mr Watkins showed her the bank, which was full of flies, and Sergeant Haines showed her the Police Station. By the end of the week she was beginning to know a good deal about Willstown.

Jim Lennon came into town on Saturday, as predicted, for his grog. He came in an International utility that Jean learned was the property of Joe Harman, an outsize in motor cars with a truck body behind the front seat, furnished with tanks for seventy gallons of petrol and fifty gallons of water. Mr Lennon was a lean, bronzed, taciturn man.

'I got an air mail letter yesterday,' he said with the deliberation of the Queenslander. 'Joe's starting on his way back from England in a ship. He said he'd be about the middle of October, so he thought.'

'I see,' said Jean. 'I want to see him before I go back to England. I've arranged to fly to Cairns on Wednesday and wait there for him.'

'Aye. There's not much for you to do, I don't suppose, waiting round here. I'd say come out and live at Midhurst, but there's less to do there.'

'What's Joe been doing in England, Mr Lennon? Did he tell you what he was going for?'

The stockman laughed. 'I didn't even know he was going. All I knew he was going down to Brisbane. Then I got a letter that he'd gone to England. *I* don't know why he went. He did say in this letter I got yesterday he'd seen a bonza herd of Herefords, belonging to a Sir Dennis Frampton. Maybe he's having bulls shipped out to raise the quality of the stock. He didn't tell me nothing.'

She gave him her address as the Strand Hotel in Cairns, and asked him to let her know when he got accurate news of Joe's arrival.

That evening as she was sitting in her deckchair on the veranda, Al Burns brought a bashful, bearded old man to her; he had disengaged the old man from the bar with some difficulty. He was carrying a sack. 'Miss Paget,' he said, 'want you to meet Jeff Pocock.' Jean got up and shook hands. 'Thought you'd like to meet Jeff,' Al said cheerfully. 'Jeff's the best alligator hunter in all Queensland. Aren't you, Jeff?'

The old man wagged his head. 'I been hunting 'gators since I was a boy,' he said. 'I reckon I knows 'gators by this time.'

Al said, 'He's got an alligator skin to show you, Miss Paget.' To the old man he said, 'Show her your skin, Jeff. I bet she's never seen a skin like that in England.'

Jeff Pocock took the sack and opened it, and took out a small alligator skin rolled up. ''Course,' he said, 'I cleaned and trimmed and tanned this one myself. Mostly we just salt them and sell 'em to the tannery like that.' He unrolled the skin before her on the floor of the veranda. 'Pretty markings, ain't they? I bet you never seen a skin like that in England.'

The sight of it brought back nostalgic memories to Jean of red buses on the Great West Road at Perivale, and Pack and Levy Ltd, and rows of girls sitting at the work benches making up alligator-skin shoes and alligator-skin handbags and alligator-skin dressing-cases. She laughed. 'I've seen hundreds of them in England,' she replied. 'This is one thing I really know about. I used to work in a factory that made these skins up into handbags and dressing-cases.' She picked up the skin and handled it. 'Ours were harder than this, I think. You've done the curing very well, Jeff.'

Two or three other men had drifted up; her story was repeated back and forth in other words, and she told them all about Pack and Levy Ltd. They were very interested; none of them knew much about the skins after they had left the Gulf country. 'I know as they make shoes of them,' said Jeff. 'I never see a pair.'

A vague idea was forming in Jean's mind. 'How many of these do you get a year?' she asked.

'I turned in eighty-two last year,' the old man said. ''Course that's a little 'un. They mostly run about thirty to thirty-six inch—width of skin, that is. That's a 'gator about eleven foot long.'

Jean said, 'Will you sell me this one, Jeff?'

'What do you want it for?'

She laughed. 'I want to make myself a pair of shoes out of it.' She paused. 'That's if Tim Whelan can make up a pair of lasts for me.'

He looked embarrassed. 'I don't want nothing for it,' he said gruffly. 'I'll give it to you.'

She argued with him for a little while, and then accepted gracefully. 'We'll want a bit of calf skin for the soles,' she said, 'and some thicker stuff for building up the heels.'

She fondled the skin in her hands. 'It's beautifully soft,' she said, 'I'll show you what to do with this.'

7

Jean made that pair of shoes working upon the dressing-table of her bedroom; to be more exact, she made three pairs before she got a pair that she could wear.

She started off upon Tim Whelan. Tim had made lasts for shoes from time to time, working for various cobblers; the outback woodworker must turn his hand to anything. Jean lent him one of her shoes and lent him her foot to measure in his carpenter's shop, and he made a pair of lasts for her in mulga wood in a couple of days. She asked Pete Fletcher about leather for the soles and heels, and he produced some pieces of tanned cow-skin which were about the right thickness for the soles, and a piece of bull's skin for building up the heels. The lining was a major difficulty at first till somebody suggested a young wallaby skin. Pete Fletcher went out and shot the wallaby and skinned it, and the tanning was carried out by a committee of Pete Fletcher and Al Burns and Don Duncan, working in the back of Bill Duncan's store. The business of this pair of shoes assumed such an importance in the life of Willstown that Jean put off her trip to Cairns for a week, and then another week.

The wallaby skin for the lining was not ready, so Jean made up the first pair with a white satin lining that she bought in the store. She knew every process of shoe-making intimately from the point of view of an onlooker, and from the office end, but she had never done it herself before, and the first pair of shoes were terrible. They were shoes of a sort, but they pinched her toes and the heels were too large by a quarter of an inch, and they hurt her instep. The satin lining was not a success, and the whole job was messy with the streaming perspiration of her fingers. Still, they were shoes, and wearable by anyone whose feet happened to be that shape.

She could not show shoes like that to the men downstairs, and so she set to work to make another pair. She got Tim to alter the lasts for her, bought another knife and a small carborundum stone from the store, and started again. For fixative she was using small tubes of Durofix, also from the store.

In all this work Annie took a great interest. She used to come and sit and watch Jean working as she trimmed and filed the soles or stretched the wet alligator hides carefully upon the lasts. 'I do think you're clever to be able to do that,' she said. 'They're almost as good as you could buy in a shop.'

The second pair were better. They fitted Jean moderately well, but the wallaby-skin lining was uneven and lumpy, and the whole job was still messy and fingermarked with sweat. Undaunted, she began upon a third pair. This time she used portions of the wallaby skin that were of even thickness, having no means of trimming the skin down, and when it came to the final assembly of the shoes she worked in the early morning when the perspiration of her hands was least. The final result was quite a creditable shoe with rather an ugly coloured lining, but a shoe that she could have worn anywhere.

She took the three pairs downstairs and showed them to Al Burns on the veranda; Al fetched two or three of the other men, and Mrs Connor came to have a look at them. 'That's what happens to the alligator skins in England,' Jean said. 'They make them up into shoes like that. Pretty, aren't they?'

One of the men said, 'You made them yourself, Miss Paget?'

She laughed. 'Ask Mrs Connor. She knows the mess I've been making in the bedroom.'

The man turned the shoe over in his hand. 'Oh my word,' he said slowly. 'It's as good as you'd buy in a shop.'

Jean shook her head. 'It's not,' she said. 'It's not really.' She pointed out the defects to him. 'I haven't got the proper brads or the proper fixative. And the whole thing's messy, too. I just made it up to show you what they do with all these skins that Jeff brings in.'

'I bet you could sell that in Cairns,' the man said, stubbornly. 'Oh my word, you could.'

Sam Small said, 'How much does a pair of shoes like that cost in England.' 'In a shop?' She thought for a minute. 'About four pounds fifteen shillings, I should say. I know the manufacturer gets about forty-five bob, but then there's purchase tax and retailer's commission to go on.' She paused. 'Of course, you can pay much more than that for a really good shoe. People pay up to ten pounds in some shops.'

'Ten pounds for a pair of shoes like that? Oh my word.'

Jeff was out of town up the river visiting his traps, so she could not show him the shoes that day. She left them with the men to take into the bar and talk over, and she went to have a bath. She had discovered how to have a bath in Willstown by that time; Annie had showed her. The Australian Hotel had a cold shower for ladies, which was usually a very hot shower because the tank stood in the sun. But if you wanted to wallow in hot water, there was another technique altogether.

Where the water from the bore ran off in a hot stream, a small wooden hut had been constructed spanning the stream, at such a distance from the bore that the temperature was just right for a bath. A rough concrete pool had been constructed here large enough for two bodies to lie in side by side; you took your towel and soap and went to the hut and locked yourself in and bathed in the warm, saline water flowing through the pool. The salts in the water made this bath unusually refreshing.

Jean lay in the warm water, locked in the little hut alone; the sunlight came in through little chinks in the woodwork and played on the water as she lay. Since she had seen Jeff Pocock's alligator skin the idea of making shoes had been in her mind. From the time that she had first met me and learned of her inheritance she had been puzzled, and at times distressed, by the problem of what she was going to do with her life. She had no background of education or environment that would have enabled her to take gracefully to a life of ease. She was a business girl, accustomed to industry. She had given up her work with Pack and Levy as was only natural when she inherited nine hundred a year, but she had found nothing yet to fill the gap left in her life. Subconsciously she had been searching, questing, for the last six months, seeking to find something that she could work at. The only work she really knew about was fancy leather goods, alligator shoes and handbags and attaché cases. She did know a little bit about the business of making and selling those.

She lay in the warm, medicated water, thinking deeply. Suppose a little workshop with about five girls in it, and a small tannery outside. Two handpresses and a rotary polisher; that meant a supply of electric current. A small motor generator set, unless perhaps she could buy current from the hotel. An air conditioner to keep the workshop cool and keep the girls' hands from sweating as they worked. It was imperative that the finished shoes should be virgin clean.

Could such a set-up pay? She lay calculating in her bath. She had discovered that Jeff Pocock got about seventy shillings for an average alligator skin, uncured. She knew that Pack and Levy paid about a hundred and eighty shillings for cured skins. It did not seem to her that it could cost more than twenty shillings to trim and tan an alligator skin, and her figures were in Australian money, too. The skins should be much cheaper than in England. Labour, too, would be cheaper; girl labour in Willstown would be cheaper than girl labour in Perivale. But then there would be the cost of shipping the shoes to

England, and an agent's fees.

She wondered if Pack and Levy would sell for her. She knew that Mr Pack had been lukewarm for a long time about the manufacturing side of the business. They did sell other people's products, too–those handbags made by that French firm, Ducros Frères. Pack and Levy sold those, although they made handbags themselves . . .

The major problem was not the business, she thought. In Willstown both labour and materials were cheap; the business end of it might well be all right. But could she train the sort of girl that she could get in Willstown to turn out first-class quality work, capable of being sold in Bond Street shops? That was the real problem.

She lay for a long time in her warm, medicated bath, thinking very deeply.

That evening as she was sitting in her deckchair on the veranda, Sam Small came to her. 'Miss Paget,' he said. 'Mind if we have a talk?'

'Of course, Sam,' she said.

'I been thinking about that pair of shoes you made,' he said. 'I been wondering if you could teach our Judy.'

'How old is Judy, Sam?'

'Fifteen,' he said. 'Sixteen next November.'

'Do you want her to learn shoe-making?'

He said, 'I been thinking that anyone who could make a dinkum pair of ladies shoes like that, they could sell them in Cairns in the shops. You see, Judy's getting to an age when she's got to do some work, and there ain't nothing here a girl can do to make a living. She'll have to go into the cities, like the other girls. Well, that's a crook deal for her mother, Miss Paget. We've only got the one girl–three boys and one girl, that's our litter. It'll be a crook deal for her mother if Judy goes to Brisbane, like the other girls. And I thought this shoe-making, well, maybe it would be a thing that she could do at home. After all,' he said, 'it looks like we've got everything you need to do it with, right here in Willstown.'

'Not buckles,' Jean said thoughtfully. 'We'd have to do something about buckles.' She was speaking half to herself.

She thought for a minute. 'It wouldn't work like that, Sam,' she said. 'You think that pair of shoes are wonderful, but they aren't. They're a rotten pair of shoes. You couldn't sell a pair like that in England, not to the sort of people who buy shoes like that. I don't think you could sell them in any first-class shop, even in Cairns.'

'They look all right to me,' he said stubbornly.

She shook her head. 'They aren't. I've been in this business, Sam–I know what a shoe ought to look like. I'm not saying that we can't turn out a decent shoe in Willstown; I'd rather like to try. But to get the job right I'll need machinery, and proper benches and hand tools, and proper materials. I see your point about Judy, and I'd like to see her with a job here in Willstown. But it's too big a thing for her to tackle on her own.'

He looked at her keenly. 'Was you thinking of a factory or something?'

'I don't know. Suppose somebody started something of the sort here. How many girls would you get to work regular hours, morning and afternoon–say for five pounds a week?'

'Here in Willstown?'

'That's right.'

'How young would you let them start?'

She thought for a minute. 'When they leave school, I suppose. That's fourteen, isn't it?'

'You wouldn't pay a girl of fourteen five pounds a week?'

'No. Work them up to that when they got skilled.'

He considered the matter. 'I think you'd get six or seven round about sixteen or seventeen, Miss Paget. Then there'd be more coming on from school.'

She turned to another aspect of the matter. 'Sam, what would it cost to put up a hut for a workshop?'

'How big?'

She looked around. 'About as long as from here to the end of the veranda, and about half as wide.'

'That's thirty foot by fifteen wide. You mean a wooden hut, like it might be an army hut, with an iron roof, and windows all along?'

'That's the sort of thing.'

He calculated slowly in his head. 'About two hundred pounds.'

'I think I'd want it to have a double roof and a veranda, like that house that Sergeant Haines lives in. It's got to be cool.'

'Ah, that puts up the cost. A house like that'ld cost you close upon four hundred, with a veranda all around.'

'How long would that take to build?'

'Oh, I dunno. Have to get the timber up from Normanton. Tim Whelan and his boys 'ld put that up in a couple of months, I'd say.'

There would be extra buildings needed for the tanning and the dyeing of the hides. 'Tell me, Sam,' she said. 'Would people here like something of that sort started? Or would they think it just a bit of nonsense?'

'You mean, if it kept the girls here in the town, earning money?'

'That's right.'

'Oh my word,' he said. 'Would they like it. They'd like anything that kept the girls at home, so long as they was happy and got work to do.' He paused thoughtfully. 'It isn't natural the way the girls go off a thousand miles from home in this country,' he said slowly. 'That's what Ma and I was saying the other night. It isn't natural.'

They sat in silence for a time. 'Takes a bit of thinking about, Sam,' she said at last.

When the Dakota came next Wednesday she left Willstown for Cairns. She took two days to get there because that was the unhurried way of the Dakota; they left Willstown in the afternoon and called at various cattle stations with the mail and correspondence lessons for the children from the school at Cairns, at Dunbar and Miranda and Vanrook. With the last of the light they put down at Normanton for the night, and drove into the town in a truck.

The hotel at Normanton was similar to the hotel at Willstown, but rather larger. Jean had tea with the pilot, a man called Mackenzie; after tea she sat with him on the veranda. She asked him if anyone made shoes in Normanton. 'I don't think so,' he said. He called out to an acquaintance. 'Ted, does anyone make shoes round here?'

Ted shook his head. 'Buy 'em from Burns Philp,' he said. 'Want a pair of shoes mended?'

Jean said, 'No–I was just curious. They all come from the cities, do they?'

'That's right.' Ted rolled himself a cigarette. 'My wife's sister, she works in a shoe factory down at Rockhampton. That's where a lot of the shoes come from.

Manning Cooper, at Rockhampton. That's where Burns Philp get 'em from.'
Jean asked, 'Was your wife's sister born round here?'
'Croydon,' he said. 'Their Dad used to keep a hotel at Croydon, but he give up; there wasn't work for two. Mrs Bridson's is the only one there now.'
'She's not married?'
'Who? Elsie Peters?'
'That's the one who works at Manning Cooper, is it?'
'No, she's not married. Got to be a charge hand now, with a lot of girls under her.'
When he had moved on Jean asked the pilot, 'Who was that?'
'Him? Ted Horner. He runs the garage here.' She noted the name for future reference.
They flew on to Cairns early the next morning; she drove into the town and went to the Strand Hotel. Cairns, she found, was a prosperous town of about twenty thousand people, situated rather beautifully on an inlet of the sea. There were several streets of shops, wide avenues with flower beds down the middle of the road; the buildings were all wood and most had iron roofs. It looked rather like the cinema pictures she had seen of American towns in the deep south, with its wide broad sidewalks shaded by verandas to enable you to look into the shop windows in the shade, but it was almost aggressively English in its loyalties. She liked Cairns from the start.
She wrote to me from there. She had written to me twice from Willstown, and at the Strand Hotel she found a letter from me waiting for her that had been there for some days, on account of her delays. She wrote,

Strand Hotel,
Cairns,
North Queensland

MY DEAR NOEL,
I got your letter of the 24th when I arrived here yesterday, and you will have got my two from Willstown by this time. I wish I had a typewriter because this is going to be a long letter. I think I'll have to get a portable soon in order to keep copies of my letters—not to you, but I'm getting involved a bit in business out here.
First of all, thank you so very much for telling me what you did about Joe Harman. You've evidently been very nice to him and, as you know, that's being nice to me. I can't get over what you say about him rushing off to England and spending all that money, just to see me again. But people out here are like that, I think. I could say an awful lot of rude things about Australians by this time, but I can say this, too. The people that I've met in the outback have all been like Joe Harman, very simple, very genuine, and very true.
And now, about Willstown. I don't know if Joe Harman will still be so keen on marrying me when he sees me; six years is a long time, and people change. I don't know if I'll be keen on marrying him. But if we were to want to marry, what he told you about Willstown is absolutely right.
It's just terrible there, Noel. There are some places in the outback where one could live a full and happy life. Alice Springs is a grand little town. But Willstown's not one of them. Noel, it's absolutely the bottom. There's nothing for a woman there at all except the washtub. I know that one ought to be able to get along without such things as radio and lipstick and ice-cream and pretty clothes. I think I *can* get along all right without them—I did in Malaya. But when it comes to no fresh milk and no fresh vegetables or fruit, it's a bit thick. I think that what Joe told you was absolutely right. I don't think any girl could come straight out from England and live happily in Willstown. I don't think I could.
And yet, Noel, I wouldn't want to see Joe try and change his way of life. He's a first-class station manager, and he'll do very well. I asked all sorts of people about the way Midhurst is run, and it's good. I don't say it couldn't be better if he travelled a bit more widely and saw what other cattle breeders do, but relative to the other stations in the Gulf country, Midhurst is pretty good and

getting better every year. The last manager let it run down, so they tell me, but Joe's done a good job in the two years that he's been there. I wouldn't want to see Joe try and make his life anywhere else, just because he'd married a rich wife who couldn't or wouldn't live in Willstown, where his work is.

Of course, you'll probably say that he could get another station near a better town, perhaps near Alice. I'm not sure that that would be very easy; I've thought a lot about that one. But if it was possible, I wouldn't like it much. Midhurst is in good country with more rainfall than in England; for a life's work it seems to me that the Gulf country is a far better prospect than anything round Alice. I wouldn't like to think that he'd left good land and gone to bad land, just because of me. That wouldn't be a very good start for a station manager's wife.

Noel, do you think I could have five thousand pounds of my capital? I'm going to take the advice you always shove at me, and not do anything in a hurry. If when I meet Joe Harman he still wants to marry me, and if I want to marry him, I'm going to wait a bit if I can get him to agree. I'd like to work in Willstown for a year or so myself before committing myself to live there for ever. I want to see if I could get to adapt myself to the place, or if it's hopeless. I don't want to think that. I would like to find it possible to live in the Gulf country even though I was brought up in England, because they are such very, very decent people living there.

I want to try and start a workshop, making shoes and handbags out of alligator skins. I told you about that in my last letter. It's work I know about, and all the materials are there to hand in the Gulf country, except the metal parts. I've written a long letter this morning to Mr Pack to ask him if he would sell for me in England if the stuff is good enough, and to let me know the maximum price that he could give for shoes delivered at Perivale. And I've asked him to make me out a list of the things I'd want for a workshop employing up to ten girls and what they cost; things like a press and a polisher with the heads for it, and a Knighton No 6 sewing machine.

The sewing-machine is a heavy duty one for leather and that's the most expensive single item. I should think the lot, including £400 for a building to work in, would cost about a thousand pounds. But I'm afraid that's not the whole story. If I'm going to start a workshop for girls, they've got to have something to spend their wages on. I want to start a shop to sell the sort of things that women want.

Not a big shop, just a little one. I want it to be a sort of ice-cream parlour with a few chromium-plated chairs and glass-topped tables. I want to sell fruit there and fresh vegetables; if I can't get them any other way I'll have them flown in from Cairns. There's plenty of money in the outback for that. I want to sell fresh milk there, too; Joe will have to play and keep a few milking cows. I want to sell sweets, and just a few little things like lipstick and powder and face cream and magazines.

The big expense here is the refrigerators and freezes, of course. I think we'd have to allow five hundred pounds for those, and then there's the building and the furniture—say £1200 the lot. That makes, say, £2500 for capital expenditure. If I have five thousand of my capital, I should be able to stock the shop and the workshop and employ five or six girls for a year without selling anything at all, and by that time the income should be coming in, I think. If it isn't, well that's just too bad and I shall have lost my money.

I want to do this, Noel. Apart from Joe Harman and me, they're decent people in Willstown, and they've got so very little. I'd like to work there for a year as a sort of self discipline and to keep from running to seed now that I've got all this money. I think I'd want to do this even if there wasn't any Joe Harman in the background at all, but I shan't make up my mind or take any definite step until I've had a talk with him.

So what I want is five thousand pounds, please, Noel. May I have it if I want to go ahead with this?

                                                                          JEAN

I got this letter five days later by the air mail. I marked the passages about her money with a red pencil, and wrote a little note upon the top, and sent it into Lester for him to read. I went into his office later in the day. 'You read that letter from the Paget girl?' I asked.

He took it up from his desk before him. 'Yes. I've just been looking at the will. Did you draft that discretionary clause yourself?'

'I did.'

He smiled. 'I think it's a masterpiece. It covers us all right, if you think she ought to have this money.'

'It's about nine per cent of her capital,' I said. 'For a commercial venture that she intends to work at whole-time herself.'

'The testator didn't know her, did he?'

I shook my head.

'She's twenty-seven years old?'

'That is correct.'

'I think that we might let her have it,' he said. 'It would be very extreme to do the other thing, to withhold it. We've got ample latitude under your discretionary clause to let her have it, and she seems to be a responsible person.'

'I'd like to think it over for a day or so,' I said. 'It seems to me to be a very small amount of capital for what she wants to do.'

I put her letter on one side for a couple of days because I never like to take any action in a hurry. After a period of reflection it seemed to me that I would be carrying out the wishes of the late Mr Douglas Macfadden if I exerted myself to see that Jean Paget did not lose her money in this venture, and I picked up my telephone and rang up Mr Pack of Pack and Levy Ltd.

I said, 'Mr Pack, this is Strachan, of Owen, Dalhousie, and Peters. I believe you've had a letter from a client of mine, Miss Jean Paget.'

'Aye, that's right,' he said. 'You're her solicitor, are you? The one that's her trustee?'

'That is correct,' I said. 'I've had a letter from her, too. I was thinking it might be a good thing if we got together, Mr Pack, and had a talk about it.'

'Well, that suits me,' he replied. 'She asked for a list of what she'd want to start up in a small way. I got a list together, but I haven't got all the f.o.b. prices in yet.'

I made an appointment with him for the following Friday when he expected to be in London on other business. He came to see me then at my office. He was a small, fat, cheerful man, very much of a works manager. He brought with him a brown paper parcel.

'Afore we start,' he said, 'these come in this morning.' He untied the parcel on my desk and produced a pair of alligator-skin shoes. I picked up one curiously.

'What are these?' I asked.

'They're what she made herself at this place Willstown,' he said. 'Did she tell you about that?'

I shook my head, and examined them with fresh interest. 'Did she make these herself, with her own hands?'

'Made 'em with her own hands in her hotel bedroom, so she said,' he replied.

I turned one over. 'Are they any good?'

'Depends on how you look at it,' he observed. 'For selling in the trade they're bloody awful. Look at this, and this, and this.' He pointed out the various irregularities and crudities. 'They're not even the same. But she knows that. If you take them as a pair of shoes made by a typist that hadn't ever made a shoe before, working on her bed with no equipment, well, they're bloody marvellous.'

I laid down the shoe and offered him a cigarette. 'She told you what she wants to do?'

He told me what he had heard from her, and I told him some of what she had written to me; we talked for a quarter of an hour. At the end of that time I asked him, 'What do you really think about her proposition, Mr Pack?'

'I don't think she can do it,' he said flatly. 'Not the way she's thinking of. I don't think she knows enough about the shoe business to make a go of it.'

I must say, I was disappointed, but it was as well to have the facts. 'I see,' I said quietly.

'You see,' he explained, 'she hasn't got the experience. She's a good girl, Mr Strachan, and she's got a good business head. But she's got no experience of making shoes to sell, and she's got no experience of keeping girls in order 'n making them bloody well work for their money. It's not even as if she was in her own country. These Australian country girls she writes about, they're just like so many foreigners to her. They may be willing, but they've never seen a factory before–they won't have the idea at all. She's got to learn her own job and teach them theirs at the same time. Well, she can't do it.'

'I see,' I said again.

'I'd like to help her,' said the little man, 'but she'll have to change her ideas a bit. She's on to a good wheeze, if she can put it over. I must say, when I read her letter where it says that she's paying seventy shillings for an alligator skin uncured, you could have knocked me down with a feather. Australian shillings, too–fifty-six bob of our money. Here have I been paying a hundred and seventy, hundred and eighty shillings for a cured skin, all these years, and thinking I was getting 'em cheap at that! I said to Mr Levy, I said, couple of bloody mugs, we are.'

'What can you suggest to help her?' I asked.

'What I thought was this,' he said. 'If she could pay the passage of a forewoman out and home, I'd let her have a girl out of my shop, say for the first year. I got a girl that's getting restless–well, a woman she is, thirty-five if she's a day. She's a married woman but she isn't living with her husband–hasn't been for a long time. She was a sergeant in the A.T.S. in the war, out in Egypt some of the time, so she knows about a hot country. Aggie Topp, the name is. You wouldn't get girls playing up in any shop with Aggie Topp in charge.'

'Does Miss Paget know her?' I inquired.

'Oh, aye, Jean knows Aggie. And Aggie knows Jean. Matter of fact, Aggie came in yesterday and handed in her notice. I handed it back to her and jollied her along, you know. She does that every two or three months, getting restless, like I said. But I asked her then, how would she like to go out to Australia for a year to work with Miss Paget. She said she'd go anywhere to get away from standing in a queue for the bloody rations. She'd go out for a year, if Jean wants her. They all liked Jean.'

I said, 'Can you spare her?'

'She won't stay long, anyway,' he said. 'I don't want to lose her and perhaps I won't. If she gets a trip out to Australia and sees that other places aren't so good as England, then maybe she'll come back and settle down with us again. Get it out of her system.'

We talked about this for a time. The woman's passages and pay while travelling would tot up to about three hundred pounds, but it seemed cheap to me if it would help the venture through the early stages. For the rest of it, Mr Pack thought Jean's estimates of capital were on the low side, but not excessively so. 'You can't afford much mechanization in the quality shoe trade,' he said. 'You got to keep changing the style all the time.'

About the style, he suggested that they air-mailed a sample to Willstown from time to time for Jean's party to copy. He was quite willing to do the selling for her. 'Mind, I don't know if she'll be able to make a go of it upon the prices we can sell at,' he said. 'I'll tell her what we can buy at, and it's up to her. But I'd like to give this thing a spin, I must say. Manufacturing's getting so bloody difficult in this country with controls and that, one feels like trying something different.'

I thanked him very sincerely, and he went away. I wrote all this out to Jean Paget by air mail, and I believe Mr Pack wrote to her by the same mail. She did not get these letters for some days after their arrival, because she had gone down to Rockhampton to look for the girl Elsie Peters who worked in the shoe factory there. She went economically by train, a slow, hot journey of some seven hundred miles; till then she had not realized how vast and sparsely populated a state Queensland was. The aeroplanes had dwarfed it for her; fifty-one hours in the train to Rockhampton expanded it again.

She found Elsie Peters, and the meeting was a complete fiasco. It only lasted ten minutes. They met in a café close outside the works; as soon as Jean broached the subject of a job in the Gulf country, Elsie told her she could save her breath. It might be a good thing, she conceded, to start something in the Gulf country, but not for her. Wild horses would not drag her back again.

Jean came away from the café relieved in one way, and yet depressed. She would not have wanted anybody in that frame of mind, but she had been counting rather heavily on this unknown woman. She was very conscious of her own lack of managerial experience; as the venture became closer difficulties loomed up which had not been quite so obvious at the birth of the idea. She spent a depressed evening in the hotel, and flew back to Cairns next day in revolt at the long train journey; she found the air fare very little more expensive.

She found our letters waiting for her at the Strand Hotel when she got back there, and her spirits revived again. She remembered the gaunt, stern Aggie very well; if Aggie was prepared to come to Queensland for a year that really was something. I think she was beginning to feel very much alone and amongst strangers while she was waiting in Cairns for Joe Harman.

She wrote temporizing letters to us, for she would not make her mind up about anything until she had seen Harman. She told me later that the three weeks that she spent in Cairns living at the Strand Hotel after she came back from Rockhampton were the worst time of her life. Each morning she woke up in the cold light of dawn convinced that she was making a colossal fool of herself, that she could never settle down in this outlandish country, that she and Harman would have nothing in common and that it would be much better not to meet him at all. The wise course was to take the next plane down to Sydney and get a cheap passage to England, where she belonged. By noon some rough Australian kindness from a waitress or the manageress had sown a seed of doubt in the smooth bed of her resolution, that grew like a weed throughout the afternoon; by evening she knew that if she left that country and that place she would be running away from things that might be well worth having, things that she might never find again her whole life through. So she would go to bed resolved to be patient, and in the morning the whole cycle would start off again.

She knew the name of Harman's ship, of course, from my letters, and she had no difficulty in finding out when it docked at Brisbane. A few discreet inquiries showed her that he must pass through Cairns to get to Willstown, and convinced her that he would have to wait for several days in Cairns because his ship docked in Brisbane on a Monday and the weekly plane into the Gulf country left at dawn on Tuesday; he could never make that connection. She had found out in Willstown that he stayed at the Strand Hotel in Cairns, and so she waited there for him.

She wrote to him care of the shipping line at Brisbane, and she had some difficulty with that letter. Finally she said,

DEAR JOE,

    I got a letter from Mr Strachan telling me that you had been to see him while you were in England, and that you were sorry to have missed me. Funnily enough, I have been in Australia for some weeks, and I will wait at Cairns here so that we can have a talk before you go on to Willstown.

    Don't let's talk too much about Malaya when we meet. We both know what happened; let's try and forget about it.

    Will you let me know your movements–when you'll be coming up to Cairns? I do want to meet you again.

Yours sincerely,

JEAN PAGET

She got a telegram on Tuesday morning to tell her he was staying to see Mrs Spears, the owner of Midhurst, and he would be flying up to Cairns on Thursday. She went to meet him at the aerodrome, feeling absurdly like a girl of seventeen keeping her first date.

I think Joe Harman was in a position of some difficulty as the Dakota drew near to Cairns. For six years he had carried the image of this girl in his heart, but, in sober fact, he didn't in the least know what she looked like. The girl that he remembered had long black hair done in a pigtail down her back with the end tied up with a bit of string, like a Chinese woman. She was a very sunburnt girl, almost as brown as a Malay. She wore a tattered, faded, blouselike top part with a cheap cotton sarong underneath; she walked on bare feet which were very brown and usually dirty, and she habitually carried a baby on her hip. He did not really think that she would look like that at Cairns, and he was troubled and distressed by the fact that he probably wouldn't be able to recognize her again. It was unfortunate that the inner light in her, the quality that made her what he called a bonza girl, didn't show on the surface.

Something of his difficulty was apparent to Jean; she had wondered if he would know her while she was making herself pretty for him in her room, and had decided that he probably wouldn't. She had no such difficulty herself for he would have changed less than she, and anyway he carried stigmata upon his hands if there were any doubt. She stood waiting for him by the white rails bounding the tarmac as the Dakota taxied in in the hot sun.

She recognized him as he came out of the machine, fair-haired, blue-eyed, and broad-shouldered. He was looking anxiously about; his gaze fell on her, rested a minute, and passed on. She watched him, wondering if she was looking very old, and saw him start to walk towards the airline office with his curious, stiff gait. A little shaft of pain struck her; that was Kuantan, and it had left its mark on him. With her intellect she had known that this must be so, but seeing it for the first time was painful, all the same.

She left the rails, and walked quickly across the tarmac to him, and said, 'Joe!' He stopped and stared at her incredulously. He had been looking for a stranger, but it was unbelievable to him that this smart, pretty girl in a light summer frock was the tragic, ragged figure that he had last seen on the road in Malaya, sunburnt, dirty, bullied by the Japanese soldiers, with blood upon her face where they had hit her, with blood upon her feet. Then he saw a characteristic turn of her head and memories came flooding back on him; it was Mrs Boong again, the Mrs Boong he had remembered all those years.

It was not in him to be able to express what he was feeling. He grinned a little sheepishly, and said, 'Hullo, Miss Paget.'

She took his hand impulsively, and said, 'Oh, Joe!' He pressed her hand and looked down into her eyes, and then he said, 'Where are you staying? How long are you here for?'

She said, 'I'm staying in the Strand Hotel.'

'Why, that's where I'm staying,' he said. 'I always go there.'

'I know,' she said. 'Mrs Smythe told me.'

There was much here that he did not understand, but first things came first. 'Wait while I get my luggage,' he said. 'We can drive in together.'

'I've got a taxi waiting,' she said. 'Don't let's go in the bus.'

In the taxi as they drove into the town she asked him, 'How was Mr Strachan, Joe?'

'He was fine,' he said. 'I stayed with him quite a long time, in his flat.'

'Did you!' She had not known that part of it because I had not told her; I had told her the bare minimum about him since it was obvious that they were going to meet. 'How long were you in England, Joe?'

'About three weeks.'

She did not ask him why he went because she knew that already, and it was hardly a matter to be entered on behind the taxi driver. He forestalled her, however, by asking, 'What have you been doing in Australia, Miss Paget?'

She temporized. 'Didn't you know I was here?'

He shook his head. 'All I knew was what Mr Strachan said, that you were travelling in the East. You could have knocked me down with a feather when I got your letter at Brisbane. Oh my word, you could. Tell me, what are you doing in Cairns?'

A little smile played around her mouth. 'What were you doing in England?'

He was silent, not knowing what to say to that. He had no lie ready. They were running through the outskirts of the town, past the churches. 'We've got a good bit of explaining to do, Joe,' she said. 'Let's leave it till you've got your room at the hotel, and then we'll find somewhere to talk.'

They sat in silence till they got to the hotel. Jean had a bedroom opening on to a veranda that looked out over the sea to the wild, jungle-covered hills behind Cape Grafton; they arranged to meet there when he had had a wash. She knew something of Australian habits by that time. 'What about a beer or two?' she asked.

He grinned. 'Good-oh.'

She asked Doris the waitress to get four beers, three for Joe and one for her; large quantities of cold liquid were necessary in that torrid place. It was symbolic of Australia, she felt, that they should hold their first sentimental conversation with the assistance of four bottles of beer.

She dragged two deckchairs into a patch of shade outside her room; the beer and Joe arrived about the same time. When the waitress had gone and they were alone, she said quietly, 'Let me have a good look at you, Joe.'

He stood before her, examining her beauty; he had not dreamed when he had met her in Malaya that she was a girl like this. 'You've not changed,' she said. 'Does the back trouble you?'

'Not much,' he said. 'It doesn't hinder me riding, thank the Lord, but I can't lift heavy weights. They told me in the hospital I won't ever be able to lift heavy weights again, and I'd better not try.'

She nodded, and took one of his hands in hers. He stood beside her while she turned it over in her own, and looked at the great scars upon the palm and on the back. 'What about these, Joe?'

'They're all right,' he said. 'I can grip anything–start up a truck or anything.'

She turned to the table. 'Have a beer.' She handed him a glass. 'You must be thirsty. Three of these are for you.'

'Good-oh.' He took a glass and sank half of it. They sat down together in the deckchairs. 'Tell me what happened to you,' he asked. 'I know you said not to talk about Malaya. It was a fair cow, that place. I don't want to remember about it any more. But I do want to know what happened to you–after Kuantan.'

She sipped her beer. 'We went on,' she said. 'Captain Sugamo sent us on the same day, after–after that. We went on up the east coast with just the sergeant in charge of us. I was sorry for the sergeant, Joe, because he was very much in disgrace, because of what happened. He never got over it, and then he got fever and gave up. He died at a place called Kuala Telang, about half way between Kuantan and Khota Bahru. That was about a month later.'

'He was the only Nip guarding you?' he asked.

She nodded.

'Well, what did you do then?'

She raised her head. 'They let us stay there all the war,' she said. 'We just lived in the village, working in the paddy fields till the war was over.'

'You mean, paddling about in the water, planting the rice, like the Malays?'

'That's right,' she said.

'Oh my word,' he breathed.

She said, 'It wasn't a bad life. I'd rather have been there than in a camp, I think–once we got settled down. We were all fairly healthy when the war ended, and we were able to make a little school and teach the children something. We taught some of the Malay children, too.'

'I did hear a bit about that,' he said thoughtfully. 'I heard from a pilot on the airline, down at Julia Creek.'

She stared at him. 'How did he know about us?'

'He was the pilot of the aeroplane that flew you out, in 1945,' he replied. 'He said that you got taken in trucks to Khota Bahru. He flew you from Khota Bahru to Singapore. He's working for T.A.A. now, on the route from Townsville to Mount Isa. That goes through Julia Creek. I met him there this last May, when I was down there putting stock on to the train.'

'I remember,' she said slowly. 'It was an Australian Dakota that flew us out. Was he a thin, fair-haired boy?'

'That'ld be the one.'

She thought for a minute. 'What did he tell you, Joe?'

'Just what I said. He said he'd flown you down to Singapore.'

'What did he tell you about me?' She looked at him, and there was laughter in her eyes.

He grinned sheepishly, and said nothing.

'Come on, Joe,' she said. 'Have another beer, and let's get this straight.'

'All right,' he said. He took a glass and held it in his hand, but did not drink.

'He said you were a single woman, Mrs Boong. I always thought the lot of you was married.'

'They all were, except me. Is that why you went rushing off to England?'

He met her eyes. 'That's right.'

'Oh, Joe! What a waste of money, when here we are in Cairns!'

He laughed with her, and took a long drink of beer. 'Well, how was I to know that you'd be turning up in Cairns?' He thought for a minute. 'What are you doing here, anyway?' he asked. 'You haven't told me that.'

She was embarrassed in her turn. 'I came into some money,' she said. 'I think Noel Strachan told you about that.'

'That's right,' he said kindly.

'I didn't know what to do with myself then,' she said. 'I didn't want to go on working as a typist in a London suburb any more. And then I got the idea into my head that I wanted to do something for the village where we lived for those three years, Kuala Telang. I wanted to give them a well.'

'A well?' he asked.

Sitting there with a glass of beer in her hand she told him about Kuala Telang, and about her friends there, and the washhouse, and the well. Then she came to the difficult bit. 'The well-diggers came from Kuantan,' she said. 'I thought that you were dead, Joe. We all did.'

He grinned. 'I bloody nearly was.'

'The well-diggers told me that you weren't,' she said. 'They told me that you'd been put into the hospital, and you'd recovered.'

'That's right,' he said. 'I tried to find out what had happened to you, but they didn't know, or if they knew they wouldn't say. I reckon they were all scared stiff of that Sugamo.'

She nodded. 'I went to Kuantan. It's very peaceful there now. People playing tennis on the tennis courts, and sitting gossiping under that ghastly tree. They told me at the hospital that you'd asked about us.' She smiled. 'Mrs Boong.'

He grinned. 'But did you come on to Australia from there?'

She nodded. 'Yes.'

'What for?'

'Well,' she said awkwardly, 'I wanted to see if you were all right. I thought perhaps you might be still in hospital or something.'

'Is that dinky-die?' he asked. 'You came on to Australia because of me?'

'In a way,' she said. 'Don't let it put ideas into your head.' He grinned. 'I'd have done the same if you'd have been an Abo.'

'Well, you're a fine one to talk about me wasting money,' he said. 'We'd have met all right if you'd have stayed in England.'

She said indignantly, 'Well, how was I to know that you'd be turning up in England, and as fit as a flea?'

They sat drinking their beer for some time. 'How did you get here?' he asked. 'Where did you come to first?'

She said, 'I knew you used to work at Wollara and I thought they'd know about you there. So I flew from Singapore to Darwin, and went down to Alice on the bus.'

'Oh my word. You went to Alice Springs? Did you go out to Wollara and see Tommy Duveen?'

She shook her head. 'I stayed about a week in Alice, and I got your address at

Midhurst from Mr Duveen over the radio, from the hospital. So then I flew up to Willstown–I sent you a wire at Midhurst to say I was coming. But they told me there, of course, that you were in England.'

He stared at her. 'Is that dinky-die? You've been to Willstown?'

She nodded. 'I was there three weeks.'

'Three weeks!' He stared at her. 'Where did you stay?'

'With Mrs Connor, in the hotel.'

'But why three weeks? Three hours would have been enough for most people.'

'I had to stay somewhere,' she said. 'If you go running off to England, people who want to see you have to hang around. You'll probably find the Australian Hotel's full of them when you get back.'

He grinned, 'My word, I will. What did you do all the time?'

'Sat around and talked to Al Burns and Pete Fletcher and Sam Small, and all the rest.'

'You must have created a riot.' He paused, thinking deeply about this new aspect of the matter. 'Did you go out to Midhurst?'

She shook her head. 'I stayed in Willstown all the time. I met Jim Lennon, though.'

The bell rang downstairs for tea. 'We'd better go down, Joe,' she said. 'They don't like it if you're late.'

'I know.' He picked up his glass to drain it, but sat with it in his hand, untouched. At last he said, 'What did you think of Willstown, Miss Paget?'

She smiled. 'Look, Joe, forget about Miss Paget. You can call me Mrs Boong or you can call me Jean, but if you go on with Miss Paget I'll go home tomorrow.'

He smiled slightly, 'All right, Mrs Boong. What did you think of Willstown?'

'We'll be late for tea, Joe, if we start on that.'

'Tell me,' he said.

She smiled at him with her eyes. 'I thought it was an awful place, Joe,' she said quietly. 'I can't see how anyone can bear to live there.' She laid her hand upon his arm. 'I want to talk to you about it, but we must go and have tea now.'

He got up from his chair, and set the glass down. 'Too right,' he said heavily. 'It's a crook kind of a place for a woman.'

They went down to tea and sat at a table together, Joe deep in gloom. When they had ordered, Jean said, 'Joe, how long have you got? When have you got to be back at Midhurst?'

He raised his head and grinned. 'When I'm ready to go back,' he said. 'I been away so long a few days more won't make any difference.' He paused. 'What about you?'

'I only came here to see if you were all right, Joe,' she said. 'I suppose I'll go down to Brisbane and start looking for a boat home next week.'

Their food came, roast beef for Joe, cold ham and salad for Jean. 'What have you been doing since you came to Cairns?' he asked presently. 'Been out to the Reef?'

She shook her head. 'I went down to Rockhampton once, and I went on one of the White Tours up to the Tableland, and stayed a night in Atherton. I've not been anywhere else.'

'Oh my word,' he said. 'You can't go home without seeing the Great Barrier

Reef.' He paused, and then he said, 'Would you like to go to Green Island for the weekend?'

She cocked an eye at him. 'What's Green Island like?'

'It's just a coral island on the reef,' he explained. 'A little round one, about half a mile across. There's a restaurant on it and little sort of bedroom huts where you can stay, in among the trees. It's a bonza little place if you like bathing. Wear your bathers all the day.'

Jean thought the little bedroom huts among the trees wanted checking up on, but the suggestion certainly had its points. They knew so little about each other; they had so much to learn, so much to talk about. Whatever else might happen if she spent a weekend in her bathing dress with Joe Harman on a coral island, they would certainly come from it knowing more about each other than they would learn under the restraints of Cairns.

'I'd like to do that, Joe,' she said. 'How would we get there?'

He beamed with pleasure, and she was glad for him. 'I'll slip out after tea and find Ernie,' he said. 'He's probably in the bar at Hides. He's got a boat, and he'll run us out there tomorrow; it'll take about three hours. We'd better start about eight o'clock, before the sun gets hot. Then I'd ask him to come out and fetch us on Monday, say.'

'All right,' she agreed. 'But look, Joe—this is to be Dutch treat.' He did not understand that term. 'I mean, you pay the boat one way and I'll pay it the other, and we both pay our own bills.' He objected strenuously. 'If we don't do that, Joe, I won't come,' she said. 'I'll think you're plotting to do me a bit of no good.'

He grinned. 'Too right.' And then he said, 'All right, Mrs Boong, we'll each pay our own whack.'

He went out after tea and came back to her on the veranda half an hour later; he had found Ernie and arranged the boat, and he had bought a large basket of fruit to take with them. In the quick dusk and the darkness they sat together for some hours, talking of everything but Willstown. She learned a lot about his early life on the various stations, and about his relations in and around Cloncurry, about his war service, and about Midhurst. 'It's got a bonza rainfall, Midhurst has,' he said. 'We got thirty-four inches in the last wet; down at Alice it's a good year if you get ten inches. I've been asking Mrs Spears if we couldn't build a couple of dams at the head of the creeks to hold back some of the water—one across the head of Kangaroo Creek and one on the Dry Gum.'

'Did she agree?'

'She'll pay for them,' he said. 'Trouble is, of course, to get the labour. You can't get chaps to come and work in the outback. It's a fair cow.'

'Why is that?' she asked. She had a very good idea, herself, but she wanted to hear his views.

'I don't know,' he said. 'They all want to go and work in the towns.'

She did not pursue the subject; there was time enough for that. They talked of pleasant, unimportant things; she found that he was very anxious to get back to Midhurst to see his horses and his dogs. 'I got a bitch called Lily,' he said. 'Her mother was a blue cattle dog and she got mated by a dingo, so Lily's half a dingo. She's a bonza dog. Well, I mated her with another blue cattle dog before I come away and she'll have had the litter now, so they'll be quarter dingo. A cross between dingo and cattle dog makes a grand dog, but you've got to get the dingo strain weak or they aren't reliable. I had a quarter dingo dog before the war at Wollara, and he was grand.'

He told her that he had about sixty saddle and pack horses on the station, but they did not seem to be as close to his heart as his dogs. 'A dog comes into the homestead and sits around with you in the evenings,' he said, and she could picture the long, lonely nights that were his normal life. 'You couldn't get along in the outback without dogs.'

At ten o'clock they went to bed, prepared for an early start in the morning. They stood together in the darkness by the entrance to her room for a moment. 'Have I changed much, Joe?' she asked.

He grinned. 'I wouldn't have known you again.'

'I didn't think you would. Six years is a long time.'

'You haven't changed at all, really,' he said. 'You're the same person underneath.'

'I think I am,' she said slowly. 'After the war I felt like an old woman, Joe. After Kuantan, I didn't think I'd ever enjoy anything again.' She smiled. 'Like a weekend at Green Island.'

'There's nothing to do there, you know,' he said. 'You bathe and go out in a glass-bottomed boat to see the coral and the fishes.'

'I know. It's going to be such fun.'

They left next morning in Ernie's fishing boat, a motor launch with a canopy. For two hours they chugged out over a smooth sea, trolling a line behind and catching two large, brilliantly coloured horse-mackerel. Green Island appeared after an hour as the tops of coconut palms visible above the horizon; as they drew near the little circular island appeared, fringed round completely with a white coral beach. There was a long landing-stage built out over the shallow water of the reef; they landed and walked down this together, pausing to look at the scarlet and blue fishes playing round the coral heads below.

There were no other visitors staying on the island and they got two of the little bedroom huts in among the trees; these huts had open sides to let the breeze blow through, with an occasional curtain for privacy. They bathed at once and met upon the beach; Jean had a new white two-piece costume and was flattered at the reception that it got. 'It's pretty as a picture,' he said. 'Oh my word.'

She laughed. 'There's not enough of it to fill a picture frame, Joe.'

'Too right,' he said. 'But there aren't any wowsers here.'

'I'll have to look out I don't get burnt,' she said. 'I bet I'm the whitest woman that ever bathed here.'

'You are in parts,' he observed. He stood looking at her, reluctant to take his eyes off her beauty. 'You've been out in the sun up top, though.'

Her shoulders and her arms were tanned; there was a hard line above her breasts, brown above and white below. 'That's where I was wearing a sarong in Malaya,' she said. 'While they were building the well. In the village we used to wear the sarong up high, under the arms. It's beautifully cool like that, and yet it protects most of you from sunburn. And it's reasonably decent, too.'

'Have you got it here?' he asked.

She nodded. 'I'm going to put it on presently.'

As they turned to go into the water she saw his back for the first time, lined and puckered and distorted with enormous scars. Deep pity for him welled up in her at the sight; this man had been hurt enough for her already. She must not hurt him any more. He glanced back at her and said, 'We'd better not go in more than about knee-deep. There's plenty of sharks round here.' And then he looked at her more closely and said, 'What's the matter?'

She laughed quickly. 'It's the sun,' she said. 'It's making my eyes water. I ought to have brought my dark glasses.'

'I'll go and get them. Where are they?'

'I don't want them, really.' She threw herself forward in a shallow dive over the sand in about two feet of water and rolled over on her back, flirting the water from her face. 'It's marvellous,' she said. He flung himself forward, wallowed for a little, and sat beside her on the coral sand in the warm sea. 'Tell me, Joe,' she said. 'Do sharks really come in close like this?'

'They'll take you in water that's only waist-deep,' he said. 'Oh my word, they will. I don't know if there are any here just now. Trouble is, you never can tell. Didn't you have sharks in Malaya?'

'I think there were,' she said. 'The villagers never went out more than about knee-deep, so we didn't. There were crocodiles in the river, too.' She laughed. 'Taking it all in all, there's nothing to beat a good swimming-pool in a hot country.'

They rolled over in the blue, translucent water; the sun came shimmering through the ripples and made silvery lights upon the coral sand around them. 'I've never bathed in a swimming-pool,' he said. 'They make them with a shallow end, do they? Where you can sit, like this?'

'Of course. They have a shallow and a deep end, with diving-boards at the deep end. Don't they have swimming-pools here, in Australia?'

'Oh my word. They have them down in places like Sydney and Melbourne. I've heard of station owners having them upon their land, too. But places like Cairns and Townsville and Mackay, they're on the sea, so they don't need a pool.'

'Mrs Maclean's got a pool at Alice Springs,' she said.

'I know. They only made it a year or two ago. I've never seen it.'

She rolled over on her back, and watched a seagull soaring in the thermals from the island. 'You could have a pool at Willstown,' she said. 'You've got all the water in the world, from the bore, running to waste right in the middle of the town. You could make a lovely swimming-pool right opposite the hotel.'

'That water isn't running to waste,' he observed. 'Oh my word. The cattle drink that, in the dry.'

'It wouldn't hurt the cattle if we borrowed it first and used it for a swimming-pool,' she said. 'It'ld taste all the sweeter.'

'Might taste sweeter if you swam in it,' he concurred. 'I don't know about me.'

He would not let her stay in the water more than a quarter of an hour. 'You'll burn,' he said. 'Midday, like this, you can burn just as easy in the sea as on the land. You want to be careful, with a skin as white as yours.' They went up from the beach into the shade of the trees and sat smoking for a time; then they went back to their huts to put on a little more covering for lunch. Australian hotels, she had discovered, are very particular about dress at mealtimes; in Cairns even on the hottest day of summer a man without a jacket and tie would not be served in the dining-room, nor would a woman in slacks.

Harman had arranged a light lunch for her, cold meat and fruit; she was touched by the care that he was taking to make her weekend a success. While struggling to eat a mango decently she asked, 'Joe, why don't places like

Willstown have more fresh fruit? Won't it grow?'

'Mangoes grow all right,' he said. 'We've got three or four mango trees at Midhurst. Aren't there any in the town? I'd have thought there must be.'

'I don't believe there are. I never saw any fruit in the hotel, or anywhere on sale.'

'Oh well, maybe you wouldn't. People don't seem to bother much about it. Some places have every shade tree a mango tree. Cooktown, in the early summer you drive over them, all along the road.'

'Don't the people like fresh fruit and vegetables? I mean, they get all sorts of skin diseases through not having them.'

'It's too hot for the old folks to work in gardens, like in other places,' he said. 'There aren't enough people in the country to grow things like that. We can't even get men to work as ringers on the stations—we have to use two-thirds boongs as stockmen, or more. There just aren't enough people. They won't come to the outback.'

She said thoughtfully, 'There were plenty of fresh vegetables at Alice Springs.'

'Ah, yes,' he replied. 'Alice is different. Alice is a bonza little town.'

They slept on their beds in the heat of the day after lunch and bathed again before tea; in the cool of the evening they went out to the end of the jetty and fished. They caught some sand snappers and three or four brilliant red and blue fish which were poisonous to eat and had to be handled with a glove because they stung; then tiring of this rather unprofitable sport they rolled up their lines and sat and watched the sunset over the heights of the Atherton Tableland on the horizon. 'It's a funny thing,' Jean said. 'You go to a new country, and you expect everything to be different, and then you find there's such a lot that stays the same. That sunset looks just like it does in England, on a fine summer evening.'

'Do you see much that's like England here?' he asked.

She smiled. 'Not on Green Island, and not much in Willstown. But in Cairns—a lot. Vauxhall and Austin motor cars parked in the streets, and politicians telling people to buy British, and the North British Insurance Company, and Tattersalls, and bank clerks in the hotel listening to "Irma". Even the newsboys selling papers in the street—"Read all about it". Listening to them with your eyes shut, they sound just the same. They used to shout exactly like that when I lived in Ealing.'

'Ealing's the place near London where you lived when you were working, isn't it?'

'That's right. It's a part of London, really—a suburb.'

'Are you going to live there again when you go home?'

'I don't know,' she said slowly. 'I don't know what I'm going to do, Joe.'

In the evening light, sitting together on the jetty and watching the sunset over the calm water, she had expected him to follow up this opening, and she was disappointed that he did not do so. She had expected more than this of him, and that she didn't get it was beginning to distress her. She had expected to spend the whole weekend on the defensive, in repelling boarders, so to speak, but so far things had worked out very differently. Joe Harman's behaviour toward her had been above reproach; he had not tried to kiss her or even to make opportunities of touching her. But for the fact that he had been to England for no other purpose than to look for her, she might have thought he wasn't interested in her at all. By the end of the day she was becoming seriously worried about his restraint. She had caused him enough pain already.

It was no better when they went to bed. She would have liked to have been kissed, in the quiet darkness under the palm trees, but Joe didn't do it. They said goodnight in the most orderly way, not even shaking hands, and they retired to their own huts with perfect decorum. Jean lay awake for some time, restless and troubled. She had taken it for granted that they would arrive at some emotional conclusion at Green Island, but if things went on as they were going they would leave on Monday with nothing settled at all. If that happened, she would have to go down to Brisbane and go home; there would be no excuse for doing anything else. The thought was almost unbearable.

She knew that her English ways were strange to him; he could not know how very willing she was to adapt herself to his Queensland life. Perhaps, too, her money stood between them. She did not think that so sincere and genuine a man would have any scruples about marrying a girl with money, but it might well make him shy of her. She had a feeling that there was a difference between herself, a strange, wealthy, English girl, and an Australian girl from Cairns. If Joe Harman had been so much interested in a girl from Cairns, Jean thought, she would have been in bed with him by then; whereas she herself had not even been kissed.

She lay awake for a long time.

Things were no better the next day. They bathed in the cool of the morning in that marvellous translucent sea; they walked out upon the reef at low tide to see the coloured coral; they paddled about in a glass-bottomed boat to see the coloured fishes, and a good six inches separated them all the time. By teatime they were finding that they had exhausted their light conversation; the restraint was heavy upon both of them, and there were long awkward pauses when neither of them seemed to know what to say.

In the evening light they decided to walk round the island on the beach. She left him at the door of her hut, and said, 'Give me a couple of minutes, Joe. I don't want to go around the beach in this frock.' She pulled one of the curtains for privacy; as she changed she thought that they had only one more day, and so much to settle that they had not started on. She would get nowhere without taking a bit of a risk, and it was worth it for Joe.

In the half light he turned as she came out of the hut, and he was back in the Malay scene of six years ago. She was wearing the same old faded cotton sarong or one very like it, held up in a roll under her arms; her brown shoulders and her brown arms were bare. She was barefooted, and her hair hung down in a long plait, tied at the end with a bit of string, as it had been in Malaya. She was no longer the strange English girl with money; she was Mrs Boong again, the Mrs Boong he had remembered all those years. She came to him rather shyly and put both hands on his shoulders, and said, 'Is this better, Joe?'

She could never remember very clearly what happened in the next five minutes. She was standing locked in his arms as he kissed her face and her neck and her shoulders hungrily while his hands fondled her body; in the tumult of feelings that swept over her she knew that this man wanted her as nobody had ever wanted her before. She stood unresisting in his arms; it never entered her head to struggle or to try to get away. But presently, when she had breath to speak, she said, 'Oh, Joe! They'll see us from the house!'

The next thing that she realized was that they were in her bedroom hut. She never knew how they got there, but thinking of it afterwards she came to the conclusion that he must have picked her up and carried her. And now a new confusion came to her. A sarong held up by a tight roll above the breasts will stay in place all day if given proper usage but it does not stand up very well to energetic man-handling; she could feel that it was getting loose and falling, and she had no other garment on at all.

Standing in his arms still unresisting, smothered by his kisses, she thought, this is It. And then she thought, It had to happen sometime, and I'm glad it's Joe. And then she thought, It's not his fault, I brought this on myself. And then she thought, I must sit down or something, or I'll be stark-naked, and at that she escaped backwards from his arms and sat down on the bed.

He followed her down, laughing, and her eyes laughed back at him as she tried to hold her sarong up with her hand to hide her bosom. Then she was in his arms again and he was hindering her. And then he said quite simply, 'Do you mind?'

She reached her right arm round his shoulders, and said quietly, 'Dear Joe. Not if you've got to. If you *can* wait till we're married, I'd much rather, but whatever you do now, I'll love you just the same.'

He looked down into her eyes. 'Say that again.'

She drew his head down to her and kissed him. 'Dear Joe. Of course I'm in love with you. What do you think I came to Australia for?'

'Will you marry me?'

'Of course I'll marry you.' She looked up at him with fondness and with laughter in her eyes. 'Anyone looking at us now would say we were married already.'

He grinned; he was holding her more gently now. 'I don't know what you must think of me.'

'Shall I tell you?' She took one of his wounded hands in hers and fondled the great scars. 'I think you're the man I want to marry and have children by.' It did not seem to matter now that the sarong had fallen to her waist. 'I'd rather wait a few months and get our lives arranged a little first, Joe. Marriage is a big thing, and there are things that ought to be done, first, before we marry. But if you say we can't wait, then I'll marry you tomorrow, or tonight.'

He drew her to him gently, and kissed her fingertips. 'I can wait. I've waited six years for this, and I can wait a bit longer.'

She said softly, 'Poor Joe. I'll try and make it easy, and not tantalize you. I oughtn't to have done this.' She freed herself from his arms and pulled up the sarong and rolled it round. 'Just get outside a minute, and I'll put on some more clothes.'

He said, 'You don't need to do that. I won't do anything, except kiss you now and then. Stay that way for tonight, as if it was Malaya.'

'Just for tonight,' she said. They went out presently and stood upon the beach in the bright moonlight, holding each other close. 'I never knew a man could be so happy,' he said once.

Half an hour later she said, 'Joe, we're both tired now, and it's time for bed. We've got an awful lot to talk about, but we'll talk better in the morning. There's just one thing I want to say tonight. If you ever feel you can't bear waiting any longer, you'll tell me, won't you? If you come to me like that, I promise we'll get married right away, or sooner than that.'

He said gently, 'I can wait a long time for you, after this.'

'Dear Joe. I won't keep you waiting any more than I can help.'

She was so tired that when she got into her hut she did not light the candle, but fell upon her bed and loosened her sarong, Malay fashion, and slept almost at once. She woke with the first light of dawn and lay reflecting upon what had happened, absurdly happy; at last, she felt things were going to go right, between them. She got up as the sun rose and peered cautiously over to Joe's hut and the restaurant building. There was no sign of any movement anywhere, so she put on her bathing dress and went down to the sea and had a bathe. Lying in the shallow water as the sun rose she discovered a number of bruises on her person, and reflected on the narrowness of her escape from a fate worse than death.

She went back very quietly to her hut and put on a frock. Then she went over to the restaurant. It stood open but there was nobody about; she put the kettle on the oil stove and made a pot of tea. Carrying a cup she went to Joe's hut and peered in cautiously.

He was lying on the bed asleep in a pair of shorts; she stood there for some minutes, watching him as he slept. The troubled lines had vanished from his face and he was sleeping easily and quietly, like a little boy; the scars upon his back stood out with an appalling and contrasting ferocity. She stood watching him for a time with fondness in her eyes, knowing that she would see him so most of the mornings of her life to come, and the thought pleased her.

She moved a little and put down the cup, and when she looked at him again he had opened his eyes, and he was looking at her. 'Morning, Joe,' she said, wondering if she ought to be running like a rabbit. 'I've made you a cup of tea.'

He leaned up on one arm. 'Tell me,' he said. 'Did what I think happened last night really happen?'

'I think so, Joe,' she said. 'I think it must have done. I've got bruises all over me.'

He stretched out one hand. 'Come here, and let me give you a kiss.'

She retreated. 'Not on your life. I'll give you a kiss when you've got up and had a bathe and got some clothes on.'

He laughed. 'Aren't you going to bathe?'

'I've bathed,' she said. 'I've been up and pottering about for an hour, while you've been sleeping. I'll come down and watch you.'

He asked, 'Did you sleep all right?'

She nodded. 'Like a log.'

'So did I.' They smiled with mutual understanding. 'Give me a minute, and I'll come down to the beach.'

She sat on the sand and chatted to him while he bathed. Then he came out and went to shave, and presently appeared in a clean shirt and a clean pair of khaki drill slacks, and she came into his arms and gave him his kiss. Then, as there was no sign yet of breakfast, they sat very close together on the beach in the cool morning breeze, talking and talking and talking. They had no difficulty in finding things to talk of now, and even their silences were intimate.

After breakfast, as they sat smoking cigarettes over a last cup of coffee, he said, 'I've been thinking. I'm going to give up Midhurst, soon as Mrs Spears can find another manager.' She listened in consternation; what was coming now? 'If we could get a grazing farm for fattening, in back of Adelaide, at Mallala or Hamley Bridge or Balaklava or some place like that, that's on the railway down from Alice Springs and not too far from the abattoir, that's what

I'd like to do. I think we might be able to find a place like that only about fifty miles from the city, so as we could get in any time.'

She sat in silence for a minute; this needed careful handling. 'Why do you want to do that, Joe? What's wrong with Midhurst?'

'It's too far from anywhere,' he said. 'All right for a single man, perhaps, but not for a married couple. Now Adelaide's a bonza city. I'm a Queenslander, but I like Adelaide better than Brisbane. I haven't seen Sydney or Melbourne, but Adelaide's a bonza city, oh my word. It's got streets and streets of shops, and trams, and cinemas, and dance halls, and it's a pretty place, too, with hills behind and vineyards growing grapes to make the wine. We could have a bonza time if we got a farm near Adelaide.'

'But Joe,' she said, 'is that the sort of work you want to do? Just buying store cattle from the outback and fattening them? It sounds awfully dull to me. Are you fed up with the outback?'

He ground his cigarette out on the floor beneath his heel. 'There's places that suit single men and places that suit married people,' he said. 'You've got to make a change or two when you get married.'

They had the breakfast table between them, separating them much too far for their newfound intimacy; she could not deal with so serious a matter as this without touching him. 'Let's go outside,' she said. So they went out and found a patch of sandy grass at the head of the beach in the shade, and sat down there together. 'I don't think that's right, Joe,' she said slowly. 'I don't think you ought to leave the outback just because we're getting married.'

He smiled at her. 'The Gulf country's no place for a woman,' he said. 'Not unless she's been brought up and raised in the outback, and sometimes not then. I've seen some married people out from England try it, and I've never known it work. The life's too different, too hard.'

She said slowly, 'I know it's very different, and very hard. I've lived in Willstown for three weeks, Joe, and so I know a bit about it.' She took his hand and fondled the great scars between her own two hands. 'I know what you're afraid of. You're afraid that a girl straight out from England, a girl like me, will be unhappy in the outback, Joe. You're afraid that I'll get restless and start making excuses to go and stay in the city, for the dentist, or for shopping, and things like that. You're afraid that if we start at Midhurst you'll be trying me too hard, and that our marriage will go wrong.'

She raised her eyes and looked at him. 'That's what you're afraid of, isn't it, Joe?'

He met her eyes. 'Too right,' he said. 'A man hasn't got a right to try and make an English girl live in a crook place like Willstown.'

She smiled. 'It isn't only English girls, Joe. Australian girls, girls born in Willstown, they run a thousand miles to get away from it.'

He grinned. 'That's right. If they can't stand it, how could you?'

'I don't know that I could,' she said thoughtfully. One had to be honest. 'Are all the towns in the Gulf country the same?'

He nodded. 'Normanton's a bit bigger; it's got three pubs instead of one, and it's got a church.'

There was a long silence. 'I'm afraid of things, too,' she said at last.

He took her hand; he could not bear that she should be afraid of anything in the new life before them. She had been brave enough last night. 'What's that?' he asked gently.

She said, 'I'm afraid of changing your job.' She paused. 'I can't believe that that would ever work out properly, that a man should change his work because his wife couldn't stand conditions that he could. You've been used to a property about two thousand square miles big, Joe, going off for three weeks at a time with packhorses and never going off your own land. What would a man like you do on a thousand acres?'

He grinned weakly; she had put her finger on the spot. 'Get accustomed to it pretty soon, I should think.'

'I know you'd do it,' she said quietly. 'You might even learn to do it reasonably well. But it could never satisfy you after the Gulf country, and cinemas won't fill the gap, or streets of shops, or dance halls. And sometimes when we squabble—we shall squabble, Joe—you'll think about your old life in the Gulf country, and how you had to give it up, because of me. And I shall know you're thinking that and blaming it on me, and that will be between us all the time. That's what I'm afraid of, Joe. I think we ought to stay up in the Gulf country, where your work is.'

'You just said you couldn't stand Willstown,' he objected. 'Burketown and Croydon—well, they're just the same.'

'I know,' she said thoughtfully. 'I'm not being very reasonable, am I? First I say I couldn't stand living in a place like that, and then I say that you oughtn't to think of living anywhere else.'

'That's right.' He was puzzled and distressed. 'We've got to try and work it out some way to find what suits us both.'

'There's only one way to do that, Joe.'

'What's that?'

She smiled at him. 'We'll have to do something about Willstown.'

8

They spent that day in a curious mixture of love-making and economic discussion. 'You can't tell me that a country with three times the rainfall of the Territory can't support a town as good as Alice,' she said once. 'I know Alice has a railway. Willstown's got rain, and I know which I'd rather have for raising cattle. If you go on doing that, Joe, I'll go off and sit by myself. We aren't married yet.' She removed his hand and kissed it.

'Rain's not the only thing you want for raising cattle,' he said. 'The better the feed, of course, the more calves live through the dry and the more you've got to sell. But there's a lot more to it than that, oh my word.'

'Tell me, Joe.' She had his hand in a firm grip.

'One thing,' he said, 'you've got to keep that water when you've got it. It's true that Midhurst gets a lot of rainfall, but it's all gone in a flash. We get rain from the middle of December till the end of February, and you'll see the creeks all running full in flood. But three weeks later, by the end of March, they'll be all dry again, and the country as dry as ever.'

'Is that what you want to build the dams for, at Kangaroo Creek and Dry Gum Creek?'

'That's right,' he said. 'I want to make a start with building little kind of barrages to hold back the water. Do a bit each year, starting at the head of each creek and working down. Get a little pool held back every two or three miles all down the creeks till they run out into the Gilbert. They wouldn't hold the water right through the dry, of course; the sun's too strong. But you could add a lot of feed to Midhurst if you had a lot of little dams like that. Oh my word, you could.'

She released his hand. 'How big is Midhurst, Joe?'

'Eleven hundred square miles.'

'How many cattle does it carry?'

'About nine thousand. Ought to carry more than that, but it's dry up at the top end. Very dry.'

'Suppose you could get all the little dams that you're imagining. How many would it carry then?'

He thought for a minute. 'I don't see why it shouldn't carry double what's on it now. That'ld be about sixteen to the mile. With a rainfall like we've got you should be able to do that.'

'You sold fourteen hundred head this year, didn't you?'

'That's right.'

'How much a head?'

'Four pound sixteen.'

She grabbed his hand again, and held it imprisoned. 'I'm trying to think, Joe. If you doubled the stock on the station you'd have another fourteen hundred to sell each year. That's—that's between six and seven thousand pounds a year more to sell. You'd be selling twelve or thirteen thousand pounds worth every year then, Joe. It'ld be worth spending a bit of capital on dams to get that rise in turnover, wouldn't it?'

He looked at her with a new respect. 'Well, that's the way I worked it out. I told Mrs Spears, I said, I want to keep a permanent gang of three men and a few Abos on this. Do a bit each year, working down from the top. Spend about fifteen hundred a year, you might say. There'd be less profit the first year, but after that it should rise steadily to nearly double. That's what I told her.'

'She agreed, did she?'

'She's agreed to spend the money. But that's only the start of it, the easy part. It may be years before I get the men.'

She looked at him incredulously. 'Years?'

'Too right,' he said heavily. 'It's all very well to think of things like that, but it's another thing to do them. Might be five years before I get the work in hand. You see, there's only three of us on Midhurst—whites, that is—me and Jim Lennon, and Dave Hope. We've got to find three more who'll work out all the week up-country, forty miles from the homestead, working with a pick and shovel mostly, and responsible enough to get on by themselves with only just a visit once a week or once a fortnight. Well, you can't get men like that. There are fewer people in the Gulf country every year. If it wasn't for the Abo stockmen, the boongs, I don't know what we'd do.'

'Are there really only three of you—whites—running Midhurst?'

He put his arm around her shoulders. 'When you come it'll be four.'

She thought it would be five or six soon after that, but she refrained from saying so. 'How many would you like to have?'

'You mean with eighteen thousand head of cattle, some time in the future?'

She nodded. 'I could use twenty on a station like that,' he said. 'That wouldn't be too many, not if you were running tame bulls in a paddock, to improve the stock. There'd be fences and stockyards and all sorts of things to make. I could use twenty white ringers, and some other hands besides.'

She said slowly, 'Pete Fletcher said that there were fifty ringers coming into Willstown, using it as their town.'

'That's about right,' he said.

'If all the stations developed like you say,' she observed, 'that means seven times as many ringers, because there are only three of you now. Three or four hundred ringers in the district, all with wives and families, and shops for them, and pubs, and garages, and radio, and cinemas. There's room here for a town of two or three thousand people, Joe.'

He smiled. 'You'll be making it as big as Brisbane next.'

She said severely, 'Joe. There was an old girl in our party in Malaya called Mrs Frith. She thought you must be Jesus Christ, because you'd been crucified. I tried to tell her that you weren't. If she saw what you're doing now she'd probably believe me.'

They talked about Mrs Frith for a time, and then reverted to more mundane matters. 'Joe,' she said, 'listen to me. Would you think it very stupid if I said I wanted to start a business in Willstown?'

He stared at her. 'A business? What sort of business could you do in Willstown?'

'Do you know what I was doing in England?' she inquired.

'Shorthand typing, wasn't it?' he asked.

She took his hand and smoothed it between her own. 'There's such a lot that you don't know about me,' she said. 'So much to tell you.' She started in to tell him about Pack and Levy, and Mr Pack, and about alligator-skin shoes, and Aggie Topp. Half an hour later she said, 'That's what I want to do, Joe. Do you think it's crazy?'

'I don't know.' And then, quite unexpectedly, he said, 'I took a walk down Bond Street, looking in the shops.'

She turned to him, surprised. 'Did you, Joe?'

He nodded. 'I asked Mr Strachan what I ought to see in London and he asked me how much history I knew and I told him that I never got much schooling. So then he said to go and see St Paul's and Westminster Abbey, and then he said to take the bus to Piccadilly Circus and walk up Regent Street and along Oxford Street and down Bond Street and back along Piccadilly; he said I'd see all the best shops that way.'

She nodded. It seemed very far away from Green Island, and the whisper of the coconut palms overhead in the sea breeze.

'I saw a lot of alligator-skin shoes,' he said. 'Sort of dressing-cases, too.' He turned to her. 'It was interesting seeing those, and wondering if they were skins that old Jeff Pocock trapped. Made me feel quite at home. Beautifully done up, they were. But the prices—oh my word. Most of them hadn't got no labels, but there was one, just a little alligator-skin case with silvery things in it, for a lady. A hundred guineas, that one was.'

She was excited. 'Joe, I bet that was made by Pack and Levy. We did all that sort of work.'

'You weren't thinking you could make that sort of stuff in Willstown?'

'Not cases, Joe. Just shoes—shoes to start with, anyway. A little workshop with six or seven girls making alligator-skin shoes. It won't cost very much, Joe–not more than I can afford to lose if it goes wrong. But I don't know–perhaps it won't go wrong. If it worked out all right, and if it paid, it'ld be a good thing for the town.'

'Six or seven girls all earning money at a job in Willstown?' he said thoughtfully. 'You wouldn't keep them six weeks. They'd all be married–oh my word, they would.'

She laughed. 'Then I'd have to find six or seven more.' She got up. 'Let's go and bathe. It'll be too hot if we don't bathe soon.'

They went and changed and lay in the clean, silvery water on the coral sand. 'Look at those bruises,' she said. 'You great bully. Hit somebody your own size.' And presently she said, 'I've got another shock for you. You won't drown if I tell you now? I want to start an ice-cream parlour.'

'Oh my word.'

'I'm going to pay these girls a lot of money, Joe,' she said seriously. 'I've got to get some of it back.'

He looked at her, uncertain if she were laughing or not. 'An ice-cream parlour in Willstown?' he said. 'It'll never pay.'

'You wait till you see what I charge for an ice-cream,' she said. 'Not only ice-cream, Joe–fruit and vegetables, quick frozen stuff, and women's magazines, and cosmetics, and all the little bits of things that women want. I've got a very pretty girl who wants to come and run it for me, a girl called Rose Sawyer who lives in Alice Springs.'

He said slowly, 'If you've got a girl like that to run it, the women won't be able to get in the shop. It'll be full of ringers.'

'That's all right,' she said, 'so long as they buy ice-cream.' She turned to him. 'Joe, did you ever spend a Sunday in Alice Springs?'

He shook his head. 'I don't think I ever did. Not since before the war, anyway.'

'I know why that is, too,' she said. 'The pubs are shut.'

He grinned. 'Too right.'

'The pub's shut in Willstown, too, on Sundays.'

'The bar's shut,' he said. 'You can usually get it out of Ma Connor, round the back.'

She rolled over in the water. 'I'll have to tip off Sergeant Haines, Joe. Sunday's the best day of all for the ice-cream parlour at Alice. All the men who are in the bar all the week come along with their wives and kids on Sunday to the ice-cream parlour and put down ice-cream sodas and Coca-Cola. That place does a roaring trade on Sundays.'

'It would,' he said thoughtfully. 'There'd be nothing else to do.'

They got out of the sea presently and went and sat in the shade; he would not let her stay in long for fear of sunburn. When they were smoking together under the trees, he said, 'It's going to cost a hell of a lot of money, all this you want to do. Three or four thousand pounds, I'd say, or more than that.'

'I've got enough,' she said.

He turned to her. 'Mr Strachan told me you were a wealthy woman,' he said quietly. 'It worried me, that did, till I got used to the idea. How much have you got? Don't tell me if you'd rather not say, but if I knew about how much I'd be able to help you more.'

'Of course,' she said. Nothing would come between them now, after last night. 'Mr Strachan says I've got about fifty-three thousand pounds. It's all in trust for me until I'm thirty-five, though. If I want to spend capital before then, I've got to ask him.'

'Oh my word.'

'It is a lot of money, isn't it?' she said. 'I'm glad that it's in trust for me in a way, because I wouldn't in the least know what to do with it. And Noel has been such a dear.' She paused. 'I want to do something useful with it,' she said. 'I don't know anything about real business. The only thing I know about at all is what Pack and Levy made. I thought if we could start a little workshop of that sort, and a shop where women could get things they like–well, even if it didn't pay very well, it'll be using money the way money ought to be used, in places like Willstown.'

He bent and kissed her. 'There's another thing, Joe,' she said. 'I don't know, but I've got a sort of feeling that there's more to it than just employing a few girls. You say the ringers are all leaving the Gulf country, and men won't come to the outback. Well, of course they won't if they can't get a girl. And all the girls go because they can't get a job. For every girl I make a job for, I believe you'll get a man to work at Midhurst. Don't you think that's true?'

'I don't know.' He stared out over the sea to the dim blue line of the Tableland. 'It'ld certainly help to have a flock of girls around. It can be lonely in the outback, oh my word.'

A poignant realization of the solitude struck her. The long nights alone in the homestead, when 'you couldn't get along in the outback without dogs'. The sensitive, intelligent face of the manager of Carlisle, Eddie Page, who had married his illiterate, inarticulate lubra. She turned to him with quick understanding and sympathy. 'I feel an awful pig asking you to wait,' she said. He took her hand and squeezed it. 'I do want to try and start this business before we get married, Joe,' she said. She smiled at him. 'You know, you're a pretty energetic lover. I don't believe you'll waste much time starting a family.'

He grinned, 'I won't go quicker than you want to.'

'I want to have them, too.' She pulled his head down to her and kissed him. 'But that means I'll only have six months for business after we get married, and then I'll have to begin thinking of other things. Joe, when do you start mustering?'

'After the wet,' he said. 'It was March this year because of the late season, but normally we'd start mustering about the middle of February.'

'How long does the muster go on for?'

'About three weeks or a month. After that there's the branding of the calves, and driving the stock down to Julia Creek.'

'Could we get married after the mustering, Joe? Say early in April?'

'Of course.'

She said thoughtfully, 'That would mean that I'd have nearly a year from now, to get it to the stage when I could leave the business for a month or two while we start your family. I think that's fair enough. If it couldn't run without me for a month by then the whole thing wouldn't be much good, and we'd better pack it up.'

He said, 'I'll be around, of course.'

She laughed. 'Handing out ice-creams and selling lipsticks to young girls. I won't ask you to do that, Joe.'

He thought about this programme. 'Jim could drive the stores alone down to

Julia Creek,' he said, 'while we're getting married. I'd send Bourneville and some of the other boongs with him. Then we could drive down in the utility and catch him up about the time he got there, and put them on the train. Have it as a kind of honeymoon.'

She smiled. 'I like your idea of a honeymoon.' He grinned. 'Is there anything to do in Julia Creek, Joe, except drink beer?'

'Oh my word,' he said. 'There's plenty to do in Julia Creek.'

'What is there to do there?'

'Put fifteen hundred cattle into railway trucks.' He grinned at her. 'There's not many English girls get a chance of a honeymoon like that,' he said.

They went and changed for lunch, and over lunch he said, 'About this tanning and dressing the alligator skins. I'd give that away.' He was very much against attempting to do that in Willstown; it was messy work, unsuitable for girls, and no men were available to do it. He told her that there was a tannery in Cairns who could dress any skins she sent them. 'A joker called Gordon runs it,' he said. 'He was over in the Gulf country last year. We could go and see him tomorrow afternoon if you like.'

'Would he have any white kid basils, do you think?'

'Might do. If not he'll probably get them.'

With his knowledge of station management he was a great help to her with suggestions for the workshop. 'I'd make it good and big, while you're at it,' he said. 'It's the transport of the wood to Willstown that's going to cost the money.' He thought for a minute. 'There's three of you new girls coming in to live in Willstown, if all goes right,' he said. 'You and this Rose Sawyer and this Aggie Topp. Why don't you make your workshop building a bit bigger and have three bed-sitting-rooms at the end, walled off from the rest of it and with a separate entrance? Then you wouldn't have to live in the hotel and you'd be all comfortable by yourselves. Then if the business grows up you can pull down the wall and throw it all into one.' This seemed to her to be a very good idea indeed.

They got a paper and pencil after lunch and jotted down a few essential things to do in Cairns when they got back there, and orders to be placed. Then they retired to their own huts and slept in the heat of the day. She was roused by Joe calling her outside her hut. 'Come on and bathe,' he was saying. 'It's nearly five o'clock.'

She pulled the sheet over quickly. 'I won't be a minute. Have you been looking in?'

'I wouldn't do a thing like that.'

'I wish I could believe you.' She pulled the curtain across and put on her bathing dress, and joined him on the beach. And lying with him in the warm blue and silvery water on the sand, she said, 'Joe, do you want us to be engaged, with a ring and everything?'

'You'd like that, wouldn't you?'

She shook her head. 'Not unless it would prevent you worrying. I'll marry you early in April, Joe—that's dinkum.' He smiled. 'But for the present, I believe we'd get on better if we weren't officially engaged.' She turned to him. 'You see, when we get back to Willstown I'll be doing some pretty odd things, things that Willstown people will think crazy. Some of them may be, because there'll probably be some mistakes. I don't want you to have to be mixed up in it, just because we're engaged. You've got a position to keep up.'

'Wouldn't it help if people thought I was with you in whatever you're doing?'

She smiled, and rolled over and kissed him. 'You're all salt. It wouldn't help if you get in a fight every Saturday night in the bar because somebody says something rude about your fiancée.' He grinned. 'They will, you know. They're bound to think I'm crackers.'

They got out of the water presently and sat in the shade of the trees, talking and talking about the future. 'Joe,' she said once, 'what do I do if a boong comes into the ice-cream parlour and wants a soda? A boong stockrider? Do I serve him in the same place, or has he got to have a different shop?'

He scratched his head. 'I dunno that it's ever happened in Willstown. They go into Bill Duncan's store. I don't think you could serve them in an ice-cream parlour, with a white girl behind the counter.'

She said firmly, 'Then I'll have to have another parlour for them with a black girl in it. There's such a lot of them, Joe—we can't cut them out. We'll have two parlours, with the freezes and the kitchen between.' She drew a little diagram on the white sand with her forefinger. 'Like this.'

'Oh my word,' he said. 'You're going to start some talk in Willstown.'

She nodded. 'I know. That's why I don't want us to be engaged till just before we're married.'

In the evening as they kissed goodnight between their bedroom huts, she said, 'We won't be able to do this in Willstown. I'll remember this Green Island all my life, Joe.'

He grinned. 'Come back here in April, if you like. Before Julia Creek.'

They left next morning, when Eddie came for them with his motorboat, and landed at Cairns early in the afternoon. They took their bags to the hotel, and then went straight to see Mr Gordon at the tannery, and spent an hour with him discussing alligator skins and other shoe materials. He advised them to dismiss the idea of kid for linings. 'Anything that can be done with kid we'll do for you with wallaby,' he said. 'You've got any amount of wallaby out there, and it's as good as kid–texture, appearance, bleaching, glazing–anything you like.' Harman arranged to send him half a dozen skins for sample treatment by the next lorry. 'Be a good thing to keep down some of these wallabies,' he said. 'They eat an awful lot of feed out on the station. Too many of them altogether.'

They spent the rest of the afternoon shopping and ordering, and got back to the hotel at dusk, tired out, having booked their passages to Willstown upon the morning plane. Jean said, 'There's one thing I must do tonight, Joe, before leaving Cairns. I must write to Noel Strachan and tell him what's happened.'

In the warm scented night of early summer by the Queensland sea, she sat down on the veranda after tea and wrote me a long letter. Joe Harman sat beside her as she wrote, smoking quietly, at peace.

She was very good about writing, and she still is; she still writes every week. I got that letter early in November; I remember it so well. It was a foggy, dark morning with a light rain or drizzle falling. I had to have the electric light on for breakfast, and the Palace stables on the other side of the road were hardly visible. In the street below the taxis went past with a wet swish of mud and water on the wet wood blocks.

It was a long letter from a very happy girl, telling me about her love. I was delighted at the news, of course. I sat reading it with my breakfast before me, and then I read it through again, and then I read it a third time. When I woke up to realities my coffee was cold and the fried egg had frozen to the dish in front of me in cold, congealed fat, but I was too absorbed in her news to want it. I went into my bedroom to put my shoes and coat on for the office, and as I opened the wardrobe to get my coat I saw her boots and skates, that I had been keeping for her till she came back for them. Old men get rather silly, sometimes, and I must say that that rather dashed me for a moment, because she wouldn't be coming back for them. She wouldn't be coming back to England ever again.

I went to the front door, and my charwoman was in the flat, just coming out of the dining-room. 'Such good news, Mrs Chambers,' I said. 'Do you remember Miss Paget, who used to come here sometimes? She's got engaged to be married, to an Australian, out in Queensland.'

'Oh, I am glad,' she said. 'Such a nice lady, she was.'

'Yes, wasn't she?' I repeated. 'Such a nice lady.'

She said, 'You didn't eat your breakfast, sir. Was everything all right?'

'Yes, quite all right, thanks, Mrs Chambers,' I said. 'I didn't want anything this morning.'

It was cold and raw out in the street, one of those yellow foggy mornings with a reeking chill that makes you cough. I walked on towards the office in a dream, thinking about wallabies and laughing black stockmen, about blue water running over the white coral sands, about Jean Paget and the trouble she had had with her sarong in that hot country where all clothes are a burden. Then there was a fierce, rending squeal right on top of me, and a heavy blow on my right arm so that I staggered and nearly fell, and I was in the middle of Pall Mall with a taxi broadside on across the road beside me. I didn't know where I was for a moment, and then I heard the white-faced driver saying, 'For Christ's sake. You can think yourself bloody lucky that you're still alive.'

'I'm sorry,' I said. 'I wasn't looking where I was going.'

'Stepping out into the road like that,' he said angrily. 'Ought to have more sense, at your age. Did I hit you?'

A little crowd was starting to collect. 'Only my arm,' I said. I moved it, and it worked all right. 'It's nothing.'

'Well, that's a bloody miracle,' he said. 'Look out where you're going to next time.' He put his gear in, straightened up his taxi, and drove on; I walked on to the office.

The girl brought in the letters for me to go through, as usual, but I put them on one side in favour of another letter that I had in my breast pocket. I had a client or two that morning, I suppose; I usually have, and I suppose I gave them some advice, but my mind was twelve thousand miles away. Lester Robinson came in once with some business or other and I said to him, 'You remember my Paget girl – the heir to that Macfadden estate? She's got herself engaged to be married to an Australian. He seems to be a very good chap.'

He grunted. 'I forget. Does that terminate our trust?'

'No,' I said. 'That goes on for some time to come. Till she's thirty-five.'

'Pity,' he said. 'It's made a lot of work for you, that trust has. It'll be a good thing when it's all wound up.'

'It's been no trouble, really,' I said. By the end of the day I think I knew her letter by heart although it was eight quarto pages long, but I took it with me to the club. I had a glass of sherry in the bar and told Moore about her engagement because he knew something about her story, and after dinner we sat down to a couple of rubbers of bridge, Dennison and Strickland and Callaghan, the four of us who play together every evening, and I told them about her.

I got up from the table at about eleven o'clock, and went into the library for a final cigarette before going back across the park to my flat. The big room was empty but for Wright, who had been in the Malay Police and knew her story. I dropped down into a chair beside him, and remarked, 'You know that girl, Jean Paget! I think I've spoken to you about her once or twice before.'

He smiled. 'You have.'

'She's got herself engaged to be married,' I told him. 'To the manager of a cattle station, in Northern Queensland.'

'Indeed?' he said. 'What's he like?'

'I've met him,' I replied. 'He's a very good chap. She's very much in love with him. I think they're going to be very happy.'

'Is she coming back to England before getting married?' he asked.

I sat staring at the rows of books upon the wall, the gold embossed carving at the corner of the ceiling. 'No,' I said. 'I don't think she's ever coming back to England, ever again.'

He was silent.

'It's too far,' I said. 'I think she'll make her life in Queensland now.'

There was a long pause. 'After all, there's no reason why she should come back to England,' I said at last. 'There's nothing for her to come back for. She's got no ties in this country.'

And then he said a very foolish thing. He meant it well enough, but it was a stupid thing to say. I got up and left him and went home to my dark, empty flat, and I avoided meeting him for some time after that. I was seventy-three years old that autumn, old enough to be her grandfather. I couldn't possibly have been in love with her myself.

9

In the months of November and December that year Jean Paget worked harder than she had ever worked before.

Rose Sawyer joined her in Willstown within a fortnight, and Aggie Topp sailed early in November. I got Mr Pack to send Aggie to see me before she left. She was a gaunt, rather prim woman, but I could see at once that Pack had been quite right; if anyone could make girls work this woman could. I gave her her ticket and a typed sheet of instructions telling her how she would get by air from Sydney to Willstown, and then I talked to her about the job. 'You know, it's very, very rough,' I said. 'It's rough, and it's hot, and Miss Paget is having to start absolutely from nothing. She's got plenty of money, but it's going to be hard, all the time. You understand that, Mrs Topp?'

She said, 'I've had two letters from Miss Paget, and she sent a photograph of the place, the main street. It don't look up to much, I must say.'

'You're quite happy to go out there, are you?'

She said, 'Oh well, I've been in rough places before. It's only for a year to start with, anyway.' And then she said, 'I always liked Miss Paget.'

I had another matter to fix up with Aggie Topp. Jean was very anxious to get hold of an air-conditioning unit, a thing about the size of a small refrigerator which stood in the room and took hot air into itself and pumped it out cold into the room; it seemed to her important to have this to prevent the girls' hands from sweating as they worked and marking the delicate leathers of the shoes. She had not been able to get hold of one in Australia and had cabled me, and I had found a firm that made them and got hold of one with a good deal of difficulty and some small payments on the side. Derek Harris is rather good at that sort of negotiation. I had it in our office standing at the foot of the stairs and I showed it to Mrs Topp, and arranged for her to take it out with her to Sydney. From Sydney it would have to be flown up with her to Cairns and Willstown at some considerable expense, but it seemed to me to be worth it since it was then the hottest time of the year.

This was the biggest commission that I got from Jean and was my own main contribution to the venture; the remainder of her cables were concerned with little bits of things that were no trouble. Aggie Topp took out with her a good deal of stuff from Pack and Levy, too; three cases full of tools and lasts and formers and all sorts of things, the bill for which came to about a hundred and forty-six pounds, which I paid for Jean in England.

Joe Harman helped her to get the buildings started on the day that they arrived in Willstown. They had a meeting with Tim Whelan and his two sons, in the carpenter's shop amongst the coffins. They had already placed orders for two lorry loads of lumber in Cairns. The men stood or sat squatting, ringer fashion, on the floor with papers on the floor before them, planning the layout of the buildings; the workshop with its three-bedroom annexe was to be built first, and after that the ice-cream parlour next to it, leaving room for the expansion of the workshop one way and of the ice-cream parlour the other way. There were no great difficulties of expansion in the built-up area of Willstown.

They sent Tim Whelan presently to find Mr Carter, the Shire Clerk, to pass the plans of the new buildings and to grant a lease of the site in the main street. 'It'll be all right there,' he said thoughtfully. 'There was a whole row of houses there in 1905 – I've got a photograph. But nobody ever paid rent for that land in my time.' Jean asked what rent would be required for the area she wanted, a difficult matter to decide in view of the fact that no plans existed and the area that she wanted was quite uncertain. 'This is a town borough,' Mr Carter said. 'You don't lease land upon an acreage basis in a town borough. If you're going to develop the land by building, then I'd say about a shilling a year for each hundred foot of frontage. It's in the main street, you see. If you wanted it for chickens or anything like that I'd have to charge five shillings.'

They adjourned to the bar of the hotel to seal the contracts; Jean sat on the steps outside with a lemonade, as was fitting for a lady with a reputation to preserve in Willstown.

She went to Brisbane a week later, flying to Cairns and flying on the same day down to Brisbane. She stayed there for three days and came back having ordered an electric generating set, a very large refrigerator, two deep freezes, a stainless steel counter, eight glass-topped tables, thirty-two chairs, two sink units, and a mass of minor shop fittings, glasses, plates, cutlery, and furnishings as well as a good deal of electrical fittings and cable. She made arrangements with the firms for all this stuff to be crated and consigned to Forsayth; in Cairns she made arrangements for the truck transport of these goods from Forsayth to

Willstown. I had arranged the necessary credits for her and she was able to pay cash for everything.

She came back to Willstown a week later having made tentative arrangements for supplies of stock for her ice-cream parlour, and found the framework of the workshop already erected; a wooden building goes up very quickly. The matter was a nine days' wonder in Willstown and old men used to stand around wondering at this midsummer madness of an English girl, a stranger to the Gulf country, who proposed to make shoes there and send them all the way to England to be sold. They were too kindly to be rude to her or to laugh at such an eccentricity, but an aura of disbelief surrounded the whole venture and made her feel very much alone in those first weeks.

She visited Midhurst at a very early stage, one Sunday when no work was going on upon her building. Joe Harman drove in to fetch her in his big utility at dawn one day, and took her back to Midhurst in time for breakfast. As soon as they were out of sight of the town they stopped for five minutes to kiss and talk.

Presently they disentangled and went on. Jean was accustomed by this time to the idea that no road in this country had a metalled surface. She had not been beyond the town hitherto; very soon she discovered that a road was where the car drove across country. The land was parched and dry with the heat of summer, covered with thin tufts of scorched grass. It was a wooded land, covered thinly with spindly, distorted eucalyptus trees averaging twenty to thirty feet in height; these trees were fairly widely spaced so that it was possible for a car or truck driven across country to find a way between them. This was the road, and when the surface of the earth became too deeply pitted and potholed with traffic the cars and trucks would deviate and choose another course. These tracks followed the same general direction, coming together at the fords where creeks, now dry and stony, had to be crossed, and fanning out again upon the other side.

Once in the twenty miles she saw half a dozen cattle, that stampeded wildly at the noise of the utility as it bounced and rocketed over the uneven ground. She asked Joe what on earth the cattle found to eat; the ground seemed to her to be completely barren. 'They get along,' he said. 'There's plenty here for them to eat, my word. This dry stuff in the tussocks, why, it's just the same as hay.' He told her that there was a waterhole a little way from their track. 'They never go more than three or four miles from water,' he said. 'Horses, now—you'll find them grazing up to twenty miles from a drink.'

Once she exclaimed at three brown, furry forms bounding away among the trees. 'Oh, Joe—kangaroos!'

He corrected her. 'Wallabies. We don't get any 'roos up in these parts.'

She stared after the flying forms, entranced. 'What's the difference between a wallaby and a kangaroo, Joe?'

'A wallaby's smaller,' he said. 'A big, buck kangaroo, he'll stand up to six feet high, but a wallaby's not more than four. A kangaroo, he's got a face like a deer. A wallaby, he's got a face like a rabbit, or a rat. I got a little wallaby to show you at the homestead.'

'A wild one?'

'He's a tame one now. He'll get wild as he grows older; then he'll go off to his own folks.' He told her that when they had shot the wallabies to send the sample skins to Cairns for her they had shot a doe with a joey, and rather than leave the small defenceless creature to die they had taken it home to rear. 'I like a wallaby about the place,' he said.

They came to Midhurst presently. A fence of two wire strands tacked to the trees, with an occasional post in the wider gaps, crossed their path, with an iron gate; beyond the gate the track became the semblance of a road. She got out of the utility and opened the gate and he drove through. 'This is the home paddock,' he said. 'For horses, mostly.' She could see horses standing underneath the trees, lean riding horses, swishing long black tails. 'I've got about three square miles fenced off like this around the house.'

The road swung round, and she saw Midhurst homestead. It was prettily situated on a low hill above the bend of a creek; this creek was not running, but there were still pools of water held along its length. 'Of course, you're seeing it at the worst time of year,' he said, and she became aware of his anxiety. 'It's a lovely little river in the winter, oh my word. But even in the worst part of the dry, like now, there's always water there.'

The homestead was a fairly large building that stood high off the ground on posts, so that you climbed eight feet up a flight of steps to reach the veranda and the one floor of the house. It was built of wood and had the inevitable corrugated iron roof. Four rooms, three bedrooms and one sitting-room, were surrounded on all four sides by a veranda twelve feet deep; masses of ferns and greenery of all sorts stood in pots and on stands on this veranda at the outer edge and killed most of the direct rays of the sun. There was a kitchen annexe at one end and a bathroom annexe at the other; the toilet was a little hut over a pit in the paddock, some distance from the house. Most of the life of the building evidently went on in the veranda and the rooms seemed to be little used; in the veranda was Joe's bed and his mosquito net, and several cane easy chairs, and the dining-room tables and chairs. Suspended from the rafters was a large canvas waterbag cooling in the draft, with an enamelled mug hung from it by a string.

Five or six dogs greeted them noisily as the utility came to a standstill before the steps. He brushed them aside, but pointed out a large blue and yellow bitch like no dog Jean had ever seen before. 'That's Lily,' he said fondly. 'She had a bonza litter, oh my word.'

He took her up into the coolness of the veranda; she turned to him. 'Oh Joe, this is nice!'

'Like it?' Puppies were surging about them, grovelling and licking their hands; odd-shaped yellow and blue puppies. Along the veranda a small animal stood erect behind a chair, peering at them around the corner. Joe took the puppies one by one and dropped them into a wire-netting enclosure in one corner. 'I let them out this morning before driving in,' he said. 'They'll be big enough to go down in the yard pretty soon.'

'Joe, who fixed up these plants? Did you?'

He shook his head. 'Mrs Spears did that, when she used to live here. I kept them going. The lubras water them, morning and evening.' He told her that he had three Abo women, wives of three of his stockriders, who shared the domestic duties of the homestead and cooked for him.

He looked around. 'There's the joey somewhere.' They found the little wallaby lolloping about on the other side of the veranda; it stood like a little kangaroo about eighteen inches high, and had no fear of them. Jean stooped beside it and it nibbled at her fingers. 'What do you feed it on, Joe?'

'Bread and milk. It's doing fine on that.'

'Don't the puppies hurt it?'

'They chase it now and then, but it can kick all right. A full-grown wallaby can kill a dog. Rip him right up.' He paused, watching her caress the little creature, thinking how lovely she was. 'It's all in fun,' he said. 'They get along all right. By and by when he gets bigger and the dogs are bigger he'll get angry with them, and then he'll go off into the bush.'

A fat, middle-aged lubra, a black golliwog of a woman, laid the table and presently appeared with two plates of the inevitable steak with two eggs on the top, and a pot of strong tea. Jean had become accustomed to the outback breakfast by this time but this steak was tougher than most; she made mental notes to look into the Midhurst cooking as she struggled with it. In the end she gave up and sat back laughing. 'I'm sorry, Joe,' she said. 'It's because I'm English, I suppose.'

He was very much concerned. 'Have a couple more fried eggs. You haven't eaten anything.'

'I've eaten six times as much as I ever ate in England for breakfast, Joe. Who does the cooking?'

'Palmolive did this,' he said. 'It's her day. Mary cooks much better, but it's her day off.'

'Who are they, Joe?'

'I've got a ringer called Moonshine,' he said. 'Palmolive's his gin. My boss Abo, he's called Bournville; he's a bonza boy. Mary's his gin. Mary cooks all right.'

'Tell me, Joe,' she said, 'do you ever get any indigestion?'

He grinned. 'Not very often. Just now and then.'

'You won't mind if I reorganize the cooking a bit when I come in?'

'Not so long as you don't do it all yourself,' he said.

'You wouldn't like me to do that?'

He shook his head. 'I'd rather see you keep time for the things you want to do, the shoes, and the ice-cream parlour, and that.'

She touched his hand. 'I want to keep time for you.'

He took her out before the heat of the day and showed her the establishment. Although the property covered over a thousand square miles, there were no more buildings round the homestead than she had seen on a four-hundred-acre farm in England. There were three or four cottages of two rooms at the most, for stockmen; there were two small bunkhouses for unmarried ringers, white and black. There was a shed housing the truck and the utility and a mass of oddments of machinery. There was a stable for about six horses, which was empty, and a saddle-room, and a butcher's room. There was a Diesel engine that drove an electric generator and pumped water from the creek. That was about all.

Once he said, 'Can you ride a horse?'

She shook her head. 'I'm afraid not, Joe. Ordinary people don't ride horses much in England.'

'Oh my word,' he said. 'You should be able to do that.'

'Could I learn?'

'Too right.'

He put his fingers to his mouth like a schoolboy and blew a shrill whistle; a black head came poking out the window of a single-room cottage. 'Bournville,' he called. 'Get out and bring in Auntie and Robin, 'n saddle up. I'll be down to help you in a minute.'

He turned to her, surveying her cotton frock. 'I dunno about your things. Could you get into a pair of my strides, or would you rather not?'

She laughed. 'Oh Joe, they'd go round me twice!'

'I wasn't always as fat as this,' he said. 'I got a pair I used to wear before the war, I can't get into now. It doesn't matter if they don't fit right; we'll only be walking the horses so you'll see what it feels like.'

He took her up into the homestead and produced a clean man's shirt and a faded pair of jodhpurs and a belt for her; she took them from him laughing, and went into his spare room and put them on, with a pair of his elastic-sided, thin-soled riding boots that were far too big for her. It gave her a queer feeling of possession to be dressed all in his clothes. She walked gingerly down into the yard with the feeling that everything was likely to fall off her, as it had done on another memorable occasion.

He helped her up into the saddle; once astride the patient fourteen-year-old Auntie the feeling of insecurity left her. They adjusted her stirrups and showed her how to set her foot; once she was fairly settled she felt very safe. She knew little about horses or saddlery at that time, but this saddle was like no saddle she had ever seen in England, even in a picture. It rose up in an arch high behind her seat and high in front of her, so that she was seated as in a hammock. There was a great horn that projected above each of her thighs and another one under each thigh, so that she was as if clamped into place. 'I don't believe that anyone could fall off from a saddle like this,' she said.

'You aren't meant to fall off,' he replied.

They walked the horses out of the yard and down the track to the creek; as they went he showed her how to hold the reins and how to use her heels. He took her up the creek for about a mile and then by a wide circuit through the bush, winding beneath the trees so far as possible to seek the shade. Once she saw four scurrying black forms vanishing among the trees and he told her that these were wild pig, and once in a wide stretch of water covered with water lilies there was a violent swirl of water as an alligator dived away from them. She saw several wallabies bounding away before their horses.

They returned to the homestead after an hour or so. Although they had walked the horses all the way Jean was drenched with sweat under the hot sun, and she had a raging thirst. In the veranda she drank several mugs of water, and then she went into the bathroom and had a shower, and changed back into her own cool clothes.

They lunched in the veranda on steak and bread and jam, a repeat of breakfast without the eggs. 'Palmolive hasn't got much imagination in the matter of tucker,' he said apologetically.

'She's looking very tired,' Jean said. 'Great black circles under her eyes. Give her the afternoon off, Joe. I'll make tea for you.'

He offered her the use of the spare room bed to sleep on after lunch, but they had seen so little of each other in the last fortnight that the time seemed too precious to waste in sleep. 'Let's sit out here,' she said. 'If I should go to sleep, Joe, it'll be just one of those things.' So they pulled two of the long cane chairs to the corner of the veranda where there might be a little breeze, and sat together close, so that they could touch hands. 'It's not always as hot as this,' he said, still anxious for her approval of the place. 'Just these two months are the bad ones. By January it'll be beginning to cool off, when the rain gets properly under way.'

'It's not too bad,' she said. 'I remember times when it was quite as hot as this in Malaya.'

She led him on to tell her about his work on the station; having seen a little of the terrain that morning she felt she could appreciate what he told her better now. 'There's not a lot to do this time of year,' he said. 'I like to get up to the top end of the station once a fortnight, if I can, in case of duffers. Make a cache or two of tucker up there, too, this time of year, and shoot the worst of the scrub bulls you see around.'

'What's a duffer, Joe?'

'Why, cattle duffers—cattle thieves. We've not had much of it this year. Sometimes the drovers coming down to Julia Creek from the Cape stations—they pick up a few as they go through the property and put them with the herd. It means faking the brands, of course, and there's the police at Julia to keep an eye open for fresh-branded beasts as they go on the train. They caught a joker at it two years ago and he got six months. We've not had much since then. Poddy-dodging, now—well, that's another matter.'

'What's poddy-dodging, Joe?' She was beginning to grow sleepy, but she wanted to know all she could.

'Why, a poddys a cleanskin, a calf born since the last muster that hasn't been branded. Some of these jokers, even your best friends, they'll come on to your station and round up the poddys and drive them off on to their own land, and then there's nothing to say they're yours. That's poddy-dodging, that is. It's a fair cow. Of course, there's always cattle crossing the boundaries because there aren't any fences, so it's a bit of a mix-up generally when you come to muster. But I've been on stations where there weren't hardly any poddys there at all when we come to muster. All the jokers on the other stations had got them.'

She said, 'But do the poddys just stay on the new land? Don't they want to go back to mother?'

He glanced at her, appreciating the question. 'That's right—they would if you let them. They'd go straight back to their own herd on their own land, even if it was fifty miles. But what these jokers do is this. They build a little corral on their land in some place where no one wouldn't ever think to look, and they drive your poddys into it. Then they leave them there for four or five days without food or water—don't give them nothing at all. Well, if you do that to a poddy he goes sort of silly and forgets about the herd, and mother. All he wants is a drink of water, same as you or I. Then you let him out and let him drink his fill at a waterhole. He's had such a thirst he won't leave that waterhole for months. He forgets all about his own place, and just stays in his new home.'

Her eyes closed, and she slept. When she woke up the sun was lower in the sky, and Joe had left her. She got up and sponged her face in the bathroom, and saw him outside working on the engine of the truck. She tidied herself up, looked at her watch, and went to investigate the kitchen.

Primitive was the word, she thought. There was a wood-burning hearth which mercifully was out, and a wick-burning oil stove; this was the cooking equipment. There was a small kerosene refrigerator. Masses of cooked meat were stored in a wire gauze meat safe with nearly as many flies inside it as there were outside. The utensils were old-fashioned and dirty and few in number; it was a nightmare of a kitchen. Jean felt that the right course would be to burn it

down and start again, and she wondered if this could be done without burning
down the house as well. There was little in the store cupboard but staple foods
such as flour and salt and soap.

She put on a kettle to boil for tea and looked around for something to cook,
other than meat. Eggs were plentiful at Midhurst and she found some stale
cheese; she went and consulted Joe, and then came back and made him a cheese
omelette with eight eggs. He cleaned his hands and came and watched her while
she did it. 'Oh my word,' he said. 'Where did you learn cooking?'

'In Ealing,' she said, and it all seemed very far away: the grey skies, the big
red buses, and the clamour of the Underground. 'I had a sort of little
kitchenette with an electric cooker. I always used to cook myself a two-course
evening meal.'

He grinned awkwardly. 'Afraid you won't find many electric cookers in the
outback.'

She touched his hand. 'I know that, Joe. But there are lots of things that
could be done here to make it a bit easier.' As they ate their tea they talked about
the kitchen and the house. 'It's just the kitchen that needs altering,' she said.
'The rest of it is lovely.'

'I'll get a toilet fixed up in the house before you come,' he promised her. 'It's
all right for me going out there, but it's not nice for you.'

She laughed. 'I don't mind that, so long as you keep up the supplies of the
Saturday Evening Post.'

He grinned, but she found him set upon this alteration. 'Some places have a
septic tank and everything,' he said. 'They put one in at Augustus when the
Duke and Duchess stayed there. I reckon that we'll have to wait a while for
that.'

They ate their tea out on the veranda as the sun went down, and sat looking
out over the creek and the bush, smoking and talking quietly. 'What are you
doing next week?' she asked. 'Will you be in town, Joe?'

He nodded. 'I'll be in on Thursday, or Friday at the latest. 'I'm going up to
the top end tomorrow for a couple of days, just see what's going on.'

She smiled. 'Looking after the poddys?'

He grinned. 'That's right. It's a bit difficult this time of year, in the dry,
because the tracks don't show so good. I got a boy called Nugget on the station
now, and he's a bonza tracker, oh my word. I'm taking him up with me. I've got
a kind of feeling that Don Curtis, up on Windermere station, he's been at my
poddys.'

'What would you do if you found tracks, then, Joe? Tracks leading off your
land and on to his?'

He grinned. 'Go after 'em and find 'em and drive 'em back,' he said. 'Hope
Don doesn't come along while we're doing it.'

He drove her into Willstown at about nine o'clock that night; they halted for
a while outside the town to say goodnight in proper style. She lay against his
shoulder with his arm around her, listening to the noises of the bush, the
croaking of the frogs, the sound of crickets, and the crying of a night bird. 'It's a
lovely place you live in, Joe,' she said. 'It just wants a new kitchen, that's all.
Don't ever worry about me not liking it.'

He kissed her. 'It'll be all ready for you when you come.'

'April,' she said. 'Early in April, Joe.'

She started up the shoe workshop in the first week of December, three or four days after Aggie Topp arrived. To start with she had five girls, Judy Small and her friend Lois Strang, and Annie, whose figure was beginning to deteriorate and who had been sacked from the hotel, and two fifteen-year-olds who had recently left school. For cleanliness and to mark the fact that they were working in a regular job she put everyone into a green overall coat in the workshop, and gave them a mirror on the wall so that they could see what they looked like.

From the first days she found that the fifteen-year-olds were the best employees. Girls straight from school were used to the discipline of regular hours of work; she seldom got the girls from outback homes to settle down to it so well as the younger ones. The monotony was irksome to the older girls who had left school for some years, or who had never been to school at all. She tried to help them by ordering an automatic changing gramophone from Cairns, with a supply of records; the music certainly intrigued and amused the whole of Willstown and may have helped the older girls a little, but not much. The big attraction of the workshop was the air-conditioner.

The air-conditioner was the best recruiting agent of the lot. In that torrid summer heat which ranged from between a hundred and a hundred and ten degrees at midday, she managed to keep the temperature of the workshop down to about seventy degrees, at which the girls could work without their hands sweating. For the girls it meant that they got respite from the heat of the day, and music to listen to, and the novelty of a clean green overall to wear, and money in their pockets at the end of the week. The workshop was popular from the first, and Jean never had any difficulty in getting as many recruits for it as she could handle. For the early months, however, she was content with five.

She spent a hectic fortnight after the workshop opened getting the ice-cream parlour furnished and stocked. She was resolved to have this open by Christmas Day, and she achieved her aim by opening on December 20th. On Joe's advice she only opened half of it at first, leaving the parlour for the Abos till it was established that they wanted ice-cream. This saved her the wages of a coloured girl and the expense of furnishing. In fact, it was not for nearly a year that the demand arose and Abo ringers started hanging round the kitchen door to buy an ice-cream soda. She opened the coloured annexe in the following September.

She stood with Joe outside in the blazing sunlit street on that first afternoon, looking at what she had done. The workshop and the ice-cream parlour stood more or less side by side on the main street. The windows of the workshop were closed to keep the cool air in, but they could hear the girls singing as they worked over the shoes. Christmas was near, and they were singing carols–'Holy Night', and 'Good King Wenceslas', and 'See Amid the Winter Snow'. The shirt was sticking to Jean's back and she shifted her shoulders to get a little air inside. 'Well, there it all is,' she said. 'Now we've got to see if we can make it pay.'

'Come on and I'll buy you a soda,' he said. 'That'll help.' They went in and bought a soda from Rose Sawyer behind the counter. 'This part of it'll pay,' he said. 'I don't know about the shoes, but this should do all right. I was talking to George Connor up at the hotel. He's getting very worried about his bar, with you starting up.'

'I don't see why he's got anything to worry about,' she said. 'I'm not going to sell beer.'

'You're going to sell drinks to ringers,' he remarked. 'If you had a bar instead of this, wouldn't it rile you?'

She laughed. 'I suppose it would. I can't see myself putting the bar out of business, Joe.'

'I can see you doing all right, all the same.' As they sat at the little chromium glass-topped table, Pete Fletcher came in shyly and sidled up to the bar and ordered an ice-cream, and began chatting with Rose Sawyer. Joe said, 'Poor old George Connor.' They laughed together, and then he said, 'I bet you don't keep Rose six months.'

Jean had seen a good deal of Rose Sawyer in the last month. 'I'll take you,' she said. 'Bet you a quid she's still there in a year from now, Joe.' They shook hands on it according to the custom of the place. 'If she is,' he said, 'it'll be a miracle.'

Now that the businesses were started, she was very tired; she felt slack and listless in the great heat, drained of all energy. She would have liked to go out with Joe to Midhurst that evening and live quietly there for a day or two, sleeping and riding and playing with the little wallaby. A cautionary instinct warned her not to offend against the rural code of morals by an indiscretion of that sort; if she was to make a success of what she had set out to do for women in that place her own behaviour would have to be above reproach. No mothers in the outback, she knew, would care to let their daughters work for her if it were known that she was spending nights alone at Midhurst with Joe Harman; no married man would care to bring his wife and daughters to an ice cream parlour run by a loose woman of that sort.

It was a Wednesday, but Sunday was no longer an off day for Jean since it was likely to be the biggest day of all for the ice-cream and soft drinks. She arranged with Joe that he should call for her at the hotel soon after dawn and take her out to Midhurst for the day. She said goodbye to him and went to her room as soon as work stopped in the workshop, pausing only to see the girls from the workshop sampling the ice-cream parlour. She went and lay down on her bed, exhausted and too tired to eat that night; it was refreshingly cool in the workshop building, for the air-conditioner had been on all day. She took off her clothes and put on her pyjamas, and slept in the coolness; she slept so for twelve hours.

She had been out to Midhurst several times since that first visit and had fitted herself out with a small pair of ringer's trousers in Bill Duncan's store for riding, with a pair of elastic-sided ringer's riding boots to match. She met Joe in the early morning with a little bundle of riding things under her arm, and got into the utility with him. As usual they drove a little way out of town and stopped for an exchange of mutual esteem; as he held her he asked, 'How are you feeling this morning?'

She smiled. 'I'm better now, Joe. It was the reaction, I suppose—getting it finished and open. I went to bed just after leaving you and slept right through. Twelve solid hours. I'm feeling fine.'

'Take things very easy today,' he said.

She stroked his hair. 'Dear Joe. It's going to be much easier from now on.'

'This bloody weather'll break soon,' he said. 'We'll get rain starting within the week, and after that it'll begin to get cool.'

They drove on presently. 'Joe,' she said, 'I had an awful row this week with the bank manager—Mr Watkins. Did you hear about it?'

He grinned. 'I did hear something,' he admitted. 'What really happened?'

'It was the flies,' she said. 'It was so hot on Friday, and I was so tired. I went into that miserable little bank to cash the wages cheque and you know how full of flies it always is. I had to wait a few minutes and the flies started crawling all over me, in my hair and in my mouth and in my eyes. I was sweating, I suppose. I lost my temper, Joe. I oughtn't to have done that.'

'It's a crook place, that bank is,' he observed. 'There's no reason why it should have all those flies. What did you say?'

'Everything,' she said simply. 'I told him I was closing my account because I couldn't stand his bloody flies. I said I was going to bank in Cairns and get the cash in by Dakota every week. I said I was going to write to his head office in Sydney and tell them why I'd done it, and I said I was going to write to the Bank of New South Wales and offer my account to them if they'd start up a branch here with no flies. I said I used a DDT spray and I didn't get flies in my workshop and I wasn't going to have them in my bank. I said he ought to be setting an example to Willstown instead of . . .' She stopped.

'Instead of what?' he asked.

She said weakly. 'I forgot what I did say.'

He stared straight ahead at the track. 'I did hear in the bar you told him he ought to set an example instead of sitting on his arse and scratching.'

'Oh, Joe, I couldn't have said that!'

He grinned. 'That's what they're saying that you told him, in Willstown.'

'Oh. . . .' They drove on in silence for a time. 'I'll go in on Friday and apologize,' she said. 'It's no good making quarrels in a place like this.'

'I don't see why you should apologize,' he objected. 'It's up to him to apologize to you. After all, you're the customer.' He paused. 'I'd go in there on Friday and see how he's getting on,' he advised. 'I know he got ten gallons of DDT spray on Saturday, because Al Burns told me.'

When they got to Midhurst he made her go at once and sit in a long chair at the corner of the veranda with a glass of lemon squash made with cold water from the refrigerator. He would not let her move for breakfast, but brought her a cup of tea and a boiled egg and some bread and butter on a tray. She sat there, relaxed, with the fatigue soaking out of her, content to have him gently fussing over her. When the day grew hot he suggested that she took the spare bedroom and lay down upon the bed leaving the double doors open at each end of the room to get the draught through; he promised, grinning, not to look if he passed along the veranda. She took him at his word and took off most of her clothes in the spare room and lay down on the bed and slept through the midday heat.

When she woke up it was nearly four o'clock and she was cool and rested and at ease. She lay for a while wondering if he had looked; then she got up and slipped her frock on and went to the shower, and stood for a long time under the warm stream of water. She came to him presently on the veranda, fresh and rested and full of fondness for him in his generosity, and found him squatting on the floor mending a bridle with palm, needle, and waxed thread. She stooped and kissed him, and said, 'Thanks for everything, Joe. I had a lovely sleep.' And then she said, 'Can we go riding after tea?'

'Still a bit hot,' he said. 'Think that's a good thing?'

'I'd like to,' she said. 'I want to be able to sit on a horse properly.'

He said, 'You did all right last time.' She had been promoted from the fourteen-year-old Auntie to the more energetic Sally and she was gradually learning how to trot. She found that trotting in that climate made her sweat more than the horse and made it difficult for her to sit down next day, but the exercise, she knew, was good for her. Starting at her age, she would never be a very good rider, but she was determined to achieve the ability to do it as a means of locomotion in that country.

They rode for an hour and a half that evening, coming back to Midhurst in the early dusk. He would not let her stay out longer than that, though she wanted to. 'I'm not a bit tired now,' she said. 'I believe I'm getting the hang of this, Joe. It's much easier on Sally than it was on Auntie.'

'Aye,' he said. 'The better the horse the less tiring for the rider, long as you can manage him.'

'I'd like to come with you one day up to the top end,' she said. 'I suppose it'll have to be after we're married.'

He grinned. 'Plenty of wowsers back in Willstown to talk about it, if you came before.'

'Do I ride well enough for that?'

'Oh, aye,' he said. 'Take it easy and you'ld get along all right on Sally. I never travel more than twenty miles in the day, not unless there's some special reason.'

He drove her into Willstown in the utility, and as they kissed goodnight he said he would be in during the following week. She went to bed that night rested and content, refreshed by her quiet day.

She went to the bank on Friday and cashed the wages cheque as usual; she found that the walls were in the process of being distempered and there was not a fly in the place. Mr Watkins was distant in his manner and ignored her; Len James, the young bank clerk, gave her her money with a broad grin and a wink. She saw Len again on Saturday afternoon, when he brought in Doris Nash for an ice-cream soda. He grinned at her, and said, 'You wouldn't know the bank, Miss Paget.'

'I was in there yesterday,' she said. 'You're having it all distempered.'

'That's right,' he said. 'You started something.'

'Is he very sore?' she asked.

'Not really,' the boy said. 'He's been wanting to decorate for a long time, but he's been scared of what the head office would say. There's not a lot of turnover in a place like this, you know. Well, now he's doing it.'

'I'm sorry I was rude,' she said. 'If you get a chance, tell him I said that.'

'I will,' he promised her. 'I'm glad you were. Haven't had such a laugh for years. I don't like flies, either.'

On the first Sunday she worked steadily in the ice-cream parlour with Rose Sawyer from nine in the morning till ten o'clock at night. They sold a hundred and eighty-two ice-creams at a shilling each and three hundred and forty-one soft drinks at sixpence. Dead tired, Jean counted the money in the till at the end of the day. 'Seventeen pounds thirteen shillings,' she said. She stared at Rose in wonder. 'That doesn't seem so bad for a town with a hundred and forty-six people, all told. How much is that a head?'

'About two and six, isn't it?'

'Do you think it's going to go on like this?'

'I don't see why not. Lots of people didn't come in today. Most of them come in two or three times. Judy must have had about ten bob's worth.'

'She can't keep that up,' Jean said. 'She'll be sick, and we'll get a recession. Come on and let's go to bed.'

She opened the ice-cream parlour after lunch on Christmas Day and took twenty pounds in the afternoon and evening. She had the gramophone from the workshop in the parlour that evening playing dance music so that the little wooden shack that was her ice-cream parlour streamed out music and light into the dark wastes of the main street, and seemed to the inhabitants just like a bit of Manly Beach dropped down in Willstown. Old, withered women that Jean had never seen before came in that night with equally old men to have an ice-cream soda, drawn by the lights and by the music. Although the parlour was still full of people she closed punctually at ten o'clock, thinking it better as a start to stick to the bar closing time and not introduce the complication of late hours and night life into a rural community.

The workshop went fairly steadily under Aggie Topp and they despatched two packing-cases of shoes to Forsayth just after Christmas to be sent by rail to Brisbane and by ship to England. She had already sent a few early samples of their work to Pack and Levy by air mail.

On Boxing Day the rain came. They had had one or two short showers before, but that day the clouds massed high in great peaks of cumulo-nimbus that spread and covered the whole sky so that it grew dark. Then down it came, a steady, vertical torrent of rain that went on and on, unending. At first the conditions became worse, with no less heat and very high humidity; in the workshops the girls sweated freely even at seventy degrees, and Aggie Topp had to postpone the finishing operations and concentrate on the earlier, less delicate stages of the manufacture of shoes.

Jean went with Joe to Midhurst for a day soon after the New Year; as usual he called for her just after dawn. This time it was a grey dawn of hot, streaming rain; she scuttled quickly from the door of her room into the cab of the utility. By that time she was getting used to being wet through to the skin, and drying, and getting wet again; the water as it fell was nearly blood temperature and the chance of a chill was slight. She said as she got into the car, 'What are the creeks like, Joe?'

'Coming up,' he said. 'Nothing to worry over yet.' A time would come when for a few weeks he would be unable to reach Willstown from Midhurst in the utility, and would have to ride in if they were to meet at all. He had been stocking up with foodstuffs for the homestead in the last week or two.

There were two creeks between Willstown and Midhurst, wide bottoms of sand and boulders that she knew as hot, arid places in the dry. Now they were wide streams of yellow, muddy water, rather terrifying to her. At the first one she said, 'Can we get through that, Joe?'

'That's all right,' he said. 'It's only a foot deep. You see that tree there with the overhanging branch? When that branch gets covered, at the fork, it's a bit deep then.'

They drove the utility ploughing through the water and emerged the other side; they forded the second creek in the same way, leaping from boulder to boulder, and went on to Midhurst. They got there as usual in time for breakfast. It was still streaming rain down in a steady torrent, too wet for any outdoor activity. They set to work after breakfast to plan out the new kitchen and the toilet he had set his heart on.

In Cairns that morning, four hundred miles to the west of them, Miss Jacqueline Bacon tripped delicately down the pavement in the rain from her home to the Cairns Ambulance and Fire Station. She wore a blue raincoat and she carried an umbrella. She hurried in between the fire engines, and shook the rain from her umbrella. She said to one of the firemen on duty, 'My, isn't it wet?'

He sucked his empty pipe and stared out at the rain. 'Fine weather for ducks.'

She went into her little office off the main hall where the gleaming fire engines stood and glanced at the clock; she had still three minutes to go. The room was furnished with a table and with a microphone and a writing-pad, and two tall metal cabinets of wireless gear; a set stood on the table before her pad. She turned three switches for the apparatus to warm up and took off her wet coat and her hat. Then she found her pencil and drew the pad to her, and a card with a long list of call signs and stations on it. She sat down and began her daily work.

She turned a switch on the face of the cabinet before her and said, 'Eight Baker Tare, Eight Baker Tare, this is Eight Queen Charlie calling Eight Baker Tare. Eight Baker Tare, Eight Baker Tare, this is Eight Queen Charlie calling Eight Baker Tare. Eight Baker Tare, if you are receiving Eight Queen Charlie will you please come in. Over to you. Over.' She turned the switch.

From the speaker in the set before her came a woman's voice. 'Eight Queen Charlie, Eight Queen Charlie, this is Eight Baker Tare. Can you hear me, Jackie?'

Miss Bacon turned the switch and said, 'Eight Baker Tare, this is Eight Queen Charlie. I'm receiving you quite well, about strength four. What's the weather like with you, Mrs Corbett? Over to you. Over.'

'Oh my dear,' the loudspeaker said, 'it's coming down in torrents here. We're having a lovely rain; Jim says we've really got it at last. I do believe it's getting cooler already. Over to you.'

'Eight Baker Tare,' said Miss Bacon, 'this is Eight Queen Charlie. We're having a lovely rain here, too. I have nothing for you, Mrs Corbett, but if you should have anybody going into Georgetown will you pass word to Mrs Cutter that her son Ronnie came up on the train from Mackay last night and he's coming on by train to Forsayth. He'll be there on Thursday morning, so he should be home on Thursday night. Is this Roger, Mrs Corbett? Over to you. Over.'

The loudspeaker said, 'That's Roger, Jackie. One of the boys or Jim will be in Georgetown later on today, and I'll see Mrs Cutter gets that message. Over.'

'Eight Baker Tare,' said Miss Bacon, 'this is Eight Queen Charlie. Roger, Mrs Corbett. I must sign off now. Listening out. Eight Easy Victor, Eight Easy Victor, this is Eight Queen Charlie calling Eight Easy Victor. Eight Easy Victor, this is Eight Queen Charlie calling Eight Easy Victor. If you are receiving me, Mrs Marshall, will you please come in. Over to you. Over.'

There was silence. Miss Bacon went on calling Eight Easy Victor for a minute, but Mrs Marshall, she knew, was in the habit of feeding the hens at the time of the morning schedule and more usually came in in the evening. She made her statutory number of calls and went on to the next. 'Eight Nan How, this is Eight Queen Charlie,' and repeated herself. 'If you are receiving me, Eight Nan How, will you please come in. Over to you. Over.'

A man's voice said, 'Eight Queen Charlie, this is Eight Nan How. Over.'

Miss Bacon said, 'Eight Nan How, this is Eight Queen Charlie. I have a telegram for you, Mr Gosling. Have you got a pencil and paper? I can wait just one minute. Only one minute, mind. Call me when you're ready. Over.'

She waited till he called her back, and then said, 'Eight Nan How, this is Eight Queen Charlie. Your telegram is from Townsville and it reads Molly had son seven last night eight pounds four ounces both doing fine. And the signature is, Bert. Have you got that, Mr Gosling? Over to you. Over.'

The speaker said, 'I got that. It's another boy. Over.'

Miss Bacon said, 'I am *so* glad it's all gone off all right. Give Molly my love when you write, won't you, Mr Gosling? Have you got anything else for me? Over.'

The speaker said, 'I'll think out a reply to this, Jackie, and give it to you on the evening schedule. Over to you. Over.'

She said, 'Okay, Mr Gosling, I'll take it then. Now I must sign off from you. Eight Item Yoke, Eight Item Yoke, this is Eight Queen Charlie calling Eight Item Yoke.' She went on with her work.

Twenty minutes later she was still at it. 'Eight Able George, Eight Able George, this is Eight Queen Charlie calling Eight Able George. Eight Able George, if you are receiving Eight Queen Charlie will you come in now. Over.'

The answer came in a sobbing torrent of words, rather impeded by the static of three hundred miles. 'Oh, Jackie. I'm so glad you've come. We're in such trouble here. Don's horse came back last night. I heard the horse come in about two o'clock in the morning and I thought, that's funny, because Don never travels at night because of the trees, you know. And then I thought, that's funny, because there was only one horse and he had Samson with him so I got up to look and I couldn't see the horse, my dear, so I got a torch and put my coat on and went out in the rain and, my dear, there it was, Don's horse, Jubilee, saddled and everything and Don wasn't there, and I'm so frightened.' The voice dissolved into a torrent of sobs.

Miss Bacon sat motionless before the microphone, one hand on the transmitter switch, listening to the carrier wave and the low sobbing at the other end, clearly distinguishable through the static. There was nothing to be done until Helen Curtis recovered herself and remembered to switch over to Receive. She glanced quickly at the list before her; she hesitated, and then left her chair and opened the door and called to the fireman on duty, 'Fred, ring up Mr Barnes and ask him to come down if he can. Something's happened at Windermere.'

She went back to her chair, and now a heterodyne squeal shrilled out, drowning the sobbing as some sympathetic, foolish woman came in on the same wave saying something unintelligible. She sat patiently waiting for the air to clear; until they remembered their routines she could do nothing for them. The heterodyne stopped and Helen Curtis was still sobbing at the microphone three hundred miles away, beneath the coloured picture of the King and Queen in coronation robes and the picture of their daughter's wedding group that stood upon the set. Then she said, 'Jackie, Jackie, are you there? Oh, I forgot. Over.'

Miss Bacon turned her switch and said, 'All right, Helen, this is Jackie here. Look, everybody, this is Eight Queen Charlie talking to Eight Able George. Will everybody please keep off the air and not transmit. You can stay listening in, but not transmit. I'll call you if you can do anything. Mrs Curtis, I've sent Fred to telephone to Mr Barnes to get him to come down. Now sit down quietly and tell me what happened and I'll take it down. Remember your routine and switch over when you want me to answer. It's going to be all right, Helen. Just tell me quietly what happened. Over to you. Over.'

The speaker said, 'Oh, Jackie, it *is* good to hear you. I've got nobody here except the boongs. Dave's on holiday and Pete's in Normanton. What happened was this. Don went up to the Disappointment Creek part of the station three days ago and he took Samson with him and he said he'd be away two days. I wasn't worried when they didn't get back because the rain, you know, and I thought they'd have to go around because the creeks would be up. And then last night Don's horse came back alone, and no sign of Samson. Samson's our new Abo stockrider. I've got a very good tracker here called Johnnie Walker, and Johnnie went out at dawn to track the horse back. But he came back an hour ago and it wasn't any good because the rain had washed the tracks out; he could only follow it about three miles and then he lost it, and now I don't know what to do.' There was a pause, and then she said, 'Oh, over.'

Miss Bacon's pad was covered with rough notes. She turned her switch and said, 'This is Jackie, Helen. Tell me, what stations are north and south of you? Over.'

'It's Carlisle, north of us, Jackie–that's Eddie Page. It's Midhurst to the south, and Pelican to the east. Midhurst is Joe Harman and Pelican Len Driver. I don't think Midhurst's got a radio, though. Over.'

Miss Bacon said, 'All right Helen, I'll call some of them. Stay listening in, because Mr Barnes will want to speak to you when he comes. Now I'm going over to Carlisle. I have telegrams for Eight Dog Sugar and for Eight Jig William, and I will give them as soon as I'm free. Eight Charlie Peter, Eight Charlie Peter, this is Eight Queen Charlie. If you are receiving me, Eight Charlie Peter, will you come in. Over.'

She turned her switch and heard the measured tones of Eddie Page, and sighed with relief. 'Eight Queen Charlie, this is Eight Charlie Peter. I heard all that Jackie. I've got Fred Dawson here, and we'll go down to Windermere soon as we can. Tell Helen we'll be with her in about four hours and see what we can do. Will you be keeping a listening watch? Over.'

She said, 'That's fine, Mr Page. We shall be on watch here till this is squared up listening every hour, from the hour till ten minutes past the hour. Is this Roger? Over.'

He said, 'Okay Jackie, that's Roger. I'll sign off now and go and saddle up. You won't be able to raise me any more; Olive can't work it. Out.'

She called Pelican next, but got no answer, so she called Eight Love Mike, the Willstown Mounted Police Station, and got Sergeant Haines at once. He said, 'Okay Jackie, I've heard all of that. I'm sending Phil Duncan and one of my trackers, and we'll see if any of the boys can come along. I'll see that someone goes round by Midhurst and tells Joe Harman. Tell Mr Barnes that Constable Duncan will be at Windermere about three or four this afternoon. Your listening watch is Roger. Good girl, Jackie. Out.'

Drama or no drama, the day's work still remained to be done. Miss Bacon said, 'Eight Dog Sugar, this is Eight Queen Charlie calling Eight Dog Sugar. I have a telegram for Eight Dog Sugar. If you are receiving Eight Queen Charlie will you please come in. Over.' She went on with her work.

At Midhurst Jean was measuring up the kitchen with Joe Harman and making a plan on a writing-pad, when they heard a horse approaching about noon. It was still raining, though less fiercely than before. They went to the other side of the house and saw Pete Fletcher handing his horse over to Moonshine; he came up to the veranda. He was wearing his broad ringer's hat and he was soaked to the skin; his boots squelched as he climbed the steps.

He said, 'Did you hear the radio?'

'No. What's that?'

'Some kind of trouble up on Windermere,' the boy said. 'Don Curtis went up with an Abo ringer to the top end of his station three days ago. Now the horse is back without him.'

'Tracked the horse back?' Joe asked at once.

'Tried that, but it didn't work. Tracks all washed out.' The boy sat down on the edge of the veranda and began taking off his boots to tip the water out of them; a little pool formed round him. 'Jackie Bacon, the girl on the Cairns radio, she got the news on the morning schedule. She called Sergeant Haines, and he sent Phil Duncan to Windermere. Phil's on his way there now, with Al Burns. I said I'd come round this way and tell you. Eddie Page is on his way to Windermere from Carlisle, with Fred Dawson.'

Joe asked, 'Who was the Abo ringer he had with him?'

'Chap called Samson from the Mitchell River. He's been with Don about a month.'

'Do they know where on the station he was going to?'

'Up by Disappointment Creek.'

'For Christ's sake,' Joe said. 'Then I know what he's been up to.' Jean, looking at him, saw his mouth set in a hard line.

'What's that?' asked Pete.

'He's been at my poddys again,' said Joe. 'The mugger's got a poddy corral up there.'

'How do you know that?' asked Pete.

'Found the sod,' said Joe. 'I'll tell you where it is. You know where Disappointment Creek runs into the Fish River?' The boy nodded. 'Well, from there you go up Disappointment Creek about four miles and you'll come to an island and a little bit of a creek running in from the north just by it. Well, go on past that about a mile and you'll see a lot of thick bush north of the creek with a little bare hill behind. You can't mistake it. The poddy corral's round the back of the thick bush, just under the bare hill. If you get up on that hill—it's only about fifty feet high—you'll see the poddy corral to the south of you.' He paused. 'If you're going on a search party I'd start off with that.'

'Thanks, Joe,' Pete said. 'I'll tell them at Windermere.'

'Aye, you'd better. I don't suppose Mrs Curtis knows anything about it.'

Jean had been hesitant to break in on a discussion about things that she knew nothing of, but now she said, 'How did you get to know about it, Joe?'

He turned to her. 'I was up at the top end just after Christmas with Bourneville, and I thought poddys were a bit scarcer than they ought to be. So then Bourneville got to tracking and the rain hadn't hardly begun then, so it was easy. The Cartwright River makes the station boundary just there, and we followed the tracks across and on to Windermere. Two horses there were, with a lot of poddys. We found the corral like I said, and there they were; been there two or three days. I let 'em out, of course, and drove them back. Had a cow of a job to get them past the first water, oh my word.'

Pete asked, 'How many were there, Joe?'

'Forty-seven.'

'All cleanskins?'

'Oh yes,' Joe was rather shocked at the implied suggestion.

'Don wouldn't go and do a thing like that,' he said.

The boy put on his boots and got up. 'What'll you do, Joe? Come along with me?'

'I don't think so,' Joe replied slowly. 'I think I'll get up to the top end of my station, where he got those poddys from. Maybe he's been after some more, and had his accident up there. That's south of the Cartwright River, and east of the new bore we made. If I can't see any trace of him on my land, then I'll follow the way he drove those poddys to his corral. Maybe I'll meet you around there somewhere tomorrow or the next day.'

Pete nodded. 'I'll tell Phil.'

'Tell him I'll be taking Bourneville with me, and I'll start as soon as I've run Miss Paget here back into town in the utility.'

Forty miles in the utility in those wet conditions would take the best part of three hours. Jean said, 'Joe, don't bother about me. I'll stay here till you come back. You get off at once.'

He hesitated. 'I may be away for days.'

'Well then, I'll ride into town on Sally. One of the boongs can come with me and bring Sally back.'

'You could do that,' he said slowly. 'Moonshine will be here, and he could go with you. I'll be taking Bourneville along with me.'

'Well, then,' she said, 'that's perfectly all right. What time's Dave coming back?'

'Should be back this afternoon,' he said. He turned to Pete. 'I've got Jim Lennon on holiday, and Dave's off visiting a girl, one of the nurses down at Normanton. But he'll be back today.'

Jean said, 'I'll stay here till Dave comes, in case anything crops up, Joe.'

He smiled at her. 'Well, that would be a help. I don't like leaving the place with just the boongs. I'll tell Moonshine he's to take you into town any time you want to go.' He turned to Pete. 'Want another horse?'

'I don't think so. 'Bout thirty miles to Windermere from here?'

'That's right. Cross over the river here, you know, and you'll find a track that leads there all the way. It's not been used much lately. If you miss it, go north to the Gilbert and follow up a mile or two and you'll find a little hut Jeff Pocock uses when he's hunting 'gators. There's a shallow about two miles up from that where you can get across. Go north from there about ten miles and you'll find their track from the homestead to Willstown. You can't mistake that.'

'Okay.'

'What about some tucker?'

The boy shook his head. 'Think I'll get on my way.'

They went down into the yard and saw him saddle up and ride away. The rain had practically stopped, but the clouds were heavy and black overhead. Joe turned to her, 'Sorry about this,' he said quietly. 'It's spoilt our day. You're sure you don't mind riding in with Moonshine?'

'Of course not,' she said. 'You must get away at once.'

She hurried in to galvanize Palmolive to prepare some lunch and food for them to take with them; down in the yard the men were saddling up. They took their riding horses and one packhorse with them, loaded with a tent and camping gear. She was distressed at the meagre quantity and poor quality of the food Joe seemed to think it necessary to take with them. He took a hunk of horrible black, overcooked meat out of the meat safe and dropped it into a sack with three loaves of bread; he took a couple of handfuls of tea in an old cocoa tin and a couple of handfuls of sugar in another. That was the whole of his provision for a journey of indefinite length. She did not interfere, seeing that he was absorbed in his preparations and not wanting to fuss him, but she stored up the knowledge for her future information.

He kissed her goodbye on the veranda and she went down with him to the yard. 'Look after yourself, Joe,' she said.

He grinned. 'See you in Willstown next week.' Then he was trotting out of the gate with Bourneville by his side and the packhorse behind on a lead, and she was left alone at Midhurst with the boongs.

It began to rain again, and she went up into the veranda. It was very quiet and empty now that Joe was gone, and Palmolive had retired to her own place. The rain made a steady drumming on the iron roof. It occurred to her that the whole business might be over. Don Curtis might have turned up at Windermere and Joe's journey might be so much wasted effort. It was absurd that Midhurst had not got a radio transmitter. It was true enough that they were only twenty miles from the hospital and so would hardly need it for their own accidents, but in a case like this it was both difficult and trying not to know what was going on. She made up her mind to have a transmitter at Midhurst when they were married. A cattle station without one in these days was a back number.

She had never been alone in Midhurst before. She wandered through from room to room, slowly, deep in thought, and the wallaby lolloped after her; from time to time she dropped her hand to caress it, and it nibbled her fingers. She spent a long time in his room, touching and fingering the rough gear and clothes that were essentially Joe. He had so few things. Yet it was in this room he had dreamed and planned that fantastic journey to England in search of her, that journey that had ended in Noel Strachan's office in Chancery Lane. Chancery Lane seemed very far away.

At about three o'clock Dave Hope arrived. He came riding from Willstown through the rain as Pete Fletcher had come in the morning; he had got a lift up on a truck from Normanton. He had heard all about the Windermere affair in Willstown, which he had left shortly before noon, and he could add further information from the radio. He told her that the Abo ringer, Samson, had returned to the homestead.

'Seems they were looking for some poddys,' he said, 'somewhere up at the Disappointment Creek end of the station. They separated and one went one way, one the other, for some reason; they left the camp standing and were going to meet back in the evening. Don didn't turn up that evening and of course the Abo couldn't track him in the dark. When the morning came the whole place was swimming in water, and he couldn't track him at all. That's how it seems to be.'

They talked about it for some time on the veranda. Somewhere thirty or forty miles from them a man must be lying injured on the ground; he might be anywhere within a circle thirty miles in diameter. He might be lying under a bush and very probably by that time he would be unconscious; looking for him would be like looking for a needle in a bundle of hay.

'You'd better go and help, Dave,' Jean said at last. 'There's nothing to do here. I'll stay here and look after things.'

He was a little doubtful. 'What did Mr Harman say I was to do?'

'He didn't say anything. I said I'd stay here till you got back. He doesn't want the station left without anyone at all, except the boongs. I'll stay here Dave, till somebody else comes. You go and join them over at Windermere. That's the best thing you can do.'

'It certainly seems crook to stay here doing nothing,' he admitted.

She got him off in the late afternoon with about two hours of daylight left. He knew Windermere station well, and was quite happy about finishing his journey in the dark. Left to herself, Jean went on with the plan of the kitchen she would have liked to see built, with a view to getting Joe to pull the old one down completely and start again from scratch. Presently Palmolive came in and cooked eggs for her tea, and fed the various animals, and watered the veranda plants.

When Palmolive had gone away, she was alone in Midhurst for the night, with only the puppies and the wallaby for company. Somewhere out in the darkness and the rain Joe Harman would be pushing on towards the top end of the property, horses and men soaked through, picking their way cautiously through the darkness. She could do nothing to help them, nothing but sit and wait.

She learned a lot that evening. She learned a little of the fortitude that a wife on a cattle station must develop, even, she thought a little grimly, a wife with fifty-three thousand pounds. She learned that a radio transmitting and receiving set was almost indispensable to such a wife; even on that first evening she would have liked to exchange a word or two with Jackie Bacon in Cairns. She learned how much a lonely person turns to animals, and queerly the memory of Olive came into her mind, the brown Abo girl who could not bear to be separated from her kitten even on a visit to the Willstown hotel. By the time she went to bed she understood Olive a bit better.

She went to bed at about nine. There were one or two old British and American magazines about the place, tattered, much read stories about a different world. She took one of these and tried to read it in bed, but the fiction failed to satisfy her or to quell her anxieties. The rain stopped, and started, and then stopped again, and presently she slept.

She slept lightly and woke many times, and dozed again. She woke before dawn to the sound of a horse in the yard. She got up at once and put her frock on and went out on the veranda, and switched on the light, and called, 'Who's that?'

A man came forward into the light at the foot of the steps, and said, 'It's me, Missy, Bourneville. Missa Hope, him come back?'

He spoke with a thick accent; she could not understand what he was saying. She said, 'Come up here, Bourneville. What is it?'

He came up to her in the veranda. He was a man of about fifty years of age, very black, with a seamed, wrinkled face and greying hair. He said again, 'Missa Hope, him come back?'

She understood this time. 'He's gone over to Windermere. He came back here, and went on to Windermere. What's happened to Mr Harman, Bourneville?'

He said, 'Missa Harman, him up top end. Him find Missa Curtis, him leg broken. Missa Harman, him send me back fetch Missa Hope, him drive utility up top end, bring Missa Curtis down.'

She was angry with herself that she could not fully understand what he was saying. The fault lay within herself; a woman of the Gulf country would understand this man at once, and it was terribly important that she should understand. She said quietly, 'I'm sorry, Bourneville. Say that again slowly.'

She got it at the second repetition. 'Mr Hope's not here,' she said. 'He's gone to Windermere.'

He was silent for a time. Then he said, 'No white feller here, drive utility?' She shook her head. 'Can you drive the utility, Bourneville?'

'No, Missy.'

'Can any of the other Abos drive the utility?'

'No, Missy.'

The thought came to her that she could drive it up to them herself, with Bourneville as a guide, but it was not a thing to be undertaken lightly. She had never owned a car, and though she had driven cars belonging to various young men from time to time and knew the movements, her total driving experience did not exceed five hours. Again, she was angry and humiliated by her own incompetence.

She lit a cigarette and thought deeply. It would benefit nobody if she attempted to drive the utility and crashed it. It was a very big vehicle, larger than any ordinary car and much bigger than anything she had ever driven before. The alternative would be to send Bourneville riding on to Willstown, perhaps to the police station; they would send a truck or a utility out with a driver who would go on to the top end. The return journey to Willstown was forty miles. It would mean at least six hours delay before the truck could arrive at Midhurst ready to start for the top end.

She asked, 'How far away is Mr Harman, Bourneville?'

He thought. 'Four mile past bore.'

Joe had once told her that the new bore was twenty-two miles from the homestead; that made the scene of the accident twenty-six miles away. She said. 'What's the track like? Can the utility get there?'

'Him bonza track in dry far as bore,' he said. She nodded; this was likely enough because the bore had only been made a few months and there must have been trucks going up to it. It would probably be possible to get along it even in this rain. Already the sky was getting grey; full daylight was not far away.

She asked, 'Are there any creeks to cross?'

He held up three fingers. 'Tree.'

'Are they deep? Can the utility go through?'

'Yes, Missy. Creeks not too deep.'

If Bourneville rode a horse beside the utility to guide her, she thought that she could make it. It was worth trying, anyway; the worst that could happen would be that she would get it stuck and have to send Bourneville back to Willstown with a note for them to send up somebody more competent. So long as he had his horse there was no risk of any great delay. She said, 'All right, Bourneville, I'll drive the utility. You come up with me on your horse.'

'Get fresh horse, Missy. Him tired.'

'All right, get a fresh horse.' Bourneville must be tired too, but she was too unaccustomed to these seamed black faces to be able to detect fatigue. 'You get some tucker,' she said. 'I get tucker, too. We'll start in half an hour.'

He went off and she put the kettle on for a cup of tea and then went and changed into her riding shirt and breeches. There was an old tin trunk in Joe's room which she had discovered the night before; it was half full of bandages and splints and various medicines. Being of tin, she thought, it would be waterproof, and she filled it up with blankets and some tins of food from the store cupboard, and a small sack of flour. That was all she could think of for provision in case she got stuck half way and had to spend a night or two in the utility.

She had a cup of tea and a small meal of meat and bread and jam; then she went down to the yard and examined the utility. The huge petrol tank had twenty gallons in it, and the sump was full of oil. She filled the radiator from the water-butt and filled the waterbag suspended from the lamp bracket. Then she sat in it; to her relief the gears were clearly marked. She switched it on and pressed the starter and jiggeted the accelerator, and was both alarmed and pleased when the engine started. Very gingerly she put it in reverse and drove it out into the yard.

They put the trunk into the back and started off, Bourneville riding ahead of her to show her the way. Partly because of Bourneville on his horse and partly because she thoroughly distrusted her own competence, she never got it into top gear all the way, and never exceeded ten miles an hour. She drove through each of the three creeks along the line that Bourneville showed her, following the agitated, plunging horse as he forced through the yellow water swirling about its legs. Once the water rose above the floorboards of the cab and she was very frightened. But she kept the utility going and the designer had anticipated such usage and had placed the ignition system above the cylinders, and it came through bounding from rock to rock with water pouring out of every hole and cranny.

Four miles beyond the bore Joe Harman sat at the mouth of his small tent. It was pitched in a clearing in a thick patch of bush in the bottom of a little valley. A heavy log stockade or corral had been built in this clearing and stood immediately behind the tent; the movable logs that formed a gate had been pulled down and the corral was empty. Joe had built a fire before the tent, and he was boiling up in a billy over it.

A man lay inside upon a bed of brushwood covered with a waterproof sheet, with a blanket over him. Joe turned his head, and said, 'What happened, Don? Did they rush you when you got the pole down?'

From the tent the man said, 'My bloody oath. They pushed the pole back on to me and knocked me down. Then about six of them ran over me.'

Joe said, 'Serve you bloody well right. Teach you to go muggering about on other people's land.'

There was a pause. Then he said, 'How many of mine did you get last year, Don?'

''Bout three hundred.'

Mr Harman laughed. 'I got three hundred and fifty of yours.'

From the tent Mr Curtis said a very rude word.

10

Jean drove the utility slowly up to the tent with Bourneville riding beside her; she took out the gear and stopped it with a sigh of relief. Joe came to her as she sat there. 'What's happened to Dave?' he asked. 'Didn't he come back?'

She told him what had happened. 'I thought I'd better have a go at driving it up myself,' she said. 'I've only driven a car about three times before. I don't think I've done it any good, Joe.'

He stepped back. 'Looks all right,' he said. 'Did you hit anything?'

'I didn't hit anything. I couldn't get the gears in sometimes and it made an awful noise.'

'Do they still work?'

'Oh, I think so.'

'That's all right, then. What were the creeks like?'

'Pretty high,' she said. 'It came over the floor of the cab.'

He grunted. 'Get along back as soon as we can. I wish this bloody rain 'ld stop.'

She asked, 'Is Mr Curtis here, Joe?'

He nodded. 'In the tent.'

'What's wrong?'

'Got his leg bust,' he said. 'Compound fracture–that's what you call it when the bone's sticking out, isn't it? I think he's got a broken ankle, too.'

She pursed her lips. 'I brought up that trunk with your splints and things.'

He asked, 'Do you know about breaks? Ever been a nurse or anything like that?'

She shook her head. 'I've not.'

'I've had a look at it and washed it,' he said. 'I set it well as I could, but it's a mess. I made a sort of long splint this morning and tied it all down on that. We'll get him down to hospital, soon as we can. It's been done two days.'

They set to work to strike camp. They removed the tent from over the injured man and he saw Jean for the first time. 'Hullo, Miss Paget,' he said. 'You don't remember me. I saw you in Willstown, day you arrived.'

She smiled at him. 'You'll be back there in a little while. In the hospital.'

Once as she worked she turned to Joe with a puzzled expression. 'Whose land are we on, Joe?'

'Midhurst,' he said. 'Why?'

She glanced at the corral. 'What's that for?'

'That?' he said. 'Oh, that's just a place we put the cattle in sometimes, for branding and that.'

She said no more, but went on with her work; once or twice a little smile played round her lips. They worked a blanket underneath the brushwood bed as the man lay upon the ground, and lowered the tailboard of the utility; then, with infinite care and great labour they lifted him on his bed into the body of the truck. The man was white and sweating when they had done and a little blood was showing on his lip where he had bitten it, but there was nothing else that they could do to ease his pain.

They started off at about nine o'clock, Joe driving the utility, Jean riding in the back with the injured man, and Bourneville following behind, riding and leading the two horses. They passed the bore and went on for about five miles till they came to the creeks. The water was considerably higher than when Jean had crossed a couple of hours earlier.

They crossed the first without difficulty, though the water was in the cab of the utility and only just below the floor of the truck body on which the sick man lay. They came through that one and went on. At the second creek the water was higher. Joe stopped on the edge and consulted with Jean and Bourneville about the crossing they had made before. It seemed shallower fifty yards above the point where Jean had crossed; Joe sent Bourneville into the water on his horse to sound the crossing. It looked good enough, so he drove the utility into the water.

It grew deep quickly, and he accelerated to keep her going. The bottom, under the swirling yellow flood, was very rough; the big car went forward leaping from boulder to boulder under the water. Then she came down heavily on something with a crunch of metal, and stopped dead.

Joe said, 'Jesus,' and pressed the starter, but the engine was immovable. Oil began to appear on the eddying yellow surface of the water, and slide away downstream in black and yellow tails. He stared at it in consternation.

Jean said, 'What's happened, Joe?'

'I've cracked the bloody sump,' he said shortly.

He got down into the water from the cab, feeling his way gingerly; it was well above his knees, close on waist deep. He called Bourneville and made Jean pass him a coil of rope from the back of the truck. The utility was only about ten yards from the bank. They made a sort of tandem harness for the three horses with lariats that they carried at the pommel of the riding saddles, and harnessed this team to the back axle of the utility, groping and spluttering under the water to do so. In ten minutes the vehicle was on dry land; a performance that left Jean awed by its efficiency.

She got down from the back and went to Joe, who was lying on his back under the front axle. She stooped down with him to look; the cast iron sump was crushed and splintered. 'Say it, Joe,' she said quietly.

He grinned at her, and said, 'It's a fair mugger.' He picked the broken pieces of cast iron from the hole, and got out from underneath. He went and got the starting-handle from the cab and turned the engine carefully. He sighed with relief. 'Crankshaft's all right,' he said. 'It's only just the sump.'

He stood in deep thought for a minute, starting-handle in his hand; the rain poured down upon them steadily. She asked, 'Where do we go from here, Joe?'

'I could patch that,' he said, 'good enough to get her home. But then we haven't got any oil. It's no good going down to fetch the truck the way these creeks are rising.' He stood watching the water for a minute or two. 'Never get the truck through by the time it got here,' he said finally. 'There's only one thing for it now. He'll have to be flown out.'

The country round about was covered with rocks and trees. 'Is there anywhere an aeroplane can land here?' she asked.

'I know one place it might,' he said. 'Five hundred yards, they want, and then a good approach.'

He took his horse and went off to the south; by the river they unpacked the tent and arranged it over Don Curtis to keep the rain off him. The wounded man said faintly once, 'Joe Harman's a clumsy mugger with a car. He's a good poddy-dodger, though.' Jean laughed. 'Pair of criminals, the two of you,' she said. 'I'm going to have a word with Mrs Curtis.'

'Don't do it,' he said. 'She don't know nothing about this.'

She said, 'Lie still, and don't talk. Joe's gone off to find a place where the aeroplane can land to fly you out.'

'Hope he makes a better job of it than he did driving this bloody truck,' said Mr Curtis.

Joe came back in a quarter of an hour. 'Think we can make something of it,' he said. 'It's only about a mile away.' With Bourneville he harnessed up the tandem team of three horses to the front axle of the truck, and with Jean at the wheel they set off through the bush, steering and manoeuvring between the trees.

They came presently to an open space, a long grassy sward with low bushes dotted about on it. It was more than five hundred yards long, but there were trees at each end. It would be possible to make an airstrip there. 'Clear off some of those bushes,' Joe said, 'and fell some of those trees. I've seen them use a lot worse places than this.'

An axe and a spade were part of the equipment of the utility; they had tools enough. Their labour was quite inadequate for the work. 'We'll have to get the boys up from Midhurst,' he said. 'Everyone that's there. And get a message down to Willstown about the aeroplane.'

She said, 'I'll ride down with Bourneville to the homestead, Joe. Then he can bring the boys back, and I'll go on to Willstown.'

He stared at her. 'You can't ride that far.'

'How far is it?'

'Forty miles, to Willstown.'

'I can get to Midhurst, anyway,' she said. 'If I can't go on I'll send Moonshine in with a note to Sergeant Haines. He's the best man to tell, isn't he?'

'That's right. If you do this, there's to be no riding alone. If you go on from Midhurst to town, you've got to take Moonshine or one of the other boys with you. I won't have you trying to cross them creeks alone, on a horse.'

She touched his arm. 'All right, Joe. I'll take someone with me.' She paused. 'We could get on the radio from Willstown,' she said. 'We could get some people over from Windermere to help you then, couldn't we?'

'That's right,' he said. 'It would be better if we had a radio at Midhurst.' He paused. 'There's one thing that they'll all want to know,' he said, 'and that's where this place is. We're about six miles west-south-west of the new bore. Can you remember that?'

'I've got that, Joe,' she said. 'Six miles west-south-west of the new bore.' She paused. 'What are you going to do?' she asked.

'I'll make a camp here.' He looked around. 'I'll pitch the tent over the back of the utility,' he said. 'We don't want to shift him again if we can help it, not until we get a stretcher. After that I'll start and fell some of those trees for the approach.'

'What about your back?' she asked.

'That'll be all right.'

She thought of swinging a two-handed axe to fell a tree. 'Have you done that, Joe?'

'No, but it'll be all right.'

She said. 'If you're going to cut down trees I'll take back what I said about not riding alone. I'll send Moonshine up with the other boongs to help you here.'

'You're not to do that,' he said. 'It's not safe for you crossing them creeks.'

'It's not safe for you to swing an axe,' she said. 'It won't help if you go and ruin your back up here, Joe.' She touched his arm again. 'Let's both be sensible,' she said. 'The work you'll do in cutting down those trees alone is only what the boongs will do in an hour when they get here. Don't take risks, Joe.'

He smiled at her. 'All right. But you're not to ride alone.'

'I'll promise that,' she said.

It was about half past ten when they put her up on Joe's horse, Robin. Robin was a much bigger horse than she had ridden before, and she was rather afraid of him. He was little, if any, wider for her to straddle than the horses she was used to, and Joe's saddle was much better than the casual saddles she had been using up till then; it was soft and worn and supple with much use and yet efficient and in very good repair. When they got the stirrups adjusted for her legs she found herself fairly comfortable.

She started off with Bourneville at a slow trot through the trees, and so began a feat of endurance which she was to look back upon with awe for years to come. She found the horse docile, responsive, and energetic; moreover, he had a very easy gait when trotting. At the same time, the bald fact remained that she had only been on a horse six times before, and never for more than an hour and a half at a time.

The rain had stopped for the moment, and they came to the creek and waded through the tumbling yellow water, Bourneville close beside her. They came through that one and went on, walking and trotting alternately. After an hour they came to the second creek and found it very deep; Bourneville made her take her feet out of the stirrups and be prepared to swim, holding to the horse's mane. That was not necessary and they came through to the other side in good order, and then the creeks were over.

'Too deep for the utility,' she said.

'Yes, Missy. Him too deep now.'

No creeks now lay between them and Midhurst; it remained only for them to ride. The rain began again and soaked her to the skin, mingling with the sweat streaming off her. Very soon the wet strides began to chafe her legs and thighs; she could feel the soreness growing, but there was nothing to be done about that. She had said that she would ride, and ride she would.

She found, on the good going that was before them now, that she could get along faster than Bourneville. She was on a much better horse, and a horse that was fresh whereas he had ridden his from Midhurst with the utility. Frequently she had to slow to a walk for him when Robin would have trotted on, and these walks helped her, easing her fatigue.

They came to Midhurst homestead at about half past two. By that time she had a raging thirst, and she was getting very tired. Moonshine and one or two of the other boys ran out and took her bridle and helped her down from Robin; she could not manage the stretch from the stirrup to the ground. She said, 'Bourneville, tell Moonshine to saddle up and come with me to Willstown. I'm going to have a cup of tea and some tucker, and then we'll start. You take all the boys back to Mr Harman. That okay?'

He said, 'Yes, Missy.' It struck her that if she was tired he must be exhausted; he had been in the saddle continuously for twenty-four hours. She looked at the seamed black face and said, 'Can you make it, Bourneville? Are you very tired?'

He grinned. 'Me not tired, Missy. Go back to Missa Harman with the boys after tucker.' He went away shouting, 'Palmolive, Palmolive. You go longa kitchen, make tea and tucker for Missy. You go longa kitchen quick.'

She sat down wearily upon the chair in the veranda, and in a very short time Palmolive appeared with a pot of tea and two fried eggs upon a steak that was almost uneatable. She ate the eggs and a corner of the steak and drank six huge cups of tea. She did not dare to change her clothes or examine her sores; once started on that sort of thing, she knew, she would never get going again. She finished eating and called out for Moonshine and went down into the yard. The black stockmen, saddling their own horses and making up the bundles for the packhorses in the rain, put her up into the saddle and she was off again for Willstown with Moonshine by her side.

The short rest had stiffened her, and it needed all her courage to face the twenty miles that lay ahead. Every muscle in her body was stretched and aching. Her legs ceased to function much to hold her in the saddle, but the big horns above and below her thighs came into play and held her in place.

They crossed the creeks, now too deep for a car, and rode on. They were following the car track, and the going was good. She was the laggard now, because Moonshine's horse was fresh and Robin was tiring. She rode the last ten miles in a daze, walking and trotting wearily; for the last five miles the black stockman rode close by her side to try and catch her if she fell. But she didn't fall. She rode into Willstown in the darkness at about seven o'clock, a very tired girl on a very tired horse with a black ringer beside her. She rode past the hotel and past the ice-cream parlour with its lights streaming out into the street, and came to a stand outside Sergeant Haines' police station and house. She had been about eight hours in the saddle.

Moonshine dismounted and held Robin's head. She summoned a last effort and got her right leg back over the saddle, and slithered down to the ground. She could not stand at first without holding on to something, and she held on to Robin's saddle. Then Sergeant Haines was there.

'Why, Miss Paget,' he said in the slow Queensland way, 'where have you come from?'

'From Joe Harman,' she said. 'He's got Don Curtis up at the top end of Midhurst with a broken leg. Look, tell Moonshine what he can do with these horses, and then help me inside, and I'll tell you.'

He told Moonshine to take the horses round to the police corral and to bed down for the night with the police trackers in the bunkhouse; then he turned to Jean. 'Come on in the house,' he said. 'Here, take my arm. How far have you ridden?'

'Forty miles,' she said, and even in her fatigue there was a touch of pride in the achievement. 'Joe Harman's up there now with Mr Curtis. All the Midhurst stockmen have gone up there to make an airstrip. It's the only way to get him out, Joe says. You can't get through the creeks with a utility.'

He took her in and sat her down in his mosquito-wired veranda, and Mrs Haines brought out a cup of tea. He glanced at the clock and settled down to listen to her in slow time; he had missed the listening watch of seven o'clock on the Cairns Ambulance radio, and now there was three quarters of an hour to wait before he could take any action. 'Six miles west-south-west of the new bore,' he said thoughtfully. 'I know, there's open country round about that part. I'll get on to the radio presently, and get the plane out in the morning.'

'Joe thought if you got on the radio some ringers might go out from Windermere and help him make the strip,' she said. 'He's talking about cutting down some trees. I don't want him to do that, because of his back.'

He nodded. 'I'll be getting Windermere at the same time.' And then he said, 'I never knew you were a rider, Miss Paget.'

'I'm not,' she said. 'I've been on a horse six times before.'

He smiled, and then said, 'Oh my word. Are you sore?'

She got up wearily. 'I'm going home to bed,' she said, and caught hold of the back of the chair. 'If I stay here any longer I won't be able to walk at all.'

'Stay where you are,' he said. 'I'll get out the utility and run you to the hospital.'

'I don't want to go to the hospital.'

'I don't care if you want to go or not,' he said, 'but that's where you're going. You'll be better off there for tonight, and Sister Douglas, she's got everything you'll want.'

Half an hour later she was bathed and in a hospital bed with penicillin ointment on various parts of her anatomy, feeling like a very small child. Back in his office Sergeant Haines sat down before his transmitter.

'Eight Queen Charlie, Eight Queen Charlie,' he said, 'this is Eight Love Mike calling Eight Queen Charlie. Eight Queen Charlie, if you are receiving Eight Love Mike will you please come in. Over to you. Over.'

He turned his switch, and the speaker on top of the set said in a girl's voice, 'Eight Love Mike this is Eight Queen Charlie answering, receiving you strength three. Pass your message. Over.'

He said, 'Eight Queen Charlie, we've got Don Curtis. Joe Harman found him at the top end of Midhurst. His injuries are compound fracture of the left leg two and a half days old, probably left ankle broken in addition. Position of the camp is six miles west-south-west of Harman's new bore. Tell me now if this is Roger. Over.'

The girl's voice from the speaker said, 'Oh, I *am* glad—we've all been so worried this end. That is Roger, but I will repeat.' She repeated. 'Over to you. Over.'

He said, 'Okay, Jackie. Now take a message for Mr Barnes. Message reads, Request ambulance aircraft at Willstown soon as possible prepared for bush landing. Just read that back to me. Over.'

She read it back to him.

'Okay, Jackie,' he said. 'Now call Windermere for me and let me speak to them. Over.'

She said, 'Eight Able George, Eight Able George, this is Eight Queen Charlie calling Eight Able George. If you are receiving me, Eight Able George, please come in. Over to you. Over.'

A tremulous woman's voice said in thirty speakers in thirty homesteads, 'Eight Queen Charlie, this is Eight Able George. I've heard all that, Jackie.

Isn't it marvellous the way prayer gets answered? Oh my dear, I'm that relieved I don't know what to say. I'm sure we all ought to go down on our bended knees tonight and thank God for His mercy. I'm sure we all ought to do that. Oh–over.'

Miss Bacon turned her switch. 'I'm sure we'll all thank God tonight, Helen. Now Sergeant Haines is waiting to speak to you. You stay listening with your switch on to Receive, Helen. Eight Love Mike, will you come in now? Over.'

In Willstown Sergeant Haines said, 'Eight Love Mike calling Eight Able George. Mrs Curtis, you've heard Joe Harman's with your husband up at the top end of Midhurst. He's got to make an airstrip for the ambulance to land on, and he's taken all his stockmen up there. Will you send everyone you have upon your station to help make this airstrip? I'll give you the position. If you have a pencil and a bit of paper write this down.' He paused. 'The place where Joe Harman is making the strip is six miles west-south-west of his new bore. Six miles west-south-west of his new bore. I want you to send every man you've got there to help him, and pass that message to Constable Duncan if he's with you. Is that Roger, Mrs Curtis? Over.'

The tremulous voice said, 'That's Roger, Sergeant. Six miles west-south-west of Joe's new bore. I've got that written down. Eddie Page is here, and I'm expecting Phil Duncan to come back tonight. I'll send everybody up there. Isn't it marvellous what God can do for us? When I think of all His mercies to us suffering sinners I could go down on my bended knees and cry.' There was a pause, and then she said, 'Oh, I keep on forgetting. Over.'

He turned his switch and said, 'It's not only God you've got to thank, Mrs Curtis.' He was very well aware that most of the housewives in a hundred thousand square miles of the Gulf country would be listening in to this conversation, and one good turn deserves another. 'Miss Paget rode forty miles down from the top end of Midhurst to bring this message about Don. You know Jean Paget, the English girl that's started the shoe workshop and the ice-cream shop? She was out at Midhurst spending the day when we heard Don was missing, and she rode forty miles to tell me where this airstrip was to be. She's only been astride a horse six times before, and the poor girl's so sore she can't stand. Sister Douglas has her in the hospital for a good rest. She'll be all right in a day or two. Over.'

She said, 'Oh my word. I don't know what to say to thank her. Give her my very dearest love, and I do hope she'll be better soon.' There was a pause, and then she said, 'I've been so troubled in my mind about that ice-cream parlour. It didn't seem right to have a thing like that in Willstown, and opening it on Sundays and Christmas Day and all. I couldn't find nothing in the Bible either for or against it, and I've been that perplexed. But now it seems God had that under His hand like everything else. I do think it's wonderful. Over.'

'That's right,' said Sergeant Haines non-committally. He had been uncertain about the shop closing hours himself and had written to his head office for guidance; it was a good long time since he had been in a district where there was a shop to close. 'Now I must sign off, Mrs Curtis. Eight Queen Charlie, this is Eight Love Mike. It's okay here if you want to close down your listening watch for tonight, Jackie. I'd like to have a listening watch in daylight hours tomorrow, from seven o'clock on. Is this Roger? Over.'

Miss Bacon said, 'That is Roger, sergeant. I'll tell Mr Barnes. If you have nothing more for me, I shall close down. Over.'

'Nothing more, Jackie. Goodnight. Out.'

'Goodnight, Sergeant. Out.'

Miss Bacon switched off her sets thankfully. There was no proper organization for a twenty-four hour listening watch at the Cairns Ambulance; in an emergency such as this everybody had to muscle in and lend a hand. She had been on duty the previous day from eight in the morning till midnight, and from eight o'clock that morning till then; Mr Barnes had taken the night watch and was preparing to do so again. She thought, ruefully, that she had missed Humphrey Bogart and Lauren Bacall; the show would be half over. But there was still one more night, and with any luck this flap would be over and she could see it tomorrow. She went to telephone to Mr Barnes.

Mr Barnes telephoned to Mr Smythe of Australian National Airways, and Mr Smythe telephoned to his reserve pilot, Captain Jimmie Cope. Mr Cope said, 'Hell, I hope it's better in the morning than it was today. We'd never have got over the Tableland today. Better say take off at six, I suppose. I'll be along at the hangar then.'

When he got to the aerodrome at dawn the old Dragon, surely the best aircraft ever built for ambulance work in the outback, was running up both engines. The clouds hung low at about five hundred feet, shrouding the hill immediately behind the aerodrome; it was raining a little. Willstown lay about four hundred miles to the west-north-west; the first seventy miles of this course lay over the Atherton Tableland with mountains up to three thousand five hundred feet in height. With no radio navigational aids he would have to fly visually all the way, scraping along between the clouds and the treetops as best he could.

He said a sour word or two to the control officer and took off down the runway with an ambulance orderly on board. Once in the air it was worse than ever. He flew at three hundred feet up the Barron River towards the mountains, hoping to find a break in the low cloud that would enable him to get up on to the Tableland through the Kuranda Gap. The grey vapour closed around him and the sides of the jungle-covered gorge drew very near his wings. There was no sign of a break ahead. He edged over to the starboard side and made a tight, dicey turn round in the gorge with about a hundred feet to spare, and headed back for the coast. He lifted his microphone and said, 'Cairns Tower, this is Victor How Able Mike Baker. I can't make it by Kuranda. I'm going up to Cooktown by the coast, and try it from there. Tell Cooktown I'll be landing there in about an hour, and I'll want twenty gallons of seventy-three octane.'

He flew on up the tropical Queensland coast at about three hundred feet, and came to Cooktown an hour later. Cooktown is a pretty little town of about three hundred people, but it was grey and rainswept when he got there. He landed on the aerodrome and refuelled. 'I'm going to try and make Willstown from here,' he said. 'There's not much high stuff on the way. If it gets too bad I shall come back. I'll be on a direct course from here to Willstown.' He said that in case a search party should be necessary.

He took off again immediately the refuelling was finished and flew inland on a compass course. In the whole of that flight he was never more than two hundred feet above the treetops. He scraped over the Great Dividing Range, petering out up in this northern latitude, with about fifty feet to spare, always on the point of turning back, always seeing a faint break ahead that made it necessary to go on. Behind him the orderly sat gripping his seat, only too well aware of danger in the flight and impotent to do anything about it. For three hours they flew like that, and then as they neared the Gulf of Carpentaria the pilot started picking up the landmarks that he knew, a river bend, a burnt patch of the bush, a curving sandy waste like a banana. He came to Willstown and flew round the few houses at a hundred feet to tell them he was there, and landed on the airstrip. He taxied in to where the truck was standing waiting for him; he was strained and tired. It was still raining.

He held a little conference with Sergeant Haines and Sister Douglas and Al Burns beside the truck. 'I'll have a crack at flying him back here,' he said. 'If it's no better this afternoon he'll have to spend the night in hospital here. I can't fly him to Cairns in this weather. It'll probably be better by tomorrow.' They gave him a freehand pencil map which the sergeant had prepared for him, showing him the creeks and Midhurst homestead, and the new bore, and the probable position of the airstrip, and he took off again. That was at about eleven o'clock.

Following this map he found the place without much difficulty. It was clear where they meant him to land, because trees had been felled upon a line he was to come in on, and bushes had been cleared for a short distance on what seemed to be a grassy meadow. He could see about ten men working or standing looking up at him; he could see a utility parked with a tent over it. He circled round under the low cloud, considering the risks. The runway that they had prepared was pitifully short, even for a Dragon. Time was also short, however; the man had had his compound fracture three days now. Sepsis and gangrene and all sorts of things would be setting in; he must not delay. He bit his lip and lined the Dragon up with the runway for a trial approach.

He came in as slowly as he dared over the trees, missing them by no more than five feet, motoring in with careful graduations of the throttles. Over the cut trees he throttled back and stuffed her down towards the grass, hoping it was smooth. He could . . . he couldn't, he could never stop her in time. With wheels no more than two feet from the ground he jammed the throttles forward, held her level for a moment, and climbed away.

He turned to the orderly behind him as he circled low under the clouds, keeping the airstrip in sight. 'Got a pencil and paper? Write this.' He thought for a moment. 'Sorry I can't make it. Strip must be about a hundred yards longer, or a hundred and fifty if you can manage it. I will come back at four o'clock this afternoon.' They put this in a message bag with coloured streamers flying from it, and flew over, and dropped it on the middle of the strip.

Back at Willstown airfield he told them what had happened. 'They've not had time to make it long enough,' the sergeant said. 'You'll find it'll be all right this afternoon.' He drove the pilot in to the hotel and Al Burns took him to the bar, but the pilot would drink nothing but lemonade till the difficult flying of the afternoon was over.

He lunched at the hotel and strolled into the ice-cream parlour after lunch. It was new since he had last been in Willstown, and he stared around him with amused wonder. He ordered an ice; Rose Sawyer told him briskly to be quick and eat it, because she was shutting up. He asked if she closed every afternoon and was told that she was going up to see Miss Paget at the hospital. Then, of course, he heard all about her ride.

At four o'clock he was back over the airstrip at the top end of Midhurst; the rain had stopped and he was able to approach at about eight hundred feet. He circled once and had a good look; they had made the strip much longer and he would have no difficulty now. He came in and touched down at the near end; the Dragon bounced on the uneven ground and landed again, and rolled bumping and swaying to a standstill.

He stopped the engines and got out; they took a stretcher from the cabin and the orderly began the business of getting Don Curtis on to the stretcher and into the cabin, helped by the ringers. The pilot lit a cigarette and gave one to Joe Harman.

Joe asked, 'Did you hear anything about Miss Paget, down in Willstown?'

The pilot said, 'She's in the hospital. Nothing much wrong, they say, just tired and sore. She must be quite a girl.'

Joe said, 'Too right. If you see anyone from the hospital, leave a message for Miss Paget, will you? Tell her I'll be in town tomorrow afternoon.'

'I'll do that,' said the pilot. 'I'll be staying there tonight. It's too late now to get to Cairns; I can't do night flying in this weather, not in this thing.'

The loading was completed now. He got into his seat; the orderly swung the propellers and they taxied back to the far end of the track. It was short, but he could make it. He opened out and took off down the runway, and cleared the trees at the far end with about fifteen feet to spare. Half an hour later he was on the ground at Willstown, helping to transfer the stretcher to the truck that was to take Don Curtis to the hospital.

In hospital that afternoon Jean Paget showed Rose Sawyer the more accessible of her wounds, great chafed raw places six inches long. 'Honourable scars,' Rose said. 'Pity you can't show them.'

'It's because everything was so wet,' Jean said. 'But I'm going to have a proper pair of riding breeches made, I think. Ringers' strides are for ringers' skins.'

'I'd never want to get up on a horse again if it'd done that to me.'

'It's going to be some time before I can,' said Jean.

Presently Rose said, 'Tell me, Jean. Do you think there'd be any work up here for a contractor?'

Jean stared at her. 'What sort of a contractor?'

'Making roads and things like that. Buildings, too.'

'Is this Billy Wakeling, from Alice?'

Rose nodded. 'He wrote me,' she said carelessly. For the bunch of seven letters that arrived by the Dakota regularly every Wednesday, this seemed to Jean to be an understatement. 'You know, his father's a contractor in Newcastle–he's got graders and bulldozers and steam shovels and all sorts of things like that. He started Billy off in Alice after the war because he said Alice was expanding and expanding places meant work for contractors. But Billy says he's fed up with Alice.'

'He's coming up here for a visit as soon as the wet's over,' she added artlessly.

'He won't get any roads or buildings to contract for here,' Jean observed. 'There's nobody to pay for them. I know what does want doing though. Joe Harman wants some little dams built up on Midhurst. I don't know if that's in his line.'

'I should think it might be,' said Rose slowly. 'After all, it's shifting muck, and that's what Billy does. He'd do it with a bulldozer in the dry, wouldn't he?'

'I haven't the least idea,' said Jean. 'Can he get hold of a bulldozer?'

'His old man's got about forty down at Newcastle,' Rose said. 'I should think he could spare one for Billy.'

'They're only little dams,' said Jean.

'Well, everything's got to start. I don't think Billy expects a contract like the Sydney Harbour Bridge, not in the first year.'

Jean asked, 'Could you scoop out a hole for a swimming-pool with a bulldozer?'

'I should think so. Yes, I'm sure you could. I went out with him once and watched one working. He let me drive it; it was awful fun. You'd scoop it out first with a bulldozer and then you'd put up wooden stuff that they call shuttering and make the concrete sides.'

'Could he do all that, too?'

'Oh, Billy can do that. Why, do you want a swimming-pool?'

Jean stared at the white painted wall. 'It was just an idea. A nice, big pool just by the bore, with diving-boards and everything, big enough for everybody to get into and have fun. You see, you've got the water there, right in the main street. You'd have a wooden thing they call a cooling tower and run the water through that to cool it off before it went into the pool. Have a lawn of grass by it, where people could lie and sunbathe if they want to. An old man taking the cash at the gate, a bob a bathe. . . .'

Rose stared at her. 'You've got it all worked out. Are you thinking of doing that, Jean?'

'I don't know. It would be fun to have it, and I believe it'ld pay like anything. Mixed bathing, of course.'

Rose laughed. 'Have all the wowsers in the place looking over the rails to see what was going on.'

'Charge them sixpence for that,' said Jean. She turned to Rose. 'Ask Billy to get hold of plans and things,' she said, 'and tell us what it would cost when he comes up after the wet. I don't believe that there's a swimming-pool in the whole Gulf country. It would be fun to have one.'

'I'll ask him. Anything else?'

Jean stretched in her bed. 'A nice hairdressing saloon and beauty parlour,' she said, 'with a pretty French brunette in it who really knew her stuff, and could make one look like Rita Hayworth. That's what I want, sometimes. But I don't think that's in Billy's line.'

'It had better not be,' said Rose.

Jean got up next day and left the hospital, and walked awkwardly to the workshop. There was an airmail letter from Mr Pack about the air freight consignment of shoes that he had received from them. His enthusiasm was temperate; he pointed out a number of defects and crudities which would require correction in production batches; most of these they were aware of and had attended to. He finished up by saying he would try and shift them, which, knowing Mr Pack, Jean and Aggie Topp interpreted as praise.

'He'll like the next lot better,' Aggie said. And then she said, 'I had two girls come along for jobs while you were away. One was Fred Dawson's daughter; he's the chief stockman or something on a station called Carlisle. She's fifteen; her mother brought her in. She's a bit young, but she'd be all right. The other was a girl of nineteen who's been working in the store at Normanton. I didn't like her so much.'

'I don't want to take on anyone else until that first batch of shoes have been sold,' said Jean. 'If Mrs Dawson comes in again, tell her that we'll let her know about the kid after the wet. I'd like to have her if I can. I don't think we want the other one, do we?'

'I don't think so. Bit of a slut, she was.'

They talked about the details of the business for an hour. 'We haven't got the overalls back yet,' said Aggie. 'I went and saw Mrs Harrison, but her back's bad again. We'll have to find someone else.' They issued the girls with a clean overall each week to work in, and the washing of these overalls was something of a problem to them.

'What we want,' said Jean, 'is one of those Home Laundry things, and do them ourselves. We could run it off the generating set. . . . Of course, it needs hot water.' She thought for a minute. 'Think about that one,' she said. 'Hire it out, do people's washing for them. Anyway, see if you can find another Mrs Harrison for the time being.'

Aggie said, 'Everybody's talking about your ride, Miss Paget.'

'Are they?'

She nodded. 'Even that girl from Normanton, she knew about it, too.'

'How on earth did she get to hear?'

'It's these little wireless sets they have up on the cattle stations,' Aggie said. 'The boys here were telling me, they all listen in to what everybody else is saying–telegrams and everything. They've got nothing else to do. You can't keep anything secret in this country.' And then she said, 'I heard the aeroplane go off this morning. Was the man very bad?'

'Not too good,' said Jean. 'Sister thinks they'll be able to save the leg. We ought to have a doctor here, of course.'

'There's not enough work to keep a doctor occupied in a place like this,' said Aggie. 'Where did they fly him to?'

'Cairns. There's a good hospital in Cairns.' She turned to the door, and paused. 'Aggie,' she said, 'how do you think a swimming-pool would go in Willstown? Would people use it?'

Joe Harman rode into the town that afternoon with Pete Fletcher. He put his horse into the stable behind the Australian Hotel and came to find Jean; he was wet and dirty in his riding clothes because the creeks were up, and though he had started spick and span from Midhurst as befits a man going in to town to see his girl, he had had to swim one of the two creeks on the way holding to the mane and saddle of his horse, which had rather spoilt the sartorial effect. He was half dry when he got to Willstown; he combed his hair and emptied out his boots, and went to the ice-cream parlour to ask Rose where Jean was.

He found her in her bedroom, writing a long letter to me. He tapped on the door and she came out to him. 'We can't talk here, Joe. I'll never hear the last of it if you come in. Let's go and have an ice-cream in the parlour.' It was borne in on her that this was literally the only place in Willstown where young men and young women could meet reputably to talk; the alternative, in the wet, would be to go into the stable or a barn. They picked a table by the wall; she looked around her at the rectangular walls and the adjacent tables with discontent. 'This won't do at all,' she said. 'I'll have some sort of booths made, little corners where people can talk privately.'

'What'll you have?' he asked.

'I'll have a banana split,' she said. 'I want feeding up. I don't know if you know it, but I've been very ill. Don't pay, Joe–have it on the house.'

He grinned. 'Think I'm the kind of man to take a girl out and let her shout?'

'If you're feeling like that, I'll have two. The bananas will be going bad by tomorrow.' She was getting fruit flown in by the Dakota every Wednesday, and she had little difficulty in selling the small quantities she got at prices that would pay for the air freight. Her trouble was that usually she could not keep it for a week.

He came back with the ices and sat down with her. 'Now Joe,' she said, 'what about that poddy corral?'

He grinned sheepishly, and looked over his shoulder. 'That's crook,' he said. 'There's no poddy corral on Midhurst.'

'There's something damn like one,' she said, laughing. 'Come clean, Joe. What happened to Don Curtis, anyway?'

'He was moseying about on my land where he hadn't got no right to be,' Joe said carefully. 'He found that corral where I'd got some poddys—my own poddys, mind you. I'd put 'em in there to consider things a bit, because they'd been wandering. Well, Don went to steal them off me, and he took down the top bar, but they were pretty wild, those poddys were; they hadn't had no water for about four days except the rain. Far as I can make out they pushed the second bar out on top of him when he went to loose it, and knocked him over on his back with the pole on top, and then they all ran over him and bust his leg. They ran out on the horse, too; Don had hitched his horse by the rein to something or other, and these poddys, they come charging down on to the horse and he bust the rein and he went too. So there Don was, and serve him bloody well right for going where he hadn't got no business to be.'

'Whose poddys were they, really, Joe?'

'Mine,' he replied firmly.

She smiled. 'Where had they been wandering?'

He grinned. 'Windermere. But they were my poddys. He pinched 'em off me. You heard me telling Pete he's got a poddy corral there.'

'Were these poddys that you had in your corral the same ones that you let out of his corral?' she asked. It seemed to be getting just a little bit involved.

'Most of 'em,' he said. 'There might have been one or two with them that we picked up as damages, you might say.' He paused. 'Things get a bit mixed up sometimes,' he observed.

'Where are the poddys now?' she asked. 'The ones that Don let out?'

'They'll be on Midhurst,' he said. 'They'll be somewhere round about the bore, I'd say. They won't stir from the first water that they find, not even in the wet.'

She ate a little of her banana split in silence. Then she said, 'Well, anyway, you're not to go after any of his poddys while he's in hospital, Joe. That's not fair. He'll come out of hospital and find there's not a poddy left.'

'I wouldn't do a thing like that.'

'I bet you would. I don't know how this game is played, Joe, but I'm quite sure that's against the rules.'

He grinned. 'All right. But he'll be after mine as soon as he gets back. That's sure as anything.'

'Why can't you let each other's poddys alone?'

'I'll let his alone, but he won't let mine alone. You see,' he said simply. 'I got about fifty more of his last year than he got of mine.'

This conversation, Jean felt, was not getting them anywhere; where poddys were concerned Joe's moral standards seemed to be extremely low. She changed the subject, and said, 'Joe, about those little dams you were talking about on Green Island. Have you got anyone to build them for you yet?'

He shook his head. 'It's no good thinking about those until the dry.'

'Could a bulldozer build them?'

'Oh my word,' he said. 'If anybody had a bulldozer he'd build the lot inside a month. But there's no bulldozer this side of the Curry.'

'There might be one,' she said. She told him about Rose Sawyer and Billy Wakeling. 'He's coming up to see her anyway,' she said, 'and she says he's looking for that sort of work to do up here. I suppose he's turning into Rose's steady. You'd better take him out to Midhurst when he comes, and have a talk to him.'

'My word,' he said. 'If we had a joker with a bulldozer in Willstown it'ld make a lot of difference to the stations.'

'It'ld make a lot of difference here in Willstown,' she observed. 'Joe, if we had a really decent swimming-pool just by the bore, with little cabins to change in and green lawns to sunbathe on, and diving-boards, and an old man in charge to mow the grass and keep it clean and nice—would people use it, Joe? If we charged, say, a bob a bathe?'

They discussed the swimming-pool for some time, and came to the conclusion that it could never pay upon the basis of a town with a hundred and fifty people. 'It's just a question of how fast this town is going to grow,' he said. 'A swimming-pool is just another thing to make it grow. There's not a town in the whole Gulf country that's got a pool.'

'The ice-cream parlour's paying, definitely,' Jean said. 'If we can keep up the quality, I feel we're home on that one. I'd like to try the swimming-pool next, I think, if I can get the money for it out of Noel Strachan.'

He smiled in curious wonder. 'What comes after the swimming-pool?'

She stared out at the wet, miry expanse of earth that was the street. 'They'll get their hair wet in the swimming-pool, so we'll have to have a beauty parlour,' she said. 'I think that's the next thing. And after that, an open-air cinema. And after that, a battery of Home Laundries for the wet wash, and after that a decent dress shop.' She turned to him. 'Don't laugh, Joe. I know it sounds crackers, but just look at the results. I start an ice-cream parlour and put Rose in it, and young Wakeling comes after her with a bulldozer, so you get your dams built.'

'You're a bit ahead of the game,' he said. 'They aren't built yet.'

'They will be soon.'

He glanced around the ice-cream parlour. 'If everything you want to do works out like this,' he said slowly, 'you'll have a town as good as Alice Springs in no time.'

'That's what I want to have,' she said. 'A town like Alice.'

I I

All that happened nearly three years ago.

I cannot deny that in that time her letters have been a great interest to me, perhaps the greatest interest in my rather barren life. I think that after the affair of Mr Curtis and the poddy dodging she became more closely integrated into the life of the Gulf country than she had been before, because even before her marriage there was a subtle change in her letters. She ceased to write as an Englishwoman living in a strange, hard, foreign land; she gradually began to write about the people as if she was one of them, about the place as if it was her place. That may be merely my fancy, of course, or it may be that I made such a study of her letters, reading and re-reading them and filing them carefully away in a special set of folders that I keep in my flat, that I found subtleties of meaning in them that a more casual reader would not have noticed.

She married Joe Harman in April after the mustering, as she had promised him. They were married by a travelling Church of England priest, one of the Bush Brothers who had been, queerly enough, a curate at St John's in Kingston-on-Thames, not ten miles from where I used to live in Wimbledon. There was, of course, no church in Willstown at that time though one is to be built next year; they were married in the Shire Hall, and all the countryside came to the wedding. They had their honeymoon, or part of it, on Green Island, and I suppose she took her sarong with her, though she did not tell me that.

In the first two years of her married life she made considerable inroads into her capital. She was very good about it; she always started off one thing and got it trading smoothly before starting on another, after the first effort when she started both the ice-cream parlour and the workshop together. She used to send me accounts of her ventures, too, prepared for her by a young man called Len James who worked in the bank. But all the same, she asked me for three or four thousand pounds every six months or so, till by the time her second son was born, the one that she called Noel after me, she had had over eighteen thousand pounds for her various local businesses. Although they all seemed to be making profits Lester and I were growing, by that time, a little concerned about our duty as trustees, broad though our terms of reference under the Macfadden will might be. Our duty was to keep her capital intact and hand it over to her when she was thirty-five, and I began to worry sometimes about the chances of a slump or some unknown disaster in Australia which would extinguish the thirty per cent of her inheritance that we had let her have. Too many eggs seemed to be going into one basket, and her investments, laudable though they might be, could hardly be classed as trustee stocks.

The climax came in February, when she wrote me a long letter from the hospital at Willstown, soon after she had given birth to Noel. She asked me if I would be one of his god-fathers, and of course that pleased me very much although there was very little prospect that I should live long enough to discharge my duties by him. Wakeling was to be the second godfather, and as he had married Rose Sawyer about six months previously and seemed to be settled in the district I felt that she would not be injuring her child by giving him an elderly godfather who lived on the other side of the world. I made a corresponding alteration to my will immediately, of course.

She went on in the same letter to discuss affairs at Midhurst. 'You know, Joe's only manager at present,' she wrote. 'He's done awfully well; there were about eight thousand head of cattle on the place when he went there, but now there are twelve or thirteen thousand. We shall be selling over two thousand head this year, too many to send down to Julia in one herd, so Joe's got to make two trips. It looks as if there'll be a steady increase for the next few years, because each year in the dry Bill Wakeling builds a couple more dams for us so we get more and more feed each year.'

She went on to tell me about Mrs Spears, the owner. 'She left the Gulf country after her husband died about ten years ago,' she said. 'and now she lives in Brisbane. Joe and I went down and stayed a couple of nights with her last October; I didn't tell you about it then because I wanted to think it over and we had to find out if we could get a loan, too.'

She told me that Mrs Spears was getting very old, and she wanted to realize a part of the considerable capital that she had locked up in Midhurst; probably she wanted to give it away during her lifetime to avoid death duties. 'She asked if we could buy a half share in the station,' she said. 'She would give us an option to buy the other half at a valuation at the time of her death, whenever that might be. It means finding about thirty thousand pounds; that's about the value of half the stock. The land is rented from the State, of course, and there's seventeen years to go upon the present lease; it means an alteration to the lease to put Joe's name into it jointly with hers.'

She told me that they had been to the bank. The bank would advance two-thirds of the thirty thousand pounds that they would have to find. 'They sent an inspector up who knows the cattle business, and he came out to Midhurst,' she wrote. 'Joe's got a good name in the Gulf country and I think he thought that we were doing all right with the property. That leaves us with ten thousand pounds to find in cash, and that's what I wanted to ask you about.'

She digressed a little. 'Midhurst's a good station,' she said, 'and we're very happy here. If we can't take it over Mrs Spears will probably sell it, and we'd have to go somewhere else and start again. I'd hate to do that and it would be a great disappointment to Joe after all the work he's put into Midhurst. I'd be miserable leaving Willstown now, because it's turning into quite a fair-sized place, and it's a happy little town to live in, too. I do want to stay here if we can.'

She went on, 'I know a cattle station isn't a trustee investment, Noel, any more than any of the other things you've let me put my money into. Will you think it over, and tell me if we can have it? If we can't, I'll have to think again; perhaps I could sell or mortgage some of the businesses I've started since I got here. I should hate to do that, because they might get into bad hands and go downhill. This town's like a young baby—I know something about those, Noel! It needs nursing all the time, till it's a bit bigger.'

Another ten thousand pounds, of course, would mean that we should have allowed her to invest half of her inheritance in highly speculative businesses in one district, which was by no means the intention of Mr Macfadden when he made his will. Legally, of course, we were probably safe from any action for a breach of trust by reason of the broad wording of the discretionary clause that I had slipped into the will. I spent a day or two thinking about this before I showed her letter to Lester, and it came to me in the end that our duty was to do what Mr Macfadden would himself have done in similar circumstances.

What would that queer recluse in Ayr have done if he had had to settle this point? He was an invalid, of course, but I did not think he was an unkind or an unreasonable man. He had not made that long trust because he distrusted Jean Paget; he did not even know her. He had made it for her good, because he thought that an unmarried girl in her twenties who was mistress of a large sum of money would be liable to be imposed upon. In that he may well have been right. But Jean Paget was a married woman of thirty with two children now, and married to a sensible and steady sort of man, whatever his ideas on poddy-dodging might be. Would Mr Macfadden, in these circumstances, still have insisted on the trust being maintained in its original form?

I thought not. He was a kindly man–I felt sure of that–and he would have wanted her to have her Midhurst station, since that was where her home and all her present interests were. He was a careful, Scottish man, however; I thought he would have turned his mind more to the details of her investment in Midhurst to ensure that she got good value for this ten thousand pounds. Looking at it from this point of view I was disturbed at the short tenure of the lease. Seventeen years was a short time for Joe Harman to regain the value of the dams that he was building on the property and all the other improvements that he was making; he could not possibly go on with capital improvements until a very much longer lease had been negotiated.

I showed her letter to my partner then, and we had a long talk about it. He took the same view that I did, that the lease was the kernel of the matter. 'I can't say that I take a very serious view of this trust, Noel,' he said. 'I think your approach is the right one, to try and put yourself in the testator's shoes when looking at this thing. He was quite content to leave the money to his sister without any question of a trust, while her husband was alive to help her. It was only after the husband's death that he wanted the trust. Well, now the daughter's got a husband to help her. If he was disposing of his money now, presumably he wouldn't bother about any trust at all.'

'That's a point,' I said. 'I hadn't thought of that one.'

'I don't suggest we disregard the trust,' he said. 'I think we ought to use it as a lever to get this lease put right for her. Tell all and sundry that we won't release her money till the leasehold is adjusted to our satisfaction. Then, so far as I'm concerned, she can have all she wants.'

I smiled. 'I wouldn't tell *her* that.'

I sat down next day and drafted a letter to her in reply. 'I do not think it is impossible to release a further ten thousand pounds,' I wrote, 'but I should be very sorry to do so until this matter of the lease had been adjusted to our satisfaction. As the thing stands at the moment, you could lose your home in seventeen years' time and lose with it all the money that you and Mrs Spears have expended on improvements such as dams and other water conservation schemes, which would pass to the State without any payment whatsoever, so far as my present information goes.' I learned later that that was incorrect.

I came to the main point of my letter next. 'No doubt you have a solicitor that you can trust, but if it would assist you I would very gladly come and visit you in Queensland for a few weeks and see this matter of the lease put into satisfactory order before you invest this money in Midhurst. It is many years since I left England and I have regretted that; I cannot expect to have many more years left in which to travel and see the world. I would like to take a long holiday and travel a little before I get too feeble, and if I could help you in this matter of the lease I should be only too glad to come and do so.' I added, 'I need hardly say that I should travel at my own expense.'

The answer came in a night letter telegram about ten days later. She urged me to come to them, and suggested that I should come out by air about the end of April, since their winter was approaching then and the weather would be just like an English summer. She said that she was writing with a list of clothes that I should have and medicines and things that I might need upon the journey. I was a little touched by that.

I saw Kennedy, my doctor, at his place in Wimpole Street next day. 'Is there any particular reason why I shouldn't fly out to Queensland?' I asked.

He looked at me quizzically. 'It's not exactly what I should advise for you, you know. Have you got to go to Queensland?'

'I want to go, very much,' I said. 'I want to go and stay out there about a month. There's business I should like to see to personally.'

'How have you been walking recently?'

There was no point in lying to him. 'I walk as far as Trafalgar Square most mornings,' I said. 'I take a taxi from there.'

'You can't quite manage the whole distance to your office?'

'No,' I said. 'I haven't done that for some time.'

'Can you walk upstairs in your club, to the first floor, without stopping?'

I shook my head. 'I always go up in the lift. But anyway, there aren't any stairs in Queensland. All the houses are bungalows.'

He smiled. 'Take off your coat and your shirt, and let me have a look at you.'

When he had finished his examination, he said, 'Well. Are you proposing to go alone?'

I nodded. 'I shall be staying with friends at the other end. They'll meet me when I get off the aeroplane.'

'And you really feel it's necessary that you should go?'

I met his eyes. 'I want to go, very much indeed.'

'All right,' he said. 'You know your condition as well as I do. There's nothing new – only the deterioration that you've got to expect. You put ten years on your age during the war. I think, on the whole, you're wise to travel by air. I think you'd find the Red Sea very trying.' He went on to tell me what I could do and what I mustn't attempt, all the old precautions that he had told me before.

I went back to my office and saw Lester, and told him what I was proposing to do. 'I'm going to take about three months holiday,' I said, 'starting at the end of April. I'm going out by air, and I don't know quite how long I shall stay for. If I find air travel too tiring on the way out, I may come home by sea.' I paused. 'In any case, you'll have to work on the assumption that I shall be away for some considerable time. It's probably about time you started to do that, in any case.'

'You really feel that it is necessary for you to go personally, yourself?' he asked.

'I do.'

'All right, Noel. I only wish you hadn't got to put so much of your energy into this. After all, it's a fairly trivial affair.'

'I can't agree with that,' I said. 'I'm beginning to think that this thing is the most important business that I ever handled in my life.'

I left London one Monday morning, and travelled through to Sydney on the same airliner, arriving late on Wednesday night. We stopped for an hour or so at Cairo and Karachi and Calcutta and Singapore and Darwin. I must say the aeroplane was very comfortable and the stewardess was most kind and attentive; it was fatiguing, of course, sleeping two nights in a reclining chair and I was glad when it was over. I stayed two nights in Sydney to rest, and took a little drive around in a hired car during the afternoon. Next day I took the aeroplane to Cairns. It was a lovely flight, especially along the coast of Queensland, after Brisbane. The very last part, up the Hinchinbrook Channel between Cairns and Townsville, must be one of the most beautiful coastlines in the world.

We landed at Cairns in the evening, and here I had a great surprise, because Joe Harman met me at the aerodrome. The Dakota, he told me, now ran twice a week to the Gulf country, partly on account of the growth of Willstown, and he had come in on the Friday plane to take me out on Monday. 'I got one or two little bits of things to order and to see to,' he said. 'My solicitor, Ben Hope, he's here in Cairns too. I thought that over the weekend you might like to hear the general set-up of Midhurst, 'n have a talk with him.'

I had not heard the slow Queensland speech since he had come to me in Chancery Lane, over three years before. He took me in a car to the hotel, a queer, rambling building rather beautifully situated, with a huge bar that seemed to be the focal point. We got there just before tea, the evening meal, and went in almost at once and sat down together. He asked me if I would drink tea or beer or plonk.

'Plonk?' I asked.

'Red wine,' he said. 'I don't go much for it myself, but jokers who know about wine, they say it's all right.'

They had a wine list, and I chose a Hunter River wine which I must say I found to be quite palatable. 'Jean was very sorry she couldn't come and meet you,' he said. 'We could have parked Joe with someone, but she's feeding Noel, so that ties her. She's going to drive into Willstown and meet the Dakota on Monday.'

'How is she?' I asked.

'She's fine,' he said. 'Having babies seems to suit her. She's looking prettier than ever.'

We settled down after tea on the veranda outside my bedroom, and began discussing the business of Midhurst. He had brought with him copies of the accounts for the station for the last three years, neatly typed and very easily intelligible. I commented upon their form, and he said, 'I'm not much of a hand at this sort of thing. Jean did these before she went into the hospital. She does most of the accounts for me. I tell her what I want to do out on the station, and she tells me how much money I've got left to spend. She's got the schooling for the two of us.'

Nevertheless, I found him quite a shrewd man, very well able to appreciate the somewhat intricate points that came up about the lease and his capital improvements. We talked for a couple of hours that night about his station and about the various businesses that Jean had started in the town. He was very interesting about those.

'She's got twenty-two girls working in the workshop,' he said. 'Shoes and attaché cases and ladies bags. That's the one that isn't doing quite so well as the others.' He turned the pages of the accounts to show me. 'It's making a profit now, but last year there was a loss of over two hundred pounds–two hundred and twenty-seven. But all the others–oh my word.' He showed me the figures for the ice-cream parlour, the beauty parlour, the swimming-pool, the cinema, the laundry, and the dress shop. 'They're doing fine. The fruit and vegetable shop, that's all right, too.' We totted up the figures and found that the seven of them together had made a clear profit of two thousand six hundred and seventy-three pounds in the previous year. 'It'ld pay her to run the workshop at a loss,' he said. 'She gets it back out of what the girls spend to make themselves look pretty for the ringers, and what the ringers spend in taking out the girls.'

I was a little troubled about the workshop. 'Can she expand it?' I asked. 'Can she lower the overhead by doing a bigger business?'

He was doubtful about that. 'She's using just about all the alligator skins Jeff Pocock and two others can bring in,' he said. 'Wallabies, they're getting scarcer than they were, too. I don't think she can get much bigger in the workshop. She doesn't want to, either. She's got a kind of hunch that in a few years' time the workshop won't be necessary at all, that the town will be so big that a workshop employing twenty girls won't be neither here nor there.'

'I see,' I said thoughtfully. 'How big is the town now?'

'There's about four hundred and fifty people living in Willstown,' he said. 'That's not counting boongs, and not counting people living out upon the stations. The population's trebled in the last three years.'

'Is that just because of the workshop?' I asked.

He said slowly, 'I think it must be—everything comes back to that, when you look at it. It's not only the workshop, you see. She's got two girls employed in the ice-cream parlour, and one lubra. Two in the beauty parlour, three in the dress shop, two in the fruit shop, three in the cinema. She employs quite a lot of people.'

I was puzzled. 'But can twenty girls in the workshop provide work for all these other girls?' I asked.

'It doesn't seem to work that way,' he said. 'We were totting it up the other day. She's never employed more than about thirty-five girls at any one time, but since she started there's been forty-two girls married out of her businesses. They mostly marry ringers. Well, that's forty-two families starting, forty-two women wanting cinema and beauty parlour and fresh vegetables and that, besides the thirty-five girls that she's still got employed. It kind of snowballs.' He paused. 'Take the bank. There's two girl clerks there that there never were before, because of the bigger business. The A.M.P. have started up an office, and there's a girl in that. Bill Wakeling's got a girl in his office.' He turned to me. 'It's a fact, there's something like a hundred girls and married women under twenty-five in Willstown now,' he said. 'When Jean came, there was two.'

'And the babies!' he said. 'There's more babies than you could shake a stick at. They've had to send a special maternity nurse to the hospital. That's another girl. She got engaged to Phil Duncan, the copper, last month, so there'll be another one.'

I smiled. 'Are there enough men to go round?'

'Oh my word,' he said. 'There's no difficulty in getting men to work in Willstown. I've had ringers coming from all over Queensland, from the Northern Territory, too, wanting a job round about Willstown. There was one chap came all the way from Marble Bar in Western Australia, two thousand miles or so. The labour situation's very different now from what it was three years ago.'

I went to bed early that night with plenty to think about. We had a conference next morning with Mr Hope, the solicitor, in his office, and wrote a letter to the Queensland Land Administration Board suggesting a meeting to discuss the lease of Midhurst. That afternoon we spent in driving around Cairns to see the sights; it seemed to me to be a pleasant little tropical town, beautifully situated. On Sunday we drove up on to the Atherton Tableland, high rolling downs farmed somewhat on the English style.

We flew to Willstown on Monday morning, in a Dakota. We landed at places called Georgetown and Croydon on the way and stayed on each aerodrome for about twenty minutes, picking up and setting down passengers and freight, as we circled Georgetown for the landing I was able to study the place. It was pathetic in a way, for you could see from the air the rectangular pattern of wide streets that once had been busy and lined with houses, now rutted with the rain and grass-grown. A few scattered houses stood at the intersections of what had once been these streets, and they were clustered rather more thickly around the hotel, the only two-storeyed building in either place. Both of these were derelict gold towns.

The people who came to meet the aeroplane in trucks were bronzed, healthy, and humorous; the men were mostly great big tanned, competent people; the women candid, uncomplaining housewives.

I sat at the window studying Croydon as we took off, till it fell away from view behind us. 'I'm kind of glad that you've seen those,' said Joe beside me. 'Willstown was like that, only a bit worse. It's no great shakes yet, of course, but it's better than Croydon, oh my word it is.'

We circled Willstown as we came in to land. It stood by quite a large river, and it was queerly like the other two towns in its layout. There were the same wide streets arranged in rectangular pattern, but the pattern was filling up with houses here. From the air the glint of the sun upon new corrugated iron roofs was everywhere, so that at one point as we circled opposite the sun I had to shut my eyes against the dazzle. All these houses seemed to be new, and a considerable number were still in the process of building. In the main street opposite the two-storeyed building that I guessed to be the hotel, a line of shrubs had been planted in a formal garden down the middle of the road, transforming the wide cattle-rack into two carriageways, and tarmac pavements had been made in this part of the town. Opposite the hotel I could see the swimming-pool with diving-boards and cabins and a lawn beside it, just as Jean had described it to me in her letters. Then the town was lost to view, and we were landing, coming in over à brand-new racetrack.

She was there to meet me in her Ford utility, her own car that she had bought for running in and out of town to see to her businesses. She was more mature now than I had remembered her; she had grown into a very lovely woman. She said, 'Oh Noel, it *is* nice to see you. Are you very tired?'

'I'm not tired,' I said. 'Three or four years older, perhaps. You're looking very well.'

'I am well,' she said. 'Disgustingly well. Noel, it was good of you to offer to come out like this. I wanted to ask you to, and then it seemed too much to ask. It's such a very long way. Come and sit in the utility. Joe's just getting your bags.'

They drove me out immediately to Midhurst. We passed through the main street of Willstown and I wanted to stop and see what she had done, but they would not let me. 'Time enough for that tomorrow or the next day,' she said. 'We'll go to Midhurst now, and you can rest a bit.'

I knew the sort of scenery that I should see upon the way to Midhurst from many readings of her letters, and it was just as I had expected it to be. There was no road in the usually accepted sense; she picked her way across country in the car following the general line of the tracks but avoiding the deep holes.

When we came to the first creek, however, I was interested to see that they had made a sort of concrete bottom or causeway across the river bed, and this causeway was marked by two massive wooden posts upon the bank at either end. 'We haven't got as far as having bridges yet,' she said. 'But this thing is a god-send in the wet, to know that you won't hit a boulder under water.'

The homestead was very much as I had expected it to be, but there was a garden now in front of it, bright with flowers, and there were great ranges of log stockades or cattle pens that I had not heard about. 'They've gone up in the last two years,' Joe said. 'We've got three Zebu bulls now, and you want more stockyards when you start breeding.' His Zebu bulls were a cross between Indian cattle and English Herefords. He told me that he was keeping a small herd of dairy cows, too, and that meant more enclosures still.

'How many hands have you got now?' I asked.

'Eleven white stockmen,' he said, 'and ten boongs. It's almost easier to get white than black in this part of the country.'

They would not let me walk that day, but put me in a long chair in the veranda with a cool drink, and I sat watching all the work of the station as it went on in the yard below. It was fascinating to sit there and watch it all, the white stockmen and the black stockmen, the cattle, the dogs, and the horses, and a half grown wallaby lolloping about with puppies teasing it by playing with its tail. I could have sat there indefinitely watching it all, and watching the grace of Jean moving round the house attending to her children and her Abo women. I did sit there for three days.

She took me into town one morning, and showed me everything that she had done. She took me to the workshop first, and she made me put a scarf on before we went in because it would be cold. It was not cold as we would know cold, but it struck chilly after the warm day outside, because she kept the air-conditioner going all the year round. 'The girls do love it so,' she said. 'There's always more of them wanting to work here than I can take on, just because of that.' They all looked very smart and pretty in their green smocks, working at the leather goods. There was a long mirror at the end of the shop, and a few pictures of hair styles and frocks cut out of illustrated magazines pinned up on the wall. 'We change those every so often,' she said. 'I like them to make the best of themselves.'

The workshop stood by itself, but she had arranged her other enterprises all in a row as a little street of shops. She had built a wooden veranda over the broad tarmac pavement to shade shopgazers from the sun or the rain. Here she had the beauty parlour with an Estonian in charge, a dark, handsome middle-aged woman, beautifully got up, with two Australian girls under her. There were four private little booths, and a glass counter and display-case full of women's things; it was all very clean and nice. Next in the row came a little shop with a battery of four Home Laundries, and three young married women sitting gossiping while they waited for their wash. Next was the greengrocer's shop, which sold seeds and garden implements as well as fruit and vegetables, and after that the dress shop. This was quite a big place, with counters and dummies clothed in summer frocks, and I was interested to see a small, secluded part served by a middle-aged woman where the elderly could buy the clothes they were accustomed to, black skirts and flannel petticoats and coarse kitchen aprons.

She took me across the road and showed me the cinema and the swimming-pool. It was quite a hot day and by that time I had had about enough, so she took me to the ice-cream parlour and we had a cool drink there. She had some business to attend to and she left me there for half an hour, and I sat watching the people as they came into the parlour, or as they passed on the sidewalk. There were far more women than men. All of them seemed to be pretty, and at least half of them seemed to be in the family way.

She came back presently, and sat with me in the parlour. 'What comes next?' I asked. 'Is there any end to this?'

She laughed and touched my hand. 'No end,' she said. 'I keep on badgering you for more money, don't I? As a matter of fact, I think I can start the next one out of the profits.'

'What's that one going to be?'

'A self-service grocer's shop,' she replied. 'The demand's shifting, Noel. When we started, it was entertainment that was needed, because everyone was young and nobody was married then. The solid, sensible things weren't wanted. What they needed then was ice-cream, and the swimming-pool, and the beauty parlour, and the cinema. They'll still need those things, but they won't expand so much more. What the town needs now is things for the young family. A really good grocer's shop selling good, varied food as cheap as we can possibly get it. And then, as soon as I can start it, we must have a household store. Do you know, you can't even buy a baby's pot in Willstown?'

I nodded at the store opposite. 'Doesn't Mr Duncan sell those?'

'He's got no imagination. He only sells big ones, that'ld hold the whole baby.'

I asked her presently, 'How do all your goods get here? They aren't all flown, surely?'

She shook her head. 'They come by train from Cairns to Forsayth, and by truck from there. There's no proper road, of course. It makes it terribly expensive, because a truck is worn out in about two years. Bill Wakeling says the Roads Commission are considering a road from here to Mareeba and Cairns–a proper tarmac road. Of course, he wants to build it. He thinks we'll get it inside two years, because the town's growing so fast. I must say, it'll be a god-send when we do. Fancy being able to drive to Cairns in a day!'

The Land Administration Board answered our letter later on that week and suggested a meeting on the following Tuesday or Wednesday, which suited our air services. I flew down to Brisbane with Joe Harman, picking up his solicitor in Cairns, and we had a conference with the Land Administration Board, which lasted most of one day, settling the Heads of Agreement. Then Harman went back to his station and Mr Hope and I stayed on in Brisbane passing the draft of the final agreement backwards and forwards to the Land Administration Board with amendments in red and green and blue and purple ink. On top of this, I was in communication with the solicitors for Mrs Spears over the option agreement for the final purchase of Midhurst; all this kept me busy in Brisbane for nearly a fortnight. Finally I was able to agree to them both, after an exchange of cables with Lester, and brought them back to Cairns. Joe Harman signed them, and we put them in the post, and my business in Queensland was done.

I went back to Willstown with Joe and stayed another week with them, not because there was any reason why I should do so, but for an old man's sentiment. I sat on the veranda with Jean, studying her drawing of the layout of the self-service grocery. We discussed whether it could not be combined with the hardware store. We went into Willstown and visited the site for it, and I spent some time with Mr Carter, the Shire Clerk, discussing with him the position in regard to the leases that she held for land. She showed me the swimming-pool and we talked about the cost of tiling over the rough concrete to make it look better, and I sat for hours in the ice-cream parlour watching those beautiful young women as they pushed their prams from shop to shop.

I asked her once if she would be coming back to England for a holiday. She hesitated, and then said gently, 'Not for a bit, Noel. Joe and I want to take a holiday next year, but we've been planning to go to America. We thought we'd go to San Francisco and get an old car, and drive down the west coast into Arizona and Texas. I'm sure we'd learn an awful lot that would be useful here if we did that. Their problems must be just the same as ours, and they've been at it longer.'

Jean touched me very much one evening by suggesting that I stayed out there and made my home with them. 'You've nothing to go back to England for, Noel,' she said. 'You're practically retired now. Why not give up Chancery Lane, give up London, and stay here with us? You know we'd love to have you.'

It was impossible of course; the old have their place and the young have theirs. 'That's very kind of you,' I said. 'I wish I could. But I've got sons, and grandchildren, you know. Harry will be coming home next year and we're all hoping that he'll get a shore appointment. He's due for a term of duty at the Admiralty, I think.'

She said, 'I'm sorry, for our sake. Joe and I talked this over, and we hoped we'd be able to get you to stay with us for a long time. Make your home here with us.'

I said quietly, 'That was a very kind thought, Jean, but I must go back.'

They drove me to the aeroplane, of course, to see me off. Leave-takings are stupid things, and best forgotten about as quickly as possible. I cannot even remember what she said, and it is not important anyway. I can only remember a great thankfulness that the Dakota on that service didn't carry a stewardess so that nobody could see my face as we circled after taking off to get on course, and I saw the new buildings and bright roofs of that Gulf town for the last time.

★   ★   ★

It is winter now, and it is nearly three months since I have been able to get out to the office or the club. My daughter-in-law Eve, Martin's wife, has been organizing me; it was she who insisted that I should engage this nurse to sleep in the flat. They wanted me to go into some sort of nursing-home, but I won't do that.

I have spent the winter writing down this story, I suppose because an old man loves to dwell upon the past and this is my own form of the foible. And having finished it, it seems to me that I have been mixed up in things far greater than I realized at the time. It is no small matter to assist in the birth of a new city, and as I sit here looking out into the London mists I sometimes wonder just what it is that Jean has done; if any of us realize, even yet, the importance of her achievement.

I wrote to her the other day and told her a queer thought that came into my head. Her money came originally from the goldfields of Hall's Creek in West

Australia, where James Macfadden made it in the last years of the last century. I suppose Hall's Creek is derelict now, and like another Burketown or another Croydon. I think it is fitting that the gold that has been taken from those places should come back to them again in capital to make them prosperous. When I thought of that, it seemed to me that I had done the right thing with her money and that James Macfadden would have approved, although I had run contrary to the strict intentions of his son's will. After all, it was James who made the money and took it away to England from a place like Willstown. I think he would have liked it when his great-niece took it back again.

I suppose it is because I have lived rather a restricted life myself that I have found so much enjoyment in remembering what I have learned in these last years about brave people and strange scenes. I have sat here day after day this winter, sleeping a good deal in my chair, hardly knowing if I was in London or the Gulf country, dreaming of the blazing sunshine, of poddy-dodging and black stockmen, of Cairns and of Green Island. Of a girl that I met forty years too late, and of her life in that small town that I shall never see again, that holds so much of my affection.

A Town like Alice

AUTHOR'S NOTE

On the publication of this book I expect to be accused of falsifying history, especially in regard to the march and death of the homeless women prisoners. I shall be told that nothing of the sort ever happened in Malaya, and this is true. It happened in Sumatra.

After the conquest of Malaya in 1942 the Japanese invaded Sumatra and quickly took the island. A party of about eighty Dutch women and children were collected in the vicinity of Padang. The local Japanese commander was reluctant to assume responsibility for these women and, to solve his problem, marched them out of his area; so began a trek all round Sumatra which lasted for two and a half years. At the end of this vast journey less than thirty of them were still alive.

In 1949 I stayed with Mr and Mrs J. G. Geysel-Vonck at Palembang in Sumatra. Mrs Geysel had been a member of that party. When she was taken prisoner she was a slight, pretty girl of twenty-one, recently married; she had a baby six months old, and a very robust sense of humour. In the years that followed Mrs Geysel marched over twelve hundred miles carrying her baby, in circumstances similar to those which I have described. She emerged from this fantastic ordeal undaunted, and with her son fit and well.

I do not think that I have ever before turned to real life for an incident in one of my novels. If I have done so now it is because I have been unable to resist the appeal of this true story, and because I want to pay what tribute is within my power to the most gallant lady I have ever met.

NEVIL SHUTE

NEVIL SHUTE

PIED PIPER

I

His name is John Sidney Howard, and he is a member of my club in London. I came in for dinner that night at about eight o'clock, tired after a long day of conferences about my aspect of the war. He was just entering the club ahead of me, a tall and rather emaciated man of about seventy, a little unsteady on his feet. He tripped over the door mat as he went in and stumbled forward; the hall porter jumped out and caught him by the elbow.

He peered down at the mat and poked it with his umbrella. 'Damned thing caught my toe,' he said. 'Thank you, Peters. Getting old, I suppose.'

The man smiled. 'Several of the gentlemen have caught their foot there recently, sir,' he said. 'I was speaking to the Steward about it only the other day.'

The old man said: 'Well, speak to him again and go on speaking till he has it put right. One of these days you'll have me falling dead at your feet. You wouldn't like that to happen—eh?' He smiled quizzically.

The porter said: 'No, sir, we shouldn't like that to happen.'

'I should think not. Not the sort of thing one wants to see happen in a club. I don't want to die on a door mat. And I don't want to die in a lavatory, either. Remember the time that Colonel Macpherson died in the lavatory, Peters?'

'I do, sir. That was very distressing.'

'Yes.' He was silent for a moment. Then he said: 'Well, I don't want to die that way, either. See he gets that mat put right. Tell him I said so.'

'Very good, sir.'

The old man moved away. I had been waiting behind him while all this was going on because the porter had my letters. He gave them to me at the wicket, and I looked them through. 'Who was that?' I asked idly.

He said: 'That was Mr Howard, sir.'

'He seemed to be very much concerned about his latter end.'

The porter did not smile. 'Yes, sir. Many of the gentlemen talk in that way as they get on. Mr Howard has been a member here for a great many years.'

I said more courteously: 'Has he? I don't remember seeing him about.'

The man said: 'He has been abroad for the last few months, I think, sir. But he seems to have aged a great deal since he came back. Getting rather frail now, I'm afraid.'

I turned away. 'This bloody war is hard on men of his age,' I said.

'Yes, sir. That's very true.'

I went into the club, slung my gas-mask on to a peg, unbuckled my revolver-belt and hung it up, and crowned the lot with my cap. I strolled over to the tape and studied the latest news. It was neither good nor bad. Our Air Force was still knocking hell out of the Ruhr; Rumania was still desperately bickering with her neighbours. The news was as it had been for three months, since France was overrun.

I went in and had my dinner. Howard was already in the dining-room; apart from us the room was very nearly empty. He had a waiter serving him who was very nearly as old as he was himself, and as he ate his dinner the waiter stood beside his table and chatted to him. I could hardly help overhearing the subject of their conversation. They were talking about cricket, reliving the Test Matches of 1925.

Because I was eating alone I finished before Howard, and went up to pay my bill at the desk. I said to the cashier: 'That waiter over there—what's his name?'

'Jackson, sir?'

'That's right. How long has he been here?'

'Oh, he's been here a long time. All his life, you might say. Eighteen ninety-five or ninety-six he come here, I believe.'

'That's a very long time.'

The man smiled as he gave me my change. 'It is, sir. But Porson—he's been here longer than that.'

I went upstairs to the smoking-room and stopped before a table littered with periodicals. With idle interest I turned over a printed list of members. Howard, I saw, had joined the club in 1896. Master and man, then, had been rubbing shoulders all their lives.

I took a couple of illustrated weeklies, and ordered coffee. Then I crossed the room to where the two most comfortable chairs in my club stand side by side, and prepared to spend an hour of idleness before returning to my flat. In a few minutes there was a step beside me and Howard lowered his long body into the other chair. A boy, unasked, brought him coffee and brandy.

Presently he spoke. He said quietly: 'It really is a most extraordinary thing that you can't get a decent cup of coffee in this country. Even in a club like this they can't make coffee.'

I laid down my paper. If the old man wanted to talk to me, I had no great objection. All day I had been working with my eyes in my old-fashioned office, reading reports and writing dockets. It would be good to take off my spectacles for a little time and unfocus my eyes. I was very tired.

I felt in my pocket for my spectacle-case. I said: 'A chap who deals in coffee once told me that ground coffee won't keep in our climate. It's the humidity, or something.'

'Ground coffee goes off in any climate,' he said dogmatically. 'You won't get a proper cup of coffee if you buy it like that. You have to buy the beans and grind it just before you make it. But that's what they won't do.'

He went on talking about coffee and chicory and things like that for a time. Then, by a natural association, we talked about the brandy. He approved of the club brandy. 'I used to have an interest in a wine business,' he said. 'A great many years ago, in Exeter. But I disposed of it soon after the last war.'

I gathered that he was a member of the Wine Committee of the club. I said: 'It must be rather interesting to run a business like that.'

'Oh, certainly,' he said with relish. 'Good wine is a most interesting study—most interesting, I can assure you.'

We were practically the only people in the long, tall room. We spoke quietly as we lay relaxed beside each other in our chairs, with long pauses between sentences. When you are tired there is pleasure in a conversation taken in sips, like old brandy.

I said: 'I used to go to Exeter a good deal when I was a boy.'

The old man said: 'I know Exeter very well indeed. I lived there for forty years.'

'My uncle had a house at Starcross.' And I told him the name.

He smiled. 'I used to act for him. We were great friends. But that's a long time ago now.'

'Act for him?'

'My firm used to act for him. I was a partner in a firm of solicitors, Fulljames and Howard.' And then, reminiscent, he told me a good deal about my uncle and about the family, about his horses and about his tenants. The talk became more and more a monologue; a word or two from me slipped in now and then kept him going. In his quiet voice he built up for me a picture of the days that now are gone for ever, the days that I remember as a boy.

I lay smoking quietly in my chair, with the fatigue soaking out of me. It was a perfect godsend to find somebody who could talk of other things beside the war. The minds of most men revolve round this war or the last war, and there is a nervous urge in them which brings the conversation round to war again. But war seems to have passed by this lean old man. He turned for his interests to milder topics.

Presently, we were talking about fishing. He was an ardent fisherman, and I have fished a little. Most naval officers take a rod and a gun with them in the ship. I had fished on odd afternoons ashore in many parts of the world, usually with the wrong sort of fly and unsuccessfully, but he was an expert. He had fished from end to end of these islands and over a great part of the Continent. In the old days the life of a country solicitor was not an exacting one.

When he spoke of fishing and of France, it put me in mind of an experience of my own. 'I saw some chaps in France doing a damn funny sort of fly fishing,' I said. 'They had a great bamboo pole about twenty-five feet long with the line tied on the end of it—no reel. They used wet flies, and trailed them about in rough water.'

He smiled. 'That's right,' he said. 'That's how they do it. Where did you see them fishing like that?'

'Near Gex,' I said. 'Practically in Switzerland.'

He smiled reflectively. 'I know that country very well—very well indeed,' he said. 'Saint-Claude. Do you know Saint-Claude?'

I shook my head. 'I don't know the Jura. That's somewhere over by Morez, isn't it?'

'Yes—not very far from Morez.' He was silent for a few moments; we rested together in that quiet room. Presently he said: 'I wanted to try that wet fly fishing in those streams this summer. It's not bad fun, you know. You have to know where the fish go for their food. It's not just a matter of dabbing the flies about anywhere. You've got to place them just as carefully as a dry fly.'

'Strategy,' I said.

'That's the word. The strategy is really just the same.'

There was another of those comfortable pauses. Presently I said: 'It'll be some time before we can go fishing out there again.' So it was I who turned the conversation to the war. It's difficult to keep off the subject.

He said: 'Yes—it's a very great pity. I had to come away before the water was fit to fish. It's not much good out there before the very end of May. Before then the water's all muddy and the rivers are running very full–the thawing snows, you know. Later than that, in August, there's apt to be very little water to fish in, and it gets too hot. The middle of June is the best time.'

I turned my head. 'You went out there this year?' Because the end of May that he had spoken of so casually was the time when the Germans had been pouring into France through Holland and Belgium, when we had been retreating on Dunkirk and when the French were being driven back to Paris and beyond. It didn't seem to be a terribly good time for an old man to have gone fishing in the middle of France.

He said: 'I went out there in April. I meant to stay for the whole of the summer, but I had to come away.'

I stared at him, smiling a little. 'Have any difficulty in getting home?'

'No,' he said. 'Not really.'

'You had a car, I suppose?'

'No,' he said. 'I didn't have a car. I don't drive very well, and I had to give it up some years ago. My eyesight isn't what it used to be.'

'When did you leave Jura, then?' I asked.

He thought for a minute. 'June the eleventh,' he said at last. 'That was the day, I think.'

I wrinkled my brows in perplexity. 'Were the trains all right?' Because, in the course of my work, I had heard a good deal about conditions in France during those weeks.

He smiled. 'They weren't very good,' he said reflectively.

'How did you get along, then?'

He said: 'I walked a good deal of the way.'

As he spoke, there was a measured *crump... crump... crump... crump*, as a stick of four fell, possibly a mile away. The very solid building swayed a little, and the floors and windows creaked. We waited, tense and still. Then came the undulating wail of the sirens, and the sharp crack of gunfire from the park. The raid was on again.

'Damn and blast,' I said. 'What do we do now?'

The old man smiled patiently: 'I'm going to stay where I am.'

There was good sense in that. It's silly to be a hero to evade discomfort, but there were three very solid floors above us. We talked about it, as one does, studying the ceiling and wondering whether it would support the weight of the roof. Our reflections did not stir us from our chairs.

A young waiter came into the room, carrying a torch and with a tin hat in his hand.

He said: 'The shelter is in the basement, through the buttery door, sir.'

Howard said: 'Do we have to go there?'

'Not unless you wish to.'

I said: 'Are you going down there, Andrews?'

'No, sir. I'm on duty, in case of incendiary bombs, and that.'

'Well,' I said, 'get on and do whatever you've got to do. Then, when you've got a minute to spare, bring me a glass of Marsala. But go and do your job first.'

Howard said: 'I think that's a very good idea. You can bring me a glass of Marsala, too–between the incendiary bombs. You'll find me sitting here.'

'Very good, sir.'

He went away, and we relaxed again. It was about half past ten. The waiter had turned out all the lights except for the one reading-lamp behind our heads, so that we sat there in a little pool of soft yellow light in the great shadowy room. Outside, the traffic noises, little enough in London at that time, were practically stilled. A few police whistles shrilled in the distance and a car went by at a high speed; then silence closed down upon the long length of Pall Mall, but for some gunfire in the distance.

Howard asked me: 'How long do you suppose we shall have to sit here?'

'Till it's over, I suppose. The last one went on for four hours.' I paused, and then I said: 'Will anyone be anxious about you?'

He said, rather quickly: 'Oh, no. I live alone, you see–in chambers.'

I nodded. 'My wife knows I'm here. I thought of ringing her up, but it's not a very good thing to clutter up the lines during a raid.'

'They ask you not to do that,' he said.

Presently Andrews brought the Marsala. When he had gone away, Howard lifted up his glass and held it to the light. Then he remarked: 'Well, there are less comfortable ways of passing a raid.'

I smiled. 'That's true enough.' And then I turned my head. 'You said you were in France when all this started up. Did you come in for many air raids there?'

He put his glass down, seven-eighths full. 'Not real raids. There was some bombing and machine-gunning of the roads, but nothing very terrible.'

He spoke so quietly about it that it took a little time for me to realise what he had said. But then I ventured,

'It was a bit optimistic to go to France for a quiet fishing holiday, in April of this year.'

'Well, I suppose it was,' he replied thoughtfully. 'But I wanted to go.'

He said he had been very restless, that he had suffered from an urge, an imperious need to get away and to go and do something different. He was a little hesitant about his reasons for wanting to get away so badly, but then he told me that he hadn't been able to get a job to do in the war.

They wouldn't have him in anything, I imagine because he was very nearly seventy years old. When war broke out he tried at once to get into the Special Constabulary; with his knowledge of the Law it seemed to him that police duty would suit him best. The police thought otherwise, having no use for constables of his age. Then he tried to become an Air Raid Warden, and suffered another disappointment. And then he tried all sorts of things.

It's very difficult for old people, for old men particularly, in a war. They cannot grow accustomed to the fact that there is little they can do to help; they suffer from frustration, and the war eats into them. Howard fell into the habit of ordering his life by the news bulletins upon the wireless. Each day he got up in time to hear the seven o'clock news, had his bath, shaved, and dressed and was down to hear the eight o'clock, and went on so all day till after the midnight news, when he retired to bed. Between the bulletins he worried about the news, and read every paper he could lay his hands upon till it was time to turn the wireless on again.

He lived in the country when the war broke out. He had a house at Market Saffron, not very far from Colchester. He had moved there from Exeter four years previously, after the death of his wife; as a boy he had been brought up in

Market Saffron and he still had a few acquaintances in the neighbourhood. He went back there to spend the last years of his life. He bought an old country house, not very large, standing in about three acres of garden and paddock.

His married daughter came back from America and lived with him in 1938, bringing her little boy. She was married to a New York insurance man called Costello, Vice-President of his corporation and very comfortably off. She'd had a spot of bother with him. Howard didn't know the ins and outs of it and didn't bother about it much; privately, he was of the opinion that his daughter was to blame for the trouble. He was fond of his son-in-law, Costello. He didn't understand him in the least, but he liked him very well.

That's how he was living when the war broke out, with his daughter Enid and her little boy Martin, that his father would insist on calling Junior. That puzzled the old man very much.

Then the war broke out, and Costello began cabling for them to go back home to Long Island. And in the end, they went. Howard backed up Costello and put pressure on his daughter, in the belief that a woman who is separated from her husband is never very happy. They went, and he was left to live alone at Market Saffron, with occasional week-end visits from his son John, a Squadron-Leader in the Royal Air Force.

Costello made a great effort, in cables many hundreds of words long, to get the old man to go too. He wasn't having any. He said that he was afraid of being in the way, that a third party would have spoilt the chance of reconciliation. But his real reason, he admitted, was that he didn't like America. He had crossed the Atlantic to stay with them when they had first been married, and he had no desire to repeat the experience. After nearly seventy years in a more equable climate he found New York intolerably hot and desperately cold in turns, and he missed the little courtesies to which he was accustomed in our feudal life. He liked his son-in-law, he loved his daughter, and her boy was one of the great interests in his life. Not all these motives were sufficient to induce him to exchange the comfort and security of England grappling in battle to the death for the strange discomforts of the land that was at peace.

So Enid and her boy sailed in October. He took them to Liverpool and saw them on the boat, and then he went back home. From then onwards he lived very much alone, though his widowed sister came and stayed with him for three weeks before Christmas, and John paid him several visits from Lincolnshire, where he had a squadron of Wellington bombers.

It was lonely for the old man, of course. In the ordinary way he would have been content with the duck-shooting and with his garden. He explained to me that he found his garden really more interesting in the winter than in the summer, because it was then that he could make his alterations. If he wanted to move a tree, or plant a new hedge, or dig out an old one–that was the time to do it. He took great pleasure in his garden, and was always moving things about.

The war spoilt all that. The news bulletins penetrated every moment of his consciousness till he could no longer take pleasure in the simple matters of his country life. He fretted that he could get nothing to do, and almost for the first occasion in his life the time hung heavily upon his hands. He poured his mind out irritably to the vicar one day, and that healer of sick souls suggested that he might take up knitting for the troops.

After that, he took to coming up to London for three days a week. He got himself a little one-room flat in bachelor chambers, and took most of his meals at the club. That made things easier for him. Travelling up to London on Tuesday absorbed the best part of a day, and travelling down again on Friday absorbed another one; in the meantime odd duties had accumulated at Market Saffron so that the week-end was comparatively busy. In this way he created the illusion that he had enough to do, and he grew happier in consequence.

'Then, at the beginning of March, something happened that made a great change in his life. He didn't tell me what it was.

After that, he shut up the house at Market Saffron altogether, and came to London permanently to live mostly at the club. For two or three weeks he was busy enough, but after that time started to lie heavy on his hands again. And still he could get nothing to do in the war.

It was spring by then, and a most lovely spring it was. After the hard winter we had had, it was like opening a door. Each day he went for a walk in Hyde Park and Kensington Gardens, and watched the crocuses as they came out, and the daffodils. The club life suited him. He felt as he walked through the park during that marvellous spring that there was a great deal to be said for living in London, provided that you could get away from it from time to time.

As the sun grew stronger, the urge came on him to get away from England altogether for a while.

And really, there didn't seem to be any great reason why he should remain in England. The war in Finland was over, and on the western front there seemed to be complete stalemate. Matters in France were quite normal, except that upon certain days of the week you could only have certain kinds of food. It was then that he began to think about the Jura.

The high alpine valleys were too high for him; he had been to Pontresina three years previously and had been very short of breath. But the spring flowers in the French Jura were as beautiful as anything in Switzerland, and from the high ground up above Les Rousses you can see Mont Blanc. He wanted passionately to get where he could see mountains. 'I will lift up mine eyes unto the hills,' he said, 'from whence cometh my help.' That's how he felt about it.

He thought that if he went out there he would be just in time to see the flowers come thrusting through the snow; if he stayed on for a month or two he would come in for the fishing as the sun got warmer. He looked forward very much to fishing in those mountain streams. Very unspoilt they were, he said, and very fresh and quiet.

He wanted to see the spring, this year–to see as much of it as ever he could. He wanted to see all that new life coming on, replacing what is past. He wanted to soak himself in that. He wanted to see the hawthorn coming out along the river-banks, and the first crocuses in the fields. He wanted to see the new green of the rushes by the water's edge poking up through the dead stuff. He wanted to feel the new warmth of the sun, and the new freshness of the air. He wanted to savour all the spring there was this year–the whole of it. He wanted that more than anything else in the world, because of what had happened.

That's why he went to France.

He had much less difficulty in getting out of the country than he had expected. He went to Cook's, and they told him how to set about it. He had to get an exit permit, and that had to be done personally. The man in the office asked him what he wanted to leave the country for.

Old Howard coughed at him. 'I can't stand the spring weather in England,' he said. 'I've been indoors most of the winter. My doctor says I've got to get into a warmer climate.' A complacent doctor had given him a certificate.

'I see,' said the official. 'You want to go down to the south of France?'

'Not right down to the south,' he said. 'I shall spend a few days in Dijon and go to the Jura as soon as the snow is off the ground.'

The man wrote out a permit for three months, upon the grounds of health. So that wasn't very difficult.

Then the old man spent a deliriously happy two days with Hardy's, the fishing tackle makers in Pall Mall. He took it gently, half an hour in the morning and half an hour in the afternoon; in between he fingered and turned over his purchases, dreamed about fishing, and made up his mind what he would buy next. . . .

He left London on the morning of April the 10th, the very morning that the news came through that Germany had invaded Denmark and Norway. He read the news in his paper in the train on the way to Dover, and it left him cold. A month previously he would have been frantic over it, jumping from wireless bulletin to newspaper and back to the wireless again. Now it passed him by as something that hardly concerned him any more. He was much more concerned whether he had brought with him enough gut casts and points. True, he was stopping for a day or two in Paris, but French gut, he said, is rotten stuff. They don't understand, and they make it so thick that the fish can't help seeing it, even with a wet fly.

His journey to Paris was not very comfortable. He got on to the steamer in Folkestone harbour at about eleven in the morning, and there they sat till the late afternoon. Trawlers and drifters and paddle-steamers and yachts, all painted grey and manned by naval ratings, came in and out of the harbour, but the cross-Channel steamer stayed at the quay. The vessel was crowded, and there weren't enough seats for lunch, and not enough food if there had been seats. Nobody could tell them what they were stopping for, although it was a pretty safe guess that it was a submarine.

At about four o'clock there were a number of heavy explosions out at sea, and soon after that they cast off and got away.

It was quite dark when they got to Boulogne, and things were rather disorganised. In the dim light the Douane took an age to pass the luggage, there was no train to meet the boat, and not enough porters to go round. He had to take a taxi to the station and wait for the next train to Paris, at about nine o'clock. It was a stopping train, crowded, and running very late. It was after one o'clock when they finally did get to Paris.

They had taken eighteen hours over a journey that takes six in normal times. Howard was tired, very tired indeed. His heart began to trouble him at Boulogne and he noticed people looking at him queerly; he knew that meant that he had gone a bad colour. However, he had a little bottle with him that he carried for that sort of incident; he took a dose of that when he got into the train and felt a good deal better.

He went to the Hotel Girodet, a little place just off the Champs-Elysées near the top, that he had stayed at before. Most of the staff he knew had been called up for military service, but they were very kind to him and made him comfortable. He stayed in bed till lunch-time the first day and rested in his room most of the afternoon, but next morning he was feeling quite himself, and went out to the Louvre.

All his life he had found great satisfaction in pictures—real pictures, as he

called them, to distinguish them from Impressionism. He was particularly fond
of the Flemish school. He spent some time that morning sitting on a bench in
front of Chardin's still-life of pipes and drinking-vessels on a stone table. And
then, he told me, he went and had a look at the artist's portrait of himself. He
took great pleasure in the strong, kind face of the man who had done such very
good work, over two hundred years ago.

That's all he saw that morning at the Louvre. Just that chap, and his work.

He went on next day towards the Jura. He was still feeling a little shaky after
the fatigue of the crossing, so that day he only went as far as Dijon. At the Gare
de Lyons he bought a paper casually and looked it over, though he had lost all
interest in the war. There was a tremendous amount of bother over Norway
and Denmark, which didn't seem to him to be worth quite so much attention. It
was a good long way away.

Normally that journey takes about three hours, but the railways were in a bad
state of disorganisation. They told him that it was because of troop movements.
The *Rapide* was an hour late in leaving Paris, and it lost another two hours on
the way. It was nearly dinner-time when he reached Dijon, and he was very
thankful that he had decided to stop there. He had his bags carried to a little
hotel just opposite the station, and they gave him a very good dinner in the
restaurant. Then he took a cup of coffee and a *cointreau* in the café and went up
to bed at about half past nine, not too tired to sleep well.

He was really feeling very well next day, better than he had felt for a long time
past. The change of air, added to the change of scene, had done that for him. He
had coffee in his room and got up slowly; he went down at about ten o'clock and
the sun was shining, and it was warm and fresh out in the street. He walked up
through the town to the Hôtel de Ville and found Dijon just as he remembered it
from his last visit, about eighteen months before. There was the shop where
they had bought their berets, and he smiled again to see the name, *AU
PAUVRE DIABLE*. And there was the shop where John had bought himself a
pair of skis, but he didn't linger there for very long.

He had his lunch at the hotel and took the afternoon train on into the Jura: he
found that the local trains were running better than the main line ones. He
changed at Andelot and took the branch line up into the hills. All afternoon the
litte engine puffed along its single track, pulling its two old coaches through a
country dripping with thawing snow. The snow slithered and cascaded off the
slopes into the little streams that now were rushing torrents for a brief season.
The pines were shooting with fresh green, but the meadows were still deep in a
grey, slushy mess. In the high spots of the fields where grass was showing, he
noticed a few crocuses. He'd come at the right time, and he was very, very glad
of it.

The train stopped for half an hour at Morez, and then went on to Saint Claude.
It got there just at dusk. He had sent a telegram from Dijon to the Hôtel de la
Haute Montagne at Cidoton asking them to send a car down for him, because
it's eleven miles and you can't always get a car in Saint Claude. The hotel car was
there to meet him, a ten-year-old Chrysler driven by the *concierge*, who was a
diamond-cutter when he wasn't working at the hotel. But Howard only found
that out afterwards; the man had come to the hotel since his last visit.

He took the old man's bags and put them in the back of the car, and they
started off for Cidoton. For the first five miles the road runs up a gorge, turning
in hairpin bends up the side of the mountain. Then, on the high ground, it runs

straight over the meadows and between the woods. After a winter spent in London, the air was unbelievably sweet. Howard sat beside the driver, but he was too absorbed in the beauty of that drive in the fading light to talk much to him. They spoke once about the war, and the driver told him that almost every able-bodied man in the district had been called up. He himself was exempt, because the diamond dust had got into his lungs.

The Hôtel de la Haute Montagne is an old coaching-house. It has about fifteen bedrooms, and in the season it's a ski-ing centre. Cidoton is a tiny hamlet—fifteen or twenty cottages, no more. The hotel is the only house of any size in the place; the hills sweep down to it all round, fine slopes of pasture dotted her and there with pine-woods. It's very quiet and peaceful in Cidoton, even in the winter season when the village is filled with young French people on their skis. That was as it had been when he was there before.

It was dark when they drew up at the hotel. Howard went slowly up the stone steps to the door, the *concierge* following behind him with the bags. The old man pushed open the heavy oak door and went into the hall. By his side, the door leading into the *estaminet* flew open, and there was Madame Lucard, buxom and cheerful as she had been the year before, with the children round her and the maids grinning over her shoulder. Lucard himself was away with the *Chasseurs Alpins.*

They gave him a vociferous French welcome. He had not thought to find himself so well remembered, but it's not very common for English people to go deep into the Jura. They chattered at him nineteen to the dozen. Was he well? Had he made a good crossing of the *Manche*? He had stopped in Paris? and in Dijon also? That was good. It was very tiring to travel in this *sale* war. He had brought a fishing-rod with him this time, instead of skis? That was good. He would take a little glass of Pernod with Madame?

And then, *Monsieur votre fils*, he was well too?

Well, they had to know. He turned away from her blindly. '*Madame,*' he said, '*mon fils est mort. It est tombé de son avion, au-dessus de Heligoland Bight.*'

2

Howard settled down at Cidoton quite comfortably. The fresh mountain air did him a world of good; it revived his appetite and brought him quiet, restful sleep at night. The little rustic company of the *estaminet* amused and interested him, too. He knew a good deal of rural matters and he spoke good, slightly academic French. He was a good mixer and the farmers accepted him into their company, and talked freely to him of the matters of their daily life. It may be that the loss of his son helped to break the ice.

He did not find them noticeably enthusiastic for the war.

He was not happy for the first fortnight, but he was probably happier than he would have been in London. While the snow lasted, the slopes were haunted for him. In his short walks along the road before the woodland paths became available, at each new slope of snow he thought to see John come hurtling over the brow, stem-christie to a traverse, and vanish in a white flurry that sped down into the valley. Sometimes the fair-haired French girl, Nicole, who came from Chartres, seemed to be with him, flying along with him in the same flurry of snow. That was the most painful impression of all.

Presently as the sun grew stronger, the snow went away. There was the sound of tinkling water everywhere, and bare grass showed where there had been white slopes. Then flowers began to appear and his walks had a new interest. As the snow passed his bad dreams passed with it; the green flowering fields held no memories for him. He grew much more settled as the spring drew on.

Mrs Cavanagh helped him, too.

He had been worried and annoyed to find an English woman staying in the hotel, so far from the tourist track. He had not come to France to speak English or to think in English. For the first week he sedulously avoided her, together with her two children. He did not have to meet them. They spent a great part of their time in the salon; there were no other visitors in the hotel in between time. He lived mostly in his bedroom or else in the *estaminet*, where he played innumerable games of draughts with the habitués.

Cavanagh, they told him, was an official in the League of Nations at Geneva, not more than twenty miles away as the crow flies. He was evidently fearful of an invasion of Switzerland by the Germans, and had prudently sent his wife and children into Allied France. They had been at Cidoton for a month; each week-end he motored across the border to visit them. Howard saw him the first Saturday that he was there, a sandy-haired, worried-looking man of forty-five or so.

The following week-end Howard had a short talk with him. To the old solicitor, Cavanagh appeared to be oddly unpractical. He was devoted to the League of Nations even in this time of war.

'A lot of people say that the League has been a failure,' he explained. 'Now, I think that is very unfair. If you look at the record of that last twenty years you'll see a record of achievement that no other organisation can show. Look at what the League did in the matter of the drug traffic!' And so on.

About the war, he said: 'The only failure that can be laid to the account of the League is its failure to inspire the nations with faith in its ideals. And that means propaganda. And propaganda costs money. If the nations had spent one-tenth of what they have spent in armaments upon the League, there would have been no war.'

After half an hour of this, old Howard came to the conclusion that Mr Cavanagh was a tedious fellow. He bore with him from a natural politeness, and because the man was evidently genuine, but he made his escape as soon as he decently could. The extent of his sincerity was not made plain to Howard till the day he met Mrs Cavanagh in the woods, and walked a mile back to the hotel with her.

He found her a devoted echo of her man. 'Eustace would never leave the League,' she said. 'Even if the Germans were to enter Switzerland, he'd never leave Geneva. There's still such great work to be done.'

The old man looked at her over his spectacles. 'But would the Germans let him go on doing it if they got into Switzerland?'

'Why, of course they would,' she said. 'The League is international. I know, of course, that Germany is no longer a member of the League. But she appreciates our non-political activities. The League prides itself that it could function equally well in any country, or under any government. If it could not do that, it couldn't be said to be truly international, could it?'

'No,' said Howard, 'I suppose it couldn't.'

They walked on for a few steps in silence. 'But if Geneva really were invaded by the Germans,' he said at last, 'would your husband stay there?'

'Of course. It would be very disloyal if he didn't.' She paused, and then she said: 'That's why he sent me out here with the children, into France.'

She explained to him that they had no ties in England. For ten years they had lived in Geneva; both children had been born there. In that time they had seldom returned to England, even on holiday. It had barely occurred to them that she should take the children back to England, so far away from him. Cidoton, just across the border into France, was far enough.

'It's only just for a few weeks, until the situation clears a little,' she said placidly. 'Then we shall be able to go home.' To her, Geneva was home.

He left her at the entrance to the hotel, but next day at *déjeuner* she smiled at him when he came into the room, and asked him if he had enjoyed his walk.

'I went as far as the Pointe des Neiges,' he said courteously. 'It was delightful up there this morning, quite delightful.'

After that they often passed a word or two together, and he fell into the habit of sitting with her for a quarter of an hour each evening after dinner in the salon, drinking a cup of coffee. He got to know the children too.

There were two of them. Ronald was a dark-haired little boy of eight, whose toy train littered the floor of the salon with its tin lines. He was mechanical, and would stand fascinated at the garage door while the *concierge* laboured to induce ten-year-old spark-plugs to fire the mixture in the ten-year-old Chrysler. Old Howard came up behind him once.

'Could you drive a car like that?' he asked gently.

'*Mais oui—c'est facile, ça.*' French came more easily to this little boy than English. 'You climb up in the seat and steer with the wheel.'

'But could you start it?'

'You just push the button, *et elle va*. That's the 'lectric starter.' He pointed to the knob.

'That's right. But it would be a very big car for you to manage.'

The child said: 'Big cars are easier to drive than little ones. Have you got a car?'

Howard shook his head. 'Not now. I used to have one.'

'What sort was it?'

The old man looked down helplessly. 'I really forget,' he said. 'I think it was a Standard.'

Ronald looked up at him, incredulous. 'Don't you *remember*?'

But Howard couldn't.

The other child was Sheila, just five years old. Her drawings littered the floor of the salon; for the moment her life was filled with a passion for coloured chalks. Once as Howard came downstairs he found her sitting in a heap upon the landing at a turn of the staircase, drawing industriously on the fly-leaf of a book. The first tread of the flight served as a desk.

He stooped down by her. 'What are you drawing?'

She did not answer.

'Won't you show me?' he said. And then: 'The chalks are lovely colours.'

He knelt down rheumatically upon one knee. 'It looks like a lady.'

She looked up at him. 'Lady with a dog,' she said.

'Where's the dog?' He looked at the smudged pastel streaks.

She was silent. 'Shall I draw the dog, walking behind on a lead?' he said.

She nodded vigorously. Howard bent to his task, his knees aching. But his hand had lost whatever cunning it might once have had, and his dog became a pig.

Sheila said: 'Ladies don't take pigs for a walk.'

His ready wit had not deserted the solicitor. 'This one did,' he said. 'This is the little pig that went to market.'

The child pondered this. 'Draw the little pig that stayed at home,' she said, 'and the little piggy eating roast beef.' But Howard's knees would stand no more of it. He stumbled to his feet. 'I'll do that for you tomorrow.'

It was only at that stage he realised that his picture of the lady leading a pig embellished the fly-leaf of *A Child's Life of Jesus.*

Next day after *déjeuner* she was waiting for him in the hall. 'Mummy said I might ask you if you wanted a sweet.' She held up a grubby paper bag with a sticky mass in the bottom.

Howard said gravely: 'Thank you very much.' He fumbled in the bag and picked out a morsel which he put into his mouth. 'Thank you, Sheila.'

She turned, and ran from him through the *estaminet* into the big kitchen of the inn. He heard her chattering in there in fluent French to Madame Lucard as she offered her sweets.

He turned, and Mrs Cavanagh was on the stairs. The old man wiped his fingers furtively upon the handkerchief in his pocket. 'They speak French beautifully,' he said.

She smiled. 'They do, don't they? The little school they go to is French-speaking, of course.'

He said: 'They just picked it up, I suppose?'

'Oh yes. We didn't have to teach it to them.'

He got to know the children slightly after that and passed the time of day with them whenever he met them alone; on their side they said: 'Good morning, Mr Howard,' as if it was a lesson that they had been taught–which indeed it was. He would have liked to get to know them better, but he was shy, with the diffidence of age. He used to sit and watch them playing in the garden underneath the pine-trees sometimes, mysterious games that he would have liked to have known about, that touched dim chords of memory sixty years back. He did have one success with them, however.

As the sun grew warmer and the grass drier he took to sitting out in the garden after *déjeuner* for half an hour, in a deck-chair. He was sitting so one day while the children played among the trees. He watched them covertly. It seemed that they wanted to play a game they called *attention* which demanded a whistle, and they had no whistle.

The little boy said: 'I can whistle with my mouth,' and proceeded to demonstrate the art.

His sister pursed up her immature lips and produced only a wet splutter. From his deck-chair the old man spoke up suddenly.

'I'll make you a whistle, if you like,' he said.

They were silent, staring at him doubtfully. 'Would you like me to make you a whistle?' he enquired.

'When?' asked Ronald.

'Now. I'll make you one out of a bit of that tree.' He nodded to a hazel bush.

They stared at him, incredulous. He got up from his chair and cut a twig the thickness of his little finger from the bush. 'Like this.'

He sat down again, and began to fashion a whistle with the pen-knife that he kept for scraping out his pipe. It was a trick that he had practised throughout his life, for John first and then for Enid when they had been children, more recently for little Martin Costello. The Cavanagh children stood by him watching his slow, wrinkled fingers as they worked; in their faces incredulity melted into interest. He stripped the bark from the twig, cut deftly with the little knife, and bound the bark back into place. He put it to his lips, and it gave out a shrill note.

They were delighted, and he gave it to the little girl. 'You can whistle with your mouth,' he said to Ronald, 'but she can't.'

'Will you make me one tomorrow?'

'All right, I'll make you one tomorrow.' They went off together, and whistled all over the hotel and through the village, till the bark crushed beneath the grip of a hot hand. But the whistle was still good for taking to bed, together with a Teddy and a doll called Mélanie.

'It was so very kind of you to make that whistle for the children' Mrs Cavanagh said that night, over coffee. 'They were simply thrilled with it.'

'Children always like a whistle, especially if they see it made,' the old man said. It was one of the basic truths that he had learned in a long life, and he stated it simply.

'They told me how quickly you made it,' she said. 'You must have made a great many.'

'Yes,' he said, 'I've made a good many whistles in my time.' He fell into a reverie, thinking of all the whistles he had made for John and Enid, so many years ago, in the quiet garden of the house at Exeter. Enid who had grown up and married and gone to live in the United States. John who had grown up and gone into the Air Force. John.

He forced his mind back to the present. 'I'm glad they liked it,' he said. 'I promised Ronald that I'd make him one tomorrow.'

Tomorrow was the 10th May. As the old man sat in his deck-chair beneath the trees carving a whistle for Ronald, German troops were pouring into Holland, beating down the Dutch Army. The Dutch Air Force was flinging its full strength of forty fighting planes against the Luftwaffe. A thousand traitors leapt into activity; all through the day the parachutists dropped from the sky. In Cidoton the only radio happened to be switched off, and so Howard whittled at his hazel twig in peace.

It did not break his peace much when they switched it on. In Cidoton the war seemed very far away; with Switzerland to insulate them from the Germans the village was able to view the war dispassionately. Belgium was being invaded again, as in the last war; the *sale Boche!* This time Holland, too, was in it; so many more to fight upon the side of France. Perhaps they would not penetrate into France at all this time, with Holland to be conquered and assimilated first.

In all this, Howard acquiesced. He could remember very clearly how the war had gone before. He had been in it for a short time, in the Yeomanry, but had been quickly invalided out with rheumatic fever. The cockpit of Europe would take the shock of the fighting as it usually did; there was nothing new in that. In

Cidoton, it made no change. He listened to the news from time to time in a detached manner, without great interest. Presently fishing would begin; the snow was gone from the low levels and the mountain streams were running less violently each day.

The retreat from Brussels did not interest him much; it had all happened before. He felt a trace of disquiet when Abbeville was reached, but he was no great strategist, and did not realise all that was involved. He got his first great shock when Leopold, King of the Belgians, laid down his arms upon the 29th May. That had not happened in the last war, and it upset him.

But on that day nothing could upset him for very long. He was going fishing for the first time next morning, and the evening was occupied in sorting out his gear, soaking his casts and selecting flies. He walked six miles next day and caught three blue trout. He got back tired and happy at about six o'clock, had dinner, and went up immediately to bed. In that way he missed the first radio broadcasts of the evacuation of Dunkirk.

Next day he was jerked finally from his complacence. He sat by the radio in the *estaminet* for most of the day, distressed and worried. The gallant retreat from the beaches stirred him as nothing had for months; for the first time he began to feel a desire to return to England. He knew that if he went, there would be nothing for him to do, but he wanted to be back. He wanted to be in the thick of things again, seeing the British uniforms in the streets, sharing the tension and anxiety. Cidoton irked him with its rustic indifference to the war.

By the 4th June the last forces had left Dunkirk, Paris had had its one and only air-raid, and Howard had made up his mind. He admitted as much that night to Mrs Cavanagh.

'I don't like the look of things at all,' he said. 'Not at all. I think I shall go home. At a time like this, a man's place is in his own country.'

She looked at him, startled. 'But surely, you're not afraid that the Germans will come here, Mr Howard? They couldn't get as far as this.' She smiled reassuringly.

'No,' he said, 'they won't get much farther than they are now. But at the same time, I think I shall go home.' He paused, and then he said a little wistfully: 'I might be able to get into the A.R.P.'

She knitted on quietly. 'I shall miss having you to talk to in the evenings,' she said. 'The children will miss you, too.'

'It has been a great pleasure to have known them,' he said. 'I shall miss them.'

She said: 'Sheila enjoyed the little walk you took her for. She put the flowers in her tooth-mug.'

It was not the old man's way to act precipitately, but he gave a week's notice to Madame Lucard that night and planned to leave on the eleventh. He did it in the *estaminet*, and provoked a lively discussion on the ethics of his case, in which most of the village took part. At the end of an hour's discussion, and a round of Pernod, the general opinion was favourable to him. It was hard on Madame Lucard to lose her best guest, the gendarme said, and sad for them to lose their English *Camarade*, but without doubt an old soldier should be in his own country in these times. Monsieur was very right. But he would return, perhaps?

Howard said that he hoped to return within a very few weeks, when the dangerous stage of the war had passed.

Next day he began to prepare for his journey. He did not hurry over it because he meant to stay his week out. In fact, he had another day's fishing and caught another two blue trout. There was a lull in the fighting for a few days after the evacuation from Dunkirk and he went through a day of indecision, but then the Germans thrust again upon the Somme and he went on preparing to go home.

On the 9th June Cavanagh appeared, having driven unexpectedly from Geneva in his little car. He seemed more worried and distrait than usual, and vanished into the bedroom with his wife. The children were sent out to play in the garden.

An hour later he tapped upon the door of Howard's bedroom. The old man had been reading in a chair and had dropped asleep, the book idle on his lap. He woke at the second tap, settled his spectacles, and said: 'Come in!'

He stared with surprise at his visitor, and got up. 'This is a great pleasure,' he said formally. 'But what brings you out here in the middle of the week? Have you got a holiday?'

Cavanagh seemed a little dashed. 'I've taken a day off,' he said after a moment. 'May I come in?'

'By all means.' The old man bustled round and cleared a heap of books from the only other chair in the room. Then he offered his guest a cigarette. 'Won't you sit down?'

The other sat down diffidently. 'What do you think of the war?' he asked.

Howard said: 'I think it very serious. I don't like the news at all.'

'Nor do I. I hear you're going home?'

'Yes, I'm going back to England. I feel that at a time like this my place is there.'

There was a short silence. Then Cavanagh said: 'In Geneva we think that Switzerland will be invaded.'

Howard looked at him with interest. 'Do you, now! Is that going to be the next thing?'

'I think so. I think that it may happen very soon.'

There was a pause. Then Howard said: 'If that happened, what would you do?'

The little sandy-haired man from Geneva got up and walked over to the window. He stood for a moment looking out over the meadows and the pine-woods. Then he turned back into the room. 'I should have to stay in Geneva,' he said. 'I've got my work to do.'

'Would that be very—wise?'

'No,' said Cavanagh frankly. 'But it's what I have made up my mind to do.'

He came back and sat down again. 'I've been talking it over with Felicity,' he said. 'I've got to stay there. Even in German occupation there would still be work for us to do. It's not going to be pleasant. It's not going to be profitable. But it's going to be worth doing.'

'Would the Germans allow the League to function at all?'

'We have positive assurances that they will.'

'What does your wife think about it?' asked Howard.

'She thinks that it's the proper thing to do. She wants to come back to Geneva with me.'

'Oh . . .'

The other turned to him. 'It's really about that that I looked in to see you,' he said. 'If we do that, things may go hardly with us before the war is over. If the

Allies win they'll win by the blockade. There won't be much to eat in any German territory.'

Howard stared at the little man in wonder. 'I suppose not.' He had not credited Cavanagh with such cool courage.

'It's the children,' the other said apologetically. 'We were thinking–Felicity was wondering . . . if you could possibly take them back to England with you, when you go.'

He went on hurriedly, before Howard could speak: 'It's only just to take them to my sister's house in Oxford, up on Boars Hill. As a matter of fact, I could send her a telegram and she could meet you at Southampton with the car, and drive them straight to Oxford. It's asking an awful lot, I'm afraid. If you feel you couldn't manage it . . . we'll understand.'

Howard stared at him. 'My dear chap,' he said, 'I should be only too glad to do anything I can to help. But I must tell you, that at my age I don't stand travel very well. I was quite ill for a couple of days in Paris, on my way out here. I'm nearly seventy, you know. It would be safer if you put your children in the care of somebody a little more robust.'

Cavanagh said: 'That may be so. But as a matter of fact, there is nobody. The alternative would be for Felicity to take the children back to England herself.'

There was a pause. The old man said: 'I see. She doesn't want to do that?'

The other shook his head. 'We want to be together,' he said, a little pitifully. 'It may be for years.'

Howard stared at him. 'You can count on me to do anything within my power,' he said. 'Whether you would be wise to send the children home with me is something that you only can decide. If I were to die upon the journey it might cause a good deal of trouble, both for your sister in Oxford and for the children.'

Cavanagh smiled. 'I'm quite prepared to take the risk,' he said. 'It's a small one compared with all the other risks one has to take these days.'

The old man smiled slowly. 'Well, I've been going seventy years and I've not died yet. I suppose I may last a few weeks longer.'

'Then you'll take them?'

'Of course I will, if that's what you want me to do.'

Cavanagh went away to tell his wife, leaving the old man in a flutter. He had planned to stay in Dijon and in Paris for a night as he had done on the way out; it now seemed to him that it would be wiser if he were to travel straight through to Calais. Actually it meant no changes in his arrangement to do that, because he had booked no rooms and taken no tickets. The changes were in his plans; he had to get accustomed to the new idea.

Could he manage the two children by himself, or would it be wiser to engage a village girl from Cidoton to travel with them as far as Calais to act as a *bonne*? He did not know if a girl could be found to come with them. Perhaps Madame Lucard would know somebody . . .

It was only later that he realised that Calais was in German hands, and that his best route across the Channel would be by way of Saint Malo to Southampton.

He came down presently, and met Felicity Cavanagh in the salon. She caught his hand. 'It's so very, very kind of you to do this for us,' she said. It seemed to him that she had been crying a little.

'Not in the least,' he said. 'I shall enjoy having them as travelling companions.'

She smiled. 'I've just told them. They're simply thrilled. They're terribly excited to be going home with you.' It was the first time that he had heard her speak of England as home.

He broached the matter of a girl to her, and they went together to see Madame Lucard. But Cidoton proved to be incapable of producing anybody willing to go with them to Saint Malo, or even as far as Paris. 'It doesn't matter in the least,' said Howard. 'After all, we shall be home in twenty-four hours. I'm sure we shall get on famously together.'

She looked at him. 'Would you like me to come with you as far as Paris? I could do that, and then go back to Geneva.'

He said: 'Not at all—not at all. You stay with your man. Just tell me about their clothes and what they say, er, when they want to retire. Then you won't need to worry any more about them.'

He went up with her that evening to see them in bed. He said to Ronald: 'So you're coming back to England with me, eh, to stay with your auntie?'

The little boy looked up at him with shining eyes. 'Yes, *please!* Are we going in a train?'

Howard said: 'Yes, we'll be a long time in the train.'

'Will it have a steam engine, or a 'lectric one?'

'Oh—a steam engine, I think. Yes, certainly a steam engine.'

'How many wheels will it have?' But this was past the old man's capacity.

Sheila piped up: 'Will we have dinner in the train?'

'Yes,' he said, 'you'll have your dinner in the train. I expect you'll have your tea and your breakfast in it too.'

'Oo . . . Oo,' she said. And then, incredulously, 'Breakfast in the train?'

Ronald stared at him. 'Where will we sleep?'

His father said: 'You'll sleep in the train, Ronnie. In a little bed to yourself.'

'Really sleep in the train?' He swung round to the old man. 'Mr Howard, please—may I sleep next to the engine?'

Sheila said: 'Me too. I want to sleep next to the engine.'

Presently their mother got them settled down to sleep. She followed the men downstairs. 'I'm fixing up with Madame Lucard to pack a hamper with all your meals,' she said. 'It'll be easier for you to give them their meals in the *wagon lit* than to bother with them in the restaurant car.'

Howard said: 'That's really very kind. It's much better that way.'

She smiled. 'I know what it is, travelling with children.'

He dined with them that night, and went early to bed. He was pleasantly tired, and slept very well; he woke early, as he usually did, and lay in bed revolving in his mind all the various matters that he had to attend to. Finally he got up, feeling uncommonly well. It did not occur to him that this was because he had a job to do, for the first time in many months.

The next day was spent in a flutter of business. The children were taking little with them in the way of luggage; one small portmanteau held the clothes for both of them. With their mother to assist him the old man learned the intricacies of their garments, and how they went to bed, and what they had to eat.

Once Mrs Cavanagh stopped and looked at him. 'Really,' she said, 'you'd rather that I came with you to Paris, wouldn't you?'

'Not in the least,' he said. 'I assure you, they will be quite all right with me.' She stood silent for a minute. 'I believe they will,' she said slowly. 'Yes, I believe they'll be all right with you.'

She said no more about Paris.

Cavanagh had returned to Geneva, but he turned up again that night for dinner. He took Howard aside and gave him the money for their journey. 'I can't tell you how terribly grateful we are to you,' he muttered. 'It just makes all the difference to know that the kids will be in England.'

The old man said: 'Don't worry about them any more. They'll be quite safe with me. I've had children of my own to look after, you know.'

He did not dine with them that night, judging it better to leave them alone together with the children. Everything was ready for his journey; his portmanteaux were packed, his rods in the long tubular travelling-case. There was nothing more to be done.

He went up to his room. It was bright moonlight, and he stood for a while at his window looking out over the pastures and the woods towards the mountains. It was very quiet and still.

He turned uneasily from the window. It had no right to be so peaceful, here in the Jura. Two or three hundred miles to the north the French were fighting desperately along the Somme; the peace in Cidoton was suddenly unpleasant to him, ominous. The bustle and the occupation that his charge of the children had brought to him had changed his point of view; he now wanted very much to be in England, in a scene of greater action. He was glad to be leaving. The peace of Cidoton had helped him over a bad time, but it was time that he moved on.

Next morning all was bustle. He was down early, but the children and their parents were before him. They all had their *petit déjeuner* together in the dining-room; as a last lesson Howard learned to soften the crusts of the rolls for the children by soaking them in coffee. Then the old Chrysler was at the door to take them down to Saint-Claude.

The leave-taking was short and awkward. Howard had said everything that there was to say to the Cavanaghs, and the children were eager to climb into the car. It meant nothing to them that they were leaving their mother, possibly for years; the delicious prospect of a long drive to Saint-Claude and a day and a night in a real train with a steam engine filled their minds. Their father and mother kissed them, awkward and red-faced, but the meaning of the parting escaped the children altogether. Howard stood by, embarrassed.

Mrs Cavanagh muttered: 'Good-bye, my darlings,' and turned away.

Ronald said: 'May I sit by the driver?'

Sheila said: 'I want to sit by the driver, too.'

Howard stepped forward. 'You're both going to sit behind with me.' He bundled them into the back of the car. Then he turned back to their mother. 'They're very happy,' he said gently. 'That's the main thing, after all.'

He got into the car; it moved off down the road, and that miserable business was all over.

He sat in the middle of the seat with one child on each side of him for equity in the facilities for looking out. From time to time one saw a goat or a donkey and announced the fact in mixed French and English; then the other one would scramble over the old man to see the wonder. Howard spent most of the drive putting them back into their own seats.

Half an hour later they drew up at the station of Saint-Claude. The *concierge* helped them out of the car. 'They are pretty children,' he said in French to Howard. 'Their father and mother will be very sad, I think.'

The old man answered him in French: 'That is true. But in war, children should stay quiet in their own country. I think their mother has decided wisely.'

The man shrugged his shoulders; it was clear that he did not agree. 'How could war come to Cidoton?'

He carried their luggage to a first-class compartment and helped Howard to register the portmanteaux. Presently the little train puffed out up the valley, and Saint-Claude was left behind. That was the morning on which Italy declared war on the Allies, and the Germans crossed the Seine to the north of Paris.

3

Half an hour after leaving Morez the children were already bored. Howard was watching for this, and had made his preparations. In the attaché case that he carried with him he had secreted a number of little amusements for them, given to him by their mother. He pulled out a scribbling-pad and a couple of coloured pencils, and set them to drawing ships.

By the time they got to Andelot, three hours later, they had had their lunch; the carriage was littered with sandwich wrappings and with orange peel; an empty bottle that had contained milk stood underneath a seat. Sheila had had a little sleep, curled up by old Howard with her head resting on his lap; Ronnie had stood looking out of the window most of the way, singing a little song in French about numerals—

> Un, deux, trois,
> Allons dans les bois—
> Quatre, cinq, six,
> Cueillir des cerises . . .

Howard felt that he knew his numerals quite well by the time they got to Andelot.

He had to rouse Sheila from a heavy slumber as they drew into the little country station where they had to change. She woke up hot and fretful and began to cry a little for no reason at all. The old man wiped her eyes, got out of the carriage, lifted the children down on to the platform, and then got back into the carriage for the hand luggage. There were no porters on the platform, but it seemed that that was inevitable in France in war-time. He had not expected it to be different.

He walked along the platform carrying the hand luggage, with the two children beside him; he modified his pace to suit their rate of walking, which was slow. At the *Bureau*, he found a stout, black-haired stationmaster.

Howard enquired if the *Rapide* from Switzerland was likely to be late.

The man said that the *Rapide* would not arrive. No trains from Switzerland would arrive.

Dumbfounded, Howard expostulated. It was intolerable that one had not been told that at Saint-Claude. How, then, could one proceed to Dijon?

The stationmaster said that Monsieur might rest tranquil. A train would run from the frontier at Vallorbes to Dijon. It was incessantly expected. It had been incessantly expected for two hours.

Howard returned to the children and his luggage, annoyed and worried. The failure of the *Rapide* meant that he could not travel through to Paris in the train from Andelot, but must make a change at Dijon. By the time he got there it would be evening, and there was no knowing how long he would have to wait there for a train to Paris, or whether he could get a sleeping berth for the children. Travelling by himself it would have been annoying: with two children to look after it became a serious matter.

He set himself to amuse them. Ronnie was interested in the railway trucks and the signals and the shunting engine; apart from his incessant questions about matters that Howard did not understand he was very little trouble. Sheila was different. She was quite unlike the child that he had known in Cidoton, peevish and fretful, and continually crying without energy. The old man tried a variety of ways to rouse her interest, without a great deal of success.

An hour and forty minutes later, when he was thoroughly worn out, the train for Dijon pulled into the station. It was very full, but he managed to find one seat in a first-class carriage and took Sheila on his knee, where she fell asleep again before so very long. Ronnie stood by the door looking out of the window, chattering in French to a fat old woman in a corner.

Presently this woman leaned forward to Howard. She said: 'Your little one has fever, is it not so?'

Startled, he said in French: 'But no. She is a little tired.'

She fixed him with beady black eyes. 'She has a fever. It is not right to bring a child with fever in the train. It is not hygienic. I do not like to travel with a child that has a fever.'

'I assure you, madame,' he said, 'you deceive yourself.' But a horrible suspicion was creeping over him.

She appealed to the rest of the carriage. 'I,' she ejaculated, '–it is I who deceive myself, then! Let me tell you, m'sieur, it is not I who deceive myself. But no, certainly. It is you, m'sieur, truly, you who are deceived. I tell you that your little one has fever, and you do very wrong to bring her in a train with others who are healthy. Look at her colour, and her skin! She has scarlet fever, or chicken-pox, or some horrible disease that clean people do not get.' She turned vehemently to the others in the carriage. 'Imagine, bringing a child in that condition in the train!'

There was a grunt from the other occupants. One said: 'It is not correct. It should not be allowed.'

Howard turned to the woman. 'Madame,' he said, 'you have children of your own, I think?'

She snorted at him. 'Five,' she said. 'But never have I travelled with a child in that condition. It is not right, that.'

He said: 'Madame, I ask for your help. These children are not my own, but I am taking them to England for a friend, because in these times it is better that children should be in their own country. I did not know the little one was feverish. Tell me, what would you do, as her mother?'

She shrugged her shoulders, still angry. 'I? I have nothing to do with it at all, m'sieur, I assure you of that. I would say, let children of that age stay with their mother. That is the place for such children. It is getting hot and travelling in trains that gives children fever.'

With a sinking heart Howard realised that there was some truth in what she said. From the other end of the carriage somebody said: 'English children are very often ill. The mothers do not look after their children properly. They expose them to currents of air and then the children get fever.'

There was general agreement in the carriage. Howard turned again to the woman. 'Madame,' he said, 'do you think this fever is infectious? If it is so, I will get out at the next station. But as for me, I think she is only tired.'

The little beady eyes of the old peasant woman fixed him. 'Has she got spots?'

'I–I don't think so. I don't know.'

She snorted. 'Give her to me.' She reached out and took Sheila from him, settled her on a capacious lap, and deftly removed her coat. With quick fingers she undid the child's clothes and had a good look at her back and front. 'She has no spots,' she said, replacing the garments. 'But fever–poor little one, she is hot as fire. It is not right to expose a child in this condition, m'sieur. She should be in bed.'

Howard reached out for Sheila and took her back; the Frenchwoman was certainly right. He thanked her for her help. 'It is clear to me that she must go to bed when we arrive at Dijon,' he said. 'Should she see a doctor?'

The old woman shrugged her shoulders. 'It is not necessary. A tisane from the chemist, and she will be well. But you must not give her wine while she has fever. Wine is very heating to the blood.'

Howard said: 'I understand, madame. She shall not have wine.'

'Not even mixed with water, or with coffee.'

'No. She should have milk?'

'Milk will not hurt her. Many people say that children should drink as much milk as wine.' This provoked a discussion upon infant welfare that lasted till they got to Dijon.

The station at Dijon was a seething mass of soldiers. With the utmost difficulty Howard got the children and his bags out of the train. He had an attaché case and a suitcase and the tin tube that held his rods with him in the carriage; the rest of his luggage with the little portmanteau that held the children's clothes was registered through to Paris. Carrying Sheila in his arms and leading Ronnie by the hand, he could not carry any of his luggage; he was forced to leave everything in a corner of the station platform and thrust his way with the two children through the crowd towards the exit.

The square before the station was a mass of lorries and troops. He threaded his way through and across the road to the hotel that he had stayed at before, startled and bewildered by the evident confusion of the town. He forced his way through to the hotel with the children; at the desk the girl recognised him, but told him that all the rooms were taken by the military.

'But, mademoiselle,' he said, 'I have a sick child to look after.' He explained.

The girl said: 'It is difficult for you, m'sieur. But what can I do?'

He smiled slowly. 'You can go and fetch Madame, and perhaps it will be possible for us to arrange something.'

Twenty minutes later he was in possession of a room with one large double bed, and apologising to an indignant French subaltern whose capitaine had ordered him to double up with another officer.

The *bonne*, a stout, untidy woman bulging out of her clothes, bustled about and made the room tidy. 'The poor little one,' she said. 'She is ill–yes? Be tranquil, monsieur. Without doubt, she has a little chill, or she has eaten something bad. All will be well, two days, three days, perhaps. Then she will be quite well again.' She smoothed the bed and crossed to Howard, sitting on a chair still holding Sheila in his arms. 'There, monsieur. All is now ready.'

The old man looked up at her. 'I thank you,' he said courteously. 'One thing more. If I put her to bed now, would you come back and stay with her while I go to get a doctor?'

The woman said: 'But certainly, monsieur. The poor little one.' She watched him as he began to undress Sheila on his lap; at the disturbance she began to cry again. The Frenchwoman smiled broadly, and began a stream of motherly French chatter to the child, who gradually stopped crying. In a minute or so Howard had surrendered Sheila to her, and was watching. The *bonne* looked up at him. 'Go and look for your doctor, monsieur, if you wish. I will stay with them for a little.'

He left them, and went down to the desk in the hall, and asked where he could find a doctor. In the thronging crowd the girl paused for a moment. 'I do not know, m'sieur . . . yes. One of the officers in the restaurant–he is a *médecin major.*'

The old man pressed into the crowded restaurant. Practically every table was taken by officers, for the most part glum and silent. They seemed to the Englishman to be a fat, untidy-looking lot; about half of them were unshaven. After some enquiry he found the *médecin major* just finishing his meal, and explained the position to him. The man took up his red velvet cap and followed him upstairs.

Ten minutes later he said: 'Be easy, monsieur. She must stay warm in bed to-morrow, and perhaps longer. But tomorrow I think that there will be no fever any more.'

Howard asked: 'What has she got?'

The man shrugged his shoulders indifferently. 'She is not infectious. Perhaps she has been hot, and playing in a current of air. Children, you understand, get fever easily. The temperature goes up quite high and very quickly. Then in a few hours, down again . . .'

He turned away. 'Keep her in bed, monsieur. And light food only; I will tell Madame below. No wine.'

'No,' said Howard. He took out his note-case. 'Without doubt,' he said, 'there is a fee.'

A note passed. The Frenchman folded it and put it in the breast pocket of his tunic. He paused for a moment. 'You go to England?' he enquired.

Howard nodded. 'I shall take them to Paris as soon as she can travel, and then to England by Saint Malo.'

There was a momentary silence. The fat, unshaven officer stood for a moment staring at the child in the bed. At last he said: 'It may be necessary that you should go to Brest. Always, there will be boats for England at Brest.'

The old man stared at him. 'But there is a service from Saint Malo.'

The doctor shrugged his shoulders. 'It is very near the Front. Perhaps there will be only military traffic there.' He hesitated, and then said: 'It seems that the *sales Boches* have crossed the Seine, near Rheims. Only a few, you understand. They will be easily thrown back.' He spoke without assurance.

Howard said quietly: 'That is bad news.'

The man said bitterly: 'Everything to do with this war is bad news. It was a bad day for France when she allowed herself to be dragged into it.'

He turned and went downstairs. Howard followed him, and got from the restaurant a jug of cold milk and a few little plain cakes for the children and, as an afterthought, a couple of feet of bread for his own supper. He carried these things through the crowded hall and up the stairs to his own room, afraid to leave the children very long.

Ronnie was standing at the window, staring out into the street. 'There's lots and lots of camions and motors at the station,' he said excitedly. 'And guns, too. Real guns, with motors pulling them! May we go down and see?'

'Not now,' said the old man. 'It's time you were in bed.'

He gave the children their supper of cakes, and milk out of a tooth-glass; Sheila seemed cooler, and drank her milk with very little coaxing. Then it was time to put Ronnie to bed in the big bed beside his sister. The little boy asked: 'Where are my pyjamas?'

Howard said: 'At the station. We'll put you into bed in your shirt for a start, just for fun. Then I'll go and get your pyjamas.'

He made a game of it with them, and tucked them up carefully one at each side of the big bed, with a bolster down the middle. 'Now you be good,' he said. 'I'm just going to get the luggage. I'll leave the light on. You won't be afraid?'

Sheila did not answer; she was already nearly asleep, curled up, flushed and tousled on the pillow. Ronnie said sleepily: 'May we see the guns and the camions tomorrow?'

'If you're good.'

He left them, and went down to the hall. The restaurant and the café were more crowded than ever; in the throng there was no hope at all of getting anyone to help him with the luggage. He pushed his way to the door and went out into the street, bewildered at the atmosphere of the town, and more than a little worried.

He found the station yard thronged with lorries and guns, with a few light tanks. Most of the guns were horse-drawn; the teams stood in their harness by the limbers as if ready to move on at any moment. Around them lorries rumbled in the darkness, with much melodious shouting in the broad tones of the southern French.

The station, again, was thronged with troops. They covered all the platforms, smoking and spitting wearily, squatting upon the dirty asphalt in the half-light, resting their backs against anything that offered. Howard crossed to the arrival platform and searched painstakingly for his luggage among the recumbent forms. He found the tin case with his rods and he found the small attaché case; the suitcase had vanished, nor could he discover any trace of the registered luggage.

He had not expected any more, but the loss of the suitcase was a serious matter. He knew that when he got to Paris he would find the registered luggage waiting for him in the *consigne*, were it six months later. But the suitcase had apparently been stolen; either that, or it had been placed in safe keeping by some zealous railway official. In the circumstances that did not seem probable. He would look for it in the morning; in the meantime they must all get on without pyjamas for the night. He made his way back to the hotel, and up to the bedroom again.

Both children were sleeping; Sheila was hot and restless and had thrown off most of her coverings. He spread them over her more lightly, and went down to the restaurant to see if he could get a meal for himself. A tired waiter refused point-blank to serve him, there was no food left in the hotel. Howard bought a small bottle of brandy in the café, and went up to the bedroom again, to dine off brandy and water, and his length of bread.

Presently he stretched himself to sleep uneasily in the arm-chair, desperately worried over what the next day would bring. One fact consoled him; he had his rods, quite safe.

Dawn came at five and found him still dozing uneasily in the chair, half-covered by the dust-cover from the bed. The children woke soon after that and began chattering and playing in the bed; the old man stirred and sat up stiffly in his chair. He rubbed a hand over his face; he was feeling very ill. Then the children claimed his attention and he got up to put them right.

There was no chance of any further sleep; already there was much tramping to and fro in the hotel. In the station yard outside his window, lorries, tanks, and guns were on the move; the grinding of the caterpillar tracks, the roar of exhausts, the chink of harness and the stamping of the teams made up a melody of war. He turned back to the children; Sheila was better, but still obviously unwell. He brought the basin to the bed and washed her face and arms; then he combed her hair with the small pocket comb that he had found in the attaché case, one of the few small toilet articles he had. He took her temperature, under the arm for fear that she might chew on the thermometer.

It came out a degree above normal; he tried vainly to recall how much he should add on for the arm. In any case, it didn't matter much; she'd have to stay in bed. He got Ronnie up, washed him, and set him to dress himself; then he sponged over his own face and rang the bell for the *femme de chambre*. He was unshaven, but that could wait.

She came presently, and exclaimed when she saw the chair and coverlet: 'Monsieur has slept so?' she said. 'But there was room in bed for all of you!'

He felt a little foolish. 'The little one is ill,' he said. 'When a child is ill, she should have room. I was quite comfortable.'

Her eyes softened, and she clucked her tongue again. 'Tonight I will find another mattress,' she said. 'Be assured, monsieur, I will arrange something.'

He ordered coffee and rolls and jam; she went away and came back presently with a loaded tray. As she set it down upon the dressing-table, he ventured: 'I must go out this morning to look for my luggage, and to buy a few things. I will take the little boy with me; I shall not be very long. Would you listen for the little girl, in case she cries?'

The woman beamed at him. 'Assuredly. But it will not be necessary for monsieur to hurry. I will bring *la petite* Rose, and she can play with the little sick one.'

Howard said: 'Rose?'

He stood for ten minutes, listening to a torrent of family history. Little Rose was ten years old, the daughter of the woman's brother, who was in England. No doubt monsieur had met her brother? Tenois was the name, Henri Tenois. He was in London, the wine waiter at the Hotel Dickens, in Russell Square. He was a widower, so the *femme de chambre* made a home for *la petite* Rose. And so on, minute after minute.

Howard had to exercise a good deal of tact to get rid of her before his coffee cooled.

An hour later, spruce and shaved and leading Ronnie by the hand, he went out into the street. The little boy, dressed in beret, overcoat, and socks, looked typically French; by contrast Howard in his old tweed suit looked very English. For ten minutes he fulfilled his promise in the market square, letting the child drink in his fill of camions, guns, and tanks. They stopped by one caterpillar vehicle, smaller than the rest.

'*Celui-ci*,' said Ronnie clearly, '*c'est un char de combat.*'

The driver smiled broadly. 'That's right,' he said in French.

Howard said in French: 'I should have called it a tank, myself.'

'No, no, no,' the little boy said earnestly. 'A tank is much bigger, monsieur. Truly.'

The driver laughed. 'I've got one myself just like that, back in Nancy. He'll be driving one of these before he's much older, *le petit chou.*'

They passed on, and into the station. For half an hour they searched the platforms, still thronged with the tired troops, but found no sign of the lost suitcase. Nor could the overworked and worried officials give any help. At the end of that time Howard gave it up; it would be better to buy a few little things for the children that he could carry in the attaché case when they moved on. The loss of a suitcase was not an unmixed disaster for a man with a weak heart in time of war.

They left the station and walked up towards the centre of the town to buy pyjamas for the children. They bought some purple sweets called *cassis* to take back with them for Sheila, and they bought a large green picture-book called *Babar the Elephant*. Then they turned back to the hotel.

Ronnie said presently: 'There's a motor-car from England, monsieur. What sort is it?'

The old man said: 'I don't suppose I can tell you that.' But he looked across the road to the filling-station. It was a big open touring car, roughly sprayed dull green all over, much splashed and stained with mud. It was evidently weeks since it had had a wash. Around it, two or three men were bustling to get it filled with petrol, oil, and water. One of them was manipulating the air hose at the wheels.

One of the men seemed vaguely familiar to the old man. He stopped and stared across the road, trying to place where they had met. Then he remembered; it was in his club six months before. The man was Roger Dickinson; something to do with a newspaper. The *Morning Record*–that was it. He was quite a well-known man in his own line.

Howard crossed the road to him, leading Ronnie by the hand. 'Morning,' he said. 'Mr Roger Dickinson, isn't it?'

The man turned quickly, cloth in hand; he had been cleaning off the windscreen. Recognition dawned in his eyes. 'I remember,' he said. 'In the Wanderers' Club . . .'

'Howard is the name.'

'I remember.' The man stared at him. 'What are you doing now?'

The old man said: 'I'm on my way to Paris, but I'm hung up here for a few days, I'm afraid.' He told Dickinson about Sheila.

The newspaperman said: 'You'd better get out, quick.'

'Why do you say that?'

The newspaperman stared at him, turning the soiled cloth over in his hands. 'Well, the Germans are across the Marne.' The old man stared at him. 'And now the Italians are coming up from the south.'

He did not quite take in the latter sentence. 'Across the Marne?' he said. 'Oh, that's very bad. Very bad indeed. But what are the French doing?'

'Running like rabbits,' said Dickinson.

There was a momentary silence. 'What did you say that the Italians were doing?'

'They've declared war on France. Didn't you know?'

The old man shook his head. 'Nobody told me that.'

'It only happened yesterday. The French may not have announced it yet, but it's true enough.'

By their side a little petrol flooded out from the full tank on to the road; one of the men removed the hose and slammed the snap catch of the filler cap with a metallic clang. 'That's the lot,' he said to Dickinson. 'I'll slip across and get a few *brioches*, and then we'd better get going.'

Dickinson turned to Howard. 'You must get out of this,' he said. 'At once. You'll be all right if you can get to Paris by tonight–at least, I think you will. There are boats still running from Saint Malo.'

The old man stared at him. 'That's out of the question, Dickinson. The other child has got a temperature.'

The man shrugged his shoulders. 'Well, I tell you honestly, the French won't hold. They're broken now–already. I'm not being sensationalist. It's true.'

Howard stood staring up the street. 'Where are you making for?'

'I'm going down into Savoy to see what the Italians are doing in that part. And then, we're getting out. Maybe Marseilles, perhaps across the frontier into Spain.'

The old man smiled. 'Good luck,' he said. 'Don't get too near the fighting.'

The other said: 'What are you going to do, yourself?'

'I don't quite know. I'll have to think about it.'

He turned away towards the hotel, leading Ronnie by the hand. A hundred yards down the road the mud-stained, green car came softly up behind, and edged into the kerb beside him.

Dickinson leaned out of the driver's seat. 'Look, Howard,' he said. 'There's room for you with us, with the two kids as well. We can take the children on our knees all right. It's going to be hard going for the next few days; we'll be driving all night, in spells. But if you can be ready in ten minutes with the other kid, I'll wait.'

The old man stared thoughtfully into the car. It was a generous offer, made by a generous man. There were four of them already in the car, and a great mass of luggage; it was difficult to see how another adult could be possibly squeezed in, let alone two children. It was an open body, with an exiguous canvas hood and no side screens. Driving all night in that through the mountains would be a bitter trial for a little girl of five with a temperature.

He said: 'It's very, very kind of you. But really, I think we'd better make our own way.'

The other said: 'All right. You've plenty of money, I suppose?'

The old man reassured him on that point, and the big car slid sway and vanished down the road. Ronnie watched it, half crying. Presently he sniffed, and Howard noticed him.

'What's the matter?' he said kindly. 'What is it?'

There was no answer. Tears were very near.

Howard searched his mind for childish trouble. 'Was it the motor-car?' he said. 'Did you think we were going to have a ride in it?'

The little boy nodded dumbly.

The old man stooped and wiped his eyes. 'Never mind,' he said. 'We'll wait till Sheila gets rid of her cold, and then we'll all go for a ride together.' It was in his mind to hire a car, if possible, to take them all the way from Dijon to Saint Malo and the boat. It would cost a good bit of money, but the emergency seemed to justify the expense.

'Soon?'

'Perhaps the day after tomorrow, if she's well enough to enjoy it with us.'

'May we go and see the *camions* and the *chars de combat* after *déjeuner*?'

'If they're still there we'll go and see them, just for a little.' He must do something to make up for the disappointment. But when they reached the station yard, the lorries and the armoured cars were gone. There were only a few decrepit-looking horses picketed beneath the tawdry advertisements for Byrrh and Pernod.

Up in the bedroom things were very happy. *La petite* Rose was there, a shy little girl with long black hair and an advanced maternal instinct. Already Sheila was devoted to her. *La petite* Rose had made a rabbit from two of Howard's dirty handkerchiefs and three little bits of string, and this rabbit had a burrow in the bedclothes on Ronnie's side of the bed; when you said 'Boo' he dived back into his burrow, manipulated ingeniously by *la petite* Rose. Sheila, bright-eyed, struggled to tell old Howard all about it in mixed French and English. In the middle of their chatter three aeroplanes passed very low over the station and the hotel.

Howard undid his parcels, and gave Sheila the picture-book about Babar the Elephant. Babar was an old friend of *la petite* Rose, and well known; she took the book and drew Ronnie to the bed, and began to read the story to them. The little boy soon tired of it; aeroplanes were more in his line, and he went and leaned out of the window hoping to see another one go by.

Howard left them there, and went down to the hall of the hotel to telephone. With great difficulty, and great patience, he got through at last to the hotel at Cidoton; obviously he must do his best to let Cavanagh know the difficulties of the journey. He spoke to Madame Lucard, but the Cavanaghs had left the day before, to go back to Geneva. No doubt they imagined that he was practically in England by that time.

He tried to put a call through to Cavanagh at the League of Nations in Geneva, and was told curtly that the service into Switzerland had been suspended. He enquired about the telegraph service, and was told that all telegrams to Switzerland must be taken personally to the *Bureau de Ville* for censoring before they could be accepted for despatch. There was said to be a very long queue at the censor's table.

It was time for *déjeuner*; he gave up the struggle to communicate with Cavanagh for the time being. Indeed, he had been apathetic about it from the start. With the clear vision of age he knew that it was not much good; if he should get in touch with the parents it would still be impossible for him to cross the border back to them, or for them to come to him. He would have to carry on and get the children home to England as he had undertaken to do; no help could come from Switzerland.

The hotel was curiously still, and empty; it seemed today that all the soldiers were elsewhere. He went into the restaurant and ordered lunch to be sent up to the bedroom on a tray, both for himself and for the children.

It came presently, brought by the *femme de chambre.* There was much excited French about the pictures of Babar, and about the handkerchief rabbit. The woman beamed all over; it was the sort of party that she understood.

Howard said: 'It has been very, very kind of you to let *la petite* Rose be with *la petite* Sheila. Already they are friends.'

The woman spoke volubly. 'It is nothing, monsieur—nothing at all. Rose likes more than anything to play with little children, or with kittens, or young dogs. Truly, she is a little mother, that one.' She rubbed the child's head affectionately. 'She will come back after *déjeuner*, if monsieur desires?'

Sheila said: 'I want Rose to come back after *déjeuner*, Monsieur Howard.'

He said slowly: 'You'd better go to sleep after *déjeuner*.' He turned to the woman. 'If she could come back at four o'clock?' To Rose: 'Would you like to come and have tea with us this afternoon—English tea?'

She said shyly: '*Oui, monsieur.*'

She went away and Howard gave the children their dinner. Sheila was still hot with a slight temperature. He put the tray outside the door when they had finished, and made Ronnie lie down on the bed with his sister. Then he stretched out in the arm-chair, and began to read to them from a book given to him by their mother, called *Amelianne at the Circus.* Before very long the children were asleep: Howard laid down the book and slept for an hour himself.

Later in the afternoon he walked up through the town again to the *Bureau de Ville*, leading Ronnie by the hand, with a long telegram to Cavanagh in his pocket. He searched for some time for the right office, and finally found it, picketed by an anxious and discontented crowd of French people. The door was shut. The censor had closed the office and gone off for the evening, nobody knew where. The office would be open again at nine in the morning.

'It is not right, that,' said the people. But it appeared that there was nothing to be done about it.

Howard walked back with Ronnie to the hotel. There were troops in the town again, and a long convoy of lorries blocked the northward road near the station. In the station yard three very large tanks were parked, bristling with guns, formidable in design but dirty and unkempt. Their tired crews were refuelling them from a tank lorry, working slowly and sullenly, without enthusiasm. A little chill shot through the old man as he watched them bungling their work. What was it Dickinson had said? 'Running like rabbits.'

It could not possibly be true. The French had always fought magnificently.

At Ronnie's urgent plea they crossed to the square, and spent some time examining the tanks. The little boy told him: 'They can go right over walls and houses even. Right over!'

The old man stared at the monsters. It might be true, but he was not impressed with what he saw. 'They don't look very comfortable,' he said mildly.

Ronnie scoffed at him. 'They go ever so fast, and all the guns go bang, bang, bang.' He turned to Howard. 'Are they going to stay here all night?'

'I don't know. I expect they will. Come on, now; Sheila will want her tea. I expect you want yours, too.'

Food was a magnet, but Ronnie looked back longingly over his shoulder. 'May we come and see them tomorrow?'

'If they're still here.'

Things were still happy in the bedroom. *La petite* Rose, it seemed, knew a game which involved the imitation of animals in endless repetition–

> My great-aunt lives in Tours,
> In a house with a cherry-tree
> With a little mouse (squeak, squeak)
> And a big lion (roar, roar)
> And a wood pigeon (coo, coo) . . .

and so on quite indefinitely. It was a game that made no great demand on the intelligence, and Sheila wanted nothing better. Presently, they were all playing it; it was so that the *femme de chambre* found them.

She came in with the tea, laughing all over her face. 'In Touraine I learned that, as a little girl, myself,' she said. 'It is pretty, is it not? All children like "my great-aunt lives in Tours"–always, always. In England, monsieur, do the children play like that?'

'Much the same,' he said. 'Children in every country play the same games.'

He gave them their milk and bread and butter and jam. Near the *Bureau de Ville* he had seen a shop selling gingerbread cakes, the tops of which were covered in crystallised fruits and sweets. He had bought one of these; as he was quite unused to housekeeping it was three times as large as was necessary. He cut it with his penknife on the dressing-table and they all had a slice. It was a very merry tea-party, so merry that the grinding of caterpillar tracks and the roaring of exhausts outside the window passed them by unnoticed.

They played a little more after tea; then he washed the children as the *femme de chambre* remade the bed. She helped him to undress them and put them into their new pyjamas; then she held Sheila on her capacious lap while the old man took her temperature carefully under the arm. It was still a degree or so above normal, though the child was obviously better; whatever had been wrong with her was passing off. It would not be right, he decided, to travel on the next day; he had no wish to be held up with another illness in less comfortable surroundings. But on the day after that, he thought it should be possible to get away. If they started very early in the morning they would get through to Saint Malo in the day. He would see about the car that night.

Presently, both the children were in bed, and kissed good night. He stood in the passage outside the room with the *femme de chambre* and her little girl. 'To-night, monsieur,' she said, 'presently, when they are asleep, I will bring a mattress and make up a bed for monsieur on the floor. It will be better than the arm-chair, that.'

'You are very kind,' he said. 'I don't know why you should be so very, very good to us. I am most grateful.'

She said: 'But monsieur, it is you who are kind . . .'

He went down to the lobby, wondering a little at the effusive nature of the French.

Again the hotel was full of officers. He pushed his way to the desk and said to the girl: 'I want to hire a car, not now, but the day after tomorrow–for a long journey. Can you tell me which garage would be the best?'

She said: 'For a long journey, monsieur? How far?'

'To Saint Malo, in Normandy. The little girl is still not very well. I think it will be easier to take her home by car.'

She said doubtfully: 'The Garage Citroën would be the best. But it will not be easy, monsieur. You understand—the cars have all been taken for the army. It would be easier to go by train.'

He shook his head. 'I'd rather go by car.'

She eyed him for a moment. 'Monsieur is going away, then, the day after to-morrow?'

'Yes, if the little girl is well enough to travel.'

She said, awkwardly: 'I am desolated, but it will be necessary for monsieur to go then, at the latest. If the little one is still ill, we will try to find a room for monsieur in the town. But we have heard this afternoon, the hotel is to be taken over tomorrow by the *Bureau Principal* of the railway, from Paris.'

He stared at her. 'Are they moving the offices from Paris, then?'

She shook her head. 'I only know what I have told you, monsieur. All our guests must leave.'

He was silent for a minute. Then he said: 'What did you say was the name of the garage?'

'The Garage Citroën, monsieur. I will telephone and ask them, if you wish?'

He said: 'Please do.'

She turned away and went into the box; he waited at the desk, worried and anxious. He felt that the net of circumstances was closing in on him, driving him where he did not want to go. The car to Saint Malo was the knife that would cut through his difficulties and free him. Through the glass of the booth he saw her speaking volubly into the telephone; he waited on tenterhooks.

She came back presently. 'It is impossible,' she said. 'There is no car available for such a journey. I regret—Monsieur Duval, the proprietor of the garage, regrets also—but monsieur will have to go by train.'

He said very quietly: 'Surely it would be possible to arrange something? There must be a car of some sort or another?'

She shrugged her shoulders. 'Monsieur could go to see Monsieur Duval perhaps, at the garage. If anybody in Dijon could produce a car for such a journey it would be he.'

She gave him directions for finding the garage; ten minutes later he was in the Frenchman's office. The garage owner was quite positive. 'A car, yes,' he declared. 'That is the least thing, monsieur, I could find the car. But petrol—not a litre that has not been taken by the army. Only by fraud can I get petrol for the car—you understand? And then, the roads. It is not possible to make one's way along the road to Paris, not possible at all, monsieur.'

'Finally,' he said, 'I could not find a driver for a journey such as that. The Germans are across the Seine, monsieur; they are across the Marne. Who knows where they will be the day after tomorrow?'

The old man was silent.

The Frenchaman said: 'If monsieur wishes to get back to England he should go by train, and he should go very soon.'

Howard thanked him for the advice, and went out into the street. Dusk was falling; he moved along the pavement, deep in thought. He stopped by a café and went in, and ordered a Pernod with water. He took the drink and went and sat down at a table by the wall, and stayed there for some time, staring at the garish advertisements of cordials upon the walls.

Things had grown serious. If he left now, at once, it might be possible to win through to Saint Malo and to England; if he delayed another thirty-six hours it might very well be that Saint Malo would be overwhelmed and smothered in the tide of the German rush, as Calais had been smothered, and Boulogne. It seemed incredible that they could still be coming on so fast. Surely, surely, they would be checked before they got to Paris? It would not possibly be true that Paris would fall?

He did not like this evacuation of the railway offices from Paris. That had an ugly sound.

He could go back now to the hotel. He could get both the children up and dress them, pay the bill at the hotel, and take them to the station. Ronnie would be all right. Sheila—well, after all, she had a coat. Perhaps he could get hold of a shawl to wrap her up in. True it was night-time and the trains would be irregular; they might have to sit about for hours on the platform in the night waiting for a train that never came. But he would be getting the children back to England, as he had promised Cavanagh.

But then, if Sheila should get worse? Suppose she took a chill and got pneumonia?

If that should happen, he would never forgive himself. The children were in his care; it was not caring for them if he went stampeding to the station in the middle of the night to start on a long, uncertain journey regardless of their weakness and their illness. That wasn't prudence. That was . . . fright.

He smiled a little at himself. That's what it was, just fright—something to be conquered. Looking after children, after all, meant caring for them in sickness. That's what it meant. It was quite clear. He'd taken the responsibility for them, and he must see it through, even though it now seemed likely to land him into difficulties that he had not quite anticipated when he first took on the job.

He got up and went back to the hotel. In the lobby the girl said to him.

'Monsieur has found a car?'

He shook his head. 'I shall stay here till the day after tomorrow. Then, if the little girl is well, we will go on by train.'

He paused. 'One thing, mademoiselle. I will only be able to take one little bag for the three of us, that I can carry myself. If I leave my fishing-rods, would you look after them for me for a time?'

'But certainly, monsieur. They will be quite safe.'

He went into the restaurant and found a seat for dinner. It was a great relief to him that he had found a means to place his rods in safety. Now that that little problem had been solved, he was amazed to find how greatly it had been distressing him; with that disposed of he could face the future with a calmer mind.

He went up to the bedroom shortly after dinner. The *femme de chambre* met him in the corridor, the yellow, dingy, corridor of bedrooms, lit only by a low-power lamp without a shade. 'I have made monsieur a bed upon the floor,' she said in a low tone. 'You will see.' She turned away.

'That was very kind of you,' he said. He paused, and looked curiously at her. In the dim light he could not see very clearly, but he had the impression that she was sobbing.

'Is anything the matter?' he asked gently.

She lifted the corner of her apron to her eyes. 'It is nothing,' she muttered. 'Nothing at all.'

He hesitated, irresolute. He could not leave her, could not just walk into his bedroom and shut the door, if she was in trouble. She had been too helpful with the children. 'Is it Madame?' he said. 'Has she complained about your work? If so, I will speak to her. I will tell her how much you have helped me.'

She shook her head and wiped her eyes. 'It is not that, monsieur,' she said. 'But – I am dismissed. I am to go tomorrow.'

He was amazed. 'But why?'

'Five years,' she said. 'Five years I have been with madame – in all seasons of the year, monsieur – five years continuously! And now, to be dismissed at the day! It is intolerable, that.' She began to weep a little louder.

The old man said: 'But why has Madame done this?'

She said: 'Have you not heard? The hotel is closing tomorrow. It is to be an office for the railway.' She raised her tear-stained face. 'All of us are dismissed, monsieur, everyone. I do not know what will happen to me, and *la petite* Rose.'

He was dumbfounded, not knowing what to say to help the woman. Obviously, if the hotel was to be an office for the railway staff, there would be no need for any chambermaids; the whole hotel staff would have to go. He hesitated, irresolute.

'You will be all right,' he said at last. 'It will be easy for so good a *femme de chambre* as you to get another job.'

She shook her head. 'It is not so. All the hotels are closing, and what family can now afford a servant? You are kind, monsieur, but it is not so. I do not know how we shall live.'

'You have some relations, or family, that you can go to, no doubt?'

'There is nobody, monsieur. Only by brother, father of little Rose, and he is in England.'

Howard remembered the wine waiter at the Dickens Hotel in Russell Square. He said a word or two of meagre comfort and optimism to the woman; presently he escaped into the bedroom. It was impossible for him to give her any help in her great trouble.

She had made him quite a comfortable bed upon a mattress laid upon the floor. He went over to the children's bed and took a look at them; they were sleeping very deeply, though Sheila still seemed hot. He sat for a little reading in the arm-chair, but he soon grew tired; he had not slept properly the night before and he had had an anxious and a worrying day. Presently he undressed, and went to bed upon the floor.

When he awoke the dawn was bright; from the window there came a great groaning clatter as a tank got under way and lumbered up the road. The children were awake and playing in the bed; he lay for a little, simulating sleep, and then got up. Sheila was cool, and apparently quite well.

He dressed himself and took her temperature. It was very slightly above normal still; evidently, whatever it was that had upset her was passing off. He washed them both and set Ronnie to dress himself, then went downstairs to order breakfast.

The hotel routine was already disarranged. Furniture was being taken from the restaurant; it was clear that no more meals would be served there. He found his way into the kitchen, where he discovered the *femme de chambre* in depressed consultation with the other servants, and arranged for a tray to be sent up to his room.

That was a worrying, trying sort of day. The news from the north was uniformly bad; in the town people stood about in little groups talking in low tones. He went to the station after breakfast with Ronnie, to enquire about the trains to Paris, leaving Sheila in bed in the devoted care of *la petite* Rose. They told him at the station that the trains to Paris were much disorganised '*à cause de la situation militaire*,' but trains were leaving every three or four hours. So far as they knew, the services from Paris to Saint Malo were normal, though that was on the Chemin de L'Ouest.

He walked up with Ronnie to the centre of the town, and ventured rather timidly into the children's department of a very large store. A buxom Frenchwoman came forward to serve him, and sold him a couple of woollen jerseys for the children and a grey, fleecy blanket. He bought the latter more by instinct than by reason, fearful of the difficulties of the journey. Of all difficulties, the one he dreaded most was that the children would get ill again.

They bought a few more sweets, and went back to the hotel. Already the hall was thronged with seedy-looking French officials, querulous from their journey and disputing over offices. The girl from the desk met Howard as he went upstairs. He could keep his room for one more night, she said; after that he must get out. She would try and arrange for meals to be sent to the room, but he would understand–it would not be as she would wish the service.

He thanked her and went upstairs. *La petite* Rose was reading about Babar to Sheila from the picture-book; she was curled up in a heap on the bed and they were looking at the pictures together. Sheila looked up at Howard, bright and vivacious, as he remembered her at Cidoton.

'*Regardez*,' she said, '*voici Jacko* climbing right up the *queue de* Babar on to his back!' She wriggled in exquisite amusement. 'Isn't he *naughty!*'

He stopped and looked at the picture with them. 'He is a naughty monkey, isn't he?' he said.

Sheila said: '*Drefully* naughty.'

Rose said very softly: '*Qu'est-ce que monsieur a dit?*'

Ronnie explained to her in French, and the bilingual children went on in the language of the country. To Howard they always spoke in English, but French came naturally to them when playing with other children. It was not easy for the old man to determine in which language they were most at home. On the whole, Ronnie seemed to prefer to speak in English. Sheila slipped more naturally into French, perhaps because she was younger and more recently in charge of nurses.

The children were quite happy by themselves. Howard got out the attaché case and looked at it; it was very small to hold necessities for three of them. He decided that Ronnie might carry that one, and he would get a rather larger case to carry himself, to supplement it. Fired by this idea, he went out of the bedroom to go to buy a cheap fibre case.

On the landing he met the *femme de chambre*. She hesitated, then stopped him.

'Monsieur is leaving tomorrow?' she said.

'I have to go away, because they want the room,' he replied. 'But I think the little girl is well enough to travel. I shall get her up for *déjeuner*, and then this afternoon she can come out for a little walk with us.'

'Ah, that will be good for her. A little walk, in the sun.' She hesitated again, and then she said: 'Monsieur is travelling direct to England?'

He nodded. 'I shall not stay in Paris. I shall take the first train to Saint Malo.'

She turned her face up to him, lined and prematurely old, beseechingly. 'Monsieur–it is terrible to ask. Would you take *la petite* Rose with you, to England?'

He was silent; he did not quite know what to say to that. She went on hurriedly.

'I have the money for the fare, monsieur. And Rose is a good little girl–oh, she is so good, that one. She would not trouble monsieur, no more than a little mouse.'

Every instinct warned the old man that he must kill this thing stone dead–quick. Though he would not admit it to himself, he knew that to win through to England would take all his energy, burdened as he was with two little children. In the background of his mind lurked fear, fear of impending, absolute disaster.

He stared down at the tear-stained, anxious face, and temporised. 'But why do you want to send her to England?' he asked. 'The war will never come to Dijon. She will be quite safe here.'

The woman said: 'I have no money, monsieur. Her father is in England, but he cannot send money to us here. It is better that she should go to England, now.'

He said: 'Perhaps I could arrange to help him to send money.' There was still a substantial balance on his letter of credit. 'You do not want her to leave you, do you?'

She said: 'Monsieur, things are happening in France that you English do not understand. We are afraid of what is coming, all of us . . .'

They were silent for a moment.

'I know things are very bad,' he said quietly. 'It may be difficult for me, an Englishman, to get to England now. I don't think it will be–but it may. Suppose I could not get her out of the country for some reason?'

She wrinkled her face up and lifted the corner of her apron to her eyes. 'In England she would be safe,' she muttered. 'I do not know what is going to happen to us, here in Dijon. I am afraid.' She began to cry again.

He patted her awkwardly upon the shoulder. 'There,' he said. 'I will think about it this afternoon. It's not a thing to be decided in a hurry.' He made his escape from her, and went down to the street.

Once out in the street, he quite forgot what he had come for. Absent-mindedly he walked towards the centre of the town, wondering how he could evade the charge of another child. Presently, he sat down in a café and ordered himself a *bock*.

It was not that he had anything against *la petite* Rose. On the contrary, he liked the child; she was a quiet, motherly little thing. But she would be another drag on him at a time when he knew with every instinct of his being that he could tolerate no further drags. He knew himself to be in danger. The sweep and drive of Germany down in France was no secret any longer; it was like the rush through Belgium had been in the last war, only more intense. If he delayed a moment longer than was necessary, he would be engulfed by the invading army. For an Englishman that meant a concentration camp, for a man of his age that probably meant death.

From his chair upon the pavement he stared out upon the quiet, sunlit *Place*. Bad times were coming for the French; he and his children must get out of it, damn quick. If the Germans conquered they would bring with them, inevitably, their trail of pillage and starvation, gradually mounting towards anarchy as they faced the inevitable defeat. He must not let his children be caught in that. Children in France, if she were beaten down, would have a terrible time.

It was bad luck on little Rose. He had nothing against her; indeed, she had helped him in the last two days. He would have found it difficult to manage Sheila if Rose had not been there. She had kept the little girl, hardly more than a baby, happy and amused in a way that Howard himself could never have managed alone.

It was a pity that it was impossible to take her. In normal times he might have been glad of her; he had tried in Cidoton to find a young girl who would travel with them to Calais. True, Rose was only ten years old, but she was peasant-French; they grew up very quickly . . .

Was it impossible to take her?

Now it seemed desperately cruel, impossible to leave her behind.

He sat there miserably irresolute for half an hour. In the end he got up and walked slowly back to the hotel, desperately worried. In his appearance he had aged five years.

He met the *femme de chambre* upon the landing. 'I have made up my mind,' he said heavily. '*La petite* Rose may come with us to England; I will take her to her father. She must be ready to start tomorrow morning, at seven o'clock.'

4

That night Howard slept very little. He lay on his bed upon the floor, revolving in his mind the things he had to do, the various alternative plans he must make if things should go awry. He had no fear that they would not reach Paris. They would get there all right; there was a train every three or four hours. But after that—what then? Would he be able to get out of Paris again, to Saint Malo for the boat to England? That was the knotty point. Paris had stood a siege before, in 1870; it might well be that she was going to stand another one. With three children on his hands he could not let himself be caught in a besieged city. Somehow or other he must find out about the journey to England before they got to Paris.

He got up at about half past five, and shaved and dressed. Then he awoke the children; they were fretful at being roused and Sheila cried a little, so that he had to stop and take her on his lap and wipe her eyes and make a fuss of her. In spite of the tears she was cool and well, and after a time submitted to be washed and dressed.

Ronnie said, sleepily: 'Are we going in the motor-car?'

'No,' said the old man, 'not today, I couldn't get a car to go in.'

'Are we going in a *char de combat*?'

'No. We're going in a train.'

'Is that the train we're going to sleep in?'

Howard shook his head patiently. 'I couldn't manage that, either. We may have to sleep in it, but I hope that we'll be on the sea tonight.'

'On a ship?'

'Yes. Go on and clean your teeth; I've put the toothpaste on the brush for you.'

There was a thunderous roar above the hotel, and an aeroplane swept low over the station. It flew away directly in a line with their window, a twin-engined, low-wing monoplane, dark green in colour. In the distance there was a little, desultory rattle, like musketry fire upon a distant range.

The old man sat upon the bed, staring at it as it receded in the distance. It couldn't possibly . . .

Ronnie said: 'Wasn't that one *low*, Mr Howard?'

They'd never have the nerve to fly so low as that. It must have been a French one. 'Very low,' he said, a little unsteadily. 'Go on and clean your teeth.'

Presently there was a tap upon the door, and the *femme de chambre* was there bearing a tray of coffee and rolls. Behind her came *la petite* Rose, dressed in her Sunday best, with a large black straw hat, a tight black overcoat, and white socks. She looked very uncomfortable.

Howard said kindly in French: 'Good morning, Rose. Are you coming with us to England?'

She said: '*Oui, monsieur.*'

The *femme de chambre* said: 'All night she has been talking about going in the train, and going to England, and going to live with her father. She has hardly slept at all, that one.' There was a twist in her smile as she spoke; it seemed to Howard that she was not far from tears again.

'That's fine,' he said. He turned to the *femme de chambre*. 'Sit down and have a cup of coffee with us. Rose will, won't you, Rose?'

The woman said: '*Merci, monsieur.* But I have the sandwiches to prepare, and I have had my coffee.' She rubbed the little girl's shoulder. 'Would you like another cup of coffee, *ma petite*?'

She left Rose with them and went out. In the bedroom Howard sat the children down, each with a buttered roll to eat and cup full of weak coffee to drink. The children ate very slowly; he had finished his own meal by the time they were only half-way through. He pottered about and packed up their small luggage; Rose had her own things in a little attaché case upon the floor beside her.

The children ate on industriously. The *femme de chambre* came back with several large, badly-wrapped parcels of food for the journey, and a very large wine bottle full of milk. 'There,' she said unsteadily. 'Nobody will starve today!'

The children laughed merrily at the poor joke. Rose had finished, and Ronnie was engulfing the last mouthful, but Sheila was still eating steadily. There was nothing now to wait for, and the old man was anxious to get to the station for fear that they might miss a train. 'You don't want that,' he said to Sheila, indicating her half-eaten roll. 'You'd better leave it. We've got to go now.'

'I want it,' she said mutinously.

'But we've got to go now.'

'I want it.'

He was not going to waste energy over that. 'All right,' he said, 'you can bring it along with you.' He picked up their bags and shepherded them all out into the corridor and down the stairs.

At the door of the hotel he turned to the *femme de chambre*. 'If there is any difficulty I shall come back here,' he said. 'Otherwise, as I said, I will send a telegram when we reach England, and Rose is with her father.'

She said quickly: 'But monsieur must not pay for that, Henri will send the telegram.'

He was touched. 'Anyway, it will be sent directly we arrive in London. *Au revoir, mademoiselle.*'

'*Au revoir, monsieur. Bonne chance.*' She stood and watched them as he guided the three children across the road in the thin morning sunlight, the tears running all unheeded down the furrows of her face.

In the station there was great confusion. It was quite impossible to find out the times or likelihood of trains, or whether, among all the thronging soldiers, there would be seats for children. The most that he could learn was that trains for Paris came in at *Quai* 4 and that there had been two since midnight. He went to the booking-office to get a ticket for Rose, but it was closed.

'One does not take tickets any more,' a bystander said. 'It is not necessary.'

The old man stared at him. 'One pays, then, on the train, perhaps?'

The man shrugged his shoulders. 'Perhaps.'

There was nobody to check tickets as they passed on to the platform. He led the children through the crowd, Sheila still chewing her half-eaten roll of bread, clutched firmly in a hand already hot. *Quai* 4 was practically deserted, rather to his surprise. There did not seem to be great competition to get to Paris; all the traffic seemed to be the other way.

He saw an engine-driver, and approached him: 'It is here that the train for Paris will arrive?'

'But certainly.'

The statement was not reassuring. The empty spaces of the platform oppressed the old man; they were unnatural, ominous. He walked along to a seat and put down all the parcels and attaché cases on it, then settled down to wait until a train should come.

The children began running up and down the platform, playing games of their own making. Presently, mindful of the chill that had delayed him, he called Ronnie and Sheila to him and took off their coats, thinking to put them on when they were in the train. As an afterthought he turned to Rose.

'You also,' he said. 'You will be better playing without your coat, and the hat.'

He took them off and put them on the seat beside him. Then he lit his pipe, and settled down to wait in patience for the train.

It came at about half past eight, when they had been there for an hour and a half. There were a few people on the platform by that time, not very many. It steamed into the station, towering above them; there were two soldiers on the footplate of the engine with the train crew.

To his delight, it was not a crowded train. He made as quickly as he could for a first-class compartment, and found one occupied only by two morose officers of the *Armée de l'Air*. The children swarmed on to the seats and climbed all over the carriage, examining everything, chattering to each other in mixed French and English. The two officers looked blacker; before five minutes had elapsed they had got up, swearing below their breath, and had removed to another carriage.

Howard looked at them helplessly as they went. He would have liked to apologise, but he didn't know how to put it.

Presently, he got the children to sit down. Mindful of chills he said: 'You'd better put your coats on now. Rose, you put yours on, too.'

He proceeded to put Sheila into hers. Rose looked around the carriage blankly. 'Monsieur–where is my coat? And my hat, also?'

He looked up. 'Eh? You had them when we got into the train?'

But she had not had them. She had rushed with the other children to the carriage, heedless, while Howard hurried along behind her, burdened with luggage. Her coat and hat had been left upon the station bench.

Her face wrinkled up, and she began to cry. The old man stared at her irritably for a moment; he had thought that she would be a help to him. Then the patience born of seventy years of disappointments came to his aid; he sat down and drew her to him, wiping her eyes. 'Don't bother about it,' he said gently. 'We'll get another hat and another coat in Paris. You shall choose them yourself.'

She sobbed: 'But they were so expensive.'

He wiped her eyes again. 'Never mind,' he said. 'It couldn't be helped. I'll tell your aunt when I send the telegram that it wasn't your fault.'

Presently she stopped crying. Howard undid one of his many parcels of food and they all had a bit of an orange to eat, and all troubles were forgotten.

The train went slowly, stopping at every station and occasionally in between. From Dijon to Tonnerre is seventy miles; they pulled out of that station at about half past eleven, three hours after leaving Dijon. The children had stood the journey pretty well so far; for the last hour they had been running up and down the corridor shouting, while the old man dozed uneasily in a corner of the compartment.

He roused after Tonnerre, and fetched them all back into the carriage for *déjeuner* of sandwiches and milk and oranges. They ate slowly, with frequent distractions to look out of the window. Sandwiches had a tendency to become mislaid during these pauses, and to vanish down between the cushions of the seats. Presently they were full. He gave them each a cup of milk, and laid Sheila down to rest upon the seat, covered over with the blanket he had bought in Dijon. He made Rose and Ronnie sit down quietly and look at Babar; then he was able to rest himself.

From Tonnerre to Joigny is thirty miles. The train was going slower than ever, stopping for long periods for no apparent reason. Once, during one of these pauses, a large flight of aeroplanes passed by the window, flying very high; the old man was shocked to hear the noise of gunfire, and to see a few white puffs of smoke burst in the cloudless sky far, far below them. It seemed incredible, but they must be German. He strained his eyes for fighters so far as he could do without calling the attention of the children from their books, but there were no fighters to be seen. The machines wheeled slowly round and headed back towards the east, unhindered by the ineffective fire.

The old man sank back into his seat, full of doubts and fears.

He was dozing a little when the train pulled into Joigny soon after one o'clock. It stood there in the station in the hot sunlight, interminably. Presently a man came down the corridor.

'*Descendez, monsieur*,' he said. 'This train goes no farther.'

Howard stared up at him dumbfounded. 'But–this is the Paris train?'

'It is necessary to change here. One must descend.'

'When will the next train leave for Paris?'

'I do not know, monsieur. That is a military affair.'

He got the children into their coats, gathered his things together, and presently was on the platform, burdened with his luggage, with the three children trailing after him. He went straight to the stationmaster's office. There was an officer there, a *capitaine des transports*. The old man asked a few straight questions, and got straight answers.

'There will be no more trains for Paris, monsieur. None at all. I cannot tell you why, but no more trains will run north from Joigny.'

There was a finality in his tone that brooked no argument. The old man said: 'I am travelling to Saint Malo, for England, with these children. How would you advise me to get there?'

The young officer stared at him. 'Saint Malo? That is not the easiest journey, now, monsieur.' He thought for a moment. 'There would be trains from Chartres . . . And in one hour, at half past two, there is an autobus for Montargis . . . You must go by Montargis, monsieur. By the autobus to Montargis, then to Pithiviers, from Pithiviers to Angerville, and from Angerville to Chartres. From Chartres you will be able to go by train to Saint Malo.'

He turned to an angry Frenchwoman behind Howard, and the old man was elbowed out of the way. He retired on to the platform, striving to remember the names of the places that he had just heard. Then he thought of his little *Baedeker* and got it out, and traced the recommended course across country to Chartres. It skirted round Paris, sixty miles farther west. So long as there were buses one could get to Chartres that way, but Heaven alone knew how long it would take.

He knew the ropes where French country autobuses were concerned. He went and found the bus out in the station yard, and sat in it with the children. If he had been ten minutes later he would not have found a seat.

Worried and distracted by the chatter of the children, he tried to plan his course. To go on to Montargis seemed the only thing to do, but was he wise to do it? Would it not be better to try and travel back to Dijon? The route that he had been given through Montargis to Chartres was quite a sensible one according to his *Baedeker*; it lay along a good main road for the whole of the hundred miles or so to Chartres. This bus would give him a good lift of thirty-five or forty miles upon the way, so that by the time he left it he would be within sixty miles of Chartres and the railway to Saint Malo; provided he could get a bus to carry him that sixty miles he would be quite all right. If all went well he would reach Chartres that night, and Saint Malo the next morning; then the cross-Channel boat and he would be home in England.

It seemed all right, but was it really wise? He could get back to Dijon, possibly, though even that did not seem very certain. But if he got back there, what then? With the Germans driving forward into France from the north, and the Italians coming up from the south, Dijon seemed to be between two fires. He could not stay indefinitely in Dijon. It was better, surely, to take courage and go forward in the bus, north and by west in the direction of the Channel and home.

The bus became filled with a hot, sweating crowd of French country people. All were agitated and upset, all bore enormous packages with them, all were heading to the west. Howard took Sheila on his knee to make more room and squeezed Ronnie standing up between his legs. Rose pressed up against him, and an enormous woman with a very small infant in her arms shared the seat with them. From the conversation of the people in the bus Howard learned that the Germans were still pouring on, but that Paris would be defended to the last. Nobody knew how far the Germans had advanced, how near to Joigny they might be. It was wise to move, to go and stay with relations farther to the west.

One man said: 'The Chamber has left Paris. It is now at Tours.' Somebody else said that that rumour was not true, and a desultory argument began. Nobody seemed to take much interest in the Chamber; Paris and the life of cities meant very little to these peasants and near-peasants.

It was suffocatingly hot in the bus. The two English children stood it better than Howard could have expected; *la petite* Rose seemed to be more affected than they were. Howard, looking down, saw that she had gone very white. He bent towards her.

'Are you tired?' he said kindly. She took her head mutely. He turned and struggled with the window at his side; presently he succeeded in opening it a little and letting in a current of warm, fresh air.

Presently the driver climbed into his seat, and the grossly overloaded vehicle lumbered from the square.

The movement brought a little more air into the bus.

They left the town after a couple of stops, carrying an additional load of people on the roof. They started out along the long straight roads of France, dusty and in poor repair. The dust swirled round the heavy vehicle; it drove in at the open window, powdering them all. Ronnie, standing between the old man's legs, clung to the window, avid for all that he could see; Howard turned Sheila on his lap with difficulty, so that she could see out too.

Beside him, presently, Rose made a little wailing cry. Howard looked down, and saw her face white with a light greenish hue; before he could do anything to help her she had vomited upon the floor.

For a moment he was startled and disgusted. Then patience came back to him; children couldn't help that sort of thing. She was coughing and weeping; he pulled out his handkerchief and wiped her face and comforted her.

'*Pauvre petite chou*,' he said awkwardly. 'You will be better now. It is the heat.'

With some struggling he moved Sheila over and lifted Rose up on his knee, so that she could see out and have more air. She was still crying bitterly; he wiped her eyes and talked to her as gently as he could. The broad woman by him smiled serenely, quite unmoved by the disaster.

'It is the rocking,' she said in soft Midland French, 'like the sea. Always I have been sick when, as a little girl, I have travelled. Always, always. In the train and in the bus, always, quite the same.' She bent down. '*Sois tranquille, ma petite*,' she said. 'It is nothing, that.'

Rose glanced up at her, and stopped crying. Howard chose the cleanest corner of his handkerchief and wiped her eyes. Thereafter she sat very quiet and subdued upon his knee, watching the slowly moving scene outside the window.

'I'm never sick in motor-cars,' said Ronnie proudly in English. The woman looked at them with new curiosity; hitherto they had spoken in French.

The road was full of traffic, all heading to the west. Old battered motor-cars, lorries, mule carts, donkey-carts, all were loaded to disintegration point with people making for Montargis. These wound in and out among the crowds of people pushing hand-carts, perambulators, wheelbarrows even, all loaded with their goods. It was incredible to Howard; it seemed as though the whole countryside were in flight before the armies. The women working in the fields looked up from time to time in pauses of their work to stare at the strange cavalcade upon the highway. Then they bent again to the harvest of their roots; the work in hand was more important than the strange tides that flowed upon the road.

Half-way to Montargis the bus heeled slowly to the near side. The driver wrestled with the steering; a clattering bump, rhythmic, came from the near back wheel. The vehicle drew slowly to a stop beside the road.

The driver got down from his seat to have a look. Then he walked slowly back to the entrance to the bus. '*Un pneu*,' he said succinctly. '*Il faut descendre—tout le monde.* We must change the wheel.'

Howard got down with relief. They had been sitting in the bus for nearly two hours, of which an hour had been upon the road. The children were hot and tired and fretful; a change would obviously be a good thing. He took them one by one behind a little bush in decent manner; a proceeding which did not escape the little crowd of passengers collected by the bus. They nudged each other. '*C'est un anglais . . .*'

The driver, helped by a couple of the passengers, wrestled to jack up the bus and get the flat wheel off. Howard watched them working for a little time; then it occurred to him that this was a good opportunity to give the children tea. He fetched his parcel of food from the rack, and took the children a few yards up the road from the crowd. He sat them down upon the grass verge in the shade of a tree, and gave them sandwiches and milk.

The road stretched out towards the west, dead straight. As far as he could see it was thronged with vehicles, all moving the same way. He felt it really was a most extraordinary sight, a thing that he had never seen before, a population in migration.

Presently Rose said she heard an aeroplane.

Instinctively, Howard turned his head. He could hear nothing.

'I hear it,' Ronnie said. 'Lots of aeroplanes.'

Sheila said: 'I want to hear the aeroplane.'

'Silly,' said Ronnie. 'There's lots of them. Can't you hear?'

The old man strained his ears, but he could hear nothing. 'Can you see where they are?' he asked, nonchalantly. A cold fear lurked in the background of his mind.

The children scanned the sky. '*V'là*,' said Rose, pointing suddenly. '*Trois avions—là.*'

Ronnie twisted round in excitement to Howard. 'They're coming down towards us! Do you think we'll see them close?'

'Where are they?' he enquired. He strained his eyes in the direction from which they had come. 'Oh, I see. They won't come anywhere near here. Look, they're going down over there.'

'Oh . . .' said Ronnie, disappointed. 'I did want to see them close.'

They watched the aircraft losing height towards the road, about two miles away. Howard expected to see them land among the fields beside the road, but they did not land. They flattened out and flew along just above the tree-tops, one on each side of the road and one behind flying down the middle. A little crackling rattle sounded from them as they came. The old man stared, incredulous–it could not be . . .

Then, in a quick succession, from the rear machine, five bombs fell on the road. Howard saw the bombs actually leave the aeroplane, saw five great spurts of flame upon the road, saw queer, odd fragments hurled into the air.

From the bus a woman shrieked: '*Les Allemands!*' and pandemonium broke loose. The driver of the little Peugeot car fifty yards away saw the gesticulations of the crowd, looked back over his shoulder, and drove straight into the back of a mule cart, smashing one of its wheels and cascading the occupants and load on to the road. The French around the bus dashed madly for the door, hoping for shelter in the glass and plywood body, and jammed in a struggling, pitiful mob in the entrance. The machines flew on towards them, their machine-guns spitting flame. The rear machine, its bombs discharged, flew forward and to the right; with a weaving motion the machine upon the right dropped back to the rear centre, ready in its turn to bomb the road.

There was no time to do anything, to go anywhere, nor was there anywhere to go. Howard caught Sheila and Ronnie and pulled them close to him, flat upon the ground. He shouted to Rose to lie down, quickly.

Then the machines were on them, low-winged, single-engined monoplanes with curious bent wings, dark green in colour. A burst of fire was poured into the bus from the machines to right and left; a stream of tracer-bullets shot forward up the road from the centre aircraft. A few bullets lickered straight over Howard and his children on the grass and spattered in the ground a few yards behind them.

For a moment Howard saw the gunner in the rear cockpit as he fired at them. He was a young man, not more than twenty, with a keen, tanned face. He wore a yellow students' corps cap, and he was laughing as he fired.

Then the two flanking aircraft had passed, and the centre one was very near. Looking up, the old man could see the bombs slung in their racks beneath the wing; he watched in agony for them to fall. They did not fall. The machine passed by them, not a hundred feet away. He watched it as it went, sick with relief. He saw the bombs leave the machine three hundred yards up the road, and watched dumbly as the debris flew upwards. He saw the wheel of a cart go sailing through the air, to land in the field.

Then that graceful, weaving dance began again, the machine in rear changing places with the one on the left. They vanished in the distance; presently Howard heard the thunder of another load of bombs upon the road.

He released the children, and sat up upon the grass. Ronnie was flushed and excited. 'Weren't they *close!*' he said. 'I did see them well. Did you see them well, Sheila? Did you hear them firing the guns?'

He was ecstatically pleased. Sheila was quite unaffected. She said: 'May I have some orange?'

Howard said slowly and mechanically: 'No, you've had enough to eat. Drink up your milk.' He turned to Rose and found her inclined to tears. He knelt up and moved over to her. 'Did anything hit you?' he asked in French.

She shook her head dumbly.

'Don't cry, then,' he said kindly. 'Come and drink your milk. It'll be good for you.'

She turned her face up to him. 'Are they coming back? I don't like the noise they make.'

He patted her on the shoulder. 'Never mind,' he said a little unsteadily. 'The noise won't hurt you. I don't think they're coming back.' He filled up the one cup with milk and gave it to her. 'Have a drink.'

Ronnie said: 'I wasn't frightened, was I?'

Sheila echoed: 'I wasn't frightened, was I?'

The old man said patiently: 'Nobody was frightened. Rose doesn't like that sort of noise, but that's not being frightened.' He stared over to the little crowd round the bus. Something had happened there; he must go and see. 'You can have an orange,' he said. 'One-third each. Will you peel it, Rose?'

'*Mais oui, monsieur.*'

He left the children happy in the prospect of more food, and went slowly to the bus. There was a violent and distracted clamour from the crowd; most of the women were in tears of fright and rage. But to his astonishment, there were no casualties save one old woman who had lost two fingers of her left hand, severed cleanly near the knuckles by a bullet. Three women, well accustomed to first aid in accidents upon the farm, were tending her, not inexpertly.

Howard was amazed that no one had been killed. From the right a dozen bullets had entered the body of the bus towards the rear; from the left the front wheels, bonnet and radiator had been badly shot about. Between the two the crowd of peasants milling round the door had escaped injury. Even the crowd in the small Peugeot had escaped, though one of the women in the mule cart was shot through the thigh. The mule itself was dying in the road.

There was nothing he could do to help the wounded women. His attention was attracted by a gloomy little knot of men round the driver of the bus; they had lifted the bonnet and were staring despondently at the engine. The old man joined them; he knew little of machinery, but it was evident even to him that all was not quite right. A great pool of water lay beneath the engine of the bus; from holes in radiator and cylinder casting the brown, rusty water still ran out.

One of the men turned aside to spit. '*Ca ne marche plus*,' he said succinctly.

It took a moment or two for the full meaning of this to come home to Howard. 'What does one do?' he asked the driver. 'Will there be another bus?'

'Not unless they find a madman for a driver.' There was a strained silence. Then the driver said: '*Il faut continuer à pied.*'

It became apparent to Howard that this was nothing but the ugly truth. It was about four in the afternoon and Montargis was twenty-five kilometres, say fifteen miles, farther on, nearer to them than Joigny. They had passed one or two villages upon the road from Joigny; no doubt one or two more lay ahead before Montargis. But there would be no chance of buses starting at these places, nor was there any reasonable chance of a hotel.

It was appalling, but it was the only thing. He and the children would have to walk, very likely the whole of the way to Montargis.

He went into the wrecked body of the bus and collected their things, the two attaché cases, the little suitcase, and the remaining parcels of food. There was too much for him to carry very far unless the children could carry some of it; he knew that that would not be satisfactory for long. Sheila could carry nothing; indeed, she would have to be carried herself a great deal of the way. Ronnie and Rose, if they were to walk fifteen miles, would have to travel light.

He took his burdens back to the children and laid them down upon the grass. It was impossible to take the suitcase with them; he packed it with the things that they could spare most easily and left it in the bus in the faint hope that one day it might somehow be retrieved. That left the two bulging little cases and the parcels of food. He could carry those himself.

'We're going to walk on to Montargis,' he explained to the children. 'The bus won't go.'

'Why not?' asked Ronnie.

'There's something the matter with the engine.'

'Oh–may I go and see?'

Howard said firmly: 'Not now. We're just going to walk on.' He turned to Rose. 'You will like walking more than riding in the bus, I know.'

She said: 'I did feel so ill.'

'It was very hot. You're feeling better now?'

She smiled. '*Oui, monsieur.*'

They started out to walk in the direction of Montargis. The heat of the day was passing; it was not yet cool, but it was bearable for walking. They went very slowly, limited by the rate at which Sheila walked, which was slow. The old man strolled patiently along. It was no good worrying the children with attempts to hurry them; they had many miles to cover and he must let them go at their own pace.

Presently they came to the place where the second load of bombs had dropped.

There were two great craters in the road, and three more among the trees at the verge. There had been a cart of some sort there. There was a little crowd of people busy at the side of the road; too late, he thought to make a detour from what he feared to let the children see.

Ronnie said clearly and with interest: 'Are those dead people, Mr Howard?'

He steered them over to the other side of the road. 'Yes,' he said quietly. 'You must be very sorry for them.'

'May I go and see?'

'No,' he said. 'You mustn't go and look at people when they're dead. They want to be left alone.'

'Dead people do look funny, don't they, Mr Howard?'

He could not think of what to say to that one, and herded them past in silence. Sheila was singing a little song and showed no interest; Rose crossed herself and walked by quickly with averted eyes.

They strolled on at their slow pace up the road. If there had been a side road Howard would have taken it, but there was no side road. It was impossible to make a detour other than by walking through the fields; it would not help him to turn back towards Joigny. It was better to go on.

They passed other casualties, but the children seemed to take little interest. He shepherded them along as quickly as he could; when they had passed the target for the final load of bombs there would probably be an end to this parade of death. He could see that place now, half a mile ahead. There were two motorcars jammed in the road, and several trees seemed to have fallen.

Slowly, so slowly, they approached the place. One of the cars was wrecked beyond redemption. It was a Citroën front drive saloon; he bomb had burst immediately ahead of it, splitting the radiator in two and blasting in the windscreen. Then a tree had fallen straight on top of it, crushing the roof down till it touched the chassis. There was much blood upon the road.

Four men, from a decrepit old de Dion, were struggling to lift the tree aside to clear the road for their own car to pass. On the grass verge a quiet heap was roughly covered by a rug.

Pulling and heaving at the tree, the men rolled it from the car and dragged it back, clearing a narrow passage with great difficulty. They wiped their brows, sweating, and clambered back into their old two-seater. Howard stopped by them as the driver started his engine.

'Killed?' he asked quietly.

The man said bitterly: 'What do you think? The filthy Boches!' He let the clutch in and the car moved slowly forward round the tree and up the road ahead of them.

Fifty yards up the road it stopped. One of the men leaned back and shouted at him: 'You—with the children. You! *Gardez le petit gosse!*'

They let the clutch in and drove on. Howard looked down in bewilderment at Rose. 'What did he mean?'

'He said there was a little boy,' she said.

He looked around. 'There's no little boy here.'

Ronnie said: 'There's only dead people here. Under that rug.' He pointed with his finger.

Sheila awoke to the world about her. 'I want to see the dead people.'

The old man took her hand firmly in his own. 'Nobody goes to look at them,' he said. 'I told you that.' He stared around him in bewilderment.

Sheila said: 'Well, may I go and play with the boy?'

'There's no boy here, my dear.'

'Yes there is. Over there.'

She pointed to the far side of the road, twenty yards beyond the tree. A little boy of five or six was standing there, in fact, utterly motionless. He was dressed in grey, grey stockings above the knee, grey shorts, and a grey jersey. He was standing absolutely still, staring down the road towards them. His face was a dead, greyish white in colour.

Howard caught his breath at the sight of him, and said very softly: 'Oh, my God!' He had never seen a child looking like that, in all his seventy years.

He crossed quickly over to him, the children following. The little boy stood motionless as he approached, staring at him vacantly. The old man said: 'Are you hurt at all?'

There was no answer. The child did not appear to have heard him.

'Don't be afraid,' Howard said. Awkwardly he dropped down on one knee. 'What is your name?'

There was no answer. Howard looked round for some help, but for the moment there were no pedestrians. A couple of cars passed slowly circumnavigating the tree, and then a lorry full of weary, unshaven French soldiers. There was nobody to give him any help.

He got to his feet again, desperately perplexed. He must go on his way, not only to reach Montargis, but also to remove his children from the sight of that appalling car, capable, if they realised its grim significance, of haunting them for the rest of their lives. He could not stay a moment longer than was necessary in that place. Equally, it seemed impossible to leave this child. In the next village, or at any rate in Montargis, there would be a convent; he would take him to the nuns.

He crossed quickly to the other side of the road, telling the children to stay where they were. He lifted up a corner of the rug. They were a fairly well-dressed couple, not more than thirty years old, terribly mutilated in death. He nerved himself and opened the man's coat. There was a wallet in the inside pocket; he opened it, and there was the identity-card. Jean Duchot, of 8 bis, Rue de la Victoire, Lille.

He took the wallet and some letters and stuffed them into his pocket; he would turn them over to the next gendarme he saw. Somebody would have to arrange the burial of the bodies, but that was not his affair.

He went back to the children. Sheila came running to him, laughing. 'He is a funny little boy,' she said merrily. 'He won't say anything at all!'

The other two had stepped back and were staring with childish intensity at the white-faced boy in grey, still staring blankly at the ruins of the car. Howard put down the cases and took Sheila by the hand. 'Don't bother him,' he said. 'I don't suppose he wants to play just now.'

'Why doesn't he want to play?'

He did not answer that, but said to Rose and Ronnie: 'You take one of the cases each for a little bit.' He went up to the little boy and said to him: 'Will you come with us? We're all going to Montargis.'

There was no answer, no sign that he had heard.

For a moment Howard stood in perplexity; then he stooped and took his hand. In that hot afternoon it was a chilly, damp hand that he felt. '*Allons, mon vieux*,' he said, with gentle firmness, 'we're going to Montargis.' He turned to the road; the boy in grey stirred and trotted docilely beside him. Leading one child with either hand, the old man strolled down the long road, the other children followed behind, each with a case.

More traffic overtook them, and now there was noticeable a greater proportion of military lorries mingled with the cars. Not only the civilians streamed towards the west; a good number of soldiers seemed to be going that way too. The lorries crashed and clattered on their old-fashioned solid rubber tyres, grinding their ancient gears. Half of them had acetylene headlamps garnishing the radiators, relics of the armies of 1918, stored twenty years in transport sheds behind the barracks in quiet country towns. Now they were out upon the road again, but going in the other direction.

The dust they made was very trying to the children. With the heat and the long road they soon began to flag; Ronnie complained that the case he was carrying hurt his arm, and Sheila wanted a drink, but all the milk was gone. Rose said her feet were hurting her. Only the limp little boy in grey walked on without complaint.

Howard did what he could to cheer them on, but they were obviously tiring. There was a farm not very far ahead; he turned into it, and asked the haggard old woman at the door if she would sell some milk. She said there was none, upon which he asked for water for the children. She led them to the well in the court-yard, not very distant from the midden, and pulled up a bucket for them; Howard conquered his scruples and his apprehensions and they all had a drink.

They rested a little by the well. In a barn, open to the court-yard, was an old farm cart with a broken wheel, evidently long disused. Piled into this was a miscellaneous assortment of odd rubbish, and among this rubbish was what looked like a perambulator.

He strolled across to look more closely, the old woman watching him, hawk-eyed. It was a perambulator in fact, forty or fifty years old, covered in filth, and with one broken spring. But it was a perambulator, all the same. He went back to the old lady and commenced to haggle for it.

Ten minutes later it was his, for a hundred and fifty francs. She threw in with that a frayed piece of old rope with which he made shift to lash the broken spring. Hens had been roosting on it, covering it with their droppings; he set Ronnie and Rose to pull up handfuls of grass to wipe it down with. When they had finished he surveyed it with some satisfaction. It was a filthy object still, and grossly expensive, but it solved a great many of his problems.

He bought a little bread from the old woman and put it with the cases in the pram. Rather to his surprise nobody wanted to ride, but they all wanted to push it; he found it necessary to arrange turns. 'The youngest first,' he said. 'Sheila can push it first.'

Rose said: 'May I take off my shoes? They hurt my feet.'

He was uncertain, revolving this idea in his head. 'I don't think that's a good idea,' he said. 'The road will not be nice to walk on.'

She said: 'But, monsieur, one does not wear shoes at all, except in Dijon.'

It seemed that she was genuinely used to going without shoes. After some hesitation he agreed to let her try it, and found that she moved freely and easily over the roughest parts of the road. He put her shoes and stockings in the pram, and spent the next quarter of an hour refusing urgent applications from the English children to copy her example.

Presently Sheila tired of pushing. Rose said: 'Now it is the turn of Pierre.' In motherly fashion she turned to the little boy in grey. 'Now, Pierre. Like this.' She brought him to the pram, still white-faced and listless, put his hands on the cracked china handles and began to push it with him.

Howard said to her: 'How do you know his name is Pierre?'

She stared at him. 'He said so—at the farm.'

The old man had not heard a word from the little boy; indeed, he had been secretly afraid that he had lost the power of speech. Not for the first time he was reminded of the gulf that separated him from the children, the great gulf that stretches between youth and age. It was better to leave the little boy to the care of the other children, rather than to terrify him with awkward, foreign sympathy and questions.

He watched the two children carefully as they pushed the pram. Rose seemed to have made some contact with the little fellow already, sufficient to encourage her. She chatted to him in childish, baby French. When she trotted with the pram he trotted with her; when she walked he walked, but otherwise he seemed completely unresponsive. The blank look never left his face.

Ronnie said: 'Why doesn't he say anything, Mr Howard? He is funny.'

Sheila echoed: 'Why doesn't he say anything?'

Howard said: 'He's been very unhappy. You must be as nice and as kind to him as ever you can.'

They digested this in silence for a minute. Then Sheila said: 'Have you got to be nice to him, too, Monsieur Howard?.

'Of course,' he said. 'Everybody's got to be as nice as ever they can be to him.'

She said directly, in French: 'Then why don't you make him a whistle, like you did for us?'

Rose looked up. '*Un sifflet?*'

Ronnie said in French: 'He can make whistles ever so well out of a bit of wood. He made some for us at Cidoton.'

She jumped up and down with pleasure. '*Ecoute*, Pierre,' she said. '*Monsieur va te fabriquer un sifflet!*'

They all beamed up at him in expectation. It was clear that in their minds a whistle was the panacea for all ills, the cure for all diseases of the spirit. They seemed to be completely in agreement on that point.

'I don't mind making him a whistle,' he said placidly. He doubted if it would be any good to Pierre, but it would please the other children. 'We'll have to find the right sort of bush. A hazel bush.'

'*Un coudrier*,' said Ronnie. '*Cherchons un coudrier.*'

They strolled along the road in the warm evening, pushing the pram and looking for a hazel bush. Presently Howard saw one. They had been walking for three-quarters of an hour since they had left the farm, and it was time the children had a rest; he crossed to the bush and cut a straight twig with his pocket-knife. Then he took them into the field a little way back from the traffic of the road and made them sit down upon the grass, and gave them an orange to eat between them. The three children sat watching him entranced as he began his work upon the twig, hardly attending to the orange. Rose sat with her arm round the little boy in grey; he did not seem to be capable of concentrating upon anything. Even the sections of the orange had to be put into his mouth.

The old man finished cutting, bound the bark back into place and lifted the whistle to his lips. It blew a little low note, pure and clear.

'There you are,' he said. 'That's for Pierre.'

Rose took it. '*Regarde*, Pierre,' she said, '*ce que monsieur t'a fait.*' She blew a note on it for him.

Then, gently, she put it to his lips. '*Siffle*, Pierre,' she said.

There was a little woody note above the rumble of the lorries on the road.

5

Presently they got back to the road and went on towards Montargis.

Evening was coming upon them; out of a cloudless sky the sun was dropping down to the horizon. It was the time of evening when in England birds begin to sing after a long, hot day. In the Middle France there are few birds because the peasant Frenchman sees to that on Sundays, but instinctively the old man listened for their song. He heard a different sort of song. He heard the distant hum of aeroplanes; in the far distance he heard the sharp crack of gunfire and some heavier explosions that perhaps were bombs. Upon the road the lorries of French troops, all making for the west, were thicker than ever.

Clearly it was impossible for them to reach Montargis. The road went on and on; by his reckoning they had come about five miles from where they had left the bus. There were still ten miles or so ahead of them, and night was coming on. The children were weary. Ronnie and Sheila were inclined to quarrel with each other; the old man felt that Sheila would burst into tears of temper and fatigue before so very long. Rose was not so buoyant as he had been and her flow of chatter to the little boy had ceased; she slipped along on her bare feet in silence, leading him by the hand. The little boy, Pierre, went on with her, white-faced and silent, stumbling a little now and then, the whistle held tight in his other hand.

It was time for them to find a lodging for the night.

The choice was limited. There was a farm on the right of the road, and half a mile farther on he could see a farm on the left of the road; farther than that the children could not walk. He turned into the first one. A placard nailed upon a post, *CHIEN MECHANT*, warned him, but did not warn the children. The dog, an enormous brindled creature, leaped out at them to the limit of his chain, raising a terrific clamour. The children scattered back, Sheila let out a roar of fright and tears, and Rose began to whimper. It was in the din of dog and children competing with each other that Howard presented himself at the door of the farm and asked for a bed for the children.

The gnarled old woman said: 'There are no beds here. Do you take this for a hotel?'

A buxom, younger woman behind her said: 'They could sleep in the barn, *ma mère*.'

The old dame said: 'Eh? the barn?' She looked Howard up and down. 'The soldiers sleep in the barn when we billet them. Have you any money?'

He said: 'I have enough to pay for a good bed for these children, madame.'

'Ten francs.'

'I have ten francs. May I see the barn?'

She led him through the cow-house to the barn behind. It was a large, bare apartment with a threshing floor at one end, empty and comfortless. The younger woman followed behind them.

He shook his head. 'I am desolated, madame, but the children must have a bed. I must look somewhere else.'

He heard the younger woman whisper something about the hay-loft. He heard the older woman protest angrily. He heard the young one say: '*Ils sont fatigués, les petits* . . .' Then they turned aside and conferred together.

The hay-loft proved to be quite possible. It was a shelter, anyway, and somewhere where the children could sleep. He made a bargain for them to sleep there for fifteen francs. He found that the women had milk to spare, but little food. He left the children in the loft and went and brought the pram in past the dog; he broke his bread in two and gave half of it to the younger woman, who would make bread and milk for the children.

Half an hour later he was doing what he could to make the children comfortable upon the hay. The younger woman came in and stood watching for a moment. 'You have no blankets, then?' she said.

He shook his head, bitterly regretful that he had left his blanket in the bus. 'It was necessary to leave everything, madame,' he said quietly.

She did not speak, but presently she went away. Ten minutes later she returned with two coarse blankets of the sort used for horses. 'Do not tell *ma mère*,' she said gruffly.

He thanked her, and busied himself making a bed for the children. She stood there watching him, silent and bovine. Presently the children were comfortable and settled for the night. He left them and walked to the door of the barn and stood looking out.

The woman by him said: 'You are tired yourself, monsieur.'

He was deadly tired. Now that his responsibilities were over for a while, he had suddenly become slack and faint. 'A little tired,' he said. 'I shall have supper and then I shall sleep with the children. *Bonne nuit*, madame.'

She went back to the farmhouse, and he turned to the pram, to find the other portion of the loaf of bread. Behind him the old woman called sharply from the door across the yard.

'You can come and have a bowl of soup with us, if you like.'

He went into the kitchen gratefully. They had a stockpot simmering upon a charcoal stove; the old woman helped him to a large bowl of steaming broth and gave him a spoon. He sat down gratefully at the bare, scrubbed table to consume it with his bread.

The woman said suddenly: 'Are you from Alsace? You speak like a German.'

He shook his head. 'I'm an Englishman.'

'Ah–an Englishman!' They looked at him with renewed interest. 'But the children, they are not English.'

The younger woman said: 'The bigger boy and the smaller girl are English. They were not talking French.'

With some difficulty he explained the position to them. They listened to him in silence, only half believing what he said. In all her life the old woman had never had a holiday; only very occasionally had she been beyond the market town. It was difficult for them to comprehend a world where people travelled to another country, far away from home, merely to catch fish. And as for an old man who took care of other people's children for them, it simply did not make sense at all.

Presently they stopped bothering him with their questions, and he finished the soup in silence.

He felt better after that, much better. He thanked them with grave courtesy and went out into the yard. Already it was dusk. On the road the lorries still rumbled past at intervals, but firing seemed to have ceased altogether.

The old woman followed him to the door. 'They do not stop tonight,' she said, indicating the road. 'The night before last the barn was full. Twenty-two francs for sleeping soldiers–all in one night.' She turned and went indoors again.

He went up to the loft. The children were all asleep, curled up together in odd attitudes; the little boy Pierre twitched and whimpered in his sleep. He still had the whistle clutched in one hand. Howard withdrew it gently and put it on the chopping machine, then spread the blanket more evenly over the sleeping forms. Finally he trod down a little of the hay into a bed and lay down himself, pulling his jacket round him.

Before sleep came to him he suffered a bad quarter of an hour. Here was a pretty kettle of fish, indeed. It had been a mistake ever to have left Joigny, but it had not seemed so at the time. He should have gone straight back to Dijon when he found he could not get to Paris, back to Switzerland, even. His effort to get through by bus to Chartres had failed most dismally, and here he was! Sleeping in a hay-loft, with four children utterly dependent on him, straight in the path of the invading German Army!

He turned uneasily in the hay. Things might not be so bad. The Germans, after all, could hardly get past Paris; that lay to the north of him, a sure shield the farther west he got. Tomorrow he would reach Montargis, even if it meant walking the whole way; the children could do ten miles in a day if they went at a slow pace and if the younger two had rides occasionally in the pram. At

Montargis he would hand the little boy in grey over to the sisters, and report the death of his parents to the police. At Montargis, at a town like that, there would be a bus to Pithiviers, perhaps even all the way to Chartres.

All night these matters rolled round in his mind, in the intervals of cold, uneasy slumber. He did not sleep well. Dawn came at about four, a thin grey light that stole into the loft, pointing the cobwebs strung between the rafters. He dozed and slept again; at about six he got up and went down the ladder and sluiced his face under the pump. The growth of thin stubble on his chin offended him, but he shrank from trying to shave beneath the pump. In Montargis there would be a hotel; he would wait till then.

The women were already busy about the work of the farm. He spoke to the older one, and asked if she would make some coffee for the children. Three francs, for the four of them, she said. He reassured her on that point, and went to get the children up.

He found them already running about; they had seen him go downstairs. He sent them down to wash their faces at the pump. The little boy in grey hung back. From the ladder Rose called to him, but he would not go.

Howard, folding up the blankets, glanced at him. 'Go on and wash your face,' he said in French. 'Rose is calling you.'

The little boy put his right hand on his stomach and bowed to him. 'Monsieur,' he whispered.

The old man stood looking at him nonplussed. It was the first time he had heard him speak. The child stood looking up at him imploringly, his hand still on his stomach.

'What's the matter, old boy?' Howard said in French. Silence. He dropped stiffly down upon one knee, till their heads were level. 'What is it?'

He whispered: '*J'ai perdu le sifflet.*'

The old man got up and gave it to him. 'Here it is,' he said. 'Quite safe. Now go on down and let Rose wash your face.' He watched him thoughtfully as he clambered backwards down the steps. 'Rose, wash his face for him.'

He gave the children their coffee in the kitchen of the farm with the remainder of the bread, attended to their more personal requirements, paid the old lady twenty francs for food and lodging. At about quarter past seven he led them one by one past the *chien méchant* and out on to the road again, pushing the pram before him.

High overhead a few aeroplanes passed on a pale blue, cloudless sky; he could not tell if they were French or German. It was another glorious summer morning. On the road the military lorries were thicker than ever, and once or twice in the first hour a team of guns passed by them, drawn by tired, sweating horses flogged westwards by dirty, unshaven men in horizon blue. That day there did not seem to be so many refugees upon the road. The cyclists and the walkers and the families in decrepit, overloaded pony-carts were just as numerous, but there were few private cars in evidence upon the road. For the first hour Howard walked continually looking backwards for a bus, but no bus came.

The children were very merry. They ran about and chattered to each other and to Howard, playing little games that now and then threatened their lives under the wheels of dusty lorries driven by tired men, and which had then to be checked. As the day grew warmer he let them take off their coats and jerseys and put them in the pram. Rose went barefoot as a matter of course; as a concession to the English children presently Howard let them take off stockings, though he made them keep their shoes on. He took off Pierre's stockings too.

The little boy seemed a trifle more natural, though he was still white and dumb. He had the whistle clutched tight in his hand and it still worked; now and again Sheila tried to get it away from him, but Howard had his eye upon her and put a stop to that.

'If you don't stop bothering him for it,' he said, 'you'll have to put your stockings on again.' He frowned at her; she eyed him covertly, and decided that he meant it.

From time to time Rose bent towards the little boy in grey. '*Siffle*, Pierre,' she would say. '*Siffle pour* Rose.' At that he would put the whistle to his lips and blow a little thin note. 'Ah, *c'est chic, ça.*' She jollied him along all morning, smiling shyly up at Howard every now and then.

They went very slowly, making not more than a mile and a half in each hour. It was no good hurrying the children, Howard thought. They would reach Montargis by evening, but only if the children took their own pace.

At about ten in the morning firing broke out to the north of them. It was very heavy firing, as of guns and howitzers; it puzzled the old man. It was distant, possibly ten miles away or more, but definitely to the north, between them and Paris. He was worried and perplexed. Surely it could not be that the Germans were surrounding Paris to the south? Was that the reason that the train had stopped at Joigny?

They reached a tiny hamlet at about ten o'clock, a place that seemed to be called La Croix. There was one small *estaminet* which sold a few poor groceries in a side room that was a little shop. The children had been walking for three hours and were beginning to tire; it was high time they had a rest. He led them in and bought them two long orange drinks between the four of them.

There were other refugees there, sitting glum and silent. One old man said presently, to no one in particular: '*On dit que les Boches ont pris Paris.*'

The wizened old woman of the house said that it was true. It had said so on the radio. A soldier had told her.

Howard listened, shaken to the core. It was incredible that such a thing could happen. Silence fell upon the room again; it seemed that no one had any more to say. Only the children wriggled on their chairs and discussed their drink. A dog sat in the middle of the floor scratching industriously, snapping now and then at flies.

The old man left them and went through into the shop. He had hoped to find some oranges, but no oranges were left, and no fresh bread. He explained his need to the woman, and examined the little stock of food she had; he bought from her half a dozen thick, hard biscuits each nine or ten inches in diameter and grey in colour, rather like dog-biscuits. He also bought some butter and a long, brown, doubtful-looking sausage. For his own weariness of the flesh, he bought a bottle of cheap brandy. That, with four bottles of the orange drink, completed his purchases. As he was turning away, however, he saw a single box of chocolate bars, and bought a dozen for the children.

Their rest finished, he led them out upon the road again. To encourage them upon the way he broke one of the chocolate bars accurately into four pieces and gave it to them. Three of the children took their portion avidly. The fourth shook his head dumbly and refused.

'*Merci, monsieur,*' he whispered.

The old man said gently in French: 'Don't you like chocolate, Pierre? It's so good.'

The child shook his head.

'Try a little bit.' The other children looked on curiously.

The little boy whispered: '*Merci, monsieur. Maman dit que non. Seulement après déjeuner.*'

For a moment the old man's mind went back to the torn bodies left behind them by the roadside covered roughly with a rug; he forced his mind away from that. 'All right,' he said in French, 'we'll keep it, and you shall have it after *déjeuner.*' He put the morsel carefully in a corner of the pram seat, the little boy in grey watched with grave interest. 'It will be quite safe there.'

Pierre trotted on beside him, quite content.

The two younger children tired again before long; in four hours they had walked six miles, and it was now very hot. He put them both into the pram and pushed them down the road, the other two walking by his side. Mysteriously now the lorry traffic was all gone; there was nothing on the road but refugees.

The road was full of refugees. Farm carts, drawn by great Flemish horses, lumbered down the middle of the road at walking pace, loaded with furniture and bedding and sacks of food and people. Between them and around them seethed the motor traffic; big cars and little cars, occasional ambulances and motor-bicycles, all going to the west. There were innumerable cyclists and long trails of people pushing hand-carts and perambulators in the torrid July heat. All were choked with dust, all sweating and distressed, all pressing on to Montargis. From time to time an aeroplane flew near the road; then there was panic and an accident or two. But no bombs were dropped that day, nor was the road to Montargis machine-gunned.

The heat was intense. At about a quarter to twelve they came to a place where a little stream ran beside the road, and here there was another block of many traffic blocks caused by the drivers of the farm wagons who stopped to water their horses. Howard decided to make a halt; he pushed the perambulator a little way over the field away from the road to where a little sandy spit ran out into the stream beneath the trees.

'We'll stop here for *déjeuner*,' he said to the children. 'Go and wash your hands and faces in the water.' He took the food and sat down in the shade; he was very tired, but there was still five miles or more to Montargis. Surely there would be a motor-bus there?

Ronnie said: 'May I paddle, Mr Howard?'

He roused himself. 'Bathe if you want to,' he said. 'It's hot enough.'

'May I really bathe?'

Sheila echoed: 'May I really bathe, too?'

He got up from the grass. 'I don't see why not,' he said slowly. 'Take your things off and have a bathe before *déjeuner*, if you want to.'

The English children needed no further encouragement. Ronnie was out of his few clothes and splashing in the water in a few seconds; Sheila got into a tangle with her Liberty bodice and had to be helped. Howard watched them for a minute, amused. Then he turned to Rose. 'Would you like to go in, too?' he said in French.

She shook her head in scandalised amazement. 'It is not nice, that, monsieur. Not at all.'

He glanced at the little naked bodies gleaming in the sun. 'No,' he said reflectively. 'I suppose it's not. Still, they may as well go on now they've started.' He turned to Pierre. 'Would you like to bathe, Pierre?'

The little boy in grey stared round-eyed at the English children. '*Non, merci, monsieur,*' he said.

Howard said: 'Wouldn't you like to take your shoes off and have a paddle, then? In the water?' The child looked doubtfully at him, and then at Rose. 'It's nice in the water.' He turned to Rose. 'Take him and let him put his feet in the water, Rose.'

She took the little boy's shoes and socks off and they went down and paddled at the very edge of the water. Howard went back to the shade of the trees and sat down again where he could see the children. Presently Sheila splashed a little water at the paddlers; he heard *la petite* Rose scolding. He saw the little boy in grey, standing in an inch of water, stoop and put his hand in and splash a little back. And then, among the children's chatter, he heard a shrill little sound that was quite new to him.

It was Pierre laughing.

Behind his back he heard a man say:

'God love a duck! Look at them bleeding kids—just like Brighton.'

Another said: 'Never mind about the muckin' kids. Look at the mud they've stirred up. We can't put that stuff in the radiator. Better go on up-stream a bit. And get a move on or we'll be here all the muckin' night.'

Howard swung round and there, before him in the field, were two men, dirty and unshaven, in British Royal Air Force uniform. One was a corporal and one a driver.

He started up. 'I'm English,' he burst out. 'Have you got a car?'

The corporal stared at him, amazed. 'And who the muckin' hell might you be?'

'I'm English. These children are English, two of them. We're trying to get through to Chartres.'

'Chartres?' The corporal was puzzled.

'Chartres, 'e means,' the driver said. 'I see that on the map.'

Howard said: 'You've got a car?'

'Workshop lorry,' said the corporal. He swung round on the driver. 'Get the muckin' water and start filling up, Bert.' The driver went off up-stream swinging his can.

The old man said: 'Can you give us a lift?'

'What, you and all them kids? I dunno about that, mate. How far do you want to go?'

'I'm trying to get back to England.'

'You ain't the only one.'

'I only want a lift to Chartres. They say that trains are running from there to Saint Malo.'

'You don't want to believe all these Froggies say. Tried to tell us it was all right goin' through a place called Susan yesterday, and when we got there it was full of muckin' Jerries! All loosing off their hipes at Bert and me like we was Aunt Sally! Ever drive a ten-ton Leyland, mate?'

The old man shook his head.

'Well, she don't handle like an Austin Seven. Bert stuck 'is foot down and I got the old Bren going over the windscreen and we went round the roundabout like it was the banking at Brooklands, and out the way we come, and all we got was two bullets in the motor generator what makes the juice for lighting and that, and a little chip out of the aft leg of the Herbert, what won't make any odds if the officer don't notice it. But fancy saying we could go through there! Susan the name was, or something of that.'

The old man blinked at him. 'Where are you making for?'

The corporal said: 'Place called Brest. Not the kind of name I'd like to call a town, myself, but that's the way these Froggies are. Officer said to go there if we got cut off, and we'd get the lorry shipped back home from there.'

Howard said: 'Take us with you.'

The other looked uncertainly at the children. 'I dunno what to say. I dunno if there'd be room. Them kids ain't English.'

'Two of them are. They're speaking French now, but that's because they've been brought up in France.'

The driver passed them with his dripping can, going toward the road.

'What are the other two?'

'They're French.'

'I ain't taking no Froggie kids along,' the corporal said. 'I ain't got no room, for one thing, and they're just as well left in their own place, to my way of thinking. I don't mind obliging you and the two English ones.'

Howard said: 'You don't understand. The two French ones are in my care.' He explained the situation to the man.

'It's no good, mate,' he said. 'I ain't got room for all of you.'

Howard said slowly: 'I see . . .' He stared for a moment absently at the traffic on the road. 'If it's a matter of room,' he said, 'will you take the four children through to Brest with you? They won't take up much room. I'll give you a letter for the R.T.O. at Brest, and a letter to my solicitor in England. And I can give you money for anything they'll want.'

The other wrinkled his brows. 'Leaving you here?'

'I'll be all right. In fact, I'll get along quicker without them.'

'You mean take them two Froggie kids along 'stead of you? Is that what you're getting at?'

'I'll be all right. I know France very well.'

'Don't talk so bloody soft. What 'ld I do with four muckin' kids and only Bert along o' me?' He swung round on his heel. 'Come on, then. Get them kids dressed toot and sweet—I ain't going to wait all night. And if I finds them messing with the Herbert I'll tan their little bottoms for them, straight I will.'

He swung off back towards his lorry. Howard hurried down to the sand spit and called the children to him. 'Come on and get your clothes on, quickly,' he said. 'We're going in a motor-lorry.'

Ronnie faced him, stark naked. 'Really? What sort is it? May I sit by the driver, Mr Howard?'

Sheila, similarly nude, echoed: 'May I sit by the driver too?'

'Come on and get your clothes on,' he repeated. He turned to Rose and said in French: 'Put your stockings on, Rose, and help Pierre. We've got to be very quick.'

He hurried the children all he could, but they were wet and the clothes stuck to them; he had no towel. Before he was finished the two Air Force men were back with him, worrying with their urgency to start. At last he had the children ready. 'Will you be able to take my perambulator?' he asked, a little timidly.

The corporal said: 'We can't take that muckin' thing mate. It's not worth a dollar.'

The old man said: 'I know it's not. But if we have to walk again, it's all I've got to put the little ones in.'

The driver chipped in: 'Let 'im take it on the roof. It'll ride there all right, corp. We'll all be walking if we don't get hold of juice.'

'My muckin' Christ,' the corporal said. 'Call this a workshop lorry! Perishing Christmas tree, I call it. All right, stick it on the roof.'

He hustled them towards the road. The lorry stood gigantic by the roadside, the traffic eddying round it. Inside it was stuffed full of machinery. An enormous Herbert lathe stood in the middle. A grinding-wheel and valve-facing machine stood at one end, a little filing and sawing machine at the other. Beneath the lathe a motor-generator set was housed; above it was a long electric switchboard. The men's kitbags occupied what little room there was.

Howard hastily removed their lunch from the pram, and watched it heaved up on the roof of the van. Then he helped the children up among the machinery. The corporal refused point-blank to let them ride beside the driver. 'I got the Bren there, see?' he said. 'I don't want no perishing kids around if we runs into Jerries.'

Howard said: 'I see that.' He consoled Ronnie and climbed in himself into the lorry. The corporal saw them settled, then went round and got up by the driver; with a low purr and a lurch the lorry moved out into the traffic stream.

It was half an hour later that the old man realised that they had left Sheila's pants beside the stream in their hurry.

They settled down to the journey. The interior of the van was awkward and uncomfortable for Howard, with no place to sit down and rest; he had to stoop, half kneeling, on a kitbag. The children being smaller, were more comfortable. The old man got out their *déjeuner* and gave them food in moderation, with a little of the orange drink; on his advice Rose ate very little, and remained well. He had rescued Pierre's chocolate from the perambulator and gave it to him, as a matter of course, when they had finished eating. The little boy received it solemnly and put it into his mouth; the old man watched him with grave amusement.

Rose said: 'It is good, that, Pierre.' She bent down and smiled at him.

He nodded gravely. 'Very good,' he whispered.

Very soon they came to Montargis. Through a little trap-door in the partition between the workshop and the driver's seat the corporal said to Howard: 'Ever been here before, mate?'

The old man said: 'I've only passed it in the train, a great many years ago.'

'You don't know where the muckin' petrol dump would be? We got to get some juice from somewhere.'

Howard shook his head. 'I'm afraid I don't. I'll ask someone for you, if you like.'

'Christ. Do you speak French that good?'

The driver said: 'They all speak it, corp. Even the bloody kids.'

The corporal turned back to Howard. 'Just keep them kids down close along the floor, mate, case we find the Jerries like in that place Susan.'

The old man was startled. 'I don't think there are any Germans so far west as this,' he said. But he made the children lie down on the floor, which they took as a fine joke. So, with the little squeals of laughter from the body of the lorry, they rolled into Montargis and pulled up at the cross-roads in the middle of the town.

At the corporal's request the old man got down and asked the way to the military petrol dump. A baker directed him to the north of the town; he got up into the driver's compartment and directed them through the town. They found the French transport park without great difficulty, and Howard went with the corporal to speak to the officer in charge, a lieutenant. They got a brusque refusal. The town was being evacuated, they were told. If they had no petrol they must leave their lorry and go south.

The corporal swore luridly, so luridly that Howard was quite glad that the English children, who might possibly have understood, were in the lorry.

'I got to get this muckin' lot to Brest,' he said. 'I don't leave it here and hop it, like he said.' He turned to Howard, suddenly earnest. 'Look, mate,' he said. 'Maybe you better beat it with the kids. You don't want to get mixed up with the bloody Jerries.'

The old man said: 'If there's no petrol, you may as well come with us.'

The Air Force man said: 'You don't savvy, mate. I got to get this lot to Brest. That big Herbert. You don't know lathes, maybe, but that's a treat. Straight it is. Machine tools is wanted back home. I got to get that Herbert home–I got to. Let the Jerries have it for the taking, I suppose! Not bloody likely.'

He ran his eye around the park. It was filled with decrepit, dirty French lorries; rapidly the few remaining soldiers were leaving. The lieutenant that had refused them drove out in a little Citroën car. 'I bet there's juice somewhere about,' the corporal muttered.

He swung round and hailed the driver. 'Hey, Bert,' he said: 'Come on along.'

The men went ferreting about among the cars. They found no dump or store of petrol, but presently Howard saw them working at the deserted lorries, emptying the tanks into a *bidon*. Gleaning a gallon here and a gallon there, they collected in all about eight gallons and transferred it to the enormous tank of the Leyland. That was all that they could find. 'It ain't much,' said the corporal. 'Forty miles, maybe. Still, that's better 'n a sock in the jaw. Let's see the bloody map, Bert.'

The bloody map showed them Pithiviers, twenty-five miles farther on. 'Let's get goin'.' They moved out on the westward road again.

It was terribly hot. The van body of the lorry had sides made of wood, which folded outwards to enlarge the floor space when the lathe was in use. Little light entered round these wooden sides; it was dim and stuffy and very smelly in among the machinery. The children did not seem to suffer much, but it was a trying journey for the old man. In a short time he had a splitting headache, and was aching in every limb from the cramped positions he was constrained to take up.

The road was ominously clear to Pithiviers, and they made good speed. From time to time an aeroplane flew low above the road, and once there was a sharp burst of machine-gun fire very near at hand. Howard leaned over to the little window at the driver's elbow. 'Jerry bomber,' said the corporal. 'One o' them Stukas, as they call them.'

'Was he firing at us?'

'Aye. Miles off, he was.' The corporal did not seem especially perturbed.

In an hour they were near Pithiviers, five and twenty miles from Montargis. They drew up by the roadside half a mile from the town and held a consultation. The road stretched before them to the houses with no soul in sight. There was no movement in the town. It seemed to be deserted in the blazing sunlight of the afternoon.

They stared at it, irresolute. 'I dunno as I fancy it,' the corporal said. 'It don't look right to me.'

The driver said: 'Bloody funny nobody's about. You don't think it's full of Jerries, corp? Hiding, like?'

'I dunno . . .'

Howard, leaning forward with his face to the trap in the partition, said over their shoulders: 'I don't mind walking in ahead to have a look, if you wait here.'

'Walk in ahead of us?'

'I don't see that there'd be much risk in that. With all these refugees about I can't see that there'd be much risk in it. I'd rather do that than drive in with you if there's any chance of being fired on.'

'Something in what he says,' the driver said. 'If the Jerries *are* there, we mightn't find another roundabout this time.'

They discussed it for a minute or two. There was no road alternative to going through the town that did not mean a ten-mile journey back towards Montargis. 'An' that's not so bloody funny, either,' said the corporal. 'Meet the Jerries coming up behind us, like as not.'

He hesitated, irresolute. 'Okay,' he said at last. 'Nip in and have a look, mate. Give us the wire if it's all okey-doke. Wave something if it's all right to come on.'

The old man said: 'I'll have to take the children with me.'

'My muckin' Christ! I don't want to sit here all the bloody day, mate.'

The old man said: 'I'm not going to be separated from the children.' He paused. 'You see, they're in my charge. Just like your lathe.'

The driver burst out laughing. 'That's a good one, corp! Just like your muckin' lathe,' he said.

The corporal said: 'Well, put a jerk in it, anyway.'

The old man got down from the lorry and lifted the children one by one down into the hot sunlight on the dusty, deserted road. He started off with them down the road towards the town, leading the two little ones by the hand, thinking uneasily that if he were to become separated from the lorry he would inevitably lose his perambulator. He made all speed possible, but it was twenty minutes before he led them into the town.

There were no Germans to be seen. The town was virtually deserted; only one or two very old women peered at him from behind curtains or around the half-closed doors of shops. In the gutter of the road that led towards the north a tattered, dirty child that might have been of either sex in its short smock, was chewing something horrible. A few yards up the road a dead horse had been dragged half up on to the pavement and left there, distended and stinking. A dog was tearing at it.

It was a beastly, sordid little town, the old man felt. He caught one of the old women at a door. 'Are the Germans here?' he said.

'They are coming from the north,' she quavered. 'They will ravish everyone, and shoot us.'

The old man felt instinctively that this was nonsense. 'Have you seen any Germans in the town yet?'

'There is one there.'

He looked round, startled. 'Where?'

'There.' She pointed a trembling, withered hand at the child in the gutter. 'There?' The woman must be mad, distraught with terror of the invaders. 'It speaks only German. It is the child of spies.' She caught his arm with senile urgency. 'Throw a stone and chase it away. It will bring the Germans to this house if it stays there.'

Howard shook her off. 'Are any German soldiers here yet?'

She did not answer, but shouted a shrill scream of dirty imprecations at the child in the gutter. The child, a little boy, Howard thought, lifted his head and looked at her with infantile disdain. Then he resumed his disgusting meal.

There was nothing more to be learned from the old hag; it was now clear to him there were no Germans in the town. He turned away; as he did so there was a sharp crack, and a fair-sized stone rolled down the pavement near the German spy. The child slunk off fifty yards down the street and squatted down again upon the kerb.

The old man was very angry, but he had other things to do. He said to Rose: 'Look after the children for a minute, Rose. Don't let them go away or speak to anyone.'

He hurried back along the road that they had entered the town by. He had to go a couple of hundred yards before he came in sight of the lorry, parked by the roadside half a mile away. He waved his hat at it, and saw it move towards him; then he turned and walked back to where he had left the children.

It overtook him near the cross-roads in the middle of the town. The corporal leaned down from the cab. 'Any juice here, do you think?' The old man looked at him uncomprehending. 'Petrol, mate.'

'Oh–I don't know. I wouldn't hang about here very long.'

'That's right,' the driver muttered. 'Let's get on out of it. It don't look so good to me.'

'We got to get juice.'

'We got close on five gallons left. Get us to Angerville.'

'Okay,' the corporal said to Howard. 'Get the kids into the back and we'll 'op it.'

Howard looked round for his children. They were not where he had left them; he looked round, and they were up the road with the German spy, who was crying miserably.

'Rose,' he shouted. 'Come on. Bring the children.'

She called in a thin, piping voice: '*Il est blessé.*'

'Come on,' he cried. The children looked at him, but did not stir. He hurried over to them. 'Why don't you come when I call you?'

Rose faced the old man, her little face crimson with anger. 'Somebody threw a stone at him and hit him. I saw them do it. It is not right, that.'

True enough, a sticky stream of blood was running down the back of the child's neck into his filthy clothes. A sudden loathing for the town enveloped the old man. He took his handkerchief and mopped at the wound.

La petite Rose said: 'It is not right to throw a stone at him, and a big woman, too, m'sieur. This is a bad, dirty place to do a thing like that.'

Ronnie said: 'He's coming with us, Mr Howard. He can sit on the other end of Bert's kitbag by the 'lectric motor.'

The old man said: 'He belongs here. We can't take him away with us.' But in his mind came the thought that it might be kind to do so.

'He doesn't belong here,' said Rose. 'Two days only he has been here. The woman said so.'

There was a hurried, heavy step behind them. 'For Christ's sake,' said the corporal.

Howard turned to him. 'They're throwing stones at this child,' he said. He showed the man the cut upon his neck.

'Who's throwing stones?'

'All the people in the village. They think he's a German spy.'

'Who—'im?' The corporal stared. 'He ain't more'n seven years old!'

'I saw the woman do it,' said Ronnie. 'That house there. She threw a stone and did that.'

'My muckin' aunt,' the corporal said. He turned to Howard. 'Anyway, we got to beat it.'

'I know.' The old man hesitated. 'What'll we do? Leave him here in this disgusting place? Or bring him along with us?'

'Bring him along, mate, if you feel like it. I ain't worried over the amount of spying that he'll do.'

The old man bent and spoke to the child. 'Would you like to come with us?' he said in French.

The little boy said something in another language.

Howard said: *Sprechen sie deutsch?*' That was the limit of the German that he could recall at the moment, but it drew no response.

He straightened up, heavy with new responsibility. 'We'll take him with us,' he said quietly. 'If we leave him here they'll probably end by killing him.'

'If we don't get a move on,' said the corporal, 'the bloody Jerries will be here and kill the lot of us.'

Howard picked up the spy, who suffered that in silence; they hurried to the lorry. The child smelt and was plainly verminous; the old man turned his face away in nausea. Perhaps in Angerville there would be nuns who would take charge of him. They might take Pierre, too, though Pierre was so little bother that the old man didn't mind about him much.

They put the children in the workshop; Howard got in with them and the corporal got into the front seat by the driver. The big truck moved across the road from Paris and out upon the road to Angerville, seventeen miles away.

'If we don't get some juice at Angerville,' the driver said, 'we'll be bloody well sunk.'

In the van, crouched down beside the lathe with the children huddled round him, the old man pulled out a sticky bundle of his chocolate. He broke off five pieces for the children; as soon as the German spy realised what it was he stretched out a filthy paw and said something unintelligible. He ate it greedily and stretched out his hand for more.

'You wait a bit.' The old man gave the chocolate to the other children. Pierre whispered: '*Merci, monsieur.*'

La petite Rose leaned down to him. 'After supper, Pierre?' she said. 'Shall monsieur keep it for you to have after supper?'

The little boy whispered: 'Only on Sunday. On Sunday I may have chocolate after supper. Is today Sunday?'

The old man said: 'I'm not quite sure what day it is. But I don't think your mother will mind if you have chocolate after supper tonight. I'll put it away and you can have it then.'

He rummaged round and produced one of the thick, hard biscuits that he had bought in the morning, and with some difficulty broke it in two; he offered one half to the dirty little boy in the smock. The child took it and ate it ravenously.

Rose scolded at him in French: 'Is that the way to eat? A little pig would eat more delicately–yes, truly, I say–a little pig. You should thank monsieur, too.'

The child stared at her, not understanding why she was scolding him.

She said: 'Have you not been taught how to behave? You should say like this'–she swung round and bowed to Howard–'*Je vous remercie, monsieur.*'

Her words passed him by, but the pantomime was evident. He looked confused. '*Dank, Mijnheer,*' he said awkwardly. '*Dank u wel.*'

Howard stared at him, perplexed. It was a northern language, but not German. It might, he thought, be Flemish or Walloon, or even Dutch. In any case, it mattered very little; he himself knew no word of any of those languages.

They drove on at a good pace through the hot afternoon. The hatch to the driver's compartment was open; from time to time the old man leaned forward and looked through between the two men at the road ahead of them. It was suspiciously clear. They passed only a very few refugees, and very occasionally a farm cart going on its ordinary business. There were no soldiers to be seen, and of the seething refugee traffic between Joigny and Montargis there was no sign at all. The whole countryside seemed empty, dead.

Three miles from Angerville the corporal turned and spoke to Howard through the hatch. 'Getting near that next town now,' he said. 'We got to get some juice there, or we're done.'

The old man said: 'If you see anyone likely on the road I'll ask them where the depot is.'

'Okay.'

In a few minutes they came to a farm. A car stood outside it, and a man was carrying sacks of grain or fodder from the car into the farm. 'Stop here,' the old man said, 'I'll ask that chap.'

They drew up by the roadside, immediately switching off the engine to save petrol. 'Only about a gallon left now,' said the driver. 'We run it bloody fine, an' no mistake.'

Howard got down and walked back to the farm. The man, a grey-beard of about fifty without a collar, came out towards the car. 'We want petrol,' said Howard. 'There is, without doubt, a depot for military transport in Angerville?'

The man stared at him. 'There are Germans in Angerville.'

There was a momentary silence. The old Englishman stared across the farmyard at the lean pig rooting on the midden, at the scraggy fowls scratching in the dust. So it was closing in on him.

'How long have they been there?' he asked quietly.

'Since early morning. They have come from the north.'

There was no more to be said about that. 'Have you petrol? I will buy any that you have, at your own price.'

The peasant's eyes glowed. 'A hundred francs a litre.'

'How much have you got?'

The man looked at the gauge upon the battered dashboard of his car. 'Seven litres. Seven hundred francs.'

Less than a gallon and a half of petrol would not take the ten-ton Leyland very far. Howard went back to the corporal.

'Not very good news, I'm afraid,' he said. 'The Germans are in Angerville.'
There was a pause. 'Bloody 'ell,' the corporal said at last. He said it very
quietly, as if he were suddenly tired. 'How many are there there?'

Howard called back the enquiry to the peasant. 'A regiment,' he said. 'I
suppose he means about a thousand men.'

'Come down from the north, like,' said the driver.

There was nothing much more to be said. The old man told them about the
petrol. 'That's not much good,' the corporal said. 'With what we've got, that
wouldn't take us more'n ten miles.' He turned to the driver. 'Let's 'ave the
muckin' map.'

Together they pored over the sheet; the old man got up into the cab and
studied it with them. There was no side road between them and the town;
behind them there was no road leading to the south for nearly seven miles.
'That's right,' the driver said. 'I didn't see no road on that side when we came
along.'

The corporal said quietly: 'An' if we did go back, we'd meet the Jerries
coming along after us from that other muckin' place. Where he picked up the
nipper what they told him was a spy.'

'That's right,' the driver said.

The corporal said: 'Got a fag?'

The driver produced a cigarette; the corporal lit it and blew a long cloud.
'Well,' he said presently, 'this puts the lid on it.'

The other two were silent.

'I wanted to get home with that big Herbert,' the corporal said. 'I wanted to
get that through okay, as much as I ever wanted anything in all my life.' He
turned to Howard: 'Straight, I did. But I ain't going to.'

The old man said gently: 'I am very sorry.'

The other shook himself. 'You can't always do them things you want to
most.' He stirred. 'Well, this won't buy baby a new frock.'

He got down from the cab on to the ground. 'What are you going to do?'
asked Howard.

'I'll show you what I'm going to do.' He led the old man to the side of the
great lorry, about half-way down its length. There was a little handle sticking
out through the side chassis member, painted bright red. 'I'm going to pull that
tit, and run like bloody 'ell.'

'Demolition,' said the driver at his elbow. 'Pull that out an' up she goes.'

The corporal said: 'Come on, now. Get them muckin' kids out of the back.
I'm sorry we can't take you any farther, mate, but that's the way it is.'

Howard said: 'What will you do, yourselves?'

The corporal said: 'Mugger off cross-country to the south an' hope to keep in
front of the Jerries.' He hesitated. 'You'll be all right,' he said, a little
awkwardly. 'They won't do nothin' to you, with all them kids.'

The old man said: 'We'll be all right. Don't worry about us. You've got to get
back home to fight again.'

'We got to dodge the muckin' Jerries first.'

Together they got the children down on to the road; then they lifted down
the pram from the top of the van. Howard collected his few possessions and
stowed them in the pram, took the corporal's address in England, and gave his
own.

There was nothing then to wait for.

'So long, mate,' said the corporal. 'See you one day.'

The old man said: 'So long.'

He gathered the children round him and set off with them slowly down the road in the direction of Angerville. There was a minor squabble as to who should push the pram, which finished up by Sheila pushing it with Ronnie to assist and advise. Rose walked beside them leading Pierre by the hand; the dirty little stranger in his queer frock followed along behind. Howard thought ruefully that somehow, somewhere, he must get him washed. Not only was he verminous and filthy, but the back of his neck and his clothes were clotted with dried blood from the cut.

They went slowly, as they always did. From time to time Howard glanced back over his shoulder; the men by the lorry seemed to be sorting out their personal belongings. Then one of them, the driver, started off across the field towards the south, carrying a small bundle. The other bent to some task at the lorry.

Then he was up and running from the road towards the driver. He ran clumsily, stumbling; when he had gone about two hundred yards there was a sharp, crackling explosion.

A sheet of flame shot outwards from the lorry. Parts of it sailed up into the air and fell upon the road and into the fields; then it sunk lower on the road. A little tongue of fire appeared, and it was in flames.

Ronnie said: 'Coo, Mr Howard. Did it blow up?'

Sheila echoed: 'Did it blow up itself, Mr Howard?'

'Yes,' he said heavily, 'that's what happened.' A column of thick black smoke rose from it on the road. He turned away. 'Don't bother about it any more.'

Two miles ahead of him he saw the roofs of Angerville. The net was practically closed upon him now. With a heavy heart he led the children down the road towards the town.

6

I broke into his story and said, a little breathlessly: 'This one's not far off.'

We sat tense in our chairs before the fire, listening to the rising whine of the bomb. It burst somewhere very near, and in the rumble of the falling debris we heard another falling, closer still. We sat absolutely motionless as the club rocked to the explosion and the glass crashed from the windows, and the whine of the third bomb grew shrill. It burst upon the other side of us.

'Straddled,' said old Howard, breaking the tension. 'That's all right.'

The fourth bomb of the stick fell farther away; then there was a pause, but for a burst of machine-gun fire. I got up from my chair and walked out to the corridor. It was in darkness. A window leading out on to a little balcony had been blown open. I went out and looked round.

Over towards the city the sky was a deep, cherry red with the glow of the fires. Around us there was a bright, yellow light from three parachute-flares suspended in the sky; Bren guns and Lewis guns were rattling away at these things in an attempt to shoot them down. Close at hand, down the street, another fire was getting under way.

I turned, and Howard was at my side. 'Pretty hot tonight,' he said.

I nodded. 'Would you like to go down into the shelter?'

'Are you going?'

'I don't believe it's any safer there than here,' I said.

We went down to the hall to see if there was anything we could do to help. But there was nothing to be done, and presently we went up to our chairs again beside the fire and poured another glass of the Marsala. I said: 'Go on with your story.'

He said diffidently: 'I hope I'm not boring you with all this?'

Angerville is a little town upon the Paris–Orleans road. It was about five o'clock when Howard started to walk towards it with the children, a hot, dusty afternoon.

He told me that that was one of the most difficult moments of his life. Since he had left Cidoton he had been travelling towards England; as he had gone on fear had grown upon him. Up to the last it had seemed incredible that he should not get through, hard though the way might be. But now he realised that he would not get through. The Germans were between him and the sea. In marching on to Angerville he was marching to disaster, to internment, probably to his death.

That did not worry him so much. He was old and tired; if an end came now he would be missing nothing very much. A few more days of fishing, a few more summers pottering in his garden. But the children–they were another matter. Somehow he must make them secure. Rose and Pierre might be turned over to the French police; sooner or later they would be returned to their relations. But Sheila and Ronnie–what arrangements could he possibly make for them? What would become of them? And what about the dirty little boy who now was with them, who had been stoned by old women mad with terror and blind hate? What would become of him?

The old man suffered a good deal.

There was nothing to be done but to walk straight into Angerville. The Germans were behind them, to the north, to the east, and to the west. He felt that it was hopeless to attempt a dash across the country to the south as the Air Force men had done; he could not possibly outdistance the advance of the invader. Better to go ahead and meet what lay before him bravely, conserving his strength that he might help the children best.

Ronnie said: 'Listen to the band.'

They were about half a mile from the town. Rose exclaimed with pleasure. '*Ecoute*, Pierre,' she said, bending down to him. '*Ecoute!*'

'Eh?' said Howard, waking from his reverie. 'What's that?'

Ronnie said: 'There's a band playing in the town. May we go and listen to it?' But his ears were keener than the old man's, and Howard could hear nothing.

Presently, as they walked into the town, he picked out the strains of 'Lieberstraum'.

On the way into the town they passed a train of very dirty lorries halted by the road, drawing in turn up to a garage and filling their tanks at the pump. The soldiers moving round them appeared strange at first; with a shock the old man realised that he was seeing what he had expected for the last hour to see; the men were German soldiers. They wore field-grey uniforms with open collars and patch pockets, with a winged eagle broidered on the right breast. Some of them were bare-headed; others wore the characteristic German steel helmet. They had sad, tired, expressionless faces; they moved about their work like so many machines.

Sheila said: 'Are those Swiss soldiers, Mr Howard?'

'No,' he said, 'they're not Swiss.'

Ronnie said: 'They wear the same kind of hat.'

Rose said: 'What are they?'

He gathered them around him. 'Look,' he said in French, 'you mustn't be afraid. They are German, but they won't hurt you.'

They were passing a little group of them. From the crowd an *Unterfeldwebel* came up to them; he wore long black boots and breeches stained with oil. 'That is the proper spirit,' he said in harsh, guttural French. 'We Germans are your friends. We bring you peace. Very soon you will be able to go home again.'

The children stared at him, as if they did not understand what he had said. Very likely this was so, because his French was very bad.

Howard said in French: 'It will be good when we have peace again.' There was no point in giving up before he was found out.

The man smiled, a set, expressionless grin. 'How far have you come?'

'From Pithiviers.'

'Have you walked so far?'

'No. We got a lift in a lorry which broke down a few miles back.'

The German said: 'So. Then you will want supper. In the *Place* there is a soup-kitchen which you may go to.'

Howard said: '*Je vous remercie.*' There was nothing else to say.

The man was pleased. He ran his eye over them and frowned at the little boy in the smock. He stepped up and took him by the head, not ungently, and examined the wound upon his neck. Then he looked at his own hands, and wiped them with disgust, having handled the child's head.

'So!' he said. 'By the church there is a field hospital. Take him to the *Sanitätsunteroffizier.*' He dismissed them curtly and turned back to his men.

One or two of the men looked at them woodenly, listlessly, but no one else spoke to them. They went on to the centre of the town. At the cross-roads in the middle, where the road to Orleans turned off to the left and the road to Paris to the right, there was a market square before a large grey church. In the centre of the square the band was playing.

It was a band of German soldiers. They stood there, about twenty of them, playing doggedly, methodically; doing their duty for their Führer. They wore soft field caps and silver tassels on their shoulders. A *Feldwebel* conducted them. He stood above them on a little rostrum, the baton held lovingly between his finger-tips. He was a heavy, middle-aged man; as he waved he turned from side to side and smiled benignly on his audience. Behind the band a row of tanks and armoured cars were parked.

The audience was mostly French. A few grey-faced, listless German soldiers stood around, seemingly tired to death; the remainder of the audience were men and women of the town. They stood round gaping curiously at the intruder, peering at the tanks and furtively studying the uniforms and accoutrements of the men.

Ronnie said in English: 'There's the band, Mr Howard. May we go and listen to it?'

The old man looked quickly round. Nobody seemed to have heard him. 'Not now,' he said in French. 'We must go with this little boy to have his neck dressed.'

He led the children away from the crowd. 'Try not to speak English while we're here,' he said quietly to Ronnie.

'Why not, Mr Howard?'

Sheila said: 'May I speak English, Mr Howard?'

'No,' he said. 'The Germans don't like to hear people speaking English.'

The little girl said in English: 'Would the Germans mind if Rose spoke English?'

A passing Frenchwoman looked at them curiously. The old man beat down his irritation; they were only children. He said in French: 'If you speak English I'll find a little frog to put into your mouth.'

Rose said: 'Oo–to hear what monsieur has said! A little frog! It would be horrible, that.'

In mixed laughter and apprehension they went on talking in French.

The field hospital was on the far side of the church. As they went towards it every German soldier that they passed smiled at them mechanically, a set, expressionless grin. When the first one did it the children stopped to stare, and had to be herded on. After the first half-dozen they got used to it.

One of the men said: '*Bonjour, mes enfants.*'

Howard muttered quietly. '*Bonjour, m'sieur,*' and passed on. It was only a few steps to the hospital tent; the net was very close around him now.

The hospital consisted of a large marquee extending from a lorry. At the entrance a lance-corporal of the medical service, a *Sanitätsgefreiter,* stood idle and bored, picking his teeth.

Howard said to Rose: 'Stay here and keep the children with you.' He led the little boy up to the tent. He said to the man in French: 'The little boy is wounded. A little piece of plaster or a bandage, perhaps?'

The man smiled, that same fixed, mirthless smile. He examined the child deftly. '*So!*' he said. '*Kommen Sie–entrez.*'

The old man followed with the child into the tent. A dresser was tending a German soldier with a burnt hand; apart from them the only other occupant was a doctor wearing a white overall. His rank was not apparent. The orderly led the child to him and showed him the wound.

The doctor nodded briefly. Then he turned the child's head to the light and looked at it, expressionless. Then he opened the child's soiled clothes and looked at his chest. Then, rather ostentatiously, he rinsed his hands.

He crossed the tent to Howard. 'You will come again,' he said in thick French. 'In one hour,' he held up one finger. 'One hour.' Fearing that he had not made himself understood he pulled out his watch and pointed to the hands. 'Six hours.'

'*Bien compris,*' said the old man. '*A six heures.*' He left the tent, wondering what dark trouble lay in store for him. It could not take an hour to put a dressing on a little cut.

Still there was nothing he could do. He did not dare even to enter into any long conversation with the German; sooner or later his British accent must betray him. He went back to the children and led them away from the tent.

Earlier in the day—how long ago it seemed!—Sheila had suffered a sartorial disaster, in that she had lost her knickers. It had not worried her or any of the children, but it had weighed on Howard's mind. Now was the time to rectify that omission. To ease Ronnie's longings they went and had a look at the German tanks in the *Place*; then, ten minutes later, he led them to a draper's shop not far from the field hospital.

He pushed open the door of the shop, and a German soldier was at the counter. It was too late to draw back, and to do so would have raised suspicion; he stood aside and waited till the German had finished his purchases. Then, as he stood there in the background, he saw that the German was the orderly from the hospital.

A little bundle of clothes lay upon the counter before him, a yellow jersey, a pair of brown children's shorts, socks, and a vest. *'Cinquante quatre, quatre vingt dix,'* said the stout old woman at the counter.

The German did not understand her rapid way of speech. She repeated it several times; then he pushed a little pad of paper towards her, and she wrote the sum upon the pad for him. He took it and studied it. Then he wrote his own name and the unit carefully beneath. He tore off the sheet and gave it to her.

'You will be paid later,' he said, in difficult French. He gathered up the garments.

She protested. 'I cannot let you take away the clothes unless I have the money. My husband—he would be very much annoyed. He would be furious. Truly, monsieur—that is not possible at all.'

The German said stolidly: 'It is good. You will be paid. That is a good requisition.'

She said angrily: 'It is not good at all, that. It is necessary that you should pay with money.'

The man said: 'That is money, good German money. If you do not believe it, I will call the Military Police. As for your husband, he had better take our German money and be thankful. Perhaps he is a Jew? We have a way with Jews.'

The woman stared at him, dumb. There was a momentary silence in the shop; then the hospital orderly gathered up his purchases and swaggered out. The woman remained staring after him, uncertainly fingering the piece of paper.

Howard went forward and distracted her. She roused herself and showed him children's pants. With much advice from Rose upon the colour and design he chose a pair for Sheila, paid three francs fifty for them, and put them on her in the shop.

The woman stood fingering the money. 'You are not German, monsieur?' she said heavily. She glanced down at the money in her hand.

He shook his head.

'I thought perhaps you were. Flemish?'

It would never do to admit his nationality, but at any moment one of the children might betray him. He moved towards the door. 'Norwegian,' he said at random. 'My country has also suffered.'

'I thought you were not French,' she said. 'I do not know what will become of us.'

He left the shop and went a little way up the Paris road, hoping to avoid the people. German soldiers were still pouring into the town. He walked about for a time in the increasing crowd, tense and fearful of betrayal every moment. At last it was six o'clock; he went back to the hospital.

He left the children by the church. 'Keep them beside you,' he said to Rose. 'I shall only be at the hospital a little while. Stay here till I come back.'

He went into the tent, tired and worn with apprehension. The orderly saw him coming. 'Wait here,' he said. 'I will tell the Herr Oberstabsarzt.'

The man vanished into the tent. The old man stood waiting at the entrance patiently. The warm sun was pleasant now, in the cool of the evening. It would have been pleasant to stay free, get back to England. But he was tired now, very, very tired. If only he could see the children right, then he could rest.

There was a movement in the tent, and the doctor was there, leading a child by the hand. It was a strange, new child, sucking a sweet. It was spotlessly clean, with short cropped hair trimmed close to its head with clippers. It was a little boy. He wore a yellow jersey and a pair of brown shorts, socks, and new shoes. The clothes were all brand new, and all seemed vaguely familiar to the old man. The little boy smelt very strong of yellow soap and disinfectant.

He wore a clean white dressing on his neck. He smiled at the old man.

Howard stared at him, dumbfounded. The doctor said genially, 'So! My orderly has given him a bath. That is better?'

The old man said: 'It is wonderful, Herr Doktor. And the clothes, too. And the dressing on his neck. I do not know how to thank you.'

The doctor swelled visibly. 'It is not me that you must thank, my friend,' he said with heavy geniality. 'It is Germany! We Germans have come to bring you peace, and cleanliness, and the ordered life that is true happiness. There will be no more war, no more wandering for you now. We Germans are your friends.'

'Indeed,' the old man said faintly, 'we realise that, Herr Doktor.'

'So,' said the man, 'what Germany has done for this boy, she will do for France, for all Europe. A new Order has begun.'

There was rather an awkward silence. Howard was about to say something suitable, but the yellow jersey caught his eye, and the image of the woman in the shop came into his mind and drove the words from his head. He stood hesitant for a minute.

The doctor gave the child a little push towards him. 'What Germany has done for this one little Dutchman she will do for all the children of the world,' he said. 'Take him away. You are his father?'

Fear lent speed to the old man's thoughts. A half-truth was best. 'He is not mine,' he said. 'He was lost and quite alone in Pithiviers. I shall take him to the convent.'

The man nodded, satisfied with that. 'I thought you might be Dutch yourself,' he said. 'You do not speak like these French.'

It would not do to say he was Norwegian again; it was too near to Germany. 'I am from the south,' he said. 'From Toulouse. But I am staying with my son in Montmirail. Then we got separated in Montargis; I do not know what has become of him. The children I was with are my grandchildren. They are now in the *Place*. They have been very good children, m'sieur, but it will be good when we can go home.'

He rambled on, getting into the stride of his tale, easily falling into the garrulity of an old man. The doctor turned away rudely. 'Well, take your brat,' he said. 'You can go home now. There will be no more fighting.'

He went back into the tent.

The old man took the little boy by the hand and led him round the church, passing on the other side of the shop that had sold children's clothes. He found Rose standing more or less where he had left her, with Sheila and Pierre. There was no sign of Ronnie.

He said anxiously to her: 'Rose, what has become of Ronnie? Where is he?'

She said: 'M'sieur, he has been so naughty. He wanted to see the tanks, but I told him it was wrong that he should go. I told him, m'sieur, that he was a very, very naughty little boy and that you would be very cross with him, m'sieur. But he ran off, all alone.'

Sheila piped up, loud and clear, in English: 'May I go and see the tanks, too, Mr Howard?'

Mechanically, he said in French: 'Not this evening. I told you that you were all to stay here.'

He looked around, irresolute. He did not know whether to leave the children where they were and go and look for Ronnie, or to take them with him. Either course might bring the other children into danger. If he left them they might get into further trouble. He took hold of the pram and pushed it ahead of him. 'Come this way,' he said.

Pierre edged up to him and whispered: 'May I push?'

It was the first time that the old man had heard the little boy volunteer a remark. He surrendered the handle of the pram. 'Of course,' he said. 'Rose, help him push.'

He walked beside them towards the parked tanks and lorries, anxiously scanning the crowd. There were German soldiers all about the transport, grey, weary men, consciously endeavouring to fraternise with a suspicious population. Some of them were cleaning up their clothes, some tending their machines. Others had little phrase books in their hands, and these were trying to make conversation with the crowd. The French peasants seemed sullen and uncommunicative.

Sheila said suddenly: 'There's Ronnie, over there!'

The old man turned, but could not see him. 'Where is he?'

Rose said: 'I see him—oh, m'sieur, what a naughty little boy. There, m'sieur, right inside the tank, there—with the German soldiers!'

A cold fear entered Howard's heart. His eyesight for long distances was not too good. He screwed his eyes up and peered in the direction Rose was pointing. True enough, there he was. Howard could see his little head just sticking out of a steel hatch at the top of the gun-turret as he chattered eagerly to the German soldier with him. The man seemed to be holding Ronnie in his arms, lifting him up to show him how the captain conned his tank. It was a pretty little picture of fraternisation.

The old man thought very quickly. He knew that Ronnie would most probably be talking French; there would be nothing to impel him to break into English. But he knew also that he himself must not go near the little boy nor must his sister; in his excited state he would at once break out in English to tell them all about the tank. Yet, he must be got away immediately, while he was still thinking of nothing but the tank. Once he began to think of other things, of their journey, or of Howard himself, he would inevitably betray them all in boyish chatter. Within five minutes of him losing interest in the tank the Germans would be told that he was English, that an old Englishman was strolling round the town.

Sheila plucked his sleeve. 'I want my supper,' she said. 'May I have my supper now? Please, Mr Howard, may I have my supper now?'

'In a minute,' he said absently. 'We'll all go and have our supper in a minute.' But that was an idea. If Sheila was hungry, Ronnie would be hungry too—unless the Germans had given him sweets. He must risk that. There was that soup kitchen that the German at the entrance to the town had spoken of; Howard could see the field-cookers a hundred yards down the *Place.*

He showed them to Rose. 'I am taking the little children down there, where the smoke is, for our supper,' he said casually. 'Go and fetch Ronnie, and bring him to us there. Are you hungry?'

'*Oui, m'sieur.*' She said that she was very hungry indeed.

'We shall have a fine hot supper, with hot soup and bread,' the old man said, drawing on his imagination. 'Go and tell Ronnie and bring him along with you. I will walk on with the little ones.'

He sent her off, and watched her running through the crowd, her bare legs twinkling. He steered the other children rather away from the tank; it would not do for Ronnie to be able to hail him. He saw the little girl come to the tank and speak urgently to the Germans; then she was lost to sight.

The old man sent up an urgent, personal prayer for the success of her unwitting errand, as he helped Pierre push the pram towards the field-cookers. There was nothing now that he could do. Their future lay in the small hands of two children, and in the hands of God.

There was a trestle table, with benches. He parked the pram and sat Pierre and Sheila and the nameless little Dutch boy at the table. Soup was dispensed in thick bowls, with a hunk of bread; he went and drew four bowls for the lot of them and brought them to the table.

He turned and Rose was at his elbow with Ronnie. The little boy was still flushed and ecstatic. 'They took me right inside!' he said in English.

The old man said gently in French: 'If you tell us in French, then Pierre can understand too.' He did not think that anyone had noticed. But the town was terribly dangerous for them; at any moment the children might break into English and betray them.

Ronnie said in French: 'There was a great big gun, and two little guns, m'sieur, and you steer with two handles and it goes seventy kilos an hour!'

Howard said: 'Come on and eat your supper.' He gave him a bowl of soup and a piece of bread.

Sheila said enviously. 'Did you go for a ride, Ronnie?'

The adventurer hesitated. 'Not exactly,' he said. 'But they said I might go with them for a ride tomorrow or one day. They did speak funnily. I could hardly understand what they wanted to say. May I go for a ride with them tomorrow, m'sieur? They say I might.'

The old man said: 'We'll have to see about that. We may not be here tomorrow.'

Sheila said: 'Why did they talk funny, Ronnie?'

Rose said suddenly: 'They are dirty Germans, who come here to murder people.'

The old man coughed loudly. 'Go on and eat your supper,' he said, 'all of you. That's enough talking for the present.' More than enough, he thought; if the German dishing out the soup had overheard they would all have been in trouble.

Angerville was no place for them; at all costs he must get the children out. It was only a matter of an hour or two before exposure came. He meditated for a moment; there were still some hours of daylight. The children were tired, he knew, yet it would be better to move on, out of the town.

Chartres was the next town on his list; Chartres, where he was to have taken train for Saint Malo. He could not get to Chartres that night; it was the best part of thirty miles farther to the west. There was little hope now that he would escape the territory occupied by Germans, yet for want of an alternative he would carry on to Chartres. Indeed, it never really occurred to him to do otherwise.

The children were very slow eaters. It was nearly an hour before Pierre and Sheila, the two smallest, had finished their meal. The old man waited, with the patience of old age. It would do no good to hurry them. When they had finished he wiped their mouths, thanked the German cook politely, collected the pram, and led them out on to the road to Chartres.

The children walked very slowly, languidly. It was after eight o'clock, long past their ordinary bed-time; moreover, they had eaten a full meal. The sun was still warm, though it was dropping towards the horizon; manifestly, they could not go very far. Yet he kept them at it, anxious to get as far as possible from the town.

The problem of the little Dutch boy engaged his attention. He had not left him with the Sisters, as he had been minded to; it had not seemed practical when he was in the town to search out a convent. Nor had he yet got rid of Pierre, as he had promised himself that he would do. Pierre was no trouble, but this new little boy was quite a serious responsibility. He could not speak one word of any language that they spoke. Howard did not even know his name. Perhaps it would be marked upon his clothes.

Then, with a shock of dismay, the old man realised that the clothes were gone for ever. They had been taken by the Germans when the little chap had been deloused; by this time they were probably burnt. It might well be that his identity was lost now till the war was over, and enquiries could be made. It might be lost for ever.

The thought distressed old Howard very much. It was one thing to hand over to the Sisters a child who could be traced; it seemed to him to be a different matter altogether when the little boy was practically untraceable. As he walked along the old man revolved this new trouble in his mind. The only link now with his past lay in the fact that he had been found abandoned in Pithiviers upon a certain day in June—lay in the evidence which Howard alone could give. With that evidence, it might one day be possible to find his parents or his relatives. If now he were abandoned to a convent, that evidence might well be lost.

They walked on down the dusty road.

Sheila said fretfully: 'My feet hurt.'

She was obviously tired out. He picked her up and put her in the pram, and put Pierre in with her. To Pierre he gave the chocolate that had been promised to him earlier in the day, and then all the other children had to have a piece of chocolate too. That refreshed them and made them cheerful for a while, and the old man pushed the pram wearily ahead. It was essential that they should stop soon for the night.

He stopped at the next farm, left the pram with the children in the road, and went into the court-yard to see if it was possible for them to find a bed. There was a strange stillness in the place. No dog sprang out to bark at him. He called out, and stood expectant in the evening light, but no one answered him. He tried the door to the farmhouse, and it was locked. He went into the cow-house, but no animals were there. Two hens scratched upon the midden; otherwise there was no sign of life.

The place was deserted.

As on the previous night, they slept in the hay-loft. There were no blankets to be had this time, but Howard, searching round for some sort of a coverlet, discovered a large, sail-like cover, used possibly to thatch a rick. He dragged this into the loft and arranged it double on the hay, laying the children down between its folds. He had expected trouble with them, excitement and fretfulness, but they were too tired for that. All five of them were glad to lie down and rest; in a short time they were all asleep.

Howard lay resting on the hay near them, tired to death. In the last hour he had taken several nips of brandy for the weariness and weakness that he was enduring; now as he lay upon the hay in the deserted farm fatigue came soaking out of him in great waves. He felt that they were in a desperate position. There could be no hope now of getting through to England, as he once had hoped. The German front was far ahead of them; by now it might have reached to Brittany itself. All France was overrun.

Exposure might come at any time, must come before so very long. It was inevitable. His own French, though good enough, was spoken with an English accent, as he knew well. The only hope of escaping detection would be to hide for a while until some plan presented itself, to lie up with the children in the house of some French citizen. But he knew no one in this part of France that he could go to.

And any way, no family would take them in. If he did know anybody, it would hardly be fair to plant himself on them.

He lay musing bitterly on the future, only half-awake.

It was not quite correct to say that he knew nobody. He did know, very slightly, one family at Chartres. They were people called Rouget—no, Rougand—Rougeron; that was it, Rougeron. They came from Chartres. He had met them at Cidoton eighteen months before, when he had been there with John for the ski-ing. The father was a colonel in the army; Howard wondered vaguely what had become of him. The mother had been typically fat and French, pleasant enough in a very quiet way. The daughter had ski'd well; closing his eyes in the doze of oncoming sleep the old man could see her flying down the slopes behind John, in a flurry of snow. She had had fair hair which she wore short and rather elaborately dressed, in the French style.

He had seen a good deal of the father. They had played draughts together in the evening over a Pernod, and had pondered together whether war would come. The old man began to consider Rougeron seriously. If by some freak of chance he should be in Chartres, there might yet be hope for them. He thought that Rougeron might help.

At any rate, they would get good advice from him. Howard became aware at this point of how much, how very much he wanted to talk to some adult, to discuss their difficulties and make plans. The more he thought of Rougeron, the more he yearned to talk to someone of that sort, frankly and without reserve.

Chartres was not far away, not much more than twenty-five miles. With luck they might get there tomorrow. Probably, Rougeron would be away from home, but—it was worth trying.

Presently he slept.

He woke several times in the night, gasping and breathless, with a very tired heart. Each time he sat upright for half an hour and drank a little brandy, presently slipping down again to an uneasy doze. The children also slept uneasily, but did not wake. At five o'clock the old man woke for good, and sitting up against a heap of hay, resigned himself to wait till it was time to wake the children.

He would go to Chartres, and look up Rougeron. The bad night that he had suffered was a warning; it might well be that his strength was giving out. If that should happen, he must get the children safe with someone else. With Rougeron, if he were there, the children would be safe; Howard could leave money for their keep, English money it was true, but probably negotiable. Rougeron might give him a bed, and let him rest a little till this deathly feeling of fatigue went away.

Pierre woke at about half past six, and lay awake with him. 'You must stay quiet,' the old man said. 'It's not time to get up yet. Go to sleep again.'

At seven o'clock Sheila woke up, wriggled about, and climbed out of her bed. Her movements woke the other children. Howard got up stiffly and got them all up. He herded them before him down the ladder to the farmyard, and one by one made them sluice their faces beneath the pump.

There was a step behind him, and he turned to meet a formidable woman, who was the farmer's wife. She demanded crossly what he was doing there.

He said mildly: 'I have slept in your hay, madame, with these children. A thousand pardons, but there was no other place where we could go.'

She rated him soudly for a few minutes. Then she said: 'Who are you? You are not a Frenchman. No doubt, you are English, and these children also?'

He said: 'These children are of all nationalities, madame. Two are French and two are Swiss, from Geneva. One is Dutch.' He smiled: 'I assure you, we are a little mixed.'

She eyed him keenly. 'But you,' she said, 'you are English.'

He said: 'If I were English, madame, what of that?'

'They are saying in Angerville that the English have betrayed us, that they have run away, from Dunkirk.'

He felt himself to be in peril. This woman was quite capable of giving them all up to the Germans.

He faced her boldly and looked her in the eyes. 'Do you believe that England has abandoned France?' he asked. 'Or do you think that is a German lie?'

She hesitated. 'These filthy politics,' she said at last. 'I only know that this farm is ruined. I do not know how we shall live.'

He said simply: 'By the Grace of God, madame.'

She was silent for a minute. Then she said: 'You *are* English, aren't you?'

He nodded without speaking.

She said: 'You had better go away, before anybody sees you.'

He turned and called the children to him, and walked over to the pram. Then, pushing it in front of him, he went towards the gate.

She called after him: 'Where are you going to?'

He stopped and said: 'To Chartres.' And then he could have bitten out his tongue for the indiscretion.

She said: 'By the tram?'

He repeated uncertainly: 'The tram?'

'It passes at ten minutes past eight. There is still half an hour.'

He had forgotten the light railway, running by the road. Hope of a lift to Chartres surged up in him. 'Is it still running, madame?'

'Why not? These Germans say that they have brought us Peace. Well then, the tram will run.'

He thanked her and went out on to the road. A quarter of a mile farther on he came to a place where the track crossed the road; here he waited, and fed the children on the biscuits he had bought the day before, with a little of the chocolate. Presently, a little puff of steam announced the little narrow-gauge train, the so-called tram.

Three hours later they walked out into the streets of Chartres, still pushing the pram. It was as easy as that; a completely uneventful journey.

Chartres, like Angerville, was full of Germans. They swarmed everywhere, particularly in the luxury shops, buying with paper money silk stockings, underclothes, and all sorts of imported food. The whole town seemed to be on holiday. The troops were clean and well disciplined; all day Howard saw nothing in their behaviour to complain of, apart from their very presence. They were constrained in their behaviour, scrupulously correct, uncertain, doubtful of their welcome. But in the shops there was no doubt about it; they were spending genuine French paper money and spending it like water. If there were any doubts in Chartres, they stayed behind the locked doors of the banks.

In a telephone-booth the old man found the name of Rougeron in the directory; they lived in an apartment in the Rue Vaugiraud. He did not ring up, feeling the matter to be a little difficult for the telephone. Instead, he asked the way, and walked round to the place, still pushing the pram, the children trailing after him.

Rue Vaugiraud was a narrow street of tall, grey shuttered houses. He rang the bell of the house, and the door opened silently before him, disclosing the common staircase. Rougeron lived on the second floor. He went upstairs slowly, for he was rather short of breath, the children following him. He rang the bell of the apartment.

There was the sound of women's voices from behind the door. There was a step and the door opened before him. It was the daughter, the one that he remembered eighteen months before at Cidoton.

She said: 'What is it?'

In the passage it was a little dark. 'Mademoiselle,' he said, 'I have come to see your father, monsieur le colonel. I do not know if you will remember me; we have met before. At Cidoton.'

She did not answer for a moment. The old man blinked his eyes; in his fatigue it seemed to him that she was holding tight on to the door. He recognised her very well. She wore her hair in the same close curled French manner; she wore a grey cloth skirt and a dark blue jumper, with a black scarf at the neck.

She said at last. 'My father is away from home. I – I remember you very well, monsieur.'

He said easily in French: 'It is very charming of you to say so, mademoiselle. My name is Howard.'

'I know that.'

'Will monsieur le colonel be back today?'

She said: 'He has been gone for three months, Monsieur Howard. He was near Metz. That is the last that we have heard.'

He had expected as much, but the disappointment was no less keen. He hesitated and then drew back.

'I am so sorry,' he said. 'I had hoped to see monsieur le colonel, as I was in Chartres. You have my sympathy, mademoiselle. I will not intrude any further upon your anxiety.'

She said: 'Is it—is it anything that I could discuss with you, Monsieur Howard?' He got a queer impression from her manner that she was pleading, trying to detain him at the door.

He could not burden a girl and her mother with his troubles; they had troubles of their own to face. 'It is nothing, mademoiselle,' he said. 'Merely a little personal matter that I wanted to talk over with your father.'

She drew herself up and faced him, looking him in the eyes. 'I understand that you wish to see my father, Monsieur Howard,' she said quietly. 'But he is away—we do not know where. And I . . . I am not a child. I know very well what you have come to talk about. We can talk of this together, you and I.'

She drew back from the door. 'Will you not come in and sit down?' she said.

7

He turned and motioned to the children. Then he glanced at the girl, and caught an expression of surprise, bewilderment, upon her face. 'There are rather a lot of us, I'm afraid,' he said apologetically.

She said: 'But . . . I do not understand, Monsieur Howard. Are these your children?'

He smiled. 'I'm looking after them. They aren't really mine.' He hesitated and then said: 'I am in a position of some difficulty, mademoiselle.'

'Oh . . .'

'I wished to talk it over with your father.' He wrinkled his brows in perplexity. 'Did you think that it was something different?'

She said, hastily: 'No, monsieur—not at all.' And then she swung round and called: 'Maman! Come quickly; here is Monsieur Howard, from Cidoton!'

The little woman that Howard remembered came bustling out; the old man greeted her ceremoniously. Then for a few minutes he stood with the children pressed close round him in the little salon of the flat, trying to make the two women understand his presence with them. It was not an easy task.

The mother gave it up. 'Well, here they are,' she said, content to let the why and wherefore pass. 'Have they had *déjeuner*? Are they hungry?'

The children smiled shyly. Howard said: 'Madame, they are always hungry. But do not derange yourself; we can get *déjeuner* in the town, perhaps?'

She said that that was not to be thought of. 'Nicole, stay with m'sieur for a little, while I make arrangements.' She bustled off into the kitchen.

The girl turned to the old man. 'Will you sit down and rest a little,' she said.

'You seem to be very tired.' She turned to the children. 'And you, too, you sit down and stay quiet; *déjeuner* will be ready before long.'

The old man looked down at his hands, grimed with dirt. He had not washed properly, or shaved, since leaving Dijon. 'I am desolated that I should appear so dirty,' he said. 'Presently, perhaps I could wash?'

She smiled at him and he found comfort in her smile. 'It is not easy to keep clean in times like these,' she said. 'Tell me from the beginning, monsieur – how did you come to be in France at all?'

He lay back in the chair. It would be better to tell her the whole thing; indeed, he was aching to tell somebody, to talk over his position. 'You must understand, mademoiselle,' he began, 'that I was in great trouble early in the year. My only son was killed. He was in the Royal Air Force, you know. He was killed on a bombing raid.'

She said: 'I know, monsieur. I have the deepest sympathy for you.'

He hesitated, not quite sure if he had understood her correctly. Some idiom had probably misled him. He went on: 'It was intolerable to stay in England. I wanted a change of scene, to see new faces.'

He plunged into his story. He told her about the Cavanaghs at Cidoton. He told her of Sheila's illness, of their delay at Dijon. He told her about the chambermaid, about *la petite* Rose. He told her how they had become stranded at Joigny, and touched lightly upon the horror of the Montargis road, because Pierre was with them in the room. He told her about the Royal Air Force men, and about the little Dutch boy they had found in Pithiviers. Then he sketched briefly how they had reached Chartres.

It took about a quarter of an hour to tell, in the slow, measured, easy tones of an old man. In the end she turned to him in wonder.

'So really, monsieur, none of these little ones have anything to do with you at all?'

'I suppose not,' he said, 'if you like to look at it that way.'

She pressed the point. 'But you could have left the two in Dijon for their parents to fetch from Geneva? You would have been able then, yourself, to have reached England in good time.'

He smiled slowly. 'I suppose so.'

She stared at him. 'We French people will never understand the English,' she said softly. And then she turned aside.

He was a little puzzled. 'I beg your pardon?'

She got to her feet. 'You will wish to wash,' she said. 'Come, I will show you. And then, I will see that the little ones also wash.'

She led him to an untidy bathroom; manifestly, they kept no servant in the flat. He looked around for a man's gear, hoping for a razor, but the colonel had been away too long. Howard contented himself with a wash, resolved at the first opportunity to see if he could get a shave.

The girl took the children to a bedroom, and washed them one by one quite thoroughly. Then it was time for *déjeuner*. By padding out the midday meal with rice, Madame Rougeron had produced a risotto; they sat down to it round the table in the salon and had the first civilised meal that Howard had eaten since Dijon.

And after lunch, sitting round the littered table over coffee, while the children played together in a corner of the salon, he discussed his future with them.

'I wanted to get back to England, of course,' he said. 'I still want to. But at the moment it seems difficult.'

Madame Rougeron said: 'There are no boats to England now, m'sieur. The Germans have stopped everything.'

He nodded. 'I was afraid so,' he said quietly. 'It would have been better if I had gone back to Switzerland.'

The girl shrugged her shoulders. 'It is always easy to be wise later,' she said. 'At the time, a week ago, we all thought that Switzerland would be invaded. I think so still. I do not think that Switzerland would be at all a good place for you to go.'

There was a silence.

Madame said: 'These other children, monsieur. The one called Pierre and the other little Dutchman. Would you have taken them to England?'

Sheila, bored with playing on the floor, came up and pulled his sleeve, distracting him. 'I want to go out for a walk. M'sieur Howard, may we go out for a walk and see some tanks?'

He put his arm round her absently. 'Not just now,' he said. 'Stay quiet for a little. We'll go out presently.' He turned to Madame Rougeron. 'I don't see that I can leave them, unless with their relations,' he said. 'I have been thinking about this a good deal. It might be very difficult to find their relations at this time.'

The mother said: 'That is very true.'

Pursuing his train of thought, he said: 'If I could get them to England, I think I'd send them over to America until the war is over. They would be quite safe there.' He explained. 'My daughter, who lives in the United States, has a big house on Long Island. She would make a home for them till the war ends, and then we could try and find their parents.'

The girl said: 'That would be Madame Costello?'

He turned to her faintly surprised. 'Yes, that is her married name. She has a little boy herself, about their age. She would be very good to them.'

'I am sure of that, m'sieur.'

For the moment the difficulty of getting them to England escaped him. He said: 'It's going to be practically impossible to find the little Dutchman's parents, I'm afraid. We don't even know his name.'

Beneath his arm, Sheila said: 'I know his name.'

He stared down at her. 'You do?' And then, remembering Pierre, he said, 'What do you think he's called?'

She said: 'Willem. Not William, just Willem.'

Howard said: 'Has he got another name?'

'I don't think so. Just Willem.'

Ronnie looked up from the floor. 'You are a story,' he said without heat. 'He has got another name, Mr Howard. He's called Eybe.' He explained. 'Just like I'm called Ronnie Cavanagh, so he's called Willem Eybe.'

'Oh . . .' said Sheila.

Madame said: 'But if he can't speak any French or English, how did you find that out?'

The children stared at her, uncomprehending, a little impatient of adult density. 'He *told* us,' they explained.

Howard said: 'Did he tell you anything more about himself?' There was a silence. 'Did he say who his daddy or his mummy were, or where he came from?'

The children stared at him, awkward and embarrassed. The old man said: 'Suppose you ask him where his daddy is?'

Sheila said: 'But we can't understand what he *says*.' The others stayed silent.

Howard said: 'Never mind, then.' He turned to the two women. 'They'll probably know all about him in a day or two,' he said. 'It takes a little time.'

The girl nodded. 'Perhaps we can find somebody who speaks Dutch.'

Her mother said: 'That might be dangerous. It is not a thing to be decided lightly, that. One must think of the Germans.'

She turned to Howard: 'So, monsieur,' she said, 'it is clear that you are in a difficulty. What is it that you want to do?'

He smiled slowly. 'I want to get to England with these children, madame,' he said. 'Only that.'

He thought for a minute. 'Also,' he said gently, 'I do not wish to get my friends into trouble.' He rose from his chair. 'It has been most kind of you to give us *déjeuner*,' he said. 'I am indeed sorry to have missed seeing monsieur le colonel. I hope very much that when we meet again you will be reunited.'

The girl sprang up. 'You must not go,' she said. 'It is not possible at all, that.' She swung round on her mother. 'We must devise something, Mother.'

The older woman shrugged her shoulders. 'It is impossible. The Germans are everywhere.'

The girl said: 'If father were here, he would devise something.'

There was a silence in the room, broken only by Ronnie and Rose chanting in a low tone their little song about the numerals. Faintly, from the town, came the air of a band playing in the main square.

Howard said: 'You must not put yourselves to inconvenience on our account. I assure you, we can get along very well.'

The girl said: 'But monsieur – your clothes alone – they are not in the French fashion. One would say at once that you are an Englishman, to look at you.'

He glanced down ruefully; it was very true. He had been proud of his taste in Harris tweeds, but now they were quite undeniably unsuitable for the occasion. 'I suppose so,' he said. 'It would be better if I got some French clothes, for a start.'

She said: 'My father would be glad to lend you an old suit, if he were here.' She turned to her mother. 'The brown suit, Mother.'

Madame shook her head. 'The grey is better. It is less conspicuous.' She turned to the old man. 'Sit down again,' she said quietly. 'Nicole is right. We must devise something. Perhaps it will be better if you stay here for the night.'

He sat down again. 'That would be too much trouble for you,' he said. 'But I should be grateful for the clothes.'

Sheila came up to him again, fretful. 'Can't we go out now and look at the tanks, Mr Howard?' she said in English, complaining, 'I do want to go out.'

'Presently,' he said. He turned to the two women, speaking in French. 'They want to go out.'

The girl got to her feet. 'I will take them for a walk,' she said. 'You stay here and rest.'

After a little demur he agreed to this; he was very tired. 'One thing,' he said. 'Perhaps while you are out it would be possible for me to borrow an old razor?'

The girl led him to the bathroom and produced all that he needed. 'Have no fear for the little ones,' she said. 'I will not let them get into trouble.'

He turned to her, razor in hand. 'You must be very careful not to speak

English, mademoiselle,' he said. 'The two English children understand and speak French very well. Sometimes they speak English, but that is dangerous now. Speak to them in French all the time.'

She laughed up at him. 'Have no fear, *cher* Monsieur Howard,' she said. 'I do not know any English. Only a phrase or two.' She thought for a minute, and said carefully, in English, 'A little bit of what you fancy does you good.' And then, in French again, 'That is what one says about the *apéritif?*'

'Yes,' he said. He stared at her, puzzled again.

She did not notice. 'And to rebuke anybody,' she said, 'you "tear him off a strip."' That is all I know of English, monsieur. The children will be safe with me.'

He said quietly, suddenly numb with an old pain: 'Who told you those phrases, mademoiselle? They are quite up to date.'

She turned away. 'I do not know,' she said awkwardly. 'It is possible that I have read them in a book.'

He went back with her to the salon and helped her to get the children ready to go out, and saw them off together down the stairs. Then he went back into the little flat; madame had disappeared, and he resorted to the bathroom for his shave. Then, in the corner of the settee in the salon he fell asleep, and slept uneasily for about two hours.

The children woke him as they came back into the flat. Ronnie rushed up to him. 'We saw bombers,' he said ecstatically. 'Real German ones, ever so big, and they showed me the bombs and they let me go and touch them, too!'

Sheila said: 'I went and touched them, too!

Ronnie said: 'And we saw the bombers flying, and taking off and landing, and going out to bomb the ships upon the sea! It was *fun*, Mr Howard.'

He said, mildly: 'I hope you said "Thank you" very nicely to Mademoiselle Rougeron for taking you for such a lovely walk.'

They rushed up to her. 'Thank you *ever* so much, Mademoiselle Rougeron,' they said.

He turned to her. 'You've given them a very happy afternoon,' he said. 'Where did you take them to?'

She said: 'To the aerodrome, monsieur.' She hesitated. 'I would not have gone there if I had realised . . . But they do not understand, the little ones.'

'No,' he said. 'It's all great fun to them.'

He glanced at her. 'Were there many bombers there?'

'Sixty or seventy. More, perhaps.'

'And going out to bomb the ships of my country?' he said gently.

She inclined her head. 'I would not have taken them there,' she said again. 'I did not know.'

He smiled. 'Well,' he said, 'there's not much we can do to stop them, so it's no good worrying about it.'

Madame appeared again; it was nearly six o'clock. She had made soup for the children's supper and she had prepared a bed in her own room for the two little girls. The three little boys were to sleep in a bed which she had made up on the floor of the corridor; Howard had been given a bedroom to himself. He thanked her for the trouble she had taken.

'One must first get the little ones to bed,' she said. 'Then we will talk, and devise something.'

In an hour they were all fed, washed, and in bed, settling for the night.

Howard sat down with the two women to a supper of a thick meat broth and bread and cheese, with a little red wine mixed with water. He helped them to clear the table, and accepted a curious, thin, dry, black cigar from a box left by his absent host.

Presently he said: 'I have been thinking quietly this afternoon, madame,' he said. 'I do not think I shall go back to Switzerland. I think it would be better to try and get into Spain.'

The woman said: 'It is a very long way to go.' They discussed the matter for a little time. The difficulties were obvious; when he had made the journey there was no sort of guarantee that he could ever get across the frontier.

The girl said: 'I also have been thinking, but in quite the opposite direction.' She turned to her mother. 'Jean Henri Guinevec,' she said, and she ran the two Christian names together to pronounce them Jenri.

Madame said placidly: 'Jean Henri may have gone already, *ma petite.*'

Howard said: 'Who is he?'

The girl said: 'He is a fisherman, of Le Conquet. In Finisterre. He has a very good boat. He is a great friend of my father, monsieur.'

They told him about this man. For thirty years it had been the colonel's habit to go to Brittany each summer. In that he had been unusual for a Frenchman. The sparse, rocky country, the stone cottages, and the wild coast attracted him, and the strong sea winds of the Atlantic refreshed him. Morgat, Le Conquet, Brest, Douarnenez, Audierne, Concarneau–these were his haunts, the places that he loved to visit in the summer. He used to dress the part. For going in the fishing-boats he had the local costume, faded rust and rose coloured sailcloth overalls and a large, floppy black Breton casque.

'He used to wear the sabots, too, when we were married first,' his wife said placidly. 'But then, when he got corns upon his feet, he had to give them up.'

His wife and daughter had gone with him, every year. They had stayed in some little pension and had gone for little, bored walks, while the colonel went out in the boats with the fishermen, or sat yarning with them in the café.

'It was not very gay,' the girl said. 'One year we went to Paris-Plage, but next year we went back to Brittany.'

She had come to know his fishermen friends through the years. 'Jenri would help us to help Monsieur Howard,' she said confidently. 'He has a fine big boat that could cross easily to England.'

Howard gave this serious attention. He knew a little of the Breton fishermen; when he had practised as a solicitor in Exeter there had been occasional legal cases that involved them, cases of fishing inside the three-mile limit. Sometimes, they came into Torbay for shelter in bad weather. Apart from their fishing peccadilloes they were popular in Devon; big burly men with boats as big and burly as they were themselves; fine seamen, speaking a language very similar to Gaelic, that a Welshman could sometimes understand.

They discussed this for some time; it certainly seemed more hopeful than any attempt to get back through Spain. 'It's a long way to go,' he said a little ruefully. It was; Brest is two hundred miles or so from Chartres. 'Perhaps I could go by train.' He would be going away from Paris.

They discussed it in all aspects. Obviously, it was impossible to find out how Guinevec was placed; the only thing to do would be to go there and find out. 'But if Jenri should have gone away,' the mother said, 'there are all the others. One or other of them will help you, when they know that you are friendly with my husband.' She spoke with simple faith.

The girl confirmed this: 'One or other of them will help.'

The old man said presently: 'It really is most kind of you to suggest this. If you would give me a few addresses, then–I would go tomorrow, with the children.' He hesitated. 'It will be better to go soon,' he said. 'Later, the Germans may become more vigilant.'

'That we can do,' said madame.

Presently, as it was getting late, she got up and went out of the room. After a few minutes the girl followed her; from the salon Howard could hear the mutter of their voices in the kitchen, talking in low tones. He could not hear what they were saying, nor did he try. He was deeply grateful for the help and encouragement that he had had from them. Since he had parted from the two Air Force men he had rather lost heart; now he felt again that there was a good prospect that he would get through to England. True, he had still to get to Brittany. That might be difficult in itself; he had no papers of identification other than a British passport, and none of the children had anything at all. If he were stopped and questioned by the Germans the game would be up, but so far he had not been stopped. So long as nobody became suspicious of him, he might be all right.

Nicole came back alone from the kitchen. 'Maman has gone to bed,' she said. 'She gets up so early in the morning. She has asked me to wish you a very good night on her behalf.'

He said something conventionally polite. 'I think I should be better in bed, myself,' he said. 'These last days have been tiring for a man as old as I am.'

She said: 'I know, monsieur.' She hesitated and then said a little awkwardly: 'I have been talking with my mother. We both think that it would be better that I should come with you to Brittany, Monsieur Howard.'

There was a momentary silence; the old man was taken by surprise. 'That is a very kind offer,' he said. 'Most generous of you, mademoiselle. But I do not think I should accept it.'

He smiled at her. 'You must understand,' he said, 'I may get into trouble with the Germans. I should not like to think that I had involved you in my difficulties.'

She said: 'I thought you might feel that, monsieur. But I assure you, I have discussed the matter with maman, and it is better that I should go with you. It is quite decided.'

He said: 'I cannot deny that you would be an enormous help to me, mademoiselle. But one does not decide a point like that all in one moment. One weighs it carefully and one sleeps upon it.'

It was growing dusk. In the half-light of the salon it seemed to him that her eyes were very bright, and that she was blinking a little. 'Do not refuse me, Monsieur Howard,' she said at last. 'I want so very much to help you.'

He was touched. 'I was only thinking of your safety, mademoiselle,' he said gently. 'You have done a very great deal for me already. Why should you do any more?'

She said: 'Because of our old friendship.'

He made one last effort to dissuade her. 'But mademoiselle,' he said, 'that friendship, which I value, was never more than a slight thing–a mere hotel acquaintance. You have already done more for me than I could have hoped for.'

She said: 'Perhaps you did not know, monsieur. Your son and I . . . John . . .

we were good friends.' There was an awkward pause.

'So it is quite decided,' she said, turning away. 'We are quite of one mind, my mother and I. Now, monsieur, I will show you your room.'

She took him down the corridor and showed him the room. Her mother had been before her, and had laid out upon the bed a long, linen nightgown, the slumber-wear of Monsieur le Colonel. On the dressing-table she had put his cut-throat razor, and a strop, and his much-squeezed tube of shaving-paste, and a bottle of scent called FLEURS DE ALPES.

The girl looked round. 'I think that there is everything you will want,' she said. 'If there is anything we have forgotten, I am close by. You will call?'

He said: 'Mademoiselle, I shall be most comfortable.'

'In the morning,' she said, 'do not hurry. There are arrangements to be made before we can start for Brittany, and one must make enquiries—on the quiet, you will understand, monsieur. That we can best do alone, my mother and I. So it will be better if you stay in bed, and rest.'

He said: 'Oh, but there are the children. I shall have to see to them.'

She smiled: 'In England, do the men look after children when there are two women in the house?'

'Er—well,' he said. 'I mean, I didn't want to bother you with them.'

She smiled again. 'Stay in bed,' she said. 'I will bring coffee to you at about eight o'clock.'

She went out and closed the door behind her; he remained for a time staring thoughtfully after her. She was, he thought, a very peculiar young woman. He could not understand her at all. At Cidoton, as he remembered her, she had been an athletic young creature, very shy and reserved, as most middle-class French girls are. He remembered her chiefly for the incongruity of her close-curled, carefully tended head, her daintily trimmed eyebrows and her carefully manicured hands, in contrast with the terrific speed with which she took the steepest slopes when sliding on a pair of skis. John, who himself was a fine skier, had told his father that he had his work cut out to keep ahead of her upon a run. She took things straight that he made traverse upon and never seemed to come to any harm. But she had a poor eye for ground, and frequently ran slowly on a piece of flat while he went sailing on ahead of her.

That was, literally, about all the old man could remember of her. He turned from the door and began slowly to undress. She had changed very much, it seemed to him. It had been nice of her to tell him in her queer, French way that she had been good friends with John; his heart warmed to her for that. Both she and her mother were being infinitely kind to him, and this proposal that Nicole should come with him to Britanny was so kind as to verge on the quixotic. He could not refuse the offer; already he had come near to giving pain by doing so. He would not press a refusal any more; to have her help might make the whole difference to his success in getting the children to England.

He put on the long nightgown and got into bed; the soft mattress and the smooth sheets were infinitely soothing after two nights spent in hay-lofts. He had not slept properly in a bed since leaving Cidoton.

She had changed very much, that girl. She still had the carefully tended curly head; the trimmed eyebrows and the manicured hands were jus: the same. But her whole expression was different. She looked ten years older; the dark shadows beneath her eyes matched the black scarf she wore about her neck. Quite suddenly the thought came into his mind that she looked like a widow. She was a young, unmarried girl, but that was what she reminded him of, a young widow. He wondered if she had lost a fiancé in the war. He must ask her mother, delicately, before he left the flat; it would be as well to know in order that he might avoid any topic that was painful to her.

With all that, she seemed very odd to him. He did not understand her at all. But presently the tired limbs relaxed, his active mind moved more slowly, and he drifted into sleep.

He slept all through the night, an unusual feat for a man of his age. He was still sleeping when she came in with his coffee and rolls on a tray at about a quarter past eight. He woke easily and sat up in bed, and thanked her.

She was fully dressed. Beyond her, in the corridor, the children stood, dressed and washed, peeping in at the door. Pierre ventured in a little way.

'Good morning, Pierre,' said the old man gravely. The little boy placed his hand upon his stomach and bowed to him from the waist. *'Bon jour*, M'sieur Howard.'

The girl laughed and ran her hand through his hair. 'It is a little boy *bien élevé*, this one,' she said. 'Not like the other ones that you have collected.'

He said a little anxiously: 'I do hope that they have not been a trouble to you, mademoiselle.'

She said: 'Children will never trouble me, monsieur.'

He thought again, a very odd young woman with a very odd way of expressing herself.

She told him that her mother was already out marketing in the town, and making certain enquiries. She would be back in half an hour or so; then they would make their plans.

The girl brought him the grey suit of her father's, rather worn and shabby, with a pair of old brown canvas shoes, a horrible violet shirt, a celluloid collar rather yellow with age, and an unpleasant tie. 'These clothes are not very chic,' she said apologetically. 'But it will be better for you to wear them, Monsieur Howard, because then you will appear like one of the little *bourgeoisie*. I assure you, we will keep your own clothes for you very carefully. My mother will put them in the cedar chest with the blankets, because of the moths, you understand.'

Three-quarters of an hour later he was up and dressed, and standing in the salon while the girl viewed him critically. 'You should not have shaved again so soon,' she said. 'It makes the wrong effect, that.'

He said that he was sorry. Then he took note of her appearance. 'You have made yourself look shabby to come with me, mademoiselle,' he said. 'That is a very kind thing to have done.'

She said: 'Marie, the servant, lent me this dress.'

She wore a very plain, black dress to her ankles, without adornment of any kind. Upon her feet she wore low-heeled, clumsy shoes and coarse black stockings.

Madame Rougeron came in and put down her basket on the table in the salon. 'There is a train for Rennes at noon,' she said unemotionally. 'There is a German soldier at the *guichet* who asks why you must travel, but they do not look at papers. They are very courteous and correct.' She paused. 'But there is another thing.'

She took from the pocket of her gown a folded handbill. 'A German soldier left this paper with the *concierge* this mornng. There was one for each apartment.'

They spread it out upon the table. It was in French, and it read:

CITIZENS OF THE REPUBLIC!

The treacherous English, who have forced this unnecessary war upon us, have been driven into disorderly flight from our country. Now is the time to rise and root out these plutocratic warmongers wherever they may be hiding, before they have time to plot fresh trouble for France.

These scoundrels who are roaming the country and living in secret in our homes like disgusting parasites, will commit acts of sabotage and espionage and make trouble for all of us with the Germans, who are only anxious to build up a peaceful régime in our country. If these cowardly fugitives should commit such acts, the Germans will keep our fathers, our husbands, and our sons in long captivity. Help to bring back your men by driving out these pests!

It is your duty if you know of an Englishman in hiding to tell the gendarmerie, or tell the nearest German soldier. This is a simple thing that anyone can do, which will bring peace and freedom to our beloved land.

Severe penalties await those who shield these rats.

VIVE LA FRANCE!

Howard read it through quietly twice. Then he said: 'It seems that I am one of the rats, madame. After this, I think it would be better that I should go alone, with the children.'

She said that it was not to be thought of. And then she said, Nicole would never agree.

The girl said: 'That is very true. It would be impossible for you to go alone, as things are now. I do not think you would get very far before the Germans found that you were not a Frenchman, even in those clothes.' She flipped the paper with disgust. 'This is a German thing,' she said. 'You must not think that French people talk like this, Monsieur Howard.'

'It is very nearly the truth,' he said ruefully.

'It is an enormous lie,' she said.

She went out of the room. The old man, grasping the opportunity, turned to her mother. 'Your daughter has changed greatly since we were at Cidoton, madame,' he said.

The woman looked at him. 'She has suffered a great deal, monsieur.'

He said: 'I am most sorry to hear that. If you could tell me something about it—perhaps I could avoid hurting her in conversation.'

She stared at him. 'You do not know, then?'

'How should I know anything about her trouble, madame?' he said gently. 'It is something that has happened since we met at Cidoton.'

She hesitated for a minute. Then she said: 'She was in love with a young man. We did not arrange the affair and she tells me nothing.'

'All young people are like that,' he said, quietly. 'My son was the same. The young man is a prisoner in German hands, perhaps?'

Madame said: 'No, monsieur. He is dead.'

Nicole came bursting into the room, a little fibre case in her hand. 'This we will carry in your perambulator,' she said. 'Now, monsieur, I am ready to go.'

There was no time for any more conversation with Madame Rougeron, but Howard felt he had the gist of it; indeed, it was just what he had expected. It was hard on the girl, terribly hard; perhaps this journey, dangerous though it might be, would not be altogether a bad thing for her. It might distract her mind, serve as an anodyne.

There was a great bustle of getting under way. They all went downstairs; Madame Rougeron had many bundles of food, which they put in the perambulator. The children clustered round them and impeded them.

Ronnie said: 'Will we be going where there are tanks, Mr Howard?' He spoke in English. 'You said that I might go with the Germans for a ride.'

Howard said, in French: 'Not today. Try and talk French while Mademoiselle Rougeron is with us, Ronnie; it is not very nice to say what other people cannot understand.'

Rose said: 'That is very true, m'sieur. Often I have told Ronnie that it was not polite to speak in English.'

Madame Rougeron said to her daughter in a low tone: 'It is clever that.' The girl nodded.

Pierre said suddenly: 'I do not speak English, m'sieur.'

'No, Pierre,' the old man said. 'You are always polite.'

Sheila said: 'Is Willem polite, too?' She spoke in French.

Nicole said: 'All of you are polite, all *très bien élevés*. Now we are quite ready.' She turned and kissed her mother.

'Do not fret,' she said gently. 'Five days—perhaps a week, and I will be home again. Be happy for me, maman.'

The old woman stood trembling, suddenly aged. '*Prenez bien garde*,' she said tremulously. 'These Germans—they are wicked, cruel people.'

The girl said gently: 'Be tranquil. I shall come to no harm.' She turned to Howard. '*En route, donc*, Monsieur Howard,' she said. 'It is time for us to go.'

They left the apartment and started down the street, Howard pushing the loaded pram and Nicole shepherding the children. She had produced a rather shabby black Homburg hat for the old man, and this, with his grey suit and brown canvas shoes, made him look very French. They went slowly for the sake of the children; the girl strolled beside him with a shawl over her shoulders.

Presently she said: 'Give me the pram, monsieur. That is more fitting for a woman to push, in the class that we represent.'

He surrendered it to her; they must play up to their disguise. 'When we come to the station,' she said, 'say nothing at all. I will do all the talking. Do you think you could behave as a much older man? As one who could hardly talk at all?'

He said: 'I would do my best. You want me to behave as a very old man indeed.'

She nodded. 'We have come from Arras,' she said. 'You are my uncle, you understand? Our house in Arras was destroyed by the British. You have a brother, my other uncle, who lives in Landerneau.'

'Landerneau,' he said. 'Where is that, mademoiselle?'

She said: 'It is a little country town twenty kilometres this side of Brest, monsieur. If we can get there we can then walk to the coast. And it is inland, forty kilometres from the sea. I think they may allow us to go there, when it would be impossible for us to travel directly to the coast.'

They approached the station. 'Stay with the children,' she said quietly. 'If anyone asks you anything, be very stupid.'

The approach to the station was crowded with German transport lorries; German officers and soldiers thronged around. It was clear that a considerable detachment of troops had just arrived by train; apart from them the station was crowded with refugees. Nicole pushed the pram through into the booking-hall, followed by Howard and the children. The old man, mindful of his part, walked with a shambling tread; his mouth hung open a little, and his head shook rhythmically.

Nicole shot a glance at him. 'It is good, that,' she said. 'Be careful you do not forget your rôle.'

She left the pram with him and pressed forward to the booking-office. A German *Feldwebel*, smart and efficient in his grey-green uniform, stopped her and asked a question. Howard, peering through the throng with sagging head and half-closed eyes, saw her launch out into a long, rambling peasant explanation.

She motioned towards him and the children. The *Feldwebel* glanced over them, shabby and inoffensive, their only luggage in an ancient pram. Then he cut short the torrent of her talk and motioned her to the booking-office. Another woman claimed his attention.

Nicole came back to Howard and the children with the tickets: 'Only as far as Rennes,' she said, in coarse peasant tones. 'That is as far as this train goes.'

The old man said: 'Eh?' and wagged his sagging head.

She shouted in his ear. 'Only to Rennes.'

He mumbled thickly: 'We do not want to go to Rennes.'

She made a gesture of irritation and pushed him ahead of her to the barrier. A German soldier stood by the ticket-puncher; the old man checked and turned back to the girl in senile bewilderment. She said something cross and pushed him through.

Then she apologised to the ticket-puncher. 'He is my uncle,' she said. 'He is a good old man, but he is more trouble to me than all these children.'

The man said: 'Rennes. On the right,' and passed them through. The German stared at them indifferently; one set of refugees was very like another. So they passed through on to the platform and climbed into a very old compartment with hard wooden seats.

Ronnie said: 'Is this the train we're going to sleep in, M'sieur Howard?' He spoke in French, however.

Howard said: 'Not tonight. We shan't be in this train for very long.'

But he was wrong.

From Chartres to Rennes is about two hundred and sixty kilometres; it took them six hours. In the hot summer afternoon the train stopped at every station, and many times between. The body of the train was full of German soldiers travelling to the west; three coaches at the end were reserved for French civilians and they travelled in one of these. Sometimes the compartment was shared with other travellers for a few stations, but no one travelled with them continuously.

It was an anxious journey, full of fears and subterfuges. When there were other people with them in the carriage the old man lapsed into senility, and Nicole would explain their story once again, how they were travelling to Landerneau from their house in Arras, which had been destroyed by the

British. At first there was difficulty with the children, who were by no means inclined to lend support to what they rightly knew to be a pack of lies. Each time the story was retold Nicole and Howard rode on a knife edge of suspense, their attention split between the listener and the necessity of preventing the children from breaking into the conversation. Presently the children lost interest, and became absorbed in running up and down the corridor, playing 'My great-aunt lives in Tours,' with all its animal repetitions, and looking out of the window. In any event, the peasants and small shopkeepers who travelled with them were too anxious to start talking and to tell the story of their own troubles to have room for much suspicion in their minds.

At the long last, when the fierce heat of the day was dying down, they pulled into Rennes. There the train stopped and everyone got out; the German soldiers fell in in two ranks in orderly array upon the platform and were marched away, leaving a fatigue party to load their kits on to a lorry. There was a German officer by the ticket-collector. Howard put on his most senile air, and Nicole went straight up to the collector to consult him about trains to Landerneau.

Through half-closed eyes Howard watched her, the children clustered round him, dirty and fretful from their journey. He waited in an agony of apprehension; at any moment the officer might ask for papers. Then it would all be over. But finally he gave her a little pasteboard slip, shrugged his shoulders and dismissed her.

She came back to Howard. 'Mother of God!' she said crossly and rather loudly. 'Where is now the pram? Do I have to do everything?'

The pram was still in the baggage-car. The old man shambled towards it, but she pushed him aside and got into the car and pulled it down on to the ground herself. Then, in a little confused huddle, she shepherded them to the barrier.

'It is not five children that I have,' she said bitterly to the ticket-collector. 'It is six.' The man laughed, and the German officer smiled faintly. So they passed out into the town of Rennes.

She said quietly to him as they walked along: 'You are not angry, Monsieur Howard? It is better that I should pretend that I am cross. It is more natural so.'

He said: 'My dear, you have done wonderfully well.'

She said: 'Well, we have got half-way without suspicion. Tomorrow, at eight in the morning, a train leaves for Brest. We can go on that as far as Landerneau.'

She told him that the German officer had given them permission to go there. She produced the ticket he had given to her. 'We must sleep tonight in the refugee hostel,' she said. 'This ticket admits us. It will be better to go there, m'sieur, like all the others.'

He agreed. 'Where is it?' he enquired.

'In the Cinema du Monde,' she said. 'I have never slept in a cinema before.'

He said: 'Mademoiselle, I am deeply sorry that my difficulties should make you do so now.'

She smiled: '*Ne vous en faites pas*,' she said. 'Perhaps as it is under German management it will be clean. We French are not so good at things like that.'

They gave up their cards at the entrance, pushed their pram inside and looked around. The seats had all been removed, and around the walls were palliasses stacked, filled with old straw. There were not many people in the place; with the growing restrictions upon movements as the Germans took over control, the tide of refugees was less than it had been. An old Frenchwoman issued them with a palliasse and a blanket each and showed them a corner where they could make a little camp apart from the others. 'The little ones will sleep quiet there,' she said.

There was an issue of free soup at a table at the end of the hall, dispensed by a German cook, who showed a fixed, beaming smile of professional good humour.

An hour later the children were laid down to rest. Howard did not dare to leave them, and sat with his back against the wall, tired to death, but not yet ready for sleep. Nicole went out and came back presently with a packet of caporal cigarettes. 'I bought these for you,' she said. 'I did not dare to get your Players; it would not be safe, that.'

He was not a great smoker, but touched by her kindness he took one gratefully. She poured him out a little brandy in a mug and fetched a little water from the drinking fountain for him; the drink refreshed him and the cigarette was a comfort. She came and sat beside him, leaning up against the wall.

For a time they talked in low tones of their journey, about her plans for the next day. Then, fearing to be overheard, he changed the subject and asked about her father.

She had little more to tell him than he already knew. Her father had been commandant of a fort in the Maginot Line not very far from Metz; they had heard nothing of him since May.

The old man said: 'I am very, very sorry, mademoiselle.' He paused, and then he said, 'I know what that sort of anxiety means . . . very well. It blackens everything for a long time afterwards.'

She said quietly: 'Yes. Day after day you wait, and wait. And then the letter comes, or it may be the telegram, and you are afraid to open it to see what it says.' She was silent for a minute. 'And then at last you do open it.'

He nodded. He felt very close to her; they had shared the same experience. He had waited and waited just like that when John had been missing. For three days he had waited; then the telegram had come. It became clear to him that she had been through the same trouble; indeed, her mother had told him that she had. He was immensely sorry for her.

Quite suddenly, he felt that he would like to talk to her about John. He had not been able to talk about his son to anybody, not since it happened. He had feared sympathy, and had shunned intrusion. But this girl Nicole had known John. They had been ski-ing companions—friends, she had said.

He blew out a long cloud of smoke. 'I lost my son, you know,' he said with difficulty, staring straight ahead of him. 'He was killed flying—he was a squadron leader, in our Royal Air Force. He was shot down by three Messerschmitts on his way back from a bombing raid. Over Heligoland.'

There was a pause.

She turned towards him. 'I know that,' she said gently. 'They wrote to me from the squadron.'

8

The cinema was half-full of people, moving about and laying down their palliasses for the night. The air was full of the fumes of the cooking-stove at the far end, and the smoke of French cigarettes; in the dim light it seemed thick and heavy.

Howard glanced towards the girl. 'You knew my son as well as that, mademoiselle?' he said. 'I did not know.'

In turn, she felt the urge to talk. 'We used to write,' she said. She went on quickly, 'Ever since Cidoton we used to write, almost each week. And we met once, in Paris–just before the war. In June, that was.' She paused, and then said quietly, 'Almost a year ago today.'

The old man said: 'My dear, I never knew anything about this at all.'

'No,' she said. 'Nor did I tell my parents.'

There was a silence while he tried to collect his thoughts and readjust his outlook. 'You said they wrote to you,' he said at last. 'But how did they know your address?'

She shrugged her shoulders. 'He would have made arrangements,' she said. 'He was very kind, monsieur; very, very kind. And we were great friends . . .'

He said quietly: 'You must have thought me very different, mademoiselle. Very rude. But I assure you, I knew nothing about this. Nothing at all.'

There was a little pause.

'May I ask one question?' he said presently.

'But yes, Monsieur Howard.'

He stared ahead of him awkwardly. 'Your mother told me that you had had trouble,' he said. 'That there had been a young who was dead. No doubt, that was somebody else?'

'There was nobody else,' she said quietly. 'Nobody but John.'

She shook herself and sat up. 'See,' she said, 'one must put down a palliasse, or there will be no room left by the wall.' She got to her feet and stirred him, and began to pull down one of the sacks of straw from the pile. He joined her, reluctant and confused, and for a quarter of an hour they worked, making their beds.

'There,' she said at last, standing back to survey their work. 'It is the best that can be done.' She eyed him diffidently. 'Will it be possible for you to sleep so, Monsieur Howard?'

He said: 'My dear, of course it will.'

She laughed shortly. 'Then, let us try.'

Over the palliasses he stood looking at her, blanket in hand. 'May I ask one more question?'

She faced him: 'Yes, monsieur.'

'You have been very good to me,' he said quietly. 'I think I understand now. That was because of John?'

There was a long silence. She stood looking out across the room, motionless. 'No,' she said at last. 'That was because of the children.'

He said nothing, not quite understanding what she meant.

'One loses faith,' she said quietly. 'One thinks that everything is false and bad.'

He glanced at her, puzzled.

'I did not think there could be anyone so kind and brave as John,' she said. 'But I was wrong, monsieur. There was another one. There was his father.'

She turned away. 'So,' she said, 'we must sleep.' She spoke practically, almost coldly; it seemed to the old man that she had set up a barrier between them. He did not resent that; he understood the reason for her curtness. She did not want to be questioned any more. She did not want to talk.

He lay down on the palliasse, shifted the rough, straw-filled pillow and pulled the blanket round him. The girl settled down upon her own bed on the other side of the children.

Howard lay awake, his mind in a tumult. He felt that he had known that there had been something between this girl and John, yet that knowledge had not reached the surface of his mind. But looking back, there had been little hints all the time that he had been with them in the flat. Indeed, she had used John's very words about a cocktail when she had said in English that: 'A little bit of what you fancy does you good.' Thinking back, he remembered the little twinges of pain that he had suffered when she had said that and yet he had not realised.

How close had their friendship been, then? They had written freely to each other; on top of that it seemed that they had met in Paris just before the war. No breath of that had reached him previously. But thinking back, he could remember now that there had been a space of two week-ends in June when he had seen nothing of the boy; he had assumed that duties with the squadron had prevented him from coming over to see him, or even from ringing up. Was that the time? It must have been.

His mind turned to Nicole. He had thought her a very odd young woman previously; he did not think of her in quite the same way now. Dimly he began to realise a little of her difficulties with regard to John, and to himself. It seemed that she had told her mother little about John; she had nursed her grief in silence, dumb and inarticulate. Then he had turned up, quite suddenly, at the door one day. To her secret grief he added an acute embarassment.

He turned over. He must let her alone, let her talk if she wanted to, be silent if she chose. If he did that, perhaps she would open out as time went on. It had been of her own volition she had told him about John.

He lay awake for several hours, turning these matters over in his mind. Presently, after a long time, he slept.

He woke in the middle of the night, to the sound of wailing. He opened his eyes; the wailing came from one of the children. He sat up, but Nicole was before him; by the time he was fully awake she was out of her bed, crouching down by a red faced, mournful little boy sitting up and crying bitterly.

It was Willem, crying as if his heart was going to break. The girl put her arm round him and spoke to him in soft, baby French. The old man rolled out of his blanket, got up stiffly and moved over to them.

'What is it?' he enquired. 'What is the matter?'

The girl said: 'I think he has had a nightmare–that is all. Presently he will sleep again.' She turned again to comfort him.

Howard felt singularly helpless. His way with the children had been to talk to them, to treat them as equals. That simply did not work at all, unless you knew the language, and he knew no word of any language that this little Dutch boy spoke. Left to himself he might have taken him upon his knee and talked to him as man to man; he could never have soothed him as this girl was soothing him.

He knelt down clumsily beside them. 'Do you think he is unwell?' he asked. 'He has perhaps eaten something that upset him?'

She shook her head; already the sobs were dying down. 'I do not think so,' she said softly. 'Last night he did this, twice. It is bad dreams, I think. Only bad dreams.'

The old man's mind drifted back to the unpleasant town of Pithiviers; it would be natural, he thought, for bad dreams to haunt the child.

He wrinkled his forehead. 'You say that he did this twice last night, mademoiselle?' he said. 'I did not know.'

She said: 'You were tired and sleeping very well. Besides your door was shut. I went to him, but each time he very soon went to sleep again.' She bent over him. 'He is almost asleep again now,' she said softly.

There was a long, long silence. The old man stared around; the long, sloping floor was lit by one dim blue light over the door. Dark forms lay huddled upon palliasses here and there; two or three snorers disturbed the room; the air was thick and hot. From sleeping in his clothes he felt sticky and dirty. The pleasant, easy life that he had known in England seemed infinitely far away. This was his real life. He was a refugee, sleeping upon straw in a disused cinema with a German sentry at the door, his companion a French girl, a pack of foreign children in his care. And he was tired, tired, dead tired.

The girl raised her head. She said very softly: 'He is practically asleep, this one. In a minute I will lay him down.' She paused, and then she said, 'Go back to bed, Monsieur Howard. I shall not be long.'

He shook his head and stayed there watching her. Presently, the little boy was sound asleep; she laid him gently down upon his pillow and pulled the blanket round him. Then she got up. 'Now,' she said quietly, 'one can sleep again, until next time.'

He said: 'Good night, Nicole.'

She said: 'Good night. Do not get up if he should wake again. He is no trouble.'

He did not wake again in the two or three hours that was left of the night. By six o'clock the place was all astir; there was no chance of any further sleep. Howard got up and straightened out his clothes as well as he could; he felt dirty and unshaven.

The girl got the children up and, with Howard, helped them to dress. She, too, was feeling dirty and unkempt; her curly hair was draggled, and she had a headache. She would have given a great deal for a bath. But there was no bath in the place, nor even anywhere to wash.

Ronnie said: 'I don't like this place. May we sleep in a farm tomorrow?'

Rose said: 'He means tonight, m'sieur. He talks a great deal of nonsense, that one.'

Howard said: 'I'm not quite sure where we shall sleep tonight. We'll see when the time comes.'

Sheila wriggling her shoulders in her Liberty bodice, said: 'I do *itch*.'

There was nothing to be done about that. To distract her mind Howard led her off with the other children to the end of the hall, where the German cook was dispensing mugs of coffee. With each mug went a large, unattractive hunk of bread. Howard left the children at a trestle table and went to draw their bread and coffee.

Nicole joined them as he brought it to the table and they all had breakfast together. The bread was hard and tasteless and the coffee bitter, acid stuff with little milk. The children did not like it, and were querulous; it needed all the tact of the old man and the girl to prevent their grumbles calling the attention of the German cook. There was some chocolate left of the provisions he had bought upon the road from Joigny; he shared this out among them and this made a little relish to the meal.

Presently, they left the Cinema du Monde and, pushing the pram before them, made their way towards the railway station. The town was full of Germans parading down the streets, Germans driving lorries, Germans lounging at the doors of billets, Germans in the shops. They tried to get chocolate for the children at several shops, but the soldiers had swept the town clean of sweets of every kind. They bought a couple of long rolls of bread and a brown sausage of doubtful origin as provision for their journey. Fruit was unobtainable, but they bought a few lettuces.

At the railway station they passed the barrier without difficulty, surrendering their billeting pass to the German officer. They put the pram into the baggage-wagon on the train for Brest, and climbed up into a third-class carriage. It was only when the train was well upon the way that Howard discovered that *la petite* Rose was nursing a very dirty black and white kitten.

Nicole was at first inclined to be sharp with her. 'We do not want a little cat,' she said to Rose. 'No, truly we do not want that cat or any other cat. You must put him out at the next station.'

The corners of the little girl's mouth drooped, and she clutched the kitten tighter. Howard said: 'I wouldn't do that. He might get lost.'

Ronnie said: '*She* might get lost, Mr Howard. Rose says it's a lady cat. How do you know it's a lady cat, Rose?'

Nicole expostulated: 'But, Monsieur Howard, the little cat belongs to somebody else. It is not our cat, that one.'

He said placidly. 'It's our cat now.'

She opened her mouth to say something impetuous, thought better of it, and said nothing. Howard said: 'It is a very little thing, mademoiselle. It won't add to our difficulties, but it will give them a good deal of pleasure.'

Indeed, what he said was perfectly correct. The children were clustered round intent upon the kitten, which was washing its face upon Rose's lap. Willem turned to Nicole, beaming, and said something unintelligible to her. Then he turned back, watching the kitten again, entranced.

Nicole said, in a resigned tone: 'As you wish. In England, does one pick up cats and take them away like that?'

He smiled, 'No, mademoiselle,' he said. 'In England only the kind of person who sleeps on straw mattresses in cinemas does that sort of thing. The very lowest type of all.'

She laughed. 'Thieves and vagabonds,' she said. 'Yes, that is true.'

She turned to Rose. 'What is her name?' she asked.

The little girl said: 'Jo-Jo.'

The children clustered round, calling the kitten by its new name, trying to make it answer. The kitten sat unmoved, washing its face with a tiny paw. Nicole looked at it for a few moments.

Then she said: 'It is like the lions, in the Zoo de Vincennes. They also do like that.'

Howard had never been to the Paris zoo. He said: 'Have they many lions and tigers there?'

She shrugged her shoulders. 'They have some. I do not know how many – I have only been there once.' And then, to his surprise, she looked up at him with laughter in her eyes. 'I went there with John,' she said. 'Naturally, one would not remember how many lions and tigers there were in the zoo.'

He was startled; then he smiled a little to himself. 'Naturally,' he said dryly. 'But did you never go there as a child?'

She shook her head. 'One does not go to see these places except when one is showing the sights of Paris to a friend, you understand,' she said. 'That was the reason that John came to Paris, because he had never seen Paris. And I said that I would show him Paris. That was how it was.'

He nodded. 'Did he like the zoo?' he asked.

She said: 'It was a very happy day that. It was a French day.' She turned to him a little shyly. 'We had arranged a joke, you see – we should speak only in French one day and in English on the next day. On the English day we did not talk very much,' she said reminiscently. 'It was too difficult; we used to say that the English day ended after tea . . .'

Mildly surprised, he said: 'Did he speak French well?' Because that was most unlike John.

She laughed outright. 'No – not at all. He spoke French very, *very* badly. But that day, on the way out to Vincennes, the taxi-driver spoke English to John, because there are many tourists in Paris and some of the drivers can speak a little English. And John spoke to him in English. Because I had a new summer hat, with carnations, you understand – not a smart hat, but a little country thing with a wide brim. And John asked the taxi-driver to tell him what the French was for' – she hesitated for a moment, and then said – 'to tell me that I was looking very pretty. And the man laughed a lot and told him, so then John knew and he could say it to me himself. And he gave the driver twenty francs.'

The old man said: 'It was probably worth that, mademoiselle.'

She said: 'He wrote it down. And then, when he wanted me to laugh, he used to get out his little book and read it out to me.'

She turned and stared out of the window at the slowly moving landscape. The old man did not pursue the subject; indeed, he could think of nothing adequate to say. He got out his packet of caporal cigarettes and offered one to Nicole, but she refused.

'It is not in the part, that, monsieur,' she said quietly. 'Not in this dress.'

He nodded; lower middle-class Frenchwomen do not smoke cigarettes in public. He lit one himself, and blew a long cloud of the bitter smoke. It was hot already in the carriage, though they had the window open. The smaller children, Pierre and Sheila, were already tired and inclined to be fretful.

All day the train ground slowly on in the hot sun. It was not crowded, and they seldom had anybody in the carriage with them, which was a relief. As on the previous day, the German troops travelling were confined strictly to their own part of the train. On all the station platforms they were much in evidence.

At towns such as Saint Brieuc, the exit from the station appeared to be picketed by a couple of German soldiers; at the wayside halts they did not seem to worry about passengers leaving the station.

Nicole drew Howard's attention to this feature. 'It is good, that,' she said. 'At Landerneau it may be possible to go through without questioning. But if we are stopped, we have still a good story to tell.'

He said: 'Where are we going to tonight, mademoiselle? I am entirely in your hands.'

She said: 'There is a farm, about five miles from Landerneau, to the south. Madame Guinevec, wife of Jean Henri—that was her home before she married. I have been there with my father, at the time of the horse fair, the fête, at Landerneau.'

'I see,' he said. 'What is the name of the people at the farm?'

'Arvers,' she said. 'Aristide Arvers is the father of Marie. They are in good circumstances, you understand, Aristide is a careful man, my father used to say. He breeds horses a little, too, for our army. Marie was Queen of Beauty at the Landerneau Fête one year. It was then that Jean Henri first met her.'

He said: 'She must have been a very pretty girl.'

'She was lovely,' Nicole said. 'That was when I was little—over ten years ago. She is still beautiful.'

The train ground on in the hot sunlight, stopping now and again at stations and frequently in between. They gave the children *déjeuner* of bread and sausage with a little lemonade. That kept them amused and occupied for a time, but they were restless and bored.

Ronnie said: 'I do wish we could go and bathe.'

Sheila echoed: 'May we bathe, Monsieur Howard?'

He said: 'We can't bathe while we're in the train. Later on, perhaps. Run along out into the corridor; it's cooler there.'

He turned to Nicole. 'They're thinking of a time three days ago—or four was it?—just before we met the Air Force men. I let them have a bathe in a stream.'

'It was lovely,' said Ronnie. 'Ever so cool and nice.' He turned and ran with his sister out into the corridor, followed by Willem.

Nicole said: 'The English are great swimmers, are they not, monsieur? Even the little ones think of nothing else.'

He had not thought about his country in that way. 'Are we?' he said. 'Is that how we appear?'

She shrugged her shoulders. 'I do not know so many English people,' she said frankly. 'But John—he liked more than anything for us to go bathing.'

He smiled. 'John was a very good swimmer,' he said reminiscently. 'He was very fond of it.'

She said: 'He was very, very naughty, Monsieur Howard. He would not do any of the things that one should do when one visits Paris for the first time. I had prepared so carefully for his visit—yes, I had arranged for each day the things that we would do. On the first day of all I had planned to go to the Louvre, but imagine it—he was not interested. Not at all.'

The old man smiled again. 'He never was one for museums, much,' he said.

She said: 'That may be correct in England, monsieur, but in Paris one should see the things that Paris has to show. It was very embarrassing, I assure you. I had arranged that he should see the Louvre, and the Trocadéro, and for a contrast the Musée de l'Homme, and the museum at Cluny, and I had a list of galleries of modern art that I would show him. And he never saw any of it at all!'

'I'm sorry about that,' said Howard. There seemed nothing else to say. 'What did you do?'

She said: 'We went bathing several times, at the Piscine Molitor in Auteuil. It was very hot weather, sunny all the time. I could not get him into one museum—not one! He was very, very naughty.'

'I expect that was very pleasant, though,' he said.

She smiled. 'It was not what I had arranged,' she said. 'I had not even got a costume. We had to go together, John and I, to buy a bathing-costume. Never have I done a thing like that before. It was a good thing I had said that we would meet in Paris, not in Chartres. In France there are conventions, Monsieur Howard, you understand.'

'I know,' he said. 'John never worried much about those. Did he get you a nice bathing-dress?'

She smiled: 'It was very beautiful,' she said. 'An American one, very chic, in silver and green. It was so pretty that it was a pleasure to be seen in it.'

'Well,' he said. 'You couldn't have worn that in a museum.'

She stared at him, nonplussed. 'But no . . .' And then she laughed. 'It would be quite ridiculous, that.' She smiled again at the thought. 'Monsieur, you say absurd things, just the same as John.'

It was four o'clock when the train pulled into the little station of Landerneau. They tumbled out of the carriage with relief, Nicole lifting each child down on to the platform except Ronnie, who insisted on getting down himself. They fetched the pram from the baggage-car and put the remainder of their lunch in it, with the kitten.

There was no guard at the *guichet* and they passed through into the town.

Landerneau is a little town of six or seven thousand people, a sleepy little place upon a tidal river running to the Rade de Brest. It is built of grey stone, set in a rolling country dotted round with little woods; it reminded Howard of the Yorkshire wolds. The air, which had been hot and stuffy in the railway carriage, now seemed fresh and sweet, with a faint savour suggesting that the sea was not so very far away.

The town was sparsely held by Germans. Their lorries were parked in the square beneath the plane-trees by the river, but there were few of them to be seen. Those that were in evidence seemed ill at ease, anxious to placate the curiosity of a population which they knew to be pro-English. Their behaviour was most studiously correct. The few soldiers in the streets were grey faced and tired looking, wandering round in twos and threes and staring listlessly at the strange sights. One thing was very noticeable; they never seemed to laugh.

Unchallenged, Howard and Nicole walked through the town and out into the country beyond, upon the road that led towards the south. They went slowly for the sake of the children; the old man was accustomed now to the slow pace that they could manage. The road was empty and they straggled all over it. It led up on to the open wold.

Rose and Willem were allowed to take their shoes off and go barefoot, rather to the disapproval of Nicole. 'I do not think that that is in the part,' she said. 'The class which we represent would not do that.'

The old man said: 'There's nobody to see.'

She agreed that it did not matter much, and they went sauntering on, Willem pushing the pram with Pierre. Ahead of them three aircraft crossed the sky in steady, purposeful flight towards the west, flying at about two thousand feet. The sight woke memories in Rose. 'M'sieur,' she cried. 'Three aeroplanes–look! Quick, let us get into the ditch!'

He calmed her. 'Never mind them,' he said equably. 'They aren't going to hurt us.'

She was only half-reassured. 'But they dropped bombs before and fired their guns!'

He said: 'These are different aeroplanes. These are good aeroplanes. They won't hurt us.'

Pierre said, suddenly and devastatingly, in his little piping voice: 'Can you tell good aeroplanes from bad aeroplanes, M'sieur Howard?'

With a sick heart the old man thought again of the shambles on the Montargis road. 'Why, yes,' he said gently. 'You remember the aeroplanes that mademoiselle took you to see at Chartres? The ones where they let you touch the bombs? They didn't hurt you, did they? Those were good aeroplanes. Those over there are the same sort. They won't hurt us.'

Ronnie, anxious to display expert technical knowledge, endorsed these statements. 'Good aeroplanes are our own aeroplanes, aren't they, Mr Howard?'

'That's right,' the old man said.

Nicole drew him a little way aside. 'I don't know how you can think of such things to say,' she said in a low tone. 'But those are German aeroplanes.'

'I know that. But one has to say something.'

She stared at the three pencil-like shapes in the far distance. 'It was marvellous when aeroplanes were things of pleasure,' she said.

He nodded. 'Have you ever flown?' he asked.

She said: 'Twice, at a fête, just for a little way each time. And then the time I flew with John over Paris. It was wonderful, that . . .'

He was interested. 'You went with a pilot, I suppose. Or did he pilot the machine himself?'

She said: 'But he flew it himself, of course, m'sieur. It was just him and me.'

'How did he get hold of the aeroplane?' He knew that in a foreign country there were difficulties in aviation.

She said: 'He took me to dance, at the flying club, in the Rue François Premier. He had a friend–*un capitaine de l'Aéronautique*–that he had met in England when he had been with our Embassy in London. And this friend arranged everything for John.'

She said: *Figurez-vous*, monsieur! I could not get him to one art gallery, not one! All his life he is used to spend in flying, and then he comes to Paris for a holiday and he wants to go to the aerodrome and fly!'

He smiled gently. 'He was like that. . . . Did you enjoy yourself?'

She said: 'It was marvellous. It was a fine, sunny day with a fresh breeze, and we drove out to Orly, to the hangar of the flying club. And there, there was a beautiful aeroplane waiting for us, with the engine running.'

Her face clouded a little, and then she smiled. 'I do not know very much about flying,' she said frankly. 'It was very chic, with red leather seats and chromium steps to make it easy to get in. But John was so rude.'

The old man said: 'Rude?'

'He said it looked like a bed bug, monsieur, but not so that the mechanics could hear what he said. I told him that I was very cross to hear him say such a thing, when they had been so kind to lend it to us. He only laughed. And then, when we were flying over Paris at *grande vitesse*, a hundred and twenty kilometres an hour or more, he turned to me and said: "And what's more, it flies like one!" Imagine that! Our aeroplanes are very good, monsieur. Everybody in France says so.'

Howard smiled again. 'I hope you put him in his place,' he said.

She laughed outright; it was the first time that he had heard that happen. 'That was not possible, Monsieur Howard,' she said. 'Never could I put him in his place, as you say.'

He said: 'I'm sorry about that.' He paused, and then he said: 'I have never flown over Paris. Is it beautiful?'

She shrugged her shoulders. 'Beautiful? I do not think that anything is beautiful seen from the air, except the clouds. But that day was marvellous, because there were those big, fleecy clouds that John called cum . . . something.'

'Cumulus?'

She nodded. 'That was it. For more than an hour we played in them, flying around and over the top and in between the white cliffs in the deep gorges of the mist. And every now and then, far down below, one would see Paris, the Concorde or perhaps the Etoile. Never shall I forget that day. And when we landed I was so sleepy that I went to sleep in the car on the way back to Paris, leaning up against John, with my head on his shoulder.'

They walked on in silence for a time. Pierre and Willem tired of pushing the pram and gave place to Rose, with Sheila trotting at her side. The kitten lay curled up in the pram, sound asleep.

Presently Nicole pointed ahead of them. 'That is the house—among those trees.'

The house that she pointed to lay about a mile ahead of them. It seemed to be a fairly large and prosperous farm, grouped round a modest country-house standing among trees as shelter from the wind. About it rolled the open pasture of the wold, as far as could be seen.

In half an hour they were close up to it. A long row of stabling showed the interests of the owner; there were horses running in the paddocks near the farm. The farm buildings were better kept and laid out than the farms that Howard had had dealings with upon his journey; this was a cut above the usual run of things.

They went up to a house that stood beside the entrance, in the manner of a lodge; here Nicole enquired for M. Arvers. They were directed to the stables; leaving the children with the pram at the gate, they went forward together.

They met their man half-way.

Aristide Arvers was a small man of fifty-five or so, thin, with sharp features and a shrewd look. Howard decided at the first glance that this man was no fool. And the second thought that came into his mind was realisation that this man could well be the father of a beauty queen, of Miss Landerneau. The delicate features, sharpening by advancing age, might well be fascinating in a young girl.

He wore a shapeless black suit with a soiled scarf wrapped round his neck in lieu of collar; a black hat was on his head.

Nicole said: 'Monsieur Arvers, do you remember me? You were so kind as to invite me here one day, with my father, Colonel Rougeron. You showed my father round your stables. After that you entertained us in your house. That was three years ago–do you remember?'

He nodded. 'I remember that very well, mademoiselle. M. le colonel was very interested in my horses for the army, being himself an artillery officer, if I remember right.' He hesitated. 'I hope you have good news of M. le colonel?'

She said: 'We have had no news for three months, when he was at Metz.'

'I am desolated, mademoiselle.'

She nodded, having nothing much to say to that. She said: 'If my father had been at home he would no doubt, have come to see you himself. As he is not, I have come instead.'

His brows wrinkled slightly, but he bowed a little. 'That is an added pleasure,' he said perfunctorily.

'May we, perhaps, go to your office?'

'But certainly.'

He turned and led them to the house. There was a littered, dusty office, full of sad-looking account-books and files, with bits of broken harness thrown aside in corners. He closed the door behind them and gave them rickety chairs; there being no other seats, he leaned backwards against the edge of the desk.

'First,' said the girl, 'I wish to introduce you to Monsieur Howard. He is an Englishman.'

The horse-breeder raised his eyebrows a little, but bowed ceremoniously. '*Enchanté*' he said.

Nicole said: 'I will come directly to the point, Monsieur Arvers. Monsieur Howard is a very old friend of my family. He is travelling with several children, and he is trying to return to England in spite of the Germans. My mother and I have talked about this, in the absence of my father, and it seemed to us that Jean Henri could help perhaps with one of his boats. Or, if that was impossible, Jean Henri might know some friend who would help. There is money enough to pay for any services.'

The man said nothing for a time. At last: 'The Germans are not to be trifled with,' he said.

Howard said: 'We appreciate that, monsieur. We do not wish that anyone should run into trouble upon our behalf. That is why mademoiselle has come to talk to you before going to your son-in-law.'

The other turned to him. 'You speak French better than most Englishmen.'

'I have had longer than most Englishmen to learn it.'

The Frenchman smiled. 'You are very anxious to return to England?'

The old man said: 'For myself, not so very anxious. I should be quite happy to live in France for a time. But I have children in my care you understand, English children that I have promised that I would escort to England.' He hesitated. 'And, as a matter of fact, there are three others now.'

'What are those other children? How many of you are there altogether? And where have you come from?'

It took nearly twenty minutes to elucidate the story. At last the Frenchman said: 'These other children, the little one called Pierre and the little Dutchman. What is going to become of them when they reach England?'

Howard said: 'I have a daughter, married, in America. She is in easy circumstances. She would make a home for those two in her house at Long Island till the war is over and we can trace their relations. They would be very happy there.'

The man stared at him keenly. 'In America? That I can well believe. You will send them over the Atlantic to your daughter? Will she be good to them–children that she has never seen? Unknown, foreign children?'

The old man said: 'My daughter has one child of her own, and now hopes for another. She is very fond of all children. They will be safe with her.'

Arvers got up suddenly from the desk. 'It is impossible,' he said. 'If Jean Henri should put his hand to this he would be in great danger. The Germans would shoot him, beyond all doubt. You have no right to suggest such a thing.' He paused, and then he said: 'I have my daughter to consider.'

There was a long, slow pause. At last the old man turned to Nicole. 'That's the end of that,' he said. He smiled at Arvers. 'I understand perfectly,' he said. 'In your place, thinking of my daughter, I should say the same.'

The Frenchman turned to the girl. 'I regret very much that I cannot help you in the way you want,' he said.

She shrugged her shoulders. '*Tant pis,*' she said. '*N'y pensez plus.*'

He looked uncomfortable. 'These children,' he said. 'Where are they now?'

They told him that they were waiting in the road, and he walked with them to the gate. It was getting towards evening. The children were playing at the edge of a pond, muddy and rather fractious. There were tear streaks around Sheila's face.

Arvers said awkwardly: 'Would it help you to stay here for the night? I do not think we have beds for so many, but something could perhaps be managed.'

Nicole said warmly: 'You are very kind, monsieur.'

They called the children and introduced them one by one to the horse-dealer; then they went towards the house. The man called his wife as they approached the door; she came from the kitchen, a stolid peasant woman. He spoke to her, told her that the party were to stay with them for the night, introduced her formally to them. Nicole shepherded the children after her into the kitchen. Arvers turned to Howard.

'You will take a little glass of Pernod, perhaps?' he said.

A little glass of Pernod seemed to the old man to be a very good idea. They went into the salon because the kitchen was full of children. The salon was a stiff and formal room, with gilt-legged furniture upholstered in red plush. On the wall there was a very large oleograph of a white-robed little girl kneeling devoutly in a shaft of light. It was entitled: '*La Première Communion.*'

Arvers brought the Pernod, with glasses and water, and the two men settled down together. They talked about horses and about country matters. Arvers had been to England once, to Newmarket as a jockey when he was a very young man. They chatted pleasantly enough for a quarter of an hour.

Suddenly Arvers said: 'Your daughter, Monsieur Howard. She will surely find so many foreign children an encumbrance? Are you so certain that they will be welcome in her home?'

The old man said: 'They will be welcome, all right.'

'But how can you possibly know that? Your daughter may find it very inconvenient to have them.'

He shook his head. 'I don't think so. But if that should be so, then she would make arrangements for them for me. She would engage some kind woman to make a home for them, because that is my wish, that they should have a good home in America–away from all this.' He motioned with his hand. 'And there is no difficulty over money, you understand.'

The Frenchman sat silent for a little time, staring into his glass.

'This is a bad time for children, this filthy war,' he said at last. 'And now that France is defeated, it is going to be worse. You English now will starve us, as we starved Germany in 1918.'

Howard was silent.

'I shall not blame your country if you do that. But it will be bad for children here.'

'I am afraid it may be,' said the old man. 'That is why I want to get these children out of it. One must do what one can.'

Arvers shrugged his shoulders. 'There are no children in this house, thank God. Or—only one.' He paused. 'That was a hard case, if you like.'

Howard looked at him enquiringly. The Frenchman poured him out another Pernod. 'A friend in Paris asked me if I had work for a Pole,' he said. 'In December, that was—just at Christmas time. A Polish Jew who knew horses, who had escaped into Rumania and so by sea to Marseilles. Well, you will understand, the mobilisation had taken five of my eight men, and it was very difficult.'

Howard nodded. 'You took him on?'

Assuredly. Simon Estreicher was his name, and he arrived one day with his son, a boy of ten. There had been a wife, but I will not distress you with that story. She had not escaped the Boche, you understand.'

The old man nodded.

'Well, this man Estreicher worked here till last week, and he worked well. He was quiet and gave no trouble, and the son worked in the stables too. Then last week the Germans came here and took him away.'

'Took him away?'

'Took him away to Germany, to their forced labour. He was a Pole, you see, m'sieur, and a Jew as well. One could do nothing for him. Some filthy swine in town had told them about him, because they came straight here and asked for him. They put handcuffs on him and took him in a camion with several others.'

'Did they take the son as well?'

'They never asked for him, and he was in the paddock at the time, so I said nothing. One does not help the Germans in their work. But it was very hard on that young boy.'

Howard agreed with him. 'He is with you, still, then?'

'Where else could he go? He is useful in the stables, too. But before long I suppose they will find out about him, and come back for him to take him away also.'

Nicole came to them presently, to call them to the kitchen for supper. She had already given the children a meal, and had put them to sleep on beds improvised upstairs by Madame Arvers. They ate together in the kitchen at a long table, together with two men from the farm and a black-haired Jewish-looking boy whom Madame called Marjan, and who said little or nothing during the meal.

The meal over, Arvers escorted Nicole and Howard back to the salon; presently he produced a set of dominoes and proposed a game. Howard settled down to it with him. The horse-dealer played carelessly his mind on other things.

Presently he returned to the subject that was on his mind. 'Are many children going to America, monsieur? I cannot comprehend how you can be so positive that they will be welcomed. America is very far away. They do not bother about our difficulties here.'

Howard shrugged his shoulders. 'They are a generous people. These children will be quite all right if I can get them there, because my daughter will look after them. But even without her, there would be many people in America willing to provide for them. Americans are like that.'

The other stared at him incredulously. 'It would cost a great deal of money to provide for a child, perhaps for years. One does not do that lightly for a foreign child of which one knows nothing.'

'It's just the sort of thing they *do* do,' said the old man. 'They would pour out their money in a cause like that.'

The horse-dealer stared at him keenly and thoughtfully. 'Would they provide for Marjan Estreicher?' he enquired at last. 'No doubt they would not do that for a Jew.'

'I don't think it would make the slightest difference in the case of a child. It certainly would make no difference to my daughter.'

Nicole moved impulsively beside him. 'Monsieur . . .' she said, but he stopped her with a gesture. She subsided into silence again, watchful.

Howard said steadily: 'I would take him with me, if that is what you want. I would send him to the United States with the other children. But before that, I should want help to get them all away.'

'Jean Henri?'

'Assuredly, Monsieur.'

The other got up, displacing the unheeded game of dominoes with his sleeve. He went and fetched the Pernod, the glasses, and the water, and poured out a drink for Howard. He offered one to the girl, but she refused.

'The risk is enormous,' he said stubbornly. 'Think what it would mean to my daughter if you should be caught.'

'Think what it would mean to that boy, if he should be caught,' the old man said. 'They would take him for a slave, put him in the mines and work him till he died. That's what the Germans do with Polish children.'

Arvers said: 'I know that. That is what troubles me.'

Nicole said suddenly: 'Does Marjan want to go? You cannot make him if he does not want to. He is old, that one.'

'He is only ten,' said Arvers.

'Nevertheless,' she said, 'he is quite grown up. We cannot take him if he does not want to go.'

Arvers went out of the room; in a few minutes he returned, followed by the boy. He said to him: 'This is the matter, Marjan. This monsieur here is going to England if he can escape the Germans, and from England the children with him are going to America. In America they will be safe. There are no Germans there. Would you like to go with them?'

The boy stood silent. They explained it to him again. At last he said in almost unintelligible French: 'In America, what should I work at?'

Howard said: 'For a time you would have to go to school, to learn English and the American way of living. At school they would teach you to earn your living in some trade. What do you want to do when you grow up?'

Without any hesitation the boy said: 'I want to kill Germans.'

There was a momentary silence. Arvers said: 'That is enough about the Germans. Tell Monsieur here what trade you wish to learn in America, if he should be so kind as to take you there.'

There was a silence.

Nicole came forward. 'Tell us,' she said gently. 'Would you like to grow up with horses? Or would you rather buy things and sell them for a profit?' After all, she thought, it would be difficult for him to go against the characteristics of his race. 'Would you rather do that?'

The boy looked up at her. 'I want to learn to shoot with a rifle from a very long way away,' he said, 'because you can do that from the hills when they are on the road. And I want to learn to throw a knife hard and straight. That is best in the darkness, in the narrow streets, because it does not make a noise.'

Arvers smiled a little ruefully. 'I am sorry, monsieur,' he said. 'I am afraid he is not making a very good impression.'

The old man said nothing.

Marjan said: 'When do we start?'

Howard hesitated, irresolute. This lad might be a great embarrassment to them; at the best he could only be described as a prickly customer. On the other hand, a deep pity for the child lurked in the background of his mind.

'Do you want to come with us?' he asked.

The boy nodded his black head.

'If you come with us, you will have to forget all this about the Germans,' said the old man. 'You will have to go to school and learn your lessons, and play baseball, and go fishing, like other boys.'

The lad said gravely: 'I could not kill a German for another two or three years because I am not strong enough. Not unless I could catch one asleep and drive a pitchfork into his belly as he slept, and even then he might reach out before he died and overcome me. But in America I could learn everything, and come back when I am fifteen years old, and big and strong.'

Howard said gently: 'There are other things to learn in America besides that.'

The boy said: 'I know there is a great deal to learn, monsieur. One thing, you should always go for the young women—not the men. If you get the young women, then they cannot spawn, and before long there will be no more Germans.'

'That is enough,' said Arvers sharply. 'Go back to the kitchen and stay there till I call you.'

The boy left the room. The horse-dealer turned to Nicole. 'I am desolated that he should have said such things,' he said.

The girl said: 'He has suffered a great deal. And he is very young.'

Arvers nodded. 'I do not know what will become of him,' he said morosely.

Howard sat down in the silence which followed and took a sip of Pernod. 'One of two things will happen to him,' he said. 'One is, that the Germans will catch him very soon. He may try to kill one of them, in which case they might shoot him out of hand. They will take him to their mines. He will be rebellious the whole time, and before long he will be beaten to death. That is the one thing.'

The horse-dealer dropped into the chair on the opposite side of the table, the bottle of Pernod between them. There was something in the old man's tone that was very familiar to him. 'What is the other thing?' he asked.

'He will escape with us to England,' said Howard. 'He will end up in America, kindly treated and well cared for, and in a year or two these horrors will have faded from his mind.'

Arvers eyed him keenly. 'Which of those is going to happen?'

'That is in your hands, monsieur. He will never escape the Germans unless you help him.'

There was a long, long silence in the falling dusk.

Arvers said at last: 'I will see what I can do. Tomorrow I will drive Mademoiselle to Le Conquet and we will talk it over with Jean Henri. You must stay here with the children and keep out of sight.'

9

Howard spent most of the next day sitting in the paddock in the sun, while the children played around him. His growing, stubbly beard distressed him with a sense of personal uncleanliness, but it was policy to let it grow. Apart from that, he was feeling well; the rest was welcome and refreshing.

Madame dragged an old cane reclining chair from a dusty cellar and wiped it over with a cloth for him; he thanked her and installed himself in it. The children had the kitten, Jo-Jo, in the garden and were stuffing it with copious draughts of milk and anything that they could get it to eat. Presently it escaped and climbed up into the old man's lap and went to sleep.

After a while he found himself making whistles on a semi-production basis, while the children stood around and watched.

From time to time the Polish boy, Marjan, appeared by the paddock gate and stood looking at them, curious, inscrutable. Howard spoke to him and asked him to come in and join them, but he muttered something to the effect that he had work to do, and sheered away shyly. Presently he would be back again, watching the children as they played. The old man let him alone, content not to hurry the friendship.

In the middle of the afternoon, suddenly, there was a series of heavy explosions over in the west. These mingled with the sharp crack of gunfire; the children stopped their games and stared in wonder. Then a flight of three single-engined fighter aeroplanes got up like partridges from some field not very far away and flew over them at about two thousand feet, heading towards the west and climbing at full throttle as they went.

Ronnie said wisely: 'That's bombs, *I* know. They go whee . . . before they fall, and then they go boom. Only it's so far off you can't hear the whee part.'

'Whee . . . Boom!' said Sheila. Pierre copied her, and presently all the children were running round wheeing and booming.

The real detonations grew fewer, and presently died in the summer afternoon.

'That was the Germans bombing someone, wasn't it, Mr Howard?' asked Ronnie.

'I expect so,' he replied. 'Come and hold this bark while I bind it.' In the production of whistles the raid faded from their minds.

In the later afternoon Nicole returned with Arvers. Both were very dirty, and the girl had a deep cut on the palm of one hand, roughly bandaged. Howard was shocked at her appearance.

'My dear,' he said, 'whatever happened? Has there been an accident?'

She laughed a little shrilly. 'It was the British,' she said. 'It was an air raid. We were caught in Brest–this afternoon. But it was the British, monsieur, that did this to me.'

Madame Arvers came bustling up with a glass of brandy. Then she hustled the girl off into the kitchen. Howard was left in the paddock, staring out towards the west.

The children had only understood half of what had happened.Sheila said: 'It was the bad aeroplanes that did that to Nicole, monsieur, wasn't it?'

'That's right,' he said. 'Good aeroplanes don't do that sort of thing.'

The child was satisfied with that. 'It must have been a very, *very* bad aeroplane to do that to Nicole.'

There was general agreement on that point. Ronnie said: 'Bad aeroplanes are German aeroplanes. Good aeroplanes are English ones.'

He made no attempt to unravel that one for them.

Presently Nicole came out into the garden, white-faced and with her hand neatly bandaged. Madame hustled the children into the kitchen for their supper.

Howard asked after her hand. 'It is nothing,' she said. 'When a bomb falls, the glass in all the windows flies about. That is what did it.'

'I am so sorry.'

She turned to him. 'I would not have believed that there would be so much glass in the streets,' she said. 'In heaps it was piled. And the fires–houses on fire everywhere. And dust, thick dust that smothered everything.'

'But how did you come to be mixed up in it?'

She said: 'It just happened. We had been to Le Conquet, and after *déjeuner* we set out in the motor-car to return here. And passing through Brest, Aristide wanted to go to the Bank, and I wanted tooth-powder and some other things–little things, you understand. And it was while Aristide was in the Bank and I was in the shops in the Rue de Siam that it happened.'

'What did happen?' he asked.

She shrugged her shoulders. 'It was an aeroplane that came racing low over the roofs–so low that one could see the number painted on the body; the targets on the wings showed us that it was English. It swung round over the Harbour and dropped its bombs near the Port Militaire, and then another of them came, and another–many of them. It was the German ships in the harbour, I think, that they were bombing. But several of them dropped their bombs in a long line, and these lines spread right into the town. There were two bombs that hit houses in the Rue de Siam, and three or more in the Rue Louis Pasteur. And where a bomb fell, the house fell right down, not five feet high, Monsieur–truly, that was all that could be seen. And there were fires, and clouds of smoke and dust, and glass–glass everywhere . . .'

There was a little silence. 'Were many people hurt?' he asked at last.

She said: 'I think very many.'

He was very much upset. He felt that something should have happened to prevent this. He was terribly concerned for her, and a little confused.

She said presently: 'You must not distress yourself on my account, Monsieur Howard. I assure you, I am quite all right, and so is Aristide.' She laughed shortly. 'At least, I can say that I have seen the Royal Air Force at work. For many months I longed to see that.'

He shook his head, unable to say anything.

She laid her hand upon his arm. 'Many of the bombs fell in the Port Militaire,' she said gently. 'One or two went wide, but that was not intended. I think they may have hit the ships.' She paused, and then she said: 'I think John would have been very pleased.'

'Yes,' he said heavily, 'I suppose he would have been.'

She took his arm. 'Come in the salon and we will drink a Pernod together, and I will tell you about Jean Henri.'

They went together into the house. Aristide was not about; in the salon Howard sat down with the girl. He was still distressed and upset; Nicole poured out a Pernod for him and added a little water. Then she poured a smaller one for herself.

'About Jean Henri,' she said. 'He is not to appear in this himself. Aristide will not have that, for the sake of Marie. But in Le Conquet there is a young man called Simon Focquet, and he will take a boat across with you.'

The old man's heart leaped, but all he said was: 'How old is this young man?'

She shrugged her shoulders. 'Twenty–twenty-two, perhaps. He is de Gaullist.'

'What is that, mademoiselle?'

She said: 'There is a General de Gaulle in England with your armies, one of our younger Generals. In France nobody knew much about him, but now he will carry on the battle from England. He is not approved by our Government of Vichy, but many of our young men are slipping away to join him, some by way of Spain and others in boats across the Manche. That is how Simon Focquet wishes to go, because he is a fishing-boy, and knows boats very well.'

'But the Germans will stop that, surely.'

She nodded. 'Already all traffic has been stopped. But the boats are still allowed to fish around the coast and by Ushant. It will be necessary to devise something.'

He said: 'Where will he get the boat?'

'Aristide has arranged that for us. Jean Henri will hire one of his boats for fishing to this young man, and Simon then will steal it when he leaves for England. Jean Henri will be the first to complain to the gendarmerie, and to the Germans, that his boat has been stolen. But Aristide will pay him for it secretly. You should pay Aristide, if you have so much money.'

He nodded. 'How much will it be?'

She said: 'Five thousand five hundred francs.'

He thought for a moment. Then he pulled out his wallet from his hip pocket, opened with the deliberation of age, and studied a document. 'I seem to have forty pounds left on my letter of credit,' he said. 'Will that be enough?'

She said: 'I think so. Aristide will want all the payment that you can make because he is peasant, Monsieur, you understand. But he wishes to help us, and he will not stop the venture for that reason.'

Howard said: 'I would see that he got the difference when the war is over.'

They talked of this for a little time. Then Nicole got up from the table. 'I must go and see the children in their beds,' she said. 'Madame Arvers has been very kind, but one should not leave everything to her.'

'I will come too,' he said. 'They have been very good children all day, and no trouble.'

The children were all sleeping in one room, the two girls in the bed and the three little boys upon a mattress on the floor, covered with rough blankets. The peasant woman was tucking them up; she smiled broadly as Nicole and the old man came in, and disappeared back into the kitchen. Ronnie said: 'My blanket smells of horses.'

Nothing was more probable, the old man thought. He said: 'I expect you'll dream that you're going for a ride all night.'

Sheila said: 'May I go for a ride, too?'

'If you're very good.'

Rose said: 'May we stay here now?'

Nicole sat down on her bed. 'Why?' she said. 'Don't you want to see your father in London?'

La petite Rose said: 'I thought London was a town.'

'So it is. A very big town.'

'I like being in the country like this,' Rose said. 'This is like it was where we used to live.'

Ronnie said: 'But we're all going to London.'

'Not all of you,' the old man said. 'You and Sheila are going to live with your Aunt Margaret at Oxford.'

'Are we? Is Rose going to live with Aunt Margaret, too?'

'No. Rose is going to live with her daddy in London.'

Sheila said: 'Is Pierre going to live with Aunt Margaret?'

'No,' he said. 'Pierre and Willem are going to America to live with my daughter. Did you know I had a grown-up daughter, older than Nicole? She's got a little boy of her own.'

They stared at him incredulously. 'What's his name?' Ronnie asked at last.

'Martin,' the old man said. 'He's the same age as Pierre.'

Pierre stared at them. 'Won't you be coming with us?'

'I don't think so,' Howard said. 'I think I shall have work to do in England.' His lip trembled. 'Won't Rose be coming?'

Nicole slipped down by his bed. 'It's going to be lovely in America,' she said gently. 'There will be bright lights at night-time, not like the black-out we have here. There is no bombing, nor firing guns at people from the air. There will be plenty to eat, and nice, sweet things like we all used to have. You will live at a place called "Coates Harbor" on Long Island, where Madame Costello has a great big house in the country. And there is a pony for you to ride, and dogs to make friends with, like we all used to have before the war when we had food for dogs. And you will learn to sail a boat, and to swim and dive like the English and Americans do, and to catch fish for pleasure. And you will feel quite safe then, because there is no war in America.'

Pierre stared up at her. 'Will you be coming with me to America?'

She said quietly: 'No, Pierre. I must stay here.'

The corners of his mouth dropped. 'I don't want to go alone.'

Howard said: 'Perhaps Rose's father will want her to go too. Then she would go with you. You'd like that, wouldn't you?'

Sheila said: 'May Ronnie and I go, Mr Howard? Can we all go with Pierre?'

He said: 'I'll have to see about that. Your Aunt Margaret may want you in England.'

Ronnie said: 'If she doesn't want us, may we go to Coates Harbor with Pierre?'

'Yes,' he said. 'If she wants you out of England you can all go to Coates Harbor together.'

'Coo,' said the little boy unfeelingly. 'I do hope she doesn't want us.'

After a time they got the children settled down to sleep; they went downstairs again and out into the garden until supper was ready. The old man said:

'You know a good deal about my daughter's house in America, mademoiselle.'

She smiled. 'John used to tell me about it,' she said. 'He had been out there, had he not, monsieur?'

He nodded. 'He was out there with Enid for a time in 1938. He thought a great deal of her husband, Costello.'

She said: 'He told me all about it very early one morning, when we could not sleep. John loved America. He was *aviateur*, you understand–he loved their technique.'

Not for the first time the old man wondered doubtfully about the nature of that week in Paris. He said absently: 'He enjoyed that visit very much.'

He roused himself. 'I am a little bit worried about Pierre,' he said. 'I had not thought of sending anybody over with him to America.'

She nodded. 'He is sensitive, that one. He will be lonely and unhappy at first, but he will get over it. If Rose could go too it would be all right.'

He faced her. 'Why not go yourself?' he suggested. 'That would be best of all.'

'Go to America? That is not possible at all, monsieur.'

A little fear stole into his heart. 'But you are coming to England, Nicole?'

She shook her head. 'No, monsieur. I must stay in France.'

He was suddenly deeply disappointed. 'Do you really think that is the best thing to do?' he said. 'This country is overrun with Germans, and there will be great hardships as the war goes on. If you came with us to England you could live with me in my house in Essex, or you could go on to America with the children. That would be much better, Nicole.'

She said: 'But monsieur, I have my mother to consider.'

He hesitated. 'Would you like to try to get hold of her, and take her with us? Life in France is going to be very difficult, you know.'

She shook her head. 'I know that things are going to be difficult. But she would not be happy in England. Perhaps I should not be happy either–now.'

'Have you ever been to England?' he asked curiously.

She shook her head. 'We had arranged that I should visit John in England in October, when he could get leave again. I think he would have taken me to see you then, perhaps. But the war came, and there was no more leave. . . . And travelling was very difficult. I could not get a visa for my passport.'

He said gently: 'Make that trip to England now, Nicole.'

She shook her head. 'No, monsieur.'

'Why not?'

She said: 'Are you going to America with the children, yourself?'

He shook his head. 'I would like to, but I don't think I shall be able to. I believe that there'll be work for me to do when I get back.'

She said: 'Nor would I leave France.'

He opened his mouth to say that that was quite different, but shut it again without speaking. She divined something of his thought, because she said:

'Either one is French or one is English, and it is not possible that one should be both at the same time. And in times of great trouble, one must stay with one's own country and do what one can to help.'

He said slowly: 'I suppose so.'

Pursuing her train of thought, she said: 'If John and I –' she hesitated – 'if we had married, I should have been English and then it would be different. But now I am not to be English, ever. I could not learn your different ways, and the new life, alone. This is my place that I belong to, and I must stay here. You understand?'

He said: 'I understand that, Nicole.' He paused for a minute, and then said: 'I am getting to be an old man now. When this war is over I may not find it very easy to get about. Will you come and stay with me in England for a little? Just for a week or two?'

She said: 'Of course. Immediately that it is possible to travel, I will come.'

They walked beside each other in silence for the length of the paddock. Presently she said: 'Now for the detail of the journey. Focquet will take the boat tonight from Le Conquet to go fishing up the Chenal as far as Le Four. He will not return to Le Conquet, but tomorrow night he will put into l'Abervrach to land his fish, or to get bait, or on some pretext such as that. He will sail again at midnight of tomorrow night and you must then be in the boat with him, for he will go direct to England. Midnight is the latest time that he can sail, in order that he may be well away from the French coast before the dawn.'

Howard asked: 'Where is this place l'Abervrach, mademoiselle? Is it far from here?'

She shrugged her shoulders. 'Forty kilometres, no more. There is a little town behind it, four miles inland, called Lannilis. We must go there to-morrow.'

'Are there many Germans in those parts?'

'I do not know. Aristide is trying to find out the situation there, and to devise something for us.'

The boy Marjan passed through the paddock on his way to the house. Howard turned and called to him; he hesitated, and then came to them.

The old man said: 'We are leaving here tomorrow, Marjan. Do you still want to come with us?'

The boy said: 'To America?'

'First we are going to try to get away to England. If we do that successfully, I will send you to America with Pierre and Willem, to live with my daughter till the war is over. Do you want to go?'

The boy said in his awkward French: 'If I stay with M. Arvers the Germans will find me and take me away. Presently they will kill me, as they killed my mother and as my father will be killed, because we are Jews. I would like to come with you.'

The old man said: 'Listen to me. I do not know if I shall take you, Marjan. We may meet Germans on the way from this place to the coast; we may have to mix with them, eat at their canteens perhaps. If you show that you hate them, they may arrest us all. I do not know if it is safe to take you, if it is fair to Rose and Ronnie and Sheila and Willem and to little Pierre.'

The boy said: 'I shall not make trouble for you. It will be better for me to go to America now; that is what I want to do. It would only be by great good luck that I could kill a German now; even if I could creep up to one in the darkness and rip him open with a sharp knife, I should be caught and killed. But in a few years time I shall be able to kill many hundreds of them, secretly, in the dark streets. That is much better, to wait and to learn how these things should be managed properly.'

Howard felt slightly sick. He said: 'Can you control yourself, if Germans are near by?'

The boy said: 'I can wait for years, monsieur, till my time comes.'

Nicole said: 'Listen, Marjan. You understand what Monsieur means? If you are taken by the Germans all these little boys and girls will also be taken, and the Germans will do to them what they will do to you. It would be very wrong of you to bring that trouble on them.'

He said: 'Have no fear. I shall be good, and obedient, and polite, if you will take me with you. That is what one must practise all the time, so that you win their confidence. In that way you can get them at your mercy in the end.'

Howard said: 'All right, Marjan. We start in the morning; be ready to come with us. Now go and have your supper and go up to bed.'

He stood watching the boy as he made his way towards the house. 'God knows what sort of world we shall have when this is all over,' he said heavily.

Nicole said: 'I do not know. But what you are doing now will help us all, I think. To get these children out of Europe must be a good thing.'

Presently they were called to the kitchen for their supper. Afterwards, in the salon, Arvers talked to them.

'Listen,' he said, 'and I will tell you what I have arranged.'

He paused. 'Lannilis is full of Germans. That is four miles from the coast, and the places at the coast itself, l'Abervrach and Portsall and places of that sort, are very lightly held or even not occupied at all. They do not interfere with the traffic of the country, and this is what I have devised for you.'

He said: 'Three miles this side of Lannilis there is a farmer called Quintin, and he is to send a load of manure tomorrow to a fisherman called Loudeac, the captain of the lifeboat at l'Abervrach, because Loudeac has a few fields on the hills and wants manure. I have arranged all that. The manure will be delivered in a cart with one horse, you understand? You, m'sieur, will drive the cart. Mademoiselle and the children will accompany you for the ride.'

Howard said: 'That seems sound enough. Nobody would suspect that.'

Aristide glanced at him. 'It will be necessary that you should wear poorer clothes. That I can arrange.'

Nicole said: 'How do we get into touch with Focquet tomorrow night?'

The horse-dealer said: 'Tomorrow night, Focquet will come at nine o'clock to the *estaminet* upon the quayside. He will appear to be slightly drunk, and he will ask for Pernod des Anges. There is no such drink. In that way you will know him. The rest I will leave to you.'

Howard nodded. 'How can we get to Quintin's farm?'

'I will take you myself so far in the car. That will be safe enough, for it is this side of Lannilis and there will be no questions asked. But there I must leave you.' He thought for a minute. 'It will be better that you should not start from Quintin's farm much before five o'clock,' he said. 'That will make it reasonable that you should be in l'Abervrach at nightfall, and even that you should spend the night there, with Loudeac.'

Nicole said: 'What about Loudeac and Quintin, monsieur? Do they know that Monsieur Howard and the children will escape?'

The man said: 'Have no fear, mademoiselle. This is not so uncommon, in these times. They know all that they wish to know, and they have been paid. They are good friends of mine.'

Howard said: 'I must now pay you, monsieur.'

They settled down together at the table.

Soon after that they went to bed; refreshed by a restful day Howard slept well. In the morning he went down for coffee feeling better than he had felt for some days.

Aristide said: 'We leave after *déjeuner*. That will be time enough. Now, I have borrowed clothes for m'sieur. You will not like them, but they are necessary.'

The old man did not like the clothes at all. They were very dirty, a coarse, stained flannel shirt, a pair of torn blue cotton trousers, a dirty canvas pullover that had once been rusty pink in colour, and a black, floppy Breton casque. Wooden sabots were the footgear provided with this outfit, but the old man struck at those, and Arvers produced a torn and loathsome pair of boots.

It was some days since he had shaved. When he came down to the kitchen Nicole smiled broadly. 'It is very good,' she said. 'Now, Monsieur Howard, if you walk with the head hanging down, and your mouth open a little–so. And walk slowly, as if you were a very, very old man. And be very deaf and very stupid. I will talk for you.'

Arvers walked round him, studying him critically. 'I do not think the Germans will find fault with that,' he said.

They spent the rest of the morning studying appearances. Nicole kept her black frock, but Arvers made her dirty it a little, and made her change to a very old pair of low-heeled shoes belonging to his wife. With a shawl belonging to Madame Arvers over her head, he passed her too.

The children needed very little grooming. During the morning they had been playing at the duck-pond, and were sufficiently dirty to pass muster without any painting of the lily. Ronnie and Willem were scratching themselves a good deal, which added verisimilitude to the act.

They started after *déjeuner*. Howard and Nicole thanked Madame Arvers for her kindness; she received their thanks with calm, bovine smiles. Then they all got into the little old de Dion van that Arvers kept for the farm and drove off down the road.

Ronnie said: 'Are we going to the train that we're going to sleep in, Mr Howard?'

'Not just yet,' he said. 'We shall get out of the car presently and say good-bye to Monsieur Arvers, and then we have a ride in a cart. You must all be very careful to speak French only, all the time.'

Sheila said: 'Why must we speak French? I want to speak English, like we used to.'

Nicole said gently: 'We shall be among the Germans. They do not like people who speak English. You must be very careful to speak only in French.'

Rose said suddenly: 'Marjan says the Germans cut his mother's hands off.'

Howard said gently: 'No more talk about the Germans now. In a little time we shall get out, and have a ride in a horse and cart.' He turned to Pierre. 'What sort of noise does a horse make?' he asked.

Pierre said shyly: 'I don't know.'

La petite Rose bent over him. 'Oh, Pierre, of course you know!

> 'My great-aunt lives in Tours,
> In a house with a cherry tree
> With a little mouse (squeak, squeak)
> And a big lion (roar, roar)
> And a wood-pigeon (coo, coo) . . .'

That lasted them all the way through Landerneau, of which they caught only glimpses through the windows at the back of the old van, and half-way to Lannilis.

Presently the van slowed, turned off the road, and bumped to a standstill. Arvers swung round to them from the driving-seat. 'This is the place,' he said. 'Get out quickly, it is not wise to linger here.'

They opened the door at the back of the van and got out. They were in a very small farmyard, the farmhouse itself little more than a workman's cottage of grey stone. The air was fresh and sweet after the van, with a clear savour of the sea. In the warm sun, and looking at the grey stone walls and roofs, Howard could have thought himself in Cornwall.

There was a cart and horse, the cart half loaded with manure, the old grey horse tied to the gate. Nobody was to be seen.

Arvers said: 'Now quickly, monsieur, before a German passes on the road. There is the cart. You have everything quite clear? You take the dung to Loudeac, who lives up on the hill above l'Abervrach, half a mile from the port. There you unload it; Mademoiselle Rougeron must bring back the cart to-morrow to this place. Focquet will be in the *estaminet* tonight at nine o'clock, and he will be expecting you. He will ask for Pernod des Anges. It is all clear?'

'One thing,' the old man said. 'This road leads straight to Lannilis?'

'Assuredly.' The horse-dealer glanced nervously around.

'How do we get through Lannilis? How do we find the road out of the town to l'Abervrach?'

The hot sun beat down on them warmly from a cloudless sky; the scent of briar mingled with the odour of manure about them. Arvers said: 'This road leads straight to the great church in the middle of the town. From the west end of the church a road runs westwards; follow that. Where it forks at the outskirts of the town, by an advertisement for Byrrh, take the right-hand fork. From there to l'Abervrach is seven kilometres.'

Nicole said: 'I have been that way before. I think I know the road.'

The horse-dealer said: 'I will not linger, mademoiselle. And you, you must move off from here at once.' He turned to Howard. 'That is all that I can do for you, monsieur. Good luck. In happier days, we may meet again.'

The old man said: 'I shall look forward to thanking you again for so much kindness.'

Arvers swung himself into the seat of the old van, reversed out into the road, and vanished in a white cloud of dust. Howard looked around; there was no movement from the house, which stood deserted in the afternoon sun.

Nicole said: 'Come, children, up you go.'

Willem and Marjan swung themselves up into the cart; the English children, with Pierre and Rose, hung back. Ronnie said doubtfully: 'Is this the cart you said we were going to have a ride in?'

Rose said: 'It is a dung-cart. It is not correct to ride in a cart full of horse-dung, mademoiselle. My aunt would be very cross with me if I did that.'

Nicole said brightly: 'Well, I'm going to. You can walk with monsieur and help lead the horse, if you like.' She bustled the other children into the cart before her; it was only half full and there was room for all of them to stand and sit upon the edges of the sides in front of the load.

Pierre said: 'May I walk with Rose and lead the horse?'

Nicole said: 'No, Pierre, you're too small for that and the horse walks too quickly. You can stroke his nose when we get there.'

Howard untied the bridle from the gate and led the horse out into the road. He fell into a steady, easy shamble beside the horse, head hanging down.

For an hour and a half they went on like that before they reached the first houses of Lannilis. In the cart Nicole kept the children happy and amused; from time to time the old man heard a little burst of laughter above the clop, clop of the hooves of the old horse. *La petite* Rose walked on beside him, barefoot, treading lightly.

They passed a good deal of German transport on the road. From time to time lorries would come up behind them and they would pull in to the right to let them pass; the grey-faced, stolid soldiers staring at them incuriously. Once they met a platoon of about thirty infantry marching towards them down the road; the *Oberleutnant* in charge looked them over, but did not challenge them. Nobody showed much interest in them until they came to Lannilis.

On the outskirts of the town they were stopped. There was a barricade of an elementary nature, of two old motor-cars drawn half across the road, leaving only a small passage between. A sentry strolled out sleepily in the hot afternoon and raised his hand. Howard pulled up the horse and stared at him, and mumbled something with head hanging and mouth open. An *Unteroffizier* came from the guard-house and looked them over.

He asked in very bad French: 'Where are you taking this to?'

The old man raised his head a little and put his hand to one ear. 'Eh?'

The German repeated his question in a louder tone.

'Loudeac,' the old man said. 'Loudeac, outside l'Abervrach.'

The *Unteroffizier* looked at Nicole. 'And madame goes too?'

Nicole smiled at him and put her hand upon Pierre's shoulder. 'It is the little one's birthday,' she said. 'It is not easy to make fête these days. But as my uncle has to make this trip this afternoon, and as the load is only half and therefore easy for the horse, we make this little journey for an outing for the children.'

The old man nodded. 'It is not easy to make a treat for children in times like these.'

The *Unteroffizier* smiled. 'Proceed,' he said lazily. 'Many happy returns of the day.'

Howard jerked up the old horse, and they passed up the street. There was little traffic to be seen, partly because the French were keeping within doors, partly, no doubt, because of the heat of the afternoon. A few houses were evidently requisitioned by the Germans; there were German soldiers lounging at the windows of bare rooms cleaning their equipment, in the manner of soldiers all over the world. None of them paid any attention to the dung-cart.

By the great church in the middle of the town three tanks were drawn up in the shade of the plane-trees, with half a dozen lorries. From one large house the

Swastika flag floated lazily in the hot summer afternoon from a short staff stuck out of a first-floor window.

They paced steadily through the town, past shops and residences, past German officers and German soldiers. At the outskirts of the town they took the right fork at the advertisement for Byrrh, and left the last houses behind them. Presently, blue and hazy in a dip between two fields, the old man saw the sea.

His heart leaped when he saw it. All his life he had taken pleasure from the sight and savour of the sea. In its misty blueness between the green fields it seemed to him almost like a portion of his own country; England seemed very close. By tomorrow evening, perhaps, he would have crossed that blue expanse; he would be safe in England with the children. He trudged on stolidly, but his heart was burning with desire to be at home.

Presently Rose became tired; he stopped the cart and helped her into it. Nicole got down and walked beside him.

'There is the sea,' she said. 'You have not very far to go now, monsieur.'

'Not very far,' he said.

'You are glad?'

He glanced at her. 'I should be very, very glad, but for one thing,' he said. 'I would like you to be coming with us. Would you not do that?'

She shook her head. 'No, monsieur.'

They walked on in silence for a time. At last he said: 'I shall never be able to thank you for what you have done for us.'

She said: 'I have benefited the most.'

'What do you mean?' he asked.

She said: 'It was a very bad time when you came. I do not know if I can make you understand.' They walked on in the hot sun in silence for a time. 'I loved John very much,' she said simply. 'Above all things, I wanted to be an Englishwoman. And I should have been one but for the war. Because we meant to marry. Would you have minded that very much?'

He shook his head. 'I should have welcomed you. Don't you know that?'

She said: 'I know that now. But at the time I was terribly afraid of you. We might have been married if I had not been so foolish, and delayed.' She was silent for a minute. 'Then John—John was killed. And at the same time nothing went right any more. The Germans drove us back, the Belgians surrendered, and the English ran back to their own country from Dunkerque and France was left to fight alone. Then all the papers, and the radio, began to say bad things of the English, that they were treacherous, that they had never really meant to share the battle with us. Horrible things, monsieur.'

'Did you believe them?' he asked quietly.

She said: 'I was more unhappy than you could believe.'

'And now? Do you still believe those things?'

She said: 'I believe this, that there was nothing shameful in my love for John. I think that if we had been married, if I had become an Englishwoman, I should have been happy for the remainder of my life.'

She paused. 'That is a very precious thought, monsieur. For a few weeks it was clouded with doubts and spoilt. Now it is clear once more; I have regained the thing that I had lost. I shall not lose it again.'

They breasted a little rise, and there before them lay the river, winding past the little group of houses that was l'Abervrach, through a long lane of jagged reefs out to the open sea. The girl said: 'That is l'Abervrach. Now you are very near the end of your journey, Monsieur Howard.'

They walked in silence, leading the horse, down the road to the river and along the water-front, past the cement factory, past the few houses of the village, past the lifeboat-house and the little quay. Beside the quay there was a German E-boat apparently in trouble with her engines, for a portion of her deck amidships was removed and was lying on the quay beside a workshop lorry; men in overalls were busy upon her. A few German soldiers lounged upon the quay, watching the work and smoking.

They went on past the *estaminet* and out into the country again. Presently they turned up the hill in a lane full of sweet-briar, and so came to the little farm of Loudeac.

A peasant in a rusty red canvas pullover met them at the gate.

Howard said: 'From Quintin.'

The man nodded and indicated the midden. 'Put it there,' he said. 'And then go away quickly. I wish you good luck, but you must not stay here.'

'That is very well understood.'

The man vanished into the house, nor did they see him again. It was getting towards evening; the time was nearly eight o'clock. They got the children down out of the cart and backed the horse till the load was in the right place to tip; then they tipped the wagon and Howard cleared it with a spade. In a quarter of an hour the job was done.

Nicole said: 'There is time enough, and to spare. If we go now to the *estaminet*, we can get supper for the little ones–coffee, perhaps, and bread and butter.'

Howard agreed. They got into the empty cart and he jerked up the horse; they moved out of the stable yard and down the road towards the village. At a turn of the road the whole entrance to the harbour lay before them, sunny and blue in the soft evening light. In the long reach between the jagged rocks there was a fishing-boat with a deep brown lug sail coming in from the sea; faintly they heard the putter of an engine.

The old man glanced at the girl. 'Focquet,' he said.

She nodded. 'I think so.'

They went on down to the village. At the *estaminet*, under the incurious glances of the German soldiers, they got out of the cart; Howard tied the bridle of the old horse to a rail.

Ronnie said in French: 'Is that a torpedo-boat? May we go and see it?'

'Not now,' said Nicole. 'We're going to have supper now.'

'What are we going to have for supper?'

They went into the *estaminet*. There were a few fishermen there standing by the bar, who looked at them narrowly; it seemed to Howard that they had divined his secret as soon as they set eyes on him. He led the children to a table in a far corner of the room, a little way away from the men. Nicole went through to the kitchen of the place to speak to Madame about supper for the children.

Supper came presently, bread and butter and coffee for the children, red wine mixed with water for Nicole and the old man. They ate uneasily, conscious of the glances at them from the bar, speaking only to assist the children in their meal. It seemed to Howard that this was the real crux of their journey; this was the only time when he had felt his own identity in question. The leaden time crept on, but it was not yet nine o'clock.

Their meal finished, the children became restless. It was still not nine o'clock, and it was necessary to spin out time. Ronnie said, wriggling in his chair: 'May we get down and go and look at the sea?'

It was better to have them out of the way than calling fresh attention to the party in the *estaminet*. Howard said: 'Go on. You can go just outside the door and lean over the harbour wall. Don't go any farther than that.'

Sheila went with him; the other children stayed quiet in their seats. Howard ordered another bottle of the thin red wine.

At ten minutes past nine a big, broad-shouldered young man in fisherman's red poncho and sea boots rolled into the *estaminet*. One would have said that he had visited competitive establishments on the way, because he reeled a little at the bar. He took in all the occupants of the estaminet in one swift, revolving glance like a lighthouse.

'Ha!' he said. 'Give me a Pernod des Anges, and to hell with the *sale Boche*.'

The men at the bar said: 'Quietly. There are Germans outside.'

The girl behind the bar wrinkled her brows. 'Pernod des Anges? It is a pleasantry, no doubt? Ordinary Pernod for m'sieur.'

The man said: 'You have no Pernod des Anges?'

'No, m'sieur. I have never heard of it.'

The man remained silent, holding to the bar with one hand, swaying a little.

Howard got up and went to him. 'If you would like to join us in a glass of the rouge,' he said.

'Assuredly.' The young man left the bar and crossed with him to the table.

Howard said quietly: 'Let me introduce you. This is my daughter-in-law, Mademoiselle Nicole Rougeron.'

The young man stared at him. 'You must be more careful of your French idiom,' he said softly out of the corner of his mouth. 'Keep your mouth shut and leave the talking to me.'

He slumped down into a seat beside them. Howard poured him out a glass of the red wine; the young man added water to it and drank. He said quietly: 'Here is the matter. My boat lies at the quay, but I cannot take you on board here, because of the Germans. You must wait here till it is dark, and then take the footpath to the Phare des Vaches—that is an automatic light on the rocks, half a mile towards the sea, that is not now in use. I will meet you there with the boat.'

Howard said: 'That is clear enough. How do we get on to the footpath from here?'

Focquet proceeded to tell him. Howard was sitting with his back to the *estaminet* door facing Nicole. As he sat listening to the directions, his eye fell on the girl's face, strained and anxious.

'Monsieur . . .' she said, and stopped.

There was a heavy step behind him, and a few words spoken in German. He swung round in his chair; the young Frenchman by his side did the same. There was a German soldier there, with a rifle. Beside him was one of the engineers from the E-boat by the quay in stained blue dungarees.

The moment remained etched upon the old man's memory. In the background the fishermen around the bar stood tense and motionless; the girl had paused, cloth in hand, in the act of wiping a glass.

It was the man in dungarees who spoke. He spoke in English with a German-American accent.

'Say,' he said. 'How many of you guys are Britishers?'

There was no answer from the group.

He said: 'Well, we'll all just get along to the guard-room and have a lil' talk with the *Feldwebel*. And don't let any of you start getting fresh, because that ain't going to do you any good.'

He repeated himself in very elementary French.

10

There was a torrent of words from Focquet, rather cleverly poured out with well-simulated alcoholic indignation. He knew nothing, he said, of these others; he was just taking a glass of wine with them–there was no harm in that. He was about to sail, to catch the tide. If he went with them to the guard-room there would be no fish for *déjeuner* tomorrow, and how would they like that? Landsmen could never see farther than their own noses. What about his boat, moored at the quay? Who would look after that?

The sentry prodded him roughly in the back with the butt of his rifle, and Focquet became suddenly silent.

Two more Germans, a private and a *Gefreiter*, came hurrying in; the party were hustled to their feet and herded out of the door. Resistance was obviously useless. The man in dungarees went out ahead of them, but he reappeared in a few minutes bringing with him Ronnie and Sheila. Both were very much alarmed, Sheila in tears.

'Say,' he said to Howard. 'I guess these belong to you. They talk English pretty fine, finer 'n anyone could learn it.'

Howard took one of them hand in hand with him on each side, but said nothing. The man in dungarees stared oddly at him for a minute, and remained standing staring after them as they were shepherded towards the guard-room in the gathering dusk.

Ronnie said, frightened: 'Where are we going to now, Mr Howard? Have the Germans got us?'

Howard said: 'We're just going with them for a little business. Don't be afraid; they won't do anything to hurt us.'

The little boy said: 'I told Sheila you would be angry if she talked English, but she would do it.'

Nicole said: 'Did she talk English to the man in the overall?'

Ronnie nodded. Then he glanced up timorously at the old man. 'Are you angry, Mr Howard?' he ventured.

There was no point in making more trouble for the children than they had already coming to them. 'No,' he said. 'It would have been better if she hadn't, but we won't say any more about it.'

Sheila was still crying bitterly. 'I *like* talking English,' she wailed.

Howard stooped and wiped her eyes; the guards, considerately enough, paused for a moment while he did so. 'Never mind,' he said. 'You can talk as much English as you like now.'

She walked on with him soberly, in sniffing, moist silence.

A couple of hundred yards up the road to Lannilis they were wheeled to the right and marched into the house that was the guard-room. In a bare room the *Feldwebel* was hastily buttoning his tunic as they came in. He sat down behind a bare trestle table; their guards ranged them in front of him.

He glanced them up and down scornfully. 'So,' he said at last. '*Geben Sie mir Ihre legitimationspapiere.*'

Howard could understand only a few words of German, the others nothing at all. They stared at him uncertainly. '*Cartes d'identité,*' he said sharply.

Focquet and Nicole produced their identity-cards; the man studied them in silence. Then he looked up. Howard put down his British passport on the bare table in the manner of a man who plays the last card of a losing hand.

The *Feldwebel* smiled faintly, took it up, and studied it with interest. 'So!' he said. '*Engländer.* Winston Churchill.'

He raised his eyes and studied the children. In difficult French he asked if they had any papers, and appeared satisfied when told that they had not.

Then he gave a few orders in German. The party were searched for weapons, and all they had was taken from them and placed on the table–papers, money, watches, and personal articles of every sort, even their handkerchiefs. Then they were taken to another room with a few palliasses laid out upon the floor, given a blanket each, and left. The window was barred over roughly with wooden beams; outside it in the road a sentry stood on guard.

Howard turned to Focquet. 'I am very sorry this has happened,' he said. He felt that the Frenchman had not even had a run for his money.

The young man shrugged his shoulders philosophically. 'It was a chance to travel and to see the world with de Gaulle,' he said. 'Another chance will come.' He threw himself down on one of the palliasses, pulled the blanket round him, and composed himself to sleep.

Howard and Nicole arranged the palliasses in two pairs to make beds for the little boys and the little girls, and got them settled down to sleep. There remained one mattress over.

'You take that,' he said. 'I shall not sleep tonight.'

She shook her head. 'Nor I either.'

Half an hour later they were sitting side by side leaning against the wall, staring out of the barred window ahead of them. It was practically dark within the room; outside the harbour showed faintly in the starlight and the last glow of evening. It was still quite warm.

She said: 'They will examine us in the morning. What shall we say?'

'There's only one thing we can say. Tell them the exact truth.'

She considered this for a moment. 'We must not bring in Arvers, nor Loudeac or Quintin if we can avoid it.'

He agreed. 'They will ask where I got these clothes. Can you say that you gave them to me?'

She nodded. 'That will do. Also, I will say that I knew Focquet and arranged with him myself.'

She crossed to the young man, now half asleep, and spoke earnestly to him for a few minutes. He grunted in agreement; the girl came back to Howard and sat down again.

'One more thing,' he said. 'There is Marjan. Shall I say that I picked him up upon the road?'

She nodded. 'On the road before you came to Chartres. I will see that he understands that.'

He said doubtfully: 'That should be all right so long as they don't cross-examine the children.'

They sat in silence for a long time after that. Presently she stirred a little by him, shifting to a more comfortable position.

'Go and lie down, Nicole,' he said. 'You must get some sleep.'

'I do not want to sleep, monsieur,' she said. 'Truly I am better sitting here like this.'

'I've been thinking about things,' he said.

'I also have been thinking.'

He turned to her in the darkness. 'I am so very sorry to have brought you into all this trouble,' he said quietly. 'I did want to avoid that, and I thought that we were going to.'

She shrugged her shoulders. 'It does not matter.' She hesitated. 'I have been thinking about different things to that.'

'What things?' he asked.

'When you introduced Focquet–you said I was your daughter-in-law.'

'I had to say something,' he remarked. 'And that's very nearly true.'

In the dim light he looked into her eyes, smiling a little. 'Isn't it?'

'Is that how you think of me?'

'Yes,' he said simply.

There was a long silence in the prison. One of the children, probably Willem, stirred and whimpered uneasily in his sleep; outside the guard paced on the dusty road.

At last she said: 'What we did was wrong–very wrong.' She turned towards him. 'Truly, I did not mean to do wrong when I went to Paris, neither did John. We did not go with that in mind at all. I do not want that you should think it was his fault. It was nobody's fault, neither of us. Also, it did not seem wrong at the time.'

His mind drifted back fifty years. 'I know,' he said. 'That's how these things happen. But you aren't sorry, are you?'

She did not answer that, but she went on more easily. 'He was very, very naughty, monsieur. The understanding was that I was to show him Paris, and it was for that that I went to Paris to meet him. But when the time came, he was not interested in the churches or in the museums, or the picture-galleries at all.' There was a touch of laughter in her voice. 'He was only interested in me.'

'Very natural,' he said. It seemed the only thing to say.

'It was very embarrassing, I assure you, I did not know what I should do.'

He laughed. 'Well, you made your mind up in the end.'

She said reproachfully: 'Monsieur–it is not a matter to laugh over. You are just like John. He also used to laugh at things like that.'

He said: 'Tell me one thing, Nicole. Did he ask you if you would marry him?'

She said: 'He wanted that we should marry in Paris before he went back to England. He said that under English law that would be possible.'

'Why didn't you?' he asked curiously.

She was silent for a minute. Then she said: 'I was afraid of you, monsieur.'

'Of me?'

She nodded. 'I was terrified. It now sounds very silly, but–it was so.'

He struggled to understand. 'What were you frightened of?' he asked.

She said: 'Figure it to yourself. Your son would have brought home a foreign girl, that he had married very suddenly in Paris. You would have thought that he had been foolish in a foreign city, as young men sometimes are. That he had been trapped by a bad woman into an unhappy marriage. I do not see how you could have thought otherwise.'

'If I had thought that at first,' he said, 'I shouldn't have thought it for long.'

'I know that now. That is what John told me at the time. But I did not think that it was right to take the risk. I told John, it would be better for everybody that we should be a little more discreet, you understand.'

'I see. You wanted to wait a bit.'

She said: 'Not longer than could be helped. But I wanted very much that everything should be correct, that we should start off right. Because, to be married, it is for all one's life, and one marries not only to the man but to the relations also. And in a mixed marriage things are certain to be difficult, in any case. And so, I said that I would come to England for his next leave, in September or October, and we would meet in London, and he could then take me to see you in your country home. And then you would write to my father, and everything would be quite in order and correct.'

'And then the war came,' he said quietly.

She repeated: 'Yes, monsieur, then the war came. It was not then possible for me to visit England. It would almost have been easier for John to visit Paris again, but he could get no leave. And so I went on struggling to get my *permis* and the visa month after month.

'And then,' she said, 'they wrote to tell me what had happened.'

They sat there for a long time, practically in silence. The air grew colder as the night went on. Presently the old man heard the girl's breathing grow more regular and knew she was asleep, still sitting up upon the bare wooden floor.

After a time she stirred and fell half over. He got up stiffly and led her, still practically asleep, to the palliasse, made her lie down, and put a blanket over her. In a short time she was asleep again.

For a long time he stood by the window, looking out over the harbour mouth. The moon had risen; the white plumes of surf upon the rocks showed clearly on the blackness of the sea. He wondered what was going to happen to them all. It might very well be that he would be taken from the children and sent to a concentration camp; that for him would be the end, before so very long. The thought of what might happen to the children distressed him terribly. At all costs, he must do his best to stay at liberty. If he could manage that it might be possible for him to make a home for them, to look after them till the war was over. A home in Chartres, perhaps, not far from Nicole and her mother. It would take little money to live simply with them, in one room or in two rooms at the most. The thought of penury did not distress him very much. His old life seemed very, very far away.

Presently, the blackness of the night began to pale towards the east, and it grew colder still. He moved back to the wall and, wrapped in a blanket, sat down in a corner. Presently he fell into an uneasy sleep.

At six o'clock the clumping of the soldiers' boots in the corridor outside woke him from a doze. He stirred and sat upright; Nicole was awake and sitting up, running her fingers through her hair in an endeavour to put it into order without a comb. A German *Oberschütze* came in and made signs to them to get up, indicating the way to the toilet.

Presently, a private brought them china bowls, some hunks of bread and a large jug of bitter coffee. They breakfasted, and waited for something to happen. They were silent and depressed; even the children caught the atmosphere and sat about in gloomy inactivity.

Presently the door was flung open, and the *Feldwebel* was there with a couple of privates. '*Marchez*,' he said. '*Allez, vite.*'

They were herded out and into a grey, camouflaged motor-lorry with a closed, van-like body. The two German privates got into this with them and the doors were shut and locked upon them. The *Feldwebel* got into the seat beside the driver, turned and inspected them through a little hatchway to the driver's compartment. The lorry started.

They were taken to Lannilis, and unloaded at the big house opposite the church, from the window of which floated the Swastika flag. Here they were herded into a corridor between their guards. The *Feldwebel* went into a door and closed it behind him.

They waited thus for over half an hour. The children, apprehensive and docile at the first, became bored and restless. Pierre said, in his small voice: 'Please, monsieur, may I go out and play in the square?'

Sheila and Ronnie said in unison, and very quickly: 'May I go too?'

Howard said: 'Not just now. You'll have to stay here for a little while.'

Sheila said mutinously: 'I don't want to stay here. I want to go out in the sun and play.'

Nicole stooped to her and said: 'Do you remember Babar the Elephant?'

The little girl nodded.

'And Jacko the Monkey? What did he do?'

Laughter, as at a huge, secret joke. 'He climbed up Babar's tail, right up on to his back!'

'Whatever did he do that for?'

The stolid, grey-faced Germans looked on mirthlessly, uncomprehending. For the first time in their lives they were seeing foreigners, displaying the crushing might and power of their mighty land. It confused them and perplexed them that their prisoners should be so flippant as to play games with their children in the corridor outside the very office of the Gestapo. It found the soft spot in the armour of their pride; they felt an insult which could not be properly defined. This was not what they had understood when their Führer last had spoken from the Sport-Palast. This victory was not as they had thought it would be.

The door opened, the sentries sprang to attention, clicking their heels. Nicole glanced upwards, and then stood up, holding Sheila in one hand. From the office the *Feldwebel* cried, '*Achtung!*' and a young officer, a *Rittmeister* of the Tank Corps came out. He was dressed in a black uniform not unlike the British battle-dress; on his head he wore a black beret garnished with the eagle and swastika, and a wreath-like badge. On his shoulder-straps an aluminium skull and crossbones gleamed dull upon the black cloth.

Howard straightened up and Focquet took his hands out of his pockets. The children stopped chattering to stare curiously at the man in black.

He had a notebook and a pencil in his hand. He spoke to Howard first. '*Wie heissen Sie?*' he asked. '*Ihr Familienname und Taufname? Ihr Beruf?*'

Somebody translated into indifferent French and the particulars of all the party were written down. As regards nationality, Howard declared himself,

Sheila, and Ronnie to be English; there was no use denying it. He said that
Willem and Marjan were of nationality unknown.

The young officer in black went into the office. In a few minutes the door was
flung open again and the party were called to attention. The *Feldwebel* came to
the door.

'*Folgen Sie mir!* Halt! *Rührt Euch!*' They found themselves in the office,
facing a long table. Behind this sat the officer who had interrogated them in the
passage. By his side was an older man with a square, close-cropped head and a
keen, truculent expression. He held himself very straight and stiff, as if he were
in a strait waistcoat, and he also wore a black uniform, but more smartly cut,
and with a shoulder-belt in black leather resembling the Sam Browne. This
man, as Howard subsequently learned, was Major Diessen of the Gestapo.

He stared at Howard, looking him up and down, noting the clothes he wore,
the Breton casque upon his head, the stained rust-coloured poncho jacket, the
dirty blue overall trousers.

'So,' he said harshly, but in quite good English. 'We still have English
gentlemen travelling in France.' He paused. 'Nice and Monte Carlo,' he said. 'I
hope that you have had a very nice time.'

The old man was silent. There was no point in trying to answer the taunts.

The officer turned to Nicole. 'You are French,' he said, fiercely and
vehemently. 'You have been helping this man in his secret work against your
country. You are a traitor to the Armistice. I think you will be shot for this.'

The girl stared at him, dumbfounded. Howard said: 'There is no need to
frighten her. We are quite ready to tell you the truth.'

'I know your English truth,' the Gestapo officer replied. 'I will find my own,
even if I have to whip every inch of skin from her body and pull out every
finger-nail.'

Howard said quietly: 'What do you want to know?'

'I want to know what means you used to make her help you in your work.'

There was a small, insistent tug at the old man's sleeve. He glanced down and
it was Sheila, whispering a request.

'Presently,' he said gently. 'You must wait a little.'

'I can't wait,' she said. 'I want to go now.'

The old man turned to the Gestapo officer. 'There is a small matter that
requires attention,' he said placidly. He indicated Rose. 'May this one take this
little girl outside for a minute? They will come back.'

The young Tank Corps officer smiled broadly; even the Gestapo man
relaxed a little. The *Rittmeister* spoke to the sentry, who sprang to attention and
escorted the two little girls from the room.

Howard said: 'I will answer your question so far as I can. I have no work in
France, but I was trying to get back to England with these children. As for this
young lady, she was a great friend of my son, who is now dead. We have known
each other for some time.'

Nicole said: 'That is true. Monsieur Howard came to us in Chartres when all
travelling to England had been stopped. I have known Focquet here since I was
a little girl. We were trying to induce him to take monsieur and the children
back to England in his boat, but he was unwilling on account of the
regulations.'

The old man stood silent, in admiration of the girl. If she got away with that
one it let Focquet out completely.

The officer's lips curled. 'I have no doubt that Mister Howard wanted to return to England,' he said dryly. 'It is getting quite too hot here for fellows of his sort.'

He said suddenly and sharply: 'We captured Charenton. He is to be executed tomorrow, by shooting.'

There was a momentary silence. The German eyed the party narrowly, his keen eyes running from one to the other. The girl wrinkled her brows in perplexity. The young *Rittmeister* of the Tank Corps sat with an impassive face, drawing a pattern on his blotting-pad.

Howard said at last: 'I am afraid I don't quite understand what you mean. I don't know anybody called Charenton.'

'No,' said the German. 'And you do not know your Major Cochrane, nor Room 212 on the second floor of your War Office in Whitehall.'

The old man could feel the scrutiny of everybody in the room upon him. 'I have never been in the War Office,' he said, 'and I know nothing about the rooms. I used to know a Major Cochrane who had a house near Totnes, but he died in 1924. That is the only Cochrane that I ever knew.'

The Gestapo officer smiled without mirth. 'You expect me to believe that?'

'Yes, I do,' the old man said. 'Because it is the truth.'

Nicole interposed, speaking in French. 'May I say a word. There is a misunderstanding here, truly there is. Monsieur Howard has come here directly from the Jura, stopping only with us in Chartres. He will tell you himself.'

Howard said: 'That is so. Would you like to hear how I came to be here?'

The German officer looked ostentatiously at his wristwatch and leaned back in his chair, insolently bored. 'If you must,' he said indifferently. 'I will give you three minutes.'

Nicole plucked his arm. 'Tell also who the children are and where they came from,' she said urgently.

The old man paused to collect his thoughts. It was impossible for him, at his age, to compress his story into three minutes; his mind moved too slowly. 'I came to France from England in the middle of April,' he said. 'I stayed a night or two in Paris, and then I went on and stayed a night in Dijon. You see, I had arranged to go to a place called Cidoton in the Jura, for a little fishing holiday.'

The Gestapo officer sat up suddenly, galvanised into life. 'What sort of fish?' he barked. 'Answer me—quick!'

Howard stared at him. 'Blue trout,' he said. 'Sometimes you get a grayling, but they aren't very common.'

'And what tackle to catch them with—quickly!'

The old man stared at him, nonplussed, not knowing where to start. 'Well,' he said, 'you need a nine-foot cast, but the stream is usually very strong, so 3X is fine enough. Of course, it's all fishing wet, you understand.'

The German relaxed. 'And what flies do you use?'

A faint pleasure came to the old man. 'Well,' he said with relish, 'a Dark Olive gets them as well as anything, or a large Blue Dun. I got one or two on a thing called a Jungle Cock, but—'

The German interrupted him. 'Go on with your story,' he said rudely. 'I have no time to listen to your fishing exploits.'

Howard plunged into his tale, compressing it as much as seemed possible to him. The two German officers listened with growing attention and with growing incredulity. In ten minutes or so the old man had reached the end.

The Gestapo officer, Major Diessen, looked at him scornfully. 'And now,' he said. 'If you had been able to return to England, what would you have done with all these children?'

Howard said: 'I meant to send them to America.'

'Why?'

'Because it is safe over there. Because this war is bad for children to see. It would be better for them to be out of it.'

The German stared at him. 'Very fine words. But who was going to pay to send them to America, may I ask?'

The old man said: 'Oh, I should have done that.'

The other smiled, scornfully amused. 'And what would they do in America? Starve?'

'Oh no. I have a married daughter over there. She would have made a home for them until the war was over.'

'This is a waste of time,' the German said. 'You must think me a stupid fellow to be taken in with such a tale.'

Nicole said: 'Nevertheless, m'sieur, it is quite true. I knew the son and I have known the father. The daughter would be much the same. American people are generous to reugees, to children.'

Diessen turned to her. 'So,' he sneered, 'mademoiselle comes in to support this story. But now for mademoiselle herself. We learn that mademoiselle was a friend of the old Englsh gentleman's son. A very great friend. . . .'

He barked at her suddenly: 'His mistress, no doubt?'

She drew herself up. 'You may say so if you like,' she said quietly. 'You can call a sunset by a filthy name, but you do not spoil its beauty, monsieur.'

There was a pause. The young Tank officer leaned across and whispered a word or two to the Gestapo officer. Diessen nodded and turned back to the old man.

'By the dates,' he said, 'you could have returned to England if you had travelled straight through Dijon. But you did not do so. That is the weak point of your story. That is where your lies begin in earnest.'

He said sharply: 'Why did you stay in France? Tell me now, quickly, and with no more nonsense. I promise you that you will talk before tonight, in any case. It will be better for you to talk now.'

Howard was puzzled and distressed. 'The little girl,' he turned and indicated Sheila, 'fell ill in Dijon. I told you so just now. She was too ill to travel.'

The German leaned across the table to him, white with anger. 'Listen,' he said. 'I warn you once again, and this for the last time. I am not to be trifled with. That sort of lie would not deceive a child. If you had wanted to return to England you would have gone.'

'These children were in my care,' the old man said. 'I could not have done that.'

The Gestapo officer said: 'Lies . . . lies . . . lies.' He was about to say something more, but checked himself. The young man by his side leaned forward and whispered deferentially to him again.

Major Diessen leaned back in his chair. 'So,' he said, 'you refuse our kindness and you will not talk. As you wish. Before the evening you will be talking freely, Mister Englishman, but by then you will be blind, and in horrible pain. It will be quite amusing for my men. Mademoiselle, too, shall be there to see, and the little children also.'

There was a silence in the office.

'Now you will be taken away,' the German said. 'I shall send for you when my men are ready to begin.' He leaned forward. 'I will tell you what we want to know, so that you may know what to say even though you be blind and deaf. We know you are a spy, wandering through the country in disguise and with this woman and these children as a cover. We know you have been operating with Charenton—you need not tell us about that. We know that either you or Charenton sent information to the English of the Führer's visit to the ships in Brest, and that you caused the raid.'

He paused. 'But what we do not know, and what this afternoon you shall tell us, is how the message was passed through to England, to that Major Cochrane'—his lip sneered—'that died in 1924, according to your story. That is what you are going to tell, Mister Englishman. And as soon as it is told the pain will stop. Remember that.'

He motioned to the *Feldwebel*. 'Take them away.'

They were thrust out of the room. Howard moved in a daze; it was incredible that this thing should be happening to him. It was what he had read of and had found some difficulty in crediting. It was what they were supposed to do to Jews in concentration camps. It could not be true.

Focquet was taken from them and hustled off on his own. Howard and Nicole were bundled into a downstairs prison room, with a heavily barred window; the door was slammed on them and they were left alone.

Pierre said, in French: 'Are we going to have our dinner here, mademoiselle?'

Nicole said dully: 'I expect so, Pierre.'

Ronnie said: 'What are we going to have for dinner?'

She put an arm round his shoulder. 'I don't know,' she said mechanically. 'We'll see when we get it. Now, you run off and play with Rose. I want to talk to Monsieur Howard.'

She turned to Howard. 'This is very bad,' she said. 'We are involved in something terrible.'

He nodded. 'It seems to be that air raid that they had on Brest. The one that you were in.'

She said: 'In the shops that day they were saying that Adolf Hitler was in Brest, but one did not pay attention. There is so much rumour, so much idle talk.'

There was a silence. Howard stood looking out of the window at the little weeded, overgrown garden outside. As he stood the situation became clear to him. In such a case the local officers of the Gestapo would have to make a show of energy. They would have to produce the spies who had been instrumental in the raid, or the mutilated bodies of people who were classed as spies.

Presently he said: 'I cannot tell them what I do not know, and so things may go badly with me. If I should be killed, you will do your best for the children, Nicole?'

She said: 'I will do that. But you are not going to be killed, or even hurt. Something must be possible.' She made a little gesture of distress.

Pursuing his thought, he said: 'I shall have to try and get them to let me make a new will. Then, when the war is over and you could get money from England, you would be able to keep the children and to educate them, those of them that had no homes. But in the meantime you'll just have to do the best you can.'

The long hours dragged past. At noon an orderly brought them an open metal pan with a meal of meat and vegetables piled on it, and several bowls. They set the children down to that, who went at it with gusto. Nicole ate a little, but the old man practically nothing.

The orderly removed the tray and they waited again. At three o'clock the door was flung open and the *Feldwebel* was there with a guard.

'*Le Vieux*,' he said. '*Marchez.*' Howard stepped forward and Nicole followed him. The guard pushed her back.

The old man stopped. 'One moment,' he said. He took her hand and kissed her on the forehead. 'There, my dear,' he said. 'Don't worry about me.'

They hustled him away, out of that building and out into the square. Outside the sun was bright; a car or two passed by and in the shops the peasants went about their business. In Lannilis life went on as usual; from the great church the low drone of a chant broke the warm summer air. The women in the shops looked curiously at him as he passed by under guard.

He was taken into another house and thrust into a room on the ground floor. The door was shut and locked behind him. He looked around.

He was in a sitting-room, a middle-class room furnished in the French style with uncomfortable, gilded chairs and Rococo ornaments. A few poor oil-paintings hung upon the walls in heavy, gilded frames; there was a potted palm, and framed, ancient photographs upon the side tables, with a few ornaments. There was a table in the middle of the room, covered over with a cloth.

At this table a young man was sitting, a dark-haired, pale-faced young man in civilian clothes, well under thirty. He glanced up as Howard came into the room.

'Who are you?' he asked in French. He spoke almost idly, as if the matter was of no great moment.

The old man stood by the door, inwardly beating down his fears. This was something strange and therefore dangerous.

'I am an Englishman,' he said at last. There was no point any longer in concealment. 'I was arrested yesterday.'

The young man smiled without mirth. This time he spoke in English, without any trace of accent. 'Well,' he said, 'you'd better come on and sit down. There's a pair of us. I'm English too.'

Howard recoiled a step. 'You're *English?*'

'Naturalised,' the other said carelessly. 'My mother came from Woking, and I spent most of my life in England. My father was a Frenchman, so I started off as French. But he was killed in the last war.'

'But what are you doing here?'

The young man motioned to the table. 'Come on and sit down.'

The old man drew a chair up to the table and repeated his question. 'I did not know there was another Englishman in Lannilis,' he said. 'Whatever are you doing here?'

The young man said: 'I'm waiting to be shot.'

There was a stunned, horrible pause. At last, Howard said: 'Is your name Charenton?'

The young man nodded. 'Yes,' he said, 'I'm Charenton. I see they told you about me.'

There was a long silence in the little room. Howard sat dumb, not knowing what to say. In his embarrassment his eyes fell upon the table, upon the young man's hands. Sitting with his hands before him on the table, Charenton had formed his fingers in a peculiar grip, the fingers interlaced, the left hand palm up and the right hand palm down. The thumbs were crossed. As soon as he observed the old man's scrutiny he glanced at him sharply, then undid the grasp.

He sighed a little.

'How did you come to be here?' he asked.

Howard said: 'I was trying to get back to England, with a few children.' He rambled into his story. The young man listened to him quietly, appraising him with keen, curious eyes.

In the end he said: 'I don't believe that you've got much to worry about. They'll probably let you live at liberty in some French town.'

Howard said: 'I'm afraid they won't do that. You see, they think that I'm mixed up with you.'

The young man nodded. 'I thought that must be it. That is why they've put us together. They're looking for a few more scapegoats, are they?'

Howard said: 'I am afraid they are.'

The young man got up and walked over to the window. 'You'll be all right,' he said at last. 'They've got no evidence against you–they can't have. Sooner or later you'll get back to England.'

There was a tinge of sadness in his voice.

Howard said: 'What about you?'

Charenton said: 'Me? I'm for the high jump. They got the goods on me all right.'

It seemed incredible to Howard. It was as if he had been listening to a play.

'We both seem to be in difficulties,' he said at last. 'Yours may be more serious than mine; I don't know. But you can do one thing for me.' He looked around. 'If I could get hold of a piece of paper and a pencil, I would redraft my will. Would you witness it for me?'

The other shook his head. 'You must write nothing here without permission from the Germans; they will only take it from you. And no document that had my signature upon it would get back to England. You must find some other witness, Mr Howard.'

The old man sighed. 'I suppose that is so,' he said. And presently he said: 'If I should get out of this and you should not, is there anything I can do? Any message you would like me to take?'

Charenton smiled ironically. 'No messages,' he said definitely.

'There is nothing I can do?'

The young man glanced at him. 'Do you know Oxford?'

'I know Oxford very well,' the old man said. 'Were you up there?'

Charenton nodded. 'I was up at Oriel. There's a place up the river that we used to walk to–a pub by a weir pool, a very old grey stone house beside a little bridge. There is the sound of running water all the time, and fish swimming in the clear pool, and flowers, flowers everywhere.'

'You mean the "Trout Inn," at Godstow?'

'Yes–the "Trout". You know it?'

'I know it very well indeed. At least, I used to, forty years ago.'

'Go there and drink a pint for me,' the young man said. 'Sitting on the wall and looking at the fish in the pool, on a hot summer day.'

Howard said: 'If I get back to England, I will do that.' He glanced round the shabby, garishly furnished room. 'But is there no message I can take to anyone?'

Charenton shook his head. 'No messages,' he said. 'If there were, I would not give them to you. There is almost certainly a microphone in this room, and Diessen listening to every word we say. That is why they have put us here together.' He glanced round. 'It's probably behind one of those oil-paintings.'

'Are you sure of that?'

'As sure as I'm sitting here.'

He raised his voice and said, speaking in German: 'You are wasting your time, Major Diessen. This man knows nothing about my affairs.' He paused and then continued: 'But I will tell you this. One day the English and Americans will come, and you will be in their power. They will not be gentle as they were after the last war. If you kill this old man you will be hung in public on a gallows, and your body will stay there rotting as a warning to all other murderers.'

He turned to Howard. 'That ought to fetch him,' he said placidly, speaking in English.

The old man was troubled. 'I am sorry that you spoke like that,' he said. 'It will not do you any good with him.'

'Nor will anything else,' the young man said. 'I'm very very nearly through.' There was a quiet finality about his tone that made Howard wince.

'Are you sorry?' he enquired.

'No, by God I'm not,' Charenton said, and he laughed boyishly. 'We didn't succeed in getting Adolf, but we gave him the hell of a fright.'

Behind them the door opened. They swung round; there was a German *Gefreiter* there with a private. The private marched into the room and stood by Howard. The *Gefreiter* said roughly: '*Kommen Sie.*'

Charenton smiled as Howard got up. 'I told you so,' he said. 'Good-bye. All the best of luck.'

'Good-bye,' said the old man. He was hustled out of the room before he had time to say more. As he passed down the corridor to the street he saw through an open door the black uniformed Gestapo officer, his face dark with anger. With a sick heart Howard walked out into the sunlit square between his guards.

They took him back to Nicole and the children. Ronnie rushed up to him. 'Marjan has been showing us how to stand on our heads,' he said excitedly. 'I can do it and so can Pierre. Willem can't, and none of the girls. Look, Mr Howard. Just look!'

In a welter of children standing on their heads Nicole looked anxiously at him. 'They did nothing?' she enquired.

The old man shook his head. 'They used me to try to make a young man called Charenton talk,' he said. He told her briefly what had happened.

'That is their way,' she said. 'I have heard of that in Chartres. To gain their end through pain they do not work upon the body. They work upon the mind.'

The long afternoon dragged into evening. Cooped in the little prison room it was very hot and difficult to keep the children happy. There was nothing for them to do, nothing to look at, nothing to read to them. Nicole and Howard found themselves before long working hard to keep the peace and to stop quarrels, and this in one way was a benefit to them in that it made it difficult for them to brood upon their own position.

At last the German orderly brought them another meal, a supper of bitter coffee and long lengths of bread. This caused a diversion and a rest from the children; presently, the old man and the girl knew very well, the children would grow sleepy. When the orderly came back for the supper things they asked for beds.

He brought them straw-filled palliasses, with a rough pillow and one blanket each. They spent some time arranging these; by that time the children were tired and willing to lie down.

The long hours of the evening passed in bored inactivity. Nicole and Howard sat on their palliasses, brooding; from time to time exchanging a few words and relapsing into silence. At about ten o'clock they went to bed; taking off their outer clothes only, they lay down and covered themselves with the blanket.

Howard slept fairly well that night, the girl not so well. Very early in the morning, in the half-light before dawn, the door of their prison opened with a clatter. The *Gefreiter* was there, fully dressed and equipped with bayonet at his belt and steel helmet on his head.

He shook Howard by the shoulder. '*Auf!*' he said. He indicated to him that he was to get up and dress himself.

Nicole raised herself on one arm, a little frightened. 'Do they want me?' she asked in French. The man shook his head.

Howard, putting on his coat, turned to her in the dim light. 'This will be another of their enquiries,' he said. 'Don't worry. I shall be back before long.'

She was deeply troubled. 'I shall be waiting for you, with the children,' she said simply. 'They will be safe with me.'

'I know they will,' he said. '*Au revoir.*'

In the cold dawn they took him out into the square and along to the big house with the swastika flag, opposite the church, where they had first been interrogated. He was not taken to the same room, but to an upstairs room at the back. It had been a bedroom at one time and some of the bedroom furniture was still in place, but the bed had been removed and now it was some kind of office.

The black uniformed Gestapo officer Major Diessen, was standing by the window. 'So,' he said, 'we have the Englishman again.'

Howard was silent. The German spoke a few words in his own language to the *Gefreiter* and the private who had brought Howard to the room. The *Grfreiter* saluted and withdrew, closing the door behind him. The private remained standing at attention by the door. The cold, grey light was now strong in the room.

'Come,' said the German at the window. 'Look out. Nice garden, is it not?'

The old man approached the window. There was a garden there, entirely surrounded by high old red-brick walls covered with fruit trees. It was a well-kept, mature garden, such as he liked to see.

'Yes,' he said quietly. 'It is a nice garden.' Instinctively he felt the presence of some trap.

The German said: 'Unless you help him, in a few minutes your friend Mr Charenton will die in it. He is to be shot as a spy.'

The old man stared at him. 'I don't know what is in your mind that you have brought me here,' he said. 'I met Charenton for the first time yesterday, when you put us together. He is a very brave young man and a good one. If you are going to shoot him, you are doing a bad thing. A man like that should be allowed to live, to work for the world when this war is all over.'

'A very nice speech,' the German said. 'I agree with you; he should be allowed to live. He shall live, if you help him. He shall be a prisoner to the end of the war, which will not be long now. Six months at the most. Then he will be free.'

He turned to the window. 'Look,' he said. 'They are bringing him out.'

The old man turned and looked. Down the garden path a little cordon of six German soldiers, armed with rifles, were escorting Charenton. They were under the command of a *Feldwebel*; an officer rather behind Charenton, who walked slowly, his hands in his trousers-pockets. He did not seem to be pinioned in any way, nor did he seem to be particularly distressed.

Howard turned to the German. 'What do you want?' he asked. 'Why have you brought me to see this?'

'I have had you brought here,' said the German, 'to see if you would not help your friend, at a time when he needs help.'

He leaned towards the old man. 'Listen,' he said softly. 'It is a very little thing, that will not injure either of you. Nor will it make any difference to the war, because in any case your country now is doomed. If you will tell me how he got the information out of France and back to England, to your Major Cochrane, I will stop this execution.'

He stepped back. 'What do you think?' he said. 'You must be realist. It is not sensible to let a brave young man die, when he could be saved to work for your country when the war is over. And further, nobody can ever know. Charenton will stay in prison till the war is over, in a month or two; then he will be released. You and your family of children will have to stay in France, but if you help us now you need not stay in prison at all. You can live quietly in Chartres with the young woman. Then, when the war is over, in the autumn, you shall all go home. There will be no enquiries about this from England, because by that time the whole organisation of British spies will have become dispersed. There is no danger for you in this at all, and you can save that young man's life.' He leaned towards Howard again. 'Just a few little words,' he said softly. 'How did he do it? He shall never know you told.'

The old man stared at him. 'I cannot tell you,' he replied. 'Quite truthfully, I do not know. I have not been concerned in his affairs at all.' He said it with a sense of relief. If he had had the information things would have been more difficult.

The Gestapo officer stepped back. 'That is mere nonsense,' he said harshly. 'I do not believe that. You know sufficient to assist an agent of your country if he needs your help. All travellers in any foreign country know that much. Do you take me for a fool?'

Howard said: 'That may be so with German travellers. In England ordinary travellers know nothing about espionage. I tell you, I know literally nothing that could help this man.'

The German bit his lip. He said: 'I am inclined to think you are a spy yourself. You have been wandering round the country in disguise, nobody knows where. You had better be careful. You may share his fate.'

'Even so,' the old man said, 'I could not tell you anything of value to you, because I do not know.'

Diessen turned to the window again. 'You have not got very much time,' he said. 'A minute or two, not more. Think again before it is too late.'

Howard looked out into the garden. They had put the young man with his back against the wall in front of a plum-tree. His hands now were bound behind his back, and the *Feldwebel* was blindfolding him with a red cotton handkerchief.

The German said: 'Nobody can ever know. There is still time for you to save him.'

'I cannot save him in that way,' the old man said. 'I have not got the information. But this is a bad, wicked thing that you are going to do. It will not profit you in the long run.'

The Gestapo officer swung round on him suddenly. He thrust his face near to the old man's. 'He gave you messages,' he said fiercely. 'You think you are clever, but you cannot deceive me. The "Trout Inn"—beer—flowers—fish! Do you think I am a fool? What does all that mean?'

'Nothing but what he said,' Howard replied. 'It is a place that he is fond of. That is all.'

The German drew back morosely. 'I do not believe it,' he said sullenly.

In the garden the *Feldwebel* had left the young man by the wall. The six soldiers were drawn up in a line in front of him, distant about ten yards. The officer had given them a command and they were loading.

'I am not going to delay this matter any longer,' said Diessen: 'Have you still nothing to say to save his life?'

The old man shook his head.

In the garden the officer glanced up to their window. Diessen lifted his hand and dropped it. The officer turned, drew himself up and gave a sharp word of command. An irregular volley rang out. The old man saw the body by the plum-tree crumple and fall, twitch for a little and lie still.

He turned away, rather sick. Diessen moved over to the middle of the room. The sentry still stood impassive at the door.

'I do not know whether I should believe your story or not,' the German said heavily at last. 'If you are a spy you are at least a clever one.'

Howard said: 'I am not a spy.'

'What are you doing in this country, then? Wandering round disguised as a French peasant?'

'I have told you that,' the old man said wearily, 'many times. I have been trying to get these children back to England, to send them to their homes or to America.'

The German burst out: 'Lies—lies! Always the same lies! You English are the same every time! Stubborn as mules!' He thrust his face into the other's. 'Criminals, all the lot of you!' He indicated the garden beyond the window. 'You could have prevented that, but you would not.'

'I could not have prevented you from killing that young man. That was your own doing.'

The Gestapo officer said, gloomily: 'I did not want to kill him. He forced me to do it, you and he between you. You are both to blame for his death. You left me with no other course.'

There was a silence. Then the German said: 'All your time you spend lying and scheming against us. Your Churchill and your Chamberlain, goading us on, provoking us to war. And you are just another one.'

The old man did not answer that.

The German pulled himself together, crossed the room, and sat down at a table. 'This story of yours about sending these children to America,' he said. 'I do not believe a word of it.'

The old man was very, very tired. He said, indifferently: 'I can't help that. That is what I meant to do with them.'

'You still say that you would have sent them to your married daughter?'

'Yes.'

'Where does she live in America?'

'At a place called Coates Harbor, on Long Island.'

'Long Island. That is where the wealthy live. Is your daughter very wealthy?'

The old man said: 'She is married to an American business man. Yes, they are quite well off.'

The German said incredulously: 'You still wish me to believe that a wealthy woman such as that would make a home in her own house for all these dirty little children that you have picked up?'

Howard said: 'She will do that.' He paused, and then he said, 'You do not understand. Over there, they want to help us. If they make a home for children, refugees from Europe, they feel that they are doing something worth while. And they are.'

The German glanced at him curiously. 'You have travelled in America?'

'A little.'

'Do you know a town called White Falls?'

Howard shook his head. 'That sounds like quite a common name, but I don't recollect it. What state is it in?'

'In Minnesota. Is that far from Long Island?'

'It's right in the middle. I should think it's about a thousand miles.' This conversation was becoming very odd, the old man thought.

The German said: 'Now about mademoiselle. Were you going to send her to America also? Is she one of your children, may I ask?'

The old man shook his head. 'I would like her to go there,' he replied. 'But she will not leave France. Her father is a prisoner in your hands; her mother is alone in Chartres. I have tried to persuade her to come with us to England, but she will not do so. You have nothing against her.'

The other shrugged his shoulders. 'That is a matter of opinion. She has been helping you in your work.'

The old man said wearily: 'I tell you over and over again, I have no secret work. I know that you do not believe me.' He paused. 'The only work that I have had for the last fortnight has been to get these children into safety.'

There was a little silence.

'Let them go through to England,' he said quietly. 'Let the young man Focquet sail with them for Plymouth in his boat, and let Mademoiselle Rougeron go with them to take them to America. If you let them go, like that, I will confess to anything you like.'

The Gestapo man stared at him angrily. 'You are talking nonsense,' he replied. 'That is an insult to the German nation that you have just made. Do you take us for a pack of dirty Russians, to make bargains of that sort?'

Howard was silent.

The German got up and walked over to the window. 'I do not know what to make of you,' he said at last. 'I think that you must be a very brave man, to talk as you have done.'

Howard smiled faintly. 'Not a brave man,' he said. 'Only a very old one. Nothing you can do can take much from me, because I've had it all.'

The German did not answer him. He spoke in his own language to the sentry, and they took Howard back to the prison room.

I I

Nicole greeted him with relief. She had spent an hour of unbearable anxiety, tortured by the thought of what might be happening to him, pestered by the children. She said: 'What happened?'

He said wearily: 'The young man, Charenton, was shot. Then they questioned me a lot more.'

She said gently: 'Sit down and rest. They will bring us coffee before very long. You will feel better after that.'

He sat down on his rolled-up mattress. 'Nicole,' he said. 'I believe there is a chance that they might let the children go to England without me. If so, would you take them?'

She said: 'Me? To go alone to England with the children? I do not think that that would be a good thing, Monsieur Howard.'

'I would like you to go, if it were possible.'

She came and sat by him. 'Is it for the children that you want this, or for me?' she asked.

He could not answer that. 'For both,' he said at last.

With clear logic she said: 'In England there will be many people, friends of yours and the relations of the English children, who will care for them. You have only to write a letter, and send it with them if they have to go without you. But for me, I have told you, I have no business in England—now. My country is this country, and my parents are here and in trouble. It is here that I must stay.'

He nodded ruefully. 'I was afraid that you would feel like that.'

Half an hour later the door of their room was thrust open, and two German privates appeared outside. They were carrying a table. With some difficulty they got it through the door and set it up in the middle of the room. Then they brought in eight chairs and set them with mathematical exactitude round the table.

Nicole and Howard watched this with surprise. They had eaten all their meals since they had been in captivity from plates balanced in their hands, helped from a bowl that stood upon the floor. This was something different in their treatment, something strange and suspicious.

The soldiers withdrew. Presently, the door opened again, and in walked a little French waiter balancing a tray, evidently from some neighbouring café. A German soldier followed him and stood over him in menacing silence. The man, evidently frightened, spread a cloth upon the table and set out cups and saucers, a large pot of hot coffee and a jug of hot milk, new rolls, butter, sugar, jam, and a plate of cut rounds of sausage. Then he withdrew quickly, in evident relief. Impassively, the German soldier shut the door on them again.

The children crowded round the table, eager. Howard and Nicole helped them into their chairs and set to work to feed them. The girl glanced at the old man.

'This is a great change,' she said quietly. 'I do not understand why they are doing this.'

He shook his head. He did not understand it either. Lurking in his mind was a thought that he did not speak, that this was a new trick to win him into some admission. They had failed with fear; now they would try persuasion.

The children cleared the table of all that was on it and got down, satisfied. A quarter of an hour later the little waiter reappeared, still under guard; he gathered up the cloth and cleared the table, and retired again in silence. But the door did not close.

One of the sentries came to it and said: '*Sie können in den Garten gehen.*' With difficulty Howard understood this to mean that they might go into the garden.

There was a small garden behind the house, completely surrounded by a high brick wall, not unlike another garden that the old man had seen earlier in the day. The children rushed out into it with a carillon of shrill cries; a day of close confinement had been a grave trial to them. Howard followed with Nicole, wondering.

It was another brilliant, sunlit day, already growing hot. Presently, two German soldiers appeared carrying arm-chairs. These two chairs they set with mathematical exactitude precisely in the middle of a patch of shade beneath a tree. '*Setzen Sie sich,*' they said.

Nicole and Howard sat down side by side, self-consciously, in silence. The soldiers withdrew, and a sentry with a rifle and a fixed bayonet appeared at the only exit from the garden. There he grounded his rifle and stood at ease, motionless and expressionless. There was something sinister about all these developments.

Nicole said: 'Why are they doing this for us, monsieur? What do they hope to gain by it?'

He said: 'I do not know. Once, this morning, I thought perhaps that they were going to let us go–or at any rate, let the children go to England. But even that would be no reason for giving us arm-chairs in the shade.'

She said, quietly: 'It is a trap. They want something from us; therefore they try to please us.'

He nodded. 'Still,' he said, 'it is more pleasant here than in that room.'

Marjan, the little Pole, was as suspicious as they were. He sat aside upon the grass in sullen silence; since they had been taken prisoner he had barely spoken one word. Rose, too, was ill at ease; she wandered round the garden, peering at the high walls as if looking for a means to escape. The younger children were untouched; Ronnie and Pierre and Willem and Sheila played little games around the garden or stood, finger in mouth, looking at the German sentry.

Presently Nicole, looking round, saw that the old man was asleep in his arm-chair.

They spent the whole day in the garden, only going back into their prison room for meals. *Déjeuner* and *diner* were served in the same way by the same silent little waiter under guard; good, plentiful meals, well cooked and attractively served. After dinner the German soldiers removed the table and the chairs, and indicated that they might lay out their beds. They did so and put all the children down to sleep.

Presently Howard and Nicole went to bed themselves.

The old man had slept only for an hour when the door was thrust open by a German soldier. He bent and shook the old man by the shoulder. '*Kommen*

Sie,' he said. '*Schnell–zur Gestapo.*'

Howard got up wearily and put on his coat and shoes in the darkness. From her bed Nicole said: 'What is it? Can I come too?'

He said: 'I don't think so, my dear. It's just me that they want.'

She expostulated: 'But what a time to choose!'

The German soldier made a gesture of impatience. Howard said: 'Don't worry. It's probably another interrogation.'

He was hustled away and the door closed behind him. In the dark room the girl got up and put on her skirt, and sat waiting in the darkness, sitting on her bed among the sleeping children, full of forebodings.

Howard was taken to the room in which they had first been interviewed. The Gestapo officer, Major Diessen, was there sitting at the table. An empty coffee cup stood beside him, and the room was full of his cigar-smoke. The German soldier who brought Howard in saluted stiffly. The officer spoke a word to him, and he withdrew, closing the door behind him. Howard was left alone in the room with Major Diessen.

He glanced at the clock. It was a little after midnight. The windows had been covered over with blankets for a blackout.

Presently the German looked up at the old man standing by the wall. 'So,' he said. 'The Englishman again.' He opened a drawer beside him and took out a large, black automatic pistol. He slipped out the clip and examined it; then put it back again and pulled the breech to load it. He laid it on the blotting-pad in front of him. 'We are alone,' he said. 'I am not taking any chances, as you see.'

The old man smiled faintly. 'You have nothing to fear from me.'

The German said: 'Perhaps not. But you have much to fear from me.'

There was a little silence. Presently he said: 'Suppose I were to let you go to England after all? What would you think then, eh?'

The old man's heart leapt and then steadied again. It was probably a trap. 'I should be very grateful, if you let me take the children,' he said quietly.

'And mademoiselle too?'

He shook his head. 'She does not want to come. She wants to stay in France.'

The German nodded. 'That is what we also want.' He paused, and then said: 'You say that you would be grateful. We will see now if that is just an empty boast. If I were to let you go to England with your children, so that you could send them to America, would you do me a small service?'

Howard said: 'It depends what it was.'

The Gestapo man flared out: 'Bargaining! Always the same, you English! One tries to help you, and you start chaffering! You are in no position to drive bargains, Mr Englishman!'

The old man persisted: 'I must know what you want me to do.'

The German said: 'It is a matter of no difficulty. . . .'

There was a short pause.

His hand strayed to the black automatic on the desk before him, and began fingering it. 'There is a certain person to be taken to America,' he said deliberately. 'I do not want to advertise her journey. It would be very suitable that she should travel with your party of children.'

The gun was now in his hand, openly.

Howard stared at him across the table. 'If you mean that you want to use my party as a cover for an agent going to America,' he said, 'I will not have it.'

He saw the forefinger snap round the trigger. He raised his eyes to the

German's face and saw it white with anger. For a full half-minute they remained motionless, staring at each other.

The Gestapo officer was the first to relax. 'You would drive me mad,' he said bitterly. 'You are a stubborn and obstinate people. You refuse the hand of friendship. You are suspicious of everything we do.'

Howard was silent. There was no point in saying more than was necessary. It would not help.

'Listen to me,' the German said, 'and try to get this into your thick head. This is not an agent who is travelling to America. This is a little girl.'

'A little girl?'

'A little girl of five years old. The daughter of my brother, who has been killed.'

The gun was firmly in his hand, resting upon the desk but pointing in the direction of the old man.

Howard said: 'Let me understand this fully. This is a little German girl that you want me to take to America, with all the other children?'

'That is so.'

'Who is she, and where is she going?'

The German said: 'I have told you who she is. She is the daughter of my brother Karl. Her name is Anna Diessen, and at present she is in Paris.'

He hesitated for a minute. 'You must understand,' he said, 'that there were three of us. My oldest brother Rupert fought in the World War, and then went to America. He now has a business, what you would call a grocery, in White Falls. He is an American citizen now.'

'I see,' said Howard thoughtfully.

'My brother Karl was Oberleutnant in the 4th Regiment Tanks, in the Second Panzer Division. He was married some years ago, but the marriage was not a success.' He hesitated for a moment and then said quickly: 'The girl was not wholly Aryan, and that never works. There was trouble, and she died. And now Karl, too, is dead.'

He sat brooding for a minute. Howard said gently: 'I am very sorry.' And he was.

Diessen said sullenly: 'It was English treachery that killed him. He was driving the English before him, from Amiens to the coast. There was a road cluttered up with refugees, and he was clearing it with his guns to get his tank through. And hiding in among these refugees were English soldiers that Karl did not see, and they threw bottles of oil on top of his cupola so they dripped down inside, and then they threw a flame to set the oil alight. My brother threw the hatch up to get out, and the English shot him down before he could surrender. But he had already surrendered, and they knew it. No man could go on fighting in a blazing tank.'

Howard was silent.

Diessen said: 'So there is Anna who must be provided for. I think it will be better if she goes to live with Rupert in America.'

The old man said: 'She is five years old?'

'Five and a half years.'

Howard said: 'Well, I should be very glad to take her.'

The German stared at him thoughtfully. 'How quickly after you reach England will the children go? How many of them are you sending to America? All of them?'

Howard shook his head. 'I doubt that. Three of them will certainly be going, but of the six two are English and one is a French girl with a father in London. I don't suppose that they would want to go–they might. But I shall send the other three within a week. That is, if you let us go.'

The German nodded. 'You must not wait longer. In six weeks we shall be in London.'

There was a silence. 'I do not want that you should think I am not confident about the outcome of this war,' Diessen said. 'We shall conquer England, as we have conquered France; you cannot stand against us. But for many years there will be war with your Dominions, and while that is going on there will be not much food for children, here or in Germany. It will be better that little Anna should be in a neutral country.'

Howard nodded. 'Well, she can go with my lot if you like to send her.'

The Gestapo officer eyed him narrowly. 'There must be no trickery. Remember, we shall have Mademoiselle Rougeron. She may return to Chartres and live with her mother, but until I have a cable from my brother Rupert that little Anna is safe with him, we shall have our eye on mademoiselle.'

'As a hostage,' said the old man quietly.

'As a hostage.' The German stared at him arrogantly. 'And another thing, also. If any word of this appears, it is the concentration camp for your young lady. I will not have you spreading lies about me as soon as you reach England. Remember that.'

Howard thought quickly. 'That has another side to it,' he said. 'If Mademoiselle Rougeron gets into trouble with the Gestapo and I should hear of it in England, this story shall be published in my country and quoted in the German news upon the radio, mentioning you by name.'

Diessen said furiously: 'You dare to threaten me!'

The old man smiled faintly. 'Let us call off this talk of threats,' he said. 'We are in each other's hands, and I will make a bargain with you. I will take your little girl and she shall travel safely to White Falls, even if I have to send her by the Clipper. On your side, you will look after Mademoiselle Rougeron and see that she comes to no harm. That is a bargain that will suit us both, and we can part as friends.'

The German stared at him for a long time. 'So,' he said at last. 'You are clever, Mr Englishman. You have gained all that you want.'

'So have you,' the old man said.

The German released the automatic and reached out for a slip of paper. 'What address have you in England? I shall send for you when we visit London in August.'

They settled to the details of the arrangement. A quarter of an hour later the German got up from the table. 'No word of this to anyone,' he said again. 'To-morrow in the evening you will be moved from here.'

Howard shook his head. 'I shall not talk. But I would like you to know one thing. I should have been glad to take your little girl with me in any case. It never entered my head to refuse to take her.'

The German nodded. 'That is good,' he said. 'If you had refused I should have shot you dead. You would have been too dangerous to leave this room alive.'

He bowed stiffly. '*Auf Wiedersehn*,' he said ironically. He pressed a button on his desk; the door opened and the sentry took Howard back through the quiet, moonlit streets to his prison.

Nicole was sitting on her bed, waiting for him. As the door closed she came to him and said: 'What happened? Did they hurt you?'

He patted her on the shoulder. 'It's all right,' he said. 'They did nothing to me.'

'What happened, then? What did they want you for?'

He sat down on the bed and she came and sat down opposite him. The moon threw a long shaft of silver light in through the window; faintly, somewhere, they heard the droning of a bomber.

'Listen, Nicole,' he said. 'I can't tell you what has happened. But I can tell you this, and you must try to forget what I am telling you. Everything is going to be all right. We shall go to England very soon, all of the children—and I shall go too. And you will go free, and travel back to Chartres to live with your mother, and you will have no trouble from the Gestapo. That is what is going to happen.'

She said breathlessly: 'But—I do not understand. How has this been arranged?'

He said: 'I cannot tell you that. I cannot tell you any more, Nicole. But that is what will happen, very soon.'

'You are not tired, or ill? This is all true, but you must not tell me how it has been done?'

He nodded. 'We shall go tomorrow or the next day,' he replied. There was a steady confidence in his tone which brought conviction to her.

'I am very, very happy,' she said quietly.

There was a long silence. Presently she said: 'Sitting here in the darkness while you were away, I have been thinking, monsieur.' In the dim light he could see that she was looking away from him. 'I was wondering what these children would grow up to be when they were old. Ronnie—I think he will become an engineer, and Marjan a soldier, and Willem—he will be a lawyer or a doctor. And Rose will be a mother certainly, and Sheila—she may be a mother too, or she may become one of your English women of business. And little Pierre—do you know what I think of him? I think that he will be an artist of some sort, who will lead many other men with his ideas.'

'I think that's very likely,' said the old man.

The girl went on. 'Ever since John was killed, monsieur, I have been desolate,' she said quietly. 'It seemed to me that there was no goodness in the world, that everything had gone mad and crazy and foul—that God had died or gone away, and left the world to Hitler. Even these little children were to go on suffering.'

There was a pause. The old man did not speak.

'But now,' she said, 'I think I can begin to see the pattern. It was not meant that John and I should be happy, save for a week. It was intended that we should do wrong. And now, through John and I, it is intended that these children should escape from Europe to grow up in peace.'

Her voice dropped. 'This may have been what John and I were brought together for,' she said. 'In thirty years the world may need one of these little ones.' She paused. 'It may be Ronnie or it may be Willem, or it may be little Pierre who does great things for the world,' she said. 'But when that happens, monsieur, it will be because I met your son to show him Paris, and we fell in love.'

He leaned across and took her hand, and sat there in the dim light holding it for a long time. Presently they lay down upon their beds, and lay awake till dawn.

They spent the next day in the garden, as the day before. The children were becoming bored and restless with the inactivity; Nicole devoted a good deal of her time to them, while Howard slept in his arm-chair beneath the tree. The day passed slowly. Dinner was served to them at six; after the meal the table was cleared by the same waiter.

They turned to put down beds for the children. The *Gefreiter* stopped them; with some difficulty he made them understand that they were going away.

Howard asked where they were going to. The man shrugged his shoulders. '*Nach Paris?*' he said doubtfully. Evidently he did not know.

Half an hour later they were taken out and put into a covered van. Two German soldiers got in with them, and they moved off. The old man tried to ask the soldiers where they were being taken to, but the men were uncommunicative. Presently, from their conversation, Howard gathered that the soldiers were themselves going on leave to Paris; it seemed that while proceeding on leave they were to act as a guard for the prisoners. That looked as if the Paris rumour was correct.

He discussed all this with Nicole in a low tone as the van swayed and rolled inland from the coast through the leafy lanes in the warm evening.

Presently they came to the outskirts of a town. Nicole peered out. 'Brest,' she said presently. 'I know this street.'

One of the Germans nodded. 'Brest,' he said shortly.

They were taken to the railway station; here they got out of the van. One of the soldiers stood guard over them while the other went to see the R.T.O.; the French passengers looked at them curiously. They were passed through the barrier and put into a third-class carriage with their guards, in a train which seemed to be going through to Paris.

Ronnie said: 'Is this the train we're going to sleep in, Mr Howard?'

He smiled patiently. 'This isn't the one I meant, but we may have to sleep in this one,' he said.

'Shall we have a little bed, like you told us about?'

'I don't think so. We'll see.'

Rose said: 'I do feel thirsty. May I have an orange?'

There were oranges for sale upon the platform. Howard had no money. He explained the requirement to one of the German soldiers, who got out of the carriage and bought oranges for all of them. Presently they were all sucking oranges, the children vying with the German soldiers in the production of noise.

At eight o'clock the train started. It went slowly, stopping at every little local halt upon the line. At eight-twenty it drew up at a little place called Lanissant, which consisted of two cottages and a farm. Suddenly Nicole, looking out of the window, turned to Howard.

'Look!' she said. 'Here is Major Diessen.'

The Gestapo officer, smart and upright in his black uniform and black field boots, came to the door of their carriage and opened it. The German sentries got up quickly and stood to attention. He spoke to them incisively in German. Then he turned to Howard.

'You must get out,' he said. 'You are not going on in this train.'

Nicole and Howard got the children out of the carriage on to the platform. Over the hill the sun was setting in a clear sky. The Gestapo officer nodded to the guard, who shut the carriage door and blew a little toot upon his horn. The train moved forward, the carriages passed by them, and went on slowly up the line. They were left standing on this little platform in the middle of the country with the Gestapo officer.

'So,' he said. 'You will now follow me.'

He led the way down the wooden steps that gave on to the road. There was no ticket-collector and no booking-office; the little halt was quite deserted. Outside, in the lane, there was a grey car, a Ford van with a utility body. In the driver's seat there was a soldier in black Gestapo uniform. Beside him was a child.

Diessen opened the door and made the child get out, '*Komm, Anna,*' he said. '*Hier ist Herr Howard, und mit ihm wirst du zu Onkel Ruprecht gehen.*'

The little girl stared at the old man, and his retinue of children, and at the dishevelled girl beside him. Then she stretched out a little skinny arm, and in a shrill voice exclaimed: 'Heil Hitler!'

The old man said gravely: '*Guten abend, Anna.*' He turned to the Gestapo officer, smiling faintly. 'She will have to get out of that habit if she's going to America,' he said.

Diessen nodded. 'I will tell her.' He spoke to the little girl, who listened to him round-eyed. She asked a question, puzzled; Howard caught the word Hitler. Diessen explained to her again; under the scrutiny of Howard and Nicole he flushed a little. The child said something in a clear, decisive tone which made the driver of the car turn in his seat and glance towards his officer for guidance.

Diessen said: 'I think she understands.' To the old man he seemed a little embarrassed.

He asked: 'What did she say?'

The officer said: 'Children do not understand the Führer. That is reserved for adults.'

Nicole asked him in French: 'But, monsieur, tell us what she said.'

The German shrugged his shoulders. 'I cannot understand the reasoning of children. She said that she is glad that she has not go to say "Heil Hitler" any more, because the Führer wears a moustache.'

Howard said with perfect gravity: 'It is difficult to understand the minds of children.'

'That is so. Now, will you all get into the car. We will not linger in this place.' The German glanced around suspiciously.

They got into the car. Anna got into the back seats with them; Diessen seated himself beside the driver. The car moved down the road. In the front seat the Gestapo officer turned, and passed back a cotton bag tied with a string to Howard, and another to Nicole.

'Your papers and your money,' he said briefly. 'See that it is all in order.'

The old man opened it. Everything that had been taken from his pockets was there, quite intact.

In the gathering dusk they drove through the countryside for an hour and a half. From time to time the officer said something in a low tone to the driver; the old man got the impression once that they were driving round merely to kill time till darkness fell. Now and again they passed through villages, sometimes past barricades with German posts on guard. At these the car stopped and the sentry came and peered into the car. At the sight of the Gestapo uniform he stepped quickly back and saluted. This happened two or three times.

Once Howard asked: 'Where are we going to?'

The German said: 'To l'Abervrach. Your fisherman is there.'

After a pause the old man said: 'There was a guard upon the harbour.'

Diessen said: 'There is no guard tonight—that has been arranged. Do you take me for a fool?'

Howard said no more.

At ten o'clock, in the first darkness, they ran softly to the quay at l'Abervrach. The car drew up noiselessly and the engine stopped at once. The Gestapo officer got out and stood for half a minute, staring around. All was quiet and still.

He turned back to the car. 'Come,' he said. 'Get out quickly—and do not let the children talk.' They helped the children from the car. Diessen said to Nicole: 'There is to be no trickery. You shall stay with me. If you should try to go with them, I shall shoot down the lot of you.'

She raised her head. 'You need not draw your gun,' she said. 'I shall not try to go.'

The German did not answer her, but pulled the big automatic from the holster at his waist. In the dim light he went striding softly down the quay; Howard and Nicole hesitated for a moment and then followed him with the children; the black-uniformed driver brought up the rear. At the end, by the water's edge, Diessen turned.

He called to them in a low tone. 'Hurry.'

There was a boat there, where the slip ran down into the water. They could see the tracery of its mast and rigging outlined against the starry sky; the night was very quiet. They drew closer and saw it was a half-decked fishing-boat. There were two men there, besides Diessen. One was standing on the quay in the black uniform they knew so well. The other was in the boat, holding her to the quay by a rope rove through a ring.

'In with you, quickly,' said Diessen. 'I want to see you get away.'

He turned to Focquet, speaking in French. 'You are not to start your engine till you are past Le Trepied,' he said. 'I do not want the countryside to be alarmed.'

The young man nodded. 'There is no need,' he said in the soft Breton dialect. 'There is sufficient wind to steer by, and the ebb will take us out.'

They passed the seven children one by one down into the boat. 'You now,' the German said to Howard. 'Remember to behave yourself in England. I shall send for you in London in a very few weeks' time. In September.'

The old man turned to Nicole. 'This is good-bye, my dear,' he said. He hesitated. 'I do not think this war will be over in September. I may be old when it is over, and not able to travel very well. You will come and visit me, Nicole? There is so much that I shall want to say to you. So much that I wanted to talk over with you, if we had not been so hurried and so troubled in the last few days.'

She said: 'I will come and stay with you as soon as we can travel. And you shall talk to me about John.'

The German said: 'You must go now, Mr Englishman.'

He kissed the girl; for a minute she clung to him. Then he got down into the boat among the children.

Pierre said: 'Is this the boat that's going to take us to America?'

The old man shook his head. 'Not this boat,' he said, with mechanical patience. 'That will be a bigger boat than this.'

'How big will that one be?' asked Ronnie. 'Twice as big?'

Focquet had slipped the warp out of the ring and was thrusting vigorously with an oar against the quayside. The stretch of dark water that separated them from France grew to a yard, to five yards wide. The old man stood motionless, stricken with grief, with longing to be back upon the quay, with the bitter loneliness of old age.

He saw the figure of the girl standing with the three Germans by the water's edge, watching them as they slid away. The ebb caught the boat and hurried her quietly out into the stream; Focquet was heaving on a halliard forward and the heavy nut-brown sail crept slowly up the mast. For a moment he lost sight of Nicole as a mist dimmed his eyes; then he saw her again clearly, still standing motionless beside the Germans. Then the gloom shrouded all of them, and all that he could see was the faint outline of the hill against the starry sky.

In deep sorrow, he turned and looked forward to the open sea. But tears blinded him, and he could see nothing of the entrance.

Ronnie said: 'May I work the rudder, Mr Howard?'

The old man did not answer him. The little boy repeated his question.

Rose said: 'I do feel sick.'

He roused himself and turned to their immediate needs with heavy heart. They had no warm clothes and no blankets to keep off the chill of the night sea. He spoke a few sentences to Focquet and found him mystified at their deliverance; he found that the young man intended to cross straight over to Falmouth. He had no compass and no chart for the sea crossing of a hundred miles or so, but said he knew the way. He thought that it would take a day and a night, perhaps a little longer. They had no food with them, but he had a couple of bottles of red wine and a beaker of water.

They pulled a sail out from the forepeak and made a resting-place for the children. The old man took Anna and made her comfortable in a corner first, and put her in the charge of Rose. But Rose, for once, displayed little of her maternal instinct; she was preoccupied with her own troubles.

In a very few minutes she was sick, leaning over the side of the boat under the old man's instructions. One by one the children followed her example as they reached the open sea; they passed Le Trepied, a black reef of rock, with so much wailing that they might just as well have had the engine running after all. In spite of the quick motion of the boat the old man did not feel unwell. Of the children, the only one unaffected was Pierre, who stood by Focquet at the stern, gazing at the moonlight on the water ahead of them.

They turned at the Libenter buoy and headed to the north. In a lull between the requirements of the children Howard said to Focquet: 'You are sure that you know which way to steer?'

The young Frenchman nodded. He glanced at the moon and at the dim loom of the land behind them, and at the Great Bear shimmering in the north. Then he put out his hand. 'That way,' he said. 'That is where Falmouth is.' He called it 'Fallmoot'. 'In the morning we will use the engine; then we will get there before evening.'

A fresh wailing from the bows drew the old man away. An hour later most of the children were lying exhausted in an uneasy doze; Howard was able to sit down himself and rest. He glanced back at the land. It was practically lost to sight; only a dim shadow showed where France lay behind them. He stared back at Brittany with deep regret, in bitter lonely sadness. With all his heart he wished that he was back there with Nicole.

Presently he roused himself. They were not home yet; he must not give way to depression. He got up restlessly and stared around. There was a steady little night breeze from the south-east; they were making about four knots.

'It is going well,' said Focquet. 'If this wind holds we shall hardly need the engine.'

The young fisherman was sitting on a thwart smoking a caporal. He glanced back over his shoulder. 'To the right,' he said, without moving. 'Put it this way. So. Keep her at that, and look always at your star.'

The old man became aware that little Pierre was at the helm, thrusting with the whole weight of his body on the big tiller. He said to Focquet: 'Can that little one steer a boat?'

The young man spat into the sea. 'He is learning. He is quick, that one. It prevents sea-sickness, to sail the ship. By the time that we reach England he will be a helmsman.'

The old man turned to Pierre. 'You can do that very well,' he said. 'How do you know which way to go?'

In the dim light of the waning moon he saw Pierre staring straight ahead. 'Focquet told me,' he replied. The old man had to strain to catch his little voice above the lapping of the waves. 'He said, to sail at those square stars up there.' He raised his little arm and pointed at the Bear. 'That is where we are going to, m'sieur. That is the way to America, under those stars. There is so much food there that you can give some to a dog and have him for your friend. Mademoiselle Nicole told me so.'

Presently he grew tired; the boat began to wander from the Bear. Focquet threw the stump of his cigarette into the sea and routed out a heap of sacking. Howard took the helm and the young man arranged a sleepy little boy upon the floor beside their feet. After a time Focquet lay down himself on the bare boards and slept for an hour while the old man sailed the boat on through the starlight.

All night they saw no ships at all upon the sea. Ships may have been near them, but if so they were sailing without lights and did not trouble them. But in the half-light of dawn, at about half past four, a destroyer came towards them from the west, throwing a deep, feathery bow wave of white foam aside as she cut through the water, bearing down on them.

She slowed a quarter of a mile away and turned from a grey, menacing spear into rather a battered, rusty ship, menacing still, but worn with much hard work. A young man in duffle coat and service cap shouted at them from the bridge, megaphone in hand: '*Vous êtes Français?*'

Howard shouted back: 'Some of us are English.'

The young man waved at him cheerfully. 'Can you get to Plymouth all right?'

'We want to go to Falmouth.' The whine of the destroyer's fans and the lapping of the waves made conversation difficult.

'You've got to go to Plymouth. Plymouth! Is that all right for you?'

Howard spoke quickly to Focquet, and then nodded to the ship. The young officer waved at him again and stepped back. There was a sudden foaming at the stern and the destroyer shot away upon her course up-Channel. They were left tossing in the creamy effervescence of her wake.

They altered course two points towards the east and started up the engine, giving them about six knots of speed. The children roused, and in failing misery began to vomit again. They were all cold, and very tired, and desperately hungry.

Presently the sun came up and the day grew warm. The old man gave them all a little drink of wine and water.

All morning they plugged on over a sunlit, summer sea. Now and again the young Frenchman asked Howard the time, studied the sun, and made a correction to his course. At noon a thin blue line of land appeared ahead of them to the north.

At about three o'clock a trawler closed them, and asked who they were, and, as they tossed beside her, showed them the high land of Rame Head on the horizon.

At about half past five they were off Rame Head. A motor-launch, a little yacht in time of peace, ranged up alongside them; an R.N.V.R. lieutenant questioned them again. 'You know the Cattewater?' he shouted to Howard. 'Where the flying-boats are? That's right. Go up there and into the basin on the north side. All refugees land at the fish quay in the basin. Got that? Okay.'

The launch sheered off and went upon her way. The fishing-boat nosed in past Rame Head, past Cawsand, past the breakwater into the shelter of the Sound. Ahead of them lay Plymouth on its hills, grey and peaceful by its harbour in the evening sunlight. Howard stared at it and sighed a little. It seemed to him that he had been happier in France than he would be in his own land.

The sight of the warships in the Sound, the land, and the calmer water revived the children a little; they began to look about and take an interest again. Under the old man's guidance Focquet threaded his way through the warships; off Drake's Island they came to the wind and lowered the brown sail. Then, under engine only, they made their way to the fish quay.

There were other boats before them at the quay, boats full of an assortment of mixed nationalities, clambering ashore and into England. They lay off for a quarter of an hour before they could get to the steps, while the gulls screamed around them, and stolid men in blue jerseys looked down upon them, and holiday girls in summer cotton frocks took photographs of the scene.

At last they were all stumbling up the steps to join the crowd of refugees in the fish-market. Howard was still in the clothes of a Breton labourer, unshaven, and very, very tired. The children, hungry and exhausted, clustered round him.

A masterful woman, trim and neat in the uniform of the W.V.S., shepherded them to a bench. '*Asseyez vous là,*' she said in very bad French, '*jusqu'on peut vous attendre.*'

Howard collapsed on to the seat and sat there half in coma, utterly exhausted. Once or twice women in uniform came to them and asked them questions, which he answered mechanically. Half an hour later a young girl brought them cups of tea, which they took gratefully.

Refreshed, the old man took more interest in his surroundings. He heard a cultured Englishwoman's voice.

'There's that lot over there, Mrs Dyson. All those children with the two men.'

'What nationality are they?'

'They seem to be a mixed lot. There's rather an attractive little girl there who speaks German.'

'Poor little thing! She must be Austrian.'

Another voice said: 'Some of those children are English.'

There was an exclamation of concern. 'I had no idea! But they're in such a *state!* Have you seen their poor little heads? My dear, they're *lousy*, every one of them.' There was a shocked pause. 'That horrible old man—I wonder how he came to be in charge of them.'

The old man closed his eyes, smiling a little. This was the England that he knew and understood. This was peace.

12

The last bomb had fallen, the last gun had fired; over in the east the fires were dying down. Then came the long notes of the 'All Clear' from different quarters of the town.

We got up stiffly from our chairs. I went over to the long window at the far end of the room, pulled back the curtains and threw back the shutters. The glass from the window fell in on the carpet with a crash; the wind blew fresh into our faces with a bitter, acrid smell of burning.

Down in the streets below tired men in raincoats, gumboots, and tin-hats were tending a small motor pump. There was a noise like a thousand jangling cut-glass chandeliers as men in the houses opposite poked the remains of broken windows from the frames, letting the glass fall on the pavements, going methodically from room to room.

A cold, grey light was spreading over London. It was raining a little.

I turned from the window. 'Did you get them over to the States?' I asked.

'Oh yes,' he said. 'They all went together. I sent a wireless telegram to the Cavanaghs offering to send Sheila and Ronnie, and Tenois asked if he might send Rose. I got a woman that I know to go with them, and take them to Coates Harbor.'

'And Anna too?'

He nodded. 'Anna went too.' We moved towards the door. 'I had a letter this week from her uncle in White Falls. He said that he had sent a cable to his brother in Germany, so that ought to be all right.'

'Your daughter must have had a bit of a shock when they arrived,' I said.

He laughed. 'Well, I don't know. I sent a cable asking if she'd have them, and she said she would. She'll be all right with them. Costello seems to be reorganising the whole place for them. He's building a swimming-pool and a new boat-house for their boats. I think that they'll be very happy there.'

We went downstairs in the grey dawn and parted in the hall. He went out a few steps ahead of me; I paused to ask the night porter about damage to the club. He said that they had had a fire-bomb on the roof, but that young Ernest had kicked it about till it went out. He said there was no gas or water coming to the building, but that the electricity had survived the blitz.

I yawned. 'I spent the night up in the smoking-room talking to Mr Howard,' I said.

The man nodded. 'I looked in once or twice and saw you sitting with him,' he said. 'I said to the steward, I said–quite a good thing you was with him. He's got to look a great deal older recently.'

'Yes,' I said. 'I'm afraid he has.'

'He went away for a long holiday a month or two ago,' the porter said. 'But I don't know as it did him a great deal of good.'

I went out, and the glass crunched tinkling beneath my feet.

NEVIL SHUTE

THE FAR COUNTRY

Into my heart an air that kills
From yon far country blows:
What are those blue remembered hills,
What spires, what farms are those?

That is the land of lost content,
I see it shining plain,
The happy highways where I went
And cannot come again.

From The Collected Poems of A. E. Housman, *published by*
Messrs. Jonathan Cape, Ltd., and reproduced by permission of The Society of Authors.

I

Tim Archer got into the utility and drove it from the Banbury Feed and General Supply Pty Ltd, down the main street of the town. The car was a 1946 Chevrolet, somewhat battered by four years of station use, a sturdy practical vehicle with a coupé front seat and an open truck body behind. In this rear portion he was carrying a forty-four-gallon drum of Diesel oil, four reels of barbed wire, a can of kerosene, a sack of potatoes, a coil of new sisal rope, a carton of groceries, and a miscellaneous assortment of spades and jacks and chains that seldom left the truck. He drove down the long tree-shaded main street, broad as Whitehall and lined with wooden stores and bungalows widely spaced, and stopped at the post office.

He was a lad of twenty-two with a broad, guileless face, with yellow hair and blue eyes, and a fair, bronzed skin. He thought and moved rather slowly; if you disliked the Victorian countryside you would have said that he looked rather like a sheep, one of the sheep he spent his life tending. His father had escaped from country life to Melbourne at an early age and had become a solicitor; Tim Archer had been sent to Melbourne Grammar School. In turn, he had escaped from city life when he was seventeen, and he had gone to learn the business of sheep upon a station at Wodonga in the north part of the state. Now he was working for Jack Dorman on a property called Leonora, twelve miles out from Banbury, and near a place called Merrijig. Leonora was hardly to be classed as a sheep station, being only eighteen hundred acres, and Merrijig was hardly to be classed as a place, being only a school and a little wooden pub and a bridge over the river. He had been at Leonora for three years, largely because he was in love in a slow, patient manner with the youngest daughter of the house, Angela Dorman. He did not see much of her because she was away at Melbourne University taking Social Studies. He wrote to her from time to time, simple, rather laboured letters about lambing and floods and bush fires and horses. She answered about one in three of these letters, because the country bored her stiff.

He got out of the utility, a big young man dressed in a check shirt open at the neck, a pair of soiled blue canvas working trousers stained and dirty from the saddle, and heavy country boots. He went into the post office and said to the girl at the counter, 'I'll take the letters for Leonora.' The mail delivery would not reach the station till late afternoon.

The girl said, 'Morning, Tim.' She handed him a bundle from the stacked table behind her. 'Going to the dance on Saturday?'

'I dunno,' he said. 'I haven't got a partner.'

'Go on,' she chaffed him. 'You don't need a partner. There'll be more girls there than men.'

'Where have all the girls sprung up from?'

'I don't know,' she said idly. 'There seem to be a lot of girls about the town just now. Mostly New Australians. They've got two new girls at the hospital–ward-maids. Lithuanians they are, I think.'

'I don't speak Lithuanian,' the young man said. 'Aussie's good enough for me–Aussie or English. Like cartridges for a twenty-two. The continental stuff's no good.' He shuffled through the letters, looking for the one that was not there. 'That all there are? Nothing for me?'

'Not unless it's there,' she said with a touch of sympathy. 'That's all there were for Leonora.'

'Okay.' He stood in silence for a moment while his mind changed topic. 'I'll have to see about the dance,' he said. 'I don't know that I'll be able to get in.'

'Come if you can,' she said. 'There's one or two Aussie girls'll be there, in among the New Australians.' He smiled slowly. 'They're having favours–paper caps, balloons, and all that.'

'I'll have to see what Jack says. He may be using the utility.' He turned to go. ''Bye.'

He went out and got into the utility and drove out of the town upon the road to Merrijig that led on to the lumber camps up at Lamirra in the forests of Mount Buller. It was October, and the spring sun was warm as he drove, but the grass was still bright green and the upland pastures were fresh and beautiful. There were wattle trees in flower still, great splashes of yellow colour on the darker background of the gum tree forests, and the gum trees themselves were touched with the reddish brown of the young shoots, making them look a little like an English wood in autumn. Tim Archer did not fully realize the beauty of the scene, the wide sunny pastures and the woods that merged into the blue mountains to the south and east, because this was where he lived and worked and scenery like that was normal to his life. He only knew that this was where he liked to be, far better than the town.

He was depressed as he drove out of town because he hadn't had a letter from Angela, as he had so often been depressed before. He was sufficiently intelligent to know that his chance of getting Angela was slender, because she liked town life and hated the country, while he was exactly the reverse. He comforted himself with the opinion that all girls were like that when they were young; they talked big about getting a job in Melbourne and doing interior decoration and going on a business trip to England, but in the end most of them came home and married and settled down in the district. He'd have to sit tight and let Angie get it out of her system, but it was going to be a long job, and the thought depressed him.

The property he worked on, Leonora, borders the road for about half a mile at Merrijig. From there the boundary of Leonora runs for a mile up the Delatite River, then up to the wooded foothills of Mount Buller, and then in a great sweep eastwards to the road again. It is a good, well-watered property of eighteen hundred acres carrying two sheep to the acre with some beef cattle. The homestead lies half a mile from the road, a small bungalow built of weatherboard with an iron roof and with verandas on three sides; there is a stockyard near the homestead and a few outbuildings. It is reached from the road by a rough, pot-holed track across the paddocks with three gates to open. Jack Dorman had occupied the property for eighteen years, first as manager and later as the owner by the courtesy of the Bank of New South Wales.

He was sitting on his horse that morning by the road gate waiting for Tim

Archer to come out of town in the utility. The horse was a rough pony, an unkempt, long-haired bay that lived out in the paddock and was never under cover, and never groomed, and seldom fed. His property was about three miles long and a mile wide, and though it was possible to drive over most of it in the utility, Jack Dorman preferred to ride over it on horseback every morning. As Tim came over the crest of a small hill he saw his boss sitting waiting for him at the road gate, and he wondered a little; the rider moved the pony up to the road gate and hooked it open for the car to enter. Tim stopped the car just inside the gate, and Dorman reined up alongside.

'Get the letters?' he enquired.

'I got them here, Mr Dorman,' the lad said, and handed up the bundle from the seat behind him.

Dorman took them, and sat on his horse looking through the envelopes. He was fifty-eight years old, but he had never strained his eyes with a great deal of reading, and he could still read small print without glasses. He took one letter from the bundle and put it in the breast pocket of his khaki shirt; on that warm day he wore no coat. He gave the rest of the letters back to Tim Archer, who wondered what the one letter was about.

'Take them into the house,' his boss said. 'Get all the rest of the stuff?'

'Not the engine oil. They hadn't got any drums, not till next week's delivery. They said I could have quart cans, but it costs more that way. I went along to the garage and had the sump checked, but she only took a pint. She's in good nick.'

'Don't ever go buying oil less than five gallons a time,' the rider said. 'Daylight robbery. There's another thing you want to watch. They'll try to kid you that you want an oil change every thousand miles, and that's a quid or so. Two thousand miles is what it says in the book. My word, you want to watch those jokers.'

'I never let them change the oil unless you say.'

'That's right. Go down and give Mario a hand out with the crutching. I'm going up to the top end.'

The lad drove on, and Jack Dorman walked his pony uphill across his pastures, heading for the highest part, where the uncleared virgin bush bordered his land on the slope of the mountain. There were no sheep in the paddocks that he crossed because most of them were in the paddocks nearer to the homestead, where Mario Ritti, his Italian man, was skilfully heaving each sheep up on to a waist-high board upon its back, holding it with shoulders and elbow while he sheared the soiled wool from its tail, gave it a dab of disinfectant, and put it on the ground again. It was heavy work, but he could do them at the rate of about one a minute or more quickly with Tim Archer helping him, but even so it would take a fortnight to work the crutching through.

Dorman rode across the top paddock to where a rocky outcrop and a few gum trees made a place to sit in the shade, a place from which you could look out over the whole valley of the Delatite. He could see most of his property from there, and the winding river with the road bridge over it, and the Hunt Club Hotel, and the track from the road to the homestead through his paddocks, and the homestead itself, small, red-roofed, and insignificant in the great panorama. He sat upon his horse, contented, looking out over all this for a minute; then he dismounted and tethered the pony to the fence by the reins. He crossed to the rocky outcrop and sat down in the shade, and opened his letter.

It was a note of account from his agent in Melbourne, a long typescript sheet covered with figures which itemized the lot numbers of the wool sold for him at auction and the price paid for each lot. A cheque was enclosed in settlement for twenty-two thousand one hundred and seventy-eight pounds, eight shillings and twopence.

He had known beforehand approximately what the sum would be, from watching the sales in the newspaper. Last year's wool cheque had been over ten thousand pounds, and the year before that about seven thousand, figures which had seemed amazing to him in their day. Those cheques, however, had meant little to him in terms of spending money; they had gone straight into the bank in reduction of the loans upon his property and stock. They had purchased his security, but nothing tangible. This time, however, it was different; this twenty-two thousand pounds was his own money, to spend or save exactly as he wished, after tax was paid.

Jack Dorman had come to Leonora as manager in 1930, when times were bad and wool was less than two shillings a pound. Before that he had been manager of stations in Gippsland and in the Benalla district, and before that again, for six years after the first war, he had been a traveller in agricultural machinery and fertilizers. In 1932 his wife's father had died at his English country home at Sutton Bassett, near Wantage, and with her legacy the Dormans had managed to buy Leonora with the very maximum assistance from the bank. Since then they had been deep in debt, head over ears in it. For the first four years it had been touch and go whether they would not go bankrupt, whether the bank would not have to foreclose on an unprofitable business and sell the land to liquidate the increasing overdraft. The demand for wool for uniforms had saved them as rearmament got under way and wool prices began to rise, and for the last twelve years Jack Dorman had been paying off the debt. On paper he had been gradually becoming a wealthy man, but this was hidden deep in the accountancy. The land and the stock on it had been gradually becoming his and not the bank's, but he still rose at dawn each day and got his two hired hands to work at the same time, and still Jane Dorman worked from dawn to dusk in the old-fashioned kitchen of the homestead, rearing her four children and cooking all the meals for the three men, and eating with them at the long kitchen table. In all those years she had no help in the house, and she had only been away from Leonora three times for a week's holiday. They had had no electricity till two years previously, when Dorman had put in a little Diesel plant. Now she was tired and old and grey at fifty-three, and the children were all out in the world except Angela, and they were rich.

Jack Dorman sat turning the wool cheque over in his hands, twenty-two thousand one hundred and seventy-eight pounds, eight shillings and twopence. Last year's cheque had virtually cleared the overdraft. His balance fluctuated a good deal, but, broadly speaking, if he had died last year the whole of the money from the sale of land and stock would have gone to his heirs, a matter of eighty or ninety thousand pounds at the inflated prices of the time. It was an academic figure to him, because neither he nor Jane would have wanted to leave Leonora; they had grown into the place and it had become a part of them. The eighty thousand pounds was quite unreal to them; if it was there at all it only concerned the children, and they might not touch a quarter of it if the bad times came again. All that concerned Jack Dorman and his wife was that last year's cheque had made them safe; however much wool slumped they could never be turned out of Leonora. They could sleep without bad dreams of wandering bankrupt with no home, nightmares that had plagued them through their thirty-two years of married life.

Jack Dorman folded the wool cheque and put it in his shirt pocket again; this one was his own. He sat on in the shade for a few minutes looking out over his property, a grey-haired, heavy man of fifty-eight, humming a little tune. He had little musical appreciation but he liked the lighter programmes on the radio; he was normally five years behind the times with the tunes that pleased him and stayed in his memory. If Jane had heard him she would have known that her stout, ageing husband was very happy.

> I don't want her, you can have her,
> She's too fat for me,
> She's too fat for me,
> Oh, she's too fat for me . . .

Twenty-two thousand pounds and a bit, and the fat lambs, and the bullocks – say twenty-six thousand pounds in all. Expenses, and income tax. . . . He drew a stub of pencil from his pocket and began figuring on the back of the wool cheque envelope. He'd whoop up his expenses this year, my word he would! He'd have to see his accountant to find out what he could get away with. He ought to have a new utility, a Mercury or an Armstrong Siddeley even. A station like this needed a Land Rover. He'd keep the Chev for the boys to use. Buildings – Mario ought to have a house and get his girl out from Italy; he'd be more settled then. Could a weatherboard shack go on the one year, or would they make him do it on depreciation? If it went on the one year the tax would pay three-quarters of the cost . . .

> I go dizzy –
> I go dumbo –
> When I'm dancing,
> With my jum – jum – jumbo . . .

Say twenty thousand for tax. He figured with his pencil. He'd have about seven thousand left after paying tax. Seven thousand pounds of his own money to spend or save that year, and the price of wool still holding nicely. He was in the money, for the first time in his life.

There must be something that the station needed, besides a Land Rover, and a new utility and a house for Mario. . . .

Presently he got on to his horse again and rode down to the homestead, humming his little tune. In the yard he unsaddled and hung saddle and bridle on a rail of the hay-barn, gave the pony a slap behind and turned it into the house paddock. Then he went into the kitchen and sat down at the long table. Jane was roasting a saddle of mutton for dinner as she had cooked mutton most days of her married life; they ate a sheep in about ten days.

'Want a cup of tea?' she asked.

'I don't mind,' he said, and she poured him one out from the teapot on the table. And then he told her, 'Got the wool cheque.'

'How much?' she asked idly.

'Little over twenty-two thousand,' he told her.

She was only mildly interested. 'That's a bit more than last year, isn't it?'

'Aye.'

She said, 'Like to peel these potatoes for me, if you're doing nothing?'

'We don't have to do anything,' he told her. 'Not with a wool cheque like that.' But he got up and began to peel them at the sink. 'You ought to have a girl to help you, make her do things like this.'

'Where do you think I'd get the girl from?' And then she asked, 'How much would we have of that to spend, after paying tax and expenses?'

'About seven thousand, near as I can figure it.' He scraped away at the potatoes. 'It's all ours this time. What do you want out of it?'

She stared around the kitchen. 'I want a Memory Tickler like Bertha Harrison's got, one of those things you hang upon the wall, with a long list of things to get in town, and tabs to turn over to remind you. She got hers in Melbourne, at McEwens.'

'That's only about five bob's worth,' he complained.

'I know, but I want it. Could we have a new stove, Jack? This one's about worn out, and the top plate's cracked.'

'We'd better have an Aga, or an Esse.'

'You've got to have coke for those,' she said. 'A wood stove's best out here, and only about a tenth the money. Another one like this would be all right.'

He said, 'Aw, look, Jane, we've got money to spend now.'

The anxious years had bitten deep into her. 'No need to chuck it away, though,' she said.

'We wouldn't be chucking it away. It'ld be cooler in the kitchen with a stove like that. It's time we spent a bit of money, anyway; my word, we haven't had a holiday for years. What do you say if we go down to Melbourne for a week and do a bit of shopping, stay at the Windsor and see some theatres? I've got a lot of things I'd like to do down there.'

'I've not got any clothes for staying in a place like that,' she said.

'We'll get some,' he replied. 'After all, we've got seven thousand pounds to spend.'

'We won't have long, if you go on like this.'

'We don't want to have it long. If we hang on to the money it'll only go to the kids after our time, and they'll have enough to spoil them, anyhow. I don't hold with leaving kids a lot of money. We never had any, and we got through.'

She poured herself a cup of tea and he left the sink and came and sat at the table with her. 'I'd like to go to Melbourne for a week,' she said thoughtfully, 'if we've really got the money. When was it we went down there last?'

'Two years ago,' he said. 'When we took Angie to the University.'

'Is it as long as that? Well, I suppose it would be. I wouldn't want to go before the Show.' The Banbury Show was in the middle of December; she always competed in the Flower section and in the Home-Made Cakes, and usually won a prize in both. 'And then there's Christmas,' she said. 'Everybody's on holiday till the middle of January.'

He nodded. 'Suppose we booked a room for a week about the middle of January?'

She smiled. 'I'd like that, Jack. Give me time to get some clothes made up. I couldn't go to the Windsor with what I've got now.'

He pulled a packet of cigarettes out of his pocket and passed it across to her; she took one and he lit it for her, and for a while they sat smoking in silence. 'We could do a lot of things,' he said. 'We could make that trip home.'

In their hard early married life a trip home to England had been her great desire, always to be frustrated by their circumstances. She was English, the daughter of an admiral, brought up in all the comfort and security of a small country house before the first war, and sent to a good school. In 1917 she had joined the W.A.A.C.s with a commission as was proper for the daughter of a senior naval officer, and in 1918 she had shocked her parents by falling in love with an Australian, a lieutenant in the first A.I.F. Her family never understood Jack Dorman and did everything they could to dissuade her from marrying him, and succeeded in preventing her from doing so till she was twenty-one, in 1919; she married him on her birthday. He was a ranker officer, for one thing, which in those days damned him from the start; he had been an N.C.O. in Gallipoli, and in France for nearly three years, and he had only recently been commissioned. He was an unpleasantly tough young man, addicted to a strange, un-English slang, and he never pulled up men for not saluting him because he didn't believe in saluting, and said so. He used to have meals with private soldiers in cafés and in restaurants, and even drink with them; he had no idea of discipline at all. All he could do, with others like him, was to win battles.

Thirty-two years had passed since those bad months of 1918, but Jane could still remember the unpleasantness as she had rebelled against her family. She was too young, too immature to be able to stand up and state her conviction that there was solid stuff in this young man, the substance for a happy and enduring marriage; she felt that very strongly, but she could never get it out in words. She could remember as if it were yesterday her father's frigid politeness to this uncouth young officer that she had brought into the house, and his blistering contempt for him in their private talks, and her mother's futile assurances that 'Daddy knows best'. She had married Jack Dorman in February 1919 in Paddington a week before sailing with him to Australia, and her parents had come to the wedding, but only just. Nobody else came except one old school friend, and Aunt Ethel.

Aunt Ethel was her father's sister, Mrs Trehearn, married to Geoffrey Trehearn, a Commissioner in the Indian Police, at that time stationed in Moulmein. Aunt Ethel had come home with her two children in 1916 to put them to school in England, and she was still in England waiting for a passage back to Burma. Aunt Ethel, alone of all Jane's relations, had stood up for her and had told the family that she was making a wise choice, and she had cut little ice with her brother Tom; indeed, in some ways she had made matters worse. Admiral Sir Thomas Foxley had little regard for the sagacity of women, and to mention the woman's vote to him in those far-off days was as a red flag to a bull.

All these things passed through Jane Dorman's mind as she sat sipping her tea in the kitchen of her homestead thirty-three years later. Seven thousand pounds to spend after paying tax, all earned in one year and earned honestly; more money than her father had ever dreamed of earning, or any of her family. Extraordinary to think of, and extraordinary that after their hard life the money should mean so little to them. Jack didn't quite know what to do with it, so much was evident, and certainly she didn't.

'I don't know about going home,' she said at last. 'I don't believe I'd know anybody there now except Aunt Ethel, and I don't suppose I'd recognize *her* now. There was a letter from her in the post today, by the way. I'd like to see the old thing again before she dies, but she's about the only one. She must be getting on for eighty now.'

'Wouldn't you like to go and see your old home?' he suggested. He knew

how much her mind had turned to that small country house when first she had
come to Australia.

She shook her head. 'Not now that it's a school. It'ld be all different. I'd
rather remember it as it used to be.' Her father had kept two gardeners and a
groom, and three servants in the house; she knew that nothing would now
resemble the gracious, easy routine of the home that she had lived in as a child.

He did not press her; if she didn't want to go to England that was all right
with him. He had only memories of a cold, unfriendly place himself, where he
had been ill at ease and that he secretly disliked. He would have liked very much
to go back to Gallipoli again, and to France and Italy–it would be interesting to
see those. His mind turned to his Italian hired man. 'There's another thing,' he
said. 'About Mario. He's got that girl of his in this town that he comes from. I
don't know how much he's got saved up now, but it might be a good thing if we
could help him with her fare. It wouldn't be so much, and we might be able to
charge it up against the tax. After all, it's all connected with the station.'

Mario Ritti was a laughing man of about twenty-eight, tall and well built,
with dark curly hair, a swarthy complexion, and a flashing eye; a peril to all the
young girls in the neighbourhood. He had been taken prisoner by the Eighth
Army at Bardia in 1942, and he had spent two years in England as a prisoner of
war, working on a farm in Cumberland where he had learned about sheep.
After the war he had got back to his own place. Chieti, a hill town in the Abruzzi
mountains near the Adriatic coast where his parents scratched a bare living
from a tiny patch of rather barren land. In Italy there were far more people than
the land could support, and Mario had put his name down almost at once for a
free immigrant passage to Australia. He had worked as a labourer and as a
waiter in a hotel in Pescara and as a house-painter till his turn came round upon
the quota three years later and he could leave for an emptier country. By the
terms of his free passage he had to work for two years as directed by the
Department of Immigration in Australia, after which he would be free to
choose his work like any other man. Jack Dorman had got him from the
Department, and was very pleased with him, and he was anxious not to lose him
at the end of the two years.

'I was thinking that we might build on to the shearer's place,' he said.
'Extend that on a bit towards the windmill and make a little place of three
rooms there. Then if we got his girl out for him he'd be settled, and the girl
could help you in the house.'

Jane laughed shortly. 'Fat lot of help she'd be, a girl who couldn't speak a
word of English having babies every year. I'd be helping her, not her helping
me. Still, if she could cook the dinner now and then, I wouldn't say no.' She sat
for a moment in thought. 'How much is her passage going to cost, and how
much has he got saved up?'

'He sends money back to Italy, to his parents,' Jack said. 'He was sending
home five pounds a week at one time, so he can't have very much. I suppose the
passage would be about fifty quid. We'd better pay that, and let him spend
what he's got saved on furniture.'

'Find out how much he's got,' his wife said. 'He ought to put in everything
he's got if we're going to do all that for him.'

'That's right.' He pushed his chair back from the table. 'Like to drive into
town this afternoon and put this cheque into the bank?'

She smiled; he was still very young at times. 'Don't you trust the postman?'

'No,' he said. 'Not with twenty-two thousand pounds. A thing like that ought to be registered.' he paused. 'We could take a drive around,' he said. 'Look in on George and Ann for tea, at Buttercup.'

'Giving up work?' she asked.

'That's right,' he said. 'Just for today.'

'Who's going to get tea here for the boys if we go gallivanting off to Buttercup?'

'They can have cold tonight,' he said.

'All right.' She reached behind her for an envelope upon the table. 'Want to read Aunt Ethel's letter?'

'Anything new in it?'

'Not really,' she said slowly. 'You'd better read it, though.'

She tossed it across to him; he unfolded it and began to read. Jane got up and glanced at the clock and put the saucepan of potatoes on to boil, and put a couple more logs into the stove. Then she sat down again and picked up the pages of the letter as Jack laid them down, and read them through again herself.

It was addressed from Maymyo, Ladysmith Avenue, Ealing, a suburb to the west of London that Jane had never seen. Till recently her old aunt had always written by air mail but lately the letters had been coming by sea mail, perhaps because there was now little urgency in any of them. Her handwriting was very bent and crabbed; at one time she had written legibly, but in the last year or two the writing had got worse and worse. The letter ran,

My dear Child,

Another of your lovely parcels came today all candied peel and currants and sultanas and glacé cherries such lovely things that we do so enjoy getting just like pre-war when you could buy everything like that in the shops without any of these stupid little bits of paper and coupons and things. I get so impatient sometimes when I go to buy the rations which mean I must be getting old, seventy-nine next month my dear but I don't feel like it it was rather a blow when Aggie died but I have quite got over that now and settled down again and last Friday I went out to bridge with Mrs Morrison because it's three months now and I always say three months mourning is enough for anyone. I'm afraid this is going to be a very long winter I do envy you your winter in our summer because it is quite cold already and now Mr Attlee says there isn't any coal because he's sold it all to America or Jugoslavia or somewhere so there won't be any for us and now the miners and the railwaymen all want more money if only dear Winston was back at No. 10 but everybody says he will be soon.

Jane turned the pages, glancing over her old aunt's ramblings that she had already deciphered once and that were clearly giving Jack some difficulty. Aggie was Mrs Agatha Harding who had shared the house at Ealing with her aunt; she was the widow of any army officer. Now she was dead, Jane supposed that her old aunt must be living alone, although she did not say so. The letter rambled on,

Jennifer came down to spend the day with me one Sunday in August and she is coming again soon she has grown into such a pretty girl reddish hair and our family nose twenty-four this year she ought to have been presented at Court long ago but everything seems to be so different now and she works in an office at Blackheath the Ministry of Pensions I think. I asked her if there was a young man and she said no but I expect there is one all the same my dear I hope he's as nice a one as Jack I often think of that time when you were so naughty and ran off and married him and Tom was so angry and how right you were only I wish you didn't have to live so far away.

Jane wished she didn't live so far away as she read that. It might be worth

while making the long journey back to England just to see this kind old lady
again, who still thought of her as a child.

It seems so funny to think of you over fifty and with all your children out in the world and so
prosperous with wool my dear I am glad for you. Our Government are so stupid about wool and
everything I went the other day to Sayers to buy a warm vest for the winter but my dear the price
was shocking even utility grade and the girl said it was all due to bulk buying of wool and the
Socialist Government so I told her to tell Mr Attlee he could keep it and I'd go on with what I've got
my dear I do hope things are cheaper with you than they are here but I suppose you can always spin
your own wool on the station and weave it can't you my grandmother always did that better than
this horrible bulk buying that makes everything so dear. My dear, thank you again for all your
lovely parcels and your letters write again soon and all my love.

Your affectionate Aunt,
ETHEL

'Keeps it up, doesn't she?' said Jack Dorman.
'Yes,' said Jane, 'she keeps it up. I don't like the thought of her living alone
though, at her age.'
'That's since this Aggie died?'
Jane nodded. 'It looks as if she's living by herself now, quite alone. I wish we
were nearer.'
He turned the pages of the letter back. 'Who's this Jennifer she speaks
about?'
'That's Jennifer Morton, her granddaughter. Her daughter Lucy married
Edward Morton—the one that's a doctor in Leicester.'
'Oh.' He did not know where Leicester was, nor did he greatly care. 'This
girl Jennifer works in London, does she?'
Jane nodded. 'Just outside London, I think. Blackheath.'
'Well, can't she go and live with the old girl?'
'I don't know,' said Jane. 'I don't suppose there's much that we can do about
it, anyway.'
Jack Dorman went out into the yard, and Jane began to lay the kitchen table
for the midday dinner. She was vaguely unhappy and uneasy; there was a
menace in all the news from England now, both in the letters from her old aunt
and in the newspapers. The most extraordinary things seemed to be going on
there, and for no reason at all. In all her life, and it had been a hard life at times,
she had never been short of all the meat that she could eat, or practically any
other sort of food or fruit that she desired. As a child she could remember the
great joints upon her father's table at Sutton Bassett, the kidneys and bacon for
breakfast with the cold ham on the sideboard, the thick cream on the table, the
unlimited butter. These things were as normal to her as the sun or the wind;
even in the most anxious times of their early married life in Gippsland they had
had those things as a matter of course, and never thought about them. If she
didn't use them now so much it was because she was older and felt better on a
sparing diet, but it was almost inconceivable to her that they should not be
there for those who wanted them.
It was the same with coal; in all her life she had never had to think about
economizing with fuel. From the blazing fireplaces and kitchen range of Sutton
Bassett she had gone to the Australian countryside, milder in climate, where
everybody cooked and warmed themselves with wood fires. Even in their
hardest times there had never been any question of unlimited wood for fuel.
Indeed, at Merrijig with the hot sun and the high rainfall the difficulty was to

keep the forest from encroaching on the paddocks; if you left a corner ungrazed for three years the bush would be five feet high all over it; in ten it would have merged back into forest. Even in the city you ordered a ton of wood as naturally as a pound of butter or a sirloin of beef.

Whatever sort of way could Aunt Ethel be living in when she could not afford a warm vest for the winter? Why *a* warm vest—why not three or four? She must do something about the washing. Was clothing rationed still? She seemed to remember that clothes rationing had been removed in England. She stopped laying the table and unfolded the letter and read the passage over again, a little frown of perplexity upon her forehead. There wasn't anything about rationing; she hadn't got the vest because it was expensive. How foolish of her; old people had to have warm clothes, especially in England in the winter. It was true that the price of woollen garments was going up even in Australia by leaps and bounds, but Aunt Ethel couldn't possibly be as hard up as that. The Foxleys had always had plenty of money. Perhaps she was going a bit senile.

She went and rang the dinner bell outside the flyscreen door, rather depressed.

The men came back to the homestead for dinner; she heard Tim and Mario washing at the basin under the tank-stand in the yard, and she began to dish up. They came in presently with Jack and sat down at the table; she carved half a pound of meat for each of them and heaped the plates high with vegetables; she gave Jack rather less and herself much less. A suet jam roll followed the meat, and cups of tea. Relaxed and smoking at the end of the meal, Tim Archer said, 'Would you be using the utility Saturday evening, Mr Dorman? There's the Red Cross dance.'

'I dunno.' He turned to Jane. 'Want to go to the dance on Saturday?'

It was a suggestion that had not been made to her for seven or eight years and it came strangely from Jack now, but everything was strange on this day of the wool cheque. She laughed shortly. 'I don't want to go to any dance,' she said. 'My dancing days are done, but let the boys go if they want to.'

'You going, Mario?'

The dark, curly-haired young man looked up with laughing eyes. 'Si, Mr Dorman.'

'Go on,' his boss grumbled. 'Talk English, like a Christian. You can if you want to.'

The young man grinned more broadly. 'Yes,' he said. 'I like to go ver' much. I like dance much.'

'I bet you do. . . .' He turned to Tim. 'If you go you've got to look after him,' he said. 'Don't let him get in any trouble, or get girls in any trouble, either.' There was some prejudice against the New Australians in the district, well founded in part, and there had been a row over Mario once before at the first dance that he attended and before he was accustomed to the social climate of Australia.

'I'll keep an eye on him, Mr Dorman.'

'All right, you can take the Chev.' He paused. 'Did you get the tickets?'

'Not yet. Thought I'd better wait and see about the ute.'

'I'll be going down to Banbury after dinner, in about an hour. I'll get them if you give me the money.'

'Thanks, Mr Dorman.' Tim hesitated. 'Would you be going by the post office?'

'I could.'

'Would you look in and tell Elsie Peters I'll be coming to the dance with Mario?'

Jack nodded. 'I'll tell her.'

Presently they got up from the table, Tim to unload the utility, Jack Dorman to go into his office, and Mario to help Jane to clear the table and wash up. A quarter of an hour later Jack Dorman, going out on the veranda, saw Mario and Tim rolling the drum of Diesel oil down from the truck on timbers to the ground. He waited till the drum was on the ground, and then said, 'Hey, Mario—come over here a minute.' They crossed to the paddock rail and stood together there in the warm sunlight.

'Say, Mario,' he said. 'I've been thinking about that girl you've got, back in Italy. You still want to get her out here to Australia?'

'Yes, Mr Dorman. I wanta ver' much. I love Lucia. We marry when she come here.'

'That's her name, is it? Lucia?'

'Yes. Lucia Tereno she is called.'

'Lucia Tereno. She lives in this town that you come from, Chieti?'

'She is from Orvieto, close to Chieti, signore.'

'Are you saving up to get her out here?'

'Si, signore.'

'How much does the ticket cost?'

'Fifty-eight pounds.'

'How much have you got saved towards it?'

'Twenty-seven pounds. I send—send money to mio padre.'

'Send money to your father, do you?'

'Yes, Mr Dorman. Evecchio.'

'What's that?'

'He—old man. Madre old also.'

The grazier stood in silence for a minute, thinking this over. At last he said, 'Look, Mario. I was thinking of building a bit of a house for you and Lucia, 'n paying for her ticket. You could spend your twenty-seven quid on furniture for it, 'n make the rest in the evenings. If I do that, will you stay with me two years after your time's up, 'n not go off to someone else for better money?'

Only about half of that got through. They discussed it for a little, the Italian gradually breaking into rapture as the proposal became clear. 'I pay her ticket and give you a three-room house on the end of the shearers' quarters. You stay with me till September 1953 at the money you get now, plus the award rises. You get all the meat you want off the station at threepence a pound, and vegetables from the garden. Capito?'

'Si, signore.'

'Talk English, you great bastard. You stay with me till September 1953 if I do this for you. Is that okay?'

'Okay, Mr Dorman. I thank you ver', ver' much.'

'You've been working well, Mario. You go on the way you're going and you'll be right. Okay, then—that's a deal. What do you want to do now—send Lucia the money for her passage right away?'

'Yes, Mr Dorman. Lucia—she very happy when she gets letter.'

'Aw, look then, Mario. You go and write her a letter in your own bloody language, 'n tell her to come out 'n marry you, 'n you're sending her the money for the ticket. You go and write that now. I'll take it into town with me this afternoon and put the money order in it, fifty-eight pounds, 'n send it off by air mail.' He got that through at the second attempt.

'Thank you ver', ver' much, Mr Dorman. I go now to write Lucia.' He went off urgently to his bunkroom.

Dorman went into the house again to change for his journey into town; he had a dark tweed suit that he wore on these occasions, and a purple tie with black stripes on it. He sat in the kitchen polishing his town shoes while Jane changed, and presently he went out into the yard to get the utility. By the car, Mario came up to him with an envelope in his hand.

'For Lucia,' he said. 'I no have stamp. Will you fix stamp on for me, please? For air mail?'

'Okay. You've told her in the letter that there's a money order going in it, fifty-eight pounds?'

'I have said that, Mr Dorman. In Italian I have said that to Lucia, and now she is to come, ver' quick.'

'I bet you've said that she's to come ver' quick, you bastard. Mind and keep your nose clean till she comes. I'll see about the timber for your house when I'm in town.'

'I thank you ver', ver' much, Mr Dorman.'

'Okay. Get down and go on with that crutching.'

He drove into the town that afternoon with Jane by his side; they parked the utility outside the bank and went in together while she cashed a cheque. She went out first and went on to the dressmaker, and Jack went into the bank manager's office to see about the draft for fifty-eight pounds payable to Lucia Tereno at Chieti, Italy. At the conclusion of that business he produced his wool cheque for the credit of his account.

The manager took it and glanced at it with an expressionless face; for the last week he had been receiving one or two like it every day. 'I'll give you the receipt slip outside, Mr Dorman,' he said. 'What do you want done with it? All into the current account?'

'That's right.'

'If you think of investing any of it, I could write to our investments section at head office and get up a few suggestions. It's a pity to see a sum like that lying idle.'

'I'll think it over,' said Dorman. 'I'm going down to Melbourne in a month or two. A good bit of it'll go in tax, and there's one or two things wanted on the station.'

The manager smiled faintly; he knew that one, too. 'I expect there are,' he said. 'Well, let me know if I can do anything.'

Dorman left the bank and went to the post office; he bought stamps and an air mail sticker for Mario's letter and handed it to Elsie Peters for the post. 'I was to tell you that Tim Archer's coming to the Red Cross dance, with Mario,' he said.

'Goody,' she replied. 'He was in this morning, but he didn't know then if he'd be able to get in to it.'

'Aye, they can have the car. If that Mario gets into any trouble they won't have it again. I said I'd get the tickets for them. Where would I do that?'

'Mrs Hayward, up by Marshall's. She's selling them. I'll get them for you if you like to give me the money, Mr Dorman, and send them out with the mail.'

He handed her a note from his wallet. 'Thanks. Anything more happened about you going home?'

She nodded, with eyes shining. 'I've got a passage booked on the *Orontes,* fifth of May. It's terribly exciting, I just can't wait. Dad did well out of the wool this year.'

'Fine,' he said. 'What part of England are you going to?'

'Ma's people all live in a place called Nottingham,' she said. 'That's in the middle somewhere, I think. I'm going to stay with them at first, but after that I want to get a job in London.'

'London's all right,' he said. 'I was in England with the first A.I.F. and I don't suppose it's altered much. From what I hear they don't get much to eat these days. We'll have to send you food parcels.'

She laughed. 'That's what Ma says. But I think it's all right. People who've been there say there's a lot of nonsense talked about food being short. It's not as bad as they make out.'

'I never heard of anyone send back a food parcel, all the same,' he observed.

'I don't think they've got as much as all that,' she said thoughtfully. 'I mean, they do like to get parcels still. I'm going to take a lot of tins with me.' She paused. 'It's going to be a beaut trip,' she said thoughtfully. 'I just can't wait till May.'

Jack Dorman went out of the post office and got into the car, and went to see the builder. He stayed with him some time talking about the three-roomed house for Mario, and arranged for him to come and measure up for the timber and weatherboarding required. This all took a little time, and by the time he got back to the dressmakers to pick up Jane she was ready for him. They did a little more shopping together, put the parcels on the ledge behind the driving seat, and drove out on the road to Buttercup.

George and Ann Pearson lived on rather a smaller property of about fifteen hundred acres; they had no river and they got the water for their stock from dams bulldozed or scooped out to form catchment pools at strategic points upon the land. They were younger than the Dormans, and they still had a young family. The youngest child was Judith, only eight years old, but old enough to catch and saddle her own pony every morning and ride six miles to school with her satchel on her back. Because this was the normal way of going to school the schoolhouse was provided with a paddock; the children rode in and unsaddled, hung their saddles and bridles on the fence, and went in to their lessons. After school they caught their ponies, the schoolmistress helping them if there were any difficulty, saddled up, and rode six miles home again.

George Pearson had rigged up a diving-board and a pair of steps to turn his largest dam into a swimming-pool, and the children were bathing in it as the Dormans drove by. They had evidently brought friends on their way back from school, because three ponies grazed beside the dam with saddles on their backs. Weeping willows seventy feet high grew round the pool, and half a dozen little bodies flashed and splashed with shrill cries from the diving-board in the bright sun.

'I'd have thought it was too cold for bathing still,' Jane observed. 'It's only October.'

'It's warm in the sun,' Jack said. 'It was up to eighty, dinner-time.'

'It's cold in the water, though,' she replied. 'George told me that it's twelve feet deep, that dam. It'll be cold just down below the surface.'

'They don't mind,' he said. He took his eyes from the track and looked again at the dam. 'I often wish we'd had a dam,' he said. 'Those kids, they get a lot of fun out of that.'

They drove on to the homestead and parked in the grassy yard. Ann Pearson came out to meet them; she was Australian born and spoke with a marked Australian accent, in contrast to her husband, who had come out as a farmer's son in 1930 and still retained a trace of Somerset in his speech. 'Didn't you see George?' she asked after the first greetings. 'He went down to the dam, with the children.'

'We didn't stop,' said Jane. 'He's probably down there.'

'Just dropped in to see if George had got his wool cheque,' Jack Dorman said, grinning.

Ann said, 'Oh, my word.' There seemed no need for any further comment.

Jack turned to Jane and said, 'It's all right. They've got enough money to give us tea.'

'Give tea to everybody in the shire,' said Ann. 'How long's it going on for, Jack? I tell you, we get sort of frightened sometimes. It can't go on like this, can it?'

'It'll be down next year,' Jack Dorman said. 'Not real low, but down to something reasonable, I'd say. It can blow a blizzard after that, for all I care.'

They got out of the car and went with her to the wide veranda, and sat down in deck-chairs. 'That's what George thinks too. I'd be quite glad if it went down a bit. It doesn't seem right, somehow. It's not good for the children, either, to see money come so easy.'

She told them that they were sailing for England in April on the P. and O. *Strathmore*; the children were going to stay with their grandmother at Nagambie. 'George booked the cabin six months ago,' she said, 'but I never really thought it'ld come off. Still, now we're going, definitely. His dad and mum, they're still alive at this place Shepton Mallet where he was brought up. I never thought I'd meet them, but now it looks as if I shall.'

She turned to Jane with a question that had been worrying her a good deal. 'When you go on those P. and O. boats travelling first-class,' she said, 'what do you wear at night? Is it a low evening dress every night, or is that just for dances?'

George Pearson came back presently with six hungry children, and they all sat down to tea at the long table in the kitchen, eleven of them, counting the hired man, a Pole from Slonim, who spoke little English. They ate the best part of two joints of cold roast mutton with a great dish of potatoes and thought nothing of it, topping up with bread and jam and two plum cakes, and many cups of tea. Then the men went out into the yard and put the three visiting children on their ponies and saw them off so that they would be home by nightfall, which comes early in Australia.

The two graziers talked quietly for a time on the veranda while their wives washed up indoors. 'Going home in April, so Ann told us,' Dorman said.

'Aye.' George smoked for a few minutes in silence. 'See the old folks once more, anyway. I don't know what it's going to be like there, now.'

'I asked Jane if she'd like to go back home, but she didn't want to. She said it'ld all be different.'

'Aye. I want to see my brother, see if he won't come out. There's still land going if you look around a bit.'

'Ninety pounds an acre.' They both smiled. 'Forty-five or fifty, if you look around,' said George. 'He'd get that for the land he's got at home.'

'All right while the wool keeps up.'

'I want to see what things are like at home,' George Pearson said. 'They may not be so bad as what you read.'

'They don't have to be,' said Dorman. 'I see where it says in the paper that you can't have a new car if you've had one since the war, and now they're selling squirrels in the butchers' shops. What's a squirrel like to look at? Is it like a possum?'

'Smaller than that,' said George. 'More the size of a rat. It's a clean feeder, though; I suppose you could eat squirrel. Gypsies used to eat them, where I come from.'

There was a slow, bewildered silence. 'I'd not know what the world was coming to, if I'd to eat a thing like that. . . .'

Everything foreign in the newspapers was puzzling to them, these days. The murders and the pictures of the bathing girls were solid, homely matters that they could understand, but the implacable hostility of the Russians was an enigma. Fortunately they were seven or eight thousand miles away, and so it didn't matter very much. Korea and the Chinese provided another puzzle; Australian boys were fighting there for no very clear reason except that a meeting of the United Nations nine thousand miles from Buttercup had said they should. Mr Menzies made a speech sometimes and told them that all this was terribly important to Australians, and failed to convince them. The only thing from all these distant places that really touched the graziers was the food shortage in England; they did not understand why that should be, but they sent food parcels copiously to their relations at home, and puzzled over their predicament. They could not understand why English people would not come to this good country that had treated them so well.

The two wives came out and joined their men on the veranda. Jane said, 'Ann's been telling me about Peter Loring falling off his horse, Jack. Did you hear about that?'

Her husband shook his head. 'That one of the Loring boys, from Balaclava?'

She nodded. 'The little one—eleven or twelve years old. You tell him, Ann.'

Ann Pearson said, 'It was a funny thing, Jack. I had to go into town early on Friday, about nine o'clock. Well, I got just up to the main road—I was all alone in the utility, and there was a pony, with a saddle on and bridle, grazing by the side of the road, and there was Peter Loring with blood all over him from scratches, sitting on the grass. So of course I stopped and got out and asked him what was the matter, and he said he fell off the pony; he was on his way to school. So I asked him if he was hurt, and he said it hurt him to talk and he felt funny.' She paused. 'Well, there I was, all alone, and I didn't know what to do, whether to take him home or what. And just then a truck came by, with a couple of those chaps from the lumber camp in it.'

Jack Dorman said, 'The camp up at Lamirra?'

'That's right. Well, this truck stopped and the men got down, and one of them came and asked what was the matter. New Australian he was, German or something—he spoke very foreign. So I told him and he began feeling the boy all over, and then the other man told me he was a doctor in his own country, but not here in Australia. He was a tall, thin fellow, with rather a dark skin, and black hair. So I asked him, "Is it concussion, Doctor?" I said. Because, I was going to say we'd bring him back here, because this was closer.'

She paused. 'Well, he didn't answer at once. He seemed a bit puzzled for the moment, and then he made little Peter open his mouth and took a look down his throat, and then he found some stuff coming out of his ear. And then he said, "It is not concussion, and the bleeding, that is nothing." He said, "He has ear disease, and he has a temperature. He should go at once to hospital in Banbury." My dear, of all the things to have, and that man finding it out so quick! Well, I felt his forehead myself, and it was awful hot, and so I asked the truck driver to go on to Balaclava and tell his mother, and I drove this doctor and Peter into town to the hospital. And Dr Jennings was there, and he said it was a sort of mastoid–otitis something, he said.'

'Pretty good, that,' said Jack Dorman.

George Pearson said, 'Dr Jennings knew all about this chap. He's a Czech, not a German. He works up at the camp there, doing his two years.'

'What's his name?'

'He did tell me, but I forgot. One of these foreign names, it was–Cylinder, or something. Not that, but something like it. Ann drove him back to Lamirra.'

His wife said, 'He was quite a quiet, well-behaved one for a New Australian. I do think it was quick of him to find out what was wrong.'

'Lucky he came along just then,' said Jack.

'My word,' said Ann with feeling. 'If he hadn't come I think I'd probably have put Peter into the utility and brought him straight back here, because it's so much closer here than Balaclava. I wouldn't have known what to do with mastoid.'

The Dormans left soon after that, and drove back to Leonora. Life went on as usual on the station, and on Saturday evening Tim Archer drove into Banbury with Mario Ritti for the Red Cross dance. He hit it off all right with Mario in spite of their very different backgrounds, but there was always a little difficulty with Mario at a dance. There was a barrier of language and experience between the Italian and the local Australian girls; he was inclined to be too bold with them, and they would not willingly have been seen with him except at a dance, where social barriers were somewhat broken down. There had been an Italian girl at one of the hotels till recently, and Mario had done most of his dancing with her, but now she had left to go to Melbourne to earn eight pounds a week in a café, and Tim was a little anxious about Mario in consequence.

There were about eighty-thousand pounds' worth of new motor-cars parked outside the Shire Hall that night, for wool had been good for a couple of years. They parked the old Chevrolet and went into the hall, neat in their blue suits, with oiled hair carefully brushed. For a time they stood with a little crowd of young men round the door while the girls sat on chairs in long lines on each side of the floor waiting to be asked to dance; only two or three couples were yet dancing, and the place was still stone cold. Tim studied the girls; Elsie Peters was there talking to Joan McFarlane. If he had been alone he would have gone and asked one or other of them to dance, but that meant leaving Mario high and dry. He felt an obligation to the Italian to get him started with at least one partner before going off to his own friends, and he did not think that either Elsie or Joan would appreciate it if he landed her with an Eyetie who spoke poor English and was full of rather obvious sex appeal.

He glanced down the row of girls beside the floor, and saw two black-haired girls sitting together. They were both rather broad in the face, and both wore woollen dresses of a sombre hue and rather an unfashionable cut. They were obviously a pair and strangers to Banbury; Tim had never seen them before. They were clearly New Australians.

He nudged Mario. 'What about that couple over there?' he asked. 'They'd be Italian, wouldn't they?'

'I do not think,' said Mario. 'I think Austrian perhaps, or Polish. I have not seen these girls before.'

'Nor have I. Let's go and ask them.' Once Mario was launched with these two, he would be able to go off and dance with his own sort.

They crossed the floor to the girls, and Tim, taking the nearest one, said, 'May I have this dance? My name's Tim Archer.' Mario bowed from the waist before the other looking as if he was going to kiss her hand at any moment, and said, 'Mario Ritti.'

Both girls smiled and got to their feet. Tim's girl was about twenty-five years old and pleasant-looking in a broad way; in later life she would certainly be stout. She danced a quickstep reasonably well, and as they moved off she said with a strange accent, 'Teem Archer?'

'That's right,' he said. 'Tim.'

She tried again. 'Tim?'

'That's right,' he said again. 'Short for Timothy.'

'Ah–I understand. Timothy.'

'What's your name?'

She smiled. 'I am Tamara Perediak.'

'How much?'

'Tamara Perediak.'

'Tamara? I never heard that name before.'

'It is a name of my country,' she said. 'Where I was born, many girls are called Tamara.'

'Are you Polish?' he asked.

She shook her head. 'I was born in the Ukraine.' He did not know where that was, but didn't like to say so. 'Now I am come from Mulheim, in the American zone, to Australia.' She called it Owstrahlia. 'I am to work here at the hospital.'

'Have you just arrived?' he asked.

'In the camp I have been three weeks, but here only three days.'

'Three days? Then you're brand-new!' They laughed together. 'How do you like Australia?'

'I like it very much, what I have seen.'

'Are you a nurse?'

She shook her head. 'I think you call it a ward-maid. I am to do scrubbing and the carrying trays, and the washing dishes, and the washing clothes.'

'Do you know anybody in Australia?'

She said, 'I have good friends that I met on the ship, but they have gone to Mildura. But I have here Natasha who came with me, who is dancing with your friend. She comes also from the Ukraine and we were together at Mulheim, working at the same canteen.'

'Natasha?'

She laughed. 'That is another name from the Ukraine. Natasha Byelev. Are our names very difficult?'

'My word!'

'Tell me,' she said presently, 'your friend, is he Australian also?'

'No,' he replied. 'He's Italian. His name's Mario Ritti.'

'Ah–an Italian. I did not think he was Australian.'

'That's right,' Tim said. 'He works at Leonora, where I work. He's on top of the world tonight, because he's got a girl in Italy and the boss is going to pay her passage out here so that Mario can get married.'

He had to repeat parts of that once or twice before its full import sunk in. 'He will pay for her to come from Italy to Australia?' she said in wonder. 'He must be a very rich man.'

'He's doing all right with the wool,' Tim said.'He's not a rich man, really.'

'Your friend is very lucky to work for such a man. Is his loved one to come soon?'

'Soon as the boss can get her on a ship. He's scared that Mario will leave when his two years are up. He wants to get him settled on the station in a house of his own, with a wife and family.'

She stared at him. 'He is to make him a house also?'

'That's right. Just a shack, you know.'

She thought about this for a minute as they danced. 'I also must work for two years,' she said. 'I am to work here in the hospital, with Natasha.'

'Do you like it?'

She shrugged her shoulders. 'I have been working so since five years, in the works canteen at Mulheim. Once I was to be a schoolteacher, but with the war that was not possible.'

'Where were you in the war?' he asked.

'In Dresden,' she said. 'When I was little girl my father and my mother left Odessa because they were not members of the Party and the life there was not good, and so they went to live in Dresden. There my father was schoolteacher, to teach the boys Russian. All before the war, and in the war, we lived in Dresden. Then the English bombed Dresden and my father and my mother were killed, both together. Our house was all destroyed. I was not there, because I worked that night in the factory outside the city and that was not bombed. But I went to go home in the morning, our house and the whole street was all destroyed, and my mother and father were dead, both of them. So then the war came to Dresden very soon after, and I went first to Leipzig and then to Kassel because the Russians were coming, and there I met Natasha and we went to Mulheim in the end to work in the canteen.'

Tim Archer said, 'You've seen a mighty lot of foreign places. I should think you'd find it a bit slow in Banbury.'

'I think it will be better to be in a slow place and live slowly for a time.' Tamara said. 'So much has happened since I was a little girl.'

Presently the dance ended and he took her back to her seat. Mario immediately asked her to dance again, and Tim escaped, and went to dance with Joan McFarlane.

At the same time, at Leonora, Jane sat with Jack before the kitchen stove in wooden arm-chairs with cushions; they generally sat there in the evening rather than in the parlour, a prim, formal room where nothing was to hand. Jack Dorman was reading the *Leader*, a weekly farming paper which was about all he ever read. Jane sat with the open letter from Aunt Ethel in her hand, worrying about it.

'I wrote to Myers with a cheque,' she said. 'They sent a statement for the parcels, seven pounds eighteen and six. I told them to keep sending them, one every month. . . .'

He grunted without looking up. 'What are you sending now?'

'I told them to keep sending the dried fruits.' she said. 'It's what she seems to like.' She turned the letter over in her hand. 'It's so difficult, because she never asks for anything, or says what she wants. She does seem to like the dried fruit, though.'

'I'd have thought that a meat parcel might be better,' he said. 'They haven't got much meat, from all I hear.'

'An old lady like her doesn't eat a lot of meat,' she replied. 'She can make cakes with the dried fruit for when she has people in to tea.'

She turned the letter over, reading it again for the tenth time. 'I can't make out about this vest,' she said, troubled. 'It almost reads as if she's short of money, doesn't it?'

'Could be,' he observed. He laid the *Leader* down, and glanced across at his wife. He could still see in her the girl he had brought out from England, stubborn in her love for him to the point of quarrelling with her parents, supported only by this aunt to whom they now sent parcels.

'Like to send her some?' he asked.

She looked up quickly, and met his eyes. 'Send her money? She might take it as an insult.'

'She might buy herself a vest,' he said.

She sat in silence for a time. 'We couldn't send her just a little money, Jack,' she said at last. 'It would have to be nothing or else quite a lot, as if it was a sort of legacy. Enough to be sure that she wouldn't take it badly. Enough to keep her for a couple of years if she's in real trouble.'

'Well, we've got a lot,' he said. 'We'll do whatever you think right.'

There was a pause. 'I feel we kind of owe it to her,' he said presently. 'To see her right if she's in any trouble. We haven't done so bad together, you and I. It might never have come to anything if she hadn't backed us up.'

'I know. That's what I feel.' She stared down at the letter in her hands. 'I'm not a bit happy about this, Jack,' she said at last. 'I don't like the sound of it at all. If we've got the money, I'd like to send her five hundred pounds.'

2

Jennifer Morton went home for the following week-end. She was the daughter of a doctor in Leicester, his only child now, for her two brothers had been killed in the war, one in the North Atlantic and one over Hamburg. She was twenty-four years old and she had worked away from home for some years; she had a clerical job with the Ministry of Pensions at their office at Blackheath, a suburb of London. Most of her life was spent in Blackheath, where she had a bed-sitting-room in a boarding-house, but once a month she went home to Leicester to see her parents, travelling up from London early on the Saturday morning, and returning late on Sunday night.

These were duty visits; she was fond enough of her father and her mother, but she had now no interests and few acquaintances in her own home town. The war and marriage had scattered her school friends. She had no particular fondness for the Ministry of Pensions or for her job in Blackheath; she would have stayed at home and worked in Leicester if there had been any useful purpose to be served by doing so. In fact, her mother and her father were remarkably self-sufficient; her mother never wanted to do anything else but to stay at home and run the house and cook her father's dinner. Her father, an overworked general practitioner, never wanted to go out at night unless, in the winter, to a meeting of the British Medical Association or, in the summer, to a meeting of the Bowls Club. This was a good thing, for the night air made her mother cough, and she seldom went out of the house after midday in the winter. As the years went on, her father and her mother settled firmly into a routine of life moulded by overwork and by poor health, a groove that left little room for the wider interests of a daughter.

Jennifer went to Leicester for her week-end once a month, but there was never very much for her to do there. She could not help her mother very much without breaking through routines that she was not familiar with; unless the water jug was on a certain spot upon the kitchen shelf, unless the saucepans were arrayed in a certain order, her mother became fussed and unable to find things, and very soon made the suggestion that Jennifer should go and sit with her father, who was usually deep in the *British Medical Journal* if he wasn't out upon a case. She came to realize that in her case the barrier of the generations was higher than usual in families because her father and her mother were so complementary; she accepted the situation philosophically, and found the interests of her life away from home.

Those interests were not very startling. She had been mildly in love when she was twenty, soon after the war, but he had gone to a job in Montreal and gradually the correspondence languished; when finally she heard that he was married it was just one of those things. She was friendly with a good many men, for she was an attractive girl, with auburn hair that had been bright red as a child, and the grey eyes that go with it, but she had been inoculated and never fell seriously in love. She knew a good deal about the London theatres, and she saw most of the films worth seeing, including the Continental ones; she could speak a little French, and she had spent two summer holidays in France with a couple of girls from her office. Now she was planning a trip to Italy for her next holiday, but that was nine months ahead, for it was October. She had bought three little books by a gentleman called Hugo, and she was teaching herself Italian out of them.

That week-end was like all the others, only more so. Though it was only October her mother was coughing as if it were January; she had not been out of doors for a week, but she had her household organized so that she could order from the shops by telephone, and what could not be done that way the daily woman did. Her father was more overworked than ever; he seemed to spend most of his time writing certificates for patients of the nationalized Health Service, who stood in queues each morning and afternoon at the surgery door. There was nothing Jennifer could do to help them and no place for her; she left them late on Sunday afternoon and travelled back to London, and so by the electric train from Charing Cross down to her own place at Blackheath. She got back to her room at about ten o'clock, made herself a cup of cocoa, washed a pair of stockings, did an exercise of Hugo, and went to bed.

She worked all next day, as usual, at her office. She left at five in the evening, and walked back through the surburban streets in the October dusk to her boarding-house. Very soon now it would be dark when she came out from work; for two months in the winter she would not walk home in daylight. She was beginning to dread those two months; in mid-winter she got a sense of suffocation, a feeling that she would never see the sun and the fresh air again.

It was raining a little that evening, and she walked back with her blue raincoat buttoned tightly round her neck. She had intended to go out to the pictures with a friend from the boarding-house after tea, but now she thought that she would stay at home and read a magazine and do her Hugo. There wasn't much joy in going to the pictures and then walking home in the rain.

She went up the steps of the shabby old brick house that was her home, spacious with its eight bedrooms, its four reception-rooms, and its range of basement kitchens, and she let herself in at the front door with her latch key. As she took off her wet coat her landlady climbed up the stairs from the kitchen.

'There was a telephone call for you about an hour ago,' she said. 'A personal call. I told them you'd be back about five-thirty.'

Jennifer looked up in surprise. 'Do you know who it was from?'

The woman shook her head. 'They didn't say.'

Jennifer went to the telephone booth and told the exchange that she would take the call, and learned that it was a call from Leicester. She hung up, and stood uncertain for a moment hoping there was nothing wrong at home. Presently she went up to her room on the first floor and changed out of her wet shoes, and then stood looking out of the window at the glistening lamplight in the wet suburban street, waiting and listening for the call. In the yellow lamplight the plane trees in the street waved a few stray leaves that still held to the twigs.

The call came through at last, and she hurried downstairs to take it. It was her mother, speaking from their home. 'Is that Jenny? How are you, dear?'

'I'm all right, Mother.'

'Jenny dear, listen to this. We had a telephone call from the district nurse, at Ealing. She said that Granny's ill. She had a fall in the street, apparently, and they took her to the hospital, but they hadn't got a bed so they took her home and put her to bed there. The nurse said somebody would have to go there to look after her. Jenny, could you go to Ealing and see what's the matter, and then telephone us?'

Jennifer thought quickly. Ealing was on the other side of London; an hour up to Charing Cross if she were lucky with the trains, and then an hour down to Ealing Broadway, and a ten minutes' walk. She could get something to eat on the way, perhaps. 'I can do that, Mummy,' she said. 'I've got nothing fixed up for tonight. I could be there by half-past eight.'

'Oh, my dear, I *am* sorry. I think you'll have to go. She oughtn't to be living alone, of course, but she won't leave the house. We'll have to fix up something better for her, after this. You'll be able to get back to Blackheath tonight, will you?'

The girl hesitated. 'I think so, Mummy. If I leave by about half-past nine I should be able to get back here. It sounds as if somebody ought to stay the night with her, though, doesn't it?'

There was a worried silence. 'I don't know what to say,' her mother said at last. 'You've got to be at work tomorrow. Oh, dear!'

'Has Daddy heard about this yet?'

'He's out still on his rounds. I couldn't get hold of him.'

'Don't worry, Mummy,' said the girl. 'I'll go over there, and give you a ring when I've seen the nurse. We'll fix up something between us.'

'What time will you be telephoning, dear?'

'It may be very late, if I've got to hurry to catch trains,' the girl said. Her grandmother was not on the telephone. 'It may be after midnight when I get back here.'

'That'll be all right, Jenny. I always hear the bell.'

'All right, Mummy. I'll go over right away and ring you back tonight, probably very late.'

She did not wait for supper, but started for the station straight way. She travelled across London to the other side and came to Ealing Broadway station about two hours later. It was raining here in earnest, great driving gusts of rain blown by a high wind down the deserted, shimmering, black streets. Her stockings and her shoes were soaked before she had been walking for three minutes.

Her grandmother lived in a four-bedroomed house called Maymyo, built in the somewhat spacious style of fifty years ago, a house with a large garden and no garage. Her husband had bought it when they had retired from Burma in 1924; he had bought it prudently because he had an idea even then that he would not survive his wife, and so he had avoided an extravagant establishment. In fact he had died in 1930, comfortable in the knowledge that her widow's pension, her small private income, and the house in perpetuity would render her secure until she came to join him.

There she had lived, surrounded by the treasures they had gathered up together in a life spent in the East. A gilded Buddha sat at the hall door, a pair of elephant tusks formed a hanger for a great brass dinner gong. Glass cases housed Indian dolls, and models of sampans and junks, and imitation mangoes out of which a wood and plaster cobra would jump to bite your finger, very terrifying. There were embossed silver and brass Burmese trays and bowls all over the place; on the walls were water-colour paintings of strange landscapes with misty forests of a bluish tinge unknown to Jennifer, with strange coloured buildings called pagodas and strange people in strange clothes. Ethel Trehearn lived on surrounded by these reminders of a more colourful world, more real to her than the world outside her door. Nothing was very interesting to her that had happened since she got on to the ship at Rangoon Strand, twenty-six years before.

Jennifer came to the house in the wet, windy night; it was in total darkness, which seemed most unusual. She pushed open the gate and went up the path through the little front garden, and now she saw a faint glimmer of light through the coloured glass panels let into the front door in a Gothic style. She stood in the porch in her wet shoes and raincoat, and pressed the bell.

She heard nothing but the tinkling of water running from a stackpipe near her feet.

She waited for a minute and then pressed the bell again. Apparently it wasn't working. She rapped with the knocker and waited for a couple of minutes for something to happen; then she tried the handle of the door. It was open, and she went into the hall.

A candle burned on the hall table, held in a brass candle-stick from Benares. Jennifer went forward and pressed the electric switch for the hall light, but no light came. She thought of a power cut, unusual at night, and stood in wonder for a moment. In any case, there was no electricity, and it was no good worrying about the cause.

She stood in the hall, listening to the house. It was dead silent, but for the tinkling of the rain. She raised her head and called, 'Granny! It's me—Jennifer. Are you upstairs?'

There was no answer.

She did not like the empty sound of the house; it was full of menace for her. She did not like the lack of light, or the long, moving shadows that the candle cast. She was a level-headed young woman, however, and she took off her coat and laid it on a chair, and picked up the candle, and went into the drawing-room.

There was nothing unusual about that room; it was clean and tidy, though stone-cold. She would have expected on a night like that to see a fire burning in the grate, but the fire was not laid; apparently her grandmother had not used the room that day. Jennifer went quickly through the dining-room and kitchen; everything was quite in order there. A tin of Benger's Food and a half-empty bottle of milk stood on the kitchen table.

She turned, and went upstairs to the bedrooms. The door of her grandmother's room was shut; she stood outside with the flickering candle in her hand, and knocked. She said again, 'Granny, it's me—Jennifer. Can I come in?' There was no answer, so she turned the handle and went into the room.

Ethel Trehearn lay on her back in the bed, and at the first glance Jennifer thought that she was dead, and her heart leaped up into her throat because she had never seen a dead person. She forced herself to look more closely, and then she saw that the old lady was breathing evenly, very deeply asleep. With the relief, Jennifer staggered a little, and her eyes lost focus for an instant and she felt a little sick; then she recovered herself, and looked around the room.

Everything there seemed to be in order, though her grandmother's day clothes were thrown rather haphazard into a chair. The old lady was evidently quite all right in bed and asleep; if she had had a fall a sleep would do her good. It looked as if somebody had been in the house looking after her, possibly the district nurse who had telephoned to Jennifer's mother. It seemed unwise to wake the old lady up, and presently Jennifer tiptoed from the room, leaving the door ajar in order that she might hear any movement.

The time was then about nine o'clock, and she had eaten nothing since lunch except a cup of tea and a biscuit at the office. She had a young and healthy appetite, and she had the sense to realize that her momentary faintness in the bedroom had a good deal to do with the fact that she was very, very hungry. She went down to the kitchen, candle in hand, to get herself a meal.

In a few minutes she had made the extraordinary discovery that there was no food in the house at all. The half bottle of milk and the tin of Benger's Food upon the kitchen table seemed to be the only edibles, except for a few condiments in a cupboard. The larder—her grandmother had no refrigerator—was empty but for a small hard rind of cheese upon a plate and three cartons of dried fruits, candied peel and sultanas and glacé cherries, open and evidently in use. There was a flour-bin, but it was empty, a bread-bin that held only crumbs. There were no tinned foods at all, and no vegetables.

Jennifer stood in the middle of the kitchen deeply puzzled, wondering what her grandmother had been eating recently, and where she had been eating it. Had she been having her meals out, or was there something blacker waiting here to be uncovered? She had been down to visit the old lady one Sunday about a month before and her grandmother had given her a very good lunch and tea, a roast duck with apple sauce with roast potatoes and cauliflower, and a mince pie to follow; for tea there had been buttered scones and jam, and a big home-made cake with plenty of fruit in it. She thought of this as she stood there in the kitchen in the flickering candle-light, and her mouth watered; she could have done with a bit of that roast duck.

One thing at least was evident; that she should have to spend the night in the house. She could not possibly go back to Blackheath and leave things as they were. Whoever had lit the candle and left the door open had done it in the expectation that some relation would arrive, and the unknown person would probably come back that night because her grandmother was clearly incapable of looking after herself. If Jennifer was to spend the night there, though, she felt she must have something to eat. Ealing Broadway was only a few hundred yards away and there would probably be a café or a coffee-stall open there; she could leave a note upon the hall table and go out and have a quick meal.

She went upstairs again and looked in on the old lady, but she was still deeply asleep. Thinking to find a place in which to sleep herself she opened the door of the guest bedroom, but it was empty. Pictures still hung upon the wall, but there was no furniture in the room at all, and no carpet on the bare boards of the floor. Unfaded patches on the wallpaper showed where bed and chest of drawers and wash-hand stand had stood.

This was amazing, because Jennifer had slept in that room less than a year before; it had been prim and neat and old-fashioned and very comfortable. What on earth had the old lady done with all the furniture? The girl went quickly to the other two bedrooms and found them in a similar condition, empty but for the pictures on the wall. There was no bed in the house except the one that her grandmother occupied; if Jennifer were to sleep there that night she would have to sleep on the sofa in the drawing-room. There did not seem to be any bedding, either; the linen cupboard held only a pair of clean sheets, a couple of towels, a table-cloth or two, and a few table-napkins.

The shadows began to close in upon Jennifer as she stood in the empty bedrooms with the flickering candle in her hand. It seemed incredible, but the old lady must have sold her furniture. And there was no food in the house. The darkness crept around her; could it be that Granny had no money? But she had a pension, Jennifer knew that, and she had always been well off. More likely that she was going a bit mental with old age, and that she deluded herself into the belief that she was poor.

She went downstairs and found a piece of writing paper in her grand-mother's desk, and wrote a note to leave on the hall table with the candle; then she put on her raincoat and went out to get a meal. She found a café open in the main street and had a sort of vegetable pie. It was dull and insipid with no meat, but she had two helpings of it and followed it up with stewed plums and coffee. Then she bought a couple of rolls filled with a thin smear of potted meat for her breakfast, and went back to the house in Ladysmith Avenue.

In the house everything was as she had left it; her note lay beneath the candle unread. She took the candle and went up to her grandmother's room, but the old lady was still sleeping deeply; she had not moved at all. The girl came out of the bedroom, and as she did so she heard movement in the hall, and saw the light from an electric torch. She came downstairs with the candle, and in its light she saw a middle-aged woman standing there in a wet raincoat, torch in hand.

The woman said, 'Are you one of Mrs Trehearn's relations?'

Jennifer said, 'I'm her granddaughter.'

'Oh. Well, I'm the district nurse. You know she had an accident?'

'I don't know very much, except that my mother got a telephone call asking somebody to come here. She rang me.'

The nurse nodded. 'I rang your mother at Leicester as soon as I could get the number out of the old dear. I'd better tell you what it's all about, and then you can take over.'

Jennifer moved towards the door. 'We'd better go in here—in case she wakes up.'

'*She* won't wake up tonight—not after what the doctor gave her.' However, they went into the drawing-room and stood together in the light of the one candle. 'She had a fall in the street this morning, just the other side of the bridge, between here and the Broadway. She didn't seem able to get up, so the police got an ambulance and took her to the hospital. Well, they hadn't got a bed, and anyway there didn't seem to be much wrong with her, except debility, you know. So as she was conscious and not injured by her fall they rang me up and sent her home here in the ambulance. I put her to bed and got in Dr Thompson. he saw her about five o'clock.'

'What did he say?'

The nurse glanced at her. 'When did you see her last?'

'About a month ago.'

'How was she then?'

'Very much as usual. She doesn't do much, but she's seventy-nine, I think.'

'Was she eating normally?'

'She gave me a very good meal, roast duck and mince pie.'

'She ate that, did she?'

'Of course. Why?'

'She doesn't look as if she's eaten anything since,' the nurse said shortly. 'She's very emaciated, and there's not a scrap of food here in the house except for some dried fruits. She vomited at the hospital, and what came up was raisins and sultanas. She couldn't be expected to digest those, at her age.'

Jennifer said, 'I simply can't understand it. She's got plenty of money.'

The nurse glanced at her. 'You're sure of that?'

'Well—I think so.'

'I rang up the electricity,' the nurse said, 'and told them that the power had failed and they must send a man to put it right because I'd got a patient in the house. They said they'd disconnected the supply because the bill hadn't been paid. You'd better see about that in the morning if you're going to keep her here.'

'I'll go round there first thing.'

'I had to go and get a candle of my own,' the nurse said. 'I brought another one round with me now.' She took it from her pocket. 'I looked for coal to light a fire, but there's not a scrap. I got a tin of Benger's Food and some milk, and I got the people next door to let me boil up some hot milk for her, and fill the hot-water-bottles. I'll take them round there and fill them again before I go.' She glanced at Jennifer. 'You're staying here tonight?'

'I wasn't going to, but I'd better. Will you be here?'

The nurse laughed shortly. 'Me? I've got a baby case tonight, but she's got an hour or two to go so I slipped round here to see if anyone had come. I'll have to get some sleep after that. I'll look round here about midday to see how you're getting on. I said I'd give the doctor a ring after that.'

Jennifer nodded. 'I'll see you then. Is she in any danger, do you think?'

'I don't think she'll go tonight,' the nurse said. 'Whether she'll pull round or not depends a lot on her digestion. I couldn't say. When she wakes, give her another cup of the Benger's. She can have as much of that as she'll take—I'll show you how to make it. But don't let her have anything else till the doctor's seen her. And keep the bottles nice and warm—not hot enough to scorch, you know, just nice and warm.'

Practical, hard-headed, and efficient, she whisked through her duties, showing Jennifer what to do, and was out of the house in a quarter of an hour. The girl was left alone with all the Indian and Burmese relics, with one candle and no fire and nowhere much to sleep.

She gave up the idea of going out in the rain at ten o'clock at night to find a public telephone to ring up her mother; that would have to wait till morning. She went up to her grandmother's bedroom and took off her wet shoes and stockings and rubbed her feet with a towel; then she found a pair of her grandmother's woollen stockings and put them on, and her grandmother's bedroom slippers, and her grandmother's overcoat. She found a travelling rug and wrapped it around her and settled down to spend the night in an arm-chair by her grandmother's bedside, chilled and uncomfortable, dozing off now and then and waking again with the cold. In the middle of the night she ate her breakfast rolls.

In the grey dawn she woke from one of these uneasy dozes, stiff and chilled to the bone. She looked at the bed and saw that her grandmother was awake; she was lying in exactly the same position, but her eyes were open. Jennifer got up and went to the bedside. The old lady turned her head upon the pillow and said in a thin voice, 'Jenny, my dear. Whatever are you doing here?'

The girl said, 'I've come to look after you, Granny. They telephoned and told us that you weren't so well.'

'I know, my dear. I fell down in the street—such a stupid thing to do. Is the nurse still here?'

'She'll be back later on this morning, Granny. Is there anything you want?'

She told her, and Jennifer entered on the duties of a sick-room for the first time in her life. Presently she took the hot-water bottles and the remains of the milk and went to the house next door, where a harassed mother was getting breakfast for a husband and three little children. As she warmed the milk and filled the water-bottles the woman asked her, 'How is the old lady this morning?'

'She's staying in bed, of course,' said Jennifer, 'but she's not too bad. I think she's going to be all right.'

'I am so sorry,' the woman said. 'I wish we'd been able to do more for her, but everything's so difficult these days. I'd no idea that she was ill. She's been going out as usual every morning. It was a terrible surprise when she came back in an ambulance yesterday.'

Jennifer was interested. 'She goes out every morning, does she?'

'That's right. Every morning about ten o'clock. She goes down to the Public

Library in the Park to read *The Times*. She told me that one day.'

Jennifer thanked her for her help, and went back with the hot milk to make a cup of Benger's, and took it up to the bedroom with the hot-water-bottles. She propped her grandmother up in bed with the pillows and helped her while she drank, but she could not get her to take more than half the cup. 'I don't want any more, my dear,' she said. 'I think I'm better without anything.'

The hot drink had stimulated her a little. 'Jenny,' she said, 'I've been thinking. Haven't you got to go to work?'

The girl said, 'That's all right, Granny. I'm going out presently to ring up Mummy to tell her how you are, and I'll ring up the office then. I'll stay with you for a few days until you're better.'

'Oh, my dear, that isn't necessary at all.'

'I'd like to, Granny. It'll be a bit of a holiday for me.'

'But Jenny, dear, you *can't* stay here. There isn't anywhere for you to sleep. Where did you sleep last night?'

'I'll be all right here, Granny,' the girl said. 'I'll fix up something in the course of the day.'

'But there isn't any electricity. You *can't* stay here.' A facile, senile tear escaped and trickled down the old, lined cheek. 'Oh, things *are* so troublesome.'

'That's all right, Granny,' the girl said. 'I'll go and see about the electricity this morning, and get them to turn it on.'

'But it's seventeen pounds, Jenny–they came and turned it off. Such a nice man, but he had to do his job. I've been getting on quite well without it.'

'Well, you're not going to get along without it any longer, Granny,' Jennifer said firmly. 'You can't when you're in bed.' She thought quickly; she had about thirty pounds in her bank, but her cheque-book was at Blackheath on the other side of London. 'I'll get them to turn it on again,' she said. 'Don't worry about it.'

'Oh, my dear, I don't know what to do. . . .'

The girl wiped the old cheeks gently with her handkerchief. 'Cheer up, Granny,' she said. 'It'll be all right. Tell me–isn't there any money?'

The old lady said, 'None at all. You see, I've lived too long.'

'Don't you believe it,' Jennifer said. 'You've got a good many more years yet. But what about the pension? That goes on until you die, doesn't it?'

'That's what Geoffrey thought, and so did I. But it was an Indian pension, dear, and when the Socialists scuttled out of India there weren't any civil servants left in India to pay into the fund. Only us widows were left drawing out of it, and now the money is all gone.'

'But wasn't it a Government pension?'

'Not for widows, dear. Geoffrey's pension was a Government pension, but that stopped when he died. This was a private fund, that we civil servants in India all paid in to. They had to halve the pensions a few years ago, and then last year they stopped it altogether and wound up the fund.'

The girl said, 'Oh, Granny! And you gave me such a lovely dinner when I came here last!'

'Of course, my dear. A young girl like you must have proper meals. Although it's all so difficult, with all this rationing. Jenny, have you had your breakfast yet?'

'Not yet. I'm going out in a few minutes, and I'll get some then.'

'I'm afraid there's nothing in the house, Jenny. I *am* so sorry.'

'Don't think about it, Granny. I'll get a few things when I'm out and bring them in.'

'Yes, do that, dear.' She·paused. 'Will you bring me the little red morocco case that's on the dressing-table?'

'This one?'

'Yes, that's it. Bring it to me here.'

The girl brought the jewel case over to the bed and gave it to her grandmother, who opened it with fingers that trembled so that they could barely serve their function. Inside there was a jumble of souvenirs, the relics of a long life. A gold locket on a gold chain, broken, with a wisp of baby's hair in it. A painted miniature portrait of a young boy in the clothes of 1880, a faded photograph of a bride and bridegroom dated 1903, a small gold sovereign purse to hang upon a watch-chain, three small gold and alabaster seals, a string of black jet beads. She rummaged among these things and many others with fingers that were almost useless and finally produced a gold ring set with five diamonds in a row, unfashionable in these days.

She gave this to Jennifer. 'I want you to do a little job for me when you are out, Jenny,' she said. 'In the New Broadway, two doors on the other side of Paul's patisserie shop, you'll find a jeweller's shop called Evans. Go in and ask to see Mr Evans himself, and give him this, and tell him that you come from me. He's a very nice man, and he'll understand. He'll give you money for it whatever it's worth I'm afraid it may not be enough to pay the electricity, but you can get a joint of beef and some vegetables, and we'll cook a nice dinner for you. Take my ration book with you—it's on the corner of the bureau in the drawing-room—and get some flour and dripping and sugar, and then we'll make a cake; there's plenty of dried fruit downstairs that dear Jane sends me from Australia. So kind of her, after all these years. And if there's enough money, get a little bottle of claret. A young girl like you ought not to look so pale.'

'You mustn't sell your ring,' the girl said gently. 'Look, I've got plenty of money to carry on with—I've got over thirty pounds in the bank. I'll use some of that, and I'll be telephoning Mummy this morning and she'll send us down some more. I expect Daddy will come down to see you tomorrow, when he hears that you're in bed.'

Her grandmother shook her head. 'Your mother hasn't got any money to spare,' she said. 'She might have had once, but now with this horrible Health Service and doctors getting less money than dentists . . . Sell the ring, my dear. I can't get it on my finger now, I'm so rheumatic, and I shan't want it any more.'

'What is it, Granny?' the girl asked, turning it over in her fingers. 'Who gave it to you?'

'Geoffrey,' the old lady said. 'Geoffrey gave it to me, when we became engaged. We went to the Goldsmiths and Silversmiths in Regent Street together to buy it . . . such a fine, sunny day. And then we went and had lunch at Gatti's; it felt so funny on the fork, because I wasn't used to wearing rings. And then we took a hansom for the afternoon and drove down to Roehampton to see the polo, because Geoffrey's friend Captain Oliver was playing. But I didn't see much of the polo, because I was looking at my new ring, and at Geoffrey. So silly . . .' The old voice faded off into silence.

'I can't sell that,' the girl said gently. 'I'm not going to sell your engagement ring.'

'My dear, there's nothing else.'

'Yes, there is,' the girl said. 'I've got thirty pounds. I'm going to spend that first. If you don't like it, you can leave me that ring in your will.'

'I've done that already, Jenny, with a lot of other things that aren't there now, because I had to sell them. I'm so very, very sorry. There was a little emerald and ruby brooch that Geoffrey got at Mandalay, and a pair of pearl ear-rings that came from Mergui. So pretty; I did want you to have those. But everything has been so troublesome. . . .'

The girl put the ring back into the jewel box. 'Leave it there for now,' she said. 'I promise you I'll come and tell you if we have to sell it. But we shan't have to; we've got plenty of money between us.'

She made her grandmother comfortable and promised her that she would be back in an hour and a half; then she went out with a shopping basket. She got a good breakfast at Lyons of porridge and fish, and as she breakfasted she made her plans. She had only twelve and threepence in her purse, and her breakfast cost her three shillings of that. Before she could lay her hands on any more money she must go to Blackheath to get her cheque-book and cash a cheque, and the fare there would be about four and three. That left her about five shillings; she had to telephone her mother, but perhaps she could reverse the charges for the call to Leicester. She must keep a margin of about two shillings for contingencies; if she could reverse the charges for the call she would have about three shillings to spend on food for her grandmother.

The sense of crisis, and the breakfast, stimulated her; she could beat this thing. She went out and stood in a call-box and rang up her parents; she was early, and the hundred-mile call came through at once. She told her father what had happened.

'She's got no money at all, Daddy,' she said. 'She just hasn't been eating—I think that's really all that's the matter with her. She's very weak, and she's in bed, of course.' She told him what the district nurse had said about her grandmother's chances. She told him about the pension.

They extended the call. 'Can you let me have some money, Daddy? I've only got a few shillings. I'm going back to Blackheath about midday and I'll get my cheque-book then, but I'm not sure if I'll be in time to cash a cheque. I may be too late. I'll be back here in Ealing this afternoon, anyway, before dark.'

He said, 'I'll send you a telegraph money order at once for ten pounds. You should get that this afternoon. Either your mother or I will come down tomorrow and be with you some time tomorrow afternoon, and we'll see what's to be done then. It's a bit of a shock, this.'

'Don't let Mummy worry over it too much,' the girl said. 'I think she's probably going to be all right. I'm going now to see if I can talk them into turning on the electricity again. It'll make a lot of difference if we can get a radiator going in her room.'

In a quarter of an hour she was talking to the manager in the office of the Electricity Commission, having got past his girl with some difficulty. He said, 'I'm sorry, Miss Morton, but we have to work to rules laid down by our head office. Two years ago I might have been able to use my own discretion in a case like this, but—well, things aren't the same as they were then. Nationalization was bound to make some differences, you know. I'm afraid the account will have to be paid before the supply can be re-connected.'

She said, 'I'm going over to Blackheath to get my cheque-book today. I can let you have the cheque first thing tomorrow morning.'

'Fine,' he said, with forced geniality. 'Then we shall be able to re-connect the supply.'

'Can't you do it today?'

'I'm afraid the account will have to be settled first.'

Jennifer said desperately, 'She's really terribly ill, and we can't even warm up hot milk in the house, or get hot water for her water-bottles. We *must* have electricity tonight.'

He got to his feet; this was too unpleasant, and he had no power to act. 'I'm sorry, Miss Morton,' he said. 'It sounds as though she would be better in the hospital–have you considered that? Perhaps the relieving officer would be the man for you to see. He's at the Town Hall.'

The red-haired girl flared into sudden anger. 'God blast you and the relieving officer,' she said. 'I only hope this happens to you one day, that you're old and dying of starvation, and you can't get anyone to help you. And it will, too.'

She turned and left the office, white with anger. She shopped carefully with her three shillings, and bought two pints of milk, a few water biscuits, and a little sugar; that finished her money. She thought deeply; she could get some more food for her grandmother and for herself on her way back from Blackheath. It was urgent to get over there at once, before the bank shut, so that she could get her money. She turned and made for Ladysmith Avenue; on the why she stopped and spent fourpence on a copy of *The Times*, thinking that it would give the old lady an interest while she was absent, and give something for her morale to hang on to during the afternoon.

When she got into the house she took *The Times* up to her grandmother's room. The old lady lay in bed exactly as Jennifer had left her; her eyes were shut, and though she was breathing steadily it seemed to the girl that the respiration was now fainter than it had been when she had been lying in the same way on the previous night. Jennifer spoke to her, but she did not answer; however, when she reached into the bed to get the hot-water-bottles the old lady opened her eyes.

'Just getting your hot-water-bottles, Granny,' the girl said. 'I'll make you another cup of Benger's, too. I brought you *The Times*.'

'So sweet of you,' her grandmother said. 'I had to give up *The Times*, but I always go down every morning to look at the Births, Deaths and Marriages. It's so easy to miss things, and then you write to somebody and find they're dead.'

The girl said, 'I'm just going to get these water-bottles filled, and make you another hot drink. I'll be back in about five minutes.'

When she got back the old lady was reading the front page of *The Times.* Jennifer packed the hot-water-bottles around her and got her to take the best part of the cup of the milk drink, and to eat about half of one biscuit. While she was coaxing her to eat the rest there was a knock at the front door; she went downstairs, and it was the postman with a heavy parcel.

She took it from him, and carried it up to show to her grandmother, with an instinct that anything that would stimulate and arouse her interest was good. 'Look what the post's brought,' she said. 'Myer's Emporium. What have you been buying?'

The old lady said, 'Oh, that's dear Jane. How sweet of her. It's a parcel from Australia, Jenny. She sends one every month.'

'It's got an English postmark, Granny,' the girl said.

'I know, my dear. She puts the order in Australia and the food comes from England somehow or other. So funny.'

'Shall I open it?'

'Please. I must write and thank her.' The parcel contained six cartons of dried fruit and a tin of lard; Jennifer now knew where the cartons she had seen in the larder came from. She asked, 'Granny, who is Aunt Jane? She isn't Mother's sister, is she?'

'No, my dear. Your mother never had a sister. She's my niece, my brother Tom's daughter.'

'She's the one who quarrelled with the family because she married an Australian?'

'Yes, dear. Tom and Margaret were very much upset, but it's turned out very well. I liked him, but Tom found him drinking white port with Jeffries, the butler, in the middle of the morning, and he used to swear dreadfully, and never saluted anybody. So different to our Army.'

Jennifer smiled. 'What was Aunt Jane like?'

'Such a sweet girl—but very stubborn. Once she decided to do a thing there was no arguing with her; she had to see it through. I sometimes think that you're a little like her, Jenny.'

Time was slipping by; if she were to get money that day she could not linger. 'I'm going over to Blackheath now,' she said. 'I'll get a few things for the night, and I'll get some money and some bits of things we need. I'll be back about tea-time, but I'll leave a note explaining everything to the nurse. Will you be all right, do you think?'

'I'll be quite all right, my dear. Don't hurry; I shall get a little sleep, I expect.'

Jennifer went downstairs and left a note on the hall table for the nurse, and travelled across London to her rooms at Blackheath. She got there about midday, packed a bag, went to the bank, and rang up her office to say that she would have to take the rest of the week off to look after her grandmother. Then she snatched a quick meal in a café, and travelled back to Ealing.

She was lucky in that when she reached the house the doctor and the nurse were both there, with her grandmother. She waited in the hall till they came down from the bedroom; a few letters had arrived, two that seemed to be bills and one air-mailed from Australia. That would be Jane Dorman, Jennifer thought, who had married the Australian who drank port with the butler and never saluted anybody, and who still sent parcels of dried fruit to her aunt after thirty years. They must have been very close at one time for affection to have endured so long.

She looked round for the candle, but she could not find it; perhaps the doctor and the nurse had it upstairs with them. She stood in the dusk of the hall, waiting.

Presently they came out of the room upstairs, and the staircase was suddenly flooded with light as the nurse turned the switch. Jennifer went forward to meet them. 'The electricity's come on!' she exclaimed.

'Of course. Didn't you go and see them?'

'They said they wouldn't turn it on until I paid the bill.'

'The man came round and turned it on this afternoon.' They left that for the moment, and the nurse said, 'This is Dr Thompson.'

He was a fairly young man, not more than about thirty; he looked tired and overworked. He said, 'You're Miss Morton? Let's go into one of these rooms.'

They went into the drawing-room; it was as cold as a tomb, but anyway the light was on. Surrounded by the Burmese relics the girl asked, 'How is she, Doctor?'

The young man glanced at her, summing her up. 'She's very ill,' he said. 'Very ill indeed. You know what's the matter with her, of course?'

Jennifer said, 'She's got no money.'

'Yes. Malnutrition. Starvation, if you like.' He glanced around the drawing-room, taking in the worn Indian carpet of fine quality, the old-fashioned, comfortable furniture, the sampler as a fire-screen, the multitude of ornaments and bric-à-brac. 'She wouldn't sell any of this stuff, I suppose.'

'She's very set in her ways,' the girl said. 'She likes to have her own things round her.'

'I know.' He glanced at her. 'Are you going to keep her here?'

'Could we get her into a hospital?'

He shook his head. 'I don't think there's a chance. I don't think any hospital would take her. You see, the beds are all needed for urgent cases; she might be bedridden for years if she gets over the immediate trouble.'

'She must have paid a lot of money into hospitals in her time,' said Jennifer. 'She was always subscribing to things.'

'I'm afraid that doesn't count for much in the Health Service. Things are different now, you know.'

'My father's coming down from Leicester tomorrow,' the girl said. 'He's a doctor. I think he'll have to decide what to do. I'll stay with her tonight in any case.'

'You'll be alone here, will you?'

'Yes.' She hesitated, and then she said, 'Do you think she'll die?'

'I hope not. Would you be very frightened if she did die, and you were alone with her?'

'I've never seen anybody die,' the girl said evenly. 'I hope that I'd be able to do what was best for her.'

'You'll be all right. . . .' He bit his lip. 'I don't think she'll die tonight,' he said. 'She's definitely weaker than when I saw her yesterday, I'm afraid. . . . Nurse here has to get some sleep tonight. I tell you what I'll do. I'll look in again myself about eleven, just before I go to bed. In the meantime, this is what she's got to have.'

He gave her her instructions, and went off with the nurse; Jennifer went up to her grandmother's bedroom. It was warm with an electric radiator burning; the old lady lay in bed, but turned her eyes to the girl.

'I see you've got the radiator going, Granny,' she said. 'That's much better.'

'It was that nice man,' she said weakly. 'I heard somebody moving around downstairs, and I thought it was you, Jenny. And then somebody knocked at my door, and it was him. He said he hoped he wasn't intruding but he thought I'd like the radiator, and he came in and turned it on and saw that it was burning properly. And then he said he hoped I'd soon be better.'

'How nice of him,' the girl said.

She made her grandmother comfortable and went out quickly to get to the shops before they shut. She bought the things that the doctor had told her to buy and a little food for her own supper. On her way back to the house she passed the Electricity Department, and saw a light still burning in the office window, though the door was locked. She stopped, and rang the bell; the manager himself came to the door of the shop.

He peered at her in the half light, his eyes dazzled by the strong light at his desk. 'It's after hours,' he said. 'The office is closed now. You'll have to come back in the morning.'

'It's me–Jennifer Morton,' she said. 'I just looked in to thank you for turning on the electricity.'

He recognized her then. 'Oh, that's all right,' he said. 'I rang up head office, and they gave permission.' In fact, he had sat for an hour staring blankly at the calendar, unable to work, and with the girl's words searing in his mind. Then he had rung up his supervisor and had repeated to him what Jennifer had said. He had added a few words of his own, saying that he had checked with the district nurse, and he was going to re-connect the supply. He had said quietly that they could take whatever action seemed best to them; if the job required behaviour of that sort from him, he didn't want the job. He was now waiting for the storm to break, uncertain of his own future, unsettled and reluctant to go home and tell his wife.

'I've got my cheque-book here,' she said. 'I can pay the bill now, if you like.'

It might soothe the supervisor if the cheque were dated on the same day as his own revolt. He showed her into the office and she sat down and wrote out the cheque; in turn he wrote out the receipt, stamped it, and gave it to her. 'How is your grandmother tonight?' he asked.

'Not too good,' she replied. 'She's got a better chance now that we can get some warmth into the house. I'm sorry I said that to you this morning. One gets a bit strung up.'

'Oh, that's all right,' he said. 'Can't you get her into the hospital?'

The girl shook her head. 'She's too old,' she said a little bitterly. 'They don't want people in there who are just dying of old age. She's lost her pension because we've left India and the fund's run dry. She can't get an old age pension under the new scheme because she hasn't contributed to it for fifteen years, or something. She's spent all her capital trying to live, and sold most of her furniture, and the bank won't give her any more upon the house. There's no place for old ladies in the brave new world.'

He tightened his lips, conscious of his own dark fears. 'I know,' he said. 'It's getting worse each year. Sometimes one feels the only thing to do is to break out and get away while you're still young enough. Try it again in Canada, perhaps, or in South Africa.'

She looked at him, startled. 'Is that what you're thinking of?'

'If I was alone I'd go, I think,' he said. 'But it's the children–that's what makes it difficult. They've got to have a home. . . .'

She had no time to stay and talk to him; she cut it short and hurried back to the house. There was a telegram there now from her father saying that he was coming down next day without her mother, who was not so well, and enclosing a telegraphed money order for ten pounds. She put that in her bag and glanced at the two bills, one for groceries and one for milk, each with a politely-worded note at the bottom that was a threat of action. No good worrying her grandmother with those. She took off her coat and hat, and went upstairs with the letter from Australia in her hand.

In the bedroom the old lady was still lying in much the same position. She was awake and she knew Jennifer, but she was breathing now in an irregular manner, with three or four deep breaths and then a pause. There was nothing that Jennifer could do about it; the only thing was to carry on and do what the doctor had told her. It was time for another drink of warm milk, this time with brandy in it.

She gave the air-mail letter to her grandmother. 'There's an air-mail letter for you,' she said brightly. 'Like me to get your glasses?'

'Please, dear. Did you see where it was from?'

'It's from Australia.'

The old lady took the spectacle case with trembling hands, fumbled a little and put the glasses on, and looked at the letter. 'Yes, that's from dear Jane. So sweet of her to keep writing, and sending me such lovely parcels. We must make a cake, Jenny. Such lovely things. . . .'

Jennifer went downstairs and warmed the milk up in a saucepan on the stove and made herself a cup of tea at the same time; she mixed the Benger's Food and added the brandy, and carried both cups up to the bedroom. She found her grandmother staring bewildered at a slip of paper in her hand, the envelope and the letter lying on the counterpane that covered her.

'Jenny,' she said weakly. 'Jenny, come here a minute. What is this?'

The girl took it from her. It clearly had to do with banking; it was like a cheque and yet it was not quite an ordinary cheque. The words were clear enough, however. 'It's a sort of cheque, Granny,' she said. 'It's made payable to you, for five hundred pounds sterling. I'm not quite sure what sterling means. It seems to be signed by the Commonwealth Bank of Australia. It's as if the bank was giving you five hundred pounds.'

The old lady said, 'It's from Jane. She says so in the letter. Oh, my dear—we'll have to send it back. Such a sweet child, but she can't possibly afford it. She ought not to have done such a thing.'

'If she's sent it to you, perhaps she *can* afford it,' the girl said.

'Oh, my dear, she's only a farmer's wife, living in quite a poor way, I'm afraid, and with all those children. Wherever would she get five hundred pounds?'

Jennifer said, 'May I see her letter, Granny?'

'Of course, my dear.'

It was written in the round schoolgirl hand that Jane Dorman had never lost. The first four pages dealt with news of the older children, news of Angela at Melbourne University, news of Jack's rheumatism, and news of the spring weather. It went on,

Jack and I have been a little worried by the part of your letter where you said you hadn't bought a new vest, and we have been wondering if rising prices are making things difficult for you. Out here everything is going up in price, too, but we station people are all making so much money that we hardly notice it. Jack's wool cheque this year was for twenty-two thousand pounds, and though most of that will go in tax of course it means that we shall still have about seven thousand for ourselves after paying all the expenses of the property.

We don't know what's the right thing to do with so much money. We can't expect it to go on, of course; wool will come down again next year and it's quite right that it should. It could fall to a quarter of the present price and not hurt us; the bank was all paid off last year and we've never spent much on ourselves, and we're too old now to do much gadding about. We're going down to Melbourne for a week or ten days after Christmas to do some shopping and Jack still talks of a trip home, but I don't suppose we'll really get much further than the Windsor Hotel.

I'm sending with this letter a little bank draft for five hundred pounds, with our dear love. It doesn't mean anything to us now, because we have more than we can ever spend. If you don't need it, will you give it to some charity in England for us? But we've been really worried about you since reading that letter about your vest, and Jack and I owe so much to you for all you did to help us thirty years ago. So if this will make things easier for you, will you take it with our very dearest love?

Your affectionate niece,

Jane

The girl laid the letter down. 'It's all right, Granny,' she said a little unsteadily. 'She's got all the money in the world. They're making twenty-two thousand pounds a year—at least, I think that's what she means.'

'Nonsense, my dear,' the old lady said weakly. 'She's only a farmer's wife. Stations, they call them in Australia, but it's only a big farm and not very good land, I'm told. She's made some mistake.'

The girl wrinkled her brows, and glanced at the letter again. 'I don't think it's a mistake—honestly. It's what she says, and I was reading somewhere about this in the paper the other day.' She laid the letter down. 'Look, drink your milk before it gets cold.'

She held the old lady upright with one arm, and raised the cup to her lips. She could not get her to drink much, and the effort seemed to tire her, because she lay back on the pillows with her eyes closed, disinclined to talk. Jennifer removed the letter and the envelope to a table at the bedside and put the bankers' draft upon the dressing-table, carefully weighted with an embossed Indian silver hand-mirror.

She went downstairs to get her own supper. Meat and eggs were out of the question, of course, but she had got herself a piece of cod and some potatoes and carrots. She put the cod on to boil because she would not encroach upon her grandmother's fat ration or open the tin of lard, and she peeled some of the potatoes and carrots to boil those. This insipid meal was normal to her life and she thought nothing of it; she had bought a pot of jam and some buns and a piece of cheese to liven it up a bit. She started all this going on the stove, and slipped upstairs to see how her grandmother was getting on.

The old lady had not moved, and she seemed to be asleep. Her breathing, if anything, was worse. To Jennifer as she stood motionless in the door, looking at her, she seemed smaller and more shrunken, further away. The room seemed suddenly a great deal colder; she shivered a little, and went in softly and turned on the second element of the electric stove.

As she ate her supper at the kitchen table she wondered what could be best done for her grandmother in the new situation presented by this five hundred pounds. Her father was coming down next day and he would decide what was the best course; she was rather ignorant about the practical points of illness and of nursing, but she knew that this five hundred pounds would make a difference. Perhaps it would be possible to get the old lady into a nursing home, or clinic. She knew that her parents had no money to spare; it was only with difficulty that they could keep up her father's considerable life insurance and endowment premiums; they had their own old age to think about. It had probably been a real difficulty for her father to send her ten pounds at a moment's notice, as he had that day.

She went up once or twice to look into the bedroom, but she did not speak; better to let her grandmother rest quietly till it was time for her next cup of milk food and brandy. She took that up after a lapse of two hours, and spoke to the old lady. 'I've made you some more Benger's, Granny,' she said quietly. 'Are you awake?'

The old eyes opened. 'I'm awake, Jenny. I've been thinking about so many things.'

The girl sat down beside her and raised her in the bed with an arm round the old shoulders, and held the cup for her to drink. 'What have you been thinking about?' she asked.

Her grandmother said, 'About when I was a girl, my dear, and how different things were then.'

Jennifer asked, 'How were they different, Granny? Drink it up.'

She took a little sip. 'It was all so much easier, dear. My father, your great-grandfather, was in the Foreign Office, but he retired early, when I was about fifteen. Before that we lived in a big house on Putney Hill, near where Swinburne lived, but when he retired, in about 1886, we moved down into the country. My father bought Steep Manor near Petersfield with about thirty acres of land. I don't think his pension and my mother's investments together amounted to more than a thousand pounds a year, but they seemed to be able to do such a lot with it, such a great, great deal.'

'Drink a little more,' the girl suggested. 'What sort of things did you do?'

'Everything that gentlefolk did do in those days, dear. My father kept three maid-servants in the house—everybody did then. And there was a gardener, and a gardener's boy who helped in the stables, and a groom. That was before the days of motor-cars, of course. My mother had her carriage with a pair of matched greys, such a pretty pair. My father and Tom and I all had our hacks, or hunters as we liked to call them, because we followed the hunt every week all through the winter.'

She sat in silence for a time; the girl held her, motionless. 'I had a chestnut mare called Dolly,' she said. 'Such a sweet little horse. I used to groom her myself, and she always knew when I was coming because I always brought her a lump of sugar or an apple, and she would put her head round, and whinny. Tom rode her sometimes, and she could jump beautifully, but I never jumped her myself except over a ha-ha or a ditch, because I rode side-saddle of course, in a habit. We thought it was very fast when girls began to ride astride in breeches just like men. I think a habit looks much nicer.'

The girl held the cup to the old lips again. 'Wasn't it dull just living in the country?' she asked.

'Oh, my dear, it wasn't dull. There was always such a lot to do, with the servants and the gardens and the greenhouses and the horses. We kept pigs and we used to cure all our own ham and bacon. And then we used to give a dance every year and all our friends did the same, and the Hunt Ball, and people coming to stay. And then there were all the people in the village to look after; everybody knew everybody else, and everybody helped each other. There was never a minute to spare, and never a dull moment.'

She took a sip of the milk that Jennifer pressed on her. 'We always had a week in London, every year,' she said. 'We used to stay at Brown's Hotel in Dover Street, generally in May or June. It was theatres and dances every night. I was presented at Court in 1892, to the Prince of Wales, and the old Queen came in for a moment and we all curtsied to her, all together. The lights, and all the men in their scarlet and blue dress uniforms, and the women in Court dress, with trains—I don't think I ever saw anything so splendid, except perhaps at the

Durbar in nineteen hundred and eleven.' She paused. 'You haven't been
presented, have you, Jenny?'

The girl said, 'No, Granny. I don't think it happens so much now.'

'Oh, my dear, how much, how very much you young girls have to miss. We
had so much, much more than you when we were young.'

Jennifer tried to get her to drink a little more, but the old lady refused it.
'Garden parties all through the summer,' she murmured, 'with tea out on the
lawn under the cedar tree. There was tennis on the lawn for those who felt like
it, but archery was what everybody went in for. We had a special strip of lawn
by the herbaceous border that we kept for archery, and the targets upon metal
stands, stuffed with straw, with white and red and blue and gold circles. Such a
pretty sport upon a sunny afternoon, dear, with the sun and the scent of
mignonette, between the cedar and the monkey-puzzle tree. . . .'

The old eyes closed; it was no good trying to get her to take any more of the
Benger's Food. The girl withdrew the cup and put it on the side table, and
gently relaxed her arm to lay the old head down upon the pillow. Her
grandmother seemed to sleep where she was put; the girl stood for a moment
looking down at her as she lay with eyes closed. It didn't look so good, but there
was nothing more that she could do for the time being, except to change the
hot-water-bottles.

When she had done that, she went downstairs again. In spite of the bad night
that she had had the night before she was not sleepy; there was a sense of
urgency upon her that banished fatigue. She considered for a moment where
she was to sleep, and put it out of her mind; the only possible place for sleep was
the sofa in the drawing-room and that was much too far from the old lady's
bedroom. It was warm up in the bedroom, and she could shade the light; she
would spend the night up there in the arm-chair again; within reach of her
grandmother.

The doctor came at about eleven o'clock as he had promised; Jennifer was
making another cup of the milk drink when he arrived, and she came out of the
kitchen to meet him in the hall.

'Good evening,' he said. 'How is she now?'

'Much the same,' the girl replied. 'If anything, I think she's a bit weaker.'

'Has she taken anything?'

'She takes about half a cup each time. I can't get her to take more than that.'

'I'll just go up and see her. You'd better come up, too.'

She was with him in the bedroom while he made his examination; the old
lady knew him, but said very little. He made it short, bade her good-night
cheerfully, and went downstairs again with Jennifer.

In the drawing-room he said, 'I'm very sorry that there isn't a nurse with
you.'

She looked at him. 'You mean, she's going?'

'She's not making any progress,' he replied. 'She's weaker every time I see
her. I'm afraid there's only one end to that, Miss Morton.'

'Do you think she'll die tonight?' the girl asked.

'I can't say. She might, quite easily. Or she might rally and go on for days or
even weeks. But her heart's getting very bad. I'm afraid you'll have to be
prepared for it to happen any time.'

He spoke to her about the practical side of death, and he spoke to her about
the continued effort to feed the old body. And then he said, 'I rang up the

relieving officer about her today. I think he'll be coming round to see you tomorrow.'

She said, 'That's somebody who doles out money, isn't it?'

'In a way,' he replied. 'He has power to give monetary relief to cases of hardship that aren't covered under any of the existing Acts. He's a municipal officer.' He paused. 'I wish I'd known about this patient earlier. I could have asked him to come round and see her months ago, but I had no idea.'

Jennifer said, 'I don't believe my grandmother would have seen him.'

'Why not?'

She shrugged her shoulders. 'She'd have looked on it as charity money. All her life she's been more accustomed to giving to charities than taking from them.'

'He's very tactful, I believe.'

'He'd have to be,' she said. 'My grandmother's a lady—the old-fashioned sort.'

There was a pause. 'In any case,' she said, 'that won't be necessary now. Granny got a cheque today for five hundred pounds, from a relation in Australia who was worried about her. There's enough money now to pay for anything she ought to have.'

'Five hundred pounds!' he said. 'That's a lot of money. Pity it didn't come three months ago.'

'I know,' she said. It's just one of those things.'

He thought for a moment. 'Would you like me to see if I can get a nurse for her tomorrow?'

'My father will be here tomorrow,' she said. 'He's a doctor. He'll be here about midday. Could we talk it over with you then? I should think a nurse would be a good thing.'

He nodded. 'I'll see if I can get one for tomorrow night. You'll need some relief by then.'

They went out into the hall, and he put on his coat. He paused then, hat in hand. 'She's got relations in Australia, has she? Do you know where they live?'

'They keep a sheep farm,' the girl said. 'Somewhere in Victoria, I think.' He nodded slowly. 'I still can't quite understand it,' she said. 'Granny thought they were quite poor, but then this money arrived for her today. They must be very well off to send a sum like that.'

'The graziers are doing very well,' he said. 'Everybody in that country seems to be doing very well.' He hesitated. 'I'm going to try it out there for a bit, myself.'

She looked at him, surprised. '*You* are? Are you leaving England?'

'Just for a bit,' he said. 'I think it does one good to move around, and there's not much future in the Health Service. I think it'll be better for the children, too, and it's not like going abroad. I've got a passage booked on the *Orion*, sailing on April the eighteenth. It's a bit of a gamble, but I've had it here.'

'Where are you going to?' she asked. 'What part of Australia?'

'Brisbane,' he said. 'I was there for a bit in 1944, when I was in the Navy. I liked it all right. I believe you could have a lot of fun in Queensland.' He hesitated for a moment, and then said, 'Don't talk about this, please, Miss Morton. It's not generally known yet that I'm going.'

'I shan't talk,' she said. 'I don't know anyone in Ealing.'

He went away, and she went back into the kitchen and stood thoughtful over the electric stove as she warmed up the milk again. The house was dead silent but for the low noise of wind and a little trickling noise of water from some gutter. She poured the milk into the cup and added the brandy, and took it up to her grandmother.

'How are you feeling now, Granny?' she asked.

The old lady did not answer, but her eyes were open and she was awake. Jennifer sat down on the bedside and lifted her with an arm around her shoulders and held the cup to her lips. She drank a little, and the brandy may have strengthened her, because presently she said in a thin voice, 'Jenny, I'm going to die.'

The girl said, 'So am I, Granny, but not just yet. Nor are you. Drink a bit more of this.'

'Have you ever seen anybody die, Jenny?'

The girl shook her head.

'I wish there was somebody here with you.'

The girl held the cup up to the lips. It was stupid to feel frightened, and she must not show it. 'Try a little more. It's good for you.'

Too weak to argue, the old lady took a tiny sip or two. Then she said, 'Jenny.' There was a long pause while she gathered strength, and then she said, 'My cheque-book. In the small left-hand drawer of the bureau. And my pen.'

'Do you want to write a cheque, Granny?' The old eyes signified assent. 'Leave it till the morning. Drink a little more of this, and then get some sleep.'

The old lady pushed the cup aside. 'No. Now.'

The girl put the cup down and went downstairs. She knew that the doctor had been right and that her grandmother would die that night. She was not frightened now; her duty was to ease the passing of the old lady and do what she wanted in the last few hours. She was calm and competent and thoughtful as she brought the pen and cheque-book and a blotting-pad to the bedside.

'Are these what you want, Granny?'

The old lady nodded slightly, and the girl put them on the sheet before her, and arranged the pillows, and lifted the old lady into a sitting position. She gave her another drink of the hot milk and brandy. Presently the old lady said, 'Bring that thing.'

The girl was puzzled. 'What thing is it?' And then she got up and fetched the draft from the dressing-table, and said, 'This?'

Her grandmother nodded weakly and took it from her and looked round, questing, till Jennifer divined what it was that she wanted, and gave her her spectacles. She put them on, and them said distinctly, 'Such a funny sort of cheque. I never saw one like it.' And then she endorsed it on the back with a hand that trembled, with a signature that was barely legible.

Jennifer held the cup up to her lips, and she drank a little more. Then, with a sudden spurt of energy, she took the cheque-book and wrote quite a legible cheque for four hundred pounds, payable to Jennifer Morton.

The girl, looking on as she wrote, said, 'Granny, you mustn't do that. I don't want it, and you'll need the money when you get well.'

The old lady whispered, 'I want you to do something for me, Jenny. Write letters now, send this to my bank and this to yours. Then go and post them.'

'I'll do that in the morning, Granny. I can't leave you alone tonight.'

The old lady gathered her ebbing strength, and said, 'Go and write them now, my dear, and bring them up and show me. And then go out and post them.'

'All right.' She could not disobey so positive and direct a command. She thought as she wrote the letters at her grandmother's bureau in the drawing-room that she could sort the matter out with her father next day and pay the money back; the thing now was to ease the old lady's passing and not disobey her. She brought the letters and the envelopes up to the bedside and showed them; the old lady did not speak, but watched her as she put the letters and the cheques into the envelopes and sealed them down. The girl said, 'There they are, Granny, all ready to post. May I post them in the morning?'

The lady shook slightly, and the old lips said, 'Now.'

'All right. I expect I'll be away about ten minutes, Granny; I'll have to go down to the Broadway. I'll be back as quick as I can.'

The old head nodded slightly, and the girl went down and put her coat on, and ran most of the way to the post office, and most of the way back. She came back into the bedroom flushed and breathing quickly, but her grandmother's eyes were closed, and she seemed to be asleep.

The girl went down to the kitchen and made herself a cup of tea, and ate a little meal of toast and jam. Then she went back to the bedroom and settled down in the chair before the electric stove.

At about half-past twelve the old lady opened her eyes and said, 'Jenny, did you post the letters?'

'I posted them, Granny.'

'There's a dear girl,' the voice from the bed said weakly. 'I've been so worried for you, but you'll be all right with Jane.'

The girl blinked in surprise, but there were more important things to be done than to ask for explanations. 'Don't try and talk,' she said. 'Let me get some more hot water in these bottles.'

Her grandmother said, 'No. Jenny . . . Jenny . . .'

The girl paused in the act of taking the bottles from the bed. 'What is it, Granny?'

The old lady said something that the girl could not catch. And then she said, 'It's not as if we were extravagant, Geoffrey and I. It's been a change that nobody could fight against, this going down and down. I've had such terrible thoughts for you, Jenny, that it would go on going down and down, and when you are as old as I am you would look back at your room at Blackheath and your office work, as I look back to my life at Steep Manor, and you'll think how very rich you were when you were young.'

It did not make sense to the girl. She said, 'I'm just going to take these bottles down and fill them, Granny. I'll be back in a few minutes.'

Her grandmother said, 'I always took a hot-water-bottle with me when we went out on shikar. Geoffrey's bearer, dear old Moung Bah, used to boil up water over the wood fire and fill it for me, while Geoffrey cleaned his gun in front of the tent. Such lovely times we had out in the jungle, dear. Such lovely places . . .' The old voice died away into silence.

The girl took the hot-water-bottles and went quickly downstairs to fill them. When she came back with them and put them in the bed around the old lady, her grandmother was lying with closed eyes; she seemed fairly comfortable, but the respiration was much worse. She was breathing in short gasps three or four times in succession; then would come a silence when for a long time she did not seem to breathe at all. It was fairly obvious to the girl that the end was coming. She wondered if she ought to go and fetch the doctor from his bed, and then she thought that there was nothing he could do; better for other and more vital patients that he should be allowed to rest. She sat down by the bedside in the chair to wait, holding her grandmother's hand, filled with deep sadness at the close of life.

The old lady spoke suddenly from the bed. Jennifer missed the first words again; she may have been half asleep. She heard, '–on twenty-two thousand a year, better than we lived at Steep. Give her my very dearest love when you see her, Jenny. I'm so happy for you now. It was so sweet of her to send those lovely fruits. Be sure and tell her how much we enjoyed them.'

There was a long, long pause, and then she said, 'So glad she sent the money for your fare. I've had so much, much more than you poor girls today.'

Jennifer was on her feet now; there was something here that had to be cleared up. She held her grandmother's hand between her own young, warm ones. 'What did you give me that money for, Granny? What do you want me to do with the four hundred pounds? Try and tell me.'

The old lips muttered, 'Dear Jane. Such lovely fruits.'

The girl stood by the bedside, waiting. If she had understood the old lady at all she was making an incredible proposal, but, after all, the doctor was going.

She said, 'Try and tell me what you want me to do with the four hundred pounds, Granny.'

There were a few faint, jumbled words that Jennifer missed, and then she heard, '–a little horse for you everything that I had at your age.'

There was very little time left now. The girl said, 'Granny! Did you give me the four hundred pounds because you want me to go to Australia to visit Aunt Jane? Is that what you're trying to say? Is that what you'd like me to do with the money?'

There was a faint, unmistakable nod. Then the old eyes closed again, as if in sleep. The girl laid the hand carefully beneath the bedclothes and sat down again to wait. There was a terrific mess here that her father must help her to clear up.

At about two o'clock her grandmother spoke again for the last time. Jennifer, bending by the old lips, heard her say, 'The dear Queen's statue in Moulmein . . . white marble. So sweet of the Burmese . . .'

About an hour later the old lady died. Jennifer, standing by the bedside, could not say within a quarter of an hour when death occurred.

3

Jennifer met her father at the front door of the house early the next afternoon. She had gone out into the wet, windy streets at about four in the morning to stand in a call-box in the Broadway to ring him up in Leicester; the telephone was by his bed and she got through to him without delay, and told him of the death. Then she had walked back to the house. She had expected to be troubled and reluctant to go back there, but in fact she found she was not worried in the least by the thought of her dead grandmother upstairs. She was calm and serious; she felt that she had done a good job and her grandmother was pleased with her; if she had still been alive the old lady would have wanted her to have a little meal and get some sleep. So she made herself a meal of tea and bread and jam in the kitchen of the silent house, turned on the radiator in the living-room, curled herself up on the sofa with a rug over her, and slept. She did not wake until the middle of the morning, when the district nurse came.

Her father came down to Ealing alone. Her mother had made arrangements to come with him, but she was coughing a good deal and far from well, and on the news of her mother's death Jennifer's father had persuaded his wife to stay at home and not risk making herself ill just for the funeral. So he came down alone, and met his daughter at the house at about two o'clock.

'I'm very sorry you had this alone, Jenny,' he said. 'I'm very sorry indeed.'

'That's all right, Daddy,' she said. 'It's a good thing I was working in London.'

He glanced around the drawing-room. 'She was very fond of this house,' he said. 'We tried once or twice to get her to come up to Leicester and live near us, but she insisted on staying here.'

The girl nodded. 'This was her own house, and she wouldn't have wanted to be a burden upon anybody. She was very independent.'

Her father said, 'We never dreamed that there was anything wrong with her pension, or her money generally. I suppose I should have come to see her more often, and gone into things a bit more.'

'She probably wouldn't have told you,' the girl said.

He asked her about the practical business of the doctor and the death certificate and the undertaker, and went out to see about these things himself. Jennifer went out to find somewhere for her father and herself to stay that night, and with some difficulty found a private hotel with a couple of bedrooms empty; then she went back to the house to wait for her father. When he came she made him tea, and they sat in the drawing-room among the Burmese relics before an electric radiator while she told him what had happened the night before.

'She insisted on giving me the cheque,' she told her father, 'and made me go out and post it to my bank. What ought I to do, Daddy? I'll have to pay it back to the executor, shan't I?'

He shook his head. 'Keep it.'

'Is that all right?'

'I think so,' he said. 'Unless she's changed her will, I'm the executor and the whole of the residuary estate goes to your mother. The four hundred pounds is probably yours, legally. But anyway, it doesn't matter.'

'Oughtn't it to go back to Aunt Jane?' She paused. 'After all, she sent it for Granny, not me.'

He pondered this. 'Did you say there was a letter from Jane Dorman.'

She went and fetched it for him from her grandmother's room, and he read it carefully. 'I don't think you need give it back,' he said. 'The intention is quite clear; she says that if Ethel didn't need it she was to give it to a charity. Well, she doesn't need it, and she's given it to you. It's yours to do what you like with, Jenny.'

The girl stared at the hot elements of the fire. 'I'm not so sure about that,' she said. 'I think it's mine to do what Granny liked.'

'What do you mean?'

She told him what had passed between them in the last hour of the old life. 'She kept saying what a rotten time girls have in England now, compared with when she was young,' she said. 'I suppose all old people are like that, that everything was better in their day. And then, it seemed quite definite, she wanted me to go and see Aunt Jane with the money. Go to Australia, I mean. It seemed as if she thought that I'd be getting back into the sort of life she knew when she was a girl, if I went out there and stayed with Aunt Jane.'

Her father said thoughtfully, 'I see. Do you want to go, Jenny?'

The girl said honestly, 'I don't know. I've not had time to think about it. I'd love to travel, of course, and see something of the world. But Granny's world . . . that's gone for ever, surely? Huntin' and shootin' and fishin', and about fifteen servants all calling you Madam. . . . If that's what happens in Australia, I don't want to go there.'

'I should be sorry to see you go to Australia, Jenny. You're the only one we've got.'

She smiled at him. 'Don't worry, Daddy. I can't see myself going.'

There was one job that had to be done before they left for the hotel, and that was to gather up all the papers in the house for examination. Edward Morton decided to start on that that evening at the hotel, but when they came to investigate the papers they found a formidable mass of stuff. The drawers of the old lady's bureau, and a sort of tallboy, were crammed full of letters and papers, the relics of a long life thrust into drawers and there forgotten. Insurance policies of 1907 were mixed up with leases of furnished houses rented on some leave in the dim past, and personal letters, and receipts, and cheque-book stubs were everywhere among the mass. They found three suitcases in the house and filled them full of all this paper, and at that there was enough left over to fill another two. Her father said, 'I'll go through these tonight, Jenny and chuck away what it's not necessary to keep. Then perhaps I'll be able to look through the rest of it tomorrow here.'

Jennifer hoped that The Poplars private hotel would be complacent about a hundredweight of waste paper, in the morning.

They got a taxi from the station and drove to The Poplars and dined together meagrely. Jenny had had two virtually sleepless nights and she could hardly keep her eyes open during the meal. As soon as it was over, she said, 'Daddy, do you mind if I go up now? I'm practically asleep.' He kissed her and wished her good-night. Then he went up to his own room and put a shilling in the slot of the gas meter and lit the stove, and pulled a chair up to the little radiants, and opened the first suit-case.

In the white-painted, rather bleak and functional bedroom the pageant of a long life gradually unrolled before him as the heap of torn papers on the floor beside him grew. It was about twenty minutes after he had started that he came upon the cookery book.

It was a small manuscript book. It began in a hand that was feminine and strange to him, and about half the recipes in the book were written in that hand; thereafter it had been written on by Ethel Trehearn, first in an unformed, almost childish hand, later maturing into the writing that he knew. On the flyleaf was the inscription,

For my dear daughter, Ethel, on the happy occasion
of her Marriage to Geoffrey Trehearn,
from her mother. June 16th, 1893.

It had been a pleasant and a practical thought of the mother to give the bride a personal cookery book as one of her wedding presents; fifty-seven years later Edward Morton smiled a little sympathetically, as he turned the leaves. How unformed the writing of the bride was in the first entry . . .

Aunt Hester's cake (very good)
Take two pounds of Jersey butter, two pounds best castor sugar, ½ gill of caramel, 2¼ lb of flour, 18 eggs, 3 lb of currants, 3 lbs of sultanas, 1½ lb of mixed peel, ½ lb of blanched sweet almonds, the grated rind of two lemons, a small nutmeg, 1 oz mixed spice, and ½ a pint of brandy.

He ran his eye down the recipe with the tolerant amusement of a doctor to the final,

–cover with almond icing and coat with royal and transparent icing. Then pipe the cake with royal icing according to taste.

What a world to live in, and how ill they must have been! His eye ran back to the ingredients. Two pounds of Jersey butter . . . eight weeks' ration for one person. The egg ration for one person for four months. . . . Currants and sultanas in those quantities; mixed peel, that he had not seen for years. Half a pint of brandy, so plentiful that you could put half a pint into a cake, and think nothing of it.

He laid the book down on his knee and stared at the stove. Funny the way that things worked out sometimes. This bride had died of starvation, with nothing to eat but currants and sultanas and candied peel in the end. He wondered, had she thought in those days of 'Aunt Hester's cake (very good)'?

Things had changed, and people no longer lived as they had done in 1893. He had eaten such cakes when he was a young man before the war of 1914, but now he could hardly remember what a cake like that would taste like. Jennifer had never eaten anything like that at all, of course, and so she couldn't miss it. Funny how the standards of living had changed, at any rate in England.

He thumbed the book through idly, glancing here and there at a page. Her mother had had little confidence in the memory or interest of her daughter before marriage, for she had written out the simplest recipes in full. 'For breakfast, bacon and eggs. For four people, take eight eggs or more if the men will want them and about a pound of streaky bacon cut in rashers . . .' He could remember breakfasts like that when he was a boy–how long it seemed since he had eaten like that! He turned the pages idly. 'Steak and Onions. Take three pounds of steak . . .'

He had not eaten a grilled steak and onions for twelve years; perhaps Jennifer at twenty-four had never eaten it at all. People seemed to keep healthy enough on the English rationed food. He was approaching sixty years of age himself and he new well, perhaps too well, that men of his years think everything was better organized when they were young. It was an old man's fancy, doubtless, that the young men were more virile in England, and the girls prettier, in 1914 than they were today. People kept healthy enough, but they had not the zest for life that they had had when he was young. Jennifer with her auburn hair looked pale and sallow most of the time, but at twenty-four she should be in her prime.

He laid the cookery book aside, too precious to destroy; though it might only be of academic interest in England now it was a pity to throw away a little book that had been prized for so many years. He turned over and tore up masses of old letters, only glancing at the signatures in case they were the autographs of famous people, and he retained one or two. Then he shook out the contents of a cardboard box that once held envelopes, and out fell dance programmes, dozens and dozens of them.

It was years since he had seen the little cards, heavily embossed with gilt and coloured lettering, with little pencils attached by a thread of silk. How thick and fine the paper was, how generous! Dance programmes with little pencils attached seemed to have gone out in England, perhaps because of fashion or perhaps because of paper rationing; if they were used, however, cards like that would cost two or three shillings each, with printing, pencils, purchase tax, and everything. Things had been cheaper, easier, and more gracious when Ethel had been young. And how many of the cards there were, how many dances she had been to! There were thirty-five or forty of them; assuming she had kept the programme of every dance that she had ever been to, which seemed unlikely, even so it was a considerable number of formal dances for a young girl to attend. She had been married at twenty-two, younger than Jennifer. He was quite sure that Jennifer had not been to thirty-five or forty formal dances. People didn't seem to give them so much now as they had in his young days; perhaps it had grown too expensive.

There were photographs almost by the hundred. He discarded the faded, sepia snapshots, hardly looking at them; there could be nothing worth keeping in those. He paused longer over the professional portraits. One was a very grand affair, hand-tinted by a photographer in Dover Street; it showed a mother and daughter in Court dress, the long trains sweeping from behind each side of the standing pair. He could see the Ethel he had first met as a middle-aged woman in the features of the girl. But what a dress, and what a train! white silk with delicate lines of a pale rose pink, showy and ornate by modern standards, it might be, but very lovely all the same. And what jewellery for a young girl to wear! That necklace, carefully worked up by the tinter, apparently of gold and rubies. Jennifer had never worn a dress or jewellery like that, and yet she came of the same family. He put the photograph aside, thinking that Jennifer might like to see her grandmother as a young woman.

There was a little bundle of letters tied with ribbon, perhaps love letters. He hesitated for a moment, thinking to throw them away unread; then he undid them and glanced at the signatures. They were all signed 'Jane'. He picked one for its embossed letterhead and glanced it through. It was dated March 5th, 1919, and it read,

S.S. *Mooltan*
In the Mediterranean

MY DARLING AUNT,

I would have written to post at Gibraltar but I've been terribly seasick ever since we left England just like being in a funny story only I didn't think it funny at all. Jack was only sick one day but I was in my bunk for five days, all through the Bay, in a cabin with five other girls all married to Australians and going out like us, all sick together except one. I felt awfully silly and very glad in a way that Jack and I couldn't have a cabin together because it would have been horrid for him with me being sick all the time. However, it seems to be over now and I've been sitting out on deck in the hot sun for two days and going into the saloon for every meal, and eating like a horse.

I wanted to write to you before now to thank you for all you have done for us over the last year. I believe you were the only one of the whole family who didn't faint at the idea of me marrying an Australian soldier and who really tried to make Jack feel at home and one of us. I'm sorry in a way that I'm leaving England and going out to live so far away, sorry that I shan't see Father and Mother again for years and years, or perhaps at all. But these last few months haven't been a very happy time as I suppose you know, and though I'm sorry to be leaving everyone and everything I know, I'm glad at the same time, if you know what I mean. I'm glad to be out of all the complications and unpleasantness and able to start fresh in a new place with Jack.

We're going to have a hard time for the first few years, much harder than if I'd been a good girl and stayed at home and married one of Father's officers, solid bone from the chin upwards. I might have done that if it hadn't been for the war, but two years in the W.A.A.C.s make one different. Jack has been promised a job with a firm called Dalgety which means going round the cattle and sheep stations selling machinery and stuff like that to the farmers in a place called Gippsland; we shan't have much money but he's got a house for us through his uncle in a little market town called Korrumburra somewhere in the depths of the country. I'll write and give you the address as soon as ever I know it; write to me sometimes, because although I'm glad to be going I expect I shall be lonely sometimes, and longing for letters.

I don't know how to thank you for being so sweet to Jack. It meant an awful lot to him to find one of my family who really liked him for himself—besides me, of course. I don't suppose I'll ever be able to do anything for you like you've done for us, like the elephant and the mouse. Only I'd like to call one of our children Ethel if there is a girl. I think I'm in the family way already but I'm not quite sure, so don't tell anybody yet.

Our very, very dearest love to you and Uncle Geoffrey.

Your affectionate niece,

JANE

Morton was tired now. He had barely sorted one of the three suitcases, but he was too tired to go on that night; the white bed beckoned him in invitation. He folded the letter carefully and put it with the others of the bundle and retied the ribbon. Better to keep that lot, or send them back, perhaps, to Jane Dorman in Australia.

He had never met Jane Dorman and he knew little of her but that she had made an unfortunate marriage with an Australian soldier after the first war, and had left the country with him, and had never been home since. That was all that he had known about her twelve hours ago; in those hours she had come alive for him, and now she was a real person. She had formed her own life and battled through, and now she had attained a point where she could send five hundred pounds to her old aunt to quell a fear for her that he had never felt. Jane Dorman, twelve thousand miles away, in her enduring affection had sensed that Ethel Trehearn was ill and short of money. Her daughter, who was his wife, and he, living no more than a hundred miles away from the old lady, had had no idea that anything was wrong.

Jane and Jack Dorman, from her recent letter, had become wealthy people now, far better off than he himself. He could hardly have found five hundred shillings for the old lady without selling something. It wasn't that he was extravagant, or Mary either. In these days, in England and in general practice, the money just wasn't there, and that was all about it.

He got into bed and turned off the light, but sleep did not come easily. How well Ethel Trehearn had lived when she was a young woman; how incredible it all seemed now! And yet, thinking back over his own youth, perhaps not quite so incredible. The standard of living had slipped imperceptibly in England as year succeeded year, as war succeeded war. His own father had been a doctor before him, but in York. He could remember how he lived as a boy in the big house in Clifton now used as part of the municipal offices of York and full of draughtsmen. They had kept a coachman and a groom before the days of motor-cars, and a horse for his father's dog-cart, and a horse for the brougham. There had been a whole-time gardener, and always two servants in the house, and sometimes three. It was unthinkable in his father's household that there should be any shortage of any food for family or servants; there always seemed to be plenty of money for anything they wanted to do, nor did his father have to work particularly hard. Only the most urgent cases ever called him out on Sunday, and all through the winter one day in each week was sacred to the shooting. It was a good life, that, that Ethel Trehearn had known as a young woman, and his father. It might some day come again in England, but not in his own time.

He turned restlessly in his bed, unable to sleep. It was easy to say that good times would come again in England, but was it true? In each year of the peace food had got shorter and shorter, more and more expensive, and taxation had risen higher and higher. He was now living on a lower scale than in the war-time years; the decline had gone on steadily, if anything increasing in momentum, and there seemed no end to it. Where would it all end, and what lay ahead of the young people of today in England? What lay ahead of Jennifer?

He lay uneasily all night, a worried and an anxious man. He got up at dawn and went out for a short walk before breakfast, as was his habit. He met Jennifer at the breakfast table and they talked of the work that lay before them, the undertaker coming at ten o'clock, the search for a second-hand furniture dealer to make an offer for the furniture left in the house, the estate agent to be found who would sell the house itself. These were easy and straightforward matters that had to be attended to before Morton went back to his practice in Leicester; more difficult was the personal matter that he must talk over with his daughter.

He broached it as they walked through the suburban streets. 'I've been thinking about you going to Australia, Jenny,' he said. 'There's a lot to be said, for and against. I don't think we want to decide anything too hastily.'

She glanced at him in surprise. 'You don't think I ought to go, Daddy?'

'I don't know,' he said. 'I don't know what to think. There's this four hundred pounds dumped into your lap, so to speak, and that's what she wanted you to do with it. It might not be a bad idea to go out for a few months and see if you like it. There should be plenty of money to pay your passage out and home.'

'I wouldn't want to stay out there, Daddy. I couldn't leave you and Mummy.'

'We wouldn't want to lose you, Jenny. But I must say, I get worried sometimes thinking of the way things are going here.'

The girl was silent. Even in her own memory the stringencies in her parents' home had increased; her own wage packet bought a good deal less than it had bought two years before. With the optimism of youth she said, 'We'll get an election and a change of Government before long. Then everything will get cheap again, won't it?'

He shook his head. 'I wish I could think so. I don't think it's anything to do with Socialism. It's been going on for thirty years, this has, this getting poorer and poorer. Too many people to feed here in England, out of too few fields. It's the food-producing countries that'll be the ones to live in in the future. You can see it now. Look at Jane Dorman!'

'That's wool, Daddy. They didn't make their money out of food. They made it out of wool.'

'Well, we've got to have wool, and we don't grow enough of our own. I'm dressed in it almost entirely. So are you.'

Jennifer thought of her winter clothes. 'Mostly, in this weather,' she agreed. They walked on for a time in silence. 'If I went out to Australia I'd have to get a job,' she said. 'I couldn't just go out and live upon Aunt Jane.'

He nodded. 'You could do that all right. I expect they want secretaries in Victoria.'

'What's the capital of Victoria, Daddy. Is it Adelaide?'

He shook his head. 'I don't know. I think that's over on the west coast somewhere. I'd have to look at an atlas.'

Later in the day, when they were having tea in the kitchen of her grandmother's house before going back to the hotel, Jennifer said, 'Of course, I'd like to go out to Australia for the trip. The only thing is, I wouldn't want to stay there.'

'You've never been out of England before, have you, Jenny?'

'I've been to France,' she said. 'I'd love to go like that, if one could look on it as just a holiday. Six months or so. But I'd never want to go and live out there.'

'Why not?'

She struggled to express herself. 'This is our place; this is where we belong. We're English, not Australian.'

He thought for a minute. 'I suppose that's right. But that's not the way the British Empire was created.'

'You don't want me to stay out there for good, do you, Daddy?'

'I want you to do what's best for you,' he said. 'I'm worried, Jenny, and I don't mind telling you. If this decline goes on, I'm worried over what may happen to you before you die.'

'That's what Granny said,' the girl replied uncertainly. 'She said that she was worried for me. Everybody seems to be worrying about me. I can look after myself.'

Her father smiled. 'All the same,' he said, 'no harm in going on a six months' trip out to Australia if it gets dropped into your lap.'

'It seems such a waste of money.'

'It's what she gave it to you for,' he said. 'But it's your money to do what you like with. Think it over.'

The funeral was on Saturday, and after it was over Jennifer went with her father to St Pancras to see him off. Then she travelled down by train to Blackheath through the drab suburbs of New Cross and Lewisham. As she went the blazing Australian deserts, the wide cattle stations, the blue seas and coral islands that she had read about in novels danced before her eyes; it seemed incredible that these things could be within her grasp, these places could be hers to go to if she wished. Only the inertia of giving up her job and going, of getting out of her rut, now stood between her and these places.

She had a duty to perform on the Sunday, the duty of writing to Jane Dorman at this queer address, 'Leonora, Merrijig, Victoria' to tell her of the death of Ethel Trehearn, and to tell her about the disposition of her five hundred pounds. She sat down on Sunday morning to write this letter; when she had finished, it was a straight, factual account of what had happened, with the unpleasant fact glossed over that the old lady's death had been virtually from starvation. She could not bring herself to tell anyone in another country that such things could happen in England. At the end she wrote,

As it stands now, I've got four hundred of your five hundred pounds, and I'm not too happy about it. She gave it me because she wanted me to go out to Australia and see if I would like to make my life out there, and to visit you. I should like to see you, of course, but as for living in Australia I think it's very unlikely that I'd like it; I suppose I'm incurably English. If I did come I'd have to get a job, of course; I'm a qualified shorthand typist with four years' experience since I got my diploma. Do you think I could get a job in Melbourne, or would that be difficult?

Do tell me if you would like to have the money back and I'll send it at once, because honestly I don't feel as though it's mine at all.

Yours sincerely,
JENNIFER MORTON

She got this off by air mail at midday on Sunday, and relaxed.

That was a time of strain and gloom in England, with the bad news of the war in Korea superimposed upon the increasing shortages of food and fuel and the prospect of heavy increases in taxation to pay for rearmament. In the week that followed Jennifer's return to work the meat ration was cut again, and now reached a point when it was only sufficient for one meagre meal of meat a week. When shortages are shared equally they are nothing like so painful as they would be in a free economy; if the Smiths can afford to buy meat and the Jones not, the strain may be intolerable, but if nobody can have the meat the lack of meat soon ceases to annoy. Nevertheless the present cut produced some serious and heated discussion at the lunch table between the men, which Jennifer listened to with interest. There were about three hundred clerical staff in that office of the Ministry of Pensions, and they mostly lunched together in one large canteen.

Forsyth, head of Department D.3. in Rehabilitation, said, 'The plain fact of it is that these Argentinos have got us where they want us. They've got the food and we've got to have it or go under.'

Morrison, in the Accounts Branch, said, 'We can't pay the prices that they're asking. The economy won't stand it.'

'We'll have to do without something, then. Free spectacles and false teeth. We've got to eat *something*.'

Somebody said something about the Minister of Food, '–that — fool. Getting the Argentinos' back up.'

Sanders, from the Assessment Branch, said, 'I don't agree at all. It's easy to sling mud at him, but he's done a marvellous job.'

'In what way?'

Sanders said, 'Well, the country's never been so healthy as it is now. Everybody gets enough to eat. The only thing that you can say against the food is that it's a bit dull sometimes. But everybody gets enough of it. Nobody dies of starvation in this country, like they do in France. That's the difference between a controlled economy and *laissez faire*.'

Jennifer thought of one old lady who had died of starvation, but she said nothing. Her grandmother could have applied to the relieving officer, of course. . . . She could not speak without showing indignation, and it was better not to make a row before the men.

Morrison said, 'There's one big difference between this country and France.' He spoke with the deliberation of an accountant, and with a slight North Country accent.

'What's that?' asked Sanders.

'You take a successful professional man,' said Morrison slowly. 'A leading surgeon, maybe, or a barrister. With taxes and costs the way they are, he really hasn't got a chance of saving for his old age, not like he could before the war. He'll save something, of course, but a man like that, he doesn't get into the big money much before he's forty-five or fifty, and in the few good years that he's got left he can't save enough to retire on in the way of life that he's accustomed to. He just can't do it, with the tax and surtax as it is. You've only got to look at the figures to see that it's impossible.'

Forsyth said, 'That's right.'

'Well, if a man like a first-class surgeon can't save properly for his old age, nobody can,' said Morrison. 'That means that nobody in England can feel safe. Everybody in this country today is worried sick for what may happen to him and to his wife when they get old, except the very lowest paid classes, who can get by on the retirement pension.'

'Well, how do you make out that things are any better in France?' asked Sanders.

'This way,' said the accountant. 'In France the man like the surgeon or the barrister is taxed much less than he is here, and the working man pays proportionately more. I don't say that's a good thing—it may be, or may not be. The fact is that it's different. In France, the leading surgeon or the leading barrister *can* save for his old age, and save enough to give him security in the way of life he's used to. He's not worried sick for what may happen to him. In France, if you're successful enough, you're all right. That means that in France you've got *some* happy and contented people. Here you've got none.'

'Yes, but hell!' said Sanders. 'That's at the expense of the under-dogs.'

'I don't say it's not,' said the accountant equably. 'I'm just saying that the French system does produce *some* happy people, and ours doesn't.'

The argument drifted inconclusively along till it was time to get back to the offices.

A day or two later, to Jennifer's interest, the subject of emigration came up. None of the older men seemed particularly interested in it. 'My nephew, he went out to Canada,' one said. 'He's an engineer; got a job in a tractor factory in Montreal. He was out there in the war with the R.A.F., so he knows the country. He's doing all right, but he says the winter's terrible.'

'It's not right, the way these young chaps go abroad,' said Sanders. 'If it goes on, the Government will have to put a stop to it.'

Jennifer spoke up with suppressed indignation. 'Why should they do that?' she asked. 'Why shouldn't people go abroad if they want to?'

Sanders was about to answer, but the accountant intervened. 'Because the country can't afford it.'

The girl said, 'They pay their own passages, don't they?'

'I'm not speaking about that, Miss Morton,' said the accountant. 'Look, suppose it was you who wanted to go to Canada.' It was uncomfortably near home, but the girl nodded. 'How much do you think you cost?'

'Me? In money?'

'That's right,' said Morrison.

'I don't quite know what you mean,' she said.

'I'll tell you, very roughly,' he said. 'When did you start working?'

'I got my first job when I was eighteen,' she told him.

'Right. For eighteen years somebody in this country fed you and clothed you and educated you before you made any money, before you started earning. Say you cost an average two quid a week for that eighteen years. You've cost

England close on two thousand pounds to produce.'

Somebody said, 'Like a machine tool.'

'That's right,' the accountant said. 'A human dictaphone and typewriter combined, all electronic and maintains itself and does its own repairs, that's cost two thousand quid. Suppose you go off to Canada. You're an asset worth two thousand quid that England gives to Canada as a free gift. If a hundred thousand like you were to go each year, it'ld be like England giving Canada a subsidy of two hundred million pounds each year. It's got to be thought about, this emigration. We can't afford to go chucking money away like that.'

She said puzzled, 'It's not really like that, is it?'

'It is and all,' said Morrison. 'That's what built up the United States. Half a million emigrants a year went from Central Europe to America for Fifty years or so. Say they were worth a thousand quid apiece. Right–that was a subsidy from Central Europe to America of five hundred million quid a year, and it went on for fifty years or so. Human bulldozers.'

He leaned forward on the table. 'Believe it or not,' he said, 'Central Europe got very poor and the U.S.A. got very rich.'

There was laughter at the table. 'It's a fact, I'm telling you,' said the accountant. 'Central Europe got very poor. If all that manpower had stayed at home in Poland and in Czechoslovakia we might have had a good deal less trouble from Hitler. We want to watch the same thing doesn't happen here. It could do, easily, if too many people start emigrating.' He paused. 'It could be the ruin of this country.'

'I don't see how you can keep people here if they want to go,' the girl said. 'After all, what's the Commonwealth or Empire or whatever they call it these days–what's it for? You can go to Australia if you want to, can't you?'

Sanders said, 'You can at present, but it's got to be controlled. People can't always do the things they want to.'

'I'm sick of the word control,' said Jennifer. 'We didn't have to have all these controls before the war.'

'No,' said Sanders. 'We had three million unemployed instead.' He leaned across the table. 'I'll give you a better reason than the money why people ought to stay here.'

'What's that?' asked Forsyth.

'To do a good job for the world,' said Sanders. 'I'll tell you. Here in England we've got the most advanced form of government of any country in the world. It's experimental, and I know there've been mistakes. Some things that have been tried out aren't so hot, like ground nuts in Tanganyika, and they've had to be written off. But what this country has tried to do, and what it's doing, is to plan for a new form of government and put it into practice, a new form of democracy where everyone will get a square deal. When we've shown it can be done, the world will copy it, all right. You see. But it can't be worked out if people are allowed to run away to other countries. It's their job to stay here and get this one right.'

Jennifer said, 'You mean, one ought to stay here because there's an experiment in Socialism going on, and if we go away we'll spoil it?'

'That's right.'

Forsyth said, 'Too bad when the guinea-pig escapes from the laboratory before the research is finished. It kind of spoils the experiment, Miss Morton.'

There was laughter, and Sanders flushed angrily. 'It's not like that at all. It's for the good of everyone to stay in England. This is the most advanced country in the world.'

Forsyth said, 'Maybe. I'd trade the brave new world for an old-fashioned capitalistic porterhouse steak.'

Jennifer said, 'If there's one thing that would make me want to go and emigrate it's what you've just said—that one's got to stay here for the sake of an experiment.'

Morrison laughed. 'She's got a bourgeois ideology,' he said. 'She's nothing but a ruddy Kulak, Sanders.'

Jennifer went back to her work that afternoon, but the incident stayed in her mind, and rankled. She had no particular aversion to Mr Sanders; indeed he was a healthy, youngish man who had been an officer in the R.N.V.R. during the war and had commanded an L.C.T. in the invasion of Normandy. What irked her was the display of Socialist enthusiasm that pervaded her office, which seemed to her slightly phoney. It was manifestly impossible for anyone who derided the Socialistic ideal to progress very far in the public service; if a young man aimed at promotion in her office he felt it necessary to declare a firm, almost a religious, belief in the principles of Socialism. Jennifer felt instinctively that Mr Sanders was less concerned with the Brave New World than the progress of Mr Sanders in the Ministry of Pensions, and she wondered what would happen to his views if an election should bring in a Conservative Government.

In the meantime she felt constrained and restricted by bureaucracy; it could not seriously be true that she would have to stay in England if she wanted to go. Abruptly the thought of going to Australia for a time became attractive to her; if they said she couldn't go, she'd darned well go.

On Monday she got a cable at her boarding-house. It read,

Deeply grieved Aunt Ethel but so glad you were with her of course keep money and do come out here and visit us plenty of jobs Melbourne about ten pounds weekly writing air mail.

JANE DORMAN

She stared at this in amazement that she could have got an answer to the letter she had written only a week before; it made Australia seem very near. Frequently when she wrote on Sunday to her parents in Leicester and missed the evening post she did not get an answer till late Thursday; true, Jane Dorman had cabled, but even so … Jennifer felt as if Jane Dorman lived in the next country, and Australia no longer seemed to be upon the far side of the world.

It wouldn't do any harm to find out about it, anyway. She made a few discreet enquiries and took Tuesday afternoon off on a pretext that she had to help her father clear up Ethel Trehearn's estate, which was totally untrue. She went up to London and visited the P. and O. office and the Orient Line next door, and Australia House, and Victoria House. She returned with a great mass of literature to study, fascinating windows opening upon a strange new world.

On the Thursday she wrote to the Orient Line and put her name down for a tourist-class passage to Australia five months ahead, the earliest date that she could get a berth. She sent ten pounds deposit, on the assurance of the company that this would be returnable if she changed her mind and didn't go. She wouldn't really go, of course, but it was nice to know she could go if she wanted to....

On the Friday she got a bulky air-mail letter from Jane Dorman in Australia, twelve days after she had written. Enclosed with it were four pages of advertisements in newspapers of situations vacant in Melbourne for secretaries and 'typistes', at salaries that made her blink. Jane Dorman wrote six pages, ending,

As regards the money, do keep it as I said in the cable. Aunt Ethel was terribly kind to us a long time ago when we first got married, and I am only so deeply grieved that I didn't realize before that she was in need of help, because now we've got so much with the wool sales as they are. Of course, we all know that it can't go on, but the debt upon the land and stock is all paid off now so everything is ours, and even if wool fell to half its present price or less we should still be all right, and safe for the remainder of our lives.

I need hardly say how much we would like to see you out here with us. We live in a country district a hundred and fifty miles from Melbourne. I don't suppose you'd want to live the sort of life we do, because it's very quiet here, rather like living in the depths of the Welsh mountains, perhaps, or in Cumberland. There's not a great deal for young people here unless they're keen on the land, and my children are all living now in the cities, Ethel and Jane in Sydney and Jack in Newcastle, about a hundred miles north of Sydney. I expect if you came here you'd want to work in Melbourne, and I am sending you some pages from the *Age* and the *Argus* to show you the sort of jobs available. Everybody is just crying out for secretaries, it seems, and you'd have no trouble at all in getting work.

I do hope that you will decide to come, and that before you take up work you will come and stay with us for as long as you like, or as long as you can stand the country. I do so want to hear about Aunt Ethel from somebody who knew her. I had not met her for over thirty years, of course, but we wrote to each other every two or three months. I can't really think of her as old, even now.

Do come and see us out here, even if it's only for the trip.

Yours affectionately,
JANE DORMAN

Jennifer had no very close friends in Blackheath, but she sometimes went to the pictures with a girl called Shirley Hyman who lived in the room below her. Shirley worked in the City and was engaged to a young man in a solicitor's office; she was with him every week-end but seldom saw him in the week. That Friday evening she was washing her hair for his benefit next day, and Jennifer went down to see her, papers in hand.

She said, 'Shirley. Have you ever thought of going to Australia?'

Miss Hyman, sitting on the floor before the gas stove drying her hair, said, 'For the Lord's sake. Whatever made you ask that?'

'I've got a relation there,' said Jennifer. 'She wants me to go out and stay.'

'What part of Australia?'

'She's outside Melbourne,' Jennifer said. 'I'd get a job in Melbourne if I went.'

'Perth's the only place I know about.'

'Have you been there?'

Miss Hyman shook her head. 'Dick's always going on about it,' she said. 'He wants us to go there when we're married. He thinks he knows a chap out there who'll take him on, as soon as he's got his articles.'

'Are you keen on it?'

'I don't quite know,' the girl said. 'It's an awful long way away. When I'm with Dick it all seems reasonable. There's not much future here and if we're going, well, it's better to go before we start a family. But . . . it's an awful long way.'

'I've been finding out about it,' Jennifer said. 'I got a letter back from my relation in twelve days. It doesn't seem so far now as it did before.'

'Is that all it took?'

'That's right.' She squatted down before the stove with Shirley and produced her papers and pamphlets. 'There's ever so many jobs, according to these advertisements.'

They turned over the brightly-coloured emigration pamphlets she had gleaned in Australia House. 'Dick's got that one–and that,' said Shirley. 'It looks all right in these things, doesn't it? But then they wouldn't tell you the bad parts, like half the houses in Brisbane having no sewage system.'

'Is that right?' asked Jennifer with interest.

'So somebody was telling Dick. He says it's all right in Perth, but I don't believe it is.'

'What do people do?' asked Jennifer. 'Go out in the woods or something?'

They laughed together. 'They've cut down all the woods,' said Shirley. 'I was reading somewhere about Australia becoming a dust bowl because they've cut down all the woods.'

'I don't think that can be right,' said Jennifer. 'They've got *some* woods left, or they couldn't have taken these pictures.' They bent together over the pictures in the pamphlet about Tasmania, showing wooded mountain ranges stretching as far as the eye could see.

'They probably kept those just to make these pictures to show mutts like us,' said Shirley sceptically. 'It's probably all desert and black people round behind the camera.'

They laughed, and sat in silence for a time.

'What do you really think about it?' Jennifer asked at last. 'Do you think it's a good thing to do?'

The girl sat playing with her hair-brush on the floor beside the stove, thoughtful and serious. 'Dick expects to be successful,' she said presently, 'and I think he will. He'd have more opportunity out there, with new things starting all the time as more people get into the country.' She raised her head and looked at Jennifer. 'And, anyway, what's the good of being successful in England? They only take it all away from you, with tax and supertax. The way he looks at it, if we stay in England he'd do best in some Government office and get a pension at the end. He wants to be on his own, though.'

There was a pause. 'I don't know what to think,' Shirley said at last. 'I'd never thought of leaving England, up until the last couple of months. It seems a horrid thing to do, as if one ought to stay and help get things right. Dick says there's too many of us in the country. I don't know. If somebody's got to get out, I wish it wasn't me.'

'Do you think it would feel strange?' asked Jennifer. 'Would people like you in Australia?'

'I don't know. There's such a lot of English people there already, I think one would find friends. People who hadn't been out there so long themselves. I think it'ld be like going to live in Scotland for a job. They talk with a funny accent, some of them, you know.'

'I don't think it could be as bad as the Scotch accent,' Jennifer said. 'I went to Edinburgh once, and I couldn't understand what some of the people were saying–porters and cab drivers, you know. I don't believe Australians are as difficult as that.'

'You're all right of course,' said Shirley. 'You could come back if you didn't like it. You could save the cost of the passage home. It's different for us. If we went out, we'd have to go for good.'

'I know,' Jennifer said slowly. 'The trouble is, I believe I might like it, and stay there for good. I don't want to do that. . . .'

The little ties that held her to her own land were still strong, ties of friendships, of places that she knew, of things she had grown up with. She went on with her work and life in Blackheath for another three days, uncertain and irresolute. On the following Tuesday she got a telegram from the Orient Line,

Can offer returned single tourist passage Melbourne in *Orion* sailing December 3rd holding open for you till midday November 23rd.

November the twenty-third was in two days' time, and if she took this she would have to sail within a fortnight. Her first reaction was that she couldn't possibly go. It was too soon; she hadn't made up her mind. She got the telegram on her return from work: Shirley Hyman was out that evening, and there was nobody else with whom she could discuss the matter.

It was impossible for Jennifer to stay in her room that evening; she was too worried and restless. She had her tea in an abstracted daze, and walked across the heath and took a train for Charing Cross, knowing that it was in her power to have done with that heath and with that train. It was not raining but the night was cold and windy; the chilly draughts whipped round her on the platform in the darkness. In Australia it would be high summer. . . .

The train was unheated owing to fuel shortages, and she was very cold by the time she got to Charing Cross. She went out of the station and turned eastwards up the Strand, and there she met a disappointment. She had hoped that the bright lights and the traffic would be stimulating and cheerful, and that England would hold out a hand there for her to hang on to. But the shop windows were all dark because of fuel rationing, and the Strand seemed sombre and deserted, with little life. She was there now, however, and very cold; she walked eastwards quickly for the exercise. She stopped now and then to look into a shop window in the light of an arc lamp, but there was no joy in it.

Warmth and feeling were coming back into her feet as she passed Waterloo Bridge. She went on past the Law Courts, down Fleet Street, empty and dark but for the street lamps and the lights and clamour from the newspaper offices. By the time she reached the bottom of Ludgate Hill she was warm and comfortable again and beginning to wonder why she had come there, and where she was heading for. There was no point in walking on into the City. She moved up the hill at a slower pace, looking for a bus-stop, and so she came to St Paul's Cathedral, an immense black mass towering up into the darkness from the blitz desolation that surrounded it.

She moved towards it, and stood staring at the mass of masonry. This was the sort of thing that Australia would never have to show her, this masterpiece of Wren. If she left England she would be leaving this for ever, and a hundred other beauties of the same kind that the new country could never show her. She stood there thinking of these things, and two devastating little words came into her mind—so what?

She had been taken inside St Paul's once as a schoolgirl. She remembered it as the biggest building that she had ever been in, and for that alone. She knew that she was probably foolish and ignorant, because there must be much more to St Paul's than that, but she stepped back till she could see the whole bulk in the fleeting moonlight as the swift clouds passed and re-passed. She would be leaving this for ever, and she must be honest with herself about it.

Would she miss it very much? She tried to examine her own feelings, and she said to herself, 'Well, there it is. Now am I getting a great thrill out of it?' She had to confess within her own mind that she wasn't. The enormous inert mass of masonry meant little to her; there was nothing in those great columns of stone to affect her decision one way or the other.

She turned back towards the West End, rather thoughtful. A bus came rattling by and stopped near her; she ran and got on to it, and rode back up Fleet Street. She got off at Charing Cross and walked on to Trafalgar Square. She stood by St Martin-in-the-Fields for a time looking round her, at the National Gallery, the Nelson Column, the Admiralty Arch, the long broad way that was Whitehall. Here was the centre of her country, the very essence of it. Here were the irreplaceable things that she would have to do without if she left England. Surely, that would be unbearable?

She felt that there must be something wrong with her, because she knew that it wouldn't be unbearable at all. In fact, she didn't much care if she never saw any of them again.

She had a queer feeling now that she was becoming a stranger in her own country, that she no longer fitted in. She had to consult her parents in Leicester about this matter of the passage, and there was so little time. She thought for a few minutes and then went diffidently into the Charing Cross Hotel and spoke to the girl at the desk, and ordered coffee and biscuits in the writing-room, and sat down to write a letter to her father and mother.

She put the matter very simply to them, and asked them to telegraph her to advise her what to do.

Then she went by Underground to St Pancras station and posted her letter in the special box upon the platform, so that it would get to them in the morning.

She got a telegram from them in answer when she returned from work next day. It read,

Think you had better go but come home for a few days first our dearest love.

DADDY and MUMMY

She sailed a fortnight later for Australia in the *Orion.*

4

The man with the crushed fingers got down awkwardly from the cab of the rickety, dust-covered truck into the timber road; his mate climbed over the tailboard and dropped down into the road beside him. He raised a hand to the driver. 'Thanks, Jack. We'll be right.' The door of the cab slammed to, the engine roared, and the truck moved on, swaying and lurching down the unmetalled road in a great cloud of dust.

The two men stood together at the entrance of the timber camp. The wooden hutments stood in a forest in a valley. A little river ran beyond the buildings and a mountain climbed up steeply beyond that, covered in eucalyptus gum trees, full of brilliantly-coloured parrots. The buildings stood among the trees for shade from the hot Victorian sunlight, blazing down out of a cloudless sky. 'This way,' the well man said. 'Down here, fourth hut along.'

They turned into the camp; the hand of the injured man was wrapped in a bloodstained rag, and he walked with it thrust into his open shirt as in a sling. He asked, 'What's the bastard's name?'

'Splinter,' said his mate. 'He'll fix you up.'

'What's the bastard's real name?'

'Splinter—that's all the name he's got. He's right, as good as any doctor.'

'Company ought to keep a mucking doctor here,' the injured man said. 'They've got no mucking right to carry on with just a first-aid box. One day some bastard's going to cop it proper, and I hope it's Mr Mucking Forrest.'

'Hurting bad?'

'Like bloody hell. I'll go down to the Jig tonight; get mucking well pissed.'

They went into the fourth hut by the door in its end, and into a central corridor of bare, unpainted, rather dirty wood. The uninjured man opened a door at random and said to a man inside, 'Say, Jack—which is Splinter's room?'

'Last on the left, down by the wash-room. Someone hurt?'

'Too right. Fred here got his hand under a log.'

'Aw, look—he may be in the canteen. See if he's in the room—if not, I'll go find him.'

The two men went down the passage to the last room and opened the door. There was a man inside sitting on the bed reading an old newspaper, a lean, swarthy, black-haired man about thirty-five years old. He looked up as they entered.

'Aw, Splinter,' said the uninjured man, 'this is Fred.' The dark man smiled, and nodded slightly. 'He got his hand mucked up.'

The man got up from the bed. 'Let me see.' He spoke with a pronounced Central European accent.

The other turned to go. 'I'll get along, Fred. You'll be right.'

The injured man withdrew his hand from his shirt and began to unwrap the bloodstained rags carefully, with fingers that trembled a little. The man called Splinter noted that, and stopped him. 'Wait, and sit down—on the bed.' He switched on the current to a china electric jug and dropped a few instruments into it to boil. Then he rolled up his sleeves and took a white enamel bowl and a bottle of disinfectant from the cupboard and went out to the bathroom; he came back with his hands washed and sterile and with warm water in the bowl. He moved the bare wooden table to a convenient position in front of the man and waited till the water in the jug boiled, opening a packet of lint while he waited, and adding a little disinfectant to the water in the bowl. Then he sat down facing his patient with the table between them, arranged the hand in a relaxed position, and began his work.

Presently, 'This is a bad injury,' he said softly. 'It must hurt you a great deal. Now, let me see if it is possible that you can move the fingers. Just bend a little, to show that you can move them. This one . . . so. And now this one . . . so. And this one . . . so. That is good. It hurts very much now, but a fortnight's holiday and it will soon be well.'

'Cripes,' said the man, 'is it going to hurt like this a mucking fortnight?'

'It will not hurt when I have done with it,' the dark man said. 'Not unless you make a hit–unless you hit it. You must wear it in a sling till it is well, and keep it carefully. I must now hurt you a little more. Will you like whisky?'

'Thanks, chum.'

The dark man produced a bottle of Australian whisky from the cupboard and poured out half a tumbler-full. The patient took it and sat drinking it neat in little gulps while the other worked. 'What is your name?'

'Fred. Fred Carter.'

'Where did you do this, Fred?'

'Up on the shoulder.'

'And how did it happen?'

'Loading two-foot sticks on a ten-wheeler.' He meant, tree-trunks two feet in diameter on to a trailer truck. 'The mucking chain broke and the stick rolled back. Whipped me crowbar back 'n pinched me mucking hand on to the next stick down.'

The dark man nodded gravely. 'Now, this will hurt you. I am sorry, but it must be done.'

Presently it was all over, the hand bandaged and in a sling. The injured man sat white-faced, the shock gradually subsiding as he smoked a cigarette given to him by the doctor and finished the whisky. 'Say, chum,' he asked, 'what's your name?'

'Zlinter,' the dark man said, 'Carl Zlinter. Most people call me Splinter here.'

'Where do you come from?'

'I am from Czechoslovakia. In Pilsen I was born.'

'How long have you been here?'

'It is fifteen months that I have come to Australia.'

'Where did you learn doctoring?'

'I was doctor in my own country, at home.'

'A real doctor?'

The dark man nodded. 'In Prague I qualified, in 1936. After that I was in hospital appointment, in Pilsen, my own town. And after that, I was doctor in the army.' He did not say which army.

'Cripes. Then you know all about it.'

The Czech smiled. 'I am not doctor any longer. I am timberman. In Australia I may not be a doctor, unless to go back to medical school for three years. So I am timberman.'

He stubbed out his cigarette and got up, and went to the cupboard and shook out some white tablets into the palm of his hand. 'Go back to your camp and go to bed,' he said. 'I will tell Mr Forrest for you, that you cannot work. Go to bed, and take three of these tablets, and the pain will go away. If it comes back in the night, take these other three. Come back and see me after tea on Sunday, and I will change the dressings for you.'

'Aw, look,' the man said. 'I was going down to the Jig tonight to get pissed.'

Carl Zlinter smiled. 'It is your hand. It will hurt very bad if you go down to the Jig, because you will hit it without knowing, and it will hurt very bad. If you go to bed it will not hurt.'

He turned to the cupboard; the bottle of whisky was about one-third full. He gave it to the man. 'Take this,' he said, 'and get pissed in bed. But go to bed.'

'Aw, look, chum, I can't take your grog. And say, how much is it?'

'There is nothing to be paid,' the Czech said. 'Mr Forrest, he pays for the dressings and the disinfectant. The whisky–you can shout for me down at the Jig one day, but not tonight.' He smiled. 'See you Sunday.'

Fred Carter went away with the bottle, and Zlinter wondered if he would go to bed, or whether he would drink the bottle and go down to the pub at Merrijig just the same. The labour camps were by the sawmills at Lamirra, four miles from Merrijig and seventeen miles from Banbury, the nearest town. By Victorian law the hotel was supposed to close its bar at six o'clock in the evening; in fact, it stayed wide open day and night, and the police connived at it. They knew that few of the timbermen would pass an open bar to go twelve miles further on to Banbury; driving past in the dark night the police would see the blazing lights, and hear the songs, and see the trucks parked outside the solitary wooden building, and they would smile as they drove past, congratulating themselves upon the simple stratagem that kept the drunks out of town.

It was a Friday evening; the timbermen worked a forty-hour week on five days, and Saturday and Sunday were holidays. Carl Zlinter was a fisherman, and December was the finest month in the year for trout-fishing in the deserted mountain streams. When Fred Carter had gone away, he set to work to prepare for the week-end; he had a spinning rod and a fly rod, but the rivers were too shallow and too swift for spinning, and he preferred to fish wet fly. He cleared away the litter of his dressings, sterilized his instruments again in the electric jug, and washed out the basin, and then set to work to make up a cast of flies, and to pack his rucksack.

The Delatite River flowed past Lamirra near his camp, but it was too small and too overgrown to fish just there, and down by Merrijig it was fished by many others. Zlinter had developed a week-end of fishing which took him into very wild, almost untrodden forest country, which he loved. His rucksack was a big, shabby thing with a light alloy frame which he had picked up in Germany in 1945 and had carried ever since; it held everything that he required for a week-end in the bush. His habit was to start out from the lumber camp early on Saturday morning and walk eight miles or so on half obliterated paths through the forest over a dividing range down into the valley of the Howqua river, untouched by any road. Here the fishing was first-class.

There was a forest ranger living in the Howqua valley, a man called Billy Slim, rather over forty years of age, who lived alone with a few horses and was glad of any company; when the solitude became oppressive he would ride out to the hotel at Merrijig and spend the evening there. Billy had a bed for anyone who came his way, and Carl Zlinter was in the habit of fishing down the Howqua to Billy's place on Saturday, staying the night with him, fishing up the river again on the Sunday and so back to the camp by the way that he had come.

So far, he was delighted with Australia. He had to work for two years in the woods in return for his free passage from the Displaced Persons' camp in Germany, and he was enjoying every minute of it. He had nobody to consider but himself. His father and mother had been killed in the Russian advance that surged through Pilsen late in 1944. He had heard nothing of his brother since 1943, and he believed him to be dead. He had never married; the war had begun soon after he was qualified, and he was not a man to marry unless he could see, at any rate a little way, into the future. He had remained unattached throughout his service in the German Army and through the long ignominy of the peace, when he had worked as a doctor in various Displaced Persons' camps. When finally the reduction of the D.P. camps gave him the chance to go to Australia with one of the last batches of emigrants, he was almost glad of the condition that he should not practise as a doctor; he would have to work for two years as a labourer wherever he might be directed, and then if he still wished to be a doctor in Victoria he would have to repeat the last three years of his medical student's course. Medicine had brought him nothing but the most intimate contact with the squalor and distress of unsuccessful war; when the time came to choose his labour he elected to be a lumberman because he loved the deep woods and the mountains, and he put medicine behind him.

On landing he had been sent to a reception camp for a few days, but as he was unattached and spoke tolerable English he had been sent on quickly to Lamirra, and he had been there ever since. He knew a good deal about camps and how to be comfortable in them, and he settled down quite happily to work out his two years in the woods he loved.

He had little regret for the loss of his medical profession. After his two years in the woods were over he would have to do something else; he did not quite know what, but in this prosperous country he was confident that he could earn a living somehow or other. In the meantime he was well clothed and fed, paid highly by the European standard, and given so much leisure that he could get in two days' trout fishing every week. Better than lying dead and putrefying in the Pripet marshes or the fields round Caen, where he had left so many of his friends. That was the old world; he was glad to put it all behind him and enjoy the new.

He left the camp at about seven o'clock that Saturday morning before the day grew hot, with his rucksack on his back and his fly rod in his hand in its cloth case. He got to the river soon after ten and put up his rod and began to fish down-stream, wading in the cool water in his normal working boots and trousers.

He caught a rainbow trout after ten minutes' fishing, a good fish about two pounds in weight that leaped into the air repeatedly to shake the fly out of its mouth. He kept his line taut and played the fish out, and landed it upon a little shoal with one hand in its gills; he never burdened himself with a net. He caught a brown trout a few minutes later; then, as the day warmed up, the fish went off the feed, and he caught nothing more.

He got to Billy's place about midday. The forest ranger lived in a clearing by the river, in a long single-storeyed building with a veranda, built, of course, of timber with an iron roof. There was a living-room which was the kitchen, with a harness room opening out of it, which in turn communicated with the stable; in winter when the snow was lying in the valley Billy Slim could feed his horses without going out into the snow. His own bedroom opened out of the living-room, and there were two bunkrooms off the veranda. He kept his house very neat and clean, having little else to do.

In one corner of the living-room there was a radio telephone set run off a large battery, with which the ranger could communicate with his headquarters in case of forest fires or similar disasters. When Carl Zlinter walked in, Billy was seated talking to the microphone; he raised a hand in greeting, then knitted his brows and bent again to his work. Giving his weekly time sheet to the girl operator on Saturday mornings was always a trouble and a perplexity to him.

'Aw, look, Florence,' he was saying. 'Tuesday . . . Oh, yes–look–Tuesday I

went upstream to Little Bend and then over the spur to the Sickle, that's down
on the Jamieson River. There was a party went in there last week from Lamirra.'
'Know who they were, Billy?'
'Naw–I didn't see them. There was four of them on horses, and two packhorses, and one of the horses was Ted Sloan's blue roan, so Ted must have been
there. One of the horses dropped a shoe and went lame on the way out. They
shot a few wallabies and camped three nights. They lit fires which they didn't
ought to; I'll see Ted about that.' He paused. 'Wednesday I had to go into the
Jig to pick up a couple of sacks of horse feed. Thursday I stayed home; I wasn't
feeling too good. Got that, Florence? Over.'

The loud-speaker said, 'Thursday's a working day, Billy. What'll I tell Mr
Bennett? I don't like to put down you got sick again. Why can't you do your
drinking at the week-end? Over.'

'Aw, look, Florence,' the ranger said, 'I didn't drink nothing down at the Jig.
You know me–I wouldn't of a Wednesday. I got one of my bad goes on the
Thursday, in the stomach, terrible griping pains. Real bad, I was. Over.'

'I don't like to put it down, Billy. Didn't you do anything about the house
that we could say? Over.'

'Aw, right ... look, Florence. I did a bit on the paddock fence in the
afternoon. Put down, Repairs to homestead and stockyards, for Thursday.
Yesterday, that's Friday, I was out all day. I went up around Mount Buller as
far as the Youth Hostel hut and then down to the King River and along by
Mount Cobbler and the Rose River; I didn't get back till after nine last night.
Today Jack Dorman's coming out with Alec Fisher from Banbury, and there's
Carl Zlinter here, one of the lumbermen from Limarra. Over.'

The loudspeaker said, 'That'll be right, Billy–I can make it up from that.
That's all I have for you. Over.'

'By-bye, Florence,' said the ranger. 'Closing down now. Out.'

He shut the set off with a sigh of relief, and turned to Carl Zlinter. 'Come
fishing?'

'If I may, I would like to spend the night.'

'You'll be right. Put your stuff in the end room; I got Jack Dorman coming
over, with Alec Fisher. Know them?'

Zlinter shook his head. 'I do not know them.'

'Aw, well, Jack Dorman, he's got a property just by the Jig. Thought maybe
you might know him. Alec Fisher, he's agent for the Australian Mercantile in
Banbury. They're coming out to do a bit of fishing.'

Zlinter smiled. 'We shall crowd you out tonight with a large party.'

'Too right. Makes a change to have a bit of company now and then.'

'Will they come on horses?'

'Might do. Alec Fisher's got a Land Rover; they can get over the track with
that. I'd never sit astride a bloody horse if I'd got a Land Rover to ride in. I'd
have thought that they'd be here by now.'

Carl Zlinter left his rucksack in the end room and went down to the river,
cleaned the two fish, and left them in Billy's larder for the evening. He had
brought a sandwich lunch with him from the camp canteen; he went down to
the river again and fished on down-stream for a little. No fish were moving in
the heat of the day; he gave it up after half an hour, and found a shade tree
standing in the middle of a grassy sward by the river, and sat down under it to
eat his lunch.

It was very quiet in the forest; a hot, windless day. A cockatoo screamed once or twice in the distance, and near at hand there was a rippling noise of water from a little fall in the river. Presently the quiet was broken by the low grinding of a vehicle coming down the horse track into the valley in low gear; he guessed that it would be the Land Rover. It passed along the track a few hundred yards upstream from him and he heard the water as it went splashing through the ford; he heard it breast the rise up from the river to the ranger's house, and then the engine stopped, and there was quiet again.

He went down to the river and drank from it after his meal, cupping up the water in his hands; then he went back and sat down under the tree again, and lit a cigarette. What a good country this was! It had all the charm of the Bohemian forests that he had loved as a young man, plus the advantage of being English. He had not learned to differentiate between English people and Australians; to him this was an English country, and England had the knack of being on the winning side in all her wars. He disliked and distrusted Russians, and his own land was gone for ever into the Russian grip. He liked south Germans and got on well with them and spoke the language fluently, more fluently than he spoke English. The Germans, however, had an unfortunate record for starting wars and losing them, which made Germany a bad country to live in. Australia had everything for Carl Zlinter; the type of country that he loved, freedom, good wages, and no war; he would willingly forgo his medical career for those good things. He revelled in the country, like a man enjoying a warm bath.

He stubbed his cigarette out on a stone, or what he took to be a stone, in the meadow beneath the tree. He looked at the stone curiously, and it was not a stone at all, but a piece of brick.

He looked about him with interest. Half buried in the grass was a low rubble of brick. Beside it, on the level grassy sward, was a series of rectangular patterns, hardly to be described as mounds, more like discolorations of the pasture. He studied these for a minute while his mind accustomed to the solitude of the Howqua, refused to accept the evidence. Then he woke up to the realization of the fact that there had been a house there at one time.

Even when he appreciated the evidence, it still seemed incredible, and for a very definite reason. He knew that this part of Australia had been first explored barely a hundred years before; he had found out sufficient of the history of the country to have become aware that it was most unlikely that the Howqua valley had seen any white man before 1850. If the evidence upon the ground before him were to be believed, a house built wholly or partly of brick had been built and lived in, and deserted, and so entirely ruined that only a bare trace upon the sward remained, all in less than a hundred years. It did not seem possible. He stood looking at the grass for a time, deeply puzzled; then he put it out of his mind for the time being, and walked over to the stream, and stepped out into the shallows and began to cast his fly. He would ask Billy Slim about it that evening.

He fished on down the river; he caught no fish and hardly expected to until the sun began to drop. He stopped presently and smoked a cigarette, and lay on his back under the gum trees, and slept for a while. When he woke up it was about five o'clock; he began to fish back up the river towards the forest ranger's house, and at once he began to catch fish, mostly small undersized brown trout that he tired as little as possible and put back into the river. Then he caught a couple of takeable fish, each about a pound and a quarter, and with that he gave

up, and took down his rod, and walked back along the forest path in the
gloaming.

When he got back to the shack the two newcomers were there, a heavy man of
fifty-five or sixty that was Jack Dorman, and a younger man, perhaps of forty-
five, Alec Fisher. They greeted him shortly; they were not unfriendly, but
waiting for this New Australian from the lumber camp to disclose himself
before showing themselves particularly cordial. They represented the
permanent population of the countryside, the men with an enduring stake in
the land. The lumbermen were here today and gone tomorrow, frequently
drunk and a nuisance to the station people; many of them were New
Australians who came for their two years' sentence on arrival from Europe and
fled to the towns as soon as they got their release, and anyway the camps
themselves were transient affairs, to be moved on to some other district as soon
as all the ripe timber from that forest had been taken out.

Carl Zlinter raised the matter of his discovery with the forest ranger over
supper. 'I have found what seems to have been formerly a house,' he said. 'In a
pasture, where two horses are. There is a big tree, and under there are bricks all
in grass and very old. Was there a house at one time?'

The ranger said, 'You mean, where the river makes a turn under a big granite
bluff? About a quarter of a mile down?'

'That is the place. There is a fast, dark pool.'

'Too right, there was a house,' the ranger said. 'That was the hotel. My dad
kept it, but that was before I was born.'

Jack Dorman said, 'Your dad kept the hotel, did he? I never knew that.'

'One of them,' the ranger said. 'There was three hotels. He kept the best one,
the Buller Arms. Two storeys, it was, with bedrooms. Used day and night,
those bedrooms were, from what I've heard.'

'Like that, was it?' said Alec Fisher.

'My word,' the ranger said, 'these gold towns were all the same. Booze and
dancing girls and all sorts.'

Carl Zlinter said, 'Was there a town then?'

'My word,' the ranger said again. 'It was a big place at one time, over three
hundred people. You'll find the adit to the mine up in the trees there, back of
the house paddock. It's blocked now; it only goes in a few feet. The battery is
still there down by the dam, in that clump of peppermint gums. There was
houses all over in this valley flat.'

'I knew there was a town here,' Alec Fisher said. 'What happened? Did the
gold run out?'

'Aw, look,' the ranger said. 'I don't think there was ever much gold there. In
1893 it started, when they found a trace of gold in the conglomerate. The Rand
mine in South Africa, that was conglomerate, so they called this one the Rand
and floated a company in Melbourne.' He paused, and ate a mouthful of trout.
'They got a little gold out, just enough to make it look a good bet. But it never
really paid. It ran on for ten years and then it bust, in 1903.'

'That's right,' said Fisher. 'Everyone was gold mad at that time.'

'My old dad,' the ranger said, 'he came out from home when he was just a kid,
back in the 'eighties some time. He came from a place called Northallerton in
England, 'n got a job in the police. Well, then when they found gold here he
gave the police away and came and started the hotel. He was a fine, big chap 'n
handy with his fists, which you needed running a hotel in these parts in those

days. He sold out in '98 or '99 and went to Jamieson 'n got married. I was born in Jamieson.'

'How did they get all the stuff in?' asked Jack Dorman. 'The track's not so good.'

'Aw, it was better then,' said Slim. 'They had a regular road up from the Jig, and brought it in in bullock wagons. I remember the road in here when I was a boy; you could have driven a car in down it, easy. But trees grow up pretty quick, 'n nobody came in here when the mine shut down.'

'People all went away,' said Fisher.

'That's right. There wouldn't have been many left here after that. There's not enough flat land to make a station, and it's a long way from the town.'

Carl Zlinter asked, 'What happened to the houses?'

'Aw, look,' said the ranger. 'There's been a fire through the valley twice at least, in 1910 and 1939. I come here first when I was just a nipper, in the first war some time. I don't remember seeing any houses. There's not much left of houses after a fire's been through,' he said. 'Only just the brick chimneys, and they soon fall down. Most of the places would have had a wooden chimney, too.'

'I remember the fire here in 1939,' said Dorman. 'A bit too close to home it was, for my liking.'

'My word,' the ranger said thoughtfully. 'A fair cow, that one. Just after I joined the Forest Service, that one was. The house was on the other side of the river then; we rebuilt it after on this side, because the land was flatter, 'n better for the paddock.' He turned to Fisher. 'Days 'n days of hot sun, 'n not a breath of wind down in the valley here. It got so that you couldn't hardly breathe for the scent from the gum leaves; it made your eyes smart, sort of distilling out in the hot sun, 'n no wind to carry it away. And then one morning I was out in the paddock lighting my pipe although I didn't really want it for the way the air made you choke, and when I lit the match the flame burned blue. There wasn't any yellow in the flame, just kind of blue, out in the open air, dead still, in the middle of the paddock.'

The men stared at him. 'My word,' said Dorman softly.

'We hadn't got no radio in those days,' the ranger said. 'I put that match out quick and saddled up, 'n rode out to the Jig. Mr Considine, he was superintendent then, 'n I got on the telephone and told him that my match turned blue, out in the open air, 'n he as good as said that I was drunk. And then he said the fire on Buller was heading down my way, 'n I'd better get anybody in the Howqua out, 'n get my own stuff out.'

He paused. 'Well, there was nobody else in, that I knew about, and nothing in the house I thought a lot of but my gun, that I got from my dad. An English gun it was, a good one that some toff had give my dad, a twelve-bore made by a firm called Gogswell and Harrison. Well, I rode back towards the Howqua, and when I got up on the ridge I could see the fire on Buller, and it was a whole lot closer now, not more'n seven or eight miles away. I sat on the horse and thought about the air down in the valley where the match went blue; it was hot as hell, 'n not a breath of wind. I didn't like to go down there a bit, my word I didn't.'

'Not worth it for a gun,' said Alec Fisher.

'I tell you,' said the ranger, 'I wouldn't have gone down for the gun. I'd have given it away. But I'd got three horses down there in the paddock, 'n I'd got to get them out. So down I went, and by the river here the air was worse than ever, sort of choking. I just grabbed the gun and left everything else, 'n let the fence rail down and drove the horses out ahead of me and up the track. I never been so frightened, oh my word.'

'Lucky to get away with it,' Jack Dorman said.

'Too right. Well, I got back on to the ridge in Jock McDougall's pasture with my horses and the gun, and there I stayed a while. I wasn't going to stay down in the valley, but I'd a right to stay as near I could to where I ought to be. So I stayed there on the ridge for a while. And about three in the afternoon, that fire on Buller, she began to jump. She come down this valley in leaps about two mile each time. She'd be blazing way off up the valley, 'n then there'd be a sort of flash and you'd see everything alight and burning two miles closer on. Then she'd rest a while, and then she'd leap on another mile or two mile down the valley. In a sort of flash.'

Alec Fisher said in wonder, 'The whole air was exploding?'

'That's right,' the ranger said. 'The whole air was exploding. That's how the old house come to be burned down. After that we built this one, next year.'

Carl Zlinter said, 'Let me understand. It was hot, so hot that the sun evaporate the eucalyptus oil out of the trees, and that explodes?'

'That's right,' said Jack Dorman. 'I've heard of that happening over in East Gippsland, by Buchan in the Cave Country.'

'But that is terrifying!'

'Too right,' said the ranger. 'It terrified me.'

'You can't do anything about a thing like that,' said Fisher. 'You can't stop a fire from spreading when it jumps two miles.'

The forest ranger said, 'Folks down in the city think you can stop a forest fire by spitting on it. They come along after and ask why you didn't put it out. Maybe you can do a bit to stop one starting, like getting campers not to light a fire in January. But only God can put it out when it gets hold.'

'We do not have fires like that in my country,' said Zlinter. 'Perhaps it is too cold, and too much rain. We have fires sometimes, but not to jump two miles.'

'Which is your country?' asked Jack Dorman. 'Where do you come from?'

'From Czechoslovakia,' the other said. 'In Pilsen I was born.'

The names meant nothing to the Australian. 'Working up at Lamirra?'

'That's right. I work there for two years.'

'Like it?'

'I like it very much. It is like Czechoslovakia, with the forests and the mountains. I would rather be working here than in the city.'

Billy Slim said, 'You don't have gum trees in your forests over there, do you?'

'No, we do not have the gum tree. There all is pines and larches, and oak trees a few, and sometimes the silver birch.'

'Get much snow in winter?' asked the ranger.

'Oh, we get much, much snow. Three feet, four feet deep from November until March. It is much, much colder in Czechoslovakia than it is here.'

'I wouldn't want four feet,' the forest ranger said. 'Four inches is enough for me.'

Carl Zlinter said, 'I am from Europe, where villages remain for many hundred years. I do not know of any village in Bohemia that has vanished with no sign left, as this one has.'

The ranger said, 'Aw, well, there's plenty left here if you look for it. Only there aren't no people living here any longer. There's the mine adit, and the battery, and down the river, 'bout a mile, there's the cemetery with all the stone headstones still standing up. The fire couldn't burn up those.'

'Where's that?' asked Alec Fisher.

'You know where there's a red stone bluff on the right side going down? Well, on past that there's a big tree-trunk lying along the bank, where I pulled it with three horses when it fell across the river. The cemetery's in behind that, on the north side.'

'Many graves there?'

'Aw, no—just a few. Just a few headstones, that's to say. Might have been more one time, with a wood cross perhaps; there wouldn't be nothing left to show those.'

Jack Dorman sat puzzled, hardly hearing what was going on, a vague memory of little Peter Loring and Ann Pearson stirring in his mind. 'Say,' he said to the Czech, 'is your name Cylinder by any chance? Are you a doctor?'

'My name is Zlinter—Carl Zlinter,' said the other. 'I am a doctor in my own country, but not here in Australia. Here I work at the timber camp.'

'That's right,' said Dorman. 'I heard about you one time. Didn't you pick up a boy that had fallen off his pony?'

Zlinter smiled. 'He had a very high temperature,' he said 'The lady was helping him when I arrived. It was not that he fell off because he could not ride. He was ill, that little boy, with a bad ear.'

'That's right. You took him into hospital.'

The Czech nodded. 'I think his mother was a stupid woman not to see that he was ill when he left from his home to go to school. It could have been a serious accident, but he was scratched a little, only.'

'You speak pretty good English,' said Jack Dorman curiously. 'D'you learn it since you came out here?'

The other shook his head. 'I learned English at school, and then for nearly five years I was in Germany, where many people now speak English, in the camps and with the officers. Also, I have been here now for fifteen months, and perhaps I have improved.'

'What's it like, coming to Australia from Europe, now?'

'It is good,' the Czech said. 'It is a good country, plenty to eat and drink, and plenty of freedom.'

'You've not got plenty of freedom, working for two years in the woods.'

The other shrugged his shoulders. 'I like the woods and the mountains. It is not cruel to me, to send me here.'

Alec Fisher said, 'Lot of people coming out here to this country now.'

'My word,' said Jack Dorman. 'My wife's got a niece, an English girl, arriving in about a fortnight's time. Seems like it's better out here now than it is in England.'

'An English migrant, like your wife's niece,' asked Zlinter, '—she will not have to work for two years, like a New Australian?'

The grazier shook his head. 'I don't think so. This girl, she's coming out just on a visit, though—paying her own passage. She say's she's going back again in six months' time.'

'It must be very expensive, to do that.'

'She got a little legacy,' the grazier said. 'She's spending it in coming out here for the trip, to see what Australia's like.'

They settled down to an evening of local gossip, with the assistance of a bottle of Scotch whisky produced by Alec Fisher.

They were all up soon after dawn, to take advantage of the cool of the day when fish feed well. They had a quick breakfast of eggs and bacon, and split up for the day's fishing. They tossed a coin for who should go alone, and Alec Fisher won; he started off up-stream. Carl Zlinter and Jack Dorman went down-stream, having arranged to fish alternate pools, leap-frogging each other.

They fished on down-stream for an hour or so, catching a few fish and exchanging a word or two when they overtook each other. Presently Carl Zlinter, going on ahead, came to a red stone bluff upon the right side of the river, and a memory of the conversation of the night before came to his mind.

Jack Dorman was not far behind him. He sat down and waited for the grazier by a little rapid; when he came, Carl said, 'There is the red bluff that Billy spoke about. Somewhere here is the cemetery of the old town of Howqua.'

The Australian grunted. 'Want to go and look for it?'

'It is a pity to be here and not to see it,' the Czech said.

'He said it was behind a tree-trunk lying along the bank, didn't he?'

'There is a tree-trunk, there. Perhaps that is the one.'

They laid the rods down on a boulder by the rapid, and pushed their way through the scrub that lined the river. Away from the water there were wattle trees in bloom among the gum trees of the forest, vivid splashes of a bright mimosa colour in the dappled sunlight. For a time they saw nothing of the cemetery; they moved down the bank in the forest, keeping near the river. Presently Jack Dorman spied a leaning headstone, and they were there.

There was not very much to see; three leaning headstones, and four or five lying on their faces on the ground, partly covered in creepers and trash. If there had been a fence at any time it had gone the way of the houses in the forest fires; if there had been wooden crosses marking graves, fire and the ants had taken them. Jack Dorman bent to read the lichened names carved on the three headstones still erect. Peter Quillam, of Tralee, Ireland. Samuel Tregarren of St Columb, Cornwall.

He came to the third headstone and stood staring at it, amazed. 'Hey, Zlinter!' he said. 'This some relation of yours?'

They stooped together at the stone. It read:

Here lies
CHARLIE ZLINTER and his dog.
Born at Pilsen, Bohemia, 1869.
Died August 18th, 1902.

The Czech read it carefully, in silence. Then he looked up at the grazier, smiling a little. 'That is my name,' he said, '–Carl Zlinter, and I was born at Pilsen in Bohemia. Of all the things that have happened in my life, this is the most strange.'

5

The Dormans left Leonora for their holiday in Melbourne on New Year's Day. They drove down in the old Chevrolet utility, leaving Mario in charge of the station and taking Tim Archer with them, sitting all three in the front seat and with four suitcases in the fruck body. Mario had had letters from Lucia; her passage was booked on the *Neptunia* for April, and he was busy with the builder working on the shack extension of the stable that they were to live in. Tim Archer came to Melbourne with them to drive the old utility back to Leonora and to see his parents; Jack Dorman had already arranged to buy another near-new Ford utility at an inflated price in Melbourne, and to drive it home.

They went with an air of festival excitement. Thinking back over their long married life, Jack and Jane had been unable to remember when they had last gone away together for a real holiday; there had been trips to Melbourne for various business reasons, always cramped and curtailed by the need for rigorous economy and by the need to get back quickly to the station. Certainly, they had not had a genuine holiday for at least ten years. Now, with two men to help them and with what was, for them, unlimited money, they were able to relax and to enjoy the fruits of thirty years' hard, grinding work.

Jane Dorman had heard from Jennifer that she was coming to Australia and that she proposed to take a job at once in Melbourne, and would like to come out to Merrijig to see them as soon as she could get a holiday. Jane thought this a bad idea; the *Orion* was due to dock in Melbourne on January 3rd and they had put forward the date of their holiday to meet the ship. There had been no time to write to Jennifer before she sailed, but Jane had written to her at Port Said and at Colombo urging her to come back with them to Leonora for a short visit before taking a job in the city; she was arriving at the hottest time of the year, Jane said, and office work in Melbourne might be trying till the end of February for anybody just arrived from England, especially if the summer was a hot one.

It was hot the day that they drove down from Merrijig; at midday the shade temperature in the country was in the nineties. Before long they stopped by the roadside for Jack Dorman to take off his coat and undo his collar; Tim Archer got out of the front seat and into the back with the luggage; the dust swirled round him there and made sweat streaks of mud upon his temples, but it was cooler so for all of them, and better travelling.

They stopped at Bonnie Doon for the cold, light Australian beer, and at Buxton for lunch. By four o'clock they were running into Melbourne, perhaps the pleasantest city in the Commonwealth, and at four-twenty they drew up in front of the Windsor Hotel.

Tim took the utility away and the Dormans went up to their bedroom, a fine, lofty room with plenty of cupboards and a bath. After the constrictions of their rather mediocre station homestead it seemed like a palace to them; the hard years fell behind them, and for the moment they were young again. 'Jack,' said Jane, 'don't let's see anyone tonight. Let's just have a very, very good dinner and go to a theatre. Any theatre.'

'Don't you want to see Angie?'

'Angie can wait till tomorrow,' said her mother. 'I want to see a theatre. Angie's probably seen them all. Let's go out alone.'

All right,' he said. 'I'll go down and see what we can get seats for.'

She said, 'And I want a bottle of champagne with dinner.'

'My word,' he said. 'What'll I order for dinner–mutton?'

'You dare! Oysters and roast duck, or as near as you can get to it.'

They went out presently and walked slowly in the heat down the tree-shaded slope of Collins Street, tacking from side to side to look at the shops. Jane said presently, 'I know what I want to buy.'

'What's that?'

'A picture.'

He stared at her. 'What sort of picture?'

'An oil painting. A very, very nice oil painting.'

'What of?'

'I don't mind. I just want a very nice picture.'

'You mean, in a frame, to hang on the wall?'

'That's right. We had lots of them at home, when I was a girl. I didn't think anything of them then, but now I want one of my own.'

He thought about it, trying to absorb this new idea, to visualize what it was that she wanted. 'I thought you might like a bracelet, or a ring,' he said. With so much money in their pockets, after so long, she should have something really good.

She squeezed his arm. 'That's sweet of you, but I don't want jewellery. I'd never be anywhere where I could wear it. No, I want a picture.'

He tried to measure her desire by yardstick. 'Any idea what it'll cost?'

'I don't know till I see it,' she said. 'It might cost a hundred pounds.'

'A hundred pounds!' he said. 'My word!'

'Well, what's the Ford going to cost you?'

'Aw, look,' he said. 'That's different. That's for the station.'

'No, it's not,' she said. 'The Chev'll do the station work for years to come. It's for you to run about in and cut a dash, and it's costing fourteen hundred pounds.'

'It's for both of us,' he said weakly, 'and it comes off the tax.'

'Not all of it,' she said. 'If you're having your Ford Custom I'm going to have my picture.'

He realized that she was set on having this picture; it was a strange idea to him, but he acquiesced. 'There's a shop down here somewhere,' he said. 'Maybe there'd be something there you like.'

When they came to the shop it was closed, but the windows were full of pictures, religious and secular. He knew better than to offer her a picture of the infant Christ in her present mood, although he rather admired it himself. He said, 'That's a nice one, that one of the harbour. The one where it says "St Ives".'

It was colourful and blue, with fishing vessels. 'It's not bad,' she said, 'but it's a reproduction. I want a real picture, an original.'

He studied the harbour scene. 'Where would that be?' he asked. 'Is it in England?'

'That's right,' she said. 'It's a little place in Cornwall.'

'Funny the way people want to buy a picture of a place so far away,' he said. 'I suppose it's because so many of us come from home.'

There was nothing in the shop window that she cared for, nor did it seem to her that there was likely to be what she wanted deeper in the shop. 'I'd like to go to picture galleries,' she said. 'They have a lot of galleries where artists show their pictures and have them for sale. Could we see some of those tomorrow, Jack?'

'Course we can,' he said. 'I've got to pick up the Custom in the morning, but we'll have all day after that.'

She smiled. 'No, we won't—you'll be wanting to drive round in the Custom. We'll go to the picture galleries in the morning and pick up the Custom in the afternoon.'

They went back to the hotel, and rested for a time in the lounge with glasses of cold beer, and dined, and went out to see *Worm's Eye View*, and laughed themselves silly. They got up late by their standards next day, and early by those of the hotel, and went down to their breakfast in the dining-room. As country folk they were accustomed to a cooked breakfast and the hotel was accustomed to station people; half a pound of steak with two fried eggs on top of it was just far enough removed from normal to provide a pleasant commencement for the day for Jack. Jane ate more modestly, three kidneys on toast and a quarter of a pound of bacon. Fortified for their day's work they set out to look at pictures with a view to buying one.

The first gallery they went to was full of pictures of the central Australian desert. The artist had modelled his style upon that of a short-sighted and eccentric old gentleman called Cezanne, who had been able to draw once but had got tired of it; this smoothed the path of his disciples a good deal. The Dormans wandered, nonplussed, from mountain after mountain picture, glowing in rosy tints, all quite flat upon the canvas, with queer childish brown scrawls in the foreground that might be construed into aboriginals. A few newspaper clippings, pinned to the wall, hailed the artist as one of the outstanding landscape painters of the century.

Jack Dorman, deep in gloom at the impending waste of money, said, 'Which do you like best? That's a nice one, over there.'

Jane said, 'I don't like any of them. I think they're horrible.'

'Thank God for that,' her husband replied. The middle-aged woman seated at the desk looked at them with stern disapproval.

They went out into the street. 'It's this modern stuff,' Jane said. 'That's not what I want at all.'

'What is it you want?' he asked. 'What's it got to be like?'

She could not explain to him exactly what she wanted, because she did not know herself. 'It's got to be pretty,' she said, 'and in bright colours, in oils, so that when it's raining or snowing in the winter you can look at it and like it. And it's got to be *like* something, not like those awful daubs in there.'

The next gallery that they went into had thirty-five oil paintings hung around the walls. Each picture depicted a vase of flowers standing on a polished table that reflected the flowers and a curtain draped behind; thirty-five oil paintings all carefully executed, all with the same motif. A few newspaper cuttings pinned up announced the artist as the outstanding flower painter of the century.

Jane whispered, 'Do you think she can do anything else?'

'I dunno,' her husband said. 'Don't look like it. Do you like any of these?'

'Some of them are quite nice,' Jane said slowly. 'That one over there . . . and that. But they aren't what I want.' She paused. 'I'd never be able to forget that there were thirty-four others just like it, if I bought one of these.'

The last exhibition that they visited that morning was of paintings and sculpture by the same artist; at the door a newspaper cutting informed them that the artist was a genius at the interpretation of Australia. The centre of the floor was occupied by a large block of polished mulga wood with a hole in it, of no recognizable shape or form, poised at eye-level on a stand that you might admire it better. Beneath it was the title, 'Design for Life'.

'Like that one to take home?' asked Jack. He glanced at the catalogue. 'It's only seventy-five guineas. . . .'

The paintings were a little odd, because this artist was a primitive, unable to paint or to draw, and hailed as a genius by people who ought to have known better. Purple houses that might have been drawn by a five-year-old child straggled drunkenly across vermilion streets that led to nowhere and meant nothing; men with green faces struggled mysteriously and perhaps discreditably with ladies who had square blue breasts. 'That's a nice one . . .' said Jack thoughtfully.

Jane said, 'Let's get out of here. People must be mad if they like things like that.'

Out in the street he said, 'There's another gallery in Bourke Street, up by William Street or somewhere.'

Jane said, 'I want a cup of tea.'

They turned into a café; over the tea she said that she was through with picture galleries. 'I know what I want,' she said, 'but it's not here. I want a picture that an ordinary person can enjoy, not someone who's half mad. I'll find it some day.'

He said tentatively, 'There might be time to go down and pick up the Ford before dinner. . . .'

'Let's do that,' she said. 'Take the taste of those foul paintings out of our mouths.'

The new utility was a very lovely motor-car, a low, flowing dark-green thing with more art in it than anything that they had seen that day. Twenty minutes before lunch-time it became their property, and they got into it, thrilled by the new possession, and drove it very carefully and slowly to park it in the Treasury Gardens. Jack Dorman locked it up whistling softly between his teeth,

> I don't want her, you can have her,
> She's too fat for me . . .

His wife caught the air, and smiled a little. 'We must ring Angie,' she said. 'See her this afternoon.' Their daughter was staying for a few days with a college friend in Toorak, the most fashionable suburb of the city.

Her father said, 'Maybe we could run her out into the country somewhere. She might like a drive. . . .'

She was in fact driving in their utility at that moment, with Tim Archer. He had picked her up in the old Chevrolet that morning and was driving her southwards to bathe in Port Phillip Bay, thirty miles from the city. He had collected a lunch of sandwiches and soft drinks and they had set off at about twelve o'clock; they were now coming to the beach that was their destination.

Angela Dorman was twenty years old; she was taking Social Studies at Melbourne University and was just about to start upon her third and last year. She was a well-built blonde girl, superbly healthy. Like many Australian girls, a country life in her early years with an abundance of good food, plenty of riding, plenty of swimming, and the good Australian climate had made her a magnificent physical specimen; she would have graced a magazine cover in any country of the world. Now she was going through that phase of youth that can find nothing good in its own country; in Australia the only places that could satisfy her were Melbourne or Sydney, and her one ambition was to escape altogether from Australia to a rose-tinted and a glamorous England.

She had known Tim Archer for three years, since he had come to work for her father at Leonora. She knew that he was devoted to her in the inarticulate, dumb manner of a dog. She found him slow and unenterprising, without much interest in the world outside Victoria; a typical country boy. For all her restlessness she had enough of her father's shrewd common sense not to throw away lightly something that she might want later on; she was sufficiently realist to know that she might not find so steady an affection easily again. She left most of his letters unanswered but she was kind to him when they met, and when he had rung her up and asked her to come swimming down past Mornington she had put off another engagement to go out with him.

They parked the old utility beside the road, took their lunch and bathing gear, and walked down through the tea trees to the beach. They had it practically to themselves, that little beach; they went back into the tea trees to change and came out in their bathers wearing dark glasses to sit and sun themselves a little before going in. Then they swam in the hot sunshine, keeping an eye open for the possible shark; although they were both strong swimmers, like most Australians they did not venture very far from shore. Sharks in Port Phillip Bay were a rarity, but then you only met one once. . . .

They came out presently, and sat drying in the sun on the hot sand till they began to burn; then they moved into the shade of the tea trees and got out their lunch. Over the cigarettes he broached the subject that was foremost in his mind.

'Coming up to Leonora soon?' he asked.

'I suppose so,' she said reluctantly. 'I'm going to spend a week or so in Sydney with Susie Martin at the end of the month. I suppose I'll have to go home for a bit before that.'

'It's nice up there now,' he offered. 'Cooler than the city.'

'There's nothing to do there,' she replied. 'It's different for you. You've got a job to do. When I come home there's nothing to do but help Mummy with the cooking and washing up. There's nobody to talk to.'

'I know,' he said patiently. 'It must seem a bit slow.'

She turned towards him. 'Don't you ever get tired of sheep—seeing the same sheep every day?'

'There's the beef cattle,' he said slowly and quite seriously. 'They make a bit of a change.'

'But don't you get *bored* up there?'

'I dunno,' he said. 'There's always something that wants doing—fences or rabbits or spreading the super. We're going to plough about eighty acres of the middle paddock in March and sow it down to rye-grass and clovers.'

'Will that make it better?'

'My word,' he said. 'If we did that all over we could carry twice the stock. Costs a lot of money, though.'

She was silent. She knew that she ought to be able to take an interest in the property that had given her the university, and pretty clothes, and leisure; she knew that the fault lay in her. 'I can't stand the country,' she said quietly.

He knew that what she said was true, and it was painful to hear her say it. 'What are you going to do when you leave the university?' he asked. 'Get a job down here in the city?'

She said, 'I want to go to England.'

'What's the matter with Australia?' he asked in his slow way.

'It's so small, so petty, and so new,' she said. 'Everything we think about or talk about—everything that's worth while—comes from England. We're such second-raters here. I want to go home and work in London and be in the centre of things and meet some first-class people. I want to be where things really happen, things that are important in the world.'

'Australia's all right,' he said. 'We've got some pretty good people here.'

'But not like England,' she said. 'It's not like things are at home.'

'You don't get enough to eat in England.'

'That's all nonsense. The children's health at home is as good as it is here.' She paused. 'The trouble is we eat too much here. Be a good thing if we all ate a bit less and sent more home.'

'What'ld you do in London?' he asked presently.

'I'd like to get a job with a hospital,' she said. 'An almoner or social work of some kind, with one of the big London hospitals. If I could get that, it'd be a job worth doing.'

'Down in the slums?' he asked. 'With very poor people?'

She nodded. 'I want to get a job where one could help—help people who need helping.'

'Couldn't you do that in Australia?'

'There's not the scope,' she said. 'There aren't any poor people here—not like there are at home.'

He knew that to be true, and he thought it was a very good thing. 'Too many people in England,' he said. 'That's the trouble. Do you know this girl Jennifer Morton that your ma's come down to meet?'

She shook her head. 'I've never seen her, nor has Ma. I don't think any of us know much about her.'

'She worked in London, so your ma was saying. She might be able to give you a few tips.'

'I want to meet her,' the girl said. 'Be somebody to talk to up at Leonora, anyway.'

He lay propped on one elbow on the warm sand, staring out at the sunlit beach and the blue sea. He was trying not to keep looking at her, but it was difficult to keep his eyes under control. 'When do you suppose you'll be going?' he asked at last.

'About this time next year,' she said. 'I've not told the parents yet, but it's what I want to do. I think they'll let me—if the wool keeps up.'

'How long do you think you'll be gone for?'

She stared down at the sand and traced a little pattern on it with one finger. 'I don't know,' she said. 'I'd rather work in London than work here. I might never come back.'

'Bit hard on your dad and ma,' he said.

'I know. That's what makes it difficult.' She paused. 'I ought to be home by five, Tim,' she said. 'I must see Dad and Ma this evening.'

'Too right. Your dad won't worry because he was taking over the new Ford today. Your ma will want to see you, though. Like me to run you straight to the hotel, or do you want to go back to Toorak first?'

She thought for a moment. 'I'd better go back to Toorak. I can't go to the Windsor straight from here, like this.'

'I'll run you back and wait while you change and take you on to the hotel.'

'Will you, Tim? That's terribly sweet of you.'

He coloured a little, and she noticed it, and knew that she had been a shade too kind. 'That's all right,' he said gruffly. 'We'd better get changed and get upon the road, if you want to be at the hotel by five.'

They changed back into their clothes in the tea trees and got into the utility, and drove back to the city with hardly a word spoken all the way.

The *Orion* docked at eight o'clock next morning, with Jennifer on board. Jane Dorman had written to her again at Fremantle, and Jennifer had replied agreeing to go to Leonora for a few days before she came back to the city to take a job. Now as the vessel docked she was uncertain if she had been wise; she knew little of the Dormans and nothing of Australia; she would have preferred to go to a hotel for a few days, and find a lodging in the suburbs, and settle down in her own way. It was impossible to refuse the evident kindness, however, and it would be interesting to see a bit of the country before starting on a city job. Moreover, it was to visit Jane Dorman that her grandmother had given her the money; but for that she would not have been there at all.

When she met the Dormans in the tourist-class saloon, in response to a loud-speaker call, she was surprised in one or two respects. For one thing, they were far smarter than she had expected them to be. Jack Dorman in a new grey suit, heavy though he might be, was better dressed than her father, and Jane Dorman, though her hands were old and worn, was very smart in a new black and white coat and skirt. Their daughter, Angela, was with them, rather younger than Jennifer, but even better turned out than her parents; Jennifer felt pale and shabby in comparison with this glorious young woman.

As she came into the saloon Jane Dorman got up to meet her; in the crowd of passengers and friends she came straight to Jennifer. 'It's Jennifer Morton, isn't it?' she said. 'I'm Jane Dorman.'

Jennifer said, 'How did you know me, Mrs Dorman?'

Jane said, 'You've got a look of your grandmother about you, my Aunt Ethel. I knew you right away.'

Then there were introductions, and enquiries about the passage, and business of the luggage. The Dormans had brought both utilities to the pier-head and Tim Archer was sitting in the Chevrolet below. Presently Jennifer was passing through the Customs, and then her suitcases and trunk were down in the new Ford utility, and she was free into Australia.

She drove to the hotel with Jack and Jane Dorman, Angela following behind in the old Chevrolet with Tim. In a blur of first impressions the width of the streets and the great number of motor-cars impressed Jennifer most; whatever else Melbourne might be, it was a beautifully laid-out city, and obviously a very prosperous one. The Dormans had engaged a room for her at the Windsor for a couple of nights; she found herself whisked up into this, and then they all had lunch together, except for Tim Archer, who had started back for Merrijig in the old utility.

Jennifer decided that it was easier to submit until the hospitality of these kind strangers had exhausted its first impetus; she felt that it would be rude and ungenerous to battle against it now. Angela disappeared after lunch upon her own affairs, and Jane and Jack Dorman took Jennifer out to the new Ford utility. They all sat together in the wide seat and started out on a long drive up into the Dandenong mountains, clothed in trees finer and taller than any that Jennifer had seen in England. At the outset she protested diffidently at the waste of their time in making this outing for her, but she was quickly told about the newness of the car and made to realize that her host would certainly have done that anyway that afternoon for his own pleasure. Indeed, the fun that Jack Dorman was getting out of his new possession was so evident that Jennifer relaxed, content to enjoy herself.

By the time they got back to Melbourne she was dazed with new impressions. By common consent they spent the evening quietly in the hotel. Jennifer was tired, and at Leonora the Dormans were in the habit of getting up at six in the morning and going to bed soon after nine each night. So for a while after dinner Jennifer sat talking quietly with Jane Dorman in a corner of the lounge of the hotel, while Jack smoked a cigar and read the *Herald.*

The girl said presently, 'I'd like to take a little time tomorrow looking for a room or a small flat to live in here. It's terribly nice of you to ask me up to Leonora, and I'd love to go back with you for a week, but after that I'll have to come back here and take a job. I thought I'd better see about that tomorrow.'

Jane said, 'I know just how you feel. We'll get you fixed up with somewhere nice to live before we go back home. I don't think you ought to be in too much of a hurry to start work, though. The temperature was over a hundred the day before yesterday, in the city here. It's the worst time of the year for anybody coming out from England, and you're bound to feel it more than we do. You'd be much more comfortable if you stay with us at Leonora for a month, and start work in the autumn. It's much cooler out there.'

The girl said awkwardly, 'I think I ought to start earning something sooner than that, even if it is a bit hot.' The austerities of England were still strong in her; to relax and rest was somehow vaguely disgraceful. 'I'm living on your money as it is,' she said.

The older woman said evenly, 'You're doing nothing of the sort, my dear. When we sent that money to Aunt Ethel we gave it to her. That was the end of it, so far as we were concerned.'

The girl said, 'I'm sorry—I oughtn't to have said that. But I would rather start earning my own living fairly soon. I don't want you to think I'm ungrateful, when you've been so very kind. But I've got to paddle my own canoe some time, and the sooner I start the better.'

'I know,' said Jane. 'So long as you know that we should love to have you for as long as you can stay with us. None of our children are home now; Angie will be coming up at the end of the week, but she won't stay longer than ten days. It's dull for young people up at Merrijig, of course—nothing ever happens there.'

'I think I'd find it rather interesting,' said Jennifer. 'If I stayed up there too long with you, I might not want to come back to the city at all.'

Jane glanced at her curiously. 'Have you ever lived in the country, at home?' The girl laughed. 'No,' she said frankly. 'I've always lived in towns–in Leicester, and then in London. I don't really know what living in the country's like. I suppose that's why I'm interested in it.'

'It can be a bit dull in the country,' Jane said. 'Long periods of doing nothing but the daily work a woman has to do, cooking and washing and cleaning the house. No one but your husband and the men to talk to, and only the radio to listen to. But . . . I don't know. I wouldn't like to live anywhere else.'

Jennifer thought about this for a minute. Then she asked, 'How many sheep have you got?'

Jane looked up in surprise. 'I don't quite know–about three thousand, I think. Jack, how many sheep are there on Leonora?'

He looked up from his paper. 'Three thousand five hundred and sixty, unless someone's been along and pinched some of 'em.'

'Then there's the beef cattle,' Jane Dorman said. 'About two hundred Herefords.'

'Two hundred and six,' said Mr Dorman, and returned to his paper.

'I suppose you sell a lot of them for meat,' said Jennifer.

'Sell about six or seven hundred fat lambs every year,' Jane replied, 'and a good few ewes. But most of the money comes from the wool clip, of course.'

'I wasn't thinking so much about the money,' the girl replied. 'It must be rather fun raising so much food.'

'Fun?'

'Don't you feel pleased at being able to turn out such a lot of meat?'

Jane smiled. 'I never thought about it. Send them to market and that's the end, so far as we're concerned, except to bank the cheque when it comes in.'

'It seems such a good thing to be doing,' said the girl.

Jane Dorman glanced at her curiously. It was the first time that she had heard it suggested that there was any ethical value in the work that she and Jack had spent their lives in. In the early years they had been looked down upon as country hicks, unable to make a living in the city and so compelled to live upon the land; in those hard days between the wars when wool was one and six a pound nobody had cared whether they lived or starved. In recent years with wool ten times the price, they had been abused as profiteers. In neither time had anyone suggested in her hearing that their work had any social value. Jennifer, she thought, came to Australia with a fresh outlook; it would be interesting to find out what it was.

She asked, 'How are things at home now, in regard to food? What's it really like, for ordinary people?'

Jennifer said, 'It's quite all right–there's really heaps of food. Of course, it's not like it is here, or on the ship. But there's heaps to eat in England.'

'Not meat, is there?'

'No. Meat *is* a bit scarce.'

'When you say scarce, Jennie, what does that mean? One hears such different stories. One day you see a picture of a week's ration of meat in England about the size of a matchbox, and then someone like you comes along and says it's quite all right. Can you get a steak?'

'Oh no–not what *you'd* call a steak.'

'What about restaurants? You can't go in and order a grilled steak?'

The girl shook her head. 'I don't think so. You might at the Dorchester or some hotel like that that ordinary people can't afford to go to. I'd never tasted a grilled steak till I got on the ship.'

'Never tasted a grilled steak?'

'No. Even if you could get the steak, I don't think you'd cook it that way, because of wasting the fat.'

Jane asked, 'But what do you cook when you go out on a picnic?'

The question rather stumped the English girl. 'I don't know,' she said, and laughed. 'Not that, anyway.'

'You eat a lot of fish, don't you?'

Jennifer nodded. 'A lot. Do you get much fish here?'

'Not much fresh fish. I don't think we've got the fishing fleets that you've got at home. We get a lot of kippers and things like that.'

'Like the English Kippers? Herrings?'

'They *are* English kippers,' Jane said. 'Scotch, rather. They all seem to come from Aberdeen.'

'Do you get those out here?'

'Why, yes. You can buy kippers all over Australia.'

'They're getting very scarce at home,' the girl said. 'I remember when I was a schoolgirl, in the war, the kippers were awfully good. But it's very difficult to get a kipper now at home.'

'Funny,' Jane said. 'We've had lots of them out here for the last two or three years. It always makes me feel very near home when we have kippers for breakfast.'

The girl asked, 'Have you ever been home since you came out here?'

Jane shook her head. 'Jack suggested we should go home on a trip a few months ago,' she said. 'But I don't know. All the people that I'd want to see are dead or gone away–it's over thirty years since I left home. And everything seems to have changed so much–I don't know that I'd want to see it now. Our old house is a school. It used to be so lovely; I don't want to see it as a school.'

'That's what everybody says,' the girl replied, 'that England used to be so much nicer. Of course, I only know it as it is now.'

'Old people have always talked like that, I suppose,' said Jane. 'And yet, I think there's something in it this time.'

There was a silence, and then Jennifer said, 'Have you been doing a lot of shopping since you came down here?'

'Oh, my dear. Do you know anything about pictures?'

Jennifer knew absolutely nothing about pictures, but she listened with interest to the results of the picture hunt to date. She went to bed early with the Dormans, thinking that these were simple and unaffected people that she was beginning to like rather well.

She went shopping with them next day, feeling rather shabby as she walked with them on a round of the best shops. Jane wanted to buy a wrist-watch for Jack Dorman to commemorate their holiday, and they all went into a shop that Jennifer alone would never have dreamed of entering, and looked at watches; finally Jane bought a gold self-winding wrist-watch for her husband for ninety-two guineas, and never turned a hair. Clothes did not appear to appeal to Jane very much–'I so seldom go anywhere, Jenny'–but shoes were another matter, and she bought thirty-eight pounds' worth in half an hour. Jack left them while this was going on, and they went on to Myer's and bought a new refrigerator for a hundred and twenty pounds and a mass of miscellaneous kitchen gadgets and equipment for fifty-three pounds eighteen shillings and sixpence. 'We get down to Melbourne so seldom,' Jane said happily.

Jennifer wandered after her relation in a daze; she had never spent a morning like that before. Jack caught up with them as they were having morning coffee and said that he'd sometimes thought that Jane should have a car of her own and not use the station utilities, and he'd found a Morris Minor that had only done a thousand miles and was a bargain at a hundred quid above list price, and would Jane like to come and look at it? They went and looked at it and bought it, and then they had lunch and started on the curtain materials and carpets. 'The homestead *is* so shabby,' Jane remarked. 'I don't know what you'll think of it, coming from England. I must brighten it up a little.'

By tea-time they were all dead tired, and they had spent about thirteen hundred and sixty pounds. Jennifer felt with all her instincts that the Dormans must be crazy, and then she reminded herself of the letter to Aunt Ethel and the statement that the wool cheque had been twenty-two thousand pounds, and thought perhaps that goings-on like this were normal to Australia. After all, Australia was on the other side of the world and so all Australians, and she herself, must now be walking upside down relative to England, so it was reasonable that all their standards should be upside down as well.

'We don't always go on like this,' said Jane. 'In fact, I don't think we've ever done it before.' Later that evening she showed Jennifer a gold and blue enamel dressing-table set that Jack had bought for her all by himself, and had presented to her rather sheepishly.

Jennifer felt that surely there must be something wrong in spending so much money; her upbringing in the austerities of England insisted that this must be so. The queer thing was that here it all seemed natural and right. The Dormans had worked for thirty years without much recompense and now had won through to their reward; in spite of the violation of all her traditions Jennifer was pleased for them, and pleased with a country that allowed rewards like that. She had been brought up in the belief that money spent by the rich came out of the pockets of the poor, and she had never seriously questioned that. But in Australia, it seemed, there were very few poor people, if any. In her two days in the country she had seen great placards at the railway stations appealing for boys of nineteen to work as railway porters at twelve pounds a week, and she had seen sufficient of the prices in the cheaper shops to realize that such boys would be much better off than she had been when working for the Ministry of Pensions in England. It was all very difficult and very puzzling, and she fell asleep that night with a queer feeling of guilty enjoyment in Australia.

They took things a little more easily next day, and bought nothing but an English grandfather clock for a hundred and eighty guineas, because it was just like one that Jane remembered in her English home, thirty years before. They took delivery of the little Morris before lunch and Jane drove it to Toorak to show it to Angela, and after lunch they all drove out in the two cars, Jane driving the Morris with Angela beside her and Jack Dorman following with Jennifer in the new Ford utility to pick up the pieces if Jane hit anything. They followed the shore of Port Phillip Bay in the hot sunshine nearly to Mornington, and had tea in a café, a Devonshire tea with splits and jam and a great bowl of clotted cream with a yellow crust. They were back in the city in time for drinks before dinner, and then to the theatre to see Sonia Dresdel in *A Message for Margaret.*

Next morning Jane and Jennifer went out early in the little car to look for a boarding-house, and found one that they had had recommended in a suburb called St Kilda, not far from the sea and about twenty minutes from the centre of the city in a tram. There was no room vacant for three weeks, which Jane Dorman considered to be a very good thing. Jennifer liked the look of the woman who kept it and bowed to the inevitable, and paid a deposit, and engaged the room. Jane and Jennifer drove back to the city and had their hair set, rather expensively.

I'll have to watch out how I spend my money,' the girl said a little ruefully. 'You're getting me into bad habits.'

'We don't go on like this at home,' said Jane. 'I think we must be a bit touched, the amount of money that we've spent in these few days. We've never done it before. Do your father and mother ever go mad like this?'

Jennifer shook her head, thinking of the hard economies her parents had to make. 'I don't think you could do it in England, even if you had the money,' she said. 'There wouldn't be the things to buy—not the cars, anyway.'

They went to the pictures that night and saw Gary Cooper; next day they left for Leonora. By a last-minute decision Angela came with them. The virtues of a utility became clear then to Jennifer, because Jack Dorman went out in the morning and loaded up the refrigerator and the grandfather clock and about a hundredweight of kitchen gear, and came back and took on board five suitcases and Jennifer's trunk. At about eleven o'clock they were ready to start.

Jane Dorman was not a fast driver, and the Morris was new to her; it was evening when they came to Leonora after a slow drive through magnificent mountain and pastoral country. Jennifer learned a great deal of Victoria as they drove; she was amazed at the brilliance of the birds. The robin was more brightly coloured than a bird had any right to be, and the red and blue parrots in the woods amazed her. Here birds, apparently, had few enemies and so no need of a protective colouring, and freed from that restraint they had let themselves go. Only the lyre bird, a sombre being with a long tail like a peacock, appeared to exercise a British discretion in colours. The rest of them, thought Jennifer, were frankly gaudy.

They saw wallabies at one point, hopping across a paddock at a distance from the road, and at another place a black and silver animal about the size of a large cat, with a bushy tail like a silver fox fur, ran across the road in front of them; she learned that this was a possum. She saw a good many rabbits, exactly like the English rabbit, and was told about their depredations and the methods that were used to keep their numbers down. The style of the small towns and villages through which they passed reminded her of movie pictures of the Middle West of the United States; the same wooden houses with wide verandas and tin roofs, the same wide streets, at one time cattle tracks. It was a gracious, pleasant country that they passed through on that drive, the grass becoming yellow in the midsummer sun, but a well-watered and a friendly country, all the same.

In the evening they came to Leonora homestead on the slopes of the Buller range above the bridge and school and hotel that was Merrijig. Jennifer was driving with Jane Dorman for the last part of the journey; she closed the last paddock gate and got back into the car, and Jane drove into the yard behind the homestead where the new Ford was already parked with Mario and Tim admiring it. They got out of the Morris, and stretched after the long journey. 'Well, this is it,' said Jane. 'Is it like what you thought it was going to be?'

Jennifer looked around her. All the buildings were severely practical, the walls of white-painted weatherboard, the roofs of corrugated iron painted with red oxide. There were numbers of great iron water tanks, cylindrical in form, disposed to catch the rain that fell upon the roofs, and there was another such tank high up on a wooden stand from which the house was supplied. The house itself had deep verandas on two sides and fly-wire doors, and screens on all the windows. Standing in the yard she had a wide view out over the basin of the Delatite, pastures and occasional woods, and behind that again the sun was setting behind a wooded mountain. It was very quiet and secure and peaceful in the evening light.

'I think it's simply lovely,' said the girl from London. 'I don't think I've ever been in such a beautiful place.'

They turned to the homestead and started on the business of getting themselves and the luggage indoors, and the refrigerator, and the grandfather clock, and began the business of preparing supper. Mario had killed a sheep and butchered it and there was cold roast mutton in the larder; salad and tinned peaches with cream and plum cake completed the impromptu meal, which they ate in the big kitchen that was the central room of the homestead.

Leonora homestead had several bedrooms, but, with Tim Archer and Mario both living in, Angela Dorman and Jennifer shared a room. Jennifer soon found that Angela was frankly curious about England; the barrage of questions began as soon as they retired.

'Have you ever seen Westminster Abbey?' Angela asked.

Jennifer was taken by surprise. 'Why–yes.'

'It's very beautiful, isn't it?'

The girl from London had to think a bit. 'It's all right,' she said at last. 'I don't know that I ever noticed it particularly.'

'It's where they have the Coronation, isn't it? Where the King and Queen get crowned?'

Jennifer wasn't quite sure if the Coronation took place there or at St Paul's; neither of them meant a great deal in her life. 'I think it is,' she said, and laughed. 'You know, it must sound awfully silly, but I'm not quite sure.'

'I'm sure it's Westminster Abbey,' said the Australian girl. 'I was reading a book about the Coronation of the King and Queen, in 1937. It had a lot of pictures taken in the Abbey. It must be marvellous to see a thing like that.'

'I should think it would be,' Jennifer agreed. 'I haven't seen it, of course. I was a kid at school, in Leicester. I remember that we got a whole holiday.'

'We got a holiday here, of course,' said Angela. 'I was only little, but I remember Banbury was all decorated with flags and bunting everywhere.'

Jennifer tried to visualise the little country town that they had passed through all decorated and rejoicing over an event that happened twelve thousand miles away, and failed. 'Really?'

'Why, of course. And then when the film came to the picture house Daddy and Mummy took me to it. It was the first film I ever saw; I think I was about Five. It came back during the war, and I saw it again then. I've seen it three times altogether.'

'I remember it was a good film,' said Jennifer. 'I saw it in England.' She reflected as she brushed her hair that Angela Dorman, then a little country schoolgirl at Merrijig, probably knew a good deal more about the Coronation ceremonies and Westminster Abbey than she did.

'Have you seen the King and Queen?' asked Angela.

Jennifer tried to remember if she had or not; surely she must have seen them some time, other than at the cinema. Surely she must have? In any case, she couldn't possibly say she hadn't. Recollection came to her just in time, and saved her from having to tell a lie. 'I saw them in the procession when Princess Elizabeth got married,' she said. 'I was standing in the Mall; they passed quite close.'

'How marvellous! The Mall—that's the avenue between Buckingham Palace and the Admiralty Arch, isn't it?.

'That's right.' It was incredible how much Angela knew about London.

'Did you see Princess Elizabeth, too?'

Jennifer nodded.

'And the Duke of Edinburgh?'

'Yes. I've seen them several times.'

'Tell me—do they look like their pictures?'

'Yes, I think so—as much as anyone looks like their picture. They look very good sorts.'

'It must be wonderful to see them close to, like that,' Angela said. 'I suppose you've seen everything there is to see in London?'

'I don't know about that,' said Jennifer. 'I lived in London for two years, but I was outside in one of the suburbs, at a place called Blackheath. I worked in an office there. I didn't see an awful lot of London, really.'

'I'm going to London next year, if the wool holds up,' said Angela. 'I want to get a job in one of the big hospitals. Have you ever seen Winston Churchill?'

'I'm not sure,' said Jennifer. 'I've seen him on the pictures so many times, one gets muddled up.' She searched for a palliative for her disgrace. 'I've seen Bob Hope.'

'Have you really? Have you seen any other film stars?'

'One or two. I saw Dennis Price once, at a dance.'

'You *are* lucky. Have you seen Ingrid Bergman? I think she's beaut.'

It went on and on, long after they were both in bed and growing sleepy. To Angela the English girl was a visitor from another planet, a beautiful rose-coloured place where everything that happened was important to the world. 'I should think you'll find it awfully dull in Melbourne, after living in London,' she said once. 'Nothing interesting ever happens here.'

Jennifer could have answered that nothing interesting ever happened in Blackheath, but she forebore to; she had not known Angela long enough to damp such a guileless enthusiasm for England and everything English. She herself, so far, had found Australia far more interesting than England. She liked the prosperous dignity of Melbourne better than the shabby austerity of London; she was deeply and inarticulately pleased with the good country she had seen that day, with the brilliant birds and the novel beasts that roamed the woods and pastures where there were so few people to disturb them. She could do without the sight and the propinquity of famous or of interesting people in return for these good things, for a time anyway.

She slept well, and woke with the first light of dawn to the sound of people moving about in the homestead; she looked at her watch and found that it was half-past five. Outside was sunshine and a man's step in the yard; she rolled sleepily out of bed and sat on the edge. Angela opened an eye and said, 'What's the time?'

'Half-past five.'

'We don't get up till eight. I never do.'

'People seem to be moving about.'

'It's only Mummy. She gets up in the middle of the night all the year round.' Angela rolled over firmly and went to sleep again.

Jennifer got up and dressed in jumper and slacks, and found Jane Dorman drinking a cup of tea at the table in the kitchen; the fire was already lit in the new stove. She poured Jennifer a cup. 'You didn't have to get up,' she said. 'Angela isn't, is she? I thought not. I often get a bit of cooking done before breakfast, in the hot weather. It's better than having the stove going in the middle of the day.'

Jennifer went out presently into the yard in the fresh morning, and found Tim Archer lifting a couple of dogs into the back of the old Chevrolet utility. They were nondescript dogs, one a sort of mongrel collie and the other a blue roan, a kind of dog that Jennifer had never seen before. She asked Tim what it was, and he said it was a 'heeler', but when she pressed him to say if that was a breed or not, he could not tell her. It was a heeler because it went for the heels of the cattle and not their heads, apparently.

'Do you use them for sheep as well?' she asked.

'My word,' he said. 'I'm going down to get the mob out of the river paddock 'n put them down the road. Want to come along?'

She got into the utility with him, and they started off across-country in it, driving over the short pastures. They went about a mile, passing through three gates, and drove round behind the sheep; here Tim stopped the utility and put the dogs out. He shouted a few orders to the dogs and got one out on one flank and one the other and got the sheep moving, seven or eight hundred of them, in the direction of the gate. They got back into the utility and drove about the paddock for a time rounding up the stragglers with the dogs; then when the mob was compact in one bunch they drove along behind them in the centre, one dog at each side. They went very slowly, at the walking pace of a sheep.

Jennifer stretched in the warm sun. 'I suppose this is the modern way of herding sheep,' she said. 'By motor-car.'

'Too right,' he said. 'It's a sight quicker and easier than messing about with a horse. The boss, he likes a horse and he'd ride if he was on this job. But to my way of thinking, by the time you've caught the horse and saddled up, you could have done the job in a utility.'

He turned to her. 'Don't they use utilities in the paddocks in England?'

She was nonplussed. 'I don't think so,' she said. 'They don't have utilities at all. Most of the farms in England are quite small, much smaller than these. It's all different here.'

'I know,' he said. 'The properties are bigger here, but you've got better land. Or else, perhaps you improve it more than we do. How do you like it here, after England?'

'I like it so far,' she said. 'It's a very, very pretty bit of country, this.'

He stared at her in surprise. 'Prettier than England?'

'It's different,' she said. 'You'd have to go a long way to find such unspoilt country in England. England might have been like this once.'

He digested this in silence for a time. Then he said, 'Angie doesn't like it here. She wants to go to England.'

'I know. She was telling me last night.'

'Do you think she'll like it there?'

'She'll like it all right,' said Jennifer. 'She's determined to. She's expecting an awful lot, and she'll have some disappointments, I should think. But—yes, she'll like it.'

They drove on for a time in silence while he digested this unpalatable opinion. The sheep baa-ed and scuffled in front of them, the dogs whimpering on either side. 'What I can't make out,' he said at last, 'is why anybody leaves England, if it's such a bonza place as that. Is it because they don't get enough to eat?'

'I don't think it's that,' said Jennifer. 'England can be difficult at times.' She paused. 'I think Angie may find that, when the glamour wears off. I shouldn't think she'd want to spend her life in England, after living here.'

'You think she'll come back here?' he asked quickly.

She laughed. 'I don't know. She might marry somebody in England and settle down there.'

'Too right,' he said quietly. 'She might do that.'

It seemed to be a difficult conversation, and Jennifer changed it, and asked him what sort of sheep they were. He told her they were Corriedales, and described to her the points that made them so. From that they passed to discussing the Hereford cattle in an adjacent paddock, and the difference between those and Shorthorns.

'I wish I knew more about all this,' she said presently. 'About the land, and how to make it grow more grass. That's important, isn't it?'

He said, 'Well, stands to reason if you grow more grass you can feed more beasts. There's a lot to be done in this part of the country to improve the pastures.'

'Aren't people doing all they can?'

'Aw, look,' he protested, 'it costs money, you know. Mr Dorman, he's ploughing up eighty acres of the river paddocks we've just come from this autumn, and sowing it down to clovers and rye-grass. He'll have to spend three hundred pounds on seed alone, let alone the labour and the tractor and that, and then the paddock will be out of grazing for six months. I'd like to see him doing a lot more than that, but it's a big thing to close a paddock for six months, with wool the price it is.'

'I see. You'd get more meat and wool later on, but not this year. You'd get less.'

'That's right. And next year the prices might not be so good. The time to close the paddocks for reseeding is when prices are low, and then you generally can't afford to do it.'

'It's terribly important to turn out more meat,' said Jennifer. 'I should have thought people would have taken a chance.'

'It's just a matter of pounds, shillings, and pence,' he said.

'It's a good thing to do as well,' she retorted. 'That ought to count for something.'

He stared at her. 'How do you mean?'

'The food's so badly needed,' she said. 'It's important to turn out as much as possible, isn't it?

'Well, I dunno.' All his life Tim Archer had lived in communities that had a surfeit of food; it was a condition of his employment on a sheep station in Victoria that he should be entitled to buy as much mutton as he wanted at threepence a pound, and this for a family meant half a sheep a week. It was hard for him to realize what this English girl was getting at. 'We don't need any more food here,' he said. 'You mean, because of people at home?'

She nodded. 'It'ld make a difference at home if people could live like you live here. It isn't till one comes away that one realizes how bad things have got in England. If anybody here wants to do something for England they can just set to and grow a bit more food.'

'I wish you'd tell Angie that,' he said with a faint smile. He could not keep from talking about Angie to this girl; every topic seemed to work round to her in the end. 'She's wanting to do something for England by going home to take a job in a London hospital.'

'She wants to see England,' Jennifer said. 'That's what she wants to go for. She'd do a better job for England by staying here at home, on Leonora, and driving the tractor to help make more food.'

'Well, you just tell her that.' He was grinning now.

'I don't mind, but it won't cut any ice. She wants to see England. But it's true, all the same. If there was a bit more food we mightn't want so many hospitals.'

Jennifer spent the morning in housework with Jane; Angela did a little bit about the house and then borrowed her mother's Morris and disappeared for the day to look up old school friends in the district, and to bring back a few vegetables and stores from Banbury. Jennifer refused an invitation to go with her, preferring on this first day to stay around the homestead and help Jane to get the lunch. It was hot in the kitchen and they let the wood stove out at about ten o'clock, and served a cold saddle of lamb for dinner with a great dish of potatoes cooked upon a Primus, and a cold jam tart.

They sat out, after washing-up, in deck-chairs on the veranda; Jack and the two men were away in one of the paddocks cutting up a dead tree for firewood. There was a little breeze from off the mountain, cool and refreshing; they sat drowsing and gossiping, looking out over the wide valley in the blazing sunshine.

Presently Jane said, 'Tell me about Aunt Ethel. What did she die of? I didn't gather that from your letters.'

It was an awkward question, and one that Jennifer was not prepared to answer directly. Ealing and the suburban house in the dark November rain seemed very far away. 'She was an old dear,' she said at last, 'but in some ways she was rather stupid. She ran out of money, and she wouldn't tell anybody about it. You see, her pension came to an end.'

She explained the matter of the pension to Jane. 'She had another old lady living with her,' Jennifer explained, 'a Mrs Harding, widow of an Army officer.'

'Is that the one she called Aggie, who died?'

'That's right,' said Jennifer. 'Aggie died last May, and that probably made things difficult because, of course, they shared expenses. My mother wrote and asked her, but she said that she'd be quite all right. Well, she wasn't all right at all. It was about that time her pension came to an end, but she never told anybody about that. She hadn't got anything to live on then, so she began selling things. Furniture that she hadn't any use for–and little bits of jewellery.'

'My dear . . .'

'We didn't know a thing about it,' the girl said. 'I went and saw her one Sunday only a month before she died, and she gave me a marvellous lunch–roast duck with all the trimmings, and a mince pie made out of some of the dried fruit parcels that you sent her . . .' It was incredible, sitting here on the veranda in the warm breeze, that those cartons had come from here. 'She had buttered scones for tea, and a great big cake. She never let on for a moment that there was anything wrong. And all the time she was–well, starving. That's what it amounted to. When she got ill, it came out that she hadn't eaten anything for days, except a few of your dried fruits.'

'My dear, I am so very, very sorry.'

'I know,' the girl said. 'She was very proud, and she wouldn't tell a soul. She needn't have let things get to such a pitch. If she didn't want to tell us, she could have got help from the Town Hall. There's an official called the relieving officer who's there to deal with cases like that, and help with money. She could have gone to him. But she wouldn't do that.'

'She didn't want to take charity, I suppose.'

The girl said, 'I think that was it. She'd have thought that was an awful thing to do.'

'I can't imagine Aunt Ethel ever taking charity. She–she was different.'

'I don't think it a very good thing to be different in England,' Jennifer said. 'It's better if you go along like everybody else.'

They talked about the details of what had happened in Ealing for a time. Presently Jane asked, 'Tell me, Jenny–is this sort of thing common now? Do old people, people of Aunt Ethel's sort–do many of them die in poverty?'

The girl said cautiously, 'I think a good many of them have a pretty bad time. It's difficult to tell, because one doesn't hear a lot about them. Old ladies who die quietly and make no fuss don't get into the newspapers. Granny didn't have to die like that. She was too proud to let anyone know that she was hard up. She could have died like that anywhere–it wasn't anything to do with England. It could have happened in Australia.'

'It could, but it doesn't,' said Jane.

'Why not?'

'I think this country's too prosperous for that to happen. An old lady who was old-fashioned and as proud as that would almost certainly have some relation, some son or grandson or nephew, who was making a whole heap of money, to whom the little assistance that she'd need would be a flea-bite. It *could* happen here, as you say, but I can't imagine it doing so.'

'She had some odd ideas,' Jennifer said presently. 'It all happened within twenty-four hours of her death, so I suppose she would be a bit funny.'

'What sort of ideas?'

The girl said, 'She was thinking of the time when she was young, and how easy and how prosperous everything was then, in England. She kept talking about that, saying what a much better time she'd had when she was a girl than I was having. I let her talk, of course; one couldn't argue.' She sat staring out across the sunlit valley to the blue hills. 'And then your letter came with the five hundred pounds, and you said that you were sending it because the wool cheque had been twenty-two thousand. I suppose you said that to make it easy for her to accept.'

Jane said, 'I thought it was best to tell her. She'd known that we were hard up for so many years.'

'I thought that was it. I think she thought a lot about your wool cheque, although she didn't say. She was lying there so still. . . . I think she got to feeling that if you had twenty-two thousand a year, you'd be living in the way that she lived in when she was young—a great big house with three servants and a butler, and grooms, and hunters, and being presented at Court—all that sort of thing. I think she thought that if I came out here to see you, I'd be getting back into the world she knew when she was young. . . .'

'Poor old dear,' Jane said softly. 'You mean, she was a bit confused.'

'I think she was,' said Jennifer. 'I don't think she could realize that all that sort of thing has gone for ever.'

'I wonder if it has!' said Jane.

Jennifer turned and stared at her. 'People don't live like that out here, do they?'

There was a short silence. 'No . . .' Jane said slowly. 'Only a very, very few—big station owners in the Western District. They have big homes, and play a lot of polo, and they hunt, and give dances, and get presented to the Governor-General. They *do* live rather in the way Aunt Ethel lived when she was young, but there aren't very many of them. Ninety-five per cent of graziers are people like ourselves, people who've always been hard up until the last few years. Since the beginning of the war the price we get for meat and wool has gone up steadily, and now we've got so much money that we don't know what to do with it. So far we've all been paying off our debts and mortgages. What happens next is anybody's guess.'

Jennifer asked, 'But will these high prices go on?'

'I don't know,' said Jane. 'We'd still be well off if they fell to half what they are now.'

'They're bound to fall, aren't they?'

'Wool's bound to fall,' she said. 'Wool will go down when the rearmament stops, but meat has been going up steadily for years. The world seems to want more and more food, and each year more and more gets eaten in Australia as our population rises, and so there's less each year to export. It's the same in the Argentine, and everywhere. That seems to mean higher and higher prices for meat. . . .'

She laid her darning in the basket, and got out her cigarette-case, and gave Jennifer one; they sat smoking in silence for a little. 'I don't know what's going to be the end of it,' she said. 'This property would fetch about ninety thousand at present-day prices, and it's all free of debt. That's heaps to leave the children when we die. We want them to work, not live on money that we leave them. We want to go on working here ourselves; it's what we like doing. And these enormous sums of money keep coming in. I don't know what we'll do with it, I'm sure.'

'Make a trip home,' suggested Jennifer.

'We've thought of that,' said Jane. 'I don't know that I really want to go to England now. I don't think I'd know anybody there at all. Jack sometimes says he'd like to make a trip to Europe and go to Gallipoli, but he doesn't really want to, I don't think.' She sat smoking in silence for a minute. 'If Angie goes next year, we might go home the year after to see her. But that wouldn't take much money, not compared with what we're making. . . .'

Jennifer smiled. 'You'll have to buy another grandfather clock.'

Jane laughed. 'I know it was stupid, Jenny, but I *did* like buying it. Made in Chester in 1806, before this country was even explored. It's a lovely thing to have.' She spoke more seriously. 'No, if things go on like this, some day I'd like to rebuild the homestead.'

'Rebuild this house?'

Jane shook her head. 'I'd like to build another house down by the river, and turn this over to a foreman. I'll show you where I want to have it. A new brick house designed by a good architect, rather like an English house, but single storey; a house with English trees and an English lawn and a garden all round it, like we used to have at home. Leave the stables and the stockyards all up here, and let the men have their meals up here with the foreman's family. I want a gracious sort of house, where Jack and I can slack off as we get older and not have to cook for the men. A house where one can have good furniture, and good pictures, and good china and glass, like we used to have at home when I was a girl.'

'An English country house,' said Jennifer thoughtfully.

'Like that in a way, but adapted to the country and the station.' She paused. 'I believe a good many people'll start doing that, if the money goes on like this.'

'So you'll get a lot of English country houses here?'

'We might,' said Jane. 'After all, the English country houses came when agriculture was doing well, and agriculture's doing well here now. We all came out from England, and we've got the English way of doing things. I don't see why we shouldn't have the same sort of houses—adapted to the times and to the labour shortage.'

'Cut out the butler,' Jennifer suggested.

Jane smiled. 'And the second parlourmaid. It'll be different, of course. More cars and travel, and no servants. But it might be something just as good.'

'You mean, there's something in what Granny was trying to say?'

'There might well be. Old people have a knack of being right, sometimes.'

Jennifer settled down at Leonora very happily. In recent years she had worked in an office, first in Leicester and then in London, and working so she had done little serious cooking or housework. It was no burden to her to take some of the cooking and cleaning off Jane for a few days; she rather enjoyed it, having nothing else to do and as a means of learning new techniques. She went out in the paddocks and the stockyards with Jack Dorman and the men whenever she got asked, and she found the management and care of stock and pastures interesting after her office life. She found a very great deal to occupy her at Leonora.

She would have found it even pleasanter if the weather had been cooler, and she came to realize the value of Jane's insistence that she should avoid the city at the height of the hot weather till she was acclimatized. It was an exceptionally hot January. Each day the sun rose in a cloudless sky at dawn and set in a cloudless sky at dusk; each night Angela and Jennifer lay with few coverings in the somewhat stuffy little bedroom of the homestead, unable to sleep till midnight for the heat. Each day thin wreaths of smoke behind the mountains told of forest fires in the high country to the south of them; each day Jack Dorman listened to the wireless forecasts, worried, for some news of rain.

'Don't like the look of it at all,' he said more than once. 'It's a fair cow.'

He was too worried and preoccupied for Jennifer to bother him with questions, and Angela knew little about the station, and cared less. She asked Tim Archer to tell her what the trouble was, and he said that the boss was worried over the condition of the top paddock, bordering on the forest. The spring up there which usually ran all through the summer had dried up some weeks before and the paddock had got very dry; on account of the lack of water they had moved the stock out. The paddock, in consequence, had been little grazed for some time and the grass was far too long for safety; if a fire should run through the forest to the Leonora boundary it would sweep across that paddock in a flash. The homestead would probably be safe enough, but fences would be destroyed; the dry wood of the posts would burn like tinder.

'The trouble is with these darn fires you don't know where they'll stop,' said Tim. 'You can't do much about it, either.'

It was on one of these cloudless days that Jane went into town with Angela in the Morris; to make a break for her Jennifer had volunteered to get the dinner so that Jane could dine at the hotel with Angela. She served the inevitable hot roast mutton with potatoes and vegetables competently, though she was dripping with sweat; Tim and Mario finished the meal, and helped her with the washing-up. Then they went out to their work, and Jack Dorman stood with her on the veranda looking at the wreaths of smoke rising almost straight up into the sky behind Buller.

He said anxiously, 'I believe that's nearer. Think I'll run up the road a bit in the Ford, 'n see if I can find out where she's burning. Like to come?'

She got into the car with him and they started up the road towards the mountain. They passed the Merrijig hotel and went on towards Lamirra and the timber camps. At Lamirra Jack Dorman stopped the car and went with Jennifer into the store, kept by an English couple who had recently come out from Portsmouth, but they knew little of the local conditions and were ignorant about the fires; they did not think that they were very near.

'Run up the road a bit to where they're cutting,' Jack said when they got outside. 'We'll get a view over the ridge up there, and see for ourselves.'

They drove on up a broad, smooth, well-engineered road winding up the mountain-side; he told her that this was a timber road made for the passage of the timber lorries getting the wood out; it was designed eventually for use as a main highway. They went on winding up the hillside, and it was cool in the forest; the great trees met high over their heads and practically the whole road was in shade. From time to time they passed a trailer truck loaded with tree-trunks coming down, sighing with air brakes; from time to time they passed a track leading off into the forest on one side or the other, and saw groups of men handling the fallen timber, who paused in their work to stare curiously at the new utility.

They stopped to ask the ganger of a group of road-makers what the fire position was. He was reassuring; he said that it had not crossed the King River and he did not think it would; the forest fire patrol were there and they had cleared a fire break three miles long to save the forest timber. Jennifer sat in the car while the men gossiped, understanding only about half of what they said; the names of mountains, rivers, people, and official bodies meant nothing to her and she did not fully understand what it was all about.

It was lovely sitting there in the car. They were at an altitude of about four thousand feet and in the speckled shade of the forest; for the first time that day she was cool and dry from sweat. She stretched luxuriously in her clothes. It was quiet in the forest, or it would have been, but for the distant and rhythmic rumbling of a bulldozer at work.

She sat listening to the bulldozer as the men talked. The noises repeated in a regular cycle; a roaring acceleration of the motor followed by a few seconds of steady running, then a period of idling, and then a few seconds of light running as the thing reversed, another idling period, and the cycle began again. It varied very little; she sat listening to it dreamily, half asleep in the coolness of the forest.

The cycle was disturbed, and woke her from her doze. A rumbling of heavy timber broke in and the roaring of the engine mounted suddenly to a climax, and then stopped dead. There was a noise of tumbling machinery and a continued rumbling of rolling logs; a few men shouted in the distance, their voices puny and lost among the greater noises. Then everything was quiet again.

The men broke off their discussion of the fire and looked in the direction of the row. 'What's going on down there?' asked Jack.

'Bulldozer at work, shifting logs,' the ganger said. 'Sounds like he's got into trouble. Those bloody things are always getting into trouble. We had one bogged up to the seat last winter; took a winch and a day's work to pull him out.'

They went on with their talk; down in the forest everything was quiet. Presently the ganger went on and Jack Dorman let the clutch in and the car moved on up-hill. 'Sounds a bit better,' he said to the girl beside him. 'We'll go up to the top of the road and have a look. He says we can see the fire from there.'

A quarter of a mile further on, a track led down the hill to the right. As they approached they saw a man running up this track towards the road, a man in a lumber jacket and dirty canvas trousers, a rough man, running clumsily up-hill, half foundered. He waved at the car when he saw it; they stopped and waited for him to come up to them.

'Aw, look,' he panted. 'Give us a run down the road to Lamirra. There's been an accident in there, and two blokes got hurt bad. I got to telephone the doctor and the ambulance at Banbury, 'n find a bloke called Splinter.'

6

Jennifer opened the door of the utility and slid across the seat towards Jack Dorman; the man tumbled in beside her and slammed the door. He was panting and streaming sweat. Jack Dorman began to turn the car. 'It's a proper muck-up,' the man said urgently. 'I got to get Splinter quick.'

The car swung round and headed down the road. 'Where d'you want to go?'

'You know the office building, other side of the bridge? They'll telephone the ambulance from there. Maybe they'll know where Splinter's working.'

'Where it says the name of the company, on a big board?'

'That's right. They'll telephone from there, and then I'll have to find Splinter.'

They did not speak again; Jack Dorman devoted his attention to the road as they went flying round the curves down into the valley. Once as they swung violently round a corner with a scream of tyres the man was flung heavily against Jennifer; he wrenched himself off her and said, 'Sorry, lady.'

'That's all right,' she said. 'Who is this man you've got to find?'

'Who? Splinter? He's the doctor here.'

Jack Dorman, eyes glued to the road, said, 'Is that the chap that goes fishing at the week-ends?'

'That's right,' the man said, 'he's just one of these D.P.s, working in the timber with the rest of us. He's a doctor in his own country, like. He's not allowed to be a doctor here.'

They came to the office building at the bottom of the stream, a small weatherboard shack of three rooms; the man flung himself from the car. 'I'll wait here a bit,' Jack Dorman called after him. ''Case you want to go back.'

They sat in the car for a few minutes, waiting. 'Where is the nearest proper doctor?' the girl asked.

'Banbury,' he said. 'There's a hospital there with an ambulance, and there's a doctor–Dr Jennings.'

'How far is that from here?'

'About seventeen miles.'

She was a little shocked; accustomed as she was to city life it was difficult to realize that there could be no doctor close at hand. 'How long will it take him to get here?'

He hesitated. 'That depends. If he's in Banbury and he's free, he might be out here in an hour. But I believe this is his Woods Point day.'

'What's that?'

'He goes to Woods Point once a week,' he said. 'They haven't got a doctor there. I think this is the day he goes there–Tuesday. I'm pretty sure it is.'

'How far is that from Banbury?'

'About forty miles.'

She said, 'You mean, it could be hours before he could get here?'

'Too right.'

'But what happens, in a case like this?'

'Just got to do the best you can,' he said. 'Most doctoring for accidents is common sense.'

They sat together in the car, waiting. Then the man that they had brought down from the woods came to the door of the office with the manager, a man called Forrest. Jack Dorman knew him slightly as an acquaintance in various local bars.

'Eh, Jim,' he said. 'Got a bit of trouble.'

Jim Forrest glanced at him in recognition, and then at the new Custom utility. He crossed the road to Dorman. 'Aw, look, Jack,' he said. 'Are you busy?'

'Not particularly.'

'Joe here, he says there's two men got hurt bad, up where you picked him up upon the road. They'll have to be fetched down and taken into hospital, unless we can get the ambulance to come out for them. Could you stand by a few minutes while we get through to Banbury? If we've got to send them in, they'll travel easier in this utility than in one of my trucks.'

'Do anything I can. I'll run them into Banbury if you want it.'

'Thanks a lot. I've got the call in now. Say, while you're waiting, could you run Joe up to Camp Four, fetch a man called Zlinter?'

'I know him. That's the chap that fishes?'

'That's right. He's a D.P. doctor, been working here for quite a while. I got him on the telephone and he's gone down to his camp by truck, pick up his stuff. I'd appreciate it if you'd slip down there 'n pick him up. Joe can show you. By the time you've got back here I'll have spoken to Banbury.'

The utility went sliding off with Joe in it again; a mile down the road it turned into the camp and ran between the rows of hutments under the gum trees, and stopped outside the fourth on the right. Joe got out and called to a man at the door. 'Hey!' he said. 'Seen Splinter anywhere about?'

The man said, 'He's inside.'

Joe vanished into the hut and Jack Dorman got out of the utility with Jennifer; together they unfastened the black twill cover of the truck-like body. Joe came out carrying in his arms a very large first-aid box. 'Put it in the back,' said Dorman.

A tall, dark man came to the door of the hut and glanced at the utility and then at Dorman; recognition came to him. 'So,' he said, 'we have already met, upon the Howqua. It is your car, this?'

'That's right.'

Carl Zlinter paused in thought. 'I have much to take,' he said. 'It will be all right to drive this car into the woods, up to the accident?'

'I should think so. The ground's pretty hard.'

'I will take everything, then, in the car.'

He went back into the hut, and reappeared with Joe, carrying five cartons roughly packed with packages of cotton-wool, dressings, splints, bandages, bottles of antiseptic; these with a worn leather case completed his equipment. It only took three or four minutes. 'Now we are ready to go,' he said.

Joe got up into the back with the stores, and Zlinter got into the front of the utility with Jennifer and Dorman. 'It is better to bring everything,' he said. 'Much will be not needed, but for the one thing left behind–it is better to take everything.'

Dorman said, 'Go back first to the office?'

'I think so. Perhaps the ambulance and doctor are already on the way. In any case, we must pass by that place.'

They slid off up the road again to the weatherboard office. The manager came out to meet them. 'Can't get through yet,' he said. 'You go on up, and I'll be along soon as the call comes through.'

Jack Dorman said, 'The doctor's day in Woods Point, isn't it?'

'I don't know.'

'Tuesday. I've an idea it is.'

Jim Forrest made a grimace. 'It would be. Will you take Zlinter up there, Jack? I'll be up there myself soon as this call comes through.' He turned to the Czech. 'Do what you can, Carl, till the doctor gets here.'

'Okay, Mr Forrest,' said Carl Zlinter. 'I will do the best that I can.'

The utility moved off and up the hill. Carl Zlinter sat in silence, mentally conning over the stores that he had brought with him, the information of the accident that he had got from Joe. A man called Bertie Hanson with a crushed leg trapped beneath the upturned bulldozer, a man called Harry Peters, the bulldozer driver, unconscious with a head injury. He was not troubled by the injuries; his long experience in the medical service of the German Army had accustomed him to front-line casualties in Russia and in Normandy. It was the lack of stores that worried him most; there was no blood plasma and no equipment for transfusion, and no dressing station. Still, he had worked and saved men's lives with less than he had now. What a clumsy fool that bulldozer driver must have been!

Jennifer sat silent between the men as the utility sped up the hill. She was somewhat at a loss, only half understanding what was going on. The tall, dark foreigner beside her had medical experience though he was not a doctor; apparently he was a lumberman, for he was dressed like one, yet in this emergency Joe, and even the manager, seemed to defer to him. She did not clearly understand what it was that had happened in the forest and nobody had enlightened her; indeed, perhaps Joe was the only one who really understood the accident, and he was inarticulate, unable to communicate exactly what he knew.

They passed the road gang and reached the track that led off the road; Jack Dorman headed the Ford down this timber lane in low gear, and they went lurching and swaying down the hill between the trees. Directed by Joe they turned presently and traversed the hillside to the right and came out into a sloping open space where all the timber had been felled. Down at the bottom of this sloping space, upon the edge of the unfelled forest, there was a bulldozer lying on its side and forepart, lying across a log about two feet in diameter. Two more tree-trunks lay above the bulldozer, one caught upon the spade, the other poised in the air above it, perilously, apparently about to fall. There were men with ropes working carefully around this game of spillikins, attempting to guy back the log poised in mid-air.

'My word,' Jack Dorman breathed. 'You wouldn't think a bulldozer could get like that. . . .' The girl from London sat silent. These things which had happened in the forest were outside all her experience.

Dorman drove the Ford slowly forward till its way was barred by scrub and timber; then he stopped it, and the dark foreigner with them got out and made his way quickly to the accident. He was wearing soiled khaki drill trousers and a grey cotton shirt open at the neck; his arms were bare to the elbow and very tanned, yet he had unmistakably the air of a doctor. Dorman followed after him with Joe, and the girl came along behind them, uncertain what she was going to see.

She saw a man pinned beneath the bulldozer by one leg bent below the knee in an unnatural attitude; he lay upon the ground beneath the log that rested one end on the bulldozer spade, most insecurely. His face was badly lacerated on one side, and there was blood congealed upon the coat that had been thrust as a pillow beneath his head. He was conscious, and the eyes looked up with recognition at Carl Zlinter.

The lips moved. 'Good old Splinter,' he muttered. 'Better than any mucking doctor in the mucking State. Get me out of this.'

The dark man dropped down on his knees beside him. 'Lie very quiet now,' he said. 'I am giving an injection which will make you sleep. Lie very quiet now, and sleep.' He opened his case, fitted up the hypodermic with quick, accurate movements, sterilized it with alcohol, broke the neck of a capsule and filled it, and sterilized the forearm of the man upon the ground, all in about thirty seconds. He drove the needle in and pressed the plunger down. 'Lie very quiet now, and go to sleep,' he said softly. 'Everything now will be all right. When you wake up you will be in hospital, in bed.'

The man's lips moved. 'Mucking German bastard,' he said faintly. 'Good old Splinter. Good old . . . mucking German bastard . . . '

Carl Zlinter got up from beside the man and crossed to the other casualty. Men parted as he came, and Jennifer saw lying on the ground the second man. He lay upon his face, or nearly so, apparently unconscious. He had been bleeding from the ears and the nose and the mouth; he lay still, breathing with a snorting sound, irregularly. Great gaping wounds were on his scalp, the fair hair matted with blood, with white bone splinters showing here and there. Jennifer bit her lip; she must not show fear or horror before these men.

'We didn't like to move him till you came, Splinter,' said somebody. 'The poor mugger's got his skull all cracked. We reckoned it was best to leave him as he was.'

The dark man did not answer, but dropped down on his knees beside the casualty and began preparing his injection. Gently he bared his arm and sterilized it, and thrust the needle in. He withdrew it and sat back on his heels, his fingers on the pulse, studying the patient. He did not touch the head at all.

Presently he got to his feet. 'We will need stretchers,' he said. 'Two bed-frames, each with a mattress. I will not wait for the ambulance. Mr Dorman, please. Will you fetch bed-frames and mattresses for us, in the utility?'

'Sure. One of you chaps come along with me 'n show me where to go.'

The utility went off up the cleared glade, and Jennifer was left with the lumbermen and the casualties. The dark foreigner went back to the first man with the trapped foot and dropped on one knee beside him; gently he lifted one eyelid, and felt the wrist. He bent to an examination of the leg beneath the bulldozer.

'Is it possible to lift this thing?' he asked.

'Aw, look,' said one, 'it's a crook job. We got to take the top stick out back-wards first 'n when we get the weight from off the butt of this one it'll roll off on top of him. We got to shore up this one first, 'n then take the top one off backwards, 'n rig a sheerlegs 'n a tackle, 'n try and get this one off backwards too. After that we might roll the dozer over, or jack it up maybe. But it's a long job, Splinter, 'n the stick'll roll off on him if we don't watch out.'

'How long will it take?'

The man said, 'It'll be dark by eight. If we can get the stuff up here, 'n lamps and that, we might get the dozer shifted about midnight.'

'Can you safely move these sticks, working in the dark, so that there can be no further accident for him?'

The man said uneasily, 'We got to get the poor mugger out of it, Splinter. But it's a crook job, working in the dark. I'd a sight rather do it in the day.'

The dark man stood in silence for a minute. The men stood round him waiting for a lead, and Jennifer could sense the trust they had in him. 'I do not think that we can save the foot, in any case,' he said. 'It is practically severed now. If we should lift the dozer by midnight and get him out of it, the leg must then come off in hospital. I think the risk now is too great to move these sticks, for nothing to be gained, but to risk injuring him more. I think it will be better if I take the leg off now and get him to the hospital. We will wait for a message first, to find out if the doctor comes.'

Somebody said softly, 'Poor old sod.' Another spat, and said, 'I wouldn't guarantee to shift them mucking sticks without one slipping.' There was a long silence after that.

Presently Carl Zlinter crossed to the other man and knelt down by him again, and very gently began to run his fingers over the skull, exploring the unnatural depressions of the scars. He lifted his head after a time, and said, 'Is there water, water in a clean billy? There is an enamel bowl in one of the cartons—use that. And a clean piece of cloth, of lint from the blue square package in the big carton. Somebody with very clean hands open it, and give me a piece of the lint.'

Water was brought in a billy and a man found the package of lint. He glanced at his hands, and then at Jennifer. 'You do it,' he said. 'You got cleaner hands than any of us here.'

She tore open the wrappings and bared the lint. She said to the dark man, 'Do you want disinfectant in the water?'

'Please. The big blue bottle, just a little. About one tablespoonful.' He glanced at her. 'Not that—the other bottle. That is good. Now give it to me here, and a small piece of the lint.'

She took the bowl and the lint to him; he dipped his hands in the solution and wiped them with the lint, and threw the lot away. She got him more lint and disinfectant while the men stood round them in a circle watching, and he began very carefully to wipe the dirt from the wounds on the man's head.

'Scissors,' he said. 'In the leather case, the middle one of the three pairs. And the forceps also. Put them in the water, in the bowl.'

She brought them to him, and stood with the men watching as he worked. The glade was very still; the sun was sinking towards the mountain and it was not now so hot as it had been. The air was fragrant with the odour of the gum trees, and from far away a faint whiff of the forest fire scented the air. In the distance a white cockatoo was screeching in some tree.

The dark foreigner worked on upon his knees, oblivious of the audience. Jennifer stood with the lumbermen looking down upon him as he worked. It was impossible for her not to share their confidence; with every movement the man showed that he knew exactly what he was doing, what the result of every tiny movement of his hand upon the scalp would be. She could feel the confidence that the men standing with her had in Splinter, and watching him at work she shared their trust. This man was good.

Presently there was a faint noise on the road above them. A man by Jennifer raised his head. 'Truck coming down,' he said. 'That'll be Mr Forrest, come to say about the ambulance.'

They listened to the approaching truck till it emerged into the glade and stopped near the wrecked bulldozer. The manager got out and came to them, and Zlinter got to his feet and went to meet him. The men crowded round, Jennifer with them.

'There's no ambulance, Zlinter,' he said. 'It's gone to Woods Point with the doctor for an appendicitis case. They don't know if it's coming back tonight or not.'

One of the men said disgustedly, 'No mucking doctor, either?' One of his mates nudged him, indicating Jennifer.

'No doctor,' said Jim Forrest. 'I'm sorry, cobber, but that's the way it is.'

'Aw, look,' said one, 'we've *got* a doctor. Old Splinter, he's a doctor, isn't he?'

'What about it, Zlinter?' asked the manager. 'What's the damage?'

'It is not good,' the dark man said. 'This man, I think we should take off the foot and take him into hospital, not to leave him here for hours while we lift the dozer.' The manager pulled him to one side. 'It is all right, he cannot hear. He is now well doped. We cannot save the foot in any case, and we must try now to control the shock, or he will die. If he is left here for many hours, I think he will die.'

'Take the foot off now, and get him out of it?'

'That is the right thing to do. He must be in a warm bed, soon, with many blankets and hot bottles; he is already very cold. I think that he is very bad, that one. I do not think that he has been a healthy man; perhaps he drinks too much.'

'What about the other one?'

They crossed to the man with the fractured skull. 'This one,' the dark man said, 'he seems more badly, but I do not think so. His skull is broken in three places, but he is a healthy man and there is yet no damage that is not repairable. I have seen men as bad as this recover, and be very good—quite well men. With him, it will be necessary to move him very carefully to where he can be operated on, to lift the pressure of the bones upon the brain. If we can so arrange that he is dealt with quickly, then I think he will have a good chance to recover and be well.'

Jim Forrest bit his lip. 'Have you done operations of that sort, Zlinter?'

'I have done such operations many times,' the man said. 'But not since the war ended.'

'Where did you do them?'

'In the war with Russia,' the man said. 'I was surgeon in the army. In France also, at the battle of Falaise. Many times I have done emergency trephine. It is not difficult, if you are very careful and very, very clean. The danger will lie in moving him to where an operation can be done. I could not do that here.'

The manager stood in silence for a minute. 'Jack Dorman will be back in a few minutes,' he said at last. 'He's bringing bed-frames and mattresses. They'll ride softer in that utility than in the truck.'

He walked a little way away from the men, deep in thought. He knew that he was in a delicate position here, and he wanted a few moments to think it over. Zlinter had no qualifications as a doctor in the State of Victoria, but he was probably competent to do a trephine operation and it seemed logical that he should be allowed to do it. Indeed, he was the only man within reach who could attempt it; without his ministrations the man might well die. The obvious place to do the operation was in Banbury hospital, but would the matron there agree to a lumberman who claimed to be an unregistered practitioner doing such an operation in her hospital? Almost certainly she would not. It might well be that while everyone was arguing the man would die. He might die anyway, upon the road to Banbury.

He went back to Carl Zlinter. 'What will you do, Zlinter?' he asked. 'Will you take them into Banbury? What's the best thing to do?'

'Will the doctor come to Banbury tonight?'

'He's operating at Woods Point on the appendicitis case this evening. If he comes back, it will be very late. We can get him on the telephone at the hotel at about six o'clock.'

'He will not be back at Banbury before ten or eleven?'

'I don't think so.'

Carl Zlinter stood in silence for a minute. He was very well aware of his position; if he operated on this fractured skull and the man died there would be trouble and he might end up in prison, a bad start to his new life in Australia. He said at last, 'I will take off the foot of the man at the dozer now—we cannot save that foot. For the other one, we must take him very carefully down to Lamirra as he is, and you must telephone again from there. I will decide then what is best to do.'

'Okay, Zlinter. What help do you want?'

'Somebody who knows, to hand me things from the case, and to keep clean and sterile as possible. The young lady was good just now.' He looked round, and saw Jennifer standing a little aside. 'Please,' he said. 'Come here.' She came towards him. 'I am going to take off that man's foot,' he said. 'Have you ever seen an operation?'

She shook her head. 'Never.'

He looked her in the eyes. 'Would you be afraid to help me? If you cannot do it, you must say so now. Can you help this man, and not faint or do anything foolish?'

'I shouldn't faint,' she replied. 'I might do something stupid, because I've never done anything like this before. But I'll do my best.'

He smiled at her, and she was suddenly confident. 'It will be nothing difficult,' he said. 'Just to keep giving me the things I shall want. I will show you the things before we begin. Just to do what I shall tell you quietly, and to keep a calm head.'

He took her to the utility, and began rummaging through his cartons for the dishes and appliances that he would need. He picked up a white rubber sheet and carried it over to the bulldozer, and laid it on the ground beside the trapped man, immediately beneath the menace of the hanging log. She helped him to arrange it neatly on the fragrant, leaf-covered ground beside the man. 'Now, come with me,' he said.

She became oblivious of the men who stood around and watched them. Her whole attention became concentrated on the job she had to do, and on this foreigner in dirty clothes who wielded so much power. He made her swab her hands and arms in disinfectant at the tailboard of the utility, and then she helped him put the instruments into the bowl and to arrange the ligatures, the dressings and the bandages neatly on the white rubber sheet. Then she went with him and knelt down beside the man, and for a time she listened while he instructed her, naming each article after him. Both became utterly immersed in the work that lay ahead.

The professional detachment of the doctor communicated itself to her, as he intended that it should, and robbed the business of all horror. She saw no sympathy and no emotion in his work upon the injured man, only a great technical care and skill, that noted impersonally every sign of feeling, every change in respiration and pulse as the work went on, and made adjustment for it. He took the leg off about eight inches below the knee with a local anæsthetic injected in several places around the leg, waited ten minutes for this to take effect, and then did the job. From the time they knelt down together by the rubber blanket till the bandaging was complete, about twenty-five minutes elapsed, and in that time Jennifer was completely oblivious of what was going on around her, concentrated only on the work in hand.

Carl Zlinter sat back on his heels. 'So,' he said. 'Now we must get him to the utility.' He raised his head. 'The mattress, please. Bring it and lay it down here.'

He got to his feet and Jennifer got up stiffly with him from her knees; she felt exhausted, drained of all energy. She was surprised to see Jack Dorman there among the men, and to see the utility parked immediately behind the bulldozer; she had not seen or heard it arrive. Carl Zlinter spoke to her. 'It was very well done, the help that you gave me,' he said. 'You have been a nurse at some time?'

She shook her head. 'No,' she said. 'I've never done anything like that before.'

He raised his eyebrows. 'So?' he exclaimed softly. 'It was well done, very well. You have a gift for this.' He glanced at her kindly. 'And now you are very tired.'

She forced a smile. 'I don't know why one should be.'

'It is the close attending,' he said. 'I also, I get tired, every time. It would be wrong if one did not grow tired, I think, for that would mean I had not done the best I could.'

She smiled at him. 'I suppose that's right. I suppose that's what it is.' And then somebody said, 'Where will they put the mattress, Splinter?'

He moved aside. 'Here. Lay it down here, like this.' She turned towards the utility, and Jack Dorman was there. 'Good show, Jenny,' he said with genuine respect. 'How're you feeling? Get into the car and sit a bit.'

'I'm all right,' she said. 'It takes it out of you, though.' She got into the car and sat with the door open, talking to him.

'I brought up a bottle of whisky from the store, 'case it was needed,' he said. He produced it. 'Let me pour you out a nip.'

'I don't want that,' she said. 'I'm all right.'

'Sure?'

'Honestly.' He slipped the bottle back into the door pocket of the car. 'I couldn't have done what you did,' he said. 'I'd have turned sick.' That wasn't true, because when it comes to the point men and women are far stronger than they think, but he thought it was true. He had seen death and wounds in plenty thirty years before, but time had wiped the details from his mind, and this had come as a fresh shock to him. He was genuinely surprised at the strength of this girl from London.

Under the direction of the Czech the men lifted the unconscious man carefully on to the mattress and carried it to the utility, and laid it in the back, assisted by Jack Dorman and the manager. Jennifer got out while this was going on and stood and watched, but there was nothing she could do to help. The evening sun was now sinking to the tops of the gum trees, flooding the glade with golden light; in the midst of her fatigue and these strange happenings she could wonder at the beauty and fragrance of the place.

Carl Zlinter came to her by the car, 'We have now to put the other man on the mattress,' he said. 'Do you feel able to help me? It is more delicate, because of the head injuries.'

'Of course,' she said. 'What do you want me to do?'

She crossed with him to the other man while the mattress was brought and laid adjacent to him. They knelt down while Zlinter carefully examined the head again, and felt the pulse, and tested the degree of unconsciousness. He made her fetch a triangular bandage and he raised the injured head while she slipped the bandage beneath it. Then very carefully they manœuvred the rubber sheet beneath the body and head, Zlinter and Forrest lifting each part an inch or so from the ground while the girl slipped the sheet under, straightening the folds as she progressed; in ten minutes the man was lying on the sheet. With three men lifting the sheet on each side of the body and Zlinter tending the head at the same time, they slipped the mattress under and carried it to the utility, and laid it in the back beside the other. Then they were ready to go.

Jack Dorman got into the utility with Zlinter and Jennifer; Forrest followed on behind them with the truck full of men, leaving the bulldozer to be sorted out and put upon its feet in the morning. Dorman drove the utility over the rough ground of the glade at no more than a walking pace, with Zlinter continually observing the effect of the motion on the wounded men through the back window; once or twice he stopped the car and got out to examine them more closely. Presently the truck drew up beside them, and it was arranged that Forrest should go on ahead and telephone the doctor at Woods Point.

The utility moved very slowly up the track towards the road. Jennifer sat silent between the men, Dorman giving the whole of his attention to getting the car over the rough road with as little motion as possible, Zlinter silent and preoccupied with the condition of the head injury. But presently he roused himself, and said, 'Please, Mr Dorman. This young lady that has been of so great help–I do not know her name. Will you make an introduction please?'

The Australian said, 'Why–sure. Jennifer Morton, my wife's niece or something.'

The girl laughed. 'Jennifer's the name,' she said. 'Jenny, if you like.' She hesitated. 'You might as well complete it,' she observed. 'Your name isn't really Splinter, is it?'

'Zlinter,' he said. 'Carl Zlinter, Miss Jennifer.' He achieved as near to a bow as he could manage in the cab of the utility, pressed up against the girl. 'They call me Splinter when it is not something ruder. I am from Czechoslovakia. You are Australian, of course?'

'I'm nothing of the sort,' the girl said. 'I'm a Pommie, from London. I've only been in the country a few days.'

'So? A few days only? I have been here for fifteen months.'

'Do you like it?'

He nodded. 'It is ver' beautiful, almost like my own country, in Bohemia, in the mountains. I would rather live there, in my own country, but I do not like Communists. If I may not live there, then I would rather live here, I think, than any other place in the world.'

'You like it as much as that?'

He smiled. 'I have been happy since coming here from Germany. I like the country, and the working in the trees.'

The utility emerged on to the made road with a lurch. Zlinter made Jack Dorman stop the car and got out to inspect his patients; what he saw was evidently not very satisfactory, because he got up on to the mattresses and crouched over the man with the fractured skull. He got down presently on to the road, and came to the window at the driver's side.

'I will ride in the back,' he said. 'The motion is not good, but if I kneel down there I can keep the head still, I think. Go very, very carefully. Very slow.'

Jennifer said, 'Can I help if I get in behind, Doctor?'

'You must not call me "Doctor",' he said. 'Not in Australia.' She did not understand that. 'There is not room for more than one person,' he said. 'I can manage alone, but please, go very, very slowly. I am afraid for splinters of the bone.'

He got back into the rear portion and knelt down between his patients; Jack Dorman let the clutch in and the car moved off at walking pace. It took them half an hour to cover the three miles down to the lumber camp in the valley; they stopped twice upon the way for Zlinter to adjust the folded blanket that served as a pillow. It was sunset when the utility crept up to the office building.

Jim Forrest came out into the road to meet them. 'The doctor's still at Woods Point,' he said. 'I got through to the hotel but he's not there; the place he's operating in isn't on the telephone. I left a message asking him to ring us here, soon as he could. I rang the hospital and asked if they could send a nurse out here. They can't do that; they've got one nurse sick and another off on holiday. As far as I can make out they've only got the sister and a couple of Ukrainian ward-maids there. The sister said we'd have to bring them into Banbury.'

There was a silence. Everybody seemed to be expecting Zlinter to say something, and Carl Zlinter apparently had nothing to say. At last he got down from the back of the utility. 'Please,' he said, 'may I come into your office, Mr Forrest?'

'Sure.' The manager led the way inside.

In the bare, rather squalid room that was the office of the lumber camp the Czech turned and faced the manager. 'This man is now very bad,' he said quietly. 'This man with the fractured skull. Mr Dorman, he drives very carefully and very slow, but I have not been able to prevent the head from moving. There are broken bones, you understand, pieces of the skull that are broken, like the shell of an egg. With every movement of the car there is a–a movement of these pieces of the skull against each other, and a rubbing on the matter of the brain.'

Jim Forrest made a grimace.

'The pulse is now worse,' Zlinter said dispassionately, 'and the colour of the face is worse also. The total condition is now seriously worse than when you saw him in the woods, by the accident. I do not think it is wise to take him into Banbury, another twelve miles, till he has had some attention.'

'You'll think he'll die upon the way?'

Zlinter shrugged his shoulders. 'I do not know. It is seventeen miles and the road is not good until the last part, so we must go very slow. It will take two hours; if we go faster there may be much damage to the brain. I cannot say if he will die or not if he is treated so. I can tell you only that I would not advise for him to go further than here till he has had attention.'

'What sort of attention, Zlinter?'

'I think the head should be examined carefully, in clean and antiseptic surroundings, with good light. I think that we shall find a portion of the bone is pressing on the brain. If that is so, that portion must be lifted or removed entirely to relieve the pressure–the operation that we call trephine. When that is done, if it needs to be done, the matter is less urgent; he must then be put into some cast or splint for the movement of the head, and taken to a hospital.'

'Could you do that–lift that bit of bone you think wants lifting?'

'I have done that operation many times. In this country, I am not allowed to practise because I am not qualified. If the man should die in the end, there would be trouble, perhaps. I think it is for you to say what is to be done.'

'If I said, "Have a go at it", would you be willing?'

'I would be willing to do what I can for him,' the Czech said.

'Even though it might mean trouble if the thing goes wrong?'

Zlinter smiled. 'I have crossed that river already,' he said. 'I am in trouble now with the other man if things go wrong, for I have taken off his leg, and that I am not allowed to do, I think. I am in one trouble now already, and another of the same kind will not matter much.'

Jim Forrest nodded. 'May as well be hung for a sheep as a lamb.' He stood in silence for a minute, looking out of the dirty window at the golden lights outside as the sun went down. It would be dark before they could get this man to Banbury, which would not make the journey any easier for him. There was no guarantee that when they got him there he would receive attention before morning; the matron certainly would not undertake an operation for trephine herself, and she would almost certainly prevent Carl Zlinter from doing anything of the sort in her hospital, even though the patient were in a dying state. Until he could get some news of when the doctor was expected back at Banbury, it might be adverse to this man in every way to take him there.

Too few doctors in the bloody country, he thought, and they tried to stop you using the ones you'd got. He was Australian to the core, bred in the country with only a few years of school in town, an individualist to the bone, a foe of all regimentation and control. He turned suddenly from the window. 'My bloody oath,' he said. 'We've got to do something, and it's no good taking him to Banbury unless the bloody doctor's going to be there. You tell me what's the best to do, Splinter, and I'll tell you to do it.'

The dark foreigner laughed. 'I think we take them to Hut Five,' he said; that was a new hut, recently constructed and so reasonably clean, and there were empty rooms. 'Two rooms we shall want, one for the amputation to lie in bed. The other with a bed and a long table from the mess-room, very clean, on which I can lay this man with the injured head while I examine him. When I have done that, I will tell you if I should go further with trephine, or if we can wait till the doctor comes. In that room I shall need a very bright light, with a long cord of flex from the lamp fitting.' The camp was lit by electricity from a Diesel generator.

'Right,' said Forrest. 'We'll get on with that, and give the bloody hospital away.' He stepped briskly out of the office to the utility and started giving orders to the men. Carl Zlinter went to the door of the utility and spoke to Jennifer.

'Mr Forrest has decided to make here a little hospital for the night,' he said. 'We shall clear two rooms, and make all as sterile as we can. I am to make an examination of the man with the broken head, and then we will decide what is the best thing to be done.' He hesitated. 'Will you be able to stay and help me?'

She said, 'Of course I'll stay if I can help at all.' She turned to Jack Dorman. 'That's all right, isn't it?'

'Sure,' he said. 'Stay as long as you like. I'll probably go back and tell Jane, and then come back here. If you're going to work long you'd better have some tea.'

Zlinter said, 'It will be a help if Miss Jennifer can stay while I examine the head. She understands more quickly than the men, the things I want. I will see she gets a meal if it is necessary to work long.'

Jennifer got out of the car. 'What have we got to do?'

Two hours later, in a little hot room that was roughly hung with sheets and that stank of carbolic, Zlinter straightened up above the patient on the table. It had taken them most of that time to rig up their little hospital and make the surroundings roughly sterile. For the last half-hour Jennifer had held the electric light bulb in the positions that he told her, and had handed him the swabs and bowls and scissors that he needed from the office table behind her. It was airless and stuffy in the little room, for they had closed the window to keep out the dust and the bugs that flew in the Australian night. The girl from London was sweating freely and her clothes were clinging to her body; she was growing very tired.

'It is not good,' said Zlinter. 'No, it is not good at all.' She could see that much, even with the untrained eye; now that the hair was cut away the huge, unnatural depression in the skull was an appalling sight.

'It is ver' hot,' the man said. 'Hang the lamp upon that nail, and we will go outside where it is cool. Perhaps there is now some news of the doctor.'

It was fresh outside the hut, and she felt better in the velvety black night. Zlinter asked the darkness if Jim Forrest was there, and from the darkness somebody said that he would go and get him. Another voice asked, 'How's he going on, Miss?'

She strained her eyes, but they were still dazzled by the light she had been holding and she could only see a dark blur of a figure. She could not give a reassuring report; she temporized, and asked, 'Which one?'

'Harry Peters,' the voice said. 'The one what got his head cracked.'

'He's going on all right,' she said. It was all that she could say.

'Bert Hanson, he's awake,' another voice said. 'I just been talking to him.'

In their preoccupation with the head injury they had rather forgotten the amputation lying in the next room where they had laid him in bed with blankets and hot bottles an hour before. Jennifer plucked Zlinter by the arm. 'Did you hear that, Mr Zlinter? They say the other man's awake!'

'Awake?' He turned back to the hut, and she followed him in. In the little room next to the head case the light was shaded with a towel roughly draped across the fixture. In the half light the man lay on his back as they had left him, but the eyes were open now, and looked at them with recognition.

'So,' said Zlinter, 'how are we now?' He took the hand and laid his finger on the pulse, and stood counting, looking at his wrist-watch.

The man's lips moved, and he said feebly, 'Good old Splinter. Mucking German bastard.'

The Czech stood silent, smiling a little as he watched the second hand move round. Then he laid the hand down. 'Do you feel any pain?' he asked.

'Kind of numb all up my leg,' the man muttered.

'No sharp pain anywhere?'

The man said something that they could not hear; Zlinter bent to him and made him repeat it. Then he straightened up. 'He's thirsty,' he said to Jennifer. 'Fetch a glass of water. There is a glass in the wash-room.' From the darkness outside a voice said audibly, 'That'll be the first time Bert's tasted bloody water in ten years.'

'Tomorrow,' Zlinter said, 'the ambulance will come to take you to hospital at Banbury, but for tonight you will stay here. Lie very quiet now, and sleep again. If there is pain, call out; I shall be in the next room and I will come at once and give you something that will stop the pain, but I do not think you will have pain again tonight.' Behind him Jennifer came with the water; he knelt and raised the head and gave the man a drink, but he took only a few sips. 'Now rest, and go to sleep again,' he said. 'It is all right now.'

There was a knock at the door, and Zlinter went out into the corridor with Jennifer; Jim Forrest was there. 'This one is doing well,' he said softly, '–the amputation. He is now conscious and resting. The other one, the head case, is not good. Will the doctor come tonight?'

The manager said, 'His appendicitis case has turned out bad, Zlinter. Peritonitis, or something. I told him what you said about not taking the head case any further before examining him, and he said to do the best you can. I asked if I should get you to ring him, but he's going back to his appendicitis. He'll be back at the hotel about ten or eleven. He said to do the best you can, and he'll be out here in the morning.'

'Did you tell him I may have to lift the bone to ease the pressure on the brain?'

'I told him that you thought an operation might be necessary tonight.'

'What did he answer, when you told him that?'

'He said, he couldn't be in two places at once, and you'd have to do the best you could. It was a crook line, and I had to make him repeat a good many times, but that's what it amounted to.'

The Czech stood silent for a minute. Then he said, 'I would like you to come in and look at him, with me. You do not mind the sight of a bad wound?'

'That'll be right.' They went into the room, and Jennifer followed. The manager, in spite of his assurance, drew his breath in sharply when he saw the extent of the injury. Zlinter moved his hand above the great depression. 'The bone here is much depressed, as you will see,' he said. 'There is hæmorrhage in the brain cavity, also.' He motioned to Jennifer to move the light; she held it above the face, putty-coloured and with a bluish tinge. 'He is a bad colour,' said Zlinter softly, 'and the breathing is bad also, and the pulse is weak. I do not think this man will live until the morning in his present state. What do you think, Mr Forrest?'

The manager said, 'I don't know. I've never seen a thing like this before, Splinter. I should think you're right. He's dying now, isn't he?'

The Czech said, 'I think he will be much improved if we can lift the bone and ease the pressure on the brain.' He motioned to Jennifer to put the light back on the nail, and took them out into the corridor. When the door was shut, he said, 'I have wanted you to see him now, Mr Forrest, so that if he should not recover from the operation you can say how he was.'

'You're going to operate, Splinter?'

The Czech nodded. 'I am going to lift the bone, and perhaps take some of it away completely.'

'Right. What do you want?'

Carl Zlinter turned to Jennifer. 'Are you too tired to go on again?'

She said, 'I'm all right.'

'It will be long, perhaps two hours.'

'I'll be all right,' she said again.

He smiled at her. 'That is good.' He turned to the manager. 'We must eat before we start again,' he said, 'especially this lady. We shall need a small meal, very quickly now, because we must not wait. Some tea, and boiled eggs, perhaps–something that will be ready soon, in a few minutes. After that we will begin the work. We shall need much boiling water.'

They went into the little room again at about a quarter to nine, freshened by a meal in the canteen and a cigarette. Heat, and not horror, was the enemy that Jennifer had to battle against in the next two hours. There was no fly-screen on the window and it was impossible to open it because of the moths and the flying beetles that crashed against the pane, attracted by the light. It was impossible to have the door open without sacrificing sterility. Both worked in a steady drip of sweat, made more intense by the heat from the high-power lamp that Jennifer held most of the time in the positions that the surgeon told her. From time to time they rested and drank lukewarm water from a pitcher before going on.

Thinking it over afterwards, Jennifer came to the conclusion that the heat made the experience easy for her. She was so miserably hot and uncomfortable that it was all that she could do to keep her wits about her, to keep on handing him the things he wanted at the time he wanted them; she had no nervous energy left with which to be upset at what she saw. She needed all her energy for what she had to do.

It was a quarter past eleven by the time the head was finally bandaged. Zlinter went out into the corridor to get some help and with Forrest and Dorman and two other men they lifted the patient in a sheet from the operating table to the bed, and laid him there. The men stood looking on while Zlinter felt the pulse.

Forrest said, 'Looking better, isn't he, Splinter?'

The Czech said, 'I think so, too. It is now a question of the operation shock. If he can live through that, I think he will recover and be a well man.'

He turned to the door. 'We will leave him for a little now. I shall come back later.' He moved them out of the room and shut the door carefully behind them, and leaned for a moment limply against the wall. He said to Jennifer, 'You must be very tired.'

She was drenched with sweat, her clothes sticking to her body at every movement. 'It was so hot in there,' she said. She felt now as though she might be going to faint. 'Let's get out into the air.'

Jack Dorman took her arm; and they moved towards the door of the hut. Zlinter stopped at the room of the other man, and went in softly to look at his amputation case. The man was lying on his back and breathing deeply, sound asleep; he did not seem to have moved since Zlinter had seen him last. He lifted the sheet and glanced at the bandaged leg, and lowered the sheet again. 'Good,' he said softly to Forrest. 'This one is all right.' He moved to the door, and then stopped for a moment. 'Do you smell anything?'

'Carbolic,' said the manager.

'I thought I could smell whisky.'

Jim Forrest laughed. 'Too right, Splinter. Jack Dorman's got a bottle in his car—it's me you're smelling. Come on and have one.'

It was cool and fresh out in the forest night after the close stuffiness of the small room, and the air smelt wonderful after the stenches of the operating table. Jennifer felt better when they got outside; Jim Forrest fetched glasses from the canteen and she drank a small, weak whisky and water with the men, and felt better still. They stood smoking together and relaxing in the cool night air, letting the freshness cool and dry their bodies and their clothes, talking in short, desultory sentences about the operation.

Once Jennifer asked, 'Will he really recover, like an ordinary man?'

The Czech said, 'He may. Not to do bulldozing again, perhaps, but for light work he may recover very well. There will be danger of paralysis, on the right side. We will see.' He turned to the manager. 'It is this man who is the student, is he not?'

'That's right,' said Jim Forrest. 'He's trying to save up to do a university course.' He paused. 'Should be able to, the money that one has to pay a bulldozer driver.'

Jennifer asked, 'What's he going to do at the university?'

'Metallurgy, I think.' He turned to the Czech. 'What about tonight, Splinter? Will he wake up?'

'I think he may, in two or three hours' time. I shall stay with him all night, myself.'

Jennifer asked, 'Will you want me again?'

He looked down at her. 'Not again tonight,' he said. 'I could not have done very much for these men without your help. I find it wonderful that you have never been a nurse.'

She smiled. 'My father's a doctor,' she said. 'Perhaps that makes a difference.'

'So?' he said. 'A doctor in England?'

'That's right,' she replied. 'He practises in Leicester.'

'And you have helped him in his practice?'

She shook her head. 'I know a little bit from living in the house, of course. One can't help learning little bits of things.'

'You have learned more than little bits of things,' he said. 'Now you must be very tired. You should go home and get some sleep.'

'You're sure you won't want me any more?'

'No,' he said. 'Nothing will happen now that will be urgent, till the doctor comes in the morning.'

She said, 'I'd like to know what happens to them.'

'Sure,' he said. 'Perhaps I may come in and tell you, at the homestead.'

Jack Dorman said, 'That's right. Come in for tea tomorrow or the next day.'

'If I can, I will do that,' he said. 'When the doctor comes, he may wish that I go to Banbury with him, to the hospital, to show what I have done and to hand over the cases in the proper way. I do not know. I will come and tell you tomorrow or the day after.'

She said simply, 'I'll look forward to you coming.'

She got into the utility, and Jack Dorman drove her home. Jane and Angela were waiting up for her with a small meal of cold meat and salad and cheese; she was hungry, but before she ate she had to rid herself of her clothes, that stank of sweat and chemicals. She went and stood under the shower, and put on clean pyjamas and a house-coat, and came back to the kitchen and ate a little cold mutton and drank a cup of tea while telling them about it.

Jack Dorman told Jane, 'It was that fellow Zlinter that Ann Pearson told us about, when Peter Loring got his mastoid. He's quite a surgeon, so it seems.'

She said, 'The one that you met over on the Howqua, who found his own grave?'

'That's right. They call him Splinter up at the camp.'

Jennifer said sleepily, 'Found his own grave?'

'That's right,' said Dorman. 'Get him to tell you about it. It's quite a story.'

She was too tired to go into that at the moment. 'He's very sure of himself,' she said reflectively. 'He knew exactly what he wanted to do, right from first to last.'

Angela asked, 'Is he good-looking?'

'Rather like Boris Karloff,' Jennifer told her. 'But he's got a nice smile.' She paused. 'I should think he's a very good doctor.'

'He wouldn't be as good as an English doctor, though, would he?' asked Angela.

Jennifer smiled at the rose-coloured dream of England. 'I don't know,' she said. 'All English doctors aren't supermen.'

'I thought the English medical schools were the best in the world,' said Angela. 'Every Aussie doctor who wants to do post-graduate work goes to England.'

'Maybe that's because they can't get dollars to go to America,' Jane said dryly.

Jennifer got up from the table. 'I think I'll go to bed,' she said. 'I should think we'd all better go to bed. I'm sorry you've had to stay up like this for me.'

'Makes a bit of a change, a thing like this. We've not had so much excitement since the cow calved,' Jane remarked. 'Don't get up tomorrow, Jenny. Sleep in late.'

'That's a damn good idea,' said Angela.

'I didn't mean you,' said her mother.

At the lumber camp after the utility had gone, Carl Zlinter sat on the steps of the hut in the cool, velvety night talking to the manager. Jack Dorman had left the remains of his bottle of whisky with them to finish off; the Czech had a second but refused a third. 'I should sleep if I drink more,' he told Jim Forrest, 'and I must stay awake tonight. Presently this man, he will wake up and I must be with him then.'

'Look,' said the manager, 'is there anything I can do? I'll stay up with you, if you like.'

'It is not necessary. There are men sleeping in the hut. If it should be needed, I will send for you. But I think it will not be needed. Everything I think will now be all right.'

Presently Jim Forrest went back to his house to bed; Carl Zlinter finished his cigarette and went back to the hut. He looked in on his amputation case; the man was still in the same position, apparently asleep; from the door Zlinter could hear the even, regular breathing. He did not go in or make any close examination; better to let him sleep. He went into his trephine case and began cleaning and tidying the room, clearing away the debris of the operation and cleaning and drying his instruments.

An hour later, at about one in the morning, the man began to come to. He became conscious; once or twice the eyes opened and closed. The colour and the breathing were now much better. Presently the lips moved; the man was trying to say something.

Carl Zlinter bent beside him. 'Don't talk, Harry,' he said. 'Don't move about. You got a blow upon your head, but you're right now. Don't try and talk or move about. Just lie quietly as you are, and rest. You're right now.'

He could not make out if the man had understood or not; the lips moved again and he bent to try and hear what he was saying. But now there was a humming in the air, unmelodious but recognizable as a tune. In one of the cubicles of the hut somebody was humming, or chanting to himself in a low tone, 'God Save the King'.

It was impossible for the Czech to hear if his patient was speaking, or if the lips were merely moving by some reflex originating from the damaged brain. He got to his feet in annoyance; the men in the hut were all good types and they knew very well that there were critically ill men in the hut with them. They should know better than to make a row like that in the middle of the night. He went out into the corridor to find out where the noise was coming from and stop it.

It was coming from the next-door cubicle, that housed his amputation case. He opened the door. In the dim, shaded light Bert Hanson was lying on his back awake, maundering through 'God Save the King' in low, alcoholic tones, and beating time with one hand. The air was heavy with the aroma of whisky. He took no notice of the doctor, but continued beating time and singing, his eyes half closed, the voice getting stronger and the tune louder with every minute.

> Thy choicess gifs insore
> On him beplea stupore . . .

Zlinter went into the room and plucked the towel from the lamp; the room was flooded with light. He saw a lump under the bedclothes, turned them back, and there was the bottle, uncorked and practically empty. He dropped it on the floor with tightened lips, wondering if his patient had drunk the whole of it. From the look of him, he probably had.

The man said genially in a strong voice, 'Good old Splinter. Good old mucking bastard!' He burst into laughter in an access of *bonhomie*. 'Come on, le's sing "God Save the King" together, and muck the mucking Germans!'

A man appeared in the corridor dressed in pyjama trousers and no top. 'Want any help, Splinter?'

'This verdamt stupid bloody fool,' said the Czech angrily, 'somebody has given him a bottle of whisky. We must try and keep him quiet, for his own sake and for the man next door.'

The next two hours were a nightmare. At an early stage Zlinter sent a man to fetch Forrest from his house; by the time he came running the pandemonium was terrific, with three men fighting to keep Bert Hanson in his bed, with Zlinter himself attempting to keep his trephine case quiet and tranquil in the next room behind a beaverboard wall. The man was frantically, fighting drunk; at one stage he got hold of the bottle and used it as a club till it broke, mercifully upon the wall beside him. It was with the greatest difficulty that they got the jagged, broken neck out of his hand.

Jim Forrest said to Zlinter at the height of it, 'You'll have to give him something. Morphia.'

The Czech said, 'I do not think that will be good. When this is over, there will be reaction, and he will be very weak. I do not think that any drug will work while there is so much alcohol, unless to give it in a great dose as would kill him later.'

'What the hell are we going to do with him?'

'Hold him, until the thing passes. If these men grow tired, get other men.'

'How's Harry going on?'

'He is going on ver' well. It would be better for him if there was less noise.'

'I'll do the best I can. But if he can't have any dope, he'll have to work it out, and he's got some way to go.'

At about three o'clock, and almost suddenly, the man stopped struggling and shouting, and entered on a stage of collapse. Carl Zlinter left his trephine case and gave his whole attention to his amputation drunk. The heart was now very weak. The man lay in a stupor of weakness, gradually sinking. At about four o'clock Zlinter gave an injection of strychnine, which only had a very temporary, slight effect.

At about half-past five, in the first light of dawn, Bert Hanson died.

7

It is the duty of the police to take note of all serious accidents occurring in their district, and Sister Fellowes at the hospital in Banbury had rung up Sergeant Russell the previous evening to tell him there had been an accident at Lamirra, and that the doctor was away at Woods Point on an operation case. The police got to the lumber camp at about half-past seven in the morning, inspired more by a genuine desire to assist than with any thought of invoking the processes of law. It was unfortunate, however, that they got there before Dr Jennings, who would probably have extended Bert Hanson's life a little upon paper and signed a death certificate which the police sergeant would have honoured; in a country chronically short of doctors it was no business of the police to go round making trouble.

As it was, they came upon the scene before the stage was set for them. They found a Czech lumberman utterly exhausted, who had conducted two major operations without any valid medical qualifications whatsoever, and they found one of the patients dead and in a shocking state of death, for there had been little time or energy to clean the body up. The other patient, on whom a major head operation had been performed, was clearly very ill and, in the view of the police sergeant, probably dying too. The whole thing was irregular and possibly criminal. In any case the coroner would have to be informed, and there must be an inquest.

Dr Jennings arrived direct from Woods Point half an hour after the police. He found them taking statements from Jim Forrest and Carl Zlinter in the canteen hut, Zlinter having refused point-blank to go to the office of the lumber company, half a mile from his patient. When the doctor came in he got up from the table. 'This can wait,' he said to the police sergeant, with small courtesy, for he was very tired. 'There are now more important things that must be done.'

He walked out of the canteen, and took the doctor over to the trephine case at once. Jim Forrest turned to the sergeant. 'He's right, Sarge. He's got to hand over his case to the doctor. Maybe I can go on telling you what happened.'

The sergeant thumbed his note-book. 'How long have you employed this man?'

'Aw, look—I couldn't say for certain. September or October, a year back, I think. Fifteen or sixteen months, maybe.'

'Has he acted as a doctor before?'

'Well, what do *you* think?' said the manager. 'If you had a doctor working as a lumberman, you'd use him if a chap got hurt, wouldn't you? Cuts and sprains and bruises and that? Anything serious gets sent into the hospital. We haven't had a real accident before this one.'

The sergeant wrote in his book. 'Did you know this man wasn't registered as a doctor in Victoria?' he asked presently.

'Sure,' said the manager. 'I got him as a labourer through the Immigration Office. If he was a doctor he'd have been doctoring.'

'When did you start using him as a doctor?'

'Aw, look—I forget. He's been a labourer all along. The men started going to him for cuts and sprains and that—things it wouldn't be worth going into Banbury for, or getting Dr Jennings out here. He started coming to me for bandages and stuff, so I made over the first-aid box to him and got a lot more stuff he said we ought to have. It just grew up, you might say.'

'But he's been working as a labourer all along?'

'That's right.'

'Did you ever make any enquiry into his medical qualifications?'

'Only what he told me, Sarge. He said he'd been a doctor in his own country, in Prague or Pilsen or some place like that. And in the German Army. He told me from the first he wasn't allowed to practise in Australia. I knew that, anyway.'

'Did you authorize him to do this operation?'

'Which one?'

'Well—both. Let's say the man who died—the amputation—first.'

'He asked me, and I told him that he'd better go ahead and take the foot off. We couldn't get a doctor. We couldn't even get a nurse out from the hospital. Look, Sarge, it was like this . . .'

Sergeant Russell said presently, 'I don't want you to think I'm making trouble, Jim. I got to get the facts right for the coroner, because there'll have to be an inquest. There's no doctor that can sign a death certificate. I got to get the facts.' He thumbed over his book and sat in silence for a minute or two, reading through his notes. 'These operations,' he said. 'The one where he took off the foot, and the one on the other fellow's head. How long did they take?'

The manager thought for a moment. 'Aw, look—I couldn't say. The foot was pretty quick—twenty minutes, maybe not so long as that. The other one was much longer—two hours, I'd say, or longer than that.'

The sergeant wrote it down. 'Did you help him?'

'No.'

Sergeant Russell raised his head and looked the manager in the eyes, sensing prevarication. 'Who did help him? He didn't do operations of that sort all on his own?'

'There was a girl there,' the manager said. 'An English girl staying with Jack Dorman. She was in the utility with him. She gave a hand.'

'That's Jack Dorman of Leonora?'

'That's right.'

'What's her name?'

'I don't know. Jack called her Jenny, I think. She was English.'

'Is she here?'

'She went back to Leonora last night, with Jack, about midnight. She's probably there now.'

'I'll look in and see her,' the sergeant said, 'on my way back.'

He glanced over his notes. 'I'll have to see this man Zlinter again,' he said. 'I'll have to know the medical degrees he's got in his own country–that'll come into it. I think that's all the questions.'

'There's one you haven't asked, Sarge,' said Jim Forrest, getting up, 'and I'd like to know the answer.'

'What's that?'

'Who gave Bert the bloody booze?' the manager said. 'I'd like to know the answer to that one.'

In the hut Dr Jennings and Carl Zlinter were debating the same point, standing and looking dispassionately at the body of Bert Hanson. 'Too bad this had to happen,' said the doctor. 'He's been an alcoholic for some time, I'd say. We'll probably find an enlarged liver at the post-mortem. Have you any idea how he got the stuff?'

The Czech shrugged his shoulders. 'There were his cobbers all around, all night, here in the corridor,' he said. 'I was operating in the next room, and I could not see. It must have been in that time. When I had finished the trephine I came in to see this one, and I then smelt whisky, and I asked Mr Forrest, and he said he had been drinking, himself, so I did not think more about it. And afterwards when I came in again, I had had a drink of whisky also, so I did not notice.'

The doctor looked at the broken bottle still lying on the floor. 'He probably drank a whole bottle.'

'I think so, too. We found the lead that is around the cork of a new bottle.'

'And there's no saying who gave it to him?'

'Mr Forrest asked this morning, but nobody would say. I do not think we shall be able to discover that.'

'I don't suppose we shall. . . .' He stood in silence for a minute, and then pulled the sheet over the body. 'There'll have to be an inquest, Zlinter,' he said at last. 'It's a pity I couldn't have got here before the police. I think I'll see the coroner before the inquest, and tell him how it all came about.'

The Czech nodded. 'They will be angry because I have done operations, I suppose.'

'It's going to have to be explained, and put in the proper light. You don't have to worry about anything, though you'll probably have to give evidence.'

'One does the best one can,' the other said. 'It is not possible to do more than that. If I had waited till you could arrive and not done anything, both men would have been dead today. We have now one alive, and would have the other but for some verdamt fool who gave the whisky.'

'I'll go and telephone for the ambulance,' the doctor said. 'You'd better come down with me to the hospital and we'll have a look at what you did on that chap's head together. Take an X-ray first, perhaps.'

Jennifer was still in bed when the police car drove up to the homestead at about half-past eight. Jack Dorman was out on his horse in one of the paddocks, but Mario was in the shearing shed, and Jane sent him to fetch her husband. She made Sergeant Russell comfortable with a cup of tea in the kitchen, and went to call Jennifer, who was awake. 'Jenny,' she said, 'you'll have to get up, my dear. You'll be sorry to hear that one of those men died, the one with the amputated foot. The police sergeant's here, and he wants to ask you a few questions about what happened.'

Jennifer sat up, dumbfounded. 'He *couldn't* have died,' she exclaimed. 'He was getting on splendidly. It was the other one who was so bad.'

'That's what he says, my dear. You'd better get up and put some clothes on and come out and see him. I've sent Mario to find Jack, to come along as well.'

Ten minutes later Jennifer was sitting at the table with a cup of tea, facing the sergeant, who told her about the whisky. 'It's just a matter of form, Miss,' he said. 'I've got to make out a report for the coroner on all this.' He asked her name and her address, which Jane told her to give as Leonora. Then he said, 'I understand you helped this man Carl Zlinter to do both operations.'

She nodded. 'That's right.'

'Had you ever helped him to do an operation before?'

She stared at him. 'Of course not. I only met him yesterday, for the first time. I've only been in this country about ten days.'

He wrote in his book. 'That's right,' he said equably. 'It's just these questions that I have to ask. Now, what made you help him this time?'

She hesitated, not knowing quite where to begin. 'Well–I suppose because my hands were cleaner than anybody else's. Look, Sergeant–this is what happened.'

Jack Dorman came into the kitchen while she was telling her story; Jane briefed him in a whisper with what was going on. He pulled up a chair and sat down to listen. Jennifer came to an end of her story, and the sergeant made a note or two, and looked back at his notes of what Jim Forrest had said. There was no real discrepancy, which was satisfactory. He said, 'That's all clear enough, Miss Morton. Now there's just one or two things arising out of that. Did this man tell you at any time that he wasn't a registered doctor?'

She wrinkled her forehead. 'I remember he told me that I mustn't call him a doctor . . . some time or other.' She sat in thought for a moment. 'I'm afraid I just can't remember,' she said. 'Such a lot happened last night, and I was so tired, I can't remember who said what. I certainly knew that he wasn't supposed to do operations, but whether he told me or someone else, I couldn't say.'

'You did know that, Miss? You knew he wasn't supposed to do operations?'

'Yes,' she said. 'I knew that.'

He made a note in his book. 'Then why did you help him to do operations?' he asked.

She stared at him. 'Well–*someone* had to help him.'

Jack Dorman broke in, 'Aw, look, Sergeant. There wasn't any other doctor–someone had to do something. Jim Forrest tried all ends up to get Dr Jennings. In the end we just had to do the best we could without a proper doctor. Jenny here gave him a hand. I'd have given him a hand myself, but she could do it so much better. You don't think we should have let 'em lie until the doctor came this morning, do you?'

The sergeant closed his book. 'It doesn't matter what I think, Jack,' he said. 'I'm just the copper. It's what the coroner thinks that matters, and he's got to have the facts. I'm not saying that in Jim Forrest's shoes I wouldn't have done the same as he did, or in this young lady's shoes, either. But if the coroner thinks different when he hears the facts of this man's death, there could be a charge of manslaughter against Carl Zlinter, oh my word. Now that's the truth of it.'

He went away, leaving them dumbfounded. Jennifer said, as they watched the car departing through the gates, 'It *can't* be like he said. They couldn't be so stupid.'

Jack Dorman scratched his head. 'What does he think we ought to have done – left 'em lying till the doctor came? It won't go any further, Jenny.'

She said, 'I'm so sorry for Carl Zlinter if they're going on like this. It must be beastly for him, and he's not deserved it.'

The fire that had burned in Lieutenant Dorman thirty years before flared up again. 'If they start anything against that chap I'll raise the bloody roof,' he said evenly. 'Pack of bloody wowsers. I never heard of such a thing.'

Jennifer said, 'If it should come to manslaughter – I can't see how it could, but if it should – I'd be in it too, wouldn't I? I mean, I helped him to do the operations.'

Jane said, 'Oh no, they'd never bring you into it, dear. You only helped – you didn't do anything yourself. I'm sure we could keep you out of it.'

'I don't want to be kept out of it,' the girl said. 'I was glad to be in it last night, and I'm glad to be in it still. I think it was the right thing to do.' She turned to Jack Dorman. 'I would like to have a talk with him about what's going to happen – with Carl Zlinter. He said he'd come round here today, but if there's a row on he may not come.'

Jack Dorman said, 'I might take a run up the road and have a talk with Jim Forrest. If Zlinter's there, I'll tell him we're expecting him.'

He got into his utility presently and went up to Lamirra; he found Jim Forrest in his office. 'Morning, Jim,' he said. 'We've had the police sergeant at our place, asking Jenny all about last night.'

'Pack of bloody nonsense,' the manager said. 'He hasn't got enough to do. I've been trying to find the bloody fool that gave Bert Hanson the whisky, but I'll never do it.'

'He had a bottle, did he?' Mr Dorman asked with interest. 'A whole bottle?'

'I don't know how full it was when he got hold of it. Probably full – we found the tinsel paper that goes round the cork. He had most of what there was, except what got spilt into the bed.'

'He took a lot, did he? In the ordinary way?'

'Oh, aye – he was a pretty fair soak. A lot of them are, of course. There's nothing else to do, in barracks, in a place like this.' He paused. 'The New Australians are the sober ones here. All saving their money for when their two years are up, to buy a house or start a business or something. But for the language trouble, they're the best men that I've got.'

'This chap Zlinter – what's he like?'

'He's right,' said the manager. 'Doesn't drink a lot – not more 'n you or I. Goes fishing all of his spare time.'

'I know. I met him on the Howqua one time, down at Billy Slim's place.' He paused. 'The sergeant was saying that if this goes wrong at the inquest, he could be up for manslaughter.'

'I know. I don't know what in hell they expect one to do. But anyway, it won't go wrong. We've got Doc Jennings on our side.'

'He's satisfied that what was done was right, is he?'

'I think so. They've gone into Banbury now with Harry in the ambulance, him and Zlinter. They took Bert Hanson in the bottom bunk; he's going to do a post-mortem on him after he's got Harry fixed up right. I said that I'd go in tomorrow afternoon and get the news.'

'I'd like to come in with you,' Dorman said. 'My girl Jenny's all mixed up in this, if it should come to manslaughter.'

The manager stared at him. 'Oh my word,' he said. 'It couldn't go that far.'

'It could if we don't watch it,' said Jack Dorman. 'Zlinter's in Banbury now with the doctor?'

'That's right. They went in in the ambulance.'

'Jenny wants to see him. I'd like to see him myself, 'n have a talk about all this.'

'I've got a truck coming out this afternoon with Diesel oil, leaving the Shell depot after dinner. I told him to get a ride out on that.'

'I'll ring the hospital and tell him to drop off at our place, and I'll bring him on here later.'

Carl Zlinter walked up from the road to Leonora homestead at about three o'clock that afternoon, dressed in a shabby grey suit of continental cut; it was hot coming across the paddocks from the road in the blazing sun, and he carried his coat over his arm. Jennifer, sitting in a deckchair on the veranda, saw him coming, and went to the last gate to meet him. 'Come and sit in the shade,' she said. 'You look very hot.'

She was wearing a clean summer frock and her legs were bare; she looked cool and pretty; the sun lit up the auburn colours in her hair. It was many years since Carl Zlinter had talked to a well-dressed girl and he was rather shy of her; in the camps that he had lived in for so long in Europe women had not dressed like that. He took courage from the memory of the sweating girl who had helped him a few hours before, and went with her to the veranda, where Jennifer introduced him to Jane. They sat down together in the deckchairs, and talked for a little about the hot road out from Banbury.

He wiped his forehead with a handkerchief. 'It is ver' beautiful here,' he said. 'For me, this is a very lovely piece of country, just this part around here, between Mount Buller and the town of Banbury, with the rivers, the Howqua and the Delatite. I would be happy if I were to stay here all my life.'

Jane was pleased. 'You like it so much as that?' She paused. 'We came here twenty years ago, and we've sometimes talked of getting another station, nearer in to Melbourne. But, well, I don't know. We've never been in the habit of going to the city much, and I wouldn't want to live anywhere else than here. If we went it would only be to see more of the children.'

'I would never want to live in any better place than here,' he said.

Jennifer smiled. 'But not as a lumberman.'

He looked at her, smiling also. 'There are worse things than to be a lumberman,' he said. 'It is not what I was educated for. But if I may not be a doctor in this country, I would rather be a lumberman, in beautiful country such as this, than work in the city.'

The girl said, 'It's such a waste for a man like you to have to work in the woods. How long will it be, after your two years are up, before you can be a doctor again?'

He said, 'I do not think that I shall ever be a doctor in Australia.'

'Why not?'

'It costs too much,' he said. 'It is necessary for a foreign doctor to do three years of medical training again, in a Melbourne hospital, before he may practise in this country. That would cost fifteen hundred pounds, and that I have not got, and I shall never have. If I should have the money, it would then be very difficult to get a place in a hospital, because the hospitals are full with your Australian doctors.' He paused. 'I do not think that I shall be a doctor again,' he said.

'But what an idiotic regulation!' the girl said.

He looked at her, smiling at her indignation for him. 'It is not so idiotic,' he said. 'There must be some rule. The doctors from some countries are ver' bad. I would not like you to be treated by a Rumanian doctor, or a doctor from Albania.'

Jane asked, 'What do you think you'll do when your two years are up?'

He shrugged his shoulders. 'I do not know. Perhaps I shall stay on and be a lumberman for ever.'

'It seems a frightful waste,' the girl repeated.

Jane changed the subject. 'Tell me,' she said, 'how's your patient getting on—the one with the fractured skull?'

'I think he will recover,' he said. 'We took an X-ray at the hospital and then we took off the dressings, that Dr Jennings could see what had been done, and he was happy; he did not want to do anything else. We made all clean and more sterile with the better equipment at the hospital. If that one does not drink a bottle of whisky I think he will be well.'

'He wouldn't want to, would he?' Jennifer asked. 'You said that he was a better type than the man with the foot.'

'Did I say that? I think that is true. Dr Jennings is to do a post-mortem on the man who died this afternoon. I think that he expects to find cirrhosis of the liver.'

'It'll be rather a good thing if he does find that, won't it?' she asked. 'If it proves he was a bad life, anyway?'

He shrugged his shoulders. 'I do not think it matters a great deal. He died because he drank a bottle of whisky after amputation.'

There was a little silence. 'The police sergeant was here today,' she said. 'He wanted me to answer a lot of questions.'

He looked up. 'I am ver' sorry. Is that because you helped me in the operating?'

She nodded. 'I'm not sorry a bit. If there's going to be a row I'm quite willing to be in it.'

'There is no reason for you to be in it,' he said. 'You did nothing but to hand things to me when I wanted them, and hold the light. I shall say to the police that you had nothing to do with the operation.'

'Don't do that,' she said. 'Just let things take their course and see what happens.'

'There is no reason for you to get into trouble with the police.'

'I don't mind getting into trouble with the police a bit,' she said. 'I think I'd rather like to. It was a good thing to have helped in, and I'm glad I did it. I'd rather like to have the chance of getting up in court, or somewhere, to say that.'

'It's her red hair, Mr Zlinter,' Jane remarked. 'Quarrelsome young person, isn't she? She might be an Australian.'

There was a step on the veranda behind them, and Jack Dorman appeared. 'How do, Zlinter,' he said. 'Go on—sit down—you don't have to get up. You're just the same as Mario.' He dropped down into a chair beside them, and laid his hat on the floor by him. 'Warming up,' he said. 'Been down to the Howqua again?'

'I was there last Saturday and Sunday,' the Czech said, 'but it is now too hot. I only caught two little fishes, and those I set free to grow bigger.'

The grazier glanced at Jennifer. 'Has he been telling you how he found his own grave?'

'Found his own grave?' she exclaimed. 'You said something about that last night.'

'You don't know nothing yet,' Jack Dorman said. 'Go on and tell her about it, Carl.'

The Czech laughed, a little embarrassed. 'It is nothing.'

The girl said, 'Do tell me.'

'It is a stupid thing,' he said. 'Have you been into the valley of the Howqua River, Miss Morton?'

'The name's Jenny,' she said. 'I've not been there yet. That's the next valley, isn't it—over those hills?'

'That is the one,' he said. 'It is very wild because there is no road to it, and very few people have been there. But once there was a town, a town for the gold miners, because there was a mine there, you understand, but now all that is finished. And the town also is finished, because the forest fires, they burnt it, so that now there is nothing of the town left to see at all, only a little machinery by the entrance to the old mine, and nothing else at all. Only the stones in the old cemetery are there still, because those the fire would not burn.'

'When did this happen, Carl?' she asked. 'When was the town there?'

'Fifty years ago,' he said. 'It was nearly fifty years since all the people went away, because the gold was finished. And after that the fires came, and there was no one living there to protect the town, and so it was all burnt.'

'All except the headstones?'

'That is right. I met Mr Dorman fishing in the Howqua a month ago, and we went together to find the stones that are on the graves. And on one stone, there is an inscription with my own name, and my town in Czechoslovakia.'

He reached for his coat on the floor beside his chair, and took a wallet from the inside pocket. 'I have copied the inscription.' He took a paper, unfolded it, and handed it to her. 'That is what is written on the stone.'

Jane Dorman leaned over, and they read it together. The girl said, 'What an extraordinary thing! Is your name Charlie?'

'Carl,' he replied, 'and I was born in Pilsen, but not in 1869.' He paused. 'It is not so very extraordinary,' he said. 'We were a large family with many branches in Pilsen, and many people from Pilsen emigrated in this last century, when times were hard. The extraordinary thing is that I should have found the grave, I myself, with the same name.' He paused, and turned to the grazier. 'I wondered if you have ever heard the name in this country, so that I could find out who this Charlie Zlinter was. He was certainly a relation of some kind.'

Jack Dorman shook his head. 'I've never heard the name,' he said. 'I don't suppose anybody in this country could tell you anything about him now. I should think you'd find out something more easily in Pilsen. Get the names of people who left for Australia at the end of the last century.'

The Czech shook his head. 'It is not possible to find out anything from Pilsen now,' he said. 'I do not even know who I could write to there, to ask. And if I did write, any letter might make trouble from the Russians. They do not like people who get letters from the West.'

'Why did it say, Charlie Zlinter and his dog?' asked Jennifer. 'Was the dog buried with him?'

'I do not know. I would like to know, ver' much.'

Jack Dorman said, 'I think you'll have a job to find out much now, after fifty years.'

'There would not be a record of deaths in the shire?'

'What about the parish register?' the girl asked.

'I doubt it,' Dorman said slowly. 'I never heard there was a church in Howqua. The nearest church would be in Banbury—if there was one there then. I shouldn't think that they'd have taken much account of what went on at Howqua. There *might* have been a shire officer there, but I rather doubt it. These gold-mining towns were pretty free and easy in those days.'

'Would there have been a policeman living in the town?' asked Zlinter.

'I shouldn't think so—not in 1902. They'd send police out from Banbury if there was any trouble.'

'It is not likely, then, that there would be any record of Charlie Zlinter anywhere?'

'It's just a chance,' said Dorman. 'If he belonged in Banbury, if he lived there, you might find something about him at the Shire Hall. It's just possible there may ·be descendants in the district—people of the same name, sons or grandsons, though I never heard the name before. Apart from that, the only thing would be to find somebody who was living in the Howqua at the time. They might remember something about this Charlie Zlinter, some old person.'

'Would it be easy to find such an old person?'

'I shouldn't think it would. Those gold-mining towns, they weren't settled places, if you know what I mean. People went there to take up claims and work the gold; if it didn't work out right for them, they went off to some other place—West Australia or South Africa, maybe, where there was gold to be found. They didn't stay around where there wasn't any gold. I think you'll have a job to find anybody who was living at Howqua then.'

The Czech said quietly, 'That is very bad luck.'

He seemed so disappointed that Jennifer asked, 'Is it very important?'

He smiled at her. 'It is not important at all,' he said. 'Only, if a member of my family had been here before me, I would have liked to know.'

Presently Jane went to the kitchen door and rang the handbell on the veranda to warn Tim and Mario that it was five o'clock and time to knock off for tea. Jack Dorman took the Czech off for a wash: he came back to the veranda presently and found Jennifer there alone.

He said, laughing, 'I must try to remember the way to behave. This will be the first time that I have eaten in a private house since I left Germany, nearly two years.'

She was appalled at the casual statement. 'Is that really true?'

'But, yes. I do not think that I know anybody in Australia yet, although I have been here for fifteen months. Hotels and bars and cinemas—I know those. This is the first time that I have entered a person's home.'

She did not know what to say. 'I suppose you don't meet many people, living up there in the camp?'

He smiled. 'Ordinary people keep away from camps, and sometimes for good reason. And I have spent much of my life in camps. Since 1939 I have lived always in camps, with practically no break—twelve years. I really do not know how ordinary people live.' He laughed.

Over the meal they talked of small, casual matters of the countryside and afterwards, in the cool of the evening, they sat on the veranda, smoking. When in the dusk he took his leave Jack Dorman offered to run him back to Lamirra. He refused that, saying that Jim Forrest was coming out of town and would pick him up upon the road; they did not press it, thinking that perhaps he meant to stop at the hotel and have a drink. On his part, he was unwilling to extend their hospitality, and preferred the four-mile walk back to Lamirra. Jennifer strolled across the paddocks with him to the road.

She knew that the matter of Charlie Zlinter and his dog was still upon his mind, and she raised the subject for him, in case he wanted to talk about it. 'It's funny about that headstone,' she said. 'Charlie Zlinter.'

'I would like to find out something about Charlie Zlinter,' he said, 'I think he must have been related to me in some way. All of the Zlinters in Pilsen are uncles or cousins of each other.'

He turned to her. 'When you leave your own place and you start again in a new country, with nobody that you know, it is wonderful to find that someone of your family has been there before,' he said. 'Even fifty years before. It makes a tie with your own home. And however good the new country may be, unless you know somebody in it you are not a part of it.'

They walked on in silence for a time. She had not met such loneliness before. 'You know some real people now, anyway,' she said. 'You know the Dormans, and me. More substantial than Charlie Zlinter. I hope you'll come and see us again some time.'

'I would like to do that,' he said. 'But also, I would like to find out about Charlie Zlinter and his dog.'

She laughed. 'I believe you've been making it all up. I don't believe there's any such person, really.'

He laughed with her. 'I promise you that it is true. I would say that I would take you there and show you the stone, but it is ten miles to walk and ten miles back. Some day when Mr Dorman goes with Mr Fisher in the Land Rover to fish in the Howqua you must come with him, and I will show you the stone.'

'That's a bargain,' she said. 'I'd like to do that some day.'

'I should be much honoured if you would,' he said.

They walked across the last paddock to the road in silence. It was nearly dark.

At the gate on to the road he turned to her. 'Now I must say good-bye. I am afraid that I have been awkward in company this evening, and I ask if you will forgive me.'

'You've not been awkward a bit,' she said. 'You've been very interesting, and very charming, Mr Zlinter. I hope you'll come again.'

He laughed diffidently. 'It is many years since I have been in company with people of good family, like you. You must forgive the awkward things I must have done. But I would like to come again, and some day I would like to take you to the Howqua to see that stone.'

'We'll fix that somehow or other,' she said. 'Good-night, Carl. Don't get run over on the way back, and don't stop at the pub too long.'

'Good night, Miss Jennifer,' he said formally. 'Thank you again for all that you have done for me. I shall not stop at the pub tonight at all.'

'I bet,' she laughed. 'Goodnight. Come and see us again.'

She walked back across the paddocks deep in thought. She found Jane sitting on the veranda with Jack Dorman; Angela was away with friends in Banbury, driving her mother's Morris. Jane said, 'I rather like Carl Zlinter.'

Jennifer dropped down into a chair. 'It's extraordinary,' she said. 'He's been in the country fifteen months, and this is the first time that he's been inside a private house.'

'Is that right?' asked Jack Dorman.

'That's what he said.'

Jane said slowly, 'Well, I can understand that in a way, although it sounds rather awful. They're a pretty rough lot up at Lamirra. Before that camp started up, Jack and I used to go down sometimes to the hotel and have a glass of beer and chat with Mrs Hawkey, the landlady, but we haven't been for a long time. Too many drunks.'

'From the lumber camp?'

'Yes–from Lamirra.'

'Of course, he's different to the ordinary lumberman,' Jack Dorman explained. 'He's an educated man.'

There was a little silence. 'I don't suppose he thinks much of Australia and Australians,' Jane said.

'He thinks it's a lovely country,' Jennifer told her. 'He doesn't want to live anywhere else. Only, he'd like to know some people. That's why he's so keen to find out something about Charlie Zlinter and his dog.'

In the dim light Jane stared at her. 'But Charlie Zlinter's dead!'

'I know. All the same, he's the only person in Australia that Dr Zlinter knows, outside the lumber camp.'

'My dear. I think that's rather touching.'

'I thought that, too,' the girl said. 'I told him he must come and see us here again–I hope you don't mind. It seemed such rotten luck.'

'Of course, Jenny. I liked him. Makes a change to talk to somebody who's lived outside the Shire of Banbury.'

'He wants to take me over to the Howqua some time, to see his tombstone,' she said. 'I'd like to see it, and I'd like to see the Howqua, but I'm not going to walk ten miles there and ten miles back in this hot weather.'

Jane said, 'You don't have to walk ten miles to get into the Howqua, surely? You can ride over on a horse.'

'I can't,' said Jennifer. 'I'd fall off.'

Jack Dorman said, 'You could probably get into the Howqua in a utility, in this dry weather. You can get in in a Land Rover any time of year. It's easy going on the track this side; the other side's a bit steep. You could leave the utility parked up in Jock McDougall's paddock on the top of the ridge, and walk down to the river. That'ld only be about two miles. Zlinter can drive, I suppose?'

'I really don't know,' Jennifer said. 'I should think he could.'

'I never met a doctor yet who couldn't drive a car,' said Jane.

'He wouldn't be used to driving on our side of the road, anyway,' said Jennifer.

'Aw, look,' Jack Dorman said, 'there's only a mile and a half of road before you turn off on the track across the paddocks up into the timber. He won't hit anything in that distance. If you want to get into the Howqua, make him drive you up to Jock McDougall's paddock and then walk. You can take the Chev.'

'That's awfully good of you,' the girl said. 'We'll ask if he can drive, if he turns up again. I'd be afraid he might smash the Chev up.'

'It's worn out, anyway. I've been thinking we should get a Land Rover to replace it.'

'That's enough of that,' said Jane. 'We've got too many cars already. I'm going to have my painting before we get another car.'

'I thought you'd forgotten about that,' he said.

'Indeed I haven't. It's just that I don't know how to get the sort of painting that I want. I'm not going to have one of those modern things we saw in Melbourne.'

Jennifer went to bed that night unreasonably happy. She was deeply grateful to Jack Dorman for his casual offer of the old utility; she had wanted to do something to ease the loneliness of Carl Zlinter, but she had been powerless to do much about it by herself. She was still happy next morning till the postman came by just before dinner, and Mario went down to pick up the mail from their box on the main road. There was a letter from her father, air-mailed from England; the happiness went from her face, and was succeeded by a troubled frown. Jane saw it, and said casually, 'Everything all right at home?'

'Not absolutely,' the girl said. 'Mummy's been in bed with bronchitis. They seem to have had terrible weather in England. Of course, it's January.'

'Not serious, is it?'

'Oh, no. The thing is that when Mummy's ill it makes things hard for Daddy. They've only got a woman who comes in in the mornings.' She paused. 'It happened last winter, and I took ten days of my holiday and went up there and ran the house. I didn't bargain on it happening again this winter.'

She said no more, but she was troubled at the thought of difficulties in the snow and rain of the Midlands, so far away. It needed a strong mental effort to picture the conditions of an English winter in the Australian summer heat, though she had left so recently.

At dinner Jack Dorman said, 'I'm going in this afternoon to meet Jim Forrest at the hospital. Anyone got anything for the post?'

'I shall have,' Jennifer said. 'I want to write an air-mail to my mother. I'll let you have it after dinner. What time are you going?'

'Not till about three.'

'I'll write it as soon as we've cleared away.'

Jack Dorman drove into Banbury in the new utility, posted Jennifer's letter before he forgot it, and drove round to the hospital. Jim Forrest's car was parked in the street; he parked behind it and went in. A New Australian ward-maid told him that Mr Forrest was with Dr Jennings in the office; he put his head in at the door.

'Come in, Mr Dorman,' said the doctor. 'I was just telling Jim here about these men.'

He was a small, brown-haired man with a sandy little moustache and blue eyes; he had been an officer in the Royal Australian Army Medical Corps in the war, and he still had the appearance of an officer in civvies. Jack Dorman went in and sat down. 'What's the news, Doctor?'

'I was telling Jim,' the doctor repeated. 'I've just finished the post-mortem. The man was an alcoholic all right. You never saw such a liver. I'm preserving part of it in spirit until after the inquest, just in case anybody wants to see it. He was full of whisky, too.'

Jim Forrest said with feeling, 'He must have been.'

'He certainly was. Matter of fact, I should have thought there was more than a bottle in him, but I suppose I'm wrong. There was certainly a lot.' He paused. 'I had a look at the amputation, while I was at it. It was carefully done. One of the ligatures was damaged a little, probably while he was struggling. But the job was done all right.'

Jim Forrest said, 'He'd have been right, but for the whisky?'

'I wouldn't say that. Sepsis might easily have set in. As I understand it, the amputation was done out in the open, to free him from the bulldozer. All I can say is that the job was well done from the surgical point of view.'

Jack Dorman said, 'It wasn't a botched job?'

'No. It wasn't a botched job. The damaged ligature was clearly the result of a blow. He probably kicked it against something in the struggle, while you were trying to keep him in bed.'

Jim Forrest nodded. 'He was thrashing about all over the place.'

There was a pause. 'As regards the other one,' the doctor said, 'the fractured skull, it's much the same story. I took an X-ray this morning. If I had been doing the job here I'd have taken an X-ray before operating, of course. If I had done so, I should probably have removed one more small piece of bone that Zlinter has left in. Working without the X-ray, as he did, I should very likely have left it, as he did. Considering the X-ray this morning, I decided to leave well alone. I don't really think that it'll make much difference, and one doesn't want to submit the patient to a further operational shock.'

He paused. 'There again, infection is the danger. Zlinter showed me what he did, and I don't think anybody could have done much more. But there's no denying that the conditions were bad for any cranial surgery.'

Jack Dorman said, 'Taking it by and large, though, he didn't do a bad job?'

'I think that's a fair statement. Taking it by and large, he didn't do at all a bad job, considering the difficulties.'

'You'll tell them that at the inquest, Doctor, will you?' asked Jim Forrest.

'That's right. That's what I shall say at the inquest.'

Jack Dorman said, 'If he can do a job like that, why can't he be a doctor properly? Get a licence, or whatever you call it?'

'There's a ruling about these immigrant doctors. In this State they've got to do the last three years of their training over again. It varies according to the State, I think. I know it's easier in West Australia.'

'Pack of bloody nonsense,' said the grazier. 'We could do with another doctor here, and now we've got one and we're not allowed to use him.'

'You've got to have a rule,' Jennings said. 'Most of these D.P. doctors are crook doctors, oh my word. You'd be the first to raise a scream if some of them got loose upon your family.'

'That's right, is it?' asked Jim Forrest. 'They're very bad?'

'I don't really know,' the doctor said. 'You'd have to ask somebody who knows about these things. I believe the truth of it is this: when they're first qualified their standard is much lower than ours. What they pick up from experience in practice may bring them up to our standard, but who's to say? Take this Zlinter, for example. He seemed to be a careful sort of chap, and since he qualified he's had a very wide experience of surgery in front-line conditions with the German Army. You've seen him at his best. He certainly knows a lot about these sort of accidents. But that's not general practice. Ninety per cent of the general practitioner's job is trying to decide if an old lady's pain is heart trouble or wind, or whether a kiddy's got scarlet fever or a sore throat. Zlinter may be useless at that sort of thing–probably is.'

He paused. 'I don't want you to think I'm against Zlinter,' he said. 'I think he's a good man. If he was qualified I'd like to see him practise in this district and take some of the work off me. But not until he's been checked over at the hospital and been passed out as competent.'

'And that takes three years?'

'I don't know if that would apply to Zlinter. I don't know if they make any exceptions. Probably not. I think he probably *would* have to do three years again.'

'It seems the hell of a long time,' the grazier said.

The doctor got up from the desk; he had still a lot of work ahead of him. 'It's better to be safe than sorry.'

The grazier went out into the street with the timber manager. 'What about a beer?' They got into their cars and drove down to the main street, and parked under the shade of the trees in front of the Queen's Head Hotel.

It had been market day in Banbury, but the market was over before dinner, and now in the late afternoon only the dregs of the crowd remained in town. The bars, which had been hot and crowded most of the day, were thinning out; the tired barmen were relaxing, watching the clock for closing time at six. Jack Dorman and Jim Forrest went into the saloon bar and ordered beers, and stood discussing what they had learned from the doctor about Zlinter.

It was still warm and the beer was very cold; they had a glass of beer, and then another, and another in the space of twenty minutes. As they stood their talk was mostly about Zlinter, how he would be situated at the end of his two years of lumber work, whether he would have a chance to qualify as a doctor, how much it would cost, whether he could raise the money on a loan from any bank, whether if he had the money he could get admission to a hospital.

The bar that they were standing in was merely a partitioned part of the long bar-room, but it was select and mostly frequented by graziers and those with money to spare. Drinks at this portion of the bar cost a trifle more, and there were little plates of onions, cheese, and other snacks, all highly spiced to induce a pleasant thirst. A yard away from Jack Dorman and Jim Forrest as they discussed Carl Zlinter was an old man sitting hunched upon a stool, a red-haired old man, now turning grey but still fiery on top; a broad-shouldered old man who must have been a very strong man in his time. He had a comical twist to his mouth and a general appearance of good humour, and he was drinking whisky, evidently determined to sit it out until the bar closed. From his appearance he had been there all the afternoon.

Presently the barman said, 'Last drinks,' and the clock stood at two minutes to six. Jim Forrest hurriedly ordered four more beers and the barman pushed the dripping glasses across the counter; the old man by their side sat sunk in reflection or in slumber, a half glass of whisky before him. They drank two beers apiece, and then, at ten past six, the barman said, 'We're closing now,' and it was time to go. He said to the old man, 'Come on, Pop. Closing now.'

The old man did not stir, but mumbled something incoherent.

Jack Dorman smiled, and put his hand on the old man's shoulder. 'Come on, Pat,' he said. 'Time to go home now. Finish up your drink. Got your jinker here?'

The old man raised his head, and very slowly lifted his glass and drank it off, with the utmost deliberation. Jim Forrest smiled, 'Who is he?'

'Pat Halloran. He's got a place five miles out on the Benalla road.' Jack knew the old man fairly well. He had come out from Southern Ireland as a stable-boy at the end of the last century, and he had been about the district ever since but for one trip home to Limerick between the wars. He was a widower and his two sons ran the property and did most of the work; he enjoyed coming into market and meeting his cronies and getting drunk, a simple pleasure that he could afford on his five-figure income. His sons drove large and powerful utilities rather too fast, but the old man had never learned to drive a car and came to town each market day in a jinker, a two-wheeled trap drawn by an old horse.

Jack Dorman smiled again, waited till the old man had drained his glass, and said, 'Come on, Pat. It's closing time; we're getting thrown out of here. Where did you leave your jinker?'

'It's in the yard out at the back,' the barman said. 'Take him out through this way, if you like.'

'Take the other arm, Jim,' said Jack Dorman. 'We'll put him in the jinker, and he'll be right.'

The old man got down from the stool, and they steadied him, one on each side. 'That's right,' he said, with a marked Irish accent. 'Sure, put me up in the jinker and I'll be right.' He paused for reflection, and they began walking him to the back premises and the yard. 'I know you,' he said. 'You're Jack Dorman, up to Leonora.'

'That's right.'

The old man turned and stared at the timber manager with bleary eyes. 'I don't know you.'

'Jim Forrest's the name. From Lamirra.'

'Oh. D'you know my name? It's Pat Halloran, from Limerick.'

'That's right,' said Jack Dorman. 'I know you and you know me. Watch these steps, now—three steps down. That's fine.'

'I'm right,' the old man said. 'Only I'm drunk. I know you. You're Jack Dorman, up to Leonora.' He swayed wildly, and they steered him into the passage, the barman holding the door open for them. 'It's a shameful thing I'm telling you,' he said seriously. 'But I'm drunk, drunk as Charlie Zlinter.'

The grazier started. 'What's that, Pat? Who am I as drunk as?'

'Drunk as Charlie Zlinter,' the old man repeated. 'I know you. You're Jack Dorman, up to Leonora. You know me, Pat Halloran, from Limerick. You know me, I know you, and you know Charlie Zlinter. Good old Charlie!'

'I don't know Charlie Zlinter, Pat,' the other said. 'Who was Charlie Zlinter?' It was quite possible that this old man could have been in the district when Howqua was a thriving township.

Pat Halloran turned bellicose. He checked in the passage; he was still a powerful man, and brought them to a standstill. 'What was that you would be saying? Who was Charlie Zlinter? Haven't I heard with my own ears you two talking all the while of Charlie Zlinter? Is it a fool that ye'd be making of me, just because I'm having drink taken? Will ye fight me, now?'

'Nobody's making a fool of you, Pat, and I won't fight you,' said the grazier. 'Come on—let's find the jinker. Tell us about Charlie Zlinter when you knew him, and I'll tell you what I know about him, and there'll be a pair of us. What did Charlie Zlinter do?'

'He got bloody drunk,' the old man said. 'I got bloody drunk. You got bloody drunk. Sure, we're all bloody drunk.'

They came into the stable yard and there was the jinker, the horse patiently waiting to take his master home. Jim Forrest untied the reins from the tethering ring, tried the girth, and looked the harness over while Jack Dorman steadied the old man. 'She's right,' he said.

The grazier said, 'The jinker's right, Pat. Can you get up in it?'

The old man grabbed the splash-board and the seat-rail, put one foot upon the step, and swung himself up into the seat, the habit of fifty years undefeated by alcohol. He took the reins, and lifted the whip from the socket. 'I'll be right, boys,' he said. 'Sure, an' I'll be wishing you a very good evening.' Now that he was in his vehicle he seemed to be at home, indeed, he looked almost sober.

The grazier stood for a moment at the wheel, looking up at the old man. 'What else did Charlie Zlinter do, Pat, besides getting drunk?'

The old man stared down at him. 'Charlie Zlinter . . .' And then he stood up in the jinker and recited, with dramatic flourishes of the whip that made the grazier retreat hurriedly,

> Charlie Zlinter and his heeler hound
> Fell into the Howqua and got bloody well drowned.
> Be warned, fellow sinners, and never forget
> If he hadn't been drunk he'd have been living yet.

He touched the horse skilfully with the whip and drove out of the yard; the grazier was left facing Jim Forrest, who was laughing. 'What the hell was all that about, Jack?'

The grazier scratched his head. 'Charlie Zlinter,' he replied. 'But I reckon it's a different Charlie Zlinter to the one we know.'

8

Carl Zlinter arrived in Banbury at about nine o'clock on Saturday morning, riding in the back of a utility that had picked him up upon the road. In that sparsely-populated district where trucks and utilities were the normal transport it was not difficult to get a ride into town in something or other; he had never had to walk more than half an hour in the direction of the town without getting picked up. He had not breakfasted, and he went and had it in a café, bacon and two eggs and coffee. They gave him a Melbourne paper two days old to read, and he sat smoking a cigarette after it, enjoying the leisure.

When he paid his bill, he said to the girl who had served him, 'Do you know a family called Shulkin? They are New Australian. The man works on the railway.'

She looked at him blankly; she came of a family of Australians that had been casual labourers for generation after generation, bad stock and mentally subnormal. She and her family were bitterly hostile to all immigrants, especially the European ones who worked too hard and were guilty of the social crime of saving money, thereby threatening the Australian Way of Life. 'Never heard of them,' she said scornfully.

He looked at her with clinical interest as he paid his bill, wondering if she were tubercular; in spite of his decision to abandon medicine he could not rid himself of interest in symptoms. A Wasserman test would be interesting, and probably positive. He smiled at her, and went out and walked down the long, wide tree-lined avenue of the main street towards the railway station.

The booking office was closed because upon this single-track line there were only two trains a day, but the stationmaster lived beside the station in a weatherboard house, and he asked there for Mr Shulkin. The stationmaster said, 'Aw, look, Stan Shulkin, he's not working today. There's a green-painted shack, the third house down this road, with an old railway coach they use for sleeping in alongside. You'll find Stan there, unless he's in the town.'

He found the shack and railway coach, a poor sort of habitation. There was a man digging in the garden, a man of about forty-five or fifty, with black hair going bald on top. Behind the railway coach he saw a fresh-faced woman with a dumpy, peasant figure hanging out some washing, and there were a couple of children playing in the background. He opened the gate and went in, and spoke to the man. 'Are you Stan Shulkin?'

The man straightened up, and said with an equally marked accent, 'I am Stanislaus Shulkin.'

The Czech said in German, 'My name is Carl Zlinter, and I work in the timber camp at Lamirra. Do you prefer to speak English?'

'Always,' the man said. 'Always I speak English. It is better for the children. The wife, she speaks it very bad. She does not try.'

Carl Zlinter said, 'You must excuse, but I have heard that you can paint very good pictures.'

The man smiled shyly across his broad face. 'I paint pictures only now one or two each year,' he said. 'There is not time and people here do not want pictures. When I came first to this place three years ago, I said, Now I will paint pictures and we shall make much money. But it did not happen in that way. Now I paint only a little.'

'You work upon the railway?'

'In the platelaying gang. It is very hard work, and not good for the hands, for painting. I do not think that I shall paint many more pictures.'

'You are Esthonian?'

'Lithuanian,' the man said. 'I am from Kaunas.'

'I am from Pilsen,' Zlinter said. 'In my country I was a doctor, but now I am a labourer.' The man nodded in comprehension. 'I have friends who want a picture. They are not artistic, but they have much land and plenty of money. They are more educated than some, and they have bought all the motor-cars that they can use, and now they want an oil-painting.'

'So?' said the Lithuanian. 'I would have thought it would have been a radio or a washing machine.'

'They will have those also,' said Zlinter, 'but the woman wants an oil painting. She has seen exhibitions of ugly pictures in Melbourne, and those she does not want. She is simple, and she wants a beautiful picture that will give pleasure to those who do not understand about pictures. There is a man called Spiegel in the camp who told me you can paint such pictures.'

'I can paint such pictures,' Shulkin said. 'I can paint any sort of picture.'

'May I see?'

Shulkin led the way into the railway coach. It had been an open coach without compartments at one time; now it had been roughly converted into three rooms with matchboarding partitions. Much of the seating still remained unchanged, and each of the three rooms still had two doors upon each side. The end room that they went into was furnished with a bed, an easel, and a great litter of old canvases and frames stacked along one side. 'I buy old canvases and frames at the sale,' the artist said. 'It is cheaper so.'

He pulled out a canvas from the heap, a beautifully executed still life of two herrings on a plate, a loaf of bread, a pat of butter, and a glass of beer, laid out in strong light on a soiled table-cloth with a dark background. 'This I did in the camp. I call it, Lithuanian Fisherman's Breakfast.'

He plucked another canvas from the heap and set it on the easel in place of the still life. 'This—a portrait of my mother.' The stern old face glowered at them from the canvas, a powerful picture finely executed. He whisked it away, and planted another canvas on the easel. 'This, the Delatite River.'

It was a bright river scene with a fine blue sky and white clouds, and a riot of golden wattles on the bank, making a delicate harmony of colour. 'So . . .' said Carl Zlinter. 'This you should show her. The others, they are beautiful in a different way, but this, or something like this, is what she wants.'

'I can paint anything she wants,' the artist remarked, 'but usually they cannot say.'

The Czech stood back, and looked critically at the river scene. 'I do not know pictures,' he said at last. 'But I would think that this is very good.' He paused. 'You must have had a great deal of experience.'

'I studied in Paris and in Rome,' the platelayer replied. 'I was Professor of Artistic Studies in the University of Kaunas.'

There did not seem to be anything to say to that. Zlinter stayed a little while and had a cup of tea. 'I will tell Mrs Dorman about you,' he said. 'If she wants a beautiful picture, she does not need to go to Melbourne for it. She can find it here, in Banbury. I will tell her this evening.'

He went off presently, and caught a bus out on the Benalla road. Twenty minutes later he was walking up to the Halloran homestead. A small girl came to the kitchen door and he asked for Mr Pat Halloran. She turned and called into the house, 'Ma, there's a feller asking for grandpa.'

'In the wood shed.'

'He's in the wood shed,' she said. 'Round there.'

In the wood shed Zlinter found a red-haired old man splitting sawn logs with a sledge-hammer and wedges, doing the work with the skill of a lifetime rather than with any great muscular effort. 'Please,' he said. 'May I speak to you?'

The old man rested on his sledge. 'An' who might you be?'

'My name is Zlinter, Charlie Zlinter,' the Czech said. 'I work in the timber camp, up at Lamirra.'

'Sure, an' you *can't* be Charlie Zlinter. Charlie Zlinter's dead these fifty years.'

'I am another one with the same name. I am trying to find out about the one who died.'

'An' what made you come here, may I ask?'

'Mr Jack Dorman, he said you were talking about Charlie Zlinter in the Queen's Head, on Thursday.'

'Who's this Jack Dorman? Jack Dorman at Leonora? Sure, an' I haven't set eyes on the man these last six months.'

'Perhaps you do not remember,' the Czech said diplomatically. 'He helped you up into the jinker on Thursday.'

'Would that be so! Well, Glory be to God, I didn't know a thing about it! Would you believe that, now?'

He evaded the rhetorical question. 'Jack Dorman said that you were speaking of this Charlie Zlinter. I have seen the grave.'

'Ye have not. Charlie Zlinter was buried in the Howqua, and the fire went through. There's nothing left there now.'

'The head-stones are left,' the other said. 'They are stone, and so they did not burn. The head-stones are there now, all of them, in the forest by the river, where there was the cemetery.'

'Do ye tell me that!'

He had gained the old man's interest, and he held it while he explained the position to him. 'This Charlie Zlinter, he was from Pilsen in Bohemia,' he said at last. 'That is on the stone. I am another Charlie Zlinter, also from Pilsen in Bohemia. I am trying to find out what I can about him.'

The old man leaned on his sledge. 'He was a bullocky,' he said at last. 'I wouldn't be able to say at this distance of time if he worked for himself or if he worked for Murphy. He drove a wagon with a team of bullocks, six bullocks, or eight would it have been? Holy Saints above, I'm losing all my memory. I couldn't say at all if it was six or eight. I was just a bit of a boy myself. I came out to this country in 1895 while the old Queen was on the throne, God rest her soul. I worked two years in the stables for Jim Pratt that had the Queen's Head in those days, and then I joined the police. There was work for a policeman in this country then.'

'Do you remember Charlie Zlinter?' the Czech asked.

'Sure, I do that. He was a German and he drove a bullock team in and out of the Howqua, from the railway here to Howqua and back again. There wasn't a fine broad highway then, with the motor-cars all racing along at sixty miles an hour. There wasn't hair nor hide of a made road at all, at all. Bullocks were the only teams to get a wagon up over the spur and down into the Howqua, passengers and machinery and food and drink and everything, all went by bullock team. Will ye believe what I tell you, the bullock drivers were the boys that made the money! The miners, they never did much in the Howqua, and in the end the company went broke. What gold there was went into the pockets of the bullock drivers. Not a breath of it did the shareholders ever see.'

'What was Charlie Zlinter like?'

'Ah, he was a fine, big fellow with dark curly hair, and he spoke English in the way you speak it. He was one for the booze, and he was one for the girls, Holy Saints above! He had a cabin in the town of Howqua, for he went there as a miner first of all, and then he had the wit to see he'd make more money with a wagon and a team. By the Mother of God, I'd think shame to repeat all that went on in that cabin. He was a big, lusty man, and drink and women were his downfall. That's the truth I'm telling you.'

He paused. 'Drink and women, drink and women,' he said. 'It's a sad, sad thing.' He shot a humorous glance at Zlinter. 'He used to drive in here the one day and back the next, twenty-two miles each day; he'd come in here the one evening and then he'd be away up to the Howqua the next day. Ten hours or so it might take him, and he had two teams, one resting and one working. He used to come to the Queen's Head Hotel, and hobble the bullocks on the green outside and feed them hay, and then he'd come into the hotel and get drunk, and he'd sleep in the wagon and away off out of it next morning, back to the Howqua. And as like as not there'd be a young girl going to the Howqua for a barmaid in Peter Slim's hotel, a girl no better than she should be, or she wouldn't be going to the Howqua . . .' He thought for a minute. 'They were fine, noble days, those times, when we were all young.'

'What did he die of?'

'Drink and drowning,' the old man said, 'drink and drowning, and his dog with him, only the dog wasn't drunk, though it might have been at that, the company it kept. It was August, and the river was running full with the melting snows. There was a girl living in the Howqua by the name of Mary Nolan, oh, a wicked girl, I'd think shame to tell you all that that girl did, and she so soft and well spoken, and pretty, too. She lodged on the other side of the river from the Buller Arms Hotel that Peter Slim kept, Billy's father, him that's the forest ranger in the Howqua now. And Charlie Zlinter, he stayed in the hotel till close on midnight, and then he made to go across the river to see this girl. Well, most part of the year ye'd cross the Howqua and never wet your feet by stepping on the stones, but in August and September, with the melting of the snows on the high mountains, it runs five or six feet deep. There was a cable bridge, a bridge of two wire ropes with planks across the way you'd walk on them, and a third one to hold on to, and Charlie Zlinter, drunk the way he was, must go across this bridge to see this girl. Ye'd think, now, for a man as drunk as Charlie to go on a bridge like that at midnight would have been enough, but he must take the dog with him. He had this heeler dog he kept for rounding up the bullocks and to guard the wagon when he was in Banbury, and he must take it with him over the river. And when he came up to the bridge the dog wouldn't go upon it, and so Charlie picked it up in his arms and started off across the bridge in the dark night, with the dog in his arms and the bridge swaying and going up and down with every step he took, and he as drunk as a lord. And that was the end of it.'

'He fell off the bridge into the water?'

'He did that. They found him half a mile down stream come the morning, him and the dog together. There was never a priest there to say a mass for him, and they buried him and the dog in the one grave, which the priest would never have allowed.' He paused. 'Aye, it was a sad thing; he was a fine, noble boy. It made a great wonder in the countryside, for he was well known on account of coming in and out of Banbury and people riding with him. And they put a poem in the paper about him, ah, a lovely, lovely poem. Did ye never hear it?'

The Czech shook his head.

The old man declaimed,

> Charlie Zlinter and his heeler hound
> Fell into the Howqua and unhappily drowned.
> Be warned, fellow sinners, and never forget
> If he hadn't been drunk he'd have been living yet.

'Ah,' he said, 'it was a lovely, lovely poem.'

'This Charlie Zlinter was almost certainly some relation of my own,' said the Czech, 'because he came from my own town. Did you ever hear anything about him–who his relations were, or who he wrote to? Did he leave any papers to say that?'

'Sure, an' I wouldn't know a thing like that at all,' the old man said. 'I was a policeman in those days, and on other duties; I only knew about him from the gossip of the time. I wouldn't know what happened to his gear. It was soon after that the mine closed down and Howqua came to an end; within the year there were only a few people living in the place. I wouldn't say that anyone took on the bullock team after he passed away. I wouldn't know. The Howqua was going down, and there wasn't the work there had been in the beginning.'

Carl Zlinter asked, 'You do not know what happened to his papers?'

'Ah, I wouldn't know at all. There's only one person left might know about a thing like that.'

'Who is that?'

'Sure, Mary Nolan herself.'

'Mary Nolan! Is she still alive?'

'Ah, she's alive. She was a wicked girl, and Father Geoghegan, he was the priest here then, he would have nothing to do with her until she came to the confession, and that she would not do, and Holy Mother of God, it's not to be wondered at. And so when the mine closed down and everybody left the Howqua what must she do but go for a barmaid at Woods Point in the hotel there, and very strict she came to be, so that there was no loose talk or dirty jokes in Mary Nolan's bar. I did hear that she made her peace with Father O'Brian from Warburton who went to Woods Point in those days, and like enough he didn't know the whole of it. And then she married a man called Williams who lived on an allotment out by Jamieson, and they lived there until he died at the beginning of the second war. And then she sold the place, and went to live at Woods Point with her brother-in-law's family; I'd say she'd be living there yet. I haven't heard she died.'

'She must be old now,' said the Czech.

'Seventy-five, maybe,' the old man said indignantly. 'She'd not be a day older than seventy-five. That's not so old at all. Sure, there's many a man fit and hearty at the age of seventy-five.'

'Do you think that Mary Nolan might have kept Charlie Zlinter's papers, or know what happened to them when he was drowned?'

'Ah, I wouldn't be saying that at all. She's the only person living in the district now that might know something, though it's a long while ago. I'll say this now, she knew Charlie Zlinter better than anyone else, and better than she had any right to as a single woman.'

Carl Zlinter left him presently, and walked back into the town and got there in time for dinner. He went to a different café for his meal where they were kinder to the New Australian, and got a lift out halfway to Merrijig in a truck driven by George Pearson on his way to Buttercup. He walked for two miles then, for it was Saturday afternoon and there were few people on the road, and finally got picked up by the storekeeper from Lamirra driving out of town in his utility. He got down at the gate of Leonora and walked across the paddocks to the homestead.

He was just in time for tea, and they made him welcome. He said to Jack Dorman, 'It is quite correct, what you have told me about Mr Pat Halloran and Charlie Zlinter. I have learned a great deal of my relative this morning.'

'What did you find out?' asked Jennifer.

He cocked an eye at her. 'I found out that he was a very bad man. I do not think that I can say all that he did with ladies in the room.'

Jane and Jennifer laughed. 'You can keep the juicy bits to tell Jack afterwards,' Jane said. 'Tell us the rest.'

Jennifer asked, 'What did he do for a living?'

'He was a bullock team driver,' said the Czech. 'He drove a wagon and a team from the railway at Banbury to the town at the Howqua River.'

'Is that what he did!' Jack Dorman exclaimed. The pieces of the puzzle were beginning to fall together now; a bullocky driver would have been well known in Banbury and his death would be remembered longer than if he were a transient miner. The verse that Pat Halloran had declaimed would not have been composed except for a man of some local reputation, good or bad. 'Did you find out anything else about him?'

Zlinter told them the story as they sat at tea. 'Mrs Williams,' Jane said thoughtfully. 'Old Mrs Joshua Williams, would that be? Used to live at Sharon, out past Jamieson?'

'I do not know,' he said. 'I did not hear the name of the station. Only that she married a man called Williams.'

'I think that must be the one.' She turned to Jack. 'You remember old Mrs Williams, the one who used to breed geese when we came here first. You remember – we got six goslings from her, and they all died but one, the first year we were here. Didn't her husband die, and she went to Woods Point?'

'I remember those bloody goslings,' Jack Dorman said emphatically. 'They were no good when we bought them, and she knew it. I'd have made a row and got my money back, but we were new here then and I didn't want to start off with a row.'

'She went to live at Woods Point, didn't she?'

'I don't remember. Easily find out.'

'I'm sure she was the one.'

They finished tea and washed the dishes, and went out on the veranda and sat down. Jack Dorman gave his guest a cigarette. 'Inquest's on Monday morning,' he said. 'You'll be there, I suppose?'

Carl Zlinter smiled, a little wryly. 'I shall be going with Mr Forrest,' he said. 'I think he will come back without me, because I shall be in prison.'

'That's not going to happen. The doctor's on your side, and it's what he says that counts.'

He shrugged his shoulders. 'I would not care a great deal if I went to prison,' he said, 'so long as it should stop at that. But in my state, if I should do a crime in this two years, I think they can send me back to Germany, into a camp. That would be very bad.'

Jennifer said, 'They'd never do that, Carl. It's not going to be like that at all.'

He shrugged his shoulders gloomily. 'It could happen.'

She laughed. 'They'd have to send me too, because I helped.'

He turned to her. 'Will you be at the inquest?'

'I'll be there. The police rang up this morning and said they wanted me.'

'It would be different for you, if this went badly,' he said. 'The worst that they could do for you would be to send you back to England, and that is your home. This place is now the home for me, and this is where I want to stay.'

'Nothing like that's going to happen,' Jack Dorman said shortly. 'They've got more sense.'

'I hope that that is true . . .'

It seemed to Jennifer that he was taking this very badly, but in his position that might be inevitable. She did not like to think of him brooding all the weekend over possible deportation back into the displaced persons' camps of Europe. 'You promised that you'd take me to see Charlie Zlinter's grave some time,' she said. 'I want to see the Howqua. What about tomorrow?'

He glanced at her, smiling; it seemed too good to be true. 'I would like to take you there, ver' much,' he said. 'But I think it is too far for you to walk.'

'Jack said he'd lend us the utility—the Chev. Could we go up tomorrow, Mr Dorman?'

'Sure,' he said. 'Sunday's the best day to take the Chev.' He turned to Zlinter. 'Say, can you drive a car?'

The Czech smiled. 'I can drive. Before the war I had a little car, an Opel, in my own country, and in the war I drove many cars and trucks. I have not driven in Australia, and I have not got a licence.'

'Ah, look—it don't matter about the licence, not up here. You can take the Chev tomorrow, if you want it.'

The dark man beamed, 'It is very, very kind. I will be ver' careful of it, Mr Dorman.'

'You won't be able to be careful of it, not up on that Howqua track. But it'll take you there all right, up on to the top, that is, by Jock McDougall's paddock. I wouldn't take it down the other side, not down into the Howqua valley—I was telling Jenny. But that cuts it down to a two-mile walk instead of ten.'

He said again, 'It is very, very kind . . .'

Presently he said, 'There is one other thing, Mrs Dorman. This morning, I visited a New Australian who can paint pictures, a man called Stan Shulkin. Do you know about him?'

'No?'

'I know about him,' said her husband. 'Chap who works on the railway.'

'That is the man. Have you seen his pictures?'

Jack Dorman shook his head. 'I remember someone saying in the pub one day there was a New Australian who can paint.'

Carl Zlinter turned to Jane. 'I think it might be interesting to you to go down to his small house and see what he can paint,' he said. 'I went there this morning. I think perhaps that he could make the sort of picture that you want.'

She laid her sewing down. 'I want a really good picture, Carl, done by a proper artist. I don't want anything done by an amateur. I want a good picture.'

'I do not know very much about pictures,' he replied. 'I saw some very fine oil paintings this morning that this man had done. I think that he could make a picture that you would enjoy.'

She wrinkled her forehead. 'Has he ever studied anywhere? I mean, it might be difficult if I went there and his pictures were too bad for what I want. You do see what I mean?'

'I understand,' he said. 'He has studied in Paris and in Rome; before the war he was Professor of Art Studies in the University of Kaunas. I think he is a very good artist.'

'But what's he doing here?'

'He works as a labourer upon the railway.'

She stared at him. 'Is that the only thing that he can find to do?'

He shrugged his shoulders. 'I do not know. He came to Australia three years ago, as a displaced person, and he was sent for his two years to work upon the railway, here in Banbury. He has stayed here since, and what else can he do? Here he has a house and easy work and a quiet life after the camps in Germany. He has tried to sell paintings a little, but not many people buy an oil painting in Banbury. I think he could paint a picture that is what you like.'

'Are his pictures pretty? Are the colours nice?'

'I saw a very beautiful picture of the Delatite River in the spring, all blue and golden, with the wattles. It looked like the river, and the colours were ver' beautiful.'

'That sounds the sort of thing,' she said. 'I'd better go and see him.' She laughed. 'It would be funny if I found the sort of picture that I want in Banbury, after searching all over Melbourne for it.'

Jennifer walked down to the road with Carl Zlinter when he went away. Jane watched them disappear across the paddocks. 'Are you going with them tomorrow?' she asked.

He grinned. 'Give 'em a break.'

'I don't know that it's a good thing,' she said. 'I don't know that her father and mother would be very pleased.'

'They shouldn't have let her come twelve thousand miles away from home by herself, then,' he said. 'Far as I remember, your father and mother weren't too pleased, either.'

'I rather like him,' she said, 'once you get used to the foreign way.'

'He's right,' he said.

As they were walking across the paddocks, Jennifer was saying, 'I don't think there's anything to be afraid of in this inquest, Carl. Honestly, I don't.'

'I do not think there is a need to be afraid,' he said, 'but I shall be happy when it is over.'

'They can't possibly make any trouble.'

He looked around him. The moon was coming up, and the bowl of the Delatite Valley was touched with a silvery light; it was very quiet. 'There is only one trouble that I would be afraid of,' he said quietly. 'That is to be sent away from this country and back to Europe.'

'Are you so fond of it as that, Carl?'

He was silent for a minute. 'Here is a beautiful, empty country,' he said, 'with freedom, and opportunity, and more than that, a King to whom every man may appeal if there is injustice. It is a great thing to have a King, a Leader, to prevent the politicians and the bureaucrats from growing stupid. The Germans had the same idea in seeking for a Führer, only they had the wrong man. The English have managed so much better. The Americans have also discovered great men for their Presidents, in some way that is difficult to understand.' He paused. 'I should be very unhappy if it happened that I had to leave this country,' he said.

'I think I should, too,' said Jennifer. 'I'm English of course, but this is very lovely. In many ways it's like what England must have been a hundred years ago.'

'From what part of England do you come?' he asked.

'From Leicester,' she said. 'That's where my home is. I worked just outside London for a time, before I came out here.'

'Leicester,' he said. 'I have heard the name, but I do not know where it is.'

'It's in the Midlands,' she told him. 'Right in the middle of England, a hundred miles or so from London.'

'What is it like there?' he asked. 'Is it beautiful?'

She shook her head. 'It's a manufacturing town,' she told him. 'One always likes the town that one was born in, I suppose, and I like Leicester well enough. But–no, I couldn't say it's beautiful. I think it's rather ugly.'

'And when you worked in London, what was that like? I have never been to London.'

'I worked outside, in one of the suburbs,' she said. 'I was in an office there. It wasn't very different from Leicester, really.'

'Why did you come to Australia?' he asked. 'Have you come here to live?'

'I'm not sure about that, Carl,' she said. 'I had a grandmother, who died and left me a little money. She didn't want me to save it; she wanted me to spend it in coming out here on a visit. I think she thought that if I came out here I'd want to stay, and that I'd have a happier life than if I lived in England. England's very different now from what it was when Granny was a girl, and she'd seen things decaying all her life. I think she had an idea that if I came out here I might be getting back into the England that she knew seventy years ago, when everything was prosperous and secure.'

'So . . .' he said. 'And how do you find it?'

'I've been here such a little time, it's hard to say. I really haven't seen anything–only a couple of days in Melbourne and this little bit of country here.'

'From what you have seen, what do you say?'

'It's a lovely country,' the girl said. 'Prosperous–yes, it's very prosperous. Secure–I suppose it is. Nobody seems to be afraid an atom bomb is going to land next door tomorrow, like we are in England.'

'No,' he said. 'All that seems very far away from here. Here we are very far from enemies, and a great distance between you and your enemy is still the best defence.' He turned to her. 'I cannot tell you how I love this country, for that reason perhaps best of all. Since I was a young man there has been this threat of war, or war itself, and death, and marching, and defeat, and camps of homeless people, and the threat of war again, and of more marching, of more death, of more parting from one's home–unending. Here in this place all that is put behind; here is a country where a man can build a home without the feeling that all will be useless and destroyed next year. Here is a country where a man can live a sane and proper life, even if it is only one little log hut in the middle of the woods for a home. I love this country for those things, because here one can gather a few toys around oneself, a fishing rod or two, some books, a little hut, a place to call one's own–and all is safe. If then a war must come in Europe, it may be my duty to go to fight again upon the side that Australia will be on, and that I do not mind, because after the war is over, if I live, I can come back to my little place here in Australia, my hut, my fishing rods, and my books, and all will be quite safe, and I can be at peace again.'

He turned to her. 'I am so sorry. I have spoken too much.'

'I'm glad you did,' she said. 'I wondered what made you so fond of this country. Now I think I understand a bit.'

'I think it is how all we homeless people feel,' he said. 'People who have lost their own country want more than anything to find a place where they can build a new home round themselves without the fear that they will ever lose it again.'

'What'll you do when your time at the camp is up?' she asked. 'Where will you make your home?'

'I do not know that,' he said. 'I think that it will be not very far from here.'
They came to the road gate. 'I have a strange idea in my head,' he said, 'but I
will not tell you now.'

'Oh, Carl! What is it?'

He laughed. 'Perhaps I will tell you tomorrow. Are you sure that it will be all
right if we go to the Howqua?'

'I'd love to, if you're free. I'm not doing anything.'

'I will come here for you at about ten o'clock.'

'I'll be ready, and I'll have the lunch packed.'

He made a stiff little bow. 'Till then. Goodnight, Miss Jennifer.'

'If we're going out tomorrow, Carl, cut out the Miss Jennifer. Everybody
calls me Jenny here.'

'All right. Good night, Jenny.'

'Good night, Carl.'

On Sunday mornings the Dorman family slept late, but Jennifer was up by
seven in the kitchen, with which she was now tolerably familiar. She was a fair
cook in an unpractised way, capable of interpreting and following a recipe with
a reasonable chance of an acceptable result. She made some pastry and cooked
half a dozen sausages and made sausage rolls in the oven, and having the oven
hot she made a few jam tarts. Surveying the results of her efforts, she came to
the conclusion that it looked a bit light for a lumberman; in the larder she found
cold mutton and some cold potatoes, and an onion, and so set to work again and
made a couple of enormous Cornish pasties. There were plenty of bananas and
grapes and passion fruit in the house so she took some of those, and then,
because the basket still looked empty, she cut a pile of honey sandwiches.

Jack Dorman came out in his dressing-gown and found her pondering. 'My
word,' he said. 'He's not going home hungry.'

She said anxiously, 'Do you think it's enough?'

'He won't starve if he gets outside that lot. What are you taking to drink?'

She smiled. 'I was wondering if you could let us have some beer.' Beer was in
short supply in that hot weather; the expanding population had beaten the
expanding beer output, as it had beaten the output of everything else in
Australia.

'I'll let you have two bottles,' he grumbled. 'I'm not going to give him any
more.'

'That's awfully sweet of you.' He fetched the bottles and put them on the
table.

'How's he getting down here from the camp?' he asked.

'He'll get a lift down, probably,' she said. 'He said he'd be here at ten
o'clock.'

'He may not find it easy on a Sunday morning,' he said. 'He'll have to start off
walking about nine or so. I'll take a run up the road in the Chev after breakfast
and pick him up, if you'll get breakfast for me before then. Jane's sleeping in.'

She glanced at the clock; it was about half-past eight. 'I'll have it on the table
in a quarter of an hour.'

Breakfast was a running meal that day; she fed Jack Dorman and then Tim
Archer and Mario, and finally Jane came out and sat down with a cup of tea. It
was still on the table when Jack Dorman came back with Carl Zlinter, whom he
had picked up on the road half a mile outside the camp.

'Morning, Carl,' said Jennifer. 'Have you had any breakfast?'

He said, 'Thank you, I have had some coffee.'

'Coffee? Is that all you've had?'

He smiled. 'In my country we do not eat a cooked breakfast.'

'But you eat a proper breakfast here, don't you, before going out in the woods?'

Jane said, laughing, 'Go on, Carl, sit down and let her cook you bacon and eggs. She wants to do it.'

He laughed with her. 'All right.'

'That's better,' said Jennifer, breaking a couple of eggs into the pan. 'I wouldn't like you to faint by the way, especially if you're driving me in the Chev.'

'He's been driving it this morning, down from the camp,' said Jack Dorman. 'You have to keep on telling him which side to drive on.'

Carl Zlinter laughed. 'It is the first time I have driven on the left side of the road, and with the steering so.'

In spite of that, he proved himself to be quite a reasonable driver when they started off in the utility half an hour later. It was still sunny and cloudless, with the promise of another hot day. Jennifer opened the last paddock gate on to the main road at Merrijig, let the Chev pass through, and closed it carefully behind. As she got back into the car she said, 'Did you bring your rod?'

He shook his head. 'I would not want to fish today. It would not be sociable.'

She laughed. 'I've never seen anybody fly-fishing. I'd like to know how it's done.'

'So?' he said. 'It is very delicate, and always one is learning something new. That is why I like it, because never do you come to the end of learning some new thing. Also, it makes you go to beautiful, deserted country, and that also I like. I will show you how to do it one day, if you like. But now, the water is too warm; the fish will not take a fly until the water grows more cold, in March.'

He drove across the bridge over the Delatite and on up the road towards the lumber camp, till after a mile or so he turned off into a paddock, and they drove on a rough track across pastures for a time, heading for the hills. Their passage stirred a great flight of white cockatoos from the trees; they wheeled above the car, brilliant against the deep blue sky before settling in the next paddock.

Presently the track left the pastures and entered the woods, and began to wind up-hill through a forest of gum trees. It was quiet in the dim aisles of the woods, and scented; fantastic parrots with brilliant red bodies and equally brilliant blue wings flew before them up the track and vanished in the glades. 'It's amazing, the colours,' the girl from London said quietly. 'Don't birds have to camouflage themselves in this country?'

He said, 'I do not think that there are any beasts of prey to worry them, such as leopards or wild cats. I do not think that birds or koala bears have many enemies in this country.'

She said, 'I never thought I'd see such lovely birds flying about wild . . .'

He smiled. 'There are many lovely things in this country that one would not see in any other place.'

The track wound up through the forest, utterly deserted. Once or twice a wallaby started at their approach and went bounding away among the trees, and once a red English fox with a great bushy tail crossed the track in front of them and vanished in the undergrowth, perhaps hunting the occasional rabbit that appeared, and looked at them, and scuttled away with flashing scut. And once Carl Zlinter said, 'You have seen a koala bear?'

'Never,' she said. 'They're little creatures, aren't they?'

He did not answer, but drove on for a few yards, stopped the car and got out quickly, and ran into the bush. He was in time to catch the koala under the armpits as it clambered unhurried up a tree to get away from him; he disengaged it gently and carried it to her on the track, a tubby little brown animal with tattered fur that struggled feebly but did not seem particularly distressed by capture.

'Oh, Carl!' she said, 'what a lovely little beast. He's just like a teddy bear.'

He did not understand the allusion. 'I think he is a very old bear, this,' he said. 'His fur is bad. You can stroke him if you like; he will not hurt you. But do not let him scratch you, because his claws will be dirty and poisonous, and a small wound may go bad.'

He held the bear from behind, gently controlling it while she stroked it. 'It's a wild one, isn't it?' she asked, puzzled.

'He is a wild bear,' he told her. 'He lives here in the forest.'

'But he seems so tame. He doesn't mind being handled or stroked a bit!'

'He has no enemies in the woods,' he said. 'No animal hunts koala bears to kill them, only men, and now that is forbidden, very strongly. Because he has no enemies, he has no fear.'

'What will happen if you let him go, Carl? Let him go, and see.'

He released the bear, and they crouched beside him; he looked from one to the other, looked around, then walked deliberately to a tree and began to climb up it, holding on with the great claws upon each foot. Jennifer walked after him and stroked him as he went till he was out of reach; he paid no attention to her. They stood watching him as he slowly made his way up the trunk above their heads.

'He is going up there for his dinner,' Carl said. 'He eats only the fresh shoots of the gum trees, and he needs several different sorts of gum tree for good health. That is why you cannot keep them in a cage as captives.'

'How did you get to know all that, Carl? Have you handled them before?'

'Many times,' he told her. 'In the woods, felling the timber, we come on them many times, sometimes one in each day, or more. It is forbidden to kill them, and they are so harmless nobody would kill them if he could help it. Sometimes as we fell the timber we find a tree with a bear in it, and that we leave, if possible, till the next day when he has gone away. Sometimes it is necessary to fell that tree with the bear in it, and usually he is only shaken and frightened a little, so then we pick him up and put him in a smaller tree, that we shall not fell, in a part where we have been to and we shall not come again. It is easy to handle them, but you must not let them scratch.'

They got back into the utility and went on up the track, winding around the contours of the hills between the trees; a rough, rutted track, more of a watercourse than a road. Presently they came out on top of the ridge; there was a cleared pasture here, or perhaps a natural clearing due to some geological formation that checked the growth of trees. Zlinter drove into it and stopped the car. 'This is Jock McDougall's paddock,' he said. 'Here we must leave the car and walk for the rest of the way, down to the Howqua.'

The paddock stood upon the summit of the ridge, with a wide view across the wooded, mountainous country to the south. In the brilliant sunlight line after line of blue hills stretched to the horizon, with here and there a thin wisp of smoke showing a fire. 'Oh, Carl,' she said, 'what a marvellous place. Are there farms and people living in this country?'

He shook his head. 'Here is nobody,' he said. 'Nobody at all.' He thought for a minute. 'There, where you see the smoke, there is a forest fire, a little one, and there there may be men trying to control it and to put it out. It could be also that somewhere in this country there would be another lumber camp, as at Lamirra, where there would be men. But, except those, there would only be the forest rangers; there would not be more than three or five people in the whole of the country that you see.'

She stared entranced. 'How far does it go?'

He shrugged his shoulders. 'The sun is behind us; we are looking to the south. Seventy or eighty miles, perhaps, the forest goes; not more. Then comes the coastal plain, I think, of farms and pastures that they call Gippsland, and then the sea.'

He stood looking over the wide, blue expanse of forest with her. 'This is another reason why I love this country,' he said quietly. 'It is a little like my own home, in Bohemia.'

She turned to him. 'Do you get homesick, Carl?'

He shook his head. 'Not now. I would not ever want to go back there to live. So much is changed, and I have changed so much myself, also. But I remember how it was at home when I was a schoolboy, and this is like the forests are at home a little, and so I am happy to be here.'

He glanced down at her. 'Do you have big forests such as this in England? You do not have them, do you?'

She shook her head. 'Not now. It might have been like this in England two hundred years ago, but it's not now. If this was England it would all be cut up into farms, with roads and filling-stations and villages and towns, and people everywhere. There's nothing like this at home.'

'Is it too big for you?' he asked. 'Does it frighten you?'

'It's strange,' she said. 'It's very, very lovely, but it's strange. If I lived here I should have to get to know what you do in a big forest, if you should be lost. Once I knew that, I don't think I'd be afraid of it.' She paused. 'It's not as if it was full of lions and tigers.'

He smiled, 'Only flies and mosquitoes, very many of those, and a few snakes. But you are right; in these forests there is nothing much to fear but your own ignorance.'

He turned back with her to the utility to take her basket, and she saw that he had put a flabby newspaper parcel on top of her basket of food, and that he had brought a grill with him. 'What's that?' she asked. 'Meat?'

He said, 'I brought some steaks with me, to make a fire and grill them in the way of this country. Have you done that? They are very good.'

She said, 'I've never done that, Carl. But we're going to have far too much food.'

He smiled. 'If there is too much, we can take it home, or give it to Billy Slim.'

'Can we make a fire in the forest, Carl, without setting everything alight, at this time of year?'

'It is necessary to be very careful,' he said. 'At the Howqua, by the river, there are stones built up to make a fireplace, and there Billy Slim allows a fire to be made. The fishermen cook steaks there sometimes; I have done that myself.'

He would not let her carry anything, and they set off down the track through the woods into the valley. As they went he told her Billy Slim's story of the match that had burned blue down in the open paddock in the valley, and the fire that jumped. 'I have not seen that in the two summers I have been here,' he said. 'One might work in the woods for fifty years, and never see that thing. Yet, I think that it is true.'

'That was the fire that burned the town that was here?' she asked.

He nodded. 'One of them. I will show you where the town was.'

Presently through the green aisles ahead of them, and below, they saw a turn of the river, and then another. They dropped down into the valley flat and came out on an open sward beside the river where no trees were growing, a meadow of perhaps five acres along the river bank. On the other side of the river, in among the trees, there was the iron roof of a weatherboard house. 'That is where Billy Slim lives,' he told her, 'the forest ranger.'

He put the basket and the grill down under a tree that stood alone in the meadow, not far from the river. 'This is where the town was,' he said.

She looked round, startled. 'Where? Here?'

'Here where we are standing, in this flat,' he said. 'There were many houses here fifty years ago, and in the trees up the hill, where we have come.'

There was absolutely nothing to distinguish the place from any other natural glade in the forest, no sign of any habitation but the forest ranger's house. 'It seems incredible that it has gone so completely,' she said, 'and so soon. How many houses were there here?'

He shrugged his shoulders. 'A hundred—perhaps more. There were three hotels.' He moved a little way from the tree. 'Can you see the line here, the rectangle? And here, another room, and here, these bricks? This was the Buller Arms Hotel, that Billy Slim's father kept. Here came the girls to serve as barmaids to the miners, the naughty girls, if that old Irishman was right.' He paused. 'Only fifty years ago, and now all is gone.'

She had great difficulty in believing it. She said, 'Carl, how have the trees recovered so quickly? These trees are very big, some of them. Have they all grown up since the last fire?'

'Fire does not kill the gum trees,' he told her. 'All other trees die in the forest fire, but not the eucalypts. After the fire when everything is burned to blackened stumps, you think the forest will be spoiled for ever. But next spring the gum trees shoot again, and in a very few years all is as it was before.' He turned and showed her blackened streaks upon the bark of the tree they stood under. 'You can see—this one has lived through the fire. Only the gum tree can live through the fire like that; all other trees are killed. I think that that is why these forests are all eucalypts.'

'Where is the cemetery?' she asked.

'It is a mile down the river, perhaps a mile and a half,' he said. 'There is a path that leads to it, but it is very overgrown. Also, it crosses the river three or four times, and it is necessary to walk through the water. Would you like for me to ask Billy Slim if he can lend a horse for you? It will be easier for you so.'

She laughed. 'I'd fall off a horse, Carl. I can't ride. How deep is the water that we've got to walk through?'

'I do not think it will be deeper than your knees.'

'Well, that's all right. I don't mind getting these shoes wet. It'll be rather nice to paddle on a day like this.' The sun blazed down upon them as they stood; it was unthinkable that wading in the river could be anything but pleasant.

They left the basket of food hung up on a branch of the tree, and started off along the meadow by the river, a clear trout stream running rippling over water-worn stones with alternate runs and pools. Presently the path led them down to the water, and was seen emerging from the river on the far side, among the bushes. 'Here is the ford,' Zlinter said. 'I will go first; I do not think it will be deep.'

He walked into the water and turned to look back at her; she followed him gingerly. The water was cool and refreshing about her ankles, plucking at her slacks; she stooped and rolled them up above the knee. Her blouse sagged open and he saw the soft curve of her breasts, because in that hot weather she had little on; he let his eyes rest for a moment in enjoyment, and then quickly averted them in case she should see him looking. She finished with her slacks and stood erect, and found him studiously looking up the river, betraying himself; she knew what he had seen and coloured slightly, but she did not mind; her own eyes had rested once or twice on his brown chest and arms with secret pleasure. She followed him across the river; as it grew deep she reached out and took his hand, and he guided her across. In the thicket on the other side, 'It would be better to put down your trousers now, or you will get your legs scratched,' and she did so, slightly turned away from him.

He went ahead of her on the narrow path, forcing the bushes aside where they grew thickly and holding them back for her to pass. The path wound along through the forest by the river, a narrow track used only by the forest ranger on his horse and by an occasional fisherman on foot. Presently they crossed the river again, and then a third time, and a fourth, as the path changed from side to side to avoid spurs and rocky outcrops.

It was very quiet in the forest. The sunlight fell in dappled patches on the undergrowth through the sparse foliage of the gum trees; an occasional parrot squawked and flew away ahead of them, but they saw no animals. They went on till they came to a red stone bluff on the north side of the river; the path wound round this, and Carl Zlinter stopped. 'It is somewhere here,' he said. 'There must have been a road here at one time, from the town, but there is nothing to see now. I think the stones are over there somewhere.'

Jennifer said, 'What's that—over there, by the white tree?'

'That is right. That is one of them.' He guided her through the undergrowth of bracken and tea tree scrub, and they came to the three stones that were still standing. He stooped beside the furthest one, and rubbed the surface of it. 'This is the one.'

She stooped beside him, and read the inscription. She had never doubted his story, but it was a satisfaction to her to see the carved letters with her own eyes. 'Charlie Zlinter and his dog,' she said quietly. 'It was nice of them to bury the dog with him.'

He looked at her and smiled. 'That old Irishman, he said the priest would not have allowed it, but he did not know.'

'Do you think he was a relation of yours, Carl?'

'Perhaps,' he said. 'I would like to think he was. I would like to think that someone of my family had been here before me, and had liked this place as I like it. I think he must have liked it here, because he had his cabin here somewhere, not in Banbury. You would think a bullock team driver who drove every day between this place and Banbury would have had his home in Banbury where there was a railway and more life, but it was not so. He had his home here.'

She looked up at him, smiling. 'Would you like to have a home here?'

He nodded soberly. 'I would like that very much. For many years I have now lived in camps, always with other men, and for at least another nine months I must still live so. I would like very much to have a little cabin in the woods by a trout river, like this one, where I could come and live at the week-end and keep some books and be alone a little. I would like that very much indeed.'

'You wouldn't be lonely?'

He shook his head. 'I have seen so much of other men, all the time, in all the camps.'

'You won't want a cabin in the woods in nine months' time,' she said. 'You'll be off somewhere qualifying to be a doctor.'

He shook his head. 'I do not think that I shall be a doctor again. It costs too much, and three years of study is too long. I do not think that I shall be a doctor.'

'What will you do when you leave the camp, then, Carl?'

He smiled. 'Perhaps I shall not leave the camp. Perhaps I shall go on as a lumberman.'

'That'ld be an awful waste,' she said. 'You ought to do something better than that.'

'It is a good life,' he replied. 'I like living in the woods, I like that very much. If I had a cabin on the Howqua here, as Charlie Zlinter had, that I could come to at the week-ends, I could be very happy as a lumberman.'

'Until the lumber camp moved on, and it was too far for you to come here for the week-ends,' she said.

'That is the danger,' he said. 'I have already thought about that. I think we shall be at Lamirra for another two years, but after that the camp may move.' He got to his feet and helped her up. 'I have shown you what we came to see,' he said. 'Charlie Zlinter and his dog, who fell into the water and got drowned. Only fifty years ago, and practically forgotten now. I wonder if anybody in Pilsen ever got to hear about it?'

'Somebody would have written, surely?'

'Perhaps. I do not know. Now, I have shown you what we came to see. Let us go back to the centre of the town, and I will take you to the restaurant, and we will see our steak cooked on the grill.'

She laughed with him. 'A silver grill.'

'No,' he said. 'In this place it would be a gold grill.'

They walked back by the way that they had come. At the meadow by the river he showed her the rough fireplace of a few stones heaped together, remote from any inflammable scrub. He gathered a few dry fallen branches from the gum trees and a handful of bark, and laid the fire and put a match to it; she was amazed to see how quickly and how easily a fire was made in that hot summer weather. He laid the grill across the stones, sprinkled the steaks with a little salt and laid them over the fire; in ten minutes from the time that the fire was lit they were ready to be eaten.

'It's awfully quick this way,' she said. 'And they're delicious.'

'It is the best way to cook meat,' he said, 'especially in this country. The fire is easily made, and the smoke of the gum tree adds a little to the flavour, also. We cook many steaks like this in the forest when we are at work.'

They ate in silence, sitting on the grass in the shade of the big tree where Billy

Slim's father had kept his hotel, where the naughty girls came to work as barmaids, where the bedrooms worked day and night and where small bags of waterworn gold once passed across the bar in payment for drinks and other recreations. In the tree above their heads a ringtailed possum peeped down at them shyly, wondering if these two intruders into his domain meant danger to his nest.

They lay smoking on the grass when they had finished eating. 'Carl,' the girl said at last. 'You promised last night that you'd tell me about your strange idea.'

He raised himself on one elbow, laughing, noting the soft curve of her neck with quiet delight. 'I have nearly told you that already.'

'What have you nearly told me?'

'That I want to build a cabin for myself, here in the Howqua valley.'

'I know that. But what's the strange idea?'

'You will say that it is sentimental.'

She raised herself and looked at him, wondering what was coming. 'Of course I shall, if it is. It may not be any the worse for that. What is it?'

He looked down at the grass. 'It was a stupid little fancy,' he said. 'It was nothing.'

'Tell me?'

He raised his head, laughing a little in embarrassment. 'It was just this. Here have been many houses, a hundred perhaps, and three hotels at least. I would like if I can to find where Charlie Zlinter had his house, and build mine there on the same place.'

She smiled. 'Why do you want to do that, Carl?'

'I do not know,' he said. 'I just want to do it. I think we are of the same family, and I have to build my cabin somewhere. I think that I would like to build it there.'

'I think that's rather nice, Carl.'

'You do not think it stupid?'

She shook her head. 'Not a bit. But how would you find out where Charlie Zlinter lived?'

'I would like to go and have a talk with Billy Slim presently,' he said. 'But I do not think that he will know, because he was not born at that time. I think it is more likely that I would learn something from Mary Nolan.'

She smiled. 'One of the naughty girls.'

He laughed with her. 'Yes, one of the naughty girls. But she will not be naughty now. She must be over seventy years old.'

'She's sort of sterilized.'

They laughed together. 'That is right.'

She rolled over and looked at him. 'She wouldn't talk about that time, would she?' She hesitated, trying to choose her words. 'I mean, Carl, if she was a naughty girl when she knew Charlie Zlinter, she wouldn't want to tell people about it when she's seventy years old.'

He stared at her, perplexed. 'I had not thought of that. You mean, she might know things about him, but she would not say, because of what they did when she was young?'

She nodded. 'I should think you'd have an awful job to get anything out of her. She'd have to know you very well before she'd talk, especially to a man.'

He lay staring over the rippling lights of the river running over stones towards a dark pool. 'It is not about personal things that I would ask her. Only about any papers that he might have had in his cabin, or about what happened to his papers and his property after he was dead.'

She smiled. 'If she hadn't been a naughty girl she couldn't know anything about the inside of his cabin,' she replied. 'She probably does know, quite a lot. She might tell another woman possibly, but she'd never tell you.'

He turned to her. 'Would you come with me to see her? Perhaps she might talk to you.'

She laughed. 'I meant another woman of her age, Carl. Not a young one like me. Not unless I was a naughty girl like she was. You'd want another woman of her age.'

'You are pretty and young, as she was when she knew Charlie Zlinter,' he said simply. 'I think she might talk to you when she would not talk to me.'

'I don't mind going to see her with you,' Jennifer said. It would mean another of these delightful days, if nothing else. 'It's just possible she might open up with me, but I don't think it's likely. What exactly is it that you want to know?'

'About any papers that would tell us who he was,' he replied. 'If there was a passport, or identity document, or letters, or photographs of home—anything that would say who he was. What happened to those things after he was dead. And where the cabin was.'

'She'd never be able to tell you that now,' she remarked. 'The place has changed so much. Billy Slim might be a better bet.'

'We will try him presently,' he said. 'We will go across the river and ask him. But will you come with me to see the old lady, one day soon?' If nothing else, it would mean another one of these lovely days with Jennifer.

'Of course I will, Carl. You mean, to Woods Point?'

He nodded. 'That is where she lives.'

'How would we get there?'

'Perhaps Jack Dorman would lend the utility again, if I pay for the petrol.'

'You'll need all your money to pay the fines if you go driving about the country without a licence.'

'I would not mind that, if I could find out the things I want her to tell me.'

She considered for a minute. 'We'd better go on Saturday,' she said. 'She's a Catholic, so Sunday might not be a very good day.'

He hesitated. 'You would not mind to do this for me?' he asked, a little shyly.

She turned to him. 'Of course not, Carl. I'd like to go and see her with you.'

They got up presently, and went to see Billy Slim. The bridge across the river to his homestead consisted of two steel cables slung across the river with planks lashed to them to form a footway; another two cables formed handrails with rabbit-wire sides from the hand-rails to the footway. Jennifer paused before going on to it, and turned to Carl. 'Do you think this is the same bridge?'

'Very likely,' he said. 'It is only fifty years.'

'I'll have to be careful not to do the same thing.'

'He was drunk, and it was dark, and he had a dog in his arms,' Zlinter said. 'It is a little different.'

'It was nice of him to carry the dog,' said Jennifer. 'He was probably rather a nice man.'

'Mary Nolan thought so.' She turned and saw a gleam of humour in his eye, and made a face at him.

They found Billy Slim asleep, that hot summer afternoon; there was a stir from the bedroom as they stepped on to the veranda, and presently he looked out at them, clad only in a pair of khaki shorts. 'Aw, look,' he said. 'I won't be more 'n a minute.' He came out presently with a shirt on. 'Just having a bit of shut-eye,' he said. 'I saw you, Splinter, earlier on today, going down the river somewhere.'

Zlinter said, 'This is Miss Jenny, who is staying with Jack Dorman.'

'This the young lady who helped you do those operations at Lamirra?'

'This is the one. How did you get to know about that?'

'Aw, everybody knows about that. I heard about it at the Jig.' To Jennifer he said, 'How do you do, Miss. I'll just put on the kettle for a pot of tea.' He busied himself with a Primus stove.

They sat down at his table. 'We have just been to see the gravestones at the cemetery,' Zlinter said. 'To see the one that has my name upon it.'

Slim paused, teapot in hand. 'I went and had a look at it myself the other day. Charlie Zlinter and his dog, just like you said.'

'I have found out a little more about Charlie Zlinter. He drove a bullock team.' He started in and told the forest ranger most of the information that he had collected from Pat Halloran, omitting the information that Mary Nolan was still alive. 'Now I would like to find out where he lived in Howqua,' he said at last.

Billy Slim set the cups before them and poured out the tea. 'You mean, where the hut he lived in was?'

'That is what I want to know.'

'You don't know the street or the number?'

The Czech said, 'I do not know anything but that he lived here, in the town of Howqua.'

The ranger sat down at the table with them and stirred his tea. 'I never saw the town myself,' he said. 'I come here first as just a little nipper some time in the first war, but that was some years after it was burnt through for the first time. The fire went through here in 1909—or was it 1910? I don't know—one or the other. There wasn't any town here when I saw the valley first, but there were a lot more stumps of brick chimneys, and iron roofing, and that sort of junk. When I come here, I picked up all the iron there was and used it as walls for sheds, with new iron on the roof; I had a stable built of it, before the second fire came through. The chimney stumps, well, they just went away in time. Fell down.'

'Were the houses in streets?' Carl Zlinter asked.

'Oh my word,' the forest ranger said, 'It was all laid out proper. Jubilee Parade ran round by the river from my dad's hotel by the big tree, and Victoria Avenue crossed it running up towards the path that you came down. Most of the houses were on one of those two streets, but there were several others, I know. I forget their names.'

Jennifer said, 'I suppose you don't know where Charlie Zlinter lived?'

The ranger shook his head. 'I don't. I don't think anyone could tell you that, not at this distance of time. What do you want to know that for?'

Carl Zlinter said, 'It was just a fancy. I would like to build a little hut here, a place where I could sleep when I come fishing and not always trouble you. A little place of one room where I could leave fishing rods and blankets, and perhaps a few tins of food. It is better when you live always in the camp to have a little place that is your own, to come away to sometimes.'

The forest ranger nodded. 'Sure,' he said, 'you could do that. You'd have to buy an allotment from the Lands Department.'

'What is that?'

'The Lands Department, in Melbourne, they own all the land, and they've got it all mapped out as town lots in the valley here. They sell these lots, see? like in any town you buy a vacant lot for a house. Well, if you've got a lot and you don't pay the rates, after a while you lose your allotment, and it goes back to the Lands Department, and they can sell it to someone else.' He paused. 'That's happened with every one of the township allotments here. They're all back with the Lands Department because everybody's gone away and stopped paying the rates, but the township's still mapped out that way, and if you want a bit of land you'll have to buy a town allotment.'

Jennifer asked, 'You mean, if you wanted to put up a hut down by the river you'd have to buy a town site?'

'That's right. You'd get so many yards frontage on the street, and so much depth.'

They laughed, and the girl said, 'No. 12, Jubilee Parade?'

'That's right.'

Carl Zlinter asked, 'How much would that cost?'

'Aw, look,' the forest ranger said, 'there's not a lot of competition for town sites in Howqua just at the moment. I wouldn't pay more than five quid for it, not unless you picked a corner site. They might make you pay ten quid for that, because of having frontage on both streets and being able to do more trade that way,' He grinned.

'How much would the rates be?'

The ranger scratched his head. 'I couldn't rightly say. The Council's been running on the cheap the last half century. They might make you pay five bob a year for the allotment.'

He could not tell them any more, and presently they left him to his lonely life and went back across the wire bridge to the meadow by the river. It was very still and quiet and beautiful in the valley; the sun was dropping towards the hill, and already the shadows were growing long. 'It's a lovely, lovely place,' the girl said. 'Whether you find out about Charlie Zlinter or not, Carl, it's a lovely place to build a little hut.'

'You like it so much, too?' he asked eagerly.

'I do,' she said. 'I think it's perfectly beautiful.'

They turned from the river and walked slowly up the track towards Jock McDougall's paddock and the utility. They talked as they went about Paris mostly; Jennifer had spent a fortnight's holiday in Paris in 1946, and Carl had spent several leaves in Paris in 1943 and 1944, so that though they had seen it under different circumstances it was a bond between them as a place that they both knew and had enjoyed. They came to the utility too soon, and stood for a time looking over the wide forest in the evening sunlight.

At last the girl said, 'It's been a wonderful day, Carl. Thank you so much for taking me.'

She held out her hand instinctively, as if she were saying good-bye, and it seemed better to say what they had to say here in the solitude and quiet of the forest than at the homestead, where there would be other people. He said, 'If I ask Jack Dorman to lend us this Chev again, will you come with me to Woods Point on Saturday?'

'Of course. I'd love to do that, Carl.'

'I will ask him when we get back.' He looked at her smiling. 'It will seem a very long time,' he said.

'Not so long as that,' she said. 'I shall see you tomorrow.'

'Tomorrow?'

She laughed up at him. 'At the inquest.'

'The inquest! I had forgotten all about it!'

'That's what I hoped you'd do,' she said, getting into the car. 'Don't start thinking about it now.'

They drove down the rough track through the woods not talking very much, but very conscious of each other. They came out in the end upon the main road to Lamirra, and then, too soon, they were at Leonora, opening each paddock gate as they passed through.

Jack Dorman met them in the yard, glancing critically at the Chev. 'Brought it home all in one piece?'

'I have not hit it against anything,' said Zlinter. 'It was very, very kind of you to lend it to us.'

Jennifer left him talking to Jack by the car, leading up to a suggestion that they should borrow it again on Saturday, and went into the house. She found Jane in the kitchen, ironing.

'There was a telegram for you from England, Jenny,' she said. 'It came over the telephone; I wrote it down.' She passed an old envelope with pencilled words written on the back across to the girl. 'Not too good news, I'm afraid.'

The girl took the paper from her. It read,

Think you should know Mummy very ill bronchitis and asthma sends you all her love with mine. Writing airmail.

DADDY

9

The telegram jerked Jennifer back into the hard, bleak winter of England, that in the heat and ease and beauty of the Australian summer she had almost forgotten. It was only about seven weeks since she had sailed from Tilbury, but in the short time that she had been in Australia she had become so steeped in the Australian scene that it was difficult for her to visualize the conditions of winter weather in England. With the shirt sticking to her back in the heat, it was difficult for her to think about the freezing fogs of Leicester, and all that they meant to her bronchial and asthmatic mother.

At Jane's suggestion she wrote her mother a telegram that they telephoned through to the post office, a telegram of sympathetic, conventional words of love. She felt as she drafted it that it was totally inadequate and for the first time she felt real regret that she had ventured so far from her home, but there was nothing to be done about that now, and no other words but the hackneyed ones to express what she would have liked to convey to her mother.

Jane said casually, 'Of course, you can telephone if you really want to. I believe it costs about two pounds a minute. They say it's very good.'

Jennifer had become so used already to the Australian way with money that she considered this seriously for a moment. 'I don't think so,' she said. 'She hasn't got the telephone in her bedroom, so she couldn't take the call herself. Unless I could speak to Mummy personally, I don't think it would be worth it.'

She sat down and wrote her a long air-mail letter instead, all about everything except Carl Zlinter and the Howqua valley.

She went into Banbury next morning with Jane and Jack Dorman in the Ford utility. The inquest was held in the police court next to the police station, a smallish room uncomfortably furnished with a jury box and a dock and a few wooden benches. The coroner was an elderly grazier, a Mr Herbert Richardson, who had been a Justice of the Peace in Banbury for many years and took the infrequent inquests that arose, as deputy coroner for the district. Jim Forrest was there with Carl Zlinter, and Dr Jennings, and a fair number of onlookers. Inquests did not happen very often in Banbury.

Mr Richardson was rather deaf and unaccustomed to an inquest; he needed a good deal of prompting by the police, but finally he opened the proceedings by inviting Sergeant Russell to tell the story of the death of Albert Hanson, which the police sergeant did with commendable detachment. The deceased, he said, had been the victim of an accident to a bulldozer in the bush above Lamirra; the manager of the Lamirra Timber Company was present in the court. The foot of the deceased had been amputated on the scene of the accident by a man called Zlinter, who was present. Mr Zlinter was not registered as a practitioner in Victoria. He was assisted in the operation by a Miss Morton, who was present, and who held no qualifications as a nurse. The man Hanson had died some hours later at the camp at Lamirra, and Dr Jennings, who was present, had seen the body shortly after death. The deceased was known to the police as an alcoholic. The circumstances leading up to the man's death appeared to the police to be irregular, but they had not yet made any charge.

On the suggestion of the police sergeant the coroner called Mr Forrest to give evidence; he took the oath and started in to tell the story, the coroner laboriously writing down his evidence in longhand. Presently he asked:

'So you authorized the man Zlinter to take off the foot of the deceased man, did you?'

'Too right,' said Mr Forrest. 'I couldn't do anything else. Zlinter said the foot would have to come off anyway, and I could see that for myself.'

'Did you know at the time that he had no medical licence to practise in Australia?'

'I knew that.'

'But you authorized him to do this operation?'

'Aw, look,' the manager said, 'what would you have done? We couldn't get a doctor, 'n we couldn't leave him there all night. If we'd tried to shift the sticks and bulldozer quick, we'd have dropped one on top of him, like as not. I reckoned I was lucky to have a doctor of any sort there, even if he was a crook one.'

The old man wrote all that down slowly. 'I see. And then when you got him to the camp, what happened then?'

The tale went on. 'And then some silly bastard went 'n give him a bottle of whisky,' the manager said at last. 'He got fighting drunk 'n it was all that we could do to keep him in the bed. My word. And then, after an hour or two of that, the doctor give him something, 'n soon after that he died.'

'When you say the doctor, you mean Mr Zlinter?'

'That's right. Mr Zlinter.'

'Who was in charge of this man when he got the whisky?'

There was an awkward pause. 'Well, we was all in charge of him, you might say. I'd got the doctor and the nurse there, 'n I was round about myself most of the night.'

'By the nurse, you mean Miss Morton?'

'That's right.'

The coroner whispered for a moment with the police sergeant. 'That will do, Mr Forrest, Call Miss . . .' He peered at a paper before him. 'Miss Jennifer Morton.'

Jennifer went to the witness stand and took the oath in a low voice. The coroner said, 'Are you a registered nurse?'

She shook her head, and said, 'No.'

'Eh, what's that? What did she say?'

Sergeant Russell said, 'She said, no, sir.' To Jennifer, 'You'll have to speak up a bit.'

The old man said, 'Were you in charge of the deceased man at the camp, before he died?'

She said, 'I–I don't think so.'

'But you were acting as a nurse?'

'Yes. I was helping Dr Zlinter.'

The coroner said testily, 'Will you please stop talking about Dr Zlinter. As I understand it, he is not a doctor at all.'

The girl flushed, and said nothing. There was a pause. At last the old man said, 'Were you supposed to be looking after this man before he died?'

'I don't think so, sir. I couldn't have been. I was helping Mr Zlinter in the next room with the other operation.'

'That was the head injury?'

'Yes. We must have been in that room for over two hours. It was in that time that he must have got the whisky.'

'And in that time you were not looking after him?'

'No, sir.'

The coroner whispered to Sergeant Russell, who shook his head. 'That will do, Miss Morton,' and Jennifer went back to her seat tired with the brief strain. The coroner said, 'Call Dr Jennings.'

The doctor took the oath. 'I understand that you examined this man shortly after death.'

'That's right.'

'What was the cause of death?'

The doctor said, 'Operational shock aggravated by an excessive amount of alcohol. I understand that the man drank a whole bottle of whisky.'

'Yes. You conducted a post-mortem?'

'I did.'

'Did you find whisky in the body?'

'I did. I found a very large amount.'

'In your opinion, if this man had not taken this unfortunate dose of whisky, would he have recovered from the operation?'

The doctor said carefully, 'I think he would have recovered. He had an enlarged liver, somewhat diseased; I have preserved a sample of that. That condition is usually due to habitual excessive drinking. Such a man would not be a good subject for an operation of any sort, and so it is a possibility that he might have died after the operation in any case. But the operation was skilfully and properly performed, and so I should say that he would have had a good chance of recovery–apart from the whisky.'

It took some time to write that down. 'The operation was properly done?'

'I examined the amputation at the post-mortem,' the doctor said. 'It was properly done, and I should have expected it to be successful.'

'I see.' The old man finished writing, thought for a minute, and then said, 'I understand that this man Zlinter did another operation on the same evening. Can you tell us anything about that one–how that is going on?'

Dr Jennings said, 'That was a much more difficult operation than the amputation. It involved the removal of a portion of the skull completely, and the lifting of two other pieces. Normally one would not like to tackle such an operation without full hospital facilities, but in this case it was done by Mr Zlinter in very difficult and improvised conditions, assisted by Miss Morton. That operation also seems to have been very well done, particularly well in the circumstances. The patient is now conscious, and likely to recover.'

There was a long pause while this was written down. 'I see. Am I to take it that these men received satisfactory medical attention, then?'

The doctor thought deeply for a minute. 'So far as the operations are concerned,' he said, 'I think they were well done. The after-care was not so satisfactory. It was probably impossible to remove the head injury to hospital until the ambulance became available. It would have been possible, perhaps, to take this man Hanson into hospital, and he wouldn't have got the whisky there. But that is being wise after the event, and I don't think one should blame Mr Zlinter for his decision to keep both men at the camp till I arrived with the ambulance.'

The coroner whispered again to Sergeant Russell. Then he said, 'Have you ever known the man Zlinter to do an operation before?'

'No sir. I have known him to do dressings and first-aid for minor injuries, which have sometimes come to me for treatment later on, at the hospital.'

'And you have been quite happy that he should do that sort of work up at Lamirra?'

'Yes, sir. I understand that he is qualified as a medical practitioner in his own country, but not in Australia. He is quite competent to do that sort of first-aid work.'

'Do you consider him competent to do the sort of operations that he did on this occasion, Dr Jennings?'

The doctor said carefully, 'As a general rule, sir, I should not regard him as competent to operate until he had complied with the regulations of the Medical Registration Board, which means that he should have to do a further period in a medical school here. In this particular emergency both these men would probably have died but for his care. That was the alternative. The operations that he performed should have saved both lives, but unfortunately one man has died through his own intemperance.' He paused. 'I should like to make it clear that I have quite a high opinion of Mr Zlinter's capabilities as a surgeon.'

The old man blinked at him. 'You have a high opinion of him?'

'Certainly, sir. If he were properly qualified in this country I should be glad to have him as a partner.'

A further bout of whispering with the police sergeant. 'That will do, Doctor, thank you. Call Mr Zlinter.'

Carl Zlinter stepped to the witness stand and took the oath. 'What is your nationality, Mr Zlinter?'

'I am a Czechoslovakian, sir.'

'And have you any medical qualifications?'

'I am a licentiate of the University of Pilsen and a Doctor of Medicine, sir.' He pulled some papers from the breast pocket of his coat. 'I have here my diploma.'

He passed it to the police sergeant and the coroner, who looked at it with interest, unable to read one single word. 'Very good.'

The coroner leaned back in his chair. 'You have heard all the evidence, Mr Zlinter,' he said. 'I think we have heard enough evidence now to determine the cause of this man's death, and I do not propose to ask you any questions. I have called you because I have some things to say to you.'

He paused, and went on slowly and deliberately, 'You have heard the evidence, and from the evidence it is fairly clear that in an emergency you performed two operations competently and well, one of which was a very serious and delicate operation. I have to thank you on behalf of the community, and at the same time I have to give you a warning. You are not licensed as a doctor in this State or in Australia at all, and if you should do any further operations, and if they should turn out badly, you would be open to a charge of manslaughter, because in this country you are not a doctor. I do not want to seem ungrateful to you, but that is the law. Before doing any further operations you must get yourself qualified, or you may find yourself in trouble. Do you understand that?'

Carl Zlinter said, 'Yes, sir. I have always understood that ver' well.'

'Well, you'd better get yourself qualified as soon as you are able to. Thank you, Mr Zlinter; you can stand down now.'

Carl Zlinter went back to his seat, and the coroner whispered again with the police sergeant. At last he raised his head, shuffled his papers, and said, 'This inquest has been called to ascertain the cause of the death of Albert Hanson. The evidence that we have heard shows that the man died of operational shock following upon an accident with a bulldozer, and that the operational shock was aggravated and intensified by a great quantity of alcohol which the man got hold of in some way that cannot be ascertained, and drank. I do not think the fact that the operation was performed by an unregistered surgeon had any particular bearing on the cause of death, but the fact that whisky was supplied to him after the operation was certainly a factor in his death. For this the management of the Lamirra Timber Company were responsible. I cannot close this inquest without expressing my opinion that some negligence occurred on the part of Mr Forrest in the aftercare of these men. It appears that no organization for the treatment of serious injuries exists at Lamirra. I think that there should be such an organization, a small hospital or dressing station where such injuries can be properly treated and isolated. If that had existed, the life of this man might have been saved. I find a verdict of accidental death, with a strong recommendation that the company should consider what I have said. I shall not be so lenient with them if this should happen again.'

He shuffled his papers together, rose from his seat and went out of the court; the people on the public benches began to stream out of the door. Jack Dorman unostentatiously got out early, and fell into step with Dr Jennings as he walked towards his car.

'All went off very well, Doctor,' he said.

The doctor nodded. 'I was sorry Jim Forrest got a rap, but I suppose somebody had to have it. I think there *was* some carelessness. Jim must have known the man was a boozer, and he might have thought some of his mates would try to slip him something.'

'Aye,' said the grazier, 'but I don't suppose Jim'll lose much sleep.'

'He should put up a dressing station of some sort.'

'Maybe he'll do that.' He hesitated. 'It was good of you to say what you did about Splinter,' he said. 'It could have gone crook for him.'

The doctor nodded. 'I know. He did a good job, as good as anybody could have done in the conditions. I thought it was only fair to make that clear.'

'When you said you'd be glad to have him as a partner,' Jack Dorman remarked, 'I suppose that was just a manner of speaking, for the police and old Bert Richardson?'

The doctor stopped and glanced at him. 'I don't know that I meant it to be taken very seriously,' he said. 'We could do with two more doctors in this district, but we're not likely to get them so long as any young chap just qualified can put his plate up in a suburb of the city and make a go of it. If Zlinter was qualified I wouldn't mind having him; he's probably quite a good doctor. However, he's not qualified, so there's an end of it.'

'He might be one day,' the grazier said.

'Are you thinking of financing him?'

Jack Dorman laughed. 'Not on your life. I was just wondering how you'd feel about it if he ever turned up in this district as a proper doctor.'

'I wouldn't mind a bit,' the doctor said. 'He certainly did those two operations very skilfully.'

Outside the court-house Jane Dorman stopped Carl Zlinter as he was about to get into the utility with Mr Forrest. 'Carl,' she said, 'what's the best way to get hold of this man Shulkin? What would be the best time to go and talk to him about pictures?'

'I think the week-end,' Zlinter said. 'In the week he will be working always, on the railway somewhere.'

Jim Forrest said, 'He won't be working today, Mrs Dorman.'

She turned to him. 'Why not?'

'The railwaymen are on strike.'

'Are they? What's it for this time?'

'It's a twenty-four-hour stoppage,' he said. 'The wharfies went to the Arbitration Court for another pound a week for something or other, and they didn't get it, so they've stopped work for a day to show their displeasure, and the railwaymen have done that too. Like what they call a Day of Mourning in India.'

'My word,' said Jane. 'Everybody's making too much money in this country, that's the trouble.'

'Too right,' said Mr Forrest.

'You think I'd find Shulkin at his home?'

'Unless he's in the pub. These twenty-four-hour stoppages, most of 'em spend the Day of Mourning in the pub.'

'I do not think that Shulkin will be in the pub,' said Zlinter. 'I think he is a serious man. I think that you will find him in his garden, or perhaps painting.'

Mr Shulkin was painting, but not in the style that Zlinter had visualized; Jane and Jennifer found him distempering a bedroom of the little weatherboard house beside the railway coach. He got down off a chair to greet them, brush in hand; a little girl about five years old, smothered in distemper and rather dirty, stared at them, finger in mouth. Jane said, 'Are you Mr Shulkin?'

He smiled. 'I am Stanislaus Shulkin.'

'Mr Zlinter was telling me that you paint pictures.'

He beamed at her, pulled forward the chair, and dusted it. 'Please–I am so sorry that you must find me like this. Carl Zlinter, he was telling me that there is–there is a lady who was wanting beautiful picture. So?'

Jane said, 'I do want a very, very nice oil painting, Mr Shulkin. The trouble is, I don't want just anything. I don't even know what I do want until I see it.'

He smiled. 'Also, you do not know if I can paint such a picture, that you will want.'

She laughed with him. 'That's right.'

'I can paint any kind of picture,' he said. 'Just like the carpenter, he can make any wood–a chair, a table, a bed, a cupboard. The good carpenter he can make all things, in all woods. So the good artist, he can paint all kinds of picture. But the good carpenter, he makes some things in some woods ver', ver' well, and the others, just like anyone could make. So the good artist. Some things I can do ver', ver' well, and others just as any artist, so-so.' He glanced at her. 'You understand me?'

'Perfectly.'

'So. Now we will go and I shall show you some pictures.'

He took Jennifer and Jane to the railway coach and showed them his pictures. For half an hour he pulled canvas after canvas out of untidy piles, set them up upon the easel, and described them. Of the ten or fifteen canvases displayed, Jane set aside three, all landscapes, one of them the Delatite river picture with the wattles that Zlinter had admired.

'These are something like it,' she said slowly, 'but not just what I want. I'm sure they're good enough in the technique, but they are not *my* picture. Do you understand what I mean?'

He nodded. 'I understand ver' well.'

She said slowly, 'Let me tell you something, Mr Shulkin. I grew up with pictures, and I never thought about them much. I was born in England and my people were well off, and there were lots of paintings in the house. I think some of them must have been very good, but I never thought about them at the time. It's only now that I'm getting old that I'm beginning to realize what a lot you miss by not having good paintings. When we couldn't have them because we hadn't enough money I never worried about them, or thought about them much. But now we've got a bit more, and I want a good picture almost more than anything.'

He nodded slowly. 'May I ask a little question, or two?'

'Of course.'

'What is it that you do?' he asked. 'What interests have you?'

'I don't do anything except the housework,' she said. 'It's a whole-time job upon a station. You can't get any help.'

'Are you interested more in flowers or in people?' he asked.

She smiled. 'Cold beef or Thursday.' She thought for a moment. 'I think, really, I like flowers more than people. They never disappoint you.'

'Do you like the high mountains and the rivers better, or the bright lights in shop windows in the coming darkness of a winter night?' he asked.

'I like the high mountains and the rivers better,' she said. 'I don't really like the city.'

He said surprisingly, 'This young lady, she is a relation of you?'

'Why, yes. This is Jennifer Morton, Mr Shulkin—she's a kind of niece. She's only just arrived from England.'

'So—she is English.' He moved round Jennifer and looked at her in profile, thoughtfully. 'Ver' interesting,' he said at last. 'Now one last question, Mrs Dorman. Do you like the picture that is full of colour or that is full of good drawing, with the colour more quiet?'

Jane thought for a long time. 'I think the picture that is full of good drawing,' she said. 'One gets such brilliant colours in this country all day long. Unless it was very unusual colour, it would be a repetition of what you see all the time, and I think one might get tired of that. I think I like the quiet colours with good drawing.'

'So,' he replied. 'Now I will say what I can do for you.' He looked at her, smiling. 'I like to paint,' he said, 'but I cannot now buy canvases and paints for pictures that nobody will buy. I would like to paint three pictures, of this size,' he raised a canvas, 'and show the three for you to choose which you like best. If you like one to buy it, you shall pay me seventy pounds for the cost of the canvases and the paints. That is all that I would need, the money that I shall have spent.'

'That sounds fair enough,' Jane said. 'But if I don't like any of the pictures, you'll have done a great deal of work for nothing.'

'I like to paint,' he said simply. 'I will have been able to paint three more pictures because you will have paid for the materials.' He paused. 'Also,' he said, 'the work is not alone for me. This young lady will require to work with me.'

'Me?' asked Jennifer.

'These pictures are to have quiet colour and good drawing,' he said equably. 'Your head also has quiet colour and good drawing. One of the pictures is to be a portrait of you, upon some landscape background of this place.'

There was a momentary silence. 'It's not a bad idea Jenny,' Jane said at last. 'You've got some lovely colours in your hair, if he could ever get them right.'

'I also have noticed those,' said Mr Shulkin. 'It will be ver' difficult, and I may not do well. But I would like to try the portrait for one picture.'

'I don't mind sitting,' said Jennifer. 'I've never done it before, though. How many times should I have to come?'

'Three times,' said Shulkin. 'If it was not possible in three sittings, then it would be impossible, and we should stop and do something different. But I think it will be possible.'

They arranged for Jennifer to come down to his cottage in the evenings after tea; he wanted her at the week-end, but she objected to that, having in mind her excursion to Woods Point with Carl Zlinter. She thought of offering to drive herself in to these sittings in Jane's little Morris; she had driven her father's car in England a little and she held an English licence. But she abandoned that idea; Jane was still proud and jealous of her little Morris, and would probably not have taken kindly to the idea, and the Chevrolet was bigger than anything that Jennifer had driven, and she was rather frightened of it. 'It won't be any trouble, driving in after tea, just three times,' Jane said. 'I should come into town more, anyway.'

The week was an uneasy one for Jennifer. Each day a letter from her father came by air mail; she knew that he must be very troubled to be writing every day. These letters had been written earlier than the cable that she had received, of course, and disclosed a crescendo of her mother's illness, worse with each letter. She got no more cables, which comforted her a little; she wrote to her mother and father every day, long cheerful letters about the Australian scene.

These troubles were half smothered by the beauty and the interest of her life at Merrijig. She went into Market one day with Jack Dorman and spent a couple of hours among the pens of sheep and pigs and cattle with the grazier and Tim Archer studying the form and characteristics and the prices of the beasts; they sold one of the homestead cows that had gone dry and bought another one, and she enjoyed every minute of it. She sat twice for Shulkin in the little railway coach, a couple of hours each time till it became too dark to work, while dumpy little Mrs Shulkin brought her cups of tea and little foreign macaroons and biscuits that she had made herself; conversation with Mrs Shulkin was difficult because she spoke practically no English. With the artist she got on very well.

Once she asked him, 'Are you glad you came to Australia, Mr Shulkin?'

He did not answer at once, being in the middle of a careful stroke. He finished it, stepped back from the canvas, and then said, 'You are just from England, no? Not Australian?'

'I'm not Australian,' she laughed. 'You can say what you like with me. I'm English.'

'So . . . the pose again, please, just for one minute. So . . .' He stepped up to the canvas, worked for a moment, and stepped back again. 'I think it was best to come to Australia from the camp in Germany,' he said. 'When I come first and I was told that my work would be on the railway, I was sad then that it had not been possible to go to the United States. But there also, I think perhaps my work would have been upon the railway, because there also they have their own teachers of fine arts. So, if it is to work upon the railway in Germany or America or Australia–' he stepped up to the easel again and began to work–'then I think Australia is good, because here is more opportunity for my children than even in America.'

He stepped back again and looked critically at his work. 'One little minute, and then you may relax. . . . Also,' he said, 'it is now three years that I have worked upon the railway, and it is not bad work. It is happier, I think, to live quietly in the country than to strain always with the mind, to teach art all day, and to think art all day, nothing, nothing, nothing but art. So, I think the mind will soon be sour, like bad milk.' He waved his hand towards the untidy stacks of canvases. 'I have here pictures that I painted before the war in Kaunas, that I took with me in the war to Germany, and so to the camps, and after here to Banbury, because I thought they were good pictures, ver' good, that would show me the great artist in Australia. But now, these pictures do not please me; they are strained, too much complicated, too much technique, too little to be said. You may rest now . . .'

He stepped back and looked critically at the picture. 'Too much art,' he said. 'Art all the day and night; I think my mind was sour. perhaps it is better to work on the railway for the living, and come to art for pleasure, not so often.' He stood with half-closed eyes staring at the portrait. 'This will be a good picture,' he said thoughtfully. 'This will be better than the paintings that I brought from Germany.'

In these sittings Jennifer could sit quietly with her own thoughts, and these were mostly on the Howqua valley and the memory of her day there with Carl Zlinter. The Howqua had a dream-like quality of unreality for her, a place so beautiful and so remote from anything she had encountered in her life before that it fell into the category of a fairy story in her mind, a fairy story with a Prince Charming, moreover. Her life up to that point had been in the somewhat bleak settings of Leicester and the London suburbs. These places were more real to her than Melbourne or Merrijig; she knew what to do with a red London bus, but it was still unreal to her that a horse should be used in this country as a normal means of locomotion. Stranger still was the story of Charlie Zlinter and his dog, whose tombstone she had felt and touched, who had driven his bullock team daily from this town named in the memory of Banbury near Oxford only fifty years ago, and who had drunk and loved in a town called Howqua that had vanished absolutely from the face of the earth, and had left only beauty in the place where it had been. This sort of thing didn't happen in Leicester or Blackheath, and as she sat quiet in the little railway coach, while the Lithuanian platelayer painted her portrait, she wondered which of her two lives was real and which was a dream.

Carl Zlinter rang up from Lamirra on Wednesday evening to ask Jack Dorman if he could borrow the utility on Saturday to go to Woods Point with Jenny. 'That'll be right,' the grazier said. 'She told us you wanted to go over there. Want to speak to her?'

When she came to the telephone she was in a slight flutter of eagerness to speak to him, which annoyed her slightly because the telephone was in the kitchen and everyone was there. She made the arrangements with him about lunch and time of starting with elaborate casualness that deceived nobody. Then he said, 'There is one other thing. I have now got a map of the town of Howqua.'

'Where on earth did you get that from, Carl?'

'It was in the Shire Hall, at Banbury,' he said. 'It belongs to the Lands Department. I went in there yesterday to see if perhaps there would be anything, and there I found this map. It is very yellow and torn, and they would not allow me to take it away, and so I went out and bought paper and I made a tracing of it.'

'Does it show where the houses were?'

'It shows all the streets and all the town allotments with their numbers,' he said. 'It does not tell us where Charlie Zlinter lived or anybody else, because there are numbers only on the map, street names and the numbers of the lots. It is ver' interesting.'

She said, 'Could you tell from it where any particular house was?'

'I think it would be possible,' he said. 'There are marks on it which a surveyor will understand, but I do not; these I have copied with great care. I will ask Mr Forrest before Saturday if he can tell me what they mean, and how to find the place where any house was from the map.'

'That's fine, Carl. I'm awfully glad.'

'What have you been doing all the week?'

'I've been sitting for my portrait–to Mr Shulkin.'

'For your portrait?'

'Yes. He's painting me. I'll tell you about it when we meet.'

'I shall want to see this portrait,' he said. 'I must visit Stanislaus.'

She laughed. 'You're not to till it's finished–if then. Good night, Carl.'

'Good night, Jenny. I will not promise anything.'

He came to the homestead on Saturday morning with his grill and his steaks in newspaper, having got a lift down from Lamirra on a truck. She was ready for him and the Chev was full of petrol; he made a half-hearted attempt to reckon with Jack Dorman, who said, 'Aw, forget it. It all goes on the farm, 'n comes off tax.' So they started for Woods Point before the day grew hot.

Jane watched the Chev go off across the paddocks to the road. 'Well, there they go again,' she said. 'I don't know what her father's going to say, or her mother.'

'From the looks of it, her mother won't be saying anything before so long,' he remarked.

'That's right,' she replied. 'It doesn't look too good, from the letters she's been getting.'

Neither of them had ever met Jennifer's mother, and they could discuss the matter dispassionately. 'What'll she do if she dies?' he asked.

'I think she might go back,' Jane said. 'She's very fond of her father, and he'd be alone.'

'She don't want to get too deep with this chap Zlinter, then.'

She stood silent for a minute. 'It's her business,' she said at last. 'She's got her head screwed on right. We can't interfere.'

As Jennifer got back into the Chev after closing the last gate, and as they started on the road for Banbury and Woods Point, Carl Zlinter said, 'Will you mind if I drive over the police sergeant when we go through Banbury?'

'Not specially,' said Jennifer. 'It might make trouble, though, because you haven't got a licence.'

'Does one need a licence to drive over police sergeants in this country?'

'My word,' she said. It was easy to fall into the idiom. 'You can go to prison if you do that without a licence. Why do you want to drive over the sergeant, anyway?'

'It was not necessary to have that inquest at all,' he said. 'He knew the answer before he started anything. It was stupid, and it caused me very much worry, so I could not sleep the night before.'

'There were a lot of things that could have stopped you sleeping the night before,' she observed. 'Too much steak, for one thing.'

'It was the inquest,' he asserted. 'I was ver' worried, for that they would send me back to Germany. I could not sleep. If we see that police sergeant we will not run over him, because I have not got a licence, but we will give him a very big fright. Now we will go and see Stanislaus Shulkin on our way to Woods Point and we will see what he has been up to.'

She turned to him, 'Carl, you're not to go and see that picture. It's not finished, and it's nothing like me, anyway.'

'So,' he said, 'If it is a bad picture of you then I will cut it with my knife so it cannot be finished. If it is good, then I will let him finish it and I will hang it in the house that I shall build in Howqua City.'

She burst into laughter. 'You *are* a fool. You can't have it; it's for Jane Dorman. He's painting three pictures for her to choose from.' She told him what was happening.

'All right,' he said. 'We will now go and see this picture, and decide what is to be done with it.' She could not move him from that, and she did not try very hard.

His mood was different from anything that she had known in him before. Hitherto she had known him as a surgeon faced with a difficult and delicate task in improvised conditions, and as a man with the threat of a manslaughter charge on his mind. She was now seeing a totally different Carl Zlinter, a man on his way out from years of life in camps, a man beginning to enjoy life who was unused to joy, a man laughing clumsily because he was unused to laughter. She did not know quite what to make of him.

Mr Shulkin was working in his garden; he stopped and came to the gate as the utility drew up. 'So,' he said, 'the model has arrived. You have come to make another sitting?'

'She has not,' said Carl Zlinter. 'She has come to ride in this utility with me to Woods Point. She has told me that you make a portrait of her, and I have come to see if it is good enough.'

Mr Shulkin said, 'I do not think that any portrait will be good enough when you have her with you. A portrait is for when you cannot see the sitter. But you may see if you want. It is not finished.'

He led the way into the railway coach and they followed him. The picture stood upon the easel. He had given more space to the background than is usual in modern portraits, using rather a wide canvas and placing the head to one side. For the background he had chosen a part of Leonora station, with the Delatite river, the paddocks, and the wooded slopes behind. He had made it a spring scene when the tips of the gum trees take a tinge of orange-red, so that the colour motif of the Leonora scene repeated the bronze lights in Jennifer's hair.

'It is not a portrait,' said Mr Shulkin, as they looked at it in silence. 'It is an order for a beautiful picture with quiet colour and good drawing, that the lady will like to live with. The portrait is nothing, nothing, only a detail of the whole picture–you understand? A bunch of flowers would have done as well, but they would not have had the fine drawing and the delicate colour of the head of this young lady.'

'It is a very lovely thing,' the Czech said quietly. The artist had painted Jennifer in profile with lips slightly parted and a faint colour in her cheeks as if a blush was just beginning; as he had said, the portrait was subordinate to the colour values of the picture as a whole, and so became the more impressive by a type of understatement.

'It's going to be a very lovely picture,' the girl said, 'but I don't believe I really look like that a bit.'

'I have seen you look like that,' the surgeon said. 'I have seen you look like that many times. It is very true of you.' The girl coloured a little, and looked very like the portrait.

Zlinter turned to the artist. 'You must do something else for Mrs Dorman,' she said. 'She has not seen this, no? I will buy this one.'

Mr Shulkin smiled broadly. 'That is not possible. I have three pictures that I must paint for Mrs Dorman, and she will choose the one that she will like the best. Already she has paid me for the materials for all the three, so this canvas is her canvas and this paint is her paint. If she will not choose this picture and she wishes to have one of the other two, or none at all, then I will sell you this picture if you can pay enough money. I am ver' expensive. I gain more than ten pounds each week on the railway; I am ver' expensive man.' He grinned.

Carl Zlinter said, 'You must now paint two more pictures, very, very good, much better than this one, so she will choose one of those. Perhaps you need not show her this one at all.'

Jennifer laughed. 'She knows all about it, Carl; I told her. You don't want it, anyway. What on earth would you do with it?'

'I would sell it to a manufacturer of soap,' he said, 'because it is so beautiful.' He paused. 'Or, I would hang it in the house that I am going to build in the Howqua. I do not know.'

'It would be better to sell it to the manufacturer of soap,' the artist said, 'because then you would have money to build the house. But I do not think that I shall sell it to you if that is what you are going to do with it.'

Jennifer said, 'What about me? Don't I have any say in this?'

Carl Zlinter said, 'You will get the soap.'

'What soap?'

'The soap that the manufacturer will give you so you will say it is the best soap in the world, and he can put it underneath the picture.'

'Don't sell it to him, Stan,' she said. 'I don't want it used as a soap advertisement.'

'I would not sell it to him in any case,' the artist replied. 'He is a bad man and not serious, only when he cuts off people's legs and they die. I do not know why you go out with him.'

They left him presently, and got going on the road to Jamieson and Woods Point. It ran through pastoral, station country to begin with, an undulating, well-watered country in a bowl of hills, the pastures becoming dried and brown in the hot sun. The road climbed slowly and became more wooded; presently they came upon a considerable river, a wide river running in a series of pools and shallows on a rocky bottom.

Carl Zlinter said, 'My word. I did not know that there was such a river here.'

He stopped the car by the roadside and they got out and looked at it; it ran completely deserted, winding through the woods and pastures, rippling in white foam at the little falls and rapids, with deep brown pools between. 'It must be full of fish, this river,' the Czech said.

'What is it, Carl? What's it's name?'

'I do not know. I think that it is perhaps the Goulburn. But I did not know the Goulburn was like this.'

The English girl asked, 'Can anybody go and fish there, Carl, or is the fishing preserved?'

He shook his head. 'It is all free fishing here. There must be very many fish in this river. I will come and fish here one day.'

'There doesn't seem to be anybody fishing,' the girl said.

'It is not like Europe, this,' he replied. 'Here, in this country, there are not very many people, and so not many fishermen. It is another reason why I am happy to be here.'

She turned to him. 'You're very fond of Australia, aren't you, Carl?'

'I have lived here fifteen months,' he said, 'and I have seen only this little corner of this big country. But now I should be sorry to live anywhere else.' He glanced at her. 'Are you happy to be here, and not in England?'

'I think so, Carl,' she said slowly. 'There are so many things, though. I've lived in towns most of my life–one does, in England–and all this is strange to me. I like it. I think I'd rather live here than in an English town.' She hesitated. 'One has so many ties with England, and it's so far away. I've been getting air-mail letters from my father all this week about my mother. She's very ill. I've been wishing I was back in England all this week.'

'I am so sorry,' he said. 'What is it that is the matter with her?'

She told him all about it, standing there with him above the Goulburn river; it was a relief to be able to tell somebody everything she thought. 'They've been a very self-contained pair, my father and mother,' she said. 'I had two brothers, but they were both killed in the war, one in a corvette and one in Bomber Command. Daddy and Mummy had so many interests that they shared, I was always a bit out of it after the war. That's why I didn't mind going away from home to work in London, and why it didn't seem too bad to come out here. But now I wish I was back. I don't know who'll be running the house for Daddy, or how he can be getting on. If Mummy were to die, I think I'd have to go back. I don't know what Daddy would do, all on his own.'

'It would be very sad for me, if you went back,' he said quietly.

'It would be very sad for me, too,' she replied. 'I'd rather stay here.' She turned to the car. 'Perhaps it won't happen. The winter will be getting on now, back in England, and that'll make it better for Mummy.'

They drove on through a tiny village and crossed the river, and went on for ten miles or so through the woods along the valley by the river. The sun was hot and the trees made dappled overhung patches of shade upon the road, and the same brilliant parrots with crimson bodies and blue wings flew in the woods ahead of them. They were delighted with the day and with the old car and with each other; twice they stopped to walk down to the river and look at its desolate grandeur, and they hardly stopped talking all the time. They laughed a great deal about silly little things that were not really funny, but they wanted to laugh.

They passed Gaffney's Creek and a small gold mine shut down for the week-end, the first that Jennifer had ever seen. From there the road wound upwards through the woods, till they came out at the summit of a col, the road going down into another valley ahead of them.

'This is Frenchman's Gap, I think,' said Carl. 'Woods Point will be about five miles further on. Shall we have our lunch here, with the gold grill?'

She laughed again at the little joke. 'It's very lovely here.' She got out of the car and looked around. 'Can we do a grill here, Carl, without setting the whole country grilling too?'

'There is here a fireplace,' he said, and he showed her the blackened stones. 'I think it will be safe if we shall make it here.'

He set to work to grill the steaks while Jennifer laid out the rest of the meal on a clean cloth upon the grass in the shade of a gum tree. 'Carl,' she said, 'tell me a bit more about Mary Nolan. Was she Irish?'

'I think perhaps she was,' he said. 'There were very many Irish people in this country at that time.'

She paused, considering her words. 'Did she have a job in Howqua, or how did she come to be there? I mean, a job apart from being a naughty girl?'

He laughed and she laughed with him. 'I do not know if she had another job,' he said. 'I have thought perhaps that she came to Howqua as a barmaid in the hotel, or perhaps she was to help one of the women with the children. I do not know, and I do not know how she happened to be living on the other side of the river. Perhaps she will tell us today.'

'Perhaps she won't,' the girl said. 'I think we're going to have a job to get anything out of her at all.'

They cooked the steaks and ate them hot from the grill, sitting on the warm grass in the shade of the trees, looking out over the blue, misty lines of hills. 'It's so different here to anything I've ever known, Carl,' she said once. 'People with so much money that they don't have to worry, who can afford to be generous if they want to, and all made honestly in farming. In this lovely, empty place. I've always lived where people were hard up, even good, clever people. It's all so different here to England.'

He nodded. 'I know. I feel like that also. I live in a camp and I must live so for nine months more, but sometimes I wake up early in the morning, and I look around, and I think of all the fine things in this country that I can do in nine months, the things that I could never do in Europe.' He looked at her a little shyly. 'I have a calendar upon the wall,' he said, 'and each day when I get up out of bed I cross off one day with a pencil, the day that has gone.'

Her eyes moistened a little. 'Oh, Carl! Do you do that?'

He nodded. 'It is a stupid thing, but that is what I do. In nine months now I shall be out of the camp life, out of it for ever, a free man.'

'When were you a free man last, Carl?' she asked. 'When did you last live a normal life, with a home?'

'In 1938,' he said. 'I lived then at my father's house, just after I became a doctor. Then came the Germans, and I joined the army.'

'It's a terribly long time,' she said softly. And then she looked up at him, and smiled, and said, 'Were you ever married?'

He smiled back at her. 'No,' he said. 'I was never married. I was spared that complication.'

She said quietly, 'You must have been very lonely, all those years.'

'I do not think so, not in the war years,' he said. 'So much was happening, so much of grief and work and pain, I think that one had no time to be lonely. After the war, in the camps, in Germany,' he shrugged his shoulders, 'perhaps one had got out of the habit of being lonely. Perhaps in Germany, where life was very hard, there was so little happiness in married life that one did not want it. I do not know. It is only in the last year, since I came here to Australia and I have seen men living happily with wives and with their children, and with no war in the country—it is only since the last year I have been a little lonely in the evenings sometimes.'

She said, 'So then you go out and catch a fish.'

He laughed. 'Yes, then I go out and catch a fish.' He got to his feet and began to put the remains of their lunch together. 'Now we must go down to Woods Point and catch Mary Nolan.'

They got back into the utility and ran down the long road into the valley before them. Woods Point proved to be a little town of wooden houses at the bottom of a valley, rather a straggling little town that had been wiped out from time to time with forest fires and so was built of fairly modern houses; these houses stood about amongst the trees around two working gold mines. There was not very much of it, a hotel, a bakery, a store or two strung haphazard along the main street; there seemed to be no reason why anyone should live there but for the gold mines.

Carl Zlinter stopped the Chev at the hotel and went in to ask where old Mrs Williams lived. He came our presently and got back into the car. 'It is just a little way,' he said. 'We must turn round.'

Jennifer said, 'You've had a beer.'

'I have found where Mary Nolan, Mrs Williams lives,' he said. 'It is not right for you to say such things.'

'It's not fair,' she said.

'It is a part of the woman's burden in this country,' he remarked, 'that they are not allowed in the bar.'

They left the utility by the roadside three hundred yards back and walked down a grassy lane, asked at a house, and were directed to the right one. A middle-aged, sandy-haired woman came to the door. Carl Zlinter asked, 'Does Mrs Williams live here, please?'

She looked at him with interest at his accent. 'That's right,' she said. 'Auntie lives here with us.'

'Would it be possible if we should have a talk with her a little?' he asked. 'My name is Carl Zlinter, and this is Miss Morton.'

To Jennifer the woman said, 'How d'you do? I'm Elsie Stevens—Mrs Stevens. What d'you want to talk to Auntie about? She's pretty old, you know, and she don't have to do much talking to get tired.'

Jennifer said, 'We've come over from Leonora station, out past Banbury. Mr Zlinter works in the timber at Lamirra. He's trying to find out about a relation of his who was in the Howqua in the old days.'

'Leonora?' The woman wrinkled her brows. 'Would that be Jack Dorman's place?'

'That's right.'

'Oh, I know,' With contact established she became more friendly. 'Did you say it was about the old days in the Howqua?'

'That's right,' the Czech said. 'There was a man there of the same name as me, who died and was drowned and buried there; I have seen the stone at the grave with his name carved upon it. It is the same name as my own, Charlie Zlinter. I was told that your aunt was living in the Howqua at that time, and I have thought that she could tell me about him, who he was and where he lived.'

The woman stood in silence for a minute. 'Well, I don't know, I'm sure,' she said at last. 'Auntie was in the Howqua for a bit before she came here, but she wouldn't remember anything about that now.'

Jennifer said, 'Could we have a talk with her, do you think? Just for a few minutes? We don't want to tire her.'

The woman said slowly, 'Well, I don't mind asking her. What did you say the name was?'

'Charlie Zlinter.'

The woman stood staring at him for a moment, while the elusive memory of a local jingle scattered through her mind. 'I've heard that name before . . . ' She paused. 'Some rhyme about a dog?'

'That's right,' said Jennifer.

Charlie Zlinter and his heeler hound
Fell into the Howqua and unhappily drowned . . .

'That's right,' the woman said. 'We used to say that when we was children, at the Sunday school. Just wait here a minute, and I'll ask Auntie.' She turned to Zlinter. 'Did you say your name was Charlie Zlinter?'

'That's right.'

'Like in the rhyme?'

'That's right. I am called Charlie Zlinter.'

'Well, isn't that funny? Just wait here a minute, and I'll tell Auntie.'

She went indoors, and they stood in the lane, waiting. Presently she came out again to them. 'Auntie wants to see you,' she said. She hesitated. 'You mustn't mind her if she talks a bit queer. And I wouldn't stay very long.'

They went into the living-room of the house. A very old woman was sitting in a chair before the fireplace with a shawl round her shoulders; she wore rather shabby black clothes. Her features were lean and long, and she was wearing steel-rimmed spectacles; her white hair was parted in the middle and done in a bun behind her head; there was still plenty of it. Her niece said to her, 'These are the people come to see you, Auntie. This is Charlie Zlinter.'

The old woman raised her head and looked at them. 'He is not,' she said, and there was still a touch of the Irish in her voice. 'He's nothing like Charlie Zlinter.'

The Czech said, 'My name, it is Charlie Zlinter like the man who lived in the Howqua and was drowned there, with his dog.' She turned towards him, and fixed him with her eyes. 'I do not know if he was a relation of me or not.'

She said, 'You talk like him. Where do you come from, the same place as he did?'

'That is right,' he said. 'I come from the same town in Bohemia.'

'Who's this?' she asked, indicating Jennifer. 'Your wife?'

'No,' he said. 'Just a friend.'

She snorted a little, as if in disbelief. 'I wouldn't know anything about Charlie Zlinter, no more than any of the other men,' she said. 'He got drowned. That's all I know.'

Carl Zlinter said, 'I am trying to find out if he left any papers or books, or any letters from his family in Pilsen, or anything to tell us who he was. I think you are the only person in this district who was living in the Howqua at that time, and I have wondered if you could tell us anything, if you remember.'

The old woman said testily, 'I knew nothing about that man, or any other of those men. Why should I know anything about his papers? There was a man there with that name; that's all I know about it.'

'Do you remember what happened after he was drowned, perhaps?' the Czech asked. 'Do you remember what happened to the things that were in his house? Who took them?'

The old woman made a gesture of irritation. 'Sure, how would I be knowing that, after all these years?' she said. 'There was many a man went away or died or was away out of it for one reason or another, and there was no keeping track of them all, if a body had wanted to. If a body had wanted to,' she repeated.

Carl Zlinter asked, 'Can you remember where he lived? Would you know where he had his house?'

'I tell you, I know nothing about the man at all,' the old woman said angrily. 'He was drunk and he got drowned, that's all I know. How would I be knowing where he lived, or what happened to his gear? I was a decent girl.' She stared at them fiercely.

'There, Auntie, there,' said her niece. 'He didn't mean nothing. He just wants to know if you remember anything about this man.'

The old woman sank back into her chair. 'I don't know nothing about Charlie Zlinter,' she said sullenly.

There was an awkward silence. Jennifer looked up at Carl Zlinter and he nodded slightly; it was developing as they had thought. He said, 'I am so sorry—when I heard that you had been in Howqua at that time I thought perhaps you might remember something.' He moved towards the door. 'I have now to take my utility to the garage before we start back; we have burst a tyre. May I leave Miss Morton here for half an hour till I have had that repaired?'

Mrs Stevens said, 'Oh, that'll be right. I was just going to give Auntie a cup of tea. You'll have a cup of tea with us while you're waiting, Miss?'

'Jenny's the name,' the girl said. 'I'd love a cup. Can I do anything?' Carl Zlinter slid out of the door behind her.

'Oh, it's nothing.' She bent to the old woman. 'You'd like a cup of tea, Auntie?' she asked, rather loudly. 'Jenny's going to have a cup of tea with us—I'm just going to put the kettle on.'

'I could drink a cup of tea,' the old lady said. Her niece disappeared into the next room, and Jennifer squatted down on a stool before her. 'I went over to the Howqua last week,' she said. 'There's nothing left there now, only the gum trees.'

'You went into the Howqua?'

The girl nodded. 'We drove the utility up to the top of the ridge, and then walked the last two miles down into the valley.'

'Eh, you'd never drive down that track in a motor-car. I heard of one man tried it once, but they had to get a team to pull him out again. Bullocks they used to use when I was there, eight bullocks to a wagon, in and out of Banbury. That was before the days of motor-cars.' She peered about her. 'What's happened to that man who was here just now, the foreigner?'

'He's gone to take the car to the garage,' Jennifer said. 'We had a flat tyre coming here; we had to change the wheel. He's gone to get it mended before we start back.'

There was a long silence. The old woman sat staring at the paper flowers in the fireplace, in red and silver tinsel. 'What did he say his name was?'

'Charlie Zlinter,' the girl said. 'It's just a coincidence, I think; he's got the same name as a man who used to work in the Howqua.'

The old woman shook her head. 'He never worked in the Howqua. He was a bullocky; used to drive a bullock team between Banbury and the Howqua.' She paused for a while. 'He talked like this fellow. Foreign, he was.'

There was another long silence; from the next room Jennifer could hear the rattling of cups. 'You're a pretty girl,' the old woman said at last. 'Too pretty for the likes of him.. Not getting up to any mischief with him, are you?'

The girl said, 'No,' and smiled, colouring a little.

'Well, mind you don't. Don't you let him do nothing till he's married you. These bullock drivers, and the miners too, they'll say anything, and then in the end you find they're married already with a wife and three children out behind some place, and you to have a fourth.'

Mrs Stevens came back with the tea and saved Jennifer from the necessity of answering that one. When the old lady was sipping her cup the girl brought her gently back to the subject by asking, 'Did the Charlie Zlinter that you knew look like this one?'

'Ah, Charlie Zlinter was fine, upstanding man,' she replied, 'twice the man of this one. He was a great strong man with black curly hair, strong enough to break the neck of an ox, and he with his bare hands alone. Broader in the shoulders he was, than this man of yours, and a champion at anything that he'd be setting his hand to. A grand, powerful man.' She sat sipping her tea and staring at the tinsel flowers, lost in memories. 'There was a slab of stone before the fireplace in his cabin,' she said, 'the way the ashes would be kept back in the fire. A slab as big as that . . . four hundredweight, he said it weighed. I've seen him lift that slab with his two hands, and carry it away. Sure, there wasn't a man in Howqua could have done the like of that. Anvils, barrels of beer, loads no two men could carry, he'd just lift them down from off the wagon to where they had to be, and he whistling a tune and thinking nothing of it.'

'It must have been a terrible loss when he got drowned,' the girl said.

'Ah,' said the old woman, 'it was a sad, sad day, and Howqua was never the same after. The mine closed down, and folks began to drift away, because with the mine shut and the gold finished there was nothing left to stay for. By the time I went out there was every other cabin in the place empty, and folks just walking in and out picking over stuff that had been left behind for that it wasn't worth the charge to take it out to Banbury upon the wagons. It's a sad, desolate thing to see houses left that way, and nobody to live in them. I did hear that the whole of Howqua came to be like that, with nobody to walk along the streets but wallabies and rabbits. That was before the fire came through the valley.'

'Which cabin did Charlie Zlinter live in?' the girl asked.

'No. 15, Buller Street,' the old woman said. 'It was just the one room with a fireplace and a bed, and a bench where he'd sit working at the bullock harness, sewing with a palm upon his hand like a sailor. He was a sailor one time, so he told me; that's how he came to be in Australia. He jumped his ship, and came up to the gold-fields, but he found that he could make more money with the wagon.'

'Did he make much money?'

'My word, the bullockies made money,' the old woman said, 'more than the miners or prospectors ever did. Everything that came to Howqua had to pass through their hands, and they charged terrible for bringing it. But they were generous as well, ah, Charlie Zlinter was an open-handed man, a kind, generous man. Many's the thing he used to bring me from the town—a new saucepan from England, or an alarm clock from America, or maybe a length of dress material if it was Christmas—anything he'd see that would take his fancy he'd bring out of town for me, as a surprise, for that I'd never be thinking. Ah, he was a grand kind man.'

'You must have been great friends,' the girl said.

'Better than we should have been, maybe,' Mary Nolan said quietly. 'But there, it didn't seem to be no harm at the time, and now it's a long while ago.'

There was a silence after she said that. Jennifer sat at her feet hoping that Carl Zlinter wouldn't come back and break the spell; she felt now that she could ask this old woman anything. She said presently, 'Did anybody live in Charlie Zlinter's cabin after he died?'

The old head shook. 'There was people leaving Howqua every day from that time on. Nobody lived in it before I left. There were houses to spare, the way you'd see doors open all along the street.'

'You're sure of that, are you—that no one lived in it?'

'Nobody lived in it before I went,' she said. 'I would have known about it if they had.'

'What happened to all his things? I mean, what *did* happen in the Howqua when a man died like that? Did the police take them?'

Mary Nolan set her cup down. 'There was a policeman, Mike Lynch was his name, from County Kerry; he lodged about the middle of Jubilee Parade, but I'm not sure if he was there. I don't think there was anything in the cabin to trouble with. Early in the morning, the day that he was found in the river, I went to his cabin in Buller Street, because he was back from Banbury. I knew that because I heard him in the dark night singing outside the hotel that Peter Slim kept, and I knew that he was having drink taken. And I thought maybe he'd have fallen asleep in his clothes or done himself an injury in the cabin, and so I went out and went to his cabin on the far side of the water before it was light, the way the neighbours wouldn't see me go. I had done that before sometimes, and cleaned him up and made him breakfast, and taken his clothes home to wash, very early in the morning, so nobody would know. But Glory be to God, the man was dead already and I crossed the bridge that he had fallen from, and never knew.'

Jennifer said, 'Did he leave any papers or books in the cabin, Mrs Williams? Can you remember anything like that?'

'Never a book,' she said. 'There wouldn't have been many books in Howqua at that time. Charlie was no scholar, but he could read labels and that—not the longer words. He did have papers of some sort with him, although he never showed me. He kept them all locked up in a tin box he called his ditty box, not very big.'

The girl asked, 'What happened to the box after he was dead? Can you remember that?'

'It wasn't there,' said Mary Nolan. 'I remember looking for it special when I found he wasn't in the cabin, and his door left open, because I knew he set store by it. Sometimes it stood on a little kind of ledge he'd made in the earth chimney, and other times it wouldn't be there at all. So when I went into the cabin I looked, but the box was away out of it, and then I looked around a little but I didn't see it. I didn't give much heed to it, because it wasn't always there. I wouldn't know what happened to that at all.'

'Could he have left it in Banbury?'

'He might. I wouldn't know at all. It could be that he had it with him when he fell into the river.'

'He had the dog in his arms,' said Jennifer. 'He wouldn't have gone to cross the river with the dog *and* the box too, would he?'

'He was a wild, reckless boy when he had drink taken,' Mary Nolan said. 'But there, he had a way with him and a body could deny him nothing. I would not say anything of what he might have done when he had drink taken.'

'What would have happened to the rest of his things?' the girl asked. 'Who looked after those?'

'Sure, and there wasn't very much,' the old lady said. 'He was buried in his Sunday suit, they told me. I never went near, because there had been tongues wagging in the Howqua about him and me, and I knew that if any of the women spoke against me I would have flown out at them, and that I would not do at Charlie's burying. So I stayed in my own cabin all the while, but they told me he was buried in his Sunday clothes. There would have been some working clothes, maybe, but nothing of value, and his wagon and the bullocks. There was a Scots boy worked for him, Jock Robertson; I think he took the wagon and the team. When the working clothes and the harness were gone from the cabin there wouldn't have been much left, and what there was nobody would want, for all the folks were starting to leave about that time.' She stared at the tinsel flowers in the grate. 'I looked into the cabin once, and the bedclothes were still upon the bed, but a possum or a rat had nested there, and the bucket still half full of water, and a loaf of bread still in the cupboard, all gone green with mould.' She shivered a little, and drew the shawl more closely round her. 'It's not good to go back afterwards to places where there has been happiness,' she said. 'It tears at your heart. I never went back again, and soon after that I left the Howqua myself. I'd say the cabin stayed like that until the fire came through.'

The girl took one of the old hands and held it in her own. 'You must have loved him very much,' she said.

'Whisht,' said the old woman, 'there's a word that you must never use until there's marrying between you, and Charlie Zlinter was a married man already in his own country. He was a kind, gracious man and I looked after him when he would let me; that's all there was between us, child. This foreigner that brought you here today and has the same name, is he a married man?'

'No,' said Jennifer. 'I asked him that.'

'Maybe you'll be luckier than I was,' Mary Nolan said. 'Maybe he's telling you the truth of it. The other Charlie Zlinter never told me any lies.'

They sat in silence for a time. The old woman was tiring, and it was evidently nearly time to go. 'One last question,' Jennifer said. 'Did Charlie Zlinter ever tell you anything about his wife—the wife he had in his own country?'

Mary Nolan shook her head. 'He wouldn't be after telling me the like of that.'

The girl stayed ten minutes longer for politeness; then she said that she would have to go and see how Zlinter was getting on with the car, or they would be late in getting home. She said good-bye to the old woman; Elsie Stevens stepped outside the door with her.

'She had a nice talk with you,' she said. 'I haven't seen her so bright for a long time.'

'I hope I haven't made her too tired,' the girl said.

'Oh, no. I think it does old people good to have a talk about old times, now and then. It comes easy to them. Did she tell you what you wanted to know?'

Jennifer shook her head. 'She couldn't tell us anything very much—except where he lived. She did tell us that. But she didn't know anything about him, really.'

'Ah, well, it isn't easy after all these years.'

She said good-bye to Mrs Stevens and walked up the lane to the utility; Carl Zlinter was sitting there in it, smoking. 'She got talking when you went away, Carl,' she said. 'She told me a lot of things, but I don't know that any of it's much good to you.'

'Shall we drive out of town, and then stop, and you can tell me what she said?'

'Let's do that. Let's go back and stop somewhere by that river, and I'll tell you all I can remember.'

They drove back over the col where they had lunched, and down to Gaffney's Creek and to the Goulburn River; presently they parked the car at a place where the river ran near the road, and walked across a strip of pasture to a bend. As they went she told him all about it. 'She didn't know much really that you didn't know already, Carl,' she said. 'There were papers in a box, a tin box, but she doesn't know what happened to that, or what was in it.' She told him what she had heard from the old woman. 'She did look for it particularly that morning, but it wasn't there.'

'She didn't know of any other place he might have put it?'

The girl shook her head. 'She thought he might have had it with him when he fell into the river—in that case, it'ld be at the bottom of the Howqua.' They walked on for a few steps in silence. 'She was so sweet,' Jennifer said quietly, 'the way she went out very early to the cabin to find where he was and clean him up. She said she often did that.'

'She must have been very much in love with him, to do that for a drunken man.'

'I think she was,' the girl said. 'Yes, I think she was.'

They came to the rocky edge of the river and sat down on a boulder in the shade to watch the water and to talk. The water made a little lilting noise from the run at the end of the pool, a cockatoo screeched now and then in the distance, and the air was fragrant with the clean scent of the gum trees in the summer sun. 'She said he lived at Number Fifteen, Buller Street,' Jennifer told him. 'Is that enough to tell you where the cabin was?'

He took a folded paper from his breast pocket, and began to spread it out. 'What's that?' she asked.

'It is the township plan that I copied in the Shire Hall,' he said. He stood up, and spread it on the flat boulder that they had been sitting on; she helped him to hold the corners down. The paper was dazzling in the bright sun. He moved his finger down the plan. 'Here is Buller Street,' he said. 'Here is Fifteen, the number on the block. I think perhaps this was the place.'

She bent to look at the faint pencil lines with him, her head very close to his own. Her hair brushed his cheek and he could smell the fragrance of her skin. 'This is Fifteen,' he said, a little unsteadily. 'The cabin must have been on this allotment.'

'Could you find the actual place on the ground from this map, Carl? Is there anything left there now to show, that's marked upon this map?' She stood up, and moved a little away from him; it was difficult for her, also, to be quite so close.

'I think that we could find the place from this,' he said. 'Here, this solid marking, this must be the Buller Arms Hotel, and that still shows upon the ground a little. This map is to the scale of two chains to each inch. Perhaps there are other markings left, that Billy Slim will know. I think it will be possible to measure out upon the ground, and find this Block Fifteen in Buller Street.'

'When are you going to do that?'

'I would like to do it tomorrow,' he said. 'Would you come with me once more to the Howqua tomorrow?'

She looked at him with laughing eyes. 'I don't know what the Dormans'll think if I keep going out with you like this, Carl.'

He smiled back at her. 'Does that matter very much? You will be going to Melbourne very soon to start your work, and then we shall not go out any more, and the Dormans will be happy.'

'I know.' Mary Nolan had told her that the other Charlie Zlinter had a way with him, and a body could deny him nothing. Perhaps these Charlie Zlinters were all the same. 'Of course I'll come with you, Charlie,' she said, unthinking.

He laughed, and met her eyes, still laughing. 'I am not Charlie Zlinter,' he said. 'I am Carl, and you are not Mary Nolan. That was fifty years ago. We are much more respectable people than that.'

She laughed with him, flushing a little. 'I don't know why I said that. I've been talking about Charlie Zlinter all the afternoon, I suppose.'

'I do not think it is a compliment,' he said. 'Charlie Zlinter was a very bad, drunken man, and he was a bullock driver.'

She looked up and met his eyes, still teasing her a little. 'Well, what about you?' she asked. 'You're a very bad man, and a lumberman. I don't see much difference.'

'I am offended,' he announced. 'A bullock driver is much lower in the social scale than a lumberman. I would not say that you were likè to Mary Nolan. I would not be so rude.'

'I hope you wouldn't.'

There was a pause; he looked from her across at the little rapids of the river, at the smooth water running to the stones. Then he turned to her again, smiling. 'I might have said it,' he remarked. 'Mary Nolan was kind to a man who was very far from his own home. I might quite well have said that you were like to Mary Nolan.'

She did not answer that, but dropped her eyes and picked a little piece of clover in the grass that she was sitting on. 'Also,' he said, 'I think that Charlie Zlinter, although he was not a very good man – he was in love with Mary Nolan. I think perhaps that is another likeness.'

'Lonely people often think that they're in love, when they aren't really,' she said quietly. 'It must take a long time to be sure you're properly in love with anybody, and not just lonely.'

'Of course.' He reached out and took her hand and held it in his own hard brown one. 'Will we be going to the Howqua tomorrow?' he asked.

She smiled at him. 'If you want to, Carl.' More and more like Mary Nolan, she thought, but she could deny him nothing. 'If you're quite sure that it's safe for a girl so like to Mary Nolan to go back into the Howqua.'

'It is very safe,' he told her. 'There is no Charlie here, only a Carl. No bullock driver, only an unregistered doctor full of inhibitions and repressions.'

She laughed, and withdrew her hand. 'I wouldn't put much trust in those,' she replied. She got to her feet. 'I'd love to come with you tomorrow, Carl,' she said. 'We'll make it all right with the Dormans, one way or another.'

They began to walk back across the paddock to the car, very near to each other but not touching; to ease the tension she began to question him about the house that he wanted to build in the Howqua valley, how big it was to be, what would it be built of, and how would he get the materials in there. He told her that it would be very small and simple, no more than twelve feet long by ten feet wide; he could afford sawn timber for a house of that description and he thought that he could get everything he needed from the sawmill at Lamirra and get a lorry driver to take it up to Jock McDougall's paddock on a Saturday; from there Billy Slim could probably get it down for him on a sledge, or he would borrow a horse and a sledge from Billy and shift it himself. He would roof it with tarred felt sheeting of some sort. He thought that he could build it in the week-ends before winter. It would be very simple inside, with just one built-in bunk and a fireplace and a table. 'It is all I need,' he said. 'Just somewhere to be at the week-ends and to leave fishing rods.'

She said, 'And you're going to build it on the site of Charlie Zlinter's house?'

'I think so. I do not really think that Charlie Zlinter was related to me, Jenny. There are many Zlinters in Pilsen. It would be pleasant if he was, but anyway, I do not think that we shall ever know. But since there was a man of my name there, if his house was in a pretty place I will build mine where he built his, because we came from the same town. I think it will be pretty; from the map Buller Street ran up the hill not far from the river, and not far from the track that leads down to the crossing now. Perhaps the track itself was Buller Street; perhaps Billy Slim will know. But if it is a pretty place, I will build there.'

Jennifer said, 'It sounds as if the house you want to build will be just about the same size as Charlie Zlinter's house.'

He nodded. 'We are very much alike, both living as single men, both working with our hands, not rich men either of us. My needs will be no more than his needs were. I think it may be very like his house.'

She thought of Charlie Zlinter's house as Mary Nolan had described it to her when she saw it last, the swinging open door, the pail half full of water, the loaf gone green with mould, and the bedclothes that a possum or a rat had made a nest in. She shivered a little. 'I'm not sure that I like the thought of building there,' she said. 'Perhaps it's an unlucky place.'

He felt for her hand, and took it in his own as they walked along together. 'We will go and see it tomorrow,' he said. 'We shall know as soon as we are there if it is a lucky or an unlucky place. I think perhaps it knew great happiness, that place, and if that is true it cannot be unlucky.'

They walked up to the road in silence, hand in hand.

At the old Chevrolet they stopped, unwilling to get into it and drive away. The sun was dropping down towards the tops of the hills; it was time that they were making their way home to Leonora. They lingered by the car a little without speaking, and now he was holding both her hands. 'It is here that we should say good-bye,' he said at last. 'I will not stay tonight long at the Dormans.' He hesitated. 'It is very impertinent and very wrong,' he said, 'but may I kiss you?'

She smiled up at him, colouring a little. 'If you want to, Carl,' she said.

He put an arm round her shoulders and they stood locked together by the car for a few minutes. Presently she drew back a little, still standing in his arms, and said softly, 'I don't want you to go away with the idea that I'm in love with you, Carl.'

He stroked her cheek, and said smiling, 'What are we doing this for, then?'

She said, 'Because I don't suppose you get a chance to do this very often in the camp. How long is it since you did this to a girl, Carl?'

He thought back over his life, holding her in his arms and caressing the soft hair behind her neck. 'In 1943—eight years.'

'Poor Carl.' She drew closer, and kissed him on the lips. 'Eight years is a long time.'

Presently he released her, and they got into the car and drove back, sitting very close together in the sunset light, through Jamieson and Banbury to Leonora station.

10

Jack and Jane Dorman stood on the veranda of their homestead next morning, watching the old utility as Carl Zlinter drove it to the road across the paddocks, with Jennifer beside him. The grazier made a little grimace, and turned away. 'She's going to tell him, I suppose,' he said.

His wife nodded. 'She didn't want to tell him here, with all of us about.'

He glanced at her. 'You think she's really serious?'

'She's serious, all right,' Jane replied. 'I must say, I think a lot of her for this. There was never a doubt in her mind about what she ought to do.'

Jack Dorman kicked the leg of a deck-chair. 'He couldn't have married her,' he said. 'Anyway, not for years. He's got another nine months to do in the camp for a start, and then another three years as a student if he wants to be a doctor. It's probably all for the best.'

Jane went to the door of the kitchen. 'Well, there's nothing we can do about it. She's not known him very long–she may forget about him. She'll have a bad time, though.'

Jennifer sat quiet by Carl Zlinter as he drove the Chev from the Lamirra road up through the paddocks on the way to Howqua, getting out at each fence to open the gate for him to drive through. She was tired and rather pale, but she had worked with Jane to get a nice lunch ready for him; whatever might have happened, it seemed to her important not to spoil his day. It was the same fine, cloudless summer January weather that they had had all the time that she had been at Leonora, the same thin wisp of smoke curled up from behind the Buller range, the same flocks of white cockatoos shrieked and wheeled in shining clouds from gum tree to gum tree in the paddocks that they drove across.

As they passed from the paddocks into the woods she roused herself, and asked him, 'How are you going to find out where the cabin was, Carl?'

He smiled down at her. 'I have a surveyor's tape and little wires with coloured marking rags on them,' he said. 'They are in the back. I have asked Jim Forrest if I might borrow these things for today.'

'Those are what you use for measuring out, are they?'

He nodded. 'I think we can measure and find where the cabin was. If Billy Slim is there, he will help us.'

They drove on up the track to Jock McDougall's paddock, and the crimson and blue parrots flew ahead of them through the woods as they had before, and a wallaby loped off among the trees till it was lost in the dappled sun and shadows of the aisles. Presently they came up to the meadow at the top of the ridge, and parked the car in the shade, and got out. Jennifer stood looking out over the wide view, at the line after line of blue, forest-covered hills merging into the distance in the bright sunlight.

'This must be one of the loveliest places in the world,' she said. 'This is where I should want a cabin, if I lived in this country.'

He smiled at her. 'It would be wet and windy and cold up here in the winter,' he said, 'with deep snow sometimes. It would be more comfortable down in the valley, by the river.'

She did not answer, but stood looking out over the blue ripples of the forests, storing her memory. He glanced at her and noticed for the first time that she was pale and drawn, almost haggard. 'You are looking tired,' he said. 'Shall I see if we can drive the Chev down to the river?'

She forced a smile; she must not spoil his day. 'I'm all right,' she said. 'I didn't sleep very well last night, that's all. A walk'll do me good. We'd better not risk getting the Chev stuck, or we might not be allowed to have it again.'

They turned to the utility and took their lunch, and the grill, and the surveyor's gear out of the back. He would not let her carry anything. 'It is quite all right,' he said. 'If there is any more argument, I will carry you too.'

She laughed. 'I'd like to see you try,' she said incautiously.

He dropped everything and caught her round the waist and lifted her quickly off the ground. For a moment she rested in his arms, feeling secure for the first time that day; then she put on the mask of flippancy again, and laughed down into his eyes. 'All right, you big brute,' she said. 'Now put me down again. I knew I wasn't going to be safe here with a Charlie Zlinter in these woods.' He put her down, kissed her on the cheek, and released her, flushing and laughing, and bent to pick up the various packages and baskets.

She stood by him, confused. 'I wouldn't like to think that this kissing business was developing into a habit,' she said.

'It is the usual thing,' he assured her. 'In my country we kiss everybody good-morning.'

'I don't believe that's true,' she replied. 'And anyway, this is Australia. If you go round kissing every girl you meet good-morning you'll find yourself in trouble.'

'I would not want to kiss every girl I meet good-morning,' he said. 'Only one.' She made a face at him, and they set off together down the track into the Howqua, all care momentarily put aside.'

When they got down on to the river flat where the house had been, they left the baskets and parcels at the end of the wire bridge, and crossed to Billy Slim's house on the other side. They found him chopping wood in the shade; he straightened up and greeted them. 'Morning, Jenny. Morning, Carl. Come fishing?'

'We have not come to fish,' the Czech said. 'You remember when last we came here we talked about the town of Howqua, and where Charlie Zlinter lived?'

'That's right. You was talking of buying an allotment.'

The Czech said, 'I have found out now where Charlie Zlinter lived.'

'Where's that?'

'Number Fifteen Buller Street.'

The forest ranger scratched his head. 'Buller Street,' he said. 'Somebody once told me where that used to be. . . . Was it up the hill, off Victoria Avenue?'

'I have here a map,' said Zlinter. 'I found one in the Shire Hall at Banbury, and I have made this copy.'

They went into the living-room of the house and spread it out upon the table. 'My word,' the ranger said. 'All the years I've been here, this is the first time

I've seen a map of Howqua. That's right, there's Buller Street, there's Victoria Avenue, and there's the river.' He studied the map for a minute. 'Aw, look,' he said. 'It must have led up the hill just a little way upstream from the track. Looks like it was the old track down into the town.'

Jennifer said, 'Perhaps that's why he lived there, because it was on the track out of the town.'

'Too right,' the ranger said. 'That's where a bullocky would want to live.'

Carl Zlinter said, 'Do you know anything left on the ground from which we could measure, to find where he lived? I have a tape.'

'Shouldn't be too difficult,' the ranger said. 'Let's get across the river and see. I'd like to have a copy of that map some time.'

'I will make you one.'

Two hours later, two hours that had been spent in measurement and argument over the dim lines on the land and the pencil tracings on the map, they reached agreement. They were standing on the slope of the hill fifty feet or so above the river overlooking the meadow where the town had been. Here there was a small space of flat land, about half the size of a tennis court, in the middle of the woods. 'This must be it,' the ranger said. 'This'll be where Charlie Zlinter lived.'

Jennifer said, 'It must have been a much larger house than I thought. Mary Nolan said that it was just a little cabin, of one room.'

'Aw, look,' the ranger said, 'this wouldn't all have been the house. He'd have to have had a place to put the wagon, and maybe a store for hay and that. The house would only be on just a little bit of this flat. If you wanted the exact place, you'd have to dig around a bit. You'd find stumps in the ground, maybe, or else the fireplace.'

'I would like to do that,' Zlinter said. 'If I come over to your place, may I borrow a pick and a spade?'

'Sure,' said the forest ranger. 'Borrow anything you like.'

Jennifer walked with them to the bridge. Carl went across with the ranger to the homestead to get pick and spade, and she picked up the lunch basket and carried it back to the forest flat where Charlie Zlinter had lived. She dropped down upon the grass in the thin shade of the gum trees and sat waiting for him to come back with the tools. She was tired, very tired with sorrow and joy too closely mixed, glad for him that he had found so beautiful a place in which to build his fishing hut, sad for herself that she was never going to see it.

He came back to her presently and found that she had laid a cloth upon the grass and put the food out on it. 'We'd better not make a fire here, had we, Carl?' she asked. 'I wouldn't like to see you start off by setting the forest on fire, and we've got masses of cold meat here that Jane gave us, without the steaks.'

He looked around. 'I would like to find Charlie Zlinter's fireplace and cook a steak on it, for ceremony,' he said.

She smiled. 'We'll dig around a bit after lunch, and cook a ceremonial steak.'

They ate together on the grassy patch of ground, examining it as they sat and speculating where the cabin had been. Presently Zlinter got up, sandwich in hand, and drove the spade into the vertical hill face, at the end of the plateau furthest from the river. The earth was blackened with soot.

'Here is the chimney,' he said quietly. 'By making the house so, against the bank, it was more easy for him; the earth bank itself would make the back of the fire, and the heat would keep it solid. What was above could easily be made of wood. In this way he would need no bricks at all.'

They discussed this as they sat eating; it seemed reasonable enough. 'Will you make your cabin like that, Carl?' she asked.

He thought about it for a minute. 'I do not know,' he said. 'In the winter, when there is no fishing, my cabin may be empty for several months, and then the earth will be wet, and there will be no fire to keep it dry. It might fall in upon the fireplace. I think it will be better if I arrange my cabin differently, and have a brick chimney away from the earth bank, perhaps on that side, over there. I do not think it would be good to build my cabin right against the earth bank, as he did. It would be better to build it here, where we are sitting now, and not use the bank at all. The water might run down and into the cabin when I am away.'

She nodded. 'Put the wall about three or four feet from the bank,' she said. 'You don't want to get the other wall too near the outer edge, though. The earth might slide there, mightn't it, with the weight of the walls?'

He measured it with his eye. 'It is to be only a little place, no more than twelve feet long,' he said. 'I have not got enough money for a palace.' She laughed. 'I think there will be plenty of room. But you are right; the inner wall should be three or four feet from the earth bank, and then there will be room outside the river wall to make a veranda and a bench to sit on and look out over the river, or perhaps a deck-chair.'

She smiled. 'You've got it all planned out, haven't you?'

He laughed, a little embarrassed. 'It is important to me, this, to have a little place that is my own.'

'I know,' she said. 'You must have that, Carl, and you've picked a lovely place for it.'

They sat smoking together after they had finished eating, discussing the cabin, where the door was to be, where the fireplace, the window, and the bed. Presently they stubbed their cigarettes out carefully and packed away the lunch; they got up and began to investigate the place more closely. Zlinter took the space and cleared the briars and the undergrowth from the vertical earth face. The sooty, blackened earth extended over about three feet of the face, showing clearly that the fireplace had been there and about centrally disposed upon the end of the flat.

He stood looking at it critically. 'The side walls, they would run outwards from the face,' he said, 'at right angles. Perhaps one was somewhere here.' He set to work and began slicing the turf and leaf-mould from the level ground; in a few minutes he was rewarded by a charred stump of rotten wood sticking up out of the soil. They examined it together.

'Here was a wall,' he said. He threw off his thin jacket and went on working in shirt and trousers only, and gradually uncovered the remnants of the charred walls, shown mostly by blackened streaks in the top soil. In half an hour he had laid bare two rectangles of blackened soil and charred stumps, and rested, wiping the sweat from his neck and arms.

'It's fascinating, Carl,' the girl said. 'It's like digging up Pompeii or something. What would this one have been?' She indicated the outer rectangle.

He shrugged his shoulders. 'Perhaps a hay-shed, or a stable. No, he could not have put eight bullocks in there. For hay, I think, and harness.'

They rested together, looking at what he had uncovered. Presently she asked, 'Where will your cabin go now, Carl?'

'I must make a drawing,' he said. 'I will do that this week, and give an order

to Mr Forrest for the timber and the planking. I think it would be best to have
the chimney there, and the door here, opposite.'

She shook her head. 'It's going to be very draughty. You won't have a warm
corner in the place, if the door's opposite the chimney.'

He nodded. 'That is true. I want to keep the outer wall for a window, to see
the height of the river when I shall get out of bed, to see if I will fish or stay in
bed.' She laughed. 'The door should be on this side, but we will put the
chimney here, on the side of the earth bank but four feet away.'

'That's like Charlie Zlinter had it, but moved out a bit.'

'That is right.'

He measured four feet with his eye from the blackened chimney marks on the
earth face, and said, 'Here will be the new fireplace.' He drove his shovel down
into the ground, to mark the place for her.

It hit with a metallic clang on stone. 'There is rock here,' he said in surprise;
till then he had encountered nothing but soft earth. He sliced away the leaves
and top soil and uncovered a smooth face of rock, level with the surface of the
ground.

Jennifer cried, 'It's Mary Nolan's stone, Carl!'

'Mary Nolan's stone?'

'She said there was a slab of stone in front of the fireplace in his cabin, to keep
the ashes back in the fire. She said it weighed four hundredweight, and he used
to lift it up and carry it about to show her how strong he was. This must be it.'

He glanced at her. 'If it weighs four hundredweight, I do not think that I will
pick it up and carry it about to show you how strong I am. I think we will do that
another day.'

She laughed. 'You're no man!'

'That is true,' he said. 'Nor are you Mary Nolan.' He went on clearing away
the soil and revealed at last an irregularly shaped slab of stone about four square
feet in area, practically level on the top. A thrust of the spade showed a white
residue of ash between it and the earth face. 'There was the fire,' he said. 'It is as
she said it was.'

'That settles it, anyway,' the girl said. 'This is Charlie Zlinter's cabin.'

He nodded. 'This is the cabin. I suppose they used to put saucepans and
kettles on that, to keep them warm before the fire.'

She wrinkled her brows. 'Would there have been a wooden floor?'

'I think so,' he said. 'I think they would have had a wooden floor, and not just
earth. This stone was to prevent the fire from coming forward to burn the floor.
I think that is a good idea.'

'If you're going to use it again, you'll have to shift it,' the girl said. 'It's right
in the middle of where your fire is to be, now. You'll have to do what Charlie
Zlinter did, Carl–pick it up and carry it about.'

He nodded. 'It will have to be moved.' He stood studying it for a moment,
and then smiled at her. 'I will pick it up and carry it about in my two hands one
day when you are not here,' he said. 'Then you can come and see it in the new
place.'

She looked up at him. 'I shan't be able to do that, Carl,' she said quietly.

He glanced at her. 'Why not?'

'I'm going away.'

'But you will be coming back again in your holidays, to stay with the
Dormans?'

She shook her head. 'I won't be coming here again, Carl. I'm going home–to England.'

He stared at her in consternation. 'To England?'

She nodded. 'I wanted to have this last day in the Howqua and tell you about it here, not at Leonora with other people about. I've got to go back to England, Carl–at once. I'm going by air on Tuesday, on the Qantas Constellation from Sydney. I've got to leave Leonora tomorrow.'

He dropped the shovel, and crossed to her and took her hand. 'What is it that has happened, Jenny?' he asked quietly. 'Is it something very bad?'

She looked up at him, blinking. 'We got a cable last night,' she said, 'soon after you'd gone. It was from Daddy. My mother died yesterday, Carl–yesterday or the day before–the times are all so muddling.' She hesitated. 'It means that Daddy's all alone there now. I've got to go.' A tear escaped and trickled down her cheek.

He put an arm around her shoulders. 'Come and sit down,' he said, 'and tell me.'

He led her to the bank and they sat down together. She was crying in earnest now with the relief from keeping up the strain of a pretence with him. He pulled out his handkerchief and glanced at it doubtfully. 'You have a handkerchief, Jenny?' he asked. 'This one is a little sweaty.' She smiled through her tears and took it; he held her with one arm round her shoulders and wiped her eyes. 'I've got one of my own somewhere,' she said, but made no effort to find it. 'I'm sorry to be such a fool, Carl. I didn't get much sleep last night.'

'I would never think you were a fool,' he said. 'Would you like to tell me what has happened, or would you rather not?'

She took his hand that held the dirty handkerchief, and held it in her own. 'I've told you most of it,' she said miserably. 'Mummy had bronchitis and asthma, and she died.'

A flicker of technical interest lightened his concern for her. 'Was she ill when you came away from England?'

'She was always ill in the winter,' the girl said. 'Not very ill, you know, but not too good. She didn't go out much in the worst winter months. I never thought that she was in any danger, or I wouldn't have come away.'

He nodded, thinking of cases he had known in the camps of Germany; a small additional strain or an infection, and the heart would give out, somewhat unexpectedly. 'The paper says that it has been a very bad winter in Europe.'

She said listlessly, 'I suppose that's it.'

They sat in silence for a minute or two. Carl Zlinter sat staring through the trees down at the river, sparkling in the afternoon sunlight, thinking of the blank space that would be coming in his life when she had gone. 'Tell me, Jenny,' he said at last, 'have you got any brothers and sisters?'

She knew what was in his mind, and she shook her head. 'I'm the only child. I've got to go home, Carl. I spoke to Daddy last night on the telephone and told him I was coming right away. I never should have come out here at all.'

'It was a very good thing for me that you did,' he said quietly. There was a pause, and then he asked her, 'Did you really speak to your father, to England, from Leonora station?'

She nodded. 'Mr Dorman said it could be done, and he arranged it all. The call came through at about four in the morning, six in the evening at home; I could hear Daddy quite well. It only cost three pounds . . .' She paused. 'The

Dormans have been awfully kind, Carl. I hadn't got quite enough money left to go home by air, and it would have taken months to get a passage home by sea. They wouldn't hear of me going any other way. They're driving me to a place called Albury tomorrow to get the train for Sydney, and Jane's coming with me to Sydney to see me off in the aeroplane. They couldn't have been kinder.'

He looked down into her face. 'Are you quite sure that it is the best thing for you to go back?' he asked. 'Could not your father come here from England, to join you?'

She shook her head. 'I thought of that, of course,' she said, 'and I tried to see it that way, but it wouldn't work. Daddy's been in practice in Leicester all his life. He doesn't like the new Health Service, but he'd never leave Leicester at a time like this. You haven't met my father, Carl. He and my mother were so wrapped up in each other, he'll be absolutely lost, for a time, anyway. But in Leicester he's got all his interests, and his friends in the Rotary Club, and the Conservative Club, and the Masons, and the British Medical Association, and all the other things he does. He'll be all right there once he's got over the first shock, if I'm there to look after him and run the house. He couldn't leave all his friends on top of this, and come out here to a strange place where he knows nobody. It wouldn't be fair to ask him.'

'But you,' he said. 'Would you rather live in England, or live here?'

'I'd rather live here, of course,' she said. 'There's no comparison. It's a pity I ever came out here and saw this country, since I've got to go back.'

'It was a very good thing for me,' he said again.

She pressed his hand. 'I'm sorry, Carl. It's just one of those things.'

They sat together in silence for a time; she had told him everything now, and he had to have time to digest what he had heard. Presently he asked her, 'Do you think you will ever come back to Australia?'

'I shall try,' she said thoughtfully. 'That's all I can say, Carl—I shall try. There may be a war and we may all get atom-bombed in England, or there may not be enough money for me to get back here,' She paused. 'If the Health Service keeps on getting worse for doctors it might be possible to get Daddy to think about trying it out here, but he's nearly sixty, and that's awfully old to uproot and leave everything and everyone you know. I don't believe I'll ever be satisfied again with England, after seeing this. I shall keep trying to get back here, Carl. I can't say if I'll ever manage it.'

His hand caressed her shoulder. 'Do you know what would have happened if you had stayed here for another year?'

She looked up at him. 'What?'

He said, 'I should have got a job as soon as I was free from the camp, and then I should have asked if you would marry me.'

She sat motionless in his arms, not looking at him, staring down towards the river. 'What sort of job, Carl?'

He shrugged his shoulders. 'I do not know. In a business office, perhaps. Any sort of job that would give enough money to be married on.' He paused, and then asked gently, 'What would you have said?'

'I don't know, Carl.' She looked up at him, unsmiling. 'One doesn't always do the right thing. I suppose I'd have said, yes. I'd like to think that I'd have had the guts to say, no.'

'Why do you say that, Jenny?'

She saw pain in his eyes. 'Maybe it's a good thing that I'm going back to

England, after all,' she said wearily. 'I'd hate to think of you taking any sort of job, just so that you could get married. I'd hate to be the girl that did that to you.' She freed herself a little from his arm and turned to face him. 'You ought to be a doctor again, Carl. I know it means another three years in a medical school, and I know you haven't got the money. Maybe you haven't tried very hard yet. But if you gave up medicine and just took any sort of job to marry me—well, I wouldn't like myself very much. With your ability, you ought to be a doctor or a surgeon.'

'It is not possible,' he said quietly. 'I have thought of this many times. For me to be a doctor means three years training in a medical school again. It would cost at least fifteen hundred pounds, and I have not got one tenth part of that money. It would mean that I would be nearly forty years old before I could work in Australia as a doctor. I know it is a waste of my experience, but wars bring much waste in the world, and this is part of it. I shall never be a doctor again.'

'I think you will,' she said. 'I don't believe you'd be happy in any other sort of job, starting at your age.'

They sat in silence for a time. At last he asked quietly, 'Shall I ever see you again, Jenny?'

She did not answer, but sat looking at the ground, and watching her he saw another tear escape and trickle down her cheek. He put his arm around her shoulders again and drew her close to him, and wiped it away with the sweaty handkerchief. 'I am sorry,' he said. 'I should not have asked that question.'

She raised her face. 'That's all right,' she said. 'It was right to ask it, Carl—one's got to face up to things. I'm going back where I belong, twelve thousand miles away upon the other side of the world, and it may be years before I manage to get back to Australia again. You've got another nine months to do in the camp, and after that you'll have no money and nothing to bring you to England.'

'I would come to England, somehow, if I thought that you would want to see me there,' he said.

'I'd always want to see you,' she said simply. 'We've not known each other very long, Carl. We don't know each other very well. If everything had gone right for us and you had wanted to marry me in a year's time, I'd probably have been a very happy person. But things haven't gone right for us, and maybe it's just as well. While you're on your own, living as a single man, you'll have a chance, somehow, somewhere, to get to be a doctor again. With a wife and perhaps a baby on your hands, you wouldn't have a hope. You'd have to take just any sort of job that offered, whether it suited you or not. I don't believe that you'd be happy. I don't believe that I'd be happy if I married you upon those terms.'

He looked down at her, smiling gently. 'I thought that I knew what you were like, what sort of a person you are,' he said. 'I now find that I know nothing about you, nothing at all.'

'That's what I said,' she replied. 'But that doesn't alter the fact that we might have been very happy if we'd married.'

He sat staring down at the river, rippling in the sun over the white stones, holding her in his arms. 'I would like to think that we shall meet again before we are too old,' he said. 'I know that what you have said is true, and that you are now to go twelve thousand miles away to the other side of the world. Perhaps it is not very likely that we shall see each other again. But I am older than you, Jenny, and I have learned this: that if you want something very badly you can sometimes make it happen. I want very badly to find you again, before we have both forgotten the Howqua valley and each other. May I write to you sometimes?'

She said, 'If you do, Carl, I shall be nagging at you all the time about becoming a doctor again.'

'You may do that,' he said quietly. 'A doctor in this country could save enough money to get to England.'

They sat almost motionless after that for a long, long time, perhaps a quarter of an hour; they had said all that there was to say. At last she stirred in his arms and sat up, and said, 'You'll go on building your cabin here just the same, Carl, won't you?'

He was doubtful. 'I am not now sure. It will cost some money even if I get the timber very cheap from Mr Forrest, and I may need all the money I can save.'

She said, 'I think you ought to go on with it, Carl. You've got another nine months in the camp, and after that it will be somewhere cheap for you to come to for a holiday. Write and tell me how you're getting on with it, and what it's like.'

'If I go on with it,' he said, 'I shall always hold the memory of you, and of this day when first we found this place of Charlie Zlinter's.'

She smiled faintly. 'Go on with it, then. I wouldn't like you to forget about me too quickly.'

Presently he asked her, 'Before I take you back to Leonora, will you tell me some things about your home, Jenny? So that I can imagine where you are when I shall write to you?'

'Of course, Carl,' she said. 'What sort of things?'

'This Leicester,' he said. 'You told me once that it was rather ugly. Is it damaged by the war?'

'It didn't get bombed very much,' she said. 'Not like some places. Nobody could call it beautiful, though. It's an industrial city, mostly boots and shoes. It's rather ugly, I suppose. I don't think anyone would choose to live there if they hadn't got associations, or a job.'

'Is there beautiful country outside the city?' he asked.

She shook her head. 'It's all just farming country, as flat as a pancake, rather grey and foggy in the winter.'

'Do you live in the city, or outside it?'

She said, 'We live in a house about a mile and a half from the centre of the city, in a fairly good part, near the university. It's a suburban street of houses in a row, all rather like the one next-door. It's not far from the shops. I shall have nothing very interesting to tell you in my letters, Carl, because very interesting things don't happen to women who keep house in Leicester. But I'll do my best.'

'One other thing,' he said. 'There is so much I ought to know about you, that I do not know. When is your birthday?'

She said laughing, 'Oh, Carl! It's in August, the twenty-fifth. And I'm twenty-four years old, in case you want to know. When is yours?'

'On June the seventeenth,' he said, 'and I am thirty-six years old. I am too old for you, Jenny.'

'That's nonsense,' she said quietly. 'We've got enough difficulties without that one.' She paused. 'There's so much we ought to know about each other, and so little time to find it out. I can't even think of all the things that I shall want to know.'

'It will be something to put into the letters from Leicester,' he said. 'All the things you want to know about me.'

He stood up, and drew her to her feet. 'I am going to take you home now, Jenny,' he said, 'back to Leonora. We have said everything there is to say, and you are very tired. Tomorrow you must start and travel for six days across the world. Before we say good-bye, will you promise me two things?'

'If I can,' she said. 'What are they?'

'I want you to go straight to bed when you get back to Leonora station and sleep.'

She pressed his hand. 'Dear Carl. I've got some packing to do, but I think there'll be time in the morning. Yes, I'll go to bed. What's the other one?'

'I want you to remember that I love you very much,' he said.

'I'll always do that, Carl.'

He left her then, and took the spade and the pick down the hill to return them to Billy Slim; she watched his lean form striding down the hill. She was so tired that she could think of nothing clearly; she only knew that she loved him, and that he was much too thin. She sank down on the grass again and sat there in the dappled sunlight under the great trees, in a stupor of misery and weariness.

When he came back to her he was calm and matter-of-fact; he picked up the basket and the grill, and raised her to her feet. 'I am going to take you home now, Jenny,' he said. 'You have long travelling ahead of you, and I have very much work. We shall neither of us help ourselves or help each other by mourning over our bad luck.'

She smiled weakly. 'Too right, Carl.' And then she said, 'I've only been three weeks in this country, but I'm getting to speak like an Australian already.'

'We are both of us Australians by our choice,' he said. 'Some day we shall be truly Australians, and live here together.'

They walked up the steep rutted track through the woods slowly, hand in hand, not speaking very much; his calm assurance comforted her, and now the years before her did not seem so bleak. They walked steadily, not hurrying, not pausing; at the end of an hour they came to the old Chevrolet utility parked in Jock McDougall's paddock.

He put the basket in the back of the utility, and turned to her, and took her in his arms. 'This is where we have to say good-bye for a little time,' he said. 'Perhaps it will not be for very long. We are both young and healthy, and for people as we are twelve thousand miles may not be quite enough to keep us apart. We will not stay here long, because we have said everything now to each other, and you are very tired. Other things we can say by letters to each other.'

She stood in his arms while they kissed for a minute or two; then he released her, and with no more spoken he put her into the utility, and got in beside her, and drove down the track towards the highway and Leonora station.

They came to the station half an hour later; she got out and opened the three gates; at the end they drove into the yard by the homestead. He stopped the car by the kitchen door. 'We will make this very short now,' he said in a low tone. 'Good-bye, Jenny.'

She said, 'Good-bye, Carl,' and got out of the car, and forced a smile at him, and went into the house. He turned back to the car, expressionless, and took the basket and put it on the edge of the veranda, and got into the car again and drove it into the shed where it belonged. He hesitated for a moment, wondering whether he should go into the house to see the Dormans, and decided against it; he would come in one evening in a few days' time to thank them for the use of the car, after Jennifer had gone. He took his grill and the measuring tape and the wire pegs from the back of the utility and made for the yard gate. He turned the corner of the house, and Jack Dorman was there, sitting on the edge of the veranda, waiting for him.

He paused, and said, 'I have put the Chev back in the shed, Mr Dorman. It was very kind of you to lend it. I do not think that we shall need to borrow it again.'

'Jenny told you she was going back to England?' The grazier held out his packet of cigarettes; the Czech took one and lit it. 'She has told me that,' he said.

'Too bad she's got to go back after such a short stay in Australia,' Jack Dorman said.

'It is bad luck,' Carl Zlinter said, 'but she is doing the right thing, and it is like her to decide the way she has.'

'That's right,' the grazier agreed.

They smoked in silence for a minute. 'What are you going to do yourself?' Jack Dorman asked at last. 'Got another nine months in the woods, haven't you?'

The other nodded. 'After that, I will try to be a doctor again. I will go and see Dr Jennings very soon, I think, and talk to him, and find if it is possible. If I may not be a doctor here, I will try other countries. In Pakistan I could be a doctor now, at once, but I do not want to live in Pakistan. I want to live here.'

'It'ld be quite a good thing to start off with Dr Jennings,' the grazier said thoughtfully. 'He thinks a lot of what you did with those two operations.'

'He was very friendly to me at the inquest,' the Czech said. 'I will go and talk to him, for a start.'

The grazier got slowly to his feet. 'Come along and see us now and then, and let's know how you're going on,' he said. 'If you need a car to get around in, there's the Chev any time.'

Carl Zlinter said, 'It is very kind of you, but I would not like to use your car.'

'We've got three cars on the station now,' the grazier said, 'and I'm getting a fourth, a Land Rover. We shan't miss the Chev if you take it. If you're going to be running in and out of town on this doctoring business, you don't want to be stuck for a car.'

'It would be a great help, certainly.'

'You'd better get yourself a licence,' said Jack Dorman. 'There's no sense in running foul of the police. You can come and take the Chev when you want it.'

Next day, in the afternoon, he drove a white-faced rather silent Jennifer with his wife to Albury to catch the Sydney express, a matter of a hundred miles or so. He said good-bye gruffly to Jennifer at the station and turned his Ford for home. He got back to Banbury by five o'clock, hot and thirsty, and ready for a few beers; he parked under the trees and went into the saloon bar of the Queen's Head Hotel.

It was full of his grazier neighbours, and old Pat Halloran, and Dr Jennings. He crossed to the doctor and drank a beer or two with him, slaking the dust from his dry throat. Presently he said, 'I had a talk with Splinter yesterday. Seems like he wants to be a doctor again after his time's up.'

'He came to see me today,' the doctor said. 'I told him that I'd write to the secretary of the B.M.A. in Melbourne about him, but I don't know that I'll do much good. The Medical Registration Board have made these rules, and that's all about it.'

'It's a pity,' said the grazier. 'He tells me that he's going to leave Australia if he can't be a doctor here. Seems like he can practise in Pakistan on the degrees he got in his own place.'

'I wouldn't be surprised,' the doctor said drily. He paused, looking at his glass of beer, in thought. 'He didn't tell me that,' he said, 'I could put that in my letter, perhaps.'

'How's the chap with the fractured skull going on?'

'He's getting on fine. Zlinter took the most appalling risk with him, operating under those conditions. I suppose he couldn't do anything else. Anyway, the patient's going on all right. He's been conscious for some days now, and he seems to be completely normal mentally. I'm going to put that in my letter, of course.'

'We should have a job for a bloke like that,' the grazier said. 'It seems all wrong that he should have to go to Pakistan.'

'Well, yes–with reservations,' Jennings said. 'He's probably a very gifted surgeon. That sort of skill seems to be born in people–either you can do it or you can't, and if you can't you'd better leave it alone. At the same time, there may be very big gaps in his knowledge and experience that we don't know about. There's only one place to check up on that, and that's in a teaching hospital.'

'It needn't take three years, though,' said the grazier.

'Well, perhaps not. I don't know much about it, Jack. Maybe they make exceptions in a case like this; maybe they don't. I'm going down to Melbourne in a fortnight's time, and I'll look in and see the secretary.'

'I'd like to know how it goes on,' the grazier said. He paused, and took a drink of beer. 'There's another thing,' he said, 'and that's that he hasn't got any money. I wouldn't mind helping a bit if that was the only thing.'

The doctor glanced up. 'That's very generous of you.'

'Aw, look,' Jack Dorman said, 'you know how it is with wool these days. The wife likes him, and Jenny likes him; he's right. If everything else was set, I wouldn't want to see the thing go crook because of the money. Keep that under your hat, though; I haven't told him, and I don't intend to for a while.'

'You wouldn't mind it if I told the secretary, though?' the doctor said. 'It all helps to build a case up, if one can say that local people are prepared to put up money. It's another thing.'

'You can tell him that,' the grazier said. 'I'll drop in and talk to him myself if they want any kind of sponsor. But don't let Zlinter know, so long as you can help it. Much better let him manage it his own way, if he can.'

On Saturday evening, five days later, the doctor posted his letter to the secretary of the British Medical Association. In his overworked routine he had little time for correspondence, and he had little practice in setting out a careful, reasoned letter. He finished a draft on Wednesday; he re-wrote it on Friday, and copied it out and posted it on Saturday, feeling that if he worked upon it any longer he would make it worse.

On Saturday evening, Carl Zlinter slept at Billy Slim's house in the Howqua valley, tired with a day of strenuous work. He had driven out that morning in a truck belonging to the timber company to deposit his load of sawn lumber and a

hundred bricks in Jock McDougall's paddock. From there he had walked down
to the forest ranger's house to borrow a horse and sledge, and he had trudged up
and down hill all the day transporting his building materials down to the flat
where Charlie Zlinter's house had been. He had driven himself hard for ten
hours, haunted by the memory of Jennifer at each turn of the road, giving
himself little time for grief. By nightfall he had got all his stuff down to the site,
and he was glad to pack up, and go and grill his steak upon the forest ranger's
fire, and chat with him for a short time before the sleep of sheer exhaustion.

On that same Saturday evening, Jennifer Morton drove in the coach from
London Airport to the airways terminal at Victoria, dazed and unhappy in the
London scene. A thin February drizzle was falling, and the air was damp and
raw after the hot Australian summer. She had bought a copy of the *Evening
Standard* at the airport and had glanced at the headlines, after which the paper
lay unheeded in her lap. The meat ration was down to matchbox size, and was
to be increased in price; the Minister for War had made a foolish speech, and
the Minister of Health an inflammatory one, full of class prejudice. She knew it
all so well, and she was so tired of these people, tired, tired, tired of everything
that she had come back to. It was a terrible mistake, she felt, to go out of
England if you had to come back. It was far better to stay quietly at home and do
the daily round, and not know what went on in other, happier countries.

She was too tired to go on to Leicester that night although she could have
done so, too miserable to face her father in his grief till she had mastered her
own troubles and grown more accustomed to the English way of life. She took a
taxi from the airways terminal to St Pancras station and got a room for the night
at the St Pancras Hotel, a clean, bare impersonal hotel room, but warm, and
with a comfortable bed. Her head was still swimming with the vista of the
countries she had flashed through, her stomach still upset with irregular meals
served at strange hours and in strange places. She could not eat anything; she
threw off her clothes and had a bath and went to bed, and lay for a long time
listening to the clamour of the London traffic, crying a little, mourning for the
brown foreigner she loved and for the clear, bright sunlight of the Howqua
valley.

On Sunday morning Carl Zlinter got up at dawn and went up early to the flat
among the gum trees, and stood for a few minutes planning his work. He
decided that it was not practical to place his house exactly where the other one
had been; he would move it laterally about a foot to clear the charred stumps of
the old posts. He came to the conclusion that he would build the brick chimney
first and make the wooden house to suit the chimney; for an inexperienced
builder it would be easier that way. He marked out the foundations for the
chimney with thrusts of his spade and considered the stone slab, reputed to
weigh four hundredweight. It now lay more or less where the fire was to be; it
would have to be moved back about three feet, and to one side. He went back to
the forest ranger's house to borrow his crowbar, resolved to work all day and
exorcise his troubles with fatigue again.

On Sunday morning Jennifer Morton came by train to Leicester station and
left her two suitcases in the cloakroom for her father to pick up in the car, and
walked in a fine, misty rain up the grey length of London Road to her home by
Victoria Park. She pushed the familiar front door open and walked into the
narrow hall; it now seemed small and rather mean to her. She opened the
drawing-room door and caught her father just getting up out of his chair at the

sound of her step, and realized that he had been asleep. He looked older than when she had gone away about ten weeks before, and the room was dirty, and the tiny fire of coal was smoking.

His face lit up when he saw her. 'Jenny!' he cried. 'I was waiting by the telephone, because I thought you'd ring from London.'

She crossed to him and kissed him. 'Poor old Daddy,' she said softly. 'I'm back now, anyhow. I wish to God I'd never gone away.'

I I

Jennifer soon found that she had a full-time job ahead of her in Leicester. In the last fortnight of her mother's life the house had been in complete confusion, with a nurse living in; because of the extra work the domestic who came in each morning had given notice and left, and it had proved impossible to replace her. The hospital nurse, as nurses will in an emergency, had done cleaning and housekeeping for her patient, jobs which were no part of her duties; since she had left, little had been done within the house. Jennifer's father had been greatly overworked in that grey winter season, and in the crisis he had taken all of his meals out to ease the burden. He had gone on taking his meals out after the funeral and the house had been let go; it was dirty and uncared for, and her mother's bedroom was still full of all her clothes and personal belongings. On top of that her father was working fourteen hours a day and requiring meals at irregular hours, and every day at surgery hours Jennifer had to monitor innumerable patients who came for a prescription of a few tablets of aspirin on the Health Service, or a certificate from her father exempting them from work. Until she came to do the job herself, Jennifer had not realized how great a burden can be thrown upon a doctor's wife in the English system of State medicine without staff and buildings adapted for the crowds of patients.

As she had realized, the loss of his wife had made an enormous gap in her father's life. She found him distracted and morose, and with a morbid interest in her mother's grave, and the choice of the tombstone, and the text to go on it. At first she fell in with these interests because they seemed to be the only ones he had, but presently she came to feel that the continual walks up to the cemetery were not good for him, and started to try to get him interested in other things. They dined several times at a hotel and went to the pictures, but neither of them enjoyed these evenings very much. Edward Morton wasn't greatly excited by the cinema, and both of them disliked the poorly-cooked and standardized meals at the hotel.

Presently she found that when her father managed to get free from patients to go to his club for a game of bridge before dinner he came back relaxed and cheerful from good company and whisky, and she began managing the patients to contrive that he should get at least two of these evenings a week. She came to look with some resentment at the surgery patients with their trivial requirements for free medicine and their endless papers to be signed. The bottom was reached, for her, when a man came for medicine and a certificate

540 The Far Country

exempting him from work because he couldn't wake up in the morning.

Presently she extended these activities, and by disciplining the patients with a sarcastic tongue she managed to free her father for lunches of the Rotary Club, for dinners of the organizations he belonged to, and even for an occasional game of bowls as summer came on. Patients began to shun this cynical, bad-tempered, red-haired girl who thought so little of their rights to free aperients and said rude things about the forms that they brought to be signed by the doctor, and they began to transfer their allegiance and their capitation fees to more accommodating practitioners, which Jennifer thought was a very good thing. With the closer insight that she now had into her father's finances she was coming to the conclusion that he could do a good deal less work and still be comfortably solvent. She was distressed to find how much he had been saving for her mother in case he had died first, and how restricted his own life had been in consequence. She was staggered to find how much her mother's illnesses had cost, how much her father had been paying out in life insurance premiums for her security.

She got him to surrender two of the policies in June.

She had no close friends in Leicester, having worked in London for some years. The two or three girls with whom she had been intimate at school had married and gone away, and though she had a number of school acquaintances in the district she did not bother much with them. She felt herself to be a transient in her own home town, and though she had only been in Australia for about a month, she felt herself to be far more Australian than English in her outlook. Controls that she had once accepted as the normal way of life now irritated her; it infuriated her when she neglected to order coal before the given date and so lost two months ration of the precious stuff. Studying to make meals more interesting for her father, she thought longingly of the claret that Jack Dorman bought in five-gallon stone jars for seven shillings a gallon, and of unlimited cream; the ration books perplexed her, and meat was a continual, bad-tempered joke.

She did her best to conceal these feelings from her father; she had not come home to England to distress him by whining about a better country on the other side of the world. All his friends and all his interests were in Leicester, and her job was to make the best of it. She was not entirely successful in her efforts; Edward Morton was no fool, and as the grief at his wife's death abated he began to take more interest in his daughter. The frequent air-mail letters that she never discussed with him showed that her interests were very far away, and the fact that most of them were in a continental handwriting intrigued him; he was quite shrewd enough to realize that in the few weeks she had spent out there a man had come into her life. He set himself to draw her out one evening, sitting by the fire when they had done the washing-up.

'What's it really like out in Australia, Jenny?' he enquired. 'Is it very different from this? I don't mean physical things, like food and drink. What's it really *like*?'

She sat staring down at the socks that she was darning. 'It's very like England in most ways,' she said. 'The people out there think of everything in terms of England. I believe they think more of the King and Queen than we do. England seems to mean an awful lot to them. I don't know how to tell you what it's really like. It's like England, only better.'

He sat digesting this for a minute or two. 'Is it like Ethel Trehearn thought that it would be, like England was half a century ago?'

' 'Not really,' she said slowly. 'There aren't the servants and the social life that she was thinking of. All that's quite different. But out there you feel perhaps it may be rather like the England she was thinking of, essentially. If you do a good job you get a good life.' She raised her eyes. 'It's all so very *English,*' she said. 'When they make some money, they spend it in the sort of way we'd spend it, if we were allowed to make any and if we were allowed to spend it.'

'You didn't feel as if you were a stranger there?'

She shook her head. 'I never felt as if I was a stranger.'

He filled and lit his pipe. 'Meet any doctors out there?'

'I met one,' she said.

'They don't have any Health Service there, do they?'

'I don't think so,' she said. 'There's no panel even, like we used to have. I think there may be some sort of a voluntary insurance scheme, but I'm really not very sure, Daddy.'

'Are there enough doctors to go round? Too many, or too few?'

'Far too few, I think. That's in the country, where the Dormans live. I don't know about the towns.'

He sat in silence for a minute, thinking it over. 'This doctor that you met—do you know what he charged a visit?'

'I don't know—he wasn't in practice.' There was no harm in telling him, and it might make things easier between them than if she were to keep up an unnecessary concealment. 'He was a D.P., a Czech doctor who's not on the register. He's the one who keeps writing to me.'

'Oh. I wasn't trying to be nosey, Jenny.'

'I know you weren't. I don't mind telling you about him.'

'What's his name?'

'Carl Zlinter,' she said. 'They call him Splinter in the lumber camp. All D.P.s have to work where they're directed for two years when they first come to Australia; he works at cutting down trees. He graduated at Prague, and then he was a surgeon in the German Army in the war.'

He opened his eyes; this daughter of his had certainly wandered far from Leicester. 'How did you meet him, Jenny?'

'There was an accident with a bulldozer in the forest,' she said. 'I was with Jack Dorman; we came along just after it had happened.' She could smell the aromatic odours of the gum tree forest, and feel the hot sunshine in her memory. She stared into the fire, too small for coal economy to warm the room. 'Two men were hurt very badly, one with a foot trapped under the bulldozer that had to be taken off upon the spot, and one with a fractured skull. There was nobody to do anything about it but Carl, and no woman to act as nurse but me, so he asked me to help him with the amputation and the trephine. He did both of them beautifully, but then the man with the amputation got hold of a bottle of whisky and got fighting drunk, and died. There was a fearful row about it, because Carl wasn't on the register, of course.'

Her father was deeply interested; in all his medical experience such a situation had never arisen in Leicester. He asked a number of questions about the operations and the treatment but refrained from more personal enquiries, and Jennifer did not take the story further than the medical side. Her father had enough information to digest without telling him about the lost township of Howqua, and Charlie Zlinter and his dog. All she said was, 'Working with him like that kind of broke the ice. He writes to me still.'

Her father smiled. 'I imagine that you couldn't be too distant after getting yourselves into a scrape like that.' Jennifer's mother had been a nurse; his mind went back to the day when he had met her first, at St Thomas's, when he was a medical student; he had stepped back suddenly and made her drop a thermometer, which broke, and then he had to pacify the sister and explain that it was his fault. Medicine was strong in Jennifer's family, but it was a pity that she had got mixed up with a foreigner who wasn't on the register.

Jennifer kept up correspondence with Jane Dorman, largely about Angela's coming visit to England; with some reluctance the Dormans had decided to let her go and take a job in the old country provided that she had a job lined up to go to before leaving Australia, and they had booked a passage for her for the following January. Jennifer and her father went to some trouble over this, and finally got the promise of a job for her at St Mary's Hospital in Paddington and put her down for a room in a hostel for young women in Marylebone; they were rewarded by an ecstatic letter from Angela and a steady flow of parcels from Jane. Tim Archer wrote rather a depressed letter about all this to Jennifer, who told him in reply that he had nothing much to worry about; in her opinion Paddington would probably cure Angela of her obsession in about two years, and what he had to do was to get himself a grazing property within that time.

From Jane she heard about her oil painting. Stanislaus Shulkin had painted a picture of the main street of Banbury in glowing sunset light, which Jane liked for its glorious colours and Jack Dorman liked for its exactitude and because it showed the Queen's Head Hotel. It now hung in the kitchen of Leonora homestead, and in planning the new house Jane Dorman was making a special place for it where she could see it as she sat before the fire. It had been much admired in the neighbourhood, and Mr Shulkin had got commissions from two of their station neighbours who had come to the conclusion that a thing like that was rather nice to have about the house.

'I don't know what he's done with the portrait he was doing of you,' Jane wrote. 'He told me that he couldn't finish it because you'd gone away, and anyway, he said it wasn't any good. I asked him once if I could see it because I never saw it at all, but he turned all arty and said that he never showed unfinished work to anyone. My own belief is that Splinter's got it, but I don't know that; perhaps you do.'

Of Carl Zlinter she said, 'We see him about once a month; he came here to tea on Sunday. Dr Jennings wrote to the British Medical Association about getting him on the register in less than three years, and Carl has been to Melbourne twice for interviews. He thinks he'll probably get some concession, and he seems very anxious now to get on to the register and be allowed to practise in Victoria, but I don't know where the money's coming from to keep him while he studies. Jack told me to see if I could find out how he stood for money, and I tried to without asking the direct question, but he wasn't a bit receptive; apparently he thinks he can manage his affairs himself and of course it's much better if he can, but where the money's coming from I can't tell you. However, there it is, and he seems quite certain that he's going to be a doctor again; the only thing that seems to worry him is that it's going to be a long job, and that he'll be so old before he's able to set up a home.'

Jennifer heard from Carl Zlinter at odd intervals, usually four or five times in a month. He wrote to her irregularly, and when the mood was on him; on one occasion she got three letters in a week, and then nothing for a fortnight. His letters contained few protestations of love; they were mostly factual accounts of what he had been doing, sometimes with touches of sly humour. As Jane had supposed, Jennifer knew all about her picture.

'I have your portrait hanging in my hut in the Howqua,' he wrote, 'and because I go there regularly even in this bad weather I see you every week-end. Last Saturday there were three inches of snow in Jock McDougall's paddock where we parked the Chev and I got my feet wet, but I had plenty of dry wood in the hut and we soon had a big fire going. Harry Peters was with me, the driver of the bulldozer who had the head injury that we operated upon. He is quite recovered now and is back on the job driving a truck, but I do not think he will be able to drive a bulldozer again safely. He does not want to; he wants to go to Melbourne and study metallurgy and get a job in a steel works, and I think he will be doing this before very long. In the meantime he comes out with me each week to Howqua.'

Jennifer wondered what on earth they found to do in the Howqua valley in the snow; he had told her in a previous letter that the fishing season was over. Perhaps they worked upon the furnishings and details of the hut. . . .

'I had a great deal of trouble with Stan Shulkin over your picture because he did not want to give it to me; he said it was too good to give to Mrs Dorman and he was going to keep it and put it in an exhibition. I told him that you would certainly bring him to court if he did that without asking your permission, and I should go at once to the Police Sergeant Russell and tell him, and then he said that I could have it if I paid him for it. I told him that he was a very greedy man because Mrs Dorman had paid him for three pictures, and then he said this was an extra that he had not shown to Mrs Dorman. However, I got it from him in the end by promising to pay him when I became qualified as a doctor, and now it hangs in the hut at the Howqua, and I look forward all the week to going there to see it again.'

He told her very little about his negotiations with the Medical Registration Board; throughout his letters there was a calm assurance that he would be a doctor again, but he had no definite ideas on how long it would take. He said once, 'I am going to Melbourne again next week to see the M.R.B. and I think it may be easier to get into a hospital in England than in Melbourne because the Melbourne hospitals are very full of Australian students. I am thinking of booking a passage to England because it may take a long time to get a passage, and they will give back the money if you do not go.'

Apparently he was not short of money, and this puzzled Jennifer a good deal. She asked in her next letter if he had really booked a passage to England, but he did not answer, nor did he answer when she asked a second time. She stopped asking after that; if he did not want to tell her things he need not; they were of different nationalities and from different backgrounds, and she knew that it would be a long time, if they ever married, before she understood him thoroughly. His letters were a great pleasure to her, and his calm assurance that all would be well was comforting.

In September she got a letter that thrilled her, and informed her at the same time. 'It has been arranged for me here that I can study for the English medical degree at Guy's Hospital in London because there is no room in the Melbourne hospitals. I do not know how long it will be necessary for me to study and I do not think that they will tell me till I get there. I have passed two examinations in

Melbourne since you left for England and these results are good in London; you see, I have been working very hard in the evenings at Lamirra and at Howqua learning again in English all the text book medicine I learned and forgot when I was a young man. So now they say that if I can get to England I may go to Guy's Hospital. I do not know how long I must work there before I become qualified, perhaps not more than a year and in any case I do not think longer than two years.

'So now I must come to England. There is a ship called the *Achilles* that is now loading sugar at Townsville in Queensland and I may be able to take a job on her as steward or on some other ship because this is the season when the sugar is sent to England. I may have to pay for the passage and if that is needed I will pay, but I have not got very much money so if I can work I would like it.

'I am leaving Lamirra at the end of this week to go by train to Townsville which I think will take three days. I am sorry to leave this place; it has been good for me after so many years in camps in Europe to work for a time in the woods. I like this country very much, and when I am qualified to work as a doctor I would like much to come back to Banbury and work with Dr Jennings if he has still no other doctor to help him.

'I am bringing your picture with me in a packing-case. I have asked Billy Slim to look after my hut at Howqua, and I have left him a little money for repairs, and if a window blows in or a sheet of iron on the roof comes loose he will mend it for me, so it will be there for me to have when I can come back to this country. And there for you also, I hope.

'I do not think that it will be possible for you to write to me again because I do not know what ship I shall go on, or when it will start or when I shall come to England. I will write to you to tell you these things as quickly as I know them, and I will come to Leicester to see you very soon.'

She read this letter over and over again in the privacy of her bedroom. The sheer tragedy of her return to England was working out in comedy; Carl Zlinter was on his way to England and she would see him again. A picture came into her mind of the dynamic energy and competence of this dark, lean man that had produced this result and in so short a time. In a barrack hut at Lamirra, a hut similar to the one that he had operated in with her, smelling of washing and whisky and raw, unpainted wood, he had studied every night at medical text books; he had then gone down to Melbourne and sat for two examinations in a language foreign to him in a strange place with strange people, and had passed them. Over and above this academic effort he had somehow or other financed himself, and he had negotiated and corresponded till he had secured himself a place in a hospital in England, twelve thousand miles away, a country that he had never been to, and an alien, enemy country. This man was shouldering his way through all these difficulties and brushing each of them aside in turn, because he wanted to practise as a doctor in the country of his choice, and because he wanted to marry her.

She could not possibly keep this news to herself. At dinner that night she said as casually as she could manage, 'Carl Zlinter's coming to England, Daddy. He's going to re-qualify at Guy's.'

He noted her shining eyes and her faint colour, and he was glad for this daughter of his, whatever changes there might be in store for him. 'That's interesting,' he said, equally casually. 'How did he manage that?'

She told him, if not all about it, as much as she thought good for him to know.

They discussed the matter for a quarter of an hour; in the end he asked:

'What's he going to do when he's qualified? Practise in England, in the Health Service?'

She shook her head. 'I shouldn't think so. He wants to go back to Australia and practise at Banbury. There's a doctor there, Dr Jennings – I told you about him. He's very overworked. Carl thinks Dr Jennings might take him as an assistant if he can get qualified before anyone else gets in.'

He was about to ask her if she would like to go back to Australia herself, but he stopped and said nothing; no sense in asking her a thing like that. He knew very well that if she were free of her responsibilities to himself she would never have come back to England; if this chap Zlinter were to ask her to marry him and go back with him to Australia, he could not possibly stand in her way.

For the first time the thought of going to Australia came into his mind as a serious possibility. Leicester without his wife was not the place it once had been for him. If Jennifer were to marry and go back to Australia he might have to choose between going with them and attempting to carry on alone in Leicester, where he had worked all his life and where all his friends were. It was not a thing to be decided lightly. He would hardly make many new friends at his age in Australia, but he would be desperately lonely if he tried to live alone at home in Leicester. In Australia he might do a little work, perhaps, and earn a little money, and so be able to come back to England every year or two to see his friends. . . .

Jennifer heard from Carl a week later that the *Achilles* had sailed without him and he was coming home upon a ship called the *Innisfail*, probably sailing in about three days' time. 'They will not take me as steward,' he wrote, 'and I shall have to pay for the journey, which is a very bad thing, but I shall have time to work; I have brought many medical books with me to read upon the journey. If I was qualified as doctor I could work as ship's doctor on the journey because they have difficulty in getting doctors now at Townsville, but although I have showed my Prague degree they will not accept it because English ships must have an English doctor. When I am an English doctor I shall be able to practise anywhere in the world, I think.'

She heard nothing more until she got an air-mail letter from Port Said nearly a month later. His ship had called for fuel at Colombo. 'We do not go very fast,' he said, 'and although we have gone steadily all the time it has taken us thirty-four days to get to this place. I think we shall arrive in London in about another fortnight, and I must then find a place cheap to live near to the hospital. As soon as it is possible I will come to Leicester, but I cannot say what day that will be on.'

He came to her on a Friday evening at the end of November. She had walked down to the chemist to pick up a parcel for her father; it was a fine, starry night with a cold wind that made her walk quickly. She was fighting her way back head-down against a freezing wind in the suburban street. She raised her head as she got near the house and saw a man peering at the houses in the half light of the street lamps, trying to read the numbers, perhaps looking for the doctor's plate upon the door. He was a tall man, rather thin, dressed in a foreign soft felt hat and in a shabby raincoat.

She cried, 'Carl!' and ran to meet him. He turned, and said, 'Jenny!' and took both her hands. She dropped the parcel and something in it cracked as it fell; it lay unheeded at their feet as he kissed her. She said presently' 'Oh, Carl! When did you get to England?'

He held her close. 'We arrived on Tuesday,' he said, 'to the London Docks. I have found a room to live in, in Coram Street, in Bloomsbury, and I have been to the hospital yesterday, and I am to start working on Monday. I do not know how long it is that I shall have to work, but I think that it will be for one and a half years. I do not think it will be longer than that.'

She said, 'Oh, Carl–that's splendid! What are you doing now? Have you come for the week-end?'

He said, a little diffidently, 'I did not know if it would be convenient if I should stay. I have brought a bag, but I have left it at the station in the cloak-room. Perhaps I could take a room at the hotel, and see you again tomorrow.'

'Of course not, Carl. We've got a spare room here–I'll make up the bed. That's where we live,' she said, nodding at the house. 'Daddy's in there now–he wants to meet you.' She stood in his arms, thinking, for a moment. 'We've got such a lot to talk about,' she said. 'Daddy's got a meeting of the committee of the Bowls Club in our house tonight; he's the chairman or the president or something. Don't let's get mixed up in that. Would you mind if we go out and have a meal, some place where we can talk? They finish about nine o'clock generally. We can come back then, and you can meet Daddy.'

He smiled down at her. 'Of course,' he said. 'Whatever you will say is good for me.'

'Wait here just a minute,' she said. 'I'll go in and put this parcel down, and tell Daddy what we're doing.' She vanished into the house and he stood waiting for her on the pavement. In the dining-room her father was laying out the table with paper and pencils before each chair for the Bowls Club meeting; when this happened they had their evening meal at the kitchen table.

She came to him in her overcoat, flushed and bright-eyed. 'Daddy,' she said. 'I got this parcel, and I dropped it and heard it crack; I believe I've bust whatever's in it. Carl Zlinter's here, and I'm going to make up the spare room for him. I'm going out to dinner with him now, and we'll be back when this committee meeting's over. Could you get your own meal, do you think? It's sausages; they're in the frig, and there's half of that jam tart we had for lunch the day before yesterday on a plate in the larder.'

He smiled at her excitement, his concern over the parcel half forgotten. 'That's all right,' he said. 'What have you done with him?'

'He's outside waiting for me.'

'Well, bring him in, and let's say how-do-you-do to him.'

'Not now,' she said. 'I'll bring him in when your committee's over, when you've got time to meet him properly. We'll be back about half-past nine or ten.'

She whisked out of the room, and the front door slammed behind her. She left her father unpacking the parcel and smiling thoughtfully; changes were coming to him again, whether he liked it or not. Jennifer joined Zlinter underneath the street lamp. 'I know a little place where we can get a meal,' she said. 'Not like we'd have got in Australia, of course, but good for here. It's quiet there, and we can talk.'

She took his arm and they went off together down the street, walking very close to each other. She took him to a café near the station, a frowsy place undecorated for some fifteen years, but reasonably warm inside, and cheap: she knew that he was short of money and she knew that he would never let her pay for her own meal. There was no meat on the menu, so they ordered fish pie and cabbage, with apple tart and custard to follow. And then they settled down, and talked, and talked, and talked.

They sat so long over their meal that the bored waitress began turning out the lights; they woke up to the fact that it was eight o'clock and the place was closing. Jennifer said, 'We'll have to go, Carl.'

He paid the bill, and helped her into her coat. He said, 'Shall we go back to the station and get my bag, and take it to your house?'

'It's too early,' she objected. 'That blasted meeting won't be over yet, and there's no fire in the drawing-room . . .' She thought for a moment. 'There's a little picture theatre, Carl,' she said. 'It's a bit of a bug-house. It's showing one of those pictures the Americans make for South America, all gigolos and black-haired beauties dancing with tambourines—a perfect stinker. The house'll be half empty. If we go in there we can talk quietly, at the back of the circle.'

They went there, and the flick was as she had described it, a noisy picture with plenty of orchestra and raucous singing. In the warmth of the circle, seated very close together, they gave no attention whatsoever to the screen. 'Tell me one thing, Carl,' she said when they were settled down, 'what are you doing about money? You told me once that you wouldn't be able to get to be a doctor again because you'd never have enough money. Are things very difficult?'

He pressed her hand between his own. 'I must be very careful,' he said. 'I have now about one thousand one hundred pounds, and on that I must live till I am qualified. Then I shall ask if you will marry me, and by that time I shall be quite broke.'

'We'll manage somehow, Carl.'

'I have not asked you yet,' he observed. 'I am only warning.'

'And I'm warning you that if you don't look out, I might say, yes.'

He leaned a little from her and undid his overcoat; he fished in an inside pocket and pulled out a little object. He put it in her hand. 'It is for you,' he said, 'one day. Perhaps not yet.'

She held it up to the reflected light from the technicolour scene; it was a ring formed of reddish gold with curious, cable-like markings around it. 'Oh, Carl!' she said, 'is this a wedding ring?'

He took it from her. 'You go too quickly,' he said. 'It is an engagement ring, but it is not for you just yet. Not till I have met your father and he had said that he agrees.'

'Well, let me see it, anyway. I promise I won't put it on.'

He gave it back to her. 'It's just like a wedding ring,' she said. 'It's gold, isn't it?'

'I know that an engagement ring, it should have precious stones,' he said. 'I could not afford to buy precious stones to put in it, Jenny. But this is solid gold, gold from the Howqua.' He smiled down at her. 'I know that it is very pure gold, because I made it myself.'

She stared at him in the dim light from the screen. 'You made it?'

'I made it,' he replied. 'Harry Peters showed me how to make a ring like this, or a bracelet of gold, or a pendant. He is the man who had the broken head, on who we did trephine. It is very lucky that we managed to save his life, or he could not have taught me how to do these things.'

'But Carl, where did you get the gold from?'

'It is Charlie Zlinter's gold,' he told her quietly. 'It would not be good for you to talk about this, perhaps, even here in England and on the other side of the world.'

In the stuffy half light of the Midland cinema she stared up at him. 'I won't say a word, Carl. Charlie Zlinter's gold?'

'There was a box,' he said. 'The box that Mary Nolan told you she had seen, a tin box that he called his ditty box. In this box he kept his valuables.'

'That's right,' said Jennifer. 'When she went back to the cabin the morning he was drowned, the door was open, and she looked for the box to put it away for him, and she couldn't find it.'

He nodded. 'Charlie Zlinter had put it away before. He was not too drunk to look after his money.'

'What do you mean?' she asked. 'Where did he put it?'

He smiled at her. 'He had a very simple place for his box, a place that would be safe from forest fires and thieves and anything. Perhaps only a very simple man, a sailor and a bullock driver, would have thought of such a simple place to keep his box, and yet that was so safe.'

'Where was that, Carl?'

'Under the stone,' he said. 'The stone that weighed four hundredweight, that only he could lift. You remember the big stone we found together, on our last day in the Howqua?'

She could remember every detail of that day, and the sheer grief of it, and the sunshine, and the clean scent of the eucalypts, and the flashing reflections from the river down below, and the brilliance of the parrots in the woods. 'Of course I do,' she said. 'Was the box under that?'

'It was under the stone,' he said. 'I found it only one week after you were gone to England, but I did not dare to say that in a letter. I think if it was known I had found gold it would be taken by the police, perhaps in England also, so you must not talk about it. I think that it is better that I use it to become a doctor.'

'I won't say a word, Carl. How much gold was there?'

'There were fifty-two coins of one pound,' he told her. 'Sovereigns, they are called. Also, there was just over five pounds in weight of washed river gold, the gold dust that they find in the river beds. Billy Slim has told me that in Howqua this gold dust was used for money. The hotel would take it for payment, and they had little scales in the bar to weigh the gold with, how much it was worth. I think also the bullock driver, he took gold for payment, too, because in the box were little brass scales also. His gold dust was in two leather bags, one large bag and one small bag.'

'Was he a relation of yours, Carl? Were there any papers to say who he was?'

He shook his head. 'I do not know. The water had been lying in the hole beneath the stone, and the box was eaten away with rust. There had been papers once, but nothing was left, nothing that I could read. There was only the rusted sides and bottom of the box, and the two leather bags, rotten and with the gold spilling out from them, and the fifty-two gold coins lying in the rust, and the little scales.' He paused. 'I do not think that we shall ever know who Charlie Zlinter was.'

'What a shame!' She sat thinking about it for a time, absently watching the coloured mime upon the screen. Presently she turned to him again. 'You must have had a job lifting that stone, Carl,' she said. 'Did you have anyone to help you?'

He shook his head. 'I was quite alone.' He hesitated. 'I might have had Billy Slim to help,' he said. 'It was lucky. It was the first time that I had been there since we said good-bye, and I was sad, and I went there to work very hard and to be quite alone, because it is good to work very hard when everything seems bad.' She pressed his hand. 'I had the timber for the house, and I borrowed Billy's crowbar, and I levered up each corner of the stone and put underneath a wedge of wood. It took nearly all the day to move it four feet back and make the new place for it, and then when it was moved away from the old hole I saw the box.'

She asked him, 'What did you do when you saw it, Carl? Were you terribly excited?'

He said quietly, 'I was very sad that we had not found it together. I stood looking at the rusty pieces and the things in the hole, and I thought, 'That must be the box that Mary Nolan talked about,' and I was not at all excited. I was very sad that you had had to go away, and that you were not there to share the discovery with me.'

She put her face up impulsively, and he leaned forward in the half light and kissed her. Presently she said, 'What do you do with gold dust when you've got it, Carl? If you can't tell anybody about it?'

He smiled down at her. 'There are several things that you can do with gold dust,' he told her, 'but they are all very wicked and if you are discovered you will go to prison. One way is that you can take out a licence to be a prospector for gold. Then you go camping up the river in deserted places, washing the gravel in a little pan to try to find gold. Presently you find it, and come back with it, and sell it to the bank.'

She laughed. 'Did you do that?'

'No,' he said. 'I thought that it would become complicated if they ask where I had found it.'

'It might,' she agreed. 'Well, what did you do?'

'Another way,' he said imperturbably, 'is to build a little hut in the middle of the woods where nobody would ever think to go.'

'Like the Howqua,' she laughed softly.

'It could be like the Howqua,' he agreed. 'And you must have a friend, a good friend who thinks he has a debt to you, who understands metallurgy and how metals can be melted.'

'Like Harry Peters,' she observed. 'I wondered why on earth you took him to the Howqua.'

'It could be like Harry Peters,' he agreed. 'And there in the hut you make a little furnace with a cylinder of gas to heat a little crucible, and these things have to be hidden very carefully from Billy Slim.'

'Oh, Carl!'

'And then,' he said, 'you bring many candles and you melt the wax, and you carve a bracelet out of candle-wax, or it could be a ring like this ring. And you put the wax bracelet in a pan of soft plaster of Paris and you let the plaster set till it is hard. And then you heat the plaster and the wax melts and runs out of a small hole you make, and so you have a mould in the middle of the plaster where the wax bracelet was. Then you pour in the melted gold and let it cool, and break the plaster away, and there is your bracelet or your ring, made of solid gold.'

She looked up, laughing. 'Is that how my ring was made, Carl?'

He pressed her hand. 'I made that ring and a hundred and five bracelets, all in four week-ends.'

'A hundred and five bracelets! What on earth did you do with them?'

'It is very tedious,' he said. 'You must take one bracelet and go to a jeweller in Melbourne, and to him you say that your Aunt Catherine has died who lived in the gold-fields fifty years ago, and you have found this bracelet in her jewel box. And then you ask if he will buy it for the weight of the gold. The proper price is fifteen pounds for each ounce of the weight, but he will only give nine or ten pounds.' He paused. 'It is very slow and difficult, because it is not safe to go to more than two or three jewellers in each town. There is a better way, that I discovered very soon.'

'What's that, Carl?'

He said, 'This third way is very simple and very easy. You must wait till a ship from India, with an Indian captain, comes to Melbourne, and you wait until the captain comes on shore. You go then to the captain in the hotel and you say, Can I sell you my gold? In Bombay he can get thirty pounds for each ounce, but he must smuggle it out of Australia and into India.'

'How much did he give you, Carl?'

'Eighteen pounds an ounce.'

'And that's where the eleven hundred pounds came from?'

He nodded. 'I think that it was worth the risk,' he said, 'because I wanted to come to England to see you, Jenny, and to be a doctor again.'

'It was worth it, Carl,' she said softly. 'We'd better forget all about it now, and never talk of it again. We don't want anybody else to get to know about that gold.'

They set talking together in low tones till half-past nine, not paying the slightest attention to the picture. Then Jennifer stirred and looked at the clock by the screen, and she said, 'Let's go home, Carl. That meeting must be over now, and Daddy will be waiting for us. We'll go round by the station and pick up your bag. Is it heavy to carry?'

He shook his head. 'It is only for the night. I have not many clothes in any case. I must now buy some, but they must be cheap.'

They went out of the theatre; in the vestibule they stopped to do up their coats. She took his arm and they went out into the street; in the darkness the freezing wind hit them with a blast. She felt his sleeve, and said, 'Is this the thickest coat you've got, Carl?'

'I must get a thicker one,' he said. 'I had not thought that England would be cold like this. It is as cold as Germany.'

They bent against the wind and walked quickly, arm in arm, to the London Road station. 'Will you tell me one thing truthfully, Carl?'

'If I know the answer, Jenny,' he said.

'Did you really have to come to England, Carl, to do your medical training? Couldn't you have done it in Australia, possibly?'

He looked down at her, smiling. 'What questions you do ask!'

'You said you'd tell me.'

'I could have done it in Australia,' he said. 'They grew so tired of seeing me in the office that at last they would have given me whatever I should want. I came to England because I wanted to find you again.'

They turned into the bleak, shabby, covered cabway of the railway station, dimly lit for gas economy. 'That's what I thought,' she said. 'It was very sweet of you to do that, Carl. To give up everything Australia has to offer and come back to Europe–after getting away once.' She paused, and looked around her at the stained and dirty brickwork, at the antiquated building, at the wet streets in the blustering, windy night.

He laughed at her gently. 'Australia is cold and wet in the winter,' he said, 'and there are dirty railway stations in Australia, too, and dirty streets.'

They walked to the cloak-room and he handed in the ticket; they stood waiting while the porter went to fetch his bag. 'Carl,' she said. 'Your hut up in the Howqua–that'll be all right, will it?' She looked up at him half fearful. 'You don't think it's like the other Charlie Zlinter's hut, with a door swinging open and a green loaf in the cupboard, and a possum or a rat nesting in the bed?'

He pressed her arm. 'I also thought of that,' he said. 'I left everything there very clean, with no bedclothes or cloths at all, and with insect powder sprinkled all over. Billy Slim is to go there once each week and light a fire and open all the windows, and he has money for repairs, also. It will be there clean and waiting for us when we can get back to it, when we can get away from Europe for a second time.'

'We'll get back to it, all right,' she said. 'Some day, somehow, we'll get back there again.'

NEVIL SHUTE

THE CHEQUER BOARD

'Tis all a chequer board of Nights and Days
Where Destiny with men for pieces plays:
Hither and thither moves, and mates, and slays,
And one by one back in the Closet lays.

'Rubáiyát of Omar Khayyám.'
Edward FitzGerald

I

I saw Mr John Turner first on June 25th last year. He came to me on the recommendation of a general practitioner at Watford: I have the letter before me.

Dear Mr Hughes,
    I should be grateful if you would make an appointment to see a patient of mine, Mr John Turner. Mr Turner has been suffering from attacks of vertigo and fainting: I have been attending him consequent on a fall which he suffered in the Strand Palace Hotel, when he was unconscious for some minutes. I have found some apraxia, and the sight of his left eye appears to have become subnormal in recent months. In view of a severe head injury which he incurred in the year 1943 I feel that an intracranial lesion may be at the root of his trouble, and it is upon this diagnosis that I would like you to see him.
    Mr Turner is married, but has no children. He is in some branch of the food business, and lives in a style corresponding with an income of £800–£1000 per annum.

Yours very sincerely,
V. C. WORTH, MB, BS

Mr Turner came to see me by appointment that afternoon; the first thing that I noticed when my receptionist showed him in was the scar. It stretched as a deep indentation from a point about an inch above the left eyebrow up in to the hair on the crown of the head, over four inches long. It was a deep cleft in his forehead, red and angry looking.

The rest of Mr Turner was not very prepossessing. He was about forty years old with a fresh complexion and sandy hair, going a little bald. He had a jaunty air of cheerfulness and bonhomie which did not fit in well with my consulting-room; he was the sort of man who would be the life and soul of the party in the saloon bar of a good class pub, or at the races. He was wearing rather a bright brown suit with a very bright tie, and he carried a bowler hat.

I got up from my desk as he came in. 'Good afternoon, Mr Turner,' I said. He said: 'Cheerio, doctor. How's tricks?'

I smiled. 'I'm all right,' I said. I motioned him to the chair before my desk. 'Sit down, Mr Turner, and tell me what you are complaining of.'

He sat down with his bowler on his knee, and grinned at me with nervous cheerfulness. 'I'm all right,' he said. 'You won't find much wrong with me, doctor. May want a bit of a tonic. You know,' he said confidentially, 'this wound on my napper frightens people. I tell you, straight, it does. Every doctor that I go to gets the wind up and says I ought to see a specialist. They'll none of them touch me. If I want my corns cutting, they say I ought to see a specialist.' He laughed heartily. 'I'm not kidding you. They get the wind up.'

I smiled at him; one has to create confidence. 'Does the wound give you any trouble?' I asked.

He shook his head. 'None at all. Throbs a bit, now and then. The only trouble I get is at the hairdressers' when they come to cut my hair—it don't half fox them.' He laughed again. 'Not that I've much to cut, now.'

I pulled my pad towards me. 'Let me get down the preliminaries first,' I said. He gave me his age, address, and occupation; it seemed that he was a flour salesman. 'Cereal Products Ltd,' he said, 'I went to them in 1935, and then went back to them again after the war.'

I picked up the letter on my desk and glanced it over. 'I see that you told Dr Worth about attacks of giddiness,' I said. 'Do those come very frequently?'

He said: 'Oh no. Might be two or three in the last month. They don't last long—just a few seconds, or maybe half a minute.' He laughed nervously. 'Sort of make you feel you want to hold on to something. I think I want a tonic, doctor. I told Dr Worth.'

'Yes,' I said, writing on my pad. 'How long since you had the first of those, Mr Turner?'

'I dunno. Couple of months, maybe.'

I glanced again at the letter. 'Dr Worth says that you had a fall in the Strand Palace Hotel,' I said. 'How did that happen?'

'Well,' he said, 'it was like this. We have to do a bit of entertaining in my line. . .it all goes on the firm, you know. Well, to cut a long story short I was in the American Bar last Thursday with Izzy Guildas and another Portuguese—Jewboys, you know, but good types all the same—and I suddenly passed out cold. Fact, I'm telling you. I passed out cold, and fell down off the little stool on the floor, clean out. When I came to I was in the lavatory lying on my back on the floor with somebody splashing water on my face, and my collar all undone. I wasn't half in a mess, I tell you.'

I said: 'How long were you unconscious, Mr Turner?'

'I dunno. Maybe three or four minutes.'

I made a note upon my pad. 'When you came to, did you feel any pain?'

'I had the hell of a headache. I was sick, too.'

'What time of day was this?'

'About eight o'clock in the evening. We were just going to have dinner. I was looking forward to that dinner.' He laughed.

'What did you do? Did you see a doctor in the hotel?'

He shook his head. 'I sat about in the lavatory for half an hour or so till I felt better, and then I went home by Underground and went to bed. The wife made me stay in bed in the morning and see Dr Worth.'

'I see,' I said. I made another note. 'Had you been drinking heavily, Mr Turner?' I asked. 'Forgive me for such a question, but I have to have the facts.'

He laughed again. 'I been tight often enough not to mind talking about it, doctor. You ask anyone who knew Jackie Turner in the war. But, matter of fact, I hadn't had a lot. I had a couple of pints at lunch, and then nothing till we went to the American Bar that evening. I had one dry Martini, and Izzy was just ordering the second round when I passed out.'

'That's quite moderate,' I said.

He took me up. 'I wish you'd tell that to the wife. She don't half carry on about the beer I drink. But I think beer's best. I started to lay off spirits the thick end of a year ago. I got a sort of throbbing, so I stick to beer, mostly.'

I made a note. 'You get this throbbing with whisky, say, but not with beer?'

'That's right.'

'Where is this throbbing, when you get it? Under the wound?'

'No-sort of right inside.'

I made another note. Then I passed him the silver box of cigarettes; he took one. I lit my own, and absentmindedly slipped the lighter back in my pocket as I glanced over my pad. 'Were you very tired that night?' I asked.

He looked up at me quickly. 'Funny you should ask that,' he said. 'I was just about all in. I dunno when I felt so tired.'

'You'd had a very heavy day?'

He shook his head. 'I'd not been doing much. I think I want a tonic. A good, stiff tonic, doctor—that's what I need. I told Dr Worth, "That all that's wrong with me," I said.'

'Do you get this feeling of exhaustion very often, Mr Turner?'

He did not answer; he was fumbling with his lighter. The cigarette was held between his lips. He had taken the lighter from his jacket pocket with his right hand and held it for a moment as if to strike it with his right thumb, but his thumb did not move. The little finger waggled to and fro instead. Then he took it in his left hand and with some difficulty rotated the knurled knob, and made a flame, and lit his cigarette. 'I'm sorry,' he said. 'What was that you said?'

'I asked if you felt tired very often.'

'I do sometimes. I didn't used to. I'm a bit run down.'

'Are you left-handed, Mr Turner?'

He stared at me. 'No.'

I said: 'I saw you had some trouble with your lighter. Let me see you light it again.'

He pulled it out of his pocket. 'You mean, light it with my right hand, doctor?' He was flushing a little.

'Yes. Can you do it with your right hand?'

He said awkwardly: 'Well, I always used to, but it doesn't seem to go, now.' He was fumbling with it. 'I don't seem able to put my thumb on to the knob.'

'How long have you had this trouble with it?'

'I dunno. Couple of months, perhaps.'

I did not want to frighten him. I said: 'All right, never mind that now.'

He stared at me uneasily. 'Rheumatism, that's what it is. I knew a chap once lost the use of every finger on his hand, every bloody finger, doctor, all through rheumatism. He got it right by taking Kruschen salts. Every morning he took salts, much as would go on a sixpence. He never had no trouble since.'

He paused, and then he said: 'I got some salts last week, and I been taking them.' He glanced at his thumb. 'It's much better than it was. It's only the lighter I can't seem to manage.'

'I'll make a physical examination of you in a minute,' I said. 'First of all, though, tell me about that wound. You got that in the war?'

'That's right,' he said.

'Mortar?'

He shook his head. 'It happened in one of them aeroplanes. Twenty millimetre. It burst right in front of me, right inside the cabin.'

I made a note. 'You were in the Royal Air Force in the war?'

He shook his head. 'I was in the Royal Army Service Corps. I was on my way home from Algiers,' he explained, 'by air. In 1943, that was. We come by Gib and then straight from Gib to the U.K., four of us, in a Hudson with a crew of three. A Jerry jumped us over the sea somewhere around Ushant, a Ju 88. He had four goes at us, but he couldn't get us down. Over and over again he come at us, and his shells bursting on the wings and in the cabin every time. I got put out on his second run, so I didn't see the end of it. They said some Spitfires came and drove him off.'

In the quiet peace of my consulting-room I made my note. 'You got back to England all right, then?'

'In a manner of speaking,' Mr Turner said. 'The second pilot made a belly landing in a field by Penzance. There was him and me and another chap all in hospital together when I come to. That's all that there was left, out of seven of us.'

I wrote again upon the pad. 'What was the hospital?'

'Penzance General Hospital.'

'That is the normal civilian hospital, is it? Not a service hospital?'

'That's right. They took us to the nearest one there was.'

I made another note. 'Who operated on you?'

There was silence. I glanced at him; he was troubled, evidently distressed that he could not remember. I tried to help him. 'Was it a civilian surgeon?'

He looked up. 'It was an Army doctor, a major. I know his name quite well. I had it on the tip of my tongue to tell you, case you wanted to know. But I can't say it now.'

'Try and think,' I said. 'It's rather important to get all the records of your case together.'

There was a long pause.

'Never mind,' I said at last. 'Do you remember what he looked like?'

'Oh aye. He was a young chap with sandy hair like me, rather thin. He knew his onions all right. The sister and the matron said he made a rattling fine job of me. Well, he did, now, didn't he?'

I smiled 'I should say so. Do you remember the date when this happened?'

'End of September 1943,' he said. 'I dunno the day.'

I made another note. 'That's good enough. I can find out all I want to from the hospital.' I glanced over the notes that I had made upon my pad, and then got up. 'Now will you please take off your shirt, Mr Turner, and let me have a look at you.'

He got up and took off his coat. When it came to unbuttoning his waistcoat the same functional disability of the right hand became apparent; he had to use the left. I stopped him, gave him a pencil, and told him to sign his name upon my blotting-pad, but he could do that all right. The disability seemed to be confined to certain familiar actions, such as unbuttoning his clothes or lighting the lighter. For these familiar actions he had no control over his fingers.

Apart from that, I did not find much physically wrong with him. Reflexes were normal. Blood pressure was rather higher than it should have been, but that might have been due to anything. Heart, lungs, stomach seemed to be quite all right. When I came to examine his eyes with the ophthalmoscope, however, I found the disc of the left eye to be blurred and pinkish. That was the only physical sign of real trouble that I found. On giving him an eye test I found the vision of that eye subnormal in all ways.

I let him put on his clothes, and we sat down again.

'Well, I think you'll have to come into hospital for a few days, for examination, Mr Turner,' I said. 'I want to take some X-ray pictures of your head, and we can do a lumbar puncture for pathological examination at the same time. That's quite a simple matter.'

He said: 'I'm all right, though, doctor?'

'That's what I'm trying to find out,' I replied. I leaned towards him. 'Look, Mr Turner—you know as well as I do that you aren't quite right at present. So far the symptoms are not serious. There is the slight functional disability of your right hand, lighting the lighter and buttoning your clothes. We've just found that your left eye isn't doing much to help you see; of course, you didn't notice that. Added to that there is the giddiness and fainting, and the exhausted feeling that you get. There's some reason for all this, you know. It may be that something under that wound of yours requires a little attention. You'll have to come in to hospital for a week for observation.'

There was a long pause. 'Okeydoke,' he said at last. 'If that's what's got to happen, well that's that. When would it be, doctor?'

'I'll have to see when I can get a bed,' I said. 'You'd like a private ward?'

'How much is that?'

'Six guineas.'

'I suppose so,' he said. 'Be nicer if the wife comes to see me.'

I nodded. 'I'll fix it up as soon as I can,' I said. 'Probably in about a fortnight. I'll write to Dr Worth and tell him what I can arrange.'

'I'll tell him what you said.' He stared down at his hat for a minute, and then looked up. 'You'd be able to see splinters and that in the X-ray?' he said.

'Were there any splinters left in the wound?' I asked.

He said: 'I think there was. I don't think they got 'em all out. They was too deep in.'

'I see,' I said thoughtfully. 'Oh yes, they'll show all right. If any of them are giving trouble, that may show, too.'

'They wouldn't, after all this time, would they?' he asked.

I got up and pressed the bell upon my desk. 'I hope not, Mr Turner,' I said. 'But that's what we've got to find out.'

He went away, and in the evening I wrote to the War Office about surgeons in the Penzance neighbourhood in September 1943 who might have operated on him after that crash. In a few days they sent me an answer. At that distance of time they could not identify the surgeon, but they gave me a list of five names of RAMC officers stationed in the district at that time who were of sufficient seniority to tackle such an operation, any one of whom might have done it.

One of them, Major P. C. Hodder, struck a chord of memory. Percy Hodder had been a medical student in the London Hospital under me in 1934. I remembered him particularly because of his great interest in the brain. He had been a thin, sandy-haired young man. I turned to the Medical Directory and looked him up; he had got his FRCS in 1938. Percy Hodder was probably my man. He was now practising in Leeds.

I sat down and wrote to him.

Three days later I received an answer.

Dear Mr Hughes,

I remember the case of Captain Turner very well; I did the operation at Penzance about the time you mention. I doubt if we could locate the X-ray photographs now, and my own case records were destroyed by enemy action in London at the time of the V bombs.

So far as I can remember, I had to leave several splinters in the brain matter as the immediate operative danger to the patient in their removal seemed greater than the risk that they would create trouble later on. I am not, therefore, greatly surprised if trouble has developed.

I shall be in London on Tuesday next, and could look in to see you at your rooms in Harley Street at about five o'clock if that would be convenient for you.

Yours sincerely,
P. C. HODDER

When we met in my consulting-room he said at once: 'If it's the Captain Turner I remember, he's had some years of useful life. I never thought he'd live to make old bones.'

I described the man to him, and his apparent injury.

'That's him all right,' said Hodder. He thought for a minute. 'So far as I remember,' he said slowly, 'there were seven or eight metallic splinters or fragments in the cerebrum. I know I left three of them in, as being altogether too deep seated to be tackled. As it was, the patient very nearly died of shock; we had a great deal of trouble in saving him after the operation. I didn't think he'd live. After that, I didn't think he'd recover all his faculties. But he did. I saw him some months later, and he seemed to be completely normal.'

He went on to tell me in some detail where he thought the other splinters were. The more I heard of it the less I liked it. The man was older now, and less able to resist operative shock.

'Not a very good prognosis,' I said at last.

He shook his head. 'I wouldn't like to try to get those out, myself,' he said. 'Would you operate, sir, in a case like that?'

I said slowly: 'I doubt it. That is, assuming that the present X-ray supports your memory of where the pieces are.'

'I think you'll find that fairly accurate,' he said. 'I remember this case particularly, because of all the circumstances.'

'You mean, the crash?' I said.

He hesitated. 'Well, yes, there was that. But they were prisoners awaiting court martial, in a detention ward. Did the patient tell you that?'

I said dryly: 'No, he didn't.'

He said: 'Well, that's what they were. There was an armed guard on the door of the ward.'

'He told me that he was on his way home from Algiers,' I said. It is not helpful when the patient tells you a pack of lies. It just wastes time.

'Well, that was true enough,' said Hodder. 'They were sent back from Algiers. There was a load of four or five of them. This man Turner and two others were wanted for some black market racket in London, selling Army stores, I think. They were found out when they got drafted to the Med. Turner was the only one of that lot who came through the crash alive. Then there was a paratrooper up for murder in a London pub. The D.A.J.A.G. sent them all back for trial in England in this Hudson, the one that got shot up and crashed.'

'Nice party,' I said. 'How many of them survived the crash?'

He wrinkled his forehead in thought. 'Three or four, I think, but they weren't all my patients. They weren't all prisoners, either. One couldn't have been a prisoner–the second pilot, the one who crash-landed the machine. He had a broken thigh; an R.A.F. doctor was treating him. I think he was taken in with the rest of them, and not moved when they put the guard on. I think there were four altogether. There was the pilot, and Turner, and the paratrooper, and the Negro. That's right. Four.'

'A Negro?' I said.

He nodded. 'There was an American Negro soldier in the ward, who'd cut his throat. He wasn't one of the party from Algiers. The hospital put him in with them, in the same ward, because he had to be under guard and he was too bad to be moved.'

'What did he want to cut his throat for?'

'I forget–some civil offence or other. The American military police were chasing him. He went into an air-raid shelter and cut his throat. But he didn't know anatomy.'

I returned to the subject in hand. 'I'm taking Mr Turner into hospital for examination,' I said. We stood together for a few minutes longer, discussing what I meant to do with him and talking generally about the case. 'I'll drop you a line later on to let you know what happens,' I said finally. 'But I doubt if it will be very satisfactory, from what you tell me.'

'I wouldn't lose much sleep over that,' said Hodder. 'I've not got a lot of use for people like Mr John Turner, myself.'

'No,' I said thoughtfully. 'They make a lot of trouble and they don't pay much dividend.'

I did not see Turner again till just before the X-ray, and then only for a few moments. I got the photographs and the reports from the pathologist and house surgeon that afternoon, and after my consultations were over for the day I sat down with the photographs at the stereoscope. As Hodder had said, there were three metallic fragments. Two were sizeable pieces not far below the dura. It might be possible to get at those if necessary, though there was the gravest danger to the patient in such an operation. The third was very small and much deeper in the cerebrum; it was surrounded by a darker infusion of the negative in the immediate vicinity. It was quite inoperable.

I sat for half an hour studying this thing and trying to think out ways and means of dealing with it. I did not want to be beaten, even in the case of Mr Turner. But presently I put the negatives and the reports back into their envelopes and said quietly to myself: 'Well, that's that.' I stubbed my cigarette out, put on my hat and coat, and went home.

I slept very badly that night. At the age of fifty-eight one does not normally lose sleep over a patient, but I lost sleep over Mr Turner. I wanted to do something for him, wanted to very badly. I had a queer inverted feeling that because this little black market racketeer was a man of no account, the case called for the very utmost limit of my skill. I put that down with diffidence because it looks absurd on paper, but that's what kept me awake. I could not sleep for running over in my mind the possible combinations of operative and anaesthetic technique, of palliative operations and of neurological treatment. I got out of bed once and went down to my study to look up some recent German work on intracranial fibrosis; I read German rather slowly, and stayed down there for an hour. Then I went back to bed, and slept a little before dawn.

I saw Turner next morning in his ward at the hospital. I took the X-ray photographs along with me. The sister showed me in to his room; after a perfunctory examination I sent her away and sat down in the chair beside his bed.

'Well, you've got three metal fragments in your head still, Mr Turner,' I said. I pulled out the negatives and showed them to him; they were quite clear without the stereoscope.

'Gosh,' he said. 'Is that me? I don't half look a guy.'

'The prettiest girl doesn't look any better, taken in this way,' I said. I picked out one of the pictures. 'This one is the side view—this shows it best. These white things are the metal pieces. These two high up, there, and that one farther in.'

He was interested. 'Where would they be on me, doctor?' He put his hand up to his head. 'Somewhere here?'

I laid two fingers on his head. 'The first two, here and here. The third one about two inches down, under here.'

I showed him the other views. He looked at them carefully and quite intelligently. 'Is this third bit the same stuff as the others, doctor?' he said presently. 'I mean, those two are sort of clear cut, but this one looks all fuzzy.'

I nodded. 'That's the one that's giving you your trouble. I should say that is fibrous matter forming round the piece of steel.'

He glanced at me quickly. 'Something that oughtn't to be there?'

'Yes,' I said. 'That is my own interpretation of these photographs. To some extent it is supported by the pathological report.'

He said weakly: 'Well, that's bloody good fun.'

There was a short silence. 'Would that be what makes me feel tired, doctor?' he said at last.

'I think so,' I replied. 'It would account for that and for the disability of your right hand. It would account for the fits of giddiness and fainting, and for your eye trouble. In fact, it fits in with most of the symptoms that you've got.'

He said: 'I suppose this means I've got to have another operation?'

I was silent for a moment. 'I'm a surgeon, Mr Turner,' I said at last. 'I've been operating all my life, and mostly on the head. What I have to tell you now is that there are limits to the things that operative technique can achieve. If you have your leg cut off in some accident, the surgeon cannot operate and give you a new, wholesome leg. In the case of the cranium there are similar limits. There are some operations that one does not usually attempt.' I paused, and looked him in the eyes. 'I've got to tell you, Mr Turner, that I think this is one of them.'

The slight grey on his rather florid face showed that he understood me. 'You mean that if you tried to get that bit out, I'd die?' he said.

I said evenly: 'I've given this a lot of thought, Mr Turner. I have to tell you that I could not undertake such an operation with any expectation of success.' I paused. 'At the same time, you must understand that that's only my personal opinion, the personal opinion of one man. If you feel you would like to have another surgeon to examine you and study these photographs, I should be very pleased to arrange it for you, or to co-operate with anyone you choose. Because one man admits defeat, it doesn't mean that everybody else does, you know.'

He said: 'You're the best in England on this sort of thing, aren't you, doctor? That's what Dr Worth told me.'

'Oh no, I'm not,' I replied. 'There are other people here in London just as experienced as I am. You could see Mostyn Collis, for example.'

He said: 'Well, what's going to happen if you leave it alone, the way it is? Will it get any worse?'

I said: 'It doesn't have to get worse, but it may. I can give you certain palliative treatment that may arrest the lesion. That means it may heal up of itself and give you no further trouble.'

'Does that often happen?'

I shook my head. 'Not very often, in my experience. I have known it occur, though.'

He asked: 'How often?'

I thought for a moment, and then I said: 'Perhaps one case in ten improves under the sort of palliative treatment that we can apply. Not more, I am afraid.'

'The other nine get worse?'

I nodded.

He whispered again: 'Bloody good fun.'

There was a long silence in the little ward. A fly buzzed on the window-pane, the knob at the end of the blind cord tapped on the window, the bright sun streamed in; from below came up the noise of London traffic. I sat by his bedside waiting for him. It's best to give the patient plenty of time, in a case like this. It's all that one can give.

At last he said: 'If it goes on getting worse, doctor, what's it going to mean? What's it going to be like?'

I knew that was coming, of course. I, too, had had time to think. 'You say you first noticed this about six months ago,' I said, 'The disability, so far, is not very great. I can't estimate the actual rate at which it will progress, you know.'

He said impatiently: 'Yes, but what do you think, doctor? I mean, I've had it, haven't I?'

I said: 'I should say that there might be a progressive loss of faculties, Mr Turner. You might be able to carry on your normal life for another six or eight months, but these attacks of fainting will grow more frequent. You ought not to drive a car again. Generally speaking, I think you must expect all the symptoms to increase as times goes on.'

He said quietly: 'After that, I'll die.'

'We've all got to do that, Mr Turner,' I replied.

2

I wrote to Dr Worth after I had explained his position to Mr Turner in the hospital. I said:

Dear Dr Worth,

I have examined Mr John Turner, and I have consulted with Mr Percy Hodder, who as a major in the R.A.M.C. performed the original operation upon Mr Turner in 1943. I have considered the pathological report resulting from a lumbar puncture, and the X-ray photographs of the cranium, which I enclose with the radiologist's report for your information.

You will see that there are three metallic fragments still lodged in the cerebrum; I have indicated with an arrow the one which I consider to be causing trouble. In my opinion no operation could be undertaken with success to remove this fragment. A lesion in this vicinity is consistent with the apraxia and vertigo from which Mr Turner suffers, and with a marked papilloedema of the left eye which is apparent on examination with the ophthalmoscope.

I have known cases of this sort to remain static for many years and even to improve, but this is not the normal course. I should expect that all symptoms would increase in severity, resulting in death within a year.

I should like to see Mr Turner again in about four months' time. In view of the wartime nature of his injury and his general position, I should waive any further fee.

Yours truly,
HENRY T. HUGHES

Mr Turner left the hospital while I was writing this. He went by Underground to Piccadilly Circus and put his bag into the cloakroom. Then he walked up Shaftesbury Avenue and turned in to Dolphin Street, and to the Jolly Huntsman. He went into the saloon bar; it was only about noon and there were few people in the place.

'Morning, Nellie,' he said. 'Gimme a pint of bitter.'

The barmaid, a cheerful woman about fifty years old, drew a tankard and wiped the bottom of it with a cloth, and passed it to him across the counter. Mr Turner took it from her, swallowed a quarter of it, and slipped on to a stool. He smacked his lips. 'First I've had for a week,' he said with satisfaction.

'You don't say,' said the barmaid mechanically. 'Elevenpence. You haven't been around here lately.'

'No,' said Mr Turner. 'What's more, I won't be around at all after a bit.'

'Going away?' she inquired idly.

'That's right,' he said. 'Going a bloody long way.' He lit a cigarette, fumbling awkwardly with the lighter in his left hand.

'There's no need to swear about it, anyway,' she said.

Only a man can know the help that barmaids give to men in trouble. 'Sorry,' he said. 'But you'd swear if you was me. I just come out of hospital. They say I'm due to pass out in a year or so. Kick the bloody bucket.'

She stared at him. 'No . . .'

'Fact,' he said. 'I'm telling you what they just told me.'

'But why? You don't look ill to me.'

'It's this conk I got on the old napper,' he said moodily. 'It's gone bad on me, after all these years.'

'Lord,' she said. 'You got to have an operation, then?'

He shook his head. 'There's bits of shell inside, going bad, or something. They can't operate, they say.'

She said again: 'Lord . . .' and then, uncertainly: 'I don't suppose they really know, Captain Turner. I mean, doctors say all sorts of things. Friend of mine, she thought she was going to have a baby, and the doctor said so too, but she never. They were all wrong. I expect they're wrong with you. I wouldn't worry my head about it, long as you feel all right.'

He took a drink of beer. 'I don't feel so good, sometimes,' he said quietly. 'They done all sorts of things to me in hospital; I reckon they know, much as anyone can do.'

There was silence.

'What are you going to do, then?' asked the woman gently, at last.

'I dunno—I got to think it out.' He blew a long cloud of smoke. 'Got to go home and tell the wife, first thing of all. She don't know nothing about it, yet.'

'Didn't they tell her nothing at the hospital?'

'She never came to see me in the hospital,' said Mr Turner briefly. 'I was only in a week.' He paused, and then he said: 'We don't get on so well—not like I thought it would be, one time. I don't reckon this is going to mean much to her, except she'll have to start and think about a job again.'

'She'll be terribly upset,' the barmaid said softly. 'You see.'

'Maybe,' said Mr Turner thoughtfully. 'I dunno.' He swallowed down the remainder of his beer. 'Got to see the firm, too, sometime, I suppose.'

'I wouldn't tell them while you can go on working,' said the barmaid shrewdly. 'Some firms turn funny, you know. Ever so mean they can be, sometimes.'

'We get three months' pay, I think,' said Mr Turner. 'Sick pay, I mean. Of course, you don't get the commission. . . . I don't know as I want to go on working, though.'

'No?'

'Well, would you? I mean, what's the sense in going on?'

'Well, I dunno,' said the barmaid. 'You got to do something.'

'I dunno what I want to do,' said Mr Turner moodily. 'I dunno that I want to go on selling flour right up to the end. I'd sort of like to chuck it up and do something better 'n that, even if there wasn't any money in it. After all, it's not for long.'

'You don't want to chuck up the job and then find you get well again,' said the barmaid practically. 'I don't think any of these doctors really know.'

'You don't want to pack up at the end and find you done nothing but sell flour all your life, either,' said Mr Turner.

He pushed his tankard to her across the bar. 'I must be getting along.'

'Want another?' she inquired.

He shook his head. 'I got to go back and have it out with the wife,' he said. 'She don't like beer.' He slid off the stool, and grinned at her. 'All be the same in a hundred years,' he said quietly. 'That's what I say.'

He went out into the busy, sunlit street. He had intended to telephone from the nearest box to his firm, Cereal Products Ltd, and possibly to go into the office that afternoon. On the pavement he hesitated, irresolute. He did not want to go into the office; he wanted to think for a little before going back. He bought an evening paper and walked slowly down towards the Circus again, and turned into the Corner House and had a steak and chips with another pint of beer.

By three o'clock he was at Watford, on his way home. He lived in a small detached villa in a row, No 15 Hyacinth Avenue. It is a fairly pleasant little house, one of many thousands around London, with a small front garden with a ceanothus tree and a larger back one with a lawn and a laburnum tree and rose bushes. He let himself in with his latchkey, and called rather gruffly: 'Mollie?' The empty house echoed back at him; he did not call again.

He went out moodily into the garden; the lawn needed cutting, but he did not feel that he could tackle that. In that suburban place of gardens it was pleasant, that warm, sunny afternoon. He did not know a great deal about gardens. His work had made great inroads on his leisure time; so many evenings had to be spent late on entertaining buyers from the provinces that he had never taken seriously to gardening. There was always something more important to be done, the sheer, insistent business of living that stood before the things he would have liked to do. A jobbing gardener came in one afternoon a week to do the garden for him.

He stood looking at the roses; they were coming into bloom. He stooped down to smell one; it had a fragrance wholly alien to the world he knew. He straightened up, and then stooped down and smelt it again. 'Be nice to have a lot of them,' he muttered to himself, and his mind travelled to a vision of a rose garden between tall trees without a house in sight, a quiet place with crazy paving and a fountain, a managing director's garden. And then he thought that he had better make the best of what he'd got, the next year's roses would not interest him much.

'Takes a bit of getting used to,' he said quietly to himself.

He went back into the house and fetched a rickety deckchair from the cupboard under the stairs, and took it out and set it up under the laburnum tree. It would be nice, he thought, to sit in his garden for a little and look at the flowers, a thing that somehow he had never had the leisure for. He took the *Evening Standard* with him; within ten minutes it was draped across his face, and presently he slept.

He woke at about five o'clock, aware in some way that his wife was coming down the garden to him. He brushed off the paper and sat up. 'Hullo,' he said, with no great cordiality.

She said: 'Hullo. You got back?'

'Aye,' he said. He did not get to his feet, but rubbed his hand over his face. It was for her to make the first approach, he felt. She had not been to see him in the hospital.

'Did they find anything wrong with you?' she asked.

'I dunno,' he said briefly. 'I'm not going to die next week, anyway.'

She said a little scornfully: 'Well, that's something off your mind.'

'Aye,' he said. 'Been to the pictures?'

'I went with Mrs Kennedy,' she said. 'It was ever so good.'

He nodded. He liked the pictures well enough, although he had not her devouring passion for them. She was ten years younger than he was, only twenty-nine. She still lived in the dream world of romance, and flew to it at every opportunity as an escape from her realities. He could not follow her; the true world was more real to him, and more interesting. That made a breach between them, increased by the many occupations of his work, and by her idleness. At one time she had been a typist in his office; they neither of them realized how much she missed the work.

'Been busy this week?' he inquired. He was bitterly resentful, deep inside him, that with so much time to spare she had not been to see him in the hospital. He had paid for a private ward for that reason only, and he had been lonely there; he liked plenty of company, and would have been happier in a public ward with many other patients.

'I been over helping Laura most mornings,' she said defensively. 'She can't do much.'

Laura was her sister, and about to produce an infant. She lived at Bushey not very far from them, and she was a thorn in Mr Turner's flesh in that she was a constant excuse for all the errors of omission that his wife fell into. Whenever the dinner was not cooked, the beds unmade, or the house dirty, it was because Laura wanted help. This had been going on for some time now because Laura produced a baby regularly once a year, and Mr Turner was getting very tired of it indeed.

'Well, put the kettle on and let's have a cup of tea,' he said. 'If you've got time for that.'

She flared out at him. 'That's no way to speak to me, after being away all week.'

'If you'd found time to come 'n talk to me in hospital during the week,' he said evenly, 'you might have got talked to better. Now go 'n put that kettle on, unless you want me to go out.'

She stared at him for a minute, and then walked slowly to the house. Mr Turner sat on in his deckchair in the garden, the great wound in his forehead throbbing a little. The sordid little quarrel had upset him. He wanted to get rid of all that sort of thing. In a short time now he would have to slough off all experience, both good and bad; since everything must go soon he wanted to get rid of the bad first in order that he might be left free to enjoy the real and the good. He wanted to get rid of Laura, and the quarrels with his wife, and the office routine. He did not want to go on nickering after small commissions. He did not want to be mixed up again in the sly, illegal deals in pastry flour for East End confectioners that had proved profitable for him in the post-war years. He had some money saved. He wanted to lay off the business of petty earning now and do something different.

He had about three thousand pounds in savings. He had never told his wife the extent of these riches because they had been amassed in a variety of dubious ways; only a small fraction came from legitimate saving out of his income. Full of ideals gleaned from the cinemas, she was so rude about his way of life in general that he could not bring himself to tell her how he had built up their joint security, and now things had reached that pitch between them when he did not even want to tell her what he had achieved to safeguard them in sickness or old age. He knew that three thousand pounds would not go far to meet her needs after his death. Safely invested, after income tax, it would not provide her with much more than a pound a week; she had been making five pounds a week in the office when they married, and five pounds ten by the end of the war when she had retired from work. She could earn that again if she went back to office life; she had not treated him so well, he felt, that he need fear to spend his money for the sake of giving her another pound a week on top of the five or six that she could earn.

The little bell rang from the house; he heaved himself up from his chair and went in to tea. She had laid it in the dining-room, tea and cold sausages, and salad, and bread and jam, and cherry cake. They usually had it cold in the summer; in winter it was a more generous meal with a hot kipper or bacon and eggs. Supper was a light meal, that took place when they wanted it.

Mollie was already seated when he came into the room. He sat down heavily and forked a sausage on to his plate; she passed him his tea and he buttered a piece of bread. 'What about a run in the car afterwards?' she said.

He considered this. He had a little ten horsepower Ford in the garage by the side of the house, seven years old; he liked driving it. It was one of their chief relaxations, marred only by the destination of their journey. She would have liked to drive out into the country and sit in the sun in some beautiful place and read a book like girls did in the pictures. He liked to drive for an hour to some country pub or roadhouse and drink beer in an atmosphere of smoke and laughter and good company.

'All right,' he said. 'Might end up at the Barley Mow.'

'Lord,' she said. 'Can't you ever get away from beer?'

'That's enough of that,' he said. 'I don't mind doing what you want to first, and after that we do what I want to. Otherwise, we better go out separate.' He paused. 'What were you thinking of?'

She said: 'I wanted to go out somewhere in the country and pick flowers.'

He glanced out of the window at their roses. 'Want any more flowers? There's flowers everywhere, this time of year.'

'Wild ones, I want,' she said. 'Hawthorn and violets and forget-me-nots, and them sort of things.'

'Okay,' he said. 'Go out past Hatfield, 'n then come home by the Barley Mow.'

She said: 'All right, if we've got to.'

He slit his sausage up the middle carefully, and spread a little mustard on it. 'One thing.' he said casually. 'You better drive.'

She stared at him. 'Don't you want to?'

'Not much,' he said, 'I don't feel like it.'

She said: 'I'm not going to drive all the way–you can't see the country, driving. I'll drive back from the Barley Mow. I'd better do that, anyway.'

He said irritably: 'You'll drive all the way, or we don't go at all.'

She said: 'For the Lord's sake! Why won't you drive some of the way?'

He said angrily: 'Because the specialist told me not to. That's why. If you think I like being driven by you, you're very much mistaken.'

She stared at him. 'Told you not to?'

'That's right. Not till I get rid of these giddy fits I been getting.'

'How long have you not got to drive for, then?'

'I dunno,' he said. 'Till I get rid of them, I suppose.'

She said no more about it, and presently they went out in the car. He sat smoking cigarette after cigarette beside her, watching the arterial road slide past. He was feeling stale and tired and upset by the slight combat with his wife; so little time was left that it was bitter that it should be marred with quarrels. He sat moody by her side, trying not to flinch each time that she cut in between two vehicles; he would have to get accustomed to that if he went on motoring, he thought.

She turned presently from the main road and went on through the byways; they knew the country within a radius of thirty miles from Watford very well from afternoon joy-riding. She drew up presently beside a watersplash in a small lane; there was a may tree in red bloom not far away beside the stream.

'Be nice to have a bit of that,' she said. 'It'ld look lovely in the drawing-room vase.'

They got out of the car and walked across the field to the tree. He had a very blunt penknife that he knew for a bad tool, but he had no means of sharpening it at home, and if he had the means he would not have had the time. One day, when he had achieved leisure, he would have liked to have a proper little workshop with a grinder and some hand tools, in a shed in the back garden, perhaps. But that meant time, and when you were out late most evenings there was hardly time to think about a thing like that, let alone do it.

With his blunt penknife they hacked off a few twigs of the may tree; the bright clusters of the flowers were thin on the twigs, but Mollie was pleased with them. She gave them to him to carry and they walked along the hedge for a little time while she looked for cowslips and for violets; he was frankly bored, and presently she agreed that he should sit upon a gate and wait for her.

He sat up on the gate, may blooms in hand, and lit a cigarette. It was quiet and pleasant in the sun, now that he had not got to walk around like a dolt looking for flowers. It was still and the sky was blue, down to the riot of colour of the hawthorn and may along the hedge. His eyes fell on the tiny flowers on the twigs that he was holding; they were delicate and perfect, and most beautiful. He realized dimly that there was some sense in what his wife was doing; if you had absolutely nothing else to do it might be possible to get great pleasure out of flowers, though that had never been his line.

She came back presently with foxgloves and daisies and violets and forget-me-nots. He said: 'You been buying up the shop?'

She disregarded that. 'I think they're ever so lovely,' she said. She passed him up the little bunch of violets. 'Don't these smell sweet?'

He put his nose to them. 'Like that place in Piccadilly,' he said. 'Coty, or some name like that.'

'That's right,' she said. 'They make scent out of violets. Other flowers, too. I don't think they get it right, though.' She buried her face in the flowers again. 'Not like these.'

'Give yourself hay fever if you go on like that,' he said. 'What about getting along to the Barley Mow?'

A shadow crossed her face. 'If we've got to. I'm not going to stay there all night.'

'They shut at ten,' he said briefly. 'It'll be quarter past nine by the time we get there. That long won't kill you.'

They drove for half an hour, and drew up at the pub. The Barley Mow is a large modern public house strategically placed at the junction of two arterial roads; it stands on the corner in two acres of grounds, one and a half acres of which is car park. Inside, the saloon bar is a discreet mixture of imitation Tudor oak and real chromium plate; it is warm in the winter and cool in the summer, and the place is split up into little corners and alcoves where a man can tell his friends a blue story without telling every lady in the room. Mr Turner loved the Barley Mow better than almost any other local he frequented.

For one thing, there always seemed to be people there that he knew. That night there was Georgie Harries and his wife, and Gillie Simmonds with a new girl friend who was on the stage, and fat old Dickie Watson, the bookmaker, with a party. All these greeted Mr Turner—'Jackie, you old sod!' 'What's it to be, Jackie?'—'Jackie, d'you get home all right last Friday? (*sotto voce*). Never see anyone so pissed in all my life'—'Evening Mrs Turner, got him on string tonight? What'll you take for it?'

It was the atmosphere that Mr Turner loved. He drank pint after pint of beer, while Mollie stood in bright forced cheerfulness with a gin and ginger, one eye on the clock. Smoke wreathed about them and the voices rose and the place grew hotter and the atmosphere thicker as the minute hand moved forward to the hour. Mr Turner stood red-faced and beaming in the midst, mug in hand, the great wound pulsing in his forehead, telling story after story from his vast repertoire. 'Well, this porter he went on the witness stand and told the Court of Inquiry that it was his first day with the Company. The chairman asks if he see the accident. He says: "Aye. I see the express run right into the trucks." The chairman asks him what he did next. "Well, sir, I turns to the ticket collector, and I says: 'That's a bloody fine way to run a railway!'"' In the shout of laughter that followed, the manager said: 'Time, ladies and gentlemen, please!' and turned out half the lights. One by one the company went out into the cool night air; starters ground in the car park, and lights shone out in beams, and the cars slipped off up the road to London.

At the little Ford Mollie said acidly: 'Good thing I'm driving you, after five pints of beer.'

'Four pints,' said Mr Turner. 'I only had four.' The air was fresh upon his face, the moon clear above him in a deep blue sky. It was perfect in the night. He felt relaxed, as if all his fatigue and distress was soaking out of him. A week was a long time to go without a bit of a blind.

'It was five,' said his wife. 'I counted them myself.'

He was relaxed and happy, and now she was nagging at him. He turned on her irritably. 'What the hell does it matter if I have four or five? I'll have fifty if I want, my girl. I won't be drinking anything this time next year, if what they said at the hospital is right.'

She stared at him. 'What did they say at the hospital?'

'They said I'm going to die before so long.' In the quiet serenity of the night that did not seem very important; it was only important that she should shut up and not spoil his evening. 'Now you get on and start her up, and shut up talking.'

She opened her mouth to give as good as she got, but said nothing. What he had told her was incredible, and yet it was what she had secretly feared for some time. Beneath her irritation with him she was well aware that his condition had deteriorated in the last six months; he was not physically the man he once had been. Moreover, it was no good arguing with him when he had just drunk five pints of beer; from past experience she knew that much. She got into the car in silence and started the engine; in silence he got in beside her and slammed the door, and they started down the long white concrete road to home.

They did not speak again till they turned into the garage of the little house at Watford forty minutes later. Closing the doors, she said to him: 'What was that they told you at the hospital?' She spoke more gently, having had time to reflect.

By this time Mr Turner was more firmly upon earth. It was quiet and still and moonlit in the garden, and it was warm. 'Let's get the deckchairs out 'n sit a bit,' he said. 'I got to tell you all about it sometime, 'cause you ought to know.'

They fetched deckchairs from the cupboard under the stairs and set them up upon the lawn. Mr Turner lit a cigarette as they sat down. 'There's bits of shell inside my head going bad on me,' he said. 'That's what they told me at the hospital. They give me about another year, as far as they can judge.'

She said: 'But, Jackie, can't they operate 'n get them out?'

'They say not.' She had not called him Jackie for some time; it was what his friends all called him, and he warmed towards her. 'They say they're too deep in.'

She said quietly: 'I'm ever so sorry.'

He laughed. 'Not half so sorry as I am!' He thought for a moment, and then said: 'I didn't mean that nasty. But I must say, I got a bit of a shock when he told me.'

'I should think so, too,' she said.

He sat in silence in the deckchair, lying back and looking at the stars. Vega burned near the deep blue zenith, with Altair on his right and Arcturus to the left. He did not know the names of any of them, but he found them comforting and permanent. They would be there when he and all others like him had gone on; it was good to sit there and lie back and look at things like that.

'It's time we had a bit of a talk about it,' he said presently. 'I mean, I dunno how long I can go on working. These giddy fits and that, they won't get any better now. Six or eight months maybe; then I'll have to go in a home or something. That means you'll have to start and think about a job again.'

'I know that,' she said slowly. 'I was thinking the same thing.'

He said: 'I got a little money saved, but not so much. It's going to take a bit, seeing me finished off. There won't be much after I'm gone–nothing to make a difference, really.' He turned to her. 'I'm sorry about that.'

'That doesn't matter,' she said quietly. 'I can brush up easy, 'n get another job.'

He nodded. 'I reckoned that you could.'

She turned to him presently. 'What about you, Jackie? Will you go on working, long as you can?'

He said slowly: 'I suppose so–I dunno. I got to sort of clean things up–one or two things I got to see about that might take a bit of time. I dunno.'

She said: 'What sort of things?'

'One thing,' he said. 'I got to try and find a nigger.'

3

She turned to him in astonishment. 'For the Lord's sake,' she exclaimed, 'what do you want with a nigger?'

It was quiet in the moonlit garden. The scent of roses was around them; in the white light the rows of similar, gabled houses were ethereal, the castles of a dream. The beer still had full hold of Mr Turner, freeing him of repressions and of irritations, making him both simple and lucid. 'You remember that time I got in prison?' he inquired.

She said quietly: 'I do.' It had been one of the disasters in her life, that had made her both cynical and bitter. She had a good deal of excuse. She had married a young vigorous man in her office back in 1939, when war broke out; they had lived together very little because he joined the Army almost immediately. He became an officer and quickly rose to captain, and she was terribly proud of him. Then he was sent out to North Africa.

Within three months he was back in England and at death's door from the wound he had got in the aeroplane. When she went down to see him at the hospital in Penzance she discovered that he was no longer a free man; there was a little matter of three truckloads of Army sugar sold in the black market to be settled first. She knew him for a warm business man in the office when she married him; she had not known that he was quite so hot as that. He was in hospital for a long time before court martial; then he got a year's imprisonment and was discharged from the Army, His Majesty having no further use for his services. He came back to her in February 1945, a perky, irrepressible little man in civvy clothes, apparently not conscious of any very great disgrace, and with that huge wound that terrified her till she got accustomed to it. From that time she had been a bad wife to him, and she knew it, and she hated him for it.

'I dunno if I ever told you much about that time,' he said. 'There was four of us all in the ward together, at that place down in Penzance. Just the four of us together.' He hesitated, and then said: 'They had a guard, you see.'

She nodded. 'I remember.'

'I'd like to know what happened to them other chaps, the three of them,' he said. 'They used to come and talk to me. Hours on end, they did.'

'Talk to you?'

'They used to come and sit inside the screen there was all round my bed, and talk to me. Hour after hour, sometimes.'

She stared at him. 'What did they do that for?'

'The doctor 'n the sisters made them do it.' He turned to her. 'I had me eyes all bandaged up after the operation 'cause they didn't want me to see anything, and they gave me things to stop me wanting to move about in bed. I was lying there all strapped up like a mummy, and I couldn't talk much, either. But I could hear things going on, 'n think about things too. Funny, being like that, it was. So as the others got well one by one the sisters made them come 'n read a book to me, but they read pretty bad, so most times they just talked. I could answer them a little, but not much. They just kept talking to me.'

'What did they talk about?'

'Themselves, mostly. They were a bloody miserable lot–the miserablest lot of men I ever saw. But they were good to me.' He paused for a moment, and repeated very quietly: 'Bloody good.'

'How do you mean?' she asked.

The beer was still strong in Mr Turner. He said: 'They were sort of kind. Do anything for me, they would. I reckon that I might have passed out that time, spite of all the doctors and the nurses, if it hadn't been for them chaps sitting with me, talking. God knows they had enough troubles of their own, but they got time for me in spite of everything.'

There was a long thoughtful pause. Presently she said: 'What's this got to do with a nigger?'

'One o' them was a nigger from America,' he said. 'The last one to go out. He was the only one I ever see clearly–Dave Lesurier, his name was.' He pronounced it like an English surname. 'Then there was Duggie Brent–he was a corporal in the paratroops. And then there was the pilot of the aeroplane, the second pilot I should say– Flying Officer Morgan. We was all in a mess one way or another, excepting him, and yet in some ways he was in a worse mess than the lot of us.'

He turned to her. 'I been thinking,' he said quietly. 'I never seen any of them from that day to this, though we was all in such a mess together that you'd have thought we might have kept up, somehow or another, just a Christmas card or something. But we never. Well, I got through all right 'n turned the corner. I got a nice house here, mostly paid for, and a good job. Folks looking at me would say I was successful, wouldn't they?'

She nodded slowly. 'They would that, Jackie. We're not up at the top, but we're a long way from the bottom.'

'Well, that's what I mean,' he said. 'A long way from the bottom. But that time I was talking of we was right down at the bottom, all four of us, me and the other three. And when I was down there they was bloody nice to me. You just can't think.'

'I see,' she said.

'I had it in my mind for a year or more I ought to try and find out what the others were doing,' he said quietly. 'Maybe some of them are dead. That nigger, he was charged with attempted rape, and they give them pretty stiff sentences for that in the American Army. The others, too. . . . But I got by all right–I never starved in the winter yet, that's what I say. We've got up a long way from the bottom, and we've got money for a nice house, and a car, 'n holidays, and after that we even save a little. And I been thinking,' he said quietly, 'I been a bloody squirt not to have done something to find out about them other chaps, and see how they was getting on. They were bloody good to me, when I needed it.'

He pulled out his cigarette case, and handed it to her. She took one and he placed one between his lips, and fumbled with his lighter in the left hand, and lit them. 'Well, there we are,' he said. In the dim, moonlit garden there was privacy. 'I've had it now. In a year's time there won't be no more of me. I don't want to go out and leave strings hanging loose. I want to find out what happened to them other three, case any of them wants a hand, or something.'

She stared at him, bewildered. This was a different Jackie from the one she knew, and she distrusted change. Injuries such as his when they went bad made people funny in the head, sometimes; this business of wanting to look for his companions in the prison ward seemed very odd to her. She tried to head him off. 'They'll be all right,' she said at last. 'I wouldn't worry too much over it.'

'I won't,' he said. 'I'm just going to find out and make sure they're all right, so as I know.'

She said helplessly: 'What are you going to do then? Write a letter?'

'I dunno an address for any of them,' he said. 'No good writing to the hospital, not after all these years. I'd better try the Air Ministry to get the pilot's address, and the War Office for the corporal, I suppose. I dunno what to do about the nigger.'

'You'll never find them after all this time,' she said. 'How would you ever find a nigger that was in the American Army, after the war, and all?'

'I dunno,' he said. There was a long pause, and then he said: 'I want to have a try.'

She sat deep in thought for a few moments. He was a bit queer, she decided. Clinically speaking, I should say that she was right; the obsession was probably related to his lesion. That did not help her in her immediate problem, what to do about it. She knew enough about her husband not to cross him directly; when once he got a fixed idea he held on to it like a dog with a bone. Moreover, for the first time in years she felt he needed her. She said: 'What were they like, these three? Was there anything particular about them?'

He grinned: 'Only they were all in such a bloody awful mess—like me.' He turned his head to her; in the white light she saw the gleam of his great wound. 'Like me to tell you about them?'

She said: 'Yes.'

He got up from his chair. 'I'm just going in to spill some of this beer. Shall I bring out a rug when I come?'

It was the first time he had offered to do anything for her for a long time. She said: 'Please. It's getting kind of chilly out here, but it's nice.'

He went into the house, and came back presently, and handed her the rug. She wrapped it round her, and settled down to listen to him talking. They sat there on the lawn in the warm summer night, in the quiet grace of the moon, and the stars faint in the bright light. It was windless, still and silent. Around them, in the dormitory suburb, the world slept.

This paratroop corporal, he said, he was a proper card. He was a young chap, not more than twenty, a short stocky young man with a thick mat of curly red hair; he wore it cut short in the army style, but even so there was a lot of it. He had the grey eyes that go with it, and like most red-haired young men, he liked a bit of fun.

His name was Duggie Brent. In full, his name was Douglas Theodore Brent, but he considered Theodore to be a cissy name, and hid it up as much as possible. His father was a butcher in Romsey, and a lay reader at the Methodist Chapel; when his son arrived it seemed proper to christen him the Gift of God. In later years his father reconsidered that.

In fact, there was nothing much the matter with Duggie Brent except that he didn't take kindly to the chapel and he took a great deal too kindly to young women. He had a way with them. He had his first girl trouble when he was fourteen, and that was only the first. By the time he was sixteen and a half his father was paying a paternity order for him, and didn't like it. When he was seventeen, in 1938, he joined the Territorials for fun, faking his age; in 1939 the war broke out and he was mobilized and sent to Durham. Every mother of girls in Romsey breathed a sigh of relief.

In the Army, they set to work to make a man of him. In that time of war they did not waste much effort in teaching him barrack square drill or dress parades. First, they gave him a rifle and taught him how to use it. Then they put a bayonet on the rifle and set him running at a line of sandbag dummies. If you gave the rifle a sharp twist after the lunge, they said, the bayonet came out easily and the wound was a lot bigger.

The next thing they gave him was a Bren gun; he discovered that you could kill a lot of people with that in a very short time, if you got them in open country. In case the enemy were so unsporting as to lie in foxholes, however, they showed him how to use a hand grenade, and how to creep up covered by his pals with the Bren gun to lob these in among the Germans in the trench. After that came the Tommy gun and, later, the Sten gun, and then he graduated in the three-inch mortar.

All this was elementary, of course, mere high school stuff. He started on his college course in 1941 at an anti-tank school, where he was taught that much the quickest way to kill the people in the tank was to set the tank and all on fire. He did an interesting and instructive little course on Ronson Lighters. He learned that you could kill a lot of people with a couple of hundred gallons of blazing oil, if you went about the matter with discretion and intelligence. After that he did a course of mines and minelaying, and then a very amusing little course in the preparation of booby-traps.

In 1942 he volunteered for the Commandos, and they really started to teach him to kill people. All that he had learned so far, he discovered, was routine stuff and unworthy of a serious student of the art of combat. Any fool could kill a German with a hand grenade which made a noise and woke up the whole neighbourhood; a man who knew his stuff could creep up in the darkness and do it with a knife from behind, grabbing the mouth and the nose with the other hand to prevent him crying out. You had to be careful not to get bitten, but like all these things it was quite easy when you got the way of it. You had to get into the right position; then you just went so, and so, and so—and there he was, kicking a bit, maybe, but very dead.

That was how an average good man who knew his stuff and took an interest in his work would do the job. If you really aimed at the top flights of the art, however, and if you were quick and agile, a knife was quite unnecessary. Duggie Brent went through a course of unarmed combat at the end of 1942, where he was taught to kill an enemy with his bare hands. This was the real peak of his military education; by the time he went back to his unit he was able to attack an armed man three stone heavier than himself, and kill him with his hands and feet alone, in perfect silence.

In 1943 he did so, in the dark outside a public house just off the New Cross Road.

It happened on his embarkation leave, and he was out of the country on a transport for North Africa before the police got on to him. It was a sordid little quarrel between men who had drunk too much to mind their words, after a winter of waiting, exasperation, and irritation with the slow progress of the war. At that time Duggie Brent was walking out with a member of the ATS whose home was at New Cross in the south-east of London. Her name was Phyllis Styles, and she was on leave from her AA station in Kent. They had tea together at a Lyons and then went to the Odeon cinema. They came out of that arm-in-arm at half past nine after three house of delicious proximity, and to round off the evening they went to the Goat and Compasses for beer.

Mike Seddon was an Irish boilermaker who had made the Goat and Compasses his evening's entertainment. The evidence did not disclose how much beer he had drunk before Brent and his girl arrived; moreover it is not significant because an Irish boilermaker can take an infinite amount of wartime beer before falling over, and as he regularly took home fifteen pounds in his wage packet he could afford it. The bar was crowded thick with people in that last hour, so that Brent and his girl and the boilermaker were thrust close together in a corner with their beer.

It was soon after Brent had transferred to the Parachute Regiment, and soon after their red beret had been introduced. Mr Seddon took exception to this sartorial idiosyncrasy. 'You young fellows running round in fancy hats,' he said scornfully. 'They don't give me a fancy hat to wear. I don't get no fancy hat. No fancy hat they don't give me. And why?' he asked the crowd, raising his voice to the injury. 'Why aren't they after giving me a fancy hat? I'll tell you. I'll tell you why I don't get no fancy hat. It's because I do a mucking job of work. That's why. That's why they don't give me no fancy hat. Because I do a mucking job of work to win the mucking war.'

There was a laugh. Corporal Brent, beer mug in hand, flushed angrily, and said: 'What the hell do you think I do, then?'

The boilermaker was on his own home ground. He came to the Goat and Compasses each evening, and he knew the temper of the crowd and their frustration with the slow building up of war effort. He glanced at the corporal's chest, innocent of decorations. He say: 'Ah, well, just tell us now, me boy. Stand up and tell the whole bloody lot of us. What are you after doing now to win the mucking war?' He turned to the crowd. 'Sit on his arse 'n polish his buttons in his fancy hat, that's what he does. I do a job of work, I do, but they don't give me no fancy hat.'

Brent opened his mouth to say that he was on embarkation leave and shut it again without speaking; there was no knowing what security snoopers might not be within hearing in that crowd. He flushed angrily. He was sensitive to the fact that he had been mobilised in the Army for three and three-quarter years, and had never been out of England, and had seen no action at all.

'I do what the sergeant and the officers tells me,' he said angrily. 'I don't have no say.'

'Don't do no work either in the mucking Army,' said Mr Seddon. 'Do some of you lads good to come and do a mucking job of work, 'stead of walking round with floosies in a fancy hat. A mucking job of work, that's what 'ld do the Army good.'

'You lay off the Army and talk clean,' the corporal said furiously. 'I got a lady with me.'

The girl laid her hand upon his arm. 'Come on, Duggie,' she said. 'Let's get out o' this.'

He shook her off. 'I'm not going to have him talking that way,' he exclaimed. 'He's got no right to talk like that.'

'That's right,' the boilermaker said, swaying a little, menacing, towards them. 'You take him away, in his fancy hat an' all. Bring him back when he's opened the Second Front 'n I'll give him a pint.' He paused a moment to consider the proposal. 'Two bloody pints,' he said. 'Bring him back when he's done a mucking job of work.'

The wrangle continued for another few minutes with both tempers rising hot; then it was closing time and the barman moved them firmly out at the tail of the crowd into the dark street.

There was no moon, and it was pitch dark in the black-out outside the pub. On the pavement the boilermaker stood swaying, fourteen or fifteen stone of him, massive and scornful. 'The Second Front,' he said. 'Sure, there'll be no Second Front at all, at all, not till they put some guts into the bloody Army. All the mucking soldiers do is walk round in a fancy hat 'n pick up tarts. Army tarts, in mucking uniform with fancy tarts' hats, too.'

The girl said quickly: 'Duggie—don't.' She pulled him by the arm. 'It don't matter what he says. He's had a bit too much.'

He shook her off. 'That's right,' he said. 'Scum o' bloody Dublin, over here to see what he can pick up, 'n tell the German consul, I suppose. The country's fair rotten with these bloody Irish bastards.' He turned away. 'Come on, Phyl—leave the mugger be.'

The boilermaker reached out and aimed a kick at him; the heavy boot caught Brent squarely at the base of the spine, infinitely painful. Duggie Brent had never learned to box like a gentleman; there had been no time to teach him that. Blind with fury and with pain he swung round and in the one movement flung his fancy hat, the maroon beret, straight in Mr Seddon's face, the opening move in unarmed combat to make your adversary blink and hide from him the terrible kick coming. In the same swing his heavy army boot landed with all his force in the pit of Mr Seddon's stomach; the boilermaker doubled up with pain. Immediately his adversary was behind him, and there was a rigid, steely arm in battledress around his neck, the elbow pressing his chin up and back against the pressure of a knee intolerable against his spine. He kicked and beat the air, but his opponent was behind him, fighting in a way that he had never known. His body was forced up against the wall and bent backwards with a fierce pain, and the arm pressing up his chin prevented him from making any but small choking sounds.

It was certainly the corporal's intention to hurt Mr Seddon, to cause him a great deal of pain. In his instruction, however, nobody had ever told him when to stop in order to avoid killing his man. To overcome the boilermaker he had to put out all his strength; I think in that last moment of fierce, straining tussle curiosity may have entered in. Suddenly there was a crack from the man's back, and he yielded suddenly to the pressure, and gave a great choke, and ceased to struggle. It was a moment or so before Brent realized what he had done.

He released his hold, and the body fell limp at his feet, twitching a little. 'Christ,' he said quietly.

He stood for a moment irresolute; then he stooped and felt the man's face. He was still breathing, and the corporal straightened up. He had injured him more than he had meant to, and that was going to mean a bloody row. There were men a hundred yards up the street passing a dim lamp, walking away; they did not seem to have noticed anything. There was nobody else about, but in the nearby public house there were still lights, faint streaks that showed round the edge of the blackout.

He crossed to the girl, standing in the middle of the road. 'Come on,' he said. 'We better get out of this. I hurt him bad.'

She said: 'Oh Duggie! We'd better do something.'

'Come on out of it,' he said. 'I'll show you.'

He hurried her away and up the New Cross Road until they found a telephone box. In the dim light of his torch he found the number of the Goat and Compasses, and rang them up. A girl's voice answered him. 'One o' your customers fell down outside on the pavement,' he said. 'He's hurt himself, or something. You'd better go and see if he's all right.' He slammed down the receiver before she could answer.

In the close intimacy of the telephone box the girl stirred by his side. 'That was ever so clever,' she said in admiration. 'I'd never have thought o' that. You *are* a one.'

He kissed her in the telephone box for a few minutes in the friendly darkness, the boilermaker all but forgotten. Then he took her home.

That night Mr Seddon died in the Miller Hospital at Greenwich. Next day Corporal Brent rejoined his unit; five days later he embarked for an unknown destination, which turned out to be North Africa. The law caught up with him two months later at a place called Blida, led to him by the unwilling evidence of Private Phyllis Styles. The police had a good deal of trouble with her before she would talk.

He was taken under guard from Blida to Algiers, kept there for a week and was then sent to England in a Hudson with several other prisoners, amongst them Captain Turner. In the hospital at Penzance he was the first upon his feet. All that he had suffered was a few flesh wounds from splinters of the same 20-mm shell that had disabled Turner, and a simple fracture of the right arm which he got in the crash landing. By that time Turner had been operated upon and lay inert with his head swathed in bandages, able to think and understand, and talk very little but with both eyes covered. He never saw Brent at all.

The ward sister had been told by the surgeon that she must keep her patient interested, so she gave Corporal Brent a book called *True Tales of Adventure* and set him down to read to Turner for an hour. The corporal disliked reading aloud and did it very badly; moreover, the true tales were thin, watery stuff compared with the adventures that he had been through. Within five minutes his stumbling voice had flagged. He turned a couple of pages, and read a paragraph in silence.

'I don't think much o' this book,' he remarked. 'You like me to go on? I will if you say.'

The swathed figure on the bed moved one hand weakly from side to side.

'Okeydoke,' said the corporal. 'I'll ask sister if she's got one with more ginger in it, next time she comes–girls and that. Maybe they'll have a copy of *No Orchids for Miss Blandish*, or one o' them. I could read you some o' that,' he said hopefully.

The figure on the bed elevated a thumb.

Brent sat in silence for a minute. 'When you get in bad with the police, 'n you get charged,' he said at last, 'they give you someone to speak for you, don't they? At the trial, I mean. Someone to take your side, who knows the ropes, like?'

From the bed there came a whisper. 'You get a lawyer given you, a barrister they call him. What you been doing, chum?'

Confession eases things. Brent said: 'I had a sort of fight with a chap, and he died. I didn't mean to hurt him, not bad like that.' He hesitated, and then said: 'They say it's murder.'

In the suburban garden the moon was bright, the night was very clear. 'I never even see his face,' said Mr Turner, 'but I got to know him well enough for all of that. I never heard what happened, or anything.' He paused. 'I dunno. Maybe he got hung. But I don't think they'd hang a chap for a thing like that, do you?'

His wife stirred beside him. 'I don't know,' she said. 'He killed the chap, from what you say.'

'Oh, he killed him all right. No doubt of that.'

'Well, if he did, they'd hang him, surely?' She thought for a moment. 'If he got off, well then, he'll be making a living somewhere, I suppose.'

He said: 'I dunno what he could do. The only thing he knew about was how to kill people–he knew plenty about that. He hadn't got a trade, or anything. Labouring–I suppose he could do that.' He turned to her. 'He was a nice chap,' he said, 'and we was all there in a mess together.'

She did not speak.

'Like to hear about the other two?'

She snuggled down into her rug, pulling it more closely round her. 'Go on,' she said. 'I never heard you talk about that time at all.'

He thought of his own trial and prison sentence. 'It's not the sort of time one talks about,' said Mr Turner, 'in the normal way.'

Flying-Officer Phillip Morgan of the R.A.F. was allowed to get up out of bed for the first time two days before Corporal Brent was removed from the ward and taken up to London to be charged. He should not have been put in a detention ward at all, and this fact was to him a permanent grievance. He was taken from the wreckage of the Hudson with a broken leg and three broken ribs and placed with the others in a small ward in the Penzance Hospital. When it became known that the other two survivors were prisoners, a guard was placed upon the ward, but there was no other bed for Flying-Officer Morgan so he had to stay there. As an educational experience it was very good for him.

He was twenty-two years old; his school and the R.A.F. had made him what he was. He had no other experience behind him; he was at a loss when faced with any problem for which he had not been trained at school or in the R.A.F. His father had been a bank manager in Kensington and had died when he was a boy; his mother was an invalid and lived in Ladbroke Square on the borders of the well-to-do part of London. He spent his holidays in that stultifying place and took no benefit from it; when war broke out he joined the R.A.F. as an aircraftsman. In that service he developed a good deal; he was commissioned in the summer of 1940 and sent for training as a fighter pilot. By the spring of 1941 he was flying Spitfires operationally in England. He survived that tour of operations and did three months' ground duty; in 1942 he did another tour in North Africa and won the D.F.C. After two tours on fighters he had a choice of occupation; he chose Transport Command and with some vague idea of fitting himself for a job in civil aviation after the war. It was in this capacity that he was flying as second pilot of the Hudson.

He was a callow and ignorant young man, but he could fly an aeroplane very well indeed. He reached the coast of Cornwall on that summer afternoon at an altitude of seven hundred feet, and losing height rapidly with one engine stopped and the other gradually failing. Behind him in the cabin there were dead and dying men; in the seat beside him the captain of the aircraft sat slumped and dead, and falling forward now and then on to the wheel, so that Morgan had to struggle with the body with one hand and fly the aircraft with the other. Beside him flew two Spitfires of the flight that had put down his assailant; they flew with their hoods open, the pilots turned towards the crippled aircraft that they were escorting, powerless to help. And yet, their very presence helped. Phil Morgan was a Spitfire pilot first and last; he loved Spitfires, and their presence was a comfort to him in his difficulties.

At the point where he crossed the coast the cliffs are nearly three hundred feet high; when he came over the fields he was not much more than four hundred feet above them. There were airstrips in the vicinity, but he had so little altitude and he was losing height so fast that he did not dare to turn towards the nearest one; he knew that he would lose more height upon a turn. He would be down in any case within a couple of minutes; he must land straight ahead of him within the next five miles. In that undulating country he had little choice of field; the one he chose was bordered by a stone wall at his end. It was only about two hundred yards long, nothing like long enough for a Hudson even in a belly landing, but the far boundary appeared to be a hedge and beyond that there was another field. The Hudson touched down belly upon grass fifty yards before the hedge, which slowed her somewhat before hitting up against the stone wall that the hedge concealed. When Flying-Officer Morgan woke up he was in hospital, and in the next bed to him was a Negro soldier of the U.S. forces. He took that as a personal affront.

He poured out his troubles to Captain Turner when he came to see him for the first time. By that time Turner's right eye was uncovered and he could see a little with it though it was very bloodshot and the light hurt it if he kept it open long; for this reason the screen was still kept around his bed. Flying-Officer Morgan could talk to Turner in the semblance of privacy; though he knew the Negro could hear every word he said the screen made it private conversation.

Almost his first words were about this urgent topic. After exchanging names, he said: 'I say, old man, do you know there's a bloody nigger in the ward with us here?'

Motionless in his bed, Turner said: 'I know. Brent told me. He's here now, is he?'

'He's right in the next bed to me. I think it's the bloody limit. I'm going to write a letter to the Air Ministry about the way that I've been treated here, and put it in through my C.O.'

'They looked after me all right,' said Mr Turner.

Morgan said: 'Well, I know, old man, but it's a bit different for me.' He hesitated for an instant, and then said: 'I mean after all, there's no reason why *I* should be kept under guard. I mean, it's a bloody insult having a sentry on the door of your ward. And then to put us in a ward with other ranks–it's a bit thick, even if they are crowded. We ought to be in an officers' ward, we two. And then on top of everything to put a bloody nigger in with us, it's too bad. I told the sister so, and the doctor too.'

'What did they say?'

'The doctor was bloody rude. Said this was a civilian hospital and we were all here on sufferance. Said if he heard any more about it, he'd tell the R.A.F. they'd got to come and take me away whether I was fit to move or not. I wish to God he would. That's no way to look at it, is it?'

'Bloody shame,' said Mr Turner mechanically. 'What's the nigger doing here, anyway? He wasn't with us in the Hudson, was he?'

'No–he's stationed somewhere near here, with the American Army. Went into an air raid shelter and cut his throat, just near the hospital here, because the military police were after him for something or other. Now he's come out all over boils and carbuncles and things, and runs a temperature all the time. Septicaemia, or something. That's what they say, but I think it's V.D. All niggers have V.D. You want to watch out, old man–don't you let them give you a cup or anything he's used. The mugger oughtn't to be in this ward at all. He ought to be in a Lock hospital.'

He paused, and then he said: 'He offered me a paper the other day, that he'd been reading and breathing all over. I soon put him in his place.'

He too, was set to read the *True Tales of Adventure* to Captain Turner, and like Corporal Brent, he found it heavy going. 'I wish they'd let us have a copy of *The Aeroplane* or *Flight*,' he said. 'If we were in a proper R.A.F. hospital instead of this stinking hole we'd have all that, and probably the American ones as well.' He went into a long dissertation on the merits of the Spitfire versus the Mustang which sent Captain Turner into a quiet doze.

He had no conversation whatsoever beyond aeroplanes, except a queer hotchpotch of schoolboy prejudices. He referred to all foreigners as dagoes, and deplored their moral habits with a frankness of speech that was novel to Mr Turner, who had not had the benefit of an English public school education. He affected superiority to these dagoes on account of their low standards of life, and he affected superiority to the Americans because they made too much money. He thought money grubbing was frightfully bad form, never having had to grub for it himself. He was not a fool, but he was wholly undeveloped and his commission in the R.A.F. which had conferred on him the status of an officer and a gentleman without much effort on his part, had bred in him a curious snobbishness. He was childlike in his ignorance of many things, and as pathetic as a child in his blunders.

Once he said: 'Are you married?'

'Aye,' said Mr Turner. 'I got married when the war broke out.'

'I suppose you knew her before the war?'

'Worked in the same office, we did,' said Mr Turner. 'Then we started going out together, evenings, 'n after a bit we got married. October 1939 that was, just before I joined up.'

'Really?' The boy stared at him in wonder. 'It must have been funny working in the office with her.'

'I dunno. It was darned distracting.'

'Most people meet girls at a party, don't they?' said the pilot. 'That's how I met Joyce. And what a party! At the Bull in Stevenage, it was. We were all as blind as bloody bats.'

'Are you married, then?' asked Mr Turner. The boy seemed so young.

'I'm married,' he replied. 'I got married just over a year ago, at the beginning of my second tour.' There was a faint tone of pride in his voice.

'Fine,' said Mr Turner. 'Got any kids yet?'

'Oh no,' the boy said. 'Joyce isn't one of those. She's got her work, you see. She's on the stage. She's awfully good, really.'

Mr Turner said: 'Got her photograph?'

Morgan was very pleased. He went hobbling across the ward and fetched his wallet from the drawer of the bed table, and brought it back with him, and showed Mr Turner the photograph beneath a sheet of cellophane. Mr Turner took it in his hand and held it sideways to the light, and looked at it with his sound eye. It showed a very luscious and provocative young woman, with downcast eyes and long hair flowing around her bare shoulders.

He gave it back to Morgan. 'I think you're a very lucky chap,' he said. 'She's perfectly lovely.'

The boy was pleased. He took the photograph back and studied it himself. 'She is, isn't she?' he said. 'She's more beautiful than that, really–it doesn't do her justice. Everybody goes mad about her.' He hesitated, and then said: 'Of course, she's been married before.'

Mr Turner was amazed. 'She has?' The girl seemed so young.

Morgan nodded. 'She was married to an awfully good friend of mine, Jack Stratton. He went for a Burton over France last year. Joyce was frightfully cut up about it, of course–it was terrible for her, poor kid. She was only twenty then, and she'd had an awfully rough deal in her life. Jack was a jolly good friend of mine, and we knew he'd want me to look after her, so we got married two months later before I went out to Egypt.'

Captain Turner thought enviously that it was grand when duty to a friend turned out like that. 'So you're her second husband,' he said. 'Well, I never.'

The boy seemed a little confused. 'Well, as a matter of fact, she was married before that,' he said. 'I'm her third husband, really. She was married first of all to a chap in 73 Squadron who bought it when they were operating in France back in 1940. She's had frightfully bad luck. It's always the best people get the worst luck, isn't it? I wonder why that it?'

He was worried about an illegal package that he had concealed in the rear fuselage of the Hudson. 'There's a stowage rack for parachute flares up in the roof, just above the little hatch in the bulkhead, aft of the gun bay, right in the rear fuselage,' he said. 'I put it there. But it'll be gone by now. Some wretched Ack Emma will have got it. It's too bad.'

'What was it?'

'Perfume that I got in Algiers, and some lipsticks, and powder, and four pairs of silk stockings, and some silk.' He hesitated, and then said: 'With a girl like Joyce, you've got to treat them right, you know. I mean, she's accustomed to pretty things, and she feels awful if she can't get them. I mean she can make herself look so stunning, she's just got to have the things.' He brooded for a minute, and then said: 'I wish I hadn't told her I was bringing her some stuff. Now I've got nothing to bring.'

'You're bringing yourself back alive. That's something.'

'Oh–yes. But she wanted some Coty.'

Turner learned that they had only lived together for a fortnight, in the Piccadilly Hotel, before he had been sent out to North Africa on his second tour; since then they had been together for half a dozen weekends only. 'She's got her work, you see.' Her work was playing the part of the chambermaid in *Smile Sweetly, Lady* at the Grafton Theatre. She had to speak three lines, smile, and exit into the bedroom.

Flying-Officer Morgan wrote a letter to her every day, long scribbled letters in pencil in an irregular, unformed hand, but he never seemed to get a reply. He talked about it once. 'Of course, there's nothing wrong or anything like that,' he said, 'but she doesn't like writing. It's about three months since I got a letter from her. It's just the way you're made, you know. When she does write, they're frightfully nice.' He showed Turner a little dog-eared sheaf of letters in his wallet, very few. 'I carry them all round with me everywhere I go, and read them over and over again till they pretty well fall to pieces.' He examined his treasures. 'I must get a bit of stamp paper for this one.'

Turner asked once if she was coming down to see him at Penzance, but he said: 'Oh, I don't expect so. She's got her work, you see. She couldn't leave that, could she?'

Mollie had left her job to come and see him, but Mr Turner said: 'Well, no, I suppose not.'

Phil Morgan did not often get a letter from his wife, but his friends wrote to him from time to time. Two days before he left hospital he came to talk to Captain Turner, troubled. 'I do wish people wouldn't write things like this,' he said. 'It's absolutely all right, of course . . .' He handed Turner one sheet of a letter:

–and we had a wizard time. We couldn't get anywhere to sleep in London because you have to book a room weeks ahead now, so we rang up Joyce and she said we could come and sleep at her flat. She had a chap called Bristow there, a two striper from 602 Squadron, and he said he had given up looking for a bedroom in London now and he always went and slept with Joyce, in a manner of speaking, of course. We got some sausage and stuff from the N.A.A.F.I. and cooked supper about one in the morning, and Bristow had a bottle of whisky and I had one of gin so we were well away. We all felt like death the next day, but it was a good party.

Captain Turner read this through; the exposed portion of his face was a poker face. 'Nothing in that,' he said. 'It was kind of friendly of your wife to look after your friends.'

'I know . . .' The boy turned to the letter in his hands. 'There's only just the sitting-room and the bedroom,' he said at last.

'Well, that's all right. Your friends wouldn't do anything you wouldn't like, 'n go and write to you about it.'

'Oh, it's not them.' He hesitated. 'It's this chap Bristow.'

'What about him?'

'Well, he's got a lot of money, and he can give her things–furs and things I simply haven't the money to get. He's awfully kind. But . . .' He hesitated, and then said: 'The poor kid's had such a packet of losing husbands, she sort of feels she's got to be safe, whatever happens. If I'd gone for a Burton on my second tour, or any time, I think this chap Bristow would be Number Four.'

'I see,' said Captain Turner thoughtfully.

'It's all perfectly all right, of course,' said Morgan. 'It's only that she's so attractive people go mad over her. It's not her fault that happens.'

'Of course not,' said Turner.

Two days later, Phil Morgan was discharged from hospital.

'I wish to God I hadn't lost that parcel,' he said. 'I don't like going up to London with nothing for her. She gets such a lot of presents . . .'

In the moonlit garden his wife stirred by Turner. 'Well, that's nothing,' she said. 'Actresses and that, they've got different standards.'

'Actresses my foot,' said Mr Turner. 'She wasn't an actress at all, till they brought in conscription for women, and she had to get a job.' He turned to her. 'You remember, we went to see *Smile Sweetly, Lady*. The chambermaid. She hadn't got much to do.'

Mollie nodded. 'Irene Morton wore a lovely pyjama suit. You remember them pyjamas? Ever so lovely they were. Silly sort of play, though. We went on and had dinner at Frascati's. Remember?'

'Aye,' said Mr Turner thoughtfully. 'Good evening, that one.'

He glanced at her. 'I sort of worried more about Phil Morgan than either of the others,' he said. 'He was married to a bitch that didn't care a sausage for him, but a chap can butt his way through all that sort of trouble.'

He paused. 'It was sort of–there was nothing *to* him, if you get me,' he said. 'There he was, twenty-two years old, and not a thought in his head beyond the perishing aeroplanes. Might have been a kid of ten. Got himself in a bloody mess through marrying a bitch like that, and probably go on getting into mess after mess, unless he got killed in an aeroplane first. But I reckon he was too good for that. He was good at flying, the only thing he was good at. I dunno what would have become of a chap like that. He just knew nothing, absolutely nothing at all.'

His wife said: 'Well, I dunno. People get more sense as they grow older, and get settled down in jobs. What about the nigger?'

'Aye,' said Mr Turner, 'he was the last one. I was much better when he got up. There was just the two of us left in the ward then, and the guard on the door just the same.' He paused, and then said: 'Funny thing about that chap,' he said. 'He didn't talk like a nigger at all. He talked just like any other Yank soldier, better than most, maybe.'

'Pretty simple, I suppose,' she said. 'I mean they don't know much, do they? I don't suppose you found much to talk about with him.'

'Well, I dunno,' he said. 'We got along all right.'

She glanced at him, puzzled. 'Was he a proper nigger, then?'

'Oh yes, he was a nigger all right. Sort of milk chocolate colour, he was, with black kinky hair. He'd got some white blood in him, I should think, but not a lot.' He paused. 'Quite young, he was–only about twenty.'

By the time he was allowed out of bed the screen had been taken away from around Turner, and the whole of his face was uncovered; he still had a dressing on the wound, but he was sitting up in bed and taking notice of things. He had spoken once or twice to the Negro before, but their beds were on opposite sides of the room, and that made conversation difficult for Turner with his wounded head and for the Negro with the deep wound in his throat. It was not until the Negro was up and in a dressing-gown that they were able to approach each other sufficiently closely for easy talk.

Turner said: 'How does it feel, now you're up?'

The Negro said: 'I don't feel so good right now. Say, if I'd known that cutting your throat gave you septicaemia, I sure would have made a job of it.'

'Or else not done it at all,' said Turner.

The Negro paused for a moment in abstraction. 'Well,' he said at last, 'that would have been another way.' He turned to Turner. 'Now I'm up and around, if you want anything, Cap'n, just say.'

'Right oh,' said Turner, and went on reading his paper.

He could not read continuously at that time, or for very long; it made his eyes ache and he had to stop. The Negro also had a paper and copies of the *Stars and Stripes* and *Yank*, but most of the time he sat in sad, thoughtful abstraction in a wicker chair, or stood in silence looking out of the window at the pleasant, undulating Cornish country scene. In the middle of the afternoon Turner said: 'What about a game of draughts? Can you play draughts?'

The other roused himself. 'Surely, Cap'n.' He got up and fetched the board and the cardboard box that held the pieces. 'You know,' he said, making conversation, 'back home we call this checkers.'

They set up the board on Turner's bed, and arranged the pieces. 'Where's your home?' said Turner, also making conversation. 'What part of the States do you come from?'

'Nashville,' said the Negro. 'Nashville, in the State of Tennessee.'

Turner thought for a moment. 'That's over somewhere in the west, isn't it? Or is that Texas?'

'No *sir*. Tennessee is in the south, between the Lakes and Florida. Not right south like Mississippi or Louisiana, just half way south.'

'I see,' said Turner, not much interested. 'Been over here long?'

'Four and a half months.' They began to play.

'Do you like it over here?'

'It's a long way from home, Cap'n,' said the Negro quietly. 'You get to feeling sometimes that you're quite a ways from home, 'n then you get lonely. But most of us colored boys like England pretty well.'

Presently Turner asked: 'What do you do in Nashville? What do you work at?'

'I got a job with the Filtair Corporation.'

'What's that?'

The Negro glanced at him, surprised. 'Why, that's quite a business, Cap'n, back in Nashville. They got over five thousand hands working now, with war contracts. Make air cleaners for autos and trucks and tanks, and airplane engines, too.' He paused, and then he said: 'My dad, he's been with them over twelve years, now. That's a long while to be with one corporation in the States, specially for a colored person.'

'What does he do there?'

'Runs the print machine, making the blueprints from the drawings. He's a draftsman really, makes a darned fine engineering drawing. We lived up in Hartford when I was a lil' boy, and he worked there as a draftsman. Then we moved back down South because his pa died and Grandma needed looking after. But I guess there's difficulties in the South you don't get in Connecticut. Pa works in the print room.'

He said that he had been sent to the James Hollis school for coloured boys in Nashville; the ex-draughtsman had given his son as good an education as a coloured boy could get. 'Pa wanted me to be a draftsman too, and I did the course at school, and I liked it well enough. But then when I left school I couldn't get a start nohow. No *sir*, not in Nashville.'

'Why not?'

The Negro looked at him. 'Things is mighty funny in some States,' he said quietly. 'In Filtair, colored people don't do drafting. I guess if I'd gone up to Hartford I'd have got a start all right, but Ma was poorly, 'n not much money, either. I got took on as a garage hand at Filtair; it's all colored in the garage. Then I got to drive a truck for them, and then they put the filters on the Type 83 bulldozer for desert service, and I got to driving that around sometimes for experimental trials. Then when I got drafted they found I knew how to drive a bulldozer, so they put me into a construction unit.' He thought for a minute. 'I guess I'd have been in a construction unit anyway,' he said. 'They don't send us on combat service.'

In the winter of 1942 he had been moved across the Atlantic; he was stationed for a month or two in Northern Ireland with his unit. An airstrip had been needed in the region of Penzance. By March 1943 his construction company, with three others, was working on a hilltop just above the little village of Trenarth, four miles from Penzance, levelling the fields, breaking down walls, demolishing farmhouses, making roads and runways. Trenarth is a little place on the railway, at the junction of the main line and the North Coast line; it is a place of about a thousand inhabitants with a small market square, a church built in the year 1356, and a public house. The construction companies were all Negro except for a few white technicians; the impact of fifteen hundred coloured soldiers on this little place was considerable.

'I like Trenarth,' he said. 'I guess we all do.'

There were some misunderstandings to be cleared up when they first arrived. A party of white American surveyors from the Eighth Air Force had come first to pick the site and mark it out, and they had told the village all about the blacks who would arrive in a few days. They said that the Negro soldiers who were coming were rather primitive, and that the villagers would have to be both careful and tolerant. They said the Negroes could speak little English and did not understand the use of lavatories. When they were hungry, they would bark like a dog, and they had small, rudimentary tails concealed within their trousers which made it difficult for them to sit down. Having drunk their beer and marked the site and had their fun with perfectly straight faces, the surveyors went away and left the village in perplexity.

Old Mr Marston, the gardener at the vicarage, raised the matter in the White Hart one night. 'I asked Mr Kendall if it's true what they were saying about these black soldiers that are coming,' he said. 'About them barking when they want their victuals. He says it's all just a story they were telling us, to get a rise out of us.'

'Aye, that's right,' said Mr Frobisher, the landlord of the pub. 'They was just pulling our legs. Negroes don't have tails, not any that I heard of.'

A mournful little man who worked as a porter at the station said: 'Well, I don't think they was pulling our legs at all. Very nice and straight they spoke to me, they did. That corporal, he said this lot come straight from Africa. Africans, they are–that's why they can't speak English. There's rum things happen in Africa, believe me.'

The general consensus of opinion was that the stories were improbable, but that it would be prudent to maintain a strict reserve when the visitors arrived.

I do not know how the story reached the Negro soldiers, but it reached them very quickly. In the March dusk, after their evening meal in the rough camp that they were making on the bleak hilltop, a few coloured men walked down into the village. They came in a little party, smiling broadly; as they passed each villager they gave a realistic imitation of a pack of hungry dogs. They thought it was a great joke, and barked at everybody, in varying tones from pekinese to bloodhound. By the time they reached the White Hart the village had come to its senses; in the bar they were accepted as interesting strangers, to whom was owed some sort of an apology.

'They were real friendly, right from that first evening,' said Lesurier. 'They made us feel like we were regular fellows.'

It was not only that the villagers were conscious of their own stupidity. At that time there had been a great deal of prominence given in the English newspapers to the assistance that America was sending in Lease-Lend, and this assistance was obvious to everybody in Trenarth in the increasing numbers of American tractors, trucks, and jeeps to be seen in the streets. Like others, Bessie Frobisher, the buxom daughter of the landlord, had half believed the stories she had heard about the Negroes, and felt in a dim way that she owed recompense to these black, soft-spoken, well-behaved strangers in the bar. So she got out her electric iron which had not functioned for a month, and brought it into the bar and put it on the counter, and said: 'Can any of you mend an iron?'

Sergeant Sam Lorimer picked it up in his enormous pink-palmed hands. 'Sure, lady,' he said. 'I can fix that for you.' He turned it over in his black hands, examining it. 'It don't get hot no more?'

She said: 'It doesn't get hot at all now. It used to be ever so good. It's a job to get anything mended now, you know.'

He called across the bar: 'Hey, Dave, lend me your screwdriver?'

Lesurier lent his screwdriver, and with that and a jack-knife they disembowelled the iron on the counter while the girl watched, picked up the broken thread of filament and made it fast, and reassembled it. They tried it in a lamp socket and it got hot at once. 'It's all okay now,' said Lorimer, 'but the filament won't last so long–it's kind of rotten. It gets that way as it gets old.'

'You can get new elements for irons like that,' said one. 'I see them that day we was in Belfast.'

'That's so,' said Lorimer. 'Maybe we could get one in Penzance.' He passed it back to Bessie. 'Well, there you are, lady. It's fixed right now, until it goes again.'

She smiled at him. 'It's ever so kind of you to take the trouble,' she said. She turned to her father. 'Dad, this gentleman's mended my iron, and it works beautifully.'

She used her normal language without thinking anything about it, but each Negro within hearing caught the word 'gentleman' and stiffened for a moment in wonder. They certainly were in a foreign country, a long ways from home.

Frobisher passed his hand over the iron to feel its warmth, and turned to Lorimer. 'Aye, it works all right,' he said. 'Will you take something on the house? A glass of beer?'

The big Negro hung his head, smiling and confused. 'Well, that's real kind of you, mister,' he said.

Within a few days they were fixing everything. They liked fixing things. They fixed the leg of the settee in the saloon bar, and they fixed the gate leading to old Mrs Pocock's cottage garden. They fixed the vicar's Austin Seven, and they fixed the bit of wall that a truck had knocked down by the war memorial. They fixed the counter-flap of Robertson's grocer's shop, and they fixed the wheel of Mr Penlee's dung-cart. When Penlee gave them tea with all his family in the farm kitchen as some recompense for what they had done to his cart, they were so overwhelmed that they turned up next Sunday in a body and limewashed his cow house.

They fixed everything that needed fixing in Trenarth in a very few weeks. In a country that had been at war for over four years with every able-bodied man and woman called up for industry or for the forces, their presence was a real help to the village; the people liked them for it, and for their unfailing courtesy and good humour. They were well paid by English standards and they brought prosperity to Trenarth which was a factor in their favour, but more important was the willing work they did; England in wartime had plenty of money, if little to spend it on. Some of them were gardeners in civil life and used to come up shyly and ask if they might work in the garden, asking for nothing but the pleasure of tending flowers. Some of them were farm hands, and wanted to do nothing better in their spare time than to help the land girls clean the muck out of the cowhouses. Inevitably they were asked in to a meal as interesting and honoured guests, and equally inevitably would take the farmer's daughter or the land girl to the pictures in Penzance.

They had a grand time, in those early days. They used to bring a couple of trucks down from the camp on Saturday afternoons to pick up the girls, and drive off to Penzance to the pictures in a great merry part, thirty or forty black young men and as many white girls all laughing and jammed together in the great trucks, having a fine time.

The vicar, Mr Kendall, held unconventional views on most of the controversial subjects in the world, which no doubt accounted for the fact that at the age of fifty-three he had progressed no farther than the living of St Jude's, Trenarth. He stood with Mr Frobisher one afternoon watching one of these expeditions as it started off, and said: 'We'll have a few black babies to look after, presently.'

Mr Frobisher rubbed his chin. 'Well, I dunno,' he said. 'It's the girls' own business if they do. Colour apart, I like these fellows well enough, I must say.'

The vicar nodded. 'I'd rather have them than some others of our gallant allies,' he said darkly.

It was in that halcyon time that Private David Lesurier became acquainted with Miss Grace Trefusis.

Miss Trefusis worked behind the counter in Robertson's grocery shop, where she spent all day making up little ounce and two-ounce parcels of rationed foods. She was nearly seventeen years old, a pretty, dark, reserved girl who had grown up late and never had much truck with boys. Lesurier, at the age of twenty-two, had played and danced with various mulatto and 'high yaller' girls back home in Nashville, but had very seldom spoken to a pure white one; he was shy of Grace, and very much attracted to her at the same time.

He saw her first at Robertson's where he was buying cigarettes. He could buy better cigarettes in the canteen up at the camp, but it pleased him to go into English shops and buy; it gave him a feeling of competence in a foreign land. From that time on he bought all his cigarettes at Robertson's, in single packets of ten that necessitated many visits.

In spite of this assiduity, he did not get on very fast with Grace. With a sixth sense she knew he came to see her. She was shy of him and did not want much to be seen about with a black boy; as he was equally shy of her and never asked for anything except: 'Ten Player's, please, ma'am,' she had little difficulty in keeping him in his place. But from his many visits a queer tenuous little friendship came into being; she grew accustomed to him and his shy 'Ten Player's, please, ma'am,' and sometimes she smiled at him. She was very young and pretty when she smiled.

Up on the hilltop the Negroes did their work efficiently and well, accelerating their own departure. In six weeks the strip was paved and usable by airplanes of the US Army Air Corps. Half of the Negroes were moved on to other work in other places; the remainder went on putting up prefabricated huts and ammunition dumps and making roadways. In their place came the first detachment of the Army Air Corps to take over the new strip.

For a week all went well. The white American soldiers mixed amicably with the Negroes, using the bar in the White Hart on friendly terms with them and chihiking with them in the street. By the end of the week, however, the detachments were of about equal strength, and a stir of uneasiness was agitating the whites.

Girls were the first and main trouble. Every eligible girl in Trenarth by that time was walking out with a black soldier, for the very good reason that there had been nobody else in the vicinity to walk out with. The white troops found to their concern that every girl was dated up by a Negro. Socially this was no great matter, for there were too few girls in Trenarth to go round in any case and there was a large camp of A.T.S. not far from Penzance willing and anxious to be taken out by the Americans. Amongst the new arrivals, however, there were a small proportion of whites from the deep South, to whom the feminine vagaries of Trenarth were genuinely distressing.

Corporal Jim Dakers, from Carthage on the Pearl River, in Leake County, Mississippi, gave expression to his feelings in the bar of the White Hart one evening. 'You'd think these English girls would have more sense of decency than to go walking with a nigger,' he proclaimed. 'What kind of a dump is this, anyway? Their folks should give them a good whipping. If they don't, well I guess there's other folks that will.'

His companions said: 'Aw, lay off, Jim. You're not in the South now.'

He said: 'It sure burns me up to see the niggers getting out of hand this way.'

Behind the bar the English landlord stood mute, faintly hostile.

There were other irritations, too. Ninety-five per cent of the white Americans of the Army Air Corps were quiet, well behaved and tactful, but unfortunately the remainder were more vocal. Corporal Stanislaus Oszwiecki, from McKeesport, Pennsylvania, considered that municipal affairs were run better at home. He returned to the bar from a visit to the urinal, and said:

'Say, what do you know? They ain't got no sewer here. Just a kinder soak pit, 'n an earth bucket.' He turned to Mr Frobisher, the landlord. 'Say, didn't nobody ever tell you guys about modern sanitation?'

The landlord took his pipe out of his mouth, and said slowly: 'You'll find all you want in the towns and cities in this country. It's not necessary in a place like this.' He spoke quietly and with restraint, because he was sensitive about the lavatory accommodation of the White Hart. As soon as the village got a more adequate water supply he meant to alter things.

'For crying out loud,' said Corporal Oszwiecki, 'he says proper sanitation isn't necessary. Say, you guys want to brush up your ideas if you're ever going to stand up to the Germans. Look what they done to you before we came–' he drew his breath in sharply–'boy, did you see Plymouth! You British want to get around a bit, 'n get some modern notions. The U.S. Army pulled you through last time, 'n it'll pull you through this time. But we aren't coming over every twenty years whenever you get into trouble. No, sir.'

The landlord sucked his pipe and said nothing. A couple of white American privates got up quietly and walked out into the street. It was quiet, peaceful in the ancient village street under the moon.

At last one said: 'Stan got a bit lit up.'

The other said: 'I certainly hate hearing that kind of talk. It's not right, 'n it don't do no good, either. And there's another thing. It don't do no good speaking about niggers in front of colored boys.'

'That's right,' the first replied. 'Back home we never talk about a nigger unless we want to start a row. We always call them colored folks, or maybe Negroes.'

It did no good at all in Trenarth, nor did the growing feeling between the white and Negro soldiers. When Colonel McCulloch of the U.S. Army and of Columbus, Georgia, arrived to take over the command of the new station, he found a tension between whites and blacks, the blacks encouraged by the sympathy and friendship of the British villagers. The South has always provided a considerable proportion of the regular officers of the U.S. Army. Colonel McCulloch was a good officer determined to pursue the war seriously, making the best of the personnel under his command.

'Reckon these colored boys got just a mite above themselves before we came,' he said. 'We'll have to put that right.'

To put it right, he set himself to reimpose the policy of segregation that had always worked well in the Southern States. He sent for a detachment of military police experienced in the segregation policy; it was not his fault that these police were all white and mostly from the South. He held a meeting with Captain Deane, the Negro officer in charge of the black troops, outranked him and beat him down on every point. Then he sent his secretary, Lieutenant Schultz, to see the landlord of the White Hart. As it was a formal call, Lieutenant Schultz wore his mosquito boots.

Schultz explained his business. 'The colonel feels that friction may arise if the colored troops use the same place of recreation as the rest,' he said. He was a big, earnest young man. 'Back in North Ireland there were quite a few cases of trouble, specially where troops used the same saloons. We had to make arrangements there for separate accommodation, same as we do at home, and the colonel's going to do that here.'

'Aye?' said Mr Frobisher.

Schultz said: 'I've been through on the telephone to Paddington station, and the railway company are fixing things so that the refreshment room up at the station stays open till ten o'clock serving drinks the same as you do, starting Thursday. The colonel says that as from Thursday next the Negro troops go to the refreshment room.'

'Not much of a place for them, that,' said Mr Frobisher slowly.

'Not for you and me, maybe,' said the lieutenant. 'But it's all right for them. You ought to see the places most of them come from, back home.'

'Aye?' said Mr Frobisher slowly. He was thinking hard.

Schultz was young and inexperienced; the way to him seemed easy. 'Well, from next Thursday you won't serve any colored soldiers in this place,' he said, 'only whites. I guess you'll probably be glad to see the last of the black boys, won't you?' The landlord did not answer. 'Anyway you won't serve them any more.'

Mr Frobisher said slowly: 'I'll serve who I like.'

There was a momentary pause. The lieutenant quickly realized that there was something here that he did not fully understand. He thought for a moment, and then said: 'The colonel sent me down to tell you what we're going to do, the way we'd get co-operation. We don't any of us want friction, fights and such-like, in this place.'

'There's been no friction here,' said Mr Frobisher. 'We've had the coloured boys here six weeks now, and never a cross word, let alone a fight. Why can't you let things be?'

'It's what the colonel says,' said Schultz, 'that they must use the refreshment room, from Thursday on.'

Mr Frobisher took the pipe out of his mouth and drew himself up, dignified in his shirtsleeves. 'I've been here twenty-seven years,' he said, 'and my father before me, and never a question of the licence or a complaint from the police. *I* say who I serve here, not your colonel. If I say I serve the coloured boys, why then, I serve the coloured boys, and that's all about it.'

Schultz was nonplussed. 'I can't go back and tell the colonel that,' he said. 'You want to think this out a bit, maybe.'

Mr Frobisher said: 'I've been thinking while you've been talking. I don't want to cross your colonel. If you feel there'll be fights if your white soldiers go on coming here along with the black boys, well, let the white boys go to the refreshment room, and let the black ones keep on coming here. That's what I say.'

The lieutenant stared at him, dumbfounded. 'Say, Mr Frobisher,' he said, 'we couldn't do that. That's the worse accommodation of the two!'

'Well then,' said the landlord, 'let 'em both keep coming here. There won't be no fights in my house, I can promise you that. Twenty-seven years I've held this licence, and I wouldn't have done that, I can tell you, if I let the men get fighting.'

'I don't think the colonel will agree to that,' said Schultz. 'He wants to get things like we have them back at home.'

'Well, he's not at home now, and that's a fact,' said Mr Frobisher. 'He's in Trenarth, and maybe we've got different ways to what you have at home. I don't want to make no difficulties for you people, but if I stopped serving any man, here in this country, because I didn't like the colour of his skin I'd soon lose my licence. That I would. I don't stop serving blacks until the licensing justices say different. Not while they behave themselves.'

The lieutenant realized that he was up against a very stubborn man. 'Well,' he said, 'I'll just have to go back and tell the colonel what you say. I guess he'd better stop off when he goes through this afternoon and have a word with you.'

'Aye,' said the landlord affably, 'ask him to look in. Maybe I'll have thought of something by that time, something else we might do.'

That happened in the morning, and if Colonel McCulloch had been able to look in that afternoon before the views of Mr Parsons got around the neighbourhood it would have been a great deal better. Unfortunately he was detained and did not come till the next day.

Ezekiel Parsons was eighty-six years old. He had been a farm labourer in his day, and had never been farther from Trenarth than Penzance. He could not read or write, and he was very deaf. Trenarth was the universe to Mr Parsons; he classed persons from villages ten miles away as foreigners equally with those from foreign countries. His wife was long dead and his family dispersed; he lived in a single attic room on the old age pension and a small allowance from his children, and sat in a corner of the public bar of the White Hart, every day, morning and evening, from opening till closing time. It was his one amusement, to sit there and watch the people. He was the oldest inhabitant, and he had long white side-whiskers.

He was well known to Jerry Bowman, the driver of the brewers' lorry delivering the casks of beer. That morning Jerry stood the old man a glass of mild, and asked: 'What do you think of all these Americans in Trenarth, Mr Parsons?'

The ancient piped in his old quavering voice: 'I like them very well, oh, very well indeed. We get on nicely with them here. I don't like these white ones that are coming in now, though. I hope they don't send us no more o' them.'

It was too good not to be repeated; it ran round both whites and blacks that afternoon. It got to Colonel McCulloch as a good story in the evening. He did not think it a good story at all. He thought it was a very bad story indeed, and he thought about it all night.

Bright and early the next morning, he sent for Lieutenant Anderson, chief of his detachment of military police. Lieutenant Anderson came from Little Rock, Arkansas, and had served there in the police; he knew a good deal about niggers. The colonel said:

'Say, Anderson, we're heading straight for trouble with these goddam niggers. They been here alone too long, and they've got the whole darned countryside with them.'

Lieutenant Anderson said: 'I guess that's right, colonel. They been here alone too long, and they've got uppity.'

The colonel said: 'That's right. Mind, we got nothing to complain of yet, beyond the fact that they go walking with these darned English girls, giving them ideas. But *I* know, and *you* know, what's the end of that. They get swelled heads, and then we'll have real trouble.'

'That's right, colonel.'

'Well now, you got to be strict with them. I don't mean go hazing them and stirring up trouble, just–strict. We got to get things back the way they should be. Keep them smart, 'n crack down on them if they're not dressed right. It won't hurt any if we make a few examples; if you get anything to go before court martial, for example, I'll see they get the limit. I had some of this before, one time, and I know what can happen if you let it slide. You want to be just, 'n give them the square deal. But when you catch them on the hop, then you got to be plenty tough.'

Lieutenant Anderson said: 'Okay, colonel. I got the idea.'

The colonel said: 'I'm going down right now to sort out this darned saloon keeper, and get that end of it straightened out.'

He drove down in his Command car to see Mr Frobisher, accompanied by Lieutenant Schultz. He found the landlord in his shirtsleeves polishing the glasses in the bar, for it was out of hours and the bar was empty.

He said: 'Say Mr Frobisher, I understand there's been a mite of disagreement between you and Schultz here over the use of this place by the colored troops. I just stopped off to tell you why we can't have that any more, so that you'd see it from our point of view.'

Mr Frobisher said: 'Aye?'

Colonel McCulloch said: 'Yeah. I've got to run the war around these parts, and I've got to do it with the troops they've given me. They've given me white troops and colored mixed for my command. I didn't ask for it that way, but that's the way it is. Well, when you get a mixed command like that you got to watch out and be mighty careful, Mr Frobisher, or they'll be fighting and shooting and God knows what.'

Mr Frobisher said: 'Aye?'

The colonel said: 'You got to be mighty careful with these niggers. Maybe you wouldn't know about that in this country. You start and treat them like you would whites, before you know it they'll be thinking they're as good as white, telling you what to do. Then you get trouble. There's only one way to deal with this, the way we do it back at home and all through the Army. Separate recreation for the colored and the whites. Keep them apart, and then you don't get trouble. Give the niggers a place of their own, and keep them in it. That's the setup I'm going to have here.'

Mr Frobisher said: 'Aye?'

'That's right. From Thursday next the niggers use the refreshment room up at the station. They won't be coming in here after Wednesday night.'

Mr Frobisher said: 'I was thinking, how would it be if your whites used the parlour of an evening, and let the blacks go on in the public bar as they've been doing?'

He led the way and showed them the parlour. It was a small room, rather dingy, with a few texts on the walls. The officers thought nothing of it. 'Can't put the boys in a dump like this,' said Schultz. Mr Frobisher did not like to hear his sitting-room referred to as a dump, but he said nothing.

'That won't do,' said the colonel. 'They'd have to use the same passage and the same door. No, from Thursday next the niggers go to the refreshment room.'

'How are you going to keep them out of here?' asked Mr Frobisher.

The colonel said: 'I'm hoping we'll get your co-operation, Mr Frobisher. If not, I'll have to put this place off limits to the colored troops, and put a policeman outside in the street.'

He went away, leaving Mr Frobisher uneasy and resentful. That evening Sergeant Lorimer, the big Negro who had mended the electric iron for the landlord's daughter, called for Bessie to take her for a walk. They had fallen into the habit of doing this once or twice a week, after which he would return with her to tea in the parlour of the pub, finishing up the evening in the bar, playing darts.

Outside the pub they met a military policeman. Lieutenant Anderson had his own ways of putting niggers in their place, and he had been genuinely shocked to see so many walking out with English girls. The M.P. said: 'See your pass, sergeant.'

He stared at the pass. 'Let's see your dog tag.'

The Negro expostulated. 'Say, what's that for?'

'So's I'll know this pass is made out for you, 'n not some other nigger,' said the policeman. 'Come on, step on it.'

To get at his identity disk, slung round his neck next to his skin, Lorimer had to undo coat and muffler, disarrange his collar and tie, open his shirt and pull out the disc from beneath his undervest. Then, while Bessie waited for him, he had to dress up again.

Twenty yards on they met another military policeman. 'C'm on, sergeant–pass and dog tag.' Again Lorimer had to undress upon the pavement.

All up and down the street, Negro soldiers walking with English girls were undressing on the pavement, while the girls stood giggling or irritated, and the Negroes struggled with their clothes in sullen fury. After the fourth encounter Lorimer and Bessie gave up their walk, thus fulfilling the intention of Lieutenant Anderson, and returned to the pub. The girl told her father all about it over tea.

'Jim here, he was ever so patient,' she said. 'They was just doing it to be nasty, seemed to me.'

'I guess they don't like to see colored people walking with English girls,' the Negro said quietly. 'They wasn't doing it to nobody except couples.'

Mr Frobisher sucked his pipe in thoughtful silence. 'I dunno,' he said at last. 'Funny sort of way o' going on.'

He was genuinely concerned at the turn that events were taking in Trenarth. He was the unofficial leader of the community; the village had a decrepit village hall, an army hut of the last war put up by the British Legion, but the main meeting place and forum for discussion was the bar of the White Hart. Mr Frobisher had run that bar for very many years, and so had presided over most of the meetings of the village upon topics that concerned them all. He felt, inarticulate, that it was up to him to take a lead in this distressing matter that was agitating the place. He was waiting upon events to show him what that lead should be.

Corporal Stanislaus Oszwiecki showed him, that same night. The bar was filled with sullen, irritated Negroes mixed with white soldiers. Corporal Oszwiecki thought this was a good time and place to give his views on the association of white girls with coloured men.

'Say,' he said, 'you hear what the Snowdrops have been doing up 'n down the street?' He told his companions in a loud tone what had been going on. 'Teach these English bitches to go walking with a nigger,' he said.

There was a momentary pause. Mr Frobisher broke it, from behind the bar. 'Not so much o' that language, *if* you please,' he said. 'If you can't talk clean, you can get outside.'

Jim Dakers said: 'Say, what kind of a place is this, anyway? It makes me sick these English floosies go around with niggers. I seen them hugging and kissing in dark corners–think o' that, man, hugging and kissing with a nigger.' He turned to Mr Frobisher. 'Say, mister, this town stinks. Stinks of nigger.'

Three white American soldiers got up and walked out in silence.

Mr Frobisher slammed down a jug upon the counter; in the silence that followed the sharp rap he said: 'If that's the way of it, I'll clear the bloody bar. Outside all the lot of you—white *and* black. Outside—every American soldier out of this house, unless you want the military police called in. Outside, all the lot of you!'

Corporal Oszwiecki said: 'Say, what is this? We don't have to go.'

Mr Frobisher left the bar and walked out into the street. Before the inn he found a couple of American military police. 'There's trouble with your soldiers in my bar,' he said. 'You'd better get every American out of my house, white and black. They'll be fighting with each other in a minute.'

The military police swung their truncheons and went in; in a few minutes the house was clear, but for a few civilians and old Ezekiel Parsons sitting in a corner. In the quiet that followed the departure of the Americans the old man piped: 'Nasty fellows, they white ones. I can't a-bear them.'

Behind the bar Mr Frobisher sat grim and silent, writing the large letters of a placard on white cardboard with a paintbrush dipped in ink.

It appeared in the bar window next morning. It read:

THIS HOUSE IS FOR ENGLISHMEN AND
COLOURED AMERICAN TROOPS ONLY

Two military policemen strolled up and looked at it. 'Say,' said one, 'that's not right. The colonel's going to put out an order that the niggers use the refreshment room. This place is for whites.'

They stared at it in silence for a moment. 'I guess it's a mistake,' the other said. 'The landlord's a bit dumb. Look, he spelt "colored" wrong.'

When Colonel McCulloch heard about the notice he knew that it was no mistake. He was down at the White Hart within half an hour; outside the inn he paused and read the notice before going in. He found Mr Frobisher in his parlour, seated at the table making out his orders.

'Say, Mr Frobisher,' he said, 'I hear that you had some trouble down here last night.'

'Aye,' said the landlord.

The colonel said: 'Well, that's just too bad. It's as I said we've got to fix up separate accommodation. The only thing is, I want the white boys to use this place, as we settled yesterday.'

'Aye?' said Mr Frobisher. 'Well, I don't.'

'Say, what's the matter with the white boys?'

The landlord thought deeply for a minute. 'There's nothing wrong with most o' them,' he said at last. 'Nine out of ten are quiet, decent lads, remarkably like us. The rest of them are kind of quarrelsome and always making trouble. You can't say you'll have one lot o' white soldiers, and not the others, though—it's all or none. I never had no trouble with the coloured boys, of any sort at all.'

The colonel said: 'When you say the white boys, ten per cent of them, make trouble, Mr Frobisher, what do you mean? What sort of trouble?'

The landlord said: 'Last night they was picking on the coloured boys—saying nasty things about niggers in their hearing, and that. It was all the whites doing it, never the black boys. I think they was out to make a fight, that's why I cleared the lot o' them out.' He turned to the colonel. 'Some of the whites with foreign names don't seem to like anything–nothing you can do will please 'em. they don't like our girls, they don't like Negroes, they don't like the beer, they don't like the lavatories, 'n they don't like the English people, either, I don't think. And they don't mind telling you about it. . . .'

'Some of them may have a lot to learn,' said Colonel McCulloch. 'Quite a few of them have never been outside the States before.' He had not himself, but he did not say so.

'Aye,' said Mr Frobisher. 'Well, they can go and do their learning up at the refreshment room, 'n come back to this house when they've learned how to behave.'

'Now that's what I've come down to talk about,' the colonel said. 'We can't have that. We can't give this place over to the colored boys and let the white boys go up to the station. That's giving the best accommodation to the niggers. You must see that we can't do that.'

'I don't know nothing about that,' said Mr Frobisher. 'You've got your troubles, and I've got mine. I got my licence to think of, that's what I've got. My licence. If I have fights and that, where do you think I'll be?'

'Why,' he said, 'I bloody near had a fight with one of your white boys myself last night, when he calls my Bessie a bitch. If I'd been twenty years younger I would ha' done, licence or no licence.' He thought for a moment. 'I'm sorry for the rest of your white boys,' he said, 'the quiet easy ones that don't feel badly about your black lads. But they just got to keep out of this house, along with the others. I can't separate them out.'

'How would it be, though, if the whites came here and send the blacks up to the station? That's the way we want it,' said the colonel.

'Have that corporal with the foreign name in my house again? Not likely,' said the landlord. 'I'll take the blacks.'

Colonel McCulloch could not make him alter that decision and returned ruefully to the camp up on the hill to take the matter up in correspondence with his general; the notice stayed in the window. That evening Mr Frobisher refused to serve white soldiers at all; as the bar-room was crowded with pleased and jubilant Negroes there was not the trouble that he had anticipated. The White Hart became firmly established as the recreation centre of the coloured soldiers, the white troops had to go to the small, ill-lit, badly furnished waiting-room, and relations between white and black deteriorated rapidly.

It was at this time of tension that Dave Lesurier made his pass at Grace Trefusis. For some time now he had thought of little else but Grace. It was clear to all the Negroes that they would not be much longer in Trenarth; the strip was made and paved and the airplanes were flying from it, and most of the roads were finished. If Dave were ever to consolidate with Grace he would have to get on with it; he had no time for the long courtship that he knew, instinctively, would be the right approach. He had been courting Grace now for a month, and he had still got no further than: 'Ten Player's, please.'

For a week he had been trying to advance to his next stage, which was 'Say, Miss Grace, would you care to take a lil' walk one evening?' But he had been unfortunate; each time the shop had been full of other people and the girl had herself been busy, though not too busy to smile as she handed him his cigarettes. He knew that she would not agree to walk out with him if other people were in hearing; he would have to wait his chance to say his piece until they were alone together. And he got no chance.

She lived with her parents at a cottage near the railway; her father was a signalman at the junction box. Standing about in the square one evening at about six o'clock, hoping for a glimpse of her, he saw her going with a friend down to the Village Hall; she recognized him, and smiled at him as she passed. It was sufficient to keep him rooted there for four hours till, in the moonlight at about ten o'clock in the evening, she came out on her way home. And she came alone.

He crossed the road, and met her in a quiet corner by the gate that led into the yard of the White Hart. He was repeating his line to himself as he crossed the road, because he was very nervous – 'Say, Miss Grace, would you care to take a lil' walk one evening?' But when he was face to face with her at the quiet corner he forgot his words.

He stood in front of her, and said: 'Say, Miss Grace.' And then he stopped. She said: 'Oh, it's you.' She smiled at him, a little nervously.

He said again: 'Say, Miss Grace . . .' And then he stopped again, because it suddenly seemed silly to ask her to take a little walk with him one evening, at ten o'clock at night. And because he was uncertain what to do, and because he had to do something, he put his arms round her and kissed her. It was very naughty of him to do that.

For a moment she yielded, too surprised to do anything else; for a moment he thought that he was going to get away with it. Then fear came to her, irrational, stark fear. When she was a little child somebody had given her a golliwog, a black doll with staring white eyes and black curly hair, dressed in a blue coat with red trousers. It had terrified her; whenever she saw it she had screamed with fright so that it had been given to a less sensitive child. Now at the age of seventeen the same stark fear came back to her. What she had been subconsciously afraid of all her life had happened. The golliwog had got her.

She started to struggle madly in his arms to free herself. She cried: 'Let me go, you beast. Let me go.' And she cried quite loud.

Chagrined, and already ashamed, he released her. He said: 'Say, I didn't mean . . . Miss Grace, I guess I done wrong . . .' But she was gone, half running, sobbing with emotion and with fright. At the corner she ran full tilt into Sergeant Burton, of Montgomery in Alabama and of the U.S. Military Police, who had heard her cry out and was coming to investigate.

He said: 'Say, lady, what's the matter?'

He was fat and forty and comfortable, and white. To her at that moment he was all security. She sobbed: 'There was a nigger there. He caught me and started messing me about.'

Sergeant Burton said: 'These goddam niggers,' and blew his whistle. He shot round the corner with surprising agility for so large a man, still whistling as he went; as Grace stood on the corner slowly composing herself two other military police shot past her, heading for the whistle. A jeep came screaming down the road in intermediate gear driven by a third, braked to a standstill with a screech of tyres by her, and two more tumbled out.

The girl was comforted by all this evidence of support, and yet at the same time she was distressed. She had started something, and she didn't quite know what. Around the corner there were men shouting, and then one reappeared and whistled again. Men came pouring out of the White Hart; American soldiers, white and black, appeared from everywhere. Grace turned from them, still weeping a little, and walked quickly up the street towards her home. She could not bear to be questioned about what had happened.

Around the corner Dave Lesurier had to act quickly. He was bitterly disappointed at the blunder he had made; as he heard what Grace had said to the sergeant he realized that he was in a very serious position. He came, if not from the deep South, from the near South, and all his youth had been conditioned by tales he had heard of Negroes lynched and murdered horribly because the whites believed they had assaulted white women. Most of the tales that had conditioned him were quite untrue because such things grow in the telling, but Dave Lesurier could hardly be expected to know that. To him, at the moment, there was real danger that if the mob got him a bonfire would be made outside the White Hart and he would be burned on it alive. He must get to hell out of it.

He dived into the yard behind him, and flung himself over the wall into Mrs Higgins's back garden, over the next wall into Polherring's timber yard; from there he gained the back alley and looked cautiously around. There was clamour in the direction he had come from, but they did not seem to be following him; he heard continuous whistling, and the sound of jeeps. And then, to his dismay, he heard shouted orders sending all American troops back to their camps.

He knew that he must rejoin them immediately and go back with the crowd. He had not heard Grace tell his name; he did not know even if she knew it. If he could catch up with the crowd and mingle in with them he might escape; to stay in Trenarth and go back alone later meant instant detection. It never occurred to him for one moment to walk out, and give himself up, and tell the truth, that he had given the girl a kiss, so what? He had not hurt her, and he had not meant to hurt her, but it never crossed his mind that anybody would believe him if he said so. He must get to hell out of it.

He edged along the alley towards the end that led into Sheep Street; from there he could gain the High Street and mix in with the crowd. When he was still in the alley he heard voices of men in the street twenty yards ahead of him; he ducked back into the deep shadow of a wall as two corporals of the military police ran up, stopped, and peered down the alley towards him. He crouched deeper in the shadow.

One said: 'Block this one – you stay right here, and block this one, and keep a look-out up 'n down this street. I'm going on around the block. We got him somewhere in this block.'

'What's he done, anyway?'

'Raped one of these darned English girls.'

'Gee. They've had it coming to them. Is he armed?'

'I guess not. Might be, though. If he don't stop on a challenge, better let him have it.'

He ran on. Peering out of the deep shade, the Negro saw the policeman at the end of the alley pull out his service automatic and cock it to bring a cartridge to the breech; he moved close to the wall and stood there, vigilant, alert, the gun ready in his hand.

Very gently, inch by inch, Lesurier moved back along the alley, keeping flat against the wall in the darkness of the shadow, testing each step on the ground before he let his weight on that foot in case of noise, feeling ahead of him with outstretched fingertips. The moon was with him, its bright light dazzling the watching policeman twenty yards away. The Negro moved back undetected.

Presently he came to a gate leading through into a garden behind him. His fingers explored it and it opened; in quick silence he went through and out of sight of the watcher at the end of the alley. Now he could hurry. He sped over the walls back into the timber yard, one side of which adjoined the High Street. Creeping over the timber, he looked down into the street.

There were no soldiers to be seen, except the military police. Under the direction of Lieutenant Anderson they seemed to be searching houses round about the White Hart. There was a picket of two policemen fifty yards away down the street in the direction of Penzance, at the corner of Sheep Street; at the moment they were looking up that street, where something seemed to be going on.

Deserted in the street, not ten yards from where he lay on the stacked timber, there was a jeep. It stood pointing in the direction of Penzance.

Lesurier thought quickly, fighting down the panic that was overwhelming him. Although the troops were all out of the village, they could not yet have got back to the camp up at the airfield, over a mile away. If he could get the jeep out of the town there was still a chance that he could catch up with the crowd and pass in with them through the guard, unidentified. If he could drive out on the Penzance road there was a chance that he could work his way round through the lanes and reach the camp in time. There was the jeep, and only two policemen at the corner fifty yards away to pass.

He took a final glance around. Then he got down from the timber and strolled nonchalantly out into the street and got into the jeep. The noise of the starter made the two men turn towards him, but the light was bad and they could not distinguish the colour of the driver. Lesurier put the jeep in gear and accelerated towards them in a normal getaway, not too fast in order not to arouse suspicion.

He was only a few yards off when they saw that it driven by a Negro, and challenged. He jammed his foot down hard in intermediate gear and drove straight at them. They leaped to one side as he roared past; then he was driving as he had never driven a jeep before, jinking and swerving all across the street. Behind him whistles shrilled and a shot rang out, missing him by twenty feet. Then he was out of Trenarth, roaring down the road towards Penzance, four miles away.

He did not know the roads. He was a bulldozer driver, and had never driven much about the countryside, though he could handle the jeep well enough. He had thought there would be a lane leading off towards the camp, and he drove on desperately looking for it. But there was no lane. He flung a glance behind him over his shoulder, and there were the headlights of cars, many cars, streaming down the road half a mile behind him. They were after him, and the hunt was up.

He knew now that when they overtook him they would shoot.

Stark panic seized him, born of the lynching stories told to him in his childhood in the South. He had done the unforgivable thing, and if the mob caught up with him they would tear him in pieces, burn him on a fire, torture him in vile ways. He put his foot hard down and dashed on through the quiet English moonlit scene in a frenzy of terror. The jeep he drove was in a poor condition; behind him the Command cars and the other jeeps were gaining on him; he had one hope now, to gain the shelter of the houses of Penzance and leave the jeep, and hide somewhere, anywhere. In his agony the thought of a well came to him; perhaps there would be a well somewhere, in some yard, that a man could get down into and hide, and let the hunt pass by. They would not think of looking down a well.

He would have been safer in a British police station, but he could not be expected to know that.

He dashed into the streets of Penzance at fifty miles an hour, his speed conditioned only by the speed at which the jeep would take the bends without going over. As he drove, he swung his head desperately from side to side, seeking for refuge. He came out by the sea not far from the harbour, and that checked him. He braked heavily and swung the jeep round into a side alley, and stopped, and ran blindly up towards the shadows. A Command car drew up with a scream of tyres, and a shot rang out, and the bullet hit the wall beside him.

He leaped for a seven foot wall and caught it with his hands, and got one leg up on it, and miraculously he was over it and in a hen run on the other side. He blundered through the wire of that and into a vegetable garden, and over another wall into a churchyard. Behind him there were lights and the American voices of excited men.

He ran through the churchyard and stopped by a wall, peering out into the street. The military police were spreading round the block that he was in, as they had done before. He was caught; in a few minutes he would be in their hands.

In those last moments all trace of confidence in military justice left him. He was the elemental, fear-crazed Negro hunted by the whites, conditioned by centuries of discrimination. The whites were after him and murderous in their intention to avenge the insult to the colour of their skin; rather than fall into their hands it was preferable to fall into the hands of death.

There was an air raid shelter built against the wall of the churchyard. Behind him the hunt was close; men were already in the far side of the churchyard at his heels. He went into the air raid shelter and drew out his knife. It was a good knife and one that he was proud of, given to him by his father back in distant Nashville when he was on leave before proceeding overseas; he kept it as sharp as a razor.

With tears streaming down his cheeks, in the smelly darkness of the shelter, he drew it hard and unskilfully across his throat.

'That's what happened,' said Mr Turner, in the quiet moonlight of the garden, four years later. 'That's how he come to be in hospital with me.'

His wife stirred in her chair; she was growing cold, but she was interested. 'What happened to him?' she inquired.

'I dunno,' he said. 'I dunno only what he told me, what I've told you now. He was for court martial when he got out, on a charge of attempted rape. That's all I know.'

She said: 'But what he done wasn't rape at all, was it? I mean, you said he kissed her.'

'That's what he told me,' said Mr Turner. 'He said that's all he did.'

'Well, they couldn't charge him with attempting rape for that.'

'I dunno,' said Mr Turner. 'Maybe they can in the American Army. I don't know but what he told me may have been a pack of lies.'

'It must have been,' she said. 'There must have been more to it than that.'

He was silent for a minute. 'I dunno that there was,' he said at last. 'I don't think he was lying. He was pretty miserable, and I think what he said was true, far as he knew it. He knew he was for court martial, and he was kind of resigned to that.'

She said: 'What was he miserable about, then? Just general disgrace?'

He said: 'It was the girl. He'd gone and spoilt everything with his own foolishness, and made her complain against him, and he'd never see her again. He used to sit staring out of the window, hour after hour without saying anything–wishing he was back in Nashville, I suppose. One time I saw him crying–tears running all down his black face. It made me feel sort of funny to see that.'

He paused, and then he said: 'I think he was in love with her. Really in love, I mean–just like he was a white lad.'

4

Mr Turner went to the London office of his firm, Cereal Products Ltd., by Underground and bus next morning. Cereal Products Ltd., has a suite of offices high up in a building in Leadenhall Street. He got there about ten o'clock, and went in to see the managing director, Mr Parkinson. He told Mr Parkinson his position frankly, as one man to another.

'I don't want any special favour, or anything o' that,' he said. 'But I want what's my due, and it's only right you should know what the doctor said, so you can make your own arrangements.'

Mr Parkinson told him what was his due. 'On your salary scale, the firm give three months sick leave on full pay. Then if you are still unfit for work, another three months on half pay.'

'And after that the firm's finished,' said Mr Turner. 'Well, that's fair enough. What about last year's summer holiday? I didn't get it then, because of that Argentine deal we did–Señor Truleja. Can I have that fortnight now?'

'I suppose so,' said the managing director. 'Yes, I think we can do that.'

'Can I put this year's fortnight to it, 'n have a month?' said Mr Turner. 'Now?'

'Yes.' He paused, and then he said: 'I got things to do.'

Mr Parkinson eyed him shrewdly. 'Three months and three months and one month makes seven months,' he said. 'The firm's not going to see much more of you, is it?'

Mr Turner said: 'It wouldn't see much more of you, either, not if you was in my shoes.'

'No. All right, go on and take your month's holiday, Turner. I'm very sorry to hear about all this.'

'Not half so sorry as I am,' said Mr Turner.

He went out, and turned into a Lyons teashop, and had a cup of coffee. He was feeling slack and unwell; the beer that he had drunk the night before, and the long sitting in the garden with his wife had done him no good. He sat there moody for a time, the great wound in his forehead pulsing intermittently. He smoked two cigarettes and then got up, paid his bill, and took a bus up to the Air Ministry in Kingsway.

'I got to try and trace an officer what served in the war,' he said to the messenger at the door.

He spent the next hour waiting in corridors and explaining his requirement to a number of uninterested people. They told him to go away and write a letter about it, but he would not do that. Finally he struck a junior clerk (female) who was much his type and very much in tune with the outrageous remarks that he saw fit to make to her, and who exerted herself to help him in his search.

She pulled a sheaf of cards from the immense card index. 'Give over,' she commanded, 'here, pay attention to this. There's five Phillip Morgans here.' She sorted them. 'He wouldn't be the Group-Captain, would he? Nor this one that got killed in April 1942. What about this one – Squadron-Leader at H.Q. Bomber Command?'

'That's not him, I shouldn't think,' said Mr Turner. 'You're busting out of your jersey, Loveliness. Want about sixteen more stitches in the next one, round about.'

'If you go on like that I won't help you any more,' she said. 'Now what about this Flight-Lieutenant Morgan that got took prisoner by the Japs in July 1944? Released from Rangoon Jail in May 1945, and demobbed.'

'What was he doing before?'

She scrutinized the card. 'Two tours in fighters, and then Transport Command.'

Mr Turner said: 'That's the boy. Got took prisoner by the Japs, did he? Well I never.'

She said: 'That's right. Last job was a Dakota squadron in South-East Asia Command. Supply drops, I suppose. Missing November 1944, reported prisoner in January 1945.'

'How can I get hold of him?'

'I dunno,' she said. 'There's next of kin here. That's all the address I've got.' She scrutinized the card. 'There's two here, wife and mother.'

'That's what'll happen to you before you're much older, Beautiful,' Mr Turner said. 'Specially the last. Let's have a look.'

He took down the addresses in his pocketbook, and left her, pleased and giggling. He lunched on a pint of beer and a snack at his favourite local off Shaftesbury Avenue, the Jolly Huntsman, and went to the address at Pont Street in the afternoon. He climbed the stairs to the tiny top floor flat; the door was opened to him by a pleasant plain woman.

He said: 'Does Mrs Morgan live here still?' He explained. 'I knew her husband in the war – I was trying to get in touch with him again.'

She wrinkled her brows. 'There's nobody of that name lives here now.'

He said: 'Pity. This was some time ago, in 1943, of course. You don't happen to have the address of the tenant before you, I suppose?'

She said: 'We've been here for eighteen months. The tenant before us was a Mrs Bristow. Bobby Charmaine, the actress, you know – that was her stage name, but she was Mrs Bristow. She might know about the people who were here before her. It's just a chance, you know.'

He said: 'Do you know how I could get in touch with her?'

'I'm afraid I don't,' she said. 'There was a divorce – she divorced Squadron-

Leader Bristow, or he divorced her just after they left here. Perhaps some theatrical agent could tell you how to get in touch with Bobby Charmaine–she's still on the stage. I saw that she had a small part in the Winter Gardens pantomime the Christmas before last, and my husband said he saw her in a touring company in Stockton-on-Tees last year. A theatrical agent might know.'

He left, and went down to the street again. He did not feel inclined to start a round of theatrical agents to get in touch with Bobby Charmaine in a second-rate touring company up at Wigan or West Hartlepool in order that he might ask her questions about her last husband but one or two. He took a bus to Kensington to see the mother.

She lived in Ladbroke Square. He found the house without difficulty, a tall old house in a terrace four storeys high, houses with basements and the stucco peeling off a little. Once it had been a smart residential neighbourhood; now it was a bit down at heels, still proud, but poor.

He rang the bell; after a long time the door was opened to him by a young woman, plainly, rather dowdily dressed. He glanced at her, and knew from the likeness that he had come to the right house.

'Excuse me,' he said, 'does Mrs Morgan live here?'

She looked him up and down, wondering what he wanted to sell. 'She does,' she said. 'What do you want?'

He hesitated. 'It's like this,' he said. 'I met a man called Flying-Officer Morgan in the war, right back in 1943, and I was trying to get in touch with him again. Phillip Morgan, the name was. I went and asked at the Air Ministry and they told me this address.'

'I see,' she said. 'You want my brother Phillip?' She did not seem to be particularly enthusiastic in the matter. She hesitated. 'I think you'd better come in,' she said at last. She led him into the narrow hall, and showed him into the room on the right, which was the dining-room. 'If you wouldn't mind waiting a few moments,' she said. 'I'll go and tell my mother.' She hesitated. 'What's the name?'

'Turner,' he said, 'Captain Turner.' He had not the slightest right to use his military title, but that never worried him.

She left him, and he stood in the dining-room, hat in hand, staring round at the depressing scene. The room was furnished in the most doleful late Victorian style, with heavy mahogany furniture of an uninspiring design. On the walls there were engravings of the Stag at Bay and of a lion and of a collie dog with a Scots shepherd, all very genteel. On the black marble mantelpiece there was a black marble clock with tarnished gilt pillars, stopped at twenty-three minutes to eleven. On the table was a white linen cloth, slightly soiled, and such tablespoons and cruets as would be needed for the next meal and could be conveniently left on the table. Mr Turner thought nothing of it at all, in comparison with his cheerful little villa at Watford.

'Fair gives you the creeps,' he thought. And then he thought, as he waited minute after minute: 'I bet something's happened to him that they don't want to talk about. She wasn't a bit keen.' The thought stiffened him to go through with the matter.

After a long ten minutes the girl came back. 'Would you come upstairs and see my mother?' she said.

He went up with her to the first floor drawing-room usual in such tall old houses. It was furnished in the same Victorian style as the dining-room had been, with mahogany furniture and heavy plush curtains. Although the day was warm all the windows were closed and a small gas fire was burning at the grate. Seated in a chair before this was an invalid lady, not very old but soured and unpleasant.

The girl said: 'This is Captain Turner, Mother, who wants to know about Phillip.'

Turner advanced jauntily into the room. He said: 'Afternoon, Mrs Morgan. I used to know your son Phillip in the war, and I wanted to get in touch with him again, talk over the old days, and all that, you know.'

She said: 'Sit down.' He sat down in a chair before her, and beamed at her expectantly, his hat upon his knee.

She said: 'Did you know my boy well?'

'Not well. We were in hospital together.'

'Did you know his wife?'

Mr Turner knew thin ice when he saw it. 'I never met her,' he said carefully. 'From what he told me, she was a very lovely girl.'

She said vehemently: 'He was a fool—oh, such a fool. But then, men are. They never know when they're well off. Always running after someone new—even the lowest of the low, Captain Turner, even the lowest of the low. Joyce was very patient with him—nobody could have had a more *angelic* wife, perfectly *angelic*. But you can't expect a girl like that to wait for ever. She has her pride, you know.'

'I suppose so,' said Mr Turner vaguely. 'Can I get in touch with him? I'd kind of like to see him again.'

'If you met him now, after having held the King's commission with him, you would be very disappointed, Captain Turner. A mother has a right to speak frankly about her son; you would be very disappointed that an officer and a gentleman could have fallen so low.'

The girl said: 'Mother, don't excite yourself.'

The invalid said: 'No.' And then there was a long silence.

Mr Turner said: 'Is he in London?'

His mother raised her head. 'He is abroad, in Burma somewhere, I believe. We do not correspond with him. If I were you, I should forget about it, Captain Turner. My son has not had a very satisfactory life.'

He said: 'I see.' If Morgan was in Burma there was not much point in going on with this. He said: 'Well, I'm sorry to have troubled you, Mrs Morgan. I just kind of thought if he was round about we might have got together for a glass of beer or something.'

She said: 'My son came home for a fortnight only, in 1945, and then went back to the East again. I am sorry that I cannot give you better news of him, but there it is.'

'Oh well, can't be helped,' said Mr Turner. He got to his feet. 'Sorry I troubled you, but it was just a thought I had, that he might have been about somewhere.'

He went downstairs escorted by the girl, leaving the invalid mother sitting over the gas fire in the sunlit room. As the girl opened the front door, he was glad to see the light and breathe fresh air after the close confinement of the house.

On the front steps, he turned to the girl. He was out of the house now, and had no further need for courtesy. 'What did he do?' he asked bluntly.

The girl hesitated, and then said: 'He left his wife, Captain Turner. I'm sorry to have to tell you this, but you'd better know about it, in case you ever meet him. He just walked out, and left her, and went back to Burma.'

'He did?' said Turner. His first reaction was that Morgan had showed more pluck and initiative than he would quite have expected. 'Well, these things happen to people,' he said. 'Sometimes there are faults on both sides.'

She said quickly: 'Oh, do you think that? Did you ever meet her?'

'I never did,' he said. 'He showed me her photograph and he talked a lot about her in the hospital. I saw her once in a play, but only on the stage.'

She said: 'It's so difficult to find out things, living alone here, like we do. What did you think of her, Captain Turner?'

He was well out in the street by that time; after the constrained atmosphere of the house it was pleasant to speak freely in the clean, fresh air. 'I thought she was the most bloody awful bitch God ever made,' he said. 'She was giving him the hell of a time, though he wouldn't admit it. He must have been crazy ever to have married her.'

She stared at him, dumbfounded. 'You don't think that?'

'I do think that, and a lot more,' he said.

She said: 'But she was always so sweet with mother.'

'I dare say.' He thought for a moment. 'Did your mother give her any money?' he inquired.

She stared at him. 'However did you know about that? You've been talking to her, Captain Turner.'

'Never met her in my life,' he said, 'and I don't want to, either.'

They stood in silence for a moment. 'I'll walk down to the end of the street with you,' she said at last. They turned and walked along the pavement together. Presently she said: 'You could write to my brother, if you want to, Captain Turner. He writes to me sometimes, and I write back. I don't tell my mother, unless there's anything very important, and that's not often. It only upsets her.'

He stopped on the pavement in the sunlit street, and got out his notebook and pencil. 'Where is he?' he asked.

'He's living at a place called Mandinaung,' she said. 'The address is Mandinaung, Irrawaddy, Burma. If you write a letter there, it will get to him all right.'

He replaced the notebook. 'I got that,' he said. 'You never know– I might be out there one day, and look him up.' For the moment he had forgotten that his future was not long.

She said: 'Oh.' They walked in silence for a few paces. 'In that case, I think I ought to tell you something, Captain Turner. My brother–' she stuck for a moment, and then said, '–my brother's living in rather a poor way, from what we can make out. He lives entirely with the natives, in this native village, Mandinaung. He is living with a native woman in a small palm shack, and he has two children by her. It practically broke my mother's heart when we heard that.'

Mr Turner said quietly: 'That's a bad one,' and walked on in silence for a moment. This then was what happened to RAF pilots who could do nothing but fly aeroplanes. They drifted to the East and sunk to living with the natives, and were lost, submerged in the vast sea of colour. A word occurred to him.

'Beachcombers,' he thought. 'That's what he'd be, a beachcomber.'

At the corner of the street, she stopped, and held out her hand. 'I'll say goodbye,' she said. 'Let me know if you hear anything of Phillip, will you? But don't write to my mother, write to me.' She paused, and then she said: 'We were good friends when we were children, and we are still, even after this.' She sighed. 'Poor Phillip–he always made a mess of things if it were possible to do so.'

Mr Turner went back to his home at Watford by Underground for tea. He got there at about five o'clock, tired and depressed. Surprisingly, his wife was there and tea was laid for him.

'I thought that maybe you'd be back,' she said. 'I'll put the kettle on–it won't be long.' She paused, and then she said: 'I got a kipper, if you'd like it.'

Kippers were his favourite delicacy; in his fatigue and his depression he felt that he could fancy a nice kipper. She cooked him two, and he ate them, and a slice of bread and jam, and two pieces of cherry cake, and drank three cups of tea, and felt a great deal better for it.

It was not his habit to discuss with his wife what he had been doing during the day; it was a long time since they had been upon such terms as that. While she gathered up the tea things and began washing up, he took a chair out in the garden and sat looking at the flowers and smoking, thinking intermittently of what he wanted to do.

He was rather shocked at what he had heard of Phillip Morgan. He had fully anticipated that the boy would not make a success of life, that he would drift into some little dead end job at four or five pounds a week; so much he was prepared for. He was not prepared to hear that he had gone completely native in a Burmese village, and he was distressed to hear it. Poverty in England in a little trivial job was one thing. Poverty in the Far East was quite another.

He stared at the flowers, and smoked cigarette after cigarette. This was what he had suspected, this was what he had set out to find. Of all the three who were in hospital with him in Penzance, Philip Morgan had seemed least fitted for the battle of life. He had wanted to find out about him, in these last months of activity he had, in order that he might help, if help should be required. Help was required all right–the boy would get no help from his mother or his wife, and very little from his sister. There was some sort of a job to be done there–Mr Turner did not quite know what. The only thing was, Burma was such the hell of a long way away.

His wife came out to him presently, and brought another chair with her, and set it up beside him. 'I went to the Commercial College and found out about courses,' she said quietly. 'I could do six weeks shorthand and typing, and brush up the bookkeeping as well, for ten guineas. That's mornings and afternoons too. The only thing is,' she said, 'if I did that, I couldn't get you dinner middle of the day.'

'I shan't want that,' he said. 'I should get on with it, while we've still got the salary coming in. Maybe after that you could get a job half time, kind of keep your hand in.'

'I believe I could do that,' she said thoughtfully. 'Mornings only. It 'ld make a bit more, too.'

She turned to him: 'I been thinking about this,' she said. 'Don't you think you ought to see another doctor, or something? I mean, surely they can do something.'

He shook his head. 'I wouldn't think that way,' he said. 'I mean, you can go on messing and messing about, and it don't do no good. They done as well as anybody could for me. I've had it, and that's all about it. I don't want to go on arguing.'

She said: 'Did you tell them at the office?'

He told her what had happened. 'I got a month's leave now,' he said. 'After that, I suppose I go back to work, and then go on till I have to start and take sick leave. After that, I got six months on pay, and then finish.'

She said: 'There'd be a war pension, or something.'

'So there would,' he said. 'I better get Dr Worth to write a letter to the Board. Maybe you'll get something out of it as well. I better see him in the morning.'

They sat together on the deckchairs in the narrow little strip of garden, and presently he was telling her about Phillip Morgan. 'Well, that's the way of it,' he said heavily at last. 'He's made a bloody muck o' things, the way I knew he would. If he was in England I'd do what I could to see him, 'n see if one could help. But out in Burma one can't do that.'

She said quietly: 'Why not?'

'Too bloody far away,' he said impatiently.

'I don't see that,' she said. 'You can fly out ever so quick, they say. Three or four days it is.'

He stared at her. 'You mean, fly out to Burma?'

'That's right,' she said. 'I don't see why you shouldn't, if you want to go.'

He said ironically: 'Don't talk so soft. What d'you think it 'ld cost?'

'I dunno, Jackie,' she said quietly. 'But you've got the money.'

There was a long silence. It was true, he had enough money for anything that he was likely to require in his lifetime, though what he spent now would mean the less for her when he was dead. Actually, he had the time, too; he had a month's holiday to run before he had to go back to the office. It was possible to go to Burma, if he wanted to, and as the thought occurred to him he knew that he wanted to go very badly.

His wife spoke again. 'Look at it this way,' she said quietly. 'I been thinking about things a lot. We neither of us had much fun since we got married, with the war and that. Well, I've got all my time to go, but you've only got a year, or maybe less than that. After you're dead, if that must happen, I'd not like to think you never had no fun at all, travelling and seeing places and that. Why don't you take a trip out there, and see if you can find him, Jackie? It's what you're interested in, and it won't cost all that.'

'Me go to Burma?' he said thoughtfully.

'That's right.'

'Well, I dunno,' he said.

There was another silence. He became resolved that he would go upon this trip. Whether he found Phillip Morgan or not, whether he could do anything for him if he did find him without encroaching further on the little store of money he could leave his wife, did not weigh greatly with Turner. He wanted to seize this opportunity to leave the office, and leave Watford, and go off to see new places, meet new people and to sort out his ideas. Abruptly, he was very conscious of the generosity of Mollie in making this suggestion.

'If I was to go,' he said, 'would you come too?'

She shook her head. 'I did think of that,' she said. 'But I'd as soon stay here. I got to brush up at the College, 'n it 'ld all cost more. I'd like us to have a holiday

together sometime, Devonshire or something. But Burma's too far off.'
'Be a bit lonely for you, staying on here all alone,' he said.
'I dunno,' she replied. 'I might go and stay with Laura for a bit. She wants help with the baby coming and all that.'
'Well,' he said, 'it all wants a bit of thinking about.' He searched his mind for something he could do for her, to match her generosity in some small measure. 'Like to go to the pictures tonight?' he said. 'I see there's Cary Grant on at the Regal.'

Four days later he left Poole upon the flying boat for Rangoon.

5

Mr Turner enjoyed his journey in the flying boat. For practically the first time in his life comfort wrapped him round, so that it was unnecessary for him to do anything but read and rest. All day the aircraft droned on across the mountains, the deserts, and the seas; he read a little, slept a little, ate a lot, and looked out of the window at the slowly moving panorama of the world. The journey did him a great deal of good; the great wound in his forehead ceased to trouble him with its throbbing, and though he sweated profusely each time they landed, he reached Rangoon rested and refreshed.

He had not come empty handed. He brought with him from England a few small packages of Crispy Wheaties, a breakfast cereal that his organisation were marketing in a big way, and he brought some samples of an older product, Mornmeal, which was full of vitamins and roughage. With these gifts from the West to the Far East he landed in Rangoon early in August in monsoon weather, and went to the hotel upon the Strand.

He was adaptable, and though the climate in that month was trying with alternative rain and sun, he did not find it insupportable by any means. He had bought readymade clothing from a tropical outfitter in London and his suits were adequate. He was a man accustomed to fending for himself and finding his own way around; the Eastern atmosphere did not impede him. He behaved in Rangoon exactly as he would have done in Manchester, and he got along quite well.

He had an introduction to the agent for his firm, a Mr S. O. Chang; he rang him up from his hotel bedroom on the first morning, and within half an hour Mr Chang was sitting with him in the hotel lounge. Mr Chang was a Chinaman and had represented Cereal Products Ltd for some years in Rangoon. In Rangoon Mr Chang had a finger in every pie that would accept his finger; he was always up to something. His interests ranged from upholstery materials for railway carriages to foundation creams for ladies, from cast-iron sluices suitable for septic tanks to breakfast cereals from England. He lived modestly in a small house up towards the jail behind the Chinese quarter; he may or may not have been wealthy, but he knew everybody in Rangoon.

They talked cereals for an hour or so. 'I come out here on sort of personal business, you might say,' said Mr Turner. 'Mr Anderson, he'll be along to see you in March. But as I was coming here, Mr Sumner said to come and have a chat with you, and show you these.'

Mr Chang beamed. 'Mr Anderson, he very welcome in Rangoon. My wife, she always ask when Mr Anderson coming. My son Hsu, he ask always also, when Mr Anderson coming. Very nice man, Mr Anderson.'

'Aye,' said Mr Turner, 'he's a proper card. Tells a good story, don't he?'

'Oh yes. Mr Anderson, he very funny man. My wife laugh and laugh.' He explained. 'My wife does not know English, so I translate stories for her. She laugh very much.'

Mr Turner split open one of the little sample packets of Crispy Wheaties on the table, and put two or three flakes in his mouth. 'Say, tell me what you think o' these, Mr Chang. I kind of like them myself, so does my wife. Sort of malty flavour, isn't it? They're going very well at home. We'll have nearly half our whole production on these by next year.'

An hour later they were finished for the time being. 'There's just one other thing,' said Mr Turner. 'I got a friend out here somewhere, chap I used to know back in England in the war, in 1943. I don't know what he's doing, but he lives in a place called Mandinaung. Mandinaung, Irrawaddy, that's the address. Is that far from here?'

Mr Chang said: 'Mandinaung is large village on the Irrawaddy river. It is about hundred, hundred and ten miles. You go by river, past Yandoon. Take two days now in the steamer, because river running very fast. One day to come back. You want to go and see your friend?'

Mr Turner hesitated. 'Is it easy to get there?'

'Very easy. Steamer all the way, twice each week, Monday, Thursday, all the way up to Henzada. Next Thursday is next steamer. You arrive Mandinaung Friday afternoon.' He looked up at Mr Turner. 'I book passage for you—leave to me. You go Thursday?'

'Hold on a minute.' He had no objection to Mr Chang earning his commission on the passage, but he did not want to be rushed. 'This chap doesn't know I'm coming, and I don't know how he's living. Would it be possible to find out anything about him—what he does, or anything?'

'Sure,' said Mr Chang. 'I have good friend who do business in Mandinaung, cheroots, Mandinaung cheroots very good, good as Danubyu. You like cheroots, Burma cheroots?'

'I wish you'd find out something about this chap,' said Mr Turner. 'Phillip Morgan, his name is. I'd like to know what he's doing, how he's living, you know, before I write to him or go up there.'

'I find out for you,' said Mr Chang. 'I ask my friend, he go there every month. Phillip Morgan. I find out for you.'

He insisted that Mr Turner should dine with him the following evening at his home, and would take no refusal. They arranged that he should fetch Mr Turner from the hotel at half past six, and then he went away. Turner sat down and wrote a cable to his wife in Watford to tell her of his safe arrival, and then, most unusually, he sat down and wrote her a long letter. He was not very good at writing, and much of his letter was concerned with a description of the plot of the detective story he had read in the aircraft on the way out, but it pleased her when she got it.

He went out presently and walked along the streets at a very slow pace, keeping well into the shade. He bought a solar topee for twice its value in a

Chinese shop, and he bought a guidebook for three times its English price from a very black Chittagonian who kept a stall, and he bought a bunch of bananas in the fruit market for almost its proper price from a young Burmese woman because he smiled at her and was friendly. Then he was tired and his head was beginning to throb so he went back to his hotel and lay down upon his bed to read the guidebook. Presently he went to sleep, and when he woke up it was afternoon. He got up and had a shower and ate some of the bananas, and went down and had a cup of tea in the hotel lounge. He spent the evening sitting in a long chair in the shade, watching the native life of the city as it moved by in the street.

He went and saw the great shrine that dominates the city next day, the Shwe Dagon, and walked around the pagoda in his stockinged feet, mystified at the profusion of strange images.

That evening Mr Chang came in a very decrepit old open motor car to fetch him to dine; they bounced erratically along to the other end of the town with Mr Chang clinging to the wheel in grim concentration and changing the worn gears with more ferocity than skill. He lived in a small suburban house, standing in a garden that was unkempt by Mr Turner's Watford standards, and suffering from the peculiarity that it had few walls, and those constructed only of venetian blind material. Outside, the jungle rats that Mr Turner knew as squirrels played in the trees, and sometimes came into the rooms.

In the main living-room there was a long table; one end was laid with a white cloth for the meal; upon the other was a jumble of well-worn Mah Jongg ivories. Mrs Chang came forward to meet them, a little woman with a wide smiling face, dressed in sandals, black satin trousers, and a very beautifully embroidered white silk shirt that reached down almost to the knees. She said something, smiling.

'My wife speaks no English,' said Mr Chang. 'She very pleased you come to our house.'

Mr Turner, in the course of a varied business life, had acquired some experience with wives who could speak no English. He had no knowledge of any language but his own, but he had made himself pleasant in the past to French wives, German wives, Dutch wives, Polish wives, Hungarian wives, and many others; a Chinese wife presented him with no problem. He worked upon the theory that all foreign wives were exactly and precisely similar to English wives, and that if you got someone to translate exactly what you would have said in Watford it worked out all right. Certainly, he had always given satisfaction. Within ten minutes Mrs Chang had produced her seven-year-old son and her five-year-old daughter, and Mr Turner was playing 'Paper wraps stone, scissors cuts paper' with the little boy.

Dinner came presently, served by a Chinese-Burman girl, a curry which Mrs Chang ate with her fingers, Mr Chang with chopsticks, and Mr Turner with a spoon and fork. Mr Chang produced a bottle of rice spirit flavoured with burnt sugar which he called Black Cat Whisky; in support of that statement he showed the black cat on the label. A glass of this set Mr Turner's head throbbing and buzzing; he refused another with some difficulty, and told them all about his head wound. Then Mrs Chang told him all about her operation for appendicitis, Mr Chang translating, so that by the end of the meal they might have been nextdoor neighbours in Watford.

The brown girl came and cleared the table, and Mr Chang produced a large paper packet of cheroots. They were very black and Mr Turner took one with some apprehension; unexpectedly it turned out very mild.

'You like my cheroots?' asked Mr Chang.

'Aye,' said Mr Turner with appreciation. 'Makes a nice smoke.'

'From Mandinaung, where your friend lives. Mandinaung cheroot.'

'It's very nice,' said Mr Turner. 'Did you find out anything about Phillip Morgan?'

'Oh yes, I find out for you. Mr Morgan very important man in Mandinaung. He just made Subdivisional Officer.'

Mr Turner stared at him in astonishment. 'What's that–Subdivisional Officer? What does that mean?'

Mr Chang said: 'Subdivisional Officer, he is Government official. Like Judge and Tax Collector and Registrar. Mr Morgan is Subdivisional Officer for five villages, but he live in Mandinaung.'

Turner said, bewildered: 'I thought he was quite poor.'

Mr Chang smiled tolerantly. 'Oh no. Mr Morgan never poor. Mr Morgan, he is owner of three motorboats trade up and down the Irrawaddy, carry passengers and goods. Now he sold those boats, and now he is Subdivisional Officer.'

Mr Turner stared at the Chinaman. 'Is he a well-known man, then?'

'Oh yes–Mr Morgan very well known in the Irrawaddy; people like him very much. He marry nice girl, Ma Nay Htohn, daughter to Maung Shway Than. Maung Shway Than is important man in Rangoon. His brother, Nga Myah, is Minister for Education in the Burman Government. All very good people.'

'Well, I'm damned,' said Mr Turner. He sat in silence for a minute, trying to readjust his ideas. 'This girl he married,' he said presently, '–Ma something, you said–is she a native? I mean, a Burmese girl?'

'Oh yes,' said Mr Chang. 'Ma Nay Htohn educated at Rangoon High School; she speak very good English. Very nice girl, very clever. She have two children now, one boy, one girl. They very happy.'

Mr Turner said mechanically: 'That's fine,' and sat trying to think out what this meant to him. It was not in the least what he had been led to expect.

Mr Chang went on to add to his information: 'Ma Nay Htohn has brother, colonel in the Burma Army, Burma Independence Army in the war. His name, Utt Nee. Utt Nee, he fight against the British in 1942 to make Burma independent. Later he fight against the Japanese also to make Burma independent, but he fight more against Japanese then against the British. He very important man also, colonel in the Burma Army.'

He grinned at Turner. 'You want to go up river to Mandinaung to see your friend? I arrange it for you, very easy.'

Mr Turner said slowly: 'Yes, I think I do want to go. I'd better write him a letter first. How long does a letter take to get there?'

'One week to get answer. Why not send telegram?'

'Can one send telegrams to Mandinaung?'

'Oh yes. It go to Danubyu, and then boy run with the message. You get answer the same day. I send it for you.'

Mr Turner said: 'Got a piece of paper?'

He thought for a moment, and then wrote:

Morgan, Mandinaung, Irrawaddy.

We met in Hospital Penzance 1943 stop I am now in Rangoon week or two on business and would like to see you again stop can we meet either Rangoon or Mandinaung. Turner, Strand Hotel, Rangoon.

He got an answer the next day at his hotel:

Sorry cannot get down to Rangoon but glad to put you up here for a few days if you can spare the time stop delighted hear from you again. Morgan.

Mr Turner stood looking at this thoughtfully, in front of the mirror in his bedroom. 'Made a bloody fool of yourself,' he said to his reflection. 'Come all this way for nothing. He don't want your help.'

He hesitated, half minded to abandon the adventure, and go downstairs, and book a passage back to England on the next aircraft. This young man that he had thought of as a beachcomber was a Government official, and one with very good connections in the country. Out here, where white faces were few, the fact that he was married to a Burmese girl did not seem quite so shattering as it had seemed in England; Mr Turner had already seen a number of girls in the street that he would not have minded being married to himself.

'Might as well go straight back home,' he said disconsolately. 'He's all right.'

He did not go. The fascination of a strange scene was upon him; he had never been to the East before, and though the purpose that had brought him there was obviously void, he might as well see everything there was to see before going home. He had said nothing to anybody, fortunately, of his desire to help Phillip Morgan make his life anew; he had described himself as on a business trip and he could stick to that story. This journey up the river to this Burmese village would be interesting, an out of the way adventure, something to tell Mollie about when he got back to Watford, something to tell buyers from the Provinces when he lunched with them at the Strand Palace Hotel. He decided that he would go, and spent some time in thinking up corroborative lies about his business in Rangoon to tell to Morgan if he showed much interest in his presence in Burma.

He set out for Mandinaung the following morning on the paddle steamer. He travelled in some comfort in a cabin with a good electric fan, and he enjoyed every minute of the journey. The Irrawaddy delta is a smiling, fertile country of tall trees and rich farm land; between the showers of rain Mr Turner sat in a deckchair upon the upper deck of the steamer watching the dug-outs and sampans on the river, the women decorously bathing with two longyis, the domestic life in villages and bamboo houses that they passed, the monkeys playing in the trees. Each minute of the day was an interest and an amusement to him, and though he was still worried that he had come upon a fool's errand, he was glad that he had come.

The steamer reached a fair-sized town called Yandoon in the evening, and berthed there for the night. Mr Turner went on shore and walked a little through the lines of bamboo and mat houses, wondering at everything he saw. He had thought that women in all Eastern countries lived in purdah and seclusion, but here the girls walked round in pairs chihiking with the young men just as they did at home. He found a well that seemed to be a social centre and sat watching for a long time a very merry scene as girls and women came down for the water and the young men drew it for them. From time to time he saw a monk in bare feet and a heavy robe of a coarse yellow cloth, and wondered. He went back to the ship to dinner, rather thoughtful. There was an atmosphere of business, good humour, and a pleasant life in Yandoon, that was different from his English conception of a native town.

He got to Mandinaung next day in the late afternoon. There was a little rickety bamboo jetty for the steamer to berth against, and on this jetty a white man was standing with a Burmese girl by his side, and few natives behind. As they drew near, he saw that it was Morgan, but a different Morgan from the one that he had known in 1943 in hospital. This was an older man, who had an air of authority about him. He was very tanned. He wore an old bush hat with a khaki shirt and faded shorts of jungle green; he had sandals on his feet. Up on the bank above the jetty an old jeep was parked, presumably his property.

The girl standing with him wore a flat, slightly conical straw sun hat, a white blouse, a green longyi wrapped around her waist and falling to her feet, and sandals. She was a pale, yellowish brown colour; she had a broad face and straight black hair, which she parted in the middle and wore made up in a knot at the back of her head, usually with a flower in it for ornament. When Mr Turner came to study her at closer range he found that she used lipstick and nail varnish like the girls in Watford, and like them made up her cheeks with a faint colour. Later still, he found she did it with the same brands of cosmetic.

A native boy carried his suitcase off the boat behind him, and he went down the gangplank to meet Morgan. 'I took you at your word,' he said. 'Seemed a shame we shouldn't meet again, being so close and all.'

'I'm jolly glad you came,' said Morgan. 'We don't see very many people out from England, up the river here. Turner, this is my wife, Ma Nay Htohn.'

Mr Turner raised his hat formally. 'I'm very pleased to meet you, Mrs Morgan.'

She smiled, and then laughed a little. 'Not Mrs Morgan,' she said, 'I am Ma Nay Htohn. We do not change our names in Burma after marriage, as you do in England. I am still Ma Nay Htohn unless we go to live in England ever. Then I suppose I shall have to be Mrs Morgan.' She held out her hand. 'I am very glad that you could spare the time to come and see us.'

She spoke English with a lilting accent, but her choice of words was perfect.

Mr Turner was confused. 'Ever so sorry,' he said. 'I got a bit to learn about the way you do things out here.'

The girl said, laughing: 'I will teach you. I hope you will be able to stay for a long time here with us.'

'Just a day or two.' He turned to Morgan. 'You've not changed a lot.'

The other studied him. 'I doubt if I'd have known you again,' he said. 'You were all bandaged up, up to the time I left the hospital. How long did you stay on after me?'

''Bout a month,' said Mr Turner. 'Bloody fed up with it, I was—just lying there day after day. After you went there was no one but the nigger to talk to.'

Morgan said quietly: 'I remember. How did you get on with him?'

Mr Turner said: 'Well, I got on with him all right. Better 'n you'd think. We used to play a lot of draughts together, I remember. Checkers, he called it.'

They turned and walked up to the jeep and got into it with the luggage; Morgan drove along a dirt road on the track that overlooked the river, out of the village. They did not drive far. A quarter of a mile from the last bamboo house they turned the corner of a wood and came upon a clearing with a mown lawn, on which stood a flagstaff; from this staff floated a blue ensign with a peacock in the fly. Behind the lawn there was a pleasant wooden house of two storeys, with a veranda and a red-tiled roof of many gables. It stood upon the river bank at a great bend, with a view over the stream, nearly a mile wide.

'This is where we live,' said Morgan.

'Nice place,' said Mr Turner, very much impressed.

Morgan said: 'We only got it built last year. You should have seen what we were living in before.'

Nay Htohn rippled into laughter. 'We use our old home for a garage,' she said. 'Show him, Phillip.'

'All right.' He stopped the jeep before the steps that led up to the veranda of the house and gave the suitcase to a manservant in a long white coat who came out to meet them; then they drove on around the house to a small bashah made of bamboo, palm leaf matting, and palm thatch. It stood looking out over the river in a pleasant place, but it was old now, and beginning to decay. Morgan drove the jeep into what had once been the main room, and they got out.

'This is where we used to live,' he said.

Mr Turner did not know quite what to say. 'Sort of country cottage,' he ventured.

'That's right,' said Morgan. 'This was the living-room, and this was the bedroom. The kitchen was that other one.' He pointed to another decrepit bashah close beside. He stared around. 'Yes, this is where we lived,' he said, 'It wasn't bad.'

The girl said softly: 'We were very happy here.'

Mr Turner looked around him. The place had a bare floor of trampled earth; there was a trench outside dug round to catch the monsoon rain. He glanced into the bedroom; the bed was a platform of thin, springy bamboo slats. There were no doors, no ceiling, no glass in the windows, no amenity of any kind.

He smiled, puzzled by the contrast between the new house and the old. 'Sort of rough living here,' he said warily.

Morgan said: 'It was rough all right.'

Nay Htohn said: 'It was as we wanted it to be. My father when we married wanted to build us a good house. But Mandinaung itself was so much ruined that we did not want to live like that. It would not have been right.'

Comprehension was beginning to dawn on Mr Turner. 'What ruined it?' he asked.

Morgan said: 'We did it a bit of no good one day with the Thunderbolts and Hurribombers, early in 1945, when we were coming down this way. It was a Jap headquarters. These places burn like fun, you know—there wasn't much left of the town when we'd done with it.'

'I suppose they do burn pretty easy.'

'They do that. When I got back here afterwards and we got married, all building materials were in short supply. Well, you see how it was. We didn't kind of fancy building a brand new slap-up house with all modern conveniences while the rest of the bloody place was flat—especially with my R.A.F. record. So we made do with a bashah for the time.' He glanced around. 'They're really quite comfortable, these places, but they get old pretty soon. This one's just about had it.'

The girl said: 'These are very good houses while you can live simply, with just the two of you. Later on, when the babies come, it is more difficult. I was glad when we could build the new house last year, with a bathroom. But I do not regret the years we spent in this small place, and the people liked it too, when they came to understand the reason why we lived here.'

They turned, and walked up to the house. They passed through the garden, a few beds full of flowering azaleas, and strange flowers that Mr Turner did not recognize that he learned later were orchids. He was diffident about asking questions. They moved in a scent of flowers brought out by the rain; beside them the azaleas and the orchids, beyond those the mimosa and the great orange and red glory of a flame tree. Mr Turner walked through these wonders in a daze.

'When did you leave England?' Morgan asked.

'Only last week– I come out by air.'

The girl walking between them said: 'Has Rita Hayworth made a new film, after *Gilda*?' She laughed. 'I am a terrible fan.'

Mr Turner scratched his head. 'I dunno,' he said. 'I don't go much, myself. You want to ask my wife; she's always going to the pictures.' He glanced at the pale brown girl beside him curiously. 'Where do you go to see a film, out here?'

'Sometimes they are shown in Danubyu,' she said. 'But every two or three months we go down to Rangoon for a few days, while Phillip does business.' She laughed. 'Then I am in the picture house all the time.'

Mr Turner said: 'Cary Grant made a good one that I saw just before I come out,' and he told her all about it.

They went up the steps on to the wide, shady veranda and into the house. There was a hall with rooms that opened out of it; the hall itself seemed to be the living-room and there was a table laid with afternoon tea, and long cane chairs with leg extensions.

Presently they were sitting down to tea. A large white cat walked slowly into the room from the veranda, and walked straight to Mr Turner as he lay in the cane chair, and jumped up on to his lap.

Mr Turner said: 'Hullo, puss,' and stroked its ear. Then he noticed Morgan and Nay Htohn staring at it.

'Well I'm damned,' said Morgan. 'Never seen it do that before. You're honoured, old boy.'

The cat stood kneading on his stomach for a moment, then settled down and began to purr. In that tropic heat its presence was uncomfortable, but Mr Turner liked a cat and was prepared to put up with it for a time. 'Took a fancy to me,' he said.

The girl said something softly to Morgan in Burmese. He smiled at her gently, and said a word or two in the same language.

'What's his name?' asked Turner.

Morgan glanced at the girl; she nodded slightly. 'I don't call him anything,' he said. 'Nay Htohn calls him Moung Payah.' He hesitated for a moment. 'That means, Your Reverence.'

'Strewth,' said Turner comfortably, 'what a name to call him.'

'As a matter of fact, you're very much honoured,' said Morgan. 'He's a most unfriendly cat in the normal way. Won't have anything to do with me or Nay Htohn. Catches a lot of rats, though.'

He turned the subject. 'How did you get to know I was out here?' he asked.

It was a question that Mr Turner had some difficulty in answering; the lie, when it came, was not very convincing. 'I kind of wondered what had happened to you,' he said. 'Then one day I met a chap in the Air Ministry who said he could find out, easy–put his girl on to look up in the records. Well, he did that, 'n wrote and told me you were out in Burma, 'n give me your last address, Ladbroke Square. Well, I didn't think no more about it–stuck the letter in the file and forgot about it, till the question of this trip come up, at the office. Then I got to thinking if there was anybody that I knew out here, and looked out the letter. And I went 'n had a talk with your mother and sister. Week before last, that was.'

The meal was over, and they were smoking. Nay Htohn got up and went into an inner room, to the sound of children. Morgan said: 'Let's go and sit out on the veranda. It's cooler there.'

They went out, and pulled other long cane chairs together, and reclined, smoking and looking out over the wide river. There was still sunshine, and it was very hot; on the far side of the river over in the direction of the Pegu Yoma the thunderheads were massing for another storm.

Morgan said: 'How was my mother?'

'She didn't seem very well to me,' said Mr Turner. ''Course, I don't know her. Sort of invalid, is she?'

'Yes.' The pilot hesitated, and then said: 'I suppose she didn't give you a very good account of me.'

Mr Turner was silent for a moment. 'Seems kind of different out here to what it did in Ladbroke Square,' he said at last. 'What she said was right enough, but it had got a twist, if you get me. Not like things really are.'

The other said quietly: 'I know. I've tried to make her see it, but it's no damn good. We don't write much now. I had to make a choice between England and Burma and–well, I chose Burma.' He paused, and then he said: 'England wasn't very kind to me, you know.'

'How did you come to get out here?' asked Mr Turner. 'I mean, settled in like this, and knowing everyone, and that?'

Morgan said: 'I'll tell you.'

He said that when he left the hospital at Penzance he went up to London to that lovely girl, his wife. She flew into his arms directly he opened the door of the little flat in Pont Street, and in her close embrace all doubts slipped away from him. Then they broke away, and she said: 'Did you bring my parcel?'

He said: 'I'm terribly sorry–I'm afraid it's gone. They've cleared away the wreck and everything.'

She said sharply: 'But it can't be gone! I mean, it's part of your luggage. It must be somewhere, if you look for it.'

'I don't know what to do about it now,' he said. 'I think it's a write-off.'

She said petulantly: 'Oh, it can't be. I mean, it had perfume in it, and silk stockings. I *need* stockings. I haven't got a thing to wear.'

Thinking to please her, he said: 'Those are lovely ones you've got on now. Your legs look wizard in them.'

She said: 'Oh, those are a pair Bill gave me, but they're *literally* the only ones I've got. You must be able to find that parcel. Can't you write to somebody about it?'

He shifted uneasily. 'You aren't allowed to bring that sort of stuff into the country, you know. Makes it a bit difficult.'

She said: 'Oh, nobody pays any attention to that.'

She did not think to ask him how he was, or to explain why she had not been able to get down to Penzance to see him, or to answer his letters. She was nice to him in a distracted sort of way, but her mind was utterly engrossed with her theatrical job, and with her clothes, and with the cabarets and night clubs that she went to, usually with Bristow. Flight-Lieutenant Bristow had a job at the Air Ministry which kept him in London; Morgan found himself an intruder into a pleasant little friendship. Whenever he went out with Joyce, Bristow was likely to go with them, and they seldom sat at home.

'It's difficult,' said Morgan, staring out over the wide river to the dim hills beyond. 'You don't know what to do when things get like that. I didn't make a song and dance about it, because I wanted to go on ops and, well, there's always the risk, you know.' He paused. 'Anyway, Bristow usually paid the bill. I hadn't got nearly enough money for all the things Joyce wanted to do.'

He sat silent for a moment. 'I suppose I was a bit of a coward,' he said. 'I was afraid to start a row.'

He was posted to an aerodrome near Exeter for ground duties after his leave, still in Transport Command. From there he could get up to London pretty frequently upon a weekend pass, and each time he returned from leave distressed and worried. Bristow was very much in evidence, and it was clear to Morgan that his wife went out with Bristow almost every night. They had little secret jokes from which he was excluded, and though the girl was still kind to him it gradually became clear that she was bored by his visits. Morgan became morose and unhappy, too inexperienced to know what to do about such things, too much tied by the R.A.F. to do very much about it anyway.

In the spring of 1944 he was put back on flying duties and sent for a short conversion course to fly Dakotas. From there he was sent to a Dakota squadron forming up in Yorkshire for supply dropping duties; while he was there he saw very little of Joyce, who now called herself Bobby Chairmaine. In July 1944 the squadron were ordered out to India, and Morgan saw his wife for the last time upon his final leave.

It was not very different from his other leaves. He was going out to the war in the Far East; he would be away for three years or so, if he came back at all. His last leave left little impression on his mind but a series of wild parties after the theatre with his wife, and Bristow, and various officers of the US Air Force—and a series of hangovers next day that lasted till the evening party started up again. During that fortnight he thought he was having a marvellous time and that everything would be all right, and that Joyce would write to him every week while he was away; he had bought her a very expensive fountain-pen, and she had promised to use it. Sometimes he wondered if they couldn't do something in the country like sailing a boat or riding a horse, which might be rather fun, but the theatre intervened, or the hangover. Then the evening party would start up, and he would have a marvellous time all over again.

The squadron left England in August 1944, and flew by night over the French battles to land at Malta in the dawn. From Malta they flew on to Cairo West, from Cairo West to Shaibah in Iraq, from Shaibah to Karachi, from Karachi to Barrackpore in Bengal. They rested at Barrackpore for a fortnight after the flight out while defects in the aircraft were made good and the crews became acclimatised. Then, as a fully operational unit, they flew down to the dirt airstrip of Cox's Bazaar, a little place on the Bay of Bengal, on the edge of Burma.

From there, they began to operate down the coast of Arakan to support the Army battling in the vicinity of Buthidaung. Each Dakota carried a load of four tons for relatively short hauls such as that; they flew in everything the Army needed from field gun ammunition and petrol to sausages and hair oil, dropping the loads by parachute from three hundred feet on ground marked out with white cloth strips by the Army, and returning immediately to Cox's for another load. They had more crews than aircraft, and the machines were worked very intensively. It was usual for the same crew to do two or even three trips in one day, flying for as much as twelve hours; then they would have two days of complete rest.

Morgan lived with the rest of his squadron in tents immediately beside the airstrip and the aircraft. There was no shade, of course; the fierce September sun beat down upon the tents and on the blazing sand that made the strip. There is surely no place hotter in the tropics than an unpaved airstrip, except perhaps a paved one. At times it was so hot that it was possible to fry an egg upon the metal tail plane of the Dakota, and this was about the only recreation that the strip provided. From time to time they would take one of the squadron jeeps and drive down to the beach, and bathe in the lukewarm Bay of Bengal from the grey, dirty sand. The water was too warm and sticky to refresh.

He lived in a continual grit of dust blown up from the surface of the strip as the aircraft took off or ran up engines on test. It got into his food, into his cigarettes and his drink, into his blankets; it formed a gritty mud upon his body with the sweat that poured off him all day. He lived dressed in a bush hat and a dirty jungle suit, which is like a battledress made of thin green material. Usually he wore the trousers only, and the top half of his body became tanned deep brown. In three months of this strange life of supply dropping he matured considerably; he grew more self-reliant in this mode of living stripped down to the elementals of the job.

At the beginning of November Phillip Morgan got a letter from his wife, the first to reach him since he had left England. Thrilled and excited, he carried it off to his tent, and sitting on the charpoy in the sweltering shade, he opened it. It read:

Phillip Darling,

This is going to be a dreadful letter to write and I really don't know how to begin but it's not as if we ever had been married really is it I mean had a home and all that. I know when Jack was killed you were too sweet in looking after me and of course he *wanted* it and so we simply had to and it's been marvellous and I'll never regret one minute of it will you?

Well now I've found somebody at last who can provide for me properly just what Jack would always have wanted for me it seems *too terrible* that he couldn't have been there first of all but that's the way things happen isn't it?

I wonder if you can guess who it is? Jack Bristow isn't it funny that his name should be Jack too it came to me like a thunderclap the other morning that this was what my first Jack would have wanted for me and of course I thought of you at once and my dear I was *miserable* and Jack and I talked it over last night when he came round after the show and he said I must write and tell you my dear I felt terrible I couldn't sleep. I asked him again this morning and he said I must and if I didn't he'd never see me again so I said I would and he said I ought to ask you to give me evidence a hotel bill or something so that I can divorce you and get the whole thing straight and then we can be married.

I feel this is a stinking mess but it's the only way I expect you can fix up something in Calcutta or something much better get it all settled up before you come home only please be quick because Jack only has another two months at the Air Ministry and it's horrible being sort of neither one thing nor the other in spite of it having been all a mistake to start with hasn't it? I do hope we'll be frightfully good friends for dear old Jack's sake.

Ever your loving,
BOBBY

Philip Morgan sat for an hour in the sweltering tent turning this *cri du coeur* over and over in his hands. He sat upon the charpoy naked to the waist; the tears made little streaks in the damp mud of dust upon his cheeks and mingled with the stream of sweat from his temples, and ran down his neck and into the sweat beads upon his chest, and were lost in the steady stream that ran down his body. At the end of the hour he lit a cigarette with hands that trembled a little; then Flying-Officer Scott who shared his tent came in from a trip over the mountains into northern Burma, and Morgan showed him the letter dumbly. Scott had the best part of a bottle of Indian gin, and sympathy, and he gave both to Morgan, and a bottle of the Wing-Commander's beer ration. Presently the sharp pain eased to a dull ache, another ache among the many aches and pains and itches that made up life upon the airstrip of Cox's Bazaar.

There was, of course, nothing that he could do about the question of divorce. There were only five European women, nurses, in the district at that time, and about seventy thousand men, and there were no hotels to provide him with a bill even if there had been any women. He was too far from England, and too much strained and occupied with war to do anything about it; he stopped writing home, and did not answer the letter. He sank into an apathy of heat and dust and sweat, and joined the morose ten per cent of men in South-East Asia Command whose wives had let them down.

He had one relaxation for his long hours of leisure that was denied to the other pilots of his squadron. Along the strip there was a squadron of Spitfires commanded by a squadron-leader who had served with Morgan in Africa; these Spitfires operated upon long-range tanks right down into the south of Burma, bombing a little, dropping parachute supplies a little, shooting up a lot. Morgan had done two tours in Spitfires, and in times of little pressure he could borrow a machine, and get up into the clean, cool air at ten or fifteen thousand feet in something that would really fly. Once or twice, when one of the Spitfire pilots was sick, he substituted for him and flew with them upon an operational sortie; he did that for the last time on November 25th, about a fortnight after he had received the letter from his wife.

The job was at extreme range for the Spitfires, to strafe Japanese river boats and shipping on the Irrawaddy river between Prome and Yandoon.

The accident, when it came, was almost unbelievably stupid. The Spitfire that he flew was old and battered, maintained for six months in the open air in the pouring rain and blazing sun of the airstrip, with only improvised appliances. Everything on it worked after a fashion; nothing worked with the mechanical reliability that Morgan was accustomed to in Spitfires. Still, he was glad of the chance to fly it, and took off with the squadron and flew into Burma. He flew on the belly tank until, not far from Zalun as he was flying down the Irrawaddy with the squadron at two hundred feet, his engine coughed and spluttered. He zoomed up and turned on the wing tanks, but the engine did not play. Instead, it went on coughing for a little, and then stopped for good.

Phillip Morgan spoke on the radio to the squadron-leader; he said: 'Orange calling Charlie. Sorry, Pete, but this thing's packing up on me. Out of juice, I

think. Looks like I'll have to put it down. I say again, I'll have to put it down.'
He switched off, and gave all his attention to the landing.

He was then at about a thousand feet, and his propeller had stopped; it stood diagonally across his view, most unusual. There were a few woods below him, the wide river and a range of paddy fields, small areas separated by earth walls a foot or so in height. There was nothing for it but these paddyfields. He swept round in a great turn in a very flat approach glide with his wheels up for the belly landing, came in across the river, dropped off height with a little flap, and put the Spitfire down in a great smother of dust on the dry fields. She bumped from wall to wall, wrecking herself considerably, and came to rest.

Phillip Morgan was unhurt, and he jumped out with his emergency pack and his revolver in his hand. A quick inspection showed him that the wing tanks were quite dry, never having been filled up before the machine took off. The petrol gauge in the cockpit, however, still showed FULL when switched to the wing tanks.

His situation was a bad one. He was in the middle of a country occupied by the enemy, and he could speak no word of the language. If he had been a hundred miles nearer to Cox's Bazaar his proper course would have been to stay near the wrecked Spitfire, in the hope that an attempt would be made to land a light aeroplane near it, an L5, to get him away. A quick calculation showed him that the range was too great for an L5 to reach him. He must depend upon himself entirely if he was not to surrender tamely; he took his pack and his revolver and ran for the nearest wood, three hundred yards across the paddy fields, and reached the shelter of it, and lay down panting.

As he rested, he considered the position. He would at any rate make an attempt to get away and back to Cox's, though he knew that his prospects were not good. Nearly five hundred miles of enemy-held country separated him from the front line, a country lightly held by the Japanese, but a country of mountain and tropical jungle. He had in his emergency pack a good kit of drugs and rations sufficient for two or three days, but nothing like sufficient for a journey such as that. Moreover, the country that he was now in was relatively thickly populated and well farmed; his forced landing must have been observed by many of the natives, if not by the Japanese. Still, he would walk on to the west and see what happened; he could not make his situation any worse. He could surrender at any time.

He pressed on westwards through the woods, using a jungle track; he could not have got through the undergrowth. It was early afternoon and very hot; the flies tormented him. He went on for about an hour, covering perhaps three miles, and sank down for a rest in an exhausted sweat. He was so blind with fatigue that he did not notice men creeping up behind him, did not know their presence till he heard a voice say: 'English,' and he swung round. There were four Burmans there with rifles in their hands, and fierce, scowling faces. They were not in any uniform.

Dispassionately, Morgan wondered if this was the end of it.

He knew from his briefings that these men could be one of several categories. They could be dacoits, who would murder him immediately for his clothes and his revolver. They could be Japanese supporters who would murder him and take his head and give it to the Japanese as evidence of loyalty, and earn a few rupees by doing so. They could be members of the Burma Independence Army who had fought against us when the Japanese invaded the country, and now were rumoured to be fighting for us. They could just be a pack of frightened farmers, uncertain what to do for the best. He could not know, and since he could not talk the language he had no means of learning.

He asked them in English who they were; either they could not or they would not tell him. They held him covered by their rifles and took his revolver from him, but left him his haversack of rations and emergency kit. Two of them got behind him and prodded him with their rifles, and made signs for him to walk; two went ahead of him in single file. They took him along the same jungle path deeper into the country, in the same general direction westwards.

They marched him for about two hours. He was quite unaccustomed to marching in the tropics, and it was a very hot afternoon. He moved blindly with sweat pouring down him, utterly exhausted at the end. He lost sense of the direction of the march; he did not know where they were going to, and did not care.

They walked into a village in the dusk, a little place of only fifteen or twenty houses. He was bundled at once into what seemed to be the village lockup, a small hut of very stout bamboos, with no window and with a rough iron hasp and padlock on the door. He sank down on the floor in exhaustion. After a quarter of an hour his perceptions had returned to him, and he could take some interest in his surroundings. His lockup stood in the garden or compound of a native house; between the lockup and the house there were men camped, and cooking over a wood fire. Presently the door opened, and a steaming bowl of boiled rice with a little fish on the top of it was shoved into him, with an earthenware chatty of water.

An hour later the door was opened again, and he was taken to the house by an armed guard. It was quite dark by that time, and the main room of the house was lit by two hurricane lamps. It was a native house of wooden posts and palm leaf thatch with the floor raised about four feet from the ground, but in it there was a table and two chairs. The place was full of young men, all armed with rifles and revolvers or automatic pistols of one sort or another; many of them also wore their dahs, long straight steel blades with clumsy wooden handles.

There was a man seated at the table, a young man with short cropped hair and a lean brown face, dressed in a longyi and a khaki jacket. On one arm he wore a white brassard with a large, five-pointed red star on it. Behind him, on the ground, a young woman sat, cross legged.

He said in quite good English: 'Sit down there.' Morgan sat down on the chair before the table, with his guards behind him. He looked at the red star and thought, Communist. That had him foxed; there had been nothing about Communists in his briefings. He did not know what that might mean for him.

The man asked him his name and rank, and what aircraft he had been flying. Morgan told him these things freely. By that time, in Burma, the regulations about prisoners giving information to the enemy had been greatly relaxed. Cases had occurred of prisoners who had been tortured by the Japanese to give information which would not have harmed the Allied cause a great deal if it had been disclosed, and who had died bravely and unnecessarily. Now it was assumed that codes and radio wavelengths were all compromised immediately a prisoner was taken, and an organization had been set up for changing them without delay. Prisoners threatened with torture were allowed to talk.

The man asked: 'Where did you fly from?'

Morgan said: 'From Cox's Bazaar.'

He was asked about his mission and he told them, to destroy Japanese military shipping on the river. Then:

'How many aeroplanes have the British got at Cox's Bazaar?'

So far, Morgan had seen no sign of any Japanese. He said: 'Before I answer that, will you tell me who you are?'

The man said: 'Answer the question. How many aeroplanes have the British got at Cox's Bazaar?'

Morgan said: 'It varies every day.' And then he said: 'I want to ask you formally to take me before an officer.'

The man said. 'You are before one now. I am a captain in the Burma Independence Army, Captain Utt Nee.' He paused, and then said: 'I have no time to waste. If you do not answer the questions it will be bad for you.'

The pilot said: 'I'll do my best, but it's not easy to answer that one. Aircraft move about very quickly. One day there might not be more than fifty on all the airstrips at Cox's. Another day there might be three hundred or more. It varies so.'

There was a stir among the men in the room. Utt Nee said: 'You are lying, Englishman. You never had three hundred aeroplanes on the whole Burma front.'

Morgan said: 'I'm not lying at all. I'm counting in the transport machines as well as the first line aircraft. If you take in all the aerodromes in Bengal, the total of aircraft on this front would be more like three thousand. There's the American Strategic Air Force that's as large as ours.' He went on to tell them more about the figures, judging the information to be valuable in making an impression on the Burmans. They asked about the numbers of tanks and guns, but although he had some idea of this he professed ignorance; the figures were not so impressive. 'I'm in the Royal Air Force,' he said. 'We see tanks and guns about in parks and on the roads, but I've no idea how many there may be. I'd only be guessing if I told you any numbers.'

The man said something in Burmese, and Morgan was taken back to the lockup. There was no bed or furniture of any kind; clearly he would have to spend the night on the bare earth, and that was not too clean. In the semi-darkness, in the few gleams of light that came in through the bamboo walls from the lighted house, he sat down in a corner leaning up against the walls, his feet stretched out along the ground, to wait for sleep.

Half an hour later the door opened again, and he got to his feet. His guards were there, but with them was the young Burmese woman that he had seen sitting on the floor behind Utt Nee. She had two blankets in her arms.

She said in English: 'I have brought you some blankets. This is a very poor place, and you will have to sleep upon the ground. If you have to stay here another night my brother will have a bed built up for you.'

He said: 'I say, that's very nice of you.' He took the blankets. 'I'll be perfectly all right with these.'

'Have they given you enough to eat and drink?' she asked.

He said: 'I got some rice—I don't want any more to eat. I'd like another jug of water.'

She spoke in Burmese to the guards, one of whom went off to get it.

He said: 'Tell me, are you people fighting the Japanese?'

'You must ask my brother that,' she replied.

He said in wonder: 'You speak English very well.'

She laughed. 'I ought to. I worked for Stevens Brothers in Rangoon for three years. I was Mr James Stevens's personal secretary. Before that I was at Rangoon High School.'

He said: 'What are they going to do with me?'

'They are talking about that now,' she replied. 'Probably they will hand you over to the Japanese.'

'The British will give you a good reward if I am taken back to them unhurt,' he observed. 'It's all written in Burmese on a sort of handkerchief in my haversack.'

She said a little scornfully: 'We know that, Mr Morgan. They will not pay much attention to your ransom money—There are more important things than that which will determine what they do with you.'

'I didn't mean to be rude,' he said awkwardly.

The guard came back with the chatty. 'Here is your water,' she said. 'Is there anything else you want?'

'I don't think so.'

'Goodnight, then,' she said, and went out. The guards locked the door behind her.

Morgan was left standing in the hut with the blankets in his arms, wondering. The girl had spoken to him just like an Englishwoman, though she was indubitably Burman. She had a lilting accent to her voice; she had a broad, yellowish face with slanting eyes, and straight black hair done in a knot behind her head. She was dressed in native costume with bare feet thrust into sandals.

He turned, and made a rough bed of the blankets on the ground, and lay down wrapping himself round as a protection against the mosquitoes, and presently he fell asleep.

Next morning he was taken out at dawn and allowed to wash in a bucket of water, and allowed to go to a latrine, and given more rice. An hour later he was taken to the house again. There were fewer people in the room this time. Again Utt Nee, the Burman with the red star on his arm interrogated him, the girl sitting on the floor behind.

He said: 'How many soldiers have the British at Cox's and nearby?'

Morgan said: 'I don't know—quite a lot. Not many English troops, but a great many I.O.R.s—the Indian Army. I should think there might be three or four divisions.'

'You mean forty or fifty thousand men?' It will go badly for you if you tell us lies.'

'I should think that's about it. I don't know much about the Army, though.'

There was a quick interchange of sentences between the men around him in Burmese.

Utt Nee said: 'If the British have so many men as that, why do they not attack?'

Morgan said: 'They are attacking in the north, and on the Chindwin. Now the war with Germany is pretty well finished, masses of stuff are coming out here. By the spring we ought to be advancing all over Burma.'

The Burman eyed him steadily. 'What do you mean, the war with Germany is finished?'

Morgan said: 'Well, we've got up to the Rhine.'

'You mean, the river Rhine? The river between Germany and France?'

There was a buzz of excited conversation in Burmese. They questioned him very intently, seeking to trip him up and make him contradict himself. They produced a small school atlas, and made him show them the position of the Rhine, and the areas occupied by the British and American forces. Presently the questions ceased, and he sat on almost unnoticed while a debate took place between the men, speaking in Burmese.

Once Utt Nee turned to him: 'Do you know Major Williams?'

Morgan shook his head blankly. 'Never heard of him.'

Presently Utt Nee made a sign to his guards, and they took him out of the room; the debate in Burmese went on hotly behind him. At the door of his lockup the guards checked; Morgan turned round, and the girl was there.

She said: 'Mr Morgan, I want to ask you a few questions myself.'

He said: 'Of course.'

'First,' she said, 'I want to warn you to speak nothing but the truth to us. It is important to us that we should know the truth of what is going on outside Burma; we have heard nothing for three years except what the Japanese choose to tell us. It is important to you also, because if my brother finds that you have told one single lie he will have you killed. He changed his name last year. He is now called Utt Nee, which means the Red Needle. Do you know why he is called that?'

Morgan grinned at her. 'Well, I can guess.'

She hesitated. 'You seem a brave man,' she said at last, 'I want you to be careful, too, and tell us nothing but the truth.'

'A prisoner of war doesn't have to talk at all,' said Morgan. 'You're a civilised people; you know that. If you mean to kill me if you think I'm telling lies, I'd better keep my mouth shut.'

She was silent for a moment. 'I believe you,' she said at last. 'I think that what you have been telling us is the truth. Some of the men in there'–she indicated the house–'think that you have been telling us a pack of lies to try and save your life.'

Morgan said: 'I can't help that. I've done my best to answer truthfully, but they asked me a great deal that I don't really know about.'

She said: 'How soon do you think the English will attack? How quickly will they get down here, into the delta?'

He replied: 'I don't know. If I told you anything at all it would only be my own opinion. If it turned out wrong, you would say that I told you lies, and have me killed.'

'But we must have something to go on. How else can we tell what to do?'

He paused for a moment, and then said slowly: 'Your brother told me that you are the Burma Independence Army. If you're the lot I'm thinking of you fought against us when the Japanese drove us out of Burma; you killed a great many of our chaps. Some of them were tortured.'

She faced him. 'That is true,' she said firmly. 'We fought to make our country free; we have been exploited by you foreigners long enough. I do not know about the tortures, but we fight our wars more bitterly than you do. You are kind to all prisoners, no matter how bad and treacherous they are. My people are not so gentle.'

The pilot glanced at her. 'Are you still fighting with the Japanese against us?'

She said vehemently: 'Never again with the Japanese.' There was a pause, and then she said: 'We are what we say, the Burma Independence Army. You

British ruled us simply to make money out of us; you took away our teak and rice and sold them for a high price, and took the money for yourselves. The Japanese promised us independence, so we fought with them to turn the British out.' She smiled cynically. 'After that we found that the Japanese only meant to turn us into a colony for their own benefit. They took everything, even the sewing-machines out of the villages, and sent them to Japan. They pay our coolies in paper money made in a note machine on the pay desk. Our country is ruined, and we are worse off than we have ever been.'

Morgan asked curiously: 'Would you like to have the British back again?'

There was a long pause. 'For myself, I would,' the girl said. 'We have learned one thing; we are not strong enough to stand alone against great nations. If we have to have foreigners in our country at all I would like it to be either the British or the Americans, and we know the British better. We have no quarrel with the British people—most Burmans get on very well with most British. But to be governed by your English sahibs who think themselves superior to us simply because of the colour of their skin—that is unbearable. We will not have it any longer. If you try to impose it upon us again, we shall murder every Englishman in the country.'

Morgan said: 'Starting with me.'

The girl broke into laughter. The guards looked at her uncertainly, with wrinkled brows; they had not understood one word of this English talk. 'It is a long time since we have had an Englishman near enough to kill. Perhaps we shall keep you as a curiosity.'

Morgan said keenly: 'What about the Japanese? Have your people killed any of them?'

The girl said: 'A few. When we hear of a very small patrol in the jungle, my brother leads a force out to surround them; then we kill them all and take their arms. In that way we are getting a few weapons for our secret army.'

She glanced up at them. 'How long will it be before the British reach here? We must know that.'

He rubbed his chin. 'I can't tell you,' he said. 'I don't know. I can only tell you that something will be starting very soon—I think it has already started in the north. When it does begin, it may go very quickly.' He paused, considering. 'This is November, and the monsoon breaks in June. I doubt if we shall get as far as this before next June—but we might.'

'What makes you think that you will advance so quickly?'

He said: 'The numbers of aircraft, and guns, ships, and machines. They are simply pouring out here now, now that the war in Europe is coming to an end. Men, too. Look at me. I was in England only four months ago. Now I'm here. And there are hundreds of thousands like me in Bengal.'

She said: 'Oh. . . . You were in England four months ago?'

He said: 'That's right.'

She said: 'How is Mr Churchill? Is he all right? He is a very great man.'

Morgan said: 'He's all right. He's still Prime Minister.'

She thought for a minute. 'How is Deanna Durbin? Is she well?'

He blinked, and then said: 'I think so. I saw her in a picture not long ago.'

She said: 'I like her pictures very much, ever since *One Hundred Men and a Girl.*' She laughed. 'And Rita Hayworth—is she all right still?'

He replied: 'I saw her in a film called *Cover Girl*, just before I left London. She was simply lovely. She dances awfully well now.'

The girl sighed. 'Here we see nothing but Japanese propaganda films, all about people looking at cherry trees and going away to war to die for the Emperor. They are very dull.'

He said: 'Never mind. It won't be long now.'

She turned to him. 'Do you know Major Williams?'

He shook his head. 'I'm afraid I don't. Who is he?'

She said: 'You are quite sure?'

'I don't know him. Who is he—is he here?'

She dropped her voice a little. 'I remember him—he was in Rangoon—he was the buyer for Everett and Fraser, a young man with red hair. They say that he is in Bassein, and that he is trying to get men to join what he calls a V Force—V for Victory, in English. My brother saw him ten days ago. He said the same as you have done, that the English would sweep forward very soon. Utt Nee did not believe him, but now you are here and you have said the same things as he did. That is why they are arguing so long in there. They do not know what to do.'

'I see,' said Morgan thoughtfully.

They stood together in silence for a minute. The guards stood patient by them; to these men time was of no importance.

He said: 'How did this Major Williams get into the country?'

She said: 'They say that a small aeroplane brought him, and flew away again, by night. I do not know if that is true.'

Morgan nodded; it was probably true enough. There was a flight of L5s, he knew, that worked on missions such as that, but it was a long flight for an L5 to come right down from Cox's to Bassein. If this Williams was in touch, however, it might well be that he could get him out by air.

He said: 'Well, it's in your hands. If you're going on playing with the Japanese, you give me up to them, dead or alive. If you decide to turn and help the British, then you'd better hand me over to this Major Williams.'

She said: 'That is what I should like to do, myself.'

He laughed. 'I'm an interested party, so I'd better not give my opinion.'

She laughed with him; beside them the guards stirred uneasily. 'Go back in there,' she said, 'I am going in to see my brother.'

Morgan lay all day in the lockup. Peering between the bamboos he could see the house; there was a continuous sound of voices from the room where he had been examined, and twice he heard voices raised in passionate argument and declamation. Once or twice he thought there was going to be a fight. From time to time Burmans came to the house and went in, or departed from it; they were all men and all incredibly young. Some of them seemed hardly more than fifteen to his inexperienced eye, and all were certainly under twenty-five. It was hot in the little hut, and flies tormented him all day.

He was fetched out again at dusk, and taken to the house. Utt Nee received him, standing by the table.

He said: 'You have been talking to my sister.'

Morgan said: 'Yes. I answer questions from anybody who asks them. I tell them the truth, so far as I know it.' Instinctively he was terrified of seeming to show interest in a native woman.

The Burman nodded. 'She has told me. You know how—how we are placed. There is this Major Williams of your Army, near Bassein. He wants us to do . . . to do certain things, and he has told us beautiful stories of what the English are about to do. When I met him I did not believe a word of it.'

Morgan was silent.

'Now you have come, and you tell us the same beautiful stories, and we do not know what we can believe. So I am sending you to this Major Williams as a proof of our good faith, upon our side. Upon his side, I am saying that he must provide us with five hundred hand grenades and fifty light machine guns, with two hundred rounds of ammunition for each gun. We cannot do what he wants us to do without grenades and guns. If he trusts us, he will give them.'

He paused. 'I send a present for a present. I give you to him as token of our good faith. As token of his good faith he must give us the grenades and guns. I will not work for him on empty words alone from an Englishman. I have had some of that before.'

Morgan said: 'How far are we from Bassein?'

The Burman said: 'About fifty miles. I shall send you to this Englishman with a small patrol under my lieutenant, Thet Shay. They will take paths that keep you away from the Japanese. I cannot go with you myself, though I should like to. I must report this to my colonel, in the direction of Pegu.'

Morgan said thoughtfully: 'You have no signals—no field telephones or radio?'

'None that we can use. That is another thing this major must supply if we are to fight with the British. We must have small radio sets, and men to work them.'

Morgan said: 'What do you want me to tell this Major Williams? Do you want me to give him your messages, or will your man, Thet Shay, do everything you want? I'll help in any way I can.'

Utt Nee sat in silence for a minute. 'Thet Shay speaks no English. I do not know how well this Englishman speaks our language. When I met him, we spoke English all the time. I know he speaks Burmese a little.'

Morgan said: 'You speak English perfectly. What were you before the war?'

'I was a student at Rangoon University. I was studying to be an engineer. I suppose you are surprised at that. You English people think of us as naked savages. But our religion and our culture is much older than yours. In your country you have only taught the common people to read and write in very recent times. In Burma every boy has learned to read and write for over a thousand years, in our religious schools. And yet you have the impudence to think yourselves superior to us. You only ever were superior to us in one thing. Do you know what that was?'

Morgan said: 'No.' He had the good sense to put up with this tirade.

Utt Nee said: 'Gunpowder. You learned the use of firearms before we did, and conquered our country.'

Morgan said: 'Well, you managed to kick us out in 1942.'

Utt Nee laughed. 'And now you will say, these crazy people are talking of co-operating with this Major Williams to help the British to come back again.'

'I don't know anything about politics,' said Morgan. 'All I know is that it's a bloody crazy world.'

Utt Nee said: 'I have lain awake night after night, wondering who is mad, the British, or my countrymen who want the Japanese to stay in Burma, or myself.' He laughed cynically. 'If we help the British to come back again, do you think that they will hang us all for fighting against them in 1942?'

Morgan rubbed his chin. 'I don't know,' he said. 'It depends how well the sense of humour's worn.'

Utt Nee said: 'For myself, I am prepared to take the risk. I see no better chance of any sort of independence for my people now. I think, too, that we are strong enough to force a decent compromise between your way and ours.'

Morgan said: 'Looks as if our Government'll have to pull the finger out and do a bit of thinking.'

There was a step behind them; Morgan turned, and saw that the girl had come up into the house. Utt Nee said: 'I have told him that I have decided to send him with Thet Shay to the Englishman.'

The girl nodded. 'It is the only thing to do.'

Morgan said: 'Let me get this straight. I see what you want; you will do nothing for this major unless he sends you five hundred grenades, fifty Tommy guns or Sten guns, and two hundred rounds for each. That's what you want to tell him?'

'Radio sets and operators,' said Utt Nee. 'We shall need those too.'

The pilot nodded. 'Radio sets and operators as well. Now, do you want me to tell the major this, or is Thet Shay going to do the talking?'

Utt Nee turned to the girl. 'Do you remember, does this major speak our language?'

The girl wrinkled her brows. 'I don't know. He worked in Rangoon all the time. If he speaks any, it will not be very much.'

Utt Nee said: 'Thet Shay will do all the negotiation, on our side. I do not think that you can help us, Mr Morgan.' He turned to the girl and said in Burmese: 'Can we rely upon Thet Shay and the Englishman understanding each other?'

She said in the same language: 'You had better ask Thet Shay that.'

Utt Nee got up, went to the opening in the house that served as a front door, and called for Thet Shay. A young man in a longyi and a khaki tunic came; there was a long three cornered conference between the leader and his lieutenant and the girl. Presently they turned and came into the room, to Morgan still sitting at the table.

'This is Thet Shay,' he said in English. Morgan half rose from the table; the Burman bowed towards him stiffly. 'We have decided this. You are to take no part in the negotiation; that will only make confusion. My sister will go with Thet Shay to interpret with the Englishman. If he says he will give us arms, then I will come to see him with Colonel Ne Win, and we will arrange the details.'

'If he says he won't give any arms,' asked Morgan, 'do you take me back and hand me over to the Japanese?'

Utt Nee laughed. 'I do not think we should do that. We are not on speaking terms with the Japanese at the moment.' He laughed again.

'Well, I hope this Major Williams sees it in your way,' the pilot said. 'I'll do what I can to help.'

Utt Nee said: 'I have told Thet Shay that you are to start at dawn. It will take you two days to get near Bassein, and perhaps another day to find this Englishman.' He walked over to the steps down to the ground, and then turned before going out. 'You can bring your blankets up and sleep here in the house,' he said. 'There will be a meal presently.'

The pilot said: 'That's very good of you. Can I have my revolver back?'

Utt Nee said: 'No.' and went out.

Morgan turned to the girl, and to Thet Shay. He said to the girl: 'Please, would you interpret for me a little? I want to tell Mr Thet Shay that I understand he is in charge of this party, that I will obey his orders, and that I will try to make no trouble.'

The girl spoke in Burmese; the young man smiled and spoke. The girl replied: 'He says that he hopes that you will get back safely to your countrymen.'

Thet Shay went away, and Morgan went to get his blankets from the lockup. When he came back, the girl was sitting on the steps; he passed her and put down his bundle in a corner of the house. He took a drink from a ewer in the corner; then he searched his pockets for a piece of paper. He had only an air letter, but the back of the sheet was large and fairly clean, and he had a pencil. He went hesitantly to the girl.

'If you're doing nothing,' he said, 'would you tell me a few Burmese words?'
She said: 'Of course. What do you want to know?'

He said: 'Just a few words, useful things, you know. One feels such a fool if one can't say anything at all.' He hesitated, pencil in hand. 'To start with, would you mind telling me your name?'

She said: 'I am called Nay Htohn. You should call me Ma Nay Htohn – that is, Miss Nay Htohn.'

He wrote it down at the top of his paper; she helped him with the spelling. He said: 'Now, what's the word for water?'

'*Ye,*' she said. He wrote it down.

'Food?'

'There is no word quite like that,' she said. 'We speak of things. The word that everybody understands is *htamin*, which is boiled rice. If you ask for htamin you will get something to eat, unless you were with starving people.'

He wrote it down, and went on to man, and woman, and latrine, and was greatly surprised when she laughed at that, just like an English girl. When he had written down about twenty words he stopped. 'I'll learn these tonight,' he said. 'If you are coming with us to Bassein, will you tell me some more tomorrow?'

She said: 'I will think of some that will be useful to you, if you stay here long.' And then she said: 'Is this the first time you have been in Burma?'

'It's the first time I have been away from England,' he replied, 'except that I was in North Africa last year.'

'How do you like it?'

He laughed. 'How would you like it, if you were a prisoner and not quite sure how you were going to be treated?' He sat down on the steps, with the whole width of the flight between them. 'I must say, it's lovely country. I'd like to come back here in peacetime, and see it properly.'

She said: 'I wish you would. The only English people who come here are the ones who want to make money out of us – Government officials who come here for their job, or traders who come to buy things from our people as cheap as they can, and sell them for a high price in the outside world. Those are the only sort of English that we ever see. We never meet the ordinary English people, people like ourselves.'

'I suppose you get missionaries out here,' he said.

'Oh, we get a lot of those. Some of them are very kind and good, especially when they start hospitals and schools, and do not try to teach us their religion.'

He said hesitantly: 'You aren't Christian, then?'

She smiled tolerantly. 'No. In Burma we are Buddhists. Surely you knew that?'

'I know that most of the people are Buddhists,' he replied. 'I thought that educated people like you and your brother might be Christians.'

She nodded. 'Some of my friends are Christian, but not very many. I studied your religion very carefully when I was at school, but I didn't like it nearly so well as ours. I don't think it is a very good one.'

He said curiously: 'What's wrong with it?'

She smiled. 'I'm not going to start a religious controversy with you, Mr Morgan. When I was at school they told us that some Englishman said once that it does not matter much what one believes so long as one believes in something. I think that's very true. For ordinary people who are not concerned with dogma there's not much difference between Buddhism and Christianity in the way that we are taught to live, only our way is much stricter than yours.'

He was a little intrigued. 'In what way?' he asked.

She said: 'Well, for one thing, you are allowed to drink wine and kill animals. I don't like that much. We have five elementary commandments; if you break them you will be reborn into a lower scale of life. You must not kill any living creature at all, you must not lie, you must not steal, you must not commit adultery, you must not touch any intoxicating drink. Those are the minimum commandments, the ones that everybody must observe if he wants to avoid being reborn as an animal. If you want to go forward you must do much more than that.'

'You really think that you can become an animal in your next life?' the pilot asked. 'You mean, like a pig?'

'You make your own destiny,' she said. 'Everyone does that. If you choose to live like a tiger or a pig, if that's the sort of life you like, you will attain your desire in your next incarnation. If you strive earnestly for wider mental powers and a better life, then next time you will be reborn higher up on the Ladder of Existence. That is what we believe.'

'I see.' He thought for a moment, and then asked: 'What happens when you get to the top of the ladder? What happens when you are as good as you can be?'

She said: 'You can only reach that point after countless thousands of lives. But ultimately, if you receive the Final Enlightenment, so that you are wholly good and completely wise, so that everything you say or do is the perfection of truth and wisdom, you are then the Buddha.'

'That's the statue in the pagodas, isn't it?' he asked.

'The statue that you see in the pagodas is the last Buddha,' she replied. 'Prince Shin Gautama. Twenty-eight souls have attained this perfection in the history of the Universe, and only four in this world; you see, it is not very easy. Prince Shin Gautama was the last, the twenty-eighth, and it is his example that we try to follow in our daily life.'

'Rather like our Christ,' he said thoughtfully.

'Exactly like your Christ,' she said. 'But you believe that your Christ was a God, the son of a God who lives somewhere in the outer relams of space and who created you for this one life. I don't quite understand that part of your religion. We have the same idea of a supremely perfect Being, but we believe that any one of us can reach that same perfection if we try hard enough to live a holy life, in age after age. We have the statue of Prince Shin Gautama in our prayer houses as an example, to remind us of what any one of us can attain to.

Frankly, Mr Morgan, I like our idea better than yours, though for practical purposes there's not much in it.'

She paused, and then she said: 'I think our religion is rather less debased than yours in some ways, too.'

He did not feel able to embark on that one. He asked: 'Is everybody in Burma a Buddhist?'

She said: 'Not everyone. Nine people out of ten are Buddhists, I should think, but the Karens are sometimes Christian, and the uneducated country people still believe in Nats, the spirits of the woods and trees, and build little houses for them. I will show you on our way, tomorrow. But when men get educated and begin to think more deeply, then they come to the Pagoda.'

Utt Nee passed them, going up the steps into the house. The girl said: 'I have been telling the Englishman all about our savage religion.'

The young man laughed. 'My sister is very religious,' he said to Morgan. 'Women think more deeply about these matters than most men. You must not let her offend you.'

The pilot said: 'She's been very kind in telling me about it. I didn't know a thing about all this before.'

The girl said, a little wistfully: 'Don't they teach anything about our country in your schools?'

Morgan said: 'We learn a little, I suppose, but only facts. The names of rivers, and about rice coming from Rangoon, and things like that.'

Utt Nee said: 'Rice will be coming here in a few minutes. You will eat with us.'

Morgan got up from his long chair on the veranda. Three men in longyis had appeared, and squatted down upon their haunches on the path at the foot of the steps. He left Turner in his chair, and went and spoke to them in Burmese. A slow conversation developed, evidently punctuated with jokes and repartee. After ten minutes there was a final sally, and the three got up and went away. Morgan came back to Turner in his chair. 'Sorry about that,' he said. 'Have a drink?'

Mr Turner hesitated. 'Got any beer?'

The other shook his head. 'It doesn't keep out here. Whisky?'

'No thanks—I got to be careful. Got a lemon squash, or anything o' that?'

'Fresh lime squash, with a bit of ice in it?'

'That'll do fine.'

Morgan called an order in Burmese back into the house, and came and sat down. 'What did them chaps want?' asked Mr Turner.

'Those? Oh, that was the headman from one of the villages and two of his pals, sort of shop stewards. I want some coolies to make up the road out to the rice mill. He came to fix the rate for the job.'

The glasses came, borne by the barefooted Burman servant. Morgan sat, glass in hand, looking out over the river. 'I was telling you about that evening before we started for Bassein,' he said. He sat in silence for a minute. 'It's a damn funny thing,' he said at last, 'but you can usually tell when there's something wrong. I couldn't speak a word of Burmese at that time, but I was pretty sure that some of those chaps were against me. Utt Nee was for me all right, and Ma Nay Htohn. Thet Shay, I think, was very doubtful if it was a good idea to turn me over to this Major Williams; some of the rest of them I'm pretty sure were hostile to the whole thing.'

He paused. 'I got an idea into my head that Utt Nee sent his sister with the party, not so much to interpret, as to see that I got there all right, and wasn't murdered on the way. I'm pretty sure that was behind it, in his mind. I asked him that straight out once, but the old devil wouldn't tell me . . .'

'Anyway,' he said, 'we pushed off before dawn the next day for Bassein.'

They went in single file along field paths between the squares of paddy, eight men, Morgan and Nay Htohn. The arms the party carried were not very impressive. Thet Shay and one other man carried Japanese rifles, and Thet Shay wore Morgan's revolver in its holster. One of the other men had an old muzzle loading rifle with a very long barrel, and one had a very modern twelve bore sporting shotgun; the other four were armed only with their dahs. None of them wore brassards or any sort of uniform. Morgan hoped they knew sufficient of the movements of the Japanese about the countryside to keep out of their way.

They marched all morning until nearly noon. They were then in a teak forest following a barely noticeable track; they halted and lay down, and boiled rice on a little fire of leaves and twigs, extinguishing the fire immediately it was done with. Morgan was very tired although he was marching light with only his blanket to carry; he was unused to marching in the tropics and was drenched with sweat. Utt Nee had given him a conical straw hat to wear and this had been a comfort in the sun, but he was very, very tired. Nay Htohn and the Burmans seemed as fresh as daisies.

They ate their rice, and curled up for a sleep, leaving one man on watch. At about three o'clock they moved off up the path again, and marched till dusk.

They camped for the night in a bamboo jungle, in a small clearing by a little stream. Again they made a little fire and extinguished it immediately their simple meal was cooked; then there was nothing to do but to lie down wrapped up in blankets and wait for sleep. Nay Htohn directed the positions of their sleeping; it did not escape Morgan's notice that the girl arranged matters so that he slept between Thet Shay and herself.

Lying upon the grass, wondering what bugs would bite him in the night, watching the fine tracery of the bamboos against the starlit sky above him, Morgan heard the girl say: 'What will happen when you get back to your Army? Will they send you back to England?'

He replied: 'I shouldn't think so. I'll probably get leave up in the hills or something, for a week or two. But I'm not back yet.'

'No. How do you live in England? Are you married?'

He said: 'Yes, I'm married.'

'Is your wife very beautiful?'

He said: 'She's the most beautiful girl I have ever seen.'

'Have you got children?'

'No.' He did not expand on that point.

'What will you do in England when the war is over? What did you do before you became an airman?'

'I didn't do anything,' he said. 'I joined the R.A.F. straight from school, when I was eighteen. I don't know what I shall do. I was going to be an architect before, but I'd only just started. I don't know.'

'Will you do that in England?'

'I don't know—I suppose I shall. I hadn't thought about it much.' He turned his head towards her. 'What will you do?'

She said: 'I might go back and be a shorthand typist in a Rangoon office, as I was before. I don't know, either.'

'Have you lived in the country for long?'

'My father moved up to Henzada when the Japanese came in, and I went there with him. That is a fairly large place. For the last year or so I have been mostly with my brother in the country districts. One cannot sit still and do nothing.'

'You must find it pretty slow, after Rangoon,' he said.

She laughed. 'I miss the pictures dreadfully. Apart from that,' she said, 'I rather like the country. Rangoon is quite dead now, and not pleasant if you do not want to go about and dine with Japanese officers.'

Presently their voices died down, and they slept uneasily on the hard ground.

At dawn they got up, cooked another meal, and marched on. That day took them to within five miles of Bassein; they camped for the night in a small spinney without a fire, eating the cold porridge-like remains of rice that they had cooked at lunch. Thet Shay and one other man went out along the path that they were following to find a nearby village, to inquire how the land lay regarding Japanese, to find the man who knew where they could make a contact with Major Williams.

They came back an hour later in a state of agitation. The Burmans and the girl clustered round Thet Shay; he had urgent and important news for them, and it was not good news. So much was obvious to Morgan. They squatted down together in an earnest conference; from time to time the men threw anxious glances in his direction. He waited for enlightenment with all the patience that he could command. Something had happened to upset their plans; so much was evident. He took the surmise fatalistically; it had been too good to be true, that he would get away from Burma easily.

Presently the girl left the group, and came and squatted down beside him. 'It is bad news,' she said quietly. 'A Japanese patrol has caught this Major Williams. They surrounded the village and took him while he was asleep. Now he is dead.'

The pilot nodded; he had been prepared for some news of the sort. 'That's a bad one,' he said quietly. 'What is Thet Shay going to do now?'

She said: 'He has sent out scouts.' Morgan glanced at the group, and noticed that three men had melted away into the darkness. 'It is very dangerous here. There are Japanese patrols everywhere in these villages.' She hesitated. 'They are on the lookout for parties such as ours, who may be trying to make contact with the Englishman.'

'Do they know anything about us?' the pilot asked.

'I do not think they do. The Englishman said nothing according to the village people, although the Japanese soldiers were very cruel to him. He took fifteen hours to die.'

Morgan bit his lip. No man is immune from fear, though he may be able to control himself. 'Nice story,' he said quietly.

She stared at him, and then laughed shortly. 'I suppose that is an English joke.'

He grinned at her. 'Well, one's got to make a joke of something.'

She said: 'You must stay very quiet. We are going to wait here until the scouts come back, and tell us which way we must go.'

She went back to the group of men; Morgan sat a short distance from them, his back against a tree, watching them and thinking. It seemed to him that they were in a most colossal jam. The Japanese had tortured this Major Williams to make him reveal his connection with the Independence Army; if they caught any members of the Independence Army they would certainly be tortured too, men or women, to make them reveal the extent of the conspiracy. Thet Shay would be tortured without doubt. Nay Htohn would be tortured.

If the party were taken with himself among them, it would be clear evidence that they were members of the Burma Independence Army. That meant torture and death for the lot of them. Nay Htohn, also, would take fifteen hours to die.

Morgan set down his glass, and called the bearer for another couple of drinks. 'Well, that's the way it was,' he said. 'The only one who might have got away with it if the Japs had caught us as a party was me. I could always plead I was an enemy in uniform doing what I could to get home–they couldn't have much against me for that.'

Mr Turner said: 'You was in a spot all right.' He paused. 'What did you do?'

The pilot said: 'Oh, I skipped off out of the party and lay up in the bushes for a couple of days to let them get away; then I walked into Bassein and gave myself up to the Japs. I mean, it was the only thing to do.'

6

It was about three in the morning, when the scouts had been back for an hour, that the pilot decided to act. The news had been altogether bad. Japanese patrols were moving upon all the paths; they had closed round behind them and no direct return along the path that they had come by was now possible. They had decided to get a little sleep, and to send out scouts again at dawn to try to find a safe escape route backwards from the trap.

There was one safe escape route which was obvious to Morgan, and it was obvious to him that several of the men would like to take it. That was, that he should be murdered there and then, buried under a tree; without him the party could split up into twos and threes and appear as peaceful villagers going about their business in the normal way. That was the safe way out for them, the way in which they could get back unquestioned and so join up with Utt Nee again. From time to time as they squatted round in conclave there was a hot argument between Thet Shay and Nay Htohn on the one side and certain of the men on the other, and in these arguments bitter, hostile glances were thrown at him. It was clear to Morgan that in the party things were moving to a crisis; that their newfound loyalty was being put to an unbearable test.

They lay down presently to sleep, with Morgan placed carefully between the girl and Thet Shay. He waited till he had heard the regular, even breathing of the girl for half an hour to indicate that she was deeply asleep; then he shook the Burman gently by the arm.

He could not talk to him in any language, but Thet Shay was intelligent and caught on to the pilot's sign language readily. Morgan said "Bassein?' in inquiry, and pointed to each path in turn in the dim light. The Burman understood him, and showed an alley between trees, with wonder and suspicion on his broad face.

The pilot nodded, pointed to himself, then to the path. He held both hands above his head in token of surrender, and said again: 'Bassein.' Then he glanced at the sleeping girl and made the sign for silence.

The next part was more difficult. He got very quietly to his feet; the Burman got up with him; they stood together in the dim starlight beneath the trees. Morgan pointed to himself and to the path for Bassein; then he pointed to the rest of the party and to the path in the opposite direction, and made a comprehensive gesture with both hands. Thet Shay nodded. Morgan went on to an elaborate pantomine of sleeping twice, and hiding in the bushes, and surrendering. He could not get that through at first, and repeated it, but he was very doubtful if the Burman understood.

He thought for a moment, and reached for his pencil. He had only the paper on which he had made his list of Burmese words; he wrote on this at right angles to the list:

I have gone into Bassein to surrender to the Japs; don't try to follow me. I shall try and hide for two days before surrendering so that you can get away. The English will send another officer to replace Major Williams, tell him about me. I will try and see you when the war is over, if I get away with it. Don't think too badly of us. We may be stupid, but we do our best.

He gave this note to Thet Shay, and indicated that he should show it to Nay Htohn when he had gone. The Burman nodded. Morgan picked up his haversack and turned to him, and held out his hand. Thet Shay took it smiling, and they shook hands, and Morgan turned and walked off softly up the path towards Bassein. He never looked back at the sleeping girl.

Mr Turner said in wonder: 'Must have took a bit of doing, that.'

Morgan laughed. 'Never been so frightened in my life. I tell you, I was simply pissed with fright. I was banking everything on getting right into Bassein before surrendering, and not meeting a patrol.' He turned to Mr Turner. 'It was the junior officers and N.C.O.s who did most of the torturing,' he said. 'If you had to surrender to the Japs, you wanted to try and pick a senior officer, and give yourself up to him. You wanted to keep clear of sergeants out on a patrol . . .'

'My Christ,' said Mr Turner. 'I'd want to keep clear of the whole bloody lot, myself.'

The two days of waiting were a bad time for Morgan. He went up the path about a mile, and then turned into a thicket and made his way into the woods. After a hundred yards or so he came out in a little glade, and he sat down there upon a fallen tree. He had no food with him, and no water.

With his intellect he did not regret those omissions. The tale that he had formulated for the Japanese was that he had been hiding and walking across country by night, guided by the stars, from where he had forced landed the

Spitfire to Bassein. His story was that he had been told at the briefing before taking off that this Major Williams was in the neighbourhood of Bassein, and that after his forced landing he had marched by night across country to get in touch with him, hiding in the woods each day. He had finally asked a group of Burmans to lead him to the Major; they had told him that the Englishman was dead, and had then run away. With nothing else to do, he had walked in and had given himself up.

The more he thought about this yarn the more it seemed convincing; he could not see how he could be tripped upon it in interrogation, if he kept his head. It was important, however, that he should not be in too good a physical condition if his story was to be that he had lived in the jungle for five or six days without much equipment. If he was half starved, crazy with thirst, and mercilessly bitten by all kinds of bugs it would be better for his story. In the next two days in the forest he suffered all three torments. He stuck it out.

At dawn, two days later, he found the path again, and wandered down it in the direction of Bassein. He went carelessly, with a raging thirst and with the high temperature of a fever on him. He was bareheaded, for he had thrown away his conical straw sun hat as not being in the part, and he was dressed in the soiled green blouse and trousers of a jungle suit. He wore no underclothes. He had canvas wellingtons upon his feet, muddy and somewhat torn, and a soiled white scarf around his neck. He carried his haversack still with the remains of his emergency kit in it, and he had a five days' growth of beard on his face. In that condition he walked straight into Bassein; it was not until he was actually walking down the main street of the town that a Japanese officer arrested him, a heavy automatic pistol in his hand.

He was taken to the military headquarters in a villa and given a drink of water, and interrogated; then he was interrogated again at the headquarters of the Kempeitai, who took all his papers from him. He played his part well, as if crushed with disappointment at his failure to escape. They did not bother a great deal about him; the arrest and imprisonment of airmen who had forced landed in the country was a normal routine to the Japanese. The only feature which made his case unusual was that he had wandered for six days about the countryside, and that was satisfactorily explained by the presence of the English major, now liquidated.

In a couple of days he was taken by river in a landing craft to Rangoon, and put in the jail there with the other prisoners, mostly R.A.F.

In Rangoon jail there was no torture, but a great deal of indignity. Minor infractions of the regulations were disciplined by the Japanese kicking the shins or slapping the face, the same treatment as was meted out by Japanese officers to privates in their own army. The food was a revolting mess of boiled rice with a few vegetables occasionally as flavouring; it was deficient in every sort of vitamin because the bulk rice supply from which it came had been more than two years in store. Old rice eaten in this way causes beriberi, and the prisoners in Rangoon jail suffered a lot from this progressive disease.

The cells were not unpleasant in that tropical climate, if prisoners had to be kept in cells at all. The jail was a fairly modern building. Morgan was put into an empty cell on the first floor of a long building that radiated with six others from a central hexagonal building which contained a well. His cell was thirteen feet long and nine feet wide, with a grating door and a grating window which permitted the cool air to blow straight through it, in itself a comfort in that climate. The walls were whitewashed, and the only furniture was a plank bed.

The cell had housed a succession of previous occupants, some of whom had been moved down to the communal prison on the ground floor after an initial period of solitary confinement, and some had died. There were calendars and messages written on the wall, half rubbed out by the Japanese guards—*F. /O. J. D. Scott, R. A. F., 698443 shot down near Prome in a Hurricane 7.2.43. I shall stay in this bloody hole until the bugs carry me out they are big enough.* Behind the door where it was not easily seen from the corridor there was written on the wall a little dictionary of a dozen elementary words necessary for prisoners, with their Japanese equivalent—Water, Food, Doctor, Cold, Hot, Latrine, Good, Bad. Below this there was a verse:

> Only one life,
>   Twill soon be past,
> Only what's done for Christ
>   Will last.

Attached to it was the signature of F./O. J. K. Davidson, of Kilburn. Morgan wondered grimly what had happened to F./O. Davidson.

Morgan had a pencil and he immediately made a calendar upon the wall to cross the days off, the first act of the prisoner in solitary confinement. Later on he added a little to the Japanese dictionary, and for a mental exercise wrote down all the counties in the United Kingdom. He also wrote down all the Burmese words that Nay Htohn had told him, with their English equivalents, in case he should forget them.

He stayed in that cell from November 23rd, 1944, until the Japanese left Rangoon before our advance on April 29th, 1945.

His life was monotonous, and his health gradually deteriorated with deficiency of vitamins, but he was not very unhappy. He used to lie for long hours on the plank bed, thinking, and what he thought about was principally Nay Htohn. His idea of women was focused about Nay Htohn. Bitterly hurt by the treatment he had received from his wife, he clung to the idea of the Burmese girl, so much more intelligent and so much wiser than any woman he had come into contact with in his short life. He wanted to see her again when he got out of prison, wanted to find out what had happened to her after he had left them, wanted her assurance that she had escaped the Japanese. He never had much doubt about it, but he wanted to see her again to make quite sure. He wanted to talk to her again, to be with her, to see her move and hear her lilting voice. It came to him, queerly, that he had been happy on that day that he had spent mostly in the bamboo lockup in that nameless village in the jungle.

As the months passed, the Royal Air Force gradually faded from his mind. He was still desperately interested in air operations, and when the massed flights of Mitchells and Thunderbolts, Liberators and Spitfires, came raiding military objectives in Rangoon he used to stand glued to the grating of his window, his heart with the aircrews, well aware from his own briefings that they would be particularly careful not to hit the jail. But as the time went by, he gradually became accustomed to the thought that he would never fly again, that by the time he was released new aircrews would have superseded him, that the very war might be over. The tropical and Burman scene became more real to him than his life in the Royal Air Force; England itself seemed very far away, a place of bitter hurt that he did not particularly want to go back to. He wanted to get back and see Nay Htohn, and listen to her talking, and watch her smile.

April 29th, 1945, was a Sunday. In the few weeks before, with the Fourteenth Army driving down past Mandalay towards Rangoon and with the Fifteenth Corps advancing down the coast of Arakan, the Japanese had grown much less severe in Rangoon jail; food had improved, and the surveillance was relaxed. A large proportion of the prisoners were suffering from dysentery, and for this reason the Japanese at night had fallen into the way of leaving the cell doors unlocked in order that the prisoners might visit the latrine, keeping guard only on the block compound. In the middle of the night an R.A.F. officer, thin and wasted and trembling hurried from his cell to the latrine outside. There was a paper pinned to the door, unusual. He could not wait, but presently when he came out he raised his hurricane lamp to look at it. It read:

English and American prisoners, you are now free. By order of the Emperor the Japanese Army has withdrawn from Rangoon, and so we have left you to regain your liberty. We shall hope to meet you again honourably on the field of battle.

The keys are on the table in the guardroom.

He stared at it amazed, and hurried back to the cells and woke the others in his building. Two senior officers ventured out of the block compound into the walled lane outside that led down from the central well towards the guardroom, half expecting to be met by a sharp squirt of submachine gun fire. But there were no Japanese; they walked down to the guardroom, and there the keys·were lying on the table, three great bunches of them. It was all quite true.

For half an hour there had been a growing clamour from the town. They unlocked the main gates and walked out into the street. From the centre of the town there was a roar of crowds rioting, and shots were going off continually. Over the houses they could see the glow of fires. It was all rather alarming to weakened, totally unarmed men isolated in a tropical city; the prisoners went back into the jail and locked themselves in. It could only be a matter of a very few days now before the Fourteenth Army marched in to relieve them.

At dawn they set about communicating with the R.A.F. aircraft on patrol above the city. Morgan and others got a long ladder and got on to the roof of their block, and with limewash painted in huge letters–JAPS GONE. They were rewarded by a Mosquito which came down to a thousand feet and circled round, photographing what they had done. Later in the morning they became apprehensive that the High Command might think their sign a Jap ruse. They searched their minds for a code message which would carry conviction, and in their impatience for release they had no hesitation in framing a rude one. They got up on the other side of the pitched roof and painted in large letters, EXTRACT DIGIT. A Thunderbolt came by and waggled its wings at them.

Firing was easier in the afternoon, and there was less noise from the city. The prisoners were urgently in need of better food; fresh meat and vegetables and fruit were probably available in the city. Under the command of a young major in the Indian Army, Morgan and three others left the jail as a compact little group and walked into the town; they were quite unarmed and went very warily. They went slowly for they were all suffering from swollen legs due to incipient beriberi. They came first to the Chinese quarter and were welcomed heartily; they found that the Chinese had erected barricades across the streets to protect their shops and go-downs from the looters who were ravaging the remainder of Rangoon. They got everything they wanted in the Chinese quarter in a couple of hours without the slightest difficulty, including a few automatic pistols stolen from the Japanese. They made arrangements for the delivery of two lorry loads of fruit and vegetables to the jail; curiously, there was plenty of petrol left behind in the town, which was only damaged by our own bombardment and by looters.

When the question of payment arose they offered chits drawn against the paymaster of the Fourteenth Army, which were accepted gladly by the Chinese banker that they dealt with. In the office he beamed at the tattered scarecrows of men in stained jungle suits facing him across the table. 'I am very glad to assist English prisoners,' he said. 'But also, this is better money than the Japanese paper money we have now. In helping you I help myself, gentlemen. Do not thank me.'

The major asked: 'Is the currency position very bad?'

The Chinaman laughed. 'I cannot describe it. During the occupation the inflation was twenty times—not less than that—twenty times at least. But last night when the Japanese left the mob broke open the banks down in the English quarter and stole all the notes. A friend of mine who has been there this morning says that notes of fifty and a hundred rupees are lying piled like dead leaves in the gutter. If that is true, then this Japanese money is completely worthless. I would rather have your chits.'

He made them drink tea with him from fine cups without handles, and showed them out with every courtesy. In the street outside, surrounded by the crowd, the major said: 'Like to take a walk up town and see if what he said about the banks is true?'

They went, walking in the middle of the street, the automatics ready in their hands. The streets were indescribably filthy; great heaps of rotting garbage lay on all the pavements. They went slowly, stopping many times to receive the greetings of various brown men in native costume who spoke excellent English. Before them rioting and crowd activity died down and the crowds melted away; behind them a long tail of interested citizens followed. They went carefully and steadily down the middle of the street, ready for anything.

They reached the banking district; it was as the Chinaman had said. Every bank had been broken open and the looting was still going on; the crowds melted away before them and resumed their reprehensible activities when they passed. Five and ten rupee notes were everywhere in the gutters and lying on the pavements; these were chicken feed, not worth the trouble of picking up. They went into several of the wrecked banks, pistols in hand, flushing the crowd before them. Great stacks of unissued paper money in bundles were standing ripped open and scattered, heaved from a burst strong room. They stood and stared in wonder at this curious sight.

'Better take a little of this back with us for current expenses,' the major said. They filled their pockets and the blouses of their jungle suits; then they commandeered a tonga and drove back to jail to rest their swollen legs. When Morgan got back to the jail he found that he had twelve thousand eight hundred and sixty rupees, about nine hundred and fifty pounds at par, in his possession. He gave a good deal of it away that evening.

Morgan lay awake for a short time that night before sleep, thinking deeply. The better food that he had eaten during the day, and the rice wine that he had drunk, had revived him, had increased his clarity of thought. Within a day or two now the British and Indian troops would reach Rangoon; messages of encouragement had been dropped into the jail by aircraft flying low that evening. When that happened the prisoners would be evacuated by air at once to India, and from there they would be sent back to England probably to be demobilized. The last thing that Morgan wanted to do was to go back to England, into the sordid mess that was his marriage. What he wanted to do was to get up into the Irrawaddy delta and find out what had become of Nay Htohn, and to meet her again. To hell, he thought, with going back to England, at any rate for a bit. He wanted to stay in Burma.

In the circumstances, discipline was very lax in Rangoon jail; parties of prisoners walked in and out of the town freely next morning. Morgan took stock of his possessions. He had his one worn jungle suit, his haversack with a few small articles of kit, his boots, his scarf, a blanket, about five thousand six hundred Japanese rupees, and a good automatic pistol with fifty-three rounds of ammunition. He felt foot-loose and free. He went down to see the Chinese banker who had helped them the day before, and asked him the best way to get to Henzada. He said that he had to get in touch with a man called Utt Nee.

The Chinaman knew all about Utt Nee. 'He is colonel in the Independence Army,' he said. 'You will be able to find somebody at Henzada who can direct you to him, if you can get there. His father is very well known in Rangoon, Maung Shway Than. He is at Henzada, or he was last month. If you find Maung Shway Than, give him my very kind regards.'

The pilot asked: 'You know him, do you?'

'Oh yes. Maung Shway Than had many important business interests in Rangoon. He has several children; Utt Nee is the eldest son. He was at Rangoon University.'

They turned to the consideration of the journey. 'You will have to go by river,' said the Chinaman. 'I do not know the situation with regard to the Japanese, but I think there are very many up by Henzada still. You can go to Yandoon in a sampan fairly easily from here; I can arrange that for you. At Yandoon you should ask for Mr Liu Sen, who is a banker we have dealings with. I will give you a letter to him, and he will help you if he can. I do not know what conditions are from Yandoon up to Henzada.'

Morgan did not go back to the jail. The Chinaman was as good as his word; he bustled around and produced a letter in Chinese for Mr Liu Sen at Yandoon. He left his office and they walked down to the waterfront; from the hundreds of sampans he picked one and they made their way from boat to boat to reach it. It was manned by a family of Chinese-Karens, a man, his wife, and two small children. They could not speak one word of English, of course.

The banker talked to them for some time, then turned to Morgan. 'These are people of my Kong,' he said. 'You can trust them. They will take you to Yandoon for two hundred Japanese rupees; it will take two days, or a little longer. I have arranged that you will pay one hundred rupees at Yandoon, but give them a hundred and twenty. The other hundred I will pay them when I get a letter from Liu Sen that you arrived there safely. Now we must buy food for the journey.'

He bought rice and vegetables and fruit for Morgan and had it taken down to the waterfront by the woman. For payment for his services the banker wanted a letter to the Officer Commanding the Fourteenth Army, saying that he had given the prisoners great help; Morgan guessed that he had had many dealings with the Japanese during the occupation and was uncertain of his own position, and anxious to establish credit. The pilot gave him a note of gratitude willingly, and left Rangoon by water at about three o'clock that afternoon.

By all civilized standards the discomfort of the sampan was extreme; to the prisoner just out of Rangoon jail it was delightful; so much do standards change. The Chinese-Karens took little notice of him, treating him mainly as a piece of cargo, as they laboured at their sweeps to bring the sampan up the river in the slack water by the river banks. Morgan sat playing with the children and watching the unaccustomed scene; he kept his money out of sight and his pistol very much in sight, and he had no trouble. The river was thronged with sampans, but when they left the main stream and entered the narrow chaungs to reach the Irrawaddy the natives motioned him to stay inside the bamboo mat shelter, in case a roving band of Japanese seeking to escape towards the east should notice him, and take a shot at him.

He slept two nights in the sampan, lying on the bare boards and eating with his hands out of a common bowl with the family. They got to Yandoon on the third day without incident; he found Mr Liu Sen, and paid off the Chinese-Karens. Mr Sen introduced him to a young man called Moung Boh Galay who held an indeterminate rank in the Independence Army and who spoke a little English; he sent him on by sampan up to Henzada with two armed Burmans as a bodyguard, with instructions to deliver him to Utt Nee. Morgan arrived in Henzada six days after leaving Rangoon, having experienced no special difficulty on the journey.

On the way up river he had learned from various people that Henzada had been bombed, but he was distressed and saddened by what he found there. It had been a Japanese headquarters; sometime in April we had turned the Royal Air Force on to it, and in two or three sharp raids they had practically obliterated the town. Once it had been a thriving place of close on twenty thousand people; now fire had swept across it, more devastating than in Europe since so much was built of wood and bamboo mat. A native town destroyed is sadder than a British city, for there is so little help for the people. These people were stricken by a clash of greater nations than they in their land, and little could be done to help them in their trouble. Here were no Army doctors and nurses to help them; here were no gifts of clothes and food from other prosperous communities. A native town blitzed means an end to civilization in that district for the time; the survivors must disperse to live as best they can from the wild fruits of the jungle, or if fortunate to work as labourers in the paddy fields.

His bodyguard made inquiries from the local people, and hearing that no Japanese were in the town, took Morgan to the headquarters of the Independence Army, a native house that stood undamaged in a palm grove on the outskirts. A young officer received him here with sullen suspicion; amongst considerable coming and going in the little house, Morgan was put through a sharp interrogation. The Independence Army at that time was worried and not a little frightened; they had been fighting for the British after fighting against them, and now that the British were back in the country the Burmans were by no means sure if they would think in terms of 1945 or 1942. Morgan was the first Englishman to reach them in the district with the exception of transient guerrilla officers, and they were distrustful of him till the policy of the British became known. They were by no means sure in Henzada that they would not have to turn and fight the British all over again, and if so, here was Flying-

Officer Morgan for them to make a start on.

In the middle of all this a young Burman passed by them; Morgan glanced at him, and he at Morgan. The pilot said: 'Thet Shay?'

The other stopped and stared, then broke into a beaming smile and came and shook him by the hand. In the babel of Burmese that followed the interrogating officer melted and became genial. 'Everything has been explained,' he said. 'I have heard of you from Colonel Utt Nee, and from Moung Thet Shay. The colonel is away up the river; we expect him back here tomorrow.'

The pilot said: 'Can I stay here till he comes? I want to see him before I go back to England.'

The Burmese talked together for a time. Then the interrogating officer turned to him again. 'It is very uncomfortable here,' he said. 'Moung Thet Shay will take you to the father of Utt Nee, who is here in Henzada and has a good house. He will be glad to put you up. His name is Moung Shway Than.'

Morgan nodded. 'I want to see him, too. I have a message for him from a business friend in Rangoon.'

Thet Shay took him through the ruined town, a place of miserable desolation and burnt posts, to a residential district out beyond what had been the railway station to the west of the town. Here they came to a large Burmese house surrounded by a fairly well tended garden. Thet Shay escorted him up the steps on to the veranda, and paused at the entrance to the main living-room, furnished in European style with cane chairs and tables. There was an old man with grey hair sitting there smoking a cheroot, a brown old man clad in nothing but a longyi. There was a very young man, or boy, reading a book.

Thet Shay said something in Burmese; Morgan stood hesitant at the entrance, feeling rather a fool. The grey-haired old Burman got to his feet, listened to Thet Shay for a minute, and then turned to Morgan. 'I am very pleased to meet you,' he said in good English. 'I remember my eldest son spoke of you.'

The pilot said: 'I'm afraid this is a bit of an intrusion. But I didn't want to leave Burma without seeing your son again. He was very kind to me when I forced landed last November, and he did his best to get me back across our lines. It wasn't his fault that I got taken by the Japs. It was just one of those things.'

Shway Than said: 'Are you free to leave Burma now? Is the port of Rangoon taken by the British?'

Morgan told him what the situation had been in Rangoon when he left. The old man said: 'So you have been in Rangoon jail. I am very sorry. You must need rest now, and good food. Come in and sit down.'

Thet Shay slipped away. Morgan dropped his haversack into a corner, and sank down into one of the cane chairs. He was already tired. 'I'm, very sorry to turn up like this,' he said, glancing down at his soiled, threadbare jungle suit, and feeling the stubble on his chin. 'I've been travelling since Monday.'

The old man said: 'You will want clean clothes, and a bath. I can provide what you need.' He spoke a few words in Burmese to the boy, who went out to the back of the house. The old man turned to Morgan. 'I am beginning to understand this now,' he said. 'You are the Englishman who surrendered to the Japanese at Bassein after the English major had been killed, are you not?'

The pilot said: 'That's right.'

The old man said: 'You saved my daughter and Thet Shay from a bad situation.

'It was the only thing to do. I didn't want them to get into a mess with the Japs on account of me.'

The old man wagged his head. 'Some men would not have seen it in that light. In this house we are very grateful to you.' He struggled to his feet. 'I do not show great gratitude by keeping you talking when you are tired and dirty. Come with me.'

He took the pilot into a cool bedroom with a bathroom opening out of it, with water in a great red chatty. On the string bed a Burman servant was laying out clothes, fine drill trousers and a shirt, and a longyi. Shway Than said: 'There are both English and Burmese clothes for you to choose from. Here are towels and soap, only Japanese soap, very bad, I am sorry. But we have English tea; it will be ready when you are.'

He went out, and the pilot stepped gratefully out of his clothes and sluiced himself with water. He thanked his stars he was not verminous. After the jail and the sampan the bedroom with the huge chatty of cool water was utter luxury; he stood about wet with the water drying on him as he shaved, and sluiced himself again. It was nearly an hour before he could tear himself away from it, till he appeared in the living-room in the shirt and trousers. He had not dared experiment with the longyi; he did not know the knot that keeps it up around the waist.

There was no sign of the old man or the boy when he looked round, but the table was laid as if for afternoon tea in England. In the entrance leading out to the veranda, with her back to him, Nay Htohn was standing. She was dressed in a green longyi and a little short cream coloured jacket over a white shirt; she had a dark red flower in her hair. He stood silent, watching her for a moment; he had not known before quite how badly he had wanted to see her again.

He made a movement, and she turned at the slight sound, and saw him. She smiled, and moved towards him quickly, and took his hand. 'My father said that you were here.' And then she stopped before him in a sort of curtsy, and kissed his hand.

He touched her on the shoulder, half blinded with a sudden watering of the eyes. 'I say, you don't have to do that,' he muttered. Then they had separated, and were staring at each other in wonder, and laughing.

She said: 'Were they cruel to you?'

He grinned at her. 'They had me in the bloody prison up till now. Not crueller than that. Nothing like—like they are sometimes. Nothing like that.'

She said: 'We had them here—they only went away last week. They lived like pigs.'

He said quickly: 'Did they trouble you?'

She shook her head. 'They were quite correct—actually, we saw very little of them. But in their officers' mess, when first they came, they were short of plates and crockery. They used to mix up all their rations, tea and flour and sugar and meat and jam and vegetables and salt and biscuit—they used to mix this all together into a sort of swill, and they served it on to the table in a bedpan.'

He laughed. 'No?'

She laughed with him. 'It is absolutely true, for weeks they ate out of the bedpan. They saw nothing wrong with it. But that was the Army; the civilians were more civilized. Still, we were very glad to see them go.'

He said: 'You got back from Bassein all right?'

She said: 'Thanks to you we did. We walked back in twos and threes, as local villagers. I carried a basket of mangoes on my head until we were past the Japanese patrols, with the revolver and all the rifle ammunition underneath the mangoes. It was terribly heavy. We had to bury the rifles, but we got them all back later on.' She glanced at him. 'You will stay with us for some days?'

'If it won't be too much nuisance, I should like to,' he replied. 'I'm a bit groggy still. My ankles keep on swelling up.'

She made him sit down in a chair, and knelt at his feet, and pressed the swollen flesh with her slim fingers. Her touch was infinitely soothing. She said: 'They gave you very bad food in the jail.'

It was a plain statement of fact, competent and comforting in its efficiency. He nodded. 'Beriberi, isn't it?'

She said: 'It is in an early stage; it will get well soon, with better food and rest. Our people get this sometimes when the crops are bad and they have to eat the old rice. But you must stay with us till you are well.'

He said: 'I don't want to be a nuisance.'

She said gravely: 'How could you be that?'

She called out in Burmese, and a man servant came in from the back quarters; he exclaimed when he saw Morgan's feet. The girl spoke to him for a time in Burmese and he went away; later on he came back with a steaming brew in a jug on a tray, with a cup, and set it down by Morgan, steaming hot. 'You must drink a great deal of that,' the girl said. 'It will do you good.' He discovered later that it was an infusion of fresh limes and rice husks, the vitamin-bearing portion of the rice. It was a country remedy for beriberi, known to the people long before the vitamin was known to anybody.

He had a long talk that evening with the girl and her father; from time to time other relations drifted in and out. He learned that there were still roving parties of Japanese about the countryside, up to three hundred strong; they were avoiding the towns and roads, which were patrolled by the Independence Army. These roving bands were short of food and cut off from their retreat towards the east by the advance of the Fourteenth Army down the middle of the country to Rangoon; a number of them were escaping down river every night in power landing craft, in an attempt to gain the sea and make a sea crossing eastwards to Tavoy. Others were trying to make their way across country, usually by night, to break through the Fourteenth Army's narrow salient in sorties to the east.

The evening meal came and they sat down seven in number to the table, a meal that consisted of a great platter of boiled rice with little bowls of curry in the middle of the table; Nay Htohn arranged special dishes for Morgan. These foods were eaten with a spoon, except for one old lady who used chop-sticks. The meal over, Morgan sat with a cheroot on the veranda in the dim light, utterly peaceful and at rest in a long chair. Nay Htohn came and knelt down on the floor by his feet; it was more natural for her to squat down on the floor than to sit up on a chair.

She had something in her hand. She said: 'I have a paper of yours here. I think perhaps you want it back.'

He said: 'A paper of mine?' It was a very dogeared, grubby piece of paper that she gave him. He held it up to the light that streamed from the room behind. It read, in his handwriting:

Ma Nay Htohn.   Water–YE
                Boiled rice–HTAMIN
                Man–

He smiled, and turned it sideways to read again what was written across the paper:

I have gone into Bassein to surrender to the Japs; don't try to follow me. I shall try and hide for two days before surrendering, so that you can get away. The English will send another officer to replace Major Williams, tell him about me. I will try and see you when the war is over if I get away with it. Don't think too badly of us. We may be stupid, but we do our best.

He smiled gently, thinking back to the tenseness of that bad time, from the ease and friendship of his chair on the veranda. He was touched that she should have thought it worth while to keep so trivial a scrap as a memento. He said: 'You must teach me some more words while I'm here.'

She hesitated, and then said: 'Have you looked inside?'

He turned the paper over, and saw that it was an old air letter, addressed to him; the sprawling, unformed handwriting gave him a great shock. He opened the tattered folds in silence, and read:

Phillip Darling,
    This is going to be a dreadful letter to write and I don't know how to begin but it's not as if we ever had been married really is it I mean had a home and all that. I know when Jack was killed you were too sweet in looking after me and everything and of course he *wanted* it and so we simply had to and it's been marvellous and I'll never regret one minute of it will you?

He read on in silence, in a wave of sudden misery.

. . . and it's horrible being sort of neither one thing nor the other in spite of it having been all a mistake to start with hasn't it? I do hope we'll be frightfully good friends for dear old Jack's sake.
                                                        Ever your loving,
                                                                BOBBY

'My Christ,' he said quietly. 'I thought the Japs had got this one.'

He glanced down at the girl beside him; she was gazing up at him, and there were tears in her eyes. 'This is an old letter from my wife,' he said. 'Did you read it?'

She said: 'I read it, but I did not let anybody else read it. It seemed so private. I thought you would not like people to see it.'

He said: 'That's terribly nice of you. I wouldn't like other people to see this. I didn't realize what it was when I wrote that message on the back of it.'

She gazed up at him. 'It meant so little to you?'

'Yes.' He thought for a moment, and then said: 'We didn't match up very well, my wife and I. And then other things happened that were more–more sort of real, crash landing the Spit, and getting taken by your people, and all that. I just didn't think about it. The Japs took all the papers in my wallet when they searched me at Bassein, and I thought they'd got this one, too.'

She took the letter, and turned it over curiously, holding it between the very tips of her fingers. 'Did she really write this filthy thing to you in India–when you were so far from home, and fighting in the war?'

'I got it a few days before I crash landed the Spit,' he said. 'She wouldn't have thought of it like that, of course.'

She looked up at him, and met his eyes. 'It is a vile letter,' she said. 'I should like to see it burnt.'

'Burn it, if you like, Nay Htohn,' he said gravely. 'I'm through with all that now. My wife and I—we're all washed up.'

She smiled suddenly. 'I have taken a copy of the message that you wrote for me. I am not going to lose that.' They laughed together, and she went and fetched a hurricane lamp from the table in the living-room, and they watched the letter shrivel and turn black and burn till there was nothing left of it.

She came and knelt beside him up against his knee, and they talked about Henzada and the Irrawaddy, and her life in Rangoon and the shorthand typing she had done for Mr Stevens in the office. And presently his hand dropped to her shoulder and caressed her; she looked up at him quickly, and smiled.

He went to bed presently, and slept for the first time in six months upon a yielding bed; to him the string charpoy was the acme of luxurious ease. He slept well, and woke in the cool of the morning infinitely refreshed. From where he lay he could see out of the open window the trees in the garden, and beyond them the glorious deep orange masses of a Flame of the Forest tree, over sixty feet in height. The bright flowers, the blue sky, the first shafts of the sunlight and the jungle rats running up and down the trunks enchanted him; he felt that he was in a lovely place, a feeling not diminished by the thought that Nay Htohn was sleeping in the same house, probably not very far away. He was suddenly convinced that if he had a nightmare of the prison and cried out, she would be with him in an instant. On that thought he drifted off to sleep again, and slept another hour.

Breakfast consisted of a repetition of supper, being rice and various curries, with a pot of tea for Morgan. He sat for an hour on the veranda afterwards smoking another cheroot and then, feeling comparatively full of beans, he walked out into the road to look at the town.

Nay Htohn came running after him, and he turned to meet her. She said: 'You ought not to walk; you should rest your legs.'

'I've got to rest my behind, too,' he pointed out. 'Besides, I want to see things.'

She said: 'May I come with you?' She hesitated. 'Some of our people are doubtful about what the British will do when they come back. You should have someone with you who can speak our language, just for a day or two.'

He said: 'Come on. What's the Burmese for a road—this road that we're on now?'

They walked through the desolate, burnt out middle of the town. Men, women, and children were living and sleeping in the charred ruins; some of them had set up little stalls to sell a few vegetables or fruits. The pilot was distressed at the sight; nothing was being done to help these people, for there was nobody to do anything. It was no hardship for them to sleep out while the fine weather lasted, but the monsoon was due to break in a fortnight. He spoke about this to Nay Htohn. 'What will they do?' he asked. 'Is there any shelter for them?'

The girl shrugged her shoulders. 'None. They will try to build bashas—look, there is a man building one. But there is very little bamboo or palm leaf in walking distance of this place—it is too crowded here. There will be a great deal of fever when the rains come and the people have no shelter.'

'That's bad. Can't they get bamboos and stuff from up the river?'

The girl said: 'There are no boats left.' That, Morgan knew, was very true. The river banks had been lined all the way up from Yandoon with holed and sunk sampans, some sunk by the Japanese and others by the R.A.F.

'There are over thirty tons of corrugated iron sheets at Taunsaw, but there is no means of bringing them here,' she observed. 'There are no lorries left, and the Japanese took most of the bullock carts.'

'Where's Taunsaw?'

'Forty miles from here, down the railway to Bassein. There is a wide chaung there, with a bridge which was blown up by the R.A.F. in January.'

'What is the matter with the railway?' the pilot asked.

'I do not know. It has not run for three years, since the British went away.'

The pilot asked: 'Is the track still all right? I mean, surely to God there must be just one truck left that will roll. If there are corrugated iron sheets at this place Taunsaw, couldn't we get a gang of coolies and let them push a truck down there or something, and get a load?'

She glanced at him curiously. 'There may be Japanese down the line.'

He grinned at her. 'There may not—or there may be the Burman Independence Army to look after them. Let's have a look at the railway.'

There were trucks standing on the weedy, grass grown rails of the metre gauge line, mostly riddled with cannon fire by the R.A.F., mostly still capable of use. In the engine shed there were three tank locomotives rusty and forlorn, sad looking little engines. Each showed two gaping holes on the sides of the boiler with a loose pipe leading to it, where the feed water clacks once had been. It was obvious that parts were missing, but the pilot did not know what the parts were, or what their function was. Steam locomotives, at that time, were a sealed book to him.

'Someone's had a nibble at them there,' he said.

A Burman in a longyi and a vest had followed them into the shed, and said something. Nay Htohn asked a question, and commenced a little conversation with the man while Morgan waited. Presently she turned to him and said:

'He says these parts were taken off when the British went away, and that the District Engineer told the Japanese the British had taken them away to India with them. He says that was not true; the District Engineer took them away and hid them himself.'

'Where's the District Engineer?'

She asked the man in Burmese. 'He is dead. He was working in the repair shops at Insein and was killed in an air-raid.'

'Too bad.' The pilot thought for a minute. 'Does he know what the parts were, or where they are now?'

She asked, and then said: 'He does not know anything more. He is only the man who cleans the carriages.'

'Are there any drivers left in Henzada?'

She asked again. 'He says that all the drivers were sent down to Rangoon to work on the main line.'

Morgan said again: 'Too bad.' There was nothing to be done about it, and they turned and went back to the house. His legs were considerably swollen again by the time they got there, and he was glad to put them up in a long chair on the veranda. Nay Htohn said: 'It is a very good chair, that. It is the Japanese Commandant's chair.'

He grinned. 'Well, that's an honour.'

She brought him a cheroot, and then she settled down upon the floor beside him with some needlework. He glanced at it, and saw that she was working on the faded, threadbare trousers of his jungle suit, now washed and pressed. She was repairing a small tear with delicate, fine stitches, using thread of the same material frayed from a seam.

He thanked her, and she turned over the blouse. It had been carefully washed, and the wings and ribbons stood out almost smartly on the faded cloth. 'Tell me,' she said, 'what do these things mean?'

He told her about the wings and how you got them, and about flying. 'And these,' she said. 'These are medals, are they not?'

He showed her the 1940 Star, and told her what it meant. And then she put her finger on the other one. 'And this?'

'That's the Distinguished Flying Cross,' he said. 'That doesn't mean a thing. They send them round with the rations.'

She looked up at him uncertainly. 'Does everybody get it?'

He was suddenly aware of the great pleasure that he was withholding from her. 'Not everybody,' he said awkwardly. 'You get it if you're lucky.'

She was puzzled. 'How, lucky?'

'Lucky enough to get away with it,' he said. 'Lucky enough to come back home again.'

She said slowly: 'Is it given for something very brave?'

He shifted uneasily. 'Not quite like that. You get it for doing something rather difficult.'

'And dangerous?'

'And dangerous. But you don't think much of it when you've got it. So many people do much more, and don't get anything.'

'Tell me,' she said, 'what was it that you did?'

He told her, and she listened to him wide-eyed, kneeling by him, the sewing on her knee. In the end she said: 'Who gave it to you? Is there a ceremony?'

'You get it from the King,' he said. 'You go to Buck House for it.'

She breathed: 'You mean, from the King Emperor? Did you see him?'

'See him? He pinned it on, and he couldn't get the pin in. He said: 'Sorry to be so damn clumsy!'

She stared at him. 'The King Emperor said that to you?'

'Yes. I thought it was decent of him.'

'What did you say?'

'Oh, I said: "That's okay, sir," or something.'

She was silent for a minute. Then she said: 'Would you mind if I tell my father?'

'If you want to.' He hesitated. 'Don't spread it round the whole place, though. I mean, it doesn't mean a thing, really, you know. Honestly, it doesn't.'

She stared at him, smiling a little. 'I believe it does,' she said. 'I believe it means a great deal.'

He changed the subject. 'I'd like to put on those clothes when you've finished them,' he said. 'It's better to be in uniform.'

The girl said: 'I will not be very long.'

He sat thinking, watching her deft grace as she knelt beside him, sewing. 'About that District Engineer,' he said. 'Did he live here? I mean, before he went to Insein and got killed?'

Nay Htohn said: 'I suppose he did.'

'Do you think his wife would be here still? I mean, the parts that he took away are probably in Henzada, if we could find them.'

She said: 'I will find out.'

That evening found them talking to an elderly Burman woman in the middle of a blackened heap of ashes that had once been a house. The woman was garrulous and distressed; Nay Htohn was sharp with her, and several times cut short her long meanderings. 'The box was buried somewhere here,' she said to Morgan. 'Underneath the house. That is, between these posts.'

They marked the place, and left the woman and walked back to the house; presently they returned with two coolies carrying a shovel and a pick. In half an hour they had found the wooden box buried a foot down; it was decayed and eaten by ants, but the six feedwater clack valves in it were all wrapped up in sacking, and were in good condition.

They returned to the house in high spirits, the coolies following behind them with the box. They set it down in the veranda; Nay Htohn went and fetched her father. 'This is very good,' he said. 'But now we have to find a man who knows about the railway, and can drive the engines. I do not think that will be very easy.'

Morgan said: 'Well I can put these valves in–that's easy enough. I should think you just screw them in and put a bit of paint or something on the threads, and away you go.'

Shway Than said: 'Do you understand railway engines?'

The pilot said: 'No. But if you can't find anyone who does, I'll bloody soon learn. After all, it's only a sort of kettle with a piston and a cylinder attached. It ought not to be difficult to get the hang of it.'

The old Burman said: 'Not difficult for you, perhaps. It would be very difficult for me.'

Morgan thought for a moment. 'One thing,' he said. 'It's going to be filthy dirty on those engines, and I've only got the one uniform. Is it possible to get an overall, or anything like that?'

Shway Than laughed. 'He will keep you busy,' he said to his daughter. 'You will have to get up early every morning now to wash his clothes.' She coloured a little.

Morgan turned to her. 'Did you wash this uniform yourself?' he asked.

Her father said: 'She would not let any of the servants touch it.'

The pilot said: 'That was very kind of you. It was so dirty.'

The girl laughed awkwardly. 'I will see what I can find for an overall.'

All the next day the pilot worked in the engine shed. He picked one of the three locomotives that seemed to be in the best condition, and fitted the two clack valves without difficulty. Then he spent some time in tracing out the lead of the various pipes and pumps, and thinking deeply; he did not want to ruin everything by making some stupid mistake and burning out the boiler. The news got around that he was working on the engines, and a few Burmans arrived to watch the progress of the work. One lad in the Independence Army turned up; Nay Htohn talked to him for a little, and then brought him to Morgan. 'He says he knows all about these engines,' she said.

The pilot looked him over; the boy did not seem to be much more than fifteen years old. 'Did he work on them?'

She said: 'No. He was only a little boy then. But he was interested in the engines and he used to play in here and watch the driver and the mechanics. He says he could drive one.'

'I'm not interested in that just at present,' said the pilot. 'Ask him if he knows how the water gets into the boiler in the first place.'

He professed to do so, and Morgan tracing out the run of the pipes to the mechanical feed pump, discovered what appeared to be a hand pump; the boy's suggestion seemed a likely one. He turned to the girl. 'What's his name?'

She replied: 'Moung Bah Too.'

Morgan elevated a thumb. 'Okay, Moung Bah Too, we'll try it your way.' Nay Htohn translated that, and the lad grinned. 'Now, what about getting us a few tons of water?'

This proved to be a major difficulty. The watertower had been thrown down and shattered by a bomb; there was no running water in the place at all. They left the engine shed and went together to the headquarters of the Independence Army, and saw the officer who had interrogated Morgan on the first day. After some negotiation by Nay Htohn the officer detailed Bah Too to round up thirty coolies with a bullock cart, to bale water from the river into casks and carry it to the locomotive. It took the remainder of the day to get the tanks half filled.

They went back wearily to the house at dusk. Utt Nee was there, having arrived from up country an hour before. He had grown in stature and in poise from the young man that the pilot remembered six months before; he now seemed more self-confident and more mature. He was very glad to see Morgan.

Later in the evening, as they sat together in the veranda after the evening meal, he was quite candid. 'It was a great help to me, when you surrendered to the Japanese,' he said. 'I had quite made up my mind that we should turn and co-operate with the British again as the best way to work towards our freedom, and that was the policy of our leaders, too. But in a loose army such as ours, you understand, it is not always easy to persuade people to do what you think right, even if you are in command. When we took you, there were many of my people who thought the British were all treacherous and selfish, who would have liked to give you to the Japanese, or perhaps to do something else with you. It had a great effect upon my people when you surrendered yourself, to save the party from trouble. I tell you, the British suddenly became quite popular. I had no difficulty after that in getting my own way, and now we have been fighting side by side with British troops for the last five months, and we have gained the victory.' He grinned. 'We are quite friendly with the British now, so friendly that they will probably hang us all as traitors.'

The pilot said: 'If they do that, you can take it out on me.'

Utt Nee laughed. 'I am not very much afraid. I am twenty-five years old, and nobody has hung me yet.'

He said that there were reports that British naval vessels were operating in the delta down below Yandoon, and that there had been one or two engagements with Japanese in landing craft escaping down the rivers to the sea. He had no information as to when the British troops were to be expected in that district; he thought the Fourteenth Army were too busy for the moment in maintaining their line down the middle of the country, and so keeping the broken Japanese Army trapped, to start mopping up operations for a time. 'You are very far ahead of your own forces,' Utt Nee said. 'When they get here in the end and find you here, and learn that you came up here in a sampan, they will be very cross.'

'They'll be bloody cross anyway,' the pilot said. 'I've probably been posted as a deserter by this time. But what the hell.'

Utt Nee said: 'They will hang both of us, then, side by side.' He translated this sally to one or two of his friends sitting in the house; it went as a very good joke.

Next day, while the coolie gang laboured to carry water to complete the filling of the tanks, Morgan with Moung Bah Too to help him oiled and lubricated the engine in every hole that seemed designed to take it. There was no shortage of lubricants although Bah Too asserted that the Japanese soldiers had eaten some of the engine grease as butter, and liked it; there was plenty of coal and wood. Utt Nee came in with several other officers about midday; they were impressed with the progress of the work, and set another gang to improvise a more efficient water supply. Later that afternoon they discovered a small motor pump belonging to the fire brigade, and thereafter they had little trouble with the water.

Next day, early in the morning, they manhandled the small locomotive to the extension smokestack and clamped it down on to the funnel, and lit the fire in the fire-box. They had some trouble in getting it to burn, knowing none of the tricks of firing a stone cold engine, but by the middle of the morning steam pressure was mounting on the gauge and Morgan, with sweat running off him in a steady stream, was anxiously experimenting with the feed pump controls in the cab.

Finally he turned to Nay Htohn, always at his side. 'She should go now,' he said. He pulled the valve control over to reverse, and unwound the handbrake. Then he showed her the regulator. 'Pull that over just a little bit, and see what happens,' he said.

She hung back, laughing. 'You do it.'

He said: 'You do it. Go on.'

Below them, on the ground, the Burmans rocked with laughter at the dispute. The girl put her hand up and moved the regulator handle an inch gingerly; nothing happened. Urged by Morgan, she moved it a little more. With a sigh and a clank the locomotive stirred and moved backwards, giving a great puff. Nay Htohn dropped her hand from the regulator in a panic; Morgan closed it, and the engine rolled out of the shed and came to rest a yard or two outside. There was a cheer from the crowd.

He pulled the whistle twice, the signal that he had arranged with Utt Nee, and the crowd cheered again, and Utt Nee and his officers arrived, and they all had a ride on the engine up and down the track. They found three trucks in good condition and greased the axle boxes; with these trucks they did a little shunting practice, forming up a train. By the evening the locomotive seemed to have settled down and to be running reasonably well; they put it back in the shed and banked the fire. Bah Too was detailed to look after it, and they went back to the house, very satisfied with the day's work.

They held a conference that evening, sitting on chairs around a table in the living-room, in the light of a couple of hurricane lamps. Moung Shway Than was in the chair; Utt Nee was there with two of his officers, Morgan, and Nay Htohn. The old man said: 'Now that we have this railway running, we can go down to Taunsaw, if the track is good enough. Does anybody know for certain if the bridge is broken?'

One of the officers said in Burmese: 'It is down and lying in the river. I was there six weeks ago, and saw it.' Nay Htohn translated in a low tone to Morgan, squatting by his chair.

They went on to discuss what they could do by going as far as Taunsaw. Corrugated iron was lying in a dump there, and there were bamboo and palm groves which would provide housing materials. It was by no means certain that the country along the line was free from Japanese, however; they decided to run what amounted to an armoured train next day.

They left next morning about an hour after dawn, the little engine pushing one truck in front and pulling two behind. These trucks were filled with armed soldiers of the Independence Army, about two hundred of them. They took with them a supply of water and fuel, breakdown gear, and food. Utt Nee would not allow Nay Htohn to go with them, fearing action with the straggling Japanese and he rode with Morgan and Bah Too upon the footplate of the engine.

They went slowly, at about fifteen miles an hour. The track was rough but adequate; in places it sagged ominously down beneath the train, to spring up again when they had passed. They were not greatly troubled about this; they had with them several plate-layers accustomed to track maintenance who had remained in Henzada; as soon as it was known that there were no enemy about these men would get on with their job and make the track sound where it needed attention.

They went cautiously, stopping every few miles to inquire about the Japanese. There was one band about three hundred strong in the vicinity; they heard of this lot on all sides, but always somewhere else and never very close at hand. They went on cautiously, and reached Taunsaw about midday. Before them lay the bridge, a fine steel girder structure broken and collapsed into the river.

They set to work there to re-water the engine, and to load the corrugated iron. It was evening by the time all this was done; they decided not to risk a night journey back to Henzada, and so they formed a lager round the train, put pickets out, and cooked a meal before nightfall, extinguishing the fire at once.

Morgan sat smoking with Utt Nee in the evening light, sitting upon the sill of one of the trucks, looking out over the river and the wrecked bridge. He felt in some way responsible for that bridge, and sorry about it. It had been a fine structure, that had cost somebody a lot of money. The railway that it carried across the river had not functioned since 1942 when the Japanese had driven us from Burma, but in 1945 we had made the bridge a target for the R.A.F., and they had smashed it up, and it now lay broken in the river. As one of the R.A.F., and seeing things from a different angle from his usual view out of the cockpit, Morgan was sorry about the bridge. It seemed, now, a wanton bit of senseless damage, rather like the nine or ten bridges on the line from Toungoo to Pegu that we had thought it necessary to destroy to put that railway out of action. One would have been sufficient, or perhaps one at each end.

Voicing his thoughts, he said: 'There's the hell of a lot of patching up needs doing in this country.'

The Burman by his side said: 'Are you thinking of the bridge?'

The pilot nodded. 'Got to be rebuilt. I don't see why we had to go and knock it down.'

Utt Nee said: 'It is a great pity. This railway was useful in this part of the country. It will be difficult for people in Bassein to trade with Henzada until we get that bridge again.'

'How long do you suppose it will take to rebuild it?'

'How long? I do not know. If some of you British soldiers stay and help us get things right, it should not be many years before this country is running again, like it was before. But if you all go home and leave us to the pukka sahibs it will take a very long time.'

The pilot said: 'We've not got very many engineers out here.'

'Engineers are necessary,' the Burman said. 'But we need people who can tell the engineers what to do.' He glanced at Morgan. 'People like you,' he said, and laughed.

The pilot was astonished. 'I couldn't tell an engineer what to do.'

Utt Nee said: 'You got this railway going.'

'Oh well–that's different,' the pilot said. 'That's just been a bit of bloody good fun.'

The Burman laughed with him. 'All work that interests you is bloody good fun,' he said. 'And yet, the railway is now running, and it was broken before you had your fun with it.' He turned to the Englishman. 'What are you going to do?' he asked. 'Are you going back to England, to live there for ever, as an architect?'

'I've got a sort of job to go to there,' the pilot said.

'There will be many jobs here for you,' said the Burman, 'if you like mending railways and things that are broken.'

Morgan sat in silence for a few minutes, staring out over the river in the gathering dusk. He had seen sufficient since he got out of jail to make him realize that this was not a casual approach. He had been living for the last week with responsible people; old Moung Shway Than was a man of influence in Rangoon in times of peace; Utt Nee held a high position in the Independence Army. This was an offer of a job, or something very like it; a job with people he could work with in a country that he was already much attached to.

He said at last: 'You wouldn't want an Englishman in any important job here. It's Burma for the Burmans now.'

Utt Nee: 'That is true, up to a point. But there are too few of us educated yet to run this country by ourselves, with no help from the British at all. There will always be important jobs for Englishmen in Burma who are not too proud to work on level terms with us and share our life, who would not think it an indignity to work under a Burman if he is the better man. I do not think you need worry about that.'

There was another long silence. Morgan said at last: 'There's another difficulty. If I were to stay here, I should ask Nay Htohn to marry me. I expect you'd rather I went back to England.'

Utt Nee shrugged his shoulders. 'I do not want to see my sister with a broken heart. You must know she is very much in love with you.'

'You wouldn't mind about a mixed marriage?' Morgan asked.

'Why should I mind, if that makes her happy? I should be very glad for her. I know several Englishmen who married Burmese girls and made them very good husbands. This is not India, you know. Our girls marry who they like. Just as in your country.'

'What about your father? Would he mind?'

'I think he would be very pleased.'

'Do you know I'm married already? That I've got a wife, back home in England?'

The Burman said: 'I know a little about that. Nay Htohn said that she was not faithful to you.'

'That's about right.' The pilot told him briefly what had happened, and answered a few questions. 'So I'm a bit shop-soiled, you might say.'

'I do not think my sister thinks of you like that. So why should you think it of yourself?' He turned to Morgan. 'Think it over,' he said quietly. 'I know a few Englishmen that I would like to see stay in our country, and I know many that we must get rid of at all costs. You have all the vigour of your people, and you are not too proud to learn our ways. If you marry Nay Htohn she will make you a good wife, and both my father and myself would like to have you with us.'

That night Morgan slept on the floor of one of the trucks covered by his blanket, his head on a gunny sack. Around him lay the Burmese soldiers that were not on guard; he could talk to them a little about very simple things, and understand them if they spoke to him slowly upon simple matters. He had become accustomed to their brown skins and their way of life. They did not seem strangers to him any more, did not seem to be incalculable creatures to be treated with distrust. He found them understandable, thinking along the same lines as he did, and laughing at the same brand of joke. They treated him with genuine liking and respect, the man who could fly aeroplanes and make the railway go.

He lay before sleep came to him, watching the stars beyond a cauliflowerlike banyan tree against the deep blue sky. England to him was represented by school life, war hardships, blitz and death, and a sordid and unprofitable marriage. Burma to him meant fun and games with railways and broken bridges and smashed boats, with people who already liked him and respected him for his achievements; it meant love from a clever girl who, in her own country, was of his own social class, or better. There was no doubt in his mind which he would do; he snuggled closer in his blanket on the hard plank floor, shifted the gunny sack beneath his head, and drifted off to sleep, thinking of Nay Htohn.

They steamed into Henzada about midday, having dropped off the platelaying gang half way down the track, and loaded up with bamboos and palm thatch. They had been careful to announce their arrival by whistling at intervals for the last five miles, and a considerable crowd was there to meet them. Nay Htohn came forward to greet Morgan as he got down from the footplate of the little engine, grimy in his old jungle suit. Moung Shway Than was with her.

The old man said: 'Did you meet any Japanese?'

'Not one,' the pilot said. 'The line is clear right down to Taunsaw; if it wasn't for the bridge we could have gone all the way to Bassein.'

He turned to the girl. 'It was a joy ride.'

She smiled. 'I was imagining . . . all sorts of things.'

He smiled at her. 'I was imagining things, too. I was thinking that we had most of the army with us on the train, and that perhaps the Japanese would have come back here while we were away.'

She laughed. 'We are still quite all right. They say that one of their motor landing craft went down the river last night full of Japanese soldiers, and that your British gunboats sank it, south of Danubyu. I do not know if that is true.'

He said: 'Are the British so close as that?'

'So they say.'

He went back to the house with her, and washed, and had a meal, and slept a little on the charpoy; in the cool of the evening he got up and found that while he had been sleeping she had washed and pressed his jungle suit again. He went out to the veranda; she was there, sitting in the evening light and sewing something, with a flower in her hair. He thanked her for washing his clothes, and then said: 'Has anything been heard of the British gunboats?'

She shook her head. 'Only that they are down by Danubyu. They may be here any time.'

He nodded: 'I shall have to go on board and report when they come.'

She said: 'Will you have to go away with them?'

'I think I shall,' he said. 'I think if I don't I shall be posted as a deserter.'

Her lip trembled, and she said: 'It will be very sad for us when you go.'

He said: 'It's better that I should go. I've got this matter of the divorce from my wife to attend to, and I'll have to go to England for that.' He glanced down at her, squatting down upon the mat beside his knee. 'But I could come back.'

She glanced up at him quickly. 'When you are at home with your own people, you will not want to come back to Henzada.'

'I don't know about Henzada,' he said. 'I should always want to come back to you.'

She said softly: 'I could make you very happy.'

He dropped his hand on to her shoulder, and caressed her neck; she turned quickly, and laid her head against his knee. Then she looked up at him and said: 'This is very bad. People can see us from the road.' But she did not move away.

He said: 'When I come back, will you marry me, Nay Htohn.'

She looked up at him, laughing. 'I would marry you now. You know that very well.'

He said: 'I've got a wife already.'

She tossed her head. 'I do not call that being married. She has not given you a child, and when you are away fighting she goes with other men. You are not married at all, really. I would be a better wife to you than that.'

He stroked her hair. 'I know. But I am married all the same, and I've got to get that straightened out. After that, Nay Htohn, I want to come back, if you'll have me.'

She breathed: 'Have you . . .' and rubbed her cheek against his knee again. And then she said: 'It is eight thousand miles from here to England, and she has another man. Why must you go away at all? I think that you could just forget about her, and stay here with me. We could be married very soon.'

He said: 'No.'

He got to his feet and raised her up; she stood up obediently and went and stood with him at the veranda rail. 'I want you to understand,' he said. 'I like this place; I like your people and your country, and I love you, Nay Htohn. I think we could be frightfully happy together, living here in Burma. And because of that, I want to start off properly, without any mess in the background. I want everything to be all tickety-boo. I want to marry you properly according to the English law so that your people will know that I'm playing straight with you. If we just married now it wouldn't be legal, and I could beat it any time and leave you flat, and Utt Nee would know that, and so would Moung Shway Than. That's not the way I want to start in Burma. I'll have to go back to England.' He thought for a minute. 'Besides, there's a war on. I think they'll probably demobilize me now, but if they want me to go on in the R.A.F. I'll have to do that till the war is over. But after that, I shall come back to Burma. I shall want you very badly then.'

She said softly: 'I want you very badly now.' He took her hand and held it, and they stood together for a minute in the dusk.

Presently she said: 'I think that you are right. Our people are suspicious of all Englishmen, and rightly so, and although I would marry you tonight and be very happy, I think that you would get on better with my people if it was a legal marriage by your laws. And there is another thing.' She hesitated. 'I think you ought to go back home to England and think carefully about this. You Westerners are brought up differently from us, and many of you have very strange ideas about your colour, and mixed marriages. I do not want to rush you into anything. If when you have been at home in England for a little you come back to me in Henzada or in Rangoon, I will marry you the day you land, Phillip. And I will make you a good wife.'

He grinned down at her. 'Nay Htohn, would it be all wrong by your standards if I was to give you a kiss?'

She glanced up at him, eyes dancing. 'You mean, in the Western fashion, as they do on the movies? I have never done that.'

He said: 'Like to try?'

'Not here.' She hesitated. 'We do not do that in Burma. Even married people do not kiss in public. We could go into your bedroom.'

'Does that make it all right? It would make it all wrong in England.'

She said demurely: 'It would be perfectly all right.' So they went into the bedroom and shut the door, and she came into his arms, and he kissed her mouth and neck, feeling her slim body lissom in his arms. And when at last he let her go she said: 'I understand why we do not do this in Burma. It is too exciting.' And they smiled together, and kissed again more gently, and went out again to the veranda, and sat talking quietly in the dim light of the stars over the flame tree. The fireflies flickered about them, and the great noise of frogs made a continuous background to their talk, and they talked on for hours.

At about ten o'clock at night a man came to the veranda and asked for Utt Nee. In the dim light they could see that he wore the brassard of the Independence Army. Nay Htohn said that her brother was down at headquarters.

The man said: 'Five British gunboats have arrived.'

The girl translated this to Morgan. She asked: 'Where are they?'

He said: 'They have not landed. The ships are lying in an ambush by the ferry, anchored close under the bank, in the shadow. We have a picket out around them. Utt Nee has sent a party two miles up the river, to the paddy mill, to watch for Japanese boats coming down the river. Then we are to warn the British by the little radio.'

She said: 'You will find Utt Nee at the headquarters.' The man slipped off into the darkness.

Morgan said: 'How far off is the ferry, where the gunboats are?'

She said: 'About a mile.'

'Like to walk down and see if we can see anything?'

She agreed, and they set out together by the shadowy paths towards the railway terminus upon the river bank. They went rather slowly, hand in hand; it was about a quarter to eleven when they reached the place. Standing upon the bank by the wrecked railway trucks they could see the gunboats just below them, not a hundred yards away, five Fairmile B type motor launches, anchored and silent, their guns trained up the river, without a light of any kind showing. They gave the pilot a great thrill, the first British forces he had seen for seven months. It was with difficulty that he restrained himself from hailing them.

He squatted down upon the bank, with Nay Htohn by his side, watching the ships. They stayed for half an hour, and were about to walk back to the house when things began to happen. There was a movement on the vessels, and a faint jangle of bells, and then a deep rumble as the engines started up; ship after ship started engines all down the line. The leading two weighed anchor and moved silently out into the middle of the stream; the other three also weighed and moved a little way upshore, keeping close in to the bank. All five lay there silent, just stemming the stream, making a great L across the river.

'Christ,' breathed the pilot. 'They've given us a grandstand seat.'

They waited tensely. There was a faint rumble of engines from up river. From the furthest of the Fairmiles a searchlight blazed out, swept a little, and focused on three landing craft about a thousand yards away, and coming down the river. A spurt of small arms fire came from them and the heavier beating of a 37 millimetre automatic gun; Morgan pressed Nay Htohn down on to the grass beside him and they lay flat, watching a naval battle. It was over in a couple of minutes. The Fairmiles turned their broadsides to bring all the guns to bear and opened fire with Oerlikons and Bofors in the glare of their searchlights; one by one the landing craft were hit and went on fire, and headed for the shore. Two came to the Henzada bank and one to the far side. At Henzada the Independence Army were lining the bank; there was much shooting, which presently died down; the fires died out upon the craft, and the Fairmiles slipped back and anchored in their old stations, to watch again.

Morgan and Hay Htohn walked back to the town, tense and alert. The walk was not without danger, for the pilot was in his jungle suit and might have been mistaken in the darkness for a Japanese, or fired at by a fugitive from the boats. They went to the headquarters and found Utt Nee there, in the centre of a group of officers; he detached himself to talk to Morgan.

'What happened to the Japs?' the pilot asked.

'We have two prisoners,' the Burman replied. 'Two, who were so badly wounded that they could not do their *hara-kiri*. The rest were either killed, or else they killed themselves. I do not know anything about the other boat, that landed on the other shore. They have got away.'

The pilot said: 'Mind if we walk down and see the boats?' An idea was already forming in his mind.

Utt Nee sent a young officer with them, and they walked down to the shore with a hurricane lamp. There were many bodies of dead Japanese where the battle had taken place; Morgan looked at them with curiosity; these were the first dead Japanese that he had seen. They picked their way between them, going warily with pistols in their hands in case any of the corpses came to life and took a shot at them, as Japanese will do. The boats were separated by about three hundred yards.

They were twin hulled, flat bottomed landing craft, with a ramp forward and a Diesel engine aft; they mounted one 37 millimetre gun as their sole fixed armament apart from small arms and mortars carried by the troops. The first one they went on board smelled badly of stale food and excrement and burning oil; casks of Diesel oil upon her deck had been on fire, but the fire had not reached the engine, which was flooded. She was holed in three places by the Bofors, and considerably punctured by the Oerlikon fire.

Morgan said quietly to Nay Htohn: 'We could repair this one.'

She stared at him in wonder. 'Repair it and use it?'

'That's right. The engine hasn't been hit. It's probably full of water, but we could get it going again. And we could patch up the hull with concrete until we can get it done properly.'

She said: 'Could you do that?'

The pilot said: 'I'd have a stab at it.'

They went on to the other landing craft. This one was in a worse state, for the engine compartment had been on fire, and that engine was probably done for. The hull, however, was not so bad as the first one.

Morgan said thoughtfully: 'I wonder what the one over on the other side is like?'

In the morning he sat in conference with Moung Shway Than, Utt Nee, and Nay Htohn. 'This is goodbye for the moment,' he said quietly. 'I've got to go and report myself on board these gunboats now, and go down to Rangoon with them; from there I shall be sent to England. I want to come back here, as soon as ever I can. I want to come back and marry Nay Htohn, if she'll have me.'

Moung Shway Than said: 'I should be very glad for you to do so. How long do you think it will be before you can get back to us?'

'I don't know–it may be three months. It should not be longer than a year. But I shall write every two or three days, and let you know what is happening with me.' He paused. 'Before I go, there is one important matter that we must discuss. These Jap landing craft can be repaired. The one down the river is the best of the two, but they must all be pulled up out of the water, and above high water level at the monsoon. If you can get them going they'll be something to replace all the sampans that have been sunk.'

Moung Shway Than said: 'I will take them over, and see that they are salvaged as much as we can. We can use the sampan builders on the work.'

The pilot said: 'Get somebody to go up and down the river and look at every one of them that you can find. Get the engines taken out and kept in a dry place, and greased; there's plenty of grease up with the locomotives, in the shed. Get the sampan builders to patch up the hulls if they can do it. I shall hope to be back here directly after the monsoon, and I'll get down to it myself then. I'm quite sure we can get some of those boats running again, if we tackle it the right way. We might get two or three going out of the lot, putting the best engines into the best hulls. If you find that we need tools, write to me in England by air mail and tell me what we need, and I'll bring them out with me.'

The old man said: 'It would be very profitable if we could get one or two of those boats running. There is no transport on the Irrawaddy now. All the river steamers have been sunk.'

Nay Htohn said: 'I will see that it is done. I will make Moung Bah Too go down the river, and see every boat. I will go myself and see that it is done. Every boat shall be pulled up out of the water and the engine shall be dried and greased, and then when you come back we will go and see them, and you can decide on each boat which parts we can use.'

Morgan thought for a moment. 'If you find any boat mechanics, or men who have run Diesel engines at any time, get hold of them.'

Utt Nee said: 'There are not many of those in Burma.. But our people are good with machinery; they only need to be shown how.'

Moung Shway Than said: 'I will take over every boat, and I will pay whatever costs may be necessary. I think it will be a very good business.'

Two hours later, Morgan was with Nay Htohn upon the river bank. 'This is not goodbye,' he said, holding her hand. 'You need not be afraid; I shall come back. This is a happy place, and I shall be back here as soon as ever I can make it.'

She said, with brimming eyes: 'I have no fear, but make it very soon.'

He went out to the leading ML in a dugout paddled by a little boy, and climbed on board her. An R.N.R. lieutenant commander met him on the deck.

'I was in Rangoon jail,' the pilot said. 'We've got the railway running half way to Bassein, if that's any good to you.'

7

The first rain drops of the storm plashed on the path below the veranda; a cool breeze drifted around Mr Turner as he sat with Morgan in the darkness. The latter stirred. 'Be time for supper in a minute,' he said. 'I told Nay Htohn we'd have an English meal.'

Mr Turner said: 'You come back here pretty soon, then?'

'Lord, yes. I shot back to England and out here again like a scalded cat.' He smiled. 'I had an advantage, of course, because I knew everybody in Transport Command. I saw the A.V.M. in Calcutta and told him I wanted to take my discharge in Burma, and about the landing craft and everything. I got flown to England in a Liberator and back to Calcutta again in a York, as part of the aircrew. I was only seventeen days in England.'

'Fixed up your divorce, then?'

'Yes. There wasn't much difficulty about that. I got the solicitor cracking on it before I left England. It wasn't legal for about two years, but we didn't wait for that. I got back to Henzada in seven weeks, seven weeks to the day from the time I left, and we got married right away. Our first kid was nearly a year old before we could get married properly, but we did it then.'

Mr Turner grinned; it was all very deplorable, but in the circles that he moved in in England he had heard of similar doings. 'What about the boats?' he asked.

Morgan said: 'That turned out pretty well. Nay Htohn had seen to that.' He turned to Turner. 'You know, Burmese girls are very good business women, better than the men. There's no flies on any of them. Nay Htohn had got all the boats pulled up out of the water, seven of them, some of them pretty badly shot up. Moung Shway Than gave them to us as a wedding present. One down by Zalun was practically undamaged and I got that going in a week. I got another going a month later, and the third sometime after that. That's all we salvaged, just the three of them.'

'What happened to them?'

'I ran them for two years,' the pilot said. 'We ran a regular service from Rangoon right up to Prome, and made a packet of money out of it. You see, the Irrawaddy Flotilla Company was short of vessels and it was some time before there was much competition; we got in on the ground floor.' He mused for a moment. 'God, they've done some work, those boats.'

'Are you still running them, then?'

'No, I sold out last year. They're still running–you'll see one of them go down tomorrow about midday. But I sold out.' He turned to Turner. 'I'm in the civil service now. I stayed out for some time, because I thought an Englishman wouldn't be very welcome–Burma for the Burmans, and all that, you know. But I got mixed up in a lot of local things. Then last year Shway Than's brother, Moung Nga Myah, had a long talk with me and persuaded me to take this job–he's in the Government, you know–Minister for Education. He said they wanted me, so I said I'd give it a crack. I think it may pan out all right.'

Mr Turner wrinkled his forehead. 'I don't get that. I thought they wasn't taking English people now.'

'It was a kind of compliment,' the pilot said. 'They've spent the last two years getting rid of all the pukka sahibs from the civil service as quick as they could, and then they came along and wanted me to join it. They sort of count me as a Burman now, I think.'

'Funny sort of setup,' said Mr Turner in wonder.

The pilot got up from his chair, and collected the glasses. 'I've got my roots deep in this country,' he said. 'Wife and kids and work and friends. I'd never want to go back and live in England again, after this. When this country gets Dominion status, I'll probably take out naturalization papers. Make a job of it.'

They went into the house to dinner, a meal served by candlelight with silver on the table, a meal of soup and casseroled chicken and a savoury. Morgan and Ma Nay Htohn were genuinely glad to have a visitor from England; in the friendship of their interest Mr Turner expanded, and talked fairly lucidly to them about conditions in London. He talked so much that he became very tired, and was glad to sit quietly after the meal with a cheroot in a long chair. The white cat, Moung Payah, walked in as soon as he sat down and jumped up on his lap, kneaded a place for himself, and settled down to purr.

Nay Htohn looked at it in wonder, and spoke again to Morgan in a low tone in Burmese.

He laughed. 'My wife can't make out about that cat,' he said. 'He never does that with anyone. He won't sit with her, or with me either.'

Mr Turner was pleased, and rubbed the cat's ear; it pressed its head against his hand in pleasure. 'Took a fancy to me all right he has,' he said. 'What was that you said you call him?'

'Moung Payah,' said Nay Htohn. 'In our language that means Mr Holiness.'

'Why d'you call him that?' He asked the question with sincerity.

The girl hesitated, and then laughed shyly. 'My people have a superstition,' she said. 'Just like in your country, if you spill salt you throw it over your shoulder to avert bad luck. You do not really believe it, but you do it. Well–like that, the country people here say that a white animal, any white animal, is a very beautiful soul upon its path up the Ladder of Existence, so fine a soul that it will one day be the Buddha.' She smiled. 'It is not part of our religion, that one–you will not find it in our holy books. It is just what the country people say. My nurse told me, when I was a little child.'

Mr Turner grinned. 'That's why you call him Mr Holiness?'

She laughed softly. 'It's a kind of joke.'

He stroked the cat's ear. 'We think black cats are lucky in England,' he said. 'Just the opposite.'

He was desperately tired. The strange scene, and all the talking he had done seemed to have exhausted him; he was confused by all the new impressions he had taken in, and the great wound in his head was throbbing painfully. A heavy weight seemed to be pressing on the nape of his neck. He made an excuse as soon as his cheroot was finished and Morgan showed him to his bedroom, a pleasant spacious room with a fan and a mosquito net. Outside the rain was pouring down in sheets; Mr Turner threw off his clothes and fell upon the bed in heavy sleep.

He woke next morning unrefreshed, and feeling slack and tired and with a headache. He took an aspirin and lay for some time watching the glory of the dawn over the river; the air was fresh and cool after the rain, and the sky cloudless. He got up presently and went down to breakfast.

He found, rather to his surprise, that quite a heavy meal of curry and rice had been provided; his previous breakfasts in the country had been light affairs. He said: 'I see you stick to the old English custom of eating hearty in the morning.'

Morgan said: 'Me? I don't usually have more than one cup of coffee and a little fruit.' And then he said: 'Oh, I see what you mean. Nay Htohn–it's her duty day. She always eats a big meal in the morning.'

Mr Turner said: 'What's a duty day?'

The girl smiled at him. 'One day in each week all good Buddhists keep a duty day; it is like your Sunday. On that day we must not eat after midday, so I eat plenty for breakfast.' She laughed.

Turner said: 'Do you go to church?'

She said: 'I go to the pagoda in the morning. It is just like the Christian Sunday, but I think our duty day is rather more strict than yours. I may not use any cosmetics on my face or fingernails.' He glanced at her, and noticed that she had no makeup on. 'We do not play the gramophone, or have any music, and I must not touch gold or silver.' She raised her hand, and Mr Turner noticed that she was eating with a wooden spoon.

Morgan laughed mischievously. 'She used to sleep on the floor, too, before we were married, but I struck at that.'

The girl laughed with him shyly. 'If you keep the duty day properly you should sleep on the floor,' she said. 'That is for humility. But I do not think that that is meant for married women, who have husbands to look after.'

Mr Turner said to Morgan: 'Are you a Buddhist?'

'I'm not anything,' the pilot said. 'Just a heretic, or an agnostic, or what-have-you.' He paused, and then he said: 'If I was to be anything, I guess I'd be a Buddhist.'

'I suppose so,' Mr Turner said. 'Religion of the country and all that. Like what you were saying last night, about making your life in Burma.'

'In a way,' said Morgan. 'But I wouldn't bother about that angle to it. A good many English people out here turn Buddhist when they get to know the ins and outs of it. It's a very pure form of religion.'

'Well, I dunno,' said Mr Turner. 'The one I was brought up to 's good enough for me.'

Nay Htohn said: 'There is very little difference, for ordinary people like ourselves.'

Mr Turner did not eat much at breakfast; the feeling of oppression was still heavy at the nape of his neck. Nay Htohn vanished into the back quarters from which came the occasional sounds of children. Morgan excused himself. 'Do you mind looking after yourself till lunchtime?' he said. 'I've got my court sitting this morning. After lunch I've got to go out to a village in the country; you might like to come with me, in the jeep.'

'I'll be all right,' said Mr Turner. 'I'm feeling a bit washed out today. I'll just sit here for a bit. Be all right if I take a walk down in the village later on?'

'Of course,' said Morgan. 'They'll be glad to see you. Take off your shoes if you go into the pagoda.'

'I know about that,' Mr Turner said, 'I saw the Shwe Dagon last week.'

He sat for an hour in the long chair, smoking and looking at the sampan traffic on the river. A brown girl came out of the house and set up a playpen in the shade and then went back and fetched a yellow little boy in a short pair of pants and put him in it, and sat sewing by him on the grass. Mr Turner got up and walked over and spoke to them; the girl stood up and smiled, but as she could speak no English and Mr Turner could speak no Burmese, and the little boy was too young to speak much of anything, they didn't get very far.

Being upon his feet, he went and fetched his sun hat and strolled out towards the village. It was only half a mile along the river bank; he took it slowly, and found the walk pleasant. He spent some time in the village, looking into the shops and smiling at the people, and he found three men building a sampan upon the bank, which interested him very much. He was interested too, in the samples of rice and millet in the shops.

He passed the pagoda, but did not go in. He paused at the gate and looked in; before the calm statue of the Buddha there were many flowers arranged in vases. On the paving before the image there were two or three rows of women kneeling in prayer; he looked at them curiously, and saw Nay Htohn. She was kneeling devoutly with a long spray of gladiolus held between her hands, salmon pink and fresh and beautiful; her lips moved in prayer; she was utterly absorbed.

Mr Turner walked on, rather thoughtfully.

He found the walk back trying. The sun was higher and it was very hot; the road along the river bank seemed very long before he reached the shade of the trees by the house, and the pressure on the nape of his neck grew unbearable. He reached the steps leading up to the veranda and walked half way up them towards his chair; then everything went red before his eyes, and he staggered, and grasped at the balustrade beside him, and missed it, and fell heavily, and rolled down the steps that he had mounted on to the path in the sun. The nurse saw him fall from where she sat beside the playpen on the lawn, and called the bearer, and came running.

They found Mr Turner quite unconscious, and with some difficulty, with the cook to help them, they carried him upstairs and laid him on the bed. The bearer fetched cold water and began to bathe his face, and the nurse went running to call Nay Htohn from the pagoda.

Mr Turner remained unconscious for three and a half hours, lying upon his back and breathing with a snoring sound. Morgan got back half an hour after Nay Htohn; beyond loosening all his clothes and bathing his head with cold water they did not know what to do. This illness was like nothing that they had experienced. At that time there was a great shortage of visiting doctors in that part of Burma. There was a hospital at Henzada, thirty-seven miles away, but the jeep track to it was very bad and it did not seem wise to attempt that with the man in his condition. By river in a sampan the journey would take a day; there was no motor vessel going up till the next day.

After an hour of vain effort to get him round, Nay Htohn said: 'We must have help, Phillip; we are doing no good. I think we ought to ask the Sayah to come over.'

Morgan thought for a moment. He knew the Sayah fairly well, the Father Superior of the local Buddhist monastery. He knew him for an honest old man, but privately he considered him to be a bit simple. Still, there was something in what his wife had said. The Sayah was the nearest approach to a doctor that Mandinaung could provide; moreover, if Turner were to die on their hands it would make matters easier all round if someone else with a position in the community had seen him. He said: 'All right. I'll go and see if he can come along, if that's what you'd like.'

She said: 'I think he ought to come. Will you go for me?'

She could not go herself; when the monk arrived she would have to keep hidden out of his sight, and ensure that he saw no female servants. When a man has taken to a life of continence and placed the world behind him, it is both rude and unkind to flaunt young women in his sight.

Morgan got into the jeep and went to the monastery; he knew the polite routine, and was shown in to the old man, sitting in quiet contemplation on a mat. He explained his business and asked for help; in a few minutes he was in the jeep with the Sayah beside him, holding his coarse yellow robe about him in the wind of their passage.

The bearer met them at the door and made obeisance; there were no women in sight. The pilot took the Sayah upstairs to the bedroom. Turner was lying as the women had left him a moment before; a bowl of water by his side and a wet cloth on his head showed their most recent ministrations. The old man went up to the bed and laid two fingers on his temples. Then he turned to Morgan, speaking in Burmese.

'He will recover very soon,' he said. 'He will be normal before sunset. I do not think he has very long to go.'

'Is he dying, then?'

'Not now. I do not think that he has very many months to come.' The old man glanced at Morgan. 'I will draw his horoscope.'

'All right. What will you want to know, Payah?'

'The date and hour of his birth, and in what part of the world. He will recover before long. I will wait till he can tell me.' He retired to a corner of the room and squatted down in meditation.

Morgan sat bathing Mr Turner's face and head. He had not expected any more from the Sayah, but his presence was a comfort and an assurance against any trouble. From the door there came a whisper from his wife, and he went out to her. She had been listening from the next room.

She whispered to him: 'Moung Payah. Tell him about Moung Payah.'

He smiled at her tenderly. He knew her very well. He knew that with her intellect she derided the divinity of the cat; he knew that with that which was still childlike in her, which he loved, she believed in it. It had not been wholly as a joke that she had called the cat Moung Payah. He said: 'Would you like me to do that?'

She said: 'Please do.'

He touched her hand and she smiled up at him, and he went back into the room. 'We have a cat,' he said simply to the old man, 'a white cat that my wife calls Moung Payah.' The old man nodded his shaven head in understanding, and Morgan went on to tell him of the liking that the cat had shown for Mr Turner.

The old man sat in meditation for a time. At last he asked: 'Is he a Christian?'

'As much as he is anything,' the pilot said in Burmese. 'In the country that he was born in, as I was, there is not much religion in the life of ordinary men. He would have been christened as a child, and confirmed when he was a boy, I suppose.'

There was another long silence. The Sayah said at last: 'Virtue is measured from the knowledge that is given to the soul in the beginning. Even if a man has kept no one of the Five Precepts for the reason that he did not know about them, he may still attain the dwellings of the Dewahs if his progress in this life has been sufficient.'

He relapsed into silence, sitting cross-legged on the floor in the corner of the room, dressed in his coarse yellow robe, his bald, shaven head bowed in meditation. Morgan turned and went on bathing Turner's face. In the house there was silence, but for his slight movements. Gradually the heavy breathing of the man upon the bed grew easier, and presently he stirred as if in sleep, and rolled over a little.

At last he woke, and stirred, and sat up on the charpoy. He saw Morgan standing with a sponge and basin by his side, and a queer old Burmese monk beside him. He said: 'I fell down.'

'That's right,' said Morgan. 'You've been unconscious for three hours.'

'Christ,' said Mr Turner. 'That's a bloody sight longer than what it was before.' He relapsed into a depressed silence.

'Better lie down a bit and take it easy,' the pilot said. 'I couldn't get a doctor. Is there anything you ought to have done?'

'I'll be all right,' Mr Turner said heavily. 'I got one of these turns before.' He paused, and then he said: 'I didn't want to make myself a bloody nuisance.'

'Don't bother about that,' said Morgan. 'I got the Sayah here to come and have a look at you; he knows more doctoring than I do. Like to tell him one or two things?'

'Sure,' said Turner heavily. 'What does he want to know?'

Morgan exchanged a few words in Burmese with the old man. 'He wants to know when you were born, what day and at what time, if you know that.'

'June the 16th, 1908,' said Mr Turner. 'Must have been about seven or eight in the evening. I know Ma was took bad at tea.'

'And the place?'

'No 17 Victoria Grove, Willesden Green.'

Morgan transmitted this information to the Sayah, who gathered his robe about him to depart. 'That all he wants to know?' Mr Turner asked in surprise.

'That's all.'

'Bloody funny kind of doctor.'

Morgan took the Sayah back to his kyaung in the jeep, and returned to the house. He found that Nay Htohn had ordered the patient to stay in bed; they kept him there for the whole of that day. He told them a little about his attack, sufficient to make them understand that it was connected with the great wound on his forehead, but he was reticent about it and told them no more than he need. When Morgan went up in the evening he found the white cat sitting on his bed. Mr Turner got real pleasure from the presence of the cat, and from the feeling that he was favoured specially.

Dawn came at about six o'clock in the morning; when Morgan came down shortly after that in the cool of the day, he found the Sayah squatting on the veranda waiting for him. The old man produced a large sheet of paper from the folds of his garment, written all over with numerals arranged in columns under the days of the week and months of the year, the whole being roughly rectangular in form. He said: 'I have drawn the zadah of the Englishman.'

Morgan knew a Burmese horoscope when he saw it. Nay Htohn had one somewhat similar to this but more carefully made out, which she affected to think little of and treasured very carefully under lock and key. He said. 'Will you interpret it for me, Payah?'

The old man squatted down on the veranda and spread the paper out upon the ground before him; Morgan drew up a chair beside him and leaned down to see the figures that his finger indicated. A faint rustle from the room behind them told him that Nay Htohn had crept up within hearing.

The Sayah said: 'I will not trouble you with that which is not important.' He laid his finger on the chart. 'When he was twenty-six years old he passed into the House of Saturn to abide there for the ten years that all must abide. That is a bad age at which to enter the house of danger, and he did many foolish things. In the eighth year he offended against the laws of his country. In the ninth year he received the wound that you now see upon his forehead.' The old man laid his finger on a numeral. 'Beside that wound, this symbol shows yourself. I do not know what that may mean; perhaps you do.'

The pilot said quietly: 'I think I do. What year was that in, Payah?'

The old man studied the chart, '1943,' he said. 'In the following year, the last year of his sojourn in the House of Saturn, the man went to prison.'

The pilot said quietly: 'I wondered about that.'

'Passing from the evil influence,' the old man said, 'he entered the House of Jupiter and lived there for three years, doing little good and little evil. From there, and early in this very year, he fell into Yahu under the Tuskless Elephant, here, where he received foreknowledge of his death.'

Morgan glanced at the old man. 'He knows when he will die?'

'He will die next year in April,' the Sayah said. 'He knows that, almost to the very month. This symbol is for knowledge, this one is for death, and this one is for April. It is very certain that he knows about his death.'

Morgan was silent for a minute. A crow flew into the veranda, picked up a crumb, and flew away. 'I know very little about him, Payah,' he said at last. 'What kind of man is he?'

The old man studied the chart and said: 'He is a good man, and will climb up to the Six Blissful Seats. He has known sin and trouble and it has not made him bitter; he has known sorrow and it has not made him sad. In these last months that have been granted to him he is trying to do good, not to avoid damnation for he has no such beliefs, but for sheer love of good. Such a man will go on up the Ladder of Existence; he will not fall back.' He laid his finger on the last numerals of the chart. 'Here is the symbol for a generous impulse, and here a great journey, and here beside it is again the symbol for yourself. I do not know what that means. Here is this illness under the gyoh of the North which means a swift recovery.' He laid the paper down. 'I cannot tell you any more.'

He got up to his feet, offered to leave the horoscope with Morgan, and was evidently pleased when the pilot told him to take it back to the monastery. In careful, polite Burmese Morgan thanked him at some length, and the old man shambled away down the road to his own place. Morgan stood thoughtful, looking after him; Nay Htohn came out and stood beside him.

'You heard all that about Turner?' he asked her in Burmese?'

'I heard,' she said. 'We are honoured to have such a good man with us.'

They stood for a minute in silence watching the retreating figure in the yellow robe. 'We must send something,' Morgan said at last. 'What had we better send?'

The girl said: 'Give them a bell. They can always use another bell.' They turned and went into the house.

They went up together to see Turner, and found him awake. They persuaded him to stay in bed for breakfast; he stayed in bed until he wearied of it in the heat of the forenoon, and came down at about eleven o'clock to sit on the veranda in his long chair. Morgan was out; Nay Htohn was watching for him, and made him comfortable in his chair with a cheroot and a long drink of iced lime squash. He sat there at ease, watching the traffic on the river.

He felt that he must leave as soon as possible, and go back to England. The fit that he had suffered had been a sharp warning to him that his time was getting short. His journey to Burma, he felt, had been a complete fiasco. He had come out from England to locate a beachcomber and set him on his feet if that were possible; instead, he had found him a man of means, happily married and holding a considerable position for a man of his age in the country of his choice. He had enjoyed every minute of the journey; he would have liked to stay and see more of the lovely country that he had come to, but there was no time for that. His time was very short; he would not waste it. If Morgan did not need his help there would be all the more for Duggie Brent, or for the Negro if he ever got in touch with him. He must get back to Watford and begin again.

He rested all day on the veranda. Morgan came back at about teatime and sat smoking with him, and Mr Turner told him something of what was in his mind. 'Them steamers down the river to Rangoon,' he said. 'I got to be thinking about getting back. The firm wouldn't half play hell if they knew I was sitting here like this with a nice drink 'n a cigar, 'n not doing a bloody thing.'

Morgan said: 'Stay a few days more, and get yourself quite right. The firm would give you sick leave.'

Turner said: 'I don't think I'd better. I've not got much time. I better be getting back to Rangoon.'

'There's a boat down the river tomorrow, if you really feel you've got to go.'

'I better take it. I can't afford to hang around.'

Morgan glanced at him. 'Did you see anyone in England about these fits you get? A doctor?'

Mr Turner said: 'Oh yes. I got examined by a specialist after the last time.'

'What did he say about it?'

Mr Turner was silent for a minute. Then he said: 'It wasn't so good.'

'Is it very bad?'

'All be the same in a hundred years,' said Mr Turner quietly. 'That's the way I look at it.'

The pilot said: 'It's kind of–fatal, is it?'

Mr Turner stared at him in admiration. 'You're a pretty sharp one,' he said. 'I never told you anything o' that, did I?'

'No. But it's right, is it?'

'Aye, it's right enough,' said Mr Turner. 'I got bits of shrapnel going bad inside my napper, 'n they can't do nothing about it. I got seven or eight months to go, not more. But I didn't want anyone to know.'

'I'm very sorry.' Morgan was silent for a minute, and then said: 'Why did you come out here, really?'

'I told you. I got business in Rangoon.'

'I know. Was it because you got a very bad account of me from my mother, by any chance?'

Mr Turner shifted uneasily in his chair. 'I thought if I was out here I might look you up,' he said evasively.

The pilot got up and walked over to the veranda rail, and stood looking out over the river. He turned presently and came back to the table by their chairs, and took another cheroot. 'When you see my mother,' he said, 'try and make her understand the way I live out here. Try and make her understand that Nay Htohn isn't a naked savage, holding me with Oriental wiles. Tell her I'm doing work I can do well. Tell her I'm prosperous and happy. Try and make her understand.'

Mr Turner said: 'I'll go and see her when I get back home next week, 'n I'll do what I can. But things look kind of different back in Notting Hill Gate, you know.'

'I know.' There was a pause. 'You're going back home at once?'

Mr Turner nodded. 'Soon as I can get a seat upon a plane.'

Morgan turned, and walked slowly to the end of the veranda, smoking and thoughtful. When he came back he said: 'It's been very, very nice seeing you here, Turner. I've had it on my mind for some time that I should have tried to find out something of what happened to you–and the other two in that ward at Penzance. I know a bit about the nigger, but I never heard a thing about you or Corporal Brent.' He stood looking down at Turner in the chair. 'I felt a bit of a squirt about that,' he said quietly. 'I've got on so well myself that I ought to have been able to spare time to poke around a bit and see if you and Brent were getting on all right. We were all in it together then. We ought to have kept up.'

'Well, that's what I thought,' Mr Turner said. 'I mean, I got a nice house at Watford 'n a bit of money saved, in spite of everything and going through a bad patch and that. And then, when the chap in Harley Street said what he did, I kind of thought I ought to get and find out, case any of you hadn't been so lucky as me.'

'That's why you came to Burma, really isn't it?' said Morgan.

Mr Turner said defensively: 'I got business to do in Rangoon as well.'

They smoked in silence for a few minutes; then he said: 'It's been nice of you 'n Mrs Morgan–I mean, your wife, to have me,' he said. 'I didn't know you'd be well off and settled like this, or maybe I wouldn't have come. I thought . . . well, things 'ld be different to what they are.' He hesitated, and then said: 'I got in prison ten months after leaving hospital; maybe you know about that. Over them trucks of sugar. I wouldn't have come if I'd known you were a proper magistrate, and that.'

Morgan grinned. 'That's all right,' he said. 'You didn't get away with it?'

Mr Turner shook his head. 'They give me a year,' he said, 'but I got two months off for good conduct. I went a bit too far that time.'

The pilot said: 'You needed money very badly?'

''Course I did. I got kind of worried.' He turned to Morgan. 'I don't know how anybody gets along these days without they do a deal now and then to get something put by for when they can't work any longer.' He paused, and then he said: 'Time was, in the old days, a chap could save for his old age, or being ill, or that, out of what he earned on a salary. But now with income tax and purchase tax 'n every other bloody sort of tax, unless you do a deal now 'n again you can't get to be safe at all. Straight, you can't.'

Morgan said thoughtfully: 'It's like that in England now, is it?'

''Course it is. Chaps working on the bench, they got security of a sort. Chaps working for the Government, they got a bloody great pension to look forward to. But chaps working on their own, like shopkeepers, or chaps working in offices like me, they ain't got nothing to speak of. You got to keep your eyes wide open for a deal all the time, and some of them deals can be pretty slippery.'

Morgan grinned. 'Like the sugar?'

'Like that bloody sugar. I knew it was a bad 'un, but what's a man to do?' He turned to Morgan. 'I was kind of worried,' he said simply. 'I mean, I'd just got married, and I thought the wife was going to have a baby. She never, but I thought she was. And I hadn't got a bean saved, fifty or sixty pounds, maybe, not more. And I got to worrying over what would happen if I got killed or badly hurt, 'n where she would be then? I mean, a chap's got to do something.'

'I suppose so.'

There was a pause. 'Well, that's all over and done with now,' said Mr Turner. 'I got three thousand pounds saved up, 'n a nice house, and furniture, and all. I wouldn't like the wife to know the way some of it come, but it's better 'n leaving her stuck with nothing at all next year. And then,' he said, 'I got to kind of thinking about us four in that room in hospital. And I thought, the wife doesn't know how much I've got so she won't miss a little bit of it 'n I could pop around before I go and see if you was all all right.'

'I was thinking on the same lines,' said Morgan slowly. 'I was thinking I ought to try and find out something about you three. I don't know anything about Corporal Brent. But I do know a little about the nigger.' He glanced at Turner. 'There was the hell of a row about that nigger,' he said thoughtfully. 'Like to hear about it?'

8

Nay Htohn came out of the house on to the veranda with her sewing in a flat rush basket. The men got to their feet. 'I was just starting in to tell Turner about that nigger at Penzance,' the pilot said.

She smiled. 'I like that story. I wish we could find out what happened to him in the end.' They sat down again, and Nay Htohn knelt down by her husband's chair, and began sewing.

Morgan said: 'I must try and get this straight–it's rather a long time ago. But I was interested at the time, of course–and it was damn funny, because when I was at Exeter after Penzance we shared a mess with some Americans, and we used to pull their legs about it.'

He paused, looking out over the wide river. Over the Pegu Yoma in the far distance the great thunderheads of the monsoon were massing for another storm; a little wind blew past them on the veranda, cool and refreshing. Jungle rats scampered up and down the trunk of the banyan tree, their tails held high; on the river beneath them sampans drifted by.

'There was an American lieutenant in the Army Air Corps who'd been stationed at this place, Trenarth,' the pilot said at last. 'He came in one day in a B25, and at lunch I heard him telling the other Goddams all about it. I guessed it was our nigger when I heard him telling them.'

Mr Turner asked: 'What did he say?'

The American had said: 'Say, Colonel McCulloch sure has got himself a mess of nigger trouble down at Trenarth. It's gotten so the boys down there don't just know who they're to take orders from, the colonel or the landlord of the pub.'

It had been just before closing time when Sergeant Burton blew his whistle as he raced around the corner of the White Hart in pursuit of Private Dave Lesurier. In the bar Mr Frobisher had already said: 'Time, gentlemen, please,' to a room full of Negroes, beaming at them as he did so. He used the words that he had used for twenty-seven years each evening to warn his patrons at five minutes to ten that they must drink up and go, at the conclusion of his licensed hours. He beamed, because he was well aware by now of the simple pleasure that the Negroes got from the words which were his common use; they would grin back at him, and drink up, and go quietly on the stroke of ten o'clock. The bar of the White Hart was therefore reeking with Anglo-American goodwill when Sergeant Burton blew his whistle, and the jeep came screaming to a standstill in the street outside, and the fun started.

The Negroes went tumbling out into the street to see what was going on, and because they had to go anyway. After the last had left Mr Frobisher walked slowly round the bar, wiping it down with a rag. Then he walked to the front door to bolt it for the night, and stood for a minute looking out into the street.

In the moonlight the street was full of American soldiers, white and black. There was whistling and the arrival of more cars with military police; somebody was standing up in the back of a command car and ordering the troops back to their camps. There was a good deal of confusion, but the doings of the military did not interest Mr Frobisher very much. He bolted the door and retired into his parlour, and put on the wireless, and lit his pipe, and sat down for a quiet smoke before bed.

Within five minutes the U.S. Military Police were hammering on his door. He heaved himself out of his chair and went to open it; he was faced by a sergeant with a couple of soldiers at his back, all armed to the teeth.

The sergeant said: 'We got to search this house for a nigger. You got any niggers in here?'

'Nobody in here but me,' said Mr Frobisher. 'Not unless my daughter's upstairs in her room.'

'Well, we got to search this house,' the sergeant said, and made as if to come in.

The landlord said slowly: 'Here, steady on a minute. What's all this about?'
'One of your village girls got raped or near raped by a nigger,' said the sergeant. 'The lieutenant said: Search all the houses in this block.'

Mr Frobisher said: 'You got a search warrant?'

The sergeant stared at him nonplussed. 'We don't need no warrant.'

Mr Frobisher said: 'Well, you can't go searching houses in this country without you've got a warrant. You ought to know better. There's no Negro in this house now, anyway. They all went at ten o'clock.'

'For crying out loud,' the sergeant said. 'You going to let us in here, or not?'

'You got to have a warrant if you're going to search my house,' said Mr Frobisher firmly.

One of the men behind pushed forward. 'Let me see what I can do, Sarge.' The sergeant gave place to him; Private Graves had lived and worked in England for five years.

'Say Mr Frobisher,' he said. 'We've got no warrant to search your house. But one of your young ladies had complained a nigger stopped her and did something to her in the street, and he's run away. We thought maybe he might be hiding in your back yard or some place. Mind if we come in and have a look?'

'Sure,' said the landlord, 'go ahead. Why didn't you say that first of all?'

Slightly bewildered, the sergeant led his men into the house; they spread out quickly, looked into the ground floor rooms, and went out into the yard. Mr Frobisher said to Private Graves: 'Take a look upstairs if you want to.' He went with him and knocked on his daughter's door. She answered from inside: 'Who's that?'

'Come on out a minute,' he said. She appeared in a kimono, and saw her father standing with an American soldier. He said: 'This gentleman wants to know if you've got a nigger in there.'

She said: 'Why, Daddy, what a thing to say. You'd better go to bed.'

He was quite unmoved. 'Well, that's what they want to know.' In a few words he told her what was happening. 'You'd better let him take a look.'

A very much abashed military policeman put his head in at the door and looked around, while Bessie regarded him as so much dirt. He went downstairs again with Mr Frobisher and the girl slammed her door. The sergeant left one military policeman in the yard and moved on to the next house; a few minutes after that there was the noise of a jeep being started up, a challenge, and two shots. In the street outside there was turmoil. Cars filled with running men and roared off in the direction of Penzance. Quite suddenly the street was quiet again, still and deserted in the bright moonlight.

Mr Frobisher shut the street door carefully, and shot the bolts one by one. Then he turned, and Bessie was standing half way down the stairs, in her kimono. 'Was that shots fired?' she asked, and there was wonder in her voice.

'Aye,' said her father heavily. 'It won't do no good, that.'

The girl said: 'Lor . . .' And then she asked: 'Who was it got assaulted, do you know?'

'I dunno.'

'Do you know which of the boys did it?'

'I dunno. One o' them called up from the cottonfields, I should think. Some o' them don't seem ever to have been educated at all, not to speak of.'

She tossed her head. 'Even so, a girl what's got her head screwed on right doesn't have to get assaulted, not unless she wants to.'

'Aye,' he said, 'that's right.' They went to bed.

Lieutenant Anderson of the U.S. Military Police did not get a great deal of sleep that night. He was a decent man, and secretly concerned at what he had found in the air-raid shelter. Easing his way cautiously around the buttress, gun in one hand and torch in the other, with a sergeant with a submachine gun at his back, he had found a young Negro sitting on a seat, his head bowed down on his knees, and drenched in his own blood. He had put away his gun in favour of a first aid kit, and rushed the lad in a command car to the nearest hospital in the next street, and left him there under guard. He then had an awkward five minutes with a British sergeant, who turned up and wanted to know all about it. Lieutenant Anderson was well aware that the British civil police had funny ideas about shooting. They went unarmed themselves, and seemed to have no difficulty in dealing with the pansy British criminals that way.

This police sergeant was a man of fifty, unimaginative and difficult. 'Was that your men shooting in the street just now?' he asked.

'That's right,' said the lieutenant.

The sergeant said ponderously: 'Well, you can't do that here.' He reached for his black notebook. 'Can I have your name and unit?'

'Say, what is this?' said the lieutenant unhappily. 'We're the military police. We don't have to make any report to you.'

'Maybe not,' said the sergeant equably, 'but I got to make a report about you. You can't go shooting off guns in the street like that, not in this country you can't. You might ha' killed somebody.'

Lieutenant Anderson realized that some explanation was required from him. 'Maybe you wouldn't know about the color difficulty,' he said patiently. 'It's kind of different when you're dealing with a nigger. They don't react until you show a gun.'

'Was this Negro armed when you found him?' asked the sergeant.

'Only just his knife,' said the lieutenant. 'But the boys wasn't to know that.'

The sergeant wrote it all down laboriously in his notebook. Again he demanded the lieutenant's name and unit, and got it, and wrote it down. 'It don't seem to be anything to do with us,' the sergeant said at last. 'I'll have to make out a bit of a report because of the firing, but I don't suppose you'll hear no more about it.' He went away at last, leaving Lieutenant Anderson irritated and slightly worried.

He drove back to his camp and, before going to bed, questioned Sergeant Burton rather closely. The sergeant, fat and forty, did not know the name of the girl, but he had seen her in the street several times, and knew where she lived. It seemed to Lieutenant Anderson that before he made out his report to Colonel McCulloch he should make the matter watertight by getting evidence from the girl, and at half past eight in the morning he was knocking on her cottage door, with Sergeant Burton at his side.

Mr Trefusis, signalman upon the railway, had already gone to work; Mrs Trefusis opened the door to them, full of feminine indignation. Gracie had come in crying shortly after ten o'clock and had been closely questioned by her mother. She had told her mother that she had been grabbed and kissed by a Negro soldier, and that she had screamed, and a sergeant of the U.S. Military Police had come running up and saved her. In her confusion and distress she thought that this was true.

'And let me tell you,' said Mrs Trefusis, arms akimbo on her hips, 'if you think you can bring them black savages into a decent town like this and let them run amuck, you're very much mistaken. It's just the mercy of Providence the poor girl isn't lying in her grave this very minute, and a lot any of you would care about it. But you ain't heard the last of this, you mark my word. Fine goings on, when decent girls can't go out after dark 'n come home safe. Fine goings on!'

Lieutenant Anderson's spirits rose; this was just what he wanted. If there was any difficulty about the charge or the shooting he could bring the colonel down, and let him listen to the mother of the victim. 'I guess we're all real sorry this has happened, lady,' he said meekly.

'And well you might be, young man,' she replied indignantly. 'This is a decent town; we don't have them goings on here, you know, however you may carry on at home where you come from. We don't want any o' your Wild West manners here. What do we have to do? Keep our girls in of an evening 'case the niggers get them? I never did hear such. The poor child hasn't slept a wink all night and didn't eat no breakfast, and now late at the shop and all. I told Mr Trefusis, I did, I said we ought to have a doctor to her, that we did. That's what I told him. But he didn't pay no attention to me.'

She stopped for breath.

The lieutenant said: 'You don't have to worry any more. We got the nigger, and you can depend upon it there won't be no more trouble of that sort, no ma'am. He'll be up for court martial that nigger will. He'll get sent up for about ten years. As for your daughter, ma'am, I'm here to tell you that we're real sorry in the U.S. Army this thing had to happen. I guess there's nothing we can do will ease the little lady's feelings, but if there's anything she needs, or anything that we can get her that 'ld take her mind off it, I'd be real glad if you'd tell me.'

Mrs Trefusis said: 'I dunno. If you've got him and he's going to be court martialled . . .'

The lieutenant laughed shortly. 'Don't you worry about that. We're going to make an example of that nigger. This isn't going to happen again.' He hesitated. 'Could I see the little lady for a minute? I'd like to know if she can identify him.'

'Come in.' She showed them into the parlour, and went to find her daughter, washing up the breakfast dishes in the scullery. 'There's a couple of American officers come in about last night, dearie,' she said. 'Ever so nice they are. Wipe your hands, and come on in and talk to them.'

The girl said: 'I don't want to see them, Ma.'

'Come on, dearie–they won't hurt you. They just want to know you can identify the nigger that they've caught.'

'I don't want to identify anybody. Why can't they leave it be?'

Her mother said firmly. 'The guilty have to take their punishment. Now wipe your hands, 'n come along. It won't take but a minute.'

'Oh, Ma!'

When she appeared behind her mother in the parlour she was practically inarticulate with embarrassment and fright. The lieutenant glanced at her, pretty and blushing and very young, and a momentary wave of fellow feeling with Lesurier swept over him; she certainly was a lovely little piece of work. It was succeeded by a virtuous resolution to make very sure the Negro got the limit.

He said: 'I'm here for the U.S. Army, Miss Trefusis, to apologize for what happened last night. We're all real sorry about it, and we hope you won't think too badly of us over it.'

The girl blushed and was silent. Her mother said kindly: 'She don't bear no ill will, do you, Gracie?' The girl whispered: 'No.'

The lieutenant said kindly: 'Did you ever see this man before, Miss Trefusis?'

Her mother said: 'Speak up, Gracie, and tell the gentleman.'

She whispered: 'I see him in the shop.'

'Did you ever go out walking with him, Miss Trefusis?'

She shook her head. Her mother said: 'She don't go out with boys. Gracie's always been a very good girl, Captain.'

The lieutenant thought: A darn sight more backward than some. I could teach her plenty.

Aloud, he said: 'Do you know his name, Miss Trefusis?'

She shook her head, and whispered: 'I heard someone call him Dave once, in the shop.'

Sergeant Burton said: 'That's right, lieutenant—Dave Lesurier.'

'You're quite sure it was the same one that troubled you last night?' the lieutenant asked. She nodded.

'Did you ever speak to him outside the shop?' he asked.

She shook her head. Her mother said: 'Speak up, Gracie, and answer the gentleman when he speaks to you.' To the lieutenant she said fondly: 'She's lost her tongue.' The girl cleared her throat, and said: 'He used to come in and buy Player's. I never spoke to him except for that.'

The lieutenant said: 'Just tell me in your own words what happened, Miss Trefusis.'

She said: 'I come out of the Hall and went along the pavement, and he was there, all alone. There was no one else about, 'n he said something, I forget what he said. And then he put his arms round me and kissed me.'

Lieutenant Anderson asked: 'Did you know he was going to do that?'

'Oh no, sir.'

'What did you do?'

'I struggled to make him let go, and cried out. And then'—she indicated the sergeant—'he come running up and the nigger let go, and I ran away.'

The sergeant was about to say something, but the lieutenant checked him. 'You never gave this nigger any encouragement?' he asked.

'Oh no, sir. I only see him in the shop.'

Lieutenant Anderson began to take his leave, well satisfied that he had got a cast iron case to give the colonel. In the jeep as he drove off, the sergeant said: 'There's just one thing about all that, Lieutenant. I heard her cry out to let go when I was round the corner, and the next I knew she come running flat out into me. She got away from the nigger before ever he saw me.'

'Shucks,' said Lieutenant Anderson, 'he'd have caught her again, easy enough, if you hadn't been there. Good thing for her you was.' They drove back to the camp.

The identity of the victim percolated through the village in the course of the morning. Bessie Frobisher, who went out every morning to do the shopping for the White Hart, came back and reported to her father that Gracie did not look very much the worse for her assault. 'Doing up the rations like she does every day,' she said. 'She hasn't got no bruises on her face, or anything.'

Jerry Bowman came at midday with a load of beer; he parked the lorry and rolled down the casks with Mr Frobisher to help him, and came into the bar for a plate of bread and cheese and a pint of his own cargo. 'Had some trouble here last night, they tell me,' he said affably.

'Aye,' said Mr Frobisher. 'Just outside here by the gate into the back yard, round the corner. They got the Negro, did they? In Penzance?'

'They've got him in the hospital,' said Mr Bowman. 'You know he cut 'is throat?'

Mr Frobisher stared at him. 'No!'

Mr Bowman told him what he had learned at the Sun in Penzance, which was not a lot. Private Dave Lesurier had got through the night with the help of a transfusion, and would live; he had not at that time developed septicaemia. In the White Hart that dinnertime the case made a first class sensation; it made a bigger one that evening when the Negroes came down after work.

Sergeant Lorimer was worried and distressed. He leaned over the bar, his great black hands clasped round a tankard, talking to Mr Frobisher and Bessie. 'It don't seem to make sense, anyway you look at it,' he said. 'If it was some of these sharecropper boys, now, it 'ld be different because some of them might not know better. Even so, colored boys have been treated real nice in this place; I don't think even the sharecropper boys 'ld do a thing like that. But Dave's got education; he's a mighty nice sort of boy, is Dave. I can't see that he'd ever do a thing like that, no sir.'

Mr Frobisher said: 'Well, what did he do, anyway? I haven't heard that yet.'

'They say up at the camp he's being charged with an attempt at rape. That's a mighty serious offence to charge a decent boy with, Mister Frobisher.'

Bessie said: 'It must have been something pretty serious, Sam, or he'd never have cut his throat. A boy don't go and do that for nothing.'

'I dunno. That boy acted mighty highstrung, now and then. He's got education.'

'Well, anyway,' said Mr Frobisher, 'I'd like to know just what it was he did.'

He thought about it for an hour or two, while he served beer across the bar and listened to the Negroes as they discussed it. He found that one and all they took it cynically. They linked it with the conduct of the military police. 'They been waiting for a case they could go to court martial on,' one said. 'They hate like hell to see us walking with white girls. Now they got one, and they'll make it plenty tough for that nigger. Yes, sir, they been out to get a colored boy upon a color charge for a court martial, 'n now they've got one. That boy's certainly going up for a long stretch.' There was sullen agreement in the bar with this view.

They displayed complete revulsion from the war. When the nine o'clock news came on the radio, one said: 'Aw, turn the blame thing off. Let the white men get on with the white man's war, 'n leave us be.' Nobody wanted to hear the news, and after an uncertain pause Mr Frobisher turned the knob to the light programme and got dance music for them.

The landlord's mind worked rather slowly, but along fairly straight lines. This thing concerned the village, and anything that concerned the village concerned him. At ten past nine he said to Bessie: 'Slip up and see Ted Trefusis, 'n ask him if he'd care to step over for a pint in the back parlour.'

Mr Trefusis came, a lean, grey-haired man, responsible and serious as a signalman must be. Mr Frobisher took him into the back parlour and brought a jug of mild in from the bar. Mr Trefusis said: 'Glad to get out of the house, straight I am. The way the wife's been going on, you'd think the end of the world was come.'

Mr Frobisher said: 'Aye?' And then he said: 'Well, I dunno that it's what one would choose to have happen in the family.'

Mr Trefusis lit a cigarette. 'No,' he said, 'but it might ha' been worse. After all, there's no harm done.'

Mr Frobisher cocked an eye at him. 'Gracie all right?'

'Be all right if her mother 'ld stop putting a lot of fool notions in her head. After all, many a girl been kissed in a dark corner before now, and will be again.'

'Aye,' said Mr Frobisher. 'That all that happened?'

'Aye. Chap come up 'n said something to her, 'n put his arms round her, 'n give her a hug and a kiss. Then when she started struggling, he let her go.'

'That's right, is it?' said Mr Frobisher. 'He let her go?'

'Aye, and she run round the corner and bumped into an American policeman. 'Course a young girl gets a bit upset about a thing like that, specially when it's a black man. But some of these things, least said soonest mended. I told her mother, I said–after all, it's not as if she come to any harm.'

'Seems to me,' said Mr Frobisher slowly, 'the man's come to more harm than Gracie has.'

'Is that right what someone told me, that he cut his throat?'

'Aye,' said Mr Frobisher, 'that's right enough. They got him in the hospital.'

'Whatever did he want to do a thing like that for?'

Mr Frobisher told him what he knew, and they discussed it for some time. 'He's for court martial soon as he comes out o' hospital,' he said.

'What's he charged with, then?' asked Mr Trefusis.

'Attempted rape.'

'O' my Gracie?'

'That's it.'

'But that ain't right. He let her go.'

'That's what he's to be charged with, all the same.'

Mr Trefusis sat silent for a minute or two, smoking and thoughtful. At last he said: 'There was a couple of Americans come to the house soon after I went to work this morning, an officer and a sergeant. God knows what the wife told them.'

There was another long silence. At last the railwayman said: 'They're kind of hard on these black fellows, aren't they?'

Mr Frobisher drew thoughtfully at his pipe. 'Well, it does seem like it,' he said at last. ''Course, we dunno what they may be like in their own place back in the States. They may have a lot of trouble with them that we don't know about. But I must say, times it seems as nothing they can do is right.'

Mr Trefusis said: 'D'you know the one they've caught, the one that cut his throat?'

'Aye, he comes in here. Decent enough sort of lad, he seemed to be, like most of them are. Always willing to lend a hand with shifting casks, or that. His sergeant was in here just this evening, speaking up for him.'

They could reach no conclusion in the matter, indeed, it seemed to be clean out of their hands. Next day it became known in the village that Dave Lesurier was being held under guard in hospital and was to come before court martial on a charge of attempted rape as soon as he was well enough. In the streets the military police redoubled their vigilance; every Negro seen to be walking with a white girl was followed by an armed military policeman, to the sullen fury of the Negro and the blazing indignation of the girl. The Negroes took to walking in the streets in bands of ten or fifteen, looking for trouble, and fights with similar bands of white American troops took place on two occasions. One night Jim Dakers was set on by a gang of Negro soldiers, and cruelly beaten up.

Mr Frobisher watched these developments with grave concern, and discussed them discreetly with the traveller from his brewery, with the vicar, and with various men of Trenarth in the forces, home on leave from various parts of the country. He learned of pitched battles with firearms between American white troops and American Negroes at Leicester and at Lancaster, reports of which were censored from the newspapers. He thought about these stories gravely while he stood behind the bar, or tapped new casks down in the cellar, or sat and smoked in his back parlour when the bar was closed. He did not think quickly and it took him a week or two to decide upon a course of action, but when he did make up his mind upon the line that he was going to take, it was not a bad one.

He sat down in his shirtsleeves one Sunday afternoon after dinner, and breathing heavily with every word, he wrote a letter to General Eisenhower. It ran:

> White Hart Hotel,
> Trenarth,
> Nr Penzance,
> Cornwall.

Dear Sir,

I take up my pen to tell you things are not as they ought to be here in Trenarth on account of there being trouble between your coloured soldiers and your white soldiers. It is not my place to say which is right but if things are not put right I think there will be shooting here like other places because there are fights and things are getting very bad. We don't want that to happen in Trenarth because in all the twenty-seven years I have held this licence we have had nothing worse than an affiliation order.

I think if you could see your way to do something about Pte David Lesurier, coloured, now being held on a charge of attempted rape of one of our young ladies it would assist and stop things getting worse because the black fellows are very sore about this charge and we think it is a bit of humbug too because the young lady struggled and he let her go at once. It is very kind of Colonel McCulloch to see that men who interfere with our young ladies get punished as they should be, but between you and me the young lady come to no harm and it would be better to forget it because the black fellows say this is a trumped up charge.

Pardon me writing when you will be very busy, but we don't want things to be let go and get so bad that there is shooting here like other places.

> Yours respectfully,
> JAMES FROBISHER, Landlord

He sealed this in an envelope and addressed it to General Eisenhower, Headquarters of the US Army, care of G.P.O., London, and posted it.

Three days later Major Mark T. Curtis arrived in Trenarth from the office of the Staff Judge-Advocate. He came nominally in connection with the application for court martial filed by Colonel McCulloch, and announced that he had come for a preliminary examination of the evidence. According to the book this seemed irregular to the colonel, but he was not one to question any officer from the Staff Judge-Advocate, and laid the whole matter before Major Curtis.

'You see the way it is,' he said at last. 'These colored boys have been alone here too long, and they're got uppity.'

'Yeah,' said the major. 'Had any other trouble of this sort here, Colonel?'

'No,' said Colonel McCulloch. 'They haven't needed to go raping. I don't know what to make of these darned English girls. You just can't keep them away from the niggers. I tell you, in this place the girls seem to prefer going with a colored man to one of our white boys. The whole place is plumb color crazy. The landlord of the pub down in the village here, he'd rather have the niggers than the white boys in his bar. Say, can you beat that?'

Major Curtis said casually: 'Does he stir up trouble?'

'I wouldn't say that,' said the colonel. 'He's made a packet of trouble for me because he won't have the white boys and I've had to find alternative accommodation for them. But I don't think he makes any trouble between whites and colored.'

The major said: 'You think this attempted rape is part of the same picture, that the colored boys got swelled heads?'

The colonel said: 'That's right. You get the colored out of place, and they'll start thinking about white women right off. That's always the way.'

The major smiled. 'I come from Maine,' he said. 'I wouldn't know about a thing like that.'

'I come from Georgia,' the colonel said. 'I do.'

'You're pretty sure about the evidence?' the major asked.

'Oh, sure. Lieutenant Anderson, he's interviewed the girl–you've got it all in his report there, in that file.' He turned the pages and picked out a paper. 'This one.'

The major read it through again. 'I'd like to have a talk with her myself,' he said. 'And with the colored man in hospital. The Staff Judge-Advocate, he's mighty anxious not to get anything irregular in these mixed cases with the British. We've got to be right all along the line.'

'Sure,' said the colonel. 'The colored is in hospital in Penzance, and I'll send a driver who knows how to contact the girl. You like anyone to come along with you?'

The major shook his head. 'Guess I'd better see them alone. They'll talk more freely.'

'Any way you like,' said the colonel.

He put a jeep at the disposal of the major, driven by a sergeant in the military police who knew the district; that afternoon Major Curtis drove into Penzance. He went with an open mind, realizing the limitations of his knowledge and wondering a little why the Staff Judge-Advocate had picked him for the job. He knew very little about Negroes. He came from Portland, Maine, and had been through the law school at Harvard; he had practised for a time in Albany and later had become junior partner in a firm of attorneys in Boston. He had defended a coloured janitor upon a charge of stealing coal, and got him off; he could not recollect any other occasion in his legal life when he had been in contact with the Negro. It seemed to Major Mark T. Curtis that in all the Staff Judge-Advocate's department there were few officers less suitable than he for this assignment, but he was an open-minded man and quite prepared to do his best with it, working from the elementary first principles of law. It never struck him that this was why he had been sent.

He found Private Dave Lesurier sitting up in bed with a dressing round his throat; he seemed to have boils all over him and he was looking thin and ill. The guard upon the door arranged with the sister for a screen around the bed, for there were other men in the ward; the major sat down on a chair behind this screen with the Negro and said: 'I'm from the Staff Judge-Advocate's office, at Headquarters. You know there's been some talk about court martialling you, Lesurier?'

The Negro said: 'Yes, sir.'

'Well, that's all in the future,' the major said. 'If you have done anything very wrong, you will not get away with it without being punished. If it comes to a court martial you will have a couple of officers who know the law to help you. Before it gets that far, we've got to make up our minds if you've done anything so bad as to make it worth while putting you on trial. That's why I've come to see you, to get your story of what happened. Do you understand me?'

The Negro said: 'Yes, sir.'

'Well now, would you like to tell me what it's all about?'

The Negro said: 'I guess you know that already.'

The officer was silent for a moment. 'Maybe I know some of it,' he said. 'I've seen a statement Miss Trefusis made, I've seen nothing from you.'

The boy said: 'If you've seen what Miss Trefusis said, I guess you've seen everything, sir.'

'There's two sides to every question, Lesurier. I want you to tell me yours.'

There was a long silence. The Negro sat studying the grey blanket on his bed covering his knees, with the red lettering upon it, PENZANCE GENERAL HOSPITAL. 'I guess there's nothing much to say,' he said at last. 'I don't want to deny it. I just grapped a holt of her, 'n kissed her. That's all there is to it.'

Major Curtis said unexpectedly: 'Have you got a girl back home?'

Lesurier looked up in surprise. 'No, sir. Not one regular one.'

'How long have you been over here?'

'Four months, sir.'

'Got to know many girls since you got over here?'

The Negro shook his head.

'None?'

The boy hesitated. 'Not unless you count Miss Trefusis,' he said.

'Apart from her, Lesurier, have you been out with any girls at all since you got over here?'

'No, sir. I haven't spoken to one since I left Nashville.'

'How old are you, Lesurier?'

'Twenty-two, sir.'

The major thought, a mighty long time for a boy of twenty-two to go without speaking to a girl. He said: 'What were you doing before you got drafted?'

He sat patiently, asking a question now and then, building up the background to the case. He heard all about the Filtair Corporation and the James Hollis School for coloured back in distant Nashville, and about the garage, and the truck driving, and the bulldozer. He had very seldom probed into a Negro's life before; in his home at Portland the help had all been white; except in sleeping cars and shoeshine parlours he had not come in contact with the coloured much. He sat patiently making the boy talk, realizing the imperfection of his own knowledge, anxious to learn.

At last he said: 'Well now. Tell me about Miss Trefusis. Where did you first meet her?'

The boy said: 'In the store.'

'I see.' The major glanced at him, and there was humour in his eye. 'Like to tell me what you said to her?'

'Sure,' said the Negro. 'I asked her for ten Player's.'

'That all you said?'

'That's all, sir.'

'Well, what happened next time you met her? Where was that?'

'In the store again, sir. I asked for another ten Player's.'

For an instant Major Mark T. Curtis felt that he was being trifled with; then, suddenly, he wasn't quite so sure. He said: 'Apart from asking her for cigarettes, when did you first speak to her?'

'I never did, sir. Only to buy Player's.'

The officer stared at him. 'Do you mean you never said a thing to her before you grabbed hold of her and kissed her, except to ask for ten Player's?'

The Negro said: 'That's right, Major. I know it sounds mighty dumb, but that's right.'

'I'll say it sounds dumb.' The major sat in silence for a moment, conning the evidence so far. Amongst white folk there were nuances in these affairs; sometimes the spoken word did not count for so much. He had not known before that coloured folks knew anything about nuances, and he was incredulous now. But his duty was to ascertain the truth.

He thought very deeply for a moment, and then said: 'Was she nice to you?'

Lesurier said evasively: 'She never spoke to me except to give me change and that.'

'I know. But when she did that, was she nice to you?'

Their eyes met for an instant; the Negro dropped his glance down to the grey blanket with the red lettering. 'She was mighty nice,' he said quietly.

'I see.' There was a short pause. 'Well now, Lesurier, what happened in the street that night? You'd arranged for her to meet you?'

'No, sir. I told you, I never said a thing to her except to buy things.'

'Well, were you waiting for her?'

'That's right, Major.'

'What for?'

'I wanted to ask her if she'd care to take a lil' walk with me one evening.'

The major felt that he was getting on to firmer ground. 'You could have asked her that in the store,' he pointed out. 'Why didn't you?'

'There was always other folk around,' the Negro said. 'I didn't think she'd like it if I asked her that with other folks around.'

'I see. So you waited for her in the street to ask her. Why did you pick ten o'clock at night, though?'

'I didn't pick it, Major. I started waiting for her around six, when I came down from the camp.'

'You hung around from six o'clock till ten to try and get a chance to speak to her alone?'

'That's right.'

'Have you got any way of proving that, Lesurier? Did you tell anyone what you were doing?'

'No, *sir*.' The Negro thought for a minute. 'I walked down from the camp with Corporal Booker Jones,' he said. 'He said to come on into the White Hart and have a lil' drink, but I said I guessed I would stick around outside. That was around six o'clock or soon after. He might remember.'

Major Curtis made a mental note of the name. 'Well now,' he said, 'in the end she came along. Was she alone?'

'Yes, sir.'

'What happened then?'

The Negro hesitated. 'I went up to her to ask her,' he said at last. 'And then I thought it was kind of late to ask her if she'd like to take a lil' walk, and I didn't know what to do. After waiting all that time, and that . . .'

'What did you do?'

The boy said: 'I gave her a kiss, Major. That's all I did.'

'Kind of sudden, wasn't it?'

The Negro said wearily: 'I guess so. It sounds mighty silly now. The only thing I got to say is that it didn't seem so silly then.'

'I see. What did she say about it?'

'Called me a beast, 'n started struggling,' the boy said heavily. 'I let her go.'

'You let her go as soon as she struggled?'

'Of course, sir,' the boy said. 'I wouldn't want to do anything she didn't like.'

Major Curtis sat with him for some time longer, drawing out the rest of the story. He questioned the Negro very closely over the attempted suicide, feeling that it must have some connection with a guilty conscience over Miss Trefusis. All he got was:

'I was just plumb scared of what them MPs would do if they caught me, after messing with a white girl, sir.'

In the end, Major Curtis said: 'You realize that what you did was very wrong, Lesurier? You just can't go around treating women that way, any women, white or colored. And especially a British girl over here. You realize that?'

The boy said: 'Sure I done wrong, Major. I know that. Will they send me up for a court martial?'

'I don't know. I'll have to see Miss Trefusis and the military police and then write the whole thing up, and make out a report. The Staff Judge-Advocate decides if you're to be court martialled, not me.'

'I don't want to make no trouble,' the boy said. 'I done wrong and I can take what's coming.' He hesitated, and then said: 'Would I get a chance to tell the little lady I'm real sorry about what I did?'

'I don't know,' said the major thoughtfully. 'That might help.'

He went down to his jeep and drove out to Trenarth. He knew from his own experience, as every soldier knows, that sex starved men may not be altogether normal; that justice is not served by trying to apply civilian standards to conditions they were not set up to govern. It seemed to him that Miss Trefusis was a casualty of the war. If she had lived in one of the big cities of Great Britain she might have been shattered by a bomb; as she lived in the country she had been kissed against her will by a Negro soldier. Both were very unpleasant experiences, and both were due entirely to the war. The landlord of the pub had described this case as a bit of humbug; Major Mark T. Curtis was inclined to agree with him.

He said to the sergeant driving him: 'Take me to the White Hart.'

'It ain't open yet, Major. Not till five-thirty.'

'That's okay—take me there. I want to see the landlord.'

His ring at the creaking bellwire roused Mr Frobisher from his afternoon nap; he came slowly to the door and shot the bolts back. He stepped aside when he saw a strange American officer, who said: 'Mr Frobisher? My name is

Curtis, Major Mark T. Curtis, from the Staff Judge-Advocate's department at Headquarters. Mind if I come in and have a talk with you?'

Mr Frobisher took him into the back parlour. 'You wrote a letter to the General,' the officer said. 'About the situation here, and about Private Lesurier. That's right, isn't it?'

'Aye,' said Mr Frobisher. He figured for a moment in surprise. 'Sunday I wrote it. What's this–Thursday. I didn't think they'd act so quick as that.'

'We don't like to leave things to get worse,' the major said. 'I've got nothing to do with the general situation between whites and colored in this place. I'm here to look into the evidence for this court martial. I want to see Miss Trefusis this afternoon, if I can, but before doing that I thought I'd come and have a talk with you. I'd like to know about the background of this girl, what sort of family she comes from, what they say about her moral character. It all adds up, you know,'

'Aye,' said the landlord. 'Well, sit down 'n make yourself comfortable. Can I get you something? I got some whisky, Major.'

Major Curtis was not the man to refuse a Scotch; he gave Mr Frobisher a Lucky Strike and they settled down to talk. 'What sort of girl is this?' he asked the landlord. 'What does her father do?'

Mr Frobisher told him.

'Run around with boys much?' asked the officer.

The landlord shook his head. 'She isn't old enough,' he said. 'I know they start young these days, but not so young as Grace Trefusis is.'

'How old is she, then?'

'Let's see,' said Mr Frobisher thoughtfully. 'She was going to school when war started, 'cause she used to pass this window every morning with the other children. Yes, 'n she was still going to school when we started the Home Guard, the L.D.V. we called it then, because I remember seeing her pass when we was drilling with pikes 'n shotguns out in the Square. Summer of 1940, that was. Well now, she was under fourteen then. She'd be sixteen and a half now, at that rate. Maybe just on seventeen.'

'Some of them get going by that time,' the major said.

'Aye,' said Mr Frobisher, 'but not this one.'

'Anyway, you wouldn't put her down as a girl of loose character?'

Mr Frobisher was rather shocked. 'Nothing like that,' he said a little curtly.

Major Curtis felt the situation needed easing a little. 'I wanted to be sure of your reaction to that,' he explained. 'There have been cases, not very many, but a few, of British women of loose character blackmailing our colored soldiers by threatening to charge them with assault. It's pretty serious with us, you know, when colored men assault white women.'

'Aye,' said Mr Frobisher, 'you'll likely get a bit o' that in the slum parts of the big cities. But not here in Trenarth.'

They discussed the girl a little more, and then the major said: 'Say, Mr Frobisher, just what did you mean in that letter by saying that you reckoned this case was a lot of humbug?'

'Well,' said Mr Frobisher, 'she come to no harm.'

'Isn't that because there was a military policeman there?'

'Not according to what her father said to me. He said he let her go as soon as she struggled.'

Major Curtis eyed him keenly. 'That's not what she said next day when

Lieutenant Anderson went to see her.'

'Aye?' said Mr Frobisher. 'Well, she was with her mother then. You'll have to sort the truth of it out for yourself.'

Major Curtis made a mental note to do so. 'You're got no strong feelings about colored men associating with white girls, then?' he asked.

'Wouldn't be no good if I did have,' said the landlord comfortably. 'If a girl takes a fancy to a black fellow and likes him, well there's nothing you or I can do to stop it.' He turned to the officer. 'One thing about these black fellows o' yours,' he said. 'They're ever so kind and considerate to the girls that go with them. Everybody's been remarking about that. Not spending money—I don't mean that. But doing things for the girls, putting themselves out for them, thinking ahead of ways to make them happy. That's the reputation that they've got in this place, and there's no good blinking it.'

'Have there been any attempts at marriage?' the major asked. He felt he'd better know the worst.

'Not yet,' said the landlord thoughtfully. 'I dunno that there may not be some though. The way your coloured fellows go talking in the bar of an evening, a lot of them would like to come back here to live when the war's over.'

Major Curtis got up to go. 'Well, thanks a lot for what you've told me, Mr Frobisher,' he said. 'And thank you for writing to the General the way you did. We certainly did appreciate that very much. Say, where would I find Miss Trefusis now?'

The landlord glanced at his watch. 'You'd catch her at the shop, if you're quick,' he said. 'Robertson's grocery shop, just up the street towards the cross. On the left-hand side. He shuts in five minutes, but you'll find her there if you go now.'

The officer said: 'Which had I better do, see her there or see her in her home?'

Mr Frobisher said: 'If you see her in her home you'll have her mother to deal with.'

'I see,' said Major Curtis. 'I'll go to the shop. Well, thanks a lot, Mr Frobisher.'

He went out into the street, and telling the driver of his jeep to wait for him, he walked towards the shop. He felt himself to be in very deep water. Even in Portland where he had been brought up, no white girl would go out with a coloured man; a marriage would have been incredible. In this village things were different. Probably never very strong, the colour bar in Trenarth had collapsed entirely with the influx of large numbers of coloured Americans. According to the landlord marriages of black men with white girls would certainly be tolerated and the girls would not lose much in social caste. In some respects the villagers seemed to find the coloured men desirable.

He entered Robertson's grocery shop with the feeling that he must be very careful not to offend. His duty was to get a fair statement from the girl of what had happened that he could put in a report for the Judge-Advocate; it would not help him to secure the truth if he showed revulsion from the standards of the village. He felt at a loss in another respect. He was there to question a very young girl, a good girl by all accounts, upon a very intimate matter. He knew practically nothing about British girls at all; he had very seldom spoken to one in his life. Certainly he had never spoken to a British village girl like this; he had no idea how she might react to any of his questions. He felt that quite unknowingly he might defeat his object by his ignorance and clumsiness, fail to secure the truth, and make the matter worse. Still, he must do his best.

He went into the shop. Most of it was given over to groceries, but there was a sub post office in one corner, behind a wire grill. At the grocery counter there was a middle-aged woman with two girls, all dressed in rather soiled white overalls, serving two or three customers. Behind the post office grille there was a middle-aged man.

The officer went up to the grille. 'Mr Robertson?' he asked.

The man looked up. 'That's me.'

'I'm looking for a young lady, Miss Trefusis,' the major said quietly. 'Is she here?'

The man nodded with understanding. 'That's her at the end,' he said in a low tone. The major turned and saw a very pretty, dark-haired girl at the other counter.

He said: 'I want to have a talk with her, about this trouble that she's had. Could I do that here?'

'Well, if you like,' the man said. 'I'm just shutting up. It'll be quiet in here in a few minutes, if you like to wait.'

Major Curtis waited; Mr Robertson came out of the post office section and closed the street door. One by one the customers were shown out; he saw the shopkeeper go to his wife, and say a word to her quietly; they glanced at him and the girl. He crossed over to the counter and said to her: 'Miss Trefusis? Could I have a word or two with you?'

She said nervously: 'With me?'

'Yes,' he said. 'I guess you know what it's about. I've been sent down from Headquarters over this court martial there's to be about your trouble. Would you tell me a few things?'

She said: 'I told one officer about it the day after, when he came. I don't want to talk about it any more.'

'I know that,' he said. 'I don't like worrying you, Miss Trefusis. But that colored boy, he's in a mighty serious position. He can go to prison for five years upon a charge like this. Well, that's fair enough and quite right if he did what he's charged with, but we want to be sure there isn't any doubt about the matter. Five years in prison is a mighty long time, if there was any mistake.'

She was silent.

'We all want to do what's proper and what's right,' he said. 'We've got to stop things like this happening, so you girls can go about your own streets safe at night. But we've got to be fair all round, fair to you and fair to him. There's just one or two things I want to ask you, to check up with his own story. Will you tell me?'

She said: 'All right.'

He smiled at her. 'How long have you worked here, Miss Trefusis?'

She looked up at him in surprise. 'Here? I come here about three years ago, after school.'

'Live in Trenarth all your life?'

She shook her head. 'We lived at Wadebridge first of all; my Dad, he works on the railway. He got moved here when I was about seven.'

Major Curtis nodded. He knew Wadebridge, another little town in Cornwall not much bigger than Trenarth. 'That about ten years back?'

'That's right.'

He glanced down at the little packages she had been making up, of butter and of cheese. 'They the day's rations?' he inquired. 'Do you spend all your time doing up those things?'

She stared at him. 'Week, you mean. We don't make up rations by the day.' She took one up. 'That's butter for a week, that is.'

'Gee,' he said. 'It doesn't look like much.'

'It's not much,' she retorted. 'Two ounces.'

'Do you get bored with it?' he asked. 'Making up those little packets all the time?'

'Well, I dunno,' she said. 'You've got to do something.'

He leaned casually against the counter; she was beginning to talk freely. 'Do you get many of our soldiers in here?' he inquired. 'Americans, I mean?'

She said: 'Not very many—just a few. I don't think there's much for them here. They aren't allowed to buy the rationed foods. Some of them come into the post office.'

He asked: 'Do any of them get fresh?'

She tossed her head. 'Some of the white ones try and be funny. I think they're awfully silly.'

'Don't the black ones ever get that way?'

She said: 'Oh no. They've got ever such good manners.'

Major Mark T. Curtis laughed within himself and thought, that's one for you. Aloud he said:

'Tell me, you knew this boy you had your trouble with a little bit, didn't you?'

She said: 'I wouldn't call it knowing him. He used to come in here for cigarettes.'

'Did you wait on him?'

'If I was about. I do the cigarettes and Maggie does the sweets. It's easier for one person to remember all the different prices of them things.'

'What did he used to buy?'

'Player's.'

'How many? Fifty or a hundred?'

'Oh no. We couldn't sell that many to one customer. He used to buy ten.'

'Just a little packet of ten Player's?'

'That's right.'

'They couldn't have lasted him long.'

'They didn't. He was in here almost every day.'

'How long did he keep on coming in like that?'

'Oh, a long time. Nigh on three weeks, maybe.'

'He didn't get fresh?'

'Oh no, sir—the black ones never do. I was telling you.'

Major Curtis said: 'Ever strike you, Miss Trefusis, that he came in to see you?'

She dropped her eyes. 'I dunno.'

The officer said: 'Be fair to him. He's in a mighty lot of trouble over this. If he kind of admired you, Miss Trefusis, well, there's nothing wrong with that.' He stopped rather suddenly, in mid oration. He had been about to say that a cat could look at a king, but it occurred to him that that might not apply to a Negro and a white girl.

She said in a low tone: 'Well, it did seem sort of funny that he came here so often.'

The major veered off on another tack, fearing to dwell too long upon a delicate point. 'Do you go to the movies much?' he asked.

She looked up, surprised. 'Oh yes, I think they're ever so nice. We close Saturday afternoons, and we go then.'

'To Penzance?'

She nodded. 'There's two lovely picture houses there, the Empire and the Regal. They get ever such good pictures.'

'Who do you go with?'

She said: 'Nellie Hunter, or Jane Penlee, mostly. Sometimes I go with Ma.'

'Are those ones that you mentioned school friends?'

'That's right.'

He smiled at her. 'Ever go with a boy?'

She shook her head. 'Not alone.'

He smiled more broadly. 'Ever been asked?'

She laughed shyly. 'Not yet.'

'Oh well,' he said, 'I guess there's plenty of time.' And still smiling at her, he asked: 'Suppose this colored boy had asked you to go to the movies with him, would you have gone?'

The smile died from her face. 'I dunno. You mean, before he done what he did?'

'That's right, Miss Trefusis. Suppose he'd brought a colored friend along with him and suggested that you brought one of your friends, and you all made a party and went to the movies together, would you have gone?'

She said: 'I wouldn't know, not after seeing how he could behave. I might have done before, when I didn't know.'

'You weren't afraid of him, before this happened?'

She shook her head.

'Was it a great surprise to you, when he behaved so badly?'

The girl said: 'Well, yes, it was. I'd never have expected him to do a thing like that. He always seemed so quiet.'

The major said: 'I had a talk in hospital with him this afternoon. He told me he wanted to ask you something that night, but things kind of went wrong. Would you like to know what it was he wanted to ask you?'

She nodded.

'He wanted to ask you if you'd like to take a little walk with him one evening. He was mighty lonely, and he wanted somebody to talk to. He didn't like to ask you in the shop, because he didn't want to embarrass you, in front of other people. So he waited for you outside. He began waiting at six o'clock that evening, hoping he'd meet you alone and be able to ask you without other people hearing. He didn't get his chance till ten o'clock at night, and he thought it was too late to ask you. I guess he got kind of confused then, and just naturally kissed you. He's mighty sorry now.'

'So he should be,' the girl said indignantly, 'doing a thing like that!' And then she said: 'Why ever didn't he say, if he wanted me to go for a walk with him? I wouldn't have been cross.'

Major Curtis said: 'It must be mighty difficult for a colored boy to ask a white girl that. He wouldn't dare to do it back in his home town.'

'Because of his colour?'

'That's right. That's one of the things that got him all confused.'

The girl said thoughtfully: 'I wouldn't have minded. I might not have gone with him, but I wouldn't have minded him asking.'

The officer said: 'There's just one thing, Miss Trefusis, where his account doesn't check up with what Lieutenant Anderson says you told him. What happened when you started struggling? Did he let you go, or did he hang on?'

She said: 'I was ever so frightened. I don't really know.' She thought for a minute. 'I ran round the corner and bumped right into another man, that fat policeman.'

'That's not what the lieutenant put in his report. He said that the Negro didn't let you go until the policeman came. It makes a big difference,' he explained, 'whether he let you go at once, or not until the policeman came.'

She said: 'I think he must have let go. I think he must have done. He wasn't all that bad.'

'It's not quite what you told Lieutenant Anderson.'

She said: 'I don't remember what I did say. Ma did most of the talking.'

'The boy himself says he let go at once.'

'I was ever so frightened,' she repeated. 'I think maybe he did. It's kind of silly to be frightened of things, isn't it?'

'I don't know about that,' the major said. 'What he did was quite enough to frighten anyone. He acted very wrongly. But he's taken a good deal of punishment, one way and another. Do you want us to go on with this court martial, Miss Trefusis?'

She looked up at him. 'I never asked you to start no court martial,' she said. 'You did that yourselves. No one ever asked me anything about it.'

He smiled. 'I guess that's so. Would you be content if we just drop the charge against him, and let the matter be?'

'I don't want you to charge him with anything,' she said. The mother flared up in her. 'If ever I see him again I'll give him a piece of my mind, acting like he did. But you don't have to send him to prison, not on my account.'

The officer said: 'I think that's real generous of you, Miss Trefusis. It's in your hands. We're over here and in your country, and we want to do right by you Britishers. If you say charge him, then he'll go for a court martial, and he'll get what he'd get if he behaved that way back in his own State, and that's plenty. If you say let him off, why then we'll reckon that he's had sufficient punishment for discipline already, and just leave the matter be.'

The girl said: 'Well, I'd say, let him off.'

He said: 'Well, that's what I think, too.' He felt mentally refreshed by the mere fact that he himself had been talking to a girl for the last twenty minutes; it was a long time since he had done that. He said: 'These boys when they're a long way from home, they get so darned lonely, Miss Trefusis, they'd give just anything to sit and talk a little with a girl. Maybe you wouldn't know about that, but it's true. You don't want to be too hard on them when these things happen.'

She said: 'It must be terrible to be so far away from everything you know.'

The major put his thumbs in his belt, and straightened up to go. 'Well, that's the way things are in wartime, and we can't change it.' He paused for a minute. 'There was just one thing,' he said. 'Lesurier said to tell you he was mighty sorry he did that to you. He didn't mean to frighten you. It just kind of happened.'

She said: 'Did he say that? I'm sorry I got frightened.' And then she hesitated, and said: 'Will he be coming back here, after he comes out of hospital?'

The major shook his head. 'Not after this. He'll be drafted to another theatre of war altogether probably.'

He said goodbye to her, and walked out and down the street to where his jeep was waiting for him in front of the White Hart. He looked in to see Mr Frobisher, and found the landlord at his tea. He refused an invitation to join the meal. 'I just stepped off to say it's all okay about the court martial,' he said. 'I had a talk with Miss Trefusis. She doesn't want us to go on with it. I'll have to make out my report in those terms for the Staff Judge-Advocate. I'd say he'll wash it out.'

'Aye?' said Mr Frobisher. 'Well, that's a good thing, to my way of thinking.'

'And to mine,' the major said. 'I just looked in to let you know.'

He went out and got into his jeep, and drove up to the camp. Mr Frobisher went back to his tea, gratified with the success he had achieved, and told his daughter Bessie all about it. Half an hour later Bessie was telling Sergeant Lorimer; an hour later it was all round the village.

Up in the camp Major Mark T. Curtis sat with Colonel McCulloch facing him across the office desk. 'I guess we'll have to drop the whole thing, Colonel,' he was saying. 'We haven't got a case.'

'Not got a case against a goddam nigger when he catches a white girl in a dark street and kisses her against her will?' the colonel asked indignantly.

'No, *sir*. If she'd been six months older, she wouldn't have taken it so seriously. As things are, she won't give evidence against him.'

Colonel McCulloch started in and told the major just exactly what he thought of British girls. It lasted for ten minutes, till the major had to leave to catch his train.

Down in the White Hart the Negroes were jubilant and, curiously, much more interested in the war; they listened to the nine o'clock news in almost complete silence. During the evening a Negro hand pulled the cardboard placard out of the window; with furtive laughter they added three words to it, and put it back again. It stayed there all next day till somebody called Mr Frobisher's attention to it, reading:

THIS HOUSE IS FOR ENGLISHMEN AND
COLOURED AMERICAN TROOPS ONLY
and General Eisenhower

Mr Frobisher took it out of the window and stuck it down beside his chair in the back parlour. It seemed to him that it had served its turn.

Next evening, when the Negroes came down to the White Hart, they came with long faces. They had spent all day packing up; they had received surprise orders for a move to some new and unknown location. In any case, their work was practically finished; they would move along and make another airfield somewhere else.

They brought a present of a ham and box of cigars for Mr Frobisher, and a huge box of candies and a dozen pairs of sheer silk stockings for Bessie. 'We been treated mighty nice since we been here,' said Sergeant Lorimer. 'The boys all say they never liked a place so much as this.'

At closing time they left for the last time. Exhausted with all the leave-taking and handshaking, Mr Frobisher stood with his daughter waving to the last of them as they went up the street towards the camp. They vanished out of sight, and Mr Frobisher moved slowly to shoot the bolts of the street door.

'Er, well,' he said, straightening up, 'that's the end o' that.'

His daughter said, a little wistfully: 'Do you think we'll ever see any of them again?'

Her father shook his head. 'Soldiers come and go in times like these,' he said. 'We'll never see them no more.'

9

Mr Turner slept quietly and well that night, his last night in Mandinaung. Morgan had sent a boy running to Danubyu with a telegram reserving him a passage on a plane for England; Mr Turner slept in the knowledge that in a week or so he would be back home in Watford telling Mollie all about it. He felt that he would like to do that. He had parted from his wife on different terms from those which were his custom; he wanted to get back to her, and see her again, and tell her all that he had done. And he was very anxious to get home to Watford before he had another fall. He knew that would happen sometime. He wanted to be with someone who would look after him when it did happen.

He woke at dawn and turned back his net, rested and at ease, and lay and watched the light creep up over the wide river. The white cat, Moung Payah, walked in at the doorless entrance to his room, jumped up on to his bed, and lay down beside him; Mr Turner said: 'Hullo, puss,' and lay stroking its head and tickling its ear. He was a little saddened at the thought that he was leaving Burma, so soon after his arrival; he would have liked to stay longer, to see more. Nay Htohn had pointed out the ridge of the Pegu Yoma on the far horizon and told him it was lovely there; she had urged him to stay a little longer, and get up into the hills of the Shan States. Others would see these places, but not he. Burma for Mr Turner was a thought of loveliness. He had seen a fringe of it and knew that it was there; he would carry that knowledge back with him to Watford, enlarged and enriched by it, content if not satisfied.

He was with Nay Htohn alone for a few minutes after breakfast, on the veranda as they waited for the steamer to come into sight around the bend of the river. 'When you see his mother,' she said quietly, 'try and make her like me. I know she does not like me now. That is curious, because we have never met. I know that it is difficult for old people in England to understand a mixed marriage like ours. It's difficult here, too. Some of my aunts think that I have done a dreadful thing in marrying an Englishman. But we have been very happy so far, and I do not fear the future. Try and make his mother understand.'

Mr Turner said: 'I'll try. I'll go and tell her just how you live, and what you have for dinner, and how you run the house, and that. But you mustn't expect too much. She's old, and she's an invalid, too. I don't think she ever goes out.'

She smiled. 'That is the trouble with the English,' she said. 'They so seldom go out, to see for themselves.'

He sat talking to Morgan and his wife until the steamer came in sight up the river; then they got into the jeep and drove down to the jetty. The steamer came in and berthed for her few minutes stay; Morgan carried Mr Turner's suitcase on board and found his cabin. They went out on deck, and found the captain waiting for Morgan to go ashore before casting off.

Morgan held out his hand. 'Well, this is goodbye,' he said. 'Thanks a lot for coming, Turner. If ever you get a chance, come out for a longer stay and I'll take you up country for a tour.' He said that because it is the sort of thing you do say, even when you know, or perhaps because you do know, that it can never happen.

Mr Turner shook his hand. 'You've seen the last o' me,' he said simply. 'I'd like to have seen the Shan Hills, an' all that, but I won't now. Still, I've seen things I never thought to see when I was working in the flour business. I'll go an' see your mother, soon as I get back.'

Nay Htohn said: 'Goodbye, Mr Turner. We are very proud to have had you staying in our house.'

He smiled, thinking that at last her perfect English had betrayed her. 'Wish I could have stayed a bit longer,' he said. 'But I got to be getting on.' He grinned. 'I haven't got much time.'

They went on to the jetty; the moorings were cast off, and the steamer pulled out into the stream. Morgan and Nay Htohn stood close together waving; Mr Turner stood upon the upper deck waving to them in turn until they dwindled in the distance, and were gone.

The captain, a Burman, paused by him, and said: 'You have been staying with Mr Morgan?'

'Aye,' said Mr Turner, 'just for a day or two. I haven't seen him since the war.'

The captain said: 'He is a very fine man, and he married into a very good family. One day he will be a member of the Government.'

Mr Turner settled down in a deckchair, smoking his cheroot and figuring the cost of it as the river scene passed by him. Cheroots in Mandinaung cost two rupees twelve annas for a hundred, or about three a penny, a price which Nay Htohn considered to be gross extortion and nearly double what they should be. They were good big cigars, mild and satisfying, with a filter tip of pith; Mr Turner considered that in a London shop they were worth a shilling of anybody's money. He had no intention of returning to London out of pocket by this journey. He travelled thoughtfully down river, and when he reached Rangoon he telephoned to his Chinese agent, Mr S.O. Chang, from his hotel bedroom, sitting on the bed as he would have done in Birmingham or Hull. He said:

'Afternoon, Mr Chang—I just got back from Mandinaung. Yes, I had a very good time. I'm leaving for England day after tomorrow, but before I go I thought it would be kind of nice to ship a few of these Burma cheroots back home, and see what I could do with them. You know, the Danubyu ones with the filter tip. Suppose a chap wanted to buy a little parcel of them, say about twenty thousand, how would he set about it?'

Mr Chang told him, thrusting his own finger deep into the pie. Mr Turner pulled it out a bit next day, and left for England at the end of the week having seen the packing cases sealed and delivered to the shipping company. He travelled home by air, as he had come, in a great flying boat from the Rangoon river. For four days he dozed across the world, rested and relaxed in the cool air as the burning deserts of Sind and Arabia passed slowly far below and gave place to the Libyan sands, the blue wastes of the Mediterranean, and the small fields of France. He ate a good deal and slept a good deal, and he got back to England at the beginning of August, just a month from the day he left.

He had not told his wife which day he was arriving because he did not know himself; from the Airway terminus he took a taxi to the Underground and travelled out to Watford carrying his bag, as he had done so many times returning from a business trip into the provinces. It was a warm afternoon, so he took a taxi at the station, and he opened his front door with his latchkey, and walked in.

The house was empty, but there was food and fresh milk in the larder, and the kettle on the gas stove was still fairly warm; he diagnosed that his wife had been there at lunchtime and had made herself a cup of tea. 'At the pictures,' he said thoughtfully, 'or else over with Laura.' He did not resent her absence, for he had not told her when he was arriving. He prowled around the house for a short time, savouring his old familiar things, and presently he found the *Daily Express*, and carried a deckchair out into the garden, and sat down to read the paper. But in a very short time it was draped across his face, and he was lying back at ease.

Funny to think that Mollie was at the pictures, and Nay Htohn, she liked the pictures, just the same. The same pictures, too. Funny to think that Nay Htohn was living seven thousand miles away, right the other side of the world. Funny the way he'd sort of felt at home in her house, spite of everything being different.

He slept.

His wife, returning from the pictures, came to the French window of the sitting-room and saw him sitting there asleep on the lawn of their long, narrow strip of garden; her heart leaped at the sight of him, for she had missed him very much. The knowledge that she would not have him for much longer had given him an added value to her; she had wanted to meet him on his way home from so long a journey, and to make him welcome. He had eluded her, and here he was, as always, asleep with a newspaper across his face, as though he had been no farther than the office or the warehouse at Gravesend. A momentary wave of disappointment swept over her, and irritation; she had wanted so much to do something special for him, and the opportunity was gone.

She walked down the garden and stood by his chair. 'Well, you're a fine one,' she said amiably, 'slinking in like that without a word, and going off to sleep with a newspaper, after being half across the world and all. Ain't you got no romance in you?'

He opened his eyes, and brushed away the paper. 'Hullo,' he said vaguely. 'I must have dropped off.'

'I'll say you did.' She smiled down at him. 'You might have let me know when you were coming. I'd have come to meet you, or something.'

He said: 'I didn't know myself.'

'Did you have a good trip? You're home much quicker than I thought you'd be, going all that way. It's only just a month since you left.'

'Aye,' he said, 'just about a month. There wasn't much to do when I got there, so I come home again.'

She said: 'Pretty hopeless, was it?'

He looked up. 'Hopeless? What d'you mean?'

'This chap that you went out to see, the pilot fellow. Couldn't you do nothing for him?'

'*For* him?' Mr Turner smiled thoughtfully. 'I got a bit of a surprise,' he said. 'It's not like we thought at all. He's got a better job than I have, and lives ever so much better, too. Great big house he lives in, with about five servants. He's all right.'

She said, puzzled: 'But I thought he lived with a native woman.' And then, curiously: 'Did you see her?'

'Aye,' said Mr Turner. 'As nice a girl as any that you'd find in Watford, or in Harrow either. It's quite different to what we thought.'

She looked at him doubtfully. 'Could she speak any English?'

'Better 'n you or me,' said Mr Turner. 'I tell you, Mr Morgan done very well for himself when he got rid of the other one and married her. Two lovely little kids, they've got.'

She said impulsively: 'But whatever colour are the children?'

'Yellowy,' he replied. 'Sort of half and half, you might say.'

'How awful!'

'I dunno,' said Mr Turner. 'Things look sort of different out there to what they do back here. Let's have a cup o' tea, and I'll tell you.'

She studied him with some concern over tea. In the month that he had been away he had changed, and not for the better. He seemed well and cheerful, but a little shrunken and with a good deal less energy. The disability of his right hand was markedly increased, and he had difficulty in using it for cutting up his food with a knife; he made increasing use of his left hand. She realized heavily that this was one of the things that must be; from now onwards he would need her more and more.

She said: 'How have you been, in yourself, Jackie? Had any pain, or any of them dizzy fits?'

He said: 'I had a fall, 'n passed out for three hours.'

'Three hours!' She was appalled. 'Was anyone with you?'

He told her how it had happened, and what had been done. 'They couldn't have been nicer,' he said. 'No one couldn't have done more. There wasn't any doctor in the place, but I didn't need one. I got over it all right.'

She said: 'You'd better see Doctor Worth, now you're back.'

'I don't want to go seeing no more doctors,' Mr Turner replied. 'I know what's coming, 'n there's no good belly-aching about it, wasting people's time.'

They took another chair out into the garden, and sat together while he told her all about his journey, and what he had seen and heard. It took an hour. She listened carefully, trying to understand the changes that had taken place in his outlook. At last she said:

'Well, what are you going to do now, Jackie? Going to try it in the office?'

She had worked herself for several years in an office. She knew that managements are generally kind to the individual, especially where the individual is known. In asking if he was going to try it in the office, she knew that in his case there would be no harsh dividing line between employment and sick leave; so long as he showed his face now and then and did a bit of work when he could manage it, he would draw his salary all right. Sick leave for Mr Turner would begin when he had not shown up for a consecutive fortnight or so, not till then.

He said: 'I think so.' He thought for a minute, and then said: 'I got to think about them other two, the corporal and the nigger. I'm not so much worried about the nigger, now; it looks like he got off all right. I would like to know about that Corporal Brent, though.'

She said: 'I wouldn't bother about the nigger any more, Jackie. He'll be back in Nashville or some place like that. He'll be all right.'

'Aye,' he said slowly, 'I think he's all right. I don't think I'll do much about him. It's just Duggie Brent now.'

His wife said: 'I expect he's all right, too.'

'Maybe,' said Mr Turner thoughtfully. 'But I'd like to know.'

In the distance they heard the church clock strike six. Mollie asked what he wanted to do that evening, and Mr Turner said at once that perhaps it would be nice to take a run out to the Barley Mow. She vetoed that, upon the score that he was tired after his journey, and won her case. Instead they talked about his journey and about her refresher course in shorthand typing, and presently they moved indoors as it grew cool and put the wireless on, and listened to *Itma* with Tommy Handley, and Lady Sonly, and Inspector Ankles, and the Colonel, and Naïve, and Mr Turner who had missed this programme very much while he had been in Burma laughed until the tears came to his eyes, while fifteen million other people in the British Islands did the same.

He went down to the office next day, only a day or two adrift upon his holiday time, and found a little work to do, and told the managing director about Mr S.O.Chang in far Rangoon. Secretly they were all rather shocked to see the change in him; if Mr Parkinson had wanted any confirmation of the sentence of death passed on Turner, he found it in the change in his appearance.

He went back to the office after lunch for a short time, and then went out and took a bus to Notting Hill Gate. He walked slowly through the streets to Ladbroke Square, and walked up the steps, and knocked on the door. Again, it was opened to him by Morgan's sister, as it had been only about five weeks before.

'Good afternoon,' he said.

The girl said: 'Oh–it's you.'

'Aye,' he said, 'it's me all right. I've been staying with your brother, out in Mandinaung, Miss Morgan. I told him that I'd come and see you when I got back home. I got some things to tell his mother.'

She stared at him. 'You say you've been staying with my brother, out in Burma?'

'That's right.'

She did not move from the door, or ask him in. 'You can't have been,' she said suspiciously. 'You were only here the other day.'

He said: 'I flew out, and flew back again; I was in Burma just on a fortnight. I was staying with your brother Thursday of last week.'

'But that's fantastic . . .' She moved aside, still only half convinced that this was not some imposition. 'Come in, Mr Turner.'

She took him up to the first floor drawing-room. The mother was not there, and one of the long windows was open, letting in fresh air and sunlight to the room. 'Yes,' he said, 'I made a very quick trip, but I got time to spend a few days with your brother, up at Mandinaung.'

'At Mandinaung? You went and saw him there?'

'That's right. He gave me a fine time.'

She stared at him. 'But could he . . . where did you stay?'

Mr Turner said: 'I don't know as you've got the right idea of how he lives, Miss Morgan. He's got a great big house, 'n servants, 'n a good job, too. It's true enough he lived in a palm hut for a while after the war, same as any young couple might live in a prefab when they start off first. But now he's built himself a great big house outside the town. Real lovely that house is,' he said, a little wistfully. 'He's living better than what I do, or what you do here.'

The girl said: 'He did mention something about a new house, once. . . .' She glanced at Mr Turner. 'I'm afraid we don't know as much about my brother as we ought to,' she said. 'There was–well, something of a breach when he married that native woman. We don't hear from him very often.' She paused, and then said: 'Did you see her?'

'Aye,' said Mr Turner, 'I saw quite a lot of her. As nice a girl as any that you'd find, in this country or any other.'

She stared at him, incredulous, and then asked, as Mollie had: 'Can she speak any English?'

He felt at a loss, not knowing where to begin. 'She speaks better'n what I do, by a long chalk,' he said. 'She's a very well educated girl, Miss Morgan, and come of a good family too. I think your brother done all right for himself, marrying her, if you ask me.'

She said: 'But they lived in a palm hut in the jungle!'

The wheel had gone the full circle, and Mr Turner started again, patiently. He talked for half an hour, telling her about the house, the meals, the furniture, the children, the servants; he told her everything that he could think of about life in Mandinaung. As he talked, there came into his mind the figure of Nay Htohn, wistful. 'That is the trouble with the English,' she had said. 'They so seldom go out, to see for themselves.' He talked to Morgan's sister with the figure of the Burman girl before his eyes, and he talked for nearly half an hour, and he was very tired by the time he had done.

A uniformed nurse came into the room, hesitated at the door on seeing Turner, and went out again. The girl said: 'My mother is ill, Mr Turner, or I should have liked her to see you, and to hear all this. But I'm afraid she is too ill to see you now.'

'That don't matter,' he said, 'I'll look in some other time, when she's up and about again.'

The girl hesitated. 'That's very kind of you,' she said at last. 'My mother had a stroke, soon after you were here before. She's very ill. If she recovers sufficiently, I will let you know. But she's made no progress in the last three weeks and the doctor tells me I must be prepared for anything.'

'Dying, eh?' said Mr Turner.

She nodded, and her eyes were very full.

'Well, there's a pair of us,' he said cheerfully. 'I'm dying, too.' The girl stared at him indignantly. 'It's a fact,' he said. 'This wound in my old napper's going wrong on me.' She glanced involuntarily at the great wound on his forehead, red and angry. 'I got till next April, not longer, and I don't reckon that I'll be in circulation after Christmas. I've had it, Miss Morgan. But what the hell? All be the same in a hundred years, that's what I say.'

She said, rather at a loss: 'I am so sorry.'

'So am I,' said Mr Turner. 'I'd like to have gone on a bit longer, but that's the way it is.' He thought for a minute. 'I think you should go out and stay with your brother,' he said at last. 'After your mother's gone, that is. I think you ought to go and see with your own eyes how different it all is to what you think. It don't cost much to go, considering what you'd get out of it.'

She said seriously: 'I'll think that over, Mr Turner. You've given me a lot to think about.'

He said: 'You won't be seeing me again, Miss Morgan, I don't suppose, because of what I told you.' He got to his feet to go. 'So just remember this. When your Ma dies, you write out to your brother, 'n go out and spend a few months with him, 'n get to know your sister-in-law. You girls are of an age and educated much the same; you'll hit it off with her all right if you can just forget what folks have told you about colour and judge for yourself from what you see with your own eyes. I don't ask more than that. Just make up your own mind from what you see with your own eyes.' He picked up his hat. 'Well, I must be getting along.'

He left the house, and travelled back to Watford on the Underground, and arrived home in time for tea. Mollie was expecting him and had a kipper for him and a great slab of cherry cake and strawberry jam, all the delicacies that Mr Turner liked the most. And relaxing in a deckchair after this repast, and looking at the roses, and smoking his pipe, Mr Turner felt that there was a great deal to be said for Watford whatever the charms of Burma. And presently, when Mollie came from washing up the tea, he said:

'Like to take a run out to the Barley Mow this evening?'

She smiled tolerantly. 'If you like.'

So presently they got out the little seven-year-old Ford and started down the arterial road in the cool evening. They got to the Barley Mow at about a quarter to nine and parked the car with all the others, and went into the saloon bar. It was full of light and smoke and good company; all his old familiar cronies were there, George Harris, and Gillie Simmonds with a new girl friend on the stage, and fat old Dickie Watson the bookie. In that atmosphere Mr Turner drank his beer and came out like the flower.

He told them the story of the temperance lecture and the glass of whisky and the worm, and he told them the one about the lecture upon psychic research and the goat. He was a very good raconteur and told a dubious story well; standing in the middle of the crowd by the bar, flushed with beer and with the great wound in his forehead red and pulsing, he was in his element. He never thought to tell them he had been in Burma but he told them about the schoolmistress and the little girl who lisped, and about the man who climbed up on the wall of the lunatic asylum and found out all about Hipposexology. He had an inexhaustible supply of these stories, all somewhat juvenile, all certain of a laugh when told as Jackie Turner told them. The men enjoyed his company tremendously; the women stood by faintly bored and brightly cheerful, with one eye covertly upon the clock.

He tired presently, more quickly than he used to, and stood listening to other people's anecdotes and stories with a mug of beer clasped in his hand. A broad shouldered young man dressed in a black coat and dark grey striped trousers told a very legal story about a man who had half his house requisitioned as a Wrennery and went on living in the other half, which was a Roman bastion and so an Ancient Monument, and immune, and what came of it all. Mr Turner found himself beside this young man presently, and said:

'You in the law business?'

The other nodded. 'I'm a junior clerk in Sir Almroth Hopkinson's chambers, in the Temple.'

Mr Turner took a sup of beer, and thought for a moment. 'Suppose one wanted to find out what happened in a trial back in 1943,' he said. 'How would one set about it?'

'Get somebody to look it up in the register.'

'Can anyone do that?'

The young man shook his head. 'You'd have to do it through a solicitor.' He glanced at Mr Turner. 'What sort of case was it?'

'A murder.'

'Murder? Do you remember the name of the prisoner?'

'Brent. Douglas Theodore Brent. A corporal he was, in the Parachute Regiment.'

'Rex *v.* Brent . . .' The young man stared at him absently. 'Wait now, Rex *v.* Brent . . . He got off didn't he? Manslaughter, was it?'

'I dunno,' said Mr Turner. 'That's what I want to find out.'

'Rex *v.* Brent,' the young man said again. 'I've heard about that case. I know. Stanier. Marcus Stanier. That's right. He was defended by a chap called Carter in Sir Phillip Bell's chambers. A man called Marcus Stanier is a clerk there now. It was he who told me about it. That's right. I could find out about it, if you like.'

'I'll be real glad if you would,' said Mr Turner. 'I was in hospital with him just before. I've always thought I'd like to know.'

They exchanged names and telephone numbers; Mr Turner learned that the young man was Mr Viner. He rang up Mr Viner the next afternoon from the office.

Viner said: 'Oh yes. I've got a copy of the transcript of the shorthand note of the trial here, Mr Turner, taken for the Judge-Advocate-General. And I've got counsel's notes for his speech. Marcus Stanier brought them over this morning; I said I'd let him have them back tomorrow. Matter of fact I've been reading it myself–it's quite an interesting case. He got six months for manslaughter.'

'That all?' said Mr Turner in surprise. 'It don't sound much. He reckoned he was charged with murder.'

'That's right,' said Mr Viner. 'But he had a very good counsel, a very unusual counsel, I may say. Would you like to see the papers?'

'I would,' said Mr Turner. 'If I slip over now, could I have a read at them?'

He went out and took a bus down to the Temple, and found the chambers with some difficulty. Mr Viner sat him down in a little badly lit outer office full of books and packets of old briefs and coats and hats, and gave him a dusty carbon copy of the shorthand transcript, Rex *v.* Douglas Theodore Brent. With it there was a dog-eared, marble paper covered book of pencilled manuscript, now smudged and faded, labelled P.C.CARTER.

The Judge was Mr Justice Lambourn, the prosecuting counsel Mr Constantine Paget, KC, with Mr Peter Melrose for his junior, and the defending counsel Mr P. C. Carter. In the opening formalities the Judge had asked: 'And for the defence?'

Major Carter stood up in the front bench. He did not wear wig and gown. He wore a uniform practically identical with that of the prisoner, with the emblem of the Parachute Regiment upon the shoulder of his rough serge battledress; the crown upon his epaulette was the only distinction between them. 'May it please your Lordship,' he said, 'I appear for the prisoner.'

The Judge glanced slowly from the counsel to the prisoner, and back to the counsel. A thin, wintry smile appeared upon his lips. He bowed slightly. 'Very well, Mr Carter. You are for the defence.' He leaned back in his seat. 'Proceed.'

Mr Constantine Paget stood up, a sheaf of papers in his hand, and opened the case for the Crown. The case concerned, he said, a Mr Michael Seddon, a boilermaker by trade, who met his death in the Miller Hospital at Greenwich as a result of injuries sustained outside a public house known as the Goat and Compasses in Albion Street, New Cross, upon the night of March 22nd, 1943. He would call evidence to prove a quarrel between the deceased man and the defendant in the public house, and to prove that this quarrel continued in the street after closing time, which was ten-thirty. He would call medical evidence relating to the injuries that the deceased sustained. He would call evidence to show the court that the defendant was a man of violent passions, and he would bring to the court the only witness of the struggle which resulted in the fatal injuries to the deceased, the young lady friend of the defendant. With this evidence he would show the court that here was a case of wilful murder, and he would ask the jury for a conviction in those terms.

He then proceeded to call the barman who gave evidence of the quarrel, and the landlord's daughter who gave evidence about the telephone call received ten minutes after closing time from an unknown caller. He called the house surgeon of the Miller Hospital for evidence of the cause of death. For the violent passions, he called a Mr Isidore Levy, a commission agent of Southampton, who deputed that in 1942 the defendant and another man had come in and wrecked his office and injured him so severely that he had to spend a week in bed, following an argument about paying out after a dog race. In cross-examination by Mr Carter, this witness admitted that he had not brought the matter to the notice of the police, for business reasons. Finally Mr Constantine Paget produced a most reluctant Phyllis Styles of the A.T.S. and put her in the box, and examined her on her sworn deposition in the police court, proving what had taken place outside the pub.

Major Carter rose to cross-examine her; she knew he was a friend of Duggie's and greeted him with a bright smile. 'Miss Styles,' he said, 'what was the original cause of this quarrel in the public house? What happened first of all?'

'He started saying ever such rude things to Duggie,' she said at once. 'He'd had a bit too much.'

The counsel said: 'Well, let's leave that for the moment. Will you tell us, what exactly did he say?'

Patiently he extracted from her, for the benefit of the jury, all that Mr Seddon had thought fit to say about the paratrooper's fancy hat. 'This hat that caused so much trouble,' he inquired. 'What sort of hat was it?'

She said: 'His beret. You know, what they all wear now.'

Major Carter reached down to the seat beside him and picked up his own magenta beret, and held it up. 'To make the matter quite clear, Miss Styles, was it a hat like that?'

She said: 'That's right, sir, just like yours. The Parachute beret.'

The counsel glanced towards the jury, and dropped his beret back on to the seat beside him; a faint smile crossed the features of the Judge. Major Carter went on and took her through the entire quarrel; the court heard all Mr Seddon's opinions of the work done by the Army and his views upon the Second Front. And after ten minutes of all this, he said:

'And now, Miss Styles, I want you to tell the court exactly what the deceased man last said before he was attacked by Corporal Brent.' He turned to the Judge. 'May it please your Lordship, it may well be that the court would wish that the witness should write down the answer to this question, rather than give a verbal answer.'

The Judge looked at the girl, slim and erect in her A.T.S. uniform. 'Would you rather write down the words that the deceased man used?' he said.

But Private Phyllis Styles had seen two years of service in an A.A. battery, and had few inhibitions. 'I don't mind saying it if you don't mind hearing it,' she replied. 'He said I was a mucking Army tart, wearing a fancy tart's hat.' She put her hand up to the gay forage cap tucked under the epaulette of her tunic, and glanced at the jury, as Major Carter had before. 'This one, he meant. Then he give Duggie a terrible kick up his behind and Duggie went for him.'

Mr Constantine Paget leaned back in his seat, stifling a smile. He was going down on this case, he could see, all on account of these blessed hats; he did not greatly care. He doubted if the jury would give murder after what the girl had said. He did not really want them to. His duty was to present the case for the Crown, but not to strive for victory at the expense of what was right. He rose slowly to his feet for re-examination of the witness, and said:

'Now, Miss Styles, what happened after the deceased man used the words that you have told us, and before he kicked Corporal Brent? The corporal said something, didn't he?'

The girl said reluctantly: 'Well, yes, he said he was the scum of bloody Dublin and one or two things like that.'

'Thank you, Miss Styles. And then what happened, after that?'

'Well, he kicked Duggie, like I said.'

'Thank you.' He turned to the Judge. 'My Lord, I have no further evidence to offer.'

Major Carter rose to his feet. 'May it please your Lordship,' he said, 'I have no witnesses with the exception of the accused man, Douglas Theodore Brent, who I propose to bring forward as a witness on his own behalf. I have no hesitation in proceeding in this way because I am convinced that he has nothing to conceal from cross-examination by my learned friend, and because by doing so I shall convince the court not only that no question of murder is involved but also that the deceased man met his death due solely to the circumstances of the war in which this country is engaged.'

The Judge raised his eyebrows. 'Very well.'

Major Carter said: 'Call Douglas Theodore Brent.'

Duggie Brent was taken from the dock by the escort and put into the witness box; he was in uniform and bareheaded. He moved with the quick grace of perfectly developed muscles; his red curly hair was as untidy as ever. In spite of his serious position, he looked tolerably cheerful.

He took his oath, and his counsel started to interrogate him. He gave his age as twenty-two, and the court heard that he had joined the Army at the age of seventeen, in 1938. After the preliminaries, his counsel said:

'Now, Corporal Brent, when you were called up in 1939, were you fully trained?'

'No, sir,' the corporal said. 'I didn't know hardly anything.'

'I see. What weapon were you taught the use of first, after you were called up?'

'The rifle, sir.'

'Yes. Were you taught to shoot with it?'

'Yes, sir.'

'What at?'

'Targets, sir.'

'What sort of targets?'

'Pictures of men advancing in open order, or behind a tank, or that.'

'Yes, pictures of men.' He paused. 'Now after that, corporal, what did they teach you to do next?'

'To attack with the bayonet, sir.'

'Yes. What did you attack?'

'Dummies, sir. Dummies representing enemy soldiers.'

'Yes. What did you have to do with these dummies?'

'Run at them, 'n run them through with the bayonet, sir.'

'As if you were trying to kill them?'

'Yes, sir.'

'I see. How long did this bayonet training go on for?'

Brent hesitated. 'About three months, I think–off and on.'

'And at the end of it, were your instructors satisfied that you could kill a man easily and quickly with the bayonet?'

'Yes, sir. I passed out top of my platoon.'

The counsel said dryly: 'They must have been very pleased with you. How old were you then?'

'Eighteen, sir.'

Mr Justice Lambourn raised his head. 'Mr Carter, is all this relevant to your case?'

The major said: 'If I may have the indulgence of the court, my Lord, I shall show presently that all this is extremely relevant to the case that is before us.'

The Judge leaned back in his chair. 'Very well, Mr Carter.'

The counsel said: 'Now Corporal Brent, what did they teach you to do after that?'

He took the corporal step by step through his whole military education, with a furtive eye upon the jury watching for the first signs of boredom. For twenty minutes he displayed to them the processes by which the corporal had been trained for four years to kill men, to kill them with grenade and flame-thrower, to kill them with the Sten gun and with the beer bottle that went off. And when at last the jury began shuffling and coughing, he said:

'Now, Corporal Brent, you volunteered for the Commandos, did you not?'

Mr Constantine Paget sat up in sudden protest at the lead, and sank back again, watchful of his colleague. It was all wrong, but it would save time.

'Yes, sir.'

'When was that?'

'In June last year, sir.'

'What unit were you sent to?'

'Number Eleven Commando Training Unit, sir.'

'What was the first thing you were taught to do there?'

'Fight with knives, sir. You remember that–you took the course.'

The major said smoothly: 'Well, yes.'

Mr Constantine Paget rose to his feet; he could not let the defence get away with that. 'My Lord,' he said, 'I really must protest. The actions of my learned friend in another place and in another capacity can have no bearing on this case.'

Mr Justice Lambourn raised his head. 'Mr Carter?'

The counsel said: 'My Lord, I did not seek the evidence to which my learned friend objects. But since the matter has been mentioned, it is right that you should know I serve the King in two capacities. I assist in the discovery of the King's justice in these courts. In another capacity and in another place, by order of the King passed to me through his officers, I teach men such as Douglas Theodore Brent to kill other men with knives. I cannot dissociate my two responsibilities to the Monarch, and it is right that this court should know the full extent of the duties that I carry out for him. Moreover, if I may have your indulgence, I shall show my learned friend that this evidence is not irrelevant to the case before us, in its wider aspects.'

There was a long, slow silence in the court. The jury sat tense and alert; there was no boredom now. At last, the Judge inclined his head, smiled faintly, and said: 'Yes, Mr Carter?' Mr Constantine Paget shrugged his shoulders testily, and sat down again.

The counsel turned to the prisoner. 'Yes, I taught you to fight with knives. Were you taught to do this noisily or quietly, Corporal Brent?'

'Quietly, sir.'

'Yes. Were you taught to approach your victim from the front?'

'No, sir. We was to creep up behind him in the dark and stick him in the back.'

'How many ways of doing this were you taught?'

'Three ways, sir.'

The counsel said: 'Yes. I taught you three different ways of creeping up behind a man in the darkness to stab him in the back.' There was dead silence in the court. 'How old were you then, Corporal Brent?'

'Twenty, sir.'

The counsel with supreme artistry bent down and shuffled with his papers, searching for a document; there was a long, painful pause. The foreman of the jury whispered something to the man next to him. Mr Constantine Paget whispered to his junior: 'Fancy letting him go on like this! Lambourn is just giving him the case.' Presently the major straightened up, a paper in his hand.

'Now, Corporal Brent,' he said, 'when you left that course, what course did you go on?'

'Unarmed combat, sir.'

'Yes, you went on to a course in unarmed combat. What did they teach you to do there?'

'We was taught how to attack an armed man just with our hands and feet, sir.'

'Yes. Were you taught to treat him gently?'

'No, sir. We was taught how to kill him.'

'Yes, you were taught how to kill a man with your bare hands, assisted by your feet. How did you get on, Corporal? What grade did you receive on passing out from this course?'

'I was graded "satisfactory", sir.'

'Who signed your grading certificate?'

'Captain Willis, sir.'

The counsel held up the paper in his hand. 'My Lord, I have this grading certificate here, signed by an officer who holds the King's commission, stating that he has trained the prisoner in the form of attack that you have heard described, and that his progress was satisfactory. If my learned friend desires, I will call Captain Willis tomorrow morning to prove this document in evidence, but on account of his urgent military duties I am anxious to avoid that course. If my learned friend can consent to treat this document as if it has been proven, it will assist the progress of the war.'

It was passed up to the Judge, who glanced at it and passed it down to the prosecution. Mr Constantine Paget glanced at it, and nodded. The Judge nodded to Major Carter, who turned to the prisoner, and said:

'Corporal Brent, did anybody ever teach you boxing?'

'No, sir.'

'Apart from this course of unarmed combat, did anybody ever teach you how. to fight with your hands, at any time?'

'No, sir.'

'Was this course the only sort of instruction you have ever had in fighting without a weapon?'

'Yes, sir.'

'Now, Corporal Brent, take your mind back to the night on which this man, Mr Seddon, met his death. When you attacked him on the pavement outside the public house, what were your feelings towards him?'

The corporal hesitated. 'I was kind of blind mad,' he said at last. 'I just went for him.'

'You were very angry with him?'

'Yes, sir. I was.'

'Why was that?'

'Well, sir, on account of what he said about my young lady, and picking on me all evening, and then kicking me up the arse.'

'Yes. Now after he kicked you, did you stop and think what you were going to do?'

'No, sir. I just went for him.'

'How did you go for him? What exactly did you do?'

'I went at him the unarmed combat way, sir, like we had been taught.'

'Yes, like you have been taught. What did you do first?'

'Well, sir, he was facing me, so I gave him a kick in the—in the lower stomach, you might say.'

'Yes, you kicked him in the lower stomach. What happened then?'

'It worked all right, sir, and he bent double, so I could get behind him and get him up against the wall, with my elbow under his chin and my knee in his back.'

'Yes. Where did you learn to do this?'

'On the unarmed combat course, sir.'

'Yes. Now when you applied the pressure with your elbow and your knees to pull his head back, what did you mean to do to him?'

The corporal said: 'Just give him a bit of a tweak, sir. That's all I meant to do. Just hurt him a bit, for saying that about my girl.'

'Yes, you just meant to hurt him slightly. In your instruction at the school of unarmed combat, had anybody told you when to stop the pressure if the man's back was not to be broken?'

'No, sir. We was taught to use all the strength we'd got and finish it.'

'Did you use all your strength on this occasion?'

'No, sir.'

'Are you quite sure of that?'

'Yes, sir. I could have pulled him a lot harder than what I did.'

'Was he struggling?'

'Yes, sir. He was a big chap and much stronger than me. I don't think I'd have stood much of a chance against him in the ordinary way.'

'Now, corporal, when you applied the moderate pressure that you did, what happened?'

'Well, he kind of collapsed, sir, and stopped struggling, so I let him go. And he fell down.'

'Were you surprised when he collapsed?'

'Yes, sir. I couldn't hardly credit it.'

'Why were you surprised?'

'Well, he was a great big chap, sir, about three stone heavier than me. And I wasn't pressing very hard.'

'After he fell down, what did you do next?'

'I went to see if he was all right, and he was sort of breathing hard and groaning.'

'Did he say anything?'

'No, sir. He didn't say nothing that I heard.'

'And what did you do then?'

'I went off to a telephone box and rang up the pub, 'n told them there was a man ill on the pavement outside.'

The counsel turned to the Bench. 'My Lord,' he said, 'I have no more questions to ask the witness.'

Mr Constantine Paget got briskly to his feet. He had little hope now of a murder verdict, and he had no intention of prolonging his cross-examination so that the case would stretch out and occupy another day; he was too busy a man for that. At the same time, he had his duties to perform, and one of those was to make quite sure that if this corporal got away with it he would at any rate remember the case. He said:

'Now, Corporal Brent, when you kicked this man in the lower stomach, did you know that that was a very dangerous thing to do?'

There was an uncertain pause. 'I can't rightly say,' the corporal said at last. 'I didn't think.'

'You didn't think! Do you know that such a kick could quite easily kill a man, in itself?'

'Yes, sir. We was told that on the course.'

'You were told that on the course. Did you know before this fight that such a kick could kill a man?'

There was another pause.

Mr Constantine Paget stared at the prisoner. 'Will you please answer the question. Did you know before you had this fight that such a kick could kill a man?'

'Yes I did. I told you.'

'When you kicked him in this way, then, did you mean to kill this man?'

'No, sir. I didn't think.'

'Why not?'

'Well, sir, he kicked me, and I kicked him.'

Mr Constantine Paget shifted his papers. 'There must have been an interval between these kicks, was there not?'

Major Carter rose to his feet. 'My Lord,' he said. The Judge said: 'If you please, Mr Paget.'

Mr Constantine Paget said testily: 'I will repeat that question in another form. Corporal Brent, was there any interval of time between these kicks?'

The corporal said hesitantly: 'I don't really know. I don't think there was.'

'Why don't you know?'

'I was sort of mad, I suppose.'

'Corporal Brent, remembering that you are giving witness upon oath, do you really mean to tell the jury that when you kicked this man you had no idea of killing him?'

'Yes, sir. I didn't go to kill him.'

Mr Constantine Paget wrapped his gown around him, and sat down. Major Carter got up.

'Now Corporal Brent, when this man kicked you, did it hurt?'

'Yes, sir. He got me right on the spine.'

'Were you in pain, then, when you went for him?'

'Yes, sir. It was hurting something cruel.'

'Is that why you cannot remember quite what you did?'

'Yes, sir.'

'How long did this pain go on for?'

'I dunno,' the corporal said. 'I remember it was pretty fierce when I was telephoning.'

Counsel glanced at the Judge. 'My Lord, I have no more questions.'

Mr Justice Lambourn glanced at the clock, and left his seat murmuring: 'Till two o'clock,' and vanished through a door behind his chair. The clerk said in a loud voice: 'The court is adjourned for one hour and ten minutes.'

After the lunch adjournment the defending counsel addressed the court. He said:

'My Lord and members of the jury, very few of the facts in this case are matters of dispute. We have heard evidence from a number of witnesses that there was a quarrel between these two men, and we have heard from the witness Phyllis Styles the words which the deceased last uttered, which brought the stinging repartee from the defendant, which caused the deceased man to launch the kick which was the first blow in this fight. If I may have the indulgence of the court for a very few moments I would like to speculate on what would have happened if this matter had occurred in peacetime, if Douglas Theodore Brent had never learned the terrible crafts that we have taught him to use against the enemy.'

He glanced up at the Judge a little anxiously, to see if he would be allowed to go on with this line. The grey wig inclined slowly. He went on with more confidence.

'I have little doubt in my own mind that a return blow would have been struck, and normal reasonable men might well agree that such a blow would have been merited. But I have little doubt also that it would have been an unskilled blow, a blow with the hands directed at the face or body. It would not have been the terrible blow that in fact occurred, the fierce, well directed kick at the lower stomach that disabled the deceased. We have heard evidence to the effect that the accused man has had no training whatsoever in the art of fighting other than that provided by the Army. In peacetime, any blow that he might have struck would have been a feeble blow, unlikely to maim or even seriously to inconvenience his powerful opponent, more than three stone heavier than himself.'

He paused. 'I want you to imagine that scene, quite a common one in certain parts of our great cities. There would no doubt have been a return blow from the deceased; there would have been a fight outside the public house that night. There might have been a black eye, a nose might have bled, and both parties might well have appeared before the magistrate next morning upon a charge of disturbing the peace. If that had happened the accused, who now stands before you in the dock upon a charge of murder, might have been fined five shillings, though in view of certain words of provocation which have been repeated in this court it might well be that he would have been convicted and bound over to keep the peace.'

He looked up. 'Members of the jury, I have done with speculation now; the matter did not take that course because at the time of Munich, at the age of seventeen, Douglas Theodore Brent joined the Territorial Army to submit himself to military discipline and training. This very young man volunteered and joined the Army before he was called up because he deemed it was his duty, being vigorous and strong, to serve his country in a time of need. The Army seems to have accepted him without any very great inquiry, and they proceeded to train him in the duties of a modern soldier.'

He paused. 'Well now,' he said at last, 'we have heard in this court today something of these duties. All soldiers are trained to kill men quickly and efficiently; we cannot overlook that this is the very substance of war. Corporal Brent was trained as an infantry soldier; he then volunteered for Commando service, and later for service in the Parachute Regiment. In those units of the Army it is necessary to teach men certain ways of killing the enemy, certain deadly and ruthless ways of ending human life, which are beyond the education of the ordinary soldier. For many months, by the delegated order of the King executed through his officers, this immature young man has learned these deadly crafts.'

He stood in silence for a minute, staring at the foreman of the jury, marshalling his thoughts; in the court there was a long, tense pause. 'I speak of what I know,' he said quietly. 'I have come here to defend this man for other reasons than because I want to take the fee marked on the brief. You have heard it stated in the evidence that I myself taught Douglas Theodore Brent to creep up in the darkness behind an unsuspecting man, and stab him with a knife, and kill him. I taught him to do that in three different ways, so that whatever method of approach was forced on him by circumstances he could kill his man immediately and without noise. I taught him more than that. With other instructors I endeavoured to secure that Douglas Theodore Brent, the man on trial before you, would act instinctively to choose the one of the three methods he was taught which would serve him best in his assault. We reasoned, we instructors, that in desperate circumstances he would have no time to stop and think. He must know his craft so well, the knife must be so familiar in his hand, that he would act instinctively in what he had to do, without the least hesitation, without any thought. Members of the jury, those are the principles that I have endeavoured to instil into the man before you.'

He paused again, Mr Constantine Paget whispered something in disgust to his junior.

The major said: 'I have dwelt upon my own association with the accused because it is a prototype of the unarmed combat instruction which he subsequently received, and which resulted lamentably in the death of Michael Seddon. Again, I ask you to consider for one moment what would have happened in peacetime if I and others like me had taught these deadly crafts to this young man before you. I do not think we would have escaped the censure of this court. We should have been involved in this matter with him, very rightly, as aiding and abetting in the crime of which he is charged. If I had taught Brent in time of peace to creep up behind a man and stab him in the back, and if he had done so in a private quarrel, I should have been implicated in his crime.'

He raised his head and faced the jury. 'I am not implicated in this crime, nor is Captain Willis who taught him the deadly methods of unarmed combat which he used, inadvertently, with such terrible effect. Why is not Captain Willis charged in this court with Corporal Brent as aiding and abetting in his crime? It is because Captain Willis did what he did by order of the King, passed indirectly to him through his various officers. The Crown protects Captain Willis, and myself, from the consequences of our acts, of our instruction to innocent men in these terrible crafts. Are we to say, then, that the Crown throws a cloak of immunity around myself and Captain Willis, but leaves Corporal Brent unprotected to face a trial for murder, for doing what we have taught him to do by instinct and without thought?'

He smiled thoughtfully. 'No, justice cannot be severed in that way. If Douglas Theodore Brent is held to be guilty of the crime of murder, then Captain Willis must be held guilty of aiding and abetting in his crime. Alternatively, if Captain Willis is held to be immune from censure because he taught these things to Corporal Brent by order of the King, then that immunity must cover Corporal Brent, who in a struggle did by instinct what he had been taught. Members of the jury, this is the truth of it. The accident of war has taught this young man to do certain things by instinct. The accident of war has turned what would have been a simple brawl into a lamentable homicide. In your deliberations you cannot escape the fact that the real and fundamental cause of this man's death was the accident of war.'

He paused. 'Members of the jury, I have nearly done. In your deliberations you may well ask—where is this thing to end? You may say, the Army is training men in the dire arts of homicide, and training them to kill at sight without thought, mercy, or compunction. The Army euphemistically describes this as a toughening process. You may well ask, how are these killers that the Army has created to be controlled if the Law be not strained and twisted to convict them? It is a reasonable question that, and one that must be answered. Upon the evidence you have no option but to find this man innocent of murder. But you may well ask—how then is the public to be protected from the homicidal crafts that he has learned in the years following the war?'

He smiled faintly. 'I cannot look into the future, but I can, perhaps, see further than you. I, too, have been through this toughening process. In civil life I serve these courts as barrister, but in recent years I, too, have been trained to kill men without mercy or compunction, instinctively, and without thought. But unlike Corporal Brent, I am thirty-seven years of age, and unlike him I have known another life, a life of peace. And I can tell you this. When the war ends and Corporal Brent puts off his uniform and puts on his civilian clothes and walks out into Civvy Street, all these dread arts will be sloughed off like his uniform. In three months after that you will find him thinking only about motorcycle races or the wallflowers in his garden, and when at times he is reminded that he once killed men in brutal physical assault, he will be filled with wonder that that same man was he. Innocent men are not so easily diverted from the life of innocence as many people think. There will be trouble with a few criminal types, who by virtue of their Army training have enlarged their repertoire of crime. Such men are few in number. The many thousands who have learned these deadly crafts for use against the enemy will soon be thinking of them in wonder and distaste, letting their knowledge sink into oblivion as soon as may be. I say again, innocent men are not easily diverted from the life of innocence.'

He gathered his papers together. 'Members of the jury, I have finished now. Upon the evidence before you, you have no option but to find the prisoner Not Guilty of the crime of murder. And, gentlemen, I do not think that you need fear for the consequences of that verdict.'

He sat down, and the Judge began to speak. The summing up of Mr Justice Lambourn came like a breath of clean, cold air into the court. He told the jury to put out of their minds the somewhat novel interpretation of the Law that they had heard from counsel, and to listen to him. It was not disputed by the defence that the deceased man, Michael Seddon, had met his death at the hands of the prisoner. Three verdicts were therefore open to them, murder, manslaughter, or homicide in self defence. If on the evidence that they had heard they came to the conclusion that the prisoner intended to kill the deceased man when he went into this struggle, or at any time in the struggle, that would constitute malice aforethought, and it would be their duty to find the prisoner guilty of the crime of murder. Alternatively, if they should think that there was no such malice, but that the deceased met his death through carelessness or negligence upon the part of the prisoner, then they should return the verdict that the prisoner was guilty of manslaughter. If they should consider that the prisoner was convinced during the struggle that Mr Seddon intended to kill him and that the only way in which he could avoid death was to kill Mr Seddon, then the proper verdict for them to return would be homicide in self defence. No other verdicts were open to them. No other considerations should be allowed to enter into their deliberations.

The jury retired for a quarter of an hour, came back into court, and returned a verdict of guilty of manslaughter. Mr Justice Lambourn sentenced him to six months imprisonment.

Mr Turner finished reading the dusty, faded carbon copy and sat down for a few minutes in the dim lobby turning it over in his hands. Duggie Brent had got away with it, thanks to a counsel with a sense of the dramatic who had made the most of an indifferent case. Presently Mr Viner looked in on him. 'Finished?' he inquired.

'Aye,' said Mr Turner. 'Pretty lucky, wasn't he?'

Mr Viner took the transcript and the counsel's notebook from him. 'I suppose you might say so,' he said thoughtfully. 'Of course, it was in the middle of the war and say what you like, the emotional aspect does come in, even with the Judge. The counsel who was a Commando and a Paratrooper himself, and all that. But really, you know, simple people doing the best they can haven't got much to fear from the Law.'

'I suppose that's right,' said Mr Turner conventionally. He thought otherwise himself and from his own experience, but he did not say so. 'Very interesting, it was,' he said. 'Thanks for letting me have a read at it.'

The young man was pleased. 'I thought you'd like to see it,' he observed. 'It *is* an interesting trial. A bit out of the ordinary.'

'Aye,' said Mr Turner. He turned towards the door, and then stopped. 'There's just one thing,' he said. 'I'm trying to find out what Duggie Brent is doing now. Do you think this counsel that he had, this Major Carter, would have kept in touch with him?'

Viner stared at him. 'I thought I told you,' he replied. He glanced down at the dog-eared, dirty manuscript book in his hand. 'This was the last brief Carter ever took. He dropped with his parachute party at Arnhem and held out at the bridgehead with his party for several days. Then he was taken prisoner. He was shot next day, while trying to escape. Too bad that had to happen. He had a great future before him in these criminal cases.'

'Aye,' said Mr Turner heavily. 'Too bad.'

IO

The months of August and September slipped past without incident for Mr Turner. He went and showed his face in the office most days, but Cereal Products Ltd., got little value out of him. Most of his time was spent in peddling samples of his cheroots in various tobacconists' shops around London. He was obsessed with the idea that his extravagance in going out to Burma must not leave his wife the poorer; whatever else he did, he must cover the cost of that journey before strength failed. And strength was failing, patently, and rather fast. He was plagued with headaches and with fits of dizziness. He was beginning to find reading difficult, but it seemed hardly worth while bothering with glasses now; it was pleasanter to sit and listen to the wireless. He had increasing difficulty with his right hand, and it was a relief to him when Mollie started to do up his collar for him every morning, and to tie his tie. And he was losing weight.

He was still interested in his search for Duggie Brent, but he did not get on very well with it. With Mr Viner's help he made contact with the solicitors who had briefed Major P. C. Carter for the defence of the Paratrooper, and learned from them, after much searching of old dusty files of letters, that Brent's father had been a butcher in Romsey. He set out one Saturday morning in the little car, with Mollie driving him, and went to Romsey, and made inquiries first at the post office, and later at the police station. He came back empty-handed. Duggie Brent's father had died two years previously, and there were no relations in the district. Nobody knew anything of Duggie Brent; it was a long time since he had been seen in Romsey, though his trial was remembered well enough. His paternity order had not been paid for a considerable time, for the girl had married and had suffered it to lapse. Mr and Mrs Turner had a nice drive down into the country, but returned to Watford very little wiser.

Over supper that evening, Turner said: 'There's one thing we never did. We could have got on to the solicitor what settled up the father's will, and that. He must have been in touch with Brent at the time.'

His wife said: 'Why not leave it be? He'll be all right. He got off from his trial, so he's just the same as any other man, now.'

'He didn't get off,' Mr Turner said. 'He got six months. But anyway, I'd kind of like to know.'

'Seems like a waste of time, if you ask me,' she said.

He was annoyed, because he knew that what she said was true. 'Well, what of it?' he inquired. 'My time's my own, an' if I like to spend it this way, why can't I? I got little enough to come.'

She said quietly: 'Okay, Jackie—please yourself. Like me to do a letter for you, then?'

She was falling into the habit of doing all his correspondence for him on the typewriter, and her sister Laura was seeing a good deal less of her in consequence. Writing for Mr Turner was becoming a matter of increasing difficulty as his infirmity progressed; he could still sign his letters, but his signature was getting very bad. Taking his letters was for her an exercise in shorthand typing, and this itself was useful to her for practice.

She wrote a letter for him to the police at Romsey reminding them of their visit, and asking if they could find out the name of the solicitor who had wound up the estate of Mr Brent, butcher. In a few days they got an answer, and wrote again to Messrs Haslett and Peabody, asking for the address of Mr Douglas Theodore Brent. The reply that they received read:

Haslett and Peabody,
Romsey,
Wilts.

Dear Sir,
    We regret we have no knowledge of the present whereabouts of Mr Douglas Brent. The last address we have, dated April, 1946, was:

c/o Badcock's Entertainments, Ltd.
Rising Sun Hotel,
Edgware, Middlesex,

Yours truly,
H.O.HASLETT

This brought the matter well into the sphere of Mr Turner. Edgware is a satellite of London not very far from Watford, and though Mr Turner did not know the Rising Sun he had no objection whatsoever to making the saloon bar of that house the object of a journey. His wife drove him there one evening early in September, two days after the arrival of this letter, resigned to an evening of forced cheerfulness and beer.

The Rising Sun hotel proved to be an old house on the outskirts of what had once been a small country town. It was now surrounded by a great area of modern little houses, dormitories for a part of the huge mass of London workers. Amongst these modern shops and houses the Rising Sun stood gaunt and shabby in old dirty brick, soon to be pulled down, no doubt, to make place for a more streamlined hostelry. Behind it was a field or parking place, now empty and dirty; one or two small caravans and piles of timber, and a circus trailer jacked up with one wheel off, showed that an entertainment business might have its headquarters there.

'Aye,' said the barmaid presently. 'Badcock's Circus, they come here in the winter. They're out on the road now, of course. Come in for the winter about the end of October they do, and go out again about Easter.'

Mr Turner said: 'I used to know a chap was with them one time, chap called Duggie Brent. Is he with them still?'

She wrinkled her brows. 'I don't remember . . . I've only been here eighteen months, you see.' And then she said: 'Oh, wait now. Was he one of them that did the Wall of Death?'

'I dunno,' said Mr Turner. 'I dunno what he did with them. I knew him in the war.'

'There was a Brent,' she said. 'That's right. Duggie Brent. Married he was, wasn't he? Chap with red hair, short and stocky, like?'

'That's the boy,' said Mr Turner eagerly. 'Is he with them still?'

'I dunno,' said the barmaid doubtfully. 'I don't think so. He hasn't been in here for a long time. Over a year, I'd say.'

Mollie asked: 'What was his wife like?'

The girl said: 'Dark–slight–wore her hair in a bang. Used to take the money in the box for the Wall of Death. Phyllis, her name was.'

Mr Turner said: 'This Wall of Death–that what they do with motor bikes?'

'That's right,' she said. 'Going round and round. He was one of the riders. But I don't think he's doing it now.' She called across the room. 'Eddie, is that red-headed boy Duggie Brent still on the Wall of Death.'

'Nah,' said Eddie. 'Left at the end of last season, 'n never turned up for this. Monty Burke and Dick Fletcher are doing the riding now.'

'How do you think I could find out where he went to?' asked Mr Turner. 'I'd like to see him again.'

The girl asked shrewdly: 'He been doing anything?'

He shook his head. 'I'm not a copper. I live over at Watford, and a pal told me this was his address. I just slipped over for a beer, 'n try and see him. We was together in the war.'

'That so?' she said. 'Well, I dunno, I'm sure. Mr Badcock might know.'

'He here now?'

She shook her head. 'They're out on the road now, won't be back before the end of next month.' She raised her voice. 'Eddie, where they playing this week?'

'Thame,' said Eddie. 'Abingdon on Monday. Newbury after that.'

Mollie had become strangely patient with Mr Turner, and raised no objection to another day spent in the little car, bouncing at forty miles an hour, hour after hour, down the long arterial roads in search of Mr Badcock. They found him after lunch in a grass field outside the small Oxfordshire town of Abingdon, among the hurly-burly of his swings and roundabouts and flip-flops and dodgem cars, and the Wall of Death and Sawing Through a Woman, and the many tables upon which you roll a penny for a girl to pick it up and drop it in a bucket by her side. Mr Badcock was a small, harassed man in a bowler hat, but he was affable enough.

'Brent?' he said. 'Duggie Brent? I know–Wall of Death. Left last season he did, when we shut down for the winter, never came back for this.' Mr Turner asked if he knew an address. The little man shook his head. 'I got a couple o' letters waiting for him, been waiting for months. I been meaning to give 'em back to the postman some day, but I put 'em away somewhere.'

'Eh,' said Mr Turner, 'it was just a thought I had. I knew he was with you, one time.'

'That's right, up till last October. He didn't show up in March for his job.'
Mr Turner asked: 'Did you expect him?'

'Well, not really. Wife was going to have a baby, and the ladies, they get funny when they get like that. Oh, thanks.' He accepted a cigarette; Mr Turner lit it for him. 'Funny thing about that Wall of Death,' he said. 'Best attraction I've got. The public, they think all the time he's going over the top, see? The riders' wives, they get all of a twitter, even the real hard pieces–straight they do. But the riders themselves, they just get bored. Round and round, a quarter of an hour, six times a day. They get proper fed up with it.' He turned to Mollie. 'You've seen it, I suppose?'

She shook her head. 'I'd like to.'

He pulled out a heavy watch from his waistcoat pocket. 'One starting in about ten minutes,' he said. 'Sorry I can't help about your friend. If you see him, say I've got a couple o' letters for him.'

They went and stood on the little gallery overlooking the vertical track of the Wall of Death, watched the riders start their motor cycles in the basin-shaped arena down below and ride up on the wall in a crescendo of open exhausts. Round and round they went, weaving in and out together, up and down the wall. Between the turns Mr Turner studied the performers. They were rather florid, beery-looking young men, professionally reckless, well aware that their performance looked a great deal more alarming than it really was. It was a job that a Commando or a Paratrooper would have turned to naturally, Mr Turner thought, full of bravado and noise and glamour. It was a job that a Commando or a Paratrooper soon got tired of, if Mr Badcock was to be believed. Studying the performance with a critical eye, Mr Turner did believe him. Duggie Brent had been there and had gone, nobody knew where.

They came down from the gallery at the conclusion of the act, dazed with the noise and rather tired. There was nothing left to stay for; they went and had a cup of tea in a cafe, and drove back to Watford. Mr Turner was very, very tired when they got home. He had a couple of sausages and a pint of beer for supper, with some bread and cheese, and went to bed at ten.

In the middle of the night his wife woke up with a start. In the dim light she saw him sitting upright in his bed; he seemed to be shivering. She was instantly awake, and said: 'What's up, Jackie?'

He said: 'Bloody bed's been turning over and over. Each time I lie down the bloody thing turns over.' He sounded infinitely tired.

She slipped out of bed, pulling on her dressing-gown. 'I'll get you one of them powders.'

She gave him his powder with a drink of water and talked to him a little: presently he lay back upon his pillows. She lay down then herself and lay awake until the regularity of his breathing told her that he was asleep; then she, too, slept herself. In the morning she woke up at seven o'clock. Jackie Turner slept on in a heavy coma, breathing irregularly and rather fast. For a time she tried to wake him by sponging his face with cold water; then she went downstairs and telephoned to Dr Worth.

He stayed in his coma till about eleven o'clock; the doctor with him for the last hour and a half. He woke with a splitting headache which the doctor mitigated for him, and lay for the remainder of the day drowsy with drugs in the little sunlit bedroom. Downstairs in the sitting-room the doctor had a word with Mrs Turner.

'I can't hold out much hope that there will not be more of these,' he said. 'It's going exactly as Mr Hughes told us it would.'

Mollie nodded. 'How long should he go on working, doctor?'

He shrugged his shoulders. 'As long as he feels he can. He couldn't go to work today or tomorrow, of course. But it's better that he should have an interest as long as he can manage it. We don't want him to get depressed with no occupation.'

She said thoughtfully. 'I don't believe he'd go like that.' And then she said: 'How long do you think it will be before he has to go into a home, or something?'

He said: 'I think by Christmas he will be permanently in bed, at this rate. Of course, you could keep him here, if you feel able to take on the work. The nurse can look in every day and do anything that might be necessary.' He hesitated, and then said: 'I don't imagine it would be for very long.'

She raised her head. 'I'd like to do that, doctor. If there's no reason why he should go into a home, he'd be much better off in his own house here while it lasts.'

He said: 'It will tie you down, you know. He ought not to be left alone.'

'I know,' she said. 'But I've not been such a good wife to him that I've not got a bit to make up, like.'

He thought for a minute. 'Mr Hughes said he wanted to see him after four months. I think that takes us to about the end of October. I'll write to Mr Hughes and make an appointment for him then.'

He gave her a few instructions about nursing and medicines, and went away. She took up the *Daily Mirror* to Mr Turner in bed, and he took it gratefully, and turned at once to the cartoon of Jane who once more had got herself into a predicament that involved the loss of much of her clothing, and chuckled over it, and laid the paper down. They had a wireless set that required no aerial or earth, and she brought it up into the bedroom and plugged it in for him to listen to a talk on Laying the Car Up for the Winter, which interested Mr Turner very much, while she went down and cooked a bloater for his lunch.

He slept a little in the afternoon, and she brought him up his tea in bed. And over tea he said: 'I been thinking about laying up the car, like it said on the wireless. It's quarter day next week, 'n we can turn the tax in and get something back on the insurance. I reckon we ought to save the money, 'n we shan't want it till the spring.'

She thought, they would not want it then, but did not say so. The car was his adventure. It would be reasonable to sell it, but she did not suggest that. Instead, she said: 'I dunno about that. What would you think if we went off in it first, 'n had a kind of holiday together, driving round? It's ever so long since we had a holiday together.'

He considered this. He liked driving in the car, and a holiday touring round and staying in hotels entirely for pleasure was a thing that he had never done since he was married. He said:

'I had my holiday this year. I got to think about work sometimes.'

She said: 'You've got your sick leave coming, Jackie.'

'Aye,' he said. 'Does Dr Worth think I ought to start that now?'

'Not really,' she admitted. 'But I think it would be fun if we went off and had a bit of holiday together like. I mean after all,' she said, 'what's the use of just going on working till you've got to stop? You've got to have a bit of fun sometimes.'

He felt that he could not have agreed with her more. 'It 'ld cost an awful lot,' he said, 'staying in hotels every night, and that.'

'It wouldn't matter for a fortnight,' she said. 'We've got that much money. Then we could come back here and put the car up like you said. We'd only lose a little bit if we did that. And the weather's lovely still.'

He said: 'Where would you want to go?'

She thought for a moment. 'Devonshire,' she said. 'Dartmoor and places like that. The heather gets ever so pretty on the hills, this time of year.'

Next day she wrote a letter for him to Mr Parkinson, the managing director of Cereal Products Ltd. They got an answer back two days later; Mr Parkinson was very sorry to hear such bad news of his illness, and had arranged with the secretary to put Mr Turner upon sick leave commencing at the end of the month. The additional ten days of full pay and commission was a gracious little act that pleased them very much.

They spent a few days planning with their maps while Mr Turner recuperated, and started off for Taunton on a Monday. They stayed the night there after a long drive in the little car, and went on to Minehead next day, and after that across Exmoor to South Molton where Mr Turner found an old friend travelling in ladies' underwear in the saloon bar, and had a glorious time with him, and learned two new stories, and got a rayon slip for Mollie very cheap. From there they went to Dartmoor and spent a couple of nights at Two Bridges, stared at the prison, and then went on through Launceston across Bodmin Moor to Bodmin.

In the hotel that night, over dinner, Mr Turner said casually: 'I see we're only about forty miles from Penzance, here.'

His wife said quietly: 'Like to go there, Jackie?' She had seen the point of his manoeuvres westwards for some days.

'Well, I dunno,' he said. 'It might be nice to go on to the very end, now we've come so far. I never seen Land's End yet.'

They decided that it would be nice to go on and see Land's End, and came to Penzance the next day in time for lunch. They took a room and went out after lunch in the small car and drove out to Land's End, and stood on the cliff looking out towards America. The sea looked very cold and grey and unfriendly, and they were glad to get back to Penzance for tea in the hotel.

Over tea Mr Turner said casually: 'We're only four miles from that place Trenarth where all that happened about Dave Lesurier, the Negro I was telling you about. Like to take a run out and see what the beer's like at the pub?'

This was his holiday, and probably his last. She knew that he had been distressed that he had only located one of his companions in the ward so far, that the quest still lay very near the surface of his mind. She was not in the least deceived by his dissimulation; he wanted to go there, she knew, in the faint hope that he might glean something from the landlord of the pub. She said quietly: 'It'll probably have changed hands by this time, Jackie.' She did not want to see him suddenly disappointed. 'There'll be another landlord after all these years.'

He said: 'Well, I dunno; it's not so long as that. Anyway, I'd kind of like to go and see the place.'

She got up. 'I'll just run up and put my things on.'

They drove out to the little town Trenarth and parked the car in the small square outside the White Hart hotel. Mr Turner stood for a few minutes looking round, while Mollie waited for him. This was the place that he had heard so much about, in hospital in 1943 from the young Negro, in Burma recently eight thousand miles away, from the young man who had married a brown girl. Nay Htohn in Mandinaung had known about this place, though she would never see it. Negroes in Memphis and New Orleans, in Nashville and St Louis, remembered this small town with pleasure. This unconsidered place, these slate-roofed, unimposing houses, and these unassuming people had formed themselves into a little thread in the weave of friendship and of knowledge that holds countries together. Mr Turner felt that Trenarth had done something for the world; it was impossible to feel otherwise when he had heard so much about it in Burma.

It seemed incredible, looking at this quiet little place, that it had once been full of Negroes from America. It seemed incredible that the landlord of this shabby little pub had once sat down in his shirtsleeves to write to General Eisenhower, and had got a hearing.

It seemed incredible that all that could have happened here.

He went into the bar with Mollie. There was a stout man of about sixty behind the bar, in shirtsleeves, a common man, but a man of authority and poise. At the first glance Mr Turner knew that the White Hart had not changed hands; he glanced at Mollie and she glanced at him in the same knowledge. Mr Turner ordered a pint of bitter for himself and a gin and French for Mollie.

The landlord served them across the bar. They stood at the bar for a moment; Mr Turner gave his wife a cigarette, and offered one to the landlord, who accepted it. 'Just passing through?' he asked.

Mr Turner blew a cloud of smoke. 'Staying in Penzance the night,' he said. 'Matter of fact, I been down here before. Not in this place. I was in hospital in Penzance for a time, back in 1943.'

'Aye?' said Mr Frobisher.

'Bit different now,' said Mr Turner.

'Aye,' said Mr Frobisher. '1943–that's when we had all them Americans in camp here, turning the place upside down.'

'That's right,' said Mr Turner. 'I was in the ward with one of them, got into trouble here. A young Negro soldier he was, Dave Lesurier.'

'Aye?' said Mr Frobisher with interest. 'You was in hospital with Dave Lesurier?'

'That's right,' said Mr Turner. 'We used to play draughts together. Checkers, he called it.'

'He calls it checkers still,' said Mr Frobisher. 'He comes in here now and again, Saturday nights, mostly.'

There was a momentary pause.

'Is he about here, then?' asked Mr Turner. 'I reckoned he'd have gone back to America.'

'He did,' said Mr Frobisher. 'And he come back again. He lives just up the road. Works over at Camborne as a draughtsman, goes there every day. It's only two stations up the line.'

'Well I'm damned,' said Mr Turner. 'You say he's living here now? I'd like to see him again.'

'Aye,' said Mr Frobisher, 'you'll find him up the road. House called "Sunnyvale", four doors up past Woodwards Stores, just past the church. You can't miss it. On the same side as Robertson's.'

Mr Turner thought for a minute. 'Does he live alone?' he asked. 'In digs, like?'

'No, he's married,' said the landlord. 'Married a Trenarth girl last year, Grace Trefusis that was.'

From Penzance hospital, in 1943, Dave Lesurier had been sent to Northern Ireland where he had joined a draft for Iceland; in Iceland he had driven a truck till V.E. day, when he had been sent back to the United States and demobilized. He had got back to Nashville in the late summer of that year a free man, to find that the Filtair Corporation was laying off hands strenuously, and that his old job in the garage was a thing of the past.

He did not regret it. It had been a dead end job at best, one which would never lead him further than the maintenance of trucks. He did not know what he wanted, except that he wanted to do more than that; as a first step he wanted to design things, to make drawings on a drawing-board of engineering parts and watch them come to life upon the fitter's bench. And he wanted to meet Grace Trefusis again, to say that he was sorry.

If there had been work for him in Nashville of a sort that he could settle down to, both these vague ambitions might have faded. In the turmoil of reconversion there was nothing for him at the time that he got home but those jobs which are traditional for the Negro; domestic or hotel service, work on a farm or on the roads, or in a shoeshine parlour. His travels had made Dave Lesurier despise these things; he was resentful of the land of opportunity that gave so small an opportunity to him. Living upon his Army money in those first few weeks at home, his mind turned back to England. Compared with the glittering, streamlined prizes of a career in his own country, the rewards that England had to offer seemed drab enough and poor, but they were more accessible to him.

He talked it all out with his father, who had been laid off due to reduction in the draughting staff at Filtair consequent on reconversion, and was doing casual tracing for a local architect for irregular payments at the wage rate of a girl. Money was tight in the Lesurier household, but his father advised him objectively. 'If you reckon you can make a living better over in Europe, son,' he said, 'you go ahead and don't you worry about your Ma and me. We'll get by all right. There'll be plenty trouble in this country before colored folks get equal opportunity with whites, at any rate down South. If they ever do you can come right back home and slip into a good job. But in the meantime, if you got a hunch you can do better over there, well, son, you go ahead and try it while you've got some money left.'

Dave Lesurier did try it. He hitchhiked to Charleston and went to the United States Shipping Board with his Army discharge papers, and after three days got a job as a mess boy in a freighter bound for Durban with machinery. He washed dishes from Charleston to Durban, from Durban to Sydney, from Sydney to Calcutta, and from Calcutta to New York. He landed back in the United States after seven months without having made much progress towards England, but with a little money saved. He shipped again then in another freighter from New York to Buenos Aires. From Buenos Aires his ship sailed for Avonmouth with a cargo of hides.

He drew his pay and left the ship at Avonmouth, only a hundred and fifty miles from Trenarth, eleven and a half months after setting out from Nashville. He was twenty-five years old then, more fully developed and self-confident than he had been when he was last in England, still anxious to become a draughtsman, still anxious to see Grace Trefusis once again, if only to say that he was sorry for his lapse three years before. A long scar, somewhat blacker than his chocolate coloured skin, reminded him of it each time he looked in a mirror.

He travelled down to Penzance by train, staring out of the window at the little fertile fields, immersed in memories of his previous journeys in troop trains about this country. At Penzance he parked the suitcase which held all his property in the station cloakroom, and went and asked a policeman where he could spend the night; he spent it in a common lodging house. In the morning he walked out to Trenarth. It was September and the weather fine and warm. He had a good suit in his bag, but he wore his seaman's clothes, blue linen slacks, a khaki shirt, and a windcheater; on his head he wore an old soft hat. He turned up in the bar of the White Hart at opening time, and the first person he saw was Bessie Frobisher behind the bar.

She greeted him warmly. 'We've wondered ever so many times if any of you boys would come back here and see us,' she said. 'We hear of some of them. Sam Lorimer, he wrote at Christmas; ever so nice it was to hear from him. He's married now and living at a place called Detroit, where they make motor cars or something.' She smiled at him. 'You married yet?'

He shook his head. 'No, *ma'am.*'

She laughed. 'Won't nobody have you?'

She asked him what he had been doing, and heard all about his wanderings. 'Fancy!' she said. Then she went and called her father. 'Dad, here's Dave Lesurier come back!' and he had to tell his story all over again. And then Mr Penlee the farmer came in, and he had to tell it a third time.

Mr Frobisher took him into the back parlour and gave him dinner, while Bessie served the bar; she had had her meal before opening time. After the pudding the Negro gave his host a cigarette, and said:

'It's been mighty nice of you to give me dinner, Mr Frobisher.' He hesitated. 'If I wanted to stop over for the night, would you have a bed? I got money to pay.'

'Aye,' said the landlord, 'I can fix you up somehow. You staying for a few days?'

'I dunno, Mr Frobisher.' The Negro hesitated. 'There was quite a bit of trouble last time I was here,' he said at last. 'Would folks remember that around these parts?'

'Aye,' said Mr Frobisher, 'they remember it all right. Proper rumpus that set up, that did.'

'If that's the way it is,' said Lesurier, 'maybe I better move along.'

'Not unless you want to,' said the landlord. 'The feeling here was you'd been treated pretty bad.'

'There wouldn't be no trouble if folks saw me here, on account of what I did?'

'I shouldn't think so,' said the landlord slowly. 'Not unless Grace Trefusis or her mother cut up nasty, and I don't see why they should.'

Lesurier asked: 'Is Miss Grace still here?'

'Aye,' said the landlord. 'She works up at Robertson's just the same. Been there all the time.'

There was a long, slow pause.

'Well, thanks a lot,' the Negro said at last, 'I'll be back around five or six tonight, Mr Frobisher, 'n let you know if I'll be wanting to stay.'

'Aye,' said the landlord, 'please yourself. The bed's there if you want it.'

Dave Lesurier went out and stood on the street corner, smoking, till the church clock struck two. Then he turned, and walked slowly up the road to Robertson's grocery shop, and went in, and walked straight up to Grace Trefusis behind the counter, and said quietly: 'Ten Player's, please.'

She looked up quickly and saw who it was, and met his eyes. Between them, for an instant, the world stood still. She was three years older now, nearly twenty; her figure had filled out, making her more mature and prettier than the frightened adolescent he had known before. She was more knowledgeable about men, too; she had been to the pictures many times and with a number of young men, and had been kissed by several in a dark corner since the Negro had initiated her into that deplorable pastime. She met his eyes, and the old fear flickered in her own for an instant, but then she smiled.

'Oh . . .' she said. 'It's you.'

In that instant all his old shyness swept back over him. He coloured hotly, and wished desperately for eloquence that he might make some flip and smart rejoinder, but no inspiration came. Instead, there was an awkward pause, and all that he could find to say to her at last was to repeat: 'Ten Player's, please.'

The last trace of fear of him left her for ever; in her more adult experience she knew that she would never be in any danger from this shy young man, coloured though he might be. The words of an American officer came into her mind, secretly treasured and remembered for three years – 'If he kind of admired you, Miss Trefusis, well there's nothing wrong with that.' That admiration had brought nothing to him but attempted suicide, hospital, and disgrace, and now, after three years, he had come back for more. She reached mechanically to the shelf for a packet of cigarettes, and said gently: 'Are you out of the Army, now?'

He swallowed, and said: 'Yes, ma'am.'

She had the packet in her hand, but she did not give it to him. 'What are you doing then?' she inquired.

He raised his head, and looked at her, and she was smiling at him in the way that she always had smiled at him when she gave him cigarettes, but she was prettier than he had ever remembered her. Courage came back to him, and he said: 'I got a job on a freighter, with the steward, 'n we docked in at Avonmouth. I thought as it was pretty close, I'd kind of come along down here.' He met her eyes again. 'I thought I'd kind of like to see if you were anywhere around here still, and tell you I been mighty sorry about that time.'

She coloured and laughed awkwardly. 'Oh, that's all right.' And then she asked curiously: 'Did you come all the way from Avonmouth just to say that?'

'Yes, ma'am,' he said simply.

She had once been as far as Exeter, nearly a hundred miles away, but Avonmouth, she knew, was much farther than that, and it seemed a very long way to her. She said weakly: 'Fancy . . .' And then she said: 'You didn't have to come all that way, just to say that.' She did not know that he had come from the United States to say it, in eleven months. 'There was an officer here once, about that time,' she said. 'He said you didn't mean nothing by it.'

'That's right,' he said. He looked at her, and she was smiling, and a slow smile spread across his own face. 'I reckon it just kind of happened.'

'Well,' she said, 'you just look out it doesn't happen again.' But she was still smiling as she said it, and he took more courage from her smile.

'I was wondering,' he said, and stopped. 'I got a lot I'd like to tell you about that time,' he said, and stopped again. And he managed to get it out, after three years. 'If I stopped over for the night,' he said, 'I was wondering if you'd care to take a lil' walk with me this evening.'

She said gently: 'That's what you wanted to ask me before, wasn't it?'

'Yes, ma'am.'

'Just for an hour?'

He nodded.

She smiled at him. 'I don't mind if I do. Six o'clock, by the gate into the churchyard?'

'I'll be waiting for you, Miss Grace.'

She laughed. 'None of your tricks, now.'

He said in horror: 'No, *ma'am!*'

'All right,' she said. 'See you then.' And, as he turned to go: 'You're forgetting your cigarettes!'

Dave Lesurier did not go down the street turning cartwheels, but he felt like it. He went and waited for the bus, and went into Penzance and got his bag, and took it back to the White Hart hotel and spent the rest of the afternoon dressing for the party. When he walked out of the White Hart that evening for his date he wore a blue suit that was a little too blue with a very marked waist, and pointed light brown shoes rather too tight for his feet, and a bright yellow tie with spots on it, and a green silk shirt and collar, and a magenta handkerchief. Grace Trefusis, when she saw him coming, thought he looked ever so smart, and wished she'd put on her best frock instead of the one that she'd been wearing for three days.

He had bought a large bunch of violets for her in Penzance, and he gave her these when he met her by the churchyard gate. 'They looked so pretty, right there in the shop,' he said diffidently, 'I thought maybe you'd like them.'

She buried her face in the little blossoms. 'Oh, they're ever so nice. Just take a smell!' He sniffed them, laughing, and they turned and walked past the churchyard wall together out towards the hill, and old Mrs Polread the sexton's wife, who had seen the whole thing from her cottage window, had a fine tale to tell Mrs Penlee when they met an hour later. 'That black boy that assaulted Grace Trefusis when the Americans were here, you know, the one that there was all that trouble over. Believe it or not, he's back here, and she's walking out with him this very minute! And he give her a bunch of violets, too, big as a plate!'

Most of that first walk they spent in talking of his plans for the future. 'I kind of thought maybe there'd be a chance of something over here,' he said. 'Drafting, or that. It's not so easy for a colored boy to get a chance at drafting in the States.' She did not really know what draughting was, but she was impressed by his sincerity of purpose. 'I thought maybe I'd take a look round a lil' bit before I get to looking for another ship. I don't want to go on as mess boy.'

He brought her back to the churchyard gate exactly at seven o'clock; she had never been treated with such courtesy and such consideration by any other young man. 'How long are you stopping here?' she asked.

'I dunno,' he said. 'Tomorrow, maybe.'

She said with studied carelessness: 'I got a half day Saturday, but I suppose you'll be gone by then.'

He said: 'I might not be, Miss Grace. If I was still here, would you like to do a movie in Penzance, or something?'

She said: 'There's ever such a good one on. Ginger Rogers, all in technicolour. I do think she's ever so nice, don't you?'

He had seen Ginger Rogers all in technicolour before he left New York; what he wanted to see now was Grace Trefusis. He said: 'I think she's swell, Miss Grace. I'd be real honored if you'd let me take you.'

She said: 'Well, look in at the shop tomorrow and say if you'll be staying over the weekend. I'd like to see that, ever so.'

'Okay, Miss Grace.'

He lifted his hat, showing his short, kinky hair, and stood bareheaded while she walked away from him towards her home, to make what explanation of her conduct that she could before her parents.

In the White Hart that evening Dave Lesurier consulted Mr Frobisher about work as a draughtsman. Mr Frobisher knew something about draughtsmen; his late wife's brother had been one. Habitually, too, he kept his ear close to the ground and gathered all the gossip of the district. 'I did hear that Jones and Porter, over Camborne way, were taking on draughtsmen,' he said thoughtfully, 'that was some time back. You might try there, perhaps.'

'What kind of work would that be, Mr Frobisher?'

'Electric switches, mostly–time switches and that, special ones to shut off under water, 'n that sort of thing. They got a lot of draughtsmen working, that I do know.'

Lesurier did not let the opportunity pass by. Next morning at eleven o'clock he was at the office of a Mr Horrocks, chief draughtsman of Jones and Porter Ltd, outside Camborne. Mr Horrocks was a thin, dark man, a little at a loss with the young Negro before him. He wanted junior draughtsmen and he was naturally inclined to take a man who came after a job, but he had never engaged a Negro and his ability was difficult to assess. On his own confession the young man had no experience in draughtsmanship except his course at school, which might mean nothing at all.

He picked a bolt up from his desk and gave it to the Negro. 'What thread is that?' he asked.

Lesurier took it with a sinking heart, and turned it over in his fingers. 'It's a quarter bolt, of course,' he said at last, 'but what the thread is I don't rightly know. It's a British thread,' he explained. 'Back home, a standard fine thread on a quarter bolt would be twenty-eight to the inch, but this looks coarser to me.'

He said, 'I'm real sorry, sir, but I don't know the British standards. But I'd soon pick them up.'

Mr Horrocks took the bolt back. 'That's a B.S.F.,' he said. 'Twenty-six to the inch.' He stood for a moment in thought; the boy's answer had not been unintelligent. 'Tell you what I'll do,' he said. 'You can start on Monday for a week on trial, if you like, at two pounds ten. At the end of the week I'll have another talk with you.'

Lesurier said: 'I certainly will do my best to please you, sir.' He hesitated, and then said: 'There wouldn't be no trouble with the other men?'

'Trouble? What about?'

'On account of the color.'

'Colour?' The chief draughtsman was puzzled for an instant. 'Oh, I see what you mean. No, of course there won't be any trouble. I'd like to see them try it on.' He made a note of Lesurier's name and temporary address. 'Are you a British subject?'

'No, sir. I'm a citizen of the United States.'

'Oh well, we'll cross that bridge when we come to it. Monday, nine o'clock.'

Dave Lesurier walked back to the station bursting with pride and apprehension, pride for having got a job as a draughtsman and apprehension that he would not be able to hold it. He went past Trenarth in the train and on to Penzance. There he bought a British engineer's pocketbook, a fat little volume, full of concentrated information, and a few drawing instruments, and an elementary book on electricity. He had learned the rudiments of electricity at the James Hollis school for coloured boys back in Nashville, enough to warn him that his knowledge was lamentably deficient for the work he had to do, or thought he had to do. It never struck him that Mr Horrocks did not really think that he was getting an experienced electrical engineer for two pounds ten a week.

He walked rather shyly into Robertson's that afternoon and waited while Grace served another customer, and said: 'Ten Player's, please.' It had become almost a joke between them by that time. She reached for the packet, and said: 'You staying tomorrow, or have you got to go?'

He said: 'I'd be real honored if you'd let me take you to the movies, Miss Grace. I got something to celebrate. I got a job. A job as draftsman.'

She stared at him. 'Not already? Wherever to?'

'Jones and Porter Limited, at a place called Camborne up the line a ways. I got took on this morning, start on Monday.'

Another customer was waiting to be served. She said: 'Oh, I am glad!' She shoved the cigarettes into his hand. 'I can't stop now. See you tomorrow, two o'clock, at the bus stop outside the church?'

He said: 'Okay, Miss Grace. I'll be there.'

He was there a quarter of an hour early, having spent the morning studying the comprehensible hardware detailed in his engineer's pocketbook, and the incomprehensible abstractions of his electrical text book. She thought again as she walked up the road towards the bus stop that he looked ever so distinguished; his brown skin and his bright blue suit and his green shirt and collar made a colour scheme that she admired very much. Whatever people might say about going out with a coloured boy, she thought, there were very few men in Trenarth who wore clothes like he did—and in that she was about right.

He was carrying a little parcel unobtrusively, and when they got into the pictures, in the friendly darkness, he offered it to her shyly, and it was a pound box of chocolates, which she called sweets and he called candies. None of her other swains had ever bought her chocolates in a beautiful box like that, all cellophane and green ribbon, and she knew that he could ill afford it, and that made the little present valuable to her. She said: 'It's ever so kind of you to think – they're lovely. Here, have one.' A woman behind leaned over and asked if she would mind not talking.

They had tea in a café after the picture, and went back in the bus. And at the bus stop in Trenarth he raised his hat to her, and said: 'I better say goodnight, Miss Grace. It certainly has been one swell day for me.'

She said: 'Oh, no. Come on, 'n see me home. I want you to meet Dad and Ma.'

He hesitated. 'Maybe they wouldn't care so much about that, Miss Grace.'

She said: 'They got to meet you some time, if you're only going to be up at Camborne. Come on, just for a minute.' She smiled at him. 'They won't eat you.'

He laughed. 'I dunno about that, Miss Grace. Maybe they will.' But he went with her to her parents' cottage, where she lived, and where Lieutenant Anderson had come three years before.

Grace Trefusis had inherited all the vigour of her mother. She took him in and said: 'Ma, this is Mr Lesurier that I was telling you about. Dad, this is Dave.'

Mr Trefusis got up and said: 'How d'you do?'

Mrs Trefusis said: 'Well!'

Grace Trefusis said: 'Now don't you start that, Ma. If Dave and I can let bygones be bygones, so can you. We've been in to see Ginger Rogers at the Regal. Ever so lovely, it was.'

Her mother said with an effort: 'How long are you staying for, Mr Lesurier?'

'I got a job here, ma'am,' he said shyly. 'At Jones and Porter, up at Camborne. I got took on for a draftsman, starting Monday.'

Mr Trefusis said: 'A draughtsman?' He looked at the young Negro with a new interest. To the signalman there was some social standing in a draughtsman's job; it was an office job that might lead to management. It was true that most draughtsmen of his acquaintance had ended up in a little sweet and tobacco shop, but some had not. 'I didn't know you was a draughtsman,' he said.

Lesurier smiled. 'I dunno as I am, sir,' he said candidly. 'I guess I'll need to work plenty hard to hold it down. But it's something to have got a start.'

'Sit down,' said the railwayman. He offered a cigarette out of a packet. 'Where d'you say you come from now?'

Lesurier left them an hour later, having promised to go back to tea next day. The Trefusis family were very thoughtful when he left them on Sunday. By that time they had grown accustomed to the milk chocolate colour of his skin, which was not unhandsome when you got accustomed to it. He was more widely travelled and better educated than any of the young men Grace had brought to the house before, for in Trenarth there was not a wide choice for her. He seemed to be infinitely considerate and kind, and they remembered this as characteristic of Negroes in the mass three years before. Moreover Mr

Trefusis, when Lesurier went away on Sunday, had a shrewd idea that he would hold his job.

Mr Horrocks began to have the same idea on Tuesday afternoon five minutes before the drawing office knocked off, when Lesurier came to him. The drawing office was on normal hours of work, but the shop was working overtime till eight o'clock at night. 'I took a lil' walk around the shop last night, sir, after hours,' he said. 'There's a whole raft o' things here that I never seen before. Would I be able to work down on the bench for the overtime hours, sir, on the assembly of the switches? I wouldn't want no money. I reckon it would make things easier to see the way the drawings go if I knew more about the job down on the bench.'

Mr Horrocks thought this was a very reasonable proposal. 'You can't go down tonight,' he said. 'There's the union to be considered.' He made a note upon his pad. 'I'll see the shop steward in the morning about it, Lesurier. I think that's a very good idea.'

Lesurier started work down on the bench on Wednesday evening and found to his surprise and pleasure that the shop steward had insisted that he should be paid, which put another twenty-seven shillings in his pay packet at the week's end. He moved into very cheap lodgings in Camborne, and got down to his work in earnest.

He did not find the office work particularly exacting. He was put under an old grey-haired draughtsman called Mr King; his work consisted principally in copying drawings that had become torn and dirty in the print room. Mr King said severely on the first morning: 'Are your hands clean?'

The Negro replied meekly: 'Yes, sir. This don't come off.' The little joke went round the drawing office directed against Mr King, who was felt to be a fussy old man, and spread down into the shop, where Mr King was regarded as an impractical obstructionist and the arch enemy of production. He may have been, but he could teach Lesurier a great deal and the Negro was wise enough to realize it. Under the stern eye of the old man he developed a neatness of drawing and a classic style of printing which was fully up to standard, and with this he began to have some inkling of what the many drawings were about, and why the radii and gauge thicknesses were made so.

He became quite popular in the office. His diversity of experience made him interesting to talk to, and he was always willing to help in tiresome jobs like entering in the part number book or checking details. He gave a cosmopolitan air to this small Cornish drawing office which the draughtsmen rather liked, and which was certainly no hindrance to the management. The managing director, showing a buying delegation from the Turkish Government around the works and walking them through the drawing office, was asked: 'You use Africans for draughting in this country?' He replied grandly: 'We use anybody in this Company who has the brains we want, white or black. As a matter of fact, he's an American. He's a very clever young designer.' It was not, of course, on this account that Jones and Porter got an order for three thousand time switches from the Turkish delegation, but Mr Porter felt that his reply had been, perhaps, a small contributory factor.

Gradually, Dave Lesurier became absorbed into the life of the community in which he moved. He spent much of his spare time with Grace Trefusis, and generally had tea with her family on Sunday afternoons. They very soon discovered that he could play the flute, and in the over-furnished little parlour of the Trefusis home he used to play hymn tunes for them on Sunday evening. On wet days they sometimes got him to go to church with them on Sunday mornings, but he was no great churchgoer and preferred to take his exercise that day. He bought a bicycle, and put it on a Jones and Porter truck that was going up to London, one Saturday, and drove to Plymouth in the truck. He spent two hours there going round the drapers' shops with a snippet of the dress that Mrs Trefusis wore on Sundays to find a scarf that matched it for a birthday present for her, and rode home in the evening fifty-five miles on his bicycle. He was always doing things like that.

In the spring Dave Lesurier and Grace Trefusis decided to get married; it was a point of dispute afterwards between them who asked who. They did it on the sea front at Penzance after a British Legion dance. Lesurier felt secure in his job with Jones and Porter by that time; he had been advanced to the full rate for his age, four pounds ten a week, and he had joined the Draughtsmen's Association. He felt that he was in control of his job, able to do the work expected of him, and a bit more. Practically the whole of his spare time had been spent with the Trefusis family while he had been in England; they had lost all sense of strangeness at his colour, and only knew him as a very courteous and pleasant young American, with whom Grace went out every Saturday.

They walked out of the dance hall arm-in-arm at midnight, reluctant to break away to fetch their bicycles and ride home. They stood on the sea front looking out over the moonlit seascape. Presently the Negro said:

'You know, it still seems darned funny to me folks don't get interfering, when they see you and me dancing together.'

The girl said: 'Why should they? It's got nothing to do with them what either of us do. You got this colour business on the brain, Dave.'

'Maybe,' he replied. 'It's how you've been brought up. I know we couldn't go on like this back home.'

'Well, this is my home, and we can,' she said. She pressed a little closer to him. 'You'd better make it yours, 'n give up worrying.'

'You mean, stay here for good?'

'That's right. You like it here, don't you?'

'I like it fine,' he said. 'I'd like nothing better than to stay right here for good.' And then he hesitated. 'But I guess there's other things to think about as well.'

'What's that?' she asked.

'Place of your own,' he said quietly. 'Being married, and having kids and that. You got to settle where you can do that.'

She said softly: 'Well, what's wrong with doing that here, Dave?'

He stared out over the sea. 'I guess no English girl wouldn't want to marry a black man.'

She said: 'You haven't asked one, Dave.'

They were standing arm-in-arm in their heavy coats; he took her other hand and drew her closer to him. 'Do you reckon you could ever get around to thinking that you'd like to marry me?' he asked.

She did not answer, but he knew her silences. 'I know it's mighty difficult for a white girl to say yes to that,' he said quietly. 'Color's color, and nobody can't get away from it. When you marry I guess you'll want babies, or you wouldn't be you. And if you marry me, they'll be black ones, not quite so black as me, perhaps, but mighty black all the same.'

She said gently: 'You aren't all that black, Dave. You don't want to go exaggerating things.'

He said: 'I don't reckon that I'd pass for white, though, even in the dark.' There was a rueful hint of laughter in his voice. 'I guess you know the way I feel about you, ever since those first times we met, in the store. There's never been another girl for me, not after that. I got enough now with this last raise to ask you, Gracie. If you kind of feel that you can't fancy it. I wouldn't blame you. Back home in some States, even saying this to you would likely get me into trouble.'

She asked: 'Do you think I'd have come out with you all these times if I cared about things like that?'

'I dunno,' he said. 'I never did know rightly what girls care about, Gracie. But getting married to a nigger is a mighty big thing for a white girl, seems to me.'

She said quietly: 'Getting married is a mighty big thing anyway, Dave. There's such a sight of things that can go wrong in a marriage, 'n I don't think colour's as important as some others—getting on all right, and respecting one another, and that. You wouldn't have asked me if you didn't think them things were right. And I think they're right, too.'

His grasp tightened on her hand. 'You mean that?'

'O' course I do,' she said. 'I'll marry you, Dave, if you want me.'

'Do I want you?' And then he said: 'You do know what it means? We'll be all right in England, maybe, but it could be mighty awkward for you if we ever had to go to the States.'

'Who's talking about going to the States?' she said. 'You don't want to go back there, do you?'

'It's my country,' he said. He stood for a minute, thoughtful, filled with nostalgic regret for the things that might have been. 'I don't reckon that I'll ever want to go back there,' he said at last. 'I got a good job here, and a darn sight more opportunity than ever I'd get at home. I don't reckon I'll ever want to go back to the States.'

Mr Turner and Mollie waited in the White Hart till half past six, to give Lesurier time to get back from his work and have his tea; then they walked up the road and found 'Sunnyvale'. It was a drab little slate cottage, but the window frames were freshly painted, and some care seemed to have been taken over the front garden. Mr Turner walked up to the door with his wife at his elbow, and knocked.

The door was opened by a young Negro. Turner said: 'Mr Lesurier, isn't it?'

'That's right.' It was nearly dark, though the room within was brightly lit by a paraffin lamp. The Negro peered at them.

'You won't remember me,' said Mr Turner, 'but I was in the White Hart, and the landlord told me you lived here. We were in hospital together back in 1943, Dave. My name's Turner.'

Lesurier exclaimed: 'Say . . . Captain Turner?'

'That's right. Not captain any longer—just Mr.'

'Come right in, Cap'n.' He led the way into the room, half parlour and half kitchen. 'Think of meeting again, after all this time!' He was introduced to

Mollie. 'Say, sit right down and make yourselves at home a minute, while I tell the wife.' He explained. 'She's bathing the baby.'

They sat down, and he vanished up a flight of wooden stairs contained in a cupboard-like structure at the side of the room; there was a murmur of voices from the room above. They looked around them. The room was fairly spacious for the size of the house, being practically the whole of the ground floor. The furniture was aged but adequate; a bright fire burned in the small kitchen range; the room was cosy and cheerful with bright, rather gaudy colours in curtains and loose covers. The lamp stood on a large kitchen table still littered with the remains of tea, but the tea things had been pushed to one side, and a pencil, and a cheap exercise book, and a thin book of trigonometrical functions, and a slide rule, and a copy of a book called *Transient Phenomena* by Steinmetz with a library tag on it showed that the draughtsman was learning the oddities of alternating current circuits. Then he appeared again, clattering down the stairs.

'She'll be right down,' he said. 'Say, I'm mighty glad to see you, Cap'n. You know,' he said, 'it's been bothering me quite a bit I never got to know what happened to you, with that wound you got, and everything. It seemed to me sometimes that we was all in a tough spot together in that ward, even the pilot with his fancy wife, 'n we ought to have kept up. But I never heard no more of you, or the pilot either.' He laughed. 'The way I was fixed myself, I didn't get much chance to make inquiries.'

'Well, I can tell you what happened to Flying-Officer Morgan,' said Mr Turner comfortably. 'He . . .' He checked himself, and looked up at the Negro. 'I met him out in Burma,' he said quietly. 'It'll interest you, this will. He got rid of that wife of his, and married a Burmese girl.'

'No!'

'Fact. I met him out there, only a couple o' months ago.'

'A colored girl?'

'That's right.'

Lesurier burst out laughing, and slapped his thigh. 'Well, what do you know about that? Say, Cap'n, do you think there could have been something catching in that ward? You know I married a white girl?'

'So Mr Frobisher said,' said Mr Turner. 'Maybe it *is* catching. For all I know, it maybe going on all over the world. If so, I shan't lose any sleep about it.'

Lesurier said: 'Say, tell me more about Mr Morgan, Cap'n. How did he come to meet this colored girl he married?'

'He met her out in Burma,' Mr Turner said. He settled down upon the worn settee to tell the Negro all about it; in the middle of their discussion Grace came downstairs, and they all stood up and were introduced. She said: 'I'm ever so pleased to meet you. I've heard Dave talk about you, Captain Turner, ever so many times, when Mr Brent was here, and wondering what happened to you.' She turned to Mollie. 'I just been putting down the baby. Like to take a peep at him before he goes to sleep?'

'Oh, I'd like to do that.' The two women went upstairs, and Mr Turner turned to the Negro. 'Did your wife say something about Brent?'

'That's right,' said Lesurier. 'Duggie Brent. He's the only one of the four of us that I knew anything about, till you came in this evening.'

'What's he doing now?' asked Mr Turner.

'Got a job at Camborne with a butcher,' said the Negro. 'Drives all round this end of Cornwall in the van, he does, selling in the villages. I'll tell you about him. But go on about Morgan.'

Mr Turner went on talking about Flight-Lieutenant Morgan and Nay Htohn in far off Mandinaung. Upstairs in the little bedroom the two women bent over the cot. The face of the baby showed as a yellowish brown patch on the white pillow.

'He's ever such a darling,' said the mother softly. 'He knows us both already, and he's ever so intelligent. Got all his father's brains, he has. He's going to have a little brother or sister in May.'

'Fancy,' said Mollie. 'My dear, I am so glad.'

Grace said: 'Well, we thought as he was kind of dark that it 'ld make things easier if he had two or three brothers 'n sisters of his own sort along with him, besides our wanting them as well.' She straightened up over the cradle. 'I dunno how you think about these things,' she said. 'Lots of folks, they think I done something terrible, marrying a Negro. But they never talk that way, not after they get to know him.' She laughed. 'Most o' them say then he's exceptional, 'n not like the others. But I dunno. I never had no regrets.'

Mollie stooped over the baby. 'He is a darling little chap,' she said, wistful at her own childlessness. 'Do you suppose he'll have much trouble at school, when he gets older, with the other children?'

Grace shook her head. 'Not if we keep him to school here,' she said. 'There's one or two more like him in Trenarth, sort of souvenirs of the Americans.' She laughed, and then she said: 'Of course, Dave says he will have trouble, on account of his colour. Like he has himself. But I dunno—I don't think trouble hurts people so much. I think it kind of brings out what's best in them, don't you? I know it has with Dave.'

Mollie nodded. 'I expect that's right.'

Grace said: 'My dear, I must tell you what the vicar said about him—it was awful. He's ever such a queer man, Mr Kendall—says the queerest things, right out in the pulpit, sometimes. I suppose that's why he's only a vicar of a little place like this, they wouldn't give him a bigger parish. Well, I asked him to come and see baby here before the christening because I thought he might not like it about the colour, and he came, and I asked him. And he said, he was about the colour of babies in the Middle East, in Palestine and that, and then he said, about the colour of Jesus Christ. And he said, if John the Baptist didn't mind about baptizing Him, he didn't mind baptizing little David here. My dear, wasn't that a terrible thing to say? He's ever such a queer man, Mr Kendall. I shouldn't think he'd ever get to be a bishop.'

Downstairs, Mr Turner was asking again about Duggie Brent. 'He's getting on all right,' the Negro said. 'He comes by here with the van Mondays and Thursdays, 'n always saves us a nice joint. Grace gets all her meat from him. It's better meat, and cheaper, too, than any she can get in Trenarth or Penzance. 'Course,' he said reflectively, 'I dare say he goes out of his way with us, because it was through us he kind of got the job, you see.'

Mr Turner asked: 'How was that, then?'

It seemed that Badcock's Fair had come to Penzance in the previous autumn, and Dave had taken Grace to it, and they had been to see the Wall of Death, and there was Duggie Brent, red-headed, dashing round the saucer on a motor bicycle and standing bowing at the bottom in the end while the audience, encouraged by the compère, showered pennies down upon the riders. They had met him after the show and had been introduced to his wife in the paybox, who was evidently going to have a baby pretty soon. They had all gone to the local for a drink, and had got on so well together that on Sunday when the show was closed down for the day the Brents had come out to Trenarth for tea with the Lesuriers.

'That was soon after our David was born,' the Negro said. 'They were kind of envious of us having a home like this, although it's not much. Phyllis didn't want to go on in the show business with the baby coming and all that, and Duggie—say, that boy certainly was fed up with the Wall of Death. But there wasn't anything else he could do, except butchering, and his father's shop in Romsey, that was sold. Well, they went on with the show but we kept thinking about it and how nice it would be if they could be neighbours, because Grace and Phyllis, they hit it off all right. So then I got to hear that Mr Sparshatt over at Camborne was starting his van round again—and say, was it wanted! The meat supply around these parts is just terrible, for all that it's a country district. Well, Grace knows Jane Sparshatt through being at school together, see? And Jane spoke to her father, 'n I wrote to Duggie at some hotel in Edgware saying how there was a job there if he wanted it, 'n he came right down, 'n Mr Sparshatt took him on for the van round. So now he drives the van round all week, selling the meat, getting back to Camborne every night, of course. He says it's a darn sight more fun than the Wall of Death, or the Parachute Corps either.'

'Got a house at Camborne, has he?'

'That's so. Got a little girl, too, Julienne Phyllis. Got another coming pretty soon, too. He's fixed 'up all right. Take over the shop someday, after Mr Sparshatt's time, I'd think.'

'Well, that's fine,' said Mr Turner. 'We all come out all right then, all the lot of us. You'd never have thought it, back in 1943, would you?'

'No,' said the Negro. 'We certainly did seem a no-good bunch of bums around that time.' He glanced at Mr Turner. 'You got on all right, then?'

'Oh, I done fine,' said Mr Turner. He hesitated for a moment, and then said: 'I had a bit o' trouble after I left hospital, but after that I went ahead in business, 'n never looked back. I got a nice house in Watford, paid for, too, 'n a good job. I been mighty lucky, taking it all round.'

'Say, that's great,' said Lesurier. 'You don't never get no trouble from the wound?'

'Not so's you notice,' said Mr Turner briefly. 'Throbs a bit, now and then, but nothing to signify.'

Lesurier did not feel that he could ask for more detail. To him, his visitor looked to be a very sick man, indeed; there was a thin grey look about him that the Negro did not understand but which seemed menacing, and he seemed only to have partial use of the right hand. He said: 'You made a mighty fine recovery, you know. Back in the hospital, one time, they didn't think you'd live.'

'Born to be hanged,' said Mr Turner comfortably. 'That's what it is.'

The women came downstairs, and Grace Lesurier made a cup of fresh tea while Dave and Mollie washed the old tea things, and they sat talking for an hour. At last the Turners got up to go. 'It's been real nice seeing you again, Cap'n Turner,' said the Negro. 'It's a pity Duggie Brent couldn't have been here, too.'

'Don't matter,' said Mr Turner. 'Long as I know he's all right, that's all I care about. I never did see him, you know. I was all bandaged up. All I ever did was hear his voice. I wouldn't know him if I met him, now.'

'Fancy . . .' said Grace.

'I'll tell him about you and Mr Morgan when I see him next,' the Negro said. 'I reckon he'll be mighty glad to hear you're going on so well. We got kind of worried, him and me, we ought to try and find out what had happened to you. It didn't seem right when we was both fixed up so nice, we shouldn't try and find out about you and Mr Morgan. And now, you're better fixed than either one of us!'

'The pilot out in Burma,' Mr Turner said, 'he's better off than all the lot of us together.'

They said goodbye at the door. 'Let's know when you're down in these parts again,' the Negro said. 'That likely to be soon?'

'Oh, aye,' said Mr Turner. 'I get down here once in a while. Next summer, maybe.'

Grace said: 'Be sure and let us know.'

They got into the little car, and drove off to Penzance. At the wheel, Mollie said: 'Why did you say we'd be down here again, Jackie?'

'Got to say something,' he said heavily. 'You didn't tell her nothing, did you?'

'No,' she said quietly. 'I thought maybe you wouldn't want it.'

'That's right,' he said. 'No good getting folks upset about things they can't do nothing about.' He paused, and then came out with his favourite cliché. 'All be the same in a hundred years,' he said. 'That's what I say.'

They drove into Penzance.

I I

After his holiday in Cornwall, Mr Turner went downhill rather rapidly. They got back to Watford without incident, but he was tired by the journey, and when his wife suggested he should stay in bed next day he made no protest. He had breakfast in bed–'Like a Lord,' as he put it–and looked at the pictures in the paper, especially Jane, but reading was now difficult for him except for the very large headlines, and he had soon done with the *Mirror*. His wife brought him up the wireless and he lay listening to that while she cleaned up the house and washed the breakfast things. She went out presently to do her shopping, and on returning to the house about half past eleven found that he had turned the wireless off, and was lying in bed doing nothing at all. As she took her coat off, she said: 'Didn't you want the wireless any longer, then?'

He said: 'I turned it off. Kind of stops one thinking.'

She sat down on the bed for a minute before going down to start to cook the dinner. 'What you been thinking about?'

He said: 'Oh, all sorts of things. Seems like I never had time for any real thinking before, thinking things out, I mean. I been having a grand time.

Ought to ha' got sick like this long ago.'

'What sort of things, Jackie?'

'I dunno,' He paused, and then he said: 'I keep on being ever so glad them chaps got themselves fixed up all right, all the lot of them. And all having babies, too, right and left, every one of them. All the whole boiling of them. Sort of makes up for you and I not having any, don't it?'

'I suppose so,' she said slowly. 'I suppose it does.'

He said: 'You aren't sorry that we never, are you, now?'

'I dunno,' she said. 'Sometimes I kind of wish we had.'

'I'm glad we didn't,' he said. 'Things being like they are, with you having to work again and that, I'm glad we never. But lying here and thinking, I'm glad them chaps don't think about it like we do.'

'They're not so sensible' she said thoughtfully.

He grinned. 'That's right,' he said. 'Chaps with a dud napper like I got ought to be sensible about not having kids, but they don't have to be.'

She went downstairs to get on with the cooking, and presently she brought him up his lunch in bed while he lay listening to the wireless. And when she came he turned it off, and said: 'I been thinking, I'd like to write a letter to Mr Morgan out in Burma, to tell him about Dave Lesurier and Duggie Brent. I know he'd like to hear, 'n Nay Htohn, she'd like to hear about them, too.' So after lunch Mollie got her pad and he lay dictating a very long letter all about Trenarth and Grace Trefusis and the disease that was catching, and about Jones and Porter, and about Duggie Brent. And tired with the effort of so much dictation, he sank into sleep while Mollie was downstairs typing it, and slept till it was time for tea, and then got up and dressed and had his tea with her downstairs and went out with her to the pictures. That was a prototype for many days that followed, perhaps the happiest of their chequered married life.

On his good days he used to get up soon after breakfast and walk out with her to help her in her shopping, and come back and write one or two business letters. He shifted the last of his parcels of cheroots during these weeks, and on casting up his accounts came to the conclusion that he had made a profit of about three hundred and forty pounds on them, which more than covered the cost of his trip out to Burma. That pleased him very much.

They did not lay the little car up for the winter, but kept it in commission for his outings. On his good days, once or twice a week, Mollie drove him to the Barley Mow for an hour before closing time. He no longer had the energy to lead the party, but these short evenings drinking beer and listening to the gossip and the stories in the warmth and light of a crowded bar were a great pleasure to him; he used to talk of them next day with reminiscent pleasure, and make plans for the next outing.

He did his football pool religiously every week. He could no longer read the small print of the announcements, but Mollie read it all out to him each week and they would make out the coupons and send them in, one for him and one for her. He did not win anything, to her regret, but she won two pounds fifteen shillings one week, and this gave them both a great deal of pleasure.

On his bad days, when headache forced him to his drugs, he stayed in bed all day, somnolent, sleepy, and thoughtful. About the middle of October he had a fall in the kitchen. He had walked all morning, shopping, with Mollie; on coming into the house the vertigo seized him; he reached for the kitchen dresser and missed it and fell, hitting the back of his head heavily upon the fender. He brought down the soup tureen with him and three plates, and Mollie, hurrying downstairs to the noise, found him lying unconscious on the floor in a litter of smashed china.

She called Mrs Pocock from next door to help her; together they managed to carry him upstairs and put him to bed. He had come round by the time Dr Worth arrived, two hours later, but after that he did not walk out in the street again.

Mrs Pocock was devoted to good works. For want of someone to confide in, and for her help in getting Mr Turner up the stairs, Mollie told her the facts of his illness; she relayed them to the vicar. They were not regular churchgoers by any means—indeed, neither of them had very often been inside the place, but the vicar was a kindly and broadminded man, and called one afternoon when Mr Turner was in bed and thinking of getting up for tea to take a run out to the Barley Mow.

Mollie brought him up to the bedroom. 'Here's Mr Holden come to see you, Jackie,' she said. To the clergyman she said: 'It's ever so kind of you to call.'

She left them together, and went downstairs to get on with the ironing. Half an hour later she heard the vicar coming out of the bedroom, and went to meet him in the hall to open the front door for him.

Mr Holden said: 'He seems to keep very cheerful, Mrs Turner.'

'That's right,' she replied. 'Nothing seems to get him down, does it?'

'No; he seems very composed.' He thought for a minute. 'Of course, it's clear that he has never been what one would call a religious man,' he said, and smiled. She wondered apprehensively what Jackie had been saying to him. 'If I can do anything practical to help you, Mrs Turner, let me know. And if you find a little later on that he would like to see me again—that sometimes does happen, you know—I will come at once. At any time.'

She said: 'That's ever so kind of you, Mr Holden. I'm sure he'll like to know that.'

He left and she turned off the iron and went up to the bedroom. 'I just let Mr Holden out,' she said. 'Like to have your tea up here, Jackie, or are you going to get up?'

'Oh, I'll get up,' he replied. 'I'm feeling all right now. I reckon we can go out, like we said.'

She asked: 'What had Mr Holden got to say?'

'I dunno—all about having Faith, and that.' He paused. 'I asked him straight out what was going to happen to me—where do I go from here? I said. But he don't know nothing, really. He talked a lot of stuff about Judgment, 'n Heaven, 'n Hell, only he didn't seem to believe in hell himself, not properly. What it all seems to boil down to is, you just got to have Faith that God'll put you where you belong, but he don't know where that is or what happens to you there. It don't seem very satisfactory to me.'

Theological discussion was a new thing between them. 'I wouldn't bother your head about it too much, Jackie,' she said gently. 'Just take it as it comes.'

He was silent for a minute, deep in thought. 'I been thinking about this,' he said at last. 'I kind of like the idea them Buddhists have the best—what Mr Morgan and Nay Htohn believe. I don't want to be judged, not yet. I done a sight o' mean things in my life, things you probably don't know nothing about in business and that. You got to these days, or you can't get by and build up any security at all, with taxes like they are. If I come up to be judged now, 'n it's either Heaven or Hell, I know which it would be.'

'You can't know that yourself, Jackie,' she said. 'That don't make sense.'

'Well, I've got a pretty good idea,' he replied. 'But these Buddhists, what they say is, if you haven't done so good in this life then you get reborn again a bit lower down, maybe as an Indian sweeper, or lower down still, as a horse or a dog. That gives you another go, like, to have another shot at it 'n try and do a bit better. And however low you get, they say, you always get reborn, and you can always have another go, and work yourself up again by living a better life. That's what Nay Htohn said. I'd like to think that it was going to be like that.'

'Maybe it will be like that, then,' she said quietly. 'I wouldn't worry about it, anyway.'

Mr Turner said: 'I don't. Can't do anything about it, now, so it's no good worrying. But I kind of like the Buddhist idea–that's how I'd like to be.' He grinned up at her. 'So if you see a little dog about next year you haven't seen before, 'n you call "Jackie", 'n it comes, just give it a nice bone.'

'And put a bottle of beer in its bowl, too, I suppose,' she said. She turned, laughing, to the door. 'Come on and get up, if you're getting up today. I'll go and put the kettle on for tea.'

Another time, he said: 'I been thinking about these coloured people that I got to know about, Nay Htohn and Dave Lesurier. You know, there don't seem to be nothing different at all between us and them, only the colour of the skin. I thought somehow they'ld be different to that. They got some things we haven't got, too–better manners, sometimes. I reckon we could learn a thing or two from them.'

His wife said: 'You got to remember that those two were different to the general run of coloured people, Jackie. They were educated ones.'

'That's so,' he said thoughtfully. 'Maybe there's some sense in paying for all this schooling.'

I saw Mr Turner on October 30th in my rooms at Harley Street, by an appointment made for him by his general practitioner, Dr Worth. I saw him at four o'clock in the afternoon upon a day when I had no further appointments, thinking that I might find it necessary to take him to the hospital for another radiological examination.

My receptionist showed him in. His wife came in with him, one hand lightly guiding his arm; she seemed to be afraid to let him move a step without her. She watched him as he lowered himself into the chair, and then said: 'I'll wait outside, doctor.'

'No, you can stay if you want to,' I replied. 'That is, if Mr Turner doesn't mind?'

'Suits me all right,' he said.

He spoke thickly, with a slurring of the consonants. He still possessed his jaunty air of cheerfulness, but one glance told me that I would have little need of radiological examination for him. Paralysis of the right arm was far advanced. The left eye was fixed and evidently useless to him, and the right one was already much affected. He had lost a great deal of weight, so that his clothes, once tight upon his body, hung upon him loosely. He still had colour in his face, but around his eyes and temples there was a grey tinge to his skin. It did not seem to me that he had very long to go.

I have been over thirty years in specialist practice. Some men say that they get hardened to these things, but I have never overcome that sadness of compassion that one must feel for a man in his position.

I offered him a cigarette, and reached over, and lit it for him.

I said: 'Well, Mr Turner, what have you been doing since I saw you last?'

NEVIL SHUTE

NO HIGHWAY

... Therefore, go forth; companion: when you find
No highway more, no track, all being blind,
The way to go shall glimmer in the mind.

Though you have conquered Earth and charted Sea
And planned the courses of all Stars that be,
Adventure on, more wonders are in Thee.

Adventure on, for from the littlest clue
Has come whatever worth man ever knew;
The next to lighten all men may be you ...

John Masefield

I

When I was put in charge of the Structural Department of the Royal Aircraft Establishment at Farnborough, I was thirty-four years old. That made a few small difficulties at first, because most of my research staff were a good deal older than I was, and most of them considered it a very odd appointment. Moreover, I wasn't a Farnborough man; I started in a stress office in the aircraft industry and came to Farnborough from Boscombe Down, where I had been technical assistant to the Director of Experimental Flying for three years. I had often been to Farnborough, of course, and I knew some of the staff of my new department slightly; I had always regarded them as rather a queer lot. On closer acquaintance with them, I did not change my views.

In spite of my appointment from outside I found them quite co-operative, but they were all getting on in years and beginning to think more about their pensions than about promotion. When I got settled in I found that each of them had his own little niche and his own bit of research. Mr Morrison, for example, was our expert on the three-dimensional concentrations of stress around riveted plate joints and he was toying with a fourth dimension, the effect of time. What he didn't know about polarised light wasn't worth knowing. He had been studying this subject for eight and a half years, and he had a whole room full of little plate and plastic models broken upon test. Every two years or so he produced a paper which was published as a R. and M., full of the most complicated mathematics proving to the aeroplane designer what he knew already from his own experience.

Mr Fox-Martin was another of them. I discovered to my amazement when I had been in the department for a week that Fox-Martin had been working since 1935 on the torsional instability of struts, with Miss Bucklin aiding and abetting him for much of the time. They were no laggards at the paper work, for in that time they had produced typescript totalling well over a million words, if words are a correct measure of reading matter that was mostly mathematical. At the end of all those years they had got the unstabilised, eccentrically loaded strut of varying section just about buttoned up, regardless of the fact that unstabilised struts are very rare today in any aircraft structure.

I knew that I had been appointed from outside the Royal Aircraft Establishment as a new broom to clean up this department, and I had to do a bit of sweeping. I hope I did it with sympathy and understanding, because the problem of the ageing civil servant engaged in research is not an easy one. There comes a time when the research worker, disappointed in promotion and secure in his old age if he avoids blotting his copybook, becomes detached from all reality. He tends to lose interest in the practical application of his work to the design of aeroplanes and turns more and more to the ethereal realms of mathematical theory; as bodily weakness gradually puts an end to physical adventure, he turns readily to the adventure of the mind, to the purest realms of thought where in the nature of things no unpleasant consequences can follow if he makes a mistake.

It is easy to blackguard these ageing men and to deride their unproductive work, easy and unprofitable and unwise. Short-term *ad hoc* experiments to solve a particular problem in the design of aircraft were the main work of my department, but I was very well aware that basic research also has a place in such a set-up, the firm groundwork of pure knowledge upon which all useful short-term work must be erected. In the great mass of typescript chaff turned out by the Fox-Martins and the Morrisons within the R.A.E. were hidden grains of truth. Callow young men entering the Establishment from the universities, avid for knowledge and enthusiastic in their early years, would read through all this guff and take it very seriously, and find and recognise the little grains of truth, and take them into their experience and use them as their tools for short-term work.

I had to steer a middle course, therefore, as every sensible new broom must do. Within the first year I had transferred two of the oldest of my scientific officers, and I had changed the line of three others. It was a busy year, because I got married soon after I went to Farnborough. Shirley was a local girl who had taught drawing and music in a little school in Farnham before the war; when the school evacuated she had become a tracer at the R.A.E. In the fourth year of the war she was sent to Boscombe Down to work in the drawing office; she had her desk and drawing board just outside my little glass cubicle, so that every time I looked up from my calculations I saw her auburn head bent over her tracings, which didn't help the calculations. I stood it for a year, high-minded, thinking that one shouldn't make passes at the girls in the office. Then we started to behave very badly, and got engaged.

We got a flat in Farnham with some difficulty and got married into it soon after I took up my new job. It was a very small flat, with just one bedroom and a sitting-room and a bathroom, and a kitchen that we had our meals in. It was big enough for all we wanted, and we were very happy. There wasn't much for Shirley to do, since I was away all day, and we didn't plan to start a family for a year or so. So she went back to teaching music and drawing in the school that she had taught in before, and one of the girls she taught was Elspeth Honey.

She told me about Elspeth one evening when we were sitting after the nine-o'clock news. Shirley was sewing a slip or something, and I was working at the first paper that I had been asked to read before the Royal Aeronautical Society, which I called 'Performance Analysis of Aircraft Flying at High Mach Numbers.' It was something of a distinction that I had been asked to read this thing, and I was very busy working on it in the evenings.

Shirley told me about Elspeth as we sat there; she was teaching her to play the piano at that time. 'She's such a funny little thing,' she said thoughtfully. 'I can't make out if she's immensely clever or just plain bats.'

I looked up, laughing. 'I've been wondering that about her father ever since I took over the department.' Because Mr Theodore Honey was another one of the old gang of budding Einsteins that I had inherited. So far I had left him alone, feeling that the work that he was doing on fatigue in light alloy structures was probably useful. But I must admit that there were moments when I had my doubts, when I wondered if Mr Honey was not sliding quietly into an inoffensive form of technical mania.

Shirley bent over her sewing. 'She *looks* so odd,' she said presently, 'with her straight black hair and her white little face, and those ugly frocks she wears. She never seems to play with the other children. And she does say the queerest things sometimes.'

'What sort of things?' I asked. I was not quite happy in my mind about her father; subconsciously I was interested in anything to do with the Honey family.

Shirley looked up from her sewing, smiling. 'Pyramidology,' she said.

I stared at her, 'What's that?'

She mocked me. 'Call yourself a scientist, and you don't know pyramidology! Even Elspeth knows that.'

'Well, I don't. What is it?'

'It's all about the Great Pyramid, in Egypt. Prophecies and all that sort of thing.'

I grinned. 'That's not the sort of science that I learned at college. Is that what they teach at your school?'

She bent to her work again, and said quietly, 'No, it's just Elspeth. She came and asked me if she could do her practising in break on the school piano, and I asked her why she couldn't do it at home. She said there wasn't time now, because she was helping her Daddy with his pyramidology. I asked her what that was, and she told me all about it. It seems that there's a sort of directional bearing from two points in the Great Pyramid which is lined up on Iceland, just like a radar beam, and that's where Our Lord will come down to earth at the end of the world, and that's going to be quite soon. But Elspeth says her Daddy found a mistake in the calculations and he's working it all out again, and she's been helping him with the sums. She says it's all terribly exciting because her Daddy thinks it will turn out that the ray goes through Glastonbury, because Jesus Christ came to live in Glastonbury when He was a young man and so He'll probably want to go back there when He comes again. But Elspeth hopes that the ray will go through Farnborough because that's the most important place in the world and, besides, it's where her Daddy works.'

Shirley said all this without a smile, concentrated on her sewing. I stared at her incredulously. 'Does Mr Honey believe all this?'

She looked up at me. 'He must do, mustn't he. Or he wouldn't have told Elspeth. It's such a pity that she hasn't got a mother. It's rather unnatural for a kid of twelve to go on like that, don't you think?'

'What happened to her mother?' Anything about Honey was of interest to me now.

'I think she died during the war. Elspeth and her father live in one of those little houses in Copse Road.'

I nodded, visualising the small villas. 'Who looks after them?'

'I don't think anybody does. I believe they've got a charwoman who comes in now and then. But Mr Honey does the cooking for them both. I know that, because Elspeth told me that she cooks the breakfast on Sundays, but next year she's going to be allowed to do it every day.'

'She's twelve, is she.'

'Just twelve–her birthday was last month. But she's small for her age. You wouldn't think to look at her that she was more than ten.'

I sat deep in thought. I was visualising my Mr Honey going home each evening to his little house to cook a high tea for his little girl, and then to spend an hour telling her about the tangled prophecies connected with the Great Pyramid, and then putting her to bed. Did he hear her say her prayers, and if so, were they all about the Pyramid? And after that, alone in his small villa, what did he do? Did he go out to the cinema? I did not think he was one to spend the evening in a pub–or was he? Did he spend the evenings pondering the energy absorption factor of light alloy structures, or checking the position of the stars in the year 2141 B.C., the datum year of the Great Pyramid? I wanted to know all I could about his background, because I had not then made up my mind if he was a useful research scientist or not. What Shirley had told me was not very reassuring.

'I was talking to Sykie about Elspeth,' she said quietly. 'Of course, Sykie doesn't really know much botany, only just enough to teach the children something elementary. Elspeth got her floored in class the other day by saying that a buttercup was pentamerous, and Sykie didn't know if that was something rude or not. And so she made Elspeth tell them what she meant, and what she meant was that the buttercup has five of everything–five sepals in the calyx, five petals in the corolla, five carpels in the pistil, and so on. Sykie looked it up in the book afterwards, and she was quite right. But then she went on to say that the Bible was septamerous because it had seven of everything, and that's why seven was a holy number. Sykie got out of that one by saying that it wasn't botany.'

'Did Mr Honey tell her that–about the Bible.'

'I suppose he must have done. She didn't learn it at the school.'

I went to the department next day resolved to give a good part of my time to checking up on Mr Honey and the progress of his research. I had not bothered him a great deal up till then, because it seemed to me that the work he was engaged on was of real importance to the modern aircraft, which was more than could be said for some of the other stuff that I had found going on in the place. Because the work was of importance to the aviation world it was imperative that it should be properly conducted, and although Mr Honey's religious beliefs were no concern of mine a man who is eccentric in one sphere of his interests may well be eccentric in another.

As I have said, Mr Honey was working on fatigue in aircraft structures. Fatigue may be described as a disease of metal. When metals are subjected to an alternating load, after a great many reversals the whole character of the metal may alter, and this change can happen very suddenly. An aluminium alloy which has stood up quite well to many thousands of hours in flight may suddenly become crystalline and break under quite small forces, with most unpleasant consequences to the aeroplane. That is the general story of the effect that we call fatigue in aircraft structures, and we don't know a great deal about it. Mr Honey's duty was to try and find out more.

I went down to his stamping ground to see what he was doing. The Farnborough buildings at that time were a mixture of the old and the new, and Mr Honey occupied a shabby little room of glass and beaverboard in the annexe to the old balloon shed. Here he sat all day and covered sheet after sheet of foolscap paper with the records of his research, or pored over the work of scientists in many languages; he could read both French and German fluently. Outside his office an area of the ground floor of the balloon shed had been allocated to his work, and here he had quite a major experiment in progress.

The Rutland Reindeer was the current Transatlantic airliner at that time, and still is, of course; the Mark I model, which went into production first, had radial engines, though now they all have jets. Two years before I came upon the scene the strength tests of the tailplane had been carried out in my department, and for this two tailplanes had been provided by the Company for test to destruction. They were quite big units, fifty-five feet in span, as big as a twin-engined bomber's wing. It had only been necessary to break one of these expensive tailplanes for the strength tests for the airworthiness of the machine, and the other one remained upon our hands until eighteen months later Mr Honey put in a plea for it, and got it.

He had set it up in the balloon shed, horizontally as it would be in flight. He had designed a considerable structure of steel girders to support it at the centre section as it would be held in the aircraft, and this structure was pivoted in such a way that it could be vibrated, or jiggeted, by a whacking great electric motor driving a whole battery of cams to simulate the various harmonics that occur in flight. He had chosen a loading for the tailplane that would reproduce the normal cruising flight conditions, and he had started up the motor a couple of months before and sat back to wait for something to happen.

All that was going on as I was settling in to my new job and as my predecessor had authorised it I had to let it take its course, though I was not too happy about it. I had a feeling that a competent researcher could have got his data from a less expensive test, and apart from that the thing was a considerable nuisance for the noise it made. It may be possible to make mechanical vibrations without making noise, but it's not often done, and this thing could be heard all over the Establishment. And apparently it was going to go on for ever, because nobody but Mr Honey thought that tail would ever break by reason of what he was doing to it. It looked much too strong.

Honey got up as I went into his office. He was a smaller man than I am, with black hair turning grey; he was dressed in a very shabby suit that had been cheap to start with. He always looked a bit dirty and down at heel, and his appearance did not help him, because he was one of the ugliest men I have ever met. He had a sallow face with the features of a frog, and rather a tired and discontented frog at that. He wore steel-rimmed spectacles with very thick glasses, and he was as blind as a bat without them. Looking at him, my wife's description of his daughter came into my mind, the dark-haired, white-faced, ugly little girl. Of course, she would be like that.

I said, 'Morning, Mr Honey. I've just come down to have a look at your tailplane. Anything happening to it yet?'

He said, 'Oh no—everything is going on quite normally, so far. We can't expect much yet, you know.' He had a few strain gauges mounted on various parts of the structure and he was reading them every three hours and graphing the readings. He showed me the curves illustrating the daily deformations of the structure as the test went on; after a few initial disturbances, due to the rivets bedding down, the curves flattening out and went along as a straight line. It was behaving just exactly as one would expect a safe structure to behave.

We stood and looked at it, and walked around it in the noise. Then we went back into his office, where the noise level was lower, and talked about it for a bit. I cannot say I was impressed with what I saw and heard. But for the expense of the set-up, I should have been very much tempted to call off the entire experiment.

'What's your prognostication, Mr Honey?' I asked presently. 'How long do you think it will go on for?'

He smiled nervously, as the pure researchers always do when you try to pin them down to something definite. 'One has to make so many assumptions,' he said. 'The mass energy absorption factor, that fact that I call U_m in my papers – that varies somewhat with each type of structure, and one really has to do a preliminary experiment to establish that.'

That sounded like an old story to me, and I was not impressed. 'You mean, with a tailplane like this you've got to break one first under a fatigue test, just like this, to establish the factor?'

'Yes,' he said eagerly, 'that's right.'

'And then,' I said, rather naughtily, 'having found out the factor you can calculate back and find out when it broke.'

He glanced at me, uncertain if I were laughing at him or not. 'Of course, you can then apply that factor to other tails of similar design, vibrated on a different range of frequencies.'

I said doubtfully, 'Yes, I suppose so, when you've built up a good deal of experience.'

I spent most of the rest of the morning going through his papers with him and getting acquainted with his theory. I knew the broad outline of his ideas already, and because I knew them I had avoided going into them in more detail until I really had to. Because, like all my other Einsteins, Mr Honey in his research upon fatigue had gone all nuclear.

When the fundamental theories about atomic fission became generally known to scientists in 1945, they came as a godsend to all middle-aged researchers. Here was a completely new field of pure thought to explore, whether it had anything to do with their immediate job or not. Each of them very soon convinced himself that in an application and extension of nuclear theory lay the solution to all his problems, whether they were concerned with the effect of sunlight on paint or the formation of sludge in engine-lubricating oil. It seemed at times that every scientist in the Establishment had made himself into an expert upon nuclear matters, all but me, who had come from the material and earthly pursuit of testing areoplanes in flight, and so had started late in the race. I didn't know much about the atom, and I was very sceptical if nuclear matters really affected my department at all.

However, Mr Honey was convinced they did, and he had built up an imposing structure of theory upon a nuclear basis. Quite simply, what he held was that when a structure like a tailplane is vibrated a tiny quantity of energy is absorbed into it, proportionate to the mass of the structure and the time that the treatment goes on for and a certain integral of strain. He had some evidence for this assertion, for he produced papers by Koestlinger of Basle University and by Schiltgrad of Upsala indicating that something of the sort does happen. Schiltgrad had made attempts to trace what happens to this lost energy, and had produced the negative result that it did not appear in any of the normal forms, as heat, electrical potential, or momentum. Mr Honey, sitting brooding over all this work, had convinced himself that this small energy flow produced a state of tension within the nucleus of aluminium of which the alloy is mainly composed, and that when this tension has built up to a certain degree one or more neutrons are released, resulting in an isotopic form of aluminium with crystalline affinities. This was the bare bones of his theory, and it was supported by about seventy pages of pure mathematics. It all seemed a bit like the Great Pyramid to me, and as difficult to criticise.

At the end of an hour or so with him I said, 'What value have you assigned to this quantity U_m for that tailplane out there?'

He said, 'Well–provisionally–just for getting a rough idea of how long the trial is likely to go on for, you see, I made a rough estimate—' He fumbled with his papers, shuffled them, dropped one on the floor and scrabbled after it, picked it up, looked at it upside down, turned it right way up, and said, 'Here it is. $2 \cdot 863 \times 10^{-7}$. That's in C.G.S. units, of course.'

I took the sheet from him and studied it. It was untidy work, half in pencil and half in ink, written in a vile hand, rather dirty. 'Those are just the rough notes,' he said nervously. 'I shall write it all up properly later on.'

I nodded. One must not, must not ever, be influenced by *gaucheries* when dealing with these people. Untidiness may be a sign of slovenly thinking in an adult man, but it can also be a sign of an immensely quick intellect that gives no time for neat and patient writing. Mr Honey was obviously nervous of me, and he was showing at his worst.

'This figure, $2 \cdot 863$,' I said at last. 'That's a pretty exact figure, Mr Honey–four-figure accuracy. When that constant goes into your theory, the time to reach fatigue failure will be directly proportional to that, won't it?' I turned to one of the final sheets of mathematics that he had displayed before me.

'That's right,' he said. 'The time to nuclear separation is directly proportional to U_m.'

'Well, I don't call that a rough estimate,' I said. 'That's a pretty detailed estimate, surely? I mean, that figure says that in a given case something may be going to happen in two thousand eight hundred and sixty-three hours. I should have said a rough estimate was one that said something would happen between two and three thousand hours.' I glanced at him.

He shifted uneasily. 'Well, naturally, I went into it as carefully as I could.' He showed me what he had based his estimate upon. It was a pile about three feet high of the Proceedings of practically every engineering learned body in Europe and America. 'I couldn't find anything about light alloy structures in fatigue prior to the year 1927,' he said dolefully. 'I don't know if there's anything else I ought to have got hold of.'

I laughed. 'I shouldn't think so, Mr Honey. If you've gone back to 1927 you've probably got everything there is.'

'I hope I have,' he said.

I turned over the sheafs of papers that were his analysis of previous trials and from which he had deduced the value of $2 \cdot 863 \times 10^{-7}$ for U_m, and I came to the conclusion that whatever bees he might have in his bonnet, he was at any rate a patient and an indefatigable worker, if rather an untidy one. At the end of ten minutes I said, 'Well, if this is what you call a rough estimate, Mr Honey, I'd like to see a detailed one.'

He flushed angrily, but did not speak. I had not meant to be offensive.

I turned over the papers before me. 'What does that mean to that tailplane out there?' I indicated the Reindeer tail upon the framework outside, booming and droning, filling the whole building with its noise. 'When do you expect something to happen?'

He said, 'There should be some evidence of nuclear separation in about 1,440 hours–taking that value for U_m.'

'That's till it breaks? It ought to break in 1,440 hours?'

He hesitated. 'I rather think that the material could be expected to suffer some change about that time,' he said, hedging. 'Under the normal loads imposed on it—yes, I think that failure would probably occur.' He shifted uneasily and said, as if in self-defence, 'The isotope is probably crystalline.'

'I see.' I stood for a moment looking at the test through his window. 'How long has it been going on for now?'

'About two months,' he said. 'We started on the twenty-sixth of May. Up till this morning it had run four hundred and twenty-three hours. It only runs in the daytime—the Director wouldn't allow it to run on night shift. It's basic research, you see.'

I calculated in my head. 'So it's got another four or five months to go?'

He said, 'Well—yes, about that time. I was expecting to learn something from it before Christmas, anyway.'

I stood silent for a minute, deep in thought. 'Well, that's all very interesting, Mr Honey,' I said at last. 'May I take what you've re-written so far and glance it over in my office? It all takes a bit of absorbing, you know.'

He sorted out a bunch of papers and gave them to me, and I tucked them under my arm, and walked back to my office in a brown study. Mr Honey was experimenting on a Reindeer tail, and what Mr Honey had lost sight of altogether was that Reindeer aircraft had come into service on the Atlantic route that summer. They were flying the Atlantic daily with full loads of passengers, from Heath Row to Gander, from Gander to New York or Montreal.

Although he didn't seem to realise it, Mr Honey had now said that the Reindeer tail was quite unsafe, that in his opinion it would break, suddenly and without warning, after 1,440 hours of flying.

It was the end of the morning. I left the paper in my office and walked up to the senior staff lunch-room. I found the Director there drinking a sherry; I waited for an opportunity when he was disengaged, and said, 'Have you got a quarter of an hour free this afternoon, sir?'

'I think so,' he replied. 'What is it, Scott?'

'It's about Mr Honey and his fatigue test,' I said. 'I'd like you to be aware of what's going on.'

'Can't help being aware of it,' he answered. 'You can hear the damn thing at the other end of the factory—it's worse than the wind tunnels. When is it coming to an end?'

'He says it's going on till Christmas,' I replied. 'I think it ought to be accelerated. But if I can come along this afternoon I'll tell you about it.'

'Quarter-past three?'

'I'll be there, sir.'

I turned away to go in to have lunch, but he detained me. 'Has Honey been all right recently?'

'All right? I think so, sir. I don't think he's had any time off.'

'I'm glad to hear that.' There was a momentary pause. 'You know,' he said, 'there has been a little trouble in the past. He seems to hold very firm ideas on certain semi-religious subjects.' I glanced at him in inquiry. 'About the lost ten tribes of Israel and their identity with Britain, and that sort of thing.'

'I hadn't heard that one,' I said. 'What I heard was something to do with the Great Pyramid.'

He laughed. 'Oh, that's another part of it—that comes in as well.' He spoke more seriously. 'No, just before you came there was a procession of these people in Woking, and it got broken up by a number of Jewish rowdies, and Honey was taken in and charged with creating a breach of the peace. He got bound over. I mention that because it's one of the matters that one has to bear in mind, that he has rather odd ideas on certain subjects.'

I nodded. 'Thank you for telling me, sir.'

'Poor old Honey,' he said thoughtfully. 'He's a man I'm very sorry for. But if you should decide at any time that a change would be desirable, I wouldn't oppose it.'

I went in to lunch aware that the Director didn't think a lot of Mr Honey. Anderson was there, who looks after radar equipment and development for civil air lines. I sat down next to him and said, 'I say, you can tell me. How many Reindeers are Central Air Transport Organisation operating now?'

He said, 'Five or six.'

'Do you know at all how many hours they've done?'

He shook his head. 'Not much, anyway. They only put them on the route last month, because they waited until four had been delivered. I shouldn't think any of the machines had done more than two or three hundred hours yet.'

I thought with relief that we had a bit of time. 'How do they like it?'

'Like the Reindeer? Oh, they're very pleased with it. It's a lovely job, you know—nice to fly in and nice to handle. I think it's going to be a great success.'

I went back to my office after lunch and sat turning over Mr Honey's papers, studying his Goodman diagrams, thinking out what I was going to say to the Director. Nuclear fission was quite outside my experience; I did not know enough about it even to read Mr Honey's work intelligently, let alone criticise it or determine for myself the truth of his prognosis. And turning over his pages, disconsolate, I saw one or two sentences that made me wonder if Mr Honey knew much more than I did, for all his pages of mathematics.

I went down to the Director that afternoon and told him all about it. 'On his estimates, he reckons that the Reindeer tail, the front spar, will fail by fatigue in 1,440 hours,' I said. 'I don't much like the sound of that. The Reindeers are in service now.'

'What is the estimate based on?' he asked.

I told him all about the nuclear fission theory and the separation of the neutron that produced an isotopic form of aluminium within the alloy. 'Quite frankly, sir,' I said, 'I don't understand all this myself. I'm not capable of criticising it. If he's correct it's very serious indeed, and all those aircraft should be grounded. But knowing something about Mr Honey—well, he may not be correct.'

He thought for a moment. 'The test will show. How long is that going on for?'

'It's only done four hundred and twenty-three hours,' I replied. 'He's not expecting it to break before next Christmas.' I paused, and then I said, 'I should think the aeroplanes are piling up hours quicker than the test. After all, they fly day and night, but the test only runs in our normal working hours.'

'What is the longest time that one of the aircraft has done?'

'I don't know, sir. One of them flew into a hill the other day, in Labrador or somewhere. I asked Anderson at lunch how many hours the rest of them had done. He said they'd only done two or three hundred hours each.'

'That gives us a little time,' he said. 'I didn't know they'd lost one of them.'

'It was in all the papers,' I told him. 'The Russian Ambassador to Ottawa was killed in it, Mr Oskonikoff or something. All the lot of them were killed.'

'Oh, that one—I remember. Was that a Reindeer?'

I nodded. 'That was the prototype Reindeer, the one we had here for the trials. But that's a clear case; it flew into the mountain. Hit just at the top of a precipice and fell about five hundred feet down into the forest, in flames. It always beats me how a pilot manages to get into that sort of position, with all the aids we give them.'

'It's the human factor,' he said. 'Still—I agree, you wouldn't expect mistakes of that sort in a decent air line.' He turned to the papers. 'I don't quite know what to say about all this, Scott. I'm like you—I can't criticise this nuclear stuff, myself. It's clearly a matter of urgency. I think we ought to put it up to I.S.A.R.B., on a high priority.'

The Inter-Services Atomic Research Board were certainly the proper people to advise us upon Mr Honey's stuff, provided they would do it quickly. 'I'm very nervous about any delay,' I said. 'Could you send it personally, sir?' I hesitated. 'I'd really like to ground those Reindeers till we get the thing cleared up, but I suppose that isn't practical.'

He stared out of the window. 'That means, stop the entire operation of C.A.T.O.'s Atlantic service . . . I think we'll have to get some supporting evidence for Mr Honey's theories before we could do that. But I agree with you, Scott, this thing has to be taken seriously. I'll send it to Sir Phillip Dolbear tonight, with a personal note.'

I went back to my office satisfied with this; I knew Dolbear to be acute and hardworking, a good chairman for the Atomic Board. I sent for Mr Honey and told him what was in the wind. I reminded him that he was playing with a real Reindeer tail, and that when he said blithely that his experiment would culminate at 1,440 hours, he really meant that real aeroplanes would crash after that flying time.

He blinked at me through his heavy glasses. 'Of course, I know that,' he said. 'But till the research work is completed, everyone is guessing in the dark. You must realise that in all this kind of work one has to feel one's way. I may be very much in error, very much indeed. There's nothing definite about it yet.'

'Do you think it could fail sooner?' I asked.

'Oh, I shouldn't think so. In fact, I've been preparing myself for a real disappointment about Christmas time. It could quite well go on till April, or even longer.'

He lived and thought in quite a different world from me if he could contemplate waiting a year for data on a thing like this. He was pure scientist all through, and I suppose I'm not. I told him that Sir Phillip Dolbear would probably want to have a talk with him in a day or two, and he went away.

At the end of the week Mr Honey went to London at the request of Sir Phillip. I sent for him next day and asked him how he had got on.

He looked uneasy and unhappy. 'I don't think he was really very much interested in the subject,' he said.

'What makes you think that?' I asked quietly. It looked as if they had not agreed too well.

He was silent for a minute. 'He was just out to pick holes in it,' he said at last. 'You aren't going to get a very good report. He's the sort of man who wants everything docketed and proved, and each stage made secure and buttoned up before you go on to the next. Well, as I told you, there's a great deal still to be confirmed in the entire basic theory. It will take years to do that. These experiments we are doing now are meant to confirm all the points that I have made assumptions on, one by one. I told him that. But he insisted on regarding the test we're doing now as a test of the Reindeer tail. I told him it was nothing of the sort. It's a test to find our errors in the theory.'

'But Mr Honey,' I said, 'this test is, in fact, a fatigue test of the Reindeer tailplane. The Reindeer is out and flying, carrying passengers across the Atlantic, and what you say is that the tailplane will break up in 1,440 hours of flying. That's a very serious thing to say. It means that all those aircraft should be grounded.'

He said unhappily. 'I never said anything of the sort. I told you I was quite prepared for a disappointment. Theoretically, and if all the assumptions I have made should be exactly and precisely correct, a separation of the neutron should occur at 1,440 hours. The purpose of this test is to show where the assumptions are wrong and to correct the theory. You're trying to turn a piece of basic research into an *ad hoc* experiment. Well, you can't do that.'

He glared at me angrily through his thick glasses. He was very much upset.

'I see your point,' I said slowly. 'But that doesn't help us in deciding what to do about the Reindeers that are in service now.'

'I don't know anything about that,' he retorted. 'It certainly won't help them to keep badgering me like this. Sir Phillip Dolbear didn't believe a word I said, and he's quite right. Nothing is proved yet, nothing is confirmed. You're trying to make me run before I can walk, and the result is I just look a fool. Well, that's not very helpful.'

'I didn't mean to do that Mr Honey,' I said. 'I'm just trying to find out what we ought to do about these aircraft that are in service now.'

'Well, I can't help you there,' he said. 'I've told you all I can, and I'm not going to be bullied into saying any more. You've got your troubles, and I've got mine.' He did not say that most of his troubles were of my making, but he meant it.

He went away, and I rang up Ferguson in the Department of Experiment and Research at the Ministry, who serves as our London office. 'Ferguson,' I said, 'this is Scott speaking. Look, we're getting a bit doubtful about the Reindeer tailplane; there's a suggestion that fatigue might crop up at a fairly early stage. It's got rather an exaggerated aspect ratio, you know. I believe I'm right in saying that C.A.T.O. are operating five or six of them on the Atlantic route. Could you get on to the Corporation or the A.R.B.–without alarming anyone unduly, because I think it may be a mare's nest–and find out how many hours flying these machines have done?'

He said at once. 'They can't have done much. They've only been operational for about a month. What number of hours represents the danger point?'

'Mr Honey's estimate is 1,440 hours. But as I say, I think it's a mare's nest.'

He laughed over the telephone. 'Oh, this is Honey, is it? In that case, I should think it might be. I'll find out from the Corporation, and let you know.' He rang back later in the morning. The longest time that any of the machines had done was 305 hours, up to the evening before.

Next day at about tea-time Shirley rang me up in the office. She said, 'Dennis, darling, I'm sorry to worry you. I've got Elspeth Honey here because she wanted to listen to the Pastoral Symphony on the wireless, and theirs is bust. I'm just going to give her tea. She wanted to let her father know where she is, because she won't be home when he gets there. I was wondering if you'd like to bring him back with you to pick up Elspeth.'

'Okay, dear,' I said. 'I'll do that.'

I rang up Mr Honey and told him, and suggested that he came back with me in my car instead of going by the bus, as he usually did. I was rather pleased to have the opportunity to do something for him, because the last time that we had spoken our relations had not been exactly cordial, and I didn't like to feel that he was nursing a grievance against me. I was aware, too, that there was a good deal of reason on his side. He met me at the car at half-past five, and we drove out on the road to Farnham.

'It's very kind of Mrs Scott to invite Elspeth like this,' he said diffidently. 'She mustn't let her make herself a nuisance.'

'Not a bit,' I said. 'She's probably company for Shirley – for my wife. It gets a bit slow for her sometimes when I'm away all day.'

'That is the trouble, of course,' he replied. 'I mean, with Elspeth. It's all right in the term time, but in the holidays it's sometimes very difficult.'

'I should think it is,' I said, thinking of his womanless menage. 'What do you do with her in the holidays?'

He said, 'There's a clergyman who runs a holiday home for children down at Bournemouth, and she goes there sometimes, but it's rather expensive. And he's started to take mental defectives now – very backward children, you know – so it's not quite so suitable as it used to be. But really, Elspeth's so good at playing by herself that I don't know that she isn't just as happy at home.'

The thought of his little girl of twelve spending her holidays alone all day in the villa in Copse Road was not an attractive one. 'It's very difficult,' I said.

'It's a great deal easier in term time,' he remarked. 'Elspeth likes being at school, and she's very fond of Mrs Scott. She talks about her a great deal.'

I was not surprised to hear that Elspeth liked being at school if her holidays were spent alone in a deserted house. 'You've met my wife, have you, Honey?' I asked. 'Miss Mansfield, who used to be a tracer in the Aerodynamics? A girl with fair, sort of auburn hair?'

He did not think that he remembered her.

At the flat we found Shirley and Elspeth sitting over tea in the sitting-room listening to the wireless; we went in quietly, not to disturb them. I made a fresh pot of tea for Honey and myself, and we sat listening to the symphony with them till it was finished. It was the first time I had seen Elspeth Honey, and this pause gave an opportunity to study her. As Shirley had said, she was an ugly child, but this ugliness seemed to me to be more associated with her unbecoming clothes and the way her hair was cut than with the child herself. She had rather sharp, pale features; she was thin; and she looked intelligent. She did not look to be a very happy child. She had fine, well-shaped hands, and when she moved she did not seem to be clumsy. If she had had a mother, I reflected, she might have been very different.

The symphony came to an end, and Shirley reached over and switched off the set. She turned to the child. 'Like it?' she asked.

The little girl nodded vigorously with closed lips. 'Mm.'

My wife got up and began to gather up the plates and put them on the trolley. 'I thought you would. They're going to do one every week. Would you like to come again?'

Honey said nervously, 'You mustn't let her be a nuisance, Mrs Scott.'
'I won't,' said Shirley. 'I like listening to symphonies.'
Elspeth said, 'I'd like that ever so. May I do the washing up?'
Shirley said, 'Of course not. I was only going to pile these things together and take them out.'
'They've got to be washed up sometime, Mrs Scott. I can do it–honestly, I can.'
Her father said, 'Do let her help you, please. She's very good at washing up.'
'I can do it,' the child repeated. 'Daddy drops things, so I always do it at home.'
My wife said, 'All right, we'll do it together.'
They took the trolley out with them, and I sat talking with Honey as we smoked. I had only half my mind on our conversation and I forget what it was about to start with. I was furtively studying the man that I was talking to and trying to sum him up, the man who said the Reindeer tail would come to bits in 1,440 hours. The man who believed that, and who also believed in the Great Pyramid and in the descent of Our Lord to earth at Glastonbury or Farnborough in the very near future. The man who lived alone, and seemed quite unconscious that by doing so he was denying most of the simple joys of childhood to his little girl. The man who took umbrage in the office at small slights; the man who lived in an unreal, scientific dream. The man who walked in some queer semi-religious procession in Woking, and got had up by the police for some brawl that arose from it. The man who said the Reindeer tail would come to bits in 1,440 hours. The man whose judgment we had to accept or to discard.
And presently he added something to the picture I was building up. He was looking at the backs of my books in the bookcase, reading the titles, as one always does in a strange house. I woke up suddenly from my abstraction to hear him say, 'I see you've got Rutherford's book there.' And he indicated *The Aryan Flow* stuck in among the novels.
When I was at college I was interested for a very short time in the movements of the races of peoples about the world, and this volume was a relic of that passing enthusiasm. I had not opened it for at least ten years, but it was there still. I said idly, 'I think it's very good.'
He got up and picked the book out of the shelf, and turned the pages. 'Sharon Turner covers much of the same ground,' he said. 'But it's Rutherford who identifies the ten tribes with the Scythians. And after all, that must have been the most difficult part, mustn't it?'
I was a little at a loss. 'I've really rather forgotten,' I said. 'It's a long time since I read it.'
'You ought to look it over again,' he said earnestly. 'It was the most wonderful migration in the world.' He stared at me through his thick glasses. 'The ten tribes, led away into captivity by Shalmaneser, King of Assyria–that's all in the Second Book of Esdras. The Persians called them Sakae–our word Saxon, of course, and Rutherford proves their identity with the Scythians. And then, from his end, Sharon Turner traces back the Anglo-Saxons all through Europe to the Scythians. It's fascinating.'
I was completely out of my depth. 'Absolutely,' I said.
He went on, 'It explains so much. The Druidic forms of worship, that were nothing but the old religion of Israel brought here in its entirety.' He paused

and then said, 'That's what impressed Joseph of Arimathea so much when first he came to England on his tin business. That's why he brought his nephew here when He was a little boy, because he saw the Child was something quite unusual, and he wanted Him to come in contact with the priests of England. That's why Our Lord came back to Glastonbury as a young man and lived here for years before His ministry, because he had to live in the precepts of the old Israel which the Druid priests had kept here undebased. That's why Joseph came back to Glastonbury with Martha and Mary and Lazarus after the death of Christ, because they wanted to settle down and found His church in the place that He had loved so well.'

The Reindeer tail, he said, would come to bits in 1,440 hours. 'I'm not very well up in all this, I'm afraid,' I said.

He put the book back carefully upon the shelf. 'It's the most fascinating story in the world,' he said quietly. 'It explains so much. That's why Simon Zelotes, His apostle, came here as soon as he could. That's why St Paul came here.' He drew himself up, a short, earnest, spectacled figure, not unimpressive. 'That's why the English are the greatest people in the world and always will be, because in the beginning we were blessed by the advice and the example and the teaching of the greatest people who have ever lived.'

Elspeth came running into the room, and saved me from the necessity of commenting on that. Her father took off his thick glasses and wiped them, and said, 'Finished the washing up?'

She nodded. 'Daddy, Mrs Scott washes up with a little mop so that you never have to put your hands into the water at all! Isn't that a good idea? May we have a little mop like that?'

He blinked at her without his glasses. 'Mop?'

She pulled him by the sleeve. 'Daddy, come and see. And they've got hot water all the time, made by the electricity!' She drew him away into our little kitchenette to see these wonders for himself.

They went away soon after that, absurdly grateful for the trivial hospitality that we had shown to them. We closed the front door behind them and went back to the sitting-room. 'I rather like your Mr Honey,' Shirley said. 'But he does look a mess.'

'That's just what he is—a mess.' I turned to her. 'Tell me, had he really never seen a mop for washing up? Or an electric water-heater?'

She laughed. 'Honestly, I don't think he had. I don't know what his own kitchen can be like!'

I lit a cigarette and flopped down in a chair. 'Tired?' she asked.

'A bit.' He said the Reindeer tail would come to bits in 1,440 hours, but he didn't know what an electric water-heater looked like. Could that possibly make sense? Did he know enough about real life to speak with confidence on anything? Was his opinion of any value whatsoever? Could one trust his judgement? I did not know, and I sat there turning it over and over in my mind.

Shirley said, 'Here you are.' I roused myself to what was going on, and the wonderful girl had been out to the kitchen and got a tumbler of whisky and soda, and she was offering it to me. I kissed the hand she gave it to me with, and said, 'Like to go to the pictures tonight?'

'I'll look and see what's on.' She picked up the paper, turned the pages, and said, 'I heard your Mr Honey holding forth very earnestly about something or other while we were washing up. What was it all about?'

I blew a long cloud of smoke. 'It was about the lost ten tribes of Israel, and the Druids, and about Jesus Christ coming to Glastonbury, and all sorts of stuff like that.' I looked up at her. 'I wish to God I could make up my mind if he's plain crackers or something different.'

'Is it important?' she asked.

'It is rather,' I told her. 'You see, he says the Reindeer tail will come to bits in 1,440 hours. And I'm supposed to be able to check up on his work. And I can't do it. I'm not good enough. . . .'

The next week was a torment of anxiety and uncertainty. I had to keep the matter to myself; I did not want to keep on badgering Mr Honey or to go wailing to the Director. Every day, I knew, the Reindeers were flying over the Atlantic piling up the hours faster than Mr Honey's test, each machine probably doing the best part of a hundred hours a week towards the point when Mr Honey said their tails would break. On the sixth day I couldn't stand it any longer, and suggested to the Director that perhaps he might give Sir Phillip a jerk up on the telephone.

On the ninth day the report came in. The Director rang through to tell me he had got it, and I went down to him. He handed it to me, and I sat down in his office to read it through.

Sir Phillip said that he had examined the work submitted to him in detail and had received certain explanations verbally from Mr Honey. He accepted, with considerable reserve, the work of Koestlinger indicating that an energy loss occurred when a material was subjected to repeated reversals of stress and that this lost energy could not be accounted for by any balance of the normal forms. It was a wild assumption on the part of Mr Honey, said Sir Phillip, that this lost energy became absorbed into the structure of the atom in the form of nuclear strain. He could only regard that as an interesting hypothesis which might perhaps be a fit subject for research at some date in the future. If ever it should be confirmed that something of the sort did happen, then he was very doubtful if the stress induced would, in fact, produce a separation of the neutron that Mr Honey postulated. He said, a little caustically, that in his experience it was not so easy to split the atom as amateurs were apt to think. If such a separation should take place, he saw no present indication that the resulting new material would be the crystallamerous isotope that Mr Honey had observed in substances broken under a fatigue test. That, he seemed to think, was little more than wishful thinking on Mr Honey's part.

In spite of all this, he recommended that the trial of the Reindeer tail should be continued, as the subject was obviously important. If it was desired that research upon the problems of fatigue should be undertaken by the I.S.A.R.B., no doubt the representative of the Ministry would bring the matter up at the next meeting of the Board, when the priority to be allocated to the investigation could be determined.

I could have wept. Sir Phillip Dolbear had seated himself firmly on the fence and had offered us no help at all. And the Reindeers were still flying the Atlantic.

I said heavily, 'Well, this doesn't take us very much further, sir.'

The Director raised his eyes from the other work that he was reading. 'I thought that myself. I had hoped that we should get more out of him.'

We discussed it glumly for a few minutes. 'I should like to think it over for the rest of the day,' I said at last. 'At the moment I can't see anything for it but to go back to our old rule-of-thumb methods of guessing if the tail was dangerously flexible, and so on. May I think it over for today, and come in and see you tomorrow morning?'

'By all means, Scott,' he said. 'I'll be thinking it over in the meantime myself. It's certainly a difficult position, but fortunately we've got time for a little thought.'

I picked up the report and turned to go. 'In any case,' I said, 'I think we must face up to the possibility of having to ground all those Reindeers after seven hundred hours. I don't think we should let them go for more than half the estimated time to failure.'

'No,' he said slowly, 'I don't think that we should although I wouldn't put too much weight on Mr Honey's estimate after this. If we said seven hundred hours, how long does that give us?'

'About three weeks from now,' I said. 'I'll find out definitely before tomorrow, sir.'

I went back to my room and dumped the report, and then went down and out of the building, and walked down to the aerodrome, to the flight office. Squadron-Leader Penworthy was there. I said, 'I say, Penworthy. You did the flying on the prototype Reindeer, didn't you?'

'Most of it,' he said.

I offered him a cigarette. 'What was the tailplane like?' I asked. I explained myself. 'I know it was quite safe, but was it very flexible? Did it have much movement of the tip in flight?'

He said, 'Well, yes—it did. It never gave us any trouble, but it's got a very high aspect ratio, you know, so you'd expect a certain amount of waggle. On the ground you can push the tip up and down about six inches with your hand.'

I nodded slowly. 'Did it have much movement in the air?'

He hesitated. 'I don't think it had any continuous movement—it wasn't dithering all the time, or anything like that. You could see it flexing in a bump, from the aft windows of the cabin.'

I turned this over in my mind. 'Was that in very bumpy weather? What time of year was it?'

He said, 'We had it flying in all sorts of weather. It was here altogether for about three months.'

'So long as that? How many hours did it do?'

'Oh,' he said, 'it did a lot. I did about two hundred hours on it myself. Before that there were the firm's trials, of course.'

A vague, black shadow was forming in my mind. 'What happened to it after it left there?'

'I flew it down to the C.A.T.O. experimental flight,' he said.

I blew a long cloud of smoke, thoughtfully. 'Any idea how many hours it did there, before they put it into service?'

He shook his head. 'I'd only be guessing. But several hundred, I should think, because they did a whole lot of proving flights over the route before they put it into regular operation. They always do a lot of time on new machines before they go on service. They're pretty good, you know.'

I stared out over the aerodrome. 'That's the machine that flew into the hill in Labrador, isn't it?'

'That's right,' he said. 'Somewhere between Goose and Montreal.'

I went back to the office with a terrible idea half formed in the back of my mind. I rang up Group-Captain Fisher of the Accidents Branch; I had had a good bit to do with him at Boscombe Down on various occasions that had not been great fun.

I said, 'You remember that Reindeer that flew into the hill in Labrador? Tell me, sir—could you let me know how many hours it had done before the crash?'

He said he'd look into the matter and let me know.

He came back on the telephone twenty minutes later. 'That figure that you asked about,' he remarked. 'The aircraft had done thirteen hundred and eighty-three hours, twenty minutes, up to the time of the take-off from Heath Row.'

I said quietly, 'Add about nine hours for the Atlantic crossing?'

'About that, I should think.'

'And say another hour from Goose on to the scene of the accident?'

'I should think so.'

'Making 1,393 hours in all?'

'That's about right.'

I put down the telephone, feeling rather sick. It was my job to stop that sort of thing from happening.

2

That afternoon the Director was in a conference; I was not able to get in to see him until six o'clock in the evening. He was tidying up his papers to go home, and I don't think he was very glad to see me at that time. 'Well, Scott, what is it?' he inquired.

'It's that Reindeer tail,' I said. 'Rather a disconcerting fact came to light this afternoon.'

'What's that?'

'You remember the prototype, the one that flew into the hill in Labrador or somewhere?' He nodded. 'Well, it had done 1,393 hours up to the moment of the crash.'

'Oh. . . . Mr Honey's figure for tail failure was 1,440 hours, wasn't it?'

'That's right, sir.' I hesitated. 'The figures seem so close I thought you ought to know at once.'

'Quite right,' he said. 'But, Scott, in fact that machine *did* come to grief by flying into a hill, didn't it?'

I hesitated again. 'Well—that's what we're told, sir, and that's what everybody seems to have accepted. The story as I've heard it is that it hit the top of a mountain and fell down into a forest. Nobody saw it happen and everyone in it was killed. So there's no direct evidence about what happened to it.'

'Marks on the ground, to show where it hit first,' he said.

'Oh yes,' I said. 'I've no doubt that there was that sort of evidence. But if the tail came off at twenty thousand feet it would have to fall somewhere.'

'Is that what you think?'

I was silent for a moment. 'I don't know,' I said at last. 'I only know that this figure of 1,393 hours, the time that this machine did till it crashed–that figure's within three per cent of Mr Honey's estimate of the time to failure of the tail. I can't check that estimate and Sir Phillip Dolbear won't.' I paused in bitter thought, and then I said, 'And that three per cent is on the wrong side. It would be.'

'It certainly is a coincidence,' he said. 'Rather a disturbing one.' We stood in silence for a minute. 'Well,' he said, 'clearly the best thing is to establish what actually did happen to that aircraft. If it was a tailplane failure, then there must be some evidence of it in the wreckage. I should make a careful check of that upon the basis of Honey's theory. After all, a fatigue fracture is quite easily recognisable.'

I nodded. 'I was thinking on those lines, sir. I think the first thing is to get hold of the accident report and talk to the people who prepared it. If you agree I'd like to go to London in the morning and see Ferguson, and go with him to see Group-Captain Fisher in the Accidents Branch.'

'Will you take Honey with you?'

'Not unless you want me to particularly,' I replied. 'He isn't very good in conference, and I'd really rather that he stayed down here and got on with the job of verifying his theory. What I'd like to do would be to see him this evening and tell him that you've authorised the trial upon the Reindeer tail to go ahead by day and night from now on. I really think we ought to run a night shift on it, sir.'

'I think we should, Scott. Can you provide the staff?'

'I'll take young Simmons away from Mallory and put him to work with Honey,' I said. 'Simmons can watch the thing at night for the time being. He can have a camp bed in the office and an alarm clock. That'll do for a week or so; I'll have Dines to put on it when he comes back from leave.'

'All right, Scott. You can tell Honey that I'll see about the night shift in the morning.'

I was greatly relieved to have got that settled: at any rate we were now doing all we could upon the technical side. 'He'll have plenty to do tomorrow, sir, getting all that cracking. I'd rather he was down here doing that than coming up with me to London.'

It was nearly half-past six by the time I left the Director. I went back to my office and rang Honey's office, but there was no reply: he had probably gone home. I asked the exchange to give me his home number, and they said he hadn't got one. I packed up my work and went down to the balloon shed on my way out, to see if by any chance he was still there working late. But his office was locked and deserted. Outside, the great span of the tailplane stood upon its testing rig beneath the loading gantries, still and silent. It was not a happy thought that there were Reindeers in the air at that moment, putting up the hours towards the point when Mr Honey said their tails would break.

It was nearly half-past seven by the time that I got home. Shirley had dinner waiting for me for half an hour, and she was not too pleased about it. 'You might have rung me up,' she said.

I told her I was sorry. 'I've got to go out afterwards and dig up Honey,' I said. 'There's a bit of drama on.'

'What's the trouble?'

'It's that Reindeer tail,' I said.

'The one that Mr Honey says will come to bits in 1,440 hours?'

I nodded. 'Do you remember seeing in the paper that a Reindeer flew into a hill in Labrador a month or so ago? With the Russian Ambassador on board it?'

'I remember the Russians kicking up a stink,' she said. 'Was that a Reindeer?'

'That was the prototype Reindeer,' I replied. 'We heard this afternoon that it had done just on fourteen hundred hours when it came to grief.'

She had not worked at Boscombe Down all those years for nothing, and she knew quite a bit about aeroplanes. 'Oh, Dennis! Do you think it was the tail?'

'I just don't know,' I said unhappily. 'If it was, I suppose the bloody Russians will say we knew that it was going to happen, and we did it on purpose.'

She smiled. 'They couldn't say that, surely. Nobody suspected there was anything wrong with the tail when that one crashed.'

'Mr Honey did,' I said. There was no end to the trouble that might come out of this thing. But the first thing to do was to make darned sure that it could never happen again.

We had dinner, and washed up; then I went out and got into the car again, and drove round to Mr Honey's little house in Copse Road. It was about a quarter-past eight when I got there; the door was locked. It was one of those suburban doors with a window in the top part; through this window I could see past the stairs down the narrow hall into the kitchen at the back. I pressed the bell; it rang, but there was no sign of life. Then as I waited there was a stir upstairs and footsteps coming down, and Honey appeared in the hall and opened the door for me.

He said, 'Oh, Dr Scott–I didn't expect to see you. Come in. I was just putting Elspeth to bed.'

I went into the hall with him. 'I'm sorry to disturb you, Honey,' I said, 'but something came up about the Reindeer tail this afternoon that I wanted to talk to you about. I've been with the Director this evening, and I've got to go to London in the morning. If you can spare a minute I'd like to have a talk about it now.'

He led the way into the front room, which would normally have been the parlour. It was furnished with a long table pushed against the wall, and with an enormous drawing-board in the bay window; on this was pinned a large-scale map of Europe and the Mediterranean Sea, but drawn to some curious projection with which I was not familiar. The other walls were lined with rather dirty, unpainted deal cupboards and bookshelves. Books and papers were everywhere, and overflowed in piles upon the floor. I noted some of the titles of the books upon the table–*Numerics of the Bible*, *The Gate of Remembrance*, *Hysteresis in Non-Ferrous Materials*, *The Apocrypha in Modern Life*, and *A Critical Examination of the Pyramid*. The room was unswept and rather dirty, with cigarette ends stubbed out on the bare boards of the floor. There were two small upright wooden chairs; he pulled one forward for me.

'I'm afraid it's not very comfortable in here,' he said apologetically.

I smiled. 'It looks as if you do a bit of work, now and again.' I turned to the matter in hand. 'What I came about was this. You know that prototype Reindeer, the one that crashed in Labrador? The one that we all thought had flown into a hill?'

He said vaguely, 'I think I do remember something about it. It was in the papers, wasn't it?'

'That's right. It crashed and everyone was killed, so no one knows exactly what did happen to it. Well, I checked up on the hours that it had flown before the crash. It had done 1,393 hours.'

He stared at me. 'Had it? There'd be nothing to say that the crash wasn't due to tailplane failure?'

'That's just the point. I think the tail might possibly have failed. The crash wasn't seen by anyone, of course. It happened in the middle of Labrador.'

A slow smile spread over his face. 'Well, that's a real bit of luck,' he said.

I was staggered. 'Luck?'

He beamed at me. 'It's just what we wanted—it will shorten down our work enormously.' He explained himself. 'I mean, if this tail that we're testing now also fails at about 1,400 hours we shall have two trials, one confirming the other. We really shall feel that we're getting somewhere then.'

I said weakly, 'Well—that's one way of looking at it.'

From one of the rooms upstairs Elspeth called out, 'Daddy, Dad-dee!' she sounded impatient.

Honey turned to me, and said nervously. 'Would you mind excusing me for just a minute? I didn't pull her blind down.'

There was no point in playing the high executive, the little tin god; I had nothing else to do that evening. 'Not a bit,' I said. 'Can I come up with you?'

'She'd be very thrilled if you came up to say good night to her,' he said. 'It would be kind of you.'

He took me up into a little bare bedroom at the back of the house; rather to my surprise it was all reasonably clean, though most unfeminine. Elspeth was lying on her back in bed, mathematically in the centre, with the sheet tucked smooth and unruffled across below her chin. Her eyes watched me as I paused in the doorway.

'Hullo,' I said, 'I've come to say good night.' And then I noticed that in bed with her, with its white-tasselled head beside her dark one on the pillow, was one of those little cottom mops that you use for washing up.

She saw me looking at it. 'Is that your dolly?' I asked, trying to be pleasant.

'No,' she said scornfully. 'That's a mop.'

Honey was busy at the window. I sat down for a moment on the end of her bed. 'Is it your best thing?' I asked. 'Is that why you've got it in bed with you?'

She nodded vigorously.

'I should use it for washing up,' I remarked. 'Then you won't have to put your hands in.'

She said, 'We've got another one for washing up. We went to Woolworth's and Daddy got two, and he said I could have this one to take to bed till we have to use it if the other one wears out. The other one's downstairs in the sink.'

Honey had finished at the window. He crossed to the bed, and bent down and kissed his daughter. 'Go to sleep now,' he said. 'Good night.'

I said, 'Good night, Elspeth. Sleep well.'

'Good night, Daddy. Good night, Dr Scott. Will you say good night to Mrs Scott for me?'

'I'll tell her. Good night from her.'

We went downstairs again to that dirty, littered room with the great drawing-board. 'It's all very well to think about the scientific value of that prototype crash,' I said, taking up from where we had left off. 'But thirty or forty people must have lost their lives in it, and if it was the tail we've got to make darned sure that doesn't happen again, Honey.'

'The important thing is to find out if the tailplane really was the cause of that accident,' he said. 'You see, it may affect the programme for this tail that we are testing now. I've been thinking. A confirmatory experiment is valuable, of course, but it may not be making the best use of the material at our disposal. We might alter the frequency, for example. It's not easy to do that in the middle of a trial, but I'd like to think around it.'

'That's for the long-term programme,' I said patiently. 'What I'm bothered about is—ought we to ground all the Reindeers that are in service now?'

'I suppose that is important, too,' he said.

'It's the most important thing of all, Honey, because it's got to be decided now, or very soon, at any rate.'

He said thoughtfully, 'Of course, we don't really *know* any more than we did yesterday. We don't *know* that that tail failed in the air.'

'An examination of the wreckage will show that, though, won't it?'

'Oh, yes. If there's a fracture of the main spars of the tail, and if the structure of the metal at the fracture should be crystalline, that would be positive evidence of failure in fatigue.'

I stood for a moment deep in thought. Somebody would have to go and have another look at that tailplane; it really ought to be brought back to Farnborough for metallurgical examination. But it was a big unit to transport and it was urgent that the matter should be settled one way or the other. Where was the wreckage now? In Montreal? Or still in Labrador? I should have to find out that, and find out quick.

'I'm going up to London in the morning to see the Inspector of Accidents,' I said at last. 'That's why I came in tonight, Honey. I shan't be in the office tomorrow. But I saw the Director this evening and told him about this, and he agreed to running your trial night and day from now on.'

'Did he? That's very good news. I only wish he'd done it earlier, though. It's a pity that you have to have an accident to impress on people the urgency of basic research.'

I disregarded that one, and went on to tell him about young Simmons and to discuss with him the detailed arrangements that he would have to make next day in my absence. Mr Honey was quite wide awake and businesslike in any matter that concerned his trial, and having worked for so long in the R.A.E. he knew all the ropes. At the end of ten minutes I was satisfied that everything would go ahead all right in my absence, and I turned to go.

'Well, I'm sorry to have disturbed you, Honey,' I said. 'I'll be away all day tomorrow, but I'll let you know what happens in London when I come in on Thursday.'

'It was good of you to come round,' he said. He came with me to the front door, and then he stopped me just as I was going out to the car. 'There's just one thing I wanted to ask you, if you could spare a minute . . .'

'Of course,' I said.

He hesitated. 'I wonder if you could tell me where you got that hot-water-heater? Are they very expensive things?'

'Why, no. They're very cheap. I don't know what they cost to buy outright, but you can hire them from the electricity company, you know. We hire ours. I forget what it costs—something quite small. Two bob a quarter, or something like that.'

'Really–so little as that? They're very useful, aren't they? I mean, with one of those you've got hot water all the time.'

'That's right,' I said. 'We couldn't do without ours. You can get a big one for the bath, you know.'

'Can you!' He paused in thought. 'I think I must see about getting one for the kitchen, anyway. It's stupid to go on boiling up kettles to wash up with.'

'It makes everything much easier,' I said. 'You know the electricity office in the High Street? Go in and tell them that you want to hire one. They'll fix you up all right.'

'I'll do that,' he said. 'Thank you for telling me. It does seem to be a thing worth having.'

I got into my car and drove home, and put it in the garage at the back of the flats, deep in thought. It seemed long odds to me that the tailplane of the prototype Reindeer would be still lying where it fell, in some Labrador forest. It was most urgent to get hold of it for technical examination; we must have a report on it within a week at the very lastest, unless we are prepared to ground the Reindeers upon Mr Honey's word alone. One thing I was resolved upon, that no Reindeer should go on flying after seven hundred hours unless this thing had been cleared up. But to achieve that end, to stop the whole British Transatlantic air service before another accident happened, I should have to show some better evidence than I had got up to date that Reindeers were unsafe.

Shirley was waiting for me in the flat. 'Did Mr Honey take it seriously?' she asked.

'And how!' I said, sinking down into my chair. 'He was as pleased as Punch about it. He thought it was a wonderful thing to have happened.' And I told her all about it.

She heard me to the end. 'He *is* a funny little man.' And then she said, 'Tell me, Dennis–do you really think, yourself, that Honey's right? Are the Reindeer tails dangerous?'

'There's not a shred of evidence that you can hang your hat on that there's anything wrong with them at all,' I said evenly. 'But–yes, I think he's probably right.'

'Why do you think that,' she asked quietly, 'if there isn't any evidence?'

'Fifteen years in the aircraft industry,' I said. 'One gets to know the smell of things like this.'

I reached for the cigarettes and gave her one, and lit one myself. We sat in silence for a time; I lay back in my chair and watched the blue clouds rising slowly to the ceiling, deep in thought. And presently she asked, 'What's Mr Honey going to do about it?'

I grinned at her. 'He's going to hire an electric hot-water-heater,' I said. 'He's already bought a mop.'

I went up to the Ministry in London first thing next morning and saw Ferguson; I told him the whole thing. He was inclined to regard it as a mare's nest, having had some experience of Mr Honey over the lunch-table while he had been at the R.A.E. himself. 'I don't want to say anything against a member of your staff, Scott,' he remarked. 'But there may be things you wouldn't know about, that you really ought to know. Poor old Honey had a lot of trouble at the end of the war, you know–he lost his wife. That changed him a lot–he's never been the same man since. It was very distressing, that.'

He paused, and glanced at me. 'Did he ever tell you about his experiments with planchette?'

I was not now surprised at anything to do with Mr Honey. 'You mean, spiritualistic stuff?' I asked. 'I've heard a lot about him, but I hadn't heard that one.'

He hesitated. 'I dare say it's all over now. It was probably an effect of the distress he suffered at the time. But he used to do a lot with that.'

I was suddenly deeply sorry for the uncouth little man. 'Trying to get in touch with her, and all that sort of thing?'

He nodded.

I thought about it for a minute. 'I hadn't heard of that,' I said at last. 'I knew that he was religious, in an eccentric sort of way. But I don't think any of that really concerns us now. What I feel is this—that we can't let this thing slide, even if we both think that Honey's as mad as a hatter. He *has* made this forecast, for what it's worth, and the prototype did crash about that time. We've got to get to the bottom of it, now.'

'Oh yes, of course we have,' he replied. 'But in the meantime, I shan't lose much sleep myself.'

He rang through to Group-Captain Fisher in the Accidents Branch, and we went down to see him. After the preliminary greeting, I said:

'Look, sir—I've come up because we want to know a bit more about that accident to the prototype Reindeer.'

He nodded. 'You rang me up for the flying time. Just under 1,400 hours, if I remember right.'

'That's right, sir. We've been studying fatigue down at Farnborough, and a suggestion has been made that the tailplane might have failed on that machine.' I started in and told him the whole thing again, of course omitting the gossip about Mr Honey. I was getting to know my story off by heart by that time, from having told it to so many people.

As I talked, the frown deepened on his face. I came to the end, and he said. 'Do I understand, then, that there is a suggestion that my staff have been completely in error in their analysis of this accident?'

I hesitated. I did not want to get on the wrong side of the Group-Captain at the start. 'I wouldn't put it quite like that,' I said. 'We feel down at our place that this new evidence requires consideration alongside of all the evidence you have gathered up to date.'

He glowered at me. 'I don't know about new evidence,' he said. 'If I understood you correctly, you have an estimate from a research worker of what he hopes will happen in a trial which is in progress now. Is that right?'

I said, 'That's about it. We have been very much impressed with the way his estimate coincides with the flying time to crash of this first Reindeer.'

'Well, I'm not,' he said. 'There's no magic in the figure 1,400.' He rang a bell upon his desk. 'In this department, when we speak of evidence we mean evidence, sworn testimony that can be proved and that would stand up in a court of law. Not supposition and impressions.' A girl appeared, and stood in enquiry at the door. 'Get me the report upon the Reindeer accident, Miss Donaldson,' he said.

We sat in silence while the girl fetched the report; he did not seem to be in a very genial mood and I did not want to put my foot in it again, so I was saying as little as possible. She brought in a bulky folder bound up in the manner of a final report and handed it to him, and went away. He turned over the pages of it on his desk in silence for a time.

He said at last, 'Well, this is the report. The actual investigation was carried out by Ottawa, of course, with our representative assisting. I suggest you take it away and read it, as a first step. Then if you want any more information, we can have another talk.'

'That's very kind of you, sir,' I said. 'I'll read this through at once and get in touch with you again.'

I went back with Ferguson to his office. When we got there, 'What's eating the old boy?' I asked. 'I've always found him very helpful in the past.'

Ferguson said, 'Well, of course—that is a final report.' He took it in his hands thoughtfully, considering it. 'It's gone to the Minister, and there was a question in the House of Commons—the Minister based his reply on this. Because of the Russians, you know.' I nodded. 'Naturally, Fisher won't exactly jump for joy if you turn up and prove that it's all wrong.'

I said irritably, 'But damn it, man—we all make mistakes. I make them, so do you, and so does every living being in the world. One just has to admit them—Fisher's not a child. If this report is based on a misapprehension it'll have to be corrected—we can't hide things up. There's no future in that.'

'I know,' he said thoughtfully. 'The trouble is that Fisher's department has been making rather a lot of mistakes recently.' He paused. 'You heard about the Zulu crash at Whitney Sutton?'

'I heard the wings came off, or something. I didn't hear why.'

'That's right,' he said. 'It was diving at round about Mach unity, and the wings came off. The ailerons came off first and then the wing broke up. Fisher's party got it all buttoned up as pilot's error of judgment. But then Cochrane from the Medical Research came in and proved pre-impact head wounds on the pilot's body. The windscreen broke up and crashed into the pilot's face—that's why it dived. It didn't do Fisher any good with the R.A.F. types.'

I was interested. 'Is that established? Is that what really happened to it?'

He nodded. 'Keep it under your hat, old boy. No point in spreading things like that about.'

I settled down in Ferguson's armchair to read the report upon the accident to the prototype Reindeer.

It had flown from London Airport on the night of March 27th with a crew of nine and a passenger list of twenty-two persons, including the Russian Ambassador to Ottawa, thirty-one people in all. It had been diverted from Gander on account of fog and had landed at Goose at about 7 a.m. G.M.T. on the morning of the 28th. It had refuelled there, and had taken off for Montreal at 9.17 in weather that was overcast and raining; the temperature was above freezing, unusual for the time of year. The crew had not reported any trouble at Goose. One wireless message of a routine character was received at 9.46 reporting that the aircraft was on course at 16,500 feet. That was the last that was heard of it.

It was three days before it was reported by one of the search aircraft, though the spot where it was finally located had been flown over several times. It was another two days before a party succeeded in getting to the wreckage. They flew up in a Norseman fitted with skis and landed in deep snow on a frozen lake called Small Pine Water; the landing was a hazardous one because of the alternate thaw and freeze: the skis mushed in beneath the icy crust. The party then had to force their way eleven miles over the snow-covered hills, thickly covered with a forest of spruce and alder. The night temperatures were as low as −45° Fahrenheit, making it a most difficult search: several of the party suffered from frostbite. In the deep snow and the forest growth they would never have found the crash at all but for the continuous guidance given by the aircraft working with them.

In the circumstances, it is hardly surprising that their investigation was, in some respects, perfunctory.

The spot where the Reindeer crashed was about 250 miles from Goose, about 50 miles west of the Moisie river and about 100 miles north of the sea coast in the Gulf of St Lawrence. It was just in Canada, in the Province of Quebec.

The bulk of the aircraft was found lying in deep snow among trees at the foot of a cliff, the estimated height of which was 340 feet. It had been on fire after the crash, and everything in it was totally destroyed. All the bodies were found within the flattened shell of the fuselage, indicating that nobody had survived the accident. The cliff face at that point ran approximately east and west along the aircraft's course, and the Reindeer had hit first at the top of this cliff, very near the edge. It had knocked down three trees, and here the starboard wing had been torn off; the wing was found at some distance from the rest of the machine, at the foot of the cliff. Two propeller blades and portions of the engine cowling were found on top of the cliff. The fuselage had then toppled over the cliff and had crashed down into the forest below, and burnt out.

From the damage to the trees it seemed that the original impact, the first touch, had been with the machine at a small angle of descent, probably not more than ten degrees below the horizontal. From that the investigators had deduced that the machine was under control up to the moment of impact, and from that that the pilot had been deliberately losing height through the overcast in order to check his position by a sight of the ground.

Ferguson, reading all this over my shoulder, said doubtfully, 'Well, that could be. But it sounds a bit odd to me. He was only an hour out from Goose. What should he want to check his position for?'

I shrugged my shoulders and turned to the photographs bound up with the report. The photographers were technicians, not sensation-mongers, and they had not gone out of their way to photograph the horrors; but it was not a pretty scene. The wreckage, of course, was hardly recognisable as an aircraft at all; in modern accidents it never is. It looked like the scrap head of a tin factory. I turned the pages one by one, examining each photograph in turn minutely.

'I don't see the port tailplane anywhere,' I said at last.

'If it's missing, it'll be referred to somewhere in the text,' said Ferguson. 'Let me have a look.'

He turned the pages till we found what we were looking for. The passage read:

The party remained on the site of the accident for three days, during which time the 31 bodies were buried in individual graves. The whole of the units of the aircraft were not accounted for, due to the dense nature of the forest at this point. It was impossible to see further than three yards in any one direction because of the thickness of the undergrowth laden with snow, and no progress was possible except along paths cut for that purpose. The daytime thaw made all work wet and difficult and greatly hampered the search. The units of the aircraft unaccounted for were the starboard aileron, the outer starboard engine No. 6, the port tailplane and elevator, the port landing wheel assembly, No. 3 propeller (parted from the engine by a fracture of the crankshaft), and about five feet of the tip of the starboard wing.

I glanced at Ferguson. 'Port tailplane and elevator,' I said. 'There we are.'

He nodded. 'It's not evidence, of course,' he said. 'It keeps the fatigue theory in the field, in that if the tailplane had been there and intact it couldn't have come off in the air. But the mere fact that the port tailplane was missing, when so much else was missing, doesn't take us very far.'

'It's beginning to tot up,' I said. 'It's one more thing.'

I settled down to read the report through carefully; when I got to the end I turned back to the beginning and read it through again, making notes as I did so. It was clear from the circumstances of the accident that the wreckage could not possibly have been removed. It would still be lying where it fell three months before, with the new growth of the forest coming up around it and through it, gradually obliterating everything. There was my evidence, all right, there in the woods. In one of the photographs I could see the broken stump of the front spar of the port tailplane. It would not be necessary, perhaps, to search the woods for the tailplane itself. If that broken spar attached to the rear fuselage showed the typical form of fatigue crystallisation of the metal at the fracture, there would be all the evidence we needed. It would, of course, be better and would make the matter more complete if we could get the tailplane, too.

In the middle of the afternoon I went down to see the Group-Captain again, ready to be firm.

'I've read through this report,' I said. 'It's very interesting, sir—and, if I may say so, the most comprehensive report I've yet seen on an accident. It's very thorough.'

He smiled. 'Got all you want from it?'

'I think so,' I said. 'I should like to take it down to Farnborough to talk it over with the Director, if you could spare this copy for a few days?'

'That's all right,' he said.

I went on. 'Well, sir—about this suggestion that's been made about tailplane fatigue. You'll hear from us officially in the next day or two, if we want anything done. My present feeling—what I shall advise the Director—is that we should send an officer out there at once to make an examination of this broken tailplane spar.' His face darkened; I opened the report and showed him the photograph. 'This one. As the port tail was missing altogether we can't rule out this theory that has arisen. Of course, if it should be proved that fatigue is present in these aircraft at such an early stage, it's a matter of the greatest urgency to put it right.'

I stared down at the photograph before us; it was horrible. 'We don't want another one like this,' I said.

Fisher said stiffly, 'If you really think that necessary after the very careful investigation that has been already made, I suppose Ottawa can arrange it. If it comes at our request, of course, financial sanction will be necessary; these expeditions to out-of-the-way places like this are very costly, you know. It's in a dollar area, too, so the Secretariat will have to submit the matter to the Treasury. But if you people insist upon it, I suppose it can all be arranged.'

'I can only state my own view, sir,' I said. 'I think it's necessary and a matter of great urgency. That's what I shall tell the Director; I can't say, of course, what he'll decide. But I should like to see an officer on his way to Ottawa tomorrow, or the day after, at the latest.'

'It all seems rather ridiculous,' he grumbled. 'The matter was most carefully gone into.'

I did not want to argue it with him, and I had given him warning of what was coming, as was only fair. I said good-bye and left the office with Ferguson. He was rather amused; in the corridor outside the office he turned to me, and grinned. 'He's putting up a good fight,' he said. 'He knows all the tricks. He'll run round to the Secretariat tonight and tell them that your journey isn't really necessary.'

'He wouldn't do a thing like that,' I said. I was a little worried at the mere suggestion. 'He's a good old stick–I've known him for years. And this thing concerns the lives of people in the air. He wouldn't want to see another stinking crash like this.'

'Of course he wouldn't,' Ferguson replied. 'But you see–he thinks you're absolutely wrong and just kicking up a stink in his department irresponsibly. People believe what they want to believe.'

I got back to Farnborough too late to see the Director. I went home with the report under my arm, tired and depressed by what had been my reading for the day. I was due to read my paper on the 'Performance Analysis of Aircraft flying at High Mach Numbers' on the following Thursday, the first paper that I had been asked to read before a learned society. When I got home I found that the advance printed copy of this thing had arrived, and that Shirley had been reading it all afternoon. She had taken it upstairs to show to Mrs Peters in the flat above; it was a great thing for us, because it was the first distinction we had managed to collect since we were married. Fingering it and turning over the pages, and discussing with Shirley the cuts that I would make when reading it, served as an anodyne; it took my mind off the Reindeer misery, so that I slept fairly well.

I went down to see the Director first thing next morning. I showed him the Reindeer accident report, and told him all about my interviews with Group-Captain Fisher. 'In spite of what he says, I think we ought to send somebody out there,' I remarked. 'I should like to see an officer from here sent out by air straight away, sir, to make a metallurgical report on that spar fracture.'

'I think you're right, Scott', he said slowly. 'I believe that's the only thing to do. Who would you send?'

'I should send Honey.'

'You have sufficient confidence in Honey, Scott?'

I said, 'I have, sir. I'm beginning to get quite a respect for Mr Honey. I'm beginning to think he's right in this thing, and he's certainly the man in the Establishment who knows most about fatigue.'

'Yes, he is that.' He turned over the pages of the report, thoughtfully. 'This place where the accident is located–I understand it's eleven miles from a lake where you can land a seaplane? That's a journey of eleven miles through the Canadian woods?'

'I think so.'

'I'm not so sure that Honey is the right man for that sort of assignment, Scott. He isn't what I should describe as an outdoor type.' He paused. 'You wouldn't rather go yourself?'

I hesitated in my turn. I would have given my eyes to go off on a trip like that and it would have been a very welcome change from my office routine. But whoever went would have to go at once. 'I'd go like a shot, sir,' I said. 'But I've got this paper to read on Thursday of next week, the one on the performance of high Mach numbers. Of course, I could cancel it.'

He said, 'I had forgotten that.' He shook his head. 'You'll have to stay for that–after all, the Royal Aeronautical Society is an important body; you can't treat them like that. No, it will have to be Honey. You really think he will get on all right upon a trip like this?'

'I'm sure he will, sir,' I replied. 'Technically, he's certainly the best man we've got to send. And as regards the physical aspects of the journey, we can warn Ottawa that we're sending over somebody who isn't very fit. They'll make things easy for him, and push him through all right.'

We stood in silence for a minute; evidently he didn't like it much. 'I only wish he had a better presence,' the Director said at last. And then he straightened up. 'All right, Scott, I'll tell Ferguson what we've decided, and I'll get on to the Secretariat about the air passage. You'd like him to fly out at once?'

'Immediately, sir. I don't think we can afford to waste a day.'

I went up to my office and sent for Mr Honey. He came in blinking through his thick spectacles; his hair was untidy, his collar was dirty, and there was a smear of what I judged to be an egg upon the front of his waistcoat. He looked even more of a mess than usual. It was certainly a problem how to clean him up without hurting his feelings and making him bloody-minded, to make him look a little more presentable before I pushed him off to Ottawa.

I told him what had happened in London and I showed him the report of the accident. He did not seem to be very interested in the factual circumstances of the crash, but he seized on the photographs and looked for a long time at the stump of the tailplane front spar. 'It has all the appearance of a fatigue fracture,' he said at last. 'Look. There's no crumpling or elongation of the metal there. There's practically no distortion of the flange at all, right up to the point of fracture. That's not natural. That's a short fracture, that's what that is. The metal must have been terribly crystalline to break off short like that.'

I could see what he meant, though the detail was very tiny in the photograph. It was one more thing.

I told him that we had decided that an officer should fly to Ottawa at once, and that we were arranging for a seaplane or amphibian to take a party up to Small Pine Water immediately for a further technical examination of the wreckage. 'I want you to go and do that, Honey,' I said. 'I don't know anybody who could do it better.'

He stared at me. 'You mean–that I should go to Canada?'

'That's right,' I said. 'I want you to go at once, starting the day after tomorrow. It really is most urgent that we should get this matter settled up and find out if that tailplane failed in fatigue or not.'

'I don't know that there's all that rush about it,' he said. 'I agree–it's information that we must have ultimately, and the sooner we get it the better, I suppose. But we've still got to go on with the trial here, and I can't possibly get out even a preliminary report for limited circulation till November.'

'I know,' I said patiently. 'But that's the other aspect of it, Honey–the long-term research. What I'm concerned about now is–have we got to ground the Reindeers that are flying now?'

He said irritably, 'Oh, the *ad hoc* trial. Surely, anybody can do that, and leave me free to get on with the stuff that really matters.'

'This is the most important thing of all at the moment, Honey,' I said firmly.

'Look. You're an older man than I am, and probably a better scientist. Perhaps I'm better as an administrator than you would be – I don't know. In any case, here I am sitting in this office and it's part of my job to decide the priorities of work in this department. I think this trip to Canada is top priority of anything that's going on at Farnborough today and I want you to drop everything else and go and do it, because I can't think of anybody who could do it better. It's not an order, because we don't work that way. But I hope you'll accept my decision about priorities, because that's what I'm here for.'

He smiled, a shy, warm smile that I had never seen before. 'Of course,' he said, 'I wasn't trying to be difficult. I only hope I shan't have to spend too long away from here.'

I thought about that for a moment. 'I know it's important to get you back as soon as ever we can,' I said. 'I don't want to see the basic work held up. I'll see that you get an air passage home immediately the job is done. I should think you'd probably be away from here for ten days or a fortnight.'

His face fell. 'So long as that?'

'I don't believe you'd do it in much less. First, you've got to get from here to Ottawa. Then there's the flight back from Ottawa to north-east Quebec, and then to reach the site of the accident is a day's trek on foot. And then the whole thing in reverse again, to get back home.'

'It's an awful waste of time,' he grumbled.

'It's not,' I said. 'That's my sphere of decisions, Honey, and I tell you that it's not a waste of time.'

'It is from the point of view of the basic research.'

'So is eating your breakfast,' I remarked. 'But you've got to do that, too.'

I went through the various arrangements that would have to be made for carrying on his trials in his absence; he was quite business-like and alert where anything to do with basic trials was concerned, and in ten minutes we were through with that. 'Now about your trip,' I said. 'It's going to mean some days of living rough in the Canadian woods, I'm afraid. You'll be with the R.C.A.F. and they'll look after you, but I understand that there's a ten or fifteen mile walk from the lake you land on to the site of the crash, and the same back again. It'll probably be quite difficult going. Have you got an outfit of clothes that would do for that, Honey?'

'I've got some good strong boots. I haven't looked at them for years, but I think they're all right.' He paused, and then he said, 'We used to do a lot of hiking on Sundays, when my wife was alive. . . .' He stared out of the window, and was silent for a moment; I did not care to interrupt him. 'We used to go in shorts. . . . I've got those somewhere, I think. Do you think shorts would be suitable?'

The thought of Mr Honey turning up in Ottawa in short hiking pants as a representative of the Royal Aircraft Establishment made me blench. 'I wouldn't take those,' I said. 'I don't believe they wear shorts in the woods, on account of the mosquitoes. I'll get a letter through to Ottawa asking them to kit you up for the trip, and we can charge it up as necessary expenses. I should take the boots with you, or . . . no, they'll supply those too. But look, Honey, go in your best suit. You're going as the representative of this Establishment. Put on a bit of dog, you know. Don't let anybody sit on you in any technical matter; you're the expert, and you're the man that counts. We'll back you up from here in anything you feel you've got to insist on.'

He nodded. 'I'll remember that,' he said.

'Now, how about your personal affairs? Are you all right with those?'

He hesitated. 'Well, no, I'm not. I've got a man from the electricity company coming in one day next week to fit up that electric hot-water-heater. And then there's Elspeth–I shall have to see if I can get somebody to come and sleep in the house, I suppose. It's rather a long time for her to be alone.'

I was a big staggered at the suggestion that he could leave Elspeth alone at all. 'What about her?' I asked. 'Have you got a relative who could come and stay with her?'

He shook his head. 'I don't think there's anybody like that.' He paused for a minute in thought, and then he said, 'Don't worry about that, Dr Scott–I'll think of something. I've left her for two days at a time, once or twice when I had to. Of course, she's older now, but I think this is much too long to do that. I think I can get Mrs Higgs–that's my charwoman–I think she'd come and sleep in while I'm away.'

The thought was distasteful to me, but it was at any rate a possible solution to his problem. If we had had a second bedroom at the flat I would have offered to put up his child myself, but we hadn't. Moreover, Honey's domestic affairs were really no concern of mine and there was a limit to the extent that I could allow them to influence me in the work of the Establishment. But I was sorry for Elspeth.

'I'll see that you get back as soon as ever we can manage it,' I said.

'That's very good of you–I really don't want to be away longer than is necessary, for a variety of reasons.' His eyes dropped to the accident report on the desk before us. 'Have you told the Rutland Company anything about this yet?'

I had forgotten all about the design staff who had produced the Reindeer, or if I had remembered them I had placed them in the background of my mind. 'I haven't told them anything about it yet,' I said slowly. 'I thought perhaps it was better to wait until the matter was rather more definite. Do you think we ought to get in touch with Prendergast now?'

'I don't want to,' he said quickly. 'I was wondering if you had.'

'No, I hadn't done anything about it.' The apprehension of a new series of difficulties swept over me. E.P.Prendergast was the Chief Designer of the Rutland Aircraft Company and the author of the Reindeer. In person he was a big, dark man with bushy black eyebrows and the face of an ascetic monk. He was about six foot four in height and broad in proportion to his height; he was nearly sixty years old, but he was still a very powerful man. He was one of the oldest and most successful chief designers in the country, and the Reindeer was the last of a long line of lovely aircraft that had come out of his office. He was a very great artist at the business of designing aeroplanes, and like all great designers in the aircraft industry he was a perfect swine to deal with.

There is, of course, a good explanation in psychology for this universal characteristic of the greatest aeroplane designers. A beautiful aircraft is the expression of the genius of a great engineer who is also a great artist. It is impossible for that man to carry out the whole of the design himself; he works through a design office staffed by a hundred draughtsmen or more. A hundred minds, each with their own less competent ideas, are striving to modify the chief designer's original conception. If the design is to appear in the end as a great artistic unity, the chief designer must be a man of immensely powerful will, capable of imposing his idea and his way of doing things on each of his hundred draughtsmen, so that each one of them is too terrified to insert any of his own ideas. If the chief designer has not got this personality and strength of will, his original conception will be distorted in the design office and will appear as just another, not-so-good aeroplane. He will not then be ranked as a good chief designer

All really first-class designers, for this reason, are both artists, engineers, and men of a powerful and an intolerant temper, quick to resist the least modification of their plans, energetic in fighting the least infringement upon what they regard as their own sphere of action. If they were not so, they could not produce good aeroplanes. For the Government official who detects an error in their work the path is not made easy, and of all men in the aircraft industry the most dangerous to cross was E. P. Prendergast. He was deeply religious in a narrow, Calvinistic way. He could be in turn a most courteous and charming host, a sympathetic and an understanding employer, and a hot-tempered friend capable of making himself physically sick with his own passion, so that he would stalk out of a conference of bitter, angry words, and retire to the toilet and vomit, and go home to bed, and return to his office three days later, white and shaken with the violence of his illness. He was about the greatest engineer in England at that time and he produced the most lovely and successful aeroplanes. But he was not an easy man to deal with, E. P. Prendergast.

The Director sent for me again that evening. He had had Ferguson working all day on the matter; cables had been passing to and fro with Ottawa and the Treasury had been persuaded that it was necessary to spend the dollars. Priority had been allocated for the passage, and it looked as if Mr Honey would get off on Sunday.

After all that, I raised the matter of the Rutland Aircraft Company. I said, 'At what stage do you think we ought to get the firm in on this thing, sir?' I paused, and then I added, 'E. P. Prendergast . . .'

He glanced at me. 'Yes . . . Prendergast.' He was silent for a minute, and I knew what he was thinking. If anybody dared to say the Reindeer tail was not above suspicion and could not produce good evidence for that assertion, E. P. Prendergast would go up in a sheet of flame. He would complain to the Minister, as he had done before, that he could not carry on his work in an atmosphere of petty back-biting and vilification by minor civil servants. He would offer, in the most dignified way, to give up his post and go to America if it would assist the Minister in his direction of the Industry. But if it was the desire of the Minister that he should continue to design British aircraft, then he must be protected from the expression of the petty jealousies of petty Government officials. As I have said, we had had some of this before.

The Director said, 'I doubt if Mr Prendergast would find Honey's theoretical work very convincing.'

'I'm damn sure he wouldn't,' I said. 'He'd chew him up and spit him out in no time.'

'I don't know that the time is quite ripe to inform the firm,' he said thoughtfully. 'After all, there's nothing they can do till it is proved that fatigue is actually taking place. We ought to have a cable from Honey in a few days which will indicate what really happened to that prototype machine. I think that would be the time when we should get the firm into the matter, when the question of some modification arises.'

'I think so, too,' I said. 'I think it's a bit early yet to worry them.'

I told Honey to make preparations for his passage on Sunday, and I put him into touch with Ferguson, who knew him well, over the matter of his passport and his money. Then I went home, and that evening over supper I told Shirley all about it. 'He's going to get the charwoman to come and sleep in the house with Elspeth,' I said.

'Oh, Dennis—the poor child! Is that the best he can do?'

'I asked him if he hadn't got a relation who could come in,' I said defensively. 'He said he hadn't got one.'

She was indignant. 'But do you mean to say she's going to be all alone for a fortnight, except for the charwoman? Dennis, you can't let him go away like that! He *must* make some better arrangement for her.'

'I can't help it if he goes away and leaves her like that,' I said irritably. 'I can't run his life for him. I'm his boss; I'm not a ruddy welfare worker.'

'I know.' She was silent for a minute, and then she said, 'Perhaps after he's gone we could go round there and see how she's getting on.'

'I think we ought to do that,' I agreed. 'It's a rotten way to leave a child, but there doesn't seem to be much else that he can do. And he's the only man to go to Canada.'

3

It was the practice of the Central Air Transport Organisation at that time to fly the Atlantic by night. The aircraft took off from London Airport at about eleven o'clock, landed at Gander in Newfoundland to refuel before dawn, and continued on to arrive at Montreal or New York about the middle of the morning.

Mr Honey travelled up to the air terminal at Victoria after supper on Sunday night. He was tired and confused with the events of the day. He had had a good deal of trouble in persuading Mrs Higgs, his charwoman, to leave her husband and come to sleep in his house; in the end she had agreed to do it 'to oblige' and for ten shillings a night. He had had little sleep the night before because he had stayed up late making every possible arrangement he could think of for the comfort and security of his small daughter while he was away. Although by normal standards he looked after her very badly, he worked hard to do his best and he took his responsibility for her quite seriously. He had had much to do at the office, too, to secure the smooth progress of his trial by day and night during his absence. With all these responsibilities he started off upon his journey tired and a little worried lest he had forgotten something that he should have done.

At Victoria, however, the C.A.T.O. travel organisation took him in its arms and wrapped him round as if with cotton-wool. While he was waiting in a deep armchair in the assembly hall a pretty stewardess brought him a cup of coffee with a couple of biscuits, and a choice of newspapers to read; he blinked and thanked her shyly. Presently his name was called out on a list, and he had to rise and walk a few steps to the motor-coach, where a rug was wrapped around to preserve him from the evening chill. He was driven to the airport and passed quickly through the emigration formalties, then he was ushered down a covered passage and into an aeroplane before he had even time to look at it. He probably would not have looked at it in any case, because he was not much interested in aeroplanes unless they had fatigue trouble. In the warm, brightly lit cabin of the aircraft he was received by a tall, dark girl in the uniform of a stewardess, one of two that served the Reindeer passengers upon their flight. She showed him to his seat and took his coat and hat from him, and saw that he was comfortably settled down with magazines within his reach. Then she pulled out the safety belt from behind the seat and showed him how to clasp it round his body, talking to him brightly and cheerfully all the time. 'It's only just for taking off and landing that you have to do this,' she said. 'Just for the first five minutes. I'll come and tell you when you can undo it.' She adjusted the strap for him with quick, expert hands. 'There–is that quite comfortable?'

He said, 'Quite, thank you. You don't have to worry about me–I know something about all this. I work with aeroplanes.'

She smiled. 'Are you the gentleman from Farnborough, sir? There was an expert from Farnborough coming across with us tonight.'

He smiled up at her through his thick glasses, that shy, warm smile that had made me wonder once before. 'That's right,' he said.

'Oh well, then–you know everything.' She smiled down at him with a new interest, but habit was strong in her and she went on with her patter. 'Captain Samuelson says we've got a very good weather report. You'll see it will be quite fine half an hour after we get started.' She said that every time and she was always right, because they flew at a high altitude above the overcast.

She left him, and turned to attend to her other passengers. The aircraft was to cross with only about fifty per cent of its designed passenger load, so the stewardesses were putting one person only into each of the double seats; Mr Honey had room to spread his paper and his briefcase on the seat beside him. He sat in warm comfort staring round at the furnishings of the long cabin, exploring the reading-light switch and the control of his reclining chair. He was impressed with the comfort and security of everything, as he was meant to be. He had never been in such a comfortable and well equipped aircraft cabin before, and for the first time he wondered idly what sort of aeroplane he was sitting in. He thought that he would ask the nice girl who had buttoned him into his safety belt, when she came to unbutton him.

He screwed round in his seat to look down the length of the wide cabin behind him, to the stewardesses' pantry and the toilets and the entrance door. The other passengers were mostly men, but there were three or four women. Mr Honey's eyes rested on a woman travelling alone; he paused, and stared at her in frank curiosity. She was seated two rows behind him, on the other side of the aisle. She was a very beautiful woman with deep auburn hair, carefully made up, wearing a most magnificent mink fur. In spite of all the trimmings her face remained keen and intelligent, giving added charm to her great beauty. Mr Honey knew her at first glance, and his heart rose in sudden emotion and he felt a tightening in his throat and tears welling up behind his eyes. She was Monica Teasdale.

When Honey had married one of the girl clerks in the Airworthiness Section back in 1934, he had married a girl as unsophisticated as he was. They were a very simple couple: they liked going for long hikes on Sundays with rucksacks on their backs; they liked amateur photography; and they did a bit of Morris dancing, too, with flying ribbons and little bells that jangled at the knee. They went a good deal to the movies, but they were discriminating picturegoers; if they didn't like the film they would walk out of it, preferring to lose their money than to sit through an unworthy show. They never walked out of anything with Monica Teasdale in it.

They loved Monica Teasdale with all the enthusiasm of very simple people; throughout their life together they did not miss one of her films. If they had been less inhibited they might have written to her to tell their admiration of her work: they talked of doing so a number of times, but when they came to frame the words upon paper once it seemed too stupid, and they never wrote. They did not do that, but they saw all of her pictures, and they remembered them and could discuss the details of the story with each other years afterwards. That went on from the day that they became engaged till Mary Honey was killed in the year 1944. That finished it abruptly; since that time Mr Honey had not been inside a picture-house.

Monica Teasdale was for Mr Honey part of his lost life, a part of the simple pleasures and enthusiasms he had shared with his young wife. She was inextricably associated in his mind with Mary Honey. As he stared at her across the aisle in the warm, bright cabin of the aircraft the tears welled up in his weak eyes behind the thick glasses of his spectacles; he had to turn away and blow his nose and take off his spectacles and polish them. The memory of his dead love was very vivid with him at that moment. He could see her sitting by the fire upon the rug one evening with a cup of cocoa in her hand, when they had just come in from seeing Monica Teasdale in *Temptation*. He could see her expression as she had looked up at him. 'Theo, darling–would you think it stupid if we went to that one again? Before it comes off?'

He stared at the back of the seat in front of him, a worn, tired little man wiping his glasses.

Behind him the door closed; the chief steward passed by him on his way to the flight deck, a sheaf of papers in his hand and carrying a black briefcase. The forward door closed behind him and the engines started one by one, deep, reassuring rumbles faintly heard as though from a great distance. Presently the cabin stirred beneath him. Mr Honey looked out of the window and saw the lights of the airport buildings pass him by as the aircraft moved down the ring road to the runway's end.

He never felt the machine leave the ground. At the runway's end she turned across the wind and cleared engines one by one; then before Mr Honey realised what was happening the runway lights were sliding past his window in acceleration and presently they fell away below. It was the first time he had ever travelled in an aeroplane with modern sound-proofing and it took him by surprise, because he had expected to be warned for the take-off by a great burst of noise. But there was no such roar, and before he realised quite what was happening the airport was below and behind. Then there was nothing to be seen out of his window but a blackness that reflected his own face and everything in the brightly lit cabin.

He leaned back in his seat and relaxed, savouring the comfort. Presently the stewardess who was attending to the passengers at his end of the cabin came up the aisle, stopping by each passenger and saying a few words, helping to tuck away the safety belt, taking orders for meals upon a little pad. She came to Mr Honey presently, and said, 'I'm sure you'd like a little supper before settling down, sir. What can I get you?' She told him what he could have.

He ordered a cup of coffee and a plate of sandwiches; she noted it. And then he said, 'I say, is that Monica Teasdale sitting over there?'

The girl nodded. 'That's right. She came over about a fortnight ago. Quite a number of film actors and actresses travel with us—American as well as British. She always travels this way.'

He said in wonder, 'She looks just like she does in her pictures, doesn't she?'

'I know. But she looks old when you see her close up, in the early morning.' The stewardess laughed, and Mr Honey laughed with her. 'But she's ever so nice.'

'One thing more,' Mr Honey asked. 'What sort of aeroplane is this?'

The girl said, 'This is one of the latest, sir—what they call the Reindeer type. That isn't what we call them on the line, of course; this one is called "Redgauntlet." But it's the Reindeer type, made by the Rutland Aircraft Company. It's the very latest thing—we've only had them in service for a few weeks.' She broke off, smiling. 'I was forgetting, sir. You must know all about them.'

He said, 'Oh, this is a Reindeer, is it?' He was not in the least perturbed, because he had complete confidence in the check that I was keeping on the flying time that all the Reindeers had done, but he looked about him with new interest. 'I must say it's very comfortable,' he said.

The stewardess said, 'I think it's lovely. I've only just come on to Reindeers; this is my first trip in one. I was working in Eagles up till last week. They're very nice, of course, but this is the most modern plane there is. You really must come down and see the galley later on, sir—it's a perfect dream. We've got everything we want, and a telephone to the flight deck. And plenty of room to work.'

She went away, and presently she came back with his coffee and sandwiches. Later she came and took away the tray, and asked him if he wanted to sleep. Although he had had a long and tiring day, Mr Honey was not ready for sleep; she adjusted the little reading-light for him and showed him the switch. 'We shall be turning off the main lights in a minute,' she said. 'If you feel sleepy, here's the switch for this one.'

He asked, 'What time do we land?'

'About seven o'clock of our time, at Gander. That's before dawn, on account of the change of time.'

The lights went down, and Mr Honey sat on, reading his magazine in a little pool of light. He looked round once or twice at Monica Teasdale but she had soon stopped reading and turned out her light, and now she lay resting or sleeping in her reclining chair, in the half darkness. Mr Honey never read a magazine in normal times, but these times were not normal; the novelty of his experiences had taken him out of his mental groove, and he found novelty in the little love stories and in the advertisements about unpleasant breath.

At about two o'clock in the morning the second pilot, a cheerful young man called Dobson, came down into the cabin and walked aft in the dim light, and went to the galley, where he stood drinking coffee and chatting to the stewardesses for ten minutes. Then he said:

'Which is the boffin?'

They laughed. 'What's a boffin?'

'The man from Farnborough. Everybody calls them boffins. Didn't you know?'

'No. Why are they called that?'

'I dunno. Because they behave like boffins, I suppose. Which of you is looking after him?'

'I am,' said Miss Corder. 'His name is Mr Honey.'

'The little half-pint size, with thick glasses?'

She nodded. 'Sitting on the starboard side, near the front.'

'I knew it. I knew that was the boffin when I saw him. You can't mistake them.'

'What about him?' asked Miss Corder. The joke was over, so far as she was concerned.

Dobson said, 'The captain sent me down to offer to show him the upper deck. Is he awake?'

She glanced down the aisle. 'I see his light's on still. Will you take him now, if he wants to go?'

He nodded. 'Get it over.'

'I'll ask him.' She walked down the aisle softly, with Dobson following behind her. 'Mr Honey,' she said, 'Captain Samuelson has asked if you would care to see the upper deck – the pilot's cockpit and the navigation and so on. Mr Dobson, here, could take you now, if you feel like it. Or would you rather go after Gander, on the run to Montreal?'

Mr Honey thought for a moment. He had no real interest in flying, though in the course of his work at the R.A.E. he had picked up a fairly comprehensive knowledge of an aeroplane's controls. If it had been that alone, he would not have bothered to leave his seat, unless from a sense of duty or politeness. He was, however, genuinely interested in the navigation. His investigations in connection with the Pyramid had led him to a study of chart projections, and he was glad of the opportunity to examine the charts prepared especially for navigation over the Atlantic. It was unlikely that the charts used for the flight overland from Gander would show many novel features. 'That's very kind of the captain,' he said. 'I think I'd rather go now.'

The stewardess introduced him to the first officer, and with Dobson he went forward through the door and up the narrow duralumin stair that led to the flight deck. He found himself standing in a fairly spacious area, well lit, with windows showing the black night outside. An engineer was seated at a desk garnished with levers, before an instrument board a yard square that was completely filled with black-faced dials. A wireless operator was seated at the instruments, to one side of him the green trace of radar showed upon its screen. Behind him was the navigator's desk, and beyond that again the two pilots' seats with the flying controls, and the windscreen that showed nothing but the black night. A man of about fifty, Captain Samuelson, sat in the port seat, but his hands were not on the controls, which made tiny movements now and then upon their own. It was very peaceful up on the flight deck.

Mr Honey asked, 'What altitude are we flying at?'

Dobson said, 'About eighteen thousand feet.' He glanced at the sensitive altimeter above the navigating table. 'Eighteen thousand five hundred. Of course, we're pressurised, you know. The pressure in here corresponds to about seven thousand feet.'

The sense of solidity and security impressed Mr Honey very much; nothing, it seemed, could ever go wrong in a thing like this. 'This is a Reindeer, isn't it?' he asked.

'That's right.'

'How do you like it?'

'Oh, it's a lovely job. I've been in this one for about six months, and I never want to go back on to anything else. As a matter of fact, this is our first trip across the Atlantic–the North Atlantic, that is. We've been operating down to Buenos Aires on loan to Anglo-Brazil Air Services for a tryout, but this is our proper route.' He turned to the chart table. 'This is about where we are now.' He indicated on the chart, 'Matter of fact, I have to keep on looking at it myself–it's extraordinary how one can get rusty. On the other route I hardly ever looked at the chart, we went backwards and forwards so often.'

Mr Honey was not interested in that gossip; he was only interested in the navigation. His eyes were on the chart: not only was the projection a new one to him, but it was crossed by a family of cycloidal lines each with a Greek letter to identify it, most intriguing. He began to ask a lot of questions about the methods of navigation; as celestial observations and radio beams and bearings were inextricably mixed up with chart work, he had a grand time, and Dobson had to think very hard indeed to answer some of the questions Honey fired at him. The second pilot was not to know that Honey had gained much of his information upon chart projections as a by-product of his Pyramid research. At last they left the chart table and went to the cockpit, where the controls were explained to Mr Honey. He was familiar with the basic aeroplane controls, of course, but the undercarriage and flap controls were new to him, and were explained to him in detail.

From the cockpit they went to the wireless and the radar, from the radar to the engine panel. The engineer explained his intricacies, and then went on to answer a few questions about the engines. 'Oh, they're very good,' he said. 'We never get much trouble with engines nowadays, you know.' Honey asked how often they did a top overhaul. 'Never do top overhauls,' the man said. 'Not in the nacelles, that is. Take 'em out and change them every six hundred hours. Six hundred hours they run–then they get taken out and overhauled in the shop. Complete overhaul, that is. This is the third lot of engines, the ones in her now. We did the change last month. Didn't take long–about three days. They should be able to do it in less time than that.'

Mr Honey stared at him through his thick glasses; something within his body seemed to have turned over. 'Do you mean you've already had two sets of engines and they've each done six hundred hours?'

'That's right,' the man said. 'Six hundred hours, they do. Then they get a complete overhaul–put another set in.'

He licked his lips, aghast. 'How many hours has the airframe done, then?'

'Airframe? Fourteen or fifteen hundred, I suppose.'

Mr Honey blinked at him dumbly. 'Let you know exactly if you're interested.' He reached for a pile of blue-jacketed log-books in a rack and picked out one, and turned the pages. 'Here we are. 1,422 hours, up to the time when we took off this evening.'

'Oh. . . .'

For a minute Mr Honey stood confused. Environment has its effect on everybody, and for a time it had a numbing effect on him, preventing him from

thinking clearly. He was moving in two worlds. Here in the aircraft everything
was firm and steady and secure; the even tremor of the engines, the faintly
heard rush of air over the outer skin, these bred confidence; there was nothing
insecure about their passage. It needed a strong mental effort to force his mind
back to the old balloon shed at Farnborough and to his untidy little office where
one calculated over months or even years to estimate when something would
break, where one set up a test to break it and confirm his calculations, where one
actually saw it crumple and sag down towards the concrete floor. It needed
mental effort to recall that at this moment the test upon the Reindeer tail was
going on, that he had estimated that that tail upon the testing gantry would
collapse about the time that this machine had flown. It needed mental effort to
identify the photographs that he had seen of the first Reindeer, split asunder
and burned out beneath that cliff in Labrador, with this firm, lovely thing that
he was standing in.

He turned to Dobson. 'Please,' he said, 'would you come over here a
minute?'

He drew him over to the navigating table and made him bend over it so that
their conversation was private. 'What is it?' Dobson asked.

Mr Honey moistened his lips, and said, 'I don't know how to put this to you,
but this aircraft is in a very dangerous condition. It's got a very serious fatigue
trouble in the tailplane. You must turn back to England at once.' He repeated
earnestly, with a rising inflection in his voice, 'At once.'

The second pilot stared at him. 'Fatigue trouble? What's that? We can't go
back to England, you know.'

'But you must.' His voice rose to a little nervous squeak. 'I tell you, this is
very serious indeed. This aeroplane should not be flying at all. The tail is liable to
fail at any moment – the front spar may fail. You've got a positive download on
the tail in this condition. You'll go into a dive quite suddenly, and there'll be no
control to get you out. I tell you, you must turn back at once. Turn back and
land at the first aerodrome in Ireland.' The young man stared at him in growing
tolerance and amusement. 'If you stop the inboard engines and reduce the
revolutions on the middle ones right down to a minimum, there's just a chance
that we may get back safely.'

'Take it easy,' Mr Dobson said. 'Whatever are you talking about? You must
have heard of an airworthiness certificate, surely? This aircraft's all okay. I'll
show you the daily inspection note, if you like.'

'This is something quite new,' said Mr Honey. 'No Reindeer is allowed to fly
more than seven hundred hours until this question of the tail has been cleared
up. And this one had flown double that, and that's right on the estimated time
for failure. I assure you, something can happen any moment now. You really
must turn back.'

'What's all this about a Reindeer not being allowed to do more than seven
hundred hours?'

'It's true. They've all got to be grounded when they reach that time.'

Dobson stared at him; impatience and hostility were beginning to appear.
'First I've heard of it.' He beckoned to the engineer, who left his seat and came
to them. 'Cousins, have you heard anything about Reindeers being grounded
after seven hundred hours?'

'Not a thing,' the engineer said in wonder. 'I never heard of that. Who says
so?'

'Chap from Farnborough,' Dobson said. He had forgotten Mr Honey's name.

'That's not right,' the engineer said scornfully. 'What do you think the Air Registration Board would have been doing?' He turned to Mr Honey. 'Who told you that?'

'It's true,' he said desperately. 'My chief, the head of my department, Dr Scott—he was arranging all about it.' They stared at him in utter disbelief. 'Please—you must pay attention to this. Stop the inboard engines and turn back. If you stop the inboard engines it will break up the harmonic and modify the effective frequency, and the amplitude will be less, too.'

The engineer turned to Dobson and said, 'What on earth is he talking about?'

The second pilot said quietly, 'All right, Cousins—I'll handle this. I'll have a word with the captain.' The engineer went back to his seat, but kept a wary eye on Mr Honey. Eccentric passengers with odd ideas about the safety of the aircraft are never very welcome on the flight deck of an airliner on passage.

Mr Honey caught the last words. 'Please do that,' he said. 'I must have a talk with the captain. It's very serious indeed, really it is. We must turn back at once.'

Dobson crossed to where Captain Samuelson was sitting at the controls, and bent beside him. 'That passenger from Farnborough that you asked me to show round is up here now, sir. He's making a good deal of trouble.'

From the navigating desk Mr Honey could see them talking quietly together; he saw the captain turn in his seat to look at him. He stood at the desk waiting for them. His agitation was subsiding; already he was becoming aware that he had not got it in him to make these men believe that what he said was true. He had had so much of this in the past; he was accustomed to being right and being disbelieved on vital issues. It was what happened to him; other people could put across their convictions and win credence, but he had never been able to do that. Now it was happening again, probably for the last time. In the black night the aircraft moved on quietly across the sky above the cloud carpet, seen faintly in the starlight far below.

Captain Samuelson got out of his seat; the second pilot slipped into it, and sat at the controls. Samuelson crossed the floor to Honey, standing by the desk. He was a small, sandy-haired man of about fifty, rather fat; he had been sitting in the pilot's seat of airliners for over twenty years.

He introduced himself to Mr Honey, and said, 'I understand from Dobson that you're not quite happy about something, Mr Honey.'

He stood in silence while Honey poured out his tale, nodding every now and then. Honey was more collected now and told his story better, and in Samuelson he had an older and a more experienced man to talk to. The Senior Captain had heard of fatigue troubles once or twice, and he even knew something of the eccentricities of scientists. He knew something of the routine of the Ministry of Supply and a good deal about the routine of the Ministry of Civil Aviation. Presently he started asking questions, and they were informed and penetrating questions. He very soon uncovered the fact that officially there was nothing wrong whatever with the Reindeer aircraft, that there was no ban upon its operation after seven hundred hours, and that there was no real evidence that the tailplane was subject to fatigue trouble at all.

Mr Honey said miserably at last, 'I've got to tell you what I know. If you don't turn back to England now and do what I say about the engines, we'll all probably be killed.'

Samuelson stood deep in thought. Once or twice before in his career he had had over-excited passengers to deal with, who had required restraint during a flight; once he had had an attempted suicide, a woman who had been found struggling to open the main entrance door during the flight. He was not antagonistic, but he could not discount the likelihood that the excitement of the journey might have inflamed the fixed ideas of a man who, from his appearance, might well be a little bit unbalanced. He was, however, disposed to pay attention carefully to everything that Mr Honey said, and for a special reason that had not been spoken of between them. Captain Samuelson had known Captain Ward, the pilot of the Reindeer that had crashed in Labrador, very well indeed.

Samuelson and Bill Ward had both been short-service officers in the Royal Air Force in 1925; Samuelson had flown Bristol Fighters in Iraq and Ward had flown Sopwith Snipes in India. They had met as civil pilots in an air circus in 1927; They had met again as minor airline pilots in Canada in 1928. In 1932 they had come together once more, as pilots on the Hillman airline operating out of Romford in Essex; shortly after that both had joined the Imperial Airways. From that time on they had met frequently, up till the time when Ward had received command of the first prototype Reindeer. Then Ward had been killed.

The accident report, when it came out, was a great shock to Samuelson; he disbelieved it utterly. He had known Ward as a fellow pilot for more than twenty years. It was incredible to him that Ward should have done what the report said he did, that he should have descended through the overcast to zero altitude above the hills of Labrador to check up his position by a sight of the ground. There were things a Senior Captain of C.A.T.O. just did not do, and that was one of them. Samuelson did not know what happened to Bill Ward, but he did know one thing very certainly. The accident report was absolutely and completely wrong.

He had been flying for more than twenty-five years. Deep in his mind lay the feeling that there was something not right with the Reindeer; that this beautiful and efficient aircraft had a weakness that would presently show up. Some unknown Gremlin in it had leaped out upon Bill Ward suddenly, so suddenly that he had been unable to send word upon the radio, and it had killed him, and thirty other people with him. His instinct, bred of nearly twenty thousand hours in the air, told him that one day that thing would happen again.

He glanced at Mr Honey thoughtfully. He saw the weak eyes behind the thick glasses, the unimpressive figure, the shabby clothes, the nervous movements of the hands, the quivering wet lips. He thought, rather sadly, that he could not change his flight plan upon this man's word alone. Mr Honey looked a crank and what he said was unsubstantiated by any evidence at all. The captain decided, heavily, he must go on. If Honey turned out to be right, well, that was just too bad.

He said, 'Look, Mr Honey, I'm going to do this. I'm going to shut down the inboard engines as you say, and I can throttle down the middle ones to nineteen hundred revs. That drops our speed by fifty miles an hour and makes us nearly two hours late at Gander. I'll do that if you think it's the right thing to do. But I'm not going to turn back.'

'You're taking a great risk if you go on. You ought to turn back now—at once—and land in Ireland,' said Mr Honey.

'That's what you think,' the captain said quietly. 'But this decision rests with me, and we're going on.'

Mr Honey met his eyes, and that shy, warm smile spread over his face, surprising to Samuelson as it had been to me. 'Well, let's wish ourselves luck,' he said.

At that moment, Samuelson very nearly became convinced. It was on the tip of his tongue to say they would turn back, but one could not chop and change. One had to take a line and stick to it. He turned to the flight engineer and gave him a few orders; then he crossed to the pilot's seat and spoke for a minute to Dobson. The second pilot got out of his seat and Samuelson slipped back into it, knocked out the automatic pilot and flew the aircraft manually while the inboard engines died and the note changed. Dobson crossed to Mr Honey at the navigating table.

'I'll take you back to the saloon,' he said. As they left the flight deck Samuelson motioned to the radio operator, demanding a signal pad.

In the saloon Dobson showed Honey to his seat with studied courtesy; then he went on down the cabin to the galley at the rear end. The tall dark stewardess was there, the one who was looking after Mr Honey.

He greeted her with a grin. 'Fun and games,' he said. 'The boffin's going mad.'

Miss Corder stared at him. 'What *do* you mean?'

'He's absolutely crackers. Says the tail's going to fall off.' She asked quietly, 'Is it?'

'No, of course it's not. It's the altitude or something, even pressurised down like this. The captain wants him specially looked after—he's a bit excited. Got any bromide with your medicines?'

She turned to the medicine chest and pulled out a drawer, and examined two or three little flasks of tablets. 'I've got these.'

He took the flask from her and read the label. 'That looks all right,' he said. 'Give him two or three of these if he gets restless. But he's quiet enough now; I don't think he'll make any trouble. Give us a ring through if it does, and one or other of us'll come down.'

She nodded. 'What does he think is going to happen?'

He shrugged his shoulders. 'Says the tail's due to fall off after this number of hours. Says we ought to turn back and land in Ireland. It's all sheer nonsense—something he's made up. It really is a most fantastic place, that Farnborough. There's not a whisper of truth in it.'

'How do you know that?' she asked.

He laughed. 'Do you think the Inspection would have let this aircraft fly if there was any danger of that sort of thing? Be your age.'

She nodded slowly. 'That's right, of course. I suppose he's been overworking or something.'

'Overdrinking. Someone's given him an egg-cup full of ginger cordial.'

She said, 'He's a nice little man.' Above her head the telephone buzzer from the flight deck rang, she lifted the hand microphone. 'Yes,' she said, 'he's here. I'll ask him to come up at once.'

She turned to Dobson. 'Captain wants you on the flight deck.'

'Okay. I like your idea of a nice little man. Ruddy little squirt, I call him, coming up with a tale like this and frightening us all into a fit.' He turned away, and moved forward up the aisle in the soft, dimmed lights of the quiet cabin, past the sleeping passengers stretched in their reclining seats. She watched him till he passed through the door at the forward end; then she moved up the aisle herself and stopped by Mr Honey. He was sitting upright in his seat, his hands playing nervously with the fringe of his overcoat upon his lap.

She said, 'Can I get you a hot drink, sir? We've got plenty of milk; would you like a cup of Ovaltine and a few biscuits?'

He said nervously, 'Oh no, thank you. I don't want anything.'

She said gently, 'Would you rather have some soup or a whisky and soda? It's better to have something when you can't sleep.'

He turned to her, roused from his obsession. Airline stewardesses are not chosen for their repellent qualities, and Miss Corder was a very charming girl. 'It's awfully kind of you,' he said. 'I'll be all right. It's—it's just a bit worrying, that's all.'

'Let me make you a hot milk drink,' she said. 'It's very good when you've got something on your mind. We've got Horlicks if you'd rather have that than Ovaltine.'

It was years since any woman had spoken in that way to Mr Honey; he was irresistibly reminded of his dead wife, and the tears welled up behind his eyes. It might have been Mary speaking to him. 'All right,' he said thickly. 'I'd like Ovaltine.'

She went away to get it, and a minute or two later the door at the forward end opened, and Captain Samuelson came into the cabin. He moved down the aisle, nodding and smiling at Mr Honey as he passed. He went on past the galley, past the toilets, and opened a door in the rear wall and went through the aft luggage bay to the end of the pressurised cabin and the concave dome of the rear wall. There was a perspex window in the dome and a switch that turned on an electric light for the inspection of the tailplane and the elevator mechanism in the space behind. He stood peering through the perspex, looking for trouble.

Mr Honey saw him go through into the luggage bay towards the tail, and smiled, a little bitterly. He got out of his seat and followed him, passing Miss Corder as she tended a saucepan of hot milk over the electric stove. She turned and saw him go through into the luggage bay, following the captain; she said, 'Oh, damn!' and turned off the current of the hot plate, and went after him. It was one of her jobs to keep the passengers from wandering about the aircraft.

In the luggage bay Mr Honey came up behind Samuelson. 'It's no good looking at it,' he said a little bitterly. 'You won't find anything wrong.' Behind him the stewardess came up, but seeing that he was talking to the captain and that Samuelson was attending to what was being said, she did not intervene.

'If what you say is right, there might be some preliminary sign,' Samuelson said. 'But there's nothing to be seen at all. No paint cracking or anything. It's all perfectly all right. Have a look for yourself.'

'I don't need to,' Mr Honey said. 'The spar flanges are perfectly all right now, or we shouldn't be here. In half a minute it may be a very different story. When it happens it happens as suddenly as that.' Captain Samuelson's brows wrinkled in a frown. 'If you cut a section of the front spar top flanges now and etched it for a microscopical examination, ten to one you'd find the structure of the metal absolutely normal. But all the same, it may be due for failure in ten minutes. There's nothing to be seen in the appearance of it that will tell you anything.'

Samuelson stood in silence for a moment, cursing his own irresolution. This little insignificant man was getting terribly plausible. He had sent a radio signal to his Flight Control reporting briefly what Honey had said and stating his decision to go on; the signal had been acknowledged but not answered. He could hardly expect such guidance from his Flight Control in view of the difficulty of the technical points that were involved and the fact that it was then the middle of the night when all right-minded technicians would be in bed and sound asleep. The most that he could hope for would be guidance when they got to Gander, by which time it would be nine o'clock in the morning in England.

'I've shut down the inboard engines,' he said at last.

'That should help it,' Mr Honey said. 'But you ought to go back while there's time. Really you should.'

Samuelson smiled brightly and confidently, more for the benefit of the stewardess than for Mr Honey. 'Oh, I don't think so,' he remarked. 'I think we're quite all right.'

He ushered Mr Honey forward out of the luggage bay, and went forward up the aisle himself to the flight deck. Mr Honey stayed at the aft end of the cabin with Miss Corder, scrutinising the structure of the fuselage so far as could be seen by reason of the cabin furnishings; he opened the doors of the toilets and investigated the methods of staying the bulkheads, peering at everything through his thick glasses.

He was behaving very oddly, Miss Corder decided. She came to him, and said, 'I should go back to your seat, sir. I'll bring you the Ovaltine in a few minutes.'

'I'll go in just one moment,' he said meekly. 'Let me have a look at your stove first.' Thinking to humour him she showed him into the galley and began to explain the operation of the various switches and ovens to him, but she found he was not interested in that at all. He examined very carefully the methods of fixing the unit to the floor and the fuselage side; then he was through, and went back to his seat. She brought him a tray with his Ovaltine and biscuits a few minutes later, full of a queer, detached pity for him in his self-induced trouble. He seemed so very helpless.

She said quietly, 'I've brought you your Ovaltine, Mr Honey. Do you like these sweet biscuits? I've got some oatmeal ones if you'd rather have those.'

He said quickly, 'Oh, thank you so much. These will do splendidly.'

She smiled down at him. 'Would you like a little drop of rum in the Ovaltine to help you sleep?'

'Oh no, thank you. I never take spirits.'

'All right. Drink it while it's hot. I'll come back presently and take the tray.'

The Reindeer moved on steadily across the starlit sky, alone in space above the overcast seen dimly far below, shrouding the black, empty wastes of sea. In the quiet cabin Mr Honey sat sipping his Ovaltine, gradually relaxing with the warmth and comfort of the drink. His hands ceased to fiddle nervously, the tight, set muscles round about his mouth relaxed, and the feeling of a tight band round his forehead eased a little. He no longer sat tense waiting for the first movement of the aircraft that would herald the steep dive to their destruction; his ears were no longer strained to hear the first crack from the tail that would be the beginning of the sequence.

It now seemed to him that he could take things as they came. There were six hours more at least to go before they came to Gander; it seemed to him most probably that they would all be dead before that time was up. The thought did not now appal him as it had. Death came to everybody in its time; it had come to Mary earlier than they had dreamed it could. If now it came to him, well, that was just one of those things; he had a simple faith that somewhere, somehow after death he would catch up with Mary once again and they would be together.

He was saddened and distressed for Elspeth. But Elspeth was twelve years old; her character was formed for good or ill; it would not alter her so much if now he had to go. Materially he knew that she would be looked after by the Ministry; she would get as good an education as if he had lived. I am almost ashamed to record that for all the little homely pleasures that make the life of a child happy, he put his trust in Shirley and myself. I do not think he quite thought that we should adopt his daughter, but he did think very certainly that we should never let her suffer the lack of a home life; he thought that when he caught up with his Mary he could tell her that their daughter would be happy. I hope we should have lived up to his expectation of us. I don't know.

Miss Corder came to take away his tray. She bent to him, and asked, 'Would you like another cup? I've got some more hot milk all ready, if you'd like it.'

He said, 'No, I've done excellently, thank you.' He blinked up at her through his thick glasses. 'It's been terribly kind of you to take all this trouble.'

She smiled at him, 'Oh no, sir. I'm so sorry you've got all this worry on your shoulders.'

This dark, kind girl would go too, when it happened. 'Are you married?' he enquired.

She stared at him in wonder; surely he wasn't one of those? She laughed. 'Me married?' she said. 'No.'

'That's a good thing,' he said quietly. 'Nor am I. There won't be a lot of trouble over us.'

The meaning of his words got through to her in a short pause. She hesitated for an instant, not knowing how to take it. She reached for a rug. 'Let me put your chair back for you and put this over you,' she said. 'Then you'll probably get a little sleep.'

She helped him to arrange his chair and tucked the rug around him; then she took the tray and went back to the galley. A quarter of an hour later she said to the other stewardess, 'I'm going up to the flight deck. Keep an eye on No. 11 for me, will you—Mr Honey. I think he's asleep.'

'That's the boffin? Is he liable to cut his throat, or anything?'

Miss Corder said, 'No, he's not. He's just a little, worried man, that's all. I'll be back in a few minutes. I just want to tell Dobson how he's going on.'

Mr Honey lay relaxed in his reclining chair. He did not want to sleep, so little time was left he had no use for that. His mind drifted to the accident as it would happen, objective and dispassionate. He began to calculate in his head, as he had calculated all his working life.

The download on the tail in this condition he knew to be about 6,000 lb. Assuming half of the tail failed only, leaving the rest of the plane intact, that meant a nose-down pitching moment of, say, 300,000 lb.-feet. He did not know the power of the one remaining elevator, but he guessed it might provide one half of that. The balance of the nose-down moment would be satisfied by an increase of speed, by diving till the forces came into equilibrium. He figured for a time and came to the conclusion that a diving speed of 420 m.p.h., attainable at perhaps 7° of flight path to the horizontal, would be somewhere near it. With the maximum control that would be left to him, the pilot would not be able to do better for them than to dive at over four hundred miles an hour until he hit the sea.

He wondered what would happen when they hit. At that small angle they might well bounce up again and not plunge straight in, though there seemed to be a likelihood that the wings would be torn off. They might bounce once or twice, reducing speed each time. The impacts and decelerations would be very violent. After that the fuselage might float for a few moments before sinking; if anybody had survived the crash they might be able to get out into the sea, to float about in lifebelts till they died of cold. There was only one chance in a million that there would be a ship in the vicinity that could help, even if anyone got out.

He put all thought of safety from him; when it happened he would die. Now that he had become used to the idea he did not mind about that much; his mind was filled with memories of Mary. His life since Mary died had not been happy; he had no great ambition to hold on to it. Mary had gone before him; somehow, somewhere he would catch up with her again. Again they would go on hiking on long summer days over the Hog's Back, drink beer in little pubs together after the day's march, make love, go Morris dancing together with little bells and ribbons at the knee, buy a new enlarger and play with it together, go to the pictures and see all their favourites, David Niven, Monica Teasdale . . .

Monica Teasdale . . .

He thought ingenuously that it would be something to tell Mary when he met her, that he had seen Monica Teasdale in the flesh; she would be thrilled. His young wife was very real to him still. His mind dwelt on the actress, on her parts that they had seen together in the years gone by, on the pleasure she had given Mary. And suddenly it seemed to him to be important that the actress should be saved in the disaster that was coming to them all. He could not meet his Mary and tell her that he had neglected to do what was possible for Monica Teasdale, whom she had loved so well. All this knowledge must be used to save Miss Teasdale's life, or at any rate to give her a fighting chance of survival. He knew one place within the aircraft where a passenger could survive the impact with the water when it came. If then she drowned, well, that was just too bad, but with his knowledge he could get her through the crash.

He leaned up on one elbow and turned to look across the aisle to where the actress was reclining. She was not asleep, she was lying there awake, smoking a cigarette. There was an empty seat beside her.

He turned back his rug and got up, and moved down the aisle to her, and said, 'Please, Miss Teasdale, may I talk to you for a few moments?'

The shadow of a frown crossed her face; one travelled by air to get away from all that sort of thing. She had been at rest before this uncouth little man with the weak eyes had come to bother her. Then her professional charm took over and she withdrew herself within its mantle, and spoke the phrases she had used so often that they came mechanically. Half of her, at least, could go on resting while she said, 'Why certainly, I'd be pleased.' She spoke with a light mid-Western accent.

He sat down beside her and plunged straight into his story. 'Miss Teasdale, my name is Honey. I'm a research worker at the R.A.E.–the Royal Aircraft Establishment–that's the British experimental station for aeroplanes at Farnborough, you know. I've been doing some experiments recently on the tailplane of the Reindeer aircraft–that's this aircraft that we're travelling in now. I'm afraid we're all in rather a dangerous position.'

She said impassively, 'Is that so?' She noted his nervous movements, his excited urgency. It was a nuisance that she had attracted an unbalanced fan; in her career she had had that before, several times. She lay listening to him with one part of her mind only, waiting for an opportunity to be delivered from the nuisance of this wretched little man, making a soothing comment now and then.

Miss Corder, coming down into the cabin from the flight deck, was surprised and concerned to see that Mr Honey's seat was empty. She spotted him immediately talking to the actress and her lips tightened; she should have thought of that. Unbalanced people always made for actresses. As she approached them Miss Teasdale raised her eyebrows slightly in appeal; the stewardess stopped by the double seat and to her horror heard the actress say lazily:

'Mr Honey, can't I use the Ladies' Toilet? It seems more kind of suitable.'

He said earnestly, 'You see, the galley stove is up against the bulkhead of the other one, and that makes the bulkhead firm–' It was at that point that Miss Corder touched him on the arm, and said, 'Mr Honey, I'm sure Miss Teasdale wants to get some sleep. Will you come back to your own seat?'

He stared up at her, hurt and affronted. 'I've been trying . . .' He glanced at the actress; she lay impassive and uninterested, her face a mask of indifference. 'I'm sorry,' he said with some dignity. 'I was only trying to help.'

'I'm sure you were,' Miss Teasdale said. 'Some other time, perhaps . . .'

Without a word Mr Honey got up and went back to his seat, his face crimson. Miss Corder followed him, and tucked the rug round him once again. 'You shouldn't have done that,' she said quietly. 'You mustn't go alarming other passengers, Mr Honey. Will you promise me not to do that again? Promise to stay quiet in this seat?'

He said bitterly, 'If you say so. There's one place in this aircraft where a human body would be safe in the deceleration of a crash. I was trying to tell her what to do if things look bad. But if she doesn't want to know, I can't do more.'

The girl said, 'If I get you a small pill to help you get some sleep, will you take it?'

He said, 'No, I don't want that.'

'Will you promise not to talk to any of the other passengers?'

He knew that she was doing her duty; he knew that she was doing it with kindness and with tact. He warmed towards her in spite of the role of prisoner and warder that they were assuming. 'All right,' he said, 'I won't talk to anyone again.' He glanced up at her thoughtfully. 'What's your name?'

She smiled down at him. 'Corder,' she said. 'Marjorie Corder. What do you want to know that for?' It was her object to make him talk, to get his mind on something different from the accident he thought was going to happen.

He said quietly, 'You've been very nice to me, Miss Corder. I'd like to do something for you. Will you listen if I tell you what I was trying to tell Miss Teasdale?'

She said, 'Of course I will. But after that, will you try and get some sleep?'

He motioned to the empty chair beside him. 'Sit down there a minute.'

She hesitated, and then sat down on the edge of the seat, turned towards him. 'What is it?' she asked.

He said evenly, 'I think this aircraft's going to crash in the next hour or so. You don't, nor does Captain Samuelson, nor anybody here. But I know more about it than the lot of you, and that is what I think. When that happens, there may be about three minutes from the time when you first know that something has gone wrong until the moment that we hit the sea.'

He paused. 'We shall most of us be killed,' he said quietly. 'We shall die with the deceleration of the crash. There's just one place to go to where a person could avoid that, and get out unhurt into the sea in a lifebelt. That doesn't give much chance for living, even then, but it's a better chance than all the rest of us will have. If I tell you where to go and what to do, will you do it?'

She said, 'Mr Honey, all this isn't going to happen, really it's not. But if it did. I've got my jobs to do.'

He said, 'If I tell you, will you listen?'

She nodded.

He said. 'You must go into the Gentleman's Toilet and sit down on the floor facing to the tail, with your back against the forward bulkhead and your head back in contact with the bulkhead, too. I was trying to tell this to Miss Teasdale, but she wouldn't listen. Get a pad of something–a towel or a blanket, and put it behind your head. The stove behind that bulkhead will hold it firm for the instant of the crash, and your body will be well supported. If you do that, you'll live through the impact. You must have your lifebelt on. When the machine comes to rest, before it sinks, pull down the emergency hatch in the toilet roof, and get out at once. Don't stay to try and help the rest of us, or you'll be trapped and drown. Get out immediately the motion stops. There's just a chance you may be picked up when dawn comes.'

She stared at him. 'Is that what you were trying to tell Miss Teasdale?'

'That's right,' he said. 'She doesn't want to know. But will you remember what to do, if what I say is true?'

She said, 'I'll remember, Mr Honey. But I don't say I'll be able to do it.'

'Do your best,' he said quietly. 'If you get through this and we don't, get yourself married and bring up a family. I think you'd be good at that.'

She coloured a little, and laughed. 'Will you go to sleep now, if I leave you?'

'No,' said Mr Honey. 'But I'll lie down, if you say.'

'I do say,' she replied. She arranged the rug around him and saw that he was comfortable; then she turned away behind him down the aisle, her forehead furrowed deep with thought. For a madman, he was damnably convincing.

She stopped by the actress and said quietly, 'I'm so sorry you were troubled in that way, Miss Teasdale. It won't happen again.'

The woman turned her head, and said, 'Don't think of it. Is the little man nuts?'

'I'm afraid so,' said the stewardess. 'He seems to have some rather odd ideas. But he's quite quiet now.'

'I'll say he's got some odd ideas,' the actress said. 'He was trying to make me go into the Men's Room and sit down on the floor. If that's not an odd idea, I'd like to hear one.'

Miss Corder felt she could not leave the matter in that state. 'He's not as mad as all that,' she explained. 'He was trying to tell you what you ought to do if–' she hesitated '–well, if anything should happen to make you feel that an accident was going to take place. It's probably true enough that in an accident the safest place would be sitting on the floor in there with your back against the bulkhead. He was trying to do his best for you.'

Miss Teasdale was more wide awake now. 'Well, that was nice of him,' she said. 'Who is the little guy anyway–apart from being nuts and apart from being a fan? Do you know anything about him?'

'Oh yes. He's a scientist from the Royal Aircraft Establishment, at Farnborough. He's an expert upon aeroplanes.'

'Well, what do you know? And he thinks that we're going to have a crash?'

Miss Corder said, 'Oh, nothing like that, Miss Teasdale. It's just that he's got into rather a nervous state. You mustn't pay any attention to him. I'm so sorry that he came and troubled you.'

The actress stared at her, and then sat up. 'He's not the only passenger that's in a nervous state right now,' she said.

4

Miss Corder had a momentary, sickening feeling that the situation amongst her passengers was getting out of control. She made a valiant effort to restore it. 'There's no need to think of it again, Miss Teasdale,' she said brightly. 'Captain Samuelson himself has had a long talk with this passenger, and I'm afraid there is no doubt that he's a little bit unbalanced. It's probably the altitude or something. But he's quite quiet now.'

'More than I am,' said the actress. She was sitting up and smoothing out her clothes. 'If I'm going to meet my Maker, I won't go with my nylons down round my ankles. Say, where in heck did my shoes get to? Oh, thanks a lot.' She studied her face in the mirror of her powder compact. 'I was a darned fool not to travel in a U.S. airplane,' she observed. 'But you haven't had so many accidents lately, and I thought I'd be safer. That's how one gets caught.'

Marjorie Corder said, 'I assure you, Miss Teasdale, there's nothing in what Mr Honey says. There's no chance of any accident. Can I get you a cup of coffee?'

The actress said a little sharply, 'Look, this scientist from Farnborough thinks this airplane's going to crack up pretty soon, and Captain Samuelson, he thinks it isn't going to crack up. And now you come along to give the casting vote, and put in with the captain's. Well, just you run along and get that cup of coffee, and bring it to me over there. You say his name is Honey? It would be. I'm going visiting with Mr Honey; bring my coffee there.'

The stewardess said anxiously, 'I wouldn't go and talk to him, Miss Teasdale–really. It'll only excite him again.'

'I can handle that, my girl,' the actress said. 'Just you go right down and get that coffee.'

Miss Corder hesitated, but there was nothing she could do against this strong-willed woman, twenty years older than herself. She went to get the coffee.

Miss Teasdale finished her appearance to her satisfaction and got up, and moved up the quiet aisle of the saloon to Mr Honey's seat. He was lying wide awake, in rather bitter reflection. He stirred as she approached, and looked up in surprise. It was about half-past three in the morning. The Reindeer was still flying steadily and quietly on course, above the overcast seen faintly down beneath them in the starlight.

Miss Teasdale said, 'Mr Honey, do you mind if I sit down here for a while?' He sat up, blinking at her through his glasses. 'I was half asleep when you were talking just now, and maybe I was just a little bit rude. I didn't mean to be, but you know how it is.'

He said, 'Oh, please—don't think of it. Do sit down.' He was a little flustered and confused. He had seen Monica Teasdale so often in the past upon the screen, had been stirred to deep emotion by her parts so many times, that he had difficulty now in knowing what to say to her in the flesh. When he had crossed the aisle to her he had been carried away by the impulse to do something for the safety of this woman; he had something definite to tell her. Now he was flustered and nonplussed.

She said, 'That's real nice of you.' She sat down and turned to him. 'Say, when you started talking about going into the Men's Room, Mr Honey, I thought you were plain nuts. But then that stewardess came along and told me one or two things, and then it seemed to me that maybe I was nuts myself for having brushed you off. Would you mind starting off and say your piece again?'

He blinked at her through the thick glasses. This was not the ethereal girl that he had known upon the screen, the Madonna-like heroine of *Temptation*. This was someone very different, but someone who was out to make amends for a discourtesy, someone who was trying to be pleasant.

He said, 'I'm sorry—I'm afraid I ought not to have alarmed you, Miss Teasdale. I was just trying to help.'

She nodded slightly. She had had this so often, but more with adolescents than with grown-up men. Fans went to every kind of trouble to speak to her, but when she stopped and met them half-way they could only stammer platitudes, with nothing to say, so that she had to help them out of their embarrassment. She set herself to help out Mr Honey, and she said,

'The stewardess, she told me that you work at airplane research, Mr Honey? Is that the sort of work they do at Langley Field?'

He turned to her, pleased and surprised. 'Not quite,' he said. 'My work is on structures, more like what they do at Wright Field. We've got the whole of that work concentrated with the flying experimental side, at Farnborough. That's about forty miles south-west of London.'

She said, 'That must be interesting kind of work.' It was a part of her technique, this art of making men talk about themselves.

He said, 'Well, yes, it is. It's rather lengthy sometimes—you go on for a long time at a thing without seeing any results.' He smiled at her, that shy, revealing smile that he pulled out so unexpectedly from time to time.

'You must feel that it's something well worth doing, though,' she said.

'Well, yes—it is. There was the wing flutter on the Monsoon in the war.' He started in to tell her all about the research he had carried out into the wing flutter, and the effect of moving the mass of the guns and ammunition boxes six inches farther back upon the chord of the wing. From that she had little difficulty in steering him on to the Reindeer tail.

When Miss Corder came back with the coffee she found them deep in conversation, with Mr Honey talking freely to the actress. She was divided in her feelings over this; it was her duty to prevent the spread of alarm from one nervous passenger amongst the rest, but at the same time she had been troubled over Mr Honey. It was pleasant to see him animated and cheerful. She was grateful to the actress that she had done that for him. She went to get another cup of coffee for the little man.

Within a quarter of an hour Miss Teasdale knew a good deal more about the Reindeer tail than Captain Samuelson. She knew more of the background of the story; she knew something about Elspeth, and a little about Shirley, and a good deal about me, as Mr Honey's boss. She knew the way the matter had arisen, the urgency with which I regarded it, the sacrifice that Honey had made in leaving his small daughter to the uncertain mercies of a charwoman. Captain Samuelson knew the bald facts of the matter; he knew nothing of the background of those facts.

Miss Teasdale said, 'That's very, very interesting, Mr Honey. Tell me, have I got this right? You reckon that the stabiliser of this airplane that we're sitting in is kind of dying of old age?'

He blinked at her. 'Well, yes. Yes. I think that's a very good way to put it. It's not very old, as structures go, but—yes, it's dying of old age. In fact, it must be just about dead by now.'

'And when it dies it breaks? What happens—does it come right off the fuselage, so that we'd have no tail at all?'

'I think half would fail first. One side—yes, I think it would come off. I think it did in the first one, the one that fell in Labrador.'

She stared down the quiet aisle of the cabin. 'You never think, somehow, this sort of thing can ever happen to you,' she said.

'It may not happen,' Mr Honey said. 'I wasn't able to convince the captain or to make him land in Ireland. But he did agree to stop the inboard engines. That helps us, certainly.'

She thought for a minute. 'How much flying time did you say the one that fell in Labrador had done?'

'1,393 hours.'

'And this plane we're riding in—how long has that done up till now?'

'About 1,426 hours. I calculated that the tail would fail about 1,440, but it's not very easy to forecast as accurately as all that. The first one went at 1,393 hours; I'm afraid the only thing that one can say is that this one might go at any time. Dr Scott intended that no Reindeer should fly over 700 hours until this thing had been thrashed out. But this one's slipped through, somehow.'

She said, 'You told the captain all this, did you?'

He nodded. 'There's no real evidence yet that the captain could act on, I suppose. We don't *know* yet that the one in Labrador did crash for that reason. That's what I'm going out to Ottawa for now. But it looks as if I may not get to Ottawa. They may have to send out someone else.'

She said, 'Looks like Mossy Bauer'll have to look around for a new star for the new picture, too.'

He turned to her. 'You mustn't think of this as certain,' he said. 'We may quite well get safely to Gander. I—I just don't know. I only know that this machine is liable to accident at any moment now. But it might go on like this for another hundred hours, or even longer.'

She nodded. 'Say, would it help any if I were to have a talk with Captain Samuelson? I mean, there's all these other people to consider.' She indicated the sleeping passengers in the other seats.'

'I don't think it would do any good at all,' Mr Honey said. 'He thinks I'm just unduly nervous, and, really, there *is* no proper evidence at all yet that the tail is liable to failure. That's what I'm going to Ottawa to find out.' He outlined to her in detail what Samuelson had done. 'I really don't think it would be much good for you to talk to him. He's the captain and he's made his decision.' He hesitated. 'And anyway, we must be very near the point of no return by now.'

She said sharply, 'The point of no return?'

'That's the point when it is shorter to go on than to go back,' Mr Honey explained. 'Sort of half-way.'

She breathed. 'I thought you meant something different. So you think there's nothing we can do but sit here with our fingers crossed?'

'I don't see what else we can do,' he said. 'If we were going to turn back we should have done it long ago.'

His coffee came, brought on a small tray by the stewardess, who put it down upon his knees and left them. Mr Honey sipped it gratefully. If death was near at hand, there were worse ways to meet it than by sitting in the utmost comfort in a warm, delicately furnished cabin, sipping a cup of very good coffee, and talking to a very beautiful woman.

'Say,' she said, 'just to pass the time, then, you can tell me what you meant about the Men's Toilet.'

He coloured and said nervously, 'I wasn't trying to be rude. It's just that the safest place in the whole aircraft in a crash is sitting on the floor in there. And at the altitude we're flying, there'd be plenty of time for you to get back there and sit down.'

She stared at him. 'Say, why would that be any safer than staying right here where we are—with the safety belts on, of course?'

'Your body gets thrown forward, very violently. If the belt holds you, it could injure you so badly that you'd die in any case. But if you're facing backwards with your spine and your head pressed up again a firm support, you can stand a far greater deceleration without injury.' He went on to tell her all the details of what she ought to do, as he had told Miss Corder.

She listened to him with attention. 'That's something to know about,' she said at last. 'Will I meet you in there when the time comes?'

He hesitated. 'I don't think so. I shall try and get to the flight cabin up forward when—when things start to happen. It's just possible that I could help the captain in some way.' He hesitated. 'I've been a long time in aircraft research,' he said. 'Something might happen after the tail fails that we could take advantage of, and that the captain might not recognise in time.'

She nodded without speaking. She had been travelling by air for twenty years and she knew a little about accidents. She knew that when a high-speed aircraft crashed those in the flight cabin were almost always killed, whereas those in the tail of the aircraft frequently escaped. She recognized that no one knew that better than Mr Honey who had sought out the safest place in the Reindeer and told her about it. She realised that this shabby, weak-eyed, insignificant little man who had been discredited by the crew was proposing to put aside the chance of safety and go to the point of maximum danger when the crisis came, following his calling to the end.

'Does anybody else know about this place in the Men's Room?' she asked. 'I mean, is there going to be a run on it? Because I'm kind of allergic to a crowd.'

He hesitated. 'I told the stewardess, Miss Corder,' he said, 'when–when I thought perhaps you didn't want to hear about it. But it's all right–the stove is quite wide enough. There'll be room for two if you crush up close together.'

The actress said, 'That's the girl who waited on us with the coffee?'

He nodded. 'She was so–so kind.'

There was a silence. Miss Teasdale sat staring up the cabin in front of her, thoughtful and silent. What she had heard bore the stamp of truth to her; in the quiet comfort of this aeroplane she realised that death might be very near. She could take that philosophically, so long as it was quick; with the Atlantic down beneath them it would be so. She would have liked to live, but she had no dependants; and as she sat there she knew that she had had the best of life. She had been born of middle-class parents in Terre Haute, Indiana; when she left school she had gone to work in an insurance office as a stenographer. Then, at the age of nineteen, she had won a beauty competition, becoming Miss Terre Haute; she had gained a screen test and her first job in Hollywood. She had been three times married, but never with success; twice she had created the divorce. The last time she had married Andy Summers, the band leader, and had divorced him after eighteen months; since then she had lived alone. She had never had a child. Twice she had visited her own state in glorious pageantry to start the Indianapolis Motor Race; these visits were to her the climax of a long career. She treasured the memory of them more dearly than her Oscars. She had a brother who ran a flourishing automobile agency in Louisville and a sister who had married an attorney and lived in Norfolk, Va.; she had not seen either of them for many years. When her star waned she planned to rent an apartment in Indianapolis, in her own state where people were proud of her, but she would spend her winters in Miami. There were indications at the box office that that time was not very far off now.

So, if it had to end, she would be missing little but old age and she could do without that, anyway.

Presently, she turned to Mr Honey. 'Why did you pick on me to give me the best seat in the house for this show?'

He said awkwardly, 'Well, you're a very well-known person, Miss Teasdale. You've given so much pleasure to so many people.'

All her life she had received compliments; they had become commonplace to her, just things that people said. With death very near, this one struck rather a new note and arrested her attention with its sincerity. She said quietly, 'You thought so much about my pictures? Do you go to the movies a great deal?' She had not taken him for an escapist.

He hesitated. 'Well–not now,' he said. 'I used to go a great deal when my wife was alive. But I've gone very little in the last five years. I'm afraid I haven't seen any of your recent films.'

'You haven't missed a lot,' she said. 'There was more adventure in the picture business in the 'thirties. Every picture that I made had something new about it then. Now–well, I don't know. Directors seem to have got cautious.'

'That's what we always said,' said Mr Honey eagerly. 'There was always something new about your pictures. I think we saw everything that you were in from the first day we got engaged right up to the end.'

She asked, 'When did your wife die, Mr Honey? Was it in the war?'

He nodded. 'It was at the time of the V.2s–the rockets, you remember. We had a flat in Surbiton.' He stared up the aisle. 'It was rather a long way from the factory, but there's a very good train service to Ash Vale. And there was always something going on in Surbiton: there was the Country Dancing Club and the Art Club and the Camera Club. We *did* have such fun . . .' He was silent for a minute, and then he said, 'I'd have been at home when it happened, only I was doing my turn firewatching at the factory. I didn't even hear about it till the morning. Elspeth was quite all right when they got her out–just a bit shocked, you know. But Mary–well, she died . . .'

She said impulsively, 'Oh, I'm sorry.' And then, to keep him talking and to ease the difficulty, she said, 'What did you do, Mr Honey? About Elspeth, I mean?'

'It was a terrible job,' he said simply. 'You see, all our furniture was gone, everything we had. We'd only just got the clothes that we were in–Elspeth was in her pyjamas. Of course, everyone was frightfully kind and we got fitted out all right, and lots of people offered to give Elspeth a home in the country right away from the bombing–places in Wales and Cornwall–all that sort of thing. But–well, there were only the two of us, and I thought that sending her away to be with strangers would do more harm than good.' The actress nodded thoughtfully. 'So I kept her with me and we managed to get digs in Farnham to start with; there wasn't much bombing there. And then we got a house, and bit by bit we got some furniture together. I think it was the best thing to do.'

'Who lives with you to keep house?' she asked.

'Nobody,' he said. 'We get along all right, Elspeth and I. Of course, now that she's growing up and can do things for herself it's getting a great deal easier.'

'How old was she when that happened?' Miss Teasdale asked.

'Eight,' he replied. 'It's bad luck to have a thing like that happen when you're only eight.'

She breathed, 'I'll say it is.'

They sat in thoughtful silence for a time. At last the actress asked, 'Was your wife a great movie fan, Mr Honey?'

He said, 'We both were, for good pictures like yours. We used to pick and choose. But Mary was terribly fond of your films.' He turned to her. 'That's really why I want you to do what I say and go and sit down in the Men's Toilet if anything happens. You will, won't you?'

There was a sudden watering behind her eyes. He certainly was the oddest little man. 'Surely,' she said gently. 'Of course I'll go.'

He stared past her through his thick glasses. 'I don't know if there's any truth in what they say in church about meeting people again,' he said. 'When the end of the world comes or when you die. Or if it all just finishes. It's an idea that kind of–helps, to think you'll meet people again. If it's true, I wouldn't want to go to Mary and tell her I hadn't done everything that could be done to help you. You see, you gave her so much pleasure.'

'I'll do just what you say,' the actress said humbly.

They sat in silence while the Reindeer moved across the night sky above the overcast, beneath the stars, in steady, effortless flight. From time to time this thing had happened to her before, that she had suddenly been brought face to face with the incredible power of the honky-tonk, of the synthetic, phoney film business. Story-teller, script writer, producer, director, cameraman, musician, cutter, actors and actresses, all came together for the purely commercial business of creating something that would sell; if they succeeded they created something that would sway the lives of men and women by the million, in all the countries of the world. That happened on the side. It was purely accidental to the business what they came together for, which was to make money.

She had few illusions about her profession; few film actresses have. In the endless, monotonous sequence of takes and retakes on the set she had a faculty for carrying through the emotion of a scene from one shot to another taken ten days later, so that given the proper opportunities by her director she could turn quite an ordinary script into a masterpiece. That, with her beauty, had made star material of her, fit for publicity. She had few other talents, but for that knack she might still have been Miss Myra Tuppen, stenographer in the Century Insurance Office in Terre Haute. At first she had attributed her screen success to her young beauty, but soon she had discovered that in Hollywood beauties were two a penny, and it was years before she got an inkling what it was that differentiated her from all the stand-ins and the walkers-on. When she discovered what it was, that she had a knack that other women had not, a tenuous knack not clearly understood even by herself, she had been terrified for years that she would lose it. That fear had left her now; she had put away a fortune in safe stocks and real estate, and now she did not greatly care if she stayed on in the commercialised entertainment business that had been her life, or not. Sometimes she felt that her life might even have been more fun if she had remained Miss Tuppen of Terre Haute instead of becoming Miss Teasdale of Beverly Hills.

When such thoughts came to her she put them away; they were the discontents of middle age, and she must not be middle-aged while she remained in business. They were nonsense anyway; life had given her everything, everything but children. That was one thing that she had had to miss; her income had been much associated with her beauty, so that she could not afford to run risks with her figure. But treasonable thoughts returned from time to time, and recently she had wondered now and then what would have happened to her if she had not gone into the movies, if she had stayed on in the office. She would have married and settled down and raised a family, no doubt. Whom would she have married? One of her brother's friends in the automobile business? She hardly thought so. One of the boys she had met in High School–Dwight Henderson? Dwight had been a nice boy; she had heard of him during the war. He was Vice-President of a corporation that made women's shoes, in New York City. Her mind turned to the Century Insurance Office, well remembered after all these years, all these experiences. It would have been funny if she had married little Eddie Stillson the lame ledger clerk. . . .

Of all the people in the office, she remembered Eddie Stillson best. His desk was next to hers; because he was a low-grade clerk the noise of her machine was supposed not to disturb his work. She had been seventeen when she went to the Century office from her school of commercial typing; she supposed now that Eddie must have been twenty-one or twenty-two, but at that time she had thought him older. He had a pasty face and he wore steel-rimmed spectacles; one leg was shorter than the other, so that he could not take much exercise, or dance. He wore a sort of iron extension fitted to his right boot. Thinking back now more than thirty years in time, she remembered Eddie Stillson as one of the kindest men that she had ever known.

It had begun on the first morning, her first morning in her first job. At the school the machines had all been modern Remingtons. In the office she had been given a worn-out Underwood. It was just different enough to spoil her work; each time she forgot and worked up speed her flying fingers would depress two keys together or print ½ instead of a stop, so that each letter that she typed was spoiled and messy with erasions. By the middle of the morning she was near to tears of apprehension and frustration, when the office boy put down upon the table by her side a glass of milk and a stick of chocolate.

'I always stop 'n take a lil' drink of something, middle of the morning,' Eddie had said, drinking his milk. 'I see they've given you the lousiest old machine in the office. Nobody else wouldn't have it.' After that, things had gone better.

She had worked in that office for two and a half years. Her evenings gradually became a whirl of dances, movies, and walks with various young men, though she found it better to cut out the walks as time went on. In all that time she never went out with Eddie Stillson. He never asked her to the movies; if he had done so she would have regarded it as a disaster, and would have told her friends about it, laughing. All she ever talked to him about was carbon papers, and the weather, and how many bits they owed the office boy for milk. Yet when opportunity came to her with a minor contract in Hollywood and she went round the office saying goodbye in a whirl of excitement and congratulations, the only leave-taking that left the smallest pang was that with Eddie Stillson, though it only took two minutes. In later years she knew he would have married her if she had so much as lifted her finger. She had sometimes thought that she would have had a very happy life if he had.

This man Honey was just such another one as Eddie Stillson, shy, insignificant, brave and kind. With her experience of married life behind her, she now knew that such men made good husbands, though girls seldom realised it. There was security in them. She wondered what kind of girl his wife had been.

In the rear of the cabin Marjorie Corder sat with the other stewardess, Miss Peggy Ryan, by the galley. She had told Peggy all about Mr Honey's apprehensions, and they had agreed facilely that they were bunk. Now she sat silent, recalling her crash drill. Although in conversation she was prepared to write off Mr Honey as a nervous crank, she was not in the least prepared to do so deep in her own mind. If things started to go wrong with the aircraft she had certain duties to perform; she sat quietly, conning her drill over. Safety belts had to be fastened; she must go up and down her end of the cabin, not hurrying, smiling reassuringly, but seeing that the passengers did fasten them, helping those who were agitated. The upholstery rip cords must be pulled, disclosing the escape hatches, but on no account must the hatches be opened till the differential pressure indicator showed zero. She must be ready to jettison the cabin doors by pulling the hinge-pins. She must be ready with her first-aid box. She must be ready at the telephone to the flight deck for taking any orders that might come by it, and all the time she must be cheerful and composed and charming. Only by the sheerest chance would she be free to fling herself down on the deck in the Men's Toilet when the crash was imminent; in any case it would be wrong for her, the stewardess, to take the only place of safety in the aircraft. She could hardly do that.

Her home was in Ealing, a suburb to the west of London; her father was a vegetable merchant in Covent Garden. She had gone to the London Hospital as a probationer early in the war, and then she had exchanged into the R.A.F. Nursing Service; she had given up nursing eighteen months before for the more varied life of an airline stewardess. She had been engaged during the war to an Ealing boy who had died in a Lancaster over Dortmund a month before her marriage; that had happened five years before, but she had not ventured into love again. She was rather older than the general run of stewardesses and had already exceeded the average length of service.

She sat quiet, thinking of the threat of death held by the Reindeer tail. It would be queer if it happened to her as it had to Donald, though his tail had been removed from the machine by A.A. fire. She still had his photograph upon the mantelpiece of her bedroom; she still heard from his mother at Christmas and on her birthday. If it had to happen to her now, it was a pity; she would go without the experience of marriage, motherhood, and children; she would go incomplete. She thought of Mr Honey and the queer thing he had said an hour or so ago–'If you get through this and we don't, get yourself married and bring up a family. I think you'd be good at that.' Funny.

Mr Honey, she thought, was a very clever little man. He could see farther through a brick wall than most; he had penetrated her secret. She would be good at that, she knew. She knew that she would be able to be patient with a crying baby, loving with a fractious child. She knew that, but that Mr Honey should have known it too was a very queer thing. Of course, he must be terribly clever to be a research scientist at a place like Farnborough, and with that there came to her the certainty that he was right about the Reindeer tail. A man who had the perspicacity to be right in one thing was very likely to be right in another, and he had been very right about her.

Captain Samuelson sat in the first pilot's seat staring at the instruments in front of him, at the silvery cloud floor ahead and below them, at the bright stars above. It was very quiet and peaceful on a fine night at that altitude; he had time for thought. Although he flew continually from continent to continent he was a very ordinary man; his interests were essentially suburban. Nothing that he had ever seen in all his travels pleased him so much as his small home in Wimbledon, chosen for its proximity to the bowls club, of which he was vice-captain. He had three children, a son of nineteen in the R.A.F. and a boy and a girl who were still at school. He did not believe that anything was going to happen to the Reindeer tail before they got to Gander; he thought that Mr Honey was a nervous crank, exaggerating the importance of his own work. At the same time, Bill Ward stood in the background of his mind. Something had killed Bill Ward, and it was not coming down through cloud to check up his position and so flying into the hill.

Samuelson was an experienced and a competent man. He had put the matter to his Flying Control in a radio signal and he had received no answer; the responsibility for the decision was left to him. He had decided to go on to Gander, anyway. When they got to Gander he would have to make another decision, whether to continue the flight normally to Dorval, the airport of Montreal, or whether to ground the aircraft and stay at Gander till he did receive instructions. The latter would be quite a serious step to take upon his own responsibility; it meant stranding passengers at Gander and delaying the mail. He could hardly stop at Gander without evidence that something really was the matter with the aircraft. Like every pilot in the world, he veered instinctively away from a policy of playing safe. If he grounded the machine at Gander and it turned out to be quite all right, people would say that he was windy, that he was getting old. . . .

Another point bulked largely in his mind. There were no facilities at Gander for a major modification to the Reindeer, but there were all the facilities required at Dorval. Unless the aircraft proved to be completely unsafe, it would have to be flown from Gander to Dorval, or else back across the Atlantic to England, before any work could be done on it; if then it had to fly from Gander he might just as well continue on his scheduled flight without delay. He thought that he would turn all his engineers on to make a thorough check on the tailplane while the aircraft was refuelled at Gander; if that was satisfactory, he would go on. He had no great confidence that instructions from his Flying Control would have reached him by the time he was ready to leave Gander. Work would only just be starting in England at that time in the morning, and to ground an aircraft on a technical suspicion such as this would need a good deal of conferring between the various technicians who were involved.

The shadow of Bill Ward stayed by his side, perturbing him. This man Honey had at any rate provided a lucid and a feasible explanation of what could have killed Bill Ward, of what could kill them all that very night, perhaps. He sighed a little, in perplexity. If only this man wasn't such an obvious nervous crank. . . .

They passed the point of no return, and as a routine matter the navigator reported to him. He nodded, and handed over the control to Dobson, and got out of his seat, and went down into the saloon, and walked the length of it into the luggage bay to have another look at the tailplane structure through the little perspex window. He stood gloomily scrutinising the structure in the light of the rear fuselage lamp, flashing the beam of his powerful torch upon each point in turn. It all seemed perfectly all right, but that infernal little man had said it would, right up to the moment when it broke. He wondered if he ought to station one of the crew to stand by that perspex window looking through it all the time, a permanent watch. But what good would that do, anyway, if Mr Honey should in fact be right? They would know at the controls as soon as something happened.

Presently he turned and went back into the main saloon. As he passed the toilets he raised his eyebrows; was everybody crackers in this ship? The film actress, Miss Monica Teasdale, was standing at the door of the Men's Toilet, holding the door open, looking in.

He smiled brightly and said, 'I'm afraid you've got that wrong, Miss Teasdale. The Ladies' is on this side.'

She said, with cool irony, 'Say, what do you know?' And then she said, 'I was just kind of looking where I'd got to go in case we had an accident, Captain.'

It was true; everybody *was* crackers in this ship, or was it he himself? 'There's not the slightest prospect of an accident, Miss Teasdale,' he said, laughing brightly. 'If ever there was anything of the sort, the stewardess would come and help you fasten your safety belt. That's what the seats and belts are designed for, to hold you safely and to prevent injury in bumpy weather, or anything like that.'

She said, 'You don't say!'

He flushed a little, irritated. 'I should go back to your seat,' he said. 'There's nothing to see in there.'

She laughed, and she was very beautiful in her laughter, so that he was mollified. 'I believe you think that I've been playing "Peeping Tom".'

In all his years of experience as an airline captain he had never had this one before. 'Of course not,' he said weakly.

'Be your age,' the actress said. 'Mr Honey told me that was the place to go to in an accident, down on the floor and facing back, with your spine pressed flat against the partition. I've been taking a look around.'

He stared at her. 'Honey said that? But why?' He opened the door and stood inside, looking at the partition.

'Something to do with the kitchen stove, he said.'

'The stove? Oh, I see what he means.' He hesitated; there was no denying that it was a very safe place, very safe indeed against deceleration. He came out into the passage, closing the door behind him. 'I'm sorry Mr Honey has been bothering you, Miss Teasdale,' he said. 'I think he must have been overworking at Farnborough, and perhaps our altitude affects him too, if he's not used to flying. There's not the slightest foundation for thinking that there's anything the matter with this aircraft, I can assure you. I'm very sorry that he's troubled you with his ideas. I suppose he must have seen your pictures at some time.'

'You don't believe in his ideas?' the actress asked.

The pilot laughed. 'Of course not, Miss Teasdale. There's not the slightest evidence that there's anything the matter.'

Her eyes dropped to the torch he carried in his hand. 'That's why you've been taking a darned good look at our stabiliser, then.'

He smiled. 'I should go back to your seat and try to get some sleep.'

'Are we going to be on time at Gander, Captain?'

'No,' he said. 'We shall be about an hour and forty minutes late.'

'Is that because you've shut down on the inboard engines?'

He cursed Mr Honey in his mind for a talkative busybody. 'Partly,' he said. 'I think Mr Honey is a little bit unbalanced, between you and me. But I have given that much weight to his ideas, because he really does come from Farnborough; I've shut down the inboard engines at his request, although it's going to make us very late.'

She nodded. 'I don't think he's unbalanced,' she said. 'I think he's as sane as you or I. I've met a few unbalanced people in my time—fans, you know—and believe me, they don't talk that way. If I were you, Captain, I'd put a good amount of weight on what he says.'

They stood for a moment, thoughtful. 'I've not neglected it,' he said at last. 'I've done everthing that he suggested, except turning back to land in Ireland. In any case, now, it's shorter to go on than to go back.'

'Okay, then,' said the actress. 'I'll just keep my fingers crossed.'

'Miss Teasdale, has Mr Honey been talking to any of the other passengers?'

She shook her head. 'He came across and spilled it all to me, but then the stewardess got after him for spreading alarm; she did everything but take him across her knee and spank him, so he won't do that again. I don't think anybody else knows a thing about all this.'

He nodded. 'I'd just as soon it didn't go any further. There's absolutely nothing in it.'

'Says you,' she said rudely. 'Still, I don't see that it's going to help any to get the other passengers worked up. You needn't worry. I'll stay with him till we land at Gander, so that he won't talk to anyone.'

'That's really good of you, Miss Teasdale. It's very helpful.'

'Don't thank me. I guess I kind of like the little man, and I'd not sleep now, anyway.' She turned to him. 'If I do that for you, Captain, will you do something for me?'

He said, 'If it's anything that I can do. What do you want?'

'If our stabiliser starts flying on its own,' she said, 'and things start going wrong, Mr Honey says he's going up to the flight deck. He's been a long time in airplane research, and maybe he could help you. If he comes up, will you listen to him and not shout him down?'

He knew that if that happened he would have little time and little inclination to listen to anybody about anything, but he said, 'Of course I will, Miss Teasdale.'

She said, 'I'll feel easier in my mind that way.'

They moved forward up the aisle past the galley. He said, 'Will you have a cup of coffee, or anything?'

She shook her head. 'Guess I'll go back and sit with Mr Honey. This is the darnedest flying trip I ever made.' She left him and moved quietly up the aisle in the dim light.

She sat down beside Mr Honey and began talking to him about other matters than the imminence of their disaster. They had said all that was to be said about that; now it remained only to wait and see if it happened. She asked him how it had happened that the aircraft had escaped our vigilance at Farnborough and in the Ministry—how it had managed to accumulate to many hours of flying unknown to any of us.

He told her what he had heard on the flight deck, about its loan to Anglo-Brazil Air Services for a trial. 'It slipped past everyone by sheer stupidity,' he said quietly. 'The Power of Evil in the world. It'll be different in fifty years from now.'

She asked, 'What'll be different?'

'Evil,' he said. 'This sort of thing won't happen after 1994. I shan't live to see that time, and you won't, even if we get through tonight. But my daughter will, when she is an old lady.'

She asked, 'What's going to happen in 1994?'

'Adam and Eve were expelled from the Garden of Eden in the year 4007 B.C.' he said. 'Sin, foolishness, and evil came into the world then and are to last six thousand years. That finishes in the year A.D. 1994 at the autumn equinox on the twenty-first of September. After that we get another chance again, I think.'

She stared at him. 'Where did you get all that from?'

'You can work it all out from the prophetic calculations in the Talmud,' he said. 'It's confirmed by the measurements to the base of the Dead End passage in the Pyramid. That's a totally different source, of course. There's no doubt at all that something absolutely cataclysmic is going to happen in the autumn of 1994. It's probably the end of this world, as we know it. The Talmud rather indicates that the millennium starts then, but that's a bit vague.'

She was startled. 'Say,' she said, 'do you believe all this?'

He said, 'Believe—that's not a scientific way to look at it. You don't believe in an hypothesis until it's proved to be true, and then it's a known fact, and doesn't have to be believed in. You don't believe in this seat you're sitting in, because it's *there*; you don't have to show your trust in it. I don't believe the end of the world is coming to us in 1994. But it's a theory that has been put forward by a number of very competent investigators, and the only theory that I know which forecasts what is going to happen to us in the future. Until a better theory turns up, one has to base one's life on that, because it's the only one.'

She stared at him. 'That kind of makes sense, when you look at it that way,' she said. 'You say the world is coming to an end in 1994? It doesn't mean a lot to you and me.'

'No,' he said. 'We shall probably just miss it. It's bad luck, after six thousand years, to miss it by ten years or so. But we prepare the people who will see it, and that's something. That's why we've got to work so hard and well, we people in the world today. We lay foundation stones.'

She thought of her work, of the endless, mean, commercial haggling on story points, of jealousies and irritations on the set, of the endless manœuvrings for star parts. 'I guess I don't lay many foundation stones,' she said bitterly.

He turned to her astonished. 'The whole world looks to you,' he said. 'People are finer and better for seeing one of your films; you give them an example. Do you really think you don't do any good? You can't think that!'

The power of the honky-tonk! She could not explain to him; if he believed that her films were conceived with a high motive, let him go on in that faith. She said quietly, 'I guess there's different ways of looking at these things. You kind of see the smutty side of any job you're working at, and maybe you forget about the rest.'

'I know. You've got to get away from a job and stand back, sometimes, and see what you've been doing in perspective.'

She turned to him. 'This daughter of yours, Mr Honey. Your little girl, Elspeth, what do you think that she's going to see in September 1994? What's going to happen then?'

It was quiet in the long saloon; the aircraft moved on steadily beneath the stars. The lights were dimmed for sleeping; it was a quiet place, a place fit for meditation before the end. 'I don't know what's going to happen,' he said quietly. 'Nobody knows. You and I will live our lives out without knowing; we may know in half an hour. But I have thought about it; I have read about it; I have worked on it—a lot. If you like, I'll tell you what I think may happen in September 1994.'

'Tell me,' she said.

He was silent for a moment. 'I think the Principle of Goodness will appear and take away all sin and evil from the world,' he said. 'I don't know how it will come about, but I think this, that to everybody in the world, Buddhist or Mohammedan, Christian or Jew, there will come a revelation of the truth, at the same time. Every religion in the world is due for a clean-up; I think they'll get it then. And when that is done, the Truth will be seen to be universal, and we shall all believe in the same things.'

She nodded slowly. 'That could be.'

'I think the revelation will be graded to our understanding,' he said. 'I think it will occur in terms that we can recognise. I shan't see it, but I think my little girl, Elspeth, will see it in the form that Our Lord will come to Glastonbury, to the place of meditation that He lived in as a boy. I think that's what the indicator sockets in the ascending passage of the Pyramid show, if you make allowance for the subsidence of the structure, as you must. I've done a great deal of work on this. I think something terrific is going to happen at Glastonbury, then.'

She stared at him; could he be nuts after all? 'Say' she said, 'where is this place Glastonbury?'

'It's a little town in Somerset,' he said. 'The legend is that Jesus Christ came there to live in meditation as a young man, before His Ministry. His great-uncle, Joseph of Arimathea, brought Him there; he used to trade in the tin business between Palestine and Cornwall. He brought Jesus there, because Glastonbury was the religious centre of the Druids, who practised the original pure form of the Hebrew religion. Jesus is supposed to have lived in Glastonbury in meditation for a long time as a young man. That's the story, and there's a good deal to support it. You can believe it or not, as you like. I think I do.'

She said in wonder, 'I never heard that one.'

He went on to tell her all about it, talking with the quiet enthusiasm of a man with a hobby that he has worked at for years. She sat listening to him, her mind in the past. Eddie Stillson had been just such another one, but his hobby was monkeys. He had read a lot about the Origin of Man and he used to talk about the Missing Link, and one day he had produced from beneath his ledgers a book that had a lot of photographs of people's skulls, thousands and thousands of years old, dug up all over the world. It had photographs of human skulls in it and monkey's skulls too, and she had listened with a sort of horrified fascination while he expounded to her all the differences and similarities. Looking back over all those years, she felt that he had meant it as a compliment to her, that he had revealed his secret interests in that way. After three marriages and thirty years of adult life, she now felt that you never really knew a man until you knew his secret interests. Mr Honey was extraordinarily like Eddie Stillson, the same insignificant appearance, the same warm, indefinable charm. It had taken her much of her life to realise it, but she had made a terrible mistake in losing touch with Eddie. When you were young and the world lay before you, you did that sort of thing. You met a man that you could really get to care about, and you thought there would be plenty of other ones, in Hollywood or wherever life took you to. It was only when you began to grow old that you realised they weren't as plentiful as all that, that you would have done better to stick to Eddie Stillson.

In the flight deck Dobson, the first officer, took a star sight with his bubble sextant through the astrodome; the navigator took another one to check it, and they plotted the position lines upon the chart. They had about two and a half hours flight to go before landing at Gander. Their hands were dirty and soiled the chart as they drew in the position line, for they had had some trouble in the flight deck. One of the electrical circuits of the undercarriage-operating mechanism had become defective and was blowing fuses with monotonous regularity; they had worked for two hours with the engineers in an attempt to rectify the fault, only to discover that it lay in the safety circuit of the retracting undercarriage mechanism and could be reached only from the ground; it was not important, so they had isolated that circuit and put it out of action. Then navigational necessities had intervened before they could wash, and they had taken their star sights with dirty hands.

Dobson walked down the saloon to the toilets; he noted with surprise that Mr Honey had got off with the actress; she was sitting by him, smiling at him, listening to what he said. He washed his hands and came out, and went into the galley, and said to Miss Corder, 'I see the boffin's got off.'

She put her head out and looked up the aisle. 'She's been sitting and talking with him for some time. How far off are we?'

'About two and a half hours. Had any more trouble with him?'

She shook her head. 'Have you had any trouble with the tail?'

He laughed. 'It's still there, so far as I know. Be still there in ten years' time, if you ask me.'

'It's funny,' she said thoughtfully. 'He was so positive that we were going to have an accident. But nothing's happened yet.'

He grinned. 'Nothing's going to happen either,' he said. 'He's got a bee in his bonnet—all those Farnborough types are the same. They just don't know what it's all about. It really is the most fantastic place. We might get some decent aircraft if it wasn't for them.'

He moved off up the aisle towards the flight deck.

The Reindeer flew on towards the last of the night, in rising moonlight. An hour later the navigator crossed to Samuelson sitting in the captain's seat and spoke a word to him. The captain spoke to Cousins, the engineer, and knocked out the automatic pilot; the engineer drew back the throttle levers a little, watching the boost gauges. The note of the engines dropped, the nose tilted down a fraction, and the Reindeer started on a slow descent, losing height at about two hundred feet a minute. Gander lay ahead.

At ten thousand feet they started up the inboard engines at reduced power and went into the cloud layer. A quarter of an hour later they were below it in diffused moonlight. They made their landfall at a rocky barren point of land that lay between two islands, seen dimly beneath them in the hazy, silvery light. At three thousand feet they flew for a quarter of an hour above fiords and inlets of the rocky coast, all full of ice. Then straight ahead of them appeared the twinkling runway lights and the cluster of lights round the airport buildings at Gander.

In the saloon the stewardesses were busy waking the passengers who were still asleep and making them do up their safety belts for the landing. Miss Corder, bending over Mr Honey, said, 'Well, we've got here all right.'

'I know,' he said. 'We're very lucky.'

Miss Teasdale had gone back to her own place. Mr Honey sat looking out of his window as they circled the airport and went off over the spruce woods and the river to turn into the runway. They turned in to land and the note of the engines died; the nose dropped a little, and he saw the flaps come down. The ground came closer and closer till the tops of the fir trees were near to the machine. Then there was the surface of the runway close beneath them; they sped over it, and suddenly a rumble and a forward tilt of the fuselage told him they were down.

Samuelson slowed the machine to a walking pace, and turned the Reindeer on to the taxiing track, towards the hangars and the airport buildings. He yawned. Cousins, the engineer, came forward to his elbow and said, 'Watch the undercart switch, sir. The safety locks are out.' He nodded.

Dobson leaned across to him, grinning, and said, 'Well, we've still got our tail.'

Samuelson nodded; he had not yet reached the point when he could joke about it. He still had to decide whether to go on normally to Montreal or to ground his aircraft at Gander, one of the most bleak and desolate airports in the world at which to strand a load of passengers, and one where there were few facilities for any serious repair. He sat gloomily considering this as they rolled up to the tarmac. He had heard nothing from his Flying Control in reply to his signal stating Mr Honey's bleat. Perhaps a signal would be waiting for him here to give him guidance and to take the onus of deciding what to do from him.

It was then shortly before dawn, about nine o'clock in the morning by British time. The stewardesses disembarked the passengers and took them to the restaurant for breakfast; the refuelling tank trucks drew up to the Reindeer and began pumping in their load. Captain Samuelson went to the Control and asked if there was any signal waiting for him; there was nothing. He tightened his lips; the responsibility for the decision lay on him.

He sent Dobson to find the local Air Registration Board Inspector. Very naturally, Mr Symes was in bed, and he was not too pleased at being woken up at that hour in the morning to make a difficult decision. He was a man of fifty-seven and Gander was his last appointment before retirement. He had never risen very high in his profession because he had never shown initiative; in his view an inspector should stick closely to the rules as they were framed for him. That quality made him valuable enough at a place like Gander, where he was far from the control of his head office; his superiors could rest content that Mr Symes would never put a foot wrong or deviate one hair's breadth from the typescripts sent to him from time to time.

Dobson stayed with him while he pulled on his trousers, putting him *au fait* with the position. 'This little squirt from Farnborough, he's clean off his rocker, I believe. I don't know what you'll make of him, but that's what we all think. Of course, if there *is* anything the matter with the tail, we'll have to stop here, but Cousins hasn't heard a thing about it, nor have any of us. Captain Samuelson wanted you to have a good look at the structure with us, and see if it's all right.'

Mr Symes grunted. 'You get some funny sort of people coming from those places,' he said. 'You remember Skues in the Airworthiness at Farnborough, back in 1928 or so? No–before your time. He always used to take his Siamese cat with him, in the offices, or into conferences–everywhere he went he took this blessed cat. . . .'

They walked together from the dormitory block where Mr Symes stayed back to the Reindeer on the tarmac. Dawn was just showing in the darkness as a grey line to the east; there was a bitterly cold north-east wind and Mr Symes had had no breakfast. Samuelson met them on the tarmac with Cousins, the engineer. A tall, wheeled gantry gave them access to the tailplane twenty feet above the ground; they commenced a meticulous examination of everything externally visible, moving the gantry from time to time. The bitter wind whipped round them mercilessly; very soon they were so cold that even holding torches became difficult.

The could find nothing wrong at all externally. They came down and went into the rear fuselage, behind the pressure cabin; clambering about in there they could see the structure of the tailplane spars where they passed through the fuselage and intersected with the fin girders. They twisted their bodies in amongst this structure, flashing their electric torches upon channels, webs, and ribs, laying the straight edges of steel rules along duralumin angles to check for any distortion, peering carefully at scratches on the paint and anodising. At the end of an hour of the most thorough examination they had finished; they had found nothing whatsoever wrong with the machine.

It was too cold to hold a conference outside or in the hangar. They went up into the heated flight deck of the Reindeer, and sent for Mr Honey from the restaurant. While they were waiting for him, Dobson and Cousins made an examination of the defective safety circuit of the undercarriage-retracting mechanism, climbing up the undercarriage legs from the ground into the engine nacelles. Mr Honey, hurrying across the tarmac to the Reindeer, saw them go back into the fuselage ahead of him; when he reached the flight deck the engineer was making his report to Samuelson.

'Port switch is burnt out, sir,' he said. 'We haven't got a spare. I've got both circuits isolated now. If Mr Symes agrees'–he indicated the inspector–'I'd suggest we go on like we are to Dorval. They've got spare switches in the stores at Dorval.'

The inspector said, 'That means no safety locks are operating on the undercarriage.'

'That's right,' the engineer replied. 'It just means being careful not to trip the operating lever while you're getting in or out of the seat. That's while she's on the ground, of course; it wouldn't matter in the air.' Mr Honey waited his turn patiently in the background, till they were ready to attend to him. The inspector and the engineer and Samuelson moved over to the control pedestal between the pilots' seats. 'This one,' the engineer said, fingering the undercarriage lever. 'It's just a matter of being careful not to put this up while the auxiliary engine's running, like it is now.' It was running to provide the heat to keep the aircraft warm. 'When the auxiliary's stopped, of course, nothing could happen if you put this up, because there wouldn't be any current.'

They talked it over for a minute or two. 'All right,' the inspector said at last to Samuelson. 'You can go on like that. But have somebody standing by it all the time you're taxiing, just to watch that nobody's coat catches in it or anything.'

Samuelson nodded. 'I'll see to that.' He turned to Mr Honey and introduced him to the inspector. 'Look, Mr Honey–we've made a very careful inspection of the tailplane, and there's nothing wrong with it at all. I don't know if you'd care to tell Mr Symes here what you told us on the way across?'

Mr Honey started wearily to tell his tale again. He had had no sleep and he was overtired, blinking more even than usual. He had not shaved and he had not been able to eat his breakfast, spoiled as it had been by his anxieties; he was feeling rather sick. He told his story badly, defeated before he started by the atmosphere of utter disbelief he sensed around him.

Mr Symes gave him some little attention because he came from Farnborough, but his mind was already made up. He was a man who had never taken any action except on physical facts; it was not his business to assess the eccentric theories of wandering scientists and take a chance on them. There were no written instructions in his files that he should take any special precautions in regard to the Reindeer tail. On the suggestion that there was something wrong with it, he had made a thorough inspection and had found everything correct. That put him in the clear, and he had no intention of imperilling his pension by a rash display of individuality at that stage of his career.

They talked for a quarter of an hour. At last Samuelson said, 'Well, if Mr Symes agrees, I think the best thing we can do now is to go on to Dorval. I'm prepared to shut down the inboard engines after climbing up to operating height, as I did coming over, if you think that will ease things, Mr Honey. At Dorval we can assess the matter properly.'

Mr Honey, nearly in tears of weariness and frustration, said, 'I assure you . . . I assure you that's the wrong thing to do. It's absolutely–' his voice cracked, and went up into a little nervous squeak– 'it's absolutely courting disaster to go on. You *must* ground this aircraft. Really you must.'

Samuelson glanced at Symes, and their eyes met in common agreement; this was not a normal, reasonable man. This was an eccentric plugging away at a fixed idea, a man whose mental balance was abnormal. 'If you would rather stay here, Mr Honey,' the captain said, 'I can make arrangements for you to finish the journey in another aircraft, probably tomorrow. But I'm afraid I can't listen to any more of this.'

The inspector nodded in agreement. This Reindeer would be off before long, and he could get back to bed and have a couple of hours more before breakfast. Then, in the course of the morning, he would write out a report upon the incident and send it in to his headquarters. Two copies would be sufficient, and one for his own file.

Honey said desperately, 'Is that your final decision? You're really going on?'

Samuelson turned aft, partly to hide a final irresolution. 'That's right,' he said. 'We're going on.'

'I assure you . . .' Mr Honey's voice died in despair; it was useless to go on trying to convince these men. He turned forward to the pilots' seats. And then, quite nonchalantly, he put his hand upon the undercarriage lever and pulled it to UP.

He did it so quietly that it did not register with anybody for an instant; Symes was the only man who actually saw him do it, and it took a second or two for the inspector to appreciate what was happening. Then he cried, 'Here–stop that!'

The note of the auxiliary motor changed as the load came on the dynamo. Samuelson turned, saw what Honey was doing, said, 'For Christ's sake!' and made a dive for the lever.

Mr Honey flung his body up against the pedestal, covering the controls. He said, half weeping, 'If you won't ground this aircraft, I will.'

The motors of the retracting mechanism groaned, the solid floor beneath their feet sagged ominously. Cousins, with quick wit, leaped for the electrical control panel and threw out the main switch to cut the current from all circuits. He was a fraction of a second too late. The undercarriage of the Reindeer was just over the dead centre. She paused for a moment; for an instant Samuelson thought that Cousins had saved her, as he struggled to pull Honey from the pedestal. Then she sagged forward, and the undercarriage folded up with a sharp whistling noise from the hydraulics. A pipe burst and fluid sprayed the ground beneath her, and she sank down on her belly on the concrete apron, all the seventy-two tons of her. By the mercy of Providence nobody was standing underneath her at the time.

The noise of the crumpling panels and propellers, a tinny, metallic, crunching noise, brought the mechanics running to the wide doors of the hangars. Marjorie Corder, going from the Reindeer to the reception and booking hall, turned at the mouth of the passage and stared aghast to see her Reindeer lying wrecked upon the tarmac. Instinctively she began to run back towards it, horrified; she met Dobson running from the machine to the Control.

She cried, 'What happened?'

He paused for an instant. 'The boffin did it,' he said furiously. 'I told you that he'd put the kiss of death on it. Well, now he has!'

5

That Monday was a bad day.

It began normally enough. I went to the office as usual. When I had left on Saturday the arrangements had been all set up that Mr Honey was to leave for Ottawa on Sunday night by C.A.T.O., I had seen nothing of him over the weekend, and I had not expected to. I went down to the old balloon shed at about ten o'clock as soon as I had cleared my desk, however, to see that he had really got away and to see that young Simmons was getting on all right with the responsibilities of the trial on the Reindeer tail.

The trial was running; I had heard it above the noise of my car when I was driving into the factory; it filled the whole district with its booming roar. In the old balloon shed it was as deafening as usual; Simmons was up upon the gantry taking readings of the strain gauges; he saw me and came down, and came up to me smiling, and proffered his foolscap pad showing the rough daily graph of the deflections. We could not talk in the noise; I ran my eye over the results, and they were absolutely normal. The trial was going smoothly.

I led him into the office and shut the door; in there we could talk. 'Everything all right?' I asked. 'Did Mr Honey get away all right?'

'Oh yes, I think so, sir. He was in most of Sunday; I was here with him. He left at about four o'clock to go home and have a meal and pick up his baggage. He was catching the eight-forty up to London from Ash Vale.'

'That's fine.' I stayed with him for ten minutes going through the work; he was a clever, competent young man who only needed guidance now and then. I soon found that I had nothing to worry about. When I couldn't think of anything more to ask him, I looked around the littered little office before leaving; there was a neat pile of stamped and addressed letters on his desk, ready for the post. I glanced idly at them the top one was addressed to Miss Elspeth Honey, No 4, Copse Road, Farnham. I lifted it, and the second bore the same address, and the third, and all of them.

Simmons said, 'Don't get them out of order, sir. I've got to post one each day, and they're all dated.'

'Dated?'

'The letters inside are dated with consecutive days, as if he was writing to her every day. I've got to post one each day.'

I stared at them in wonder. 'How many are there?'

'Twenty-one, sir.' He said that he was reckoning to be away three weeks.'

'Are all the letters different?'

'I don't know—I think they must be.' He picked up one of them and fingered it, 'From the feel, they've each got two sheets of paper, too.'

I was staggered by the magnitude of the work, because Honey had only had about three days' notice of his journey, and these three days had been very busy ones for him. I said, 'Well, I'm damned!'

Simmons smiled and said, 'He must be a very devoted father.'

The telephone bell rang then. It was the exchange trying to locate me; Ferguson had been on the line from the Ministry, but while looking for me they had lost the connection. I said I would go back and take it from my office.

I got through to Ferguson ten minutes later. He said, 'Scott, rather an awkward thing has just come up. C.A.T.O. have had a radio signal from the *Reindeer* that left last night for Gander, the one with Honey on board. It seems that that machine has done over fourteen hundred hours, and Honey has been making a good deal of trouble during the flight. The pilot asks what action he should take.'

I had an awful feeling of apprehension in my stomach, suddenly. I said, 'That's terrible. That aircraft must be grounded at once. How on earth did it get through? I thought you told me none of them had done more than three or four hundred hours.'

He said anxiously, 'I know, old man–I did tell you that. I got that from C.A.T.O. The trouble is, this aircraft wasn't operating with them at that time.' He went on to tell me about its loan for trial operations with A.B.A.S.

I bit my lip. It was the position that I had been anxious to avoid at any cost. 'Has it landed yet at Gander?' I asked.

'I haven't heard that it has,' he said. 'I should think it must have, by this time. Wait a minute–no–oh hell, their time's all different of course. I don't know exactly when it took off.'

'Look, Ferguson,' I said. 'It's got to be stopped at Gander. It mustn't fly one minute longer. Can you get through now to C.A.T.O. and ground it, ground it positively and for good at Gander?'

He hesitated. 'I'd have to see the Director for that.'

I said, 'I'll have to see my own Director. But we've got to jump at this decision, now just you and me. We can clue up the official side later. Will you get through to C.A.T.O. and tell them that?'

'It's a bit awkward,' he said slowly. 'I don't know that we're justified in taking a snap decision, quite . . . I mean, it might be very awkward if it turned out later there was nothing wrong with it. I think it should go through the proper channels.'

I said bitterly, 'We won't look quite so good at the court of inquiry if that tail fails in the air while you and I are looking for our senior officers. If you won't ring up C.A.T.O., I will.'

He said doubtfully, 'I could get through to them and say that's what you recommend, explaining that it's not official yet.'

'Will you tell them that I insist on grounding that machine?' I said. 'That's what I'm telling you. And that's what I should tell a court of inquiry.'

'You're taking a great deal of responsibility upon yourself,' he said resentfully.

'I am.'

'Have you got any evidence at all upon this tailplane yet?'

'Nothing,' I said. 'Nothing to call evidence.'

'But you insist that I ring up C.A.T.O. and have that aircraft grounded here and now, before consulting anyone?'

'I do.'

'All right,' he said. 'I'll get through to them now.'

I put down the telephone, sick and angry at the position that we had been forced into. I picked it up again and asked for the Director's office. The operator said, 'I've got an outside call for you, Dr Scott.'

'Hold it,' I said. 'Put me through to the Director's office now. I'll take that outside call immediately I've finished.'

The Director's girl told me he was up in London for a meeting of the Aeronautical Research Committee. I swore; I should have thought of that. I could not now shelve my responsibility. I asked for the waiting call, thinking it was C.A.T.O., but it was Shirley.

She said urgently, 'Dennis, please, can you come and help me? I'm speaking from the call-box at the end of Copse Road. It's Elspeth Honey. I found her lying in a heap at the foot of the stairs in their house; she's quite unconscious and she's awfully cold. Please, do come at once.'

I hesitated. I could not take in properly the substance of what she was saying; my mind was full of the blazing row that I had landed myself in by grounding a C.A.T.O. aircraft at a place like Gander, without any previous notice and without any real evidence that there was anything the matter with it at all. I knew that it was only a question of minutes now before the storm burst; Ferguson must be already speaking to Carnegie, the Technical Superintendent. I forced my mind back to what Shirley was saying. 'Is she ill?' I asked foolishly. 'Couldn't you ring up the doctor–Dr Martin? His number's in the book.'

She said desperately, 'I've rung up Dr Martin–he's out on his rounds–I can't get hold of him till lunch time. I can't remember the name of anyone else. I've got her lying down and covered up with rugs–she's on the floor. There's nowhere else to put her downstairs–there's no couch or anything. I couldn't carry her up those stairs by myself. The old woman next door is boiling kettles up for hot-water bottles, but Dennis–she's looking awful–she's so blue. I'm frightened that she might be going to pass out. Do please come, Dennis.'

I could not leave her in the lurch; moreover, this was Honey's daughter. If the child Elspeth was really dangerously ill it would react straight back upon the grounding of the Reindeer. I should have to send Honey a cable, and he would obviously want to come home on the first available plane. If he did that, it would mean that the first Reindeer crash in Labrador would remain an enigma; we should not secure the evidence that we required to justify grounding the one at Gander. All this was running through my mind while I was listening to Shirley, and coupled with it was the thought that I had counted on two quiet days for finally rehearsing the paper that I was to read before the Royal Aeronautical Society on Thursday night upon the 'Performance Analysis of Aircraft Flying at High Mach Numbers.'

It was a blazing mess–just one thing after another. I said, 'All right, darling, I'll be with you in ten minutes. Keep her warm. I'll come right away, in the car.'

I put down the receiver and rang the bell for Miss Learoyd. But before she came, the telephone bell rang again, and it was Carnegie.

He said, 'Is that Dr Scott? Look, Dr Scott, I've had the most extraordinary request from Ferguson. He says you want to ground one of our Reindeers and ground it at Gander. Is that right?'

I said, 'That's right. We're getting rather concerned about the possibility of fatigue trouble in the tailplane. We've got people working on it on the highest priority now, and we've sent a member of the staff to Canada to have another look at the prototype Reindeer structure that crashed in Labrador. We've come to the conclusion that until this matter is cleared up no Reindeer ought to fly more than 700 hours. It was rather a shock when I heard this morning that one of your machines had done 1,400.'

'Well, it's very disconcerting having this sprung upon us at a moment's notice,' he said. 'I can't think what the Ministry are up to. They haven't said a word to us about it and the A.R.B. don't know a thing about it, either.'

'It's not the Ministry,' I said. 'It hasn't got as far as them yet, on an official level, that is to say. Ferguson knows all about it, of course. It's all come up very recently, very recently indeed.'

He asked, 'The firm–Rutlands–do they know anything about it?'

I said, 'Not yet.'

'The only people who know anything about it, then, are your department down at Farnborough?' He was becoming hostile.

'That's right,' I said. 'Everything starts down here. As a matter of fact, we thought we had plenty of time to get the whole thing sorted out before any question of grounding your existing machines arose. We were told that none of your Reindeers had done more than 400 hours. Then we sent one of our staff across last night by C.A.T.O., and he seems to have discovered in the air that the machine that he was flying in had done over 1,400, which just about coincides with our theoretical estimate of the time to failure of the tailplane in fatigue.'

He broke in, 'Who told you that?' Who told you that none of our machines had done more than 400 hours?'

I hesitated. 'Ferguson,' I said at last. Obviously everything was going to come out now. 'We put the inquiry through him.'

'It didn't come to me,' he retorted. 'I must say I would rather like to know why that was. Who did Ferguson get his information from–the office boy? If you people would only have the courtesy to come to the right person when you want to know anything, you might get the right answer.'

It would not do to tell him at this stage that I had asked Ferguson to get the information without calling too much attention to the inquiry. I said, 'Look, Mr Carnegie, let's settle on the action now and we can have the inquest and the slanging match later. I understand the Reindeer that our Mr Honey is travelling in is at or near Gander at this moment. We say it must be grounded right away, wherever it is. You must take my word for it that the machine is in a dangerous condition.'

There was a long silence. I said at last, 'Are you there, Carnegie?'

'I was just thinking,' he replied. 'I know nothing whatever about this, because you haven't thought fit to take me into your confidence. But at the same time I am responsible for the technical state of the aircraft of this organisation. What you suggest that I should do is to tell the Traffic side that this Reindeer is no longer airworthy, when I myself know of no technical reason why it shouldn't go on flying. Is that what you want?'

Put in that way it sounded very awkward. 'Yes I suppose so,' I said. 'I'm sorry to put you in that position, but we're all in a difficulty together over this.'

He said evenly, 'I'm sorry, too. And what's more, I won't do it. If you want that aircraft grounded without giving us more technical reasons than we have had up to date, you'll have to do it on a higher level.'

'Look, Mr Carnegie,' I said. 'I'll give you all the technical reasons that you want as soon as we can get together, but we can't do that over the phone. I'll come to you, or you come to me, and we'll have a session on it, this evening, if you like. But we've got to stop that Reindeer flying now, this minute.'

He said, 'All right. Get your Director to ring up my Chairman – Sir David's in his office. If you're making it a question of confidence because of the time element, then that's the way to do it.'

I bit my lip. 'I can't do that,' I said. 'The Director's in London, at a meeting of the Aeronautical Research Committee.'

He was on that one like a knife. 'Does he know anything about this?'

'He knows of our suspicions about fatigue trouble,' I said. 'He doesn't know that one of the machines has done 1,400 hours.'

'Well, don't you think you'd better take him into your confidence first of all, even if you don't take us?'

I became angry. 'Look, Mr Carnegie,' I said. 'All that can be settled later. I'm telling you now that in the view of this Establishment that Reindeer is in a grossly unsafe condition and should not fly one moment longer. The time is now eleven-fifteen, when I have told you that. If there's an accident, that will be my evidence at the court of inquiry. Whether you ground it now is entirely up to you, but you'll get a letter grounding it in the post tomorrow. That's all I've got to say to you.'

He said evenly, 'Well, Dr Scott, I hear what you say. And I will think it over and discuss it with my Chairman. The only thing I have to say now is that it's most difficult for us to do our job and keep the airline running if you people are allowed to carry on like this.'

I put down the receiver, breathing rather quickly, and glanced at my watch. We had been talking for ten minutes, and I had told Shirley that I would be with her by that time. I rang for Miss Learoyd again, and when she came I was at the door with my hat on. 'Miss Learoyd,' I said, 'I've got to go out for an hour, but I'm expecting several rather urgent calls. Will you sit in here and taken them, and tell everyone that I'll ring them – oh, say at two o'clock.' I left her, and hurried away down to my car.

I stepped on it on my way to Farnham, because I was anxious to get Shirley settled up and get back to my office and my row. I could not imagine what had happened to Elspeth Honey, and I had an unpleasant feeling that whatever had happened to her was partly my fault, for having sent her father off to the other side of the world at such short notice that he hadn't had time to make proper arrangements for her.

The door of the house was ajar; I parked the car and went in. I heard Shirley's voice upstairs, and went up. Elspeth was lying in her bed, which was tumbled and slept in; she was an unpleasant greyish colour with a huge bruise on her forehead close up to the hair; she seemed to be unconscious. Shirley was there with an elderly woman, Mrs Stevens from next door.

Shirley and I withdrew on to the landing. 'What happened?' I asked.

She said, 'I really don't know, but I think she must have fallen downstairs some time in the night. I was just a bit worried, Dennis, because she didn't turn up at school this morning, and you know I never thought much of this charwoman arrangement. So I came round here at break, but the front door was locked, of course, and I couldn't get in. Well then I looked through the window in the door, and darling–there she was, lying in a heap at the foot of the stairs, in her pyjamas. I couldn't make her hear, or anything, so I went round to the back and broke the kitchen window and got in, and there she was.'

I said, 'I'm frightfully sorry. But wasn't the charwoman here last night?'

'I don't think she can have been. But I don't know. I don't even know who she is.'

'How is she now?'

She shrugged her shoulders. 'Very much the same. I think she's warmer than she was–she was terribly cold. Mrs Stevens helped me to carry her upstairs to bed, and we've got three hot bottles in bed with her. I do wish the doctor would come.'

I stood by the door looking in. The little dark-haired girl lay in bed with eyes half open but immobile, like a dead rabbit; she looked very like her father. My wife said softly, 'Poor little brat. It *is* a shame.'

There was nothing more that we could do, for the moment, till Dr Martin turned up. I stood there with them in silence. Back in my office the telephone, I knew, would be ringing almost continuously as various infuriated people tried to find me; the storm would be mounting as frustrations multiplied because I was not at the office. Too bad; they would have to multiply. I had to tackle each of my responsibilities in turn; one thing at a time.

The doctor came at last; I knew him slightly. We told him all we knew; then he went in to her with Shirley. He came out after ten minutes, and we went down to the sitting-room, so called, that was Honey's drawing office.

'Well,' he said, 'she's got concussion, of course. I can't find any fracture. You think she fell downstairs; the bruising supports that. She was alone in the house . . . I think that's very wrong, if I may say so.' He stared at us severely. 'A child of that age is much too young to be left alone at night.'

'I quite agree with you,' I said. 'Unfortunately, her father is abroad and the arrangements that he made for her seem to have broken down.'

He nodded. 'Well, she needs care now. She'll probably wake up before long, and when she does there may be a good deal of vomiting. She must stay in bed for at least a week. I'll look in again this afternoon. Who is in charge of her?'

There was an awkward pause. 'I don't think anybody is,' said Shirley. 'There's only us.'

I explained. 'I'm the head of his department at the R.A.E.'

'Well, who is going to look after her?'

I said doubtfully, 'Couldn't she go into a hospital?'

'Not here,' the doctor said. 'I haven't got a bed. We might be able to get her into Guildford or Woking.'

Shirley said, 'Dennis, we can take her. I mean, we *are* mixed up in it, in a sort of way. And if it's only being sick and that sort of thing–well, I can cope with that. I think we ought to take her. I'd hate to think of her waking up in hospital amongst strangers.'

I said, 'Yes, old thing–but where? You couldn't keep her here?'

She turned to the doctor. 'Could we take her to our flat? Can she be moved?'

In the end we telephoned for the ambulance and put her on the stretcher unconscious as she was, and took her to the flat and put her in bed. We both skated over the implications of that, because Shirley and I only had one bed between us and we put Elspeth in that one, and there was no other bed in the flat. We shelved the problem of where we were going to sleep ourselves till bedtime got a little nearer, and that was the quiet evening on which I had planned to sit down and run over my lecture on the 'Performance Analysis of Aircraft Flying at High Mach Numbers.'

By the time all that was done and sorted out it was ten minutes past two; I had had no lunch and had to get into my car and dash back to the office to catch up with my blazing row.

Miss Learoyd had a whole list of people who had left their numbers asking or demanding I should ring them. There was Ferguson and Seabright in the Ministry, and Carter in the Ministry of Civil Aviation, and Sir David Moon of C.A.T.O., and Drinkwater in the Air Registration Board and–my heart sank–Mr Prendergast of the Rutland Aircraft Company, the designer of the Reindeer.

I asked Miss Learoyd to see if she could locate the Director. She asked his secretary, who told her that after his committee meeting he had intended to come back by Kew Gardens, to look at the flowers.

I sighed, and put in a call first of all to Ferguson. But before it came through, the exchange asked me if I would take an incoming call. It was from Sir David Moon, the Chairman of C.A.T.O.

He said, 'Is that Dr Scott?'

'This is Scott speaking,' I replied.

'Is a Mr Honey a member of your department, Dr Scott?'

'Yes,' I said. 'He's not here at the moment. He's in Canada.'

'I am very well aware of that,' he said. 'I have been trying to make contact with your Director, but he seems to be away. Are you aware of what your Mr Honey has been doing, Dr Scott?'

'No–I haven't heard from him yet. There's hardly been time.' I wondered what on earth the trouble was.

'Then you don't know that he has been responsible for destroying one of our aircraft?'

I had a sudden sickening feeling in my stomach. 'Destroying one of your aircraft? Whatever do you mean, sir?'

'I understand that he deliberately raised the undercarriage while the machine was standing on the ground at Gander. I need hardly say that the damage is very extensive indeed.'

I was staggered. 'But–but how could he have done that? There must be some mistake, sir. Our people don't make errors of that sort.'

'I tell you, this wasn't an error,' he said forcibly. 'It was done deliberately and maliciously, according to the report we have received.'

'I'm afraid I just can't believe that,' I said. 'I know Mr Honey very well. He's not a fool. You say this happened at Gander?' I was beginning to recover from the shock and think.

'That is correct.'

'What sort of aircraft was it?' I inquired.

'A Reindeer.'

'The Reindeer that he had flown over in last night? The one that was on loan to A.B.A.S. and had flown 1,400 hours?'

'I don't know how many hours it had flown. Thanks to the antics of your officer, it will be a long time before it flies again.'

I said, 'If that's the machine, Sir David, this may possibly be true. Have you see Mr Carnegie since I spoke to him this morning, insisting that that aircraft should be grounded?'

He said, 'Yes, I have. And I may tell you here and now, Dr Scott, that this organisation will not tolerate technical secrecy where our aircraft are concerned. If you suspect at any time that there are latent defects in the aircraft that we operate, it is your duty to come forward and tell us immediately. I understand from Mr Carnegie that you have been considering a defect in the tailplane of the Reindeer for some weeks behind closed doors, till suddenly you came forward this morning and demanded that a certain aircraft should be grounded and put out of service at ten minutes' notice, without disclosing any technical reason for your action. Now, is that correct or not?'

'Broadly speaking,' I said slowly, 'that is quite correct. It came as a complete surprise to us this morning to learn that a Reindeer had done 1,400 hours. When we got that news quick action became necessary, and we decided that it must be grounded right away. Tell me, this machine that had the undercarriage accident at Gander—was that the same machine?'

'It was the machine that flew across last night,' he said. 'The one that had your representative on board.'

'Then it *was* the same machine,' I replied. 'You say that Mr Honey was responsible for retracting the undercarriage while the aircraft was standing on the ground?'

'That is so. The signal that we have received states that in the most explicit terms.'

'I can only say I'm very sorry this has happened,' I said. 'Where is Mr Honey now?'

'I presume that he's at Gander.'

I thought quickly. This new row over the smashed Reindeer was likely to overshadow the one about grounding the Reindeer; there would be a thumping repair bill to be paid by somebody. If it was true that Honey, a Government servant, had pulled up the undercarriage deliberately, inevitably the Treasury would come in at some stage or another; there was no knowing where the thing would end. Honey would have to come back to this country to tell us his end of it and the investigation of the crash in Labrador would have to wait for a few days. There was probably no urgency about that now, in any case.

'I think we ought to get Mr Honey back at once and hear his account,' I said.

He snorted. 'By all means, Dr Scott, so long as you don't ask for a passage for him in one of our aircraft. Get him back by all means.'

Gander is a day's journey in the train from St John's and the train goes twice a week; a steamer leaves St John's for Liverpool about once a month and takes a week or so to make the crossing.

I said, 'I think we ought to get him back without any delay.'

'Dr Scott,' he said, 'I have to make myself very clear. The signal that we have received suggests that Mr Honey is mentally unbalanced. He has already gravely damaged one of our aircraft. We do not consider him a fit person to travel by air, and I very much doubt if any other line will take him in the face of our refusal. If you consider that he should be brought back to this country by air, then your proper course is to send an aircraft of R.A.F. Transport Command for him. And I should recommend you to send suitable medical attendants with it, to look after him upon the journey.'

This was simply terrible. I said, 'I can't believe that it is quite so bad as that, Sir David.'

He replied, 'I think I should like to speak to your Director, Dr Scott. Would you kindly put me through?'

'I'm afraid he isn't in,' I said. I could not say that he had snatched an afternoon to go and see the flowers in Kew Gardens. 'He's been up in London at a meeting of the Aeronautical Research Committee. I'm expecting him in later this afternoon.'

'Oh. Can I reach him on the telephone?'

'I don't think you can. He's probably on his way back here now.'

'Very well. Would you kindly ask him to telephone me immediately he arrives. I shall wait for his call in this office until six o'clock.'

'I'll tell him that, Sir David,' I said. 'I'll get him to call you up immediately he comes in.'

I put down the receiver in a cold sweat, but within half a minute the bell was ringing again, and it was Ferguson to tell me that Honey had ruined a Reindeer at Gander by pulling up its undercart. I said, 'I know. I've just had Sir David Moon upon the telephone.'

He said, 'Whatever can he have been thinking of? Do you think he's mad?'

'I don't know if he's mad or not,' I said angrily. 'I know that Reindeer had done 1,400 hours and that I asked you this morning to have it grounded. Well, now we hear that Honey's grounded it, so his action seems to be exactly in accordance with my own.'

'I don't think this is a time for flippancy, old man,' he said. 'The consequences of this thing are going to be very serious indeed.'

'I quite agree with you,' I said forcibly. 'The implications here are very serious indeed. We are the research establishment concerned, and we have asked that a certain aircraft should be grounded, because we think it dangerous to fly. There's been some hours of argument, and now we hear that our representative who is with the aircraft has taken energetic action to prevent that aircraft flying any farther. If it turns out that Honey did that as the only way to stop that Reindeer taking off from Gander, I shall support him. The lives of people are at stake in this affair, a fact that you chaps up in London tend to forget sometimes.'

'There's no need to talk like that,' he replied. 'We're just as much concerned to keep the airlines safe as you are. What worries us is that up to the present you don't seem to have any real technical justification for the action that you are taking.'

'That depends on what you regard as technical justification,' I replied. 'We suspect that trouble may occur at about 1,400 hours, and to some extent the first Reindeer accident confirms that. Till the matter is cleared up, no Reindeer is to fly more than 700 hours. Now, that's my attitude and I'm sticking to it. My staff work under me, and that's their attitude.'

'Is the Director back yet?' he inquired.

'No,' I said. 'I think he's looking at the flowers in Kew Gardens, if you really want to know where he is. And if you want the full story, Elspeth Honey, Honey's twelve-year-old daughter, fell downstairs last night, and she's unconscious with concussion and shock in my bed, and God knows where I'm going to sleep tonight.'

'I say, old man, I'm sorry about that. Can I do anything to help?'

'Yes, you can,' I said. 'You can keep these ruddy blood-hounds off my track and give me time to get things sorted out. We'll have to have a meeting of some sort tomorrow, I suppose, but I would like to get Honey back in time for it and hear what really happened at Gander. That bloody old fool Moon has just told me that he won't bring Honey back by air in case he wrecks another aeroplane. Will you see if you can get that one sorted out, and get Honey back here pronto?'

He said doubtfully, 'I'll do what I can. But I'm afraid they're taking rather a firm line.'

He rang off, and then Carter in the Ministry of Civil Aviation rang through to tell me that Mr Honey had ruined a Reindeer by pulling up its undercarriage while it was standing on the ground.

I got rid of him after ten minutes, and in a momentary breathing space I rang up Shirley. She said, 'Oh, Dennis dear, I'm so glad you are there. Dr Martin's been again. Yes, she's sort of half awake now, but I don't think she knows where she is; she hasn't said anything. Dr Martin said to keep her absolutely quiet–complete rest. He's given me a list of things we've got to get, but I can't leave her to go out to the chemist. Could you possibly get them on the way home, if I give you the list now?'

I blinked. 'What time do the shops shut?'

'I'm not quite sure. Five o'clock, don't they?'

I could not possibly leave the office by that time. I said, 'All right, dear–let's have the list and I'll do something about it. But I shan't be home before seven at the earliest. There's the hell of a row going on here, and I'm in a perfect shambles.'

'Oh, I *am* sorry, Dennis. Well, we've got to get another hot-water bottle and a bedpan and some tablets of Veganin . . .'

She went on with the list and I wrote it all down on my blotter and rang off, and then I rang for Miss Learoyd, and said, 'Miss Learoyd, can you drive my car?' But then the telephone bell rang again, and she waited while I answered it.

It was Seabright from the Ministry ringing up to tell me that Honey had crashed a Reindeer at Gander by pulling up its undercart.

Ten minutes later I resumed my conversation with Miss Learoyd. She said, 'I'm afraid I can't drive, Dr Scott.'

I said, 'Oh well, then, never mind.' Test pilots never have anything to do but stand around on the tarmac and goop at the aeroplanes; I rang through to the flight office and got hold of Flight-Lieutenant Wintringham, and said, 'Wintringham, are you doing much for the next hour?' He said he wasn't, and I got him to come up to my office and gave him the list for the chemist and the key of my car, and got him to go out and get the stuff and take it round to Shirley. Then Drinkwater in the A.R.B. came on the telephone to tell me that a member of my department had damaged an aeroplane of C.A.T.O. at Gander by pulling up its undercarriage.

And then Miss Learoyd, bless her, came in with a cup of tea.

I asked her to find out if the Director had come to life yet, but she came back in a couple of minutes and said he had not returned; his girl would let us know immediately he came in. I sighed and pulled my IN basket towards me, full of the arrears of work, but a quarter of an hour later I was speaking on the telephone again, this time to E.P.Prendergast, designer of the Reindeer.

He said, 'Is that Dr Scott?'

'Speaking, Mr Prendergast,' I said. 'It's very nice to hear you again.'

'Dr Scott, Mr Carnegie of C.A.T.O. rang me up before lunch and told me rather a curious story about trouble with the Reindeer tail. He said you want to ground all our machines. Is that correct?'

'Not quite,' I said. 'We're not quite happy that the crash of the first Reindeer was, in fact, due to pilot's error of judgment. Obviously I can't tell you the whole story over the phone, but we suspect that trouble with fatigue may crop up in the tailplane, due to the particular harmonic modes induced in cruising flight. We thought it wise to ground one Reindeer that has flown rather a long time until the matter is investigated further. We are quite happy to allow the others to go on, for the time being.'

'This is the very first that I have heard of it,' he said, 'when Mr Carnegie rang through today and told me that a Reindeer had been grounded at a moment's notice, and asked if it was done with my approval. I told him that of course it wasn't.'

'I know,' I said. 'I feel we owe you some explanation for that.' I searched my mind hurriedly to think up some sort of explanation that I could give. 'The matter came up very suddenly, I am afraid, and in connection with a piece of basic research upon fatigue, for which we used the second Reindeer tail that you delivered for experimental purposes.'

'I see, Dr Scott. Don't you think it would have been more courteous, if you suspected trouble with the aircraft designed by this company, to have taken us into your confidence? It is just possible that we might have been able to assist you. After all, we did give the design a great deal of consideration in this office, and we are not wholly inexperienced in problems of fatigue.'

I could not tell the truth, that Prendergast had become so difficult in recent years that one was most reluctant to approach him upon anything. I said, 'The thing moved very quickly from the basic research stage to the stage of immediate urgency. As a matter of fact, we had no idea until last night that any Reindeer had done anything like 1,400 hours. Our information was that they had all done about 400, and at that the matter was not urgent.'

'I see. Of course, you have your own way of doing things. I must say, I should appreciate it if we could be told before long what you think is the matter with our product.'

'Of course, Mrs Prendergast,' I replied. 'I want to have a meeting on the thing as soon as possible, at which everybody will be represented. I'm going to fix that up as soon as ever I can get Mr Honey back from Gander, possibly tomorrow. But apart from that rather formal meeting, if you could come down here one morning we should be only too pleased to go into the matter thoroughly with you. In fact, I think a private meeting of that sort might well precede the formal conference.'

'I think it might,' he said. 'I think it might have happened some considerable time ago.' He paused. 'I think perhaps that it would be as well if I come down immediately,' he said. 'Would ten-thirty tomorrow morning be convenient for you?'

I hesitated. 'I think that maybe just a trifle too soon for us,' I said. 'Mr Honey has been doing all the work on this research, and I should very much prefer that he were present at our meeting. At present he's at Gander in Newfoundland, and I am expecting him to cross by air tonight.' I did not think it wise to mention that C.A.T.O. had flatly refused to bring him back, because I hoped that Ferguson would get around that one. 'If I could give you a ring tomorrow morning, perhaps, and fix the date then?'

'Do I understand that Mr Honey is the only man at Farnborough who is conversant with the trouble that the Reindeer tail is supposed to be having?' he asked.

'Not at all, Mr Prendergast,' I replied. 'I am conversant with it myself, although I have not been able to work on problems of fatigue over a period of years, as Mr Honey has. You'll naturally want the fullest information that's available in this department, and so I think perhaps that we should wait till he gets back.'

'Mr Honey has been doing all the work on this research, then?'

'That's correct.'

'Mr Theodore Honey? A small man, with glasses?'

'That's right.'

'And you expect to get him back by air by tomorrow morning, from Gander?'

I could see myself being driven into a corner. 'I expect so. The Ministry are arranging for a passage now.'

'Oh. Are you aware, Dr Scott, that C.A.T.O. have refused to carry this man in their aircraft, on the grounds that the mental instability from which he suffers makes him a danger to the safety of the other passengers? Are you aware of that?'

I coloured hotly at his tone. 'I know that has been said in the heat of the moment,' I replied. 'It's perfect nonsense. I have told Mr Ferguson that we take a most serious view of allegations of that sort, and that Honey must come home by air at once.'

'I might reply that I take a serious view of allegations against the structural safety of the Reindeer, Dr Scott. I understand that Mr Honey has already destroyed one Reindeer standing on the ground at Gander. In the circumstances the action of C.A.T.O. appears to me to be not unreasonable.'

I checked an angry retort. 'I think we'll have to leave that matter to be settled later, Mr Prendergast,' I said. 'What we have to decide now is the date when we shall meet. May I give you a ring tomorrow morning, making a proposal? I shall be able to see my way a little bit more clearly then.'

'If you wish it so,' he said. 'But I must make it clear to you, Dr Scott, that until these allegations, as you call them, about Mr Honey's health have been cleared up I shall be most unwilling to accept the results of his work, or even to waste much time in studying them.' He paused. 'I have worked in this industry for nearly forty years, Dr Scott. I have watched the personnel engaged in research come and go. I know the members of your staff. Probably I have known all of them longer than you have, I may even know some of them better. Take Mr Honey, for example. Did he not write a paper, published in the *Journal of the Interplanetary Society* in 1932 or 1933, advocating the construction of a rocket projectile for an exploratory journey to the moon?'

I felt rather helpless. 'I haven't the least idea,' I said. 'If he did, what of it?'

'I merely call your attention to the lines on which his mind appears to run,' he replied. 'I believe he has been Chairman of the Surbiton branch of the Society for Psychic Research, and that much of his leisure time has been spent in the detection of ghosts. I understand that he had been in trouble with the police arising out of his activities with the British Israelites. He has more than once forecast the coming dissolution of the world to members of my staff, over the lunch table. We now have a–er, an allegation by the officials of C.A.T.O. that

Mr Honey is mentally unbalanced. I must say that I should like to see that allegation disposed of before I am required to waste much of my time in an examination of his work upon the Reindeer tailplane.'

I said, 'Very well, Mr Prendergast. The most that I can do is to let you know tomorrow morning when we shall be ready to meet you to discuss the Reindeer tail. If then you prefer not to attend the meeting that we offer, that, of course, is your affair entirely. As regards these allegations against Mr Honey, we shall of course investigate them fully, and if we find that they have substance in them we shall reconsider our position. If we find that they are irresponsible slanders, we shall maintain our attitude, which is that till this matter is cleared up to the complete satisfaction of all parties, no Reindeer aircraft should fly more than 700 hours.' I put a little vehemence into the last words.

'Will you please transfer this call to your Director?' he asked.

'I'm afraid I can't do that,' I said. 'He isn't here this afternoon.'

'That is a great pity, Dr Scott. I had hoped to avoid troubling the Minister. Would you ask the Director to telephone to me as soon as it may be convenient to him?'

'Certainly,' I said. 'I don't suppose that that will be until tomorrow morning, by which time I hope the matter will have become rather clearer.'

He rang off, and I sat staring at the piles of work in my IN basket. The attack was developing, and it was going to take the form that Mr Honey was mad, and all his work upon the Reindeer tail was worthless rubbish. Inevitably it would come out that we had put it up to the Inter-Services Atomic Research Board, and that Sir Phillip Dolbear had thought nothing of it; that was bound to happen at some stage of the affair. Moreover, we had nothing positive to put upon the credit side. I had a hunch that he was right, a hunch derived from a study of the accident report on the first Reindeer and from a study of the little man himself. But could my hunch stand up against the formidable array of evidence now massing up that Honey was irresponsible and that his work was therefore worthless? Would the truth emerge that the Reindeer tail was quite safe after all? And if so, what would my position be?

The only other thing that happened on that most unpleasant afternoon was that Ferguson came through again, to say that C.A.T.O. were adamant that they would not carry Mr Honey back across the Atlantic in one of their aircraft. He said that they were taking a firm stand upon the question of safety. They had no facilities in the aircraft or upon their staff for the control of passengers who might become unbalanced in the air, and in view of this man's record they would have nothing more to do with him. 'They just won't carry him, and that's all about it,' Ferguson said. 'I don't see that we can force them, in the circumstances. And I don't see that we can ask a foreign or Dominion line to take him, either. We'd have to go back to the Treasury for that and that would mean explaining all the circumstances there.'

I bit my lip. 'We must get him back,' I said. 'Until we have him here, we can't have a really effective meeting on the technicalities of this fatigue story. And everybody's clamouring for a meeting now.'

He said, 'Well, the only other way would be to get him back by means of R.A.F. Transport Command. And that's really going just a bit above my head, you know. I think that that would have to be put through by your Director, on a higher level.'

'All right,' I said. 'That's how we'll have to do it.'

The Director came into his office soon after five; Miss Learoyd got the news, and I went down at once to see him. He was in a calm and cheerful frame of mind, and greeted me warmly. 'Good afternoon, Scott,' he said. 'I came back by Kew and spent an hour in the Gardens. You really ought to go and see them now – the rose gardens are perfect, and they've got the most magnificent hedge of sweet-peas that I have ever seen in all my life. You really ought to go. It's very delightful there at most times of the year, of course, especially in spring, but really I think I prefer the formal effects that you can get in a made garden in July. I think I do. However. You've got something for me?'

'I'm afraid I have,' I said. 'I've got a major row.'

He made me sit down, and I told him all about it. It took a quarter of an hour. 'Well, there it is,' I said at last. 'I think that the immediate thing is to get Honey back here at once, and for that I'm afraid we'll have to ask for the assistance of Transport Command.'

'I see,' he said thoughtfully. 'You wouldn't let him go on now and do his job in Labrador?'

I met his eye. 'Do you think that anything he did in Labrador would be accepted as a valuable contribution, sir – after this?'

He stared out of the window. 'It's a question of fact. . . . But I think that I agree with you, it might be better to recall Honey and send out somebody to Labrador whose findings would be readily accepted by our critics.' He turned to me. 'We depend entirely on the evidence from the Labrador crash, do we not? We have nothing else to show, except Honey's theoretical investigations, which Sir Philip Dolbear won't accept?'

I shook my head. 'Nothing, unless you count this photograph.' I had the accident report with me; I opened it upon his table and we studied the one print that showed the port tailplane front spar fracture at the fuselage. The print was an enlargement from a Leica frame, carried up already to a size at which the detail was becoming fuzzy; it would obviously go no bigger without losing definition. At that, the bit that interested us was no more than one-eighth of an inch long, and the really vital part considerably less than that. We studied it together with a magnifying glass. 'It certainly looks like a fatigue fracture,' he said quietly. 'It might come up more clearly in the stereoscope.'

He turned to me. 'That's all the evidence we've got to go upon, until we get this portion back from Labrador?'

I nodded. 'That's right, sir. That, and what we think of Mr Honey as a reliable research worker.'

'And what do you think of that now?'

There was a long pause. 'I think the same as I did,' I said heavily at last. 'I think that there's a very fair chance that he's right. The fact that one Reindeer last night flew up to 1,430 hours or so before he wrecked it means nothing, of course; it might have been due to fail in the next hour. We don't yet know the full story of why he raised the under-carriage. But if, as I suppose, he felt it was the only way to stop that aircraft flying any more, I think that he was right. In his shoes I should probably have done the same, if I had had the guts. That hasn't shaken my opinion of his work.'

'It was a very extreme step to take,' he said thoughtfully. 'It's obviously going to make a lot of trouble.'

'It makes a lot of trouble when airliners crash, and people lose their lives,' I said.

He walked to the window and looked out upon the aerodrome, deep in thought. 'I made a mistake in this thing, Scott,' he said at last. 'I should have sent somebody upon this job who had more personality. I ought to have sent you. Honey's an inside man. I can quite see that in the circumstances that obtained at Gander, when the aircraft was due to fly on, he would have had difficulty in enforcing his point of view. Probably, in view of what both you and he feel on the likelihood of this fatigue trouble, he did as well as he could be expected to. He probably did right. But it will make a lot of trouble for us; I can see that coming.'

'I'm very sorry about that, sir,' I replied.

He smiled. 'It's none of your making.'

'I feel it is,' I said. 'If I could have handled things a bit more cleverly, all this could have been avoided.'

He shrugged his shoulders. 'We'll get over it.'

'What about Honey?' I asked. 'I presume that he's at Gander now. Will you start up something with Transport Command to get him back?'

He glanced at the clock. 'Not tonight. I think I'd like to sleep upon it, Scott, and take some action in the morning. It won't hurt Honey to stay there for another twelve hours or so.' He smiled at me. 'You sleep on it, too. Take your wife out tonight and forget about all this.'

I moved with him towards the door. 'I can't do that,' I said. 'I've got another spot of Honey trouble on my plate at home.' And I told him all about little Elspeth Honey falling downstairs in the middle of the night.

'But wasn't anybody looking after her?' he asked.

'I don't know,' I said. 'That's one of the things that hasn't been cleared up.'

I went back to my office and started my day's work, and for a merciful two hours I had respite from the telephone, so that by seven o'clock I had got well down into my IN basket. I gave it up then, and went home. Shirley was in the bedroom; she heard me in the little hall and came out to meet me.

'She's much better,' she said in a quiet voice. 'She's awake now.' We went into the sitting-room. 'Flight-Lieutenant Wintringham brought along the stuff from the chemist, and I've given her some of the Veganin, because her headache was so bad. She's been sick, but the doctor said that would happen. I think she's getting on as well as can be expected.'

I grunted. 'Well, that's one thing going on well, anyway.' I glanced at her. 'Her father's in a stinking mess over at Gander.'

'Mr Honey is? Why, Dennis?'

'I'm not quite certain why,' I said. 'But what happened was this. He pulled up the undercart of a Reindeer while it was standing on the ground. Retracted it.'

She stared at me. 'You mean, so that it sat down on its tummy?'

I nodded wearily. 'That's right.'

She said, 'What a naughty little man!' And then she laughed, and freed from the strain of the day, I hesitated for a moment, and then laughed with her. 'Oh,' she said, 'I would like to have seen him doing it!'

'All very well,' I said at last. 'But you just wouldn't believe the trouble that it's made.'

'Is the damage very serious, Dennis?'

'I simply don't know, yet.' I thought for a moment; somebody had once told me that the contract price of each Reindeer was £453,000. 'I suppose the repair bill will be something like fifty thousand pounds,' I said ruefully.

'Oh, Dennis, how bad of him! However did he come to do it?'

I started to tell her, and she went and got me a drink, so that I finished telling her about it in a more cheerful frame of mind. And then we went into the bedroom to see Elspeth.

She was lying in our bed, drowsy with the drug, but she opened her eyes when we came in. 'Hullo, Elspeth,' I said. 'How are you getting on?'

She said, 'I put on Daddy's warm dressing-gown and I trod on it and fell down.' And then she said, 'Will you tell Daddy that I want him?'

'He's coming back at once,' I said. 'He doesn't know you're ill yet, but he's coming home tomorrow or the day after at the latest.'

The little girl said, 'Was there a burglar?'

'A burglar—in your house last night do you mean? I don't think so.' Beside me Shirley shook her head. 'There was nobody there this morning but you, and everything was quite all right.'

She said, 'I heard a burglar, so I put on Daddy's warm dressing-gown, but I trod on it and I fell down.'

'Don't worry about burglars now,' I said. 'You just get well again before your daddy gets back. He won't want to find you in bed, will he?'

She shook her head slightly on the pillow. The little movement drew my attention to the mop, its white cotton head, now rather grubby, on the pillow near her own. Shirley had found it in her bed and brought it round, to comfort her in her loneliness amongst strangers.

'Are you quite warm now?' I asked.

She said, 'I've got three hot-water bottles, all rubber ones.'

'Fine. Do you want any supper?'

'No, thank you, Dr Scott. I was sick three times and Mrs Scott held my head. May I go back and sleep in our house tonight?'

'I don't think that's a very good idea,' I said. 'I think you'd better stay with us till you're quite well again.'

'I must go back to our house,' she said in agitation, 'because it's empty and there'll be a burglar because of Daddy's work. It's very valuable, and burglars come and break into empty houses and steal valuable things. Please, Dr Scott, may I go back and sleep in our house? I'm quite all right now.'

'Your daddy's work will be quite safe,' I told her. 'Burglars don't come to steal that sort of valuable thing, because they can't sell it. They come and steal silver spoons and things like that.'

'Would they steal electro-plate, Dr Scott? It's just like silver.'

'No,' I said, 'they never steal electro-plate.'

'But there *was* a burglar last night, Dr Scott, because I heard him. And I put on Daddy's warm dressing-gown and I trod on it, and I fell down.'

This was where I had come in. I told her that I'd have a talk with Shirley and decide who was going to sleep where that night, and I left her, and went and found Shirley in the kitchen. 'I simply must eat something,' I said. 'I haven't had any lunch.'

'Oh, Dennis! Look, supper will be ready in about ten minutes. Have a couple of biscuits, and go in and eat them with Elspeth.'

I took the biscuits, but before I got to Elspeth there was a little wail, and Elspeth was in trouble again. What's more, she hadn't got her basin handy. I called to Shirley, 'All right, you go on cooking; I can cope with this.' And I did, and I can testify that there's no better anodyne to worry than coping with a vomiting child.

Presently supper was ready; I went to it with a reduced appetite, partly on account of the biscuits. While we were eating I told Shirley about the burglars. 'That poor kid's got burglars on the brain, Dennis. She's been talking about them ever since she woke up. She's terribly upset that somebody will come and steal Mr Honey's work on the Great Pyramid.'

'Is that what's on her mind?'

She nodded.

'But that's absurd,' I said weakly.

'I know it is. But that's what's on her mind. She's got a great sense of responsibility.' She turned to the dresser and picked up a dirty halfsheet of notepaper. 'I do think it's a blasted shame,' she said vehemently. 'I went round to get her night things while Wintringham was here, and this is what I found in the kitchen.'

It was an ill-written note. It read:

Dear Miss,
　I find I wont be able to come tonight as my husband is took poorly.
　　　　　　　　　　　　　　　　　　　　Yours respectfully,
　　　　　　　　　　　　　　　　　　　　　　E. Higgs.

I gave it back to her. 'Just like that,' I said.

'Just like that,' she said angrily. 'I'm keeping it to show to Mr Honey.'

I thought for a minute. 'About these bloody burglars,' I said, 'I've got to sleep somewhere, anyway, and so have you. I could sleep round there tonight if that would help.'

'I think it would help, Dennis,' she said. 'As a matter of fact, I don't quite know where else you *are* to sleep tonight, unless you went to a hotel. I thought I'd sleep on the sofa here.'

'All right,' I said. 'I'll go around and sleep there.' At any rate, I thought, it would be quiet, and I could take the 'Performance Analysis of Aircraft Flying at High Mach Numbers' with me.

'I'm awfully sorry,' Shirley said. 'But I think it might be quite a good thing if you did sleep there. I kicked the glass out of the kitchen window this morning, to get in to her, so there really might be a burglar tonight. I mean, the house is wide open.'

I went round there after supper, in the dusk. I found a piece of three-ply and a hammer and some tacks, and tacked the plywood up to the frame of the broken window; then I carried my bag up to the front bedroom, Honey's room, and made the bed. I took the typescript of my thesis from the bag and went down to the sitting-room, meaning to settle down in the one armchair that the house possessed and concentrate upon it.

The house was still and quiet, but I could not concentrate. The Honey matter was so urgent that here, surrounded by all Honey's personal belongings, I could not bring my mind to bear upon the aircraft flying at high Mach numbers. That afternoon various responsible people had stated bluntly their opinion that Mr Honey was mad. I had taken my stand on my opinion that his work was valuable; very soon the matter would be decided one way or the other. If I was right there would be a complete disruption of C.A.T.O.'s Atlantic service. If events should prove that Honey's work was worthless, my position would be very much in question; It would hardly be possible for me to continue in charge of the Department after having been proved wrong in such a major row as this was going to be.

Probably I should have to leave the R.A.E., leave Government service altogether, having put up such a black as that. I should have to start again in industry; possibly it would be better to make a complete break and emigrate and start again in aviation in Australia, or in Canada perhaps. If Honey's work was worthless, that would be my future: to leave the country, go down in salary and in prestige, and start again in a strange place. But then, was Honey's work worthless?

My eyes strayed to his books, untidily arranged upon three long shelves. The *Psychology of the Transfiguration* rubbed shoulders with *An Experiment With Time*, and next came *A Discussion of the Infinite*. Then there was *The Serial Calculus Applied to Numerical Analysis* and then, surprisingly, *Great Motion Pictures, Past and Present*. I picked this out in curiosity and opened it; upon the flyleaf there was written, 'Mary with all my love, from Theo, March 16th, 1939'. I put it back, a little thoughtfully. There had been a human side at one time, long ago.

There was more such evidence farther along the shelf. Between *The Pyramid in History* and *The Stability of a Harmonic Series* there stood a large gift volume, richly illustrated and interspersed with musical scores, called *Country Dancing*. This was inscribed 'Theo dear, from Mary, September 2nd, 1936'. It was a well-used book that lay open at any page; clearly it had seen some service on a music stand. Beside that was another well-worn, paper-covered volume called *Rambles in Old World Sussex*. I thought of the short hiker's pants and the good strong boots; they would be upstairs somewhere, probably with a rucksack. It would be interesting, I thought, to look and see if the good strong boots had been used recently, if Honey still went hiking, if he took any exercise at the week-ends. It would all add up.

The thought got me out of my chair and set me wandering about the empty house. On the kitchen table somebody had put three or four letters. All were bills or receipts saving one, addressed to Miss Elspeth Honey in her father's handwriting, the first from the pile standing on his office desk. I put it on one side to take to her in the morning.

The little house was rather dirty and rather bare of furniture. Upstairs there were three bedrooms, but one, although it had a bed set up in it, was clearly never used and served more for a box-room. At the back of the house looking over the small gardens of the row was Elspeth's room, which I had seen: a small, bare, rather bleak little room. On the mantelpiece there was a photograph of a dark-haired young woman with a pleasant, rather appealing expression. I stared at it in thought for a minute; would that be the mother who had died? I came to the conclusion that almost certainly it was.

I went into Honey's room, the room I was to sleep in. There was no such photograph there, and that seemed odd to me until it struck me that he might have taken it away with him in his bag, to Canada. In a cupboard in his room I found the strong hiking boots. There was mud on them, but it was very old and dry and flaked to dust beneath the pressure of my fingers. They had not been worn for years.

There was a small writing table, or bureau, by the window. I had lost all scruples by that time about intruding into his privacy; too much lay at stake for that. Here, alone in his house, I had the opportunity of learning more of Honey than I should ever get again. I wanted to find written arguments by him, essays, theses, papers for learned societies, or anything of that sort. I wanted to see how his mind worked, whether the conclusions and the inferences that he drew from given facts were reasonable on other matters than the Reindeer tail.

The bureau yielded nothing much to help me. He kept his cheque-book and his unpaid bills and his receipts there; I did not hesitate to look into his affairs. I found them in good order. There were two life insurance policies and his Will, which I did not read because I could guess very well what would be in it. His bills were paid up to date, but this was evidently not usual, because a study of the counterfoils in his cheque-book showed that he had had a field-day at them before leaving for Canada. He had a credit of about three hundred pounds in the bank. I found no evidence of anything but a modest and a frugal life.

In a drawer, at the back, there were a large number of letters, faded, all in the same girlish hand, tied up in bundles with red tape out of the office. I did not look at any of those.

I went downstairs again to his living-room, more like a drawing-office than a parlour, and there in a big cupboard was a row of files containing what I was in search of. These files were all labelled on the back—PYRAMID DEDUCTIONS, MIGRATION (ANIMALS), and MIGRATION (MEN). Then there was one called HEBRAIC FORMS IN DRUID RITUAL, and another, PSYCHIC PHENOMENA. I was interested to notice one called INTERPLANETARY (MASS ATTRACTION OF CELESTIAL BODIES), and another, INTERPLANETARY (VEHICLES). And there was one simply entitled OSMOSIS. In all there must have been about fifteen of them.

I pulled a few of them out of the cupboard and sat down at his table to study them.

An hour later I sat back, filling a pipe, very thoughtful. In the year 1932 he was already writing about the bi-fuel propulsion of rockets and had demonstrated clearly how a three-stage rocket projectile could be constructed which would have sufficient energy and range to escape from the gravitational field of the Earth, with an intent to reach the Moon. He had made weight estimates and he had gone in some detail into the technique of launching. He had not dealt with matters of control, so far as I could discover. His work here seemed to parallel very closely the early German investigations; indeed, in point of date, it seemed to me that he was some years in advance of German work. I could not say that there was evidence of madness in this work of his, but there was sad evidence that we had not made use of genius that lay under our hand, in the last war.

OSMOSIS was the same story, so far as I could understand the technicalities involved, which were quite outside my beat. It had arisen, queerly, from the design of a radio valve for use in centimetre wave reception; this had apparently been a little mental relaxation from his normal work. In the course of it the properties of the metal thorium had seemed to him unusual when in the presence of argon, and upon this he had built up a considerable research, apparently all carried out in this front sitting-room. It had not been completed, for some reason that I was unable to discover, perhaps because of prior publication by some other research worker. But the work was careful, reasonable and probably correct.

In the other subjects I was quite out of my depth; I knew nothing about the

Pyramid and the Hebraic forms left me cold, except that they were interesting as evidence of his wide interests. Everybody, however ignorant, is attracted by psychic phenomena, or ghosts, and though I was growing sleepy I pulled that towards me, and opened it at random.

The first part of this set of papers consisted of a series of temperature recordings taken in a house that was troubled by a poltergeist. The evidence was that the house, a modern villa occupied by the manager of a motor garage and his wife, was the scene of various unexplainable occurrences. At a time when the family was at dinner and there was nobody else in the house, the barometer which normally hung in the hall had been thrown with a clatter into the kitchen sink, through a closed door. In similar circumstances a disused paraffin lamp, normally kept in the loft, was thrown downstairs; and kitchen plates were broken with a crash under the bed of the main upstairs bedroom. Unlike the majority of such cases, there was no adolescent in the house. In every instance observers had noticed an apparent fall of temperature at the time of the occurrence. Honey had installed three recording thermographs, probably borrowed from the R.A.E., at different points in the house, and a mass of these records occupied the first part of the file. I could not find that the research had yielded much result.

The rest of the file was filled with records of communications by planchette; in some cases these were transcripts of the questions and answers and in other cases the actual sheets covered with scrawled automatic writing were preserved. Most of them were concerned with a Roman aqueduct and water distribution system in the neighbourhood of Guildford; Honey had apparently selected this as a test case because the details of its plan had been lost in the passage of the centuries, and anything discovered by planchette could be verified fairly easily by excavation. He had amassed a thick bundle of communications from a spirit called Armiger, who was apparently a Roman soldier, but much of the other side of the investigation, the verifying excavations, was missing.

Next came a thin sheaf of papers filed in an envelope; upon the cover was the one word MARY. I hesitated over this, and finally passed on, leaving them unread.

Last came a draft for a thesis, perhaps a paper he had read before the local Society for Psychic Research; it was entitled AUTOMATIC WRITING. It was a carefully prepared description of the Guildford experiments, which showed considerable verification by digging of the facts stated by the planchette. What interested me most, however, as in every technical paper that one scans through quickly, was the paragraph headed 'Conclusions'. Here Honey said:

It is beyond question that information can be obtained by automatic writing which is not obtainable in any other way, provided that the matter is approached in a spirit of serious inquiry, and that the investigator is not put off by the somewhat bizarre donors of information on the other side. It is not possible to obtain information upon any subject that one chooses. It is difficult, if not impossible, to obtain information benefiting the inquirer. The information which appears to come most readily is that benefiting mankind as a whole, or which will benefit a third party who is not aware of the inquiry.

I put the files back thoughtfully, and went to bed.

6

I went to see the Director when I got in first thing next morning. 'I had E.P.Prendergast upon the telephone last night, at my house,' he said. 'He's very much upset.'

'I suppose he told you that Honey's off his head,' I replied. 'I had him yesterday afternoon.'

'Yes, he said that. Of course, Honey lays himself wide open to that sort of thing, and that makes it rather difficult for us. Prendergast has been digging up a lot of Honey's activities in regard to ghosts. I must say, that was news to me.'

'It was news to me, too, yesterday,' I said. 'I know a bit more about it now.' There was nothing to be gained by concealing things; I told the Director that by no design of mine I had been forced to spend the night in Honey's house, and that I had spent the evening going through his private papers. He smiled gently. 'Very wise, if somewhat unconventional,' he said. 'And what do you think of him now, Scott?'

It was sunny and fresh that morning. 'I think exactly as I did,' I said. 'I think that there's a very fair chance that he's right about the Reindeer tail. I think he has a very logical mind. The fact that his interests spread very wide doesn't mean that he's mad. It means that he's sane.'

'And so you feel inclined to maintain your attitude?'

'I do indeed,' I said. 'I don't think we should dream of letting any Reindeer fly more than 700 hours.'

He smiled again, 'Well, I don't mind a fight.' He glanced at me. 'I think we must get Transport Command to fetch Honey back for us,' he said. 'I'll see to that this morning. Then there arises the problem of who to send to Labrador in place of him. When are you reading your paper before the Royal Aeronautical Society, Scott?'

'On Thursday,' I said.

He nodded. 'I want to come to that. But afterwards I think you had better go to Labrador yourself and get this thing cleared up. If we have the formal meeting on Thursday morning at the Ministry and then you read your paper on Thursday night, you should be able to get the night plane to Ottawa after that?'

'If C.A.T.O. will consent to carry me,' I said. 'I think Honey is as sane as you or I, so they'll probably look a bit old-fashioned at me.'

He laughed. 'I want you to go yourself. It's getting on to quite a high level, this thing is, and it's obviously going to make some difficulties.'

'Well, I'd be very glad to go,' I said. 'I'm beginning to feel a trip to Canada would do me good.'

I went out of his office; on my way back to my own place I had to cross the road outside the main administrative block. A very large blue Daimler limousine was just drawing up to the door, driven by a chauffeur; everything about it shone in the sunlight, including the buttons on the man. I wondered sardonically which of the aircraft firms had thought fit to send their representative to us that way, until I saw the only passenger in it was a woman. I passed on without thinking any more about it.

Five minutes later, in my office, Miss Learoyd came in and said. 'There's a lady downstairs wants to see you, Dr Scott. Miss Teasdale.'

I stared at her. 'Who the hell's Miss Teasdale?'

'I don't know. Shall I ring down and ask what her business is?'

I nodded. 'Yes, do that. I'm very busy today.' I was, but I was rather intrigued; in my job it was quite unusual to have a stranger as a visitor, and especially a woman.

Miss Learoyd came back in a minute, round-eyed. 'It's Monica Teasdale, Dr Scott. She says she's come to see you about Mr Honey.'

The name was vaguely familiar in some way, and anything about Honey now concerned me very much indeed. I wrinkled my brows. 'Who is Monica Teasdale?' I asked.

Miss Learoyd gazed at me reproachfully. 'Wouldn't she be the film actress?'

I stared at her. 'Well, I don't know . . .' The thought offended me; I was too busy to be bothered by that sort of person. On the other hand, the Honey matter was now vitally important, and if a movie star had anything to say about him, I should see her. 'You'd better tell them to send her up,' I said at last.

Miss Learoyd, pop-eyed, showed her in a few minutes later; I got up from my desk and met Monica Teasdale in the flesh, whom I had seen upon the screen so many times. She was an older woman than I had thought; she still had the same beauty and appeal, still the same slight figure, the same unwrinkled face, but there was an indefinable sense of age about her; she was not the young girl that I knew upon the screen. Later, I learned to my surprise that she was over fifty.

She came forward with a dazzling smile, with hand outstretched. 'Dr Scott?' she said. 'Dr Scott, I heard so much about you from Mr Honey that I thought, maybe, since there's a mite of trouble going on, I'd come right down and see you and tell you all about it.'

I said, 'Well, Miss Teasdale–that's very good of you. Er–have you known Mr Honey long?' And then I said, 'Would you sit down?'

She said, 'I only met him night before last, flying over to Gander in an airplane.'

I was amazed. 'But . . . did you go to Gander?'

'Sure I did,' she said. 'I was at Gander with him yesterday, up till around midnight when my plane took off for London.'

'Then you know about the accident to the Reindeer?'

'Surely,' she said. 'I actually saw it happen. I could have died laughing.'

It was satisfactory, perhaps, to hear that somebody had got some fun out of this business. I leaned over and offered her a cigarette, which she refused, and said, 'But how did you get back here, then?'

She said, 'I flew right back last night. Out there, your Mr Honey's got himself in quite a spot, Doctor. I guess you know he pulled the landing wheels up, so 'Redgauntlet' couldn't take off from Gander.' I nodded. 'Well, after that there was some trouble, as you'd suppose, and folks were going around declaring that he's mentally deranged–that's what they're saying out there.' I nodded. 'Well, I don't think he's mentally deranged at all, but it's got so that no airline will carry him away from Gander, and as there *is* no other way to get away from Gander, it looks like he'll stay there for quite a while. And that worried him a lot, because he thought he ought to get back and report to you, and tell you what he did.'

'I see,' I said thoughtfully. 'How do you come in on this, Miss Teasdale?'

'I got to kind of like the little man,' she said frankly. 'Seems like he's getting a raw deal. I said that I'd come right back myself and tell you just what happened. At first I couldn't get a passage–they said all the planes were full up, but I got a call long distance to New York–four hours it took to come through, would you believe it!–and I spoke to Solly Goldmann and I said, 'Solly, this is Monica, I've just *got* to get a seat on that Trans World Airline plane this evening back to London. I've just *got* to, Solly. Don't you ask me why, I'll tell you when I see you on the lot, but just you go right round and see the President for me and say that Monica's set down at Gander by the British and she's just *got* to get back to London on that plane tonight.' That's what I said. Well, then I stuck around with Mr Honey, and sure enough when that plane landed around nine o'clock they had a seat for me, and here I am.'

'Did anybody else come back with you from Gander?' I inquired. 'Any of the crew?'

She shook her head. 'They're all sitting around grieving about their airplane, and trying to think of ways of getting it up on its wheels again. They say it weighs seventy tons, and that's a mean load to handle at a place like Gander, seemingly, where all the tools they've got is one jack from the tool-box of a Ford. I expect they'll be there some time with it.'

I asked her, 'Would you tell me exactly what did happen, Miss Teasdale? I'd like to know it all, right from the start.'

'Surely,' she said 'I only came into the story half-way through, but we were barely clear of Ireland, only an hour or so out, when Mr Honey first discovered that that airplane had flown twice the hours it should have done.' She settled down to tell me the whole tale. Honey had briefed her well; she had a little paper of notes in her handbag and she had a letter for me, half a dozen lines scrawled in his vile handwriting, telling me I could depend on her story, and asking me to cable him instructions whether to go on by land or to come back. In half an hour I had the picture very clearly in my mind of what had happened.

'It's been most kind of you to come back here and tell us all this,' I said at last. 'It's really very helpful.'

She said, 'Well, it seemed kind of wrong to go on to the Coast and leave it so.' She glanced at me. 'I like your Mr Honey,' she said quietly. 'I think he's a nice person.'

'It's good of you to say so,' I replied. 'I'm afraid he's interrupted your journey, though.'

She shrugged her shoulders. 'Guess I'd rather be sitting in this office than lying dead some place, even if I am back in England when I meant to be over on the Coast today.'

'You think that there was danger in going on?' I asked curiously. 'Honey convinced you, did he?'

'I don't know anything about these things,' she said. 'Out there at Gander they're all saying that he's nuts. Well, I don't think that–and I've met some crackpots in my time, believe me. I'm just as glad I didn't have to fly on in that airplane, after hearing what he said.' She paused, and then she said, 'I reckon

Captain Samuelson, the pilot of the plane, he was kind of relieved, too, when it sat down on its belly, though he was as mad as hell.'

I nodded thoughtfully. 'Miss Teasdale,' I said, 'would you mind waiting here a minute, while I go and see my chief–the Director of this Establishment? I think he might like to meet you.'

'Sure,' she said. 'Go right ahead.'

I went down to the Director; fortunately he was free. 'About this Honey business, sir,' I said rather desperately. 'I've got a film star here who knows a lot about it. Miss Monica Teasdale.' I had a feeling that my blazing row was getting altogether out of control.

He looked at me, smiling. 'Do you want me to see her, Scott?'

'I think you ought to,' I said. 'She travelled over with Honey and knows all about what happened on the crossing and at Gander. She came back specially to tell us all about it, and so far as I can make out she's the only witness who has come back to this country.'

'Are you going to put this lady from Hollywood up against Sir David Moon and E. P. Prendergast?' he asked. But he was grinning, and I knew that he was pulling my leg.

'I think you ought to see her,' I said stubbornly. 'I don't suppose you'll ever get another chance of moving in such high society.'

'By all means bring her down,' he said. 'I've never met a film star in the flesh.'

She came into his office with a radiant smile and hand a little bit outstretched, a perfect gesture from a very lovely woman. 'Say,' she said, 'it's just terribly nice of you to see me, and I'll try not to waste any of your time. I just wanted to tell you what a marvellous front your Mr Honey put up out at Gander, and how grateful to him I feel as a passenger.'

She launched into the story, as she had with me, and talked for about ten minutes. At the end of that the Director thanked her, talked to her about a few casual matters, asked if she would like to see the less secret parts of the Establishment, and asked me to show her round. I took her out on to the tarmac where the aeroplanes were parked awaiting test, and walked her round a little, and introduced her to Flight-Lieutenant Wintringham, who was properly impressed. And while we were chatting in among the aircraft, he inquired, 'How's Elspeth this morning?'

'Better,' I said. 'She's got a headache and she was sick again during the night–Shirley was up with her a good bit. But she's going on all right.'

'Honey know anything about it yet?'

'No,' I said. 'He's got enough on his plate out at Gander without bothering him with that.' It was common knowledge by that time what had happened.

He laughed boyishly. 'I would like to have seen him do it.'

'Miss Teasdale did,' I said. 'She saw the whole thing happen.'

He turned to her. 'You did?' But she was already speaking to me.

'Who is this Elspeth, anyway?' she asked. 'Not Mr Honey's little girl?'

'That's right,' I replied. 'She fell downstairs the night he went away, the night that you flew over to Gander, Sunday night. She's been rather bad.'

She stared at me. 'How did that happen? Mr Honey told me that he'd got the hired woman to come and stay in the house.'

'She didn't turn up,' I explained. 'Elspeth was alone in the house. She thought she heard a burglar in the middle of the night and got up to see, and fell downstairs and knocked her head. She was unconscious for over twelve hours;

my wife found her about eleven o'clock on Monday morning, lying in a heap at the foot of the stairs. But she's getting on all right now.'

She stared at me in horror. 'The poor child! Where is she now?'

'As a matter of fact, she's lying in my bed,' I said ruefully. 'My wife's looking after her. I slept round at Honey's house last night, and I suppose I'll do the same tonight.'

She said slowly, 'I'm just terribly sorry to hear this, Dr Scott. I know how anxious Mr Honey's going to be when he gets to hear of it—he just thinks the world of his little girl. Is there anything that I can do?'

I smiled. 'It's quite all right, thanks. We shan't tell him about it till he gets back here, I don't think. She's getting on quite well, and it would only upset him.'

She said, 'Your Mr Honey was mighty nice to me, Doctor. Isn't there any little thing that I can do at all?'

I thought for a minute, wondering how far this actress was sincere or putting on an act. It would thrill Shirley to meet her, in any case. 'What are you doing for the rest of today, Miss Teasdale?' I inquired.

'Nothing,' she said. 'I'm completely free.'

'There is just one thing you could do,' I said. 'My wife's tired out; she got practically no sleep last night, sitting up with Elspeth. If you could go and sit with Elspeth while Shirley takes a nap on the sofa, it really would be very kind indeed.'

She said, 'Why, certainly.' She was more Miss Myra Tuppen than Miss Monica Teasdale at that moment; far from the honky-tonk, the simple past was opening before her. 'I'd be real glad to do that. Tell me, where do I go? And will you call your wife and tell her that I'll come right over?'

We went back to the offices and I rang up Shirley and told her simply that a friend of Honey's, a Miss Teasdale, was coming over to sit with Elspeth while Shirley got some sleep. I didn't feel equal to explaining to my tired wife upon the telephone that I was sending her a movie queen. Then we went down and she got into her enormous car, and I told the chauffeur where to find my little flat, and Wintringham and I were left as they moved off.

'The old devil!' he said with a note of admiration in his voice. 'Fancy Honey collecting a Popsie like that!'

It did seem rather curious when you came to think of it.

I went up to my office, but Miss Learoyd said the Director wanted me, and I went down again. He said, 'What have you done with our distinguished visitor, Scott?'

'I've sent her off to sit with Elspeth Honey while my wife gets some sleep,' I said. 'She seemed to want to help, so I took her at her word.'

He raised his eyebrows, 'And she went?'

I grinned. 'She did. Just like an ordinary woman.'

'Really . . .' He asked me about Elspeth, and I told him. And then he said, 'You know, the thing that interested me most in Miss Teasdale's story was the reaction of the pilot, Samuelson. He didn't seem to be sorry that it was impossible to fly that aircraft any farther.'

'I know,' I said. 'I think that wants looking into. He couldn't have diagnosed anything wrong with the machine, though, from his own experience. I wonder if old Honey shook his confidence a bit?'

'Maybe,' he said. 'About Honey, Scott. I've been talking to the Air Ministry.

There's an old Lincoln from the Navigation School due to fly from Winnipeg back here one day this week, and they're instructing it to land at Gander and pick Honey up. I've got a draft signal here from us to him that I'd like you to look at.'

We got that off, and I went back to my office to deal with my overflowing IN basket.

Shirley, wearily cooking up a cup of arrowroot for Elspeth to see if she could keep that down, heard a ring at the door and thought it was the butcher; she was so tired she had already forgotten all about Miss Teasdale. She went with her overall on and a wisp of hair hanging down across her eyes and an enamel tray in her hand to receive the joint, and there was a most lovely and most beautifully turned out woman standing at the head of the dark staircase that led up to our flat. Her face was vaguely familiar and her voice soft and husky and slightly Middle West.

She said, 'Say, it's Mrs Scott, is it?'

Shirley said, 'Oh . . . of course. My husband rang me up.' She fumbled with the tray in her hands. 'I'm so sorry—I thought it was someone else. Please, do come in.'

Miss Teasdale said, 'I was visiting with Dr Scott this morning, and he told me what a time you're having with Mr Honey's little girl, and he suggested I could come and sit with her a while so you could get some sleep. I'd be glad to do that, if it suits you, Mrs Scott. I'm free all day.'

Shirley said mechanically, 'Oh, you don't need to bother—really.' She hesitated. 'Would you come in?'

Miss Teasdale took hold firmly as they went into the sitting-room. 'My dear, you're looking real tired,' she said. I'm a kind of friend of Mr Honey. I'm quite free to stay here up till ten o'clock tonight, or all night if it suits. Just show me where things are and where the little girl is, and then you get off to bed and get some sleep.'

Shirley stared at her. 'Aren't . . . don't I know you?'

'Sure you know me, if you ever go to pictures,' said the actress. 'But that doesn't mean I can't look after a sick child, same as anybody else.'

'Monica Teasdale?'

'That's right.'

'But—do you know Mr Honey?'

'Surely. Now you just—' She stopped and glanced out of the window at the Daimler. 'Just one thing first of all, my dear,' she said quietly. 'We don't want any trouble here with Press or fans or anything. I don't think anybody noticed when I came in. Do you mind—would you go down and tell the chauffeur he's to go right back because I'm staying here a while? Say I'll call them at the office later in the day.'

Shirley went down to the car in a state of tired bemusement, the chauffeur touched his cap to her, and the great car moved off. When she got back to the flat Miss Teasdale was not in the sitting-room; Shirley went down the passage to the bedroom and there she was, standing in the doorway, leaning reflectively against the jamb, looking in at Elspeth, who was sleeping in our double bed, with a basin at her side.

She turned at Shirley's step. 'She's just the image of her father,' she said quietly.

Shirley stopped by her; together they stood looking at the sleeping child.

'She is and she isn't,' she said. 'She's got his features, but she's awfully well proportioned. Look at her hands. I think she may be beautiful when she gets older.'

The actress said quietly, 'That could be.' And then she said, 'Did you know her mother?'

Shirley shook her head. 'I only met Mr Honey a few days ago.' She drew away from the door. 'Don't let's wake her.'

They moved back to the sitting-room. 'Say, is that the only bed you've got?' the actress asked.

Shirley nodded. 'It's only a small flat,' she said. 'We've not been married very long.'

'Kind of difficult for nursing a sick child, isn't it?'

'It's a bit hard on Dennis—my husband. He had to go and sleep in Mr Honey's house last night.'

'Where did you sleep then?'

Shirley laughed. 'I didn't sleep much, anyway. I lay down on the sofa for a bit.'

'Well, you lie right down on that sofa again and get some sleep. I'll sit in the bedroom to be near her if she wakes.' She was tired herself after two nights sitting up in an aircraft, but she did not want to sleep. She could rest sufficiently by sitting quiet by the sleeping child.

Shirley said, 'It's awfully kind of you—I would like to lie down a bit. Let me get some lunch first.' They went together to the kitchen; the actress watched, a little helplessly, while Shirley got out the cold meat and salad and put on a kettle. And then she said, 'Would you like for me to take her up to Claridge's? We've got a suite there permanently reserved where she could have a bedroom and a private nurse and everything . . .'

Shirley said quickly, 'Oh thank you, but that wouldn't do. She'd be worried to death—she wants to get back into her father's house. She's worrying that all their things will get stolen. It wouldn't do to move her up to London—honestly it wouldn't.'

'Okay,' said the older woman. 'It was just an idea.' She watched Shirley for a minute, and then said, 'What were you doing before you got yourself married?'

'I was a tracer.'

'In a drafting office?'

Shirley nodded. 'That's where I met Dennis.'

There was a long pause. 'I was a stenographer,' the older woman said. 'But that was quite a while ago.' She stood in thought, her mind full of memories of Eddie Stillson, the lame ledger clerk.

Shirley stared at her . 'Really? I thought you were always in films.'

'You don't get born that way,' Miss Teasdale said. 'How old are you?'

Shirley said, 'Twenty-four.'

'Well, I've been in pictures all your life, and maybe a bit longer. But I was a stenographer one time, in an insurance office.'

Shirley said curiously, 'How did you come to meet Mr Honey, Miss Teasdale?'

'It was this way.' They sat down to lunch at the dining-table in the little kitchen; as she heard all about it Shirley studied her visitor. She had never before sat and talked with any American; she was overwhelmed by the sophisticated, carefully tended beauty of the actress and confused by the real kindliness of the woman that lay under the sophistication. Above all, she was tired, too tired to take much in.

Miss Teasdale said, 'Now, you go right into that sitting-room and lie down with a rug over you, and let me see you make yourself real comfortable and warm.'

Shirley said, 'I'll just wash these things up first.'

'Wash–oh, the dishes. No, you leave those where they are. I'll see to them.'

It was too incongruous; the woman was not dressed for housework, her nails too carefully manicured for washing dishes, her costume too good. Shirley said, 'No–really, it won't take me a minute.'

'You do what I say.' Shirley was too tired to argue any more; she took off her overall and gave it to the actress, showed her the rusty tin that contained soda. 'This double saucepan's got arrowroot in it,' she said. 'Keep it warm and give Elspeth a cup if she wakes up. The sugar's here. She'd better not have anything else, and if she's sick, just empty the bowl down the lavatory and wash it out, you know. Dr Martin may look in this afternoon. It's awfully kind of you.'

She went into the sitting-room and let down the end of the sofa; under the disciplinary eye of the older woman she lay down and pulled a rug over her. In ten minutes she was fast asleep.

Back in the kitchen, Monica Teasdale started gingerly upon the washing up. She had not done that in years because her negro house servants were genuinely fond of her, and had seldom let her down, but long ago Myra Tuppen had done it after every meal as a matter of course. The greasy feel of hot wet plates stirred memories in her. Old tunes came creeping back into her mind as she stood there at the sink, the dance tunes of her early youth, *Redwing, That Mysterious Rag.* . . . She stood there with these old tunes running through her head, washing the dishes mechanically, a middle-aged woman who had crept back into the past, when everything was bright and promising and new . . .

She finished washing the dishes without breaking anything, and found places for them in the cupboard where they seemed to fit. Then she took off her overall and did up her face in the small mirror of her flapjack. If she had married Eddie Stillson this would have been her life, the kitchen and children in Terre Haute or in some other city of the Middle West. She had done better for herself than that, or had she? She had seen India and China and the Philippines in films upon location, but Eddie Stillson's wife could have learned as much as she about those countries by seeing the films. She had travelled once or twice in Europe for her holidays between the wars, but Eddie Stillson's wife could have learned as much by reading the *Geographic Magazine*–possibly more. She had, however, tangible experiences that Eddie Stillson could not have provided. Twice she had started the Indianapolis Motor Race, in her own State. She had adventured three times into marriage. She had met interesting people in all walks of life; she had entertained Ambassadors. Now as her career was drawing to its close a life of idleness alone in an apartment lay ahead of her. All her experience and all the money she had earned had not secured for her a home and quiet interests for her old age, had not brought her children and grandchildren. She could never have those now, even if she married again. She smiled, a little cynically; for the fourth time. If ever she ventured into matrimony again she would look for very different qualities in a man.

She moved quietly to the sitting-room door and looked in; Shirley was asleep upon the sofa. she glanced around our room, thoughtfully, noting the second-

hand carpet, the ten-year-old radio, the bookcases I had made in the evenings
out of the planks of packing-cases stained with permanganate of potash. There
were many flowers in the room because Shirley was fond of them; one spray of
roses in a tall glass bottle etched with the legend MANOR FARM DAIRY. With a
little pang she recognised the room for what it was, something she had never
really known, the beginning of a home. Somehow, it seemed easier for folks to
make a place like that when there wasn't very much money. When you built a
bookcase with your own hands instead of ordering it by telephone from the
department store complete with books, it was a little tenuous link that bound
you to the home.

She was forgetting her charge; she moved down the short corridor to the
bedroom. Elspeth had turned over in bed; as the actress came to the door she
moved and blinked sleepily, her hair over her eyes, only half awake. Miss
Teasdale said, 'It's all right, honey. Mrs Scott's having a nice sleep and I said I'd
stay around and look after you.'

Elspeth said, 'What's your name?'

'Teasdale–Monica Teasdale. You'd better call me Monica.'

The child asked directly, 'Then why did you call me Honey?'

The actress laughed. 'Why, that's what we call folks back in America, in
Indiana where I was raised. I didn't mean it for your name.'

'My name's Elspeth,' said the child. 'I've been sick six times.'

'Well, don't you be sick again till Mrs Scott wakes up, or maybe I'd not know
what to do about it.'

'Why don't you call her Shirley?'

'I don't know–I only just met her today. That's her name, is it?'

The child nodded. Then she said, 'May I get up and go along the passage?'

'Surely,' said Miss Teasdale quickly. 'Wait–you'd better put something on.'
She looked around a little helplessly.

'It's hanging up behind the door,' the child said. Miss Teasdale looked and
found a very small, worn dressing-gown; Elspeth slipped it on, and put her feet
in bedroom slippers, and went off. The actress moved to the bed, and smoothed
out the bedclothes and pulled out the hot-water bottles, which were cold, and
then Elspeth was back again and climbing into bed.

The actress watched the little active figure in pyjamas getting into bed,
watched with her hands full of hot-water bottles and with her heart full of
regret. She said, 'How do you feel now?'

The child said, 'My head aches when I move about.'

'Sure, it will do after giving it a bump like that. Does it hurt when you stay
still?'

'Not till I think of it. It hurts then.'

Miss Teasdale laughed. 'I'll get these bottles filled.'

'I don't want them, please. They're too hot.'

'Okay. Mrs Scott left arrowroot upon the stove for you. Think you could take
a cup of that?'

'No, thank you.'

The actress said, 'Come on, honey, try a little bit. It'll do you good.'

Elspeth said, 'It can't do me any good if I sick it all up.'

'You won't.'

'I did last time.'

'You won't this time.'

She went into the kitchen and found a cup and saucer and a tin of biscuits, and came back to the bedroom with the arrowroot and crackers on a little tray. The child obediently ate the food and said, 'Do you live in America?'

'Most of the time,' the actress said.

'My daddy's in America—not really in America. He's in Canada. He went on Sunday.'

'I know it. I travelled over with him—that's how I met him. Then I had to come back again directly, and he asked me if I'd come and see how you were getting on.'

Elspeth accepted this without much interest. 'When's he coming home?'

'Quite soon now, I think. Maybe this week.'

'He's been away an awfully long time.'

'Only since Sunday, honey. This is Tuesday.'

'It seems an awfully long time,' the child said.

There was a jigsaw puzzle started upon my drawing-board. 'Say,' said the actress, 'that's an elegant picture. Going to be Southampton Docks, isn't it, with all the liners?' She fetched the board, and they began doing it together.

When I got home that night at about half-past six I found Shirley just waking up upon the sofa; she sat up sleepily as I came in and asked what time it was. We went together to the bedroom. Miss Teasdale got up as we came in. She had been reading to Elspeth; the bed was littered with books from our bookcase: *The Oxford Book of English Verse*, *Puck of Pook's Hill*, and *The Earthly Paradise*. Elspeth had not been sick again, and they had a cup of tea together and some bread and butter. 'We finished the puzzle,' said the actress. 'We've been reading for a while.'

Elspeth said to Shirley, 'She does read well, Mrs Scott. She reads much better than Miss Lansdowne or anybody at school. You sort of actually see things happening when she's reading out loud.'

Miss Teasdale laughed, a little self-consciously, which was odd in so sophisticated a woman. 'I guess I've had some practice,' she said quietly.

'She says she'll teach me to read like that when I get bigger,' Elspeth said.

'Sure I will, honey.' She gathered up the books. 'You've got a nice selection of good books,' she said. 'This author, William Morris—I've never met his work before. Elspeth wanted me to read her some of this.'

Shirley took over to give Elspeth a bath and make her ready for bed; I took Miss Teasdale into the sitting-room and mixed her a drink. 'It's been terribly kind of you to come and help us out like this,' I said, lighting her cigarette. 'Shirley slept five hours this afternoon.'

She nodded. 'I might say it's kind of you folks to look after Mr Honey's little girl,' she said. 'As I see it, you hadn't any call to do so.'

I laughed. 'Well, it was I who sent her father off.'

She nodded. 'Surely.' And then she said, 'I don't know if you'll believe me if I say it's been a real pleasure to me, sitting here this afternoon, playing and reading with Elspeth.'

She hesitated. 'Some women have a lot to do with children, and some don't,' she said. 'I'm one of the ones who don't.'

I nodded. It seemed difficult to pursue that subject with this exotic woman. 'We fixed up about Mr Honey coming back from Gander,' I said, 'An R.A.F. Lincoln is going to pick him up one day this week and bring him over.'

She nodded. 'And what happens after that?'

I laughed. 'Then we're going to have the hell of a row.'

'Say, not over what he did at Gander, pulling up the wheels?'

'Oh, not with him,' I said. 'We're on his side–I think he did quite right. The trouble is we haven't any evidence to prove it.'

I told her briefly what the row was all about, and mentioned that I should be going out to Labrador myself. Then I asked her plans, and persuaded her to stay and have supper with us. 'It'll probably only be the same bit of cold meat you had for lunch,' I said. 'We might cook up a Welsh rarebit or something, afterwards.' She called her office in Wardour Street and ordered the car for nine o'clock to take her back to Claridge's. Summoning the company's car forty miles out into the country to pick her up at that time of night seemed the most natural thing in the world to her.

She was interested in Honey, and kept leading the conversation round to him. She wanted to know what place he held in the organisation of the R.A.E., what we thought about him in the office. I had some difficulty in answering that one. 'He's an inside man,' I said, using the words that the Director had used about him to me. 'He's deeply interested in research and he doesn't concern himself very much with user problems. Opinions vary about him; lots of people think he's crackers.'

'Do you?' she asked.

I laughed. 'No–I think he's very good, within his own sphere. But I shan't send him out upon a job again. From now on he stays in the laboratory, where he belongs.'

'I don't think that's fair,' she said. 'He wants to get around and meet more people.'

I smiled at her. 'He can do that at the week-ends. I don't want any more Reindeers broken up.' That seemed badly phrased, and I regretted it as soon as the words were out of my mouth. 'I mean, a man who was more interested in operations would have found some other means of stopping that thing flying on.'

'I don't know about that,' she objected. 'The little man was in a mighty tough spot. Nobody believed him.'

'That's what I mean,' I said. 'He's an inside man. If he'd been an athletic type six foot two in height and weighing fourteen stone, with a red face and a fist like a ham, they'd have believed him all right, and he wouldn't have had to crash the aeroplane.'

'Maybe,' she said thoughtfully.

'He hated going, anyway,' I said. 'I had to force him and now I'm sorry that I did. I thought he was the best man to send. He's only really happy on his own research.'

Later on, while we were eating the cold meat and salad, she said, 'Have you got a lot of scientists like Mr Honey in your organisation, Doctor?'

'Hundreds,' I said. 'I'm one of them. We're all bats in our own way.'

She said, 'He knows an awful lot about a lot of things. I never mixed with scientists before. He was telling me about the end of the world coming, all from the Great Pyramid. Say, do you believe in that?'

'No,' I said, 'I don't. But then I didn't really believe him first of all when he said the Reindeer tail was going bad on us. Now I think I do.' I turned to her. 'There's no doubt that he's got a very penetrating mind,' I said. 'He's full of scientific curiosity. We'd have done better in the war if we'd paid some attention to his crazy notions.' I was thinking of the rockets.

'I think he's a great little man,' she said quietly. 'With a brain like that and at the same time so simple and so kind.'

Her car came for her at nine o'clock. She said to Shirley almost diffidently, 'Mrs Scott, do you think I might come down tomorrow and sit with Elspeth? I certainly would like to do that.'

Shirley said, 'Oh please, don't bother. It's been terribly nice of you to help us out today, but we'll be all right now. I think she'll sleep tonight.'

The actress said, 'It wouldn't be a trouble. I'd be glad to do it. I did enjoy being with her this afternoon.'

Shirley said doubtfully, 'Would you really like to? Haven't you got more important things to do?'

Miss Teasdale shook her head. 'I've got nothing fixed. I've got to be back on the West Coast in ten days from now, but up till then I'm free. I certainly would like to spend another day with her.'

Shirley laughed. 'I won't say no to that. She's got to stay in bed a week, and keeping her amused is going to be a job.'

'Okay,' said the actress. 'I'll be with you in the morning, around eleven o'clock.'

We stood and watched the car move off. Elspeth was still occupying our only bed, so it was necessary for me to go and sleep in Honey's house again, while Shirley slept on the sofa. 'I rather like the sofa,' she said. 'I'll be all right there if Elspeth doesn't keep on being sick all night again.'

We went back into the house to get my bag with my night things in it. Shirley walked round to the little villa in Copse Road with me; it was only ten minutes away and she felt that she could leave Elspeth for that time. 'I was round there this morning,' she said as we went. 'Isn't it simply foul?'

I hadn't noticed anything much wrong with it. 'It hasn't got much furniture in the sitting-room,' I said.

'I don't mean that. Didn't you see the kitchen floor? It's absolutely filthy; and the scullery's disgusting. It can't have been properly washed out for years.'

We reached the house, and she took me and showed me all the horrors. They didn't seem very bad to me, but then I am a man. Shirley said, 'We can't send Elspeth back here with the place like this—it isn't healthy.' She thought for a minute. 'I'll come round tomorrow and have a go at it.'

'You don't have to do that,' I said. 'It's not our house and we've not made it dirty.'

'We can't leave it like this,' she said firmly. 'If Miss Teasdale turns up, I'll come round here tomorrow.'

'What about the school?'

'I've only got one period tomorrow.'

'I shouldn't bank upon Miss Teasdale,' I said. 'You'll probably get a phone call saying she can't make it.'

Shirley said, 'I think she'll come. Do you know–' She stopped.

'What?'

'Oh–nothing. It was just a stupid idea.'

'What's that?'

She hesitated. 'It would be funny if there was something between her and Mr Honey, wouldn't it?'

I stared at her. 'There couldn't be . . .'

'I suppose there couldn't. But one or two things she said made me kind of wonder.'

She went away, and I got in a couple of hours upon the 'Aircraft Flying at High Mach Numbers' before I got too sleepy.

Next morning, in the office, the Director sent for me. 'I have arranged a meeting for eleven o'clock tomorrow morning,' he said, 'at the Ministry. It's going to be quite a big meeting, with representatives of C.A.T.O. and the Company, and M.C.A., as well as the M. of S. and ourselves. You'll bring up everything we're likely to require?'

'Very good, sir. You'll be coming up yourself?'

'Oh, I think so. I think we shall need all the weight that we can muster, Scott.'

'What about Honey, sir?' I asked. 'Will he be back?'

'I rather doubt it. I think we may have to get along without him. I only know that the Lincoln is picking him up at Gander one day this week.'

'Pity,' I said. 'It would have been better if we could have had him there.'

He nodded. 'Carnegie wanted to see Sir Phillip Dolbear's letter about Honey's work. I sent him a copy of that yesterday.'

I made a grimace. It was impossible to hide up evidence like that, but it wasn't going to make it any easier for us to persuade them that the Reindeer tail was dangerous.

'They're getting back the pilot of the Reindeer, Captain Samuelson, in time for the meeting, I understand. We should get an informed account from him upon exactly what took place.'

'I don't like that,' I said. 'We're going to get the Organisation's account of what happened, but not our own. If we're going to have the pilot of the aircraft, we should have Honey too.'

He shrugged his shoulders. 'We've got to work on the assumption we shall get a fair account. You wouldn't suggest bringing in Miss Monica Teasdale, I suppose?'

I grinned. 'I don't think she could add much to our meeting, except glamour.'

He said grimly. 'Well, we may need light relief before this thing blows over.' He paused. 'I forgot to say, the Treasury are sending somebody, to hold a watching brief for the expenditures involved.'

I left him, and went down to the old balloon shed to see how the Reindeer tail on test was getting on. It was now running day and night; the graphs showed nothing yet that we could cite as any evidence of trouble. I had hoped that something would have turned up in the readings that I could take with me to the meeting as an evidence of abnormality, as a warning. There was nothing of that sort at all.

'I don't think there will be, sir,' young Simmons said. 'Mr Honey was convinced that it would go on like this right up to the end.'

While I was down there, Miss Learoyd rang through. 'There's a lady waiting in the Reception to see you,' she said. 'A Miss Corder.'

I said, 'Do you know who she is?'

'She's got a letter to give you from Mr Honey, sir.'

I blinked; another woman from Honey. 'All right,' I said. 'Have her shown up and ask her to wait. I'll be up in a few minutes.'

When I got up to my office there was a tall, dark girl sitting on an upright chair against the wall, waiting for me. She was dressed quietly in a dark blue coat and skirt; she wore a very simple hat. She was quite young, very attractive, and with the most beautiful features and colouring.

'I'm sorry to have kept you waiting,' I said. 'It's Miss Corser, is it?'

She had risen to her feet as I entered. 'Corder,' she said. 'I have a letter for you, sir, from Mr Honey.' She opened her bag and gave it to me. 'He said that it was very urgent, so I thought it would be better if I brought it down by hand.'

'Oh—thank you,' I said. 'When did he give you this?'

'Last night, sir,' she said, 'at about ten o'clock—just before I left Gander.' She explained, 'I was one of the stewardesses on the Reindeer that got damaged at Gander, the one that Mr Honey crossed in. Most of the aircrew are staying at Gander with the aircraft, but we stewards were recalled to London. I suppose they'll put me in another aircraft; there's no point in keeping us with the machine till it's repaired. So as I was to come back last night, Mr Honey asked me if I would bring this letter with me and let you have it immediately I landed. I thought I'd better bring it down at once.'

'You landed this morning?'

'Yes, sir.'

She stood silent, holding her bag in her hands before her while I opened and read the letter.

It was not a very long one. He said that I must know all the facts by that time from Miss Teasdale. He had been thinking it all over, and while he did not see what else he could have done, he realised that his action must have let down the reputation of the R.A.E. He said that for some time past he had felt that perhaps he was out of place in the department, and it might well be that this was the time when he should make a break and find some other employment. He did not want to embarrass me in any way, but he would like me to consider that letter as his resignation.

I said quietly, 'Oh, damn . . .' and read it through again, biting my lip. It was another complication in this business; if Honey resigned, how could I maintain my attitude of taking a firm line by showing confidence in his judgment? He would have to be persuaded to withdraw his resignation and fight this thing through with me, and now he was in Gander, inaccessible. I raised my eyes, and the dark stewardess was staring at me in distress.

I said, 'Well . . . thank you for bringing me this, Miss Corder. I'll have to think it over.' I paused, and then said, 'Do you know what's in it?'

'I think so—more or less.' She stared at me appealingly. 'It's his resignation, isn't it?'

I nodded. 'That's right. I didn't want him to resign.'

'You didn't want him to? He thought you'd all be so angry with him.'

I cursed the comedy of misunderstandings. 'I'm not angry with him,' I replied. 'I wish he hadn't had to stop it flying in that way, but if that was the only way to ground it, then I think he did quite right. I'm backing him up all I can. Probably lose my own job over this before we're through.'

'Oh,' she said, relieved. 'I wish he'd known that.'

I chucked the letter on to my desk. 'You'll have a cup of tea?' She protested, but I opened the door and told Miss Learoyd to see if she could raise two cups of tea, and coming back I made the stewardess sit down beside my desk. I offered her a cigarette, which she refused. 'Tell me,' I said, 'how is Honey, in himself? Is he worrying about this very much?'

'He is, rather,' she said. 'You see, he hasn't anything to do, and the crew said some horrid things to him after it happened. Not Captain Samuelson, but some of the others.' I sat watching her as she talked, wondering who did the picking of the stewardesses and where they found such very charming girls. 'I thought a little exercise might take his mind off it, sir, so I got him to take me for a long walk yesterday, and I think that helped. He's very fond of hiking.'

I smiled. 'You've been looking after him, have you?'

'He was the only passenger I had left,' she replied. 'All the others went on, the same day.'

I nodded. 'Tell me just what happened.'

7

When the Reindeer settled down upon the tarmac she went slowly; the men standing in the flight deck staggered and reached for something to hang on to, but they were not thrown down. They stood petrified for an instant after the fuselage reached the ground, listening aghast to the rending and crashing noise of crumpling propeller blades and duralumin panels as the weight came on to yielding parts of the structure; then there was silence, and they came to life again.

Samuelson was the first to speak. He said dully, 'Well, that's the bloody limit.' And then he turned to Symes, the inspector. 'Come outside, Mr Symes.'

He turned away without a word to Mr Honey, who got up from the control pedestal that he had been embracing, his face scarlet and with tears running down his cheeks. The inspector looked him up and down, snorted, and followed the captain down into the saloon and so to the ground, to view the damage from outside.

In the control deck Dobson turned to Honey. 'You bloody little squirt,' he said. 'Pleased with what you've done?'

Mr Honey made a helpless gesture with his hands, but said nothing. Behind them the note of the auxiliary motor dropped and died; the engineer had switched if off, in case of fire.

Dobson said again, 'Pleased with what you've done?'

Honey raised his head. 'It was the only thing to do. You wouldn't believe me. If you'd gone on everybody might have been killed.'

Cousins, the engineer, pressed forward passionately. He loved his aircraft. He had worked upon it for three months before it flew; since then he had lived in it for much of the time, and he had tended it lovingly; he existed for nothing else. 'Nonsense,' he said passionately. 'There was nothing wrong with that tail, and you know it. Who the hell are you, anyway? Just a bloody penpusher and slide-rule merchant. What the hell do you know about aircraft?'

Dobson said, 'That's right. Have you ever flown anything? Ever piloted anything yourself? Come on, speak up.'

'No,' said Honey helplessly, 'I've never been a pilot.'

'What the hell do you know about aeroplanes, then, if you've never had to do with them? You say you come from Farnborough. God, I've heard some tales about that place, but this beats everything.'

Cousins laughed bitterly. 'That's what they do there, come around and smash things up. He'll get an O.B.E. for this, you see.' He turned to Honey passionately. 'Get out of here, you dirty little swine, before I sock you one.'

Honey turned and went down into the saloon without a word. From the ground Samuelson called up to Dobson to bring down a signal pad. The two pilots stood in front of the wrecked Reindeer drafting a quick signal to their Flight Control in London; then Dobson went hurriedly with it to the control tower, passing Miss Corder on the way.

Mr Honey stood around upon the tarmac for an hour, with nobody paying any attention to him. There was a bitter north-east wind and he grew colder and colder; presently he got back into the fuselage and sat down in his seat, miserable and chilled. Miss Corder, coming to the aircraft presently to clean up and remove the unused food, observed him sitting in the unlit cabin half-way down the aisle.

She went up to him, 'I should go into the lounge, sir,' she said. 'In the restaurant building. All the other passengers are there.'

He said dolefully, 'I don't think they'd be very pleased to see me.'

She said, 'Oh . . . But have you had any breakfast?'

He shook his head. 'I don't want any.'

'But you must have some breakfast!' She thought for a moment. 'I know,' she said. 'There's a little private office you can use. Come with me.'

He followed her obediently out of the aircraft and across the tarmac and into the main building by a side door. She took him to a little room marked on the door PASSPORTS AND IMMIGRATION. It was rather a bare room with a deal table, ink-stained, and a few hard chairs, but it was warm and it was private. She said, 'Stay here and make yourself comfortable, Mr Honey. I'll bring you some breakfast.'

She came back presently with a tray of eggs and bacon and coffee and toast and marmalade, and set it down before him on the table. 'There,' she said. 'Get that in you and you'll feel better.'

He said warmly, 'It's terribly kind of you to look after me like this, especially when I've made such a lot of trouble.'

She smiled at him. 'You've not made any trouble for me,' she said.

'What about the other passengers? What's going to happen to them?'

'We've had a signal that a Hermes is coming up to fetch them,' she said. 'It's arriving about two o'clock.' She hesitated, and then said, 'Will you be going on with them, sir?'

'I don't know. I should like to have a talk with Captain Samuelson as soon as he can spare the time.'

She nodded. 'I'll tell him. Now, eat your breakfast. I'll be along for the tray presently.'

Mr Honey was hungry, and made quite a substantial meal. When it was over he lit a cigarette, feeling more at ease. Samuelson, coming in to see him, found him sitting in a chair beside the radiator.

'Morning, Mr Honey,' he said. 'You wanted to see me?'

Honey got up from his chair. 'I wanted to apologise for all the trouble that I've caused you,' he said simply. 'Not for the Reindeer—that had to be grounded anyway. But I'm sorry about the work I've had to put on you and for the inconvenience to all the other passengers.'

The pilot laughed shortly. 'Don't bother about me. If I wasn't doing this I'd be doing something else.'

Mr Honey asked, 'Is the aircraft very much damaged?'

'I don't know. Until we raise her up we can't make a proper inspection, and that won't be for some time. There's no equipment here to lift an aircraft of this size. We've got no air bags. They'll have to be shipped from England. The whole job may take months.'

The scientist said nothing.

The captain said, 'I've had to send a full report about it all to Headquarters, Mr Honey. The other passengers are going on to Montreal this afternoon, but I'm rather doubtful if C.A.T.O. will carry you–after this. I think you may have to go down to St John's and go on by boat.'

Mr Honey blinked at him. 'Oh . . .'

'Well, look at it from their point of view. They don't have to carry you if they're afraid of you damaging their equipment.'

'I don't make a habit of doing this,' said Honey unhappily. 'I don't do it every time.'

'No. Well, it will all have to be sorted out in London. I expect we'll get some signals as the day goes on.'

'I don't know what the R.A.E. will want me to do,' said Mr Honey, 'after this. They may cable me and tell me to come home and not go to Labrador.'

'I see . . .' The pilot glanced at him. 'You were going out to reopen an inquiry on Bill Ward's crash?'

'Er–the Reindeer that fell in Labrador.'

'That's right. The one that is supposed to have flown into the hill. Bill Ward's crash.'

'That's the machine. I was to inspect the spar fractures in the tailplane and bring samples back for metallurgical examination.'

'You think the tail came off that aircraft in the air, don't you?'

'It might have done,' said Mr Honey. It had flown nearly 1,400 hours, which comes in very close accord with the estimated time to failure.'

The pilot stared out of the window. 'Bill Ward never flew into a hill,' he said. 'He couldn't have done. I knew that part of the accident report was utter nonsense from the first.'

Mr Honey blinked at him. 'You think that something else happened? Something like a tailplane failure?'

The pilot said, 'I just don't know, and it's not for me to guess. But strictly between you and me, Mr Honey, I'm not sorry personally that you've taken a strong line, in spite of all the trouble that it's going to mean for both of us. If I'd been able to, I'd have taken that machine on to Montreal. But as things are, I can't say that I'm sorry. I don't aim to be the bravest pilot in the world. Just the oldest.'

He went away, and crossing the waiting-room he had to run the gauntlet of the passengers. He answered a number of questions about transport on to Montreal; then came the film actress, Miss Teasdale.

She said, 'Say, Captain, I don't see Mr Honey anywhere around. Is he here some place?'

He told her where she could find him, and presently she tapped at Mr Honey's door. He called out, 'Er–come in,' and she opened the door and stood there looking at him quizzically.

'Well,' she said, 'you certainly have got the strength of your convictions, haven't you?'

He smiled weakly. 'You've got to do what you can. Won't you come in and sit down? I'm afraid it's not very clean in here.'

She seated herself on a hard chair on the other side of the table, and lit a cigarette with a gold lighter. 'How do you think your people back at Farnborough will react now?' she asked.

Honey said, 'I don't know and I don't much care. You've got to do the best you can,' he repeated a little desperately. 'You've got to do what you think is the right thing to do.'

She nodded. He was terribly like what Eddie Stillson had been, thirty years ago—always worrying about doing the right thing. She asked, 'This Dr Scott that you were speaking of. He's the boss, isn't he? How will he take it?'

Honey said, 'I think he'll be all right. He's quite a young man, much younger than I am. I think he'll see it was the only thing to do. But he's not the head of the Establishment by any means—and then there's the Ministry over the whole lot of us. I'm afraid there'll be a great deal of trouble.'

She laughed. 'I'll say there'll be some trouble. You should hear the second pilot talking, Mr Dobson. He takes it kind of personally.' She paused. 'What do you plan to do now, Mr Honey? Will you go on to Labrador?'

He shook his head. 'I can't make up my mind. But from what the captain said I can't go anywhere—by air, that is. He says the company won't take me.'

She nodded. There had been some very frank talk in the waiting-room about the passenger who had become mentally deranged by the excitement of the flight. 'It's just a lot of hooey,' she said. 'But if they won't carry you by air you can't make them, though your office might be able to.'

'I don't know what to do,' he said irresolutely. 'If I write a letter it would take about three days to get to Farnborough. I suppose I ought to try and send a cable somehow, and ask what I'm to do.'

'What do you want to do, yourself?' she asked. 'Go on to Ottawa or go back to Farnborough?'

He replied, 'Oh, I'd like to go back. I didn't want to come away at all. You see, there's nobody looking after Elspeth except Mrs Higgs, and she isn't very reliable. I'd much rather go back to Farnborough. After all, the basic work is more important than this sort of thing.'

They talked about his movements for some time. She learned that he had little interest in his mission to Canada; the travelling, the change of scene, did not excite him. He regarded it as so much time wasted from the progress of his real work, as a distraction which he had been forced by discipline to submit to. She found him restless and unhappy, uncertain whether he could exploit the damage to the Reindeer as an excuse to give up his mission in Canada and to return to the work he loved, and to his home.

'I don't know what to do,' he said. 'I can't make up my mind. And one can't put it all into a cable, either.'

They sat talking of his difficulties for some time. For many years the actress had been out of touch with the hard realities of life. She had not been short of money for thirty years and she would never be again. All her working life had been spent in the facile world of honky-tonk, a synthetic emotion and of phoney glamour. Now she was getting a glimpse into a new world, a world of hard, stark facts, a world in which things had to be exactly right or people would be

killed. There was no place for glamour or emotion in a world that had to say if
the Reindeer tail was going to break or not. She was beginning to perceive that
little insignificant men like Mr Honey were the brains behind the world, just as
lame Eddie Stillson had been the coming brain of the Century Insurance office.
The perception brought out everything that was still good in her; nineteen-
year-old Myra Tuppen came to life again, suppressing Monica Teasdale. As
she sat talking to Mr Honey the desire to help him grew; she felt that she could
play a small part in a bigger production than any she had starred in. And help
she could; in travelling Monica Teasdale had unquestioned priority.

She said, 'Say, Mr Honey, how would it be if I went back to England and
took a letter to your Dr Scott? It would get to him first thing tomorrow
morning, that way. I'd be real pleased to go, if it would help any.'

He was staggered at the suggestion. Unused to travelling himself, it seemed
extraordinary to him. 'You mean, you'd fly back to England? But you're going
on to Montreal, aren't you?'

She shrugged her shoulders. 'I'm not dated up. I've got to be in Hollywood
on the twenty-seventh, but that's eleven days from now. I was reckoning I'd
stop off in Indianapolis for a few days before flying on home, but I'd just as
soon stop over those few days at Claridge's in London. I kind of like London,
for all it's such a dirty town.'

He blinked at her. 'But it would be so expensive for you to go back.'

She said simply, 'I wouldn't pay. All my travelling goes on to the expense
account. Honestly, Mr Honey, I'd be real glad to do that if it would help.'

He was bewildered by this woman, whom with his dead wife he had adored
upon the movies; bewildered by her hard competence, by her sophistication, by
her carefully tended beauty and her luxurious clothes, by the incongruous
kindliness and small-town warmth of her consideration. He had never met
anyone in the least like her before, never had dealings with anybody from her
world. He said uncertainly, 'Well, that would be very helpful, certainly, Miss
Teasdale. But it seems an awful lot to ask you to do.'

She said, 'I'm interested in this thing, Mr Honey, and I'd like to see it
through. And if I can help any by going back instead of stopping in the Middle
West a week, I'd like to do it. After all, it is kind of important, this, and
Indiana's no novelty to me.'

He said, 'But can you get a passage back today?'

Her lips tightened. 'I can try.'

She left him to think out a letter to me that she could take with her, and found
Dobson, and smiled dazzlingly at him so that he took her meekly to the Control,
where she was very charming and just terribly sorry to be such a nuisance, but
could she get a call down to New York? She delighted the Control Officer for
four hours with her conscious charm, and left his office in the end with her
return passage to London arranged and little lines of strained fatigue around
her lovely eyes. Time was, she thought a little bitterly, when she could do that
sort of thing just naturally. With the last remnants of her energy she charmed
Dobson into arranging a bedroom for her use, and went and pulled the shade
down and lay down upon the bed to rest.

Marjorie Corder was busy all the morning cleaning up the galley and the
passengers' quarters of the wrecked Reindeer and in arranging lunch for the
stranded passengers. She found time to visit Mr Honey with a cup of coffee in
the middle of the morning, and to bring him a selection of magazines. She

arrived just after Samuelson had visited him again, to break the news to him that C.A.T.O. had refused to carry him any farther in their aircraft. She found him worried and distressed; he told her all about it.

'I don't know what to do,' he said. 'I suppose I'll have to try and get away from here by train. But now they say there isn't a train till Thursday.'

'Drink your coffee while it's hot,' she suggested. 'It'll all come out all right, you see.'

He sipped it obediently. 'What are you doing?' he inquired. 'Are you going on with the passengers to Montreal?'

She shook her head. 'We shall stay here till we get some orders. The aircrew always stay with their own machine. The Hermes that's coming up will have its own steward.' She smiled. 'So after all the rest have gone on, I shall only have you to look after.'

He said diffidently, 'I'm terribly sorry to make so much trouble.'

She stood looking down upon him kindly. 'Last night you told me where to go if anything happened,' she said, 'where it would be safe. I don't suppose I'd have gone, but it was nice of you to tell me. I'm glad to be able to do something in return. It's my job to see that you're made comfortable, of course, but I'd want to do that anyway, for what you tried to do for me.'

He said awkwardly, 'I didn't do anything.'

She said, 'You'd rather have your lunch in here, sir, wouldn't you? You don't want to mix with the other passengers?'

He said, 'Er–if it's not an awful lot of trouble.'

'Of course it's not,' she said. 'I'll bring it you about one o'clock. There's cold meat or hot Irish stew, and I saw some cold salmon in the larder, but there's not enough of that to go round so I think the staff are having it. Would you like a salmon mayonnaise?'

He said, 'I'd love that, if it's going.' And he gave her one of his shy, warming smiles.

She nodded. 'There's treacle tart afterwards or semolina pudding.'

'Treacle tart, please.'

She nodded. 'And coffee?'

'Please.'

'Bottle of beer?'

'Well–if there is one–yes, that would be very nice.'

She nodded. 'Have you got enough to smoke?'

'Well–I would like another packet of cigarettes. Player's, if they've got them.'

'I'll get you those at once.'

She brought his cigarettes and a box of matches, and a few minutes later she took an easy chair from the lounge and carried it along the passage and put it in the office for him. Mr Honey sat reading the *Cosmopolitan* and smoking his cigarettes in some comfort, warmed by the solicitude of the girl. He felt in better spirits now, ready to face whatever might be coming to him.

The Hermes from Quebec came in and landed before lunch; Mr Honey stood at his window and watched it taxi in. Miss Corder brought him his tray of lunch, with the salmon and the bottle of beer. 'All the other passengers are having their lunch now,' she said. 'They're going on in the Hermes as soon as it's refuelled. All except Miss Teasdale, who's decided that she wants to go back to England.'

He said, 'She's very kindly offered to take a note back to Dr Scott for me. It seems an awful imposition, but she offered to, and it really is a great help.'

The girl said, 'I should think she's very nice, when you get to know her.'

'I think she is,' said Honey. 'Of course, one thinks one knows her from seeing her films, but really, she's quite a different person altogether.' He laughed. 'It's a bit confusing.'

Miss Corder said, 'I think her films are lovely. I never miss one if I can help it.'

She went out, and Mr Honey ate his lunch, and presently stood at his window watching the Hermes load up with its passengers and taxi out towards the runway's end, watched it as it left the ground and slid off into the distance. He turned again to the *Cosmopolitan*; presently the stewardess came back to take his tray.

'You don't have use this office any longer, sir, unless you want to,' she said. 'There's nobody here now except the crew and Miss Teasdale.'

He said, 'Well—I'll sit in the lounge. Where is Miss Teasdale?'

'I think she's lying down, sir. Shall I bring your coffee to the lounge?'

'Oh—yes, please do.'

He stayed in the lounge all afternoon. Three or four aircraft landed to refuel, and there was a stream of passengers from them in and out, stretching their legs and gossiping together over cups of coffee or short drinks. Mr Honey sat insignificant in a corner, unhappy. Now that the first excitement had passed, he was miserably anxious about his own position; clearly there was going to be a most appalling row about the Reindeer, and he was quite unused to rows and hated them. Personal unpleasantness always upset his work; he could not think clearly if his mind was full of hard things that had been said about him, and he liked thinking clearly. Rows frightened him; he would go to considerable lengths to avoid them. For the first time in years the thought of resigning his position at the R.A.E. entered his mind.

If things got too nasty, he could always do that. He could resign and not go there any more. True, it would be a terrible wrench to part from the work he loved; true he would have to find another job. But he was not unknown in the intimate, unpublicised, middle world of science; he was on blinking and smiling terms with the heads of several other research departments. Perhaps a little niche would open out for him at the National Physical Laboratory or the Admiralty Research Laboratory. He knew people at both places, and he could be happy there, though not so happy as he now felt he had been while dealing with fatigue in light alloy structures.

By tea-time he was in a state of deep dejection. When Marjorie Corder brought him his tea, unasked, she noticed his preoccupation. 'Haven't you been out?' she asked. 'Have you been sitting here all the time?'

He nodded. 'I've had a lot to think about.'

'It's nice outside,' she said. 'There's a cold wind, but if you wrap up well it's rather lovely.'

He was not listening to her words; he only heard her sympathy 'I wish they'd cable and say what I'm to do,' he muttered. 'I'm afraid I shall have to resign.'

'Resign your job?' she said. She looked down at him with deep compassion; he was such an unhappy little man and yet so terribly clever. 'You mustn't think of that. They'll understand, back at your office.'

'I think I'll have to,' he said miserably. 'I think it's the only thing to do.'

She said gently, 'Look, I got you some buttered toast, and there's anchovy paste here and jam. I got you strawberry jam, but would you rather have apricot? There's apricot if you'd rather have that.'

He roused, and smiled at her. 'No–I like strawberry, thank you.'

She poured out his tea for him. 'Is that how you like it? I brought you a piece of cherry cake and a piece of madeira, but there's more of either if you want it.'

'Oh, thank you very much, but I don't think I shall want any more. I don't think I shall get through all of this.'

'Well, let's see you try.'

She went away and had her own tea in the staff room, but in her turn she was preoccupied. She recognised in Mr Honey a man of moods, capable of deep depression; all geniuses, she had read, were men like that. She was not a very talented girl herself, nor very highly educated; she had had to go to work too early. She was firmly convinced that Mr Honey was a genius and that he was right about the Reindeer tail. She could not help him in the matter of the Reindeer directly, but she might be able to do something to ease the burdens on his mind. It shocked her that he should be talking of resigning from the R.A.E. She felt dimly that if that were to happen her country would have suffered an irreparable loss, because he was the cleverest man that she had ever met. He had seen through into her secret places at one glance, and had known that she would be good with children.

When she went to take his tray, she asked, 'Do you play chess, Mr Honey?'

He looked up in surprise. 'Chess? I haven't played for years. My–my wife and I used to play in the evenings, sometimes. It's a very good game.'

'I can play a little,' she said. 'I'm not very good. Would you like a game or would you rather read?'

He roused. 'No–I'd like a game of chess. Are you sure that you can spare the time, though?'

'I've only got two passengers left now,' she said, 'you and Miss Teasdale, and she's still lying down. I'll bring the things along.' She took his tray.

She played three games with him, and beat him once; she suspected that he had contrived to be mated by her, and she liked him for it. In the course of the two and a half hours she had learned a good deal about Elspeth. 'What do you do about her clothes, Mr Honey?' she asked curiously. 'Who buys those for you?'

He said, 'Oh, whenever she needs anything I take her to a shop in Farnham. The woman that keeps it is really very helpful, and I buy what she says.'

She stared at him. 'But do you just take what's in the one shop?'

He replied, 'Well, yes, I do. I suppose one ought to go to other shops sometimes, but it's so much easier to do it that way.' He hesitated. 'I've sometimes thought that Elspeth isn't dressed quite like the other girls at school,' he admitted. 'I suppose I ought to learn a bit more about what schoolgirls wear. Do you think if I took in *Vogue*, or some paper like that, it would help?'

She was at a loss. 'I don't think that's quite the right sort of paper,' she said. 'I'll think of something and let you know, if you like.'

'I wish you would,' he said. 'She's getting so big now that I think I ought to do something.' He paused, and then he said, 'Mrs Higgs gives me a lot of advice, but I don't know that Elspeth isn't outgrowing that.'

'Who's Mrs Higgs?'

'She's the charwoman. She's got a lot of children of her own, and she's really been very helpful.'

'Oh. . . .'

Later on she asked him, 'What do you do at the week-ends?'

He said, 'Well, we don't do very much. Cleaning the house up takes us a lot of time, of course, and then there's the garden to be done and cooking. It just seems to go.' He turned to her. 'There never seemes to be time for anything. When—when Mary was there we always had time to do things on a Sunday–photography or hiking in the summer. But now there just doesn't seem to be time.'

She nodded. 'Are you fond of hiking?'

'We used to do a lot,' he said.

'Staying in Youth Hostels?' she inquired, her eyes gleaming.

'Sometimes. Have you done that?' He was interested.

She nodded. 'I had a lovely holiday in the Lake District once,' she said thoughtfully. 'Four of us, staying in Youth Hostels every night, for a fortnight. It *was* fun.' She turned to him. 'That was when I was engaged,' she said simply.

'Oh . . .' He glanced at her hand, but there was no ring. She saw his glance. 'That was a long time ago,' she said. 'He was in Bomber Command and got shot down over Dortmund. I thought the end of the world had come. But I suppose it hadn't.'

'My dear,' said Mr Honey, 'I'm so very sorry.'

She roused herself. 'Your move,' she said.

She went away after the third game to assist in serving dinner, and presently Miss Teasdale appeared, looking fresh and radiant and about eighteen years old. She said, 'Say, Mr Honey, I just heard my plane's coming in around nine o'clock, so we'll have time for dinner before I go.' She ordered an Old-fashioned for herself and persuaded him to join her; beer was his normal drink and he took the novelty gingerly, and under the influence he pulled out his wallet and showed her a photograph of Elspeth.

'My,' said the actress, 'doesn't she look cute?'

He agreed. 'I think she's more intelligent than children of her age usually are,' he said. 'She's only twelve, but she's got a very good grasp of crystallography.'

She stared at him. 'What's that?'

He smiled. 'Everything,' he said. 'All matter is built up of the associations that result in crystals, like miniature universes. It's an extraordinary thing that schools don't teach more about it.' He turned to her. 'Schools only teach results,' he said. 'All the basic knowledge that Elspeth has, she seems to have got from me.'

'I'd believe that,' she replied. 'Say, does she get around at all–parties with boy friends and that sort of thing?'

'Who–Elspeth? She's only just a child.' He was amazed. 'She's only twelve years old.'

Miss Teasdale laughed. 'From what you say about her crystal–crystall–what you said, she sounds to be about forty. Still, maybe English children don't get around so early as they do at home. Has she got a flapjack?'

'What's that?'

She stared at him. 'For powder.' She rummaged in her bag. 'Like this.'

He was at a loss. 'No,' he said weakly. 'Ought she to have one?'

She laughed. 'It's not obligatory. I guess she ought to have it when she wants it.'

'I really don't think she's old enough for that,' he said. 'I don't think any of the older children at her school have those.'

'Maybe not.' And then she said, 'Tell me about this Dr Scott that I'm to go and see. And how do I get to this place you work at, Farnborough?'

He told her, and wrote a short letter for her to give to me, and presently they dined together. Then her plane landed to refuel and the lounge was filled with passengers stretching their legs after the flight up from New York. In the bustle he said good-bye to her as her luggage was carried out. 'I'll tell him just the way you're fixed,' she said. 'Leave it to me. And I'll say that you'd appreciate it if you could get back to your work in England.'

'Do please tell him that,' he said earnestly. 'I really feel I'm much more use in the Establishment than on this sort of thing.'

The passengers departed and the plane taxied away for the take-off for England in the dusk. Mr Honey was left reading the *Saturday Evening Post* in the deserted lounge. At ten o'clock the stewardess came up softly behind him. 'I've got a bedroom ready for you, sir,' she said. 'Would you like me to show you which it is? It's just over the road.'

He said, 'Oh, thank you,' and got up and went with her out into the night. It was cold and bright and brilliantly starry out on the road. To the north the sky was shot with spears of glimmering white light reaching up towards the zenith. They paused for a minute, looking at it. 'That's the aurora,' the girl said. 'They call it Northern Lights here. We often see it.'

He said, 'It's associated with the cosmic rays, I believe. It would be interesting to find out more about it.' And then he said, unusually for him, 'It's very beautiful.'

'It's wild,' the girl said 'and uncanny. I don't like it much.' She took him into a two-storeyed wooden hutment, one of a row upon the other side of the road, and opened a door. He saw rather a bare bedroom, but his bag had been unpacked for him, and his hairbrush and shaving things laid out neatly on the dressing-table, and his pyjamas put to air upon the radiator so that they would be warm for him to get into, and the bed was turned down invitingly. 'I put a hot-water bottle in the bed,' she said. 'I hope you'll find everything all right, sir.'

He had not been treated like that for years. 'Oh, thank you,' he said. 'It all looks most comfortable. Did you do all this for me?'

She smiled. 'It's what I'm here for, sir.' She hesitated. 'I hope you don't mind—I've taken two pairs of your socks to darn. They've both got holes in the toe. I'll bring them with your tea in the morning.'

He said, 'Oh please, you don't have to bother. They won't show.'

The girl said, 'I've got nothing else to do, and you can't go around like that.' She hesitated. 'I did notice your pyjama coat has a great tear in the back,' she said. 'If you let me have that tomorrow I'll mend it for you. It must be terribly uncomfortable wearing it like that.'

He flushed. 'It's so old,' he said. 'I ought to get another suit, but there never seem to be any coupons.'

She asked curiously, 'Who mends your clothes when you're at home?'

'Oh, I do that myself,' he said. 'It's really very little trouble, and Elspeth's getting quite good at it, too. We get along splendidly, only the coupons are so short.'

Coupons, she knew, were always short for the bad managers. 'I'll take your jacket anyway tomorrow,' she said. 'The material's quite good–it'll patch all right.'

'I don't like putting you to so much trouble,' he said.

'I'd like to do it,' the girl said. 'I like mending things.'

She went away, and Mr Honey went to bed in greater comfort than he had experienced for many years. He stood for a few moments in his torn pyjamas before opening the window, looking at the Northern Lights, noting the form of the radiation. Then he got into bed; with his feet resting snugly on the hot-water bottle he was able to relax and think about the geographical distribution of the cosmic rays, a subject that was beginning to intrigue him. He lay in warm comfort doing mental calculations of the strength of the earth's magnetic field in various latitudes and computing its effect upon the distribution of the protons and the positrons as they approach the planet, till sleep came to him.

He was roused at eight o'clock in the morning by the stewardess, who brought him a cup of tea and a few slices of bread and butter on a tray. She pulled his curtains and let in the sunlight. 'It's going to be a lovely day, sir,' she said. 'What would you like for breakfast?'

He smiled at her. 'What can I have?'

'Orange or pineapple juice,' she said. 'Porridge or cereals. Eggs anyway you like. Bacon, cold ham, sausages. Buckwheat cakes and syrup with a sausage on the side–that's very good. Toast, hot rolls . . .'

He considered this. 'Could I have porridge and bacon and eggs?'

'Two eggs?'

'Well–yes, if I can.'

'Coffee or tea?'

'Er–coffee, I think.'

She nodded. 'What time would you like it? It's eight o'clock now.'

'Oh, I don't take long. Half-past eight?'

'Very good, sir.' She paused, and then she said, 'I want to go out for a walk this morning–it's such a lovely day. Would you like to do that?'

He considered this. 'Well–yes, I would. It seems rather stupid to be in Newfoundland and see nothing of the country, doesn't it? May I come with you?'

'Of course,' she said. 'The Gander River's only about two miles away and there's a road down to that, but there's nothing much to do there except bathe, and it's frightfully cold still. But going the other way, out past the restaurant, there's a path that takes you to a lake; it's awfully pretty there. That's where people go to fish. Do you do any fishing, sir?'

He shook his head. 'I'm afraid I don't.'

'The staff, the people stationed here, go fishing there on their days off,' she said. 'They catch salmon and trout and all sorts of things. But apart from that, it's terribly pretty. We could go there, if you like.'

He said eagerly, leaning up upon one elbow in his bed, 'Do let's. I haven't done that sort of thing for years.'

She hesitated. 'Would you like to take out lunch? I could cut some sandwiches.'

He said doubtfully, 'It'd be fun . . . But do you think I ought to be away all day? I mean, there might be a cable for me from the office.'

She smiled. 'It could wait. We'd be back anyway by four, and if you're ordered to go on or to go back, you won't miss a plane because they all come through at night. I think a day out in the country would do you good.'

He said, 'I think it would.'

She nodded. 'I'll see about the sandwiches. Oh, and here are your socks–I did them last night.'

He took them gratefully. 'It's terribly kind of you to do all this for me.'

'Not a bit,' she said. 'Let me have your pyjama jacket when we get back and I'll do that for you.' She glanced at the tear. 'You can't go on wearing it like that.'

'I know,' he said ruefully. 'It got bigger in the night.'

When she was gone he sat in bed sipping his tea and fingering his socks, full of pleasure. He had not been looked after like that since Mary died; since then he had battled on alone, doing everything for himself and most things for his little girl. When Mary had been killed he had resigned himself to a life of celibacy; it had never entered his head, as practical politics, that he should go looking for another girl. He would not have known how to set about it. He had not married Mary; she had married him, to the surprise and consternation of her friends in the office, who thought she might have done a great deal better for herself than that. Mary had just happened in his life, a rare, sweet interlude that he had done very little to provoke; when she had gone he had slipped back quietly into his bachelor ways, more complicated now that there was Elspeth to look after.

He got up presently, and as he dressed looked ruefully at his pyjama jacket; not only was it very badly torn but it was indisputably dirty. He could not hand it over to her to be mended in that state; he washed it ineffectively in the basin in his room and hung it over the radiator to dry. As a consequence he was late for breakfast and it was nearly ten o'clock before he was ready to start off.

He met her in the lounge. 'I say,' he said diffidently, 'I hope I haven't kept you waiting.'

'Not long,' she said. She had a small blue stewardess's bag in her hand. 'I've got the sandwiches, and I brought a thermos of coffee, too.' She hesitated. 'I didn't ask you what sort of sandwiches you like,' she said. 'I made some chicken ones and some sardine and some cheese. Is that all right?'

'Oh–of course,' he said. 'That's fine.' Food did not mean a great deal in his life; his meals were either canteen meals at the factory or scrappy messes that he cooked himself at home; moreover, his mind was usually too full of other matters for him to pay much attention to what he was eating. 'I like all those,' he said.

She was relieved. 'I had an awful feeling that perhaps you wouldn't like sardine . . .'

They set out walking down the path away from the hangars; as they went he asked her how she knew the way so well. He learned a little of her life. She made three Atlantic crossings, on the average, each week; most times she came to Gander for a short stop to refuel. Sometimes, on the rare occasions of easterly gales in the Atlantic, the flight had been delayed there for a day or longer; once before she had been stranded there for several days due to defective motors in the aircraft. 'But we shan't have to stop here for weather in the future, I don't think,' she said. 'The Reindeer carries so much petrol we can make the crossing even against the worst gales in the winter. That's what Captain Samuelson was saying.'

Mr Honey said, 'Well, that will save a lot of trouble. But we've got to get its tailplane right, first of all.'

She nodded. 'How long do you think that will take, sir?'

He smiled up at her. 'Please–don't you think you might stop calling me sir? I mean, you're doing so much for me that you don't have to.'

She laughed. 'All right. But how long do you think the Reindeers will be grounded for?'

'I don't know,' he said vaguely. 'These things usually seem to take three or four months to put right. But that's supposing that what I think is correct.' His face clouded, and he was in distress again. 'It's just an estimate,' he said. 'I didn't want people to take me up on it like this. I should have had more time, and now there's all this row . . .'

She said sympathetically, 'I know. But it had to be done this way, didn't it?'

He shook his head. 'We should have gone on working in the department in the proper way until we had some positive results to show.'

She smiled. 'I'm glad you didn't.'

'Why?'

She said gently, 'I should have been killed.'

He blinked up at her, taller than he was, slim and lovely against a background of Newfoundland fir trees and blue sky. It was Mary all over again, incredible that girls like that should come to death. He stared at her, confused by the clash of the theoretical and the practical in his work. 'Jean Davenport and Betty Sherwood were the stewardesses in Captain Ward's Reindeer,' she said. 'That one that fell in Labrador. If you'd gone on working in the proper way, I should have been killed too.'

He said a little timidly, 'Did you know them?'

'Of course I did. I knew them very well.'

'Oh. Were they people like you?'

She glanced at him curiously. 'They were both fair. Betty was smaller than me. I suppose Jean was much the same.'

'But were they young, like you?'

'I suppose they were about twenty-five,' she said. 'It's not a job for people much older than that. Most of us are round about that age.'

They walked on for a time in silence through the woods. 'I suppose Dr Scott was right,' he said at last. 'But there ought to be more time for scientific work. One can't produce results all in a hurry, out of the hat, like this.'

She said, 'It must be terribly difficult.'

He glanced up at her, distressed. 'I don't know what to do. There must be a tremendous row going on in England because I damaged this Reindeer. You see, there isn't any proof yet. Sir Phillip Dolbear didn't believe a word I said.'

She was sorry for him; if it would help him to tell her all about it she wanted him to do so. 'Who is Sir Phillip Dolbear?' she asked.

She listened while he told her the whole story. 'You see,' he said at last, 'there isn't any proof at all–it just rests on my estimate. I was on my way to Labrador to find out if the fracture at the tailplane of the crashed one is crystalline–if it supports the theory of failure in fatigue. They never meant me to do anything like this. They'll all be very angry about it, I know. But it seemed the only thing to do.'

'It *was* the only thing to do,' she said gently. 'It was playing safe. Captain Samuelson isn't angry about it. And after all, he's been flying nearly thirty years and he does know about things.'

He shook his head. 'I told them they'd do better to send someone else. I always do this sort of thing all wrong.'

To distract his mind she said, 'Look, there's the lake. It's lovely, isn't it?'

It lay blue and shimmering before them under the summer sky, fringed with tall fir trees, its shores broken up into little rocky bays. Waterfowl were dotted about upon its surface; three or four deer, grazing on a rocky sward beside the water half a mile away, looked up as they stopped and vanished into the woods. 'There are all sorts of wild things here,' she said. 'There's a stream running out at the far end where there were beavers last year. And there are bears here, too.'

He stared at her. 'Are they dangerous?'

She laughed. 'The only time I saw one he ran like a rabbit. They say they're all right unless you feed them; then they come after more and you get clawed. But if you let them alone they're quite harmless.'

The path ran alongside the lake, made by the fishermen from the airfield; they passed a couple of rough dorys moored to the bank. They went on and came to the place where the deer had been and studied their tracks, and on until they came to the beaver stream. But the beavers were gone and only fragments of their dam remained.

They laid out their lunch by the stream, on a bare rock. 'It's so quiet here,' she said. 'You might be a thousand miles from anywhere.'

'Apart from the airport,' Mr Honey said, 'we probably are.'

She nodded. 'It's a mistake to leave the path, they say,' she remarked. 'You can quite easily get lost in these woods, and that's not so funny. All this country looks the same.'

'Do people ever get lost?' he asked in wonder.

'Oh yes. Two of the boys from the airport got lost last year. One of them died; it was eight days before they were found.'

He thought this over for a minute. 'You have a very adventurous life,' he said at last. 'What will you do? Can you go on as a stewardess indefinitely?'

She smiled. 'I suppose you could if you wanted to,' she said. 'I don't know that I should want to, though.'

'Don't you like it?'

She picked up a twig of fir, and absently scratched a little furrow in the earth. 'It's been quite fun,' she said. 'It's been fun meeting people and going to new places. I went into it after the war when I was restless, with Donald being killed, and everything. But now—well, I don't know. I sometimes feel I'd like to give it up.'

'You'd find it rather difficult to settle down,' he said. 'After this.'

She said, 'When you've seen all the new places you've got no more new places to see. And anyway, one new place is just like another new place. . . . I used to like meeting new people every trip—and I still do. But those things, meeting new people, seeing new places, they aren't everything. And while you go on in that sort of life you can't have any real friends or any real home. Because you're never there . . .'

'You don't get worried about the risks?' he asked.

She shook her head. 'There's so little danger in flying now. I know Jean and Betty bought it in the first Reindeer, but that sort of thing happens so seldom.'

She flashed a smile at him. 'Thanks to people like you.' He was confused, and she went on, 'No–it's fun living this sort of life, but there's nothing *permanent* about it, if you understand. Sometime I'd like to be a bit more permanent. . . .'

'You'll be looking for another job?' he asked.

'I suppose so.'

He said, 'So shall I.'

She glanced at him. 'Are you going to leave Farnborough?'

He nodded. 'I've decided to resign.'

'Oh. . . .' There was a pause, and then she said 'Do you think that's necessary? Surely they'll understand?'

He shook his head. 'They've got nothing tangible on this fatigue at all–just my own hypotheses, which nobody really believes in but myself. And there's certain to be a row about this Reindeer, because I'm a Government servant and so the Government will have to pay for its repair. And that means the Treasury and–oh, all sorts of things. I thought it all out last night. I want to write a letter to Dr Scott putting in my resignation, and get it to him as soon as I can.'

She was convinced in her own mind that he was doing the wrong thing, but she knew too little of the problems that confronted him to argue. She said, 'But what will you do? What sort of a job would you look for, Mr Honey?'

He said, 'I think they might take me on at the National Physical Laboratory–I know a lot of people there. And the work might be quite similar. . . . I should try that first of all. Or else I might try teaching.'

She was distressed for him. With her wider knowledge of the world she new one thing very certainly; that Mr Honey would not be much good at keeping order in a class of boys. He would be ragged unmercifully, grow bitter and morose. She said, 'I should think the other one would be better.'

'I think it might be more interesting,' he said thoughtfully. 'There's such a lot of new stuff coming up about the earth's magnetic field and its relation to cosmography. It's all getting rather exciting.'

'I'm sure it must be,' she said. 'Look, try one of these chicken ones–they're rather nice.'

He brought his mind back to the matter in hand. 'They're very nice,' he said. 'Things you make yourself always taste better than what you get in a canteen, don't they?'

She said, 'You take a lot of your meals in the canteen, do you?'

He said, 'Well, yes, we do. We get our own breakfast, but then I always have lunch at the factory, and Elspeth has hers at school. There's a very good British Restaurant in Farnham and we go there sometimes in the evening, but it shuts at six and that sometimes isn't very convenient. It's such a lot of work getting meals at home, you know, when you're both working all day.'

She nodded slowly. 'It isn't very good, having so many meals out, is it?'

He said, 'It makes it rather expensive. I think you're right in a way–I get a lot of indigestion that I didn't seem to get before. But one can always take magnesia for that.'

She laughed. 'That's expensive, too.'

They sat by the lake for a couple of hours, talking, finding out about each other. In the middle of the afternoon they recalled the cables and the signals that might be waiting for them in the airport office from the outside world, and got up reluctantly and walked slowly back up the path.

At the edge of the airport clearances they stopped for a moment. 'It was terribly kind of you to suggest coming out like this,' Mr Honey said. 'I haven't had a day like this for years.'

'Nor I,' she said. 'I'm getting rather tired of aeroplanes, I think, and racketing around the world. A quiet day like this is rather a relief.'

Mr Honey hesitated, uncertain how to put in words what he wanted very badly to say. 'Do you think we might do it again some time in England,' he asked timidly, 'one Sunday? There are some lovely walks along the Hog's Back . . .'

She smiled down at him, 'I'd love to do that, Mr Honey,' she said. 'I'll give you my address.'

They went back together to the airport, rather quiet. In the C.A.T.O. office there was a signal ordering her to take passage on the night aircraft for London; there was a cable for Honey telling him to stay at Gander till an R.A.F. aircraft arrived later in the week to bring him back to England.

He wrote a short letter to me giving in his resignation, and gave it to Marjorie Corder to deliver; at dusk he walked with her to the plane.

'It's been terribly kind of you to do all that you have for me,' he said. And then he added wistfully, 'We'll meet again in England, won't we?'

For some odd reason, tears welled up behind her eyes. 'Of course, Mr Honey,' she said quietly. 'Of course we will.'

8

I sat fingering Mr Honey's letter of resignation while Miss Corder was telling me what had been going on at Gander; I was only listening to her with half my mind. With the other half I was wondering if I dared put his letter in the wastepaper basket and tell him not to be a bloody fool when I saw him, or whether I ought to show it to the Director. I sat fingering it uncertainly as she talked.

I looked down at it when she had finished, and read it through again. 'I see,' I said thoughtfully. And then I said, 'I wish he hadn't written this.'

She said, 'He was so positive that you would all be very angry with him.'

'So we are,' I said. I raised my eyes and grinned at her. 'He's been a silly fool. There *must* have been other ways of stopping that thing flying on without wrecking it. But if that was the best he could manage, then he did quite right to wreck it. I should never have forgiven him if he'd let it fly on.'

She stared at me, puzzled, trying to absorb that one. 'I don't think he's quite the person to deal with things of that sort,' she said.

I nodded. 'You're quite right. He's an inside man. The fault was mine for ever sending him.' I waggled the letter in my fingers. 'But that doesn't help me in deciding what to do about this.'

She was silent.

I glanced at her. 'Did he write this reluctantly, because he thought it was the thing to do in the circumstances? Or does he really want to leave and get another job?'

'He doesn't want to leave,' she said. 'He thought that things would be so unpleasant for him if he came back here—well, he'd rather go somewhere else. He talked of going to some place called the National Physical Laboratory to try and get a job on cosmic radiations or something.'

I nodded; it was a likely story. He was quite capable of taking cosmic radiations in his stride. 'Things won't be unpleasant for him here,' I said. 'That Reindeer had to be stopped flying, and he stopped it.' I fingered the letter in my hand. 'I should be very sorry to lose him,' I said thoughtfully. 'I've got a feeling that he's working on the right lines in this matter of fatigue, and that we'll find in a few months' time that his estimates are very near the truth.' I raised my head and looked at her, thinking of what I should have to say at our formal conference next day. 'He's a valuable man in this department. I don't want to take this letter seriously. I think it would be a loss to the Establishment, and even to the country, if he left his work upon fatigue just at this stage.'

She said, 'If he's as important as all that, I can't understand why you don't look after him a bit better.'

I stared at her. 'How do you mean?'

She said firmly, 'He gets a terrible lot of indigestion and he's always taking pills for it. He'll be getting a duodenal ulcer if you don't look out, and then he won't be able to work for you at all.'

The indigestion was news to me, and there didn't seem to be much that I could do about that, but it fitted in with his complexion, and one bit more was added to the picture of him in my mind. 'I can't help that,' I said. 'I wish his home life was a little easier for him, but that's just one of those things.'

She got up to go. 'I know, sir,' she said. 'It was stupid of me to say that. I know you can't help him in that way.' She hesitated. 'I told him that I'd go and see his daughter, Elspeth, while I was down here,' she said. 'There's only a charwoman looking after her. He lives in Copse Road, Farnham. What's the best way for me to get there, sir? Is there a bus?'

I blinked; another lovely woman to see Elspeth Honey. 'She's not there now,' I said. 'As a matter of fact, you'll find her in my flat. She had a bit of an accident.' And I told her shortly what had happened.

Miss Corder was upset. 'The poor kid!' she said. 'I *am* glad Mr Honey doesn't know about this—he'd be terribly worried. I mean, on top of all the other trouble.' She asked a few more questions, and then said,

'It's awfully kind of Mrs Scott to have done so much, sir. I was wondering if I could help at all? I went into the office at the airport this morning, and they've given me a few days' leave. I'm a nurse, you know. I trained at the London Hospital.' She paused. 'If I can help, I really would like to. Mr Honey was so kind to me, and I'm quite free.'

I thought quickly. There was some substance in this offer; Miss Teasdale, charming and good-hearted as she was, was not a trained nurse. But here was a trained nurse who felt herself to be under some obligation to Honey, and who was free for some days and anxious to assist. In fairness to Shirley I could not pass this over.

'It's very nice of you to say that,' I replied. 'As a matter of fact, Miss Monica Teasdale came down and helped a bit yesterday, and I think she's coming again today. But she's just an amateur; I know my wife would be awfully glad of your help.'

I told her how to get to my flat and that I would ring up Shirley; then I showed her out, because I had a lot to do that day. At the door she turned to me.

'You won't let him resign, will you, Dr Scott?' She looked up at me appealingly; she was a very lovely girl. 'He's not the sort for changes and adventures. He'd be much happier going on quietly here.'

I nodded. 'I don't want to lose him,' I said. 'I'll do what I can.'

She went, and I read Honey's letter of resignation again. Then I asked Miss Learoyd to find out if the Director was free; he was, and I went down to see him, forgetting all about my call to Shirley.

I said, 'Good morning, sir. I've got a letter from Mr Honey here, resigning his position with us. With your permission I'm going to tear it up and forget I ever had it.'

He smiled, and stretched out his hand. 'Let me see.'

He read it carefully, and then said, 'Why, particularly, do you want to destroy it?'

'We've got this conference tomorrow, sir,' I said. 'I still think he's probably right about this Reindeer tail, and as a member of my staff I'm going to back him up. But if we accept this letter, then he's not a member of my staff any longer, and I don't know where we are. We'll all look pretty good fools and the right decisions probably won't be made.'

He said thoughtfully, 'You are quite sure about him still?'

I was silent for a moment, thinking. 'I don't want to be stupid about this,' I said at last. 'I don't want to back him automatically, just because he *is* a member of my staff. I've got a strong feeling that he's probably right about the Reindeer tail, but that's not evidence. I'm basing my opinions more on the quality of his other work, the stuff I found in his private files. He's a fine mathematician, he's very well informed on physical chemistry, and he's got a very clear analytical mind. Apart altogether from the Reindeer tail, I think it would be a great loss if he left us, sir.'

He handed me back the letter. 'All right, tear it up.' He paused, and then said, 'How did that get here?'

I grinned. 'The stewardess from the Reindeer flew over last night and brought it down to me by hand. Miss Corder. She's a very beautiful young woman.'

He smiled. 'Stewardesses usually are. What have you done with her?'

'Sent her off to see Elspeth. It's just a procession of girl friends from Honey—two in two days.' I turned to him. 'Old Honey with his face like a frog. What's he got that we haven't, sir?'

He laughed. 'I can't tell you that—but I'm not a bit surprised. Mrs Honey, who got killed, you know, she was a very beautiful girl.' He paused, reflectively. 'She used to work in the Airworthiness Department, when we had that here. Really lovely, she was.'

I stood in thought for a moment; every little thing I could find out about Honey was important to me at that time. I was staking my career on my opinion that his work was valuable, that he was a credible person. 'When Mrs Honey was alive,' I said slowly, 'was he just the same as he is now? Or was he any different?'

The Director did not understand. 'He was younger,' he replied.

'I know. But was he different in himself? Was he always as touchy and difficult in the office?'

'Oh, I see what you mean. Yes, he was very different. He was much tidier in his dress and he had a better colour. Now you mention it, I don't think he was so difficult in the office. He used to make little jokes. He probably got better food at home and more exercise.'

The heavy boots came into my mind, and the indigestion. 'I should think that's right,' I said thoughtfully.

'Mary Honey did a great deal for him,' said the Director. 'It was a tragedy when she got killed. She was such a lovely girl.'

All this drove the thought of telephoning Shirley clean out of my mind; when I got back to my office I pulled my IN basket towards me and started on it, my mind still running upon what I had learned of Honey's past life. In consequence, when Shirley opened the door of my flat, she opened it on a completely strange young woman, who said, 'Good morning, Mrs Scott. I'm Miss Corder–Marjorie Corder.'

Shirley stared at her blankly; she had Miss Teasdale in the bedroom sitting with Elspeth, and she herself was just about to go round for a day of cleaning in Honey's house.

The stewardess said, 'Didn't Dr Scott ring you?'

'No. Ought he to have done?'

She explained. 'I've just come from him. I brought a note to him from Mr Honey in Newfoundland–I flew across last night. I told Mr Honey I could come and see his little girl, and Dr Scott told me to come here.'

Shirley's brain reeled; another beautiful stranger had flown the Atlantic with a message from Mr Honey and was diving deep into his private life. She said weakly, 'Do you know Miss Monica Teasdale? She's here.'

'I thought she might be. I was with her at Gander–I'm the stewardess, you see. Dr Scott told me that she might be here.'

Shirley nodded. 'She came yesterday. She's in the bedroom reading to Elspeth, now. Do come in.' She took Miss Corder into the sitting-room and explained to her.

The stewardess laughed, flushing a little. 'You won't want the two of us fussing round, Mrs Scott,' she said. 'I'd just like to look in and see Elspeth for a moment, and then I'll go away. Unless there's anything I can do to help you?'

Shirley said, 'Oh–no, not really. I was just going round to clean up Mr Honey's house a bit, but I've got nothing else to do.'

'What's the matter with it? Is it dirty?'

'Perfectly filthy. The kitchen floor simply makes you sick.'

The stewardess laughed. 'Well, I can do that, Mrs Scott. I'm used to scrubbing.'

If there is one job Shirley loathes, it is scrubbing a floor. 'Would you really like to come and help?' she asked. 'I was going to take some lunch round there and make a day of it.'

'I'd love to.'

They made their plans together; then Shirley took Marjorie down the corridor to our bedroom, where Monica Teasdale was reading *Just So Stories* to Elspeth Honey, lying in bed. She looked up in surprise at the stewardess.

'Good morning, Miss Teasdale,' Marjorie said. 'I came over last night and brought another note from Mr Honey to Dr Scott. He asked me to come on and see Elspeth when I was down here.'

Elspeth from her bed said, 'Is Daddy coming home soon?'

'My name's Marjorie,' the stewardess said. 'I saw your daddy last night. Yes, he's coming back soon. In two or three days, perhaps.'

'Why can't he come sooner?'

'He's got to wait for an aeroplane to bring him. It's a long way, across the Atlantic.'

'Didn't an aeroplane bring you?'

'Yes, but he was to wait for a special one, in two or three days' time.'

'Couldn't he have come on the same one that you came on?'

She shook her head. 'He's got to wait for a particular one, that has to do with his work.'

That satisfied Elspeth. 'My Daddy works on things to do with aeroplanes,' she said. 'He works at Farnborough. He's terribly clever.'

'I know,' said the stewardess, 'I know that.'

Miss Teasdale asked, 'They've fixed that difficulty there was about his passage home?'

The stewardess said, 'He's coming on an R.A.F. aircraft of the School of Navigation. It's coming across some time this week.'

Shirley said, 'I'm just taking Marjorie down with me to your house, Elspeth, so that we can do some cleaning before your father gets back. Is there anything you want from there? We could bring it when we come.'

She shook her head. 'May I sleep at home tonight, Mrs Scott?'

'I don't think tonight, dear. Better stay here till you feel quite well.'

The child said in distress, 'If nobody's there, there'll be a burglar.'

'Don't worry about that,' Shirley said. 'Dennis–Dr Scott–slept there last night, and I expect he'll be there again tonight. One or other of us will be there. We won't leave the house empty.'

Elspeth said, 'I do want to go back.'

'You shall, the very minute you're well.'

Miss Teasdale said, 'You'll just have to hurry up and get well, honey.'

Elspeth snuggled down in bed. 'I like the way you always call me honey.'

Shirley collected scrubbers and soap and Vim and a dustpan and brush, and put them in a basket with the lunch, and started out with Marjorie Corder to Copse Road. As they walked through the suburban streets, the stewardess said, 'She's very anxious to get back into her own house, isn't she?'

'I know,' said Shirley. 'It's a sort of fixed idea. She feels responsible for all her father's papers, and she's terribly afraid a burglar will get in and steal them. As if anybody would want to steal that sort of stuff! But that's what she thinks. That's how she came to fall downstairs–she thought she heard a burglar.'

They came to the little house in Copse Road and opened it, and went through it with curious disdain. The products of Honey's creative research in the many files in the front room meant nothing to them, except that they were papers to collect a lot of dust. There was little in the house that they approved of. 'My dear, that kitchen!' Shirley said. 'The whole place wants doing out from top to bottom, really.'

Marjorie nodded. 'I'll start off on the kitchen floor, and after that I think I'll wash the walls,' she said. 'It wouldn't be a bad room if it was cleaned up. It's got quite a nice outlook.'

Shirley said, 'If you make a start on that I'll slip round to the builder and tell him to come and put some glass in this window, where I kicked it out. After that, I think I'd better start off in the bedrooms and turn those out, and work down.' She paused. 'I'll get some Harpic for that ghastly lavatory . . .'

They worked together till the middle of the afternoon; then Shirley left to do her own housekeeping. Marjorie stayed on in the house, partly because she was not yet tired and partly because the glazier was working on the window. She roamed through the house for a little, smoking a cigarette, touching and feeling things, rather as I had done two nights before. She stared in wonder at the many files and books and drawing instruments, relating them to the man she had known at Gander. This was what the home of a genius looked like. A genius who had no woman to look after him.

There was one small rug on the bare boards of the front room, that mixture of drawing-office and study. She took this rug up and fetched a bucket of hot water from the kitchen, and got down on her knees again to scrub the floor. Better to make a job of the whole house, while she was at it. And this was where he did his work, and so the most important room of all.

There was a step on the path outside, and the front door opened. She raised her head and knelt back on her heels, thinking to see Shirley again. But it was Miss Teasdale, delicately gowned and perfectly made up, who stood in the doorway looking down at Marjorie as she knelt on the scrubbing mat.

'Say,' she said, 'Mrs Scott just told me all that you've been doing. She's back in the apartment now for a while, so I just stepped around to see.'

Marjorie flushed a little. 'I was just going to start scrubbing this floor.'

'So I see.' The actress stared around her curiously. 'Is this some kind of a laboratory?'

'It's his study, where he does his work.'

Standing in the door, Miss Teasdale glanced out into the kitchen and the stairs leading to the rooms above. 'Which is the sitting-room, then?'

'This is it. It's the only sitting-room there is.'

She stared around her, at the drawing-board, the deal cupboards and shelves loaded with books and files, the bare floor. 'The little girl,' she said at last. 'Where does she go?'

The stewardess said, 'They've got a couple of armchairs in the kitchen–basket ones. I think they sit in there a good deal.' She stared around her. 'It doesn't have to be like this,' she said. 'I'm sure it doesn't. He could be much more comfortable.'

The actress glanced at the pail of steaming water. 'I see you're doing all you can to make it so.'

'Me? All I'm doing is to get rid of some of the dirt. But he could have curtains in this room and a carpet on the floor and some decent lampshades, as a start.'

The actress smiled. 'Kind of wants a woman round about the place?'

Their eyes met. Marjorie said evenly, 'I think he does.'

'Okay,' said Miss Teasdale. 'Just so as we know.' She turned and wandered into the kitchen. It was scrubbed and clean and smelling of antiseptic soap. The window was open and the sun streaming in; on the wooden table there was a small vase of flowers. A little pang struck at her heart again, as many pangs had in the last two days. Kitchens had been like that back in her youth in Indiana, before they got to look hygienic, like a hospital. She called over her shoulder, 'You've done a swell job in here.'

Marjorie got up from her knees in the sitting-room and came and stood behind the actress. 'It's clean now, anyway,' she said. 'But it's all so old-fashioned. It must seem terrible to you.'

'Maybe.' The actress stood for a moment in thought. 'I kind of like a scrubbed table,' she said at last. 'I haven't seen one in years. But they were all that way when I was young, and it carries you back.'

'All right if you haven't got to scrub them yourself,' the stewardess said. 'But the metal ones are so much easier.'

Miss Teasdale glanced at her. 'Kind of interested in housework, aren't you?'

Unaccountably, beside this sophisticated woman Marjorie Corder felt like a child. 'Everybody's interested in that,' she said defensively. 'Besides, I was a nurse once, before I went to the Air Transport Organisation. I know a lot about scrubbing.'

'Going to stay with the airline? Or leave and marry the boy friend?' She glanced at the stewardess's hand. 'Or isn't there a boy friend?'

The girl shook her head. 'Not now.'

'No? I'd have thought there'd have been plenty.'

'I got inoculated,' Marjorie said. 'There was one once, but he was killed. He was a bomber pilot.'

'In the war?'

She nodded.

'That was quite a while ago,' the actress said. And then she said, 'I see.'

Miss Corder flushed, in spite of herself. 'I don't know what it is you see,' she said. 'I've got this other floor to do.' And she went back to the sitting-room, and went down on her knees beside the pail.

'Okay,' the older woman said. 'You don't have to get worked up about it. Guess I'll go along now and get Mrs Scott to telephone the office for my car.'

Marjorie raised her head. 'All right,' she said. 'Tell her I'll be round in about half an hour for my coat.'

Miss Teasdale walked back slowly to our little flat, deep in thought; it did not now seem very important to her whether she was recognised or not. One or two women and three men, glanced at her curiously in the street, but no one spoke. She reached the garden gate just as I drove up from the factory; I had left early that night, resolved to get in a couple of hours more upon my lecture that evening, somehow and in some place. I had to give it the following night; indeed, the next day, with our full-dress meeting upon Reindeer fatigue in the morning and my lecture in the evening and flying to Montreal that night, was likely to be quite a heavy one.

I took her into the flat and telephoned for her car; it would take an hour or so to come from London. I poured her out a glass of sherry.

'Tired?' I said. She looked rather limp.

'Just a bit.' She roused herself. 'I walked around to see where Mr Honey lives. Miss Corder, she's still there scrubbing the floor. Says she'll be another half an hour. She's got energy, that kid has.'

'Well,' I said, 'she's young.' I could have bitten my tongue out an instant later for having said that.

The actress nodded briefly. Presently she said, 'Say, Dr Scott—this research on airplanes you and Mr Honey do. Can that be done any place? I mean, suppose a man had money, enough money to set up a swell laboratory, say, at some place like Palm Beach, and maybe another one in Vermont for the summer months. Could the work be done that way?'

'Research on aeroplanes?' I asked. 'You mean, the sort of things that we do here in Farnborough?'

'That's right. Fatigue, is that it?'

I shook my head. 'I don't think you could do any effective work upon fatigue effects in airframes in a private laboratory,' I said. 'You'd have no access to the secret information, for one thing, so you'd never be up to date. But apart from that, the expense would be prohibitive to any private individual.'

'What's that about secret information?'

'All the work done on military aeroplanes is secret,' I said. 'If the wings start coming off our latest bomber in a dive, we don't tell the world about it. Not until we get it put right, anyway. But at Farnborough, all that experience is at our disposal when we're dealing with the Reindeer tail—in fact, we should ourselves be working on the secret troubles of the bomber at the same time. A private research worker would always be behind, for that reason alone.'

'He wouldn't cut any ice, working that way?'

'I don't see how he could. Research on aeroplanes is a big business, too. I don't know what this fatigue story on the Reindeer is going to cost before we're through with it. Apart altogether from the repair of the one at Gander, what's going on at Farnborough may cost thirty thousand pounds before we're through with the first stage of it.'

She opened her eyes. 'A hundred and twenty thousand dollars. That's quite a lot of money. How long would that be spread over?'

'About a year,' I said. 'But I don't think it could be done at all upon a private basis. There's the buildings and the plant to be considered too, you see.'

She nodded. 'Like the stages.'

I did not understand her. 'No, I mean the actual buildings to house the experimental work.'

'That's right. Like the stages that we put up the sets in, ready to start shooting the scene.'

I thought of the great barnlike buildings I had read about. 'Yes—just like that,' I said. 'You'd need something just about as big as that, and a corresponding staff.'

She turned the conversation and asked me about my lecture that I was to give upon the 'Performance Analysis of Aircraft Flying at High Mach Numbers.' Elspeth had told her about it, it seemed, and had confused Miss Teasdale with her erudition. The child, it seemed, knew quite a lot about high Mach numbers and the difficulties that aeroplanes get into in those regions. The actress had no idea what a Mach number was, high or low, and was hazy about the meaning of the word analysis. But she was a very beautiful and charming woman; I did not find the explanations tedious.

Shirley came in while that was going on, and almost immediately Miss Corder followed her. I poured them both out a glass of sherry. Monica Teasdale said, 'Dr Scott's been telling me about his lecture tomorrow night, Mrs Scott. Elspeth told me first. She said it was a great distinction for a young man like Dr Scott to be asked to read a paper to the Royal Aeronautical Society.' She glanced at me mischievously. 'I'm just repeating what she said.'

'I can quite believe it,' I replied. 'That child's got the mind of a woman of forty.'

Shirley said artlessly, 'I do wish I could come up and hear it.'

I stared at her; it had never entered my head that she would not be coming to London. 'Aren't you coming?' I suppose there was disappointment in my voice, because we had worked at it a good deal together. And then, it struck me that she was talking with a purpose.

'I *can't*, Dennis,' she said. 'There's Elspeth.'

Miss Teasdale sat motionless, staring at the sherry in her glass. The faint lines upon her face seemed suddenly deeper.

Marjorie Corder burst out, 'But Mrs Scott, of course you must go! I've got a few days' leave. I'd love to come down again tomorrow and sit with her, or stay the night if you like. She'll be perfectly all right with me. If anything should happen, I *am* a nurse, you know.'

The actress sat silent, motionless.

Shirley said, 'Would you – really?'

'Of course, Mrs Scott. I'd love to do that.' The girl was bright-eyed and eager.

Shirley said, 'It really is most awfully kind of you – I do want to go, terribly.' And then we all said what a good idea it was and Shirley said, 'And after the lecture we can go on and have dinner somewhere, and then I'll come to the Airways place at Victoria and see you off.'

I grinned. 'Fine,' I said. 'But you'll miss the last train home.'

'Then I'll stay in Town, and make a night of it,' she said. She turned to Marjorie Corder. 'Did you really mean that you'd spend the night here with Elspeth? It means sleeping on the sofa, I'm afraid.'

'Of course, Mrs Scott. I'd love to do that.'

Presently I suggested that we'd better go and tell Elspeth about it, and we all walked down to see her in the bedroom. 'Guess what's going to happen tomorrow,' I said.

The child's face lit up. 'Am I going back to our house?'

Marjorie sat down on the bed and took her hand. 'Not quite that,' she said gently. 'But Mrs Scott wants to go to London to hear Dr Scott give his lecture, so I said I'd come and spend the night here and look after you. Would you like that?'

The stewardess, as I have mentioned before, was a very charming young woman. She made a sweet picture, sitting talking to the sallow little girl. Elspeth said, rather shyly, 'Yes.' And then she said, 'Will Dr Scott be coming back after the lecture?'

'No,' said Marjorie. 'He's got to fly to Montreal and he's leaving that night from London, and Mrs Scott's going to see him off and stay the night in Town. So there'll be just you and me alone down here tomorrow night.'

Elspeth said in distress, 'But that means there'll be nobody at all in our house, and there'll be a burglar.'

We stared at each other in consternation. We had all heard about this burglar in the last few days, sufficiently to realise that it was the sort of phobia that a child has to be led out of, that it may not be very good to repress. In Elspeth's case she certainly would not sleep while that house remained empty, and she was a mild concussion case.

Shirley said, 'Oh dear. I never thought of that.'

There was a momentary silence.

Marjorie Corder said slowly, 'Mrs Scott, would you think this very awful? I don't believe Mr Honey would mind me sleeping in his house, in the circumstances. They won't want me at Air Transport before the week-end, and Mr Honey will probably be back himself by then. What I was thinking was, we might move Elspeth back into her own house and her own bed tomorrow morning. I'd be very glad to sleep there tomorrow night and look after her there, and the next night, too, if that would help. I'm sure Mr Honey will be back in a day or two.'

I said, 'It'll only be a couple of days at the most. There's a Lincoln from the Navigation School picking him up this week.'

Shirley said slowly, 'I don't think it would matter a bit. After all, he did ask you to come and see if Elspeth was getting on all right. I don't think he could possibly mind if you moved in for a night or two to look after her, as things are. But surely, it's a great tie for you?'

The girl said, 'I'd like to do that, honestly.'

I said that I thought it would be a darned good idea. Shirley had had quite enough of sleeping on the sofa, I thought, and if I was to go away to Labrador upon this trip, I did not want to leave her with a sick child on her hands. If this Miss Corder who was a trained nurse wanted to take over and move Elspeth back into her own place and look after her there, I was all for it, and the sooner the better.

Everyone was very pleased about the decision we had taken, except possibly Miss Teasdale, who said very little. We made all the arrangements; Marjorie was to come down first thing in the morning. Shirley was to drive me to the station in the car and then bring back the car and transfer Elspeth back into her own house.

Soon after that, the stewardess went off to catch the bus to the station for the train that was to take her up to London. As soon as she was gone, Miss Teasdale said, 'I guess I'll have to say good-bye, now, to you folks. I don't see any reason to come down again tomorrow.' She was brightly cheerful.

Shirley said in disappointment, 'Oh, can't you stay and see Mr Honey when he gets back? You've done such a lot for him.'

She smiled. 'It's you folks have done everything–all I did was read a while with Elspeth. I certainly did enjoy doing that. But now she's going to be all fixed up, and as for me, I've no right to be over this side at all. I'm due back on the Coast in five days' time.'

She was emphatic that she had to go, and she went through into the bedroom again to say good-bye to Elspeth. 'One day,' she said, 'when you're a little older, I want you to come over to the States and spend a holiday with me. We'll go on a ranch up in the mountains, riding and swimming all day. In the spring, when all the flowers are out. Would you like that?'

The child nodded. 'Mm.'

'Okay, honey,' said the actress brightly. 'We'll look forward to it.' She paused, and then she said, 'If I write you sometimes, would you like to write me back and say what you've been doing?'

Elspeth nodded again. 'I'll write four pages,' she said.

'Okay, honey,' said Miss Teasdale again, 'that's a deal. I must go now.' She stooped and kissed the little sallow face. 'Tell your daddy I'm sorry that I couldn't wait to see him. Tell him I'll look forward to seeing you both again next time I'm over on this side.'

'How long will that be?' the child asked.

'A couple of years, maybe. But we'll write in the meantime, won't we?'

Elspeth nodded vigorously.

Miss Teasdale turned to the door, and waved her hand brightly. 'Good-by-ee,' she said, with rising American inflection.

As we walked down the passage there was a ring at the door, and it was the chauffeur. We went into the sitting-room, where she gathered up her things. And then she said, 'It's been swell knowing you folks. Going around the way I do, one never gets to know the real English people, the way you live and work. But this two days has been just like it used to be at home, as if you were all Hoosiers. It certainly has been grand knowing you.'

I forget what we said in reply; it doesn't matter. We walked down with her to her car, and this time there was a little crowd of ten or fifteen people on the pavement for the news had leaked. Two little girls with autograph albums stopped her as she crossed the pavement and said, 'Miss Teasdale, would you sign my book?' She smiled brilliantly, professionally, at them, scrawled her name, and got into the car; we stood and watched it as it slid away, conscious of the eyes of the small crowd now focused upon us, friends of the great.

Shirley asked, 'Dennis, what's a Hoosier?'

'Blowed if I know,' I said.

We went in and had supper, and gave Elspeth hers, and made her bed for her, and put her down to sleep. Then we washed up the supper things, and then I had to pack a suitcase with everything I would need for a fortnight or three weeks in Ottawa and Labrador. By half-past nine I was finished, and could take my overnight bag and the printed script of my paper and go round to Honey's house to do a final trial reading of the thing, and finally, to sleep.

Shirley came with me to the gate of the front garden of our little block of flats. 'Good night, Dennis,' she said softly. 'Don't stay up later than midnight, will you?'

It was reasonable that I should get a good night's sleep. 'All right,' I said.

She stood for a moment, looking down the road in the dusk, in the direction that Miss Teasdale's car had gone. 'That poor woman,' she said thoughtfully.

I asked her, 'Why do you say that?'

She kicked absently at a tuft of grass. 'I don't know. I think she's having rather a tough time.' She turned back to the house. 'Mind now, don't stay up too late.'

I went off down the road, and the 'Performance Analysis of Aircraft Flying at High Mach Numbers' put the matter from my mind.

9

I travelled up to London next morning with the Director for our meeting at the Ministry of Supply. It took place in one of those long, bleak conference rooms you sometimes find in economical Government offices, furnished only with a long table and about twenty hard seats. It was a very hot day, with the sun streaming in across the table. Our Chairman was Stanley Morgan, the Director of Research and Development. Ferguson was seated by his side, and on his other hand was a chap from the Secretariat that I did not know, and next to him there was a lean, cadaverous beggar from the Treasury whose name I never learned. Then there was Carter from the Ministry of Civil Aviation with some stooge or other. Next was Sir David Moon, the Chairman of C.A.T.O., with Carnegie beside him, and next to them and in their party was a little sandy-haired man, rather stout, who turned out to be Samuelson, the Captain of the Reindeer that Honey had had his fun with. There were two chaps from the Air Registration Board, and Group-Captain Fisher of the Accident Branch, with somebody to help him. Next came E. P. Prendergast, the designer of the Reindeer, looking like thunder, and with him was a chap in a black jacket who turned out to be the legal adviser to the Company. Finally, there was the Director and myself. I don't know what he felt like. I know I felt like a bag fox about to be let loose in front of a pack of hounds.

The Chairman opened the meeting by saying that as there was no formal agenda he would lay down terms of reference right away. The meeting had been called to discuss the airworthiness of the Reindeer aircraft with particular reference to tailplane failure by fatigue. He hoped that as a result of our discussions we would reach agreement upon whether any steps were necessary to restrict the operation of the aircraft, either now or in the future. He wished to emphasise that any decisions taken must be taken upon sound technical grounds alone. At the same time, he said, the matter was of grave political importance. The Reindeer aircraft was now maintaining more than half of the British Transatlantic passenger service, and by the end of the year would be doing the lot. If those aircraft had to be taken out of service the consequences would be very serious indeed. He was sure that the technicians present, of whom he was one, appreciated these hard facts. With that, he would ask the Director of the R.A.E. to give a short account of the investigations which had been proceeding on the Reindeer tail.

The Director said that the matter arose from certain basic researches into the question of fatigue, for which the second Reindeer tailplane submitted for structural tests, and unbroken in those tests, was used. This choice had been entirely fortuitous; the tailplane happened to be there, and so we used it. The research was directly in the hands of Mr Honey, working under Dr Scott; it was unfortunate, he said dryly, that circumstances prevented Mr Honey from being present at that meeting. Sir David Moon tightened his lips and looked annoyed, but said nothing.

The Director went on to outline what had happened up to the point where the Reindeer crash in Labrador came into the picture. Here he called on me to speak. 'I was very much impressed with the coincidence of flying times,' I said carefully. 'The Reindeer crashed in somewhat mysterious circumstances when it had flown for 1,393 hours. Mr Honey's estimate of the time to tailplane failure, under normal weak mixture cruising conditions, was 1,440 hours—that is, $3\frac{1}{2}$ per cent greater than the point at which an accident occurred. $3\frac{1}{2}$ per cent is nothing in investigations of that sort, of course. Clearly, it is very possible that the accident may be related to the estimate.'

Group-Captain Fisher said, 'If I may say a word, Mr Chairman, Dr Scott speaks of the Reindeer accident—the *first* Reindeer accident, perhaps I should say—as having taken place in somewhat mysterious circumstances. I cannot agree with that. The accident was very fully investigated and was fully explained. There is no mystery about that accident at all.'

Morgan said, 'Quite so, Captain Fisher. I think we may come on to that a little later.'

Prendergast raised his head. 'I should like to say a word, Mr Chairman. I quite agree that the coincidence of flying times deserved attention, provided that one has confidence in the estimate produced by Dr Scott and Mr Honey.

May we hear a little of the nature of this research and of the substance of this estimate?'

The Chairman said, 'I was about to ask the R.A.E. if they would deal with that next.'

The Director said, 'A point of difficulty arises here at once, sir. This estimate was produced by Mr Honey as an incidental to a programme of pure research into fatigue problems. In the course of this research Mr Honey has made a completely new approach to the fatigue problem. It is a very great pity that he could not have been brought here to tell you about it himself. However, I will do my best to outline it to you.'

He paused, and then he said, 'Mr Honey's work is nuclear. He bases it on the small energy loss of materials under strain detected first by Koestlinger and further investigated by Shiltgrad at Upsala University. That work is public property. Mr Honey related these investigations to certain work of a more secret character recently carried out at the N.P.L. which, with your permission, sir, I propose to gloss over.'

The Chairman nodded.

'Arising out of these investigations,' the Director went on, 'Mr Honey produced a completely novel theory of the fatigue effects in light alloy structures, which involved a considerable extension of the accepted nuclear theory. If confirmed by experimental tests, this theory would present for the first time a firm basis for designing structures to resist fatigue, instead of the somewhat hit and miss empirical design factors that we have used to date. Accordingly we put in hand a test upon the Reindeer tail left over from the airworthiness investigations, to confirm or to disprove the theory. That test has now run for about five hundred and ten hours, and on the present rate of progress, running twenty-three hours a day, we expect to reach Mr Honey's figure of 1,440 hours running time about the end of August.'

There was some discussion of the trial programme then and the nature of the test. I produced some photographs of it from my attaché case and circulated them around the table. Prendergast seized them at once and began studying them intently.

The Director went on. 'At the R.A.E. we do not pretend to expert knowledge upon every branch of natural science. There are bodies in this country charged with the investigation of nuclear matters; we are not one of them. When nuclear matters come our way we submit them to the appropriate authority, and in this case we submitted Mr Honey's thesis to the Inter-Services Atomic Research Board for guidance. In addition, Mr Honey visited Sir Phillip Dolbear to discuss the matter. The letter from the Board is there, sir.'

The Chairman picked it up. 'Well, yes. I think I'd better read it to the meeting.'

He did so.

At the conclusion he smiled wryly. 'Well, gentlemen,' he said. 'We all appreciate that the Inter-Services Atomic Research Board has a very full programme, but unfortunately this letter does not take us very much further. In its concluding paragraph it expresses the willingness of the Board to put fatigue problems upon their programme, indicating that they consider that an extension of the nuclear theory may yield useful results in assessing the effects of fatigue; at the same time they clearly don't think very much of Mr Honey's work in this field. They do not go so far as to say that his work is inaccurate or worthless. They refer to it'–he glanced at the letter–'as a wild assumption, which needs much experimental verification.'

I said, 'Which is what we are trying to do.'

'Exactly, Dr Scott. Well, gentlemen, I must confess I don't see what further steps the R.A.E. could have taken in the matter. The confirmatory trial is running night and day, and such assistance as could be obtained has been obtained, from the I.S.A.R.B. I understand that in the circumstances the R.A.E. have a recommendation to make.'

The Director glanced at me.

'I have an opinion,' I said. 'A recommendation, if you like, sir, I don't think any Reindeer should fly more than 700 hours until this thing has been cleared up.'

The Chairman nodded. 'Any comments upon that?'

Carnegie, the technical superintendent of C.A.T.O., said, 'Well, sir, I should like to ask one or two questions. First of all, why seven hundred hours? What is the magic in that number?'

I said, 'It's half the estimated time to failure.'

'No, it's not,' he said. 'Half the estimated time to failure is seven hundred and twenty hours.'

I swallowed. 'All right,' I said. 'Make it seven hundred and twenty hours, if you like. But I don't think any aircraft carrying passengers should fly more than half the estimated time to failure.'

Sir David Moon said, 'I don't want anyone to think this is a trivial point. Twenty more hours flying, on an average of six aircraft only, means twelve more Atlantic flights, which would earn a revenue of over sixty thousand pounds. I am very grateful to Dr Scott for allowing us to make that money by his concession.'

I flushed at his tone. The battle was evidently on.

'I have another question,' said Carnegie. 'Who decided this ratio of one half? We are all agreed that safety comes first, up to a point. If safety precautions are unreasonable, of course, they can stop aviation altogether, and we can all go home.'

He paused. 'I should like to suggest that it is perfectly safe to permit these aircraft to fly up to two-thirds of Mr Honey's estimated time failure–that is, to 960 hours. As operations are going, some of the aircraft will reach seven hundred hours before the test reaches 1,440 hours. As far as I can see, when the test has reached 1,440 hours the first aircraft will have flown about 910 hours, and after that the test should keep ahead of the aircraft if it runs twenty-three hours a day, operating as at present. Two-thirds seems to me to present a fair margin of safety.'

Prendergast said, 'I would certainly agree with that.'

The Chairman turned to me. 'Dr Scott.'

'I don't agree,' I said. 'I should like to. But we know too little about fatigue problems and their onset. All estimates that I have ever seen upon fatigue in built-up structures–and there aren't many to see–have been very much in error, and in the majority of cases failure has taken place before the estimate. I think a factor of two is necessary in a case like this–seven hundred and twenty hours. I shouldn't like to see the aircraft flying on to nine hundred and sixty hours.'

Carnegie said, 'I take it, Dr Scott, that that is just your personal opinion.'

'My personal opinion,' I agreed. 'That's what I think.'

Prendergast said, 'Dr Scott, am I not right in saying that another Reindeer, the one that there has been some trouble with at Gander, has flown 1,429 hours, without any trouble at all?'

'I think that's about right,' I said.

'Well, in view of that, do you still feel that so large a factor of safety as two is desirable?'

'For all we know that one may be on the point of failure.' I replied. 'If it is, then I think a factor of two is necessary. We know too little about fatigue problems to sail nearer the wind than that, where passenger services are concerned. If it were a military aircraft, I might take a different view.'

Sparkes, of the Air Registration Board, spoke up. 'Mr Chairman, with every respect, the allocation of factors of safety is our responsibility, and not that of the R.A.E.'

'Certainly,' I said. 'I'm just telling you what I think.'

There was a short pause.

Then Sir David Moon said, 'Mr Chairman, nobody here wishes to subject the travelling public to any undue risk. But this factor of safety seems to be a matter of opinion. Opinions should be based upon the consideration of all the factors involved, including both the technical factors *and* the operational ones. Now, here there is a political issue. If these aircraft are grounded at 720 hours, the British Transatlantic air service will virtually come to an end, probably for several months, with the most deplorable results to the prestige of this country. If they are allowed to go on flying up to 960 hours and therefore to two-thirds of the time currently run by the test at Farnborough, there is a very good prospect that it may not be necessary to interrupt the services at all.' He paused. 'I should like to ask Dr Scott if he has taken that into consideration.'

The Chairman glanced at me.

I stuck my chin out. 'No, I haven't,' I said. 'This is a technical matter. For safety, I think this thing should carry a factor of two. That is, the aircraft should be grounded at 720 hours, subject to the further investigation of the fatigue problem.'

Sir David Moon said, 'That's a very positive statement, Dr Scott.'

'It is,' I agreed.

Prendergast leaned forward. 'Dr Scott,' he said. 'Is it not the fact that we have no evidence that there is any fatigue trouble in the Reindeer tail at all? Let me put it another way. Mr Honey has produced a theory of fatigue which is unsupported as yet by any experimental evidence. This theory states that the Reindeer tail is dangerous. That is all we have to go upon?'

'Not quite,' I said. I opened the accident report lying on the table before me. 'The tailplane of the first Reindeer crash is still lying in Labrador, and a metallurgical examination of that in the region of the fracture will show if that tail failed in fatigue or not. Here's a photograph of that crash, and I've drawn a pencil circle round the sump of the front spar. It's very tiny, I'm afraid, but it looks not unlike a fatigue fracture to me.'

There was a pause while the report was passed eagerly round the table. Group-Captain Fisher said irritably, 'Nobody can possibly tell anything from that – it's only about a sixteenth of an inch long. The accident was very carefully sifted and all the parts examined. There's no question about what happened.'

Prendergast said, 'Have any steps been taken to recover these parts for examination?'

The Director said, 'We sent out Mr Honey to investigate the matter on the spot. Unfortunately circumstances have prevented him from doing so. Instead, Dr Scott is flying to Ottawa this evening to recover the parts and to carry out any other investigations that may be necessary, in conjunction with the Accidents Investigation Branch.'

The Chairman said, 'Dr Scott is going out there personally? That seems a very good thing.'

Prendergast said, 'But at this moment, all the evidence we have upon this matter is this photograph and Mr Honey's theories?'

I nodded. 'That is correct.' I knew that it was coming now, and it did.

He said, 'Dr Scott, leaving aside the photograph, have you got confidence in Mr Honey's theory of fatigue?'

'I'm not sure that that is quite a fair question,' I said slowly. 'I'll tell you quite frankly that I don't understand it very well, and I doubt if anybody in this room would understand it any better. I have a bowing acquaintance with nuclear theory, as many of us have. I don't know enough about it to criticise the work of somebody who has made a deep study of nuclear matters, as Mr Honey certainly has. I'm sorry, gentlemen, but that's the way it is.'

The Chairman said, 'I think that is a reasonable answer. Dr Scott's appointment does not call for experience in nuclear matters—indeed, no appointment at the R.A.E. has called for that experience up to the present. The R.A.E. very properly applied for advice to the I.S.A.R.B., and it is unfortunate for us that no very definite advice has been forthcoming. However, there it is, and we must make the best of it.'

Prendergast said, 'Making the best of it, Mr Chairman, may I ask another question? Dr Scott, are you satisfied with Mr Honey's work in general? In technical matters have you got confidence in him as a credible person?'

It was a very hot conference room. I was beginning to perspire.

The Chairman said, 'Well, that's rather an unusual question.'

Sir David Moon said, 'These are rather unusual circumstances, Mr Chairman. So far as I can make out there is grave danger that we may be called upon to suspend the entire operation of the British Transatlantic air service because Mr Honey has produced a theory of fatigue which the I.S.A.R.B. think nothing of, and which nobody else has checked. Some of my staff have had experience with Mr Honey recently, as you know, and we are not at all impressed. Indeed, so little impressed were we with his mental stability that we have felt compelled to refuse him any further passages in our aircraft.'

There was a tense pause. I said, 'I should like to answer Mr Prendergast's question, if I may, sir. I have complete confidence in Mr Honey. I think his work, in general, is very advanced and very competent. I think that in this matter he is very likely to be right.'

And I thought to myself as I said that, there goes your job.

Prendergast said slowly, 'I am astonished.'

The Chairman said, 'I think we should accept the opinion of Dr Scott, Mr Prendergast. Mr Honey is a member of his staff, and he is better known to Dr Scott than to anybody in this room.'

Sir David Moon said, 'With every respect, Mr Chairman, I should like to say a word about that. In C.A.T.O. we also know a good deal about Mr Honey. We consider him to be a man with an obsession on this question of fatigue that impels him to the most extravagant acts. I do not think I need go into what happened at Gander; I imagine we are all aware that Mr Honey has wrecked one of our aircraft in deference to his theory.'

'No,' I said. 'In deference to me. I told Mr Honey before he left England that no Reindeer was to fly more than seven hundred hours.'

Carnegie exclaimed, 'You did?' He turned to the Chairman. 'Really, sir, I think that was a little bit high-handed. This meeting has been called to consider that very point.'

I said, 'In emergencies, somebody has to say something. At that time we had no idea that any Reindeer had flown more than four hundred hours. But Mr Honey knew my views, and he acted on them to the best of his ability. I don't think he was backing up his theory by preventing that Reindeer from flying on. He was doing his best to ensure the safety of the travelling public.'

Sir David Moon said, 'Nobody questions that Mr Honey was doing his best, Dr Scott. What we feel in C.A.T.O. is that it was the best of an unbalanced man. I do not know if you quite realise the seriousness of his acts. I have no exact figures yet of the cost of repair of the Reindeer which is now lying at Gander, nor of the loss to which my Organisation will be subjected due to that aircraft being out of service for a period of many weeks. It does not seem possible to me that the sum of those two figures will be less than eighty thousand pounds. I do not feel that my Organisation should be liable for that amount.'

The Chairman pursed his lips and wrote down the figure on his pad.

'We feel in C.A.T.O. that that large financial loss has been forced upon us lightly and unreasonably by an employee of the State who, let us say, thinks differently from ordinary people.' Sir David glanced at the chap from the Treasury, who made a note upon his pad in turn. The legal representative of the Rutland Aircraft Company was already scribbling busily; clearly there was going to be a fine dog-fight over who was to pay for that aircraft. 'Having had this experience of Mr Honey and his obsessions we are quite unwilling to accept him as a passenger again in any of our aircraft. And, equally, we shall be most reluctant to accept any reductions of our services based upon the uncorroborated work of this man, in view of our experience with him.'

Prendergast said, 'As one who has known Mr Honey by repute for a great many years, may I say a word, sir?' The Chairman nodded.

The designer said, 'I have worked in this industry for thirty-nine years. I came into it as a boy two months after Bleriot flew the English Channel, and I have been working in it ever since. At that time the R.A.E. was still known as the Balloon Factory. I have seen that establishment grow from practically nothing to its present size, and all that time I have been in close and intimate touch with it. I have seen scientists come and go at the R.A.E.; I know them, and I know their ways, and many of them have been most able and devoted men. But I can tell this meeting frankly I consider Mr Honey to be exceptional. Scientists, like other men, are subject to mental disturbances, perhaps more so in view of the continuous mental efforts that they are required to make. Some scientists grow senile at an early age, they develop kleptomania and steal small articles from little shops'–he was speaking very slowly–'or they behave indecently in the Park, or they engage in treasonable activities, or they slip into religious mania.'

The Director flushed. All these were true incidents that had bedevilled him within the last three years.

'All my life I have watched these men in their careers,' Prendergast continued. 'I fancy that I know the initial symptoms of a scientific mental decline by this time, and I could make a tolerably good guess of what the future holds for Mr Honey.' The Chairman stirred restively, but Prendergast was Prendergast, senior in age and in experience to the lot of us. 'We have here a man,' he continued, 'who takes a deep interest in psychic phenomena – that is, gentlemen, in ghosts. Mr Honey believes in ghosts; he has been chairman of a body dealing with psychic research. Apart from that, Mr Honey will forecast the date of the coming dissolution of the world to anyone who cares to listen to him, based, I believe, on the structure of the Great Pyramid. If you take fright at that, and wish to escape from a planet which is doomed to destruction' – there was infinite sarcasm in his tone – 'Mr Honey is your man again, because he has been concerned with the Interplanetary Society and at one time produced designs for a rocket-propelled Space Ship, I think he called it, for a projected journey to the moon.'

There were smiles around the table. I spoke up in a cold fury. 'I don't know much about the ghosts or the end of the world,' I said. 'I have looked over his work on interplanetary rockets, which was carried out in his own time in the years 1935 and 1936. So far as I can see, modern developments in guided missiles are following exactly on the lines that he forecast.'

Prendergast glared at me. 'I wish I could believe that certain other forecasts made by Mr Honey would come equally true,' he said harshly. 'As it is, they appear to me to be a particularly offensive form of blasphemy. Are you aware that Mr Honey expects Our Lord to descend to Earth in this country in the year 1994? Are you aware of that, Dr Scott?'

I said angrily, 'Are you aware that He won't?'

The Chairman said, 'Gentlemen, I don't think any of this is really relevant to our consideration of what action we should take, if any, in regard to the Reindeer.'

Prendergast said, 'Our action depends upon our confidence in Mr Honey's work, sir. For my part, I have no confidence at all. The eccentricities that I have mentioned are plain indications of mental decline. Unless fresh evidence, as from the Reindeer crash in Labrador, should be produced, I don't think we should take any action at all, though I would agree to Mr Carnegie's proposal to limit the flying time to two-thirds of the time done by the test.'

The Chairman said, 'Well, Mr Prendergast, as I understand the matter no question of grounding any aircraft upon Mr Honey's estimate alone is likely to arise. It has already been decided to send a representative of the R.A.E., Dr Scott, to make a fresh investigation of the wreckage in Labrador, in conjunction with the Accidents Department. How long do you suppose that that will take?' He turned to the Director.

'It should not take longer than a fortnight,' the Director said. 'That is, assuming that there is no further obstruction in regard to the air transport of my staff.' He said that very quietly.

Sir David Moon said, 'Sir, any action that we may have taken has been for the protection of the travelling public. If we consider any passenger, *any* passenger, to be mentally unstable, we refuse to carry him. We do not wish to obstruct the R.A.E. in any way.'

The Director said gently, 'I should like to say a word upon this question of mental instability, if I may. A wiser man than I once said that an unusual man is apt to look unusual, gentlemen. I will admit that Mr Honey sometimes presents an unusual, an untidy appearance in his manner and his clothes. I do not condone that, but I should be sorry to see the R.A.E. staffed entirely by correct young men in neat, conventional, civil service clothes, with neat, conventional, civil service minds.' A smile ran around the table. 'In my department,' he went on, 'we seek for original thinkers, for the untiring brain that pursues its object by day and by night. If the untiring brain refuses to leave its quest to attend to such matters as the neat arrangement of collar and tie or to removing food stains from its waistcoat, I do not greatly complain.'

He paused. 'As regards Mr Honey's other interests, I would say this. You cannot limit a keen intellect or try to fetter its activity. At times, perhaps, I have no job on hand for a few weeks that will wholly occupy the energies of some member of my staff, but I cannot put the untiring brain into cold storage or prevent the thinker from thinking. If there is a hiatus in the flow of work my research workers will start researching on their own, into the problems of thought transference, or ghosts, or the Lost Tribes of Israel, or the Great Pyramid and the coming dissolution of the world. That, gentlemen, does not mean that they are going mad. It means that I have picked my men well, because the true research worker cannot rest from research.'

Prendergast said acidly, 'May I ask if other members of your staff destroy aircraft when they are not fully occupied?'

The Chairman said hastily, 'I think, Mr Prendergast, we can pass on.'

Prendergast interrupted hotly, 'With every respect, I think we should hear more about the circumstances in which Mr Honey wrecked the Gander aircraft. We have the captain of the aircraft here, Captain Samuelson. May we not hear what he has to say about Mr Honey, sir?'

'If you wish,' the Chairman said reluctantly. 'Captain Samuelson?'

The pilot hesitated. 'Well, sir, I don't know what to say. At the time I thought he was off his head, but having heard all this it seems there's something on the other side as well. I think it's a matter for the doctors,' he concluded weakly.

'Exactly,' said the Chairman. 'Well now, gentlemen—'

Samuelson spoke again. 'Excuse me, sir,' he said. 'May I add just one more thing?'

'Certainly.'

'Well, I've heard a great deal this morning that I don't really understand,' the pilot said. 'I mean, I'm just the b.f. who knows how to fly the thing. But one thing I'm quite certain of, and that's that that first accident report is wrong.' He pointed to the folder lying on the table before me. 'That thing says that Bill Ward came down through the overcast to check his position, and flew into a hill at about fifteen hundred feet. I never heard such bloody nonsense in all my life. I've known Bill Ward for twenty years. He was as senior as I am in the Organisation. It's just bloody nonsense to suggest that he'd have done a thing like that.'

Group-Captain Fisher, red as a turkey cock, said, 'The whole weight of the evidence supports that explanation of the accident.'

The pilot said, 'I don't give a mugger about that, sir. It's plain bloody nonsense. Senior pilots in the Organisation just don't do that sort of thing.

Whatever happened to that Reindeer, it wasn't that.'

Sir David Moon stared down the table at his pilot thoughtfully. 'I think that we should give that view a great deal of consideration,' he said.

The Chairman said, 'I think we should. Well, gentlemen, I think we have heard all that can be said upon the matter at this stage. The R.A.E. will recover the relevant parts of the wreckage of the first machine and will report to me, if possible within a fortnight.' He glanced at the calendar. 'That is, by the 25th. We cannot settle anything this morning, or, indeed, until we have that report upon the first machine. In the meantime, I will see Sir Phillip Dolbear and see if any interim investigation is possible, on high priority. If any action then seems necessary, we must have another meeting.'

Prendergast said sullenly, 'Very good, sir. If any action on our part is required, no doubt somebody will consent to let us know, sometime.'

The chap from the Air Registration Board said, 'It looks as if a little preliminary investigation for the modifications that may be required would be justified.'

Prendergast said sourly, 'It's rather difficult to do that when there is no fault apparent in the present structure. Certainly, I can invent a weakness and get out a modification to put it right, if that is what you wish.'

On that the meeting broke up; the various members stood about in little groups. Sir David Moon went down to the end of the room and stood in close conversation with his pilot, Samuelson; in a lull in the conversation I heard the little sandy-haired man expostulating, 'I tell you, it's all a lot of bloody nonsense, sir.' Group-Captain Fisher was complaining to the Chairman, who was trying to brush him off; he did so just as I was leaving the room with the Director, and bustled over to us.

'You're crossing over to Ottawa tonight, then, Scott?' he said.

'Yes, sir,' I replied.

'Fine,' he said. 'Do your best to get this settled quickly, one way or the other. It's very disturbing to everybody when these things drag on in uncertainty.'

I left then, and went to the Royal Aero Club for lunch. The Director had to go back to the R.A.E., so I lunched alone in the snack-bar and sat for half an hour smoking in the lounge over a cup of coffee. I was very tired. The last few days had been a bit of a strain and the tensions in the meeting that morning had left me feeling slack and ill. Hanging over my head was the lecture in the evening; it should have been the great day of my life, but now it was just another hour of tension to be battled through. I sat trying to rest and read an illustrated magazine till it was time to go back to the Ministry to see about my journey to Canada.

I went to see Ferguson first of all. 'I thought old Prendergast was going to break a blood-vessel this morning,' he said cheerfully. 'Specially when you picked him up on Jesus Christ. I must say, we do have fun at our meetings. That chap from the Treasury said he'd never been at one quite like it.'

I went with him to the Secretariat and spent an hour in various departments getting my passport and my tickets and my money. We got back to his office at about a quarter to four, and his secretary was waiting for me with a message from the Director of Research and Development, our chairman this morning. 'Dr Scott, Mr Morgan wants to see you . . .'

When I got into his office, he said, 'Sit down, Scott. I want to have a talk with you about this morning's meeting. How well do you know Mr Honey?'

'Not very well,' I said. 'This matter of fatigue is the first job of his that I've investigated. He was working on it when I took over the department.'

'Is he a friend of yours? Do you know him personally?'

'No,' I said. 'He's been to my house a couple of times, and I've had his daughter staying with me for the last two days.' I told him about Elspeth.

'I take it that you're friendly with him, then?'

'Not specially,' I said. 'I think he has rather a hard time, living alone after the death of his wife and all that, sir. And I think he's an able little man. As regards his daughter, I hope we'd do that much for any of my staff who got into a jam.'

'You think he's able?'

'I do, sir.'

He drummed on the table for a moment, staring out of the window. 'Well, I hope you're right,' he said at last. He raised his head and looked at me kindly. 'There's going to be a row about this Reindeer, either way,' he said. 'If it proves that there is real trouble in the tailplane, that you and Honey are right, then there's going to be Parliamentary trouble over the suspension of the North Atlantic service. People will start saying that this country can't build aircraft so we'd better give up trying.'

'We can plough through that one, sir,' I said.

He nodded. 'Of course we can. But if it goes the other way, and it turns out to be a mare's nest—that there's nothing wrong with the tailplane at all, then there'll be trouble of a different sort. Then the Treasury will come in over the payment for the aircraft Honey wrecked at Gander. I rather wish you hadn't thrown your weight on his side quite so definitely this morning, Scott.'

'There'll be a row about that, will there, sir?'

'I'm rather afraid there will. I had the Treasury man with me for half an hour after lunch. He's very much concerned about the action that Honey saw fit to take.'

'Too bad,' I said wearily. 'But I can't help that. Honey knew my views and what he did was certainly influenced by what he knew my attitude to be. You can't go through life sitting on the fence. You've got to make decisions, and sometimes you're pretty sure to make them wrong. If you're going to chuck Honey to the lions, sir, you'll have to chuck me too.'

He said doubtfully, 'Oh, I don't think it will come to that.' He stared out of the window for a minute; it was hot in his office and I was sweating a little. 'You must have thought about this for a long time,' he said. 'What makes you so positive that he is right?'

I could not relate the sum of tiny things that had built up my judgment, the strong hiking boots, the rocket thesis, the quality of his discourse upon automatic writing, his spartan mode of life, the beauty and intelligence of the women who had loved him. 'I don't know,' I said. 'I've just got a hunch that he's right.'

'From your experience?'

I knew he understood. 'That's right, sir,' I said eagerly. 'I just kind of smell trouble here. Honestly, I think there's something the matter with the Reindeer tail.'

'I believe I agree with you,' he said slowly. He smiled. 'Well, we'll keep our fingers crossed and hope you bring something definite back with you from Canada.' He stood up and held out his hand. 'Good luck. You've got everything you want for the journey—money and tickets and all that?'

'Everything,' I said. 'I'll come ·back with the evidence all right, sir'–I smiled–'for or against.'

I went back to Ferguson's office. 'What did he want?' he asked casually.

'He wanted to break it to me that if the Reindeer hasn't got fatigue trouble I could start looking for another job,' I said. 'But he didn't get around to putting it in so many words.'

I left the office and walked slowly across the Green Park towards the club. I was tired and dispirited; everything was massing up on me as if for a disaster. I had backed Mr Honey in his fatigue theory because one has to take a positive line. I had thought it out and come to the conclusion that he was probably right, and I had plumped for that, but I could not overlook the other side of the question. What if he were wrong? He had never seen a washing-up mop or an electric hot-water heater; he had walked in a provocative procession and had been taken up by the police and charged with creating a breach of the peace. Lucky that Prendergast did not bring out that one at the meeting! Suppose, in fact, he was a stupid, trivial man; suppose in fact, I found nothing wrong at all with the wreckage in Labrador? My name would then be mud; it would take a long time to live down the stink that this would make in official circles. Probably it would mean that there would be no more promotion for me at the R.A.E. In that case I would do better to get out of the country, go down to the bottom and start again, perhaps in Australia or New Zealand.

I sat for a long time on a bench in the park tired and trying to rest, wondering miserably if my life in my own country was coming to an end.

Presently I got up and went back to the club. Shirley was waiting for me there, and I ordered tea. 'We got Elspeth moved all right,' she said. 'She's back in her own room now, with Miss Corder looking after her. She's a nice girl that, Dennis.'

'She is,' I said. 'Where's she sleeping?'

She looked at me reproachfully. 'In the little spare room, of course. All in among the suitcases. You didn't think she'd sleep in Mr Honey's bed?'

'Not yet,' I said. She aimed a kick at my ankle under the table. 'Is Elspeth happy to be back in her own place?'

'Oh yes. Marjorie was going to wash the stairs and the hall this afternoon, and she can talk to Elspeth while she's doing that. After tea they were going to make toffee.'

'Where's she going to get the sugar from?'

'Mr Honey's got about thirty pounds of it in the larder. It's their jam sugar ration for about four years. He doesn't know how to make jam.'

'She'd better make him some.'

'She's going to do that tomorrow. There are strawberries in the shops now, and they're reasonably cheap.'

She turned to me. 'How did the meeting go, Dennis?'

'Not too well,' I said. 'There's going to be the hell of a row if these machines have got fatigue and a worse one if they haven't.'

'Oh, darling, I *am* sorry.'

Presently we left the club and walked across the park to the lecture hall; my lecture was at half-past six, but I had to go through the slides with the lantern operator first. Then came a period of waiting and nervous, distracted talk with various people in the industry while the hall filled up, till there was an audience of six or seven hundred people. Finally I went through with the President on to the platform, with the Secretary behind me, and sat nervously trying to control my twiddling fingers while the President introduced me as the lecturer on the 'Performance Analysis of Aircraft Flying at High Mach Numbers.'

When I got on my feet, all my nervousness vanished after the first few words. I was very tired and stale, but I knew my subject, and the familiar graphs and diagrams followed each other on the screen without a hitch. I spoke for about fifty minutes; at the end I was a little hoarse, and was glad to sit down and take a drink of water, happy that the damn thing was over. There was applause, of course; there always is. It seemed a terribly long time before it stopped; the next fence was the discussion, and then it would be over. To my dismay I saw Prendergast get heavily to his feet in the second row. I waited with sick anticipation for what he was going to say.

He said, 'Mr President and gentlemen. I have worked in this industry for nearly forty years, and during that time I have attended most of the meetings of this Society. I have several points on which I wish to cross swords with the lecturer, but at the outset I wish to pay my tribute to his clarity. I have very seldom listened to a lecture that explained so difficult a subject in such simple language. I am left with the feeling that the most inexperienced student in this hall must have learned as much as I have this evening, and I have learned a great deal which will be of value to me.'

I sat blinking as I listened to this incredible man. He changed like a chameleon, but I sat back sick with relief that he was not going to go for me in public as he had that morning at the meeting. The fact that he then proceeded to tear to pieces my analysis of the critical area of the pressure plate based upon the harmonic surges that occur when passing through the compressibility zone did not worry me a bit; it was done constructively and in one instance at least suggested a line well worth further investigation. Morgan was there and I could see that he was pleased. Other speakers took their tone from Prendergast, and the discussion went on for another three-quarters of an hour. I replied to the various points as best I could, and then it was all over.

Shirley met me in the lobby. 'Dennis, it was marvellous,' she said. 'Everybody said it was awfully good. Was that Mr Prendergast who spoke first?'

'That's right,' I said.

'What a nice man he must be. I can't think why people say such horrid things about him.'

I could, but I did not want to spoil her pleasure in the good reception that my talk had had, and so I marched her off back to the club and there we had dinner with a bottle of red Algerian wine to celebrate our success, and to put me to sleep on the plane, and a glass of port to follow. Then it was time to get a taxi and take my suitcase to the Airways terminal. On the steps I kissed Shirley good-bye.

'Back in about a fortnight,' I said. 'Look after yourself.'

'You look after yourself,' she said a little tremulously. 'Don't go and get eaten by a moose in Labrador, or anything, Dennis.'

I said I wouldn't, and we parted, and I went into the hall and showed my passport and my tickets. And as I turned away, a woman in a great fur came up behind me with a swirl, and it was Monica Teasdale.

'Evening, Miss Teasdale,' I said. 'Are you crossing over tonight?'

She stretched out a hand in her most dazzling, professional gesture, that made me feel that everybody in the hall was taking note of us. 'Say, Dr Scott, isn't this nice? Are you going over too?' And then she said, 'Did you give your lecture? How did it go?'

'All right,' I said. 'They didn't throw any eggs.'

There were several sleek young men with shiny black hair and flashing eyes with her to see her off, and one portly old gentleman with a very hooked nose; I drifted away and left her to her other life. We travelled down in different seats of the bus; at the airport I did not speak to her. I was amused to note that we were to travel in a Reindeer; I decided to ask no question about that one and to refuse any invitation from the captain that I should go to the flight deck. What the eye doesn't see, the heart doesn't grieve over.

We took off, and as we climbed up on our way to the Atlantic I relaxed for the first time that day. The Algerian wine was doing its work; as I leaned back in the reclining chair fatigue came soaking out of me in great waves. Three rows ahead of me I could see Miss Teasdale's auburn hair; as on Honey's trip, the aircraft was only half full. After half an hour or so, when I was beginning to doze, she got up and went aft down the cabin; on her return she stopped beside me.

'Say, Dr Scott,' she asked, 'is this a Reindeer, too?'

I sat up. 'I'm afraid it is,' I said. 'But I don't think you need be afraid of anything going wrong this time.'

She smiled, 'Will we be landing at Gander again?'

'I imagine so,' I said.

She laughed. 'You'll be interested to meet your Mr Honey there,' she said. 'Mind if I sit down a little while and visit with you?' ·

'Do–please.' I picked my papers off the seat, and she sat down beside me. 'I hope Honey will be on his way home by this time. The Lincoln that was to pick him up was due through Gander today.'

'He won't be at Gander when we land?'

'I hope not. I hope he'll be at home.'

She was silent. I glanced at her after a moment, and was surprised to see the hard lines of age and suffering on her face as she stared up the cabin. People had told me that she was over fifty, but I had never really believed it till then.

I said, 'Are you going back to the west coast?'

She nodded. 'I'll go from Montreal to Chicago, and pick up with the airline there. I kind of like this way of travelling, unless there's business in New York.'

'When will you be over here again?' I asked. 'Do let us know, so that Honey can bring Elspeth up to see you.' It's extraordinary how cruel one can be, quite unintentionally, when one is too tired to be careful any more.

She turned to me, and she was every day of fifty. 'I don't just know when that will be,' she said. 'Maybe not for some years. I guess a person ought to stay in her own place.'

I was more awake now to the situation. 'Don't think like that,' I said. 'We've loved having you, and it's been terribly kind of you to spend so much time with Elspeth. It's taken a lot off Shirley.'

She said quietly, 'It's been real nice getting out of Wardour Street and Claridge's a little while, and getting to know you folks in your homes. I never knew that British people lived so much like folks in the U.S. But I guess if you've been born American you're better off in your own country. Maybe you British think the same way.'

'I think that's true, after a certain age,' I said. 'If you're going to make your life in a new country you should go before you're twenty-five. After that you start to get associations, little grooves and anchors, that make it difficult to change.'

She nodded. 'I know it. Not only living places, either–that goes for what you do. Take pictures, now. You get set in pictures when you're young and maybe you think you can give up and get right out of it any time you say, like marrying and bringing up a family like any other woman. But then when you come down to hard brass tacks, you find you can't. So many little grooves and anchors, like you said.'

I said thoughtfully, 'You mean you've got to make the pattern of your life before you're twenty-five. I never thought of that, but I dare say it's true.'

'I'd say that's true,' she replied. 'By that age you either go for marrying and raising a family and making a home or you go for a job and forget about the other. If it happens later, maybe it works out, maybe it doesn't. But if you want to be sure, then you've just got to drop the job and do the other by the time you're twenty-five.' She was about to add something, but checked herself.

I was fully awake by that time. I smiled; the woman wanted to talk. 'Marjorie Corder,' I said.

She turned to me. 'You're clever,' she said. 'I guess that's why they made you boss of your department, all about fatigue and things like that. Well, there's a case for you. I'd say she's around twenty-four or twenty-five. And now she's switching over.'

I glanced at her. 'You think she wants to marry Mr Honey?'

'She's moved into his house already,' she said bitterly.

There was a long pause. 'I don't say that I blame her,' she went on at last. 'He's a grand little guy, and he deserves a young wife.' Her face was lined and old. 'I guess she knows she wouldn't find a man like that so easily again; she's been around, that girl has, and she's got to know about men. I guess she's in love with him all right.'

There was a long silence. My eyes drooped with fatigue; sleep was not far away. But presently the actress said, 'It's funny the way those little quiet men get you. I knew a man one time, oh, years and years ago, before éver I went into pictures. In the office, that was, back in Terre Haute. He was so kind, but he was lame and I was a young fool and thought I'd meet ones like him around every corner, and get married when I wanted to. Well, I did get married, but it wasn't like it might have been if I had married Eddie Stillson. I'd have had about four kids then and no money, and a lot of work and worry and been old and tired and worn out by this time.'

'Sorry?' I inquired.

'Sometimes,' she said. 'I never did my stuff. Seems I've always been a kind of passenger.'

There was another of those long, slow pauses. 'It's too late to do anything about it now,' she said. 'That kind of man, he's got a right to have a family when he marries. It wouldn't be good for him to marry somebody like me, not now. That kind of man, he's got a right to a young wife, who'll have some children for him, and not mind living in a little house like that and working, with just two weeks in a summer camp some place each year. I couldn't do that, now.

'You can't put back the clock,' she said. 'You may want to, terribly badly. But some things you just can't do, and that's one of them.'

I was desperately tired, and closed my eyes for a moment to think this over. When I opened them again the lights in the saloon were dimmed and Miss

Teasdale, the World's Pin-Up Girl, had gone back to her own seat three rows ahead of me. I turned on my pillow and slept again, and when next I woke the stewardess was standing over me, telling me to fasten my belt. We were going into Gander.

We came round in a great sweep, low over the forests in the moonlight. The approach lights came in view, the flaps came down and the runway appeared immediately beneath our wheels; then we were down and rolling towards the hangars and the office buildings. We drove up near the Reindeer lying on its belly on the tarmac.

As soon as we were allowed to disembark I went to the reception hall and asked for Honey at the C.A.T.O. desk. But he had left about tea-time the day before in a Lincoln for Shawbury; he must have been already in the British Isles when I took off for Gander. Probably by that time he would already have arrived back in Farnborough. I went and had a wash and a shave and then crossed the road to the restaurant; as I went in I passed Miss Teasdale coming out, fresh and blooming like a rose.

I stopped. 'I was terribly rude last night,' I said. 'I went clean off to sleep while we were talking.'

She laughed, and passers-by stared at me with interest and with envy. She said, 'You must have been tired after a day like that. I felt real sorry for you.'

'I've just heard that Honey left for home yesterday,' I said. 'He'll be there by now.'

'You see he stays there,' she said. 'He's a great little guy, but not the sort to go wandering around the world alone.'

'Too true,' I said. The sight of the first Reindeer lying on its belly was still fresh in my mind. 'What's the breakfast like in here?'

She laughed. 'I had just a cup of coffee—I never take more in the morning. The people at the next table had buck-wheat cakes and syrup, with a sausage on the side.'

I asked anxiously, 'Can I get porridge, do you think?'

She laughed. 'I wouldn't know about that. You're on our side of the Atlantic now.'

I did not speak to her again. I breakfasted in a hurry on cornflakes and bacon and eggs, and then went out with one of the C.A.T.O. officials to the tarmac to inspect the first Reindeer. It was a sad sight, the propellers, flaps, and engine cowlings crushed and distorted, and the belly of the fuselage on which it rested badly crumpled. The air bags to raise it had not yet arrived and were not expected for another week; when they came they would be placed under the delicate wing structure and inflated; by bearing on so large an area they would gently lift the great thing without further damage. The A.R.B. inspector, Symes, appeared while I was looking at it, and the official introduced me.

He grunted. 'We got rid of your Mr Honey yesterday,' he said. Evidently he did not think much of Honey.

I asked, 'Have you made any examination of the tail?'

'It's perfect,' he replied. 'There's not a sign of trouble of any sort. Of course, I know that this fatigue may not give very much warning, but I'd stake my reputation that that tail's as perfect as when it left the factory. About the only thing that is,' he said gloomily, looking at the aircraft. 'Just wanton destruction, I call it.'

'There are two views on that,' I said. 'It's just possible that he might turn out to be right.'

'I've been in this industry since 1917,' he said. 'I don't say that fatigue never does occur. What I say is, that you don't very often meet it.'

We climbed up into the fuselage and went aft through the luggage bay. They had taken out a panel from the pressure bulkhead and I was able to crawl in and get all round the spars with an electric torch. What the inspector had said was quite true; the structure seemed in perfect condition. I knew that that meant nothing in the case of fatigue trouble, but it was depressing all the same. The evidence was running all in favour of the diehards.

Mr Symes clearly did not believe in the least that there was anything the matter with the machine at all, apart from what Honey had done to it. I had to leave them, because the passengers were being marshalled out to the other Reindeer, the one that I had come from England in. I followed them and we took off for Montreal.

We landed there at about 10 o'clock in the morning, local time. Miss Teasdale was surrounded in the reception hall by a little crowd of friends and fans; I was met by a flight-lieutenant of the R.C.A.F., who had a four-seat Beaver waiting to fly me down to Ottawa. The actress was busily engaged and I was reluctant to keep my officer waiting; moreover, I had nothing more to say to her. I left her to her other life, and went with him to the Beaver and took off for Ottawa.

We got there in about an hour and there was a car to meet me. We drove straight to the Bureau of Civil Aviation, and in half-an-hour I was sitting in conference with the Director, a Group-Captain Porter, and the Inspector of Accidents, Squadron-Leader Russell.

A small population in a big country seems to breed a clearer-headed sort of man than we get in England, although they may be less well informed. These men knew all about my business and they were very ready to accept the possibility of fatigue in the Reindeer tail. Indeed, they were very interesting in opinions of the onset of fatigue at sub-zero temperatures. When operating a certain high-speed jet-propelled medium bomber at temperatures exceeding thirty degrees below zero they had had two cases of structural failure by fatigue, one of a vertical fin and one of an elevator. They were convinced that temperature came into it, a new idea to me. They suggested that the life of Mr Honey's Reindeer had been prolonged by the fact that it had operated mostly in the tropics.

All this was very stimulating, and they were not less helpful in the practical investigation of the crash in Labrador. They had a Norseman seaplane all laid on for the journey, and all the equipment and provisions for a week or ten days in the woods already loaded into it. The pilot was to be a civilian bush-pilot called Hennessey, a thick-set tough who knew that country intimately; Russell and an assistant of his called Stubbs were coming with us, making a party of four. The programme was that we should fly up and land on Small Pine Water, about eleven miles from the wreck; from there a trail made by previous visitors to the scene led over the hills and through the forests. It was, of course, quite impossible to put a landplane down in such country.

'They say the trail's pretty well defined,' Russell said. 'There was our party first of all, and then there was a funeral party went up there, and then the Russians sent a third party to bring away the body of their ambassador for

burial in Russia. They had the hell of a job carrying a coffin down that trail.'
'Our people were all buried up there, were they?' I inquired.
'Oh yes. It wasn't practical to bring the rest of them away. There were over thirty, and all would have had to be carried eleven miles. No, we buried them all up there; a padre went up for the funeral service.'

They were all ready to start, and were only waiting for me. We lunched and then they took me to a sort of store and fitted me out with a bush shirt, breeches, and high laced boots that buckled close below the knee. 'The mosquitoes are liable to be mighty bad this time of year,' Hennessey said. They had hammocks for sleeping in, provided· with a sort of roof of waterproof fabric with a mosquito net attached.

I transferred some small personal kit from my suitcase into a small kitbag; then I was ready and we drove down to the dock, where the Norseman was moored. It was only about three o'clock in the afternoon, and we were all ready to start. 'I guess we'll make Ivanhoe by sundown,' Hennessey said. 'Tank up there, 'n have plenty up at the lake.'

The others agreed with this programme. 'How far is this place Ivanhoe?' I inquired.

Russell said, 'About five hundred and fifty miles. It's on the north shore of the St Lawrence, about a hundred miles from the crash.'

I said good-bye to the Director and thanked him for all his help; then we got into the machine. Hennessey started the engine and someone on the pontoon swung the wing-tip round; we taxied out into the lake, running up the engine in short bursts as we went. Then we headed into wind and took off after a long run, about fifty seconds. The machine was very heavily loaded for its power.

We circled the city and steadied on our course back over the route I had flown that morning. The machine was equipped for hard commercial work in the Canadian north, mostly for carrying freight. The passenger seats were small and rather hard, designed to be quickly removable; they wasted no weight upon blinds, and the cabin on that sunny afternoon became very hot. I sat drowsing and sweating and tired, but unable to sleep as we droned back past Montreal towards Quebec, a slow, interminable journey. Finally as the sun was getting down to the horizon we came to Ivanhoe, a little town of white wooden houses on the shore of an inlet of the sea. Behind it stretched the fir woods, apparently pathless, impenetrable. Such roads as there were came to an end immediately outside the town. There were three churches, with white wooden steeples, a little dock with a few fishing vessels and another seaplane moored to it, a small air-strip suitable for very little aeroplanes. That was all there was of Ivanhoe.

We saw all this as we circled round for the landing; then Hennessey put her down on the water gently; he was a very good pilot, on that aircraft anyway. She touched with a quick slapping of the small waves on the bottom of the floats; the floats bit down into the water and she leaned forward and decelerated, and slowed, and floated on the water off the town, pitching a little. Hennessey turned her, and we taxied into the pontoon.

A sergeant in the gay red tunic of the Royal Canadian Mounted Police was there to meet us; he knew Hennessey, and said, 'Guess you folks 'll have to sleep in the store tonight. Hotel's full of summer visitors.'

In the fading light he took us to a sort of marine store, a wooden shed full of old ships' ropes and other· gear. There were big hooks down each wall, especially put there, it seemed, for slinging hammocks; it was frequently used as a dormitory. We slung ours, Stubbs assisting me and showing me how to do it, and made the seaplane fast at the pontoon; then we walked into the little town and sat down at the counter of the only café and ordered dinners of steak and onions and fried potatoes, from a girl who spoke nothing but French. Over the ice-cream and coffee we talked a little.

The crash was about four months old, but Hennessey had been up there within the last month as a guide to the party of Russians who had come from the Embassy to disinter the body of their Ambassador and carry him away. 'Great big jars of stuff they had with them,' he said, 'and a kind of zinc tank with a lid you could screw down on a rubber gasket. He didn't smell so bad after they got him all sealed down. Eight handles it had, for carrying, but gee, that was a mean load. I never want another like that again. Eleven miles, and a rough trail at that.'

He stared at his cup. 'I'm not sure even now they got the right one. It was the right grave, but when we buried them they weren't too easy to identify, and it didn't seem to matter which got which cross; they were all there together. We tossed a dime for which cross to put on some of them. Still, it wouldn't make a row of beans, anyway.'

We went back to the store in the soft darkness; at the pontoon near by the Norseman loomed with a great shadowy wing over the water. We undressed partially and got into our hammocks, but for a long while I could not sleep. I was overtired, and lay restless, wondering what the Director was saying to Honey in my absence, wondering what the next day would bring for me, wondering if corrosion would have destroyed the evidence for which I sought. Then, unhappily, I wondered if temperature did enter into this fatigue problem. If so, it might well mean a year's investigation before we could say definitely if the Reindeer was, in fact, unsafe. In that case it would be quicker to take the aircraft out of service and modify them whether they were dangerous or not, but what a stinking row there would be about that!

I rolled insecure, sleepless, overtired, and unhappy for most of the night. The store was full of rats, who scurried all around incessantly.

Early in the morning we were up and breakfasting in the same café, served by the same French-speaking girl. Then we began the weary task of filling six forty-gallon drums of petrol into the tanks of the Norseman through a semi-rotary pump. Each barrel had to be rolled from the petrol store a hundred yards away down to the pontoon, and the empties rolled back again. It took us about two hours, and by that time the sun was high and hot and we were tired and sweating. At last it was finished, and we got into the machine and started up the engine, and took off.

Small Pine Water is about an hour's flight from Ivanhoe. We left the St Lawrence and flew approximately north-east, over a desolate country covered in fir woods and fallen timber like spillikins, on hills which grew gradually higher beneath us as we went on inland. Presently Russell asked me if I would like to see the scene of the accident from the air before we landed on the lake. I said I would, and Hennessey brought the Norseman down to about five hundred feet above the tree tops and began circling around. But there was very little to be seen from the air. I saw a cliff that the aircraft had evidently hit, but it was not very conspicuous or very high. I saw a few shells of dulled duralumin between the fronds of new vegetation, and there was a little clearing where a few trees had been felled; in this clearing there were planted two rows of neat white crosses. That was all that could be seen from the air, and we turned back and landed on the lake.

When we were down, we turned and taxied into a beach. People had been here before us, for trees had been felled and undergrowth cleared at the landing. There were oil stains on the ground and a few empty tins, and burnt ashes in a fireplace built of stones, and stuck up in the fork of a tree there was a bundle tied around with sacking. The floats of the Norseman grounded upon rotting and decayed vegetation on the bottom of the lake about a couple of yards from the shore. We stopped the engine and got out on to the float, and walked along, and splashed through the shallow water to the shore. We took mooring lines with us and made the seaplane fast to screw pickets; immediately the flies were all around us in a cloud.

It was then about noon. We unloaded all the gear out of the Norseman on to the beach, and Stubbs set about cooking a meal. It was arranged that he should stay there at the beach to look after the aircraft while Hennessey and Russell and I walked the eleven miles up to the crash, carrying upon our backs the packs containing our hammocks, blankets, ammunition, and food for two days. In addition each of us carried an axe and Hennessey carried a rifle, Russell a shot-gun.

I am ashamed to say how much that walk distressed me. It was a very hot summer afternoon, for one thing. My pack weighed about fifty pounds and it was comfortable enough on a light duralumin frame carrier. But I was out of condition with years of office work, whereas both Russell and Hennessey were wiry and perfectly fit. They took an easy pace to avoid tiring me too much and several times they offered to carry my pack for me, but pride made me refuse. It took us nearly five hours to get there, blind and drenched with sweat and tormented by flies.

The country that we passed through was appalling. It was a forest of spruce and alder; in some parts the trees were not more than three feet apart. It was full of rotting trunks of fallen trees, and these trees and the decaying vegetation round them made a queer, stifling aroma that was more a gasp than a smell. For much of the way the ground was soft muskeg in which the feet sank up to six inches. It was impossible to see more than a few yards in any direction; at the same time the trees were fairly small, so that they gave little shelter from the sun. The trail wound in and out among the fallen trunks marked here and there by a fading blaze upon a standing tree, but it was difficult to discern except to the practised eye, and in no way resembled a path. In places it was swampy, and here if you put a foot down incautiously you would go in knee deep. And always the flies were an incessant torment.

When finally we came out into the clearing with the double row of wooden crosses I was practically foundered. I slid the pack from my back and sat down on it for a moment with my head swimming and the flies in a great cloud around me. I thanked God in my fatigue that circumstances had prevented Honey from coming on this trip; I might be quite unfit for it, but I was certainly a great deal fitter than he was. Russell and Hennessey set about making a fire and boiling up a kettle for tea; by the time that was well under way I was feeling better, and able to assist them a bit by gathering the wood.

Tea refreshed us all, though none of us could eat anything. While Hennessey put the things together and began to arrange a camp Russell and I walked over to the wreck. It lay about two hundred yards away, under the stony cliff that had appeared in the photographs. New vegetation had grown up and was covering it over; by next year it would have merged into the forest.

We came first to the bow, to the smashed cockpit where Bill Ward had died, to the broken control columns, the scattered instruments, the flattened and corroded boxes of the radio and radar gear. Then came the broken wing and the engines, and the cabin with smashed seats and burnt upholstery, and the galley stove and lavatory behind it, practically undamaged amongst all the wreckage. I reflected that Honey had been quite right about that; was it to prove that he was right about fatigue as well?

Then we came to the tail.

The seaboard side was more or less intact; the port tailplane and elevator were missing completely, as in the photographs and the description of the accident report. I went straight to the broken stumps of the spars still attached to the rear fuselage, that in the tiny detail of the photographs had suggested a fatigue fracture.

They were not as they had been in the photograph. A clean, recent saw-cut had been made to cut both spars through close up to the fuselage. The evidence had been removed.

Russell was dumbfounded, and shouted to Hennessey, who came running. We showed him what had happened. 'Oh, aye,' he said, 'the Russians did that. They cut them bits off with a hacksaw 'n took them away. They took some other bits as well.'

He eyed us with mounting anxiety. 'We thought it was all so much junk,' he said. 'Not important, were they?'

10

Mr Honey travelled back across the Atlantic in a Lincoln of the Empire Air Navigation School that had been wandering about the north of Canada doing something or other with the lines of flux at the Magnetic Pole. Now it was on its way back to Shawbury and the R.A.F. navigators were glad to oblige by giving Mr Honey a lift back to England. Originally they had been bound straight for their base in Shropshire, but being navigators they rather enjoyed going out of their way in bad visibility on tortuous courses that would test their skill. They landed Mr Honey at Farnborough outside his own office door at half-past one in the morning, put him out upon the runway, kissed their hands to him, and took off again for Shawbury in the darkness. Mr Honey was left holding his suitcase in the middle of Farnborough aerodrome in the middle of the night.

Characteristically, he went into the office. He walked in, blinking, to the bright lights of the old balloon shed where the night shift test upon the Reindeer tail was clattering and booming away, and there was young Simmons entering the routine hourly strain readings upon the routine graphs of the distortion of the structure, all of which went along as a perfectly straight horizontal line as the strain graphs of a safe structure should. He blinked at the great clattering thing, sniffed, savoured the familiar atmosphere; everything was all right, and he was home again.

He stayed about half an hour, examining the records; he had only been away for four days, but so much had happened in that time he felt that it was several months, that something must have changed, some catastrophe must have happened to his trial during his absence. But finally he satisfied himself that it was going on all right, and asked if Simmons had been posting the letters to Elspeth properly.

The boy hesitated. 'Well, yes I have, sir,' he said, 'but I don't know that they've been getting to her. You know she fell downstairs the night you went away, and she's been staying with Dr Scott ever since, I think.'

He told Honey what he knew, which was not very much, and satisfied him that Elspeth was not very ill. Honey said warmly, 'It was very kind of Dr Scott to do that. Is he at home now?'

'I think he flew to Canada this evening, sir. He was going to, after his lecture on the "Performance of Aircraft flying at High Mach Numbers". We all went up to that. It was awfully good.'

It seemed to Honey that there was not much else he could do but go home and go to bed; he could hardly burst in on Shirley in the middle of the night and demand to see Elspeth, who was apparently being well looked after. As regards getting home, there was a little difficulty. There were no buses at that hour and no R.A.E. transport. Simmons had a motorbicycle, but Honey could not ride it and Simmons could not leave the Reindeer trial. In the end Honey left the suitcase in his office, and set out to walk the four miles to his home through the deserted lanes and streets.

He got there at about half-past three, walked up the path through the front garden, and let himself into the house with his latchkey. He went into the front sitting-room and snapped on the light. The familiar room was somewhat changed in the short time that he had been away; there was a smell of soap that he could not at first identify, and there was a vase of roses on the table. He wondered who could have done a thing like that, and then he remembered that something had happened to Elspeth and other people must have been in the house.

A door opened upstairs, and he heard someone moving on the landing. He went out into the hall and looked up the one flight, blinking, and at the head of the stairs there was a young woman standing looking down, a very pleasant-looking young woman in pyjamas and a kimono. He did not recognise her at first; I don't know what he thought about it. Something that his Fairy Godmother had done for him, perhaps.

She said, 'Mr Honey! We didn't expect you back so soon.'

He said, 'Who is it?'

'It's me,' she said. 'Marjorie Corder.' She laughed a little awkwardly. 'I'd have stayed up if I'd known that you were coming home tonight, but we didn't think you could be here before tomorrow.'

She came downstairs to him. 'You must think it terribly funny for me to be here,' she said. 'But Elspeth was so anxious to get back here, and Mrs Scott couldn't have her for tonight. So I said I'd sleep here with her.' She broke off. 'Did you know she had an accident?'

'They told me something at the office. What did happen?' he asked. 'Simmons—he's my assistant there—he said Mrs Scott had taken her into their flat.'

She told him briefly what had been going on. 'Dr Scott wouldn't let anybody cable you about it,' she said, 'because you couldn't have got home any sooner and he thought it would only worry you. She's quite all right now—she's upstairs, asleep. She's going to get up a bit tomorrow.'

He said, 'I'll just go up and see her.'

She smiled. 'Don't wake her up, will you? She's sleeping so nicely.'

'I won't wake her up,' he said.

She stopped him as he turned to the stairs. 'Have you had any supper?'

He thought back vaguely over the last few hours. 'We had some sandwiches and things in the aircraft,' he said.

'But when did you have your last proper meal?'

He thought for a minute. 'Gander, I suppose.'

She nodded. 'I'll get you something—you must be hungry. Scrambled eggs all right? Cocoa? Or Bovril?'

'Cocoa, please,' he said. 'But please don't bother—'

'But of course,' she said. 'You must have something.'

He went upstairs and peeped in on Elspeth, who was sleeping, with the washing-up mop in bed with her. On the table by her bedside, pulled forward where she could see it, was another little vase of roses and the photograph of her mother, his Mary, that somebody had taken from the mantelpiece arranged specially for his daughter, in case she should be lonely amongst so many strangers. Mr Honey closed the door quietly with more moisture even than was usual in his weak eyes, washed his hands, and went down again to the kitchen.

He found Miss Corder at the gas-stove cooking for him; there was a cleaner, fresher air about the kitchen which seemed strange to him and which he did not understand. 'Please let me do that,' he said. 'There's no need for you to stay up now. I'll be all right.'

She turned half round from the stove. 'I feel an awful pig going to bed at all,' she said. 'If we'd thought that there was any chance of you getting back tonight I'd have had a decent meal ready for you.'

He said weakly. 'It's terribly nice of you,' and began to lay the table. 'When did you get here?'

'Yesterday,' she said. 'I brought your letter down to Dr Scott and then I heard that Elspeth was in bed, so I came round to see what I could do. And then she was so anxious to get back here, and Mrs Scott wanted to be up in London tonight to see her husband off to Canada, so I said I'd sleep here with Elspeth until you came back. I do hope you don't mind. It did seem the best thing to do.'

'Of course I don't mind,' he said warmly. 'It's so very, very kind of you to take the trouble.'

She brought the scrambled eggs on toast to the table for him on a warm plate, and poured out cocoa for them both. As she supped she told him what they had been doing. 'Dr and Mrs Scott have been so kind,' she said, 'but really, Elspeth's much happier round here. She likes being in her own room and her own bed. I was doing the stairs this afternoon and we could talk, and then after that I made some toffee with her on the gas-ring in her room, and we played Sevens.'

Mr Honey realised dimly that nobody had played with Elspeth like that for many years; perhaps that was what was wrong with her. He said, 'You did the stairs? Do you mean, brushed them down?'

'I washed them,' the girl said. 'They did need it. I hope you don't mind. I did this room, too.'

Mr Honey glanced around the kitchen; so that was what had happened to it. 'It's awfully nice,' he said ingenuously. 'What did you do to the walls to make them like that?'

'I washed those, too,' she said. 'It didn't take long. An awful lot of dirt came off.'

He looked at her in slight distress. 'I didn't know it had got so bad.'

'Of course not,' she said gently. 'One wouldn't, living in the house the whole time. It's only when you come in fresh that it hits you in the eye.'

'I did tell Mrs Higgs to do some scrubbing, only last week,' he said. 'Or sometime. I suppose she didn't do it.'

'I don't think she can have,' the girl said positively. 'I should give her the sack if I were you. She doesn't seem to be very reliable.'

'The one I had before used to steal things,' Mr Honey said. 'Mrs Higgs is very honest, and she's given me a lot of help with Elspeth's clothes.'

The girl compressed her lips and took a drink of cocoa. 'Do you think I might look through Elspeth's clothes tomorrow?' she said. 'I don't want to barge in. But she tells me that she hasn't got any light cotton frocks for summer. Not one.'

'Ought she to have?' asked Mr Honey. 'I wear the same myself all the year round. You mean, like her party frock? I told her she could wear that when it's hot.'

Miss Corder moistened her lips and started off from the beginning to inform Mr Honey what a child should wear. As they talked the cocoa cooled; the streak of light appeared at the black window. Presently she gathered the cups together.

'Let me have a look at her clothes while you're at work tomorrow,' she said. 'Then I'll make you out a list of what she ought to have.'

He said, 'I would be so grateful. It's so hard to find out, and one doesn't think, I suppose.' He hesitated. 'Could you stay with her till I get back tomorrow evening, possibly? I can fix up something else by then.'

'I could stay till Sunday night if you like,' she said. 'They won't want me at the Airways before Monday.'

His face lit up. 'I know Elspeth would like that,' he said. 'It would be horribly dull for her to be in bed alone here, even if I could get back for lunch.' And then he looked troubled. 'I don't know if that would do, though, would it?'

She said, 'You mean, for me to sleep here?'

'That's right.'

She considered for a minute. 'Not if the neighbours are going to start talking,' she said. 'I suppose they wouldn't like it at the R.A.E. either.'

He stared at her. 'I wasn't thinking of that. It wouldn't matter what anyone at the R.A.E. thought, and I don't even know the neighbours. Elspeth knows the people in No. 23, I think, but I don't know any of them.'

She laughed. 'Well that's all right then. Were you thinking about me?'

He nodded. 'You don't want to get a bad reputation,' he said awkwardly.

She smiled. 'Would it be all right if I put on my nurse's uniform?'

He stared at her. 'Well, I suppose it would. That's rather funny, when you come to think of it.'

'I'll do that if you like,' she said. 'It means I'll have to go back home and get it.' She paused. 'If you like, I'll sleep at home and come over each day.'

He smiled slowly. 'It's an awfully long way.'

She met his eyes. 'I think so, too. I don't mind if you don't.'

'I don't mind,' he said. 'I was just thinking about you.'

'Think about yourself,' she said gently. 'Think about what *you* want for a change, what *you* want out of life.' She put the plates together on the draining-board. 'I'll do these in the morning before breakfast. You go to bed now, or you won't be fit to go into the office in the morning. And I know you're dying to do that.'

He smiled. 'I did look in for just a minute after we landed, this evening.'

'I might have known it. Go on up to bed. It's all made up and ready for you.'

In the door he paused. 'Good night, Marjorie,' he said.

'Be off with you,' she laughed. 'Good night, Theodore.'

He was very tired, but he lay awake in bed for some time thrilled and excited by the thought that Marjorie had come to stay with him, to take some of the aching responsibility for Elspeth off his shoulders, if only for three days. He was deeply grateful to her; from the first moment in the Reindeer when she had talked to him about the weather they would have upon the crossing, he had known that she was naturally kind. He had been right in that; at the first hint of trouble she had come to his house to help him in his absence; she had cared for his little daughter and played with her, she had washed his floors and made him supper in the middle of the night when he had turned up hungry. Now she was going to go through Elspeth's clothes and tell him what to buy.

Only one woman in his life had treated him like that before. Some girls radiated kindness; this one was fit to set beside the memory of Mary.

He drifted into sleep.

She would not let him help in getting breakfast; instead she sent him up to sit with Elspeth, who was wide awake and sitting up in bed. She told him what had happened to her. 'There was a burglar,' she said, 'so I put on your warm dressing-gown and then I fell downstairs. And then when I woke up I was in Mrs Scott's bed and I was sick seven times and once the basin wasn't there and Dr Scott wiped it up and said it didn't matter.'

Honey said, 'Oh dear. I *am* sorry that happened.'

She reassured him. 'He didn't mind a bit, Daddy, honestly he didn't. He said he could remember being sick in a motorcar when he was a little boy and he wasn't ill at all. He was just sick. I do like Dr Scott. He's nice, isn't he?'

He nodded. 'You like Mrs Scott too, don't you?'

'I like them both, and Monica and Marjorie. Can Marjorie stay till Sunday, Daddy? She said she could if you said yes. Then she's got to go to Canada in the aeroplane but she's coming back on Thursday and she said she'd come down and see me again. Would that be all right?'

He said, 'Who's Monica?'

'Monica Teasdale. She was nice, too, but she's old. She reads out loud awfully well and she kept calling me honey. Why did she do that, Daddy?'

'I don't know. Is she still here?'

The child shook her head. 'She went away the day before yesterday. She said I was to come and spend a holiday with her and go on a dude ranch. What's a dude ranch, Daddy?'

'I don't know,' he said vaguely. 'Something they do in America, I suppose.'

Marjorie called him for his breakfast, a better one than he had tasted in that

kitchen for years. She took up a tray and got Elspeth started; then she came
down and smoked a cigarette while he finished his. And presently she pushed
him off to the office just as Mary used to do, and he with difficulty restrained a
crazy impulse to turn and kiss her in the doorway, as he had used to kiss Mary.
He walked down to the bus with his old felt hat crammed untidily on his head
and his brief-case in his hand, very thoughtful.

He went to the Director's office as soon as he got to the R.A.E., and stood for
a few minutes nervously explaining what had happened at Gander. 'I didn't
know what else to do,' he said unhappily. 'Dr Scott had said that it was so
important that the aircraft shouldn't fly if there was any risk. And I couldn't
make them understand why it shouldn't go on. But I do realise that it has made
a very awkward situation, sir. I sent my resignation in to Dr Scott.'

The Director said, 'I know – he came and saw me about it. He tore your letter
up.'

'My letter of resignation, sir?'

'Yes. It's not going to help anybody if you resign and afterwards it turns out
you were right, Honey. It only makes the matter worse. Leave that for the
present and go on with the trial on the Reindeer tail. I won't pretend that I was
pleased when I heard what you did at Gander – it's made a lot of trouble. But if
it turns out you were justified – well, there's an end of it, of course. And that we
ought to know quite soon. I'm expecting a cable from Scott tomorrow or the
next day, when he's been up to the wreckage.'

There followed two halcyon days for Mr Honey. At the office he dived
straight back into his routine; while he had been absent a report had come in of
some work carried out in Oslo on the strain energy absorption of copper alloys
with particular reference to high tension electrical conductors, and this report
blew a small sidewind on the fatigue investigations. He plunged deep into
consideration of what this might mean, and dismissed the Reindeer altogether
from his mind; it was for other people, me particularly, to deal with trivial
matters like the fate of C.A.T.O.'s North Atlantic Air Service, while he got on
with the real work, the stuff that really mattered. That did not prevent him,
however, from leaving the office punctually at half-past five. He found that
Shirley had been round to tea with Marjorie and Elspeth and that they had all
been playing Monopoly on Elspeth's bed, a game new to Mr Honey. Elspeth
insisted that he should play too, and ruined him without the slightest difficulty,
and by the time they all woke up to the time it was half-past seven.

He supped simply on a fish pudding and stewed fruit with a milk pudding, all
cooked by Miss Corder, and it was with a sense of internal well-being and ease
unusual for him after a meal that he sat down with her when they had done the
washing-up to study Elspeth's clothes. 'She's all right for winter things,'
Marjorie said, 'but really, she's got practically nothing for the summer. Those
flannel pyjamas that she wears must be lovely in the winter, but she's awfully
hot in them now. And she's got no frocks at all. . . .'

He went through the list with her and she priced the various garments for
him. 'She doesn't need all these at once, of course,' she said. 'In fact, two frocks
would do to start with if you could get the washing done at home.' She turned to
him. 'I was thinking we might get her up on Sunday for a bit. If we could get
her some of these things tomorrow afternoon for her to get up into, it'll give her
a tremendous lift.'

Mr Honey said, 'We'd better get them all at once, hadn't we? I'll have to go to the bank, but I think there's plenty of money. Plenty for this, anyway.'

'I think we'd better get just what she needs for the moment,' the girl said. 'Later on, when she can get about, it would be fun to take her up to London to the big shops; I saw some lovely children's frocks in Barker's the other day, awfully cheap. And she'd get a great thrill out of buying her own frocks in a big shop.'

The week-end passed in quiet, happy intimacy. On Saturday afternoon the Transatlantic stewardess and the research scientist on whose work depended all the lives of people travelling in Reindeer aircraft went out with a string bag to go shopping together down the High Street of the little Hampshire town, and came back loaded with brown paper parcels like any other suburban couple living in more regular circumstances, to have tea in the kitchen and turn over their purchases on Elspeth's bed, and watch the child's delight. Then Honey went down quietly to the front room to consider his more recent calculations on the Pyramid, and presently became immersed in them till Marjorie put her head into the door to tell him supper was ready. And after that, he told her all about it.

On Sunday morning they got Elspeth up after breakfast in her new print frock and sat her in a chair in the garden while Mr Honey mowed the lawn and Marjorie weeded and cooked alternately. They made Elspeth lie down on her bed after dinner while they dozed in the garden in deckchairs, and then they all had tea together on the lawn. Then it was time for Marjorie to go: in order to be at Heath Row by eight-thirty in the morning she would have to sleep at home in Ealing.

Elspeth said, 'Please, will you come down on Thursday, like you said?'

She glanced at Honey. 'If your father says I may.'

He said, 'Oh please do. I do wish you could stay on now. It makes such a difference. . . .'

She shook her head. 'I wish I could. But I'm almost sure they'll have a trip for me tomorrow. That means Montreal on Tuesday morning and back again on Wednesday afternoon. I ought to be able to get down here again by tea-time on Thursday,' she said to Elspeth. 'But don't worry if I'm late, because I might not get down till Friday morning. But I will come. I promise you.'

They left Elspeth sitting in the garden with a rug round her and went together to the front door. 'Let her have a little of the semolina pudding for her supper, with some of the jam,' she said. 'I wouldn't give her any more. And she ought to be in bed by seven–it's her first day up, you know. I'd give her her supper in bed.'

He said, 'I do wish you were staying. It's such a help, and it's been so lovely having someone. . . .' He hesitated awkwardly. 'Someone to talk to.'

She met his eyes. 'If by any chance they don't want me at the airport,' she said, 'may I come back?'

He said earnestly. 'Please do.'

She nodded. 'I'll do that if they don't want me, Theodore. But I'm afraid they'll have a trip for me, and in that case it'll probably be Thursday evening.'

He said simply, 'We shall be looking forward to that, both of us.'

She left him, and walked down the road to catch the Green Line bus for London. She hated the thought of going back to work. For her the run to Montreal held little charm; she was tired of serving coffee and biscuits with a smile, like any waitress in a café. The glamour of an airline stewardess was dead for her; she could not rate it equal in importance with the job of making something out of Elspeth Honey, of broadening her warped, one-sided life. For Honey himself she had a deep respect, verging upon love. He seemed to her to be the most unassuming, the bravest, and the cleverest man she had ever met, and she knew that her own qualities could help him tremendously. She was shrewd enough to know that she would never equal him in mental power, but with her cooking and her care behind that power he could do great things.

On Monday morning Mr Honey went into the office thinking mainly of the strain energy absorption factor of copper-tungsten alloys, with a side thought or two to Marjorie Corder; I think he had forgotten all about C.A.T.O. and my mission in Labrador. It was quite a surprise when he received a message in the middle of the morning that the Director would like to see him; he blinked and wondered what it could be all about, and then remembered that there was some trouble going on about the Reindeer, trouble that was really nothing to do with him at all. He went to the office unwillingly, reluctant to be dragged into the Reindeer controversy again.

The Director said, 'Oh, Honey, I want you to keep *au fait* with what Dr Scott is doing about this Reindeer accident. Quite a lot has happened over the week-end. To begin with, this radiogram came in on Saturday night.'

He passed the slip across the table. Mr Honey took it, blinking. It was headed IVANHOE P.Q.

'What does this word Ivanhoe mean, sir?' he asked puzzled. 'Isn't that a book or something?' It seemed to him to be some kind of code, and he was intrigued.

'It's a small town on the Gulf of St Lawrence,' the Director said patiently. 'It *is* a book as well, but it's the name of the place Scott sent that cable from.'

'Oh.'

The message read:

Have visited crashed Reindeer but broken stubs of tailplane spars have been removed with hacksaw stop local evidence states that these and other portions of the wreckage were removed by Russian personnel visiting the scene to recover body of M. Oskonikoff for reburial at Moscow stop suggest demand these parts from Russians as difficult country will make finding of port tailplane uncertain if not impossible stop cable further instructions to me at Ivanhoe–Scott.

Mr Honey handed this back to the Director. 'It's very unfortunate if these parts have been lost,' he said.

'Very,' said the Director dryly. 'I spoke to D.R.D. about it yesterday morning as a matter of urgency and, to cut a long story short, a cable about the matter went off yesterday to our Embassy in Moscow. But I'm sorry to say that the Russians don't seem to be very co-operative in the matter.'

I doubt if he knew more than that himself; it was weeks later that I got something of the story of what had happened in Moscow. The story as I heard it was that Sir Malcolm Howe had rung up M. Serevieff immediately he got the cable and asked for the parts to be sent to England for a further examination. M. Serevieff had countered by saying that he was glad that Sir Malcolm had raised the matter, which was one of some moment. It was certainly the case that the Russian burial party had included certain members of their Accidents Bureau; he could not say whether any parts had been removed and anyway, that was a matter of no importance. What *was* important was that the British Government had tried to trick the Russians, to conceal the evidence of their crime. The body handed to the Russian mission in Labrador was not that of M.

Oskonikoff; the dentures did not correspond, and expert examination of the body in Moscow had proved it to be that of a considerably younger man. Would the Ambassador kindly explain this action of the British Government? His manner left no room for doubting that the Russians thought that the accident had been contrived to secure the murder of their Ambassador in a remote place where detection would be difficult, and that the substitution of another body was all part of the plot. Indeed, M. Serevieff said so, in so many words.

I need hardly say that this charge raised considerable stir in diplomatic circles, to the extent that it was impossible even to try any further to make the Russians disgorge the bits that they had taken from the crash. I don't know how it all ended; I doubt if anyone outside the Foreign Office and the Cabinet knows that. I only know that, on that Monday morning, the Director with Mr Honey blinking at his elbow concocted the following cable, which reached me a couple of hours later at Ivanhoe, in the telegraph office of the Royal Canadian Mounted Police:

Foreign Office consider it inadvisable to press for recovery of Reindeer parts from Russians as wider issues are involved stop it is therefore imperative to locate and examine missing port tailplane however long this takes rely on you to do your utmost. R.A.E.

They sent that one off to me, and Mr Honey went blithely back to his office and the copper-tungsten alloy papers, relieved that he had not been called upon to do something in a matter that held little interest for him.

I got that cable about breakfast time, when by reason of the difference in local time Mr Honey was just going home to lunch to get Elspeth out of bed for the afternoon. The Mounties called me into their office as we were walking from the store where we had slept again in our hammocks, walking down the sunlit main street of that small Canadian lumber town to the café with the French-speaking waitress. I took the message slip from them and read it in dismay, and showed it to Hennessey and Russell and Stubbs in the middle of the street.

Russell went up in a sheet of flame, rather naturally. 'My Christ!' he said. 'The British Foreign Office must be nuts. They just don't know the way we're fixed out here! If that tailplane came off in the air the way you think it did, it might be twenty miles away from the rest of the machine. How do they think we're going to find that in this type of country? Do they suppose a street cleaner 'll find it and bring it in?'

I stared at him in despair. 'I don't know what they think.'

We went and sat down at the stainless bar and ordered flakes and eggs and bacon from the French girl. I studied the message again, and compared it with the copy I had kept of my previous one to the Director. I pointed out to them, 'See, I said "finding of port tailplane uncertain if not impossible".'

'You're darn right,' said Hennessey.

'Well, now they come back with this,' I said. I turned to them. 'It just means we've got to do our best to find the thing. After all, it's quite a big unit—over twenty feet long. It might be visible from the air.'

Hennessey said doubtfully, 'It's a chance. It's a pretty thickly wooded section of the country, though, and spruce and alder, they grow pretty fast this time of year. And all the leaves on, too.'

We talked about it for an hour, and then worked out the following programme. We would go up to the lake again in the Norseman, and trek up again to the scene of the crash, prepared to camp there for four days. We would mark out an area half a mile each way of the crash, one square mile in all, with the crashed Reindeer in the centre, and we would search that area minutely whatever the difficulties. If we did not discover the port tailplane there would be a strong presumption that the unit had come off in the air; it was too big a thing for the Russians to have removed *in toto*. That in itself would lend some substance to the theory of failure in fatigue.

After that area had been searched, we would then return to the lake and begin an air search of the district, flying the Norseman low above the tree-tops endeavouring to see the fallen tailplane, flying on closely parallel strips as in an air survey. None of us had much confidence in this procedure, but it was the only thing we could do.

'One thing,' said Russell. 'We'd better set to work and draft a cable to your chief telling him not to expect too much.' We set to work to do so.

Back in England, Mr Honey hurried home to lunch with Elspeth. He did not normally go home to lunch because the journey from the office to his house took half an hour, or three-quarters if he was unlucky with his bus, and this meant over an hour spent travelling alone, whereas his nominal lunch-time was an hour only. So he hurried to get Elspeth out of bed and give her a cold lunch and get her settled in a chair with a book to read before he had to hurry off again back to the office. She told him, 'Mrs Scott came and sat with me a little this morning, Daddy. She said she'd come in and give me tea, and you weren't to worry because she'd be able to stay here till you got back.'

He said, 'That's very kind of her.'

Elspeth nodded. 'She said she'd bring some rock cakes round with her, too.'

'Don't let her do this washing up,' he said. 'And don't you do it, either. I'll just leave the things stacked here, and then I'll do it with the supper things this evening.'

He hurried back to the office, and got in three-quarters of an hour late. In the normal course this would not have mattered and no one would have known, because he worked in a watertight compartment and he was apt to stay late in the evenings so that I, for one, would never have bothered him about small irregularities in timekeeping. As luck would have it, the Director had sent for him at five minutes past two to meet E. P. Prendergast, who had turned up at the R.A.E. shortly before lunch to investigate these allegations about the Reindeer tail. The Director had had to hold Prendergast in play with smooth words till Honey had showed up at ten minutes to three, and neither the Director nor Mr Prendergast were very pleased about it.

Mr Honey said breathlessly, 'I'm sorry I'm late, sir. I had some personal matters that kept me.'

The Director said, 'This is Mr Prendergast of the Rutland Aircraft Company, Honey. He has come down to look into this matter of the Reindeer tail.' Mr Honey gazed at the great bulk of the designer apprehensively; Mr Prendergast did not seem to be in a very good temper. 'I have told him the outlines of what we have been doing here. I think, perhaps if he went with you to your office and you went through the work in detail with him, and bring him back here after that, it would be best.'

Prendergast said, 'Certainly. I shall be most interested to hear what Mr Honey has to say about the Reindeer tail.'

That was the last thing he said for the next hour, according to Honey.

Whatever the little man showed him or explained, the designer did nothing but grunt. This was one of his more offensive techniques; he would stand in silence listening to a halting explanation and then grunt, a grunt expressing an ill-tempered scepticism or plain disbelief. They stood under the great clattering bulk of the Reindeer tail while Honey nervously expounded the harmonics that were being imposed on it; they stood in the office while Honey, nearly in tears by that time, endeavoured to explain his hypothesis of nuclear strain to a designer who knew nothing of the atom and cared less, grunting in disbelief of this newfangled nonsense. He only spoke once, so far as Honey remembers; that was to say, 'I understand, then, that there is no experimental evidence at all yet that confirms the truth of all this theory?'

Honey said unhappily, 'It's too early. You can't rush basic research like everybody here is trying to do.'

The designer grunted.

When finally Mr Honey took Prendergast back to the Director's office he was in a state of acute nervous tension, noticed by the Director, who released him as soon as was polite. As the door closed behind him the designer relaxed, and smiled for the first time that afternoon. 'Queer customer,' he said.

The Director said politely, 'I hope he gave you all the information you need?'

Prendergast grunted. 'He gave me plenty of information. Whether any of it's any good is another matter.' However, when he came to go away he was quite cordial to the Director, almost benign.

The Director did not have time to speculate on that, because as the door closed behind Prendergast, his secretary brought in my cable in reply from Ivanhoe. This read:

Propose search for tailplane an area one square mile around crash intensively estimate this will take four days stop thereafter propose search from air by strip flying an area approximately 100 square miles this may take a fortnight stop am pessimistic of flight search yielding results owing to density of forest growth and recommend all possible pressure on the Russians to surrender parts removed. Scott.

The Director sent for Honey again, who appeared white and nervous and trembling a little in frustrated rage after his hour with Prendergast. The Director showed him his cable; Honey read it without properly taking it in.

'It's no good putting pressure on me, sir,' he said, nearly weeping, handing it back. 'I can't make this test go any faster.'

The Director said, 'I'm not putting pressure on you, Honey. But you're in charge of the Reindeer tail investigation in Dr Scott's absence. I want you to realise the very difficult position that Dr Scott is in, that's all.'

Honey flushed angrily. 'He's not in a difficult position. I'm the one who's in a difficult position, with everybody trying to extract *ad hoc* data from an incomplete piece of basic research. I can't do my work if you keep badgering me like this—I'll have to give up and go somewhere else. First of all it was Sir Phillip Dolbear and now Prendergast. I've got nothing to show to anybody yet, and every time I'm made to look a fool. And Dr Scott's as bad as any of them.' He was very much upset.

The Director said, 'Mr Honey, I don't think you quite realise how much you owe to Dr Scott. At last Thursday's meeting with D.R.D. he expressed complete confidence in your estimate of this fatigue failure, in the face of the most damaging attacks, I may say, from both C.A.T.O. and the company. He staked his own reputation on your work. He told the meeting that he thought that you were right, and when he left this country he was confident that if he brought back the parts in question they would prove beyond all doubt that you were right in your diagnosis of the cause of this accident; and that he was right in standing up and putting his whole reputation on your side. Well, now he finds he can't produce that evidence unless he finds this tailplane, and in that country that seems to be like looking for a needle in a bundle of hay.'

Honey stared at the cable through his thick glasses. 'Oh,' he said, 'is that what this means? It wasn't very clear.'

'That's exactly what that means,' the Director said shortly. 'If you were as good a friend to Dr Scott as he had been to you, you'd talk about him rather differently.'

Mr Honey flushed crimson. 'I'm sorry,' he said weakly. And then he waved the cable in his hand. 'May I take this tonight and think about it?' he inquired. 'I'll let you have it back in the morning, sir.'

The Director shrugged his shoulders; he was tired of Mr Honey. 'If you like.'

Mr Honey went back to his office distressed and confused. He was a sensitive little man and absurdly grateful to Shirley and to me for the little trivial things that we had done to help him; the Director had hurt him very deeply by what he had said. He stood for ten minutes in humiliated unhappiness in his office, re-reading my cable and re-orientating his ideas; then he went out and caught his bus back home, lost in deep thought.

His ruminations were rudely interrupted at his own front gate, and he was jerked into another world. Elspeth had been watching for him, and she came rushing down the path to meet him, flushed and excited in her new frock. 'Daddy,' she cried, 'the water heater's come! The men came with it just after you went, and they worked all the time and made a new pipe and fixed it on the wall over the sink, and it's making hot water! They're coming in to paint the pipe tomorrow!'

She dragged him by the arm to show him this wonder in the kitchen. In the front door Marjorie Corder came forward to meet him, with Shirley behind her. 'I came back,' she said simply. 'They didn't want me for another week at the airport, so I came back.'

She did not tell him that she had put in for a week's leave, and got it, after some argument.

Mr Honey said, 'Oh, I *am* glad,' and Shirley standing close behind the girl saw the radiance on his frog-like features, and understood why Marjorie had bothered to come back. And then they all went into the kitchen and admired the hot-water heater, and gave it its first job to do by doing the lunch wash-up.

He pressed Shirley to stay to supper, and as she was alone in our flat she was glad to do so, so they set to and made a shepherd's pie and put it in the oven to cook. And while that was doing they all had a game of Monopoly with Elspeth, which Mr Honey played unusually badly even for him, so that he was ruined in ten minutes. His mind was so obviously remote from the game that when they were dishing up the supper, Marjorie asked him quietly in a corner by the gas-stove, 'Is anything wrong, Theo?'

'Nothing much,' he said heavily. 'It's been rather a bad day. I had the designer of the Reindeer on my hands most of the afternoon, a Mr Prendergast. He was very difficult.'

Shirley overheard this. 'Everyone says he's difficult. I thought he was such a nice man at the lecture. I hope you told him where he got off.'

Honey smiled weakly. 'He's not a very easy man to tell that to. And there were other things, too. . . .' He hesitated, and then decided to unburden himself to them. 'We've had a lot of cables from Dr Scott over the week-end,' he said. 'He can't find the fractured pieces of the tail.'

Shirley said sharply, 'But they *must* be there!' and Marjorie said, 'Oh, Theo!' Both girls were very well acquainted with the issues that were involved, but none of them had even considered before what it would mean if I failed to find a fatigue fracture in the first Reindeer crash. They pressed Honey for more details of what had happened, and he told them a stumbling and confused narrative, and showed them the crumpled copy of my last cable that he had brought from the Director's office. A sense of disaster descended on them and spoilt their party; they talked through supper in depressed tones with long pauses between each remark. Elspeth, who did not understand what it was all about, asked, 'What's the matter with Dr Scott in Labrador, Daddy?'

Marjorie, to relieve him, said, 'He's lost something, and he can't find it. Something very important.'

'What can't he find, Daddy?'

Honey said, 'A piece of an aeroplane.'

'Is it a very important piece?'

'Very important,' Honey said. 'He's in dreadful trouble.' Shirley, watching him, was interested to see that he had suddenly lost his air of impotent worry. He looked, she said, like a dog just coming on the scent. A funny sort of simile, but that's how she described him.

Elspeth said, 'Oh, poor Dr Scott.'

'Poor Dr Scott,' Honey repeated with deep, emphatic sympathy. 'He's in terrible trouble. And he's been so kind to us, hasn't he? Would you like to try and find it for him with the little trolley?' The two girls stared uncomprehending at them across the cooling food upon the table.

Elspeth nodded vigorously, 'Mm.'

Honey got up from the table, his entire attention fixed upon his little white-faced daughter. 'All right, let's go into the other room and get the little trolley.'

He got up from the table and took Elspeth by the hand entirely oblivious to the two girls. They moved to the door; Marjorie half rose from her seat. 'Where are you going?' she asked.

Honey turned in the doorway, 'Please,' he said sternly, and there was a confidence of command about him that was new to both of them. 'You may come with us if you sit very quiet at the back of the room, but you mustn't speak at all or interrupt in any way. If you feel you can't control yourselves, you must stay here.'

He went out into the front room; the girls glanced at each other in mystification, and then followed him. They found him pinning a fresh sheet of paper down upon the drawing-board and laying it horizontal on the table at a comfortable height for Elspeth sitting in a chair before it. Then he pulled the heavy curtains to shut out the daylight and switched on a powerful desk reading-lamp upon the table. Next he went to the cupboard and got out two instruments. The first was a small affair of rotating black and white segments, worked by a small air turbine from a rubber bulb held in the palm of his hand; by pressing the bulb he could make the black and white segments alternate at varying speeds. The second instrument was a planchette, a little flat triangular trolley of three-ply wood about nine inches wide, supported on two tiny castoring wheels and a pencil at the third corner. He put this down upon the drawing-board and Elspeth laid the tips of her fingers upon it; Marjorie noted with a shock that she was evidently well accustomed to this routine.

Then he arranged the powerful light to focus only on the rotating black and white segments immediately in front of his little daughter; the rest of the room was in darkness.

'Is that light too strong?' he asked quietly.

'No, Daddy, it's all right.' she said. It was the first time they had spoken.

'All right,' he said. 'Just look at the whizzer.' The segments started to turn white and black in turn before her eyes in the bright light.

He said softly, 'Poor Dr Scott, he's in such terrible trouble. He wiped up the mess you made when you were sick, didn't he?' The black and white segments were changing places more quickly now.

Her eyes fixed upon them, Elspeth whispered, 'Yes.'

'He's been so kind,' he said quietly. 'He showed us how to get the hot-water heater so that we'll have hot water all the time now.'

She repeated, 'He's so kind.' Her eyes were fixed upon the changing segments in the brilliant light.

'He showed us how to use the washing-up mop, so that we don't have to use the rag,' Honey said in an even tone.

The little girl said drowsily, 'We don't have to use the rag now.'

In the darkness at the back of the room the two young women sat motionless, tense. In Marjorie there was a great tumult of feelings. She was deeply shocked at what was going on; every fibre in her being revolted at the use that Honey was making of his child. At the same time, she could not interrupt; there was a power and a competence about him in this matter that she dared not cross. She must stay quiet now and see it out, but never, never, never should this happen again.

Honey said quietly, 'Poor Dr Scott, he's been so kind to us, and now he's in such terrible trouble, because he can't find what he's looking for. He's so unhappy. It's lost in the forest, all among the trees, in the wild land where no people have ever been.' The black and white segments were changing places quickly now; the white-faced little girl was sitting with glazed eyes, motionless. 'Try and help poor Dr Scott find what he's looking for. Try and help him. He's been so kind to us. It's in the forest, lying somewhere in the trees, where nobody has ever been. It's a big metal piece, nearly as big as this house.'

The faint whirring of the segments was the only sound in the room. The blackness was oppressive, intense, around the girls. Shirley found later that her palms were bleeding from the unconscious pressure of her finger-nails, so great was the tension.

'Poor Dr Scott,' Honey repeated monotonously, 'he's so unhappy, in the forest, looking for it, and he can't find it. Try and help him find it. Try and help him. Try now. Try.'

Beneath the child's fingers the planchette began to stir, and crept across the paper in uneven, jerky spasms.

I I

Mr Honey went to the Director's office in the morning with the greatest reluctance. He did not like contact with any of his superior officers, ever, on any subject. He regarded technical executives as mean creatures who had abandoned scientific work for the fleshpots, for the luxuries of life that could be bought with a high salary. He had no opinion of any of us, judged as men; for this reason he preferred his own company or the company of earnest young men fresh from college who were not yet tainted with commercialism. He went cynically on this occasion, already embittered by the anticipation of disbelief. It had always been so when he had put forward new ideas; he had not got the happy knack of making people credit him from the start.

He had to wait some time in the outer office, because the Director was engaged. When finally Mr Honey got in to see him he was rather short of time and rather overwhelmed by the pressure of other work; later that morning he would have to entertain and show round a commission of French scientists on a visit to our aeronautical research establishments. He said, 'Well, Honey, what is it?'

Mr Honey said, 'Is it possible to get in touch with Dr Scott, sir?'

'We can send cables to him. There is a routine in force by which Ottawa can get in contact with the radio in his aeroplane once a day.' The procedure was that a cable from the R.A.E. was telephoned to Ferguson at the Ministry of Supply. It was then radioed to the Department of Civil Aviation in Ottawa, who relayed it to the Royal Canadian Air Force post at Rimouski on the lower St Lawrence. We could reach Rimouski on the two-way radio in the Norseman, and made contact with them each day at six in the evening to receive or transmit any message of urgency.

Mr Honey hesitated. 'I should like to send him a cable, sir. I've got a message here that might be helpful to him.'

'What sort of message, Honey?'

'It's about this tail unit that he's trying to find, sir. I think I've got something that might help.'

The Director stared at him. 'What sort of thing?'

'Automatic writing,' Mr Honey said reluctantly. 'I've had a great deal of experience with that—not in office time, of course. It gives really remarkable results in certain cases.'

The Director wrinkled his brows. 'Automatic writing? You mean produced by someone in a mental trance?'

Mr Honey said eagerly, 'That's right, sir. I got it through my daughter, Elspeth, last night. She's only twelve, but she's really got a remarkable gift. Of course, children do produce the most amazing results sometimes. They don't often retain their powers in later life, though.'

The Director was too busy to allow Mr Honey much latitude to discourse on his researches in that field. 'What is it that you've got?'

Mr Honey produced a small roll of drawing paper, cut from the large sheet he had pinned down on the drawing-board the night before. 'Well, this is what was actually produced,' he said. He unrolled it on the desk.

It was covered all over with pencil jabs, squiggles, and irregular traces. Some of these appeared to form themselves into letters, and some into half words, thus in one part of the paper the letters ING were fairly clear, and in another there was a very definite capital R. Mr Honey turned the paper round. 'This is what I mean, sir.'

Across one corner the squiggles ran consecutively in a fairly straight line. They were certainly writing, jerky and uneven though the letters were; it was not too difficult to decipher the message. It read, UNDER THE FOOT OF THE BEAR.

'I'm sure that means something,' Mr Honey said. 'I think we ought to cable it to Dr Scott.'

The Director grunted, not unlike the grunts that Mr Prendergast had dispensed the day before, and Honey winced. 'We should have to table some explanation of how the message was produced,' he said.

'Oh, yes sir. We must let Dr Scott have all the facts, of course.'

The Director suffered an instinctive feeling of revulsion, and I don't blame him. He was in charge of a large Government research establishment of the most serious character. Honey was suggesting that he should send out, in the name of that establishment, a message which could only imply his own confidence in a spiritualistic message produced by a little girl of twelve, the daughter of an official who was believed by many to be mentally unbalanced. This message had to be sent through the Ministry of Supply, who were his parent body, and through Canadian Government organisations. Inevitably its subject-matter would attract attention; it would become the subject of a tea-time joke up in the Ministry. People would start saying he was mentally unbalanced too if he sent out a thing like that.

He said slowly, 'I don't think we should bother Dr Scott with this, Honey. It's too unscientific for us to put forward as evidence.'

That touched Honey on the raw; he was the scientist and the Director a renegade who had deserted the pure field of science for the fleshpots of administration. 'It's not unscientific at all,' he said hotly. 'It's the product of a carefully controlled piece of research extending over a good number of years. The fact that aeronautical people don't know much about research in that field doesn't prove that it's unscientific. They don't know much about cancer research, either.'

The Director was very busy that morning, but he had a few moments to try and placate the angry little man before him. 'I didn't mean that in any derogatory sense, Honey,' he said. 'But it's not the sort of science that usually emanates from this Establishment, and not the sort that anybody here could possibly endorse.'

'That doesn't mean it isn't true,' Honey retorted.

The Director turned the paper over in his hands. 'Before you can say if it's true or not, you've got to decide what it means,' he observed. 'UNDER THE FOOT OF THE BEAR. The Bear means Russia, I suppose. I told you yesterday that the Russians had refused to release these parts that they have taken from the wreck of the Reindeer in Labrador. Would it not be correct to say that those parts are, in fact, under the foot of the Bear?'

Mr Honey stared at him. 'I don't know,' he said weakly. 'I never thought of that.'

The Director said, 'I merely put that out as a suggestion, Honey, that if this message does, in fact, mean anything, it may merely refer to something we already know about.'

Honey said, 'That might possibly be so. But Elspeth knew nothing about the Russians, sir. I didn't discuss that with her.'

'You knew about it, though,' the Director said. 'Might not thought transference come in? I merely put that forward as a suggestion.'

Honey was silent. He could not think of any answer to that one.

The Director handed him back the paper. 'I don't think we could send that out through official channels in the name of the R.A.E., Honey,' he said. 'If you feel strongly about it you could write a private letter to Scott, care of the Department of Civil Aviation in Ottawa.'

'Would he get that up in this place where he is, sir?'

'I should rather doubt it. I shouldn't think he'd get it till he returns to Ottawa.'

Honey said irritably, 'What's the use of that? It wouldn't be any help to him to let him have this after the job is over.'

The Director did not think that it would be any help to me anyway, but all he said was, 'I'm sorry, Honey, but that's the only thing I can suggest. Now, if you don't mind, I have a great many things to do this morning.'

Mr Honey said hotly, 'And I bet they're none of them more important than this,' and flounced out of the room. The Director stared after him a little sadly. Was Prendergast right, after all? He had had doubts of Honey's mental stability himself from time to time, but my faith in the little man had reassured him and had made him stalwart in his defence at the D.R.D. meeting. Now I, the buffer, was away in Canada and he had had a taste of Honey direct from the cup, pure and undiluted. He sighed as he turned to other work. Was another problem looming up before him, another scientist upon his staff who would start pilfering from small shops or behaving rudely in the park?

Mr Honey went back to his office in frustrated rage, not for the first time. He was convinced from his experience in psychic matters that the words they had received were an indication that would be helpful in the future and were not a mere record of current knowledge; he had received too many in connection with the excavation of the Roman acqueduct not to know the style. The flat denial of official methods of communication was sheer frustration to him, because a little reflection showed him that there was, in fact, no possible means of getting into touch with me except through the official channels. He could give no attention to his work, could think of nothing but the grievance that he suffered from, the disregard with which his seniors treated him. He raged inwardly all through lunch, thinking of other jobs that he was going to apply for so that he could shake the dust of the R.A.E. from off his feet. In the middle of the afternoon he came suddenly to his senses. He had done nothing and now he was exhausted by his rage, with a nervous headache. He would do no work that day, and in his present mood he would not stay upon the scene of his frustration for mere office discipline. If the R.A.E. didn't like his way of doing things, well, they could get along without him; he would be leaving before long in any case.

At half-past three he put on his hat and went home.

He got back to Copse Road in time for tea. Marjorie was in the kitchen laying out a tray with tea for two. She said, 'Oh, Theo, you're back early. You're just in time for tea.' She explained. 'I thought Elspeth had better stay in bed today, so we're having it upstairs. I'll cut some more bread and butter.'

He was naïvely surprised. 'Isn't Elspeth well?'

The girl hesitated. 'She's all right,' she said. 'She was just tired, and I thought she'd better stay in bed.' She did not want to hurt him or to remind him that they had had some difficulty in getting Elspeth out of her trance the night before; Marjorie had carried her upstairs and put her to bed still in a dazed state, and had sat with her holding her hand till she was sleeping naturally. She had certain things to say to Mr Honey about that, but they could wait a favourable chance. She said, 'You must have got off early.'

'I know,' he said. 'Everything went wrong at the office today and it didn't seem to matter, so I thought I'd come home.'

He sounded tired and depressed, and she could guess the reason. She had talked it all over with Shirley that morning, who knew more than she about the workings of the R.A.E. 'They won't pay any attention to him,' Shirley had said. 'Dennis might, if he was home, although I'm not too sure about that. But everybody else regards him as a joke, you know.'

Marjorie had flushed. 'If that's the way they think about him, the sooner they accept his resignation the better,' she said angrily.

'Dennis believes in him,' said Shirley gently. 'And Dennis is his boss. But planchette at the R.A.E. . . . . It's going to take a bit of stomaching, you know.'

'I suppose it is,' said Marjorie slowly. 'They ought to listen to him, if they're proper scientists.'

'We'll see,' Shirley had said. 'I don't think they're as scientific as all that.'

And so Marjorie said hesitantly to Mr Honey, 'Couldn't you get them to do anything, Theo?'

He shook his head. 'They're so stupid. It's maddening having to work under fools like that. . . .'

'Oh, Theo, I am sorry!' And then, to ease his burden and divert his mind, she said, 'This tray's all ready to go up. If you'll take it, I'll bring up the teapot and the hot water.'

They went up together to the bedroom and had tea with Elspeth. Elspeth was reading *Swallows and Amazons*, bought for her that morning by Marjorie, the first child's book that she had had for over a year with the exception of those she got at school. She told her father all about it. 'It's ever so exciting, Daddy,' she said. 'They did all sorts of things in boats, without any grown-ups with them at all! Can we go somewhere in the holidays and sail a boat, Daddy? Marjorie says there's a sort of series of books all about the same children. May I have another for my birthday?'

He sat looking at Arthur Ransome's pictures with her, his troubles assuaged and sunk into the background of his mind. Presently Marjorie took the tray down to the kitchen to begin washing up, and after a few minutes Mr Honey went down to dry for her. And there he asked, 'Aren't you going to let her get up at all today?'

She was filled suddenly with a great pity for the two of them; he was so completely innocent of any will to hurt. There were things she had to say to him. By the draining-board, piled with the soiled dishes, she reached impulsively for his hand; it was the first time that they had done that.

'Theo,' she said, 'I don't want to be beastly to you. Please don't take offence at this. But honestly, you oughtn't to have done that last night with Elspeth. It's terribly bad for her.'

He blinked through his thick glasses. 'Oh, do you think so? She's done it quite a lot of times before.'

'I know she has,' the girl said. 'But, Theo, she must never do it again. It's a terrible thing to make any child do. And Elspeth's only just getting over concussion. . . .' He was silent and distressed. 'I know it was important,' she said gently. 'But Elspeth is important, too. You could warp her whole life by making her do this sort of thing, at her age. You could make her grow up morbid and neurasthenic. She might get fits of depression; she might even become suicidal. Things like that do happen, Theo, I know. I've been a nurse. One always thinks they happen to other people, that they can't happen to you. But they can. And, Theo, children's brains aren't balanced like ours are. They—well, they're just *young*. They can't throw off unhealthy influences like we can. You could do terrible harm to her. Honestly, Theo, she must never do that again.'

She stood holding his hand, looking at him in appeal. She knew that this was a crux in their relations. She knew that she could help him, and she wanted to help him more than anything in the world, but she could only help him if he would accept her ruling in the matters that were properly her sphere. If he took her interference as a slight or turned the matter off with a laugh, she might as well go home.

He stared at her with blurred eyes behind his thick spectacles. 'I never thought of it like that,' he said unhappily.

She squeezed his hand in sympathy with his distress. 'Of course you didn't. But you do want to watch out, Theo—honestly you do. She doesn't seem to know any other children and she talks quite like an old woman sometimes. It's not natural, you know. It's not as she should be.'

He said miserably, 'I know. I know she's not like other children, but I don't see what one can do about it.' He glanced at the girl beside him. 'I know one thing. It makes a very great deal of difference to her having you here.'

'That's only natural,' she replied. 'She's got somebody to talk to, instead of being alone all day.' Gently she freed her hand. 'But do remember, Theo—try and treat her as a child, not quite so much as a grown-up. It's better for her—really it is.'

'I suppose it must be,' he said. 'But living alone as we do, it's so difficult to know where to begin.'

'I know it is, she said. She stood in thought for a moment. She could not tell him to start playing with his child; he was as he was, and her words could not change his character. If Elspeth got played with it would be through other people, through herself. She turned to the draining-board. 'Let's just wash these few things.'

He dried for her as she washed; as they worked together they talked about the water-heater, about children's books, and about Elspeth's clothes, and presently she said, 'Tell me some more about the R.A.E., Theo; wouldn't they pay any attention to the message?'

He shook his head, his face clouded. 'I saw the Director. I don't think he believed in it at all. He wouldn't let me send a cable through official channels, and there *is* no other way to get a cable to Dr Scott except through the official channels. They're just afraid of being laughed at, by sending out a cable dealing with matters they don't understand.' He laid down the plate that he was drying and stared out of the window, the cloth drooping unheeded from his hand. 'I'm sure this does mean something,' he said quietly. 'It always did before, when we were finding out about the aqueduct. It's a very well established means of getting information, this—only those fools haven't bothered to learn about it.'

She was impressed again by his sincerity of purpose. 'Is there no possible way of letting Dr Scott know, so that he could form his own judgment?' she asked.

He snorted in disgust. 'They said I could write him a private letter. And when I asked when that would get to him they said when he got back to Ottawa! That's after the job is all over!'

'Oh, Theo!'

She took the drying-up cloth from his hand as he stood in abstraction, and dried the last two plates, unnoticed by Mr Honey. Presently she asked, 'Where, exactly, is Dr Scott, Theo?'

He said vaguely, 'In Canada, I think—or else in Labrador. Sometimes they say one and sometimes the other.'

'It's on the north side of the St Lawrence River, isn't it?'

She said thoughtfully, 'Mrs Scott would probably know.'

She sent him to play a game of dominoes with Elspeth after tea, and told him she was going out to the post. Instead, she walked round to see Shirley in our flat. She said, 'Mrs Scott, can you tell me just where Dr Scott is now? You were quite right about the people at the R.A.E. They've not been very helpful.'

'Won't they send his message?'

Marjorie shook her head. 'He's awfully disappointed.'

Shirley said, 'I had a night letter from Dennis, from a place called Ivanhoe. He said they were about a hundred miles due north of it, and ten miles to the west of Small Pine Water, and I could look it up on the map. Well, I looked in the atlas, but the map's all just plain white paper north of Ivanhoe.' She pulled out the atlas and they studied it together. 'There's Ivanhoe.'

'That doesn't help much.'

'No.'

Marjorie frowned, staring at the map. 'However did it come to get up there? I've been on the Montreal route for three months, but we don't go north of the St Lawrence at all. We go just south of the Gaspe peninsula, *here*. We don't come to the St Lawrence till we're nearly into Montreal.'

'Dennis said that this machine went to Goose because there was fog at Gander. Goose is up here somewhere, isn't it? It doesn't seem to be marked either—I do think this is a rotten atlas. But I know he told me once the crash was on the line between Goose and Montreal.'

'I see. . . .' Marjorie hesitated for a minute, and then said, 'I wonder, might I use your telephone?'

'Of course.'

She called up Directory Inquiries, and then rang a Wimbledon number. She asked, 'Is that Captain Samuelson's house? Is he there?'

A woman's voice said, 'Well, he's out now.'

Marjorie said. 'Would he be at home if I came round—oh, say in an hour and a half? I'm speaking from Farnham. I'm one of his stewardesses, Miss Corder. I do want to see him this evening, if possible. It's rather important.'

'Well, I don't know if he'll be home before dark. He's down at the Bowls Club and there's been a tournament today. He's the vice-captain of the club, you know, and so he couldn't leave before the end, could he? You could go down there and see him on the greens, of course.'

Marjorie said, 'Oh, that would do. The club isn't very far away from your house?'

'It's only just around the corner. That's why we had to have this house, so that he could get his bowls. I'd rather we lived nearer to the shops.'

'Oh, thank you so much,' Marjorie said. 'I'll be along at about seven o'clock.'

She rang off and turned to Shirley. 'Thank you ever so much,' she said. 'I'm going to Wimbledon to see Captain Samuelson. I believe C.A.T.O. could get a message to them. . . .' She was silent for a minute, standing in thought. 'I wonder if I might ask something?'

Shirley glanced at her.

'I wonder–could you go in and sit with Elspeth, Mrs Scott? Captain Samuelson knows Mr Honey, and I would like Mr Honey to come with me to see him.'

Shirley said, 'I was only going to the pictures. You're going up this evening?'

'I think so. There's a train every half-hour from Aldershot, isn't there?'

They walked back together to the house in Copse Road. Marjorie said, 'Theo, I'm going up to Wimbledon to have a talk with Captain Samuelson. He lives there; I've just rung his wife up. I'd like to have a talk about this thing, getting in touch with Dr Scott. C.A.T.O. have got their own communications service, you know. There might be some way of getting a message or a letter to Dr Scott through them without it going through official channels at all. Captain Samuelson, would know, and I believe he'd help us. Anyway, it's worth trying. Will you come with me?'

He blinked at her. 'That never entered my head. Do you think C.A.T.O. would help?'

She did not tell him what was really in her mind; it was too long a shot. 'I don't know,' she said. 'They send wireless messages about the aircraft all over the place, of course–to machines in flight and everything. I don't see why they shouldn't be able to get in touch with Dr Scott, if they wanted to. But Captain Samuelson will know.'

Mr Honey nodded. 'I'd like to come,' he said. 'I thought Samuelson was very reasonable. Not like that other pilot, the young one.'

She laughed. 'Peter Dobson!'

An hour and a half later they were at the door of the house in Wimbledon, with the sun dropping down towards the horizon. It was a commonplace, medium-sized house in a suburban road; from somewhere within came the noise of children going to bed, with resonance from the bathroom. The door was opened to them by his wife. 'Oh, Miss Corder,' she said, 'he's still down at the club. There's been a tournament today, and when there's a tournament there's just no knowing when he'll be home. If I were you I should go down and catch him there.' She gave them the directions.

At the Bowls Club they found a few spectators drifting away; out upon the greens there were three or four groups of middle-aged and elderly men in shirt-sleeves, very intent upon their game. They walked round the green till they saw·

the rather stout, sandy-haired figure of the Transatlantic pilot. Marjorie called, 'Captain Samuelson!'

He raised his head, stared in surprise, and crossed the lawn to them. 'Miss Corder—what are you doing here?' He glanced at her companion. 'I know you. Wait—yes. Mr Honey, isn't it? You got back all right from Gander, then?'

Honey said, 'The Royal Air Force brought me back.'

'Fine.'

Marjorie said, 'Captain Samuelson, I've got something I want to ask you about. I wonder if we could go somewhere and talk for a few minutes?'

He glanced back at his game. 'Well—we can talk here, if it's not very long.'

'I'll be as quick as I can.' She told him what had happened, about the deadlock in Labrador over the location of the missing tailplane, about Mr Honey's trials with planchette. She told her story quickly and well, far better than Mr Honey could have done. 'Nobody can say, of course, whether this information will actually help Dr Scott or not. But it does seem to be all wrong that it shouldn't get to him at all.'

The pilot nodded. 'I see that. But what am I supposed to do about it?'

She hesitated. 'I know you'll think this a terrible suggestion,' she said diffidently. 'But I was wondering if you could fly over Dr Scott's camp on your way tomorrow, and drop a letter to them.'

'Oh, you were, were you?' His manner was not encouraging. 'Where is this place? North of the St Lawrence, isn't it?'

She said, 'There's a lake called Small Pine Water, about a hundred miles north of a place called Ivanhoe, on the St Lawrence.'

He nodded. 'I know Ivanhoe.'

'Well, there's this lake a hundred miles north of it and the crash was eleven miles west of the south end of that lake. That's where they are.'

Behind them came the clink of woods upon the green. The pilot said, 'Well, I can't go rushing off there, Miss Corder. That's a hundred and seventy miles or so off our course.'

'It wouldn't mean that much extra distance, would it?' she pleaded. 'Honestly, it does seem a thing that ought to be done. And, after all, it *was* an Organisation aircraft that crashed.'

He said testily, 'Well, yes, I know it was. But if I go off wandering about the world instead of sticking to the route, I'll get myself the sack, Miss Corder, and quite right, too. You can't run airlines in that way.'

There was a long, slow pause. A bee droned past them; from the lawn somebody called, 'Samuelson!' The pilot raised his head and glanced in that direction. 'In about three minutes,' he called. 'Roll for me, Doc.' He stood looking down, kicking the turf at the edge of the path irritably. 'The Russians took away the spar stumps, did they? And you reckon that you've found the other part by planchette?'

'I don't quite go so far as that,' Mr Honey said cautiously. 'All I've got is a sentence—"UNDER THE FOOT OF THE BEAR." But that was produced under well controlled conditions, conditions that were identical with those of another research, in which we got some quite remarkable results.'

'I see.' The pilot stood deep in thought, his mind back on what had happened at D.R.D.'s meeting. Many people, Prendergast amongst them, took the view that this small man with the weak eyes was off his head; others, Dr Scott, and the Director, were emphatic that he wasn't. He had oscillated from one view to the other, himself, several times; on the balance he was now inclined to believe in Mr Honey. But God, what types that Farnborough place did produce!

He asked, 'Do you still think Bill Ward had this fatigue trouble?'

Mr Honey blinked. 'Bill Ward?'

'The machine that crashed in Labrador. Do you still think that that one had fatigue trouble?'

'Oh, I see. Well, yes, I think that's very probable,' Mr Honey said. 'I think that's very likely indeed. In fact, I should be rather surprised, if they ever find these parts, if they don't show a very marked fatigue fracture.'

The pilot stared at the gabled line of the suburban roofs behind the almond trees. 'That bloody old fool–that Group-Captain the Accidents Department, I've forgotten his name–he said it was pilot's error of judgment. I've never heard such cock in all my life.'

'I shouldn't think it was that,' said Mr Honey. 'It would be a very remarkable coincidence if the pilot had made an error of judgment just at the time when we could reasonably anticipate a failure in fatigue.'

Samuelson said keenly, 'At the same time, I suppose you can't prove that it was failure by fatigue unless Scott comes back with that tail?'

'Well, no. I think you'd have to have some evidence from the crashed parts if you're going to upset the accident investigation.'

Marjorie Corder said, 'Surely the organisation would be interested in finding out what actually happened? Enough to let you go off your course a bit to drop a letter?'

'I don't know about the Organisation. . . .' The pilot stood in silence, staring out across the level greens. Bill Ward was dead, and vilified after his death when he could not defend himself. Small, stupid people said that he had come down from altitude to check up his position, and had hit a hill, like any pupil on his first cross-country. He had been furious when first he heard of that report; he was furious still. He had spoken his mind at D.R.D.'s meeting; he would speak his mind again, at any time, to anybody who would listen. That was not how Bill Ward had met his death.

Professional pride was very strong in him, and the memory of Bill Ward in many a pilot's room, in many countries.

'All right,' he said. 'Let's have your letter and I'll see what I can do.'

We searched that square mile of Labrador forest for three days, and it was a terrible job.

Before I went there I thought that Labrador was a country of rocks and sparse, scattered trees. I mentioned that to Russell once, who told me that it was, all except this particular bit. That bit was dense jungle–there is no better word. On the first day we did no more than cut a trail round our square mile, blazing the trees and cutting a track through the undergrowth as we went, sinking deep in the swampy muskeg in the bottoms and clambering over hills strewn with rotten, fallen trees. The flies were sheer torment all the time; we had fly-nets to protect our faces and streamed with sweat in them; our hands and wrists grew puffed and swollen with the bites.

The others were more used to these conditions than I was and they were certainly in better training, but I found that I could keep pace with them in the work. The very novelty of these conditions was a stimulus to me; moreover, I knew that as a scientist from Farnborough I was expected to be a passenger, useless in the woods, and I was determined to show them that a scientist can also be tough. I found that I could do as much as they did or a bit more, but there is no doubt that at the end of the three days I was far more exhausted than they were. I couldn't have kept up much longer.

On the second and third days we split up into two pairs and set to work to traverse the area in twenty-yard strips; in places the vegetation was so dense that even that left quite a possibility that we could pass each side of the tailplane and never see it. We found the starboard aileron and the No. 6 engine. We did *not* find the port landing wheel assembly, the No. 3 propeller, or the port tailplane and elevator. The position on the evening of the third day was therefore still inconclusive; we had not found the parts that we were looking for, but that was not to say they were not in the immediate vicinity. The port landing wheel and the No. 3 propeller were almost certainly lying somewhere very near us, and we had not found them.

That evening we were tired to death; I was so tired myself that I could eat nothing, though I drank some tea. Only a small piece of our self-imposed task remained to be done. We planned to finish that in the forenoon and get down to the Norseman on the lake shore after dinner, and fly down to Ivanhoe and rest for a couple of days before commencing the air search. I remember I was deeply depressed that night and hardly slept at all.

We were all anxious to get finished with the wretched job. The fourth morning we were up at dawn and started off after a cup of tea and a few biscuits. It was better early in the day; it was cool and the flies did not get going in full strength until the day was well advanced. We worked for a couple of hours and knocked off for breakfast a little after eight, with only a trifle left to do. We were still sitting smoking when the Reindeer flew over at about a quarter to ten.

She came from the south-east, flying very low, only about five hundred feet above the tree-tops. She passed to the east and north of us and came round in a great circle to the west; then they evidently saw our camp, because they turned directly for us and flew over. From the port window of the cockpit someone waved to us and we ran out into the clearing in among the crosses of the graves and waved back to them; she flew over us so low that we could see the faces of the passengers at the windows.

I cannot describe what a beautiful sight she was, that summer morning, above the fronds of the spruce trees, shining in silvery silhouette against the bright blue sky. She was flying well throttled back, a great shining lovely thing that slipped through the air without effort, with only a murmur of noise. I stood and watched her, fascinated by her beauty. Down in the forest we were tired and hot and grimy and bitten to death by bugs of every sort, but up there they were clean and well fed and comfortable and safe, up in the clear air in that lovely, lovely thing. I remember looking at her perfect lines and at the great clean grace of her, and thinking it was worth while, after all, to bear with Prendergast, who could turn out so wonderful a design as that.

They went well over to the east and turned again, and now they came so low that they were not a hundred feet above the trees. We stood out in the little glade amongst the graves and as she came to us I saw someone's head half out of the starboard window of the cockpit, and I recognised Samuelson, whom I had met in London a few days before at D.R.D.'s meeting. I doubt if he would have recognised me. His arm was out of the window and he was holding something with coloured streams flying from his hand, and as they approached he let this go, and it came parabolically down to us, its bright tails flashing in the sun. It landed on the edge of the clearing and Stubbs ran to get it; the Reindeer opened up her engines and climbed away from us towards the west.

Stubbs came back with the message bag and gave it to Russell, who opened it. It contained one letter, addressed to me in the uncouth scrawl that I had come to know as Mr Honey's writing. I slit it open; there were two sheets of notepaper. As I read it, I sighed with disappointment. It was just sheer stupidity; it seemed that he had been playing with planchette, and he sent me an incomprehensible message that he thought must be important. Honey again. . . .

I raised my eyes, and the other three were standing there looking at me eagerly, waiting to hear what it was all about. I smiled wryly. 'I don't think it's very important,' I said. I hesitated, embarrassed. 'One of my staff has been messing about with spiritualistic stuff–planchette. He got a message that he thought might be useful to us.'

Russell laughed. 'Oh!'

'I know,' I said ruefully. 'You know what people are.'

'What's the message?'

'"Under the foot of the bear,"' I said.

'That's all? Just "Under the foot of the bear"?'

'That's all,' I said. He turned away; I think he was as disappointed as I was. When we had seen the message bag flash down we had expected something that would help us.

'Which foot?' asked Hennessey, with ox-like stupidity. He was a good bush pilot, but he was pretty slow sometimes.

'I don't know,' I said irritably.

'The one he stands on, I suppose,' he said. 'That's what it must mean.'

Russell knew him better than I did. He turned back suddenly. 'Say, is there a place round here that's called Bear anything?'

'Dancing Bear Water,' Hennessey replied. 'That's the only Bear I know of round these parts. But it's the heck of a long way from here.'

I stared at him. 'Which way is it?'

He looked towards the sun. 'Over that way,' he said, pointing. 'East–east with a bit of north in it, maybe. Thirty–forty miles.'

Russell said quickly, 'Back along the course to Goose, from here?'

'I dare say it would be,' he replied. 'It's right next to Piddling Dog.' He turned to me. 'I guess these names sound kind of funny to you,' he explained. 'This section of the country was mapped out first by an air survey, back in 1929. Nobody hadn't ever been here, only a few Indians, maybe. When they got the survey all laid out in Ottawa they found they'd got the heck of a lot of lakes they didn't know about, so they set down to give 'em all names from what they looked like on the map. I got a map down in the Norseman that shows Dancing Bear. Just like a bear it is, with a little island for the eye, 'n everything.'

And there, that afternoon, we found the port tailplane of the crashed Reindeer. We saw it first from about a thousand feet as we flew over; it was standing nearly vertical between the spruce trees, about a quarter of a mile due south of the sole of the foot of the Dancing Bear. It was about thirty-seven miles from the crash. We might have found it ultimately in our air survey if we had gone so far, but I think we might have stopped short of that.

We landed on the lake and taxied in to the shore, and beached the Norseman on a little bit of shingle. The going was fairly easy upon land and we reached the tailplane in about a quarter of an hour. And when we got to it, it was a clear case if ever I saw one; a fatigue fracture of the top front spar flange, the metal short and brittle and crystalline at the break. The rear spar had been twisted off after failure, and the metal there was good.

Bill Ward must have kept her in the air for five or six minutes after losing half his tail, before they hit the trees and they all died. One thing puzzled us a lot at first; how was it that they had not managed to get out a wireless signal in that time? Then we found the insulators of a wireless aerial on the tip of the tailplane, and that too was explained.

12

I got back to England three days later, and I was very tired indeed. I had slept very little, because the itching of the bites that I had got on the woods was with me still when I got home; indeed, they took a fortnight to subside completely. Moreover, the strain and tension of the travelling and the research were having their effect, preventing sleep. I should have asked some doctor to prescribe for me, but I could not wait for that. I felt it urgent to get back to Farnborough without delay.

We landed at Heath Row from Montreal about midday. A car was there to meet me; I had a packing-case for luggage and we got it into the back seat with difficulty, and drove to Farnborough. I went straight to the main office block, to the Director's office.

I got in to see him at once. 'Good morning, sir,' I said. 'You got my cable?'

He got up from his chair. 'Yes, thanks.' He looked at me, and then said, 'Rather a hard trip?'

'It was anxious for a time,' I said. 'I thought at one time that we weren't going to find it.'

'You brought some samples back with you?' he asked.

'Oh yes. They're in a crate outside. I couldn't transport the whole thing, of course, so I cut off all the bits that seemed to matter. I've told the Transport to take them to the Metallurgical. It's absolutely clear, sir. It's a straightforward fatigue fracture of the front spar, the top spar flange.' And I told him what it looked like.

'Really. . . .' He stood in silence for a moment. 'Well, that's very satisfactory from our point of view,' he said. 'We come well out of it. That's not what matters, though. It's shocking bad for C.A.T.O. and bad for the country. This means that all those machines will have to come back for modification, and that means the end of the British Transatlantic service for the time being, I'm afraid. But there's nothing for it, now.'

I made a small grimace. 'It's just one of those things. It's a frightful shame. That Reindeer's a delightful thing to travel in.'

'You crossed in one, did you?'

'Both ways. It's a lovely job.'

'I know it is,' he said. 'Still, I don't know that I'd have fancied it myself, in the circumstances.'

I laughed. 'You have to shut your mind to that,' I said. 'Be like an ordinary passenger. Forget about the structure and take an interest in the stewardess.'

He glanced at me quizzically. 'I understand that Mr Honey has been doing some of that.' It's extraordinary how the Director gets to know what's going on.

'A very good thing, too,' I said.

'Oh, very.' He turned the conversation back to business. 'I'll wait until those parts are ready for me to see and we've all seen them,' he said. 'Then I'll ring up D.R.D. and I expect he'll want to call another meeting.'

'Had we better let Prendergast know, unofficially?' I suggested. 'He had a bit of a drip last time because we kept him in the dark.'

He nodded. 'Yes, we'd better do that. Will you get in touch with him, Scott?'

We stood talking over details for a few minutes. Then I said, 'There's just one more thing, sir. I got a note in Ottawa from Captain Samuelson, the pilot of the Reindeer, asking me not to broadcast the fact that he'd dropped that note from Honey to us. It seems that he went a long way out of his course without telling the Organisation anything about it, and he'd rather like to keep it dark.' I grinned. 'If Sir David Moon had seen him assing about down among the tree-tops in the middle of Labrador, he'd have had twins.'

'I see. . . .'

'I spoke to Russell and Group-Captain Porter,' I said. 'They won't let it out from Ottawa.'

The Director said slowly, 'I think it might be rather a good thing to gloss over all the automatic writing side of this business.' I smiled. 'After all, you went out to find and to examine this wreckage, and you found it and you examined it. That's all that matters to anybody. I'm quite sure the Foreign Office would very much object to any publicity about the Russian element.'

'And we should very much object to any publicity about planchette,' I said.

'Exactly,' he replied. 'Until that type of research becomes one of the regular activities of this Establishment, which I hope won't be in my time, the less said about it the better.'

I nodded. 'I should think so, sir.' I turned towards the door. 'Everything has been all right in my party while I've been away, I hope?'

He said, 'So far as I know.' He glanced down at his desk. 'There's a new job coming on. They're having trouble with the Assegai.'

'They were bound to do that,' I said. The Assegai was one of the jet interceptor fighters coming into squadron use. For rapid climb it had the new Boreas engine; in level flight at over thirty thousand feet it was probably capable of exceeding the speed of sound. Because the forces on the structure were still very much a matter of guesswork in the trans-sonic range, its speed in level flight was supposed to be limited to Mach ·90. People who knew the fighter pilots said from the start that those young men would never pay attention to that sort of restriction, and they hadn't.

'They lost one of them about a month ago,' the Director said, 'and then they lost another one last week. All with structural failure of the wing. Then the day before yesterday they lost a third, but this time the pilot got out safely with his parachute. Apparently he was looking out along the wing and saw the whole thing happen. He says he saw a line of light along the leading edge before it broke.'

I stared at him. 'A line of light?'

'That's what he says he saw. It seems he's very positive about it.'

I was dumbfounded. 'But what could cause that?'

He smiled. 'I don't know, Scott. That's what we've got to find out.'

I said ruefully, 'Well, that's a new one.'

'I said that it had better wait till you came back,' the Director said. 'They'll send the pilot here to see you and tell you the whole story in his own words, as soon as you like. Who would you put on it?'

'Morrison,' I said. 'It's right up his street.'

He nodded. 'I think so. The only thing is, Morrison is having trouble—oh, that's since you went away. His wife has got T.B.; she's got to go into a sanatorium. I think that you may have some difficulty in getting any useful work out of him for a month or so.'

'I'm very sorry to hear about Mrs Morrison,' I said. 'I'll have a talk with him. He's certainly the man who ought to handle anything like this.'

I went back to my office. My desk was piled high with dockets and papers that had come in during my absence, waiting for my attention. I told Miss Learoyd to put them all on the side table, and I rang down for Mr Honey and asked him if he would come up and see me. When he came I told him all about it, the success of his fatigue estimate and the success of his automatic writing. He did not seem very greatly interested in either, except technically; success did not thrill him in the least. He regarded a success merely as a convenient platform from which to plan a further advance.

He was, however, viciously pleased at the effect the news would have on Prendergast. 'These ignorant fools in the design offices,' he said angrily, 'they don't know what they're doing, half the time. They come down here and strut about and treat you like so much dirt. If only they'd pay some attention to the people who know something about the job, they wouldn't have these accidents.'

He displayed a characteristic reaction to the news that the entire British Transatlantic service would be suspended for an indefinite time by the grounding of the Reindeer fleet. He asked if we could get hold of the tailplanes of two of the grounded aircraft for further experiments. It seemed a golden opportunity to him. 'If they can't fly they won't want their tailplanes,' he pointed out. 'It really would be a great assistance if we could carry through a complete research on tailplanes of one type.'

He was deeply grateful to Shirley and to me for the little we had done for Elspeth. 'I don't know what to say to thank you,' he muttered. 'If Mrs Scott hadn't come round that morning and found her, I–I don't know what would have happened.'

'Forget about it,' I said gently. 'You'd have done the same of us. But, Honey, if you don't mind my saying so, you ought to make some arrangements that Elspeth isn't left alone quite so much. It's taking a bit of a risk.'

'I know it is,' he replied. 'As a matter of fact . . .' and then he stopped. He began again. 'I've got somebody staying with me now, for a little while. I do agree with you, it's very bad for Elspeth so much alone.'

'It's none of my business,' I said, 'but it's a bit hard on the kid.'

He said ingenuously, 'I'm very hopeful that I'll be able to do something before long.'

I thought of Marjorie Corder, and kept my face as straight as a judge. 'That's fine.'

They rang through from the Metallurgical Section a few minutes after that and said that my crate was there, and they were opening it. I rang the Director, and we all went down together to inspect the bits that I had brought back with me from Labrador. There was a little surface corrosion, as one might expect from parts that had been lying for some months in thawing snow, but there was general agreement that the evidence was absolutely clear. I went back to my office and rang up Prendergast.

'Good afternoon, Mr Prendergast,' I said. 'This is Scott speaking. Yes, this morning. Oh yes, thank you–not quite a holiday, you know, but very interesting, all the same. Look, Mr Prendergast–I'm sorry to say that we found a very definite fatigue fracture. I brought the parts back with me–yes, I cut the spars beyond the fractures and brought the fractures back. They're here now, if you'd like to come down and see them.' And I told him where the fractures were.

He said, 'Really? How very, very interesting. I should very much like to see those pieces.' He spoke very pleasantly; I was amazed. He went on to discuss the repetitive stresses on the tail for a little; he was cordial, benign, and considerate. 'I had a most interesting visit to your department while you were away,' he said. 'Mr Honey showed me the research that you have going on. I was very much impressed.'

So had Mr Honey been, but I would not tell him that. I said, 'I'm very sorry about the Reindeer, Mr Prendergast. I'm afraid this is bound to mean that all those aircraft will be grounded now at seven hundred and twenty hours.'

He said genially, 'Oh well, worse things happen at sea. I expect we shall get over it, one way or another.'

Well, that was one way of looking at it. I wondered if Sir David Moon would take it quite so philosophically when he was told that all his Reindeers were going to be grounded for an indefinite period, but that was none of my business. I talked to Prendergast for a few minutes more, and the extraordinary man was as smooth as silk when I had expected him to be as a raging demon. I put the telephone down, wondering if I should ever understand designers.

It was five o'clock, and I was very tired. I had to start something going on the Assegai before I could relax, and I rang through to Mr Morrison. After some delay the girl answered the call. She said that Mr Morrison wasn't in the office; he had not been in that day. His wife was very ill; he had taken her to the sanatorium at Bognor Regis. No, she didn't know if he was coming in tomorrow.

The Assegai, it seemed, was going to be my baby.

I had a wife; I had not see her for ten days and about nine thousand miles. I rang up Shirley at our flat and said, 'Darling, I'm back.'

She said, 'Oh, Dennis, *dear*. Where are you now? In the office?'

'That's right. Will you come and fetch me with the car? I've done all that I'm going to do.'

She came, and we drove home together to the flat, and mixed a drink. Everything was strangely as I knew it; it was curious to think of all that I had seen and done since I had been home last. We had a vast amount to talk about; I had to tell her what had gone on in Canada and she had to tell me what had gone on in Mr Honey's little house in Copse Road. 'I crossed over in the same machine as Monica Teasdale,' I said. 'We had a long talk in the middle of the night.'

'That poor woman,' she said softly. 'I did like her. Was she very much cut up, Dennis?'

'I think she was,' I said. 'It's hard to tell with an American, especially an actress like that. You can't tell if she's putting on an act.'

She was silent for a minute. 'I can't help thinking about her,' she said at last. 'She was awfully fond of him, you know. I think it was heroic of her, to go away like that. Do you think we'll ever see her again, Dennis?'

'No,' I said, 'I don't think so. Only on the screen.' I rubbed my wrists and hands; they were itching again like fire.

Shirley said, 'Dennis, come and let me put something on those bites. I've got some cream that will soothe them.' We went into the bedroom and she put it on for me, and then she said. 'What about our holiday, Dennis? You really must take one this year; you're looking awfully tired. The Reindeer must be just about cleaned up, isn't it? Couldn't we go away now, before anything else crops up?'

I grinned at her. 'Too late,' I said. 'It's cropped.' And I told her about the Assegai.

'Oh, Dennis! Someone else must deal with that. You can't go on for ever without a holiday.'

'I'll have to hold the fort till Morrison gets back,' I said. 'I don't suppose that'll be so long. I'm seeing the pilot in a day or two.' I stared out of the window of our little bedroom. 'I can't make out why there should be a light,' I said. 'It doesn't make sense.'

She laid her hand upon my arm. 'Forget about it now,' she said gently.

I roused myself to talk of matters that were more up Shirley's street. 'How's Marjorie Corder getting on with Honey?'

'Oh, she's a dear. You know, I wouldn't be surprised if they got married.'

'So they ruddy well ought to,' I replied. 'From what you tell me they've been living in sin for the last week.'

She turned on me. 'Oh, Dennis, they haven't! Mr Honey wouldn't know how.'

'Don't you be too sure about that,' I said. 'Are they engaged?'

'I don't think so,' she said. 'Not yet. But her leave's up at the end of the week. Perhaps they will be then.'

As a matter of fact, they got engaged that night. Mr Honey went back to his little house that evening anxious to justify himself in Marjorie's eyes. What she had said about his treatment of Elspeth had made a deep impression on him. He regarded her as a woman of the world and more knowledgeable than he: somebody who travelled repeatedly to Canada and the United States and liked it. He had a deep respect for her. Curiously, she seemed to have a deep respect for him, and in this she was unusual; most people treated him with very little respect. He did not want to lose her regard.

He went into the kitchen and beamed at her through his thick glasses. 'Dr Scott's come back,' he said. 'The message we sent got to him all right. Captain Samuelson flew over and dropped it.'

Her face lit up. 'Oh Theo, I *am* glad. Was it any good?'

'Yes, it was. There's a lake there called Dancing Bear and they found the tailplane just south of its foot.'

'Theo! So it was under the foot of the bear, after all?'

He nodded. 'I knew it must be something like that. It was just the same with the aqueduct. You couldn't understand the message till you'd thought about it for a bit. But in this case, of course, we hadn't got the data. We didn't know there was a lake called that.'

'It's wonderful!' she exclaimed. There was a light of admiration in her eyes that he could not mistake.

He coloured a little. 'Well,' he said diffidently, 'it just comes of proceeding in the proper scientific manner. So many people start off right, but then when they come up against something they don't understand, they turn round and say the whole research was started on wrong lines. But I *am* glad this turned out to be useful, because of Elspeth.' He looked at her appealingly. 'You don't really think it did her any harm, do you?'

She laid her hand impulsively upon his arm. 'Of course not, Theo–don't worry about that. We must find her and tell her–she'll be thrilled!'

He said, 'Do you think that's wise?'

She stared at him. 'But don't you want to tell her?'

He blinked at her through his glasses. 'Well, what do you think, Marjorie? Won't it impress it on her mind? I thought you wanted to forget all about that sort of thing.'

'Wouldn't you tell her at all?' she said thoughtfully. 'Just forget about it?'

'Well, yes–I think I would. After all, it's not important any longer. Tell her in some years' time, when she's a bit older. She hasn't talked about it again, has she?'

The girl shook her head. 'That's very sweet of you, Theo,' she said soberly. 'You really are the kindest man I've ever met.'

He coloured; it was a long time since anyone had said that sort of thing to him. 'There's another thing,' he said unsteadily. 'It *was* a fatigue fracture.'

'Oh, Theo! So you were right in that, too?'

He blinked. 'I thought it must have been. It's really very satisfactory, because it adds another trial without wasting our time, if your understand. This trial I'm doing at the R.A.E. becomes a confirmatory experiment–it means that we're about six months further ahead than we thought we were. If this one confirms the results of the first, the Labrador accident, we really will be on a firm foundation, so that we can go ahead with confidence.'

She did not understand what all that meant, but it was evidently something very near his heart, and so she said, 'How splendid!'

He beamed at her. 'It's really very satisfactory,' he repeated. 'I think we're on the way to getting something useful now.'

She thought for a minute, and then asked. 'Theo, what's going to happen to the Reindeer if it gets fatigue like this? Can they go on using it?'

'The Reindeer? Oh, you mean the machines they're using now. They've got to stop, I think. Dr Scott said something about grounding them all. I think he said they could go on to 720 hours–that's half the estimated time to failure.'

'Oh. . . .' With her knowledge of the Organisation she tried to visualise how the Montreal and New York services could be run without Reindeers, and failed. 'I suppose they aren't safe any longer.'

'I should think they'd be all right up to 720 hours,' he said. 'But after that they ought to stop. I think Dr Scott's quite right in that.'

She said slowly, 'Then the one at Gander must have been very dangerous, Theo.'

He laughed, almost boyishly; his success and her approval had lifted years of care and grief and worry off his shoulders. 'You know, I think it was. I'm rather surprised we got across all right, really I am. It did 1,430 hours, that one, without breaking. The only thing is, Dr Scott says the Canadians are quite certain that fatigue fractures are governed by the temperature, that they come sooner when it's cold. That's one of the parameters I haven't dealt with yet, that and the question of electrical conductivity. It might possibly explain why that one didn't break, because it had been operating in the tropics, you see. There's a whole field to explore,' he said enthusiastically. 'All sorts of things.' He was like a little boy let loose in a toy shop, uncertain which of the attractive treasures to pick up first.

Marjorie said, 'If you hadn't pulled up its undercarriage, Theo, I should have gone on flying in it. And I should have been killed, like Betty Sherwood and Jean Davenport.'

He stared at her dumbly, blinking in distress at the idea.

She said thoughtfully, 'I wonder how many lives you've saved, Theo? How many people are now living who would be dead by now, or just about to die, but for your courage and your genius?'

He blinked at her in silence. Much more important to him at that moment was the curve of her throat as it slid into her dress and a small curl of hair beside her ear.

'You're a great man, Theo,' she said quietly. 'This was all your doing. But for your work and your devotion other Reindeers would have crashed and other people would have been killed–hundreds, perhaps. Captain Samuelson would have been killed, as Captain Ward was killed. I should have died, as Betty and Jean died. I happen to know about it, so does Captain Samuelson. The passengers who would have died but for your courage and your work, they'll never know. But I can speak for them. Thank you, Theo, for all that you've done for them, and for their wives, and for their children.'

Mr Honey was never a very articulate man. He just put his arm round her shoulders and kissed her. As Marjorie put it to Shirley, that kind of broke the ice. By the time Elspeth, who was reading Arthur Ransome lying on her bed upstairs, awoke to the fact that she was hungry and came down to see what was happening about tea, her father was engaged to Marjorie Corder. Elspeth, who had been expecting that to happen for some time, thought it was a very good idea.

Marjorie went round and saw Shirley alone at tea-time on the following afternoon. 'I know it's no good trying to kid you and Dr Scott,' she said candidly. 'You think I've worked for this, that it's been all my doing. Well, up to a point, it has.'

Shirley smiled. 'I don't think anyone that Mr Honey married could expect to be exactly passive in the matter,' she observed. 'Any girl would have had to have done most of the work.'

Marjorie nodded. 'I think that's true. But that doesn't mean that we aren't going to be terribly happy together.'

'My dear, I know you will,' said Shirley. 'I can tell you one thing–he's an awfully kind man.'

'I know,' the stewardess said softly. 'You wouldn't think it, but he's brave too—and just terribly clever.' She turned to Shirley. 'I'm not a very clever person,' she said, 'and I don't really understand very much about his work. But I do know this—it's just about as important as a man's work can be. I've only known him a short time, but in that time I've seen him save hundreds of lives—literally hundreds. When you think of what might have happened to the Reindeers if he hadn't found out this about fatigue—'

'I know,' said Shirley. It was in her mind to say that I had had a bit to do with it as well, and so had Marjorie herself and Captain Samuelson, but she did not want to be ungracious or to spoil her pleasure.

'All my life,' the girl said, 'ever since Donald got killed, I wanted to be in aviation. That's why I manœuvred to get this job with the Organisation, to be a stewardess. I love being on aerodromes and seeing aeroplanes. It's a sort of bug that gets in you, you know.'

Shirley nodded. 'I've got it, too.'

The stewardess said, 'Serving teas and drinks and asking passengers to fasten safety belts and helping them to do it—that's one way to work in aviation. It's all right if you can't do anything more important. But then when I met Theo, when he pulled the undercart up out at Gander, I started wondering if that was really the best thing I could do. He's such a—such a *big* little man,' she said. 'His work is so vastly more important than mine, and he does need someone's help so very, very much.'

'My dear,' said Shirley softly.

Marjorie said, 'I never went to college and I won't be able to do much to help him in his work. I don't think he'd want that, anyway. But I can help him for all that, in all the things he can't do properly himself. And I can make him young again, I think, and make him enjoy things. If I can do that, he's bound to do better work even than he does now. And I think that's a better way to work in aviation than just serving teas and drinks and telling passengers when to do up their safety belts. . . .'

D.R.D. called his second meeting on the Reindeer tail two days later, at 11.30 in the same room in the Ministry of Supply. I killed two birds with one stone, that day, by arranging for the pilot of the Assegai to meet me an hour previously in Ferguson's room.

His name was Flying-Officer Harper. He was a dark-haired, fresh-faced boy of twenty-one or twenty-two, who adopted the pose that everything was a joke and nothing really mattered, whether being crossed in love or being killed in an Assegai. He came into the room warily, as if walking into a trap.

'Flying-Officer Harper?' I said. 'Good morning. My name is Scott and I'm from Farnborough. We've got to start a special investigation into these accidents that you've been having with the Assegai, and I asked if you could meet me here to tell me just what happened.' I motioned him to a chair and gave him a cigarette. 'Tell me, what happened first of all?'

'Well,' he said, 'the wing came off.'

'I know. Any idea why it came off?'

'I suppose it just isn't strong enough.'

'Tell me just what happened,' I said. 'It's my job to try and make it stronger. First of all, what height were you at?'

'About thirty-five thousand, I should think. Anyway, between thirty and forty thousand.'

'Were you alone or were there other machines about?'

'There were other machines up at the time, but nobody near me. Nobody else saw what happened.'

'What were you doing? Were you flying level or diving?'

'I was in a shallow dive, sir.'

'What speed were you going at?'

'I don't know,' he said evasively. 'The air-speed indicator goes all haywire—it was flipping about all over the scale.'

'What was the Machmeter showing?'

'I never look at that,' he said. 'It's no bloody good, that thing. Half the time its U/S.'

One had to be patient. I said, 'Would you say that you were near the speed of sound?'

He said reluctantly, 'I might have been. It's rather difficult to tell.'

I smiled. 'What about the restriction on the speed of the Assegai? The one about not doing more than ·90 Mach?'

He laughed cynically. 'That's just a bit of bloody nonsense. Nobody pays any attention to that.'

'You mean, in combat practice you go faster than that in Assegais?'

'Of course. Everybody does. It's just a lot of nonsense put out by the boffins, that.'

I grinned. 'What's the fastest you have ever been in an Assegai?'

He said proudly, 'I got it up to 1·2 on that Machmeter thing. That was in about a thirty-degree dive. I believe you'd get her faster than that if you started at about fifty thousand.'

1·20 Mach is getting on for a thousand miles an hour. 'Did you have any trouble getting through the speed of sound?' I asked.

'It's just like being inside a kettledrum,' he said. 'Everything's sort of hammering at you, very quick, and it gets bloody hot. Then as you go through it all gets smooth again. Then it's the same as you slow down and come back through.'

I stared at him. It had never been contemplated that ordinary squadron pilots would do that. 'Have you done that often?' I asked.

He shrugged his shoulders. 'Half a dozen times,' he said. 'It's rather fun.'

'Does everybody do this?' I asked.

'Of course they do,' he said. 'Wingco hands out a raspberry if he hears anyone talking about it. But everybody does it.'

R.A.F. discipline was no concern of mine; my job was simply to do what I could to see that aircraft were built strong enough to be safe in the way that they were used. I said 'Let's say that you got out of control when flying at Mach ·90 and inadvertently approached the speed of sound. I suppose it was around that region that this accident happened?'

He grinned. 'That's right. I got out of control.'

'Well now, what happened?'

'She stuck in it,' he said. 'In the kettledrum, I mean. I suppose I wasn't going fast enough to go through. I think you've got to make it quick or not at all. I tried to get out of it by slowing down, but the stick was jammed or something, and everything you touched was vibrating like one of those electric shocking coils, you know. Everything was getting bloody hot to touch, and I thought, "Oh, Momma!!"' He laughed. 'Well, then I looked at the port wing, and there was a sort of line of light right from the root to the tip, right along the leading edge, and then there was a bloody great bang and the whole wing was gone—just like that. Well, then I pulled the blind down over my face and the seat ejected all right, and there I was sitting in the air with bits of metal all round me. So I pulled the chute and came down normally.' He paused. 'I can't think of anything else.'

He had had a most miraculous escape. I thought about it for a minute, and then said, 'This line of light along the leading edge. What did it look like?'

'It looked sort of incandescent,' he replied. 'Like the crack of light you see at a furnace door.'

I could not make head or tail of that. 'Do you remember how it ran?' I asked. 'I've got an Assegai wing down at Farnborough. If you came down there, could you mark that wing with a pencil to show exactly where you saw the crack of light? Or don't you remember well enough for that?'

He said, 'Oh, yes, I could do that. I know just how it went.'

Well that was something to start from; at any rate we had a description of the symptoms, if the cause of the disease was quite obscure. I talked to Harper for some time, but he could add little more. He treated it as rather a joke, regardless of the fact that his Assegai had cost the taxpayer about twenty thousand pounds. He was taking his girl friend to see *Lovely Lady* at the Hippodrome that evening, so I fixed for him to come to Farnborough next day and draw his line upon my Assegai wing.

I went on down to D.R.D.'s meeting, in the same conference room as the previous one. I had had the bits of spar that I had brought from Labrador sent up from Farnborough and placed at the end of the table, in case there should be any argument about it from the diehards. As each member came in for the meeting he made for these bits of structure and examined them. E.P.Prendergast pulled out a pocket magnifying glass and examined the fractures for a long time, grunting sourly when anybody spoke to him; he was in no genial mood that day. Carnegie and Sir David Moon examined the parts gloomily, talking in low tones. Group-Captain Fisher came in just before the meeting opened, red-faced and irritable; he did not examine the parts because he had seen them the afternoon before.

D.R.D. opened the meeting by saying that the representative of the R.A.E. had brought back certain parts from the Reindeer accident in Labrador, some of which were on the table. Technical opinion was unanimous that they indicated a fatigue fracture of the front spar flanges of the port tailplane. He would ask Dr Scott to outline his investigation to the meeting.

'There's not much to say,' I remarked. 'When we reached the scene of the accident we discovered that the spar fractures at the fuselage had been removed for examination by the Russian burial party who had come to exhume the body of their ambassador.' There were incredulous smiles and raised eyebrows round the table. D.R.D. nodded shortly. 'It therefore became necessary to locate the tailplane itself. We found this thirty-seven miles east-north-east of the scene of the accident—that is, back along the course to Goose. These fractures on the table, there, were cut from the tailplane as it lay. There was, of course, no means of bringing the whole unit down to the coast for shipment. I think that's all about it, I'm sorry not to have both parts of the fracture to show you, but I understand that political difficulties have prevented that.'

D.R.D. said, 'I'm afraid that is so.' Then he turned to the Inspector of

Accidents. 'I don't know if you have had an opportunity to consider the matter, Group-Captain?'

The old man raised his head. 'Not yet,' he said definitely. 'I have not received any report of this investigation from Ottawa, and until I do so the matter must remain *sub judice*, so far as I am concerned.' He was so ill advised as to go on, clutching at a straw. 'I understand that the wreckage from which these parts were cut was found thirty-seven miles from the main crash. That seems to me to be a very long way away. It is at least possible that these parts do not belong to the Reindeer at all, but to some other accident. I think that point wants some investigation.'

With that, I think, the bowler-hat descended firmly on his head. Prendergast stuck out his great jowl and said, 'What on earth do you mean?'

D.R.D. interposed hastily. 'The identification of these pieces is clearly part of the procedure, Mr Prendergast.'

The designer grunted offensively. 'I should have thought that was hardly necessary, since I am present at this meeting. I am not accustomed to wasting my time investigating casual bits of aircraft junk. These are all portions of the front and rear spar structures of the Reindeer tailplane.'

D.R.D. said, 'Well, that settles that. It seems that this first machine had flown 1,393 hours up to the time of the accident, and these samples clearly show that the cause of the disaster was a fatigue failure of the nature postulated by the investigation undertaken by the R.A.E. We now have to consider what action we must take.' He turned to me. 'Dr Scott?'

'I have not changed my views,' I said. 'Action must be taken by some other body. But I think that some modification to the present design of the tail structure is clearly necessary, and until that has been carried out no Reindeer should fly more than 720 hours. That's my opinion.'

Carnegie said, 'Based on Mr Honey's work and on this evidence?'

'That's right,' I replied. 'Some rather unfortunate things were said about Mr Honey at our last meeting. I should like to point out that he's the only one among the lot of us who has been consistently right all through. If he hadn't damaged that second Reindeer at Gander, you'd have had another accident, beyond all doubt.'

There was a glum silence. It was broken by Carnegie, who said, 'That aircraft might as well stay at Gander, if we can't use it. In fact, I suppose it will have to. I suppose I may take it that that one, which has flown something over 1,440 hours, is grounded from now on.'

D.R.D. said, 'That is an executive decision, to be taken as a result of this meeting. But I think it's very likely.'

Sir David Moon said, 'Mr Chairman, the news that we have heard this morning is bad news for us, as you can suppose. It entails laying up our fleet of Reindeer aircraft for a major modification, probably for a matter of months, if our past experience is any guide. That means, this country must cease to operate a Transatlantic service, unless we care to do so by reverting to the obsolete and uneconomic types that we lately discarded. And, in fact, there are too few of those now available to enable us to maintain our services. That is a very heavy blow to us, and to this country.' He was speaking quietly and seriously. 'We do not question its necessity, but we ask for a hand in framing what restrictions on the Reindeer are deemed necessary, with a view to making the optimum use of the aircraft.'

I was not paying much attention; I was thinking of the Assegai. The Reindeer was over, so far as I was personally concerned; what happened now was for others to decide. The Assegai was vital and urgent. It had never been intended that the Assegai should be flown in the trans-sonic region, but the young men were doing it and doing it every day. It had already killed two of them. It might well be impossible to prevent the fighter pilots from getting the most out of their machine; they were not of the temperament to submit to restrictions based on safety. Either the Assegai must be taken away from them or it must be strengthened, and strengthened quickly, to withstand the forces that they put on it. What those forces were was very little known. It was a complete mystery to me, at that time, why one thin line along the leading edge should have become incandescent. And till we found the answer to that one, the Assegai would go on killing the young men.

I came back to the meeting with a start. D.R.D. was saying. 'The first thing is to find out what modifications are necessary.' He glanced down the table at the designer. 'Perhaps Mr Prendergast can give us some indication of what will be involved?'

Prendergast reached for his attaché case, pulled out a whiteprint, and opened it upon the table. 'I have given this matter a good deal of attention, personally,' he said ponderously. 'Clearly, there is no alternative to increasing the mass of the spar flanges at the root and for several feet out from the root, and it is desirable that the elastic modulus of the spar flange should be increased as well. I propose to insert a steel channel section, nesting into the existing duralumin flange.' And he went on to talk about families of nesting sections, one of his structural fetishes, and fitted bolts in reamed holes prepared on the spar drilling jig. He showed us his drawing.

Carnegie asked gloomily, 'What's the delivery of these special steel sections?'

'Enough for two machines will be available on Thursday next,' the designer said. 'The remainder will follow on after that as required.'

We stared at him incredulously. Carnegie asked, 'Do you mean to say that we can get these special steel sections without any delay at all?'

'I am not accustomed to having my word doubted, Mr Carnegie,' said the designer haughtily. 'I have been thirty-seven years in this industry, and I hope I know what I am talking about. I have chosen this particular solution, one of several, because it seemed to offer certain production advantages, though at a small cost in extra weight. We already have the necessary dies, prepared as part of our policy of laying by the dies required for all our nesting sections.' He glared down the table at the Treasury official. 'And I may say, in passing, that we experience continual and increasing difficulty in obtaining payment for dies which are not immediately required for our contracts. If it were not for our foresight and prudence in preparing these dies in the face of all the obstructions thrown in our path by the officials of this Ministry, I should not be able to assist you in this way.' The Treasury official made a note upon his pad. E.P. Prendergast swelled himself out like a frog. 'The great company which I have the honour to represent,' he said, 'has placed the full facilities of its Sheffield steel plant behind this matter, with overriding priority, in anticipation of our requirements. I see no reason to suppose that we shall be held up for materials.'

D.R.D. remarked. 'Well, I'm sure we all feel that this is very satisfactory, Mr Prendergast. Have you been able to prepare any estimate of the time that the modification is likely to take?'

'I have.' The designer pulled a paper from his case. 'In the first place, I have assumed that you will give me verbal authority to commence work now–this morning–upon the preparation of the necessary parts, which are, in fact, already in hand.' The man from the Treasury frowned, and then laughed. 'I also assume that you sanction night-shift work upon this contract, and overtime except Sundays. Am I correct?'

D.R.D. was somewhat at a loss. 'I think so.'

The designer grunted offensively. 'Well, you must make up your minds if you want this work done or not.'

Ferguson leaned over and whispered to D.R.D., who said, 'Yes. We can give verbal instructions to proceed, Mr Prendergast.'

Sir David Moon said, 'Mr Chairman, in view of the extreme urgency of this matter to us, may I ask if Sunday work can be authorised?'

E.P. Prendergast stuck out his great jowl and said, 'On no account would I agree with that. If you want work done on Sundays, you must go elsewhere. It is uneconomic upon any account, and it strikes at the root of family life, which is the basis of the greatness of this country.' We stared at him, blinking. 'God comes before the Reindeer, gentlemen,' he said.

D.R.D. said smoothly, 'Of course. On the assumptions you have made, Mr Prendergast, how long do you suppose this job will take?'

The designer consulted his paper. 'We can accept the first machine for modification on Monday the 18th, and the work will be completed by the evening of the 21st. Thereafter we can modify one machine in each four complete working days.'

We stared down the table at him. Sir David Moon said,

'Am I to understand that each aircraft will only be out of service for four days?'

'That does not include the time of the delivery flights to and from our Stamford works,' said Prendergast.

Carnegie said impulsively, 'But that's fantastic!'

Prendergast glared at him. 'I am not accustomed to that language in relation to my statements,' he said harshly. 'If you are unable to accept our estimates, you must take your work elsewhere.'

All good designers are difficult men or they could not be good designers; I think everybody at the table was more or less aware of that. We set ourselves to mollify the great man, and I say that with sincerity. A great man he was, a great designer and a superlative engineer. But not an easy man to deal with. No.

In the end Sir David Moon said, 'This represents a different picture altogether, Mr Chairman. If the company can do the necessary modifications in so short a time, there will be no need to interrupt our present schedule of services at all.' Prendergast nodded. 'We can allocate the machines off service one by one for this work to be done. The general public need not know anything at all about it.'

D.R.D. said, 'I think that's very desirable. It never does any good to have a garbled version of these troubles in the newspapers.'

The Director leaned across to me. 'They'd only print half the story, anyway,' he remarked. 'They wouldn't believe the other half.'

The meeting broke up. I said to him, 'I had a chat with that Assegai pilot, sir. It was at the speed of sound, of course; it stuck for several seconds in the region of high drag. He said he'd been through to the supersonic zone several times. He was quite positive about the incandescent line along the leading edge. He's coming down tomorrow to sketch it on the wing.'

He nodded. 'Morrison back yet?'

'Not yet,' I said, 'I think he's coming in tomorrow. I hope he sees more daylight in this matter than I do.'

He smiled gently. 'It'll come,' he said.

Honey got married to Marjorie Corder about a month later, and on the third day of his honeymoon the test tail broke, at 1,296 hours only, which gave him something to think about. Flight-Lieutenant Wintringham said it was a wedding present for him. He came hurrying back from Bournemouth, where they were staying, to view the body, and I sent him back to his honeymoon with a flea in his ear. But I don't know what kind of a honeymoon they had after that, because he came back to the office with a considerable extension to his nuclear theory of fatigue, expressed in twenty-six pages of pure mathematics.

That autumn I was restless after office hours. I had nothing much to work at in the evenings and I was very worried about the Assegai. I tried reading Shirley's novels, but I can't take any interest in those things; real life always seems to me to be so much more stimulating. I tried listening to the wireless and got fed up with that. And it was much too soon to write another paper for the Society.

One evening Shirley laid her sewing down. 'Dennis, I wish you or somebody would write up some of these things that happen, like the Reindeer tail. I mean, write literally all about it, not just the scientific part. All about Monica Teasdale, and Elspeth, and planchette, and the Director going to Kew Gardens—all the bits that made it fun. We shall forget what really happened in a few years' time and we'll have lost something worth having. I'd like to try and save some of the fun we're having now, to look at when we're old.'

I stared at her thoughtfully. 'That's not a bad idea,' I said. 'It'll be better than sitting worrying about the Assegai.'

AUTHOR'S NOTE

This book is a work of fiction. None of the characters are drawn from real persons. The Reindeer aircraft in my story is not based on any particular commercial aircraft, nor do the troubles from which it suffered refer to any actual events.

In this story I have postulated an inefficient Inspector of Accidents, with a fictitious name and a fictitious character. Only one man can hold this post at a time, and I tender such apologies as may be necessary to the distinguished and efficient officer who holds it now. I would add this. The scrupulous and painstaking investigation of accidents is the key to all safety in the air, and demands the services of men of the very highest quality. If my story underlines this point, it will have served a useful purpose.

NEVIL SHUTE